U0050541

檸 檬 樹 出 版

Your Book of Choice

實用英語會話大全

字頻/大考/英檢/多益，四類字級解析應用版

A COLLECTION OF PRACTICAL ENGLISH CONVERSATIONS

王琪 編著

🍋 檸檬樹

出版前言

學習外語最大的功能與成就感，莫過於能夠「達成溝通」。如果以學習的完成度來說，「表達、對話」可說是語言學習的集大成表現。

因為，「構成表達內容」的要素很多，舉凡「單字、片語、文法、句型」等等皆是，必須將這些基本要素恰當地「使用、銜接、組合」，才能夠構成句子，呈現想要「說」或「寫」的內容。

不過，真實的情況往往是 —— 我們還未熟練這些基本要素，卻已經開始、或者必須開始進行表達。即使單字、片語記憶量不夠多、不夠熟練；即使文法、句型還似懂非懂，無法融會貫通 —— 表達，卻已經在嘗試、練習之中，逐步展開。

曾經嘗試外語表達的人，應該都有這樣的察覺 —— 一旦「單字、片語、文法、句型」能力越完備，對於句子的構成、掌握、理解能力，就能夠越純熟。而對於會話表達產生最直接影響的，應該屬「單字」了。

「單字」是構成句意的基礎，沒有單字當作基礎，表達便難以成立。

因此 —— 本書著重於「會話內容的要角」——「單字」，並適時補充「句型接續、文法時態、片語、可替換字詞」等等，其他「支撐、豐富句意」的要件。強調「不能籠統學習英語會話，必須具體掌握每一個構句單字」並踏實學習。

因此 —— 全書 5,073 個會話句子，逐一拆解構句單字，具體明辨「字義、發音、詞性」；並透過「字頻／大考／英檢／多益」四類英語單字字級標準，明確定義出「單字的難易程度、使用頻度」。

透過「左頁會話‧右頁單字」互相對應，學習表達的同時，能夠務實增強單字能力，掌握會話句的字詞運用，直接從「靈活運用單字」的角度，達成從「字」到「句」融會貫通。

另外，在內容的取材與選擇，也兼顧「真實會話情境」的需求。
全書 8 大類會話，延伸出豐富多樣的 158 種主題。

例如「想法／主張」包含「贊成」「反對」「建議」「喜惡」等；「表達善意」包含「打招呼」「寒暄」「提醒」「讚美」「鼓勵」「祝賀」等。各主題兼具「兩種會話立場內容」：【立場 1】自我表達，開場攀談【立場 2】利用提問延續話題、回應與附和。藉此熟練外語互動，並能掌握字詞在兩種立場中的不同活用方式。

‧第 1 類：【立場 1】自我介紹　　【立場 2】我想認識你
‧第 2 類：【立場 1】我的日常生活　【立場 2】你的日常生活
‧第 3 類：【立場 1】我的喜怒哀樂　【立場 2】你的喜怒哀樂
‧第 4 類：【立場 1】我的想法／主張【立場 2】你的想法／主張
‧第 5 類：【立場 1】表達善意　　　【立場 2】回應對方的善意
‧第 6 類：【立場 1】出國旅遊　　　【立場 2】聽懂外國人說什麼
‧第 7 類：【立場 1】辦公室英語　　【立場 2】和同事&客戶溝通
‧第 8 類：【立場 1】開啟聊天話題　【立場 2】如何讓話題持續

期望結合「會話表達」與「單字說明&級等分析」，體驗會話與單字的多元性，具體了解學習內容的「實用性」與「程度領域」，以務實的步伐，提升自己的會話能力。

檸檬樹出版社 敬上

本書版面說明

【左頁】主題名稱・主題會話

主題名稱
· 紅底：表示【立場1】自我表達，開場攀談
（※翻頁後，主題名稱變成「灰底」）
· 灰底：表示【立場2】利用提問延續話題、回應與附和

MP3 音軌

· 052-01-05
表示：
單元 052
【立場1】
第 5 句

· 052-02-08
表示：
單元 052
【立場2】
第 8 句

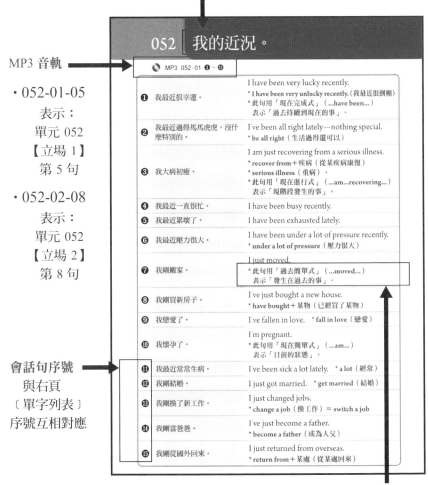

會話句序號
與右頁
〔單字列表〕
序號互相對應

註解補充：文法、時態、句型、片語、可替換字句

【右頁】會話句單字列表・單字級等分析

字頻／大考／英檢／多益，四類字級程度對應
・字頻：以「數字」表示「出現頻次」
・大考：以「數字」表示「級數」
・英檢：區分為「初級」「中級」「中高（＝中高級）」
・多益：以「◎」表示「屬於多益測驗常考字」

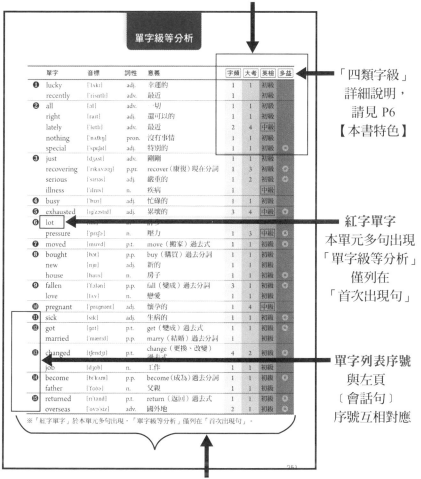

除「疑問詞、介係詞、連接詞、助動詞」，其餘均列入單字標示級等解析

本書特色

迷信單字量，未必保證「能夠完成溝通表達」！
本書運用 4,702 個單字，
形成 5,073 句同時滿足「陳述」與「提問」的「兩種立場英語會話」；

其中 50% 以上單字，
屬於各字級認定的「初級、常用」及「高頻」單字，
會話實例證明，最基本的字彙「使用度高、活用度廣」；

不能籠統學習英語會話！
具體掌握構句各單字，將「基本單字」發揮最大活用，
就能擁有「互動不冷場」的英語會話力！

■ 說明：全書四類字級&單字數量分析

（1）【字頻】（＝日常運用出現頻次）

分為「1～8 級」，「1 級」為最高出現頻次。此級等為：彙整多種字彙來源，包括「英語演說、書籍雜誌、報導文刊」等，利用電腦篩選字詞，並排序字頻表；同時參考台灣現行英語詞彙學習標準，以及外語學習環境等因素，加以篩選調整而成。

● 本書【字頻】單字數統計

1 級〔2811 字〕占全書單字數 <u>59.8%</u>

2 級〔733 字〕、3 級〔316 字〕、4 級〔165 字〕、5 級〔90 字〕
6 級〔92 字〕、7 級〔62 字〕、8 級〔45字〕

（2）【大考】（＝大考中心定義級等）

分為「1～6 級」，「6 級」為最高級。此級等為：「大學入學考試中心」編製的「高中英文參考詞彙表」，其中「1～2 級」屬於「教育部公布的常用 2000 字詞」。

●本書【大考】單字數統計

1 級〔1863 字〕、2 級〔807 字〕占全書單字數 56.8%

3 級〔534 字〕、4 級〔344 字〕、5 級〔138 字〕、6 級〔100 字〕

（3）【英檢】（＝全民英檢參考字）

分為「初級、中級、中高級」。此級等為：「語言訓練測驗中心」的「全民英檢參考字表」作為統計依據，檢定結果可供台灣的學校及公民營機構參考受試者的英語程度。

●本書【英檢】單字數統計

初級〔2750 字〕占全書單字數 58.5%

中級〔903 字〕、中高級〔342 字〕

（4）【多益】（＝多益測驗常考字）

針對求職英語能力需求所開發的付費考試。此級等整理出「多益測驗常用單字」作為統計依據，提供學習者「此是否為多益常考字」之參考。

●本書【多益】單字數統計

屬於多益測驗常考字〔2258 字〕占全書單字數 48%

■ **兩種立場英語會話：**
　【立場 1】── 自我表達，開場攀談
　【立場 2】── 利用提問延續話題、回應與附和

各主題會話兼具「真實會話情境」所需的「陳述」與「提問」兩種立場，具備「自我表達」及「用英語詢問對方，讓話題延續」雙重功能。全書內容豐富多樣，完備「可順利開場、接話」的內容，堪稱「足以應付任何狀況」的「英語表達語句庫」；自己有話可說，也有能力加碼問、延續對話不冷場！

【立場 1】自我表達，開場攀談（例如：單元 075 我的建議。）

〔我可以提個意見嗎？〕May I make a suggestion?
〔我建議大家先冷靜下來。〕I suggest that everyone calm down first.
〔這樣也許行得通。〕This way might work.
〔我想不出什麼好建議。〕I can't think of any good suggestions.
〔我在想這麼做是不是比較好？〕I am considering whether this is a
　　　　　　　　　　　　　　　　　　better way to do it.

【立場 2】利用提問延續話題、回應與附和（例如：單元 075 你的建議？）

〔這件事你有什麼看法？〕Do you have any opinion on this matter?
〔你有什麼好建議嗎？〕Do you have any good suggestions?
〔你可以幫忙想想辦法嗎？〕Can you help think of a solution?
〔謝謝你提供建議。〕Thank you for offering your suggestion.
〔你的建議很有可行性。〕Your suggestion is quite feasible.

■ 會話句涵蓋 8 大領域，158 種主題，
   足以應付各種「真實會話情境」！

全書內容涵蓋 8 大領域，再區分為 158 種會話主題；從「生活各層面」
到「職場互動」，從「個人自我表達」到「海外各種問題」，完備各種真
實會話情境必備的英語短句與單字，便於「逐句學習」與「檢索查詢」。
※ 8 大領域實用會話：

1 自我介紹　　2 日常生活　　3 喜怒哀樂　　4 想法主張
5 表達善意　　6 出國旅遊　　7 職場英語　　8 聊天話題

■ 中籍＋美籍配音員【會話句中英順讀 MP3】，
   可以完全拋開紙本，隨時訓練「聽力」與「口說」！

全書「5073 會話句，一句一音軌」，以「先唸中文、再唸英文」順讀錄製。
MP3 音軌「完全對應書中會話句序號」，例如「單元 032-01 第 8 句」
音軌編號即為「032-01-08」，「想聽哪一句，可以準確點選收聽」。可
以完全拋開書本，徹底體驗「用聽的學英語會話」！
※ 全書 MP3 共「5074 音軌」（5073 會話句＋片頭曲目）：
因各音響器材「可確實讀取的音軌數上限，依廠牌、機型而有差異」，
建議使用電腦讀取此光碟，以確保完整收聽。

■ 補充說明：「現在分詞」「動名詞」的縮寫表示

「現在分詞」「動名詞」常通稱為「V-ing」。本書參考《Collins English
Dictionary》將「現在分詞」以「p.pr.」表示，「動名詞」則歸為「名詞」，
以「n.」表示。

特別補充 —— 英語詞性簡介

1 | 名詞 | 用於指稱「人」「地點」「事物」…等

■ 我的童年在家鄉度過。（單元 003）

I spent my | childhood | in my | hometown | .

* 「childhood」指「事物」。

* 「hometown」指「地點」。

2 | 代名詞 | 用於「代替名詞」，以避免相同單字重複出現

■ 這個行李箱和我的一樣，但不是我的。（單元 110）

This suitcase looks the same, but | it | 's not mine.

* 「it」代替前面出現的「suitcase」。

3 | 動詞 | 用於敘述「名詞、代名詞」的「動作、行為、狀態」

■ 我們公司允許員工隨性打扮。（單元 017）

Our company | allows | us to | dress | casually for work.

* 「allows」指「公司的動作」。

* 「dress」指「員工的動作」。

■ 我的心好像被挖空了。（單元 060）

My heart | seems | empty.

* 「seems」指「心好像被挖空的狀態」。

特別補充 —— 英語詞性簡介

4 形容詞 用於修飾「名詞」或「代名詞」

■ 我的油錢很可觀。（單元 036）

My fuel expenses are quite considerable .

* 修飾句中作為主詞的名詞「fuel expenses」。

■ 是臨時出狀況嗎？（單元 058）

Anything unexpected happened?

* 修飾句中作為主詞的代名詞「anything」。

5 副詞 用於修飾「動詞、形容詞」或「整個句子」

■ 我這陣子很沮喪。（單元 053）

I have been very depressed lately .

* 「very」修飾形容詞「depressed」。

* 「lately」修飾整個句子，指「最近的情況」。

■ 我很需要你的意見。（單元 075）

I really need your comments.

* 「really」修飾句中的動詞「need」。

6 感嘆詞 用於表示「驚喜」「悲傷」「生氣」…等情感

■ 差點就過關了，真是的！（單元 061）

I almost made it, darn it!

* 「darn」表現出話中「生氣」或「遺憾」的情感。

■ 天啊！我怎麼忘記了？（單元 097）

Gosh ! How could I forget about that?

* 「gosh」表現出話中「驚訝」的情感。

特別補充 —— 英語詞性簡介

7 疑問詞　用於詢問對方「人」「地點」「事物」「時間」…等

■ 這些年都在忙什麼？（單元 095）

What have you been doing for the past few years?

＊「what」表示詢問對方「事物」。

■ 什麼時間跟你聯絡比較方便？（單元 139）

When is the best time to contact you?

＊「when」表示詢問對方「時間」。

疑 問 詞 彙 整

疑問詞	音標	意義	疑問詞	音標	意義
how	[haʊ]	如何	which	[hwɪtʃ]	哪一個、哪一些
what	[hwɑt]	什麼	who	[hu]	誰、什麼人
when	[hwɛn]	何時	why	[hwaɪ]	為什麼
where	[hwɛr]	哪裡			

8 介係詞　用於表示「時間」「地點、「方向」…等

■ 請給我高樓層的房間。（單元 112）

Please give a room on the upper floors.

＊「on」表示句中房間的地點「the upper floors」。

■ 捷運末班車大概是晚上十二點。（單元 148）

The last train boards at about twelve pm.

＊「at」表示句中末班車的時間「about twelve pm」。

介 係 詞 彙 整

介係詞	音標	意義	介係詞	音標	意義
about	[əˋbaʊt]	關於	into	[ˋɪntu]	進入
above	[əˋbʌv]	在…上面	like	[laɪk]	像…
according to	[əˋkɔrdɪŋ tu]	根據	near	[nɪr]	在…附近
after	[ˋæftɚ]	在…之後	next	[nɛkst]	貼近
against	[əˋgɛnst]	反對、倚靠	of	[ɑv]	…的、具…特質
along	[əˋlɔŋ]	沿著	on	[ɑn]	在…上面、由…支付
among	[əˋmʌŋ]	在…之中	over	[ˋovɚ]	高於、在…之上
around	[əˋraʊnd]	圍繞、在…附近	per	[pɚ]	每一…
as	[æz]	作為、如同	regarding	[rɪˋgɑrdɪŋ]	關於
at	[æt]	在…地點、在…時間點	through	[θru]	穿過、憑藉
before	[bɪˋfor]	在…以前	throughout	[θruˋaʊt]	遍及、貫穿
behind	[bɪˋhaɪnd]	在…背後	to	[tu]	往、對於
beside	[bɪˋsaɪd]	在…旁邊	toward	[təˋwɔrd]	向、朝/接近
besides	[bɪˋsaɪdz]	除…之外	under	[ˋʌndɚ]	在…下面
between	[bɪˋtwin]	在…之間	underneath	[ʌndɚˋniθ]	在…底下
beyond	[bɪˋjɑnd]	在…那一邊、超出於	until	[ənˋtɪl]	到…為止
by	[baɪ]	經由、在…旁邊	up	[ʌp]	在…之上
down	[daʊn]	沿著、在…下方	via	[ˋvaɪə]	經由
during	[ˋdjʊrɪŋ]	在…期間	with	[wɪð]	以…、和…一起
for	[fɔr]	為了、對於	within	[wɪˋðɪn]	在…範圍內
from	[frɑm]	從…	without	[wɪˋðaʊt]	沒有
in	[ɪn]	在…之內			

特別補充 —— 英語詞性簡介

9 連接詞 用於連接「單字」「片語」「句子」…等

■ 行李外有寫我的姓名及電話。（單元 110）

My name 　and　 phone number are on my luggage.

*「and」連接兩個名詞：「name」和「phone number」。

■ S 號太小，M 號又太大。（單元 116）

The small is too small, 　but　 the medium is too big.

*「but」連接兩個句子：

「the small is too small」和「the medium is too big」。

連 接 詞 彙 整

連接詞	音標	意義	連接詞	音標	意義
after	[ˈæftɚ]	在…之後	so	[so]	所以
and	[ænd]	和…	than	[ðæn]	比…
as	[æz]	像…一樣	that	[ðæt]	無意義，用於引導「從屬子句」
because	[bɪˈkɔz]	因為	till	[tɪl]	直到…為止
before	[bɪˈfor]	在…以前	until	[ənˈtɪl]	直到…為止
but	[bʌt]	但是	when	[hwɛn]	當…時
either	[ˈiðɚ]	（與 or 連用）或	whenever	[hwɛnˈɛvɚ]	無論何、每當
if	[ɪf]	如果	where	[hwɛr]	在…處
once	[wʌns]	一旦	whether	[ˈhwɛðɚ]	是否
or	[ɔr]	或者	while	[hwaɪl]	在…的同時
since	[sɪns]	自從			

特別補充 —— 英語詞性簡介

10 助動詞 輔助動詞，用於「改變句意」或「時態」

■ 我不敢吃生食。（單元 045）

Ew, I don't want to eat raw food.

＊「don't」為助動詞「do」的否定形態，將句意改變為「否定句」。

■ 你這支電話是最近申請的嗎？（單元 130）

Have you just recently started using this number?

＊「have started」為「現在完成式」，表示「結果持續到現在」。

＊ 將「have」放到句首形成「疑問句」。

助 動 詞 彙 整

助動詞	音標	意義	助動詞	音標	意義
can	[kæn]	可以	had	[hæd]	have 的過去式
cannot	[`kænɑt]	can 的否定	may	[me]	可能
can't	[kænt]	can 的否定	might	[maɪt]	may 的過去式
could	[kʊd]	can 的過去式	must	[mʌst]	必須
couldn't	[`kʊdnt]	could 的否定	should	[ʃʊd]	應該
do	[du]	無意義，用於「疑問句、否定句」	shouldn't	[`ʃʊdnt]	should 的否定
don't	[dont]	do 的否定	will	[wɪl]	將
did	[dɪd]	do 的過去式	won't	[wont]	will 的否定
didn't	[`dɪdnt]	did 的否定	would	[wʊd]	will 的過去式
have	[hæv]	已經	wouldn't	[`wʊdnt]	would 的否定
haven't	[`hævnt]	have 的否定			

特別補充 —— 英語時態用法說明

1 ｜現在簡單式｜和會話的關係

使用型態：（1）be 動詞現在式 （2）一般動詞現在式

（1）描述＆詢問：經常如此的事

■ 我們隨時有專人為您服務。（單元 137）
Our expert staff ｜is｜ always at your service.
＊「隨時有專員為您服務」屬於「經常如此的事」。

■ 我沒有一份工作做得長久。（單元 069）
I ｜don't keep｜ jobs for very long.
＊「沒有一份工作做得久、從沒有工作做得久」屬於「經常如此的事」。

■ 你常買名牌嗎？（單元 143）
｜Do｜ you buy name-brand items often?
＊「常買名牌嗎」屬於詢問「經常…嗎」。

（2）描述＆詢問：目前的狀態

■ 我的父親已經退休。（單元 046）
My father ｜is｜ retired.
＊「已經退休」屬於「目前的狀態」。

■ 我懷孕了。（單元 052）
｜I'm｜ pregnant.
＊「懷孕了」屬於「目前的狀態」。

■ 你記得他大概什麼時候打的嗎？（單元 132）
｜Do｜ you remember when he called?
＊「你記得…嗎」（你目前記得…嗎）屬於詢問「目前狀態…嗎」。

特別補充 —— 英語時態用法說明

2 過去簡單式 和會話的關係

使用型態：（1）be 動詞過去式 （2）一般動詞過去式

（1）描述＆詢問：發生在過去的事

■ 我和我先生是同班同學。（單元 009）
My husband and I were classmates in school.
* 和老公「以前是同班同學」，屬於「發生在過去的事」。

■ 我今天中午吃很少。（單元 040）
I had a small lunch.
*「稍早前的午餐」屬於「發生在過去的事」。

■ 我想你不是故意的。（單元 081）
I am sure you didn't mean it.
* 意思指「我想你之前的⋯、當時的⋯，並不是故意的」，「之前的⋯」
  或「當時的⋯」屬於「發生在過去的事」。

■ 你的老闆白手起家嗎？（單元 050）
Did your boss start his own business?
*「老闆以前是白手起家嗎」屬於詢問「發生在過去的事」。

■ 我不在時有人打來嗎？（單元 132）
Did anyone call while I was out?
*「之前我不在的時候，有人⋯嗎」屬於詢問「發生在過去的事」。

（2）描述＆詢問：過去經常如此的事

■ 我整天以淚洗面。（單元 060）
I cried all day.
*「整天、頻繁地傷心流淚」，屬於「過去某時點經常如此的事」。

特別補充 —— 英語時態用法說明

3 現在完成式 和會話的關係

使用型態： 助動詞 have / has ＋ 動詞過去分詞

（1）描述＆詢問：過去某時點發生某事，且結果持續到現在，
   或結果對現在仍有影響

■ 工作中我學到很多東西。（單元 021）
I have learned a lot from my work.
*「從工作中學到很多」（過去某時點發生的事），「且結果對現在仍有
 影響」（當時讓我學到很多，直到現在這些能力都對我有影響）。
* 在美式英語中，此用法也能和「過去簡單式」通用。例如：
 我被加薪了。（單元 023）
   I've gotten a raise. ＝ I got a raise.（過去簡單式）

（2）描述＆詢問：過去持續到現在的事

■ 我一直都很健康。（單元 033）
I have always been very healthy.
*「從過去到現在都很健康」屬於「過去持續到現在的事」。

■ 你從小住在這裡嗎？（單元 004）
Have you lived here since you were young?
*「從小到現在都…嗎」屬於詢問「過去持續到現在都…嗎」。

（3）描述＆詢問：過去到現在發生過、經歷過的事

■ 珍妮打了好幾通電話找你。（單元 132）
Jenny has already called you several times.
*「剛才」（過去的時點）到「現在」這一段時間，珍妮打了幾次電話找你。

■ 久仰大名。（單元 133）
I've heard a lot about you.
*「以前」（過去的時點）到「現在」這一段時間，曾經聽過你的大名。

特別補充 —— 英語時態用法說明

4 [現在完成進行式] 和會話的關係

使用型態： [助動詞 have / has] + [been] + [動詞-ing 型態]

（1）描述＆詢問：從過去開始、且直到現在仍持續中的事

■ 我從小就離鄉背井。（單元 003）
I [have been living] away from my hometown ever since I was young.
＊「小時候開始」（從過去開始）就離開家鄉，直到現在仍然如此。

■ 我來公司五年了。（單元 020）
I [have been working] with this company for five years.
＊「五年前開始」（從過去開始）在這間公司上班，直到現在仍在這間公司。

■ 我和男朋友交往五年。（單元 048）
My boyfriend and I [have been dating] each other for five years.
＊「五年前開始」（從過去開始）交往，直到現在仍持續交往中。

（2）描述＆詢問：現階段持續發生的事

■ 最近看起來氣色很好喔！（單元 055）
[You've been looking] good these days!
＊「最近看來氣色很好」指「現階段、最近這一段時間，氣色都持續很好」。

■ 他最近常常請假。（單元 134）
Lately he [has been asking] for a lot of time off.
＊「最近常請假」指「現階段、最近這一段時間，都持續常請假」。

■ 最近睡得好嗎？（單元 152）
[Have] you [been sleeping] well lately?
＊「最近⋯嗎」意即詢問對方「現階段、最近這一段時間，都持續⋯嗎」。

特別補充 —— 英語時態用法說明

5 現在進行式 和會話的關係

使用型態： be 動詞現在式 + 動詞-ing 型態

（1）描述＆詢問：說話當下正在做的事

■ 我在想這麼做是不是比較好？（單元 075）

I am considering whether this is a better way to do it.

＊「說話當下正在想…」屬於「說話當下正在做的事」。

（2）描述＆詢問：現階段發生的事

■ 我努力減少臉上細紋。（單元 026）

I am trying to reduce my facial wrinkles.

＊「現階段正在努力於…」屬於「現階段發生的事」。

（3）描述＆詢問：現階段逐漸變化的事

■ 我的女友越來越任性。（單元 067）

My girlfriend is getting more and more wild.

＊「以前不是這樣」，但「現階段卻變成…」，屬於「現階段逐漸變化的事」。
＊ 此用法經常使用「get 或 become＋比較級」，例如「getting more and more」。

（4）描述＆詢問：現階段經常發生、且令人厭惡的事

■ 你總是給我惹麻煩。（單元 083）

You are always making trouble for me.

＊「現階段經常…，且令人感到厭惡」。此用法經常搭配「always」。

（5）描述＆詢問：已排定時程的個人未來計畫

■ 我今年年底要結婚。（單元 009）

I am getting married toward the end of this year.

＊「我已排定年底要結婚」屬於「已排定時程的個人未來計畫」。

特別補充 —— 英語時態用法說明

6 　過去進行式　 和會話的關係

使用型態：　 be 動詞過去式 　 + 　 動詞-ing 型態

描述 & 詢問：過去的當下正在做的事

■ 買的時候就已經說了「貨出概不退換」。（單元 120）

When you 　 were buying 　 it, we told you that it couldn't be returned.

＊「當你在買的時候，我說…」指「過去的當下你正在買，我說…」。

■ 吉米有說找我什麼事嗎？（單元 132）

Did Jimmy say why he 　 was calling 　 me?

＊「吉米找我的時候」（過去的當下）「他是否正在說…嗎」（詢問當下
正在做的事）。

特別補充 —— 英語時態用法說明

7　未來簡單式 ❶　和會話的關係

使用型態：　助動詞 will　＋　動詞原形

（1）描述＆詢問：在未來將發生的事

■ 我的父母親希望我趕快結婚。（單元 046）
My parents hope that I　will get　married soon.
*「目前」我還沒結婚，父母親希望「在未來我將趕快結婚」。

（2）描述＆詢問：有意願做的事

■ 我一定會報答你。（單元 079）
I　will　definitely　pay　you back.
*「我一定會…」表示「我有意願…」。

（3）描述＆詢問：根據直覺預測未來發生的事

■ 你這樣會累出病來的。（單元 072）
You　will wear　yourself out and get sick.
* 未必有明確證據，根據自己的經驗或直覺預測，未來可能會累出病來。

（4）描述＆詢問：某人經常性的習慣

■ 有時候我到便利商店買午餐。（單元 038）
Sometimes I　will go　to the convenience store to buy lunch.
* 可以用「現在簡單式」表示「經常如此的事」。但如果某種行為屬於「某人經常性的習慣」，就適合使用「未來簡單式」。
* 例如上方句子即表示「有時候到…買午餐」是「某人經常性的習慣」。

特別補充 —— 英語時態用法說明

8 未來簡單式 ❷ 和會話的關係

使用型態： be 動詞 ＋ going to ＋ 動詞原形

（1）描述＆詢問：未排時程、但預定要做的事

■ 我很多同事最近要離職。（單元 051）
Many of my colleagues are going to quit .
＊沒有排定時程，但「很多同事預定要離職」。

■ 我老了一定會去拉皮。（單元 146）
I'm going to tighten my skin when I get older.
＊沒有排定時程，但「老了要去拉皮」。

■ 接下來幾天是你負責接待我嗎？（單元 136）
Are you going to be my guide for the next few days?
＊沒有排定時程，詢問「接下來幾天你預定要做…嗎」。

（2）描述＆詢問：根據現況預測未來發生的事

■ 再說下去我就要睡著了。（單元 064）
I'm going to fall asleep if you keep talking.
＊根據「現況」（目前我正在聽你說話的狀況）預測，如果你繼續說下去，
　未來我將會睡著。

特別推薦 —— 行動學習 APP

■ 可累計與保存個人學習記錄的【行動學習 APP】

將書籍內容，結合「文字、音訊、個人學習記錄」等功能，規劃具體、便捷的學習動線，整合設計為『可累計與保存個人學習記錄的行動英語會話單字教室』。讓消費者享受科技帶來的學習便利、流暢、與舒適。全書 8 大領域分為 8 篇，透過三支 APP 呈現：

・（1）【自我介紹篇 APP】：收錄書籍「第 1 篇」「第 2 篇」
・（2）【生活表達篇 APP】：收錄書籍「第 3 篇」「第 4 篇」「第 5 篇」
・（3）【溝通聊天篇 APP】：收錄書籍「第 6 篇」「第 7 篇」「第 8 篇」

■【行動學習 APP】功能介紹（1）：學習路徑便捷順暢

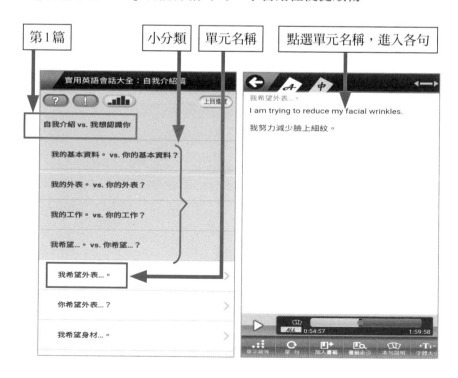

■【行動學習 APP】功能介紹（2）：可切換「四類單字級等顯示」

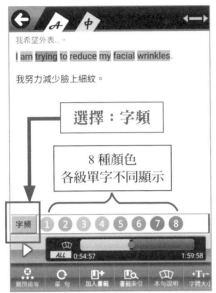

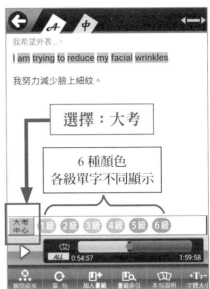

■【行動學習 APP】功能介紹（3）：可進行「個人化學習設定」

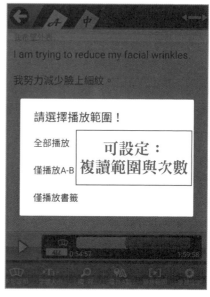

久按會話句單字，可查詢單字

收錄文法、時態、片語等補充

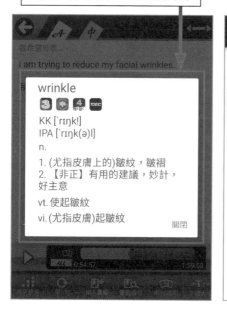

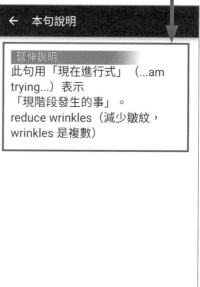

■【行動學習 APP】功能介紹（4）：具備「書籤」及「關鍵字搜尋」

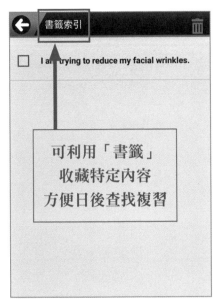

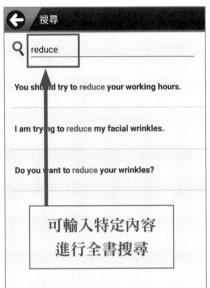

■【行動學習 APP】購買＆免費試閱說明

※ 　步驟 1

掃描下方 QR code 安裝【語言導航家 APP】。

語言導航家 APP 圖示　　　　　　iOS　　　　　　Android OS

※〔裝置版本需求〕：iOS 9.0（含）以上／Android OS 5.0（含）以上。

※ 步驟 2 ── 從【語言導航家 APP】搜尋「實用英語會話大全」

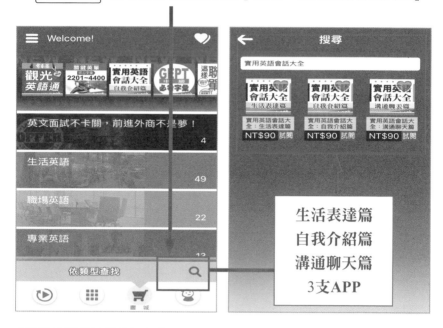

可選擇【購買】或【免費試閱】

從書櫃查看【購買或試閱】的APP

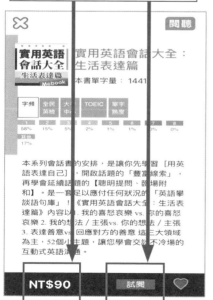

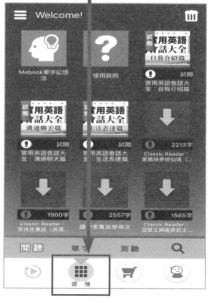

不論「付費版」或「免費試閱版」，只要登入會員，均能使用：

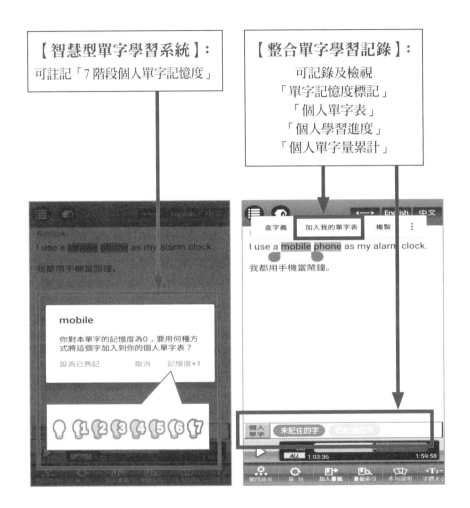

・【學習功能完備】：可根據自己的學習節奏與程度，進行個人化設定。

・【手機／平板閱讀模式】：提供不同載具最佳閱讀體驗。可離線使用。

・【字體】：可依需求調整字體大小。

目錄

特別補充 —— 英語時態用法說明

8 大類，158 種主題會話　　　　　　（下頁起）

1 自我介紹 vs. 我想認識你

2 我的日常生活 vs. 你的日常生活

3　我的喜怒哀樂 vs. 你的喜怒哀樂

4 我的想法／主張 vs. 你的想法／主張

5　表達善意 vs. 回應對方的善意

6 出國旅遊 vs. 聽懂外國人說什麼

7 辦公室英語 vs. 和同事&客戶溝通

8　開啟聊天話題 vs. 如何讓話題持續

001　我的名字。

🔊 MP3　001-01　❶～⓱

❶	我叫凱蘿・陳。	My name is Carol Chen. = I am Carol Chen.
❷	我姓林。	My last name is Lin. = My surname is Lin. = My family name is Lin. * **last name = surname = family name**（姓氏）
❸	你可以叫我湯姆。	You can call me Tom.
❹	家人暱稱我為「糖果」。	My family calls me Candy.
❺	朋友都叫我「小貓」。	All my friends call me Kitty.
❻	我沒有英文名字。	I don't have an English name.
❼	我的英文名字是老師取的。	My English name was given to me by my teacher. * 名字＋**was given to me by**＋某人 　（某人幫我取名字）
❽	同事習慣叫我的英文名字—詹姆斯。	My colleagues usually call me by my English name—James.
❾	我不喜歡我的綽號。	I don't like my nickname.
❿	我的名字常被唸錯。	People often pronounce my name wrong. = People often say my name incorrectly.
⓫	有一個朋友和我同名。	One of my friends has the same name as me. * **A has the same name as B**（A 和 B 同名）
⓬	我的名字是爺爺取的。	My name was given to me by my grandfather.
⓭	我的名字是算命來的。	My name was chosen by a fortune teller. * **be chosen by**＋某人（被某人選擇） * **fortune teller**（算命師）
⓮	我的名字的涵意是「勇敢」。	My name means "brave."
⓯	我的名字很大眾化。	My name is quite common.
⓰	我很想改名字。	I'd really like to change my name. * **would like to**（想要）
⓱	我非常喜歡我的名字。	I like my name very much.

	單字	音標	詞性	意義	字頻	大考	英檢	多益
❶	name	[nem]	n.	名字	1	1	初級	◎
❷	last	[læst]	adj.	最後的、姓的	1	1	初級	◎
	surname	[`sɜ,nem]	n.	姓氏	6			
	family	[`fæməlɪ]	n.	家庭	1	1	初級	
❸	call	[kɔl]	v.	稱呼	1	1	初級	◎
❺	all	[ɔl]	adj.	所有的	1	1	初級	
	friend	[frɛnd]	n.	朋友	1	1	初級	
❻	have	[hæv]	v.	有	1	1	初級	
	English	[`ɪŋglɪʃ]	adj.	英文的	1	1	初級	
❼	given	[`gɪvən]	p.p.	give（給）過去分詞	2	1	中高	◎
	teacher	[`titʃɚ]	n.	老師	1	1	初級	
❽	colleague	[`kɑlig]	n.	同事	1	5	中級	◎
	usually	[`juʒuəlɪ]	adv.	經常	1		初級	◎
❾	like	[laɪk]	v.	喜歡/想要	1	1	初級	
	nickname	[`nɪk.nem]	n.	綽號	3	3	中級	
❿	people	[`pipl]	n.	person（人）複數	1	1	初級	
	often	[`ɔfən]	adv.	常常	1	1	初級	
	pronounce	[prə`naʊns]	v.	發音	2	2	初級	
	wrong	[rɔŋ]	adv.	錯誤地	1	1	初級	◎
	say	[se]	v.	說、唸	1		初級	
	incorrectly	[,ɪnkə`rɛktlɪ]	adv.	不正確地	5			
⓫	one	[wʌn]	pron.	一個人	1	1	初級	
	same	[sem]	adj.	相同的	1	1	初級	
⓬	grandfather	[`grænd.fɑðɚ]	n.	祖父	2	1	初級	
⓭	chosen	[`tʃozn]	p.p.	choose（選擇）過去分詞	4	2	初級	◎
	fortune	[`fɔrtʃən]	n.	時運、命運	1	4	中級	◎
	teller	[`tɛlɚ]	n.	講述者	4	5	中高	◎
⓮	mean	[min]	v.	表示…意思	1	2	初級	◎
	brave	[brev]	adj.	勇敢的	2	1	初級	
⓯	quite	[kwaɪt]	adv.	相當地	1	1	初級	
	common	[`kɑmən]	adj.	大眾化的	1	1	初級	
⓰	really	[`rɪəlɪ]	adv.	很	1		初級	
	change	[tʃendʒ]	v.	改、換	1	2	初級	◎
⓱	very	[`vɛrɪ]	adv.	十分	1	1	初級	
	much	[mʌtʃ]	adv.	非常	1	1	初級	

※「紅字單字」於本單元多句出現，「單字級等分析」僅列在「首次出現句」。

001 你的名字。

❶	你貴姓？	What is your last name? = What is your surname? = What is your family name?
❷	你叫什麼名字？	What is your name?
❸	我該怎麼稱呼你？	What should I call you?
❹	請問你的名字怎麼拼？	May I ask how to spell your name?
❺	你有英文名字嗎？	Do you have an English name?
❻	你有綽號嗎？	Do you have a nickname?
❼	我可以叫你吉米嗎？	Can I call you Jimmy?
❽	請問你是林先生嗎？	Are you Mr. Lin?
❾	你的家人怎麼叫你？	What does your family call you?
❿	你的名字是誰取的？	Who gave you your name?
⓫	你的名字有特殊的涵意嗎？	Does your name have any special meaning?
⓬	你喜歡你的名字嗎？	Do you like your name?
⓭	你想改名字嗎？	Do you want to change your name? * **change one's name**（改名）
⓮	大家都會唸你的名字嗎？	Is everyone able to pronounce your name? * **be able to**＋動詞原形（能夠）
⓯	你知道有任何人跟你同名嗎？	Do you know anyone with the same name as you? * **as**＋某人（如同某人）
⓰	你的名字真好聽。	Your name sounds nice.
⓱	你的名字非常特別。	Your name is very special. = You have a very special name
⓲	你和我的朋友同名。	You have the same name as my friend.

	單字	音標	詞性	意義	字頻	大考	英檢	多益
❶	last	[læst]	adj.	最後的、姓的	1	1	初級	
	name	[nem]	n.	名字	1	1	初級	◎
	surname	[ˋsɝ͵nem]	n.	姓氏	6			
	family	[ˋfæməlɪ]	n.	家庭	1	1	初級	
❸	call	[kɔl]	v.	稱呼	1	1	初級	◎
❹	ask	[æsk]	v.	詢問	1	1	初級	
	spell	[spɛl]	v.	拼字	2	1	初級	◎
❺	have	[hæv]	v.	有	1	1	初級	
	English	[ˋɪŋglɪʃ]	adj.	英文的	1	1	初級	
❻	nickname	[ˋnɪk͵nem]	n.	綽號	3	3	中級	
❽	Mr.	[ˋmɪstɚ]	n.	先生		1	初級	
❿	gave	[gev]	p.t.	give（給）過去式	1	1	初級	
⓫	any	[ˋɛnɪ]	adj.	任何的	1	1	初級	
	special	[ˋspɛʃəl]	adj.	特別的	1	1	初級	◎
	meaning	[ˋminɪŋ]	n.	意義	1	2	初級	◎
⓬	like	[laɪk]	v.	喜歡	1	1	初級	
⓭	want	[wɑnt]	v.	想要	1	1	初級	
	change	[tʃendʒ]	v.	改、換	1	2	初級	
⓮	everyone	[ˋɛvrɪ͵wʌn]	pron.	每個人、大家	1		初級	
	able	[ˋebl̩]	adj.	能夠的	1	1	初級	◎
	pronounce	[prəˋnaʊns]	v.	發音	2	2	初級	
⓯	know	[no]	v.	知道	1	1	初級	◎
	anyone	[ˋɛnɪ͵wʌn]	pron.	任何人	1	2	初級	
	same	[sem]	adj.	相同的	1	1	初級	
⓰	sound	[saʊnd]	v.	聽起來	1	1	初級	◎
	nice	[naɪs]	adj.	好的	1	1	初級	
⓱	very	[ˋvɛrɪ]	adv.	十分	1	1	初級	
⓲	friend	[frɛnd]	n.	朋友	1	1	初級	

※「紅字單字」於本單元多句出現，「單字級等分析」僅列在「首次出現句」。

🔊 MP3 002-01 ❶～❻

❶	我今年 25 歲。	I am twenty-five years old this year.
❷	我未滿 18 歲。	I am not yet eighteen years old. * be not yet ＋ 年齡（未滿…歲）
❸	我快 50 歲了。	I am almost fifty years old. * be almost ＋ 年齡（快要…歲）
❹	我 30 多歲。	I am thirty-something years old. ＝ I am in my thirties. * be ＋ 10、20、30、40、… 90-something years old ＝ be in one's ＋ 該數字的複數型態（在該數字的年齡層）
❺	我剛過 40 歲的生日。	I just had my fortieth birthday.
❻	我屬羊。	I was born in the Year of the Goat.
❼	我和你同年。	I was born in the same year as you.
❽	我生於 1980 年。	I was born in 1980.
❾	我同事都比我年輕。	All my colleagues are younger than me.
❿	我跟我妹妹相差 10 歲。	There is a ten-year age difference between my younger sister and me. * a ten-year age difference（相差 10 歲）
⓫	我比我哥哥小 3 歲。	I am three years younger than my older brother.
⓬	我早過了適婚年齡。	I have already passed the age for marrying. ＝ I'm too old to get married. * the age for marrying（適婚年齡）
⓭	我年紀不小了。	I am not young anymore.
⓮	我看起來比實際年齡年輕。	I look younger than my actual age. * actual age（實際年齡）
⓯	年齡是女人的祕密。	Age is a woman's secret. ＝ A woman's age is her secret.
⓰	我討厭人家問我年齡。	I hate it when people ask me my age. ＝ I am not very comfortable when people ask me my age. * 第二句是比較婉轉的說法

單字級等分析

	單字	音標	詞性	意義	字頻	大考	英檢	多益
❶	twenty-five	[ˌtwɛntɪˋfaɪv]	n.	二十五				
	year	[jɪr]	n.	年	1	1	初級	
	old	[old]	adj.	…歲	1	1	初級	
	this	[ðɪs]	adj.	這個	1	1	初級	
❷	yet	[jɛt]	adv.	還沒	1	1	初級	◎
	eighteen	[ˋeˋtin]	n.	十八	2	1	初級	
❸	almost	[ˋɔl.most]	adv.	幾乎	1	1	初級	
	fifty	[ˋfɪftɪ]	n.	五十	2	1	初級	
❹	thirty-something	[ˋθɝtɪˋsʌmθɪŋ]	n.	三十多歲				
	thirty	[ˋθɝtɪ]	n.	三十	2	1	初級	
❺	just	[dʒʌst]	adv.	剛剛	1	1	初級	
	had	[hæd]	p.t.	have（經歷）過去式	1	1	初級	
	fortieth	[ˋfɔrtɪɪθ]	adj.	四十的				
	birthday	[ˋbɝθ.de]	n.	生日	1		初級	
❻	born	[bɔrn]	p.p.	bear（出生）過去分詞	1	1	初級	
	goat	[got]	n.	山羊	2	1	初級	
❼	same	[sem]	adj.	相同的	1	1	初級	
❾	all	[ɔl]	adj.	所有的	1	1	初級	
	colleague	[ˋkɑlig]	n.	同事	1	5	中級	◎
	younger	[ˋjʌŋgɚ]	adj.	young（年輕的）比較級	1	1	初級	
❿	there	[ðɛr]	adv.	有	1	1	初級	
	ten-year	[ˋtɛnˋjɪr]	adj.	十歲的				
	age	[edʒ]	n.	年齡	1	1	初級	◎
	difference	[ˋdɪfərəns]	n.	差距	1	2	初級	◎
	sister	[ˋsɪstɚ]	n.	姐姐、妹妹	1	1	初級	
⓫	three	[θri]	n.	三	1	1	初級	
	brother	[ˋbrʌðɚ]	n.	哥哥、弟弟	1	1	初級	
⓬	already	[ɔlˋrɛdɪ]	adv.	已經	1	1	初級	◎
	passed	[pæst]	p.p.	pass（超過）過去分詞	1	1	初級	◎
	marrying	[ˋmærɪɪŋ]	n.	marry（結婚）動名詞	1	1	初級	
	too	[tu]	adv.	太過	1	1	初級	
	get	[gɛt]	v.	成為（某種狀態）	1	1	初級	◎
	married	[ˋmærɪd]	p.p.	marry（結婚）過去分詞	1	1	初級	
⓭	young	[jʌŋ]	adj.	年輕的	1	1	初級	
	anymore	[ˋɛnɪmor]	adv.	不再	1		中高	
⓮	look	[lʊk]	v.	看起來	1	1	初級	
	actual	[ˋæktʃʊəl]	adj.	實際的	1	3	中級	◎
⓯	woman	[ˋwʊmən]	n.	女人	1	1	初級	
	secret	[ˋsikrɪt]	n.	秘密	1	2	初級	◎
⓰	hate	[het]	v.	討厭	1	1	初級	
	people	[ˋpipl̩]	n.	person（人）複數	1	1	初級	
	ask	[æsk]	v.	詢問	1	1	初級	
	very	[ˋvɛrɪ]	adv.	非常	1	1	初級	
	comfortable	[ˋkʌmfətəbl̩]	adj.	舒服的	1	2	初級	◎

※「紅字單字」於本單元多句出現，「單字級等分析」僅列在「首次出現句」。

🔵 MP3 002-02 ❶～⓱

❶	你幾歲？	How old are you?
❷	你滿 20 歲了嗎？	Are you twenty years old yet?
❸	你應該快 30 歲了吧？	You'll be in your thirties soon, right?
❹	你的生日是哪一天？	When is your birthday?
❺	你是哪一年出生的？	What year were you born? = What is your birth year?
❻	你的生肖是什麼？	What year were you born in? * be born in＋某年（出生於某年）
❼	你們兩個誰的年齡比較大？	Which of the two of you is older? * Which of＋某幾個人＋is...? （某幾個人之中，哪個是…？）
❽	你跟你弟弟相差幾歲？	How much younger than you is your brother?
❾	你姊姊比你大幾歲？	How much older than you is your sister?
❿	你可以考駕照了嗎？	Are you old enough to take the driver's license exam? * driver's license（駕照） * be old enough to＋動詞原形（年齡足夠做某事）
⓫	我們的年紀差不多。	We are about the same age.
⓬	你看起來總是這麼年輕。	You always look so young.
⓭	你的身材保養得真好！	You are in really good shape. * be in good shape（身材好）
⓮	你跟我姊姊同年。	You and my older sister were born in the same year.
⓯	我們的生日同一天。	We share the same birthday. * share＋形容詞＋名詞（有同樣的…）
⓰	你聽誰的歌長大的？	Whose songs did you listen to while growing up? * while＋動詞-ing（在…的時候） * grow up（成長）
⓱	你看起來好年輕，像一個大學生。	You look so young, like a university student. * like＋某身分（像是某身分的人）

	單字	音標	詞性	意義	字頻	大考	英檢	多益
❶	old	[old]	adj.	…歲	1	1	初級	
❷	twenty	[ˋtwɛntɪ]	n.	二十	1	1	初級	
	year	[jɪr]	n.	歲數	1	1	初級	
	yet	[jɛt]	adv.	還沒	1	1	初級	◎
❸	thirty	[ˋθɝtɪ]	n.	三十	2	1	初級	
	soon	[sun]	adv.	不久	1	1	初級	
	right	[raɪt]	int.	對吧？	1	1	初級	
❹	birthday	[ˋbɝˏde]	n.	生日	1		初級	
❺	born	[bɔrn]	p.p.	bear（出生）過去分詞	1	1	初級	
	birth	[bɝθ]	n.	出生、誕生	1	1	中級	
❼	two	[tu]	pron.	兩個人	1	1	初級	
	older	[ˋoldɚ]	adj.	old（老的）比較級	1	1	初級	
❽	much	[mʌtʃ]	adv.	…得多	1	1	初級	
	younger	[ˋjʌŋgɚ]	adj.	young（年輕的）比較級	1	1	初級	
	brother	[ˋbrʌðɚ]	n.	哥哥、弟弟	1	1	初級	
❾	sister	[ˋsɪstɚ]	n.	姐姐、妹妹	1	1	初級	
❿	enough	[əˋnʌf]	adv.	足夠地	1	1	初級	◎
	take	[tek]	v.	接受	1	1	初級	◎
	driver	[ˋdraɪvɚ]	n.	駕駛	1	1	初級	◎
	license	[ˋlaɪsns]	n.	執照	2	4	中級	◎
	exam	[ɪgˋzæm]	n.	測驗	2	1	初級	
⓫	about	[əˋbaʊt]	adv.	大約	1	1	初級	
	same	[sem]	adj.	相同的	1	1	初級	
	age	[edʒ]	n.	年齡	1	1	初級	◎
⓬	always	[ˋɔlwez]	adv.	總是	1	1	初級	
	look	[lʊk]	v.	看起來	1	1	初級	
	so	[so]	adv.	這麼	1	1	初級	
	young	[jʌŋ]	adj.	年輕的	1	1	初級	
⓭	really	[ˋrɪəlɪ]	adv.	很、十分	1		初級	
	good	[gʊd]	adj.	良好的	1	1	初級	◎
	shape	[ʃep]	n.	身材	1	1	初級	◎
⓯	share	[ʃɛr]	v.	有同樣的…	1	2	初級	◎
⓰	song	[sɔŋ]	n.	歌曲	1	1	初級	
	listen	[ˋlɪsn]	v.	聽	1	1	初級	
	growing	[ˋgroɪŋ]	p.pr.	grow（成長）現在分詞	1	1	初級	◎
	up	[ʌp]	adv.	增長、向上	1	1	初級	
⓱	university	[ˏjunəˋvɝsətɪ]	n.	大學	1	4	初級	
	student	[ˋstjudnt]	n.	學生	1	1	初級	

※「紅字單字」於本單元多句出現，「單字級等分析」僅列在「首次出現句」。

003   我的家鄉。

🔘 MP3 003-01 ❶～⓮

❶	我是台灣人。	I am Taiwanese.
❷	我是高雄人。	I am a Kaohsiung native.
❸	我來自台灣的中部。	I come from central Taiwan. * **come from**＋某處（來自某處）
❹	我在台灣東部出生。	I was born in eastern Taiwan.
❺	我非常愛我的家鄉。	I love my hometown very much.
❻	我的童年在家鄉度過。	I spent my childhood in my hometown. * **spend one's childhood**（度過童年）
❼	我 10 歲就離開家鄉。	I left my hometown when I was ten.
❽	我從小就離鄉背井。	I have been living away from my hometown ever since I was young. * **away from**＋某處（遠離某處） * 此句用「現在完成進行式」（...have been living...）表示「從過去開始、且直到現在仍持續中的事」。
❾	我對家鄉沒什麼印象了。	I don't have much of an impression of my hometown. ＝ I only have a vague impression of my hometown. * **not have much of**＋名詞（沒有太多的…）
❿	我常回家鄉探望父母。	I often go back to my hometown to visit my parents. * **visit**＋人／地點（探望某人、拜訪某地點）
⓫	我的家鄉是繁榮的大城市。	My hometown is a prosperous city. * **prosperous**（繁榮的）可替換為： **bustling**（喧鬧的）、**populous**（人口稠密的）
⓬	我的家鄉盛產稻米。	My hometown is rich in rice. * **be rich in**＋某物（盛產某物）
⓭	家鄉永遠是我最眷戀的地方。	I will always be most attached to my hometown. * **be attached to**＋人事物（眷戀某人事物）
⓮	我的家鄉非常美麗。	My hometown is beautiful. * **beautiful**（美麗的）可替換為：backward（落後的）

	單字	音標	詞性	意義	字頻	大考	英檢	多益
❶	Taiwanese	[ˌtaɪwəˈniz]	n.	台灣人	4		初級	
❷	Kaohsiung	[ˈkauˈʃjuŋ]	n.	高雄			初級	
	native	[ˈnetɪv]	n.	本地人	1	3	中級	◎
❸	come	[kʌm]	v.	來自	1	1	初級	
	central	[ˈsɛntrəl]	adj.	中部的	1	2	初級	◎
	Taiwan	[ˈtaɪˈwɑn]	n.	台灣			初級	
❹	born	[bɔrn]	p.p.	bear（出生）過去分詞	1	1	初級	
	eastern	[ˈistən]	adj.	東部的	1	2	初級	
❺	love	[lʌv]	v.	喜愛	1	1	初級	
	hometown	[ˈhomˈtaun]	n.	家鄉	2	3	中高	
	very	[ˈvɛrɪ]	adv.	非常	1	1	初級	
	much	[mʌtʃ]	adv.	很	1	1	初級	
❻	spent	[spɛnt]	p.t.	spend（度過）過去式	6	1	初級	◎
	childhood	[ˈtʃaɪl.hud]	n.	童年	1	3	初級	
❼	left	[lɛft]	p.t.	leave（離開）過去式	1	1	初級	
	ten	[tɛn]	n.	十	1	1	初級	
❽	living	[ˈlɪvɪŋ]	p.pr.	live（居住）現在分詞	1	1	中高	
	away	[əˈwe]	adv.	離開	1	1	初級	
	ever	[ˈɛvə]	adv.	從來	1	1	初級	
	young	[jʌŋ]	adj.	年輕的	1	1	初級	
❾	have	[hæv]	v.	擁有	1	1	初級	
	impression	[ɪmˈprɛʃən]	n.	印象	1	4	中級	◎
	only	[ˈonlɪ]	adv.	只有	1	1	初級	
	vague	[veg]	adj.	模糊的	2	5	中級	◎
❿	often	[ˈɔfən]	adv.	常常	1	1	初級	
	go	[go]	v.	去	1	1	初級	
	back	[bæk]	adv.	回原處	1	1	初級	◎
	visit	[ˈvɪzɪt]	v.	拜訪	1	1	初級	◎
	parents	[ˈpɛrənts]	n.	parent（雙親）複數	2	1		
⓫	prosperous	[ˈprɑspərəs]	adj.	繁榮的	3	4	中級	◎
	city	[ˈsɪtɪ]	n.	城市	1	1	初級	
⓬	rich	[rɪtʃ]	adj.	富於…的	1	1	初級	
	rice	[raɪs]	n.	稻米	1	1	初級	
⓭	always	[ˈɔlwez]	adv.	總是	1	1	初級	
	most	[most]	adv.	最	1	1	初級	
	attached	[əˈtætʃt]	p.p.	attach（眷戀）過去分詞	6	4	中高	◎
⓮	beautiful	[ˈbjutəfəl]	adj.	美麗的	1	1	初級	

※「紅字單字」於本單元多句出現，「單字級等分析」僅列在「首次出現句」。

003　你的家鄉？

❶	你的家鄉在哪裡？	Where is your hometown?
❷	你來自哪裡？	Where are you from?
❸	你在哪裡出生？	Where were you born?
❹	你想念家鄉嗎？	Do you miss your hometown?
❺	要不要聊聊你的家鄉？	Do you want to talk about your hometown? ＝ Would you like to talk about your hometown?
❻	你的家鄉有什麼特產？	What is the signature product of your hometown? * **signature product**（特產）
❼	你的家鄉以什麼聞名？	What is your hometown famous for? * **be famous for**＋某物（以某物聞名）
❽	你幾歲離開家鄉的？	How old were you when you left your hometown?
❾	你想回家鄉看看嗎？	Would you like to visit your hometown? * **would like to**（想要）
❿	你的家鄉近來有什麼改變嗎？	Has your hometown experienced any changes recently? * 此句用「現在完成式問句」（**Has...experienced...?**）表示「從過去到現在是否發生過、經歷過某事」。
⓫	你常回家鄉嗎？	Do you return to your hometown often?
⓬	你幾年沒回家鄉了？	How long has it been since you last returned to your hometown? * **How long has it been since**＋子句（自從…已經有多久）
⓭	家鄉還有親人嗎？	Do you have any relatives left in your hometown?
⓮	你打算返鄉定居嗎？	Do you plan to return to and settle down in your hometown? * **settle down**（定居）

	單字	音標	詞性	意義	字頻	大考	英檢	多益
❶	hometown	[ˈhomˌtaʊn]	n.	家鄉	2	3	中高	
❸	born	[bɔrn]	p.p.	bear（出生）過去分詞	1	1	初級	
❹	miss	[mɪs]	v.	想念	1	1	初級	
❺	want	[wɑnt]	v.	想要	1	1	初級	◎
	talk	[tɔk]	v.	談論	1	1	初級	◎
	like	[laɪk]	v.	想要	1	1	初級	
❻	signature	[ˈsɪgnətʃɚ]	n.	特徵	2	4	中級	◎
	product	[ˈprɑdəkt]	n.	產品	1	3	初級	◎
❼	famous	[ˈfeməs]	adj.	有名的	1	2	初級	◎
❽	old	[old]	adj.	…歲	1	1	初級	
	left	[lɛft]	p.t.	leave（離開）過去式	1	1	初級	
❾	visit	[ˈvɪzɪt]	v.	拜訪	1	1	初級	◎
❿	experienced	[ɪkˈspɪrɪənst]	p.p.	experience（經歷）過去分詞	1	2	中高	
	any	[ˈɛnɪ]	adj.	任何的	1	1	初級	
	change	[tʃendʒ]	n.	改變	1	2	初級	◎
	recently	[ˈrisntlɪ]	adv.	最近	1		初級	
⓫	return	[rɪˈtɜn]	v.	返回	1	1	初級	◎
	often	[ˈɔfən]	adv.	常常	1	1	初級	
⓬	long	[lɔŋ]	adv.	多久	1	1	初級	
	last	[læst]	adv.	上一次、最近一次	1	1	初級	◎
	returned	[rɪˈtɜnd]	p.t.	return（返回）過去式	1	1	初級	◎
⓭	have	[hæv]	v.	擁有	1	1	初級	
	relative	[ˈrɛlətɪv]	n.	親戚	1	4	初級	◎
	left	[lɛft]	p.p.	leave（留下）過去分詞	1	1	初級	
⓮	plan	[plæn]	v.	計畫	1	1	初級	◎
	settle	[ˈsɛtl]	v.	定居	1	2	中級	◎
	down	[daʊn]	adv.	定下	1	1	初級	

※「紅字單字」於本單元多句出現，「單字級等分析」僅列在「首次出現句」。

004　我的家。

❶	我住在台北市。	I live in Taipei City. * live in＋城市（住在某城市）
❷	我家總共 4 個人。	There are four people in my family.
❸	我是單親家庭的孩子。	I grew up in a single-parent family. * grow up（成長）
❹	我是獨生子。	I am the only son in my family. * the only son（獨生子） * the only daughter（獨生女）
❺	我們家人感情很好。	My family is close.
❻	我排行老大。	I am the oldest child in my family. * the oldest child（老大） * the second child（老二）
❼	我住公寓。	I live in an apartment. * live in＋房屋類型（住在某種房子）
❽	我們家三代同堂。	My family has three generations living together. * three generations living together（三代同堂） * live together（居住在一起）
❾	我貸款買房子。	I bought a house with a loan. * with a loan（用貸款的方式）
❿	我跟父母同住。	I live with my parents. * live with＋某人（和某人住一起）
⓫	我和妹妹共用房間。	I share a room with my sister.
⓬	我一個人租房子住。	I rent a house and live alone.
⓭	我們家是雙薪家庭。	Our family is a double-income household. * double-income household（雙薪家庭）
⓮	我 3 年前搬到這裡。	I moved here three years ago.
⓯	我家樓下是 7-11。	Downstairs from my house is a 7-11. * downstairs from＋地點（某地點的樓下）
⓰	我家靠近捷運站。	My house is near the MRT station.
⓱	我住在郊區。	I live in the suburbs.

	單字	音標	詞性	意義	字頻	大考	英檢	多益
❶	live	[lɪv]	v.	居住	1	1	初級	
	Taipei	[ˋtaɪˋpe]	n.	台北			初級	
	city	[ˋsɪtɪ]	n.	城市	1	1	初級	◎
❷	there	[ðɛr]	adv.	有…	1	1	初級	
	four	[for]	n.	四	1	1	初級	
	people	[ˋpipḷ]	n.	person（人）複數	1	1	初級	
	family	[ˋfæməlɪ]	n.	家庭	1	1	初級	
❸	grew	[gru]	p.t.	grow（成長）過去式	1	1	初級	◎
	up	[ʌp]	adv.	增長、向上	1	1	初級	
	single-parent	[ˋsɪŋgḷˋpɛrənt]	adj.	單親的	6			
❹	only	[ˋonlɪ]	adj.	唯一的	1	1	初級	
	son	[sʌn]	n.	兒子	1	1	初級	
❺	close	[klos]	adj.	感情好的	1	1	初級	◎
❻	oldest	[ˋoldɪst]	adj.	old（老的）最高級	1	1	初級	
	child	[tʃaɪld]	n.	小孩	1	1	初級	
❼	apartment	[əˋpɑrtmənt]	n.	公寓	1	2	初級	◎
❽	have	[hæv]	v.	擁有	1	1	初級	
	three	[θri]	n.	三	1	1	初級	
	generation	[ˌdʒɛnəˋreʃən]	n.	世代	1	4	初級	◎
	living	[ˋlɪvɪŋ]	p.pr.	live（居住）現在分詞	1	1	中高	
	together	[təˋgɛðɚ]	adv.	在一起	1	1	初級	
❾	bought	[bɔt]	p.t.	buy（購買）過去式	1	1	初級	
	house	[haʊs]	n.	房子	1	1	初級	◎
	loan	[lon]	n.	貸款	1	4	中級	◎
❿	parents	[ˋpɛrənts]	n.	parent（雙親）複數	2	1		
⓫	share	[ʃɛr]	v.	共用	1	2	初級	◎
	room	[rum]	n.	房間	1	1	初級	
	sister	[ˋsɪstɚ]	n.	姐姐、妹妹	1	1	初級	
⓬	rent	[rɛnt]	v.	承租	2	3	初級	◎
	alone	[əˋlon]	adv.	單獨地	1	1	初級	
⓭	double-income	[ˋdʌbḷˋɪnˏkʌm]	adj.	雙薪的				
	household	[ˋhaʊsˏhold]	n.	家庭	1	4	中級	◎
⓮	moved	[muvd]	p.t.	move（搬家）過去式	1	1	初級	◎
	here	[hɪr]	adv.	這裡	1	1	初級	
	year	[jɪr]	n.	年	1	1	初級	
	ago	[əˋgo]	adv.	在…以前	1	1	初級	
⓯	downstairs	[ˌdaʊnˋstɛrz]	adv.	…的樓下	2	1	初級	◎
⓰	MRT	[ˋɛmˋɑrˋti]	n.	Mass Rapid Transit（捷運）縮寫		2	初級	◎
	station	[ˋsteʃən]	n.	車站	1	1	初級	◎
⓱	suburb	[ˋsʌbɚb]	n.	郊區	2	3	中級	◎

※「紅字單字」於本單元多句出現，「單字級等分析」僅列在「首次出現句」。

MP3 004-02 ❶～❻

❶	你有兄弟姊妹嗎？	Do you have any brothers or sisters?
❷	你們家有幾個人？	How many people are in your family? * **How many people are in…?** （…有多少人？）
❸	你和家人感情好嗎？	Do you get along well with your family? * **get along well with**＋某人 （和某人相處融洽）
❹	你住哪裡？	Where do you live?
❺	你一個人住嗎？	Do you live alone?
❻	你的房子是買的嗎？	Did you buy your house?
❼	你租房子嗎？	Do you rent a house?
❽	你們家是單親家庭嗎？	Do you come from a single-parent family? * **single-parent family**（單親家庭）
❾	你住的地方有多大？	How big is the place you live in? * **How big is**＋地點？ （某地點有多大？）
❿	你住公寓嗎？還是大廈？	Do you live in an apartment or a large building? * **large building**（大廈）
⓫	你跟家人住一起嗎？	Do you live with your family?
⓬	你從小住在這裡嗎？	Have you lived here since you were young? * 此句用「現在完成式問句」（**Have...lived...?**） 表示「從過去到現在是否持續某事」。
⓭	你喜歡住郊區?還是住市區?	Do you like to live in the suburbs or the city?
⓮	你搬過家嗎？	Have you ever moved house? * **Have you ever**＋過去分詞？ （你是否有…經驗）
⓯	你有自己的房間嗎？	Do you have your own room?
⓰	你家靠近捷運站嗎？	Is your house near an MRT station?

	單字	音標	詞性	意義	字頻	大考	英檢	多益
❶	have	[hæv]	v.	擁有	1	1	初級	
	any	[ˋɛnɪ]	adj.	任何的	1	1	初級	
	brother	[ˋbrʌðɚ]	n.	哥哥、弟弟	1	1	初級	
	sister	[ˋsɪstɚ]	n.	姐姐、妹妹	1	1	初級	
❷	many	[ˋmɛnɪ]	adj.	許多的	1	1	初級	
	people	[ˋpipl̩]	n.	person（人）複數	1	1	初級	
	family	[ˋfæməlɪ]	n.	家庭	1	1	初級	
❸	get	[gɛt]	v.	相處	1	1	初級	◎
	along	[əˋlɔŋ]	adv.	一起	1	1	初級	
	well	[wɛl]	adv.	融洽地	1	1	初級	◎
❹	live	[lɪv]	v.	居住	1	1	初級	
❺	alone	[əˋlon]	adv.	單獨地	1	1	初級	
❻	buy	[baɪ]	v.	購買	1	1	初級	
	house	[haʊs]	n.	房子	1	1	初級	◎
❼	rent	[rɛnt]	v.	承租	2	3	初級	◎
❽	come	[kʌm]	v.	來自	1	1	初級	
	single-parent	[ˋsɪŋgl̩ˋpɛrənt]	adj.	單親的	6			
❾	big	[bɪg]	adj.	大的	1	1	初級	
	place	[ples]	n.	地方	1	1	初級	◎
❿	apartment	[əˋpɑrtmənt]	n.	公寓	1	2	初級	◎
	large	[lɑrdʒ]	adj.	高大的	1	1	初級	◎
	building	[ˋbɪldɪŋ]	n.	建築物	1	1	初級	◎
⓬	lived	[lɪvd]	p.p.	live（居住）過去分詞	1	1	初級	
	here	[hɪr]	adv.	這裡	1	1	初級	
	young	[jʌŋ]	adj.	年輕的	1	1	初級	
⓭	like	[laɪk]	v.	喜歡	1	1	初級	
	suburb	[ˋsʌbɝb]	n.	郊區	2	3	中級	◎
	city	[ˋsɪtɪ]	n.	市區	1	1	初級	◎
⓮	ever	[ˋɛvɚ]	adv.	曾經	1	1	初級	
	moved	[muvd]	p.p.	move（搬家）過去分詞	1	1	初級	◎
⓯	own	[on]	adj.	自己的	1	1	初級	◎
	room	[rum]	n.	房間	1	1	初級	
⓰	MRT	[ˋɛmˋɑrˋti]	n.	Mass Rapid Transit（捷運）縮寫		2	初級	◎
	station	[ˋsteʃən]	n.	車站	1	1	初級	◎

※「紅字單字」於本單元多句出現，「單字級等分析」僅列在「首次出現句」。

005 　我的個性。

❶	我活潑外向。	I am a lively and outgoing person.
❷	我害羞內向。	I am a shy and introverted person.
❸	我話不多。	I'm not a talkative person.
❹	我喜歡交朋友。	I like to make friends. * make friends（結交朋友）
❺	我很有正義感。	I have a strong sense of justice. * have a strong sense of＋名詞（有強烈的…意識） * sense of justice（正義感）
❻	我勇於接受挑戰。	I have the courage to take on a challenge. * take on a challenge（接受挑戰）
❼	我喜歡幫助別人。	I like to help others. * help others（幫助別人）
❽	我天性樂觀。	I am naturally optimistic. * I am naturally＋形容詞（我天生具有…特性） * pessimistic（悲觀的）
❾	我個性隨和。	I have an easygoing personality.
❿	我脾氣很好。	I have a good temper. * have a good temper（脾氣好） * have a bad temper（脾氣不好）
⓫	我害怕孤獨。	I am afraid of loneliness. * be afraid of＋名詞（害怕…）
⓬	我幽默愛搞笑。	I am funny and like to joke around. * joke around（搞笑）
⓭	我容易緊張。	I get nervous easily. * get nervous（緊張）
⓮	我有一點固執。	I am a bit of a stubborn person. * a bit of a＋形容詞＋名詞（程度上稍微有點…） * stubborn person（固執的人）
⓯	我是急性子。	I am a rash person.

	單字	音標	詞性	意義	字頻	大考	英檢	多益
❶	lively	[ˋlaɪvlɪ]	adj.	活潑的	3	3	中級	
	outgoing	[ˋaʊtˏgoɪŋ]	adj.	外向的	4	5	中高	
	person	[ˋpɝsn]	n.	人	1	1	初級	
❷	shy	[ʃaɪ]	adj.	害羞的	2	1	初級	
	introverted	[ˋɪntrəˏvɝtɪd]	adj.	內向安靜的				
❸	talkative	[ˋtɔkətɪv]	adj.	話多的	7	2	初級	◎
❹	like	[laɪk]	v.	喜歡	1	1	初級	
	make	[mek]	v.	成為、變成	1	1	初級	
	friend	[frɛnd]	n.	朋友	1	1	初級	
❺	have	[hæv]	v.	擁有	1	1	初級	
	strong	[strɔŋ]	adj.	強烈的	1	1	初級	
	sense	[sɛns]	n.	意識	1	1	初級	◎
	justice	[ˋdʒʌstɪs]	n.	正義	1	3	中級	◎
❻	courage	[ˋkɝɪdʒ]	n.	勇氣	2	2	初級	
	take	[tek]	v.	接受	1	1	初級	
	challenge	[ˋtʃælɪndʒ]	n.	挑戰	1	3	中級	◎
❼	help	[hɛlp]	v.	幫助	1	1	初級	
	other	[ˋʌðə]	pron.	其他人	1	1	初級	
❽	naturally	[ˋnætʃərəlɪ]	adv.	天生地	1		中級	
	optimistic	[ˏɑptəˋmɪstɪk]	adj.	樂觀的	2	3	中高	◎
❾	easygoing	[ˋizɪˏgoɪŋ]	adj.	隨和的	6			
	personality	[ˏpɝsnˋælətɪ]	n.	個性	1	3	中級	
❿	good	[gʊd]	adj.	良好的	1	1	初級	◎
	temper	[ˋtɛmpə]	n.	脾氣	3	3	中級	◎
⓫	afraid	[əˋfred]	adj.	害怕	1	1	初級	
	loneliness	[ˋlonlɪnɪs]	n.	孤獨	3		中級	
⓬	funny	[ˋfʌnɪ]	adj.	搞笑的	1	1	初級	
	joke	[dʒok]	v.	開玩笑	1	1	初級	
	around	[əˋraʊnd]	adv.	四處	1	1	初級	
⓭	get	[gɛt]	v.	變得	1	1	初級	◎
	nervous	[ˋnɝvəs]	adj.	緊張的	1	3	初級	
	easily	[ˋizɪlɪ]	adv.	容易地	1		中級	
⓮	bit	[bɪt]	n.	少許	1	1	初級	
	stubborn	[ˋstʌbən]	adj.	固執的	3	3	中級	◎
⓯	rash	[ræʃ]	adj.	個性急躁的	4	6	中高	◎

※「紅字單字」於本單元多句出現，「單字級等分析」僅列在「首次出現句」。

🔊 MP3 005-02 ❶～❸

❶	你一向這麼樂觀嗎？	Have you always been this optimistic? * 此句用「現在完成式問句」（Have...been...?）表示「從過去到現在是否持續某事」。 * this＋形容詞（這麼的…、如此的…）
❷	你容易緊張嗎？	Do you get nervous easily?
❸	你總是這麼沈默嗎？	Have you always been such a silent person? * such a＋形容詞＋名詞（這麼的…、如此的…） * silent person（安靜的人）
❹	你說話都是這麼直接嗎？	Do you always speak this directly?
❺	你從小就這麼內向嗎？	Have you been this introverted since childhood? * Have you been...since childhood?（你從小就…嗎）
❻	你喜歡結交朋友嗎？	Do you like to make friends?
❼	你擅長交際嗎？	Do you have good communication skills? * communication skills（溝通技巧）
❽	你勇於發表意見嗎？	Do you have the courage to express your opinions? * have the courage to＋動詞原形（勇於做某事） * express one's opinion（發表意見）
❾	你是急性子嗎？	Are you an impatient person? * impatient（個性急躁的） = rash = short-tempered
❿	你覺得自己固執嗎？	Do you think that you are stubborn?
⓫	你喜歡嘗試新事物嗎？	Do you like to try new things?
⓬	你的個性隨和嗎？	Do you have an easygoing personality?
⓭	你害怕面對壓力嗎？	Are you afraid of facing pressure? * be afraid of＋動詞-ing（害怕…） * face pressure（面對壓力）

	單字	音標	詞性	意義	字頻	大考	英檢	多益
❶	always	[ˈɔlwez]	adv.	總是	1	1	初級	
	this	[ðɪs]	adv.	這麼	1	1	初級	
	optimistic	[ˌɑptəˈmɪstɪk]	adj.	樂觀的	2	3	中高	◎
❷	get	[gɛt]	v.	變得	1	1	初級	◎
	nervous	[ˈnɝvəs]	adj.	緊張的	1	3	初級	
	easily	[ˈizɪlɪ]	adv.	容易地	1		中級	
❸	such	[sʌtʃ]	adv.	這麼、如此	1	1	初級	
	silent	[ˈsaɪlənt]	adj.	沉默的	1	2	初級	◎
	person	[ˈpɝsn]	n.	人	1	1	初級	
❹	speak	[spik]	v.	講話	1	1	初級	
	directly	[dəˈrɛktlɪ]	adv.	直截了當地	1	1	中高	◎
❺	introverted	[ˈɪntrəvɝtɪd]	adj.	內向安靜的				
	childhood	[ˈtʃaɪldˌhʊd]	n.	童年	1	3	初級	
❻	like	[laɪk]	v.	喜歡	1	1	初級	
	make	[mek]	v.	成為、變成	1	1	初級	
	friend	[frɛnd]	n.	朋友	1	1	初級	
❼	have	[hæv]	v.	擁有	1	1	初級	
	good	[gʊd]	adj.	良好的	1	1	初級	◎
	communication	[kəˌmjunəˈkeʃən]	n.	溝通	1	4	中級	◎
	skill	[skɪl]	n.	技巧	1	1	初級	◎
❽	courage	[ˈkɝɪdʒ]	n.	勇氣	2	2	初級	
	express	[ɪkˈsprɛs]	v.	表達	1	2	初級	◎
	opinion	[əˈpɪnjən]	n.	意見	1	2	初級	◎
❾	impatient	[ɪmˈpeʃənt]	adj.	個性急躁的	3		中級	◎
❿	think	[θɪŋk]	v.	認為	1	1	初級	
	stubborn	[ˈstʌbən]	adj.	固執的	3	3	中級	◎
⓫	try	[traɪ]	v.	嘗試	1	1	初級	
	new	[nju]	adj.	新的	1	1	初級	
	thing	[θɪŋ]	n.	事物	1	1	初級	
⓬	easygoing	[ˈizɪˌgoɪŋ]	adj.	隨和的	6			
	personality	[ˌpɝsnˈælətɪ]	n.	個性	1	3	中級	
⓭	afraid	[əˈfred]	adj.	害怕的	1	1	初級	
	facing	[ˈfesɪŋ]	n.	face（面對）動名詞	8	1	初級	
	pressure	[ˈprɛʃə]	n.	壓力	1	3	中級	◎

※「紅字單字」於本單元多句出現，「單字級等分析」僅列在「首次出現句」。

MP3 006-01 ❶～❸

❶	我的興趣是聽音樂。	My hobby is listening to music. * **My hobby is** ＋ 動詞-ing （我的興趣是…）
❷	我的興趣是看各種展覽。	My interest is attending various exhibitions. * **My interest is** ＋ 動詞-ing （我的興趣是…）
❸	我很喜歡出國旅行。	I really like to travel abroad.
❹	我習慣每天散步。	Taking a walk is my daily habit. * **Taking a walk is...**（散步是…） * 此句用動名詞（**taking a walk**）當主詞
❺	我習慣假日去戶外走走。	I usually go out during the holidays. * **during** ＋ 時間詞（在…期間）
❻	我習慣睡前看書。	I have the habit of reading before bed. * **before bed**（睡覺之前）
❼	我常常跟朋友看電影。	I often go to the movies with my friends.
❽	我常常跟家人去爬山。	I frequently go hiking with my family.
❾	我超愛講手機。	I love talking on my cell phone. * **love** ＋ 動詞-ing（喜歡…） * **talk on cell phone**（講手機）
❿	我喜歡跟人聊天。	I like to chat with others. * **like to** ＋ 動詞原形（喜歡…）
⓫	我最近迷上網路遊戲。	Lately I've gotten into online gaming. * 此句用「現在完成式」（…**have gotten**…）表示 　「過去某時點發生某事，且結果持續到現在」。 * **get into** ＋ 名詞（沉迷…）
⓬	品嚐美食是我的嗜好之一。	Enjoying gourmet food is one of my hobbies. * **gourmet food**（精緻美食）
⓭	我最大的嗜好是釣魚。	Fishing is my biggest hobby.

單字級等分析

	單字	音標	詞性	意義	字頻	大考	英檢	多益
❶	hobby	[ˋhɑbɪ]	n.	嗜好	3	2	初級	
	listening	[ˋlɪsənɪŋ]	n.	listen（聽）動名詞	3	1	初級	
	music	[ˋmjuzɪk]	n.	音樂	1	1	初級	
❷	interest	[ˋɪntərɪst]	n.	興趣	1	1	初級	◎
	attending	[əˋtɛndɪŋ]	n.	attend（參加）動名詞	1	2	初級	◎
	various	[ˋvɛrɪəs]	adj.	各種的	1	3	中級	◎
	exhibition	[ˌɛksəˋbɪʃən]	n.	展覽	1	3	中級	◎
❸	really	[ˋrɪəlɪ]	adv.	很、十分	1		初級	
	like	[laɪk]	v.	喜歡	1	1	初級	
	travel	[ˋtrævl]	v.	旅遊	1	2	初級	◎
	abroad	[əˋbrɔd]	adv.	國外地	2	2	初級	◎
❹	taking	[ˋtekɪŋ]	n.	take（執行）動名詞	4	1	初級	
	walk	[wɔk]	n.	散步	1	1	初級	
	daily	[ˋdelɪ]	adj.	每日的	1	2	初級	◎
	habit	[ˋhæbɪt]	n.	習慣	1	2	初級	◎
❺	usually	[ˋjuʒʊəlɪ]	adv.	經常	1		初級	◎
	go	[go]	v.	去	1	1	初級	
	out	[aut]	adv.	出外、向外	1	1	初級	
	holiday	[ˋhɑləˌde]	n.	假日	1	1	初級	
❻	have	[hæv]	v.	擁有	1		初級	
	reading	[ˋridɪŋ]	n.	read（閱讀）動名詞	1		中級	
	bed	[bɛd]	n.	就寢時間	1	1	初級	
❼	often	[ˋɔfən]	adv.	常常	1	1	初級	
	movie	[ˋmuvɪ]	n.	電影	1	1	初級	
	friend	[frɛnd]	n.	朋友	1	1	初級	
❽	frequently	[ˋfrikwəntlɪ]	adv.	頻繁地	1			◎
	hiking	[ˋhaɪkɪŋ]	n.	hike（登山）動名詞	5	3	中級	
	family	[ˋfæməlɪ]	n.	家人	1	1	初級	
❾	love	[lʌv]	v.	喜愛	1			
	talking	[ˋtɔkɪŋ]	n.	talk（講話）動名詞	3			
	cell	[sɛl]	adj.	cellular（蜂巢式的）縮寫	1	2	初級	
	phone	[fon]	n.	電話	1	2	初級	◎
❿	chat	[tʃæt]	v.	聊天	2	3	中級	
	other	[ˋʌðɚ]	pron.	其他人	1	1	初級	
⓫	lately	[ˋletlɪ]	adv.	最近	2	4	中級	
	gotten	[ˋgɑtn]	p.p.	get（變得）過去分詞	1	1	初級	◎
	online	[ˋɑnˌlaɪn]	adj.	線上的	1		初級	◎
	gaming	[ˋgemɪŋ]	n.	遊戲	4			
⓬	enjoying	[ɪnˋdʒɔɪɪŋ]	n.	enjoy（品嘗）動名詞	1	2	初級	
	gourmet	[ˋgurme]	n.	美食家	3			◎
	food	[fud]	n.	食物	1	1	初級	◎
	one	[wʌn]	pron.	一個（人或事物）	1	1	初級	
⓭	fishing	[ˋfɪʃɪŋ]	n.	fish（釣魚）動名詞	1	1	中級	
	biggest	[ˋbɪgɪst]	adj.	big（大的）最高級	1	1	初級	

※「紅字單字」於本單元多句出現，「單字級等分析」僅列在「首次出現句」。

🔊　MP3 006-02 ❶～⓯

❶	你有什麼嗜好嗎？	What is your hobby?
❷	你常看電影嗎？	Do you go to the movies frequently? * go to the movies（看電影）
❸	你有看書的習慣嗎？	Do you read regularly? * 動詞原形＋regularly （有規律地做某事）
❹	你常出國旅行嗎？	Do you travel abroad often?
❺	你偏愛哪一類型的電影？	What kind of movies do you prefer? ＝ What kind of movies is your favorite? * What kind of＋人事物 （什麼類型的人事物）
❻	你喜歡看哪一類的書？	What kind of books do you read?
❼	你喜歡看表演嗎？	Do you like to watch performances?
❽	你的嗜好真昂貴。	Your hobby is very expensive.
❾	你喜歡聽哪一種音樂？	What kind of music do you like?
❿	你常聽音樂嗎？	Do you listen to music very often? * listen to music（聽音樂）
⓫	我想你應該有很多CD。	I bet you own a lot of CDs. * I bet＋子句（我敢斷言…、我敢肯定…）
⓬	你喜歡看電視嗎？	Do you like to watch TV?
⓭	你常看哪些電視節目？	What kind of TV shows do you usually watch? * TV show（電視節目）
⓮	你習慣上網聊天嗎？	Do you have the habit of chatting online? * have the habit of＋動詞-ing（習慣…）
⓯	你的嗜好該不會就是吃東西吧？	Eating wouldn't be your only hobby, would it? * wouldn't be... （猜測該不會是…） * would be... （猜測應該是…）

	單字	音標	詞性	意義	字頻	大考	英檢	多益
❶	hobby	[ˋhɑbɪ]	n.	嗜好	3	2	初級	
❷	go	[go]	v.	去	1	1	初級	
	movie	[ˋmuvɪ]	n.	電影	1	1	初級	
	frequently	[ˋfrikwəntlɪ]	adv.	頻繁地	1			◎
❸	read	[rid]	v.	閱讀	1	1	初級	
	regularly	[ˋrɛgjələlɪ]	adv.	規律地	2			◎
❹	travel	[ˋtrævl̩]	v.	旅遊	1	2	初級	
	abroad	[əˋbrɔd]	adv.	國外	2	2	初級	
	often	[ˋɔfən]	adv.	常常	1	1	初級	
❺	kind	[kaɪnd]	n.	種類	1	1	初級	◎
	prefer	[prɪˋfɝ]	v.	偏愛	1	2	初級	
	favorite	[ˋfevərɪt]	adj.	最喜歡的	1	2	初級	
❻	book	[bʊk]	n.	書籍	1	1	初級	◎
❼	like	[laɪk]	v.	喜歡	1	1	初級	
	watch	[wɑtʃ]	v.	觀看	1	1	初級	◎
	performance	[pɚˋfɔrməns]	n.	表演	1	3	中級	
❽	very	[ˋvɛrɪ]	adv.	非常	1	1	初級	
	expensive	[ɪkˋpɛnsɪv]	adj.	昂貴的	1	2	初級	◎
❾	music	[ˋmjuzɪk]	n.	音樂	1	1	初級	
❿	listen	[ˋlɪsn̩]	v.	聽	1	1	初級	
⓫	bet	[bɛt]	v.	斷言、確信	1	2	中級	◎
	own	[on]	v.	擁有	1	1	初級	◎
	lot	[lɑt]	n.	許多				
	CD	[ˋsiˋdi]	n.	compact disc（光碟）縮寫		4	初級	
⓬	TV	[ˋtiˋvi]	n.	television（電視）縮寫		2	初級	
⓭	show	[ʃo]	n.	節目	1	1	初級	◎
	usually	[ˋjuʒʊəlɪ]	adv.	經常	1		初級	
⓮	have	[hæv]	v.	擁有	1	1	初級	
	habit	[ˋhæbɪt]	n.	習慣	1	2	初級	◎
	chatting	[ˋtʃætɪŋ]	n.	chat（聊天）動名詞	2	3	中級	
	online	[ˋɑn͵laɪn]	adv.	在網路上	1	1	初級	◎
⓯	eating	[ˋitɪŋ]	n.	eat（吃）動名詞	2	1	初級	
	only	[ˋonlɪ]	adj.	唯一的	1	1	初級	

※「紅字單字」於本單元多句出現，「單字級等分析」僅列在「首次出現句」。

MP3 007-01 **❶**～**⓰**

❶	我精通四國語言。	I am fluent in four languages. * **be fluent in**＋語言（精通某語言）
❷	我的英語能力很強。	My English is quite good.
❸	我很會跳舞。	I am good at dancing. * **be good at**＋動詞-ing／名詞（擅長…）
❹	所有運動都難不倒我。	There is no sport too difficult for me. * **too difficult**（太過於困難） * **for me**（對我來說）
❺	我跑得很快。	I can run very fast.
❻	我彈得一手好鋼琴。	I am good at playing the piano. * **play the**＋樂器（彈奏某種樂器）
❼	我有救生員執照。	I have a lifeguard license.
❽	我是電腦高手。	I am a computer expert.
❾	我游自由式。	I swim freestyle. * **breaststroke**（蛙式） * **butterfly stroke**（蝶式） * **backstroke**（仰式）
❿	我是一個好廚師。	I am a good cook.
⓫	大家都說我唱歌很好聽。	Everyone says that I am a good singer. * **Everyone says that**＋子句（大家都說…）
⓬	我擅長做各式糕點。	I am good at making various cakes and desserts. * **make cakes and desserts**（做蛋糕甜點）
⓭	我會開車。	I can drive a car.
⓮	我是空手道黑帶。	I have a black belt in karate. * **black belt in karate**（空手道黑帶）
⓯	我對畫畫很拿手。	I am good at painting.
⓰	我會自己做衣服。	I can make my own clothes. * **make clothes**（做衣服）

	單字	音標	詞性	意義	字頻	大考	英檢	多益
❶	fluent	[ˈfluənt]	adj.	精通的	5	4	中級	◎
	four	[for]	n.	四	1	1	初級	
	language	[ˈlæŋgwɪdʒ]	n.	語言	1	2	初級	◎
❷	English	[ˈɪŋglɪʃ]	n.	英語	1	1	初級	
	quite	[kwaɪt]	adv.	相當	1	1	初級	
	good	[gʊd]	adj.	擅長的	1	1	初級	◎
❸	dancing	[ˈdænsɪŋ]	n.	dance（跳舞）動名詞	2	1	中級	
❹	there	[ðɛr]	adv.	有…	1	1	初級	
	sport	[sport]	n.	運動	1	1	初級	
	too	[tu]	adv.	過於	1	1	初級	
	difficult	[ˈdɪfəˌkəlt]	adj.	困難	1	1	初級	◎
❺	run	[rʌn]	v.	跑步	1	1	初級	◎
	very	[ˈvɛrɪ]	adv.	非常	1	1	初級	
	fast	[fæst]	adv.	快速地	1	1	初級	
❻	playing	[ˈpleɪŋ]	n.	play（彈奏）動名詞	3	1	初級	
	piano	[pɪˈæno]	n.	鋼琴	2	1	初級	
❼	have	[hæv]	v.	擁有	1	1	初級	
	lifeguard	[ˈlaɪfˌgɑrd]	n.	救生員	6	3	中高	
	license	[ˈlaɪsns]	n.	執照	2	4	中級	◎
❽	computer	[kəmˈpjutɚ]	n.	電腦	1	2	初級	
	expert	[ˈɛkspɚt]	n.	高手	1	2	初級	◎
❾	swim	[swɪm]	v.	游泳	2	1	初級	
	freestyle	[ˈfriˌstaɪl]	n.	自由式	5			
❿	cook	[kʊk]	n.	廚師	1	1	初級	◎
⓫	everyone	[ˈɛvrɪˌwʌn]	pron.	每個人	1		初級	
	say	[se]	v.	說	1	1	初級	
	singer	[ˈsɪŋɚ]	n.	歌手	2	1	初級	
⓬	making	[ˈmekɪŋ]	n.	make（製作）動名詞	2	1	中高	
	various	[ˈvɛrɪəs]	adj.	各種的	1	3	中級	◎
	cake	[kek]	n.	蛋糕	1	1	初級	
	dessert	[dɪˈzɝt]	n.	甜點	2	2	初級	◎
⓭	drive	[draɪv]	v.	駕駛	1	1	初級	◎
	car	[kɑr]	n.	車	1	1	初級	◎
⓮	black	[blæk]	adj.	黑色的	1	1	初級	
	belt	[bɛlt]	n.	腰帶、皮帶	1	2	初級	
	karate	[kəˈrɑtɪ]	n.	空手道	6			
⓯	painting	[ˈpentɪŋ]	n.	paint（繪畫）動名詞	1	2	初級	
⓰	make	[mek]	v.	製作	1	1	初級	
	own	[on]	adj.	自己的	1	1	初級	◎
	clothes	[kloz]	n.	cloth（衣服）複數	1	2	初級	

※「紅字單字」於本單元多句出現，「單字級等分析」僅列在「首次出現句」。

🔊 MP3 007-02 ❶〜⓰

❶	你的拿手科目是什麼？	Which is your best subject?
❷	你最擅長什麼？	What do you excel in? * excel in＋名詞（擅長…）
❸	你會說幾種語言？	How many languages do you speak? * How many＋名詞複數形…? （…有多少數量？）
❹	你會說英文嗎？	Do you speak English?
❺	你精通電腦嗎？	Are you good with computers? * be good with＋名詞（擅長…）
❻	你會演奏什麼樂器？	What musical instruments can you play? * What＋某物品＋…？（什麼物品…？） * musical instrument（樂器）
❼	你會游泳嗎？	Do you know how to swim? * Do you know how to＋動詞原形? （你知道如何…嗎）
❽	你幾歲開始學鋼琴？	When did you begin learning to play the piano? * violin（小提琴）
❾	你會做菜嗎？	Can you cook?
❿	你的拿手菜是什麼？	What is your best homemade dish? * best homemade dish（拿手菜）
⓫	你是 KTV 高手嗎？	Are you a KTV master?
⓬	你擅長運動嗎？	Are you good at sports? * painting（繪畫） * photography（攝影）
⓭	你是舞林高手嗎？	Are you an expert dancer?
⓮	你會開車嗎？	Can you drive a car?
⓯	你是說話高手嗎？	Are you a good speaker?
⓰	你是談判高手嗎？	Are you a good negotiator?

	單字	音標	詞性	意義	字頻	大考	英檢	多益
❶	best	[bɛst]	adj.	最擅長的、最好的	1	1	初級	
	subject	[ˋsʌbdʒɪkt]	n.	科目	1	2	初級	◎
❷	excel	[ɪkˋsɛl]	v.	擅長	3	5	中高	◎
❸	many	[ˋmɛnɪ]	adj.	許多的	1	1	初級	
	language	[ˋlæŋgwɪdʒ]	n.	語言	1	2	初級	◎
	speak	[spik]	v.	會說某種語言	1	1	初級	
❹	English	[ˋɪŋglɪʃ]	n.	英文	1	1	初級	
❺	good	[gʊd]	adj.	擅長的	1	1	初級	◎
	computer	[kəmˋpjutɚ]	n.	電腦	1	2	初級	
❻	musical	[ˋmjuzɪkl̩]	adj.	音樂的		3	中級	◎
	instrument	[ˋɪnstrəmənt]	n.	儀器、器具	1	2	初級	◎
	play	[ple]	v.	彈奏	1	1	初級	
❼	know	[no]	v.	知道	1	1	初級	◎
	swim	[swɪm]	v.	游泳	2	1	初級	
❽	begin	[bɪˋgɪn]	v.	開始	1	1	初級	
	learning	[ˋlɝnɪŋ]	n.	learn（學習）動名詞	1	4	中級	
	piano	[pɪˋæno]	n.	鋼琴	2	1	初級	
❾	cook	[kʊk]	v.	做菜	1	1	初級	◎
❿	homemade	[ˋhomˋmed]	adj.	自製的	3			
	dish	[dɪʃ]	n.	菜餚	1	1	初級	
⓫	KTV	[ˋkeˋtiˋvi]	n.	是以下二字的縮寫：karaoke（卡拉 OK 歌唱）television（電視）			初級	
	master	[ˋmæstɚ]	n.	高手	1	1	初級	◎
⓬	sport	[sport]	n.	運動	1	1	初級	
⓭	expert	[ˋɛkspɚt]	adj.	專家的	1	2	初級	◎
	dancer	[ˋdænsɚ]	n.	舞者	2	1	中級	
⓮	drive	[draɪv]	v.	駕駛	1	1	初級	◎
	car	[kɑr]	n.	車	1	1	初級	◎
⓯	speaker	[ˋspikɚ]	n.	說話者	1	2	初級	
⓰	negotiator	[nɪˋgoʃɪ͵etɚ]	n.	談判者	3		中高	◎

※「紅字單字」於本單元多句出現，「單字級等分析」僅列在「首次出現句」。

🔘 MP3 008-01 ❶～⓮

❶	同事覺得我是開心果。	My colleagues think that I am a funny person. * 某人＋think that＋子句（某人認為…）
❷	朋友喜歡找我訴苦。	My friends like to talk about their problems with me. * talk about one's problems（訴苦）
❸	老闆誇我幹勁十足。	My boss speaks highly of my energetic performance. * speak highly of＋人事物（稱讚…） ＝ praise＋人事物
❹	主管說我很細心。	My manager says that I am very careful with details. * be careful with details（用心處理細節、細心）
❺	父母親覺得我太孩子氣。	My parents think that I am too childish.
❻	老闆誇我工作認真。	My boss speaks highly of my earnest attitude toward work. * attitude toward＋某事（對某事的態度）
❼	男朋友覺得我太依賴。	My boyfriend thinks that I am too dependent.
❽	長輩讚美我聰明。	Older people praise my cleverness.
❾	大家都說我很有耐性。	Everyone says that I am a patient person. * everyone says that＋子句（大家都說…）
❿	有人說我是溫室裡的花朵。	Some people say that I am a sheltered person. * sheltered person（受保護的人，比喻溫室裡的花朵）
⓫	有人覺得我太嚴肅。	Some people think that I am too serious. * serious（嚴肅的）可替換為：stubborn（固執的）
⓬	朋友要我別太情緒化。	My friends tell me not to be overly emotional. * 某人＋tell me not to＋動詞原形（某人勸我別…）
⓭	大家都說我是小迷糊。	Everyone says that I am a muddle-headed person.
⓮	大家都說我脾氣好。	Everyone says that I have a good temper. * have a good temper（脾氣好） * have a bad temper（脾氣不好）

	單字	音標	詞性	意義	字頻	大考	英檢	多益
❶	colleague	[ˋkɑlig]	n.	同事	1	5	中級	◎
	think	[θɪŋk]	v.	認為	1	1	初級	
	funny	[ˋfʌnɪ]	adj.	搞笑的	1	1	初級	
	person	[ˋpɝsn]	n.	人	1	1	初級	
❷	friend	[frɛnd]	n.	朋友	1	1	初級	
	like	[laɪk]	v.	喜歡	1	1	初級	
	talk	[tɔk]	v.	談話	1	1	初級	◎
	problem	[ˋprɑbləm]	n.	問題	1	1	初級	◎
❸	boss	[bɔs]	n.	老闆	1	1	初級	
	speak	[spik]	v.	說話	1	2	初級	
	highly	[ˋhaɪlɪ]	adv.	高度地	1	4	中級	
	energetic	[ˌɛnɚˋdʒɛtɪk]	adj.	充滿活力的	3	3	中級	
	performance	[pɚˋfɔrməns]	n.	表現	1	3	中級	◎
❹	manager	[ˋmænɪdʒɚ]	n.	主管	1	3	初級	◎
	say	[se]	v.	說	1	1	初級	
	very	[ˋvɛrɪ]	adv.	十分	1	1	初級	
	careful	[ˋkɛrfəl]	adj.	細心的	1	1	初級	◎
	detail	[ˋditel]	n.	細節	1	3	中級	◎
❺	parents	[ˋpɛrənts]	n.	parent（雙親）複數	2	1		
	too	[tu]	adv.	過於	1	1	初級	
	childish	[ˋtʃaɪldɪʃ]	adj.	幼稚的、孩子氣的	5	2	初級	
❻	earnest	[ˋɝnɪst]	adj.	認真地	3	4	中級	◎
	attitude	[ˋætətjud]	n.	態度	1	3	中級	◎
	work	[wɝk]	n.	工作	1	1	初級	
❼	boyfriend	[ˋbɔɪˌfrɛnd]	n.	男朋友	2		中級	
	dependent	[dɪˋpɛndənt]	adj.	依賴的	2	4	中級	◎
❽	older	[ˋoldɚ]	adj.	old（老的）比較級	1	1	初級	
	people	[ˋpipl]	n.	person（人）複數	1	1	初級	
	praise	[prez]	v.	稱讚	2	2	初級	
	cleverness	[ˋklɛvɚnɪs]	n.	聰明、伶俐	8			
❾	everyone	[ˋɛvrɪˌwʌn]	pron.	每個人	1		初級	
	patient	[ˋpeʃənt]	adj.	耐心的	1	2	初級	◎
❿	some	[sʌm]	adj.	有些	1	1	初級	
	sheltered	[ˋʃɛltɚd]	adj.	受保護的	5	4	中級	◎
⓫	serious	[ˋsɪrɪəs]	adj.	嚴肅的	1	2	初級	◎
⓬	tell	[tɛl]	v.	勸告	1	1	初級	
	overly	[ˋovɚlɪ]	adv.	過度地	3			
	emotional	[ɪˋmoʃənl]	adj.	情緒化的	1	6	中級	◎
⓭	muddle-headed	[ˋmʌdlˋhɛdɪd]	adj.	頭腦迷糊的				
⓮	have	[hæv]	v.	擁有	1	1	初級	
	good	[gʊd]	adj.	良好的	1	1	初級	◎
	temper	[ˋtɛmpɚ]	n.	脾氣	3	3	中級	◎

※「紅字單字」於本單元多句出現，「單字級等分析」僅列在「首次出現句」。

❶	有人說你情緒化嗎？	Does anyone think that you are moody? * moody（情緒化的）＝ emotional
❷	你的朋友怎麼形容你？	How do your friends describe you? * How do＋某人＋…?（某人平時如何…？）
❸	朋友覺得你善變嗎？	Do your friends feel that you are a fickle person? * 某人＋feel that＋子句（某人覺得…）
❹	有人說你很固執嗎？	Does anyone say that you are stubborn?
❺	我想你應該讓老師傷透腦筋。	I bet you give your teachers a lot of trouble. * I bet＋子句（我敢斷言…） * give＋某人＋a lot of trouble（給某人帶來麻煩）
❻	老師對你的成績滿意嗎？	Is your teacher satisfied with your performance at school? * be satisfied with＋某事物（對某事物感到滿意）
❼	主管滿意你的表現嗎？	Is your manager pleased with your performance? * be pleased with＋某事物（對某事物感到滿意）
❽	孩子嫌你囉唆嗎？	Does your child think you are a nag?
❾	有人說你太沈默嗎？	Does anyone say that you are too quiet?
❿	男朋友覺得你體貼嗎？	Does your boyfriend think you're considerate?
⓫	父母親一定以你為榮。	Your parents must be very proud of you. * be proud of＋某人（以某人為榮）
⓬	你一定是個好爸爸。	You must be a good father. * You must be＋某種人（我猜想你一定是個…）
⓭	你一定是個賢妻良母。	You must be an excellent wife and a loving mother. * an excellent wife and a loving mother（賢妻良母）
⓮	朋友常找你訴苦嗎？	Do your friends usually complain to you about things? * complain＋某人＋about...（向某人抱怨…）

	單字	音標	詞性	意義	字頻	大考	英檢	多益
❶	anyone	[ˈɛnɪ.wʌn]	pron.	任何人	1	2	初級	
	think	[θɪŋk]	v.	認為	1	1	初級	
	moody	[ˈmudɪ]	adj.	情緒化的	5		中高	
❷	friend	[frɛnd]	n.	朋友	1	1	初級	
	describe	[dɪˈskraɪb]	v.	描述	1	2	初級	◎
❸	feel	[fil]	v.	覺得	1	1	初級	
	fickle	[ˈfɪk!]	adj.	善變的	6			
	person	[ˈpɝsn̩]	n.	人	1		初級	
❹	say	[se]	v.	說	1	1	初級	
	stubborn	[ˈstʌbən]	adj.	固執的	3	3	中級	◎
❺	bet	[bɛt]	v.	斷言	1	2	中級	◎
	give	[gɪv]	v.	給	1	1	初級	
	teacher	[ˈtitʃə]	n.	老師	1	1	初級	
	lot	[lɑt]	n.	許多	1			
	trouble	[ˈtrʌb!]	n.	麻煩	1	1	初級	◎
❻	satisfied	[ˈsætɪs.faɪd]	adj.	滿意的	2	2	中高	◎
	performance	[pəˈfɔrməns]	n.	表現	1	3	中級	
	school	[skul]	n.	學校	1	1	初級	
❼	manager	[ˈmænɪdʒə]	n.	主管	1	3	初級	◎
	pleased	[plizd]	adj.	滿意的	2		初級	◎
❽	child	[tʃaɪld]	n.	小孩	1	1	初級	
	nag	[næg]	n.	愛嘮叨的人、囉嗦的人	5	5	中高	
❾	too	[tu]	adv.	過於	1	1	初級	
	quiet	[kwaɪət]	adj.	安靜的	1	1	初級	◎
❿	boyfriend	[ˈbɔɪ.frɛnd]	n.	男朋友	2		中級	
	considerate	[kənˈsɪdərɪt]	adj.	體貼的	7	5	中級	◎
⓫	parents	[ˈpɛrənts]	n.	parent（雙親）複數	2	1		
	very	[ˈvɛrɪ]	adv.	十分	1	1	初級	
	proud	[praud]	adj.	驕傲的	1	2	初級	◎
⓬	good	[gʊd]	adj.	良好的	1	1	初級	◎
	father	[ˈfɑðə]	n.	父親	1	1	初級	
⓭	excellent	[ˈɛkslənt]	adj.	傑出的	1	2	初級	◎
	wife	[waɪf]	n.	妻子	1	1	初級	
	loving	[ˈlʌvɪŋ]	adj.	令人喜愛的	2	1	中高	
	mother	[ˈmʌðə]	n.	母親	1	1	初級	
⓮	usually	[ˈjuʒuəlɪ]	adv.	經常	1		初級	◎
	complain	[kəmˈplen]	v.	訴苦、抱怨	1	2	初級	◎
	thing	[θɪŋ]	n.	事物	1	1	初級	

※「紅字單字」於本單元多句出現，「單字級等分析」僅列在「首次出現句」。

MP3 009-01 ❶～⓯

❶	我單身。	I am single.
❷	我完全不想結婚。	I really don't want to get married. * get married（結婚）
❸	我前年結婚。	I got married two years ago.
❹	我上個月訂婚。	I got engaged last month. * get engaged（訂婚）
❺	我今年年底要結婚。	I am getting married toward the end of this year. * 此句用「現在進行式」（...am getting...）表示「已排定時程的個人未來計畫」。 * toward（接近、將近） * the end of this year（今年底）
❻	我結婚十年了。	I've been married for 10 years already.
❼	我的婚姻很幸福。	I have a happy marriage.
❽	我是個家庭主婦。	I am a housewife. * I am a professional woman.（我是職業婦女）
❾	我和我先生是同班同學。	My husband and I were classmates in school. * 此句用「過去簡單式」（...were...）表示「發生在過去的事」。 * A and B were＋某身分（A 和 B 當時是某種身分）
❿	我是奉子成婚。	I got married because I was pregnant.
⓫	我結婚不到半年就懷孕。	I became pregnant less than six months after marriage. * become pregnant（懷上孩子） * less than＋一段時間（某段時間以內）
⓬	這是我的第二段婚姻。	This is my second marriage.
⓭	我離婚好幾年了。	I've been divorced for quite a few years.
⓮	我跟婆婆關係很糟。	I have a bad relationship with my mother-in-law. * have a bad relationship with＋某人（和某人關係不睦）
⓯	我後悔結婚。	I regret getting married. * regret＋動詞-ing（後悔…）

	單字	音標	詞性	意義	字頻	大考	英檢	多益
❶	single	[ˋsɪŋɡḷ]	adj.	單身的	1	2	初級	◎
❷	really	[ˋrɪəlɪ]	adv.	確實	1		初級	
	want	[wɑnt]	v.	想要	1	1	初級	◎
	get	[ɡɛt]	v.	成為	1	1	初級	◎
	married	[ˋmærɪd]	p.p.	marry（結婚）過去分詞	1		初級	
❸	got	[ɡɑt]	p.t.	get（成為）過去式	1	1	初級	◎
	two	[tu]	n.	二	1	1	初級	
	year	[jɪr]	n.	年	1	1	初級	
	ago	[əˋɡo]	adv.	在…以前	1	1	初級	
❹	engaged	[ɪnˋɡedʒd]	p.p.	engage（訂婚）過去分詞	4	3	中高	◎
	last	[læst]	adj.	上一個、前一個	1	1	初級	◎
	month	[mʌnθ]	n.	月	1	1	初級	
❺	getting	[ˋɡɛtɪŋ]	p.pr.	get（成為）現在分詞	1	1	初級	◎
	end	[ɛnd]	n.	末端	1	1	初級	
	this	[ðɪs]	adj./pron.	這個	1	1	初級	
❻	already	[ɔlˋrɛdɪ]	adv.	已經	1	1	初級	◎
❼	have	[hæv]	v.	擁有	1	1	初級	
	happy	[ˋhæpɪ]	adj.	幸福的	1	1	初級	
	marriage	[ˋmærɪdʒ]	n.	婚姻	1	2	初級	
❽	housewife	[ˋhaʊs͵waɪf]	n.	家庭主婦	4	4	中級	
❾	husband	[ˋhʌzbənd]	n.	丈夫	1	1	初級	
	classmate	[ˋklæs͵met]	n.	同學	2		初級	
	school	[skul]	n.	學校	1	1	初級	
❿	pregnant	[ˋprɛɡnənt]	adj.	懷孕的	1	4	中級	
⓫	became	[bɪˋkem]	p.t.	become（變為）過去式	1	4	初級	◎
	less	[lɛs]	adv.	少於…	1	1	初級	
	six	[sɪks]	n.	六	1	1	初級	
⓬	second	[ˋsɛkənd]	adj.	第二的	1	2	初級	◎
⓭	divorced	[dəˋvɔrst]	p.p.	divorce（離婚）過去分詞	3	4	中高	◎
	quite	[kwaɪt]	adv.	相當	1	1	初級	
	few	[fju]	adj.	少數的	1	1	初級	
⓮	bad	[bæd]	adj.	不好的	1	1	初級	
	relationship	[rɪˋleʃən͵ʃɪp]	n.	關係	1	2	中級	◎
	mother-in-law	[ˋmʌðərɪn͵lɔ]	n.	婆婆、岳母	4			
⓯	regret	[rɪˋɡrɛt]	v.	後悔	2	3	初級	

※「紅字單字」於本單元多句出現，「單字級等分析」僅列在「首次出現句」。

009 你已婚／未婚？

❶	你不想結婚嗎？	Wouldn't you like to get married? * Wouldn't you like to＋動詞原形？（你不想要…嗎） * Would you like to＋動詞原形？（你想要…嗎）
❷	你結婚了嗎？	Are you married?
❸	你考慮相親嗎？	Have you considered a matchmaker?
❹	你什麼時候要結婚？	When will you get married? * get married（結婚）
❺	你先生如何向你求婚的？	How did your husband propose to you? * How did＋某人＋…?（某人當時用什麼方法…？）
❻	你結婚幾年了？	How many years have you been married?
❼	你的新婚生活如何？	How's your life as a newlywed going? * How's＋某種生活＋going?（某種生活過得如何？） * life as a newlywed（身為新婚夫妻的生活）
❽	你後悔結婚嗎？	Do you regret getting married? * regret＋動詞-ing（後悔…）
❾	你和太太怎麼認識的？	How did you meet your wife?
❿	你何時要訂婚？	When will you get engaged? * get engaged（訂婚）
⓫	你打算幾年後生小孩？	How many years until you have a child? * have a child（生孩子）
⓬	你想要生幾個小孩？	How many children would you like to have? * would like to（想要）
⓭	你跟公婆相處得如何？	How are you getting along with your in-laws? * 此句用「現在進行式」（…are…getting…）表示「現階段發生的事」。 * get along with＋某人（和某人和睦相處）
⓮	你為什麼離婚？	Why did you divorce? * When did you divorce?（你什麼時候離婚的？）
⓯	你想再婚嗎？	Would you like to get married again? * get married again（再婚）

	單字	音標	詞性	意義	字頻	大考	英檢	多益
❶	like	[laɪk]	v.	想要	1	1	初級	
	get	[gɛt]	v.	成為…	1	1	初級	◎
	married	[ˋmærɪd]	p.p.	marry（結婚）過去分詞	1		初級	
❸	considered	[kənˋsɪdəd]	p.p.	consider（考慮）過去分詞	1	2	初級	◎
	matchmaker	[ˋmætʃˏmekə]	n.	媒人				
❺	husband	[ˋhʌzbənd]	n.	丈夫	1	1	初級	
	propose	[prəˋpoz]	v.	求婚	1	2	初級	◎
❻	many	[ˋmɛnɪ]	adj.	許多的	1	1	初級	
	year	[jɪr]	n.	年	1	1	初級	
❼	life	[laɪf]	n.	生活	1	1	初級	
	newlywed	[ˋnjulɪˏwɛd]	n.	新婚夫妻	5	6	**中高**	
	going	[ˋgoɪŋ]	p.pr.	go（進行、進展）現在分詞	4	1	初級	
❽	regret	[rɪˋgrɛt]	v.	後悔	2	3	初級	
	getting	[ˋgɛtɪŋ]	n.	get（成為）動名詞	1	1	初級	◎
❾	meet	[mit]	v.	認識	1	1	初級	
	wife	[waɪf]	n.	妻子	1	1	初級	
❿	engaged	[ɪnˋgedʒd]	p.p.	engage（訂婚）過去分詞	4	3	**中高**	◎
⓫	have	[hæv]	v.	生育	1	1	初級	
	child	[tʃaɪld]	n.	小孩	1	1	初級	
⓬	children	[ˋtʃɪldrən]	n.	child（小孩）複數	1	1	初級	
⓭	getting	[ˋgɛtɪŋ]	p.pr.	get（相處）現在分詞	1	1	初級	◎
	along	[əˋlɔŋ]	adv.	一起	1	1	初級	
	in-law	[ˋɪnˏlɔ]	n.	姻親、岳父母、公婆				
⓮	divorce	[dəˋvors]	v.	離婚	2	4	中級	◎
⓯	again	[əˋgɛn]	adv.	再次	1	1	初級	

※「紅字單字」於本單元多句出現，「單字級等分析」僅列在「首次出現句」。

🔘 MP3 010-01 ❶～❹

❶	我的身高 160 公分。	I am 160 centimeters tall. * I am＋身高＋tall（我身高…）
❷	我很久沒量身高了。	I haven't measured my height in a long time. * haven't＋過去分詞（過去的某時點到現在都未曾…） * in a long time（很長一段時間）
❸	我很滿意自己的身高。	I am fine with my height. * be fine with...（滿意…）
❹	我的身高中等。	I am of average height. * of（具…特點）
❺	我的身高遺傳自父親。	I inherited my father's height. * I inherit＋某人的某特徵 （我的某種特徵遺傳自某人）
❻	我跟你一樣高。	I am just as tall as you. * A＋be as tall as＋B（A 和 B 一樣高）
❼	我比姊姊矮 3 公分。	I am three centimeters shorter than my elder sister. * be...shorter than＋某人（比某人矮…）
❽	我比弟弟高 5 公分。	I am five centimeters taller than my younger brother. * be...taller than＋某人（比某人高…）
❾	我是矮個子。	I am a short person.
❿	我羨慕比我高的人。	I envy people who are taller than me.
⓫	我是我們家最高的。	I am the tallest one in my family. * the tallest one in...（在…最高的）
⓬	我的身高只有 145 公分。	I am only 145 centimeters tall. * be only＋身高（身高只有…）
⓭	我的身高超過 190 公分。	My height is over 190 centimeters. * be over＋身高（身高超過…）
⓮	我上國中後才突然長高。	I suddenly grew taller after starting junior high. * grow taller（長高） * after＋動詞-ing（在…之後）

單字級等分析

	單字	音標	詞性	意義	字頻	大考	英檢	多益
❶	centimeter	[ˈsɛntə.mitɚ]	n.	公分	4	3	初級	
	tall	[tɔl]	adj.	身高…/高的	1	1	初級	◎
❷	measured	[ˈmɛʒɚd]	p.p.	measure（測量）過去分詞	4	4	初級	◎
	height	[haɪt]	n.	身高	1	2	初級	◎
	long	[lɔŋ]	adj.	長的	1	1	初級	
	time	[taɪm]	n.	時間	1	1	初級	◎
❸	fine	[faɪn]	adj.	滿意的	1	1	初級	◎
❹	average	[ˈævərɪdʒ]	adj.	普通中等的	1	3	中級	◎
❺	inherited	[ɪnˈhɛrɪtɪd]	p.t.	inherit（遺傳）過去式	5	5	中級	◎
	father	[ˈfɑðɚ]	n.	父親	1	1	初級	
❻	just	[dʒʌst]	adv.	恰好	1	1	初級	
❼	three	[θri]	n.	三	1	1	初級	
	shorter	[ˈʃɔrtɚ]	adj.	short（矮的）比較級	1	1	初級	◎
	elder	[ˈɛldɚ]	adj.	較年長的	2	2	初級	
	sister	[ˈsɪstɚ]	n.	姐姐、妹妹	1	1	初級	
❽	five	[faɪv]	n.	五	1	1	初級	
	taller	[ˈtɔlɚ]	adj.	tall（高的）比較級	1	1	初級	◎
	younger	[ˈjʌŋgɚ]	adj.	young（年輕的）比較級	1	1	初級	
	brother	[ˈbrʌðɚ]	n.	哥哥、弟弟	1	1	初級	
❾	short	[ʃɔrt]	adj.	矮的	1	1	初級	
	person	[ˈpɜsn]	n.	人	1	1	初級	
❿	envy	[ˈɛnvɪ]	v.	羨慕	4	3	初級	
	people	[ˈpipl]	n.	person（人）複數	1	1	初級	
⓫	tallest	[ˈtɔlɪst]	adj.	tall（高的）最高級	1	1	初級	◎
	one	[wʌn]	pron.	一個人	1	1	初級	
	family	[ˈfæməlɪ]	n.	家庭	1	1	初級	
⓬	only	[ˈonlɪ]	adv.	只有	1	1	初級	
⓮	suddenly	[ˈsʌdnlɪ]	adv.	突然地	1		初級	
	grew	[gru]	p.t.	grow（成長）過去式	1	1	初級	◎
	starting	[ˈstɑrtɪŋ]	n.	start（開始）動名詞	2	1	初級	
	junior	[ˈdʒunjɚ]	adj.	年紀較輕的	1	4	中級	
	high	[haɪ]	adj.	中學	1	1	初級	

※「紅字單字」於本單元多句出現，「單字級等分析」僅列在「首次出現句」。

010　你的身高？

❶	你的身高多少？	How tall are you? * how tall...（…多高）
❷	你覺得自己夠高嗎？	Do you think you are tall enough? * be＋形容詞＋enough（足夠…的）
❸	你希望再長高一點嗎？	Do you wish you were taller than you are now? * Do you wish＋過去式子句…? （可以的話，你希望…嗎）
❹	你的家人都像你這麼高嗎？	Is everyone in your family as tall as you? * everyone in your family（你們家的人）
❺	你跟他誰比較高？	Who is the taller, you or him?
❻	你跟我弟弟一樣高。	You are as tall as my younger brother. * A＋be as tall as＋B（A 和 B 一樣高）
❼	你跟你哥哥身高相差多少？	What is the difference in height between you and your elder brother? * What is the difference in...?（…的差距是多少？） * between A and B（A 和 B 之間）
❽	你又長高了。	You've grown taller again. * 此句用「現在完成式」（...have grown...）表示「過去某時點發生某事，且結果持續到現在」。
❾	你看起來比你爸爸高。	You look taller than your father. * be...taller than＋某人（比某人高…）
❿	你不瞭解矮個子的痛苦。	You cannot understand the pain of being a short person. * be a short person（身為一名矮個子）
⓫	你的身高真令人嫉妒！	Your height makes people jealous! * make people＋形容詞（使人覺得…）
⓬	你的身高適合打籃球。	Your height is perfect for playing basketball. * be perfect for＋動詞-ing（非常適合…）
⓭	你的女朋友好嬌小。	Your girlfriend is so petite.
⓮	你的身高可以去當模特兒。	You could be a model with your height. * with your height（運用身高）

	單字	音標	詞性	意義	字頻	大考	英檢	多益
❶	tall	[tɔl]	adj.	身高…/高的	1	1	初級	◎
❷	think	[θɪŋk]	v.	認為	1	1	初級	
	enough	[ə`nʌf]	adv.	足夠	1	1	初級	◎
❸	wish	[wɪʃ]	v.	希望	1	1	初級	
	taller	[`tɔlə]	adj.	tall（高的）比較級	1	1	初級	◎
	now	[naʊ]	adv.	現在	1	1	初級	
❹	everyone	[`ɛvrɪ.wʌn]	pron.	每個人	1		初級	
	family	[`fæməlɪ]	n.	家庭	1	1	初級	
❻	younger	[`jʌŋgə]	adj.	young（年輕的）比較級	1	1	初級	
	brother	[`brʌðə]	n.	哥哥、弟弟	1	1	初級	
❼	difference	[`dɪfərəns]	n.	差異	1	2	初級	◎
	height	[haɪt]	n.	身高	1	2	初級	
	elder	[`ɛldə]	adj.	較年長的	2	2	初級	
❽	grown	[gron]	p.p.	grow（成長）過去分詞	6	1	初級	◎
	again	[ə`gɛn]	adv.	再次	1	1	初級	
❾	look	[lʊk]	v.	看起來	1	1	初級	
	father	[`fɑðə]	n.	父親	1	1	初級	
❿	understand	[ʌndə`stænd]	v.	了解	1	1	初級	
	pain	[pen]	n.	痛苦	1	2	初級	
	short	[ʃɔrt]	adj.	矮的	1	1	初級	◎
	person	[`pɜsn]	n.	人	1		初級	
⓫	make	[mek]	v.	使得	1	1	初級	
	people	[`pipl]	n.	person（人）複數	1	1	初級	
	jealous	[`dʒɛləs]	adj.	嫉妒的	3	3	初級	◎
⓬	perfect	[`pɜfɪkt]	adj.	完美的	1	1	初級	◎
	playing	[`pleɪŋ]	n.	play（打球）動名詞	3		初級	
	basketball	[`bæskɪt.bɔl]	n.	籃球	1	1	初級	◎
⓭	girlfriend	[`gɜl.frɛnd]	n.	女朋友	2		中級	
	so	[so]	adv.	如此地	1	1	初級	
	petite	[pə`tit]	adj.	個子嬌小的	5			
⓮	model	[`mɑdl]	n.	模特兒	1	2	初級	◎

※「紅字單字」於本單元多句出現，「單字級等分析」僅列在「首次出現句」。

011　我的身材。

❶	我的體重 48 公斤。	My weight is 48 kilograms.
❷	我的體重不到 60 公斤。	My weight is not quite 60 kilos. * **be not quite**（尚未達到）
❸	我是胖子。	I am a fat person.
❹	我很苗條。	I am very slim.
❺	我羨慕吃不胖的人。	I envy those who eat a lot but don't get fat. * **those who**＋子句（某些⋯的人） * **eat a lot**（吃很多） * **get fat**（變胖）
❻	我是中等身材。	I have an average figure. * **have**＋形容詞＋**figure**（是⋯的身材）
❼	我比我哥哥重 10 公斤。	I am 10 kilos heavier than my elder brother. * **be heavier than**＋某人（體重比某人重）
❽	我比我妹妹瘦。	I am thinner than my young sister. * **be thinner than**＋某人（體重比某人輕）
❾	我的胸圍 34 吋。	My chest measurement is 34-inches. * **waist**（腰部） * **hip**（臀部）
❿	我的手臂肉肉的。	My arms are fleshy.
⓫	我的大腿太粗。	My thighs are too big. * **thighs**（大腿）可替換為：**waistline**（腰圍）
⓬	我靠運動維持身材。	I exercise to maintain my figure. * **exercise to**＋動詞原形（藉由運動來達成⋯） * **maintain one's figure**（保持身材）
⓭	我覺得自己很胖。	I think I am fat.
⓮	我覺得自己太瘦。	I think that I am too skinny. * 某人＋**think that**＋子句（某人認為⋯）
⓯	我最近胖了。	I've gained some weight recently. * **I've lost some weight recently.**（我最近瘦了） * 此句用「現在完成式」（...have gained...）表示 「過去某時點發生某事，且結果持續到現在」。

	單字	音標	詞性	意義	字頻	大考	英檢	多益
❶	weight	[wet]	n.	體重	1	1	初級	◎
	kilogram	[ˈkɪlə.græm]	n.	公斤		3	初級	
❷	quite	[kwaɪt]	adv.	相當	1	1	初級	
	kilo	[ˈkilo]	n.	kilogram（體重）簡寫				
❸	fat	[fæt]	adj.	肥胖的	1	1	初級	
	person	[ˈpɝsn]	n.	人	1	1	初級	
❹	very	[ˈvɛrɪ]	adv.	十分	1	1	初級	
	slim	[slɪm]	adj.	苗條的	2	2	初級	◎
❺	envy	[ˈɛnvɪ]	v.	羨慕	4	3	初級	
	those	[ðoz]	pron.	那些人	1	1	初級	
	eat	[it]	v.	吃	1	1	初級	
	lot	[lɑt]	n.	許多	1	1	初級	
	get	[gɛt]	v.	變得	1	1	初級	◎
❻	have	[hæv]	v.	擁有	1	1	初級	
	average	[ˈævərɪdʒ]	adj.	普通中等的	1	3	中級	◎
	figure	[ˈfɪgjə]	n.	身材	1	2	初級	◎
❼	heavier	[ˈhɛvɪə]	adj.	heavy（重的）比較級	1	1	初級	
	elder	[ˈɛldə]	adj.	較年長的	2	1	初級	
	brother	[ˈbrʌðə]	n.	哥哥、弟弟	1	1	初級	
❽	thinner	[ˈθɪnə]	adj.	thin（瘦的）比較級	1	1	初級	◎
	younger	[ˈjʌŋgə]	adj.	young（年輕的）比較級	1	1	初級	
	sister	[ˈsɪstə]	n.	姐姐、妹妹	1	1	初級	
❾	chest	[tʃɛst]	n.	胸部	1	3	中級	
	measurement	[ˈmɛʒəmənt]	n.	尺寸	2	2	中高	◎
	inch	[ɪntʃ]	n.	英吋				
❿	arm	[ɑrm]	n.	手臂	2	4	中高	
	fleshy	[ˈflɛʃɪ]	adj.	肉肉的	6			
⓫	thigh	[θaɪ]	n.	大腿	2	5	中高	
	too	[tu]	adv.	過於	1	1	初級	
	big	[bɪg]	adj.	大的	1	1	初級	
⓬	exercise	[ˈɛksə.saɪz]	v.	運動	1	2	初級	◎
	maintain	[menˈten]	v.	維持	1	2	初級	◎
⓭	think	[θɪŋk]	v.	認為	1	1	初級	
⓮	skinny	[ˈskɪnɪ]	adj.	非常瘦的	2	2	初級	
⓯	gained	[gend]	p.p.	gain（增加）過去分詞	1	2	初級	◎
	some	[sʌm]	adj.	有些	1	1	初級	
	recently	[ˈrisntlɪ]	adv.	最近	1		初級	

※「紅字單字」於本單元多句出現，「單字級等分析」僅列在「首次出現句」。

011 你的身材？

🔊 MP3 011-02 ❶～⓮

❶	你的體重多少？	What is your weight? = How much do you weigh?
❷	你希望自己多重？	How much is your ideal weight? * **How much is...?**（…是多少） * **ideal weight**（理想體重）
❸	你是不是又胖了？	Did you get fat again?
❹	你如何保持身材？	How do you keep your shape? * **keep one's shape**（保持身材）
❺	你怎麼瘦到皮包骨？	How did you become just skin and bones? * **just skin and bones**（瘦到只剩下皮包骨）
❻	你為什麼想減肥？	Why do you want to lose weight?
❼	你胖了幾公斤？	How many kilograms did you gain? * **How many kilograms did you lose?** （你瘦了幾公斤？）
❽	你應該不到 40 公斤。	You probably don't even weigh 40 kilograms. * **not even**（甚至沒有） * **weigh**＋重量（重達…）
❾	你知道她的三圍嗎？	Do you know her measurements?
❿	我想他至少有 90 公斤。	I think that he weighs at least 90 kilograms. * **at least**（至少）
⓫	你看起來完全沒有贅肉。	You look like you have no fat on your body. * **You look like**＋子句（你看起來像是…） * **have no fat**（沒有贅肉） * **on your body**（在你身上）
⓬	我真羨慕你的好身材。	I am jealous of your good figure. * **be jealous of**＋某事物（羨慕某事物）
⓭	你的身材真好！	What a great figure you have! * **What**＋形容詞＋名詞＋**you have.**（你擁有…）
⓮	十年來，你的身材絲毫未變。	Your figure hasn't changed a bit in the past ten years. * **hasn't changed**（從過去到現在都不曾改變） * **hasn't changed a bit**（絲毫未變） * **in the past**＋數字＋**years**（過去…年之間）

單字級等分析

	單字	音標	詞性	意義	字頻	大考	英檢	多益
❶	weight	[wet]	n.	體重	1	1	初級	◎
	much	[mʌtʃ]	adv. /adj.	許多地/許多的	1	1	初級	
	weigh	[we]	v.	重達…	1	1	中級	◎
❷	ideal	[aɪˋdiəl]	adj.	理想的	2	3	中級	◎
❸	get	[gɛt]	v.	變得	1	1	初級	◎
	fat	[fæt]	adj./n.	肥胖的/脂肪	1	1	初級	
	again	[əˋgɛn]	adv.	再次	1	1	初級	
❹	keep	[kip]	v.	保持	1	1	初級	◎
	shape	[ʃep]	n.	身材	1	1	初級	
❺	become	[bɪˋkʌm]	v.	變得	1	1	初級	◎
	just	[dʒʌst]	adv.	僅僅	1	1	初級	
	skin	[skɪn]	n.	皮膚	1	1	初級	
	bone	[bon]	n.	骨頭	1	1	初級	
❻	want	[wɑnt]	v.	想要	1	1	初級	
	lose	[luz]	v.	減少	1	2	初級	◎
❼	many	[ˋmɛnɪ]	adj.	許多的	1	1	初級	
	kilogram	[ˋkɪləˏgræm]	n.	公斤		3	初級	
	gain	[gen]	v.	增加	1	2	初級	◎
❽	probably	[ˋprɑbəblɪ]	adv.	可能	1		初級	◎
	even	[ˋivən]	adv.	甚至	1	1	初級	◎
❾	know	[no]	v.	知道	1	1	初級	◎
	measurement	[ˋmɛʒəmənt]	n.	三圍	2	2	中高	◎
❿	think	[θɪŋk]	v.	認為	1	1	初級	
	least	[list]	n.	最少	1	1	初級	◎
⓫	look	[lʊk]	v.	看起來	1	1	初級	
	have	[hæv]	v.	擁有	1	1	初級	
	body	[ˋbɑdɪ]	n.	身體	1	1	初級	
⓬	jealous	[ˋdʒɛləs]	adj.	羨慕的	3	3	初級	◎
	good	[gʊd]	adj.	良好的	1	1	初級	◎
	figure	[ˋfɪgjə]	n.	身材	1	2	初級	◎
⓭	great	[gret]	adj.	很好的	1	1	初級	◎
⓮	changed	[tʃɛndʒd]	p.p.	change（改變）過去分詞	4	2	初級	◎
	bit	[bɪt]	n.	些許	1	1	初級	
	past	[pæst]	adj.	過去的	1	1	初級	
	ten	[tɛn]	n.	十	1	1	初級	
	year	[jɪr]	n.	年	1	1	初級	

※「紅字單字」於本單元多句出現，「單字級等分析」僅列在「首次出現句」。

🔘 MP3 012-01 ❶～⓰

❶	我變白了。	I've become fair-skinned. * 此句用「現在完成式」(...have become...) 表示 「過去某時點發生某事，且結果持續到現在」。
❷	我的皮膚白皙。	I have fair skin. * have＋顏色＋skin（膚色是…）
❸	我很容易曬黑。	My skin tans easily. * tan（曬黑）= get a tan
❹	我曬黑了。	I've got a tan.
❺	我的膚質很好。	My skin is very good.
❻	我的臉色蒼白。	My face looks pale. * look＋形容詞（看起來…）
❼	我的膚質不容易上妝。	My skin does not take to makeup easily. * take to＋某物質（吸收某物質）
❽	我是油性肌膚。	I have oily skin. * dry（乾性的）
❾	我的皮膚很光滑。	My skin is very smooth.
❿	我是混合性肌膚。	I have a combination of skin types. * a combination of...（綜合的…） * skin type（膚質）
⓫	我的皮膚容易過敏。	My skin is easily irritated. * be irritated（引發過敏）
⓬	我有黑眼圈。	I have bags under my eyes.
⓭	我的皮膚很有光澤。	My skin shines.
⓮	我容易長痘痘。	I break out in pimples very easily. * break out in＋長在皮膚上的東西（從皮膚冒出…）
⓯	我一熬夜就臉色暗沈。	My skin darkens if I stay up late at night. * 子句＋If I＋動詞（如果我…，就會…） * stay up late（熬夜） * at night（晚上）
⓰	冬天我經常脫皮。	My skin frequently peels in winter. * in＋spring、summer、fall、winter（在某季節中）

	單字	音標	詞性	意義	字頻	大考	英檢	多益
❶	become	[`bɪkʌm]	p.p.	become（變為）過去分詞	1	1	初級	◎
	fair-skinned	[`fɛr.skɪnd]	adj.	白皙皮膚的				
❷	have	[hæv]	v.	擁有	1	1	初級	
	fair	[fɛr]	adj.	皮膚白皙的	1	2	初級	◎
	skin	[skɪn]	n.	皮膚	1	1	初級	◎
❸	tan	[tæn]	v./n.	曬黑／棕褐膚色	4	5	中高	
	easily	[`izɪlɪ]	adv.	容易地	1		中級	
❹	got	[gɑt]	p.p.	get（變成）過去分詞	1	1	初級	◎
❺	very	[`vɛrɪ]	adv.	十分	1	1	初級	
	good	[gʊd]	adj.	良好的	1	1	初級	◎
❻	face	[fes]	n.	臉色	1		初級	
	look	[lʊk]	v.	看起來	1	1	初級	
	pale	[pel]	adj.	蒼白的	2	3	初級	◎
❼	take	[tek]	v.	吸收	1	1	初級	◎
	makeup	[`mek.ʌp]	n.	化妝品	2	4		◎
❽	oily	[`ɔɪlɪ]	adj.	油性的	5			
❾	smooth	[smuð]	adj.	光滑的	1	3	中級	◎
❿	combination	[.kɑmbə`neʃən]	n.	綜合	1	4	中級	◎
	type	[taɪp]	n.	類型	1	2	初級	◎
⓫	irritated	[`ɪrə.tetɪd]	p.p.	irritate（引發過敏）過去分詞	6	6	中高	◎
⓬	bag	[bæg]	n.	黑眼圈	1	1	初級	
	eye	[aɪ]	n.	眼睛	1	1	初級	
⓭	shine	[ʃaɪn]	v.	發出光澤	2		初級	
⓮	break	[brek]	v.	冒出	1	1	初級	◎
	out	[aʊt]	adv.	出現、顯露	1	1	初級	
	pimple	[`pɪmpl̩]	n.	青春痘	7	5	中高	
⓯	darken	[`dɑrkn̩]	v.	變暗	4			
	stay	[ste]	v.	保持、堅持	1	1	初級	◎
	up	[ʌp]	adv.	醒著地	1	1	初級	
	late	[let]	adv.	晚地	1	1	初級	◎
	night	[naɪt]	n.	晚上	1	1	初級	
⓰	frequently	[`frikwəntlɪ]	adv.	頻繁地	1			◎
	peel	[pil]	v.	脫皮、剝落	2	3	中級	
	winter	[`wɪntə]	n.	冬天	1	1	初級	

※「紅字單字」於本單元多句出現，「單字級等分析」僅列在「首次出現句」。

012 你的皮膚？

❶	你怎麼都曬不黑？	How come you don't tan? * How come＋子句（怎麼會…？）
❷	你希望肌膚白皙嗎？	Do you want your skin to be whiter?
❸	你打算曬成古銅色嗎？	Do you want to have a bronze-colored skin tone? * bronze-colored skin tone（古銅色的肌膚）
❹	你的皮膚容易過敏嗎？	Do you have sensitive skin? * have＋形容詞＋skin（有…的皮膚）
❺	你不怕曬黑嗎？	Aren't you afraid of getting too tan? * Aren't you afraid of＋動詞-ing＋...? （你不害怕…嗎）
❻	你怎麼長這麼多痘痘？	How come you have so many pimples?
❼	你的皮膚白裡透紅。	Your skin looks very healthy with a touch of rose. * with a touch of rose（臉色帶著少許的紅潤） * a touch of（少許）
❽	你的皮膚真好！	Your skin is very good!
❾	你的皮膚越來越好了。	Your skin is getting better and better. * be getting＋比較級（越來越…）。 此句用「現在進行式」（...is getting...） 表示「現階段逐漸變化的事」。
❿	你變白了。	Your skin is whiter.
⓫	你完全沒有皺紋。	You don't have any wrinkles. * don't have any＋名詞複數形（沒有任何…）
⓬	你曬黑了。	You've gotten a suntan.
⓭	你的臉色很蒼白。	Your face looks very pale. * rosy（紅潤的） * florid（氣色好的）
⓮	你得好好保養皮膚。	You should take good care of your skin. * take good care of＋人事物（仔細照顧某人事物）
⓯	你的痘痘變少了。	Your acne is getting better. * get better（好多了）

單字級等分析

	單字	音標	詞性	意義	字頻	大考	英檢	多益
❶	come	[kʌm]	v.	怎麼…	1	1	初級	
	tan	[tæn]	v./adj.	曬黑/棕褐色的	4	5	中高	
❷	want	[wɑnt]	v.	想要	1	1	初級	◎
	skin	[skɪn]	n.	皮膚	1	1	初級	◎
	whiter	[`hwaɪtɚ]	adj.	white（白皙的）比較級	1	1	初級	
❸	have	[hæv]	v.	擁有	1	1	初級	
	bronze-colored	[`brɑnz͵kʌlɚd]	adj.	古銅色的				
	tone	[ton]	n.	色調	1	1	中級	◎
❹	sensitive	[`sɛnsətɪv]	adj.	容易過敏的	1	3	中級	
❺	afraid	[ə`fred]	adj.	害怕的	1	1	初級	
	getting	[`gɛtɪŋ]	n.	get（變成）動名詞	1	1	初級	◎
	too	[tu]	adv.	過於	1	1	初級	
❻	so	[so]	adv.	如此	1	1	初級	
	many	[`mɛnɪ]	adj.	許多的	1	1	初級	
	pimple	[`pɪmpl̩]	n.	青春痘	7	5	中高	
❼	look	[lʊk]	v.	看起來	1	1	初級	
	very	[`vɛrɪ]	adv.	十分	1	1	初級	
	healthy	[`hɛlθɪ]	adj.	健康的	1	2	初級	◎
	touch	[tʌtʃ]	n.	少許	1	1	初級	◎
	rose	[ros]	n.	臉色紅潤	2	1	初級	
❽	good	[gʊd]	adj.	良好的	1	1	初級	◎
❾	getting	[`gɛtɪŋ]	p.pr.	get（變成）現在分詞	1	1	初級	◎
	better	[`bɛtɚ]	adj.	good（良好的）比較級	1	1	初級	
⓫	any	[`ɛnɪ]	adj.	任何的	1	1	初級	
	wrinkle	[`rɪŋkl̩]	n.	皺紋	3	4	中級	◎
⓬	gotten	[`gɑtn̩]	p.p.	get（變成）過去分詞	1	1	初級	◎
	suntan	[`sʌntæn]	n.	曬黑				
⓭	face	[fes]	n.	臉色	1	1	初級	
	pale	[pel]	adj.	蒼白	2	3	初級	◎
⓮	take	[tek]	v.	採取	1	1	初級	◎
	care	[kɛr]	n.	照顧	1	1	初級	◎
⓯	acne	[`æknɪ]	n.	青春痘、粉刺	6	5	中高	

※「紅字單字」於本單元多句出現，「單字級等分析」僅列在「首次出現句」。

013　我的臉蛋。

❶	我的臉圓圓的。	I have a round face. * square（方形的） * long（長的）
❷	我的臉很大。	My face is big. * My face is small.（我的臉很小）
❸	我的臉比手掌還小。	My face is smaller than my palm. * be...smaller than＋某事物（比某事物小…）
❹	我的臉型像爸爸。	My face is shaped like my father's. * A is shaped like B（A 的形狀像 B）
❺	我是娃娃臉。	I have a baby face. * baby face（娃娃臉）
❻	我的面貌姣好。	I have a good-looking face. * 形容詞-looking（相貌…的）
❼	我的長相普通。	I am an ordinary-looking person.
❽	我的額頭很高。	I have a high forehead. * high（高的）可替換為：low（低的）
❾	我的臉頰肉肉的。	My cheeks are chubby.
❿	我有雙下巴。	I have a double chin. * double chin（雙下巴）
⓫	我的下巴尖尖的。	I have a sharp chin. ＝ My chin is narrow.
⓬	我立志當小臉美女。	I am determined to be a beauty with a cute face. * be determined to be＋某種人（決心要成為某種人） * with＋某特徵（附帶某種特徵）
⓭	大家都說我的圓臉很有親和力。	Everyone says that my round face looks friendly. * Everyone says that＋子句（大家都說…）
⓮	我總是笑臉迎人。	I always have a smiling face. * a smiling face（帶著笑容的臉）
⓯	我看起來很兇。	I look very mean. * look very＋形容詞（看起來很…）
⓰	我常常面無表情。	I usually am expressionless.
⓱	我的顴骨突出。	I have distinct cheekbones.

	單字	音標	詞性	意義	字頻	大考	英檢	多益
❶	have	[hæv]	v.	擁有	1	1	初級	
	round	[raʊnd]	adj.	圓圓的	1	1	初級	
	face	[fes]	n.	臉	1	1	初級	
❷	big	[bɪg]	adj.	大的	1	1	初級	
❸	smaller	[ˈsmɔlə]	adj.	small（小的）比較級	1	1	初級	◎
	palm	[pɑm]	n.	手掌、掌部	2	2	中級	
❹	shaped	[ʃept]	p.p.	shape（形狀為…）過去分詞	5	1	中高	◎
	father	[ˈfɑðə]	n.	父親	1	1	初級	
❺	baby	[ˈbebɪ]	adj.	娃娃的	1	1	初級	
❻	good-looking	[ˈgʊdˈlʊkɪŋ]	adj.	面貌姣好的	4		中高	
❼	ordinary-looking	[ˈɔrdnˌɛrɪˈlʊkɪŋ]	adj.	長相普通的				
	person	[ˈpɜsn]	n.	人	1	1	初級	
❽	high	[haɪ]	adj.	高的	1	1	初級	
	forehead	[ˈfɔrˌhɛd]	n.	額頭	2	3	中級	
❾	cheek	[tʃik]	n.	臉頰	1	3	中級	
	chubby	[ˈtʃʌbɪ]	adj.	肉肉的	6	5	初級	
❿	double	[ˈdʌbl]	adj.	雙重的	1	2	初級	◎
	chin	[tʃɪn]	n.	下巴	2	2	初級	
⓫	sharp	[ʃɑrp]	adj.	尖銳的	1	1	初級	◎
	narrow	[ˈnæro]	adj.	窄的	1	2	初級	◎
⓬	determined	[dɪˈtɜmɪnd]	p.p.	determine（立志）過去分詞	3		中級	◎
	beauty	[ˈbjutɪ]	n.	美女	1	1	中級	
	cute	[kjut]	adj.	小巧可愛的	2	1	初級	
⓭	everyone	[ˈɛvrɪˌwʌn]	pron.	每個人	1		初級	
	say	[se]	v.	說	1	1	初級	
	look	[lʊk]	v.	看起來	1	1	初級	
	friendly	[ˈfrɛndlɪ]	adj.	有親和力的	1	2	初級	
⓮	always	[ˈɔlwez]	adv.	總是	1	1	初級	
	smiling	[ˈsmaɪlɪŋ]	adj.	帶著笑臉的	3	1	初級	
⓯	very	[ˈvɛrɪ]	adv.	十分	1	1	初級	
	mean	[min]	adj.	不友善的	1	1	初級	◎
⓰	usually	[ˈjuʒʊəlɪ]	adv.	經常	1		初級	◎
	expressionless	[ɪkˈsprɛʃənlɪs]	adj.	面無表情的	7			
⓱	distinct	[dɪˈstɪŋkt]	adj.	明顯的	2	4	中級	◎
	cheekbone	[ˈtʃikˌbon]	n.	顴骨	5			

※「紅字單字」於本單元多句出現，「單字級等分析」僅列在「首次出現句」。

013 你的臉蛋？

❶	你為什麼不喜歡笑？	Why don't you like to smile? * **Why don't you...?**（你為什麼不…？） * **like to ＋動詞原形**（喜歡…）
❷	你的臉型很漂亮。	You have a beautiful facial structure. * **facial structure**（臉型）
❸	你的臉好小。	Your face is so small.
❹	你的臉型比較方正。	The shape of your face is somewhat square. * **shape of one's face**（臉型）
❺	你的臉變圓了。	Your face looks rounder than before. * **than before**（和以前相比）
❻	你圓圓的臉很可愛。	Your round face looks very cute. * **look very ＋形容詞**（看起來很…）
❼	你有一張娃娃臉。	You have a baby face.
❽	你長得很甜。	You look so sweet.
❾	你的臉比你媽媽的還大。	Your face is bigger than your mother's.
❿	你跟你家人的臉型完全不同。	Your face is shaped totally differently from your family members'. * **be shaped ＋副詞**（形狀…） * **be differently from ＋人事物**（和某人事物不同） * **your family member**（你的家人）
⓫	娃娃臉讓你看起來更年輕。	Having a baby face makes you look younger. * **having a baby face**（有張娃娃臉） * **make ＋某人 ＋動詞原形**（使某人變得…）
⓬	你的笑容很迷人。	Your smile is very charming.
⓭	你的顴骨很高。	You have high cheekbones.
⓮	你的表情看起來很嚴肅，發生了什麼事？	You look so serious; what happened? * **What happened?**（怎麼了、發生什麼事）

單字級等分析

	單字	音標	詞性	意義	字頻	大考	英檢	多益
❶	like	[laɪk]	v.	喜歡	1	1	初級	
	smile	[smaɪl]	v./n.	微笑/笑容	1	1	初級	
❷	have	[hæv]	v.	擁有	1	1	初級	
	beautiful	[ˋbjutəfəl]	adj.	美麗的	1	1	初級	
	facial	[ˋfeʃəl]	adj.	臉部的	3	4	中級	
	structure	[ˋstrʌktʃɚ]	n.	結構	1	3	中級	◎
❸	face	[fes]	n.	臉	1	1	初級	
	small	[smɔl]	adj.	小的	1	1	初級	◎
❹	shape	[ʃep]	n.	形狀	1	1	初級	◎
	somewhat	[ˋsʌm.hwɑt]	adv.	稍微有些	1	3	中級	
	square	[skwɛr]	adj.	方形的	1	2	初級	◎
❺	look	[lʊk]	v.	看起來	1	1	初級	
	rounder	[ˋraʊndɚ]	adj.	round（圓圓的）比較級	1	1	初級	
	before	[bɪˋfor]	adv.	以前	1	1	初級	
❻	round	[raʊnd]	adj.	圓圓的	1	1	初級	
	very	[ˋvɛrɪ]	adv.	十分	1	1	初級	
	cute	[kjut]	adj.	小巧可愛的	2	1	初級	
❼	baby	[ˋbebɪ]	adj.	娃娃的	1	1	初級	
❽	so	[so]	adv.	如此	1	1	初級	
	sweet	[swit]	adj.	甜美的	1	1	初級	
❾	bigger	[ˋbɪgɚ]	adj.	big（大的）比較級	1	1	初級	
	mother	[ˋmʌðɚ]	n.	母親	1	1	初級	
❿	shaped	[ʃept]	p.p.	shape（形狀為…）過去分詞	5	1	中高	◎
	totally	[ˋtotlɪ]	adv.	完全	1			◎
	differently	[ˋdɪfərəntlɪ]	adv.	不同地	2			
	family	[ˋfæməlɪ]	n.	家庭	1	1	初級	
	member	[ˋmɛmbɚ]	n.	成員	1	2	初級	◎
⓫	make	[mek]	v.	使得	1	1	初級	
	younger	[ˋjʌŋgɚ]	adj.	young（年輕的）比較級	1	1	初級	
⓬	charming	[ˋtʃɑrmɪŋ]	adj.	迷人的	2	3	中級	
⓭	high	[haɪ]	adj.	高的	1	1	初級	
	cheekbone	[ˋtʃik.bon]	n.	顴骨	5			
⓮	serious	[ˋsɪrɪəs]	adj.	嚴肅的	1	2	初級	◎
	happened	[ˋhæpənd]	p.t.	happen（發生）過去式	1	1	初級	

※「紅字單字」於本單元多句出現，「單字級等分析」僅列在「首次出現句」。

014 我的五官。

❶	我的輪廓很深。	I have a distinct face.
❷	我的眼睛像媽媽。	My eyes look like my mother's. * **look like...**（看起來像…、長得像…）
❸	我的眼皮浮腫。	My eyelids are swollen.
❹	我的眼睛很小。	My eyes are small.
❺	大家都說我的眼睛大。	Everyone says that my eyes are big. * **everyone says that**＋子句（大家都說…）
❻	我的眼睛細長。	My eyes are long and thin. * 形容詞＋and＋形容詞（…且…） * **long and thin**（細長的） 　可替換為：**round**（圓的）
❼	我是單眼皮。	My eyelids are single-folded. * **double-folded**（雙眼皮的）
❽	我的眼睫毛很長。	My eyelashes are very long. * **short**（短的）
❾	我的鼻子很挺。	I have a high-bridged nose.
❿	我的眼珠是黑色。	My eyes are black. * **dark brown**（深棕色的）
⓫	我的眉毛濃密。	My eyebrows are thick.
⓬	我有近視。	I am nearsighted. * **farsighted**（遠視的）
⓭	我經常修眉毛。	I trim my eyebrows frequently.
⓮	我的嘴唇很厚。	My lips are thick.
⓯	我的嘴巴很大。	My mouth is large.

	單字	音標	詞性	意義	字頻	大考	英檢	多益
❶	have	[hæv]	v.	擁有	1	1	初級	
	distinct	[dɪˋstɪŋkt]	adj.	明顯的	2	4	中級	◎
	face	[fes]	n.	臉	1	1	初級	
❷	eye	[aɪ]	n.	眼睛	1	1	初級	
	look	[lʊk]	v.	看起來	1	1	初級	
	mother	[ˋmʌðə]	n.	母親	1	1	初級	
❸	eyelids	[ˋaɪˌlɪds]	n.	eyelid（眼皮）複數	4	5	中高	
	swollen	[ˋswolən]	adj.	浮腫的	4		中高	
❹	small	[smɔl]	adj.	小的	1	1	初級	◎
❺	everyone	[ˋɛvrɪˌwʌn]	pron.	每個人	1		初級	
	say	[se]	v.	說	1	1	初級	
	big	[bɪg]	adj.	大的	1	1	初級	
❻	long	[lɔŋ]	adj.	長的	1	1	初級	
	thin	[θɪn]	adj.	薄的/稀疏的	1	2	初級	◎
❼	single-folded	[ˋsɪŋglˋfoldɪd]	adj.	單眼皮的				
❽	eyelashes	[ˋaɪˌlæʃəs]	n.	eyelash（眼睫毛）複數	5	5	中高	
	very	[ˋvɛrɪ]	adv.	十分	1	1	初級	
❾	high-bridged	[ˋhaɪˌbrɪdʒt]	adj.	鼻梁高的				
	nose	[nos]	n.	鼻子	1	1	初級	
❿	black	[blæk]	adj.	黑色的	1	1	初級	
⓫	eyebrows	[ˋaɪˌbraʊs]	n.	eyebrow（眉毛）複數	2	2	中級	
	thick	[θɪk]	adj.	濃密的/厚的	1	2	初級	
⓬	nearsighted	[ˋnɪrˋsaɪtɪd]	adj.	近視的		4	中高	
⓭	trim	[trɪm]	v.	修剪	2	5	中高	◎
	frequently	[ˋfrikwəntlɪ]	adv.	頻繁地	1			◎
⓮	lips	[lɪps]	n.	lip（嘴唇）複數	1	1	初級	
⓯	mouth	[maʊθ]	n.	嘴巴	1	1	初級	
	large	[lɔrdʒ]	adj.	大的	1	1	初級	

※「紅字單字」於本單元多句出現，「單字級等分析」僅列在「首次出現句」。

014　你的五官？

🔊 MP3 014-02 ❶～⓱

❶	你的雙眼炯炯有神。	Your eyes are bright and piercing.
❷	你的眼睛很漂亮。	Your eyes are very beautiful.
❸	你有雙水汪汪的大眼睛。	What big, bright eyes you have. = You have a pair of big, bright eyes. * What＋形容詞＋名詞＋you have.（你擁有…）
❹	你是典型的瞇瞇眼。	Your eyes look typically thin and narrow. * thin and narrow（又細又窄的）
❺	你是雙眼皮嗎？	Do you have double-folded eyelids? * single-folded（單眼皮的）
❻	你的眼皮腫腫的。	Your eyelids look swollen.
❼	你的藍色眼珠很美。	Your blue eyes are very beautiful.
❽	你的眼神很銳利。	You have sharp eyes.
❾	你想做雷射手術消除近視嗎？	Do you want to have LASIK surgery to cure your nearsightedness? * want to＋動詞原形（想要…） * have LASIK surgery（做雷射手術）
❿	你有近視嗎？	Do you have a problem with nearsightedness? * have a problem with＋某困擾（有某種困擾）
⓫	你的酒窩很可愛！	Your dimples are very cute!
⓬	你的眉色很深。	The color of your eyebrows is very dark. * color of eyebrows（眉毛顏色）
⓭	你的眉型很美。	Your eyebrow shape is very beautiful. * eyebrow shape（眉毛形狀）
⓮	你的嘴唇很性感。	You have sexy lips.
⓯	你的鼻子真挺！	You have quite a sharp nose!
⓰	你的鼻子像你爸爸。	Your nose looks like your father's. * look like...（看起來像…、長得像…）
⓱	你是櫻桃小嘴。	You have a small mouth.

	單字	音標	詞性	意義	字頻	大考	英檢	多益
❶	eye	[aɪ]	n.	眼睛	1	1	初級	
	bright	[braɪt]	adj.	明亮的	1	1	初級	
	piercing	[ˈpɪrsɪŋ]	adj.	眼神銳利的	5	6	中高	◎
❷	very	[ˈvɛrɪ]	adv.	十分	1	1	初級	
	beautiful	[ˈbjutəfəl]	adj.	美麗的	1	1	初級	
❸	big	[bɪg]	adj.	大的	1	1	初級	
	have	[hæv]	v.	擁有/動（手術）	1	1	初級	
	pair	[pɛr]	n.	一對	1	1	初級	◎
❹	look	[lʊk]	v.	看起來	1	1	初級	
	typically	[ˈtɪpɪklɪ]	adv.	典型地	1		中高	
	thin	[θɪn]	adj.	細的	1	2	初級	◎
	narrow	[ˈnæro]	adj.	窄的	1	2	初級	◎
❺	double-folded	[ˈdʌblˈfoldɪd]	adj.	雙眼皮的				
	eyelids	[ˈaɪˌlɪds]	n.	eyelid（眼皮）複數	4	5	中高	
❻	swollen	[ˈswolən]	adj.	浮腫的	4		中高	
❼	blue	[blu]	adj.	藍色的	1	1	初級	
❽	sharp	[ʃɑrp]	adj.	眼神銳利的/尖挺的	1	1	初級	◎
❾	want	[wɑnt]	v.	想要	1	1	初級	◎
	LASIK	[ˈlesɪk]	n.	雷射手術，是以下三字的縮寫：Laser-Assisted（雷射輔助的）in Situ（原位）Keratomileusis（角膜磨鑲術）				
	surgery	[ˈsɝdʒərɪ]	n.	手術	1	4	中級	◎
	cure	[kjʊr]	v.	治療	2	2	初級	◎
	nearsightedness	[ˈnɪrˈsaɪtɪdnɪs]	n.	近視				
❿	problem	[ˈprɑbləm]	n.	問題	1	1	初級	◎
⓫	dimple	[ˈdɪmpl]	n.	酒窩	7			
	cute	[kjut]	adj.	可愛的	2	1	初級	
⓬	color	[ˈkʌlɚ]	n.	顏色	1	1	初級	
	eyebrows	[ˈaɪˌbraʊs]	n.	eyebrow（眉毛）複數	2	2	中級	
	dark	[dɑrk]	adj.	深的	1	1	初級	
⓭	shape	[ʃep]	n.	形狀	1	1	初級	◎
⓮	sexy	[ˈsɛksɪ]	adj.	性感的	2	3	中級	
	lips	[lɪps]	n.	lip（嘴唇）複數	1	1	初級	
⓯	quite	[kwaɪt]	adv.	相當	1	1	初級	
	nose	[nos]	n.	鼻子	1	1	初級	
⓰	father	[ˈfɑðɚ]	n.	父親	1	1	初級	
⓱	small	[smɔl]	adj.	小的	1	1	初級	◎
	mouth	[maʊθ]	n.	嘴巴	1	1	初級	

※「紅字單字」於本單元多句出現，「單字級等分析」僅列在「首次出現句」。

015 我的頭髮。

❶	我是長髮。	I have long hair. * short（短的） * straight（直的）
❷	我有瀏海。	I have bangs.
❸	我的髮型旁分。	My hair is parted to one side. * be parted（被分開） * to one side（到其中一邊）
❹	我的髮長及腰。	I have waist-length hair. * I have shoulder-length hair.（我的頭髮到肩膀）
❺	我的頭髮有自然捲。	My hair is naturally curly. * be naturally＋形容詞（天生…）
❻	我的髮型中分。	My hair is parted in the middle. * in the middle（在中間）
❼	我把頭髮燙直了。	I had my hair straightened. * have＋某物＋過去分詞（使某物…）
❽	我染了頭髮。	I had my hair dyed.
❾	我的髮質很好。	I have good hair quality. * hair quality（髮質） * good（良好的）可替換為：poor（粗糙的）
❿	我將頭髮染成紅色。	I dyed my hair red. * dye＋某物＋顏色（將某物染成某顏色）
⓫	我每天洗頭。	I wash my hair every day.
⓬	我每星期上一次美容院。	I go to the beauty shop once a week. * beauty shop（美容院）
⓭	我的頭髮又硬又粗。	My hair is coarse and thick. * My hair is silky and soft.（我的頭髮又細又軟）
⓮	我常綁馬尾。	I usually wear my hair in a ponytail. * wear one's hair in＋髮型（使用某髮型） * a braid（一條辮子）
⓯	我經常改變髮型。	I change my hairstyle frequently.
⓰	我很喜歡我的新髮型。	I like my new hairdo very much.

	單字	音標	詞性	意義	字頻	大考	英檢	多益
❶	have	[hæv]	v.	擁有	1	1	初級	
	long	[lɔŋ]	adj.	長的	1	1	初級	
	hair	[hɛr]	n.	頭髮	1	1	初級	
❷	bang	[bæŋ]	n.	瀏海	2	3	中級	
❸	parted	[`pɑrtɪd]	p.p	part（使分開）過去分詞	1	1	初級	◎
	one	[wʌn]	n.	一	1	1	初級	
	side	[saɪd]	n.	邊	1	1	初級	
❹	waist-length	[`west.lɛŋθ]	adj.	長及腰的				
❺	naturally	[`nætʃərəlɪ]	adv.	天生地	1		中級	
	curly	[`kɝlɪ]	adj.	捲的	4			
❻	middle	[`mɪdl]	n.	中間	1	1	初級	
❼	had	[hæd]	p.t.	have（使某物…）過去式	1	1	初級	
	straightened	[`stretnd]	p.p.	straighten（弄直）過去分詞	2	5	中高	
❽	dyed	[daɪd]	p.p.	dye（染髮）過去分詞	8	4	中級	
❾	good	[gʊd]	adj.	良好的	1	1	初級	◎
	quality	[`kwɑlətɪ]	n.	品質	1	2	初級	
❿	dyed	[daɪd]	p.t.	dye（染髮）過去式				
	red	[rɛd]	n.	紅色	1	1	初級	
⓫	wash	[wɑʃ]	v.	洗	1	1	初級	
	every	[`ɛvrɪ]	adj.	每一	1	1	初級	
	day	[de]	n.	天	1	1	初級	
⓬	go	[go]	v.	去、前往	1	1	初級	
	beauty	[`bjutɪ]	n.	美容	1	1	中級	
	shop	[ʃɑp]	n.	店	1	1	初級	◎
	once	[wʌns]	adv.	一次、一回	1	1	初級	
	week	[wik]	n.	週、一星期	1	1	初級	
⓭	coarse	[kors]	adj.	粗糙的	3	4	中級	◎
	thick	[θɪk]	adj.	濃厚的	1	2	初級	
⓮	usually	[`juʒʊəlɪ]	adv.	經常	1		初級	◎
	wear	[wɛr]	v.	留成…	1	1	初級	◎
	ponytail	[`ponɪ.tel]	n.	馬尾	4			
⓯	change	[tʃendʒ]	v.	改變	1	1	初級	◎
	hairstyle	[`hɛr.staɪl]	n.	髮型	6	5	中高	
	frequently	[`frikwəntlɪ]	adv.	頻繁地	1			◎
⓰	like	[laɪk]	v.	喜歡	1	1	初級	
	new	[nju]	adj.	新的	1	1	初級	
	hairdo	[`hɛr.du]	n.	髮型	7	5		
	very	[`vɛrɪ]	adv.	十分	1	1	初級	
	much	[mʌtʃ]	adv.	非常	1	1	初級	

※「紅字單字」於本單元多句出現，「單字級等分析」僅列在「首次出現句」。

🔊 MP3 015-02 ❶～❶❺

❶	你喜歡直髮還是捲髮？	Do you like straight or curly hair?
❷	你染頭髮嗎？	Do you dye your hair?
❸	你喜歡長髮還是短髮？	Do you like long or short hair?
❹	你每天花多少時間弄頭髮？	How much time do you spend doing your hair? * spend＋動詞-ing（花時間…） * do one's hair（整理頭髮、弄頭髮）
❺	你有在護髮嗎？	Do you condition your hair? * condition＋名詞（修護…）
❻	你每天洗頭嗎？	Do you wash your hair every day?
❼	何不大膽嘗試染個金髮？	Why not be bold and try dyeing your hair blonde? * Why not...?（何不…呢？） * dye＋某物＋顏色（將某物染成某顏色）
❽	你什麼時候剪頭髮的？	When did you cut your hair? * cut one's hair（剪頭髮）
❾	你頭髮習慣分哪一邊？	Which way do you part your hair? * Which way...?（…是哪一邊？）
❿	你的頭髮真美！	What beautiful hair you have! * What＋形容詞＋名詞＋you have.（你擁有…）
⓫	你想改變髮型嗎？	Would you like to change your hairdo? * hairdo（髮型）＝ hairstyle * change one's hairdo（換髮型）
⓬	你的新髮型很適合你。	Your new hairstyle suits you. * 某事物＋suit＋某人（某事物適合某人）
⓭	我覺得你比較適合短髮。	I think short hair suits you better. * suit you better（更適合你）
⓮	你打算把頭髮留長嗎？	Do you plan to grow your hair long? * grow hair long（把頭髮留長）
⓯	你的髮型數十年不變。	Your hairstyle hasn't changed in decades. * 此句用「現在完成式」（...hasn't changed...） 表示「過去持續到現在的事」。

	單字	音標	詞性	意義	字頻	大考	英檢	多益
❶	like	[laɪk]	v.	喜歡/想要	1	1	初級	
	straight	[stret]	adj.	直的	1	2	初級	◎
	curly	[ˋkɝlɪ]	adj.	捲的	4			
	hair	[hɛr]	n.	頭髮	1	1	初級	
❷	dye	[daɪ]	v.	染髮	4	4	中級	
❸	long	[lɔŋ]	adj.	長的	1	1	初級	
	short	[ʃɔrt]	adj.	頭髮	1	1	初級	
❹	much	[mʌtʃ]	adj.	許多的	1	1	初級	
	time	[taɪm]	n.	時間	1	1	初級	◎
	spend	[spɛnd]	v.	花時間	1	1	初級	◎
	doing	[ˋduɪŋ]	n.	do（做）動名詞	1	1	初級	
❺	condition	[kənˋdɪʃən]	v.	修護	1	3	中級	◎
❻	wash	[wɑʃ]	v.	洗	1	1	初級	
	every	[ˋɛvrɪ]	adj.	每一	1	1	初級	
	day	[de]	n.	天	1	1	初級	
❼	bold	[bold]	adj.	大膽的	2	3	中級	◎
	try	[traɪ]	v.	嘗試	1	1	初級	
	dyeing	[ˋdaɪɪŋ]	n.	dye（染髮）動名詞	4	4	中級	
	blonde	[blɑnd]	adj.	金色的	3	5	中高	
❽	cut	[kʌt]	v.	剪	1	1	初級	
❾	way	[we]	n.	邊	1	1	初級	
	part	[pɑrt]	v.	使分開	1	1	初級	◎
❿	beautiful	[ˋbjutəfəl]	adj.	美麗的	1	1	初級	
	have	[hæv]	v.	擁有	1	1	初級	
⓫	change	[tʃendʒ]	v.	改變	1	2	初級	◎
	hairdo	[ˋhɛr.du]	n.	髮型	7	5		
⓬	new	[nju]	adj.	新的	1	1	初級	
	hairstyle	[ˋhɛr.staɪl]	n.	髮型	6	5	中高	
	suit	[sut]	v.	適合	1	2	初級	◎
⓭	think	[θɪŋk]	v.	認為	1	1	初級	
	better	[ˋbɛtɚ]	adv.	well（良好地）比較級	1	1	初級	
⓮	plan	[plæn]	v.	計畫	1	1	初級	◎
	grow	[gro]	v.	留頭髮	1	1	初級	◎
⓯	changed	[tʃendʒd]	p.p.	change（改變）過去分詞	4	2	初級	◎
	decade	[ˋdɛked]	n.	十年	1	3	中級	◎

※「紅字單字」於本單元多句出現，「單字級等分析」僅列在「首次出現句」。

MP3 016-01 ❶～❸

❶	我不會化妝。	I don't know how to put on makeup. * **not know how to**＋動詞原形（不會做…） * **put on**（塗抹）＝ **wear** ＝ **apply** * **makeup**（化妝品）＝ **cosmetics**
❷	臉色不好時我會上妝。	I apply makeup when my complexion looks bad.
❸	我想學化妝。	I'd like to learn how to put on makeup. * **would like to**＋動詞原形（想要…）
❹	我大學時開始化妝。	I started to use makeup when I was a college student. * **start to**＋動詞原形（開始做…）
❺	我經常使用睫毛膏。	I apply mascara regularly. * **eye shadow**（眼影）
❻	大家都說我上妝前後判若兩人。	Everyone says that I become another person when I put on makeup. * **become another person**（變成另一個人） * **when I put on makeup**（在我有上妝時）
❼	我從不戴任何飾品。	I never wear any jewelry. * **wear**＋配件（穿戴某配件）
❽	我只戴我的結婚戒指。	I only wear my wedding ring. * **wedding ring**（結婚戒指）
❾	這條項鍊對我深具意義，我總是戴著它。	I always wear this necklace which means a lot to me. * **mean a lot**（意義重大） * **to me**（對於我）
❿	我喜歡戴耳環。	I like to wear earrings. * **like to**＋動詞原形（喜歡…）
⓫	我戴眼鏡。	I wear glasses.
⓬	我們公司規定上班一定要化妝。	Our company requires its employees to wear makeup to work. * **require**＋某人＋**to**＋動詞原形（要求某人…）
⓭	我不喜歡戴眼鏡。	I don't like to wear glasses.

	單字	音標	詞性	意義	字頻	大考	英檢	多益
❶	know	[no]	v.	知道	1	1	初級	◎
	put	[pʊt]	v.	塗抹	1	1	初級	
	makeup	[`mekˌʌp]	n.	化妝品	2	4		◎
❷	apply	[ə`plaɪ]	v.	塗抹	1	2	初級	◎
	complexion	[kəm`plɛʃən]	n.	臉色、氣色	4	6	中高	
	look	[lʊk]	v.	看起來	1	1	初級	
	bad	[bæd]	adj.	不佳的	1	1	初級	
❸	like	[laɪk]	v.	想要/喜歡	1	1	初級	
	learn	[lɝn]	v.	學習	1	1	初級	
❹	started	[`stɑrtɪd]	p.t.	start（開始）過去式	1	1	初級	
	use	[juz]	v.	使用	1	1	初級	◎
	college	[`kɑlɪdʒ]	n.	大學	1	3	初級	◎
	student	[`stjudnt]	n.	學生	1	1	初級	
❺	mascara	[mæs`kærə]	n.	睫毛膏	6			
	regularly	[`rɛgjələlɪ]	adv.	定期地	2			◎
❻	everyone	[`ɛvrɪˌwʌn]	pron.	每個人	1		初級	
	say	[se]	v.	說	1	1	初級	
	become	[bɪ`kʌm]	v.	變成	1	1	初級	◎
	another	[ə`nʌðə]	adj.	另一個	1	1		
	person	[`pɝsn]	n.	人	1	1	初級	
❼	never	[`nɛvə]	adv.	從不	1	1	初級	
	wear	[wɛr]	v.	穿戴/塗抹	1	1	初級	◎
	any	[`ɛnɪ]	adj.	任何的	1	1	初級	
	jewelry	[`dʒuəlrɪ]	n.	飾品	2	3		
❽	only	[`onlɪ]	adv.	只有	1	1	初級	
	wedding	[`wɛdɪŋ]	adj.	結婚的	1	1	初級	
	ring	[rɪŋ]	n.	戒指	1	1	初級	
❾	always	[`ɔlwez]	adv.	總是	1	1	初級	
	this	[ðɪs]	adj.	這個	1	1	初級	
	necklace	[`nɛklɪs]	n.	項鍊	3	2	初級	
	mean	[min]	v.	具…意義	1	2	初級	◎
	lot	[lɑt]	n.	許多	1			
❿	earrings	[`ɪrˌrɪŋs]	n.	earing（耳環）複數	3		中級	
⓫	glasses	[`glæsɪz]	n.	glass（眼鏡）複數	2	1	中級	
⓬	company	[`kʌmpənɪ]	n.	公司	1	2	初級	◎
	require	[rɪ`kwaɪr]	v.	要求	1	2	初級	◎
	employee	[ˌɛmplɔɪ`i]	n.	員工	1	3	中級	◎
	work	[wɝk]	v.	工作	1	1	初級	◎

※「紅字單字」於本單元多句出現，「單字級等分析」僅列在「首次出現句」。

016　你的裝扮？

🔵 MP3 016-02 ❶〜❸

❶	你每天化妝嗎？	Do you wear makeup every day?
❷	你怎麼學會化妝的？	How did you learn to put on cosmetics? * **How did you...?**（你當時是如何…？）
❸	你的耳環真漂亮。	Your earrings are very beautiful.
❹	你幾歲開始化妝的？	How old were you when you began to apply cosmetics? * **begin to＋動詞原形**（開始做…）
❺	你的妝很時髦。	The makeup you put on looks very fashionable. * **the makeup you put on**（你化的妝）
❻	擦口紅讓你比較有精神。	Wearing lipstick makes you more energetic. * **wearing lipstick**（擦口紅，在此句是動名詞當主詞）
❼	你的彩妝很自然。	Your makeup looks very natural.
❽	有時候化妝是一種禮貌。	Sometimes, applying makeup is a matter of good manners. * **a matter of...**（關於…） * **good manners**（有禮貌）
❾	這個顏色的眼影很適合你。	This color of eye shadow really fits you. * **color of...**（…的顏色） * **fit＋某人**（適合某人）
❿	越來越多的年輕女生開始化妝。	More and more young ladies are beginning to put on cosmetics. * **begin to＋動詞原形**（開始…） * 此句用「現在進行式」（...are beginning...）表示「現階段發生的事」。
⓫	你可以教我化妝嗎？	Can you teach me how to put on makeup?
⓬	你戴隱形眼鏡嗎？	Do you wear contact lenses? * **contact lenses**（隱形眼鏡）
⓭	適度化妝可以為自己加分。	An appropriate amount of makeup can really add to your looks. * **an appropriate amount**（適量） * **add to one's looks**（為某人外貌加分）

	單字	音標	詞性	意義	字頻	大考	英檢	多益
❶	wear	[wɛr]	v.	塗抹/穿戴	1	1	初級	◎
	makeup	[`mek.ʌp]	n.	化妝品	2	4		◎
	every	[`ɛvrɪ]	adj.	每一	1	1	初級	
	day	[de]	n.	天	1	1	初級	
❷	learn	[lɜn]	v.	學習	1	1	初級	
	put	[put]	v.	塗抹	1	1	初級	
	cosmetics	[kɑz`mɛtɪks]	n.	化妝品	4	6		
❸	earrings	[`ɪr.rɪŋs]	n.	earing（耳環）複數	3		中級	
	very	[`vɛrɪ]	adv.	十分	1	1	初級	
	beautiful	[`bjutəfəl]	adj.	美麗的	1	1	初級	
❹	old	[old]	adj.	…歲	1	1	初級	
	began	[bɪ`gæn]	p.t.	begin（開始）過去式	1	1	初級	
	apply	[ə`plaɪ]	v.	塗抹	1	2	初級	◎
❺	look	[luk]	v./n.	看起來/外表、外貌	1	1	初級	
	fashionable	[`fæʃənəbl̩]	adj.	時髦的	3	3	初級	
❻	wearing	[`wɛrɪŋ]	n.	wear（塗抹）動名詞	7	1	初級	◎
	lipstick	[`lɪp.stɪk]	n.	口紅	3	3	中級	
	make	[mek]	v.	使得	1	1	初級	
	energetic	[ˌɛnɚ`dʒɛtɪk]	adj.	充滿活力的	3	3	中級	
❼	natural	[`nætʃərəl]	adj.	自然的	1	2	初級	
❽	sometimes	[`sʌm.taɪmz]	adv.	有時	1	1	初級	
	applying	[ə`plaɪɪŋ]	n.	apply（塗抹）動名詞	2	2	初級	◎
	matter	[`mætɚ]	n.	事情、問題	1	1	初級	◎
	good	[gud]	adj.	良好的	1	1	初級	◎
	manner	[`mænɚ]	n.	禮貌	2	3		◎
❾	this	[ðɪs]	adj.	這個	1	1	初級	
	color	[`kʌlɚ]	n.	顏色	1	1	初級	
	eye	[aɪ]	n.	眼睛	1	1	初級	
	shadow	[`ʃædo]	n.	陰影	1	3	中級	◎
	really	[`rɪəlɪ]	adv.	很、十分	1		初級	
	fit	[fɪt]	v.	適合	1	2	初級	◎
❿	more	[mor]	adj.	many（許多的）比較級	1	1	初級	
	young	[jʌŋ]	adj.	年輕的	1	1	初級	
	lady	[ledɪ]	n.	女士	1	1	初級	
	beginning	[bɪ`gɪnɪŋ]	p.pr.	begin（開始）現在分詞	1	1	初級	
⓫	teach	[titʃ]	v.	教導	1	1	初級	
⓬	contact	[`kɑntækt]	n.	接觸	1	2	初級	◎
	lenses	[`lɛnzɪz]	n.	lens（鏡片）複數	2	3	中級	
⓭	appropriate	[ə`proprɪ.et]	adj.	適度的	1	4	中級	◎
	amount	[ə`maunt]	n.	數量	1	2	初級	◎
	add	[æd]	v.	加分	1	1	初級	◎

※「紅字單字」於本單元多句出現，「單字級等分析」僅列在「首次出現句」。

017 我的穿著。

🔊 MP3 017-01 ❶～❹

❶	我看場合穿衣服。	I dress for the occasion. * **dress for...**（因應…穿衣服）
❷	我穿套裝上班。	I wear a suit to work.
❸	假日時我穿得很休閒。	I dress casually on weekends. * **dress casually**（穿著休閒、穿著隨興）
❹	我們公司允許員工隨興打扮。	Our company allows us to dress casually for work. * **allow＋某人＋to＋動詞原形**（允許某人…）
❺	上班時我穿制服。	I wear a uniform at work. * **at work**（工作時）
❻	出席宴會我會穿上小禮服。	I wear semi-formal clothes when I attend a banquet. * **semi-formal clothes**（小禮服）
❼	我喜歡簡單大方的穿著。	I like simple and tasteful clothing.
❽	我最愛 T 恤及牛仔褲。	I love T-shirts and jeans the most. * **love＋某事物＋the most**（最喜愛某事物） * **pants**（長褲） * **shorts**（短褲）
❾	我偏愛長裙。	Long skirts are my favorite.
❿	我有各種款式的牛仔褲。	I have every style of jeans. * **every style of...**（各個款式的…）
⓫	我喜歡寬鬆的衣服。	I like loose-fitting clothes. * **form-fitting**（合身的）
⓬	我經常為了搭配衣服而苦惱。	I usually struggle to decide what to wear. * **struggle to＋動詞原形**（掙扎於…） * **what to wear**（要穿什麼）
⓭	我每個月的置裝費約 5000 元。	My monthly clothing budget is about NT$5000. * **clothing budget**（置裝費）
⓮	我喜歡穿高跟鞋。	I like to wear high heels. * **high heels**（高跟鞋） * **sneakers**（運動鞋） * **leather shoes**（皮鞋） * **canvas shoes**（帆布鞋） * **boots**（靴子）

單字級等分析

	單字	音標	詞性	意義	字頻	大考	英檢	多益
❶	dress	[drɛs]	v.	穿著	1	2	初級	
	occasion	[oˋkeʒən]	n.	場合	1	3	中級	◎
❷	wear	[wɛr]	v.	穿	1	1	初級	◎
	suit	[sut]	n.	西裝、套裝	1	2	初級	◎
	work	[wɝk]	v./n.	工作	1	1	初級	◎
❸	casually	[ˋkæʒjuəlɪ]	adv.	隨意地	3			◎
	weekend	[ˋwikˋɛnd]	n.	週末	1	1	初級	
❹	company	[ˋkʌmpənɪ]	n.	公司	1	2	初級	◎
	allow	[əˋlaʊ]	v.	允許	1	1	初級	
❺	uniform	[ˋjunəˌfɔrm]	n.	制服	2	2	初級	
❻	semi-formal	[ˋsɛmɪˋfɔrml]	adj.	半正式著裝的				
	clothes	[kloz]	n.	cloth（衣服）複數	1	2	初級	
	attend	[əˋtɛnd]	v.	參加	1	2	初級	◎
	banquet	[ˋbæŋkwɪt]	n.	宴會	4	5	中高	◎
❼	like	[laɪk]	v.	喜歡	1	1	初級	
	simple	[ˋsɪmpl]	adj.	簡單的	1	1	初級	◎
	tasteful	[ˋtestfəl]	adj.	有品味的	7		中級	
	clothing	[ˋkloðɪŋ]	n.	衣服	1		中級	
❽	love	[lʌv]	v.	喜愛	1	1	初級	
	T-shirt	[ˋtiˌʃɝt]	n.	T恤	2	1	初級	
	jeans	[dʒinz]	n.	jean（牛仔褲）複數	2	2	初級	
	most	[most]	adv.	最	1	1	初級	
❾	long	[lɔŋ]	adj.	長的	1	1	初級	
	skirt	[skɝt]	n.	裙子	2	2	初級	
	favorite	[ˋfevərɪt]	adj.	最喜歡的	1	2	初級	◎
❿	have	[hæv]	v.	擁有	1	1	初級	
	every	[ˋɛvrɪ]	adj.	各種的	1	1	初級	
	style	[staɪl]	n.	風格	1	3	初級	◎
⓫	loose-fitting	[ˋlusˋfɪtɪŋ]	adj.	寬鬆的				
⓬	usually	[ˋjuʒuəlɪ]	adv.	經常	1		初級	◎
	struggle	[ˋstrʌgl]	v.	掙扎	1	2	初級	◎
	decide	[dɪˋsaɪd]	v.	決定	1	1	初級	◎
⓭	monthly	[ˋmʌnθlɪ]	adj.	每月的	2	4	初級	◎
	budget	[ˋbʌdʒɪt]	n.	費用、預算	1	3	中級	◎
⓮	high	[haɪ]	adj.	高的	1	1	初級	
	heels	[hils]	n.	heel（高跟鞋）複數	2	3	中級	

※「紅字單字」於本單元多句出現，「單字級等分析」僅列在「首次出現句」。

017 你的穿著？

MP3 017-02 ❶～⓮

❶	你喜歡穿裙子還是褲子？	Do you like to wear skirts or pants? * **like to＋動詞原形（喜歡）**
❷	你偏好什麼樣的穿著？	Which style of clothing do you like? * **Which style of...?（什麼樣的…？）**
❸	你會注意當季的流行資訊嗎?	Do you pay attention to the current season's fashion news? * **pay attention to（留意）** * **current season（當季）**
❹	你上班穿制服嗎？	Do you wear a uniform to work?
❺	你今天穿的衣服很適合你。	The clothes you are wearing today really suit you. * **服飾＋you are wearing（你現在穿的服飾）**
❻	這是新衣服嗎？	Are these new clothes?
❼	你想嘗試高跟鞋嗎？	Would you like to try high heels? * **Would you like to＋動詞原形＋...?（你是否想要…？）**
❽	你很會搭配衣服。	You really know how to put together an outfit. * **you really know＋子句（你很了解…）** * **put together an outfit（搭配一套衣服）**
❾	你的鞋子很好看。	Your shoes are beautiful.
❿	你真是天生的衣架子。	You really are born to wear anything. * **be born to wear anything（天生衣架子）**
⓫	你穿西裝真帥！	You look terrific in that suit! * **in that suit（穿著那件西裝）**
⓬	女人的衣服永遠少一件。	Women's wardrobes are always short one item. * **be short...（缺少…）** * **one item（一個品項）**
⓭	你的置裝費一定很可觀。	Your clothing budget must be considerable.
⓮	你的鞋子跟衣服很搭。	Your shoes really match your clothes. * **A match B（A 和 B 很相搭）**

單字級等分析

	單字	音標	詞性	意義	字頻	大考	英檢	多益
❶	like	[laɪk]	v.	喜歡/想要	1	1	初級	
	wear	[wɛr]	v.	穿	1	1	初級	◎
	skirt	[skɝt]	n.	裙子	2	2	初級	
	pants	[pænts]	n.	pant（複數）褲子	3	1	初級	
❷	style	[staɪl]	n.	風格	1	3	初級	◎
	clothing	[ˈkloðɪŋ]	n.	衣服	1	2	中級	
❸	pay	[pe]	v.	給予	1	3	初級	◎
	attention	[əˈtɛnʃən]	n.	注意	1	2	初級	◎
	current	[ˈkɝnt]	adj.	當前的	1	3	初級	◎
	season	[ˈsizn]	n.	季度	1	1	初級	◎
	fashion	[ˈfæʃən]	n.	流行、時尚	1	3	中級	◎
	news	[njuz]	n.	資訊	1	1	初級	◎
❹	uniform	[ˈjunəˌfɔrm]	n.	制服	2	2	初級	◎
	work	[wɝk]	v.	工作	1	1	初級	◎
❺	clothes	[kloz]	n.	cloth（衣服）複數	1	2	初級	
	wearing	[ˈwɛrɪŋ]	p.pr.	wear（穿）現在分詞	7	1	初級	
	today	[təˈde]	adv.	今天	1	1	初級	
	really	[ˈrɪəlɪ]	adv.	很、非常/真的	1	1	初級	
	suit	[sut]	v./n.	適合/套裝、西裝	1	1	初級	
❻	these	[ðiz]	pron.	這些	1	1	初級	
	new	[nju]	adj.	新的	1	1	初級	
❼	try	[traɪ]	v.	嘗試	1	1	初級	
	high	[haɪ]	adj.	高的	1	1	初級	
	heels	[hils]	n.	heel（高跟鞋）複數	2	3	中級	
❽	know	[no]	v.	知道	1	1	初級	◎
	put	[pʊt]	v.	放置	1	1	初級	
	together	[təˈgɛðɚ]	adv.	一起	1	1	初級	
	outfit	[ˈaʊtˌfɪt]	n.	裝扮	2	6	中高	◎
❾	shoes	[ʃuz]	n.	shoe（鞋子）複數	2	1		
	beautiful	[ˈbjutəfəl]	adj.	美麗的	1	1	初級	
❿	born	[bɔrn]	p.p.	bear（出生）過去分詞	1	1	初級	
	anything	[ˈɛnɪˌθɪŋ]	pron.	任何事物	1	1	初級	
⓫	look	[lʊk]	v.	看起來	1	1	初級	
	terrific	[təˈrɪfɪk]	adj.	非常好的	2	2	初級	◎
	that	[ðæt]	adj.	那個	1	1	初級	
⓬	women	[ˈwɪmɪn]	n.	woman（女人）複數	1	1	初級	
	wardrobe	[ˈwɔrˌrob]	n.	衣櫥、衣櫃	3	6	中高	◎
	always	[ˈɔlwez]	adv.	總是	1	1	初級	
	short	[ʃɔrt]	adj.	缺少的	1	1	初級	
	one	[wʌn]	n.	一個	1	1	初級	
	item	[ˈaɪtəm]	n.	品項	1	2	初級	◎
⓭	budget	[ˈbʌdʒɪt]	n.	費用、預算	1	3	中級	◎
	considerable	[kənˈsɪdərəbl]	adj.	數字可觀的	2	3	中級	◎
⓮	match	[mætʃ]	v.	相搭	1	2	初級	◎

※「紅字單字」於本單元多句出現，「單字級等分析」僅列在「首次出現句」。　　109

018　我的工作。

🔊 MP3 018-01 ❶～❸

❶	我還在唸書。	I am still in school. = I am still a student.
❷	我是朝九晚五的上班族。	I am part of the 9-to-5 workforce. * 9-to-5 workforce（朝九晚五的工作者）
❸	我和朋友經營一間店。	My friends and I manage a shop.
❹	我自己創業當老闆。	I've started my own business and am my own boss. * 此句用「現在完成式」（...have started...）表示「過去某時點發生某事，且結果持續到現在」。
❺	我的工作完全與所學無關。	My job has nothing to do with what I learned in school. * have nothing to do with...（與…完全無關） * have something to do with...（與…有些關係）
❻	我是在家工作的 SOHO 族。	I work at home. * at home（在家裡）
❼	我在電視台上班。	I work at a TV station. * work at＋某種公司（在某種公司上班）
❽	我從事服務業。	I work in the service industry. * work in＋產業（在某產業上班）
❾	我是公務員。	I am a public servant. * public servant（公務員）
❿	我們公司在台北市中心。	Our firm is located in downtown Taipei. * be located in（位於） * downtown＋城市（…市中心）
⓫	我嘗試過很多不同的工作。	I have tried my hand at various professions. * try one's hand at＋某事（嘗試做某事）
⓬	我的工作是目前最熱門的行業。	My job is currently the most fashionable profession.
⓭	我同時兼差好幾份工作。	I currently hold more than one job. * hold one job（有一份工作） * more than（多於）

	單字	音標	詞性	意義	字頻	大考	英檢	多益
❶	still	[stɪl]	adv.	仍然	1	1	初級	◎
	school	[skul]	n.	學校	1	1	初級	
	student	[`stjudnt]	n.	學生	1	1	初級	◎
❷	part	[pɑrt]	n.	一部分	1	1	初級	◎
	workforce	[`wɜk.fɔrs]	n.	上班族				
❸	friend	[frɛnd]	n.	朋友	1	1	初級	
	manage	[`mænɪdʒ]	v.	經營	1	3	中級	◎
	shop	[ʃɑp]	n.	店	1	1	初級	◎
❹	started	[`stɑrtɪd]	p.p.	start（開始）過去分詞	1	1	初級	
	own	[on]	adj.	自己的	1	1	初級	◎
	business	[`bɪznɪs]	n.	公司、企業	1	2	初級	◎
	boss	[bɔs]	n.	老闆	1	2	初級	
❺	job	[dʒɑb]	n.	工作	1	1	初級	
	have	[hæv]	v.	擁有	1	1	初級	
	nothing	[`nʌθɪŋ]	pron.	沒有事情	1	1	初級	
	do	[du]	v.	關聯	1	1	初級	
	learned	[`lɜnɪd]	p.t.	learn（學習）過去式	4	4	中級	
❻	work	[wɜk]	v.	工作	1	1	初級	◎
	home	[hom]	n.	家	1	1	初級	
❼	TV	[`ti`vi]	n.	television（電視）縮寫		2	初級	
	station	[`steʃən]	n.	電台、電視台	1	1	初級	
❽	service	[`sɜvɪs]	n.	服務	1	1	初級	
	industry	[`ɪndəstrɪ]	n.	產業	1	2	初級	◎
❾	public	[`pʌblɪk]	n.	公共的	1	1	初級	
	servant	[`sɜvənt]	n.	公僕	2	2	初級	
❿	firm	[fɜm]	n.	公司	1	2	初級	◎
	located	[`loketɪd]	p.p.	locate（位在）過去分詞	1	2	中高	◎
	downtown	[.daun`taun]	adj.	市中心的	2	2	初級	◎
	Taipei	[`taɪ`pe]	n.	台北				
⓫	tried	[traɪd]	p.p.	try（嘗試）過去分詞	7	1	初級	
	hand	[hɛnd]	n.	技能、技藝	1	1	初級	
	various	[`vɛrɪəs]	adj.	各種的	1	3	中級	◎
	profession	[prə`fɛʃən]	n.	職業	2	4	中級	◎
⓬	currently	[`kɜəntlɪ]	adv.	當前地	1			◎
	most	[most]	adv.	最	1	1	初級	
	fashionable	[`fæʃənəbl]	adj.	熱門的	3	3	初級	◎
⓭	hold	[hold]	v.	擁有⋯工作	1	1	初級	
	more	[mor]	adv.	多於	1	1	初級	
	one	[wʌn]	n.	一	1	1	初級	

※「紅字單字」於本單元多句出現，「單字級等分析」僅列在「首次出現句」。

018　你的工作？

MP3 018-02 ❶～❶

❶	你從事什麼工作？	What do you do for a living? * for a living（謀生）
❷	你自己創業嗎？	Do you run your own business? * one's own business（自己的公司）
❸	你和朋友共同創業嗎？	Do you jointly run a company with your friend? * jointly run（共同經營）
❹	你在哪間公司上班？	Which company do you work for? * work for＋公司（在某公司上班）
❺	你們公司是做什麼的？	What's your company's main business? * main business（主要的業務項目）
❻	你們公司有多少員工？	How many employees are in your firm? * firm（公司）＝ company
❼	你們公司在哪裡？	Where is your firm located?
❽	你們公司很有名。	Your company is very well known. * well known（知名的，眾所皆知的）
❾	你屬於哪一個部門？	Which department do you belong to? * belong to＋部門（屬於某部門）
❿	你的職務是什麼？	What is your job title? * job title（職稱）
⓫	很多人擠破頭想進你們公司。	A lot of people would do anything to work for your company. * would do anything（願意做任何事）
⓬	你有兼職的工作嗎？	Do you still hold any part-time jobs?
⓭	你的工作跟所學相關嗎？	Does your current job relate to what you learned in school? * relate to...（與…相關）
⓮	你的工作是目前最熱門的產業。	Your job is currently the most popular one on the market. * on the market（市面上）
⓯	你怎麼找到這份工作的？	How did you find this job?
⓰	你們公司打算徵人嗎？	Does your company plan to recruit new employees? * plan to＋動詞原形（計畫…） * new employee（新人）

	單字	音標	詞性	意義	字頻	大考	英檢	多益
❶	do	[du]	v.	從事/做	1	1	初級	
	living	[ˋlɪvɪŋ]	n.	生計	1	1	中高	
❷	run	[rʌn]	v.	經營	1	1	初級	
	own	[on]	adj.	自己的	1	1	初級	◎
	business	[ˋbɪznɪs]	n.	公司/業務	1	2	初級	◎
❸	jointly	[ˋdʒɔɪntlɪ]	adv.	共同地	4			◎
	company	[ˋkʌmpənɪ]	n.	公司	1	2	初級	◎
	friend	[frɛnd]	n.	朋友	1	1	初級	
❹	work	[wɝk]	v.	工作	1	1	初級	◎
❺	main	[men]	adj.	主要的	1	2	初級	◎
❻	many	[ˋmɛnɪ]	adj.	許多的	1	1	初級	
	employee	[ˏɛmplɔɪˋi]	n.	員工	1	3	中級	◎
	firm	[fɝm]	n.	公司	1	2	初級	◎
❼	located	[ˋloketɪd]	p.p.	locate（位於）過去分詞	1	2	中高	◎
❽	very	[ˋvɛrɪ]	adv.	十分	1	1	初級	
	well	[wɛl]	adv.	良好地	1	1	初級	◎
	known	[non]	p.p.	know（知道）過去分詞	2	1	初級	◎
❾	department	[dɪˋpartmənt]	n.	部門	1	2	初級	◎
	belong	[bəˋlɔŋ]	v.	屬於	1	1	初級	
❿	job	[dʒɑb]	n.	工作	1	1	初級	
	title	[ˋtaɪtl̩]	n.	稱謂	1	2	初級	◎
⓫	lot	[lɑt]	n.	許多	1	1		
	people	[ˋpipl̩]	n.	person（人）複數	1	1	初級	
	anything	[ˋɛnɪˏθɪŋ]	pron.	任何東西	1	1	初級	
⓬	still	[stɪl]	adv.	仍然	1	1	初級	◎
	hold	[hold]	v.	擁有	1	1	初級	
	any	[ˋɛnɪ]	adj.	任何的	1	1	初級	
	part-time	[ˋpartˋtaɪm]	adj.	兼職的	2		中高	◎
⓭	current	[ˋkɝənt]	adj.	當前的	1	3	初級	◎
	relate	[rɪˋlet]	v.	有關聯	4	3	中級	◎
	learned	[ˋlɝnɪd]	p.t.	learn（學習）過去式	4	4	中級	
	school	[skul]	n.	學校	1	1	初級	
⓮	currently	[ˋkɝəntlɪ]	adv.	當前地	1			◎
	most	[most]	adv.	最	1	1	初級	
	popular	[ˋpapjələ]	adj.	有名的	1	2	初級	
	one	[wʌn]	pron.	一個	1	1	初級	
	market	[ˋmarkɪt]	n.	市場	1	1	初級	
⓯	find	[faɪnd]	v.	找到	1	1	初級	
	this	[ðɪs]	adj.	這個	1	1	初級	
⓰	plan	[plæn]	v.	計畫	1	1	初級	◎
	recruit	[rɪˋkrut]	v.	招募	2	6	中高	◎
	new	[nju]	adj.	新的	1	1	初級	

※「紅字單字」於本單元多句出現，「單字級等分析」僅列在「首次出現句」。

019　我的工作內容。

❶	我的工作內容一成不變。	The nature of my job is unchanging.
❷	我的工作很繁瑣。	My work is very complicated. * simple（簡單的）
❸	我需要經常出差。	I have to go on business trips regularly. * go on a business trip（出差） = take a business trip
❹	我必須控管產品的品質。	I manage quality control. * quality control（品管）
❺	我的工作是負責協助我的上司。	My job is assisting my manager. * My job is＋動詞-ing（我的工作是…）
❻	我的工作需要長時間盯著電腦螢幕。	At work, I have to stare at a computer for long periods of time. * stare at＋人事物（注視某人事物） * long periods of time（長時間）
❼	我必須向客戶介紹新產品。	I have to introduce our clients to our new products. * introduce＋某人＋to＋產品（介紹產品給某人）
❽	我負責解決客戶的所有問題。	I am in charge of dealing with all the problems that are brought up by our clients. * be in charge of＋動詞-ing（負責） * deal with（處理） * bring up（提及）
❾	我在公司從基層做起。	I started out at the bottom of the company. * start out（開始職業生涯） * 此句用「過去簡單式」（...started...）表示「發生在過去的事」。
❿	接聽電話是我的工作之一。	Answering telephones is part of my job. * Answering telephones is...（接聽電話是…） * 此句用動名詞（answering telephones）當主詞。
⓫	我常常一整天都在開會。	I am often in meetings for the whole day. * be in meetings（在開會） * for the whole day（一整天）
⓬	我負責行銷企畫。	I am in charge of planning and marketing.

	單字	音標	詞性	意義	字頻	大考	英檢	多益
❶	nature	[`netʃɚ]	n.	性質	1	1	初級	◎
	job	[dʒɑb]	n.	工作	1	1	初級	
	unchanging	[ʌn`tʃɛndʒɪŋ]	adj.	沒有變化的	7			
❷	work	[wɜk]	n.	工作	1	1	初級	◎
	very	[`vɛrɪ]	adv.	非常	1	1	初級	
	complicated	[`kɑmplə.ketɪd]	adj.	繁複的	1		中級	◎
❸	have	[hæv]	v.	必須	1	1	初級	
	go	[go]	v.	去、前往	1	1	初級	
	business	[`bɪznɪs]	n.	商務	1	2	初級	◎
	trip	[trɪp]	n.	旅行	1	1	初級	◎
	regularly	[`rɛgjələlɪ]	adv.	定期地	2			◎
❹	manage	[`mænɪdʒ]	v.	負責	1	3	中級	◎
	quality	[`kwɑlətɪ]	n.	品質	1		初級	◎
	control	[kən`trol]	n.	管制	1	2	初級	◎
❺	assisting	[ə`sɪstɪŋ]	n.	assist（協助）動名詞	1	3	中級	◎
	manager	[`mænɪdʒɚ]	n.	上司	1	3	初級	◎
❻	stare	[stɛr]	v.	凝視	1	3	中級	◎
	computer	[kəm`pjutɚ]	n.	電腦	1	2	初級	
	long	[lɔŋ]	adj.	長的	1	1	初級	
	period	[`pɪrɪəd]	n.	時期、期間	1	2	初級	◎
	time	[taɪm]	n.	時間	1	1	初級	
❼	introduce	[.ɪntrə`djus]	v.	介紹	1	2	初級	◎
	client	[`klaɪənt]	n.	客戶	1	3	中級	
	new	[nju]	adj.	新的	1	1	初級	
	product	[`prɑdʌkt]	n.	產品	1	3	初級	◎
❽	charge	[tʃɑrdʒ]	n.	掌管、責任	1	2	初級	◎
	dealing	[`dilɪŋ]	n.	deal（處理）動名詞	2	1	中高	
	all	[ɔl]	adj.	所有的	1	1	初級	
	problem	[`prɑbləm]	n.	問題	1	1	初級	◎
	brought	[brɔt]	p.p.	bring（帶來）過去分詞	1	1	初級	
	up	[ʌp]	adv.	出現	1	1	初級	
❾	started	[`stɑrtɪd]	p.t.	start（開始）過去式	1	1	初級	
	out	[aʊt]	adv.	出現	1	1	初級	
	bottom	[`bɑtəm]	n.	底層	1	1	初級	◎
	company	[`kʌmpənɪ]	n.	公司	1	2	初級	◎
❿	answering	[`ænsɚɪŋ]	n.	answer（接聽）動名詞	3	1	初級	
	telephone	[`tɛlə.fon]	n.	電話	1	2	初級	
	part	[pɑrt]	n.	一部分	1	1	初級	
⓫	often	[`ɔfən]	adv.	常常	1	1	初級	
	meeting	[`mitɪŋ]	n.	會議	1	2	初級	
	whole	[hol]	adj.	整個的	1	1	初級	◎
	day	[de]	n.	天	1	1	初級	
⓬	planning	[`plænɪŋ]	n.	企劃	1	1	初級	◎
	marketing	[`mɑkɪtɪŋ]	n.	行銷	1	1	中高	◎

※「紅字單字」於本單元多句出現，「單字級等分析」僅列在「首次出現句」。

🔊 MP3 019-02 ❶～❶⑤

❶	你的工作內容是什麼？	What are your job responsibilities? * job responsibility（工作義務、職務內容）
❷	你的工作有趣嗎？	Is your job interesting?
❸	你的工作有挑戰性嗎？	Is your job challenging?
❹	你的工作必須用到英文嗎？	Does your job require the use of English? * English（英文）可替換為：computers（電腦）
❺	你有一個工作團隊嗎？	Do you work with a team? * with a team（和團隊一起）
❻	你都是獨立作業嗎？	Do you work independently?
❼	你用 Skype 和客戶聯絡嗎？	Do you use Skype to contact your clients? * contact one's clients（聯絡客戶）
❽	你必須公司大小事一手包嗎？	Are you responsible for every issue, large and small, in your company? * be responsible for（負責） 　= be in charge of
❾	你有助理嗎？	Do you have an assistant?
❿	你有整天接不完的電話嗎？	Do you have phone calls that never stop coming? * stop＋動詞-ing（停止）
⑪	你在公司從基層做起嗎？	Did you start out at the bottom of your company? * bottom of company（公司底層）
⑫	你必須經常出差嗎？	Do you need to take frequent business trips? * take a business trip（出差）
⑬	你必須經常拜訪客戶嗎？	Do you need to visit clients frequently? * visit a client（拜訪客戶）
⑭	你有開不完的會嗎？	Do you have meetings that never seem to end? * seem to＋動詞原形（似乎…）
⑮	你的工作一成不變嗎？	Does your work never change?

	單字	音標	詞性	意義	字頻	大考	英檢	多益
❶	job	[dʒɑb]	n.	工作	1	1	初級	
	responsibility	[rɪ‚spɑnsə`bɪlətɪ]	n.	責任	1	3	中級	◎
❷	interesting	[`ɪntərɪstɪŋ]	adj.	有趣的	1		中級	
❸	challenging	[`tʃælɪndʒɪŋ]	adj.	挑戰性的	2	3	中級	◎
❹	require	[rɪ`kwaɪr]	v.	要求	1	2	初級	◎
	use	[juz]	n./v.	運用/使用	1	1	初級	◎
	English	[`ɪŋglɪʃ]	n.	英文	1	1	初級	
❺	work	[wɜk]	v.	工作	1	1	初級	
	team	[tim]	n.	團隊	1	2	初級	
❻	independently	[‚ɪndɪ`pɛdəntlɪ]	adv.	獨立地	3			
❼	contact	[kən`tækt]	v.	聯絡	1	2	初級	◎
	client	[`klaɪənt]	n.	客戶	1	3	中級	◎
❽	responsible	[rɪ`spɑnsəbl]	adj.	負責的	1	2	初級	◎
	every	[`ɛvrɪ]	adj.	每個	1	1	初級	
	issue	[`ɪʃʊ]	n.	事務	1	5	中級	
	large	[lɑrdʒ]	adj.	大的	1	1	初級	
	small	[smɔl]	adj.	小的	1	1	初級	
	company	[`kʌmpənɪ]	n.	公司	1	2	初級	
❾	have	[hæv]	v.	擁有	1	1	初級	
	assistant	[ə`sɪstənt]	n.	助理	1	2	初級	◎
❿	phone	[fon]	n.	電話	1	1	初級	◎
	call	[kɔl]	n.	電話、通話	1	1	初級	◎
	never	[`nɛvɚ]	adv.	從不	1	1	初級	
	stop	[stɑp]	v.	停止	1	1	初級	◎
	coming	[`kʌmɪŋ]	n.	come（來電）動名詞	2	1	中級	
⓫	start	[stɑrt]	v.	開始	1	1	初級	
	out	[aʊt]	adv.	出現、顯露	1	1	初級	
	bottom	[`bɑtəm]	n.	底層	1	1	初級	◎
⓬	need	[nid]	v.	需要	1	1	初級	
	take	[tek]	v.	採取	1	1	初級	
	frequent	[`frikwənt]	adj.	頻繁的	2	3	中級	◎
	business	[`bɪznɪs]	n.	商務	1	2	初級	◎
	trip	[trɪp]	n.	旅行	1	1	初級	◎
⓭	visit	[`vɪzɪt]	v.	拜訪	1	1	初級	◎
	frequently	[`frikwəntlɪ]	adv.	頻繁地	1			◎
⓮	meeting	[`mitɪŋ]	n.	會議	1	2	初級	
	seem	[sim]	v.	似乎	1	1	初級	
	end	[ɛnd]	v.	結束	1	1	初級	
⓯	change	[tʃendʒ]	v.	改變	1	2	初級	◎

※「紅字單字」於本單元多句出現，「單字級等分析」僅列在「首次出現句」。

MP3 020-01 ❶～❸

❶	我每天九點上班，六點下班。	I arrive to work at nine am and leave at six pm. * **arrive to work**（到班）
❷	我每天工作八小時。	I work eight hours a day.
❸	我們公司午休是一個小時。	Our company's lunch break is one hour long. * **lunch break**（午休） * 時間＋**long**（…的時間長度）
❹	公司午休時間是十二點到下午一點。	The company's lunch break is from 12:00 pm to 1:00 pm. * **from**＋時間＋**to**＋時間（從…時間，到…時間）
❺	我的工作時間不固定。	My work schedule is not fixed.
❻	我們公司採輪班制。	Our company adopts a shift-work system. * **shift-work system**（輪班制） 　＝ **shift rotation system**
❼	我已經好幾個月沒休假了。	It's been several months since my last vacation. * **since last vacation**（自從上次休假以後）
❽	我們公司週休二日。	Our company has a two-day weekend. * **two-day weekend**（週休二日）
❾	我從不遲到早退。	I have never arrived late or left early. * 此句用「現在完成式」（…**have never arrived**… **or left**…）表示「過去持續到現在的事」。 * **arrive late**（遲到） * **leave early**（早退）
❿	我一年有七天年假。	I get a seven-day annual leave. * **annual leave**（年假）
⓫	我經常假日也到公司加班。	I often have to work overtime even on holidays. * **work overtime**（加班）
⓬	我經常加班到深夜。	I often work late into the night. * **late into the night**（直到深夜） * **into**（進入到）
⓭	我來公司五年了。	I have been working with this company for five years. * 此句用「現在完成進行式」（…**have been working**…）表示「從過去開始、且直到現在仍持續中的事」。

	單字	音標	詞性	意義	字頻	大考	英檢	多益
❶	arrive	[əˋraɪv]	v.	到達	1	2	初級	◎
	work	[wɜk]	v.	工作	1	1	初級	◎
	nine	[naɪn]	n.	九	1	1	初級	
	am	[ˋeˋɛm]	adv.	上午	1	4	初級	
	leave	[liv]	v./n.	離開/休假日	1	1	初級	◎
	six	[sɪks]	n.	六	1	1	初級	
	pm	[ˋpiˋɛm]	adv.	下午	1	4		
❷	eight	[et]	n.	八	1	1	初級	
	hour	[aʊr]	n.	小時	1	1	初級	
	day	[de]	n.	天	1	1	初級	
❸	company	[ˋkʌmpənɪ]	n.	公司	1	2	初級	◎
	lunch	[lʌntʃ]	n.	午餐	1	1	初級	
	break	[brek]	n.	休息	1	1	初級	◎
	one	[wʌn]	n.	一	1	1	初級	
	long	[lɔŋ]	adv.	時間長…	1	1	初級	
❺	schedule	[ˋskɛdʒʊl]	n.	時程、行程	1	3	中級	◎
	fixed	[fɪkst]	adj.	固定的	2	2	中高	◎
❻	adopt	[əˋdɑpt]	v.	採取	1	3	初級	◎
	shift-work	[ˋʃɪftˏwɜk]	adj.	輪班的				
	system	[ˋsɪstəm]	n.	體制、制度	1	3	初級	◎
❼	several	[ˋsɛvərəl]	adj.	幾個的	1	1	初級	◎
	month	[mʌnθ]	n.	月	1	1	初級	
	last	[læst]	adj.	上次的	1	1	初級	◎
	vacation	[veˋkeʃən]	n.	假期	1	2	初級	◎
❽	two-day	[ˋtuˏde]	adj.	兩天的				
	weekend	[ˋwikˏɛnd]	n.	週末	1	1	初級	
❾	never	[ˋnɛvɚ]	adv.	從不	1	1	初級	
	arrived	[əˋraɪvd]	p.p.	arrive（到達）過去分詞	1	2	初級	◎
	late	[let]	adv.	晚地	1	1	初級	◎
	left	[lɛft]	p.p.	leave（離開）過去分詞	1	1	初級	
	early	[ˋɜlɪ]	adv.	提早	1	1	初級	
❿	get	[gɛt]	v.	得到	1	1	初級	◎
	seven-day	[ˋsɛvnˏde]	adj.	七天的				
	annual	[ˋænjʊəl]	adj.	一年的、年度的	1	4	中級	◎
⓫	often	[ˋɔfən]	adv.	常常	1		初級	
	overtime	[ˏovɚˋtaɪm]	adv.	超時地	3			◎
	even	[ˋivən]	adv.	甚至	1	1	初級	
	holiday	[ˋhɑləˏde]	n.	假日	1	1	初級	
⓬	night	[naɪt]	n.	晚上	1	1	初級	
⓭	working	[ˋwɜkɪŋ]	p.pr.	work（工作）現在分分詞	2	1	初級	◎
	this	[ðɪs]	adj.	這個	1	1	初級	
	five	[faɪv]	n.	五	1	1	初級	
	year	[jɪr]	n.	年	1	1	初級	

※「紅字單字」於本單元多句出現，「單字級等分析」僅列在「首次出現句」。

020　你的工作時間？

❶	你的上班時間是幾點到幾點？	What is your work schedule? * **work schedule**（工作時間）
❷	你們公司什麼時候午休？	When does your office take a lunch break? * **take＋某事**（進行某事）
❸	你常工作到很晚嗎？	Do you usually work late into the night?
❹	你們公司午休時間多長？	How long is your company's lunchtime? * **How long is...?**（…時間是多久？）
❺	你幾點到公司？	What time do you arrive at the office? * **arrive at**（到達）可替換為：leave（離開）
❻	你今晚要加班嗎？	Do you need to work overtime tonight? * **need to＋動詞原形**（需要…）
❼	你一天工作幾小時？	How many hours a day do you work?
❽	你經常假日加班嗎？	Do you have to work on holidays a lot? * **a lot**（經常）
❾	你工作幾年了？	How long have you been working? * **How long have you been...?**（…時間持續多久？）
❿	你們要輪班嗎？	Do you have to work different shifts? * **work different shifts**（輪流換班）
⓫	你在這間公司多久了？	How long have you been working in your current company?
⓬	你經常請假嗎？	Do you often ask for leave? * **ask for leave**（請假）
⓭	你經常遲到嗎？	Are you often late for work?
⓮	你上早班還是夜班？	Do you work the day shift or the night shift? * **day shift**（日班、早班） * **night shift**（晚班）
⓯	你們是週休二日嗎？	Do you have two-day weekends?
⓰	你們公司要打卡嗎？	Does your company require you to punch in and out? * **punch in and out**（上下班打卡）

	單字	音標	詞性	意義	字頻	大考	英檢	多益
❶	work	[wɜk]	n./v.	工作	1	1	初級	◎
	schedule	[ˋskɛdʒʊl]	n.	時程、行程	1	3	中級	◎
❷	office	[ˋɔfɪs]	n.	常常	1	1	初級	◎
	take	[tek]	v.	執行	1	1	初級	◎
	lunch	[lʌntʃ]	n.	午餐	1	1	初級	
	break	[brek]	n.	休息	1	1	初級	◎
❸	usually	[ˋjuʒʊəlɪ]	adv.	經常	1		初級	◎
	late	[let]	adv.	晚地	1	1	初級	◎
	night	[naɪt]	n.	晚上	1	1	初級	
❹	long	[lɔŋ]	adj.	時間長…	1	1	初級	
	company	[ˋkʌmpənɪ]	n.	公司	1	2	初級	◎
	lunchtime	[ˋlʌntʃˌtaɪm]	n.	午休時間	5		中高	
❺	time	[taɪm]	n.	時間	1	1	初級	◎
	arrive	[əˋraɪv]	v.	到達	1	2	初級	◎
❻	need	[nid]	v.	需要	1	1	初級	
	overtime	[ˌovəˋtaɪm]	adv.	超時地	3			◎
	tonight	[təˋnaɪt]	adv.	今晚	1	1	初級	
❼	many	[ˋmɛnɪ]	adj.	許多的	1	1	初級	
	hour	[aʊr]	n.	小時	1	1	初級	
	day	[de]	n.	一天/白天	1	1	初級	
❽	have	[hæv]	v.	必須/擁有	1	1	初級	
	holiday	[ˋhɑləˌde]	n.	假日	1	1	初級	
	lot	[lɑt]	n.	許多				
❾	working	[ˋwɜkɪŋ]	p.pr.	working（工作）現在分詞	2	1	中級	◎
❿	different	[ˋdɪfərənt]	adj.	不同的	1	1	初級	◎
	shift	[ʃɪft]	n.	輪班	1	4	中級	◎
⓫	current	[ˋkɜnt]	adj.	目前的	1	3	初級	◎
⓬	often	[ˋɔfən]	adv.	常常	1	1	初級	
	ask	[æsk]	v.	尋求	1	1	初級	
	leave	[liv]	n.	休假	1	1	初級	◎
⓯	two-day	[ˋtuˋde]	adj.	兩天的				
	weekend	[ˋwikˋɛnd]	n.	周末	1	1	初級	
⓰	require	[rɪˋkwaɪr]	v.	需要	1	2	初級	◎
	punch	[pʌntʃ]	v.	打（卡）	2	3	中級	
	in	[ɪn]	adv.	進班	1	1	初級	
	out	[aʊt]	adv.	下班	1	1	初級	

※「紅字單字」於本單元多句出現，「單字級等分析」僅列在「首次出現句」。

021 我的工作心得。

MP3 021-01 ❶～❹

❶	我熱愛我的工作。	I love my job.
❷	我是個工作狂。	I am a workaholic.
❸	工作給我很大的壓力。	Work puts me under a lot of pressure. * put＋某人＋under pressure（帶給某人壓力） * a lot of（許多的、大量的）
❹	我做這份工作游刃有餘。	I am more than good enough to do this job. * more than（超過） * good enough（足夠勝任）
❺	我以我的工作為榮。	I am proud of my work. ＝ I am proud of what I do. * be proud of（引以為傲）
❻	我覺得我的工作很有挑戰性。	I think my work is full of challenges. * be full of（充滿）
❼	我的工作可以讓我一展長才。	My job enables me to show my abilities. * enable me to＋動詞原形（讓我能夠…） * show one's ability（展現才華）
❽	工作中我獲得很多成就感。	I derive a great sense of achievement from my job. * derive A from B（從 B 當中，獲得 A）
❾	我覺得自己不適合這份工作。	I don't think I am suitable for this job. * I don't think＋子句（我不認為…） * A be suitable for B（A 適合 B）
❿	我總有忙不完的工作。	I always have too much work to finish. * too much work to finish（要完成的工作太多）
⓫	工作中我學到很多東西。	I have learned a lot from my work. * 此句用「現在完成式」（... have learned...） 表示「過去某時點發生某事，且結果持續到現在」。
⓬	我試著提高我的工作效率。	I have been trying to improve my work efficiency. * I have been＋動詞-ing（我一直…）
⓭	我喪失工作熱忱。	I have lost my enthusiasm for work. * lose enthusiasm（失去熱忱）
⓮	工作使我認識很多朋友。	Work has helped me meet many friends. * meet friends（認識朋友）

122

	單字	音標	詞性	意義	字頻	大考	英檢	多益
❶	love	[lʌv]	v.	喜愛	1	1	初級	
	job	[dʒɑb]	n.	工作	1	1	初級	
❷	workaholic	[ˌwɜkəˈhɔlɪk]	n.	工作狂	8			
❸	work	[wɜk]	n.	工作	1	1	初級	◎
	put	[pʊt]	v.	施加	1	1	初級	
	lot	[lɑt]	n.	許多				
	pressure	[ˈprɛʃɚ]	n.	壓力	1	3	中級	◎
❹	more	[mor]	adv.	多於	1	1	初級	
	good	[gʊd]	adj.	勝任的	1	1	初級	◎
	enough	[əˈnʌf]	adv.	足夠地	1	1	初級	
	do	[du]	v.	做	1	1	初級	
	this	[ðɪs]	adj.	這個	1	1	初級	
❺	proud	[praʊd]	adj.	驕傲的	1	2	初級	◎
❻	think	[θɪŋk]	v.	認為	1	1	初級	
	challenge	[ˈtʃælɪndʒ]	n.	挑戰	1	3	中級	◎
❼	enable	[ɪnˈebl]	v.	讓…能夠	1	3	中級	◎
	show	[ʃo]	v.	展現	1	1	初級	◎
	ability	[əˈbɪlətɪ]	n.	能力	1	2	初級	◎
❽	derive	[dɪˈraɪv]	v.	獲得	2	6	中高	◎
	great	[gret]	adj.	很大的	1	1	初級	◎
	sense of achievement	[sɛns ʌv əˈtʃivmənt]	n.	成就感				◎
❾	suitable	[ˈsutəbl]	adj.	適合的	2	4	中級	◎
❿	always	[ˈɔlwez]	adv.	總是	1	1	初級	
	have	[hæv]	v.	擁有	1	1	初級	
	too	[tu]	adv.	太過	1	1	初級	
	much	[mʌtʃ]	adj.	許多的	1	1	初級	
	finish	[ˈfɪnɪʃ]	v.	完成	1	1	初級	◎
⓫	learned	[ˈlɜnɪd]	p.p.	learn（學習）過去分詞	4	4	中級	
⓬	trying	[ˈtraɪɪŋ]	p.pr.	try（嘗試）現在分詞	6	1	初級	
	improve	[ɪmˈpruv]	v.	增進	1	2	初級	◎
	efficiency	[ɪˈfɪʃənsɪ]	n.	效率	2	4	中級	◎
⓭	lost	[lɔst]	p.p.	lose（失去）過去分詞	1	2	中高	◎
	enthusiasm	[ɪnˈθjuzɪˌæzəm]	n.	熱忱	2	4	中級	◎
⓮	helped	[hɛlpt]	p.p.	help（幫助）過去分詞	1	1	初級	
	meet	[mit]	v.	認識	1	1	初級	
	many	[ˈmɛnɪ]	adj.	許多的	1	1	初級	
	friend	[frɛnd]	n.	朋友	1	1	初級	

※「紅字單字」於本單元多句出現，「單字級等分析」僅列在「首次出現句」。

🔊 MP3 021-02 ❶～❸

❶	你喜歡你的工作嗎？	Do you like your job?
❷	你的工作讓你學以致用嗎？	Does your job allow you to use what you have learned? * allow＋某人＋to＋動詞原形（允許某人…） * what you have learned（你所學的東西）
❸	你覺得這份工作適合自己嗎？	Do you think this job is suitable for you? * Do you think...?（你是否認為…） * A suitable for B（A 適合 B）
❹	你的工作能讓你一展長才嗎？	Does your job allow you to display your talent? * display talent（展現才華）＝ show abilities
❺	你從工作中學到什麼？	What have you learned from your job?
❻	你以工作為榮嗎？	Are you proud of your job? * be proud of（引以為傲）
❼	你曾試著改變工作方法嗎？	Have you ever tried to change your work methods? * Have you ever...?（你是否曾經…）
❽	工作時你最大的挫折是什麼？	What was the most discouraging thing you ever experienced while working? * ...thing you ever experienced（你經歷過的…事）
❾	你希望成為一個怎麼樣的職場人？	What kind of working person do you want to be? * What kind of＋人事物＋...?（什麼樣的人事物…？） * working person（工作者、職場人）
❿	你覺得自己不斷在進步嗎？	Do you feel like you are constantly improving? * feel like＋子句（感覺…）
⓫	你對工作充滿幹勁嗎？	Are you very enthusiastic about your work? * be enthusiastic about＋某事（對某事有熱忱）
⓬	你是工作狂嗎？	Are you a workaholic?
⓭	工作中你能接觸不同行業的人嗎？	Do you come in contact with people from other fields when working? * come in contact with＋某人（與某人互相來往） * people from other fields（其他領域的人）

單字級等分析

	單字	音標	詞性	意義	字頻	大考	英檢	多益
❶	like	[laɪk]	v.	喜歡	1	1	初級	
	job	[dʒɑb]	n.	工作	1	1	初級	
❷	allow	[əˋlaʊ]	v.	允許	1	1	初級	◎
	use	[juz]	v.	使用	1	1	初級	◎
	learned	[ˋlɝnɪd]	p.p.	learn（學習）過去分詞	4	4	中級	
❸	think	[θɪŋk]	v.	認為	1	1	初級	
	this	[ðɪs]	adj.	這個	1	1	初級	
	suitable	[ˋsutəbl]	adj.	適合的	2	3	中級	◎
❹	display	[dɪsˋple]	v.	展現	1	2	中級	◎
	talent	[ˋtælənt]	n.	才能	1	2	初級	◎
❻	proud	[praʊd]	adj.	驕傲的	1	2	初級	
❼	ever	[ˋɛvɚ]	adv.	曾經	1	1	初級	
	tried	[traɪd]	p.p	try（嘗試）過去分詞	7	1	初級	
	change	[tʃendʒ]	v.	改變	1	2	初級	◎
	work	[wɝk]	n.	工作	1	1	初級	
	method	[ˋmɛθəd]	n.	方法	1	2	初級	
❽	most	[most]	adv.	最	1	1	初級	
	discouraging	[dɪsˋkɝɪdʒɪŋ]	adj.	挫折的	6	4	中級	◎
	thing	[θɪŋ]	n.	事	1	1	初級	
	experienced	[ɪkˋspɪrɪənst]	p.t.	experience（經歷）過去式	2	2	中高	◎
	working	[ˋwɝkɪŋ]	p.pr.	work（工作）現在分詞	2	1	中級	
❾	kind	[kaɪnd]	n.	種類	1	1	初級	◎
	working	[ˋwɝkɪŋ]	adj.	工作的	2	1	中級	
	person	[ˋpɝsn]	n.	人	1	1	初級	
	want	[wɑnt]	v.	想要	1	1	初級	◎
❿	feel	[fil]	v.	覺得	1	1	初級	
	constantly	[ˋkɑnstəntlɪ]	adv.	不斷地	1			
	improving	[ɪmˋpruvɪŋ]	p.pr.	improve（增進）現在分詞	3	2	初級	◎
⓫	very	[ˋvɛrɪ]	adv.	十分	1	1	初級	
	enthusiastic	[ɪn͵θjuzɪˋæstɪk]	adj.	熱忱的	2	5	中級	◎
⓬	workaholic	[͵wɝkəˋhɔlɪk]	n.	工作狂	8			
⓭	come	[kʌm]	v.	著手	1	1	初級	
	contact	[ˋkɑntækt]	n.	接觸	1	2	初級	◎
	people	[ˋpipl]	n.	person（人）複數	1	1	初級	
	other	[ˋʌðɚ]	adj.	其他的	1	1	初級	
	field	[fild]	n.	領域	1	2	初級	◎

※「紅字單字」於本單元多句出現，「單字級等分析」僅列在「首次出現句」。

MP3 022-01 ❶～⓬

❶	我每天樂在工作。	I find pleasure in my work every day.
❷	我全心投入工作。	I devote myself to work. * devote oneself to＋某事物（致力於某事物）
❸	我會在時間內完成工作。	I will finish my work in time. * in time（在時間內）。此句用「未來簡單式」 （...will finish...）表示「有意願做的事」。
❹	我不遲到早退。	I never arrive late for work, or leave early.
❺	上班時間我不做私事。	I don't engage in my personal affairs while working. * engage in（從事） * personal affair（私人事務）
❻	我會盡力完成公司交付的工作。	I will do my best to finish the tasks that are assigned to me by my company. * do my best（盡力） * assign to＋某人（指派給某人）
❼	我努力滿足客戶需求。	I always strive to satisfy my customers' needs. * strive（努力）可替換為：spare no effort（不遺餘力） * customer's needs（客戶的需求）
❽	我小心做事避免出錯。	I work very carefully in order to avoid making mistakes. * in order to（為了） * avoid＋動詞-ing（避免…） * make a mistake（犯錯）
❾	我不隨便請假。	I don't ask for time off without a good reason. * ask for time off（請假） * good reason（正當理由）
❿	我希望從工作中學習與成長。	I hope to learn and grow from my work. * I hope to＋動詞原形（我希望…）
⓫	我希望今日事今日畢。	I never put off till tomorrow what should be done today. * put off（延遲） * what should be done（該完成的事）
⓬	我不讓個人情緒影響工作。	I don't let my personal emotions influence my work. * I don't...（我不做…） * influence＋某事（影響某事）

	單字	音標	詞性	意義	字頻	大考	英檢	多益
❶	find	[faɪnd]	v.	找到	1	1	初級	
	pleasure	[ˋplɛʒɚ]	n.	樂趣	1	2	初級	◎
	work	[wɝk]	n./v.	工作	1	1	初級	◎
	every	[ˋɛvrɪ]	adj.	每一	1	1	初級	
	day	[de]	n.	天	1	1	初級	
❷	devote	[dɪˋvot]	v.	致力、奉獻	2	4	中級	◎
	myself	[maɪˋsɛlf]	pron.	我自己	1		初級	
❸	finish	[ˋfɪnɪʃ]	v.	完成	1	1	初級	◎
	time	[taɪm]	n.	時間	1	1	初級	◎
❹	never	[ˋnɛvɚ]	adv.	從不	1	1	初級	
	arrive	[əˋraɪv]	v.	到達	1	2	初級	◎
	late	[let]	adv.	晚地	1	1	初級	◎
	leave	[liv]	v.	離開	1	1	初級	◎
	early	[ˋɝlɪ]	adv.	提早	1	1	初級	
❺	engage	[ɪnˋgedʒ]	v.	從事	1	3	中級	◎
	personal	[ˋpɝsnl]	adj.	私人的	1	2	初級	◎
	affair	[əˋfɛr]	n.	事務	1	2	初級	◎
	working	[ˋwɝkɪŋ]	p.pr.	work（工作）現在分詞	2	1	中級	◎
❻	do	[du]	v.	做	1	1	初級	
	best	[bɛst]	n.	最好、佳	1	1	初級	
	task	[tæsk]	n.	工作、任務	1	2	初級	◎
	assigned	[əˋsaɪnd]	p.p	assign（指派）過去分詞	5	4	中級	◎
	company	[ˋkʌmpənɪ]	n.	公司	1	2	初級	◎
❼	always	[ˋɔlwez]	adv.	總是	1	1	初級	
	strive	[straɪv]	v.	努力	2	4	中級	
	satisfy	[ˋsætɪs.faɪ]	v.	滿足	2	2	初級	◎
	customer	[ˋkʌstəmɚ]	n.	客戶	1	2	初級	◎
	need	[nid]	n.	需求	1	1	初級	◎
❽	very	[ˋvɛrɪ]	adv.	十分	1	1	初級	
	carefully	[ˋkɛrfəlɪ]	adv.	小心地	1			
	order	[ˋɔrdɚ]	n.	目的	1	1	初級	◎
	avoid	[əˋvɔɪd]	v.	避免	1	2	初級	◎
	making	[ˋmekɪŋ]	n.	make（犯下）動名詞	2	1	中高	
	mistake	[mɪˋstek]	n.	錯誤	1	1	初級	◎
❾	ask	[æsk]	v.	尋求	1	1	初級	
	off	[ɔf]	adj./adv.	休假的/取消、停止	1	1	初級	
	good	[gʊd]	adj.	正當的	1	1	初級	◎
	reason	[ˋrizn]	n.	理由	1	1	初級	◎
❿	hope	[hop]	v.	希望	1	1	初級	
	learn	[lɝn]	v.	學習	1	1	初級	
	grow	[gro]	v.	成長、進步	1	1	初級	◎
⓫	put	[pʊt]	v.	延後	1	1	初級	
	tomorrow	[təˋmɔro]	n.	明天	1	1	初級	◎
	done	[dʌn]	p.p.	do（做）過去分詞	1	2	初級	
	today	[təˋde]	adv.	今天	1	1	初級	◎
⓬	let	[lɛt]	v.	讓	1	1	初級	
	emotion	[ɪˋmoʃən]	n.	情緒	1	2	初級	◎
	influence	[ˋɪnfluəns]	v.	影響	1	2	初級	◎

※「紅字單字」於本單元多句出現，「單字級等分析」僅列在「首次出現句」。

🔵 MP3　022-02　❶～⓯

❶	你樂在工作嗎？	Do you find pleasure in your work? * **find pleasure in...**（以⋯為樂）
❷	你認真工作嗎？	Do you take your job seriously? * **take＋某事物＋seriously**（認真看待某事物）
❸	從工作中，你希望學到什麼？	What do you hope to learn from your job? * **from job**（從工作中）＝ **from work**
❹	你常請假嗎？	Do you often ask for leave? * **ask for leave**（請假）
❺	你經常遲到早退嗎？	Do you often arrive late to work and leave early? * **leave early**（早退）
❻	你可以臨危不亂嗎？	Can you remain calm in a crisis? * **remain calm**（保持冷靜） * **in a crisis**（在危機中）
❼	工作低潮時，你會怎麼辦？	How do you deal with bad times at work? * **deal with**（處理） * **bad times**（不好的時機）
❽	你會努力吸取專業知識嗎？	Do you work hard to gain professional knowledge? * **work hard**（努力） * **gain knowledge**（獲得知識）
❾	你會主動要求加薪嗎？	Do you actively request raises?
❿	被同事抹黑，你怎麼處理？	How do you handle colleagues who try to discredit you? * **handle＋某人**（對付某人） * **discredit you**（惡意中傷你）＝ **harm your reputation**
⓫	你積極參與會議嗎？	Do you actively participate during meetings? * **during meetings**（在會議中）
⓬	你勇於發問嗎？	Are you brave enough to ask questions? * **be brave enough**（有足夠勇氣）
⓭	你擅長危機處理嗎？	Are you good at dealing with crises? * **be good at＋動詞-ing**（擅長⋯）
⓮	你勇於開發新產品嗎？	Do you strive to develop new products? * **develop products**（開發產品）
⓯	你有創新的精神嗎？	Do you have an innovative spirit?

	單字	音標	詞性	意義	字頻	大考	英檢	多益
❶	find	[faɪnd]	v.	找到	1	1	初級	
	pleasure	[ˈplɛʒɚ]	n.	樂趣	1	2	初級	◎
	work	[wɝk]	n./v.	工作	1	1	初級	◎
❷	take	[tek]	v.	看待	1	1	初級	◎
	job	[dʒɑb]	n.	工作	1	1	初級	
	seriously	[ˈsɪrɪəslɪ]	adv.	認真地	1		中高	◎
❸	hope	[hop]	v.	希望	1	1	初級	
	learn	[lɝn]	v.	學習	1	1	初級	
❹	often	[ˈɔfən]	adv.	常常	1	1	初級	
	ask	[æsk]	v.	尋求/發問	1	1	初級	
	leave	[liv]	n./v.	休假日/離開	1	1	初級	◎
❺	arrive	[əˈraɪv]	v.	到達	1	2	初級	◎
	late	[let]	adv.	晚地	1	1	初級	◎
	early	[ˈɝlɪ]	adv.	提早	1	1	初級	
❻	remain	[rɪˈmen]	v.	保持	1	3	初級	
	calm	[kɑm]	adj.	冷靜的	2	2	初級	
	crisis	[ˈkraɪsɪs]	n.	危機	1	2	初級	
❼	deal	[dil]	v.	處理	1	1	初級	◎
	bad	[bæd]	adj.	不好的	1	1	初級	
	time	[taɪm]	n.	時機	1	1	初級	
❽	hard	[hɑrd]	adv.	努力地	1	1	初級	
	gain	[gen]	v.	獲得	1	2	初級	◎
	professional	[prəˈfɛʃən!]	adj.	專業的	1	4	中級	◎
	knowledge	[ˈnɑlɪdʒ]	n.	知識	1	2	初級	◎
❾	actively	[ˈæktɪvlɪ]	adv.	主動地	2			
	request	[rɪˈkwɛst]	v.	要求	1	3	中級	◎
	raise	[rez]	n.	加薪	1	1	初級	◎
❿	handle	[ˈhænd!]	v.	處理、對付	1	2	初級	◎
	colleague	[ˈkɑlig]	n.	同事	1	5	中級	◎
	try	[traɪ]	v.	嘗試	1	1	初級	
	discredit	[dɪsˈkrɛdɪt]	v.	抹黑、惡意中傷	4		中高	
⓫	participate	[pɑrˈtɪsəˌpet]	v.	參與	1	3	中級	◎
	meeting	[ˈmitɪŋ]	n.	會議	1	2	初級	
⓬	brave	[brev]	adj.	勇敢的	2	1	初級	
	enough	[əˈnʌf]	adv.	足夠地	1	1	初級	◎
	question	[ˈkwɛstʃən]	n.	問題	1	1	初級	
⓭	good	[gʊd]	adj.	擅長的	1	1	初級	
	dealing	[ˈdilɪŋ]	n.	deal（處理）動名詞	2	1	中高	◎
	crises	[ˈkraɪsiz]	n.	crisis（危機）複數	1	2	初級	
⓮	strive	[straɪv]	v.	努力	2	4	中級	◎
	develop	[dɪˈvɛləp]	v.	開發	1	2	初級	◎
	new	[nju]	adj.	新的	1	1	初級	
	product	[ˈprɑdəkt]	n.	產品	1	3	初級	◎
⓯	have	[hæv]	v.	擁有	1	1	初級	
	innovative	[ˈɪnoˌvetɪv]	adj.	創新的	2	6	中高	◎
	spirit	[ˈspɪrɪt]	n.	精神	1	2	初級	◎

※「紅字單字」於本單元多句出現，「單字級等分析」僅列在「首次出現句」。

023 我的工作異動。

❶	我失業了。	I lost my job. * 此句用「過去簡單式」（...lost...） 　表示「發生在過去的事」。
❷	我被加薪了。	I got a raise. = I've gotten a raise.
❸	我們公司大幅精簡人事。	Our company cut down on personnel. * cut down on（減少）
❹	我被減薪了。	My salary has been cut. * 此句用「現在完成式」（...has been...）表示 　「過去某時點發生某事，且結果持續到現在」。
❺	我被升職了。	I have been promoted. = I got a promotion.
❻	我被降職了。	I have been demoted. = I got demoted.
❼	我換工作了。	I switched jobs. * switch（更換、改變）= change
❽	我將被派往海外。	I will be assigned abroad.
❾	我將被調到總公司。	I will be transferred to headquarters. * another branch（其它分公司）
❿	我被調到其他部門。	I have been assigned to another department. * be assigned to＋部門（被指派到某部門）
⓫	我才剛通過試用期。	I've just made it through the trial period. * make it through（成功通過） * trial period（試用期）
⓬	我將增加兩名助手。	I will have two additional assistants.
⓭	我的部門來了一位新同事。	There is a new employee in my department.
⓮	我有一個新主管。	I have a new manager.
⓯	我明年要退休。	I will retire next year.
⓰	我被裁員了。	I got laid off. * get laid off（被解雇）

	單字	音標	詞性	意義	字頻	大考	英檢	多益
❶	lost	[lɔst]	p.t.	lose（失去）過去式	1	2	中高	◎
	job	[dʒɑb]	n.	工作	1	1	初級	
❷	got	[gɑt]	p.t.	get（獲得）過去式	1	1	初級	◎
	raise	[rez]	n.	加薪	1	1	初級	◎
	gotten	[ˈgɑtn]	p.p.	get（獲得）過去分詞	1	1	初級	◎
❸	company	[ˈkʌmpənɪ]	n.	公司	1	2	初級	◎
	cut	[kʌt]	p.t.	cut（減少）過去式	1	1	初級	
	down	[daʊn]	adv.	向下	1	1	初級	
	personnel	[ˌpɜsnˈɛl]	n.	人事	1	5	中高	◎
❹	salary	[ˈsælərɪ]	n.	薪水	1	4	中級	◎
	cut	[kʌt]	p.p.	cut（減少）過去分詞	1	1	初級	
❺	got	[gɑt]	p.t.	get（被…）過去式				
	promoted	[prəˈmotɪd]	p.p.	promote（升遷）過去分詞	1	3	中級	◎
	promotion	[prəˈmoʃən]	n.	升遷	2	4	中級	◎
❻	demoted	[dɪˈmotɪd]	p.p.	demote（降職）過去分詞	7		中級	
	demotion	[dɪˈmoʃən]	n.	降職	7		中級	
❼	switched	[swɪtʃt]	p.t.	switch（更換）過去式	1	3	中級	◎
❽	assigned	[əˈsaɪnd]	p.p.	assign（指派）過去分詞	5	4	中級	◎
	abroad	[əˈbrɔd]	adv.	國外地	2	2	初級	◎
❾	transferred	[træsˈfɜd]	p.p.	transfer（調動）過去分詞	1	4	中級	◎
	headquarter	[ˈhɛdˌkwɔrtə]	n.	總公司	2	3	中級	
❿	another	[əˈnʌðə]	adj.	其他的	1	1		
	department	[dɪˈpɑrtmənt]	n.	部門	1	2	初級	◎
⓫	just	[dʒʌst]	adv.	才	1	1	初級	
	made	[med]	p.p.	make（達到）過去分詞	1	1	初級	
	trial	[ˈtraɪəl]	n.	試用	1	2	初級	◎
	period	[ˈpɪrɪəd]	n.	時期、期間	1	2	初級	◎
⓬	have	[hæv]	v.	擁有	1	1	初級	
	two	[tu]	n.	二	1	1	初級	
	additional	[əˈdɪʃənl]	adj.	額外的	1	3	中級	◎
	assistant	[əˈsɪstənt]	n.	助理	1	2	初級	◎
⓭	there	[ðɛr]	adv.	有…	1	1	初級	
	new	[nju]	adj.	新的	1	1	初級	
	employee	[ˌɛmplɔrˈi]	n.	員工	1	3	中級	◎
⓮	manager	[ˈmænɪdʒə]	n.	主管	1	3	初級	◎
⓯	retire	[rɪˈtaɪr]	v.	退休	1	4	中級	◎
	next	[nɛkst]	adj.	下一個	1	1	初級	
	year	[jɪr]	n.	年	1	1	初級	
⓰	laid	[led]	p.p.	lay（解雇）過去分詞	1	1	初級	
	off	[ɔf]	adv.	開除	1	1	初級	

※「紅字單字」於本單元多句出現，「單字級等分析」僅列在「首次出現句」。

023 你的工作異動？

❶	你為什麼離職？	Why did you leave your job?
❷	你想換工作嗎？	Do you want to change jobs?
❸	你的新工作是什麼？	What is your new job?
❹	聽說你升官了？	I heard that you got promoted. * 此句用「過去簡單式」（...heard...） 　表示「發生在過去的事」。 * I heard that＋子句（我聽說了⋯） * got promoted（升遷）可替換為：got a raise（加薪）
❺	你滿意新的職稱嗎？	Are you satisfied with your new title? * be satisfied with（滿意）
❻	你通過試用期了嗎？	Have you made it through the trial period? * Have you＋過去分詞＋...?（你是否已經⋯了）
❼	你是不是被挖角？	Have you been approached by other companies? * be approached by＋公司（被某公司接洽、挖角）
❽	你願意到大陸發展嗎？	Are you willing to develop in China? * Are you willing to...?（你是否願意⋯）
❾	你什麼時候遞辭呈的？	When did you hand in your resignation? * hand in＋某物（遞交某物）
❿	你什麼時候要退休？	When will you retire?
⓫	你為什麼被炒魷魚？	Why did you get fired? * get fired（被開除） 　= get dismissed 　= get laid off
⓬	你們公司今年有調薪嗎？	Did your company give raises this year? * give raises（給予加薪）
⓭	你習慣新主管了嗎？	Have you gotten used to your new manager? * get used to＋某人（適應某人）
⓮	你們公司面臨財務危機嗎？	Is your company facing any financial difficulties? * financial difficulty（財務困難）
⓯	你的新同事何時就任？	When will your new colleague begin work? * begin work（開始上班）

	單字	音標	詞性	意義	字頻	大考	英檢	多益
❶	leave	[liv]	v.	離開	1	1	初級	◎
	job	[dʒɑb]	n.	工作	1	1	初級	
❷	want	[wɑnt]	v.	想要	1	1	初級	◎
	change	[tʃendʒ]	v.	更換	1	2	初級	◎
❸	new	[nju]	adj.	新的	1	1	初級	
❹	heard	[hɜd]	p.t.	hear（聽說）過去式	1	1	初級	
	got	[gɑt]	p.t.	get（被…）過去式	1	1	初級	◎
	promoted	[prə`motɪd]	p.p.	promote（升遷）過去分詞	1	3	中級	
❺	satisfied	[`sætɪs.faɪd]	adj.	滿意的	2	2	中高	
	title	[`taɪtl]	n.	職稱	1	2	初級	
❻	made	[med]	p.p.	make（達到）過去分詞	1	1	初級	
	trial	[`traɪəl]	n.	試用	1	2	初級	
	period	[`pɪrɪəd]	n.	時期、期間	1	2	初級	
❼	approached	[ə`protʃt]	p.p.	approach（接洽）過去分詞	1	3	中級	◎
	other	[`ʌðɚ]	adj.	其他的	1	1	初級	
	company	[`kʌmpənɪ]	n.	公司	1	2	初級	◎
❽	willing	[`wɪlɪŋ]	adj.	願意的	1	2	初級	
	develop	[dɪ`vɛləp]	v.	發展	1	2	初級	◎
	China	[`tʃaɪnə]	n.	中國	4	3	初級	
❾	hand	[hænd]	v.	遞交	1	1	初級	
	resignation	[ˌrɛzɪg`neʃən]	n.	辭呈	3	4	中級	◎
❿	retire	[rɪ`taɪr]	v.	退休	1	4	中級	◎
⓫	get	[gɛt]	v.	被…	1	1	初級	◎
	fired	[faɪrd]	p.p.	fire（解雇）過去分詞	7	1	初級	◎
⓬	give	[gɪv]	v.	給	1	1	初級	
	raise	[rez]	n.	調薪	1	1	初級	◎
	this	[ðɪs]	adj.	這個	1	1	初級	
	year	[jɪr]	n.	年	1	1	初級	
⓭	gotten	[`gɑtn]	p.p.	get（變成）過去分詞	1	1	初級	◎
	used	[juzd]	p.p.	use（習慣）過去分詞	1	2	初級	◎
	manager	[`mænɪdʒɚ]	n.	主管	1	3	初級	◎
⓮	facing	[`fesɪŋ]	p.pr.	face（面臨）現在分詞	8	1	初級	
	any	[`ɛnɪ]	adj.	任何的	1	1	初級	
	financial	[faɪ`nænʃəl]	adj.	財務的	1	4	中級	◎
	difficulty	[`dɪfə.kʌltɪ]	n.	困難	1	2	初級	◎
⓯	colleague	[`kɑlig]	n.	同事	1	5	中級	◎
	begin	[bɪ`gɪn]	v.	開始	1	1	初級	
	work	[wɜk]	n.	工作	1	1	初級	◎

※「紅字單字」於本單元多句出現，「單字級等分析」僅列在「首次出現句」。

MP3 024-01 ❶～❾

❶	我想做個規律上下班的上班族。	I want to work the same hours every day. * want to＋動詞原形（想要…） * work the same hours（工作時間規律）
❷	我想在時尚界工作。	I want to work in the fashion industry. * work in＋產業（在某產業上班） * fashion industry（時尚產業）
❸	我想做自己有興趣的工作。	I want a job that I am interested in. * a job that＋子句（…的工作） * be interested in（有興趣）
❹	進入演藝圈一直是我的夢想。	To get into show business has always been a dream of mine. * 此句用「現在完成式」（…has…been…）表示「過去持續到現在的事」。 * To get into＋行業（進入某行業） * 此句用不定詞（To get into show business）當主詞。 * show business（演藝圈） * dream of mine（我的夢想）
❺	我想當公務員。	I want to be a public servant. * be＋身分（成為某身分的人） * public servant（公務員） * teacher（老師） * lawyer（律師） * doctor（醫生） * nurse（護士）
❻	我希望自己創業。	I hope to start my own business. * I hope to＋動詞原形（我希望…） * one's own business（自己的公司）
❼	我希望工作與所學相關。	I wish my job was related to what I learned in school. * I wish＋過去式子句（可以的話，我希望…） * be related to（相關）
❽	我想開一間店。	I want to open a shop. * I want to open a coffee shop.（我想開一間咖啡廳） * open a shop（開店）
❾	我想當個自由的 SOHO 族。	I want to be free and work from home. * work from home（在家工作）

	單字	音標	詞性	意義	字頻	大考	英檢	多益
❶	want	[wɑnt]	v.	想要	1	1	初級	◎
	work	[wɜk]	v.	工作	1	1	初級	◎
	same	[sem]	adj.	相同的	1	1	初級	
	hour	[aʊr]	n.	時刻、時間	1	1	初級	
	every	[ˋɛvrɪ]	adj.	每一	1	1	初級	
	day	[de]	n.	天	1	1	初級	
❷	fashion	[ˋfæʃən]	n.	流行、時尚	1	3	中級	◎
	industry	[ˋɪndəstrɪ]	n.	產業	1	2	初級	◎
❸	job	[dʒɑb]	n.	工作	1	1	初級	
	interested	[ˋɪntərɪstɪd]	adj.	有興趣的	1	1	初級	◎
❹	get	[gɛt]	v.	掙得	1	1	初級	◎
	show	[ʃo]	n.	演藝	1	1	初級	◎
	business	[ˋbɪznɪs]	n.	產業、行業	1	2	初級	◎
	always	[ˋɔlwez]	adv.	一直	1	1	初級	
	dream	[drim]	n.	夢想	1	1	初級	
	mine	[maɪn]	pron.	我的	1	2	初級	
❺	public	[ˋpʌblɪk]	adj.	公共的	1	1	初級	
	servant	[ˋsɝvənt]	n.	公僕	2	2	初級	
❻	hope	[hop]	v.	希望	1	1	初級	
	start	[stɑrt]	v.	創辦	1	1	初級	
	own	[on]	adj.	自己的	1	1	初級	◎
❼	wish	[wɪʃ]	v.	希望	1	1	初級	
	related	[rɪˋletɪd]	p.p.	relate（有關）過去分詞	2	3	中級	◎
	learned	[ˋlɝnɪd]	p.t.	learn（學習）過去式	4	4	中級	
	school	[skul]	n.	學校	1	1	初級	
❽	open	[ˋopən]	v.	開張	1	1	初級	
	shop	[ʃɑp]	n.	店鋪	1	1	初級	◎
❾	free	[fri]	adj.	自由的	1	1	初級	
	home	[hom]	n.	家	1	1	初級	

※「紅字單字」於本單元多句出現，「單字級等分析」僅列在「首次出現句」。

024 我想從事的工作。（2）

❿	我一直希望到外商公司上班。	I have always hoped to work in a foreign trading company. * have always hoped（一直以來都希望） * work in＋某種公司（在某種公司上班） * foreign trading company（外商公司） * publishing house（出版社）
⓫	我想到國外工作。	I want to work abroad. * abroad（國外）= overseas
⓬	我希望在大城市工作。	I wish I worked in a big city. * I wish＋過去式子句（可以的話，我希望…） * work in＋城市（在某城市上班）
⓭	我希望從政。	I hope to work in politics. * I hope to＋動詞原形（我希望…） * politics（政治）可替換為：the government（政府）
⓮	我希望從事媒體相關工作。	I hope to have a job related to the mass media. * have a job（得到一份工作） * (be) related to（關於） * mass media（大眾媒體）
⓯	我想從事 3C 產業。	I want to work in the 3C industry. * I want to work in＋產業（我想從事某產業）
⓰	我想從事服務業。	I want to work in the service industry. * service industry（服務業）
⓱	我想從事必須與人接觸的工作。	I want a job that requires contact with people. * require＋名詞（需要…） * contact with（聯繫）
⓲	我只想在家當一個家庭主婦。	I just want to be a housewife.
⓳	我希望公司有員工旅遊。	I wish my firm had employee trips. * employee trip（員工旅遊）
⓴	我打算換工作。	I plan to change my job. * change my job（換工作）

	單字	音標	詞性	意義	字頻	大考	英檢	多益
⑩	always	[ˋɔlwez]	adv.	一直	1	1	初級	
	hoped	[hopt]	p.p.	hope（希望）過去分詞	1	1	初級	
	work	[wɜk]	v.	工作	1	1	初級	◎
	foreign	[ˋfɔrɪn]	adj.	國外的	1	1	初級	◎
	trading	[ˋtredɪŋ]	adj.	貿易的	2	2	初級	◎
	company	[ˋkʌmpənɪ]	n.	公司	1	2	初級	◎
⑪	want	[wɑnt]	v.	想要	1	1	初級	
	abroad	[əˋbrɔd]	adv.	國外地	2	2	初級	◎
⑫	wish	[wɪʃ]	v.	希望	1	1	初級	
	worked	[wɜkt]	p.t.	work（工作）過去式	1	1	初級	◎
	big	[bɪg]	adj.	大的	1	1	初級	
	city	[ˋsɪtɪ]	n.	城市	1	1	初級	◎
⑬	hope	[hop]	v.	希望	1	1	初級	
	politics	[ˋpɑlətɪks]	n.	政治	1	3	中級	
⑭	have	[hæv]	v.	得到	1	1	初級	
	job	[dʒɑb]	n.	工作	1	1	初級	
	related	[rɪˋletɪd]	p.p.	relate（關聯）過去分詞	2	3	中級	◎
	mass media	[mæs ˋmidɪə]	n.	大眾媒體				
⑮	3C	[ˋθriˋsi]	n.	是以下三字的縮寫：computer（電腦）communication（通訊）consumer electronics（消費電子）			初級	
	industry	[ˋɪndəstrɪ]	n.	產業	1	2	初級	◎
⑯	service	[ˋsɜvɪs]	n.	服務	1	1	初級	◎
⑰	require	[rɪˋkwaɪr]	v.	需要	1	2	初級	◎
	contact	[ˋkɑntækt]	n.	接觸、聯繫	1	2	初級	◎
	people	[ˋpipl̩]	n.	person（人）複數	1	1	初級	
⑱	just	[dʒʌst]	adv.	只是	1	1	初級	
	housewife	[ˋhaʊsˌwaɪf]	n.	家庭主婦	4	4	中級	
⑲	firm	[fɜm]	n.	公司	1	2	初級	◎
	had	[hæd]	p.t.	have（擁有）過去式	1	1	初級	
	employee	[ˌɛmplɔɪˋi]	n.	員工	1	3	中級	◎
	trip	[trɪp]	n.	旅遊	1	1	初級	◎
⑳	plan	[plæn]	v.	計畫	1	1	初級	◎
	change	[tʃendʒ]	v.	更換	1	2	初級	◎

※「紅字單字」於本單元多句出現，「單字級等分析」僅列在「首次出現句」。

🔊 MP3 024-02 ❶～⓫

❶	你希望從事哪一行？	What kind of career do you hope to have? * **What kind of...?**（哪一種…？）
❷	你可以接受一成不變的工作嗎？	Can you accept a job that is always the same? * **Can you accept...?**（你是否能接受…） * **always the same**（總是不變）
❸	你曾經夢想當一個大明星嗎？	Have you ever dreamt of being a superstar? * **Have you ever...?**（你是否曾經…） * **dream of** ＋動詞-ing（夢想…） * **be a superstar**（成為巨星）
❹	你希望工作與所學相關嗎？	Do you wish your work was related to what you studied in school? * **Do you wish** ＋過去式子句? 　（可以的話，你是否希望…） * **what you studied in school** 　（你在學校所學的事） 　＝ **what you learned in school**
❺	你希望擁有一間小店嗎？	Do you hope to own a small shop? * **Do you hope to** ＋動詞原形?（你是否希望…） * **own a shop**（擁有一間店） * **shop**（店鋪）＝ **store**
❻	你希望自己創業嗎？	Do you hope to start your own business?
❼	你想當 SOHO 族嗎？	Do you want to work from home?
❽	你能接受需要輪班的工作嗎？	Can you accept a job with shifts?
❾	你能接受 24 小時的工作嗎？	Can you accept a 24-hour job? * **24-hour job**（24 小時的工作）
❿	你希望工作充滿挑戰嗎？	Do you wish your work was full of challenges? * **be full of** ＋名詞複數形（充滿…）
⓫	工作對你有什麼意義？	What meaning does your job hold for you? * **hold** ＋名詞＋ **for you**（對你來說，具有…）

	單字	音標	詞性	意義	字頻	大考	英檢	多益
❶	kind	[kaɪnd]	n.	種類	1	1	初級	◎
	career	[kəˋrɪr]	n.	職業	1	4	初級	◎
	hope	[hop]	v.	希望	1	1	初級	
	have	[hæv]	v.	從事	1	1	初級	
❷	accept	[əkˋsɛpt]	v.	接受	1	2	初級	◎
	job	[dʒɑb]	n.	工作	1	1	初級	
	same	[sem]	adj.	相同的	1	1	初級	
❸	ever	[ˋɛvɚ]	adv.	曾經	1	1	初級	
	dreamt	[drɛmt]	p.p.	dream（夢想）過去分詞	1	1	初級	
	superstar	[ˋsupɚˌstɑr]	n.	巨星	3			
❹	wish	[wɪʃ]	v.	希望	1	1	初級	
	work	[wɜk]	n./v.	工作	1	1	初級	◎
	related	[rɪˋletɪd]	p.p.	relate（關聯）過去分詞	2	3	初級	◎
	studied	[ˋstʌdɪd]	p.t.	study（學習）過去式	6	1	中級	◎
	school	[skul]	n.	學校	1	1	初級	
❺	own	[on]	v./adj.	擁有/自己的	1	1	初級	◎
	small	[smɔl]	adj.	小的	1	1	初級	
	shop	[ʃɑp]	n.	店鋪	1	1	初級	
❻	start	[stɑrt]	v.	創辦	1	1	初級	
	business	[ˋbɪznɪs]	n.	公司、企業	1	2	初級	◎
❼	want	[wɑnt]	v.	想要	1	1	初級	◎
	home	[hom]	n.	家	1	1	初級	
❽	shift	[ʃɪft]	n.	輪班	1	4	中級	◎
❾	24-hour	[ˋtwɛntɪforˋaʊr]	adj.	24 小時的				
❿	full	[fʊl]	adj.	充滿的	1	1	初級	
	challenge	[ˋtʃælɪndʒ]	n.	挑戰	1	3	中級	◎
⓫	meaning	[ˋminɪŋ]	n.	意義	1	2	初級	◎
	hold	[hold]	v.	具有	1	1	初級	

※「紅字單字」於本單元多句出現，「單字級等分析」僅列在「首次出現句」。

024　你想從事的工作？（2）

⑫	你希望到國外工作嗎？	Do you hope to work overseas?
⑬	你想朝傳播業發展嗎？	Do you want to work in mass media?
⑭	你想從政嗎？	Do you want to work in politics?
⑮	你希望到外商公司上班嗎？	Do you wish you could work for a foreign company? * **Do you wish＋過去式子句？** 　（可以的話，你是否希望…） * **foreign company**（外商公司） 　= **foreign trading company**
⑯	你對 3C 產業有興趣嗎？	Do you have any interest in the 3C industry? * **Do you have interest in…?**（你對…有興趣嗎） * **have interest in＋某事物**（對某事物有興趣） 　= **be interested in＋某事物**
⑰	你對服務業有興趣嗎？	Are you interested in the service industry? * **Are you interested in…?**（你對…有興趣嗎）
⑱	你動過不要工作的念頭嗎？	Have you ever thought about not working? * **Have you ever…?**（你是否曾經…） * **think about**（考慮）
⑲	你必須繼承家業嗎？	Do you have to inherit your family business? * **have to**（必須） * **inherit＋某物**（繼承某物） * **family business**（家族事業）
⑳	你喜歡與人接觸的工作嗎？	Do you like jobs that require working with people? * **require＋動詞-ing**（需要…）
㉑	你希望公司有員工旅遊嗎？	Do you wish your company had employee trips?
㉒	你會找時間充電嗎？	Do you take time to reinvigorate yourself? * **Do you…?**（你平常是否會…） * **take time to＋動詞原形**（花時間…） * **reinvigorate oneself**（讓自己再度充滿活力）
㉓	你應該試著縮短工作時間。	You should try to reduce your working hours. * **You should…**（你應該…） * **reduce**（減少）= **shorten** = **cut down** * **working hours**（工作時間）

	單字	音標	詞性	意義	字頻	大考	英檢	多益
⑫	hope	[hop]	v.	希望	1	1	初級	
	work	[wɜk]	v.	工作	1	1	初級	◎
	overseas	[ˋovəˋsiz]	adv.	海外地	2	2	初級	◎
⑬	want	[wɑnt]	v.	想要	1	1	初級	◎
	mass media	[mæs ˋmidɪə]	n.	大眾媒體				
⑭	politics	[ˋpɑlətɪks]	n.	政治	1	3	中級	
⑮	wish	[wɪʃ]	v.	希望	1	1	初級	
	foreign	[ˋfɔrɪn]	adj.	國外的	1	1	初級	◎
	company	[ˋkʌmpənɪ]	n.	公司	1	2	初級	◎
⑯	have	[hæv]	n.	擁有/必須	1	1	初級	
	any	[ˋɛnɪ]	adj.	任何的	1	1	初級	
	interest	[ˋɪntərɪst]	n.	興趣	1	1	初級	◎
	3C	[ˋθriˋsi]	n.	是以下三字的縮寫： computer（電腦） communication（通訊） consumer electronics （消費電子）			初級	
	industry	[ˋɪndəstrɪ]	n.	產業	1	2	初級	◎
⑰	interested	[ˋɪntərɪstɪd]	adj.	有興趣的	1	1	初級	◎
	service	[ˋsɜvɪs]	n.	服務	1	1	初級	◎
⑱	ever	[ˋɛvə]	adv.	曾經	1	1	初級	
	thought	[θɔt]	p.p.	think（考慮）過去分詞	1	1	初級	◎
	working	[ˋwɜkɪŋ]	n.	work（工作）動名詞	2	1	中級	◎
⑲	inherit	[ɪnˋhɛrɪt]	v.	繼承	2	5	中級	◎
	family	[ˋfæməlɪ]	n.	家庭	1	1	初級	
	business	[ˋbɪznɪs]	n.	公司、企業	1	2	初級	◎
⑳	like	[laɪk]	v.	喜歡	1	1	初級	
	job	[dʒɑb]	n.	工作	1	1	初級	
	require	[rɪˋkwaɪr]	v.	需要	1	2	初級	◎
	people	[ˋpipl]	n.	person（人）複數	1	1	初級	
㉑	had	[hæd]	p.t.	have（擁有）過去式	1	1	初級	
	employee	[ˌɛmplɔɪˋi]	n.	員工	1	3	中級	◎
	trip	[trɪp]	n.	旅遊	1	1	初級	◎
㉒	take	[tek]	v.	花費	1	1	初級	◎
	time	[taɪm]	n.	時間	1	1	初級	◎
	reinvigorate	[ˌriɪnˋvɪgəˌret]	v.	恢復活力	7			
	yourself	[juəˋsɛlf]	pron.	你自己	1		初級	
㉓	try	[traɪ]	v.	嘗試	1	1	初級	
	reduce	[rɪˋdjus]	v.	減少	1	3	中級	◎
	hour	[aur]	n.	時刻、時間	1	1	初級	

※「紅字單字」於本單元多句出現，「單字級等分析」僅列在「首次出現句」。

025　我喜歡的工作環境。

🔘 MP3 025-01 ❶~❷

❶	我希望公司福利完善。	I wish my company had more benefits. * I wish＋過去式子句（可以的話，我希望…） * have more benefits（有更多福利）
❷	我希望到員工 100 人以上的大公司。	I wish I could work in a large company with more than 100 employees. * more than＋人數（人數超過…）
❸	我希望錢多事少。	I wish I had less work and more income. * I wish I had...（可以的話，我希望擁有…） * less work and more income（錢多事少）
❹	我希望到員工 20 人以下的小公司。	I wish I could work in a small company with less than 20 employees. * less than＋人數（人數低於…）
❺	我希望公司重視員工培訓。	I wish my company would focus on employee training. * focus on（重視） * employee training（員工訓練）
❻	我希望公司交通便利。	I wish my firm was conveniently located. * be conveniently located（在交通便利的地方）
❼	我希望公司離家近。	I wish my firm was close to my home. * be close to＋地點（離某地點很近）
❽	我希望公司有完善的升遷制度。	I wish my firm had a complete system for promotion. * system for promotion（升遷制）
❾	我希望能準時下班。	I wish I could leave work on time.
❿	我希望每年有 10 天年假。	I wish I had ten days' leave every year. * leave（休假日）＝ vacation
⓫	我希望有豐厚的年終獎金。	I hope to get a substantial year-end bonus. * year-end bonus（年終獎金）＝ annual bonus
⓬	我希望同事好相處。	I wish my colleagues were easier to get along with. * be easier to（容易） * get along with（相處融洽）

單字級等分析

	單字	音標	詞性	意義	字頻	大考	英檢	多益
❶	wish	[wɪʃ]	v.	希望	1	1	初級	
	company	[ˈkʌmpənɪ]	n.	公司	1	2	初級	◎
	had	[hæd]	p.t.	have（擁有）過去式	1	1	初級	
	more	[mor]	adj.	many（許多的）比較級	1	1	初級	
	benefit	[ˈbɛnəfɪt]	n.	福利	1	3	中級	◎
❷	work	[wɝk]	v./n.	工作	1	1	初級	◎
	large	[lɑrdʒ]	adj.	大的	1	1	初級	◎
	more	[mor]	adv.	多於	1	1	初級	
	employee	[ˌɛmplɔɪˈi]	n.	員工	1	3	中級	◎
❸	less	[lɛs]	adj.	little（少的）比較級	1	1	初級	
	income	[ˈɪn.kʌm]	n.	收入	1	2	初級	◎
❹	small	[smɔl]	adj.	小的	1	1	初級	◎
	less	[lɛs]	adv.	少於	1	1	初級	
❺	focus	[ˈfokəs]	v.	重視	1	2	初級	◎
	training	[ˈtrenɪŋ]	n.	訓練	1	1	中級	◎
❻	firm	[fɝm]	n.	公司	1	2	初級	◎
	conveniently	[kənˈvinjəntlɪ]	adv.	方便地	5			◎
	located	[ˈloketɪd]	p.p.	locate（位於）過去分詞	1	2	中高	◎
❼	close	[klos]	adj.	近的	1	1	初級	◎
	home	[hom]	n.	家	1	1	初級	
❽	complete	[kəmˈplit]	adj.	完整的	1	2	初級	◎
	system	[ˈsɪstəm]	n.	制度、體制	1	3	初級	◎
	promotion	[prəˈmoʃən]	n.	升遷	2	4	中級	◎
❾	leave	[liv]	v./n.	離開/休假日	1	1	初級	◎
	time	[taɪm]	n.	時間	1	1	初級	◎
❿	ten	[tɛn]	n.	十	1	1	初級	
	day	[de]	n.	天	1	1	初級	
	every	[ˈɛvrɪ]	adj.	每一	1	1	初級	
	year	[jɪr]	n.	年	1	1	初級	
⓫	hope	[hop]	v.	希望	1	1	初級	
	get	[gɛt]	v.	獲得/相處	1	1	初級	◎
	substantial	[səbˈstænʃəl]	adj.	豐厚的	1	5	中高	◎
	year-end	[ˈjɪrˈɛnd]	adj.	年終的	7			◎
	bonus	[ˈbonəs]	n.	獎金	2	5	中高	◎
⓬	colleague	[ˈkɑlig]	n.	同事	1	5	中級	◎
	easier	[ˈizɪɚ]	adj.	easy（簡單的）比較級	1	1	初級	
	along	[əˈlɔŋ]	adv.	一起	1	1	初級	

※「紅字單字」於本單元多句出現，「單字級等分析」僅列在「首次出現句」。

025 你喜歡的工作環境？

❶	你希望薪水多少？	How much do you hope your salary will be? * **How much do you hope...?** （你希望有多少…呢）
❷	你希望多久調薪一次？	How often do you hope to get a raise? * **How often do you hope...?** （你希望多久一次…呢）
❸	你希望年終獎金幾個月？	How much of an annual bonus do you hope to receive?
❹	你希望幾點上班？	What time would you like to start work? * **What time...?**（…是幾點？） * **would like to**（想要）
❺	你希望公司附近有捷運站嗎？	Do you wish there was an MRT station around your office? * **around＋某地**（在某地點附近）
❻	你希望公司分紅配股嗎？	Do you wish your firm offered bonuses and stock options? * **offer bonuses**（分紅、提供紅利） * **offer stock options**（配股、提供股票選擇權）
❼	你希望到大公司還是小公司？	Do you hope to work in a big company or a small one?
❽	你希望上下班不打卡嗎？	Do you wish you didn't have to punch in and out of work? * **have to**（需要） * **punch in and out**（上下班打卡）
❾	你希望月休幾天？	How many days off do you wish you had per month? * **How many＋名詞複數形＋...?**（有多少…呢） * **days off**（day off〔休假日〕複數） * **per...**（每一…）
❿	你希望天天準時下班嗎？	Do you wish you could leave work on time every day? * **leave work**（下班） * **on time**（準時地）
⓫	你希望公司有更完善的升遷制度嗎？	Do you wish your company had a more complete system for promotion?

	單字	音標	詞性	意義	字頻	大考	英檢	多益
❶	much	[mʌtʃ]	adj.	許多的	1	1	初級	
	hope	[hop]	v.	希望	1	1	初級	
	salary	[ˈsælərɪ]	n.	薪水	1	4	中級	◎
❷	often	[ˈɔfən]	adv.	常常	1	1	初級	
	get	[gɛt]	v.	獲得	1	1	初級	◎
	raise	[rez]	n.	調薪	1	1	初級	◎
❸	annual	[ˈænjʊəl]	adj.	每年的	1	4	中級	◎
	bonus	[ˈbonəs]	n.	紅利、獎金	2	5	中高	◎
	receive	[rɪˈsiv]	v.	收到	1	1	初級	◎
❹	time	[taɪm]	n.	時間	1	1	初級	◎
	like	[laɪk]	v.	想要	1	1	初級	
	start	[stɑrt]	v.	開始	1	1	初級	
	work	[wɝk]	n./v.	工作	1	1	初級	◎
❺	wish	[wɪʃ]	v.	希望	1	1	初級	
	there	[ðɛr]	adv.	有…	1	1	初級	
	MRT	[ˈɛmˈɑrˈti]	n.	Mass Rapid Transit（捷運）縮寫		2	初級	◎
	station	[ˈsteʃən]	n.	車站	1	1	初級	◎
	office	[ˈɔfɪs]	n.	公司	1	1	初級	◎
❻	firm	[fɝm]	n.	公司	1	2	初級	◎
	offered	[ˈɔfɚd]	p.t.	offer（提供）過去式	7	2	初級	◎
	stock	[stɑk]	n.	股票	1	6	中級	◎
	option	[ˈɑpʃən]	n.	選擇權	1	6	中級	◎
❼	big	[bɪg]	adj.	大的	1	1	初級	
	company	[ˈkʌmpənɪ]	n.	公司	1	2	初級	◎
	small	[smɔl]	adj.	小的	1	1	初級	◎
	one	[wʌn]	pron.	一個	1	1	初級	
❽	have	[hæv]	v.	必須	1	1	初級	
	punch	[pʌntʃ]	v.	打（卡）	2	3	中級	
	in	[ɪn]	adv.	進班	1	1	初級	
	out	[aʊt]	adv.	下班	1	1	初級	
❾	many	[ˈmɛnɪ]	adj.	許多的	1	1	初級	
	day	[de]	n.	天	1	1	初級	
	off	[ɔf]	adj.	休假的	1	1	初級	
	had	[hæd]	p.t.	have（擁有）過去式	1	1	初級	
	month	[mʌnθ]	n.	月	1	1	初級	
❿	leave	[liv]	v.	離開	1	1	初級	◎
	every	[ˈɛvrɪ]	adj.	每一	1	1	初級	
⓫	more	[mor]	adv.	更加	1	1	初級	
	complete	[kəmˈplit]	adj.	完整的	1	2	初級	◎
	system	[ˈsɪstəm]	n.	體制、制度	1	3	初級	◎
	promotion	[prəˈmoʃən]	n.	升遷	2	4	中級	◎

※「紅字單字」於本單元多句出現，「單字級等分析」僅列在「首次出現句」。

MP3 026-01 ❶〜❻

❶	我希望變美。	I wish I could become more beautiful. * **I wish I could＋動詞原形** （可以的話，我希望能…）
❷	我希望自己是眾人目光的焦點。	I wish I could be the focus of everyone's attention. * **the focus of attention**（目光焦點）
❸	我希望皮膚完美無瑕。	I wish I had flawless skin. * **I wish I had＋名詞**（可以的話，我希望擁有…） * **flawless**（沒有瑕疵的）＝ **perfect**
❹	我希望看起來更年輕。	I wish I could look younger. * **look＋比較級**（看起來更…）
❺	我希望雀斑變少。	I wish I had fewer freckles. * **pimple**（青春痘）
❻	我希望眼睛大一點。	I wish I had bigger eyes.
❼	我羨慕膚色白皙的人。	I envy people with fair skin. * **envy＋某人**（羨慕某人）＝ **be jealous of＋某人** * **with＋某特徵**（有某種特徵）
❽	我羨慕別人的小臉。	I am jealous of people with small faces.
❾	我希望變成雙眼皮。	I wish I had double-fold eyelids.
❿	我想要又長又翹的眼睫毛。	I want to have long, raised eyelashes.
⓫	我希望鼻子變挺。	I wish I had a pronounced nose.
⓬	我想要性感渾厚的嘴唇。	I want to have thick, sexy lips.
⓭	我努力減少臉上細紋。	I am trying to reduce my facial wrinkles. * 此句用「現在進行式」（...am trying...）表示「現階段發生的事」。 * **reduce wrinkles**（減少皺紋）
⓮	我希望沒有黑眼圈。	I wish I didn't have bags under my eyes.
⓯	我希望看起來有自信。	I wish I looked more self-confident.

	單字	音標	詞性	意義	字頻	大考	英檢	多益
❶	wish	[wɪʃ]	v.	希望	1	1	初級	
	become	[bɪˋkʌm]	v.	變得	1	1	初級	◎
	more	[mor]	adv.	更加	1	1	初級	
	beautiful	[ˋbjutəfəl]	adj.	漂亮的	1	1	初級	
❷	focus	[ˋfokəs]	n.	焦點	1	2	初級	◎
	everyone	[ˋɛvrɪˏwʌn]	pron.	每個人	1		初級	
	attention	[əˋtɛnʃən]	n.	注意	1	2	初級	◎
❸	had	[hæd]	p.t.	have（擁有）過去式	1	1	初級	
	flawless	[ˋflɔlɪs]	adj.	沒有瑕疵的	5			◎
	skin	[skɪn]	n.	皮膚	1	1	初級	◎
❹	look	[lʊk]	v.	看起來	1	1	初級	
	younger	[ˋjʌŋgɚ]	adj.	young（年輕的）比較級	1	1	初級	
❺	fewer	[ˋfjuɚ]	adj.	few（少的）比較級	1			
	freckles	[ˋfrɛkls]	n.	freckle（雀斑）複數	5			
❻	bigger	[ˋbɪgɚ]	adj.	big（大的）比較級	1	1	初級	
	eye	[aɪ]	n.	眼睛	1	1	初級	
❼	envy	[ˋɛnvɪ]	v.	羨慕	4	3	初級	
	people	[ˋpipl]	n.	person（人）複數	1	1	初級	
	fair	[fɛr]	adj.	白皙的	1	2	初級	◎
❽	jealous	[ˋdʒɛləs]	adj.	羨慕的	3	3	初級	◎
	small	[smɔl]	adj.	小的	1	1	初級	◎
	face	[fes]	n.	臉	1	1	初級	
❾	double-folded	[ˋdʌblˋfoldɪd]	adj.	雙眼皮的				
	eyelids	[ˋaɪˏlɪds]	n.	eyelid（眼皮）複數	4	5	中高	
❿	want	[wɑnt]	v.	想要	1	1	初級	◎
	have	[hæv]	v.	擁有	1	1	初級	
	long	[lɔŋ]	adj.	長的	1	1	初級	
	raised	[rezd]	adj.	揚起的	3	1	初級	◎
	eyelashes	[ˋaɪˏlæʃəs]	n.	eyelash（眼睫毛）複數	5	5	中高	
⓫	pronounced	[prəˋnaʊnst]	adj.	明顯的	3	2	初級	
	nose	[noz]	n.	鼻子	1	1	初級	
⓬	thick	[θɪk]	adj.	濃厚的	1	2	初級	
	sexy	[ˋsɛksɪ]	adj.	性感的	2	3	中級	
	lips	[lɪps]	n.	lip（嘴唇）複數	1	1	初級	
⓭	trying	[ˋtraɪɪŋ]	p.pr.	try（嘗試）現在分詞	6	1	初級	
	reduce	[rɪˋdjus]	v.	減少	1	3	中級	◎
	facial	[ˋfeʃəl]	adj.	臉部的	3	4	中級	
	wrinkles	[ˋrɪŋkls]	n.	wrinkle（皺紋）複數	3	4	中級	◎
⓮	bags	[bægs]	n.	bag（黑眼圈）複數	1	1	初級	
⓯	looked	[lʊkt]	p.t.	look（看起來）過去式	1	1	初級	
	self-confident	[ˏsɛlfˋkɑnfədənt]	adj.	自信的	8	1		

※「紅字單字」於本單元多句出現，「單字級等分析」僅列在「首次出現句」。

026　你希望外表⋯？

❶	你滿意自己的長相嗎？	Are you satisfied with your appearance? * be satisfied with＋名詞（滿意⋯）
❷	你希望減少細紋嗎？	Do you want to reduce your wrinkles? * want to＋動詞原形（想要⋯）
❸	你最不滿意的五官是哪一個？	What is the facial feature that you are most dissatisfied with? * What is...?（哪個是⋯？） * facial feature（五官） * be dissatisfied with（不滿意）
❹	你羨慕小臉的人嗎？	Are you envious of people who have smaller faces than you? * be envious of（羨慕）＝ envy
❺	你希望皮膚更白嗎？	Do you wish you had whiter skin? * Do you wish you had...? （可以的話，你是否想擁有⋯）
❻	你打算曬成古銅色嗎？	Do you plan to get a bronze tan? * plan to＋動詞原形（計畫⋯） * get a tan（曬黑）
❼	你希望自己看起來充滿自信嗎？	Do you wish you looked full of confidence? * full of confidence（充滿信心）
❽	你打算整型嗎？	Do you plan to have plastic surgery? * have plastic surgery（做整型手術）
❾	你希望自己看起來成熟穩重嗎?	Do you want to look mature and dignified?
❿	你打算利用雷射除斑嗎？	Do you plan to have your blemishes removed by laser? * have＋某物＋過去分詞（使某物⋯） * have...removed（除掉⋯）
⓫	你希望自己看起來更年輕嗎？	Do you wish you looked younger? * look younger（看起來更年輕）
⓬	你希望自己看起來比同年齡的人年輕嗎？	Do you wish you looked younger than people the same age as you? * the same age as you（和你同年齡）

	單字	音標	詞性	意義	字頻	大考	英檢	多益
❶	satisfied	[ˈsætɪsˌfaɪd]	adj.	滿意的	2	2	中高	◎
	appearance	[əˈpɪrəns]	n.	長相	1	2	初級	◎
❷	want	[wɑnt]	v.	想要	1	1	初級	◎
	reduce	[rɪˈdjus]	v.	減少	1	3	中級	◎
	wrinkles	[ˈrɪŋkls]	n.	wrinkle（皺紋）複數	3	4	中級	◎
❸	facial	[ˈfeʃəl]	adj.	臉部的	3	4	中級	
	feature	[ˈfitʃɚ]	n.	特徵、特色	1	3	中級	◎
	most	[most]	adv.	最	1	1	初級	
	dissatisfied	[dɪsˈsætɪsˌfaɪd]	adj.	不滿意的	4		初級	◎
❹	envious	[ˈɛnvɪəs]	adj.	羨慕的	6	4	中級	
	people	[ˈpipl]	n.	person（人）複數	1	1	初級	
	have	[hæv]	v.	擁有/做（手術）/讓…	1	1	初級	
	smaller	[ˈsmɔlɚ]	adj.	small（小的）比較級	1	1	初級	◎
	face	[fes]	n.	臉	1	1	初級	
❺	wish	[wɪʃ]	v.	希望	1	1	初級	
	had	[hæd]	p.t.	have（擁有）過去式	1	1	初級	
	whiter	[ˈhwaɪtɚ]	adj.	white（白的）比較級	1	1	初級	
	skin	[skɪn]	n.	皮膚	1	1	初級	◎
❻	plan	[plæn]	v.	計畫	1	1	初級	◎
	get	[gɛt]	v.	變成	1	1	初級	◎
	bronze	[brɑnz]	adj.	古銅色的	2	5	中高	
	tan	[tæn]	n.	曬黑	4	5	中高	
❼	looked	[lʊkt]	p.t.	look（看起來）過去式	1	1	初級	
	full	[fʊl]	adj.	充滿的	1	1	初級	
	confidence	[ˈkɑnfədəns]	n.	自信	1	4	中級	◎
❽	plastic	[ˈplæstɪk]	adj.	整形的	1	3	中級	◎
	surgery	[ˈsɝdʒərɪ]	n.	手術	1	4	中級	◎
❾	look	[lʊk]	v.	看起來	1	1	初級	
	mature	[məˈtʃʊr]	adj.	成熟的	2	3	中級	◎
	dignified	[ˈdɪgnəˌfaɪd]	adj.	莊重的	4			
❿	blemishes	[ˈblɛmɪʃəs]	n.	blemish（斑點）複數	7			
	removed	[rɪˈmuvd]	p.p.	remove（除掉）過去分詞	1	3	中級	◎
	laser	[ˈlezɚ]	n.	雷射	2	5	中級	
⓫	younger	[ˈjʌŋɡɚ]	adj.	young（年輕的）比較級	1	1	初級	
⓬	same	[sem]	adj.	相同的	1	1	初級	
	age	[edʒ]	n.	年齡	1	1	初級	◎

※「紅字單字」於本單元多句出現，「單字級等分析」僅列在「首次出現句」。

027　我希望身材…。

🔊 MP3 027-01 ❶～⓰

❶	我希望永遠保持好身材。	I hope that I can maintain my figure forever. * **hope that**＋子句（希望…） * **maintain figure**（保持身材）
❷	我希望身材更完美。	I wish I had a more attractive body. * **I wish I had**＋名詞（可以的話，我希望擁有…） * **more attractive**（更迷人的）
❸	我希望維持目前體重。	I hope that I can maintain my current weight. * **maintain one's weight**（維持體重）
❹	我想減肥。	I want to lose some weight. * **want to**＋動詞原形（想要…）
❺	我想減重 5 公斤。	I want to lose five kilos.
❻	我想增胖 3 公斤。	I want to gain three kilos.
❼	我希望長高。	I wish I were taller. * **I wish**＋過去式子句（可以的話，我希望…）
❽	我希望別再長高了。	I hope that I won't get any taller. * **get taller**（變得更高）
❾	我希望身上毫無贅肉。	I wish that I didn't have any excess weight. * **excess weight**（多餘的體重）
❿	我希望有雙美腿。	I wish that I had a pair of beautiful legs. * **a pair of**（一雙）
⓫	我希望胸部豐滿。	I wish I had a larger bust. * **larger bust**（胸部更大）
⓬	我希望消除小腹。	I wish that I could get rid of my gut. * **get rid of**（擺脫、甩掉）
⓭	我希望雙腿纖細。	I wish my legs were slim and slender.
⓮	我希望手臂結實。	I wish I had sturdy arms.
⓯	我想要小蠻腰。	I want to have a small waist. * **small waist**（小蠻腰）
⓰	我希望臀部小而翹。	I wish I had a small and shapely butt.

	單字	音標	詞性	意義	字頻	大考	英檢	多益
❶	hope	[hop]	v.	希望	1	1	初級	
	maintain	[menˋten]	v.	維持	1	2	初級	◎
	figure	[ˋfɪgjɚ]	n.	身材	1	2	初級	◎
	forever	[fɚˋɛvɚ]	adv.	永遠	1	3	中級	
❷	wish	[wɪʃ]	v.	希望	1	1	初級	
	had	[hæd]	p.t.	have（擁有）過去式	1	1	初級	
	more	[mor]	adv.	更加	1	1	初級	
	attractive	[əˋtræktɪv]	adj.	迷人的	2	3	中級	◎
	body	[ˋbɑdɪ]	n.	身材	1	1	初級	
❸	current	[ˋkɝənt]	adj.	目前的	1	3	初級	◎
	weight	[wet]	n.	體重	1	1	初級	◎
❹	want	[wɑnt]	v.	想要	1	1	初級	◎
	lose	[luz]	v.	減少	1	2	初級	◎
	some	[sʌm]	adj.	一些	1	1	初級	
❺	five	[faɪv]	n.	五	1	1	初級	
	kilo	[ˋkilo]	n.	kilogram（公斤）簡寫				
❻	gain	[gen]	v.	增加	1	2	初級	◎
	three	[θri]	n.	三	1	1	初級	
❼	taller	[ˋtɔlɚ]	adj.	tall（高的）比較級	1	1	初級	◎
❽	get	[gɛt]	v.	變成	1	1	初級	◎
	any	[ˋɛnɪ]	adv.	絲毫	1	1	初級	
❾	have	[hæv]	v.	擁有	1	1	初級	
	excess	[ɪkˋsɛs]	adj.	多餘的	3	5	中高	◎
❿	pair	[pɛr]	n.	雙、對	1	1	初級	
	beautiful	[ˋbjutəfəl]	adj.	美麗的	1	1	初級	
	leg	[lɛg]	n.	腿	1	1	初級	
⓫	larger	[ˋlɑrdʒɚ]	adj.	large（大的）比較級	1	1	初級	◎
	bust	[bʌst]	n.	胸部	3		中高	
⓬	rid	[rɪd]	p.p.	rid（擺脫）過去分詞	2	3	中級	
	gut	[gʌt]	n.	小腹	2	5	中高	
⓭	slim	[slɪm]	adj.	苗條的	2	2	初級	◎
	slender	[ˋslɛndɚ]	adj.	纖細的	3	2	初級	◎
⓮	sturdy	[ˋstɝdɪ]	adj.	肌肉結實的	3	5	中高	◎
	arm	[ɑrm]	n.	手臂	2	4	中高	
⓯	small	[smɔl]	adj.	小的	1	1	初級	◎
	waist	[west]	n.	腰	2	2	初級	
⓰	shapely	[ˋʃeplɪ]	adj.	豐滿好看的	8			
	butt	[bʌt]	n.	屁股	2			

※「紅字單字」於本單元多句出現，「單字級等分析」僅列在「首次出現句」。

MP3 027-02 ❶～⓬

❶	你希望自己的體重多少公斤？	How many kilograms do you wish you were? * **How many...do you wish you were?** （你希望…是多少？）
❷	你希望自己再瘦一點嗎？	Do you wish you were a bit thinner? * **Do you wish＋過去式子句?** （你是否希望…？） * **a bit＋比較級**（稍微再…）
❸	你覺得自己的體重標準嗎？	Do you think your weight is average? * **average**（中等的）＝ **normal**
❹	你希望身高多少？	How tall do you wish you were? * **How tall...?**（…是多高？）
❺	你滿意你的身材嗎？	Are you satisfied with your figure? * **be satisfied with**（滿意）
❻	你希望自己永遠吃不胖嗎？	Do you wish you could eat as much as you wanted and never gain weight? * **eat as much as you want** （想吃多少就吃多少） * **as much as＋過去式子句** （如同原本…的一樣多） * **never gain weight**（不會變胖）
❼	你羨慕模特兒的好身材嗎？	Do you envy the good figure of models? * **good figure**（好身材）
❽	誰是你心目中的完美身材代表？	Who do you think has the most ideal body? * **Who do you think...?**（你認為…的是誰？） * **ideal body**（理想身材）
❾	你希望能更強壯嗎？	Do you wish you were a bit stronger?
❿	你最不滿意全身哪一個部位？	Which part of your figure are you most dissatisfied with? * **be dissatisfied with**（不滿意）
⓫	你努力消除贅肉嗎？	Are you trying to get rid of excess fat? * **excess fat**（贅肉、多餘的脂肪）
⓬	你希望穿得下 S 號的衣服嗎？	Do you wish you could wear size small clothes? * **size small clothes**（S 號的衣服）

	單字	音標	詞性	意義	字頻	大考	英檢	多益
❶	many	[ˋmɛnɪ]	adj.	許多的	1	1	初級	
	kilogram	[ˋkɪləˌgræm]	n.	公斤		3	初級	
	wish	[wɪʃ]	v.	希望	1	1	初級	
❷	bit	[bɪt]	n.	稍微	1	1	初級	
	thinner	[ˋθɪnɚ]	adj.	thin（瘦的）比較級	1	2	初級	◎
❸	think	[θɪŋk]	v.	認為	1	1	初級	
	weight	[wet]	n.	體重	1	1	初級	◎
	average	[ˋævərɪdʒ]	adj.	普通中等的	1	3	中級	◎
❹	tall	[tɔl]	adj.	身高…	1	1	初級	◎
❺	satisfied	[ˋsætɪsˌfaɪd]	adj.	滿意的	2	2	中高	◎
	figure	[ˋfɪgjɚ]	n.	身材	1	2	初級	◎
❻	eat	[it]	v.	吃	1	1	初級	
	much	[mʌtʃ]	adv.	許多	1	1	初級	
	wanted	[ˋwɑntɪd]	p.t.	want（想要）過去式	5	1	初級	◎
	never	[ˋnɛvɚ]	adv.	從不	1	1	初級	
	gain	[gen]	v.	增加	1	2	初級	
❼	envy	[ˋɛnvɪ]	v.	羨慕	4	3	初級	
	good	[gʊd]	adj.	良好的	1	1	初級	◎
	model	[ˋmɑdl]	n.	模特兒	1	2	初級	◎
❽	have	[hæv]	v.	擁有	1*	1	初級	
	most	[most]	adv.	最	1	1	初級	
	ideal	[aɪˋdiəl]	adj.	理想的	2	3	中級	◎
	body	[ˋbɑdɪ]	n.	身材	1	1	初級	
❾	stronger	[ˋstrɔŋgɚ]	adj.	strong（強壯的）比較級	1	1	初級	
❿	part	[pɑrt]	n.	部分	1	1	初級	◎
	dissatisfied	[dɪsˋsætɪsˌfaɪd]	adj.	不滿意的	4			◎
⓫	trying	[ˋtraɪɪŋ]	p.pr.	try（嘗試）現在分詞	6	1	初級	
	get	[gɛt]	v.	變成	1	1	初級	
	rid	[rɪd]	p.p.	rid（擺脫）過去分詞	2	3	中級	
	excess	[ɪkˋsɛs]	adj.	多餘的	3	5	中高	◎
	fat	[fæt]	n.	脂肪	1	1	初級	
⓬	wear	[wɛr]	v.	穿	1	1	初級	◎
	size	[saɪz]	n.	尺寸	1	1	初級	◎
	small	[smɔl]	adj.	小的	1	1	初級	
	clothes	[kloz]	n.	cloth（衣服）複數	1	2	初級	

※「紅字單字」於本單元多句出現，「單字級等分析」僅列在「首次出現句」。

🌐 MP3 028-01 ❶〜❷

❶	我對未來有很多計畫。	I have many plans for my future. * plan for＋某事（對某事的計畫） * for my future（針對我的未來）
❷	我對未來沒有想法。	I don't have any plans for my future.
❸	我打算出國留學。	I intend to study abroad. * intend to＋動詞原形（打算）
❹	我只想走一步算一步。	I just want to take life one step at a time. * want to＋動詞原形（想要） * take life one step at a time（走一步算一步）
❺	我希望闖出一番事業。	I hope to develop a career for myself. * hope to＋動詞原形（希望） * develop a career（發展職業生涯）
❻	我計畫 5 年後創業。	I plan to have my own business in five years. * plan to＋動詞原形（計畫） * have one's own business（擁有自己的公司）
❼	我希望 27 歲前結婚。	I hope that I can get married before I turn 27. * get married（結婚） * before I turn＋歲數（在我…歲以前）
❽	30 歲後我想開一間店。	I want to open a store after I turn 30. * after I turn＋歲數（在我…歲以後）
❾	我想當頂客族。	I want to be a DINK (Double Income, No Kids).
❿	我計畫 60 歲退休。	I plan to retire at age 60. * at age＋歲數（在…歲的時候）
⓫	我希望 30 歲前生小孩。	I hope to have a child before I turn 30. * have a child（生孩子）
⓬	我想生兩個小孩。	I intend to have two children.
⓭	一生中我一定要環遊世界。	I absolutely must travel around the world at some point in my life. * travel around the world（環遊世界） * at some point in my life（在我人生的某個時刻）
⓮	我希望有經濟基礎再結婚。	I hope to get married after I have some economic stability. * have economic stability（經濟穩定）

	單字	音標	詞性	意義	字頻	大考	英檢	多益
❶	have	[hæv]	v.	擁有/生育	1	1	初級	
	many	[ˋmɛnɪ]	adj.	許多的	1	1	初級	
	plan	[plæn]	n./v.	計畫	1	1	初級	◎
	future	[ˋfjutʃɚ]	n.	未來	1	2	初級	
❷	any	[ˋɛnɪ]	adj.	任何的	1	1	初級	
❸	intend	[ɪnˋtɛnd]	v.	打算	1	4	中級	◎
	study	[ˋstʌdɪ]	v.	學習	1	1	初級	◎
	abroad	[əˋbrɔd]	adv.	國外地	2	2	初級	◎
❹	just	[dʒʌst]	adv.	只是	1	1	初級	
	want	[wɑnt]	v.	想要	1	1	初級	◎
	take	[tek]	v.	看待	1	1	初級	◎
	life	[laɪf]	n.	人生	1	1	初級	
	one	[wʌn]	n.	一	1	1	初級	
	step	[stɛp]	n.	腳步	1	1	初級	◎
	time	[taɪm]	n.	時間	1	1	初級	◎
❺	hope	[hop]	v.	希望	1	1	初級	
	develop	[dɪˋvɛləp]	v.	發展	1	2	初級	◎
	career	[kəˋrɪr]	n.	職業	1	4	初級	◎
	myself	[maɪˋsɛlf]	pron.	我自己	1		初級	
❻	own	[on]	adj.	自己的	1	1	初級	◎
	business	[ˋbɪznɪs]	n.	公司、企業	1	2	初級	◎
	five	[faɪv]	n.	五	1	1	初級	
	year	[jɪr]	n.	年	1	1	初級	
❼	get	[gɛt]	v.	變成	1	1	初級	
	married	[ˋmærɪd]	p.p.	marry（結婚）過去分詞	1		初級	
	turn	[tɝn]	v.	成為…歲數	1	1	初級	◎
❽	open	[ˋopən]	v.	開張	1	1	初級	
	store	[stor]	n.	店鋪	1	1	初級	◎
❾	DINK	[dɪŋk]	n.	頂客族				
	double	[ˋdʌbl̩]	adj.	雙重的	1	2	初級	◎
	income	[ˋɪn͵kʌm]	n.	收入	1	2	初級	◎
	kid	[kɪd]	n.	小孩	1	1	初級	
❿	retire	[rɪˋtaɪr]	v.	退休	1	4	中級	◎
	age	[edʒ]	n.	年齡	1	1	初級	◎
⓫	child	[tʃaɪld]	n.	小孩	1	1	初級	
⓬	two	[tu]	n.	二	1	1	初級	
	children	[ˋtʃɪldrən]	n.	child（小孩）複數	1	1	初級	
⓭	absolutely	[ˋæbsə͵lutlɪ]	adv.	絕對、勢必	1		中級	◎
	travel	[ˋtrævl̩]	v.	旅遊	1	2	初級	◎
	world	[wɝld]	n.	世界	1	1	初級	
	some	[sʌm]	adj.	某個	1	1	初級	
	point	[pɔɪnt]	n.	時刻、階段	1	1	初級	◎
⓮	economic	[͵ikəˋnɑmɪk]	adj.	經濟的	1	1	中級	◎
	stability	[stəˋbɪlətɪ]	n.	穩定	2	1	中高	

※「紅字單字」於本單元多句出現，「單字級等分析」僅列在「首次出現句」。

🎧 MP3 028-02 ❶～❻

❶	你希望成為怎麼樣的人？	What kind of person do you hope to become? * **What kind of...?**（什麼樣的…？）
❷	十年後，你希望成為什麼樣子？	What kind of person do you hope to be in ten years? * **in＋一段時間**（在某段時間以後） * **hope to＋動詞原形**（希望）
❸	你計畫幾歲結婚？	When do you plan to get married? * **get married**（結婚）
❹	你想過你的未來嗎？	Have you ever considered your future? * **Have you ever...?**（你是否曾經…）
❺	你有計畫生小孩嗎？	Do you plan to have a child? * **plan to**（打算）＝ **intend to** ＝ **have plans to** * **have a child**（生小孩）
❻	你打算出國留學嗎？	Do you have plans to study abroad?
❼	你打算一輩子單身嗎？	Do you plan to be single for the rest of your life? * **the rest of your life**（你剩餘的人生）
❽	你計畫幾歲退休？	When do you plan to retire?
❾	你計畫生幾個小孩？	How many children do you plan to have? * **How many＋名詞複數形＋...?**（多少個…？）
❿	你想從事什麼樣的工作？	What kind of career would you like to have? * **would like to**（想要）
⓫	你退休後想做什麼？	What do you want to do after you retire?
⓬	你打算創業嗎？	Do you intend to start your own business? * **start one's own business**（創業）
⓭	你希望找什麼樣的人生伴侶？	What kind of life partner do you hope to find? * **life partner**（另一半、人生伴侶）
⓮	你打算移民嗎？	Do you plan to immigrate to another country? * **immigrate to＋國家**（移民到某國家）
⓯	你準備考證照嗎？	Are you prepared for the certification tests? * **be prepared for**（準備好） * **certification test**（證照考試）

	單字	音標	詞性	意義	字頻	大考	英檢	多益
❶	kind	[kaɪnd]	n.	種類	1	1	初級	◎
	person	[ˋpɝsn]	n.	人	1	1	初級	
	hope	[hop]	v.	希望	1	1	初級	
	become	[bɪˋkʌm]	v.	變為	1	1	初級	◎
❷	ten	[tɛn]	n.	十	1	1	初級	
	year	[jɪr]	n.	年	1	1	初級	
❸	plan	[plæn]	v./n.	計畫	1	1	初級	◎
	get	[gɛt]	v.	變成	1	1	初級	◎
	married	[ˋmærɪd]	p.p.	married（結婚）過去分詞	1		初級	
❹	ever	[ˋɛvɚ]	adv.	曾經	1	1	初級	
	considered	[kənˋsɪdɚd]	p.p.	consider（考慮）過去分詞	1	2	初級	◎
	future	[ˋfjutʃɚ]	n.	未來	1	2	初級	
❺	have	[hæv]	v.	生育/擁有/從事	1	1	初級	
	child	[tʃaɪld]	n.	小孩	1	1	初級	
❻	study	[ˋstʌdɪ]	v.	學習	1	1	初級	◎
	abroad	[əˋbrɔd]	adv.	國外地	2	2	初級	◎
❼	single	[ˋsɪŋgl]	adj.	單身的	1	2	初級	◎
	rest	[rɛst]	n.	剩餘	1	1	初級	
	life	[laɪf]	n.	人生	1	1	初級	
❽	retire	[rɪˋtaɪr]	v.	退休	1	4	中級	◎
❾	many	[ˋmɛnɪ]	adj.	許多的	1	1	初級	
	children	[ˋtʃɪldrən]	n.	child（小孩）複數	1	1	初級	
❿	career	[kəˋrɪr]	n.	職業	1	4	初級	◎
	like	[laɪk]	v.	想要	1	1	初級	
⓫	want	[wɑnt]	v.	想要	1	1	初級	
⓬	intend	[ɪnˋtɛnd]	v.	打算	1	4	中級	◎
	start	[stɑrt]	v.	開創	1	1	初級	
	own	[on]	adj.	自己的	1	1	初級	◎
	business	[ˋbɪznɪs]	n.	公司、企業	1	2	初級	
⓭	partner	[ˋpɑrtnɚ]	n.	伴侶	1	2	初級	◎
	find	[faɪnd]	v.	找到	1	1	初級	
⓮	immigrate	[ˋɪmə.gret]	v.	移民	6	4	中高	
	another	[əˋnʌðɚ]	adj.	其他的	1	1	初級	
	country	[ˋkʌntrɪ]	n.	國家	1	1	初級	
⓯	prepared	[prɪˋpɛrd]	p.p.	prepare（準備）過去分詞	3	1	中級	◎
	certification	[.sɝtɪfəˋkeʃən]	n.	證照	3		中級	
	test	[tɛst]	n.	考試	1	2	初級	

※「紅字單字」於本單元多句出現，「單字級等分析」僅列在「首次出現句」。

029 我的理財規畫。

MP3 029-01 ❶～⓰

❶	我每天記帳。	I keep track of my expenses every day.
❷	我每個月儲蓄薪水的三分之一。	I save one-third of my salary every month. * save＋金額（儲蓄…金額）
❸	我投資股票。	I invest in stocks.　* invest in（投資）
❹	我打算 30 歲買房子。	I plan to buy a house when I am 30.
❺	我每個月儲蓄 5000 元。	I save five thousand every month.
❻	我希望 25 歲擁有第一個 100 萬。	I hope to have earned my first million by the time I'm 25.　* by（在…時間以前） * hope to have＋過去分詞（從以前就希望…，但尚未達成）
❼	我做期貨買賣。	I do futures trading.　* futures trading（期貨交易）
❽	我希望 10 年內付清車貸。	I hope to pay off my car loan within ten years. * pay off（付清、清償）、within＋時間（…時間以內）
❾	我跟會。	I've joined a credit cooperative. * 此句用「現在完成式」（...have joined...）表示 　「過去某時點發生某事，且結果持續到現在」。
❿	我不隨便花錢。	I don't spend money carelessly.
⓫	我把錢在銀行定存。	I deposit my money in a savings account. * savings account（儲蓄帳戶）
⓬	我為自己買保險。	I bought insurance for myself. * buy insurance（買保險）
⓭	我完全不懂理財。	I don't know how to manage my money at all. * I don't know how...（我不懂…）、manage money（理財）
⓮	我必須準備小孩的教育費。	I have to save for my child's education. * save for＋某事物（為了某事物儲蓄）
⓯	我花錢完全不做規畫。	I spend money without thinking. * without thinking（不經過思考）
⓰	我貸款創業。	I took out a loan to start my own business. * take out a loan（辦理貸款）

	單字	音標	詞性	意義	字頻	大考	英檢	多益
❶	keep track of	[kip træk ʌv]	v.	記錄				◎
	expense	[ɪkˋspɛns]	n.	支出	1	3	中級	◎
	every	[ˋɛvrɪ]	adj.	每一	1	1	初級	
	day	[de]	n.	天	1	1	初級	◎
❷	save	[sev]	v.	儲蓄	1	1	初級	

❷	one-third	[ˋwʌnˋθɝd]	n.	三分之一	2	4	初級	
	salary	[ˋsælərɪ]	n.	薪水	1	1	中級	◎
	month	[mʌnθ]	n.	月	1		初級	
❸	invest	[ɪnˋvɛst]	v.	投資	1	4	中級	◎
	stock	[stɑk]	n.	股票	1	6	中級	◎
❹	plan	[plæn]	v.	計畫	1	1	初級	
	buy	[baɪ]	v.	購買	1	1	初級	
	house	[haʊs]	n.	房子	1	1	初級	◎
❺	five	[faɪv]	n.	五	1	1	初級	
	thousand	[ˋθaʊznd]	n.	千	1	1	初級	
❻	hope	[hop]	v.	希望	1	1	初級	
	earned	[ɝnd]	p.p.	earn（賺得）過去分詞	5	2	初級	◎
	first	[fɝst]	adj.	第一個	1	1	初級	
	million	[ˋmɪljən]	n.	百萬	1	2	初級	
	time	[taɪm]	n.	時間	1	1	初級	◎
❼	do	[du]	v.	做	1	1	初級	
	future	[ˋfjutʃɚ]	n.	期貨	1	2	初級	◎
	trading	[ˋtredɪŋ]	n.	交易、買賣	2	2	初級	
❽	pay	[pe]	v.	付錢	1	3	初級	◎
	off	[ɔf]	adv.	清、完	1	1	初級	
	car	[kɑr]	n.	車	1	1	初級	
	loan	[lon]	n.	貸款	1	4	中級	◎
	ten	[tɛn]	n.	十	1	1	初級	
	year	[jɪr]	n.	年	1	1	初級	
❾	joined	[dʒɔɪnd]	p.p.	join（加入）過去分詞	1	1	初級	◎
	credit	[ˋkrɛdɪt]	n.	信用	1	3	中級	
	cooperative	[koˋɑpə,retɪv]	n.	合作社	2	4	中級	
❿	spend	[spɛnd]	v.	花費	1	1	初級	◎
	money	[ˋmʌnɪ]	n.	金錢	1	1	初級	◎
	carelessly	[ˋkɛrlɪslɪ]	adv.	漫不經心地	7			
⓫	deposit	[dɪˋpɑzɪt]	v.	儲蓄	2	3	中級	◎
	savings	[ˋsevɪŋz]	n.	儲蓄	2	3		◎
	account	[əˋkaʊnt]	n.	帳戶	1	3	中級	◎
⓬	bought	[bɔt]	p.t.	buy（購買）過去式	1	1	初級	
	insurance	[ɪnˋʃʊrəns]	n.	保險	1	4	中級	◎
	myself	[maɪˋsɛlf]	pron.	我自己	1		初級	
⓭	know	[no]	v.	知道	1	1	初級	◎
	manage	[ˋmænɪdʒ]	v.	管理	1	3	中級	◎
	all	[ɔl]	n.	完全	1	1	初級	
⓮	have	[hæv]	v.	必須	1	1	初級	
	child	[tʃaɪld]	n.	小孩	1	1	初級	
	education	[,ɛdʒʊˋkeʃən]	n.	教育	1	2	初級	◎
⓯	thinking	[ˋθɪŋkɪŋ]	n.	think（思考）動名詞	1	1	中級	
⓰	took	[tʊk]	p.t.	take（辦理）過去式	1	1	初級	◎
	out	[aʊt]	adv.	辦理出…	1	1	初級	
	start	[stɑrt]	v.	開創	1	1	初級	
	own	[on]	adj.	自己的	1	1	初級	◎
	business	[ˋbɪznɪs]	n.	公司、企業	1	2	初級	◎

※「紅字單字」於本單元多句出現，「單字級等分析」僅列在「首次出現句」。

MP3 029-02 ❶〜⓰

❶	你如何理財？	How do you manage your money? * money（金錢）可替換為：finances（財務）
❷	你一個月存多少錢？	How much do you save per month? * per＋名詞（每一…）
❸	你如何運用薪水？	How do you make use of your salary? * make use of（運用）
❹	你定期儲蓄嗎？	Do you save money regularly?
❺	你有投資房地產嗎？	Do you invest in real estate? * real estate（房地產） * funds（基金） * stocks（股票）
❻	你每天記帳嗎？	Do you keep track of your finances every day?
❼	你有貸款嗎？	Do you have a loan?
❽	你很清楚錢花到哪裡去了嗎？	Do you know exactly how you spend your money? * know exactly...（清楚知道…）
❾	你看理財雜誌嗎？	Do you read magazines about financial management? * magazines about＋題材（某題材的雜誌）
❿	你做什麼投資？	What do you invest in?
⓫	你每個月的薪水都花個精光嗎？	Do you blow your salary every month? * blow（花光）＝ spend all of ＝ use up
⓬	你跟會嗎？	Are you part of a credit cooperative? * be part of...（…的一員） * credit cooperative（互助會）
⓭	你用錢有計畫嗎？	Do you have any spending plans for your money? * spending plan（支出計畫）
⓮	你希望退休時有多少現金？	How much cash do you hope to have when you retire?
⓯	沒錢的時候你怎麼辦？	What would you do if you didn't have any money?
⓰	你有什麼賺錢的好方法嗎？	Do you know any good ways of making money? * good way（好方法） * make money（賺錢）

單字級等分析

	單字	音標	詞性	意義	字頻	大考	英檢	多益
❶	manage	[ˋmænɪdʒ]	v.	管理	1	3	中級	◎
	money	[ˋmʌnɪ]	n.	金錢	1	1	初級	◎
❷	much	[mʌtʃ]	adv.	許多地	1	1	初級	
	save	[sev]	v.	儲蓄	1	1	初級	◎
	month	[mʌnθ]	n.	月	1	1	初級	
❸	make	[mek]	v.	做出	1	1	初級	
	use	[juz]	n.	運用	1	1	初級	◎
	salary	[ˋsælərɪ]	n.	薪水	1	4	中級	◎
❹	regularly	[ˋrɛgjələlɪ]	adv.	定期地	2			◎
❺	invest	[ɪnˋvɛst]	v.	投資	1	4	中級	◎
	real	[riəl]	adj.	不動產的	1	1	初級	
	estate	[ɪsˋtet]	n.	地產	1	5	中級	
❻	keep track of	[kip træk ʌv]	v.	記錄				◎
	finance	[faɪˋnæns]	n.	財務	2	4	中級	◎
	every	[ˋɛvrɪ]	adj.	每一	1	1	初級	
	day	[de]	n.	天	1	1	初級	
❼	have	[hæv]	v.	擁有	1	1	初級	
	loan	[lon]	n.	貸款	1	4	中級	◎
❽	know	[no]	v.	知道	1	1	初級	◎
	exactly	[ɪgˋzæktlɪ]	adv.	清楚地	1		中級	◎
	spend	[spɛnd]	v.	花費	1	1	初級	◎
❾	read	[rid]	v.	閱讀	1	1	初級	
	magazine	[mægəˋzin]	n.	雜誌	1	2	初級	
	financial	[faɪˋnænʃəl]	adj.	理財的	1	4	中級	◎
	management	[ˋmænɪdʒmənt]	n.	管理	1	3	中級	◎
⓫	blow	[blo]	v.	花光	1	1	初級	
⓬	part	[pɑrt]	n.	一員	1	1	初級	◎
	credit	[ˋkrɛdɪt]	n.	信用	1	3	中級	◎
	cooperative	[koˋɑpəˌretɪv]	n.	合作社	2	4	中級	
⓭	any	[ˋɛnɪ]	adj.	任何的	1	1	初級	
	spending	[ˋspɛndɪŋ]	n.	spend（花費）動名詞	1	1	初級	
	plan	[plæn]	n.	計畫	1	1	初級	
⓮	cash	[kæʃ]	n.	現金	1	2	初級	◎
	hope	[hop]	v.	希望	1	1	初級	
	retire	[rɪˋtaɪr]	v.	退休	1	4	中級	◎
⓯	do	[du]	v.	做	1	1	初級	
⓰	good	[gʊd]	adj.	良好的	1	1	初級	◎
	way	[we]	n.	方法	1	1	初級	
	making	[ˋmekɪŋ]	n.	make（賺）動名詞	2	1	中高	

※「紅字單字」於本單元多句出現，「單字級等分析」僅列在「首次出現句」。

🔘 MP3 030-01 ❶ ～ ⓰

❶	我習慣早起。	I am used to getting up early. * be used to＋動詞-ing（習慣…） * get up（起床）＝ wake up
❷	我通常 8 點起床。	I usually wake up at eight o'clock.
❸	我早上都會自己醒來。	I wake myself up every morning. * wake myself up（讓自己醒來）
❹	星期六日我睡到很晚。	I get up late on weekends. * get up late（晚起）
❺	我習慣睡到自然醒。	I am used to waking up naturally.
❻	我每天都要別人叫我起床。	I need someone to wake me up every day. * need＋人事物＋to＋動詞原形 　（需要某人事物做某事）
❼	我常因為爬不起來而遲到。	I am usually late because I can't get out of bed. * get out of＋某地（離開某地）
❽	我都用手機當鬧鐘。	I use a mobile phone as my alarm clock. * as＋物品（作為某物品）
❾	我需要鬧鐘叫我起床。	I need an alarm clock to wake me up. * alarm clock（鬧鐘）
❿	我喜歡賴床。	I like to stay in bed. * stay in bed（賴床）＝ lie around in bed
⓫	鬧鐘根本叫不醒我。	An alarm clock can't wake me up at all.
⓬	起床後我仍然覺得沒睡飽。	Even after I get up, I still feel like I didn't get enough sleep. * get enough sleep（睡眠充足）
⓭	我一睡著誰都叫不醒我。	As long as I'm asleep, nobody can wake me up. * as long as＋子句（一旦…）
⓮	我剛起床會一直打呵欠。	I always yawn just after getting up.
⓯	起床後 30 分鐘我就出門。	I go out 30 minutes after I wake up. * 30 minutes after...（在…之後的30分鐘）
⓰	我常常被隔壁鄰居吵醒。	I usually get woken up by noise from my neighbors. * get woken up（被弄醒）

	單字	音標	詞性	意義	字頻	大考	英檢	多益
❶	used	[juzd]	p.p.	use（習慣）過去分詞	1	2	初級	◎
	getting	[ˋgɛtɪŋ]	n.	get（起床）動名詞	1	1	初級	◎
	up	[ʌp]	adv.	起來	1	1	初級	
	early	[ˋɝlɪ]	adv.	早地	1	1	初級	
❷	usually	[ˋjuʒʊəlɪ]	adv.	經常	1		初級	◎
	wake	[wek]	v.	醒來	1	2	初級	
	eight	[et]	n.	八	1	1	初級	
	o'clock	[əˋklɑk]	n.	…點鐘	2	1	初級	
❸	myself	[maɪˋsɛlf]	pron.	我自己	1		初級	
	every	[ˋɛvrɪ]	adj.	每一	1	1	初級	
	morning	[ˋmɔrnɪŋ]	n.	早上	1	1	初級	
❹	get	[gɛt]	v.	起床/被…	1	1	初級	◎
	late	[let]	adv.	晚地	1	1	初級	◎
	weekend	[ˋwikˏɛnd]	n.	週末	1	1	初級	
❺	waking	[ˋwekɪŋ]	n.	wake（醒來）動名詞	5	2	初級	
	naturally	[ˋnætʃərəlɪ]	adv.	自然地	1		中級	
❻	need	[nid]	v.	需要	1	1	初級	◎
	someone	[ˋsʌmˏwʌn]	pron.	某人、有人	1	1	初級	
	day	[de]	n.	天	1	1	初級	
❼	out	[aʊt]	adv.	向外	1	1	初級	
	bed	[bɛd]	n.	床	1	1	初級	
❽	use	[juz]	v.	使用	1	1	初級	◎
	mobile	[ˋmobɪl]	adj.	行動的	2	3	中級	◎
	phone	[fon]	n.	電話	1	1	初級	◎
	alarm	[əˋlɑrm]	n.	鬧鐘	2	1	初級	
	clock	[klɑk]	n.	時鐘	1	1	初級	◎
❿	like	[laɪk]	v.	喜歡	1	1	初級	
	stay	[ste]	v.	賴床	1	1	初級	◎
⓫	all	[ɔl]	n.	完全	1	1	初級	
⓬	even	[ˋivən]	adv.	甚至	1	1	初級	◎
	still	[stɪl]	adv.	仍然	1	1	初級	◎
	feel	[fil]	v.	覺得	1	1	初級	
	enough	[əˋnʌf]	adj.	足夠的	1	1	初級	◎
	sleep	[slip]	n.	睡眠	1	1	初級	
⓭	long	[lɔŋ]	adv.	一旦	1	1	初級	
	asleep	[əˋslip]	adj.	睡著的	2	2	初級	
	nobody	[ˋnobɑdɪ]	pron.	沒有人	1	2	初級	
⓮	always	[ˋɔlwez]	adv.	總是	1	1	初級	
	yawn	[jɔn]	v.	打呵欠	4	3	中級	◎
	just	[dʒʌst]	adv.	剛剛	1	1	初級	
⓯	go	[go]	v.	去	1	1	初級	
	minute	[ˋmɪnɪt]	n.	分鐘	1	1	初級	◎
⓰	woken	[ˋwokən]	p.p.	wake（醒來）過去分詞	1	2	初級	
	noise	[nɔɪz]	n.	聲響	1	1	初級	
	neighbor	[ˋnebɚ]	n.	鄰居	1	2	初級	

※「紅字單字」於本單元多句出現，「單字級等分析」僅列在「首次出現句」。

030　你的起床？

🔊 MP3 030-02 ❶～⓱

❶	你通常幾點起床？	What time do you usually wake up? * **What time...?**（幾點…？）
❷	你每天早上會自己醒來嗎？	Do you get up by yourself every morning? * **by oneself**（藉由自己）
❸	假日你都比平常晚起嗎？	Do you always sleep in when you have the day off? * **sleep in**（比平常晚起） * **day off**（非工作日）
❹	你會賴床嗎？	Do you lie around in bed? * **lie around in bed = stay on bed**（賴床）
❺	你一向晚起嗎？	Do you always get up late? * **Do you always...?**（你是否一直都是…）
❻	你要我叫你起床嗎？	Do you need me to wake you up?
❼	你沒聽到鬧鐘響嗎？	Didn't you hear the alarm clock ringing? * **Didn't you...?**（你剛才沒有…嗎） * **hear＋名詞＋動詞-ing**（聽見…）
❽	你用鬧鐘嗎？	Do you need to use an alarm clock?
❾	鬧鐘叫得醒你嗎？	Do alarm clocks wake you up?
❿	家人會叫你起床嗎？	Does your family wake you up?
⓫	你常被吵醒嗎？	Does noise usually wake you up?
⓬	你還要睡多久？	How long do you still need to sleep? * **How long...?**（…多久時間？） 　= **How much time...?**
⓭	你清醒了嗎？	Are you awake?
⓮	你都睡到這麼晚嗎？	Do you always get up so late?
⓯	你今天起得真早！	You got up really early today! * **early**（早的）可替換為：**late**（晚的）
⓰	你每天折被子嗎？	Do you make your bed every day? * **make one's bed**（折被子）
⓱	你應該多準備幾個鬧鐘。	You should set more than one alarm clock. * **more than＋數量**（多於某數量）

	單字	音標	詞性	意義	字頻	大考	英檢	多益
❶	time	[taɪm]	n.	時間	1	1	初級	◎
	usually	[ˈjuʒʊəlɪ]	adv.	經常	1		初級	◎
	wake	[wek]	v.	醒來	1	2	初級	
	up	[ʌp]	adv.	起來	1	1	初級	
❷	get	[gɛt]	v.	起床	1	1	初級	◎
	yourself	[jʊəˈsɛlf]	pron.	你自己	1		初級	
	every	[ˈɛvrɪ]	adj.	每一	1	1	初級	
	morning	[ˈmɔrnɪŋ]	n.	早上	1	1	初級	
❸	always	[ˈɔlwez]	adv.	總是	1	1	初級	
	sleep	[slip]	v.	睡覺	1	1	初級	
	have	[hæv]	v.	擁有	1	1	初級	
	day	[de]	n.	天	1	1	初級	
	off	[ɔf]	adj.	休假的	1	1	初級	
❹	lie	[laɪ]	v.	躺	1	1	初級	
	around	[əˈraʊnd]	adv.	環繞	1	1	初級	
	bed	[bɛd]	n.	床	1	1	初級	
❺	late	[let]	adv.	晚地	1	1	初級	◎
❻	need	[nid]	v.	需要	1	1	初級	◎
❼	hear	[hɪr]	v.	聽到	1	1	初級	
	alarm	[əˈlɑrm]	n.	鬧鐘	2	2	初級	
	clock	[klɑk]	n.	時鐘	1	1	初級	◎
	ringing	[ˈrɪŋɪŋ]	p.pr.	ring（鳴、響）現在分詞	4	1	初級	
❽	use	[juz]	v.	使用	1	1	初級	◎
❿	family	[ˈfæməlɪ]	n.	家人	1	1	初級	
⓫	noise	[nɔɪz]	n.	聲響	1	1	初級	
⓬	long	[lɔŋ]	adv.	長地	1	1	初級	
	still	[stɪl]	adv.	仍然	1	1	初級	◎
⓭	awake	[əˈwek]	adj.	清醒的	2	3	中級	
⓮	so	[so]	adv.	這麼	1	1	初級	
⓯	got	[gɑt]	p.t.	get（起床）過去式	1	1	初級	◎
	really	[ˈrɪəlɪ]	adv.	很、十分	1		初級	
	early	[ˈɝlɪ]	adv.	早地	1	1	初級	
	today	[təˈde]	adv.	今天	1	1	初級	◎
⓰	make	[mek]	v.	整理	1	1	初級	
⓱	set	[sɛt]	v.	設定	1	1	初級	◎
	more	[mor]	adv.	多於、更多	1	1	初級	
	one	[wʌn]	n.	一	1	1	初級	

※「紅字單字」於本單元多句出現，「單字級等分析」僅列在「首次出現句」。

165

031 我的睡眠。

MP3 031-01 ❶～⓱

❶	我習慣晚睡。	I am used to going to bed late. * **be used to**＋動詞-ing（習慣…）
❷	我每天晚上 10 點就寢。	I go to bed at ten pm every night. * **go to bed**（就寢）＝ **go to sleep**
❸	我都是一覺到天亮。	I always sleep right through until dawn. * **sleep right through until dawn**（一覺到天亮） * **right through**（從頭到尾）
❹	我很容易被吵醒。	I am easily awakened by noise. * **be awakened**（被弄醒）
❺	我每天睡足 8 小時。	I sleep a full eight hours every day.
❻	我經常失眠。	I frequently get insomnia. * **get insomnia**（失眠）
❼	我很容易入睡。	I fall asleep easily. * **fall asleep**（入睡）
❽	我睡覺常作夢。	I usually dream while sleeping. * **while**＋動詞-ing（在…的時候）
❾	沒事的話我可以睡一整天。	I can sleep for a full day if there's nothing going on. * **there's nothing**（沒有事情） * **go on**（發生）
❿	我會認床。	I have to sleep in my own bed. * **have to**（必須） * **sleep in**＋床（睡在某張床）
⓫	我的睡相不好看。	I don't look good when I sleep.
⓬	我睡覺會打鼾。	I snore in my sleep.
⓭	我嚴重睡眠不足。	I have serious sleep deprivation. * **sleep deprivation**（睡眠不足）
⓮	我經常熬夜。	I often stay up late. * **stay up late**（熬夜）
⓯	我習慣裸睡。	I am used to sleeping naked. * 動詞＋**naked**（裸著身體…）
⓰	我睡覺會踢被子。	I kick the quilt off while sleeping.
⓱	我有午睡的習慣。	I have a habit of taking naps. * **a habit of**＋動詞-ing（…習慣） * **take naps**（午睡）

	單字	音標	詞性	意義	字頻	大考	英檢	多益
❶	used	[juzd]	p.p.	use（習慣）過去分詞	1	2	初級	◎
	going	[ˋgoɪŋ]	n.	go（去）動名詞	4	1	初級	
	bed	[bɛd]	n.	睡眠	1	1	初級	
	late	[let]	adv.	晚地	1	1	初級	◎
❷	go	[go]	v.	去	1	1	初級	
	ten	[tɛn]	n.	十	1	1	初級	
	pm	[ˋpiˋɛm]	adv.	下午	1	4		
	every	[ˋɛvrɪ]	adj.	每一	1	1	初級	
	night	[naɪt]	n.	晚上	1	1	初級	
❸	always	[ˋɔlwez]	adv.	總是	1	1	初級	
	sleep	[slip]	v./n.	睡覺/睡眠	1	1	初級	
	right	[raɪt]	adv.	直接地	1	1	初級	
	dawn	[dɔn]	n.	黎明	2	2	初級	
❹	easily	[ˋizɪlɪ]	adv.	容易地	1		中級	
	awakened	[əˋwekənd]	p.p.	awaken（弄醒）過去分詞	3	3	中級	
	noise	[nɔɪz]	n.	聲響	1	1	初級	
❺	full	[fʊl]	adj.	滿的/整個的	1	1	初級	
	eight	[et]	n.	八	1	1	初級	
	hour	[aʊr]	n.	小時	1	1	初級	
	day	[de]	n.	天	1	1	初級	
❻	frequently	[ˋfrikwəntlɪ]	adv.	頻繁地	1			◎
	get	[gɛt]	v.	患上	1	1	初級	◎
	insomnia	[ɪnˋsɑmnɪə]	n.	失眠	5			
❼	fall	[fɔl]	v.	變成	1	1	初級	◎
	asleep	[əˋslip]	adj.	睡著的	2	2	初級	
❽	usually	[ˋjuʒʊəlɪ]	adv.	經常	1	1	初級	◎
	dream	[drim]	v.	作夢	1	1	初級	◎
	sleeping	[ˋslipɪŋ]	p.pr.	sleep（睡覺）現在分詞	3	1	初級	
❾	there	[ðɛr]	adv.	有…	1	1	初級	
	nothing	[ˋnʌθɪŋ]	pron.	沒事	1	1	初級	
	going	[ˋgoɪŋ]	p.pr.	go（發生）現在分詞	4	1	初級	
❿	have	[hæv]	v.	必須/擁有	1	1	初級	
	own	[on]	adj.	自己的	1	1	初級	◎
⓫	look	[lʊk]	v.	看起來	1	1	初級	
	good	[gʊd]	adj.	良好的	1	1	初級	◎
⓬	snore	[snor]	v.	打鼾	4	5	中高	
⓭	serious	[ˋsɪrɪəs]	adj.	嚴重的	1	2		◎
	deprivation	[ˏdɛprɪˋveʃən]	n.	缺乏、不足	4			
⓮	often	[ˋɔfən]	adv.	常常	1	1	初級	
	stay	[ste]	v.	保持、堅持	1	1	初級	◎
	up	[ʌp]	adv.	醒著地	1	1	初級	
⓯	sleeping	[ˋslipɪŋ]	n.	sleep（睡覺）動名詞	3	1	初級	
	naked	[ˋnekɪd]	adj.	裸體的	2	2	中級	◎
⓰	kick	[kɪk]	v.	踢	1	1	初級	
	quilt	[kwɪlt]	n.	被子	3	4	中級	
	off	[ɔf]	adv.	移除	1	1	初級	
⓱	habit	[ˋhæbɪt]	n.	習慣	1	2	初級	◎
	taking	[ˋtekɪŋ]	n.	take（從事）動名詞	4			
	nap	[næp]	n.	午睡	3	3	中級	◎

※「紅字單字」於本單元多句出現，「單字級等分析」僅列在「首次出現句」。

031　你的睡眠？

❶	通常都幾點睡覺？	What time do you usually go to sleep? * **What time...?**（幾點…？）
❷	你一天睡幾個小時？	How many hours of sleep a night do you get? * **How many hours...?**（…是幾個小時呢） * **a night**（一個晚上）
❸	你很早睡嗎？	Do you go to bed early? * **Do you go to bed late?**（你很晚睡嗎）
❹	你常熬夜嗎？	Do you usually stay up late? * **stay up late**（熬夜）
❺	你容易入睡嗎？	Do you fall asleep easily? * **fall asleep**（睡著）
❻	你容易被吵醒嗎？	Are you a light sleeper? * **deep**（睡得沉的）
❼	你的睡眠品質好嗎？	Do you get good-quality sleep?
❽	你常作夢嗎？	Do you often have dreams? * **have a dream**（作夢）＝ dream
❾	你會認床嗎？	Can you sleep in other beds? ＝ **Do you need to sleep in your own bed?**
❿	睡前你會聽音樂嗎？	Do you listen to music before going to bed? * **listen to music**（聽音樂）
⓫	你睡覺會打鼾嗎？	Do you snore?
⓬	你會踢被子嗎？	Do you kick the blanket off while sleeping? * **kick＋物品＋off**（踢除某物品）
⓭	你睡眠不足嗎？	Is your sleep insufficient?
⓮	你會裸睡嗎？	Do you sleep in the nude? * **in the nude**（裸體狀態）
⓯	你開燈睡覺嗎？	Do you sleep with a light on? * **with a light on**（在燈光開著的狀態下）
⓰	你有午睡的習慣嗎？	Do you have a habit of taking naps? * **a habit of＋動詞-ing**（…習慣） * **take naps**（午睡）
⓱	你經常失眠嗎？	Do you have a lot of sleepless nights? * **sleepless night**（睡不著的夜晚）

	單字	音標	詞性	意義	字頻	大考	英檢	多益
❶	time	[taɪm]	n.	時間	1	1	初級	◎
	usually	[ˈjuʒʊəlɪ]	adv.	經常	1		初級	◎
	go	[go]	v.	去	1	1	初級	
	sleep	[slip]	v./n.	睡覺/睡眠	1	1	初級	
❷	many	[ˈmɛnɪ]	adj.	許多的	1	1	初級	
	hour	[aʊr]	n.	小時	1	1	初級	
	night	[naɪt]	n.	晚上	1	1	初級	
	get	[gɛt]	v.	取得	1	1	初級	◎
❸	bed	[bɛd]	n.	睡眠	1	1	初級	
	early	[ˈɝlɪ]	adv.	早地	1	1	初級	
❹	stay	[ste]	v.	保持、堅持	1	1	初級	◎
	up	[ʌp]	adv.	醒著地	1	1	初級	
	late	[let]	adv.	晚地	1	1	初級	◎
❺	fall	[fɔl]	v.	變成	1	1	初級	◎
	asleep	[əˈslip]	adj.	睡著的	2	2	初級	
	easily	[ˈizɪlɪ]	adv.	容易地	1		中級	
❻	light	[laɪt]	adj./n.	睡得淺的/燈光	1	1	初級	
	sleeper	[ˈslipɚ]	n.	睡眠者	4	1		
❼	good-quality	[ˈgʊdˈkwɑlɪtɪ]	adj.	品質良好的				
❽	often	[ˈɔfən]	adv.	常常	1	1	初級	
	have	[hæv]	v.	作（夢）/擁有	1	1	初級	
	dream	[drim]	n.	夢	1	1	初級	
❾	other	[ˈʌðɚ]	adj.	其他的	1	1	初級	
	need	[nid]	v.	需要	1	1	初級	◎
	own	[on]	adj.	自己的	1	1	初級	◎
❿	listen	[ˈlɪsn]	v.	聽	1	1	初級	
	music	[ˈmjuzɪk]	n.	音樂	1	1	初級	
	going	[ˈgoɪŋ]	p.pr.	go（去）動名詞	4	1	初級	
⓫	snore	[snor]	v.	打鼾	4	5	中高	
⓬	kick	[kɪk]	v.	踢	1	1	初級	
	blanket	[ˈblæŋkɪt]	n.	被子、毯子	2	3	初級	◎
	off	[ɔf]	adv.	移除	1	1	初級	
	sleeping	[ˈslipɪŋ]	p.pr.	sleep（睡眠）現在分詞	3	1	初級	
⓭	insufficient	[ˌɪnsəˈfɪʃənt]	adj.	不足的	3		中高	
⓮	nude	[njud]	n.	裸體	3	5	中高	
⓯	on	[ɑn]	adj.	開啟著	1	1	初級	
⓰	habit	[ˈhæbɪt]	n.	習慣	1	2	初級	◎
	taking	[ˈtekɪŋ]	n.	take（從事）動名詞	4			
	nap	[næp]	n.	午覺	3	3	中級	◎
⓱	lot	[lɑt]	n.	許多	1			
	sleepless	[ˈsliplɪs]	adj.	失眠的	6			

※「紅字單字」於本單元多句出現，「單字級等分析」僅列在「首次出現句」。

032　我的美容。

❶	我很重視皮膚保養。	I pay a lot of attention to skin care. * **pay attention to**（重視）
❷	我很重視保養品的成分。	I pay a lot of attention to the ingredients of skin care products. * **a lot of**（許多）、**skin care product**（保養品）
❸	我沒有固定使用同一個品牌的保養品。	I don't use a specific brand of skin care products.
❹	我每週用面膜敷臉一次。	I apply a facial mask once a week. * **apply a facial mask**（敷面膜）
❺	我早晚各洗一次臉。	I wash my face once in the morning and once in the evening.
❻	我每天徹底卸妝。	I completely remove my makeup every day. * **remove makeup**（卸妝）
❼	避免毛孔粗大，我只用冷水洗臉。	I only wash my face with cold water to avoid enlarging my pores. * **with**（使用）、**to avoid**＋動詞-ing（為了避免…）
❽	我定期做皮膚去角質。	I exfoliate my skin regularly.
❾	夏天出門我一定擦防曬乳。	In the summertime, I am sure to put on sunblock when I go out. * **be sure to**（必定）、**put on**（塗擦）＝ **apply**
❿	為了美容，我不熬夜不抽煙。	To maintain my appearance, I never stay up late or smoke. * **maintain one's appearance**（保持外貌）
⓫	我很喜歡做 spa。	I like to go to the spa. * **like to**＋動詞原形（喜歡）
⓬	洗完手我立刻擦護手霜。	Right after I wash my hands, I apply hand cream. * **right after**（在…之後，立刻）
⓭	冬天我會加強皮膚保濕。	In the winter, I work on moisturizing my skin. * **work on**＋動詞-ing（努力） * **moisturize**＋部位（保濕某部位）

	單字	音標	詞性	意義	字頻	大考	英檢	多益
❶	pay	[pe]	v.	給予	1	3	初級	◎
	lot	[lɑt]	n.	許多	1			
	attention	[ə`tɛnʃən]	n.	注意	1	2	初級	◎
	skin	[skɪn]	n.	皮膚	1	1	初級	◎
	care	[kɛr]	n.	保養	1	1	初級	◎
❷	ingredient	[ɪn`ɡrɪdɪənt]	n.	成分	1	4	中級	◎
	product	[`prɑdəkt]	n.	產品	1	3	初級	◎

❸	use	[juz]	v.	使用	1	1	初級	◎
	specific	[spɪˋsɪfɪk]	adj.	特定的	1	3	中級	◎
	brand	[brænd]	n.	品牌	1	2	中級	◎
❹	apply	[əˋplaɪ]	v.	塗抹	1	2	初級	◎
	facial	[ˋfeʃəl]	adj.	臉部的	3	4	中級	
	mask	[mæsk]	n.	面膜	2	2	初級	
	once	[wʌns]	adv.	一次	1	1	初級	
	week	[wik]	n.	一周	1	1	初級	
❺	wash	[wɑʃ]	v.	清洗	1	1	初級	
	face	[fes]	n.	臉	1	1	初級	
	morning	[ˋmɔrnɪŋ]	n.	早上	1	1	初級	
	evening	[ˋivnɪŋ]	n.	晚上	1	1	初級	
❻	completely	[kəmˋplitlɪ]	adv.	完全地	1			
	remove	[rɪˋmuv]	v.	移除	1	3	中級	◎
	makeup	[ˋmek,ʌp]	n.	化妝	2	4		◎
	every	[ˋɛvrɪ]	adj.	每一	1	1	初級	
	day	[de]	n.	天	1	1	初級	
❼	only	[ˋonlɪ]	adv.	只有	1	1	初級	
	cold	[kold]	adj.	冷的	1	1	初級	
	water	[ˋwɔtə]	n.	水	1	1	初級	
	avoid	[əˋvɔɪd]	v.	避免	1	2	初級	◎
	enlarging	[ɪnˋlɑrdʒɪŋ]	n.	enlarge（讓…變大）動名詞	3	4	中級	◎
	pore	[por]	n.	毛孔	5		中高	
❽	exfoliate	[ɛksˋfolɪ,et]	v.	去角質				
	regularly	[ˋrɛgjələlɪ]	adv.	定期	2			◎
❾	summertime	[ˋsʌmə,taɪm]	n.	夏天	5			
	sure	[ʃur]	adj.	必定的	1	1	初級	
	put	[put]	v.	塗抹	1	1	初級	
	sunblock	[ˋsʌn,blɑk]	n.	防曬乳				
	go	[go]	v.	去	1	1	初級	
	out	[aut]	adv.	向外	1	1	初級	
❿	maintain	[menˋten]	v.	維持	1	2	初級	◎
	appearance	[əˋpɪrəns]	n.	外表	1	2	初級	◎
	never	[ˋnɛvə]	adv.	從不	1	1	初級	
	stay	[ste]	v.	保持、堅持	1	1	初級	◎
	up	[ʌp]	adv.	醒著地	1	1	初級	
	late	[let]	adv.	晚地	1	1	初級	◎
	smoke	[smok]	v.	抽菸	1	1	初級	
⓫	like	[laɪk]	v.	喜歡	1	1	初級	
	spa	[spɑ]	n.	spa美體中心	3			
⓬	right	[raɪt]	adv.	立即、馬上	1	1	初級	
	hand	[hænd]	n.	手	1	1	初級	
	cream	[krim]	n.	乳霜	1	2	初級	
⓭	winter	[ˋwɪntə]	n.	冬天	1	1	初級	
	work	[wɝk]	v.	工作	1	1	初級	◎
	moisturizing	[ˋmɔɪstʃə,raɪzɪŋ]	n.	moisturize（保濕）動名詞				

※「紅字單字」於本單元多句出現，「單字級等分析」僅列在「首次出現句」。

🔊 MP3 032-02 ❶～❹

❶	你怎麼保養皮膚？	How do you take care of your skin? * take care of（保養）
❷	你現在是用哪一個品牌的保養品？	Which brand of skin care products are you using right now? * What brand of＋名詞＋...?（是哪一個品牌的…？） * 此句用「現在進行式」（...are...using...）表示「現階段發生的事」。
❸	你定期敷臉嗎？	Do you apply a facial mask regularly?
❹	你用過瘦身霜嗎？	Have you ever used weight-loss cream? * Have you ever...?（你是否有…經驗）
❺	夏天出門一定要做好防曬。	In the summertime you should do your best to protect against the sun. * do one's best（盡力）、protect against（防禦）
❻	你的皮膚需要去角質。	You need to have your skin exfoliated. * have＋部位＋過去分詞（讓某部位接受…動作）
❼	你怎麼卸妝？	How do you remove the cosmetics you put on?
❽	你應該注重皮膚清潔。	You should pay attention to the cleanliness of your skin.
❾	你應該用溫水或冷水洗臉。	You should use either warm or cold water to wash your face.　* either A or B（A 或 B）
❿	你做過 spa 嗎？	Have you ever been to a spa?
⓫	熬夜是美容大敵。	Staying up late is the arch-enemy of beauty. * stay up late（熬夜，staying up late 是動名詞當主詞）
⓬	眼睛周圍的皮膚要輕柔對待。	You should treat the skin around your eyes gently.　* around one's eyes（眼睛周圍）
⓭	你應該加強皮膚保濕。	You should work on moisturizing your skin.
⓮	選擇適合自己的保養品最重要。	The most important thing is to choose the most suitable care products.

	單字	音標	詞性	意義	字頻	大考	英檢	多益
❶	take	[tek]	v.	採取	1	1	初級	◎
	care	[kɛr]	n.	保養	1	1	初級	◎
	skin	[skɪn]	n.	皮膚	1	1	初級	◎
❷	brand	[brænd]	n.	品牌	1	2	中級	◎
	product	[ˈprɑdəkt]	n.	產品	1	3	初級	◎
	using	[ˈjuzɪŋ]	p.pr.	use（使用）現在分詞	1	1	初級	◎

❷	right	[raɪt]	adv.	正值	1	1	初級	
	now	[nau]	adv.	現在	1	1	初級	
❸	apply	[əˈplaɪ]	v.	塗抹	1	2	初級	◎
	facial	[ˈfeʃəl]	adj.	臉部的	3	4	中級	
	mask	[mæsk]	n.	面膜	2	2	初級	
	regularly	[ˈrɛgjələlɪ]	adv.	定期地	2			◎
❹	ever	[ˈɛvə]	adv.	曾經	1	1	初級	
	used	[ˈjuzd]	p.p.	use（使用）過去分詞	1	2	初級	◎
	weight-loss	[ˈwet`lɔs]	adj.	減重的				
	cream	[krim]	n.	乳霜	1	2	初級	
❺	summertime	[ˈsʌmə͵taɪm]	n.	夏天	5			
	do	[du]	v..	做	1	1	初級	
	best	[bɛst]	n.	最好、最佳	1	1	初級	
	protect	[prəˈtɛkt]	v.	保護	1	2	初級	◎
	sun	[sʌn]	n.	太陽、陽光	2	1	初級	
❻	need	[nid]	v.	需要	1	1	初級	◎
	have	[hæv]	v.	使某物…	1	1	初級	
	exfoliated	[ɛksˈfolɪ͵etɪd]	p.p.	exfoliate（去角質）過去分詞				
❼	remove	[rɪˈmuv]	v.	移除	1	3	中級	◎
	cosmetics	[kɑzˈmɛtɪks]	n.	化妝品	4	6		
	put	[put]	v.	塗抹	1	1	初級	
❽	pay	[pe]	v.	給予	1	3	初級	◎
	attention	[əˈtɛnʃən]	n.	注意	1	2	初級	◎
	cleanliness	[ˈklɛnlɪnɪs]	n.	乾淨	6			
❾	use	[juz]	v.	使用	1	1	初級	◎
	warm	[wɔrm]	adj.	溫暖的	1	1	初級	
	cold	[kold]	adj.	冷的	1	1	初級	
	water	[ˈwɔtə]	n.	水	1	1	初級	
	wash	[wɑʃ]	v.	清洗	1	1	初級	
	face	[fes]	n.	臉	1	1	初級	
❿	spa	[spɑ]	n.	spa美體中心	3			
⓫	staying	[ˈsteɪŋ]	n.	stay（保持、堅持）動名詞	1	1	初級	
	up	[ʌp]	adv.	醒著地	1	1	初級	
	late	[let]	adv.	晚地	1	1	初級	◎
	arch-enemy	[͵ɑrtʃˈɛnəmɪ]	n.	首要敵人				
	beauty	[ˈbjutɪ]	n.	美容	1	1	中級	
⓬	treat	[trit]	v.	對待	1	2	初級	◎
	eye	[aɪ]	n.	眼睛	1	1	初級	
	gently	[ˈdʒɛntlɪ]	adv.	輕柔地	1			
⓭	work	[wɜk]	v.	致力	1	1	初級	◎
	moisturizing	[ˈmɔɪstʃə͵raɪzɪŋ]	n.	moisturize（保濕）動名詞				
⓮	most	[most]	adv.	最	1	1	初級	
	important	[ɪmˈpɔrtnt]	adj.	重要的	1	1	初級	◎
	thing	[θɪŋ]	n.	東西	1	1	初級	
	choose	[tʃuz]	v.	選擇	1	2	初級	◎
	suitable	[ˈsutəbl]	adj.	適合的	2	3	中級	◎

※「紅字單字」於本單元多句出現，「單字級等分析」僅列在「首次出現句」。

🔵 MP3 033-01 ❶～❹

❶	我一直都很健康。	I have always been very healthy. * 此句用「現在完成式」（…have…been…）表示「過去持續到現在的事」。
❷	我很容易感冒。	I catch colds easily. * catch colds（感冒）
❸	我從小就體弱多病。	I have been weak and sickly since childhood. * have been＋形容詞＋since…（自從…一直…）
❹	我習慣看西醫。	I am used to seeing Western doctors. * be used to＋動詞-ing（習慣做…） * Western doctors（西醫） * traditional Chinese doctors（中醫）
❺	我常頭痛。	I often get headaches. * get headaches（頭痛）
❻	我討厭吃藥。	I dislike taking medicine. * dislike＋動詞-ing（討厭做…） * I dislike getting shots.（我討厭打針）
❼	我有經痛的毛病。	I'm having menstrual pains. * 此句用「現在進行式」（…am having…）表示「現階段發生的事」。
❽	我每天吃綜合維他命補充營養。	I take vitamins every day to supplement my diet. * take vitamins（吃維他命） * supplement diet（補充飲食）
❾	我腸胃不好。	I have a bad digestive system. * digestive system（腸胃系統）
❿	我有蛀牙。	I have cavities.
⓫	我很重視養生。	I pay a lot of attention to my health. * pay attention to（重視） * a lot of（許多）
⓬	我每年做健康檢查。	I get a physical examination each year. * physical examination（健康檢查）
⓭	我是過敏體質。	I have allergies.
⓮	我動過一次手術。	I had an operation once. * have an operation（動手術）

	單字	音標	詞性	意義	字頻	大考	英檢	多益
❶	always	[ˋɔlwez]	adv.	一直	1	1	初級	
	very	[ˋvɛrɪ]	adv.	十分	1	1	初級	
	healthy	[ˋhɛlθɪ]	adj.	健康的	1	2	初級	◎
❷	catch	[kætʃ]	v.	染上	1	1	初級	
	cold	[kold]	n.	感冒	1	1	初級	
	easily	[ˋizɪlɪ]	adv.	容易地	1		中級	
❸	weak	[wik]	adj.	虛弱的	1	1	初級	◎
	sickly	[ˋsɪklɪ]	adj.	多病的	6			
	childhood	[ˋtʃaɪld.hʊd]	n.	童年	1	3	初級	
❹	used	[juzd]	p.p.	use（習慣）過去分詞	1	2	初級	◎
	seeing	[ˋsiɪŋ]	n.	see（看〔病〕）動名詞	7	1	初級	
	Western	[ˋwɛstən]	adj.	西式的	1	2	初級	
	doctor	[ˋdɑktə]	n.	醫生	1	4	初級	◎
❺	often	[ˋɔfən]	adv.	常常	1	1	初級	
	get	[ɡɛt]	v.	患上	1	1	初級	◎
	headache	[ˋhɛd.ek]	n.	頭痛	2		初級	
❻	dislike	[dɪsˋlaɪk]	v.	討厭	3	3	中級	
	taking	[ˋtekɪŋ]	n.	take（服用）動名詞	4			
	medicine	[ˋmɛdəsn]	n.	藥物	1	2	初級	◎
❼	having	[ˋhævɪŋ]	p.pr.	have（擁有）現在分詞	1	1	初級	
	menstrual	[ˋmɛnstruəl]	adj.	月經的	6			
	pain	[pen]	n.	痛苦	1	2	初級	
❽	take	[tek]	v.	服用	1	1	初級	◎
	vitamin	[ˋvaɪtəmɪn]	n.	維他命	2	3	中級	
	every	[ˋɛvrɪ]	adj.	每一	1	1	初級	
	day	[de]	n.	天	1	1	初級	
	supplement	[ˋsʌpləmənt]	v.	補充	2	6	中高	◎
	diet	[ˋdaɪət]	n.	飲食	1	3	初級	◎
❾	have	[hæv]	v.	擁有	1	1	初級	
	bad	[bæd]	adj.	不健全的	1	1	初級	
	digestive	[dəˋdʒɛstɪv]	adj.	消化的	5			◎
	system	[ˋsɪstəm]	n.	系統	1	3	初級	◎
❿	cavity	[ˋkævətɪ]	n.	蛀牙	3	6	中高	
⓫	pay	[pe]	v.	給予	1	3	初級	◎
	lot	[lɑt]	n.	許多				
	attention	[əˋtɛnʃən]	n.	注意	1	2	初級	◎
	health	[hɛlθ]	n.	健康	1	1	初級	
⓬	physical	[ˋfɪzɪkl]	adj.	身體的	1	4	中級	
	examination	[ɪɡ.zæməˋneʃən]	n.	檢查	2	1	中級	◎
	each	[itʃ]	adj.	各個、每一	1	1	初級	
	year	[jɪr]	n.	年	1	1	初級	
⓭	allergy	[ˋæləndʒɪ]	n.	過敏	3	5	中高	◎
⓮	had	[hæd]	p.t.	have（接受）過去式	1	1	初級	
	operation	[.ɑpəˋreʃən]	n.	手術	1	4	初級	◎
	once	[wʌns]	adv.	一次	1	1	初級	

※「紅字單字」於本單元多句出現，「單字級等分析」僅列在「首次出現句」。

🔘 MP3 033-02 ❶～❻

❶	你常生病嗎？	Do you get sick often? * **get sick**（生病）
❷	你覺得自己健康嗎？	Do you think you're healthy?
❸	你看西醫還是中醫？	Do you go to see a traditional Chinese doctor or a Western doctor?
❹	你定期做健康檢查嗎？	Do you regularly go in for a physical? * **physical**（健康檢查）= **physical examination**
❺	你常感冒嗎？	Do you often catch colds?
❻	你容易頭疼嗎？	Do you get headaches easily?
❼	你有蛀牙嗎？	Do you have any cavities?
❽	你害怕打針嗎？	Are you afraid of having an injection? * **Are you afraid of＋動詞-ing＋…?** 　（你害怕…嗎） * **Are you afraid of taking medicine?** 　（你害怕吃藥嗎） * **have an injection**（打針）
❾	你動過手術嗎？	Have you ever had an operation? * **Have you ever …?**（你是否有…經驗）
❿	生理期你會不舒服嗎？	Do you feel uncomfortable during your period? * **during one's period**（生理期時）
⓫	你有職業病嗎？	Do you have any occupational sicknesses? * **occupational sickness**（職業病）
⓬	你如何保養身體？	How do you keep yourself in good health? = **How do you preserve your health?**
⓭	你經常全身痠痛嗎？	Do you often feel soreness throughout your whole body? * **throughout one's whole body**（全身）
⓮	你擔心癌症嗎？	Are you worried about cancer? * **be worried about**（擔心）= **be concerned about**
⓯	你容易過敏嗎？	Do you have bad allergies?
⓰	你每天吃維他命嗎？	Do you take vitamins every day?

	單字	音標	詞性	意義	字頻	大考	英檢	多益
❶	get	[gɛt]	v.	變成/患上	1	1	初級	◎
	sick	[sɪk]	adj.	生病的	1	1	初級	◎
	often	[ˋɔfən]	adv.	常常	1	1	初級	
❷	think	[θɪŋk]	v.	認為	1	1	初級	
	healthy	[ˋhɛlθɪ]	adj.	健康的	1	2	初級	◎
❸	go	[go]	v.	去	1	1	初級	
	see	[si]	v.	看（病）	1	1	初級	
	traditional	[trəˋdɪʃənl]	adj.	傳統的	1	2	初級	◎
	Chinese	[ˋtʃaɪˋniz]	adj.	中式的	1		初級	
	doctor	[ˋdɑktɚ]	n.	醫生	1	4	初級	◎
	Western	[ˋwɛstɚn]	adj.	西式的	1	2	初級	
❹	regularly	[ˋrɛɡjələlɪ]	adv.	定期	2			◎
	physical	[ˋfɪzɪkl]	n.	健康檢查	1	4	中級	
❺	catch	[kætʃ]	v.	染上	1	1	初級	
	cold	[kold]	n.	感冒	1	1	初級	
❻	headache	[ˋhɛd͵ek]	n.	頭痛	2		初級	◎
	easily	[ˋizɪlɪ]	adv.	容易地	1		中級	
❼	have	[hæv]	v.	擁有	1	1	初級	
	any	[ˋɛnɪ]	adj.	任何	1	1	初級	
	cavity	[ˋkævətɪ]	n.	蛀牙	3	6	中高	
❽	afraid	[əˋfred]	adj.	害怕	1	1	初級	
	having	[ˋhævɪŋ]		have（接受）動名詞	1	1	初級	
	injection	[ɪnˋdʒɛkʃən]	n.	注射	3	6	中級	◎
❾	ever	[ˋɛvɚ]	adv.	曾經	1	1	初級	
	had	[hæd]	p.p.	have（接受）過去式	1	1	初級	
	operation	[͵ɑpəˋreʃən]	n.	手術	1	4	初級	◎
❿	feel	[fil]	v.	感到	1	1	初級	
	uncomfortable	[ʌnˋkʌmfɚtəbl]	adj.	不舒服的	2		中高	
	period	[ˋpɪrɪəd]	n.	生理期	1	2	初級	◎
⓫	occupational	[͵ɑkjəˋpeʃənl]	adj.	職業的	3			
	sickness	[ˋsɪknɪs]	n.	疾病	3		中級	
⓬	keep	[kip]	v.	維持	1	1	初級	◎
	yourself	[juɚˋsɛlf]	pron.	你自己	1		初級	
	good	[ɡʊd]	adj.	良好的	1	1	初級	◎
	health	[hɛlθ]	n.	健康	1	1	初級	
	preserve	[prɪˋzɝv]	v.	保養	1	4	中級	◎
⓭	soreness	[ˋsornɪs]	n.	疼痛	8			
	whole	[hol]	adj.	整個的	1	1	初級	◎
	body	[ˋbɑdɪ]	n.	身體	1	1	初級	
⓮	worried	[ˋwɝɪd]	adj.	擔心的	2	1	中級	◎
	cancer	[ˋkænsɚ]	n.	癌症	1	2	初級	◎
⓯	bad	[bæd]	adj.	嚴重的	1	1	初級	◎
	allergy	[ˋælɚdʒɪ]	n.	過敏	3	5	中高	
⓰	take	[tek]	v.	服用	1	1	初級	◎
	vitamin	[ˋvaɪtəmɪn]	n.	維他命	2	3	中級	
	every	[ˋɛvrɪ]	adj.	每一	1	1	初級	
	day	[de]	n.	天	1	1	初級	

※「紅字單字」於本單元多句出現，「單字級等分析」僅列在「首次出現句」。

🔊 MP3 034-01 ❶～⓰

❶	我喜歡運動。	I like to exercise. * **like to＋動詞原形**（喜歡）＝ **like＋動詞-ing**
❷	我每天運動。	I exercise every day.
❸	我討厭運動。	I dislike exercising. * **dislike＋動詞-ing**（討厭）
❹	我很少運動。	I seldom exercise.
❺	我每週運動三次。	I exercise three times a week.
❻	我是個體育白癡。	When it comes to athletics, I'm completely ignorant. * **When it comes to＋某事物**（關於某事物） * **completely ignorant**（完全沒有知識）
❼	我的運動神經很發達。	I am very athletic.
❽	運動完我立即補充水分。	I rehydrate immediately after exercise. * **after exercise**（運動後）
❾	醫生說我缺乏運動。	The doctor said I don't get enough exercise. * **某人＋said＋子句**（某人曾說…）。子句用「現在簡單式」（...don't get...）表示「經常如此的事」。 * **not get enough exercise**（運動不足）
❿	游泳是我最愛的運動。	Swimming is my favorite sport.
⓫	我喜歡各種球類運動。	I like playing every sport with a ball.
⓬	我偶爾打保齡球。	Every once in a while I go bowling. * **every once in a while**（偶爾）
⓭	我定期上健身房。	I work out at the gym regularly. * **work out**（健身）
⓮	做家事就是我的運動。	My exercise consists of doing the housework. * **consist of...**（由…組成）
⓯	我最近迷上瑜珈。	Recently, I have become very interested in yoga. * 此句用「現在完成式」（...have become...）表示「過去某時點發生某事，且結果持續到現在」。 * **interested in＋某事物**（對某事物有興趣）
⓰	走路是我最常做的運動。	Walking is the exercise I do most often. * **do most often**（最常做）

	單字	音標	詞性	意義	字頻	大考	英檢	多益
❶	like	[laɪk]	v.	喜歡	1	1	初級	
	exercise	[ˈɛksə͵saɪz]	v./n.	運動	1	2	初級	◎
❷	every	[ˈɛvrɪ]	adj.	每一	1	1	初級	
	day	[de]	n.	天	1	1	初級	
❸	dislike	[dɪsˈlaɪk]	v.	討厭	3	3	中級	
	exercising	[ˈɛksə͵saɪzɪŋ]	n.	exercise（運動）動名詞	1	2	初級	◎
❹	seldom	[ˈsɛldəm]	adv.	很少	2	3	初級	◎
❺	three	[θri]	n.	三	1	1	初級	
	time	[taɪm]	n.	次數	1	1	初級	◎
	week	[wik]	n.	一周	1	1	初級	
❻	come	[kʌm]	v.	關於…、談到…	1	1	初級	
	athletics	[æθˈlɛtɪks]	n.	運動	4		中高	
	completely	[kəmˈplitlɪ]	adv.	完全地	1			
	ignorant	[ˈɪgnərənt]	adj.	無知的	3	4	中級	◎
❼	very	[ˈvɛrɪ]	adv.	十分	1	1	初級	
	athletic	[æθˈlɛtɪk]	adj.	擅長運動的	2	4	中級	◎
❽	rehydrate	[riˈhaɪdret]	v.	補充水分				
	immediately	[ɪˈmidɪtlɪ]	adv.	立即地	1		中級	◎
❾	doctor	[ˈdɑktə]	n.	醫生	1	4	初級	◎
	said	[sɛd]	p.t.	say（說）過去式	4	1	初級	
	get	[gɛt]	v.	獲得	1	1	初級	◎
	enough	[əˈnʌf]	adj.	足夠的	1	1	初級	◎
❿	swimming	[ˈswɪmɪŋ]	n.	swim（游泳）動名詞	2	1	中級	
	favorite	[ˈfevərɪt]	adj.	最喜歡的	1	2	初級	◎
	sport	[sport]	n.	運動	1	1	初級	
⓫	playing	[ˈpleɪŋ]	n.	play（打球）動名詞	3	1	初級	
	ball	[bɔl]	n.	球類	1	1	初級	
⓬	once	[wʌns]	n.	一回、一次	1	1	初級	
	while	[hwaɪl]	n.	一段時間	1	1	初級	
	go	[go]	v.	從事	1	1	初級	
	bowling	[ˈbolɪŋ]	n.	保齡球	3	2	初級	
⓭	work	[wɜk]	v.	健身	1	1	初級	◎
	out	[aʊt]	adv.	完全、徹底	1	1	初級	
	gym	[dʒɪm]	n.	健身房	2	3	初級	◎
	regularly	[ˈrɛgjələlɪ]	adv.	定期地	2			◎
⓮	consist	[kənˈsɪst]	v.	由…組成	1	4	中級	◎
	doing	[ˈduɪŋ]	n.	do（做、從事）動名詞	1	1	初級	
	housework	[ˈhaʊs͵wɜk]	n.	家事	6	4	中級	
⓯	recently	[ˈrisntlɪ]	adv.	最近	1		初級	
	become	[bɪˈkʌm]	p.p.	become（變為）過去分詞	1	1	初級	◎
	interested	[ˈɪntərɪstɪd]	adj.	有興趣的	1	1	初級	◎
	yoga	[ˈjogə]	n.	瑜珈	3	5	中高	
⓰	walking	[ˈwɔkɪŋ]	n.	走路	2	1	初級	
	do	[du]	v.	做、從事	1	1	初級	
	most	[most]	adv.	最	1	1	初級	

※「紅字單字」於本單元多句出現，「單字級等分析」僅列在「首次出現句」。

034　你的運動？

❶	你每週運動幾次？	How many times a week do you exercise? * **How many times...?**（…多少次？）
❷	你喜歡運動嗎？	Do you like to exercise?
❸	你常做什麼運動？	What do you usually do for exercise? * **What do you...?**（你平常會做什麼…？） * **for exercise**（作為運動）
❹	你的運動神經好嗎？	Are you athletic?
❺	你通常什麼時間運動？	When do you usually exercise?
❻	你到健身房運動嗎？	Do you go to the gym to exercise?
❼	你覺得自己的運動量夠嗎？	Do you think you get enough exercise? * **get enough exercise**（運動充足）
❽	你會游泳嗎？	Can you swim?
❾	你經常走路嗎？	Do you walk often? = Do you take walks often? * **walk**（走路）= **take walks**
❿	運動絕對有益健康。	Exercise is definitely good for one's health. * **be good for**（有好處）
⓫	你喜歡慢跑嗎？	Do you like to jog?
⓬	你可以把爬樓梯當運動。	You can climb stairs for exercise. * **climb stairs**（爬樓梯） * **do housework**（做家事）
⓭	我想你缺乏運動。	I guess you don't exercise enough. * **I guess**＋子句（我猜想…）
⓮	你運動是為了維持身材嗎？	Do you exercise to stay in shape? * **stay in shape**（維持身材）
⓯	你應該養成運動的好習慣。	You should develop good exercise habits. * **develop a habit**（培養習慣）
⓰	你應該穿雙好鞋運動。	You should wear a good pair of sneakers for exercise. * **a pair of**（一雙）

	單字	音標	詞性	意義	字頻	大考	英檢	多益
❶	many	[ˈmɛnɪ]	adj.	許多的	1	1	初級	
	time	[taɪm]	n.	次數	1	1	初級	◎
	week	[wik]	n.	一周	1	1	初級	
	exercise	[ˈɛksɚˌsaɪz]	v./n.	運動	1	2	初級	◎
❷	like	[laɪk]	v.	喜歡	1	1	初級	
❸	do	[du]	v.	做、從事	1	1	初級	
	usually	[ˈjuʒʊəlɪ]	adv.	經常	1	1	初級	◎
❹	athletic	[æθˈlɛtɪk]	adj.	擅長運動的	2	4	中級	◎
❻	go	[go]	v.	去	1	1	初級	
	gym	[dʒɪm]	n.	健身房	2	3	初級	◎
❼	think	[θɪŋk]	v.	認為	1	1	初級	
	get	[gɛt]	v.	獲得	1	1	初級	◎
	enough	[əˈnʌf]	adj./adv.	足夠的/足夠地	1	1	初級	◎
❽	swim	[swɪm]	v.	游泳	2	1	初級	
❾	walk	[wɔk]	v./n.	走路	1	1	初級	
	often	[ˈɔfən]	adv.	常常	1	1	初級	
	take	[tek]	v.	執行、做	1	1	初級	◎
❿	definitely	[ˈdɛfənɪtlɪ]	adv.	絕對	1		中高	◎
	good	[gʊd]	adj.	良好的	1	1	初級	
	one	[wʌn]	pron.	一個（人或物）	1	1	初級	
	health	[hɛlθ]	n.	健康	1	1	初級	◎
⓫	jog	[dʒɑg]	v.	慢跑	3	2	初級	
⓬	climb	[klaɪm]	v.	爬	1	1	初級	◎
	stair	[stɛr]	n.	樓梯	6			
⓭	guess	[gɛs]	v.	猜想	1	1	初級	
⓮	stay	[ste]	v.	維持	1	1	初級	◎
	shape	[ʃep]	n.	身材	1	1	初級	◎
⓯	develop	[dɪˈvɛləp]	v.	培養	1	2	初級	◎
	habit	[ˈhæbɪt]	n.	習慣	1	2	初級	◎
⓰	wear	[wɛr]	v.	穿戴	1	1	初級	◎
	pair	[pɛr]	n.	一雙	1	1	初級	◎
	sneakers	[ˈsnikɚs]	n.	sneaker（運動鞋）複數	3	5	初級	◎

※「紅字單字」於本單元多句出現，「單字級等分析」僅列在「首次出現句」。

035   我的寵物。

❶	我喜歡養寵物。	I like pets. * like＋名詞（喜歡）
❷	我有養寵物。	I have a pet. * I don't have a pet.（我沒有養寵物）
❸	我們都叫牠小白。	We call it Snowball.
❹	我養狗。	I have a dog. * cat（貓） * fish（魚） * rabbit（兔子） * bird（鳥）
❺	牠是男生。	It is a male. * female（母的）
❻	牠是我領養的。	I adopted it. * I bought it.（牠是我買來的） * I found it on the street.（牠是我在路上撿來的）
❼	我的狗狗是朋友送的。	My dog was given to me by my friend. * A was given to me by B（A是B給我的）
❽	我每天帶狗狗去散步。	I take my dog for a walk every day. * take for a walk（帶去散步）
❾	我養牠7年了。	I have had it for seven years. * for...year(s)（持續…年）。 * 此句用「現在完成式」（...have had...） 　表示「過去持續到現在的事」。
❿	我的狗一個禮拜洗一次澡。	I bathe my dog once a week. * bathe＋動物（為某動物洗澡）
⓫	牠現在3歲。	It is three years old.
⓬	牠是我們全家的寶貝。	It is our family's baby.
⓭	我餵牠吃飼料。	I feed it pet food. * pet food（飼料）
⓮	牠很貪吃。	It likes to eat.
⓯	牠很受寵。	It is spoiled. * It is very obedient.（牠很聽話）
⓰	我很喜歡跟我的寵物玩。	I like to play with my pet. * play with＋動物（和某動物玩耍）

	單字	音標	詞性	意義	字頻	大考	英檢	多益
❶	like	[laɪk]	v.	喜歡	1	1	初級	
	pet	[pɛt]	n.	寵物	2	1	初級	
❷	have	[hæv]	v.	養	1	1	初級	
❸	call	[kɔl]	v.	稱呼	1	1	初級	◎
❹	dog	[dɔg]	n.	狗	1	1	初級	
❺	male	[mel]	adj.	公的	1	2	初級	
❻	adopted	[ə'dɑptɪd]	p.t.	adopt（領養）過去式	4	3	初級	◎
❼	given	['gɪvən]	p.p.	give（給）過去分詞	2	1	中高	◎
	friend	[frɛnd]	n.	朋友	1	1	初級	
❽	take	[tek]	v.	執行、做	1	1	初級	◎
	walk	[wɔk]	n.	散步	1	1	初級	
	every	['ɛvrɪ]	adj.	每一	1	1	初級	
	day	[de]	n.	天	1	1	初級	
❾	had	[hæd]	p.p.	have（養）過去分詞	1	1	初級	
	seven	['sɛvn]	n.	七	1	1	初級	
	year	['jɪr]	n.	年/歲	1	1	初級	
❿	bathe	[beð]	v.	洗澡	3	1	中級	
	once	[wʌns]	adv.	一次	1	1	初級	
	week	[wik]	n.	一周	1	1	初級	
⓫	three	[θri]	n.	三	1	1	初級	
	old	[old]	adj.	…歲	1	1	初級	
⓬	family	['fæməlɪ]	n.	家庭	1	1	初級	
	baby	['bebɪ]	n.	寶貝	1	1	初級	
⓭	feed	[fid]	v.	餵食	1	1	初級	◎
	food	[fʊd]	n.	食物	1	1	初級	◎
⓮	eat	[it]	v.	吃	1	1	初級	
⓯	spoiled	[spɔɪlt]	p.p.	spoil（寵愛）過去分詞	6	3	中級	◎
⓰	play	[ple]	v.	玩	1	1	初級	

※「紅字單字」於本單元多句出現，「單字級等分析」僅列在「首次出現句」。

035 你的寵物？

❶	你有養寵物嗎？	Do you have a pet?
❷	你會想要養寵物嗎？	Do you want to own a pet? * **own a pet**（養寵物）= **have a pet**
❸	你養什麼寵物？	What kind of pets do you have? * **What kind of pets...?**（…是什麼寵物？）
❹	牠是你買的嗎？還是別人送的？	Did you buy it, or did someone give it to you? * **Did you..., or...?**（當時你是…，還是…）
❺	你的寵物叫什麼名字？	What's your pet's name? * **What is...?**（…是什麼？）
❻	牠年紀多大了？	How old is it? * **How old…?**（…幾歲？）
❼	你飼養牠多久了？	How long have you had it? * **it**（牠）可替換為：**him**（他）、**her**（她）
❽	牠是公的還是母的？牠是什麼顏色？	Is it male or female? What color is it?
❾	你每天遛狗嗎？	Do you walk your dog every day? * **walk**＋動物（帶某動物散步）
❿	你喜歡你的寵物嗎？	Do you like your pet?
⓫	牠幾天洗一次澡？	How often does it take a bath? * **How often...?**（…多久一次？） * **take a bath**（洗澡）
⓬	你都餵牠吃什麼？	What do you feed it?
⓭	牠有被寵壞嗎？	Does it ever act spoiled? * **act spoiled**（恃寵而驕）
⓮	牠會亂叫嗎？	Does it bark a lot? * **bark a lot**（經常吠叫）
⓯	牠會咬人嗎？	Does it bite?
⓰	牠的食量大不大？	Does it eat a lot?
⓱	你會送牠去美容嗎？	Do you send it to the pet salon? * **send to**＋地點（送到某地點） * **pet salon**（寵物美容院）
⓲	你的寵物乖不乖？	Is your pet well behaved? * **be well behaved**（很乖巧）

	單字	音標	詞性	意義	字頻	大考	英檢	多益
❶	have	[hæv]	v.	養	1	1	初級	
	pet	[pɛt]	n.	寵物	2	1	初級	
❷	want	[wɑnt]	v.	想要	1	1	初級	◎
	own	[on]	v.	擁有	1	1	初級	◎
❸	kind	[kaɪnd]	n.	種類	1	1	初級	◎
❹	buy	[baɪ]	v.	購買	1	1	初級	
	someone	[ˋsʌmˌwʌn]	pron.	有人、某個人	1	1	初級	
	give	[gɪv]	v.	給	1	1	初級	
❺	name	[nem]	n.	名字	1	1	初級	◎
❻	old	[old]	adj.	…歲	1	1	初級	
❼	long	[lɔŋ]	adv.	久的	1	1	初級	
	had	[hæd]	p.p.	have（養）過去分詞	1	1	初級	
❽	male	[mel]	adj.	公的	1	2	初級	
	female	[ˋfimel]	adj.	母的	1	2	初級	
	color	[ˋkʌlə]	n.	顏色	1	1	初級	
❾	walk	[wɔk]	v.	散步	1	1	初級	
	dog	[dɔg]	n.	狗	1	1	初級	
	every	[ˋɛvrɪ]	adj.	每一	1	1	初級	
	day	[de]	n.	天	1	1	初級	
❿	like	[laɪk]	v.	喜歡	1	1	初級	
⓫	often	[ˋɔfən]	adv.	常常	1	1	初級	
	take	[tek]	v.	執行、做	1	1	初級	◎
	bath	[bæθ]	n.	洗澡	2	1	初級	
⓬	feed	[fid]	v.	餵食	1	1	初級	◎
⓭	ever	[ˋɛvə]	adv.	曾經	1	1	初級	
	act	[ækt]	v.	表現出…行為	1	1	初級	
	spoiled	[spɔɪlt]	p.p.	spoil（寵愛）過去分詞	6	3	中級	◎
⓮	bark	[bɑrk]	v.	吠叫	3	2	初級	
	lot	[lɑt]	n.	許多	1			
⓯	bite	[baɪt]	v.	咬、啃	2	1	初級	
⓰	eat	[it]	v.	吃	1	1	初級	
⓱	send	[sɛnd]	v.	送到	1	1	初級	
	salon	[səˋlɑn]	n.	美容院	3		中高	
⓲	well	[wɛl]	adv.	良好地	1	1	初級	◎
	behaved	[bɪˋhevd]	p.p.	behave（表現好）過去分詞	2	3	初級	◎

※「紅字單字」於本單元多句出現，「單字級等分析」僅列在「首次出現句」。

🔘 MP3 036-01 ❶～⓰

❶	我搭捷運上班。	I take the MRT to work. ＝ I go to work by MRT. * take＋交通工具（搭乘某交通工具）
❷	捷運後我轉公車。	I transfer to a bus after taking the MRT. * transfer to＋交通工具（轉乘某交通工具）
❸	我不常搭公車。	I rarely take the bus.
❹	我偶爾搭計程車上班。	Sometimes I take a taxi to work.
❺	我騎機車上學。	I ride a motorcycle to school. * bicycle（腳踏車）
❻	我開車上班。	I drive to work. * take the train（搭火車） * walk（走路）
❼	我害怕搭飛機。	I am afraid of flying. * be afraid of＋動詞-ing（害怕）
❽	我有車。	I have a car.
❾	我容易暈車。	I get carsick easily. * airsick（暈機） * seasick（暈船）
❿	我剛貸款買車。	I just bought a car with a loan. * with a loan（以貸款的方式）
⓫	我有汽車駕照。	I have a driver's license. * driver's license（駕照）
⓬	我用悠遊卡搭捷運。	I take the MRT using EasyCard.
⓭	我的油錢很可觀。	My fuel expenses are quite considerable. * fuel expense（燃料費）
⓮	上個月我收到三張罰單。	I got three traffic violation tickets last month. * traffic violation ticket（交通違規罰單）
⓯	我定期保養愛車。	I have my car serviced regularly. * have＋某物＋serviced（維修保養某物）
⓰	假日我常開車兜風。	I usually go for drives on my days off. * go for drives（開車兜風） * days off（day off〔非工作日〕的複數）

	單字	音標	詞性	意義	字頻	大考	英檢	多益
❶	take	[tek]	v.	搭乘	1	1	初級	◎
	MRT	[ˋɛmˋɑrˋti]	n.	Mass Rapid Transit（捷運）縮寫		2	初級	◎
	work	[wɝk]	v.	工作	1	1	初級	◎
	go	[go]	v.	去	1	1	初級	
❷	transfer	[trænsˋfɝ]	v.	轉乘	1	4	中級	◎
	bus	[bʌs]	n.	公車	1	1	初級	
	taking	[ˋtekɪŋ]	n.	take（搭乘）動名詞	4			
❸	rarely	[ˋrɛrlɪ]	adv.	很少	1		中級	◎
❹	sometimes	[ˋsʌm͵taɪmz]	adv.	有時候	1	1	初級	
	taxi	[ˋtæksɪ]	n.	計程車	2	1	初級	
❺	ride	[raɪd]	v.	騎	1	1	初級	
	motorcycle	[ˋmotɚ͵saɪkl]	n.	機車	3	2	初級	
	school	[skul]	n.	學校	1	1	初級	
❻	drive	[draɪv]	v./n.	開車/兜風	1	1	初級	◎
❼	afraid	[əˋfred]	adj.	害怕的	1	1	初級	
	flying	[ˋflaɪɪŋ]	n.	fly（搭飛機）動名詞	2	1	初級	
❽	have	[hæv]	v.	擁有/使某物…	1	1	初級	
	car	[kɑr]	n.	車	1	1	初級	◎
❾	get	[gɛt]	v.	患上	1	1	初級	◎
	carsick	[ˋkɑr͵sɪk]	n.	暈車			中級	
	easily	[ˋizɪlɪ]	adv.	容易地	1		中級	
❿	just	[dʒʌst]	adv.	剛剛	1	1	初級	
	bought	[bɔt]	p.t.	buy（購買）過去式	1	1	初級	
	loan	[lon]	n.	貸款	1	4	中級	◎
⓫	driver	[ˋdraɪvɚ]	n.	駕駛員	1	1	初級	◎
	license	[ˋlaɪsns]	n.	執照	2	4	中級	◎
⓬	using	[ˋjuzɪŋ]	p.pr.	use（使用）現在分詞	1	1	初級	◎
⓭	fuel	[ˋfjʊəl]	n.	燃料	1	4	中級	◎
	expense	[ɪkˋspɛns]	n.	費用	1	3	中級	◎
	quite	[kwaɪt]	adv.	相當	1	1	初級	
	considerable	[kənˋsɪdərəbl]	adj.	金額可觀的	2	3	中級	◎
⓮	got	[gɑt]	p.t.	get（獲得）過去式	1	1	初級	◎
	three	[θri]	n.	三	1	1	初級	
	traffic	[ˋtræfɪk]	n.	交通	1	2	初級	◎
	violation	[͵vaɪəˋleʃən]	n.	違反	2	4	中級	◎
	ticket	[ˋtɪkɪt]	n.	罰單	1	1	初級	◎
	last	[læst]	adj.	上一個	1	1	初級	
	month	[mʌnθ]	n.	月	1	1	初級	
⓯	serviced	[ˋsɝvɪst]	p.p.	service（維修、保養）過去分詞	1	1	初級	◎
	regularly	[ˋrɛgjəlɚlɪ]	adv.	定期地	2			◎
⓰	usually	[ˋjuʒʊəlɪ]	adv.	經常	1		初級	◎
	day	[de]	n.	天	1	1	初級	
	off	[ɔf]	adj.	休假的	1	1	初級	

※「紅字單字」於本單元多句出現，「單字級等分析」僅列在「首次出現句」。

036 你的交通工具？

🔵 MP3 036-02 ❶～⓳

❶	你怎麼去上班？	How do you get to work?
❷	你搭捷運上班嗎？	Do you get to work by MRT? * by＋交通工具（利用某交通工具）
❸	你開車上班嗎？	Do you drive to work?
❹	你打算換車嗎？	Do you plan to change cars? * plan to＋動詞原形（打算）
❺	你有車嗎？	Do you have a car?
❻	你容易暈船嗎？	Do you get seasick easily?
❼	你害怕搭飛機嗎？	Are you afraid of flying?
❽	你出過車禍嗎？	Have you ever been in a car accident before? * Have you ever...?（你是否有…經驗）
❾	你有汽車駕照嗎？	Do you have a driver's license?
❿	你有悠遊卡嗎？	Do you have an EasyCard?
⓫	你通常搭公車嗎？	Do you usually take the bus?
⓬	你害怕晚上一個人開車嗎？	Are you afraid of driving alone at night? * Are you afraid of...?（你是否害怕…）
⓭	你害怕晚上搭計程車嗎？	Are you afraid of taking a taxi at night?
⓮	你的油錢一個月多少？	How much is your monthly fuel cost? * How much...?（…多少錢？） * fuel cost（燃料費）
⓯	你喜歡開車兜風嗎？	Do you like to drive?
⓰	你多久保養一次愛車？	How often do you service your car? * How often...?（…多久一次？） * service＋某物（保養某物）
⓱	你常吃罰單嗎？	Do you get traffic tickets often? * get traffic ticket（被開交通罰單）
⓲	這是你剛買的車嗎？	Is this the car you just bought? * the car＋過去式子句（…的汽車）
⓳	你喜歡轎車、休旅車還是跑車？	Do you like sedans, SUVs or sports cars? * sports car（跑車）

	單字	音標	詞性	意義	字頻	大考	英檢	多益
❶	get	[gɛt]	v.	抵達/患上/得到	1	1	初級	◎
	work	[wɜk]	v.	工作	1	1	初級	◎
❷	MRT	[ˈɛmˌɑrˈti]	n.	Mass Rapid Transit（捷運）縮寫		2	初級	◎
❸	drive	[draɪv]	v.	開車	1	1	初級	◎
❹	plan	[plæn]	v.	計畫	1	1	初級	◎
	change	[tʃendʒ]	v.	更換	1	2	初級	◎
	car	[kɑr]	n.	車	1	1	初級	◎
❺	have	[hæv]	v.	擁有	1	1	初級	
❻	seasick	[ˈsiˌsɪk]	n.	暈船				
	easily	[ˈizɪlɪ]	adv.	容易地	1		中級	
❼	afraid	[əˈfred]	adj.	害怕的	1	1	初級	
	flying	[ˈflaɪɪŋ]	n.	fly（搭飛機）動名詞	2	1	初級	
❽	accident	[ˈæksədənt]	n.	事故	1	3	初級	◎
❾	driver	[ˈdraɪvɚ]	n.	駕駛員	1	1	初級	◎
	license	[ˈlaɪsns]	n.	執照	2	4	中級	◎
⓫	usually	[ˈjuʒʊəlɪ]	adv.	經常	1		初級	◎
	take	[tek]	v.	搭乘	1	1	初級	◎
	bus	[bʌs]	n.	公車	1	1	初級	
⓬	driving	[ˈdraɪvɪŋ]	n.	drive（開車）動名詞	2	1	初級	◎
	alone	[əˈlon]	adv.	單獨地	1	1	初級	
	night	[naɪt]	n.	晚上	1	1	初級	
⓭	taking	[ˈtekɪŋ]	n.	take（搭乘）動名詞	4			
	taxi	[ˈtæksɪ]	n.	計程車	2	1	初級	
⓮	much	[mʌtʃ]	adv.	許多地	1	1	初級	
	monthly	[ˈmʌnθlɪ]	adj.	每月的	2	4	初級	◎
	fuel	[ˈfjuəl]	n.	燃料	1	4	中級	◎
	cost	[kɔst]	n.	費用	1	1	初級	◎
⓯	like	[laɪk]	v.	喜歡	1	1	初級	
⓰	often	[ˈɔfən]	adv.	常常	1	1	初級	
	service	[ˈsɜvɪs]	v.	維修、保養	1	1	初級	◎
⓱	traffic	[ˈtræfɪk]	n.	交通	1	2	初級	◎
	ticket	[ˈtɪkɪt]	n.	罰單	1	1	初級	◎
⓲	this	[ðɪs]	pron.	這個	1	1	初級	
	just	[dʒʌst]	adv.	剛剛	1	1	初級	
	bought	[bɔt]	p.t.	buy（購買）過去式	1	1	初級	
⓳	sedan	[sɪˈdæn]	n.	轎車	3			
	SUV	[ˈɛsˈjuˈvi]	n.	sport utility vehicle（休旅車）縮寫				
	sports	[sports]	adj.	運動的	1	1	初級	

※「紅字單字」於本單元多句出現，「單字級等分析」僅列在「首次出現句」。

🔊 MP3 037-01 ❶～❻

❶	我喜歡上網。	I like to go online.
❷	我覺得網路很方便。	I think that the Internet is very convenient. * **I think that**＋子句（我覺得…）
❸	我幾乎每天上網。	I go online almost every day.
❹	我偶爾利用網路購物。	Sometimes I shop online.
❺	我對上網沒興趣。	I don't have any interest in going online. ＝ I am not interested in going online. * **have interest in**（有興趣）＝ **be interested in**
❻	我常上網跟朋友聊天。	I usually go on the Internet to talk with my friends.
❼	我每天上網 1 個小時。	I go online for an hour every day.
❽	我透過網路結交很多朋友。	I've made a lot of friends via the Internet. * 此句用「現在完成式」（...have made...）表示 　「過去某時點發生某事，且結果持續到現在」。 * **via**＋工具（透過某工具）
❾	我偶爾跟朋友玩視訊。	Sometimes I will use a webcam with my friends. * **Sometimes I will**＋動詞原形（我平常習慣做…） * 此句用「未來簡單式」（...will...） 　表示「某人經常性的習慣」。
❿	我常用網路搜尋資料。	I usually use the Internet to search for information.
⓫	我用 email 聯絡客戶。	I use email to contact my clients.
⓬	我從網路下載東西。	I download material from the Internet.
⓭	我經常因為上網而熬夜。	I always stay up late because of the Internet. * **stay up late**（熬夜） * **because of**＋名詞（因為）
⓮	我很迷線上遊戲。	I am obsessed with online games. * **be obsessed with**（沉迷）
⓯	我有兩個電子郵件信箱。	I have two email addresses. * **email address**（電子郵件信箱）
⓰	我常泡網咖。	I hang out at Internet cafés a lot. * **Internet café**（網咖） * **hang out**（在某地逗留，且不做正事）

單字級等分析

	單字	音標	詞性	意義	字頻	大考	英檢	多益
❶	like	[laɪk]	v.	喜歡	1	1	初級	
	go	[go]	v.	做、從事	1	1	初級	
	online	[ˈɑn.laɪn]	adv./adj.	在網路上/網路上的	1		初級	◎
❷	think	[θɪŋk]	v.	認為	1	1	初級	
	Internet	[ˈɪntɚ.nɛt]	n.	網路	1	4	初級	
	very	[ˈvɛrɪ]	adv.	非常	1	1	初級	
	convenient	[kənˈvinjənt]	adj.	方便的	2	2	初級	◎
❸	almost	[ˈɔl.most]	adv.	幾乎	1	1	初級	
	every	[ˈɛrvɪ]	adj.	每一	1	1	初級	
	day	[de]	n.	天	1	1	初級	
❹	sometimes	[ˈsʌm.taɪmz]	adv.	有時候	1	1	初級	
	shop	[ʃɑp]	v.	購物	1	1	初級	◎
❺	have	[hæv]	v.	擁有	1	1	初級	
	any	[ˈɛnɪ]	adj.	任何的	1	1	初級	
	interest	[ˈɪntərɪst]	n.	興趣	1	1	初級	◎
	going	[ˈgoɪŋ]	n.	go（做、從事）動名詞	4	1	初級	◎
	interested	[ˈɪntərɪstɪd]	adj.	有興趣的	1	1	初級	◎
❻	usually	[ˈjuʒʊəlɪ]	adv.	經常	1		初級	◎
	talk	[tɔk]	v.	聊天	1		初級	◎
	friend	[frɛnd]	n.	朋友	1		初級	
❼	hour	[aʊr]	n.	小時	1	1	初級	
❽	made	[med]	p.p.	make（結交）過去分詞	1	1	初級	
	lot	[lɑt]	n.	許多	1		初級	
❾	use	[juz]	v.	使用	1	1	初級	◎
	webcam	[ˈwɛb.kæm]	n.	視訊攝影機				
❿	search for	[sɝtʃ fɔr]	v.	搜尋				◎
	information	[.ɪnfəˈmeʃən]	n.	資訊	1	4	初級	◎
⓫	email	[ˈimel]	n.	電子郵件	2	4		◎
	contact	[kənˈtækt]	v.	聯絡	1	2	初級	◎
	client	[ˈklaɪənt]	n.	客戶	1	3	中級	◎
⓬	download	[ˈdaʊn.lod]	v.	下載	3	4	中高	◎
	material	[məˈtɪrɪəl]	n.	資料	1	6	初級	◎
⓭	always	[ˈɔlwez]	adv.	總是	1	1	初級	
	stay	[ste]	v.	保持、堅持	1	1	初級	◎
	up	[ʌp]	adv.	醒著地	1	1	初級	
	late	[let]	adv.	晚地	1	1	初級	
⓮	obsessed	[əbˈsɛst]	adj.	沉迷的	3		中高	◎
	game	[gem]	n.	遊戲	1	1	初級	
⓯	two	[tu]	n.	二	1	1	初級	
	address	[əˈdrɛs]	n.	地址	1	1	初級	◎
⓰	hang	[hæŋ]	v.	逗留、徘徊	1	2	初級	◎
	out	[aʊt]	adv.	在外	1	1	初級	
	café	[kəˈfe]	n.	咖啡店				

※「紅字單字」於本單元多句出現，「單字級等分析」僅列在「首次出現句」。

🔵 MP3 037-02 ❶～⓰

❶	你喜歡上網嗎？	Do you like to go online? * like to＋動詞原形（喜歡）
❷	你經常上網嗎？	Do you regularly go online?
❸	你的電子信箱帳號是什麼？	What is your email account? * email account（電子信箱帳號） 　= email address
❹	你每天收 email 嗎？	Do you check your email every day? * check email（收email、檢查email）
❺	你有電子信箱嗎？	Do you have an email address?
❻	你上網跟朋友聊天嗎？	Do you talk with friends online? * talk with＋某人（和某人聊天） 　= chat with＋某人
❼	你每天花多少時間上網？	How much time do you spend online every day? * How much time...?（…多少時間？）
❽	你玩過視訊嗎？	Have you ever used a webcam before? * Have you ever...?（你是否有…經驗）
❾	你從網路下載東西嗎？	Do you download things from the Internet?
❿	你會上網找資料嗎？	Do you search for information online?
⓫	你上網都在做什麼？	What do you do when you go online?
⓬	你有網友嗎？	Do you have any Internet friends? * Internet friend（網友）= online friend
⓭	你在網路上買過東西嗎？	Have you ever bought anything online? * Have you ever sold anything online? 　（你在網路上賣過東西嗎）
⓮	你用臉書嗎？	Do you use Facebook?
⓯	你去過網咖嗎？	Have you ever been to an Internet café before? * Have you ever been to＋某地? 　（你是否曾經去某地）
⓰	你玩線上遊戲嗎？	Do you play online games?

	單字	音標	詞性	意義	字頻	大考	英檢	多益
❶	like	[laɪk]	v.	喜歡	1	1	初級	
	go	[go]	v.	做、從事	1	1	初級	
	online	[ˋɑn͵laɪn]	adv./adj.	在網路上/網路上的	1		初級	◎
❷	regularly	[ˋrɛgjələlɪ]	adv.	定期地	2			◎
❸	email	[ˋimel]	n.	電子郵件	2	4		
	account	[əˋkaunt]	n.	帳號	1	3	中級	◎
❹	check	[tʃɛk]	v.	收、檢查	1	1	初級	◎
	every	[ˋɛvrɪ]	adj.	每一	1	1	初級	
	day	[de]	n.	天	1	1	初級	
❺	have	[hæv]	v.	擁有	1	1	初級	
	address	[əˋdrɛs]	n.	地址	1	1	初級	◎
❻	talk	[tɔk]	v.	聊天	1	1	初級	◎
	friend	[frɛnd]	n.	朋友	1	1	初級	
❼	much	[mʌtʃ]	adj.	許多的	1	1	初級	
	time	[taɪm]	n.	時間	1	1	初級	◎
	spend	[spɛnd]	v.	花費	1	1	初級	◎
❽	ever	[ˋɛvɚ]	adv.	曾經	1	1	初級	
	used	[juzd]	p.p.	use（使用）過去分詞	1	2	初級	◎
	webcam	[ˋwɛb͵kæm]	n.	視訊攝影機				
	before	[bɪˋfor]	adv.	過去、以前	1	1	初級	
❾	download	[ˋdaun͵lod]	v.	下載	3	4	中高	◎
	thing	[θɪŋ]	n.	東西	1	1	初級	
	Internet	[ˋɪntɚ͵nɛt]	n.	網路	1	4	初級	
❿	search for	[sɝtʃ fɔr]	v.	搜尋				◎
	information	[͵ɪnfɚˋmeʃən]	n.	資訊	1	4	初級	◎
⓫	do	[du]	v.	做	1	1	初級	
⓬	any	[ˋɛnɪ]	adj.	任何的	1	1	初級	
⓭	bought	[bɔt]	p.p.	buy（購買）過去分詞	1	1	初級	
	anything	[ˋɛnɪ͵θɪŋ]	pron.	任何東西	1	1	初級	
⓮	use	[juz]	v.	使用	1	1	初級	◎
⓯	café	[kəˋfe]	n.	咖啡店				
⓰	play	[ple]	v.	玩	1	1	初級	
	game	[gem]	n.	遊戲	1	1	初級	

※「紅字單字」於本單元多句出現，「單字級等分析」僅列在「首次出現句」。

🔊 MP3 038-01 ❶～⓮

❶	我很少去便利商店。	I seldom go to the convenience store.
❷	我常到便利商店買東西。	I often go shopping at the convenience store. * **go shopping**（購物）
❸	我利用便利商店繳費。	I pay my bills at the convenience store.
❹	我每天去便利商店買報紙。	I go to the convenience store to buy a newspaper every day.
❺	便利商店讓我的生活更方便。	Convenience stores make my life more convenient. * **make life more convenient**（讓生活更方便）
❻	我喜歡便利商店的便當。	I like the boxed lunches from the convenience store. * **boxed lunch**（便當） * **from＋店家**（來自某店家）
❼	我偶爾到便利商店傳真。	Sometimes I go to the convenience store to send a fax. * **Sometimes I...**（我平常有時候會…）
❽	我住的地方離便利商店很遠。	I live far away from any convenience store. * **far away from＋某地**（離某地很遠）
❾	我常利用便利商店的提款機。	I usually use the ATM in the convenience store.
❿	我最常到便利商店買口香糖。	I mostly buy gum from the convenience store. * **gum**（口香糖）可替換為：**cigarettes**（香菸）
⓫	我常利用便利商店寄宅配。	I usually use the convenience store's home delivery service. * **home delivery service**（宅配服務）
⓬	我喜歡嘗試便利商店的新產品。	I like to try out the convenience store's new products. * **like to＋動詞原形**（喜歡） * **try out**（嘗試）
⓭	有時候我到便利商店買午餐。	Sometimes I will go to the convenience store to buy lunch. * **Sometimes I will＋動詞原形**（我平常習慣做…）。 * 此句用「未來簡單式」（...will...） 　表示「某人經常性的習慣」。
⓮	我覺得逛便利商店是種樂趣。	I think shopping in the convenience store is fun. * **I think＋子句**（我認為…），子句用動名詞 　（**shopping in the convenience store**）當主詞

	單字	音標	詞性	意義	字頻	大考	英檢	多益
❶	seldom	[ˋsɛldəm]	adv.	很少	2	3	初級	◎
	go	[go]	v.	去	1	1	初級	
	convenience	[kənˋvinjəns]	n.	便利	2	4	中級	◎
	store	[stor]	n.	商店	1	1	初級	◎
❷	often	[ˋɔfən]	adv.	常常	1	1	初級	
	shopping	[ˋʃɑpɪŋ]	n.	shop（購物）動名詞	1	1	中級	◎
❸	pay	[pe]	v.	付款	1	3	初級	◎
	bill	[bɪl]	n.	帳單	1	2	初級	◎
❹	buy	[baɪ]	v.	購買	1	1	初級	
	newspaper	[ˋnjuz͵pepɚ]	n.	報紙	1	1	初級	
	every	[ˋɛvrɪ]	adj.	每一	1	1	初級	
	day	[de]	n.	天	1	1	初級	
❺	make	[mek]	v.	使得…	1	1	初級	
	life	[laɪf]	n.	生活	1	1	初級	
	more	[mor]	adv.	更加	1	1	初級	
	convenient	[kənˋvinjənt]	adj.	方便的	2	2	初級	◎
❻	like	[laɪk]	v.	喜歡	1	1	初級	
	boxed	[bɑksd]	adj.	盒裝的	7			
	lunch	[lʌntʃ]	n.	午餐	1	1	初級	
❼	sometimes	[ˋsʌm͵taɪmz]	adv.	有時候	1	1	初級	
	send	[sɛnd]	v.	傳送	1	1	初級	
	fax	[fæks]	n.	傳真	3	3	中級	◎
❽	live	[lɪv]	v.	居住	1	1	初級	
	far	[fɑr]	adv.	遠地	1	1	初級	
	away	[əˋwe]	adv.	離…遠地	1	1	初級	
	any	[ˋɛnɪ]	adj.	任何的	1	1	初級	
❾	usually	[ˋjuʒʊəlɪ]	adv.	經常	1		初級	◎
	use	[juz]	v.	使用	1	1	初級	
	ATM	[ˋeˋtiˋɛm]	n.	自動提款機，是以下三字的縮寫：automated（自動的）teller（出納）machine（機器）	4	4	中高	
❿	mostly	[ˋmostlɪ]	adv.	大部分地	1	4	中級	
	gum	[gʌm]	n.	口香糖	3	3	中級	
⓫	home	[hom]	n.	家	1	1	初級	
	delivery	[dɪˋlɪvərɪ]	n.	配送	2	3	中級	◎
	service	[ˋsɝvɪs]	n.	服務	1	1	初級	◎
⓬	try	[traɪ]	v.	嘗試	1	1	初級	
	out	[aʊt]	adv.	完全、徹底	1	1	初級	
	new	[nju]	adj.	新的	1	1	初級	
	product	[ˋprɑdəkt]	n.	產品	1	3	初級	◎
⓮	think	[θɪŋk]	v.	認為	1	1	初級	
	fun	[fʌn]	adj.	有趣的	1	1	初級	

※「紅字單字」於本單元多句出現，「單字級等分析」僅列在「首次出現句」。

🔵 MP3 038-02 ❶～⓯

❶	你常去便利商店嗎？	Do you go to the convenience store frequently?
❷	你喜歡逛便利商店嗎？	Do you like shopping in the convenience store? * like＋動詞-ing（喜歡）
❸	你喜歡便利商店的食物嗎？	Do you like the food in the convenience store? * like＋名詞（喜歡）
❹	你到便利商店提款嗎？	Do you withdraw money from the ATM in the convenience store? * withdraw money（提款）
❺	你吃過便利商店的便當嗎？	Have you ever eaten a boxed lunch from the convenience store? * Have you ever…?（你是否有…經驗）
❻	你到便利商店影印嗎？	Do you make copies in the convenience store? * make a copy（影印）
❼	你有 7-11 的 i-cash 卡嗎？	Do you have a 7-11 i-cash card? * Do your have＋物品?（你是否擁有某物品）
❽	你利用便利商店繳費嗎？	Do you pay your bills at the convenience store?
❾	你家附近有便利商店嗎？	Is there a convenience store around your home? * Is there…?（是否有…） * around＋某地（某地附近）
❿	你喜歡 7-11 還是全家？	Do you like 7-11 or Family Mart? * like A or B（喜歡 A 或 B）
⓫	你寄過便利商店的宅配服務嗎？	Have you ever used the convenience store's home delivery service?
⓬	你每天在便利商店買報紙嗎？	Do you buy newspapers in the convenience store every day?
⓭	你到便利商店買早餐嗎？	Do you go to the convenience store to buy breakfast?
⓮	很多便利商店全年無休。	Many convenience stores are open all year round. * be open all year round（全年無休）
⓯	在台灣，便利商店隨處可見。	Convenience stores are everywhere in Taiwan. * be everywhere（位在各個地方、到處都有）

	單字	音標	詞性	意義	字頻	大考	英檢	多益
❶	go	[go]	v.	去	1	1	初級	
	convenience	[kən'vinjəns]	n.	便利	2	4	中級	◎
	store	[stor]	n.	商店	1	1	初級	◎
	frequently	['frikwəntlɪ]	adv.	頻繁地	1			◎
❷	like	[laɪk]	v.	喜歡	1	1	初級	
	shopping	['ʃɑpɪŋ]	n.	shop（購物）動名詞	1	1	中級	◎
❸	food	[fud]	n.	食物	1	1	初級	◎
❹	withdraw	[wɪð'drɔ]	v.	提款	1	4	中級	◎
	money	['mʌnɪ]	n.	金錢	1	1	初級	◎
	ATM	['e'ti'ɛm]	n.	自動提款機，是以下三字的縮寫：automated（自動的）teller（出納）machine（機器）	4	4	中高	◎
❺	ever	['ɛvɚ]	adv.	曾經	1	1	初級	
	eaten	['itn]	p.p.	eat（吃）過去分詞	1	1	初級	
	boxed	[bɑksd]	adj.	盒裝的	7			
	lunch	[lʌntʃ]	n.	午餐	1		初級	
❻	make	[mek]	v.	做、製作	1	1	初級	
	copy	['kɑpɪ]	n.	影印、拷貝	1	2	初級	◎
❼	have	[hæv]	v.	擁有	1	1	初級	
	card	[kɑrd]	n.	卡片	1	1	初級	◎
❽	pay	[pe]	v.	付款	1	3	初級	◎
	bill	[bɪl]	n.	帳單	1	2	初級	◎
❾	there	[ðɛr]	adv.	有…	1	1	初級	
	home	[hom]	n.	家	1	1	初級	
⓫	used	[juzd]	p.p.	use（使用）過去分詞	1	2	初級	◎
	delivery	[dɪ'lɪvərɪ]	n.	配送	2	3	中級	◎
	service	['sɝvɪs]	n.	服務	1		初級	◎
⓬	buy	[baɪ]	v.	購買	1	1	初級	
	newspaper	['njuzˌpepɚ]	n.	報紙	1	1	初級	
	every	['ɛvrɪ]	adj.	每一	1	1	初級	
	day	[de]	n.	天	1	1	初級	
⓭	breakfast	['brɛkfəst]	n.	早餐	1	1	初級	
⓮	many	['mɛnɪ]	adj.	許多的	1	1	初級	
	open	['opən]	adj.	營業的	1	1	初級	
	all	[ɔl]	adj.	全部的	1	1	初級	
	year	[jɪr]	n.	年	1	1	初級	
	round	[raund]	adv.	整個地、循環地	1	1	初級	
⓯	everywhere	['ɛvrɪˌhwɛr]	adv.	各個地方	1		初級	
	Taiwan	['taɪ'wɑn]	n.	台灣			初級	

※「紅字單字」於本單元多句出現，「單字級等分析」僅列在「首次出現句」。

🔊 MP3 039-01 ❶～❻

❶	我每天吃早餐。	I have breakfast every day. * **have breakfast**（吃早餐）= **eat breakfast**
❷	我從不吃早餐。	I never eat breakfast.
❸	我常因睡過頭而沒吃早餐。	I often skip breakfast because I oversleep. * **skip**＋某餐（略過某餐） * **because**＋子句（因為）
❹	我不吃早餐會沒體力。	I have no energy without breakfast. * **have no energy**（沒有活力） * **have energy**（有活力）
❺	我常在公車上吃早餐。	I often have my breakfast on the bus.
❻	我在家裡吃早餐。	I have my breakfast at home. * **at home**（在家） * **at school**（在學校）
❼	我媽媽每天幫我做早餐。	My mom makes me breakfast every day. * 某人＋**makes me breakfast**（某人為我做早餐）
❽	我吃三明治當早餐。	I have sandwiches for breakfast. * **for breakfast**（當作早餐）
❾	我自己做早餐。	I make myself breakfast. * **make myself breakfast**（自己做早餐）
❿	我到便利商店買早餐。	I get my breakfast from the convenience store.
⓫	我喜歡中式早餐。	I like Chinese-style breakfasts. * **Western-style**（西式的）
⓬	我今天早餐很豐盛。	I had a sumptuous breakfast. * **sumptuous**（豐盛的）可替換為：**simple**（簡單的）
⓭	我的早餐常換花樣。	I'll have various kinds of breakfasts. * **various kinds of**（各式各樣的）。 * 此句用「未來簡單式」（...will...） 　表示「某人經常性的習慣」。
⓮	我每天早上都吃吐司夾蛋。	I have a piece of toast with egg every morning. * **a piece of**（一份） * **toast with egg**（烤吐司加蛋）
⓯	我覺得早餐是一天中最重要的一餐。	I think that breakfast is the most important meal of the day.
⓰	我的早餐一成不變。	My breakfast is always the same.

	單字	音標	詞性	意義	字頻	大考	英檢	多益
❶	have	[hæv]	v.	吃/擁有	1	1	初級	
	breakfast	[ˋbrɛkfəst]	n.	早餐	1	1	初級	
	every	[ˋɛvrɪ]	adj.	每一	1	1	初級	
	day	[de]	n.	天	1	1	初級	
❷	never	[ˋnɛvɚ]	adv.	從不	1	1	初級	
	eat	[it]	v.	吃	1	1	初級	
❸	often	[ˋɔfən]	adv.	常常	1	1	初級	
	skip	[skɪp]	v.	掠過	2	3	中級	◎
	oversleep	[ˋovɚˋslip]	v.	睡過頭		5	中高	
❹	energy	[ˋɛnɚdʒɪ]	n.	活力	1	2	初級	
❺	bus	[bʌs]	n.	公車	1	1	初級	
❻	home	[hom]	n.	家	1	1	初級	
❼	mom	[mɑm]	n.	母親	1	1		
	make	[mek]	v.	做、製作			初級	
❽	sandwich	[ˋsændwɪtʃ]	n.	三明治	2	2	初級	
❾	myself	[maɪˋsɛlf]	pron.	我自己	1		初級	
❿	get	[gɛt]	v.	購買、取得	1	1	初級	◎
	convenience	[kənˋvinjəns]	n.	便利	2	4	中級	◎
	store	[stor]	n.	商店	1	1	初級	◎
⓫	like	[laɪk]	v.	喜歡	1	1	初級	
	Chinese-style	[ˋtʃaɪˋnizˏstaɪl]	adj.	中式的				
⓬	had	[hæd]	p.t.	have（吃）過去式	1	1	初級	
	sumptuous	[ˋsʌmptʃʊəs]	adj.	豐盛的	6			
⓭	various	[ˋvɛrɪəs]	adj.	各種的	1	3	中級	◎
	kind	[kaɪnd]	n.	種類	1	1	初級	◎
⓮	piece	[pis]	n.	一份	1	1	初級	◎
	toast	[tost]	n.	吐司	3	2	初級	◎
	egg	[ɛg]	n.	蛋	1	1	初級	
	morning	[ˋmɔrnɪŋ]	n.	早上	1	1	初級	
⓯	think	[θɪŋk]	v.	認為	1	1	初級	
	most	[most]	adv.	最	1	1	初級	
	important	[ɪmˋpɔrtnt]	adj.	重要的	1	1	初級	◎
	meal	[mil]	n.	餐	1	2	初級	
⓰	always	[ˋɔlwez]	adv.	一直	1	1	初級	
	same	[sem]	adj.	同樣的	1	1	初級	

※「紅字單字」於本單元多句出現，「單字級等分析」僅列在「首次出現句」。

039 你的早餐？

❶	你每天吃早餐嗎？	Do you have breakfast every day?
❷	你通常幾點吃早餐？	What time do you usually have breakfast? * **What time do you...?**（你平常幾點…呢）
❸	你為什麼不吃早餐？	Why don't you want to have breakfast? * **Why don't you...?**（你為何不…呢）
❹	你自己弄早餐嗎？	Do you make breakfast yourself?
❺	你的早餐吃什麼？	What did you have for breakfast? * **What did you...?**（詢問對方當時的具體行為）
❻	你在辦公室吃早餐嗎？	Do you have breakfast at the office?
❼	你在早餐店吃早餐嗎？	Do you have your breakfast at the breakfast shop? * **breakfast shop**（早餐店）
❽	你常因睡過頭而沒吃早餐嗎？	Do you skip your breakfast due to oversleeping? * **due to＋動詞-ing**（因為）
❾	你常吃西式早餐還是中式早餐？	Do you usually eat a Western-style or Chinese-style breakfast?
❿	你覺得早餐很重要嗎？	Do you take breakfast seriously? * **take＋某事物＋seriously**（認真看待某事物）
⓫	你早餐吃漢堡嗎？	Do you have hamburgers for breakfast? * **sandwich**（三明治）
⓬	你在公車上吃早餐嗎？	Do you have your breakfast on the bus?
⓭	你到便利商店買早餐嗎？	Do you get your breakfast from convenience stores? * **get breakfast**（買早餐）
⓮	你今天早餐很豐盛嗎？	Did you have a sumptuous breakfast? * 此句用「過去簡單式問句」（Did...?） 　表示「在過去是否發生某事？」。
⓯	你的早餐常換花樣嗎？	Do you often try different kinds of breakfasts? * **different kinds of**（各種不同的） 　＝**various kinds of**
⓰	你不吃早餐有精神嗎？	Will you still have energy if you skip breakfast? * **Will you＋動詞＋if you＋動詞...?** 　（如果你…，是否…？）

	單字	音標	詞性	意義	字頻	大考	英檢	多益
❶	have	[hæv]	v.	吃/擁有	1	1	初級	
	breakfast	[ˋbrɛkfəst]	n.	早餐	1	1	初級	
	every	[ˋɛvrɪ]	adj.	每一	1	1	初級	
	day	[de]	n.	天	1	1	初級	
❷	time	[taɪm]	n.	時間	1	1	初級	◎
	usually	[ˋjuʒʊəlɪ]	adv.	經常	1		初級	◎
❸	want	[wɑnt]	v.	想要	1	1	初級	◎
❹	make	[mek]	v.	做、製作	1	1	初級	
	yourself	[jʊəˋsɛlf]	pron.	你自己	1		初級	
❻	office	[ˋɔfɪs]	n.	公司、辦公地點	1	1	初級	◎
❼	shop	[ʃɑp]	n.	商店	1	1	初級	◎
❽	skip	[skɪp]	v.	略過	2	3	中級	◎
	due	[dju]	adj.	因為	1	3	中級	◎
	oversleeping	[ˋovəˏslipɪŋ]	n.	oversleep（睡過頭）動名詞		5	中高	
❾	eat	[it]	v.	吃	1	1	初級	
	Western-style	[ˋwɛstənˏstaɪl]	adj.	西式的	7			
	Chinese-style	[ˋtʃaɪˋnizˏstaɪl]	adj.	中式的				
❿	take	[tek]	v.	看待	1	1	初級	◎
	seriously	[ˋsɪrɪəslɪ]	adv.	認真地	1		中高	◎
⓫	hamburger	[ˋhæmbɝgə]	n.	漢堡	3	2	初級	
⓬	bus	[bʌs]	n.	公車	1	1	初級	
⓭	get	[gɛt]	v.	購買、取得	1	1	初級	◎
	convenience	[kənˋvinjəns]	n.	便利	2	4	中級	◎
	store	[stor]	n.	商店	1	1	初級	◎
⓮	sumptuous	[ˋsʌmptʃʊəs]	adj.	豐盛的	6			
⓯	often	[ˋɔfən]	adv.	常常	1	1	初級	
	try	[traɪ]	v.	嘗試	1	1	初級	
	different	[ˋdɪfərənt]	adj.	不同的	1	1	初級	
	kind	[kaɪnd]	n.	種類	1	1	初級	◎
⓰	still	[stɪl]	adv.	仍然	1	1	初級	◎
	energy	[ˋɛnədʒɪ]	n.	活力	1	2	初級	

※「紅字單字」於本單元多句出現，「單字級等分析」僅列在「首次出現句」。

MP3 040-01 ❶～❶

❶	我今天中午吃很少。	I had a small lunch. * **I had a big lunch.**（我今天中午吃很多） * 此句用「過去簡單式」（…had…） 　表示「發生在過去的事」。
❷	我今天午餐很簡單。	I had a simple lunch. * **simple**（簡單的）可替換為：**sumptuous**（豐盛的）
❸	我今天跟同事一起吃午餐。	I had lunch with my coworkers. * **with＋某人**（和某人一起）
❹	我今天午餐吃便當。	I had a boxed lunch for lunch.
❺	我常約客戶吃午餐。	I often invite my clients to have lunch with me. * **invite＋某人＋to**（邀約某人） * **have lunch with me**（和我一起吃午餐）
❻	我通常在下午兩點前吃完午餐。	I usually finish my lunch before two pm. * **before＋某時間**（在某時間之前）
❼	我們公司免費供應午餐。	There's a free lunch offered by our company. * **某物＋offered by＋公司**（由公司提供的某物）
❽	我今天在員工餐廳吃午餐。	I had lunch at the employee cafeteria. * **employee cafeteria**（員工餐廳）
❾	我中午習慣吃飯。	I'm used to having rice for lunch. * **be used to＋動詞-ing**（習慣）
❿	我自己帶便當。	I bring my own lunch box.
⓫	我偶爾吃商業午餐。	I have a business lunch from time to time. * **business lunch**（商業午餐） * **from time to time**（偶爾）
⓬	我們常在學校附近吃午餐。	We often have lunch somewhere near the school. * **somewhere near…**（在…附近的某個地方）
⓭	我經常忙到沒時間吃午餐。	I'm often too busy to have lunch. * **too busy to＋動詞原形**（忙碌到無法做某事）
⓮	我今天午餐只吃沙拉。	I had only a salad for lunch.
⓯	中午吃太飽我會想睡覺。	If I eat too much for lunch I get sleepy. * **If I＋動詞＋I＋動詞**（如果我…，就會…）

	單字	音標	詞性	意義	字頻	大考	英檢	多益
❶	had	[hæd]	p.t.	have（吃）過去式	1	1	初級	
	small	[smɔl]	adj.	少量的	1	1	初級	◎
	lunch	[lʌntʃ]	n.	午餐	1	1	初級	
❷	simple	[ˈsɪmpl]	adj.	簡單的	1	1	初級	◎
❸	coworker	[ko.wɜkɚ]	n.	同事				
❹	boxed	[bɑksd]	adj.	盒裝的	7			
❺	often	[ˈɔfən]	adv.	常常	1	1	初級	
	invite	[ɪnˈvaɪt]	v.	邀請	1	2	初級	◎
	client	[ˈklaɪənt]	n.	客戶	1	3	中級	◎
	have	[hæv]	v.	吃	1	1	初級	
❻	usually	[ˈjuʒʊəlɪ]	adv.	經常	1		初級	◎
	finish	[ˈfɪnɪʃ]	v.	吃光、結束	1	1	初級	◎
	two	[tu]	n.	二	1	1	初級	
	pm	[ˈpiˈɛm]	adv.	下午	1	4		
❼	there	[ðɛr]	adv.	有…	1	1	初級	
	free	[fri]	adj.	免費的	1	1	初級	
	offered	[ˈɔfɚd]	p.p.	offer（提供）過去分詞	7	2	初級	◎
	company	[ˈkʌmpənɪ]	n.	公司	1	2	初級	◎
❽	employee	[ˌɛmplɔɪˈi]	n.	員工	1	3	中級	◎
	cafeteria	[ˌkæfəˈtɪrɪə]	n.	自助餐廳	3	2	初級	◎
❾	used	[juzd]	p.p.	use（習慣）過去分詞	1	2	初級	◎
	having	[ˈhævɪŋ]	n.	have（吃）動名詞	1	1	初級	
	rice	[raɪs]	n.	米飯	1	1	初級	
❿	bring	[brɪŋ]	v.	攜帶	1	1	初級	
	own	[on]	adj.	自己的	1	1	初級	◎
	box	[bɑks]	n.	餐盒	1	1	初級	◎
⓫	business	[ˈbɪznɪs]	n.	商業、商務	1	2	初級	◎
	time	[taɪm]	n.	次、回	1	1	初級	◎
⓬	somewhere	[ˈsʌm.hwɛr]	adv.	某個地方	1	2	初級	
	school	[skul]	n.	學校	1	1	初級	
⓭	too	[tu]	adv.	太過	1	1	初級	
	busy	[ˈbɪzɪ]	adj.	忙碌的	1	1	初級	
⓮	only	[ˈonlɪ]	adv.	只有	1	1	初級	
	salad	[ˈsæləd]	n.	沙拉	1	2	初級	
⓯	eat	[it]	v.	吃	1	1	初級	
	much	[mʌtʃ]	adv.	許多地、大量地	1	1	初級	
	get	[gɛt]	v.	變成	1	1	初級	◎
	sleepy	[ˈslipɪ]	adj.	想睡的	3	2	初級	

※「紅字單字」於本單元多句出現，「單字級等分析」僅列在「首次出現句」。

040 你的午餐？

MP3 040-02 ❶～❶

❶	你吃午餐了嗎？	Did you have lunch yet? * 此句用「過去簡單式問句」（Did...?） 　表示「在過去是否發生某事？」。
❷	你要一起吃午餐嗎？	Do you want to join us for lunch? * want to＋動詞原形（想要） * join us（來和我們作伴）
❸	你通常一個人吃午餐嗎？	Do you usually have lunch alone? * have lunch alone（獨自吃午餐）
❹	你和同事一起吃午餐嗎？	Do you have lunch with your coworkers?
❺	你們公司供應午餐嗎？	Is lunch provided by your company? * be provided by...（由…提供）
❻	你的午餐通常吃什麼？	What do you usually have for lunch?
❼	你自己帶便當嗎？	Do you bring your own lunch box? * bring lunch box（帶便當）
❽	你通常忙到幾點吃午餐？	What time can you usually have lunch? * What time can you...? 　（通常在幾點，你能夠…？）
❾	你今天中午吃飯還是吃麵？或是別的？	Did you have rice or noodles for lunch? Or something else?
❿	你中午要和客戶聚餐嗎？	Do you need to have lunch with your clients? * need to＋動詞原形（需要）
⓫	你中午有約人吃飯嗎？	Do you have an appointment with anyone for lunch? * have an appointment（有約會）
⓬	你中午只吃水果嗎？	Do you only have fruit for lunch?
⓭	你的午餐都吃這麼少嗎？	Do you usually have so little for lunch? * so little（這麼少）可替換為：so much（這麼多）
⓮	你在公司附近吃午餐嗎？	Do you have lunch near the office?
⓯	你的午餐吃得太油膩了！	You're having too much greasy food for lunch! * greasy food（油膩食物）。 * 此句用「現在進行式」（...are having...） 　表示「現階段發生的事」。

單字級等分析

	單字	音標	詞性	意義	字頻	大考	英檢	多益
❶	have	[hæv]	v.	吃/擁有	1	1	初級	
	lunch	[lʌntʃ]	n.	午餐	1	1	初級	
	yet	[jɛt]	adv.	尚未	1	1	初級	◎
❷	want	[wɑnt]	v.	想要	1	1	初級	◎
	join	[dʒɔɪn]	v.	加入	1	1	初級	◎
❸	usually	[ˈjuʒʊəlɪ]	adv.	經常	1		初級	◎
	alone	[əˈlon]	adv.	單獨地	1	1	初級	
❹	coworker	[ˈko͵wɝkɚ]	n.	同事				
❺	provided	[prəˈvaɪdɪd]	p.p.	provide（提供）過去分詞	2		中高	
	company	[ˈkʌmpənɪ]	n.	公司	1	2	初級	◎
❼	bring	[brɪŋ]	v.	攜帶	1	1	初級	
	own	[on]	adj.	自己的	1	1	初級	◎
	box	[bɑks]	n.	餐盒	1	1	初級	◎
❽	time	[taɪm]	n.	時間	1	1	初級	◎
❾	rice	[raɪs]	n.	米飯	1	1	初級	
	noodles	[ˈnudls]	n.	noodle（麵食）複數	3	2	初級	
	something	[ˈsʌmθɪŋ]	pron.	某事物	1	1	初級	
	else	[ɛls]	adj.	其他的	1	1	初級	
❿	need	[nid]	v.	需要	1	1	初級	◎
	client	[ˈklaɪənt]	n.	客戶	1	3	中級	◎
⓫	appointment	[əˈpɔɪntmənt]	n.	約會	2	4	中級	◎
	anyone	[ˈɛnɪ͵wʌn]	pron.	任何人	1	2	初級	
⓬	only	[ˈonlɪ]	adv.	只有	1	1	初級	
	fruit	[frut]	n.	水果	1	1	初級	
⓭	so	[so]	adv.	這麼	1	1	初級	
	little	[ˈlɪtl]	adv.	少地	1	1	初級	
⓮	office	[ˈɔfɪs]	n.	公司、辦公地點	1	1	初級	◎
⓯	having	[ˈhævɪŋ]	p.pr.	have（吃）現在分詞	1	1	初級	
	too	[tu]	adv.	過於	1	1	初級	
	much	[mʌtʃ]	adj.	許多的	1	1	初級	
	greasy	[ˈgrizɪ]	adj.	油膩的	4	4	中級	
	food	[fud]	n.	食物	1	1	初級	◎

※「紅字單字」於本單元多句出現，「單字級等分析」僅列在「首次出現句」。

041　我的晚餐。

❶	我買晚餐回家吃。	I bring food home for dinner.
❷	我通常在家吃晚餐。	I usually have dinner at home. * **have dinner at**＋某地（在某地吃晚餐）
❸	我很少跟家人一起吃晚餐。	I seldom have dinner with my family. * **have dinner with**＋某人（和某人共進晚餐）
❹	我自己下廚煮晚餐。	I cook dinner myself.
❺	我常跟家人上館子吃晚餐。	I often eat out for dinner with my family. * **eat out**（外食、在外用餐）
❻	我常跟朋友共進晚餐。	I often have dinner with my friends.
❼	我習慣很晚吃晚餐。	I'm used to having a late dinner. * **be used to**＋動詞-ing（習慣） * **have a late dinner**（很晚吃晚餐）
❽	朋友邀我今晚一起吃飯。	My friend asked me to dinner tonight. * **ask me to**＋動詞原形（邀約我…）
❾	我常忙到沒空吃晚餐。	I'm often too busy to have dinner. * **too busy to**＋動詞原形（忙碌到無法做某事）
❿	我偶爾吃泡麵當晚餐。	I have instant noodles for dinner sometimes. * **instant noodles**（泡麵）
⓫	我很久沒回家吃晚餐了。	I haven't gone home for dinner in a long time. * 此句用「現在完成式」（...haven't gone...） 　表示「過去持續到現在的事」。
⓬	晚餐我總是吃太多。	I always eat too much for dinner.
⓭	我總是草草解決我的晚餐。	I always take care of my dinner in a hurry. * **take care of dinner**（解決晚餐、吃晚餐） * **in a hurry**（草草、倉促）
⓮	我偶爾在高級餐廳吃晚餐。	I'll go to a fancy restaurant for dinner occasionally. * **fancy restaurant**（高級餐廳） * 此句用「未來簡單式」（...will...） 　表示「某人經常性的習慣」。
⓯	為了減肥我晚餐吃得少。	I eat a light dinner to lose weight. * **eat a light dinner**（吃少量的晚餐）
⓰	週末我回家和父母共進晚餐。	On weekends, I go back to my parents' for dinner. * **go back to my parents'**（回父母家）

	單字	音標	詞性	意義	字頻	大考	英檢	多益
❶	bring	[brɪŋ]	v.	攜帶	1	1	初級	
	food	[fud]	n.	食物	1	1	初級	◎
	home	[hom]	n.	家	1	1	初級	
	dinner	[ˋdɪnɚ]	n./v.	晚餐/吃晚餐	1	1	初級	
❷	usually	[ˋjuʒʊəlɪ]	adv.	通常	1		初級	◎
❸	seldom	[ˋsɛldəm]	adv.	很少	2	3	初級	◎
	family	[ˋfæməlɪ]	n.	家人	1	1	初級	
❹	cook	[kʊk]	v.	煮飯	1	1	初級	◎
	myself	[maɪˋsɛlf]	pron.	我自己	1		初級	
❺	often	[ˋɔfən]	adv.	常常	1	1	初級	
	eat	[it]	v.	吃	1	1	初級	
	out	[aʊt]	adv.	在外	1	1	初級	
❻	friend	[frɛnd]	n.	朋友	1	1	初級	
❼	used	[juzd]	p.p.	use（習慣）過去分詞	1	2	初級	◎
	having	[ˋhævɪŋ]	n.	have（吃）動名詞	1	1	初級	
	late	[let]	adj.	晚的	1	1	初級	◎
❽	asked	[æskt]	p.t.	ask（邀約）過去式	1	1	初級	
	tonight	[təˋnaɪt]	adv.	今晚	1	1	初級	
❾	too	[tu]	adv.	過於	1	1	初級	
	busy	[ˋbɪzɪ]	adj.	忙碌的	1	1	初級	
❿	instant	[ˋɪnstənt]	adj.	速食的	2	2	初級	◎
	noodles	[ˋnudl̩z]	n.	noodle（麵食）複數	3	2	初級	
	sometimes	[ˋsʌm͵taɪmz]	adv.	有時候	1	1	初級	
⓫	gone	[gɔn]	p.p.	go（去）過去分詞	1	1	初級	
	long	[lɔŋ]	adj.	長的	1	1	初級	
	time	[taɪm]	n.	時間	1	1	初級	◎
⓬	always	[ˋɔlwez]	adv.	總是	1	1	初級	
	much	[mʌtʃ]	adv.	許多地、大量地	1	1	初級	
⓭	take	[tek]	v.	採取	1	1	初級	◎
	care	[kɛr]	n.	處理	1	1	初級	◎
	hurry	[ˋhɝɪ]	n.	急忙、倉促	2	2	初級	◎
⓮	go	[go]	v.	去	1	1	初級	
	fancy	[ˋfænsɪ]	adj.	高級的	2	3	初級	◎
	restaurant	[ˋrɛstərənt]	n.	餐廳	1	2	初級	
	occasionally	[əˋkeʒənl̩ɪ]	adv.	偶爾	1			
⓯	light	[laɪt]	adj.	少量的	1	1	初級	
	lose	[luz]	v.	減少	1	2	初級	◎
	weight	[wet]	n.	體重	1	1	初級	◎
⓰	weekend	[ˋwik`ɛnd]	n.	週末	1	1	初級	
	back	[bæk]	adv.	返回	1	1	初級	◎
	parents	[ˋpɛrənts]	n.	parent（雙親）複數	2	1		

※「紅字單字」於本單元多句出現，「單字級等分析」僅列在「首次出現句」。

🔘 MP3 041-02 ❶～❼

❶	你吃晚餐了嗎？	Did you have your dinner? * 此句用「過去簡單式問句」（Did...?） 　表示「在過去是否發生某事？」。
❷	你為什麼不吃晚餐？	Why didn't you have your dinner? * Why didn't you...?（為何你當時不做…？）
❸	你真的不吃晚餐嗎？	Do you really not want any dinner? * not want any＋某物（不想要某物）
❹	你通常幾點吃晚餐？	What time do you usually have dinner? * What time...?（幾點…？）
❺	你都這麼晚吃晚餐嗎？	Do you always have your dinner this late?
❻	你的晚餐通常吃什麼？	What do you usually have for dinner?
❼	你會自己下廚煮晚餐嗎？	Do you cook dinner yourself? * cook oneself（自己下廚）
❽	你常在外面吃晚餐嗎？	Do you often go out for dinner?
❾	你每天回家吃晚餐嗎？	Do you go home for dinner every day?
❿	晚餐吃這麼多，你不怕胖嗎？	You ate so much for dinner, aren't you worried about your weight? * aren't you worried about...?（你不擔心…嗎）
⓫	你晚上常跟朋友聚餐嗎？	Do you often have dinner with your friends? * friends（朋友）可替換為：family（家人）
⓬	加班時你怎麼解決晚餐？	What do you do for dinner when you have to work overtime? * What do you do...?（你會怎麼做…？） * work overtime（加班）
⓭	你常去餐廳吃晚餐嗎？	Do you often go to restaurants for dinner?
⓮	你的晚餐吃得少嗎？	Do you have light dinners?
⓯	你的晚餐會吃泡麵嗎？	Do you have instant noodles for dinner?
⓰	今晚你想吃什麼嗎？	What would you like for dinner? * would like（想要） * for dinner（作為晚餐）
⓱	晚上你有吃飽嗎？	Did you get enough to eat at dinner?

	單字	音標	詞性	意義	字頻	大考	英檢	多益
❶	have	[hæv]	v.	吃/必須	1	1	初級	
	dinner	[ˈdɪnɚ]	n.	晚餐	1	1	初級	
❸	really	[ˈrɪəlɪ]	adv.	真的	1		初級	
	want	[wɒnt]	v.	想要	1	1	初級	◎
	any	[ˈɛnɪ]	adj.	任何的	1	1	初級	
❹	time	[taɪm]	n.	時間	1	1	初級	◎
	usually	[ˈjuʒʊəlɪ]	adv.	通常	1		初級	◎
❺	always	[ˈɔlwez]	adv.	總是	1	1	初級	
	this	[ðɪs]	adv.	這麼	1	1	初級	
	late	[let]	adv.	晚地	1	1	初級	◎
❼	cook	[kʊk]	v.	煮飯	1	1	初級	◎
	yourself	[jʊɚˈsɛlf]	pron.	你自己	1		初級	
❽	often	[ˈɔfən]	adv.	常常	1	1	初級	
	go	[go]	v.	去	1	1	初級	
	out	[aʊt]	adv.	在外	1	1	初級	
❾	home	[hom]	n.	家	1	1	初級	
	every	[ˈɛvrɪ]	adj.	每一	1	1	初級	
	day	[de]	n.	天	1	1	初級	
❿	ate	[et]	p.t.	eat（吃）過去式	1	1	初級	
	so	[so]	adv.	如此	1		初級	
	much	[mʌtʃ]	adv.	許多地、大量地	1		初級	
	worried	[ˈwɜɪd]	adj.	擔心的	2	1	中級	◎
	weight	[wet]	n.	體重	1	1	初級	◎
⓫	friend	[frɛnd]	n.	朋友	1	1	初級	
⓬	do	[du]	v.	做	1	1	初級	
	work	[wɜk]	v.	工作	1	1	初級	◎
	overtime	[ˌovɚˈtaɪm]	adv.	超時地	3			◎
⓭	restaurant	[ˈrɛstərənt]	n.	餐廳	1	2	初級	
⓮	light	[laɪt]	adj.	少量的	1	1	初級	
⓯	instant	[ˈɪnstənt]	adj.	速食的	2	2	初級	◎
	noodles	[ˈnudl̩s]	n.	noodle（麵食）複數	3	2	初級	
⓰	like	[laɪk]	v.	想要	1	1	初級	
⓱	get	[gɛt]	v.	獲得	1	1	初級	◎
	enough	[əˈnʌf]	adv.	足夠地	1	1	初級	◎
	eat	[it]	v.	吃	1	1	初級	

※「紅字單字」於本單元多句出現，「單字級等分析」僅列在「首次出現句」。

MP3 042-01 ❶～❶

❶	我最愛喝可樂。	Coke is my favorite. ＊某物＋**is my favorite**（某物是我的最愛）
❷	我只喝開水。	I drink only water.
❸	我每天至少喝 2000cc 的水。	I drink at least two liters of water every day. ＊**at least**（至少）
❹	我每天早上喝牛奶。	I have milk every morning.
❺	我偏愛冷飲。	I'm partial to cold drinks. ＊**be partial to**（偏愛）
❻	我從不喝冰飲。	I never touch iced drinks. ＊**I never touch**＋某物（我從不碰某物） ＊此句用「現在簡單式」（...**touch**...） 　表示「經常如此的事」。
❼	我經常嘗試各種不同的飲料。	I'm always trying all kinds of drinks. ＊**all kinds of**（各式不同的） ＊此句用「現在進行式」（..**am trying**...） 　表示「現階段發生的事」。
❽	我冬天常喝熱巧克力。	I often drink lots of hot chocolate during winter. ＊**during**＋季節（在某季節）
❾	我習慣飯後喝一杯茶。	I'm used to having a cup of tea after meals. ＊**be used to**＋動詞-**ing**（習慣） ＊**after meals**（用餐後）
❿	我很少喝運動飲料。	I seldom drink sports drinks.
⓫	我每天喝一杯鮮榨果汁。	I have a glass of fresh juice every day. ＊**fresh juice**（新鮮果汁）
⓬	我一直都不喝汽水。	I've never drunk any soda. ＊此句用「現在完成式」（...**have never drunk**...） 　表示「過去到現在持續的事」。
⓭	我喝咖啡提神。	I drink coffee to wake myself up. ＊**wake myself up**（讓自己清醒）
⓮	我不喝酒。	I never drink. ＊**I drink sometimes.**（我偶爾會喝酒）
⓯	我都喝黑咖啡。	I drink my coffee black.
⓰	我酒量很差。	I can't hold my liquor. ＊**I can hold my liquor.**（我酒量很好）

	單字	音標	詞性	意義	字頻	大考	英檢	多益
❶	Coke	[kok]	n.	可樂	6	1	初級	
	favorite	[ˈfevərɪt]	adj.	最喜歡的	1	1	初級	◎
❷	drink	[drɪŋk]	v.	喝/喝酒	1	1	初級	
	only	[ˈonlɪ]	adv.	只有	1	1	初級	
	water	[ˈwɔtɚ]	n.	開水	1	1	初級	
❸	least	[list]	n.	最少	1	1	初級	◎
	two	[tu]	n.	二	1	1	初級	
	liter	[ˈlitɚ]	n.	公升	5	6	初級	
	every	[ˈɛvrɪ]	adj.	每一	1	1	初級	
	day	[de]	n.	天	1	1	初級	
❹	have	[hæv]	v.	喝	1	1	初級	
	milk	[mɪlk]	n.	牛奶	1	1	初級	
	morning	[ˈmɔrnɪŋ]	n.	早上	1	1	初級	
❺	partial	[ˈpɑrʃəl]	adj.	偏愛的	2	4	中級	◎
	cold	[kold]	adj.	冷的	1	1	初級	
	drink	[drɪŋk]	n.	飲料	1	1	初級	
❻	never	[ˈnɛvɚ]	adv.	從不	1	1	初級	
	touch	[tʌtʃ]	v.	碰	1	1	初級	◎
	iced	[aɪst]	adj.	冰的	5	1	初級	
❼	always	[ˈɔlwez]	adv.	總是	1	1	初級	
	trying	[ˈtraɪɪŋ]	p.pr.	try（嘗試）現在分詞	6	1	初級	
	all	[ɔl]	adj.	所有的	1	1	初級	
	kind	[kaɪnd]	n.	種類	1	1	初級	◎
❽	often	[ˈɔfən]	adv.	常常	1	1	初級	
	lot	[lɑt]	n.	許多				
	hot	[hɑt]	adj.	熱的	1	1	初級	
	chocolate	[ˈtʃɑkəlɪt]	n.	巧克力	1	2	初級	
	winter	[ˈwɪntɚ]	n.	冬天	1	1	初級	
❾	used	[juzd]	p.p.	use（習慣）過去分詞	1	2	初級	◎
	having	[ˈhævɪŋ]	n.	have（喝）動名詞	1	1	初級	
	cup	[kʌp]	n.	一杯	1	1	初級	
	tea	[ti]	n.	茶	1	1	初級	
	meal	[mil]	n.	用餐	1	2	初級	
❿	seldom	[ˈsɛldəm]	adv.	很少	2	3	初級	◎
	sports	[sports]	adj.	運動的	1	1	初級	
⓫	glass	[glæs]	n.	一杯	1	1	初級	
	fresh	[frɛʃ]	adj.	新鮮的	1	1	初級	
	juice	[dʒus]	n.	果汁	1	1	初級	
⓬	drunk	[drʌŋk]	p.p.	drink（喝）過去分詞	2	3	中級	
	any	[ˈɛnɪ]	adj.	任何的	1	1	初級	
	soda	[ˈsodə]	n.	汽水	2	1	初級	
⓭	coffee	[ˈkɔfɪ]	n.	咖啡	1	1	初級	
	wake	[wek]	v.	清醒	1	2	初級	
	myself	[maɪˈsɛlf]	pron.	我自己	1	1	初級	
	up	[ʌp]	adv.	起來	1	1	初級	
⓯	black	[blæk]	adj.	（咖啡）不加牛奶的	1	1	初級	
⓰	hold	[hold]	v.	忍受	1	1	初級	
	liquor	[ˈlɪkɚ]	n.	酒	3	4	中級	

※「紅字單字」於本單元多句出現，「單字級等分析」僅列在「首次出現句」。

🔊 MP3 042-02 ❶～⓱

❶	你要喝茶、喝咖啡還是喝水？	Do you want tea, coffee or water? * **Do you want A or B?**（你想要 A 或 B？）
❷	你每天喝水嗎？	Do you drink water every day?
❸	你常喝哪些飲料？	What do you usually drink?
❹	你喜歡冷飲還是熱飲？	Do you like cold or hot drinks? * **Do you like A or B?**（你喜歡 A 或 B？） * **cold drinks**（冷飲） * **hot drinks**（熱飲）
❺	你喜歡可樂嗎？	Do you like Coke?
❻	你喝茶會失眠嗎？	Can you sleep after drinking tea? * **Can you...?**（你是否能夠…） * **after drinking tea**（在喝茶之後）
❼	你一天喝多少水？	How much water do you drink per day? * **How much＋不可數名詞...?**（…有多少？）
❽	你每天喝咖啡嗎？	Do you have coffee every day?
❾	你喝酒嗎？	Do you drink alcohol? * **drink alcohol**（喝酒）= **drink**
❿	你喝運動飲料嗎？	Do you drink sports drinks?
⓫	你喜歡嘗試不同口味的飲料嗎？	Do you like to try different-flavored drinks? * **Do you like to try...?**（你是否喜歡嘗試…？）
⓬	你喝優酪乳嗎？	Do you drink yogurt? * **milk**（牛奶）
⓭	每人每天應該攝取 2000cc 的水分。	Everyone should drink two liters of water every day.
⓮	你喜歡喝汽水嗎？	Do you like soda?
⓯	你的酒量好嗎？	Can you hold your liquor? * **hold one's liquor**（酒量好）
⓰	你曾經喝醉嗎？	Have you ever got drunk? * **Have you ever...?**（你是否有…經驗） * **get drunk**（喝醉）
⓱	小孩子大多愛喝甜的飲料。	Most kids prefer sweet drinks. * **sweet drinks**（甜飲）

單字級等分析

	單字	音標	詞性	意義	字頻	大考	英檢	多益
❶	want	[wɑnt]	v.	想要	1	1	初級	◎
	tea	[ti]	n.	茶	1	1	初級	
	coffee	[ˋkɔfɪ]	n.	咖啡	1	1	初級	
	water	[ˋwɔtɚ]	n.	開水	1	1	初級	
❷	drink	[drɪŋk]	v./n.	喝/飲料	1	1	初級	
	every	[ˋɛvrɪ]	adj.	每一	1	1	初級	
	day	[de]	n.	天	1	1	初級	
❸	usually	[ˋjuʒʊəlɪ]	adv.	通常	1		初級	◎
❹	like	[laɪk]	v.	喜歡	1	1	初級	
	cold	[kold]	adj.	冷的	1	1	初級	
	hot	[hɑt]	adj.	熱的	1	1	初級	
❺	Coke	[kok]	n.	可樂	6	1	初級	
❻	sleep	[slip]	v.	睡覺	1	1	初級	
	drinking	[ˋdrɪŋkɪŋ]	n.	drink（喝）動名詞	2	1	初級	
❼	much	[mʌtʃ]	adj.	許多的	1	1	初級	
❽	have	[hæv]	v.	喝	1	1	初級	
❾	alcohol	[ˋælkə.hɔl]	n.	酒	1	4	中級	
❿	sports	[spɔrts]	adj.	運動的	1	1	初級	
⓫	try	[traɪ]	v.	嘗試	1	1	初級	
	different-flavored	[ˋdɪfərənt`flevɚd]	adj.	不同口味的				
⓬	yogurt	[ˋjogɚt]	n.	優酪乳	3	4	中級	
⓭	everyone	[ˋɛvrɪ.wʌn]	pron.	每個人	1		初級	
	two	[tu]	n.	二	1	1	初級	
	liter	[ˋlitɚ]	n.	公升	5	6	初級	
⓮	soda	[ˋsodə]	n.	汽水	2	1	初級	
⓯	hold	[hold]	v.	忍受	1	1	初級	
	liquor	[ˋlɪkɚ]	n.	酒	3	4	中級	
⓰	ever	[ˋɛvɚ]	adv.	曾經	1	1	初級	
	got	[gɑt]	p.p.	get（變成）過去分詞	1	1	初級	◎
	drunk	[drʌŋk]	adj.	喝醉的	2	3	中級	
⓱	many	[ˋmɛnɪ]	adj.	許多的	1	1	初級	
	kid	[kɪd]	n.	小孩	1	1	初級	
	prefer	[prɪˋfɝ]	v.	偏愛	1	2	初級	◎
	sweet	[swit]	adj.	甜的	1	1	初級	

※「紅字單字」於本單元多句出現，「單字級等分析」僅列在「首次出現句」。

MP3 043-01 ❶～⓰

❶	心情不好我就食不下嚥。	I can't eat when I'm sad. * **I can't eat**（我會吃不下） * **when ＋子句**（在…時）
❷	我喜歡重口味。	I prefer strong-flavored food.
❸	我沒有胃口。	I have no appetite. * **I have a good appetite.**（我胃口很好）
❹	我挑食。	I'm picky on food. * **I'm not picky on food.**（我不挑食） * **be picky on food**（挑食）= **be picky about food**
❺	我的食量很大。	I eat like a horse.
❻	我喜歡吃辣。	I enjoy spicy food. * **I enjoy ＋食物**（我愛吃某食物）
❼	我吃東西的速度很快。	I eat quickly.
❽	我吃素。	I'm a vegetarian.
❾	我吃得很清淡。	I have a light diet.　* **light diet**（清淡的飲食）
❿	我喜歡嘗試沒吃過的食物。	I like to try food I've never tried before. * **food (that) ＋子句**（…的食物） * 子句用「現在完成式」（...have never tried...） 　表示「過去到現在不曾有的經驗」。
⓫	我經常暴飲暴食。	I often eat and drink excessively. * **eat and drink excessively**（暴飲暴食）
⓬	我習慣睡前吃宵夜。	I'm used to having night snacks. * **have night snacks**（吃宵夜）
⓭	我的三餐定時定量。	I have three square meals a day. * **have three square meals**（三餐定時定量）
⓮	我通常只吃八分飽。	I normally don't eat until I'm full. * **I normally...**（我通常…） * **eat until I'm full**（吃到最飽）
⓯	我的晚餐經常外食。	I often dine out.　* **dine out**（在外面吃晚餐）
⓰	我的食量變大了。	I'm eating more now. * 此句用「現在進行式」（...am eating...） 　表示「現階段發生的事」。

	單字	音標	詞性	意義	字頻	大考	英檢	多益
❶	eat	[it]	v.	吃	1	1	初級	
	sad	[sæd]	adj.	心情不好的	1	1	初級	
❷	prefer	[prɪˋfɝ]	v.	偏愛	1	2	初級	◎
	strong-flavored	[ˋstrɔŋˋflevəd]	adj.	重口味的				
	food	[fud]	n.	食物	1	1	初級	◎
❸	have	[hæv]	v.	擁有/吃	1	1	初級	
	appetite	[ˋæpə͵taɪt]	n.	胃口	2	2	中級	◎
❹	picky	[ˋpɪkɪ]	adj.	挑食的	7			
❺	horse	[hɔrs]	n.	馬	1	1	初級	
❻	enjoy	[ɪnˋdʒɔɪ]	v.	享受	1	2	初級	
	spicy	[ˋspaɪsɪ]	adj.	辣的	3	4	中級	
❼	quickly	[ˋkwɪklɪ]	adv.	快速地	1			
❽	vegetarian	[͵vɛdʒəˋtɛrɪən]	n.	素食者	4	4	中級	◎
❾	light	[laɪt]	adj.	清淡的	1	1	初級	
	diet	[ˋdaɪət]	n.	飲食	1	3	初級	◎
❿	like	[laɪk]	v.	喜歡	1	1	初級	
	try	[traɪ]	v.	嘗試	1	1	初級	
	never	[ˋnɛvɚ]	adv.	從未	1	1	初級	
	tired	[traɪd]	p.p.	try（嘗試）過去分詞	7	1	初級	
⓫	often	[ˋɔfən]	adv.	常常	1	1	初級	
	drink	[drɪŋk]	v.	喝	1	1	初級	
	excessively	[ɪkˋsɛsɪvlɪ]	adv.	過度地	5			
⓬	used	[juzd]	p.p.	use（習慣）過去分詞	1	2	初級	◎
	having	[ˋhævɪŋ]	n.	have（吃）動名詞	1	1	初級	
	night	[naɪt]	n.	夜間	1	1	初級	
	snack	[snæk]	n.	點心	2	2	初級	◎
⓭	three	[θri]	n.	三	1	1	初級	
	square	[skwɛr]	adj.	定量的	1	2	初級	◎
	meal	[mil]	n.	一餐	1	2	初級	
	day	[de]	n.	一天	1	1	初級	
⓮	normally	[ˋnɔrml̩ɪ]	adv.	通常	1		中級	
	full	[fʊl]	adj.	吃飽的	1	1	初級	
⓯	dine	[daɪn]	v.	用餐	3	3	中級	◎
	out	[aʊt]	adv.	在外	1	1	初級	
⓰	eating	[ˋitɪŋ]	p.pr.	eat（吃）現在分詞	2	1	初級	
	more	[mor]	adv.	更多地	1	1	初級	
	now	[naʊ]	adv.	現在	1	1	初級	

🎵 MP3 043-02 ❶～❽

❶	你的食量大嗎？	Are you consuming a lot of food? * 此句用「現在進行式問句」(Are...consuming...?) 　表示「詢問對方現階段是否發生某事？」。 * consume a lot of food（吃很多食物）
❷	你都吃的這麼清淡嗎？	Do you always have such light meals? * greasy（油膩的）
❸	你吃素嗎？	Are you a vegetarian? * Are you＋身分?（你是某身分的人嗎）
❹	你的食慾好嗎？	Do you have a good appetite? * have a good appetite（食慾好、胃口好）
❺	你挑食嗎？	Are you a picky eater? * picky eater（挑食的人）
❻	你經常在外吃晚餐嗎？	Do you usually dine out?
❼	你自己下廚嗎？	Do you cook for yourself?
❽	你能吃辣嗎？	Can you handle spicy food? * handle spicy food（能吃辣）
❾	你三餐定時定量嗎？	Are you having three square meals?
❿	你吃東西速度快嗎？	Do you eat quickly?
⓫	你習慣吃宵夜嗎？	Are you used to having nighttime snacks? * Are you used to＋動詞-ing?（你是否習慣做…？）
⓬	你喜歡嘗試各種食物嗎？	Do you like to try different kinds of food? * Do you like to try＋名詞?（你是否喜歡嘗試…？）
⓭	你都吃這麼少嗎？	Do you always eat like a bird? * eat like a bird（食量小） * eat like a horse（食量大）
⓮	你是不是沒胃口？	You have no appetite, do you?
⓯	你經常暴飲暴食嗎？	Do you usually eat and drink excessively?
⓰	你習慣吃零食嗎？	Are you used to having snacks?
⓱	你是有厭食症嗎？	Are you anorexic? * Are you＋形容詞?（你是否…？）
⓲	你應該要多吃一點。	You should eat more.

	單字	音標	詞性	意義	字頻	大考	英檢	多益
❶	consuming	[kən`sumɪŋ]	p.pr.	consume（吃）現在分詞		4	中高	◎
	lot	[lɑt]	n.	許多				
	food	[fud]	n.	食物	1	1	初級	◎
❷	always	[`ɔlwez]	adv.	總是	1	1	初級	
	have	[hæv]	v.	吃	1	1	初級	
	such	[sʌtʃ]	adv.	這麼	1	1	初級	
	light	[laɪt]	adj.	清淡的	1	1	初級	
	meal	[mil]	n.	一餐	1	2	初級	
❸	vegetarian	[ˌvɛdʒə`tɛrɪən]	n.	素食者	4	4	中級	◎
❹	good	[gʊd]	adj.	良好的	1	1	初級	◎
	appetite	[`æpə.taɪt]	n.	胃口	2	2	中級	◎
❺	picky	[`pɪkɪ]	adj.	挑食的	7			
	eater	[`itɚ]	n.	食客	5			
❻	usually	[`juʒʊəlɪ]	adv.	經常	1		初級	◎
	dine	[daɪn]	v.	用餐	3	3	中級	◎
	out	[aʊt]	adv.	在外	1	1	初級	
❼	cook	[kʊk]	v.	煮飯	1	1	初級	◎
	yourself	[jʊɚ`sɛlf]	pron.	你自己	1		初級	
❽	handle	[`hændl]	v.	應付	1	2	初級	◎
	spicy	[`spaɪsɪ]	adj.	辣的	3	4	中級	
❾	having	[`hævɪŋ]	p.pr.	have（吃）現在分詞	1	1	初級	
	three	[θri]	n.	三	1	1	初級	
	square	[skwɛr]	adj.	定量的	1	2	初級	◎
❿	eat	[it]	v.	吃	1	1	初級	
	quickly	[`kwɪklɪ]	adv.	快速地	1			
⓫	used	[juzd]	p.p.	use（習慣）過去分詞	1	2	初級	◎
	having	[`hævɪŋ]	n.	have（吃）動名詞	1	1	初級	
	nighttime	[`naɪt.taɪm]	adj.	夜間的	4			
	snack	[snæk]	n.	點心	2	2	初級	◎
⓬	like	[laɪk]	v.	喜歡	1	1	初級	
	try	[traɪ]	v.	嘗試	1	1	初級	
	different	[`dɪfərənt]	adj.	不同的	1	1	初級	◎
	kind	[kaɪnd]	n.	種類	1	1	初級	◎
⓭	bird	[bɜd]	n.	鳥	1	1	初級	
⓯	drink	[drɪŋk]	v.	喝	1	1	初級	
	excessively	[ɪk`sɛsɪvlɪ]	adv.	過度地	5			
⓱	anorexic	[ˌænə`rɛsɪk]	adj.	厭食的				
⓲	more	[mor]	adv.	更多地	1	1	初級	

※「紅字單字」於本單元多句出現，「單字級等分析」僅列在「首次出現句」。

🔊 MP3 044-01 ❶～⓮

❶	我愛吃的食物很多。	There are many kinds of food that I love. * **many kinds of...**（很多類型的…） * 某物＋**that I love**（我喜愛的某物）
❷	我不能一天不吃水果。	I can't go one day without fruit. * **go one day without**＋某物（度過沒有某物的一天）
❸	我是標準的肉食主義者。	I'm a total meat lover. * **a total**＋某食物＋**lover**（標準的某食物愛好者）
❹	我喜歡吃蔬菜。	I like vegetables. * **rice**（米飯）、**seafood**（海鮮）
❺	我超愛吃辣。	I'm crazy about spicy food. * **be crazy about**＋某物（熱愛某物）
❻	我對甜食和零嘴來者不拒。	I love all kinds of sweets and snacks. * **all kinds of**（各式各樣的）
❼	我喜歡到夜市吃小吃。	I love going to the night market for snacks. * **for snacks**（為了小吃）
❽	我偏愛中國料理。	I have a weakness for Chinese food. * **have a weakness for**＋某物（無法抗拒某物）
❾	我喜歡焗烤食物。	I love food cooked au gratin. * **food cooked au gratin**（焗烤食物）
❿	我偏愛油炸食物。	I prefer deep-fried foods.
⓫	我最近迷上義大利麵。	I've been crazy about spaghetti lately. * **I've been**＋形容詞（我已經處於…狀態）
⓬	夏天一定要吃刨冰。	Shaved ice is a must in summertime. * **shaved ice**（刨冰） * 某物＋**is a must**（某物是不可或缺的東西）
⓭	冬天我喜歡吃熱騰騰的食物。	I love steaming hot food in wintertime. * **steaming hot food**（熱騰騰的食物）
⓮	我喜歡台灣特有的木瓜牛奶。	I like papaya milk, which is peculiar to Taiwan. * **papaya milk**（木瓜牛奶） * **pearl milk tea**（珍珠奶茶） * **be peculiar to**＋某地（某地特有的）

	單字	音標	詞性	意義	字頻	大考	英檢	多益
❶	there	[ðɛr]	adv.	有…	1	1	初級	
	many	[ˋmɛnɪ]	adj.	許多的	1	1	初級	
	kind	[kaɪnd]	n.	種類	1	1	初級	◎
	food	[fud]	n.	食物	1	1	初級	◎
	love	[lʌv]	v.	喜愛	1	1	初級	
❷	go	[go]	v.	度過	1	1	初級	
	one	[wʌn]	n.	一	1	1	初級	
	day	[de]	n.	天	1	1	初級	
	fruit	[frut]	n.	水果	1	1	初級	
❸	total	[ˋtotl]	adj.	完全的	1	1	初級	◎
	meat	[mit]	n.	肉類	1	1	初級	
	lover	[ˋlʌvɚ]	n.	愛好者	1	2	初級	
❹	like	[laɪk]	v.	喜歡	1	1	初級	
	vegetable	[ˋvɛdʒətəbl]	n.	蔬菜	1	1	初級	◎
❺	crazy	[ˋkrezɪ]	adj.	狂熱的、著迷的	1	2	初級	
	spicy	[ˋspaɪsɪ]	adj.	辣的	3	4	中級	
❻	all	[ɔl]	adj.	全部的	1	1	初級	
	sweet	[swit]	n.	甜的	1	1	初級	
	snack	[snæk]	n.	甜點	2	2	初級	◎
❼	going	[ˋgoɪŋ]	n.	go（去）動名詞	4	1	初級	
	night	[naɪt]	n.	夜晚	1	1	初級	
	market	[ˋmɑrkɪt]	n.	市場	1	1	初級	◎
❽	have a weakness	[hæv ə ˋwiknɪs]	v.	無法抗拒				◎
	Chinese	[ˋtʃaɪniz]	adj.	中國的	1		初級	
❾	cooked	[kʊkt]	p.p.	cook（煮飯）過去分詞	3	1	初級	◎
	au gratin	[ˌou·ˋgrætæn]	adj.	焗烤的				
❿	prefer	[prɪˋfɝ]	v.	偏愛	1	2	初級	◎
	deep-fried	[ˋdip.fraɪd]	adj.	油炸的	8			
⓫	spaghetti	[spəˋgɛtɪ]	n.	義大利麵	4	3	初級	
	lately	[ˋletlɪ]	adv.	最近	2	4	中級	
⓬	shaved	[ʃevd]	p.p.	shave（刨）過去分詞	7	3	中級	
	ice	[aɪs]	n.	冰	1	1	初級	
	must	[mʌst]	n.	不可或缺的東西	1	1	初級	◎
	summertime	[ˋsʌmɚ.taɪm]	n.	夏天	5			
⓭	steaming	[ˋstimɪŋ]	adj.	冒出熱氣的	4	2	初級	
	hot	[hɑt]	adj.	熱的	1	1	初級	
	wintertime	[ˋwɪntɚ.taɪm]	n.	冬天	8			
⓮	papaya	[pəˋpaɪə]	n.	木瓜	6	2	初級	
	milk	[mɪlk]	n.	牛奶	1	1	初級	
	peculiar	[prˋkjuljɚ]	adj.	特有的	2	4	中級	◎
	Taiwan	[ˋtaɪˋwɑn]	n.	台灣			初級	

※「紅字單字」於本單元多句出現，「單字級等分析」僅列在「首次出現句」。

044　你喜歡的食物？

❶	你喜歡什麼樣的食物？	What kind of food do you like? * **What kind of**＋名詞**...?**（是什麼樣的…？）
❷	你喜歡吃飯、吃麵還是麵包？	Do you like rice, noodles or bread? * **Do you like A, B or C?**（你喜歡A或B或C？）
❸	你喜歡肉類還是海鮮？	Do you like meat or seafood?
❹	你最喜歡什麼水果？	What kinds of fruit do you like the best?
❺	你喜歡喝湯嗎？	Do you like soup?
❻	你喜歡吃辣嗎？	Do you like something hot? * **something hot**（辣的東西） * **hot**（辛辣的）＝ **spicy**
❼	你偏好哪一國的料理？	Which nation's cuisine do you prefer? * **Which nation's cuisine...?** 　（哪一個國家的料理…？）
❽	你喜歡中式還是西式的食物？	Do you prefer Chinese style or Western style food? * **Do you prefer A or B?**（你比較喜歡 A 還是 B？）
❾	你喜歡速食嗎？	Do you like fast food?
❿	你常到夜市吃東西嗎？	Do you often eat at the night market?
⓫	你喜歡熱騰騰的食物嗎？	Do you like your food steaming hot?
⓬	你喜歡重口味的食物嗎？	Do you like strongly flavored food? * **strongly flavored food**（重口味的食物）
⓭	你喜歡吃麥當勞還是肯德基？	Do you like McDonald's or KFC?
⓮	你喜歡義式料理嗎？	Do you like Italian food?
⓯	你喜歡又酸又辣的食物嗎？	Do you like spicy and sour food? * **spicy and sour**（又辣又酸）
⓰	你喜歡燒烤的食物嗎？	Do you like roasted food? * **deep-fried**（油炸的）
⓱	你喜歡吃生的東西嗎？	Do you like to eat raw food? * **raw food**（生食）
⓲	哇，我以前不知道你這麼愛甜食！	Wow, I didn't know you were such a lover of sweet food! * **I didn't know**＋子句（我以前不知道…）

	單字	音標	詞性	意義	字頻	大考	英檢	多益
❶	kind	[kaɪnd]	n.	種類	1	1	初級	◎
	food	[fud]	n.	食物	1	1	初級	◎
	like	[laɪk]	v.	喜歡	1	1	初級	
❷	rice	[raɪs]	n.	米飯	1	1	初級	
	noodles	[ˈnudls]	n.	noodle（麵食）複數	3	2	初級	
	bread	[brɛd]	n.	麵包	1	1	初級	
❸	meat	[mit]	n.	肉類	1	1	初級	
	seafood	[ˈsiˌfud]	n.	海鮮	3		中級	
❹	best	[bɛst]	adv.	最好地	1	1	初級	
❺	soup	[sup]	n.	湯	2	1	初級	
❻	something	[ˈsʌmθɪŋ]	pron.	某事物	1	1	初級	
	hot	[hɑt]	adj.	辣的/熱的	1	1	初級	
❼	nation	[ˈneʃən]	n.	國家	1	1	初級	◎
	cuisine	[kwɪˈzin]	n.	料理	3	5	中高	◎
	prefer	[prɪˈfɝ]	v.	偏愛	1	2	初級	◎
❽	Chinese	[ˈtʃaɪˈniz]	adj.	中式的	1		初級	
	style	[staɪl]	n.	風格	1	3	初級	◎
	Western	[ˈwɛstən]	adj.	西式的	1	2	初級	
❾	fast	[fæst]	adj.	速食的	1	1	初級	
❿	often	[ˈɔfən]	adv.	常常	1	1	初級	
	eat	[it]	v.	吃	1	1	初級	
	night	[naɪt]	n.	夜晚	1	1	初級	
	market	[ˈmɑrkɪt]	n.	市場	1	1	初級	◎
⓫	steaming	[ˈstimɪŋ]	adj.	冒出熱氣的	4	2	初級	
⓬	strongly	[ˈstrɔŋlɪ]	adv.	濃烈地	1			
	flavored	[ˈflevəd]	adj.	口味的	8	3	中級	
⓮	Italian	[ɪˈtæljən]	adj.	義式的	1			
⓯	spicy	[ˈspaɪsɪ]	adj.	辣的	3	4	中級	
	sour	[saur]	adj.	酸的	2	1	初級	◎
⓰	roasted	[ˈrostɪd]	adj.	燒烤的	3	3	中級	◎
⓱	raw	[rɔ]	adj.	生的	1	3	中級	◎
⓲	wow	[waʊ]	int.	哇！	2		中級	
	know	[no]	v.	知道	1	1	初級	◎
	such	[sʌtʃ]	adv.	這麼	1	1	初級	
	lover	[ˈlʌvɚ]	n.	愛好者	1	2	初級	
	sweet	[swit]	adj.	甜的	1	1	初級	

※「紅字單字」於本單元多句出現，「單字級等分析」僅列在「首次出現句」。

045　我討厭的食物。

❶	我很挑食，很多東西不吃。	I'm picky; there is a lot of food that I won't eat. * **be picky**（挑食） * **food that I won't eat**（我不願意吃的食物）
❷	我從來不吃青菜。	I never touch green vegetables.
❸	我討厭油膩的食物。	I hate greasy food. * **hate＋名詞**（討厭…） 　＝ **detest＋名詞 ＝ dislike＋名詞**
❹	我討厭食物沒有嚼勁。	I don't like food that's not chewy. * **food that's not＋形容詞**（不具…特質的食物）
❺	我討厭吃米飯。	I detest rice.
❻	我最討厭吃苦瓜了。	I hate bitter gourd the most.
❼	我不愛喝湯。	I don't like soup.
❽	我不吃零食。	I don't eat snacks.
❾	我不喜歡吃酸的食物。	I'm not fond of sour food. * **be not fond of**（不喜歡） * **be fond of**（喜歡）
❿	我討厭蔥的味道。	I hate the smell of green onions. * **the smell of＋食物**（某食物的味道）
⓫	我覺得臭豆腐很臭。	I think that stinky tofu is really smelly. * **stinky tofu**（臭豆腐） * **really smelly**（很臭的）
⓬	我不敢吃生食。	Ew, I don't want to eat raw food. * **I don't want to...**（我不想要…）
⓭	我討厭魚腥味。	I hate fishy food. * **fishy food**（有魚腥味的食物）
⓮	我小時候最怕吃青椒。	I hated to eat green peppers when I was little. * **I hate to...**（我討厭…） * **when I was little**（我小時候） * 此句用「過去簡單式」（...hated...） 　表示「發生在過去的事」。
⓯	我不吃肥肉。	I don't eat fat.
⓰	我不吃冷掉的食物。	I don't eat food that's cold.
⓱	我討厭吃速食。	I dislike fast food.

單字級等分析

	單字	音標	詞性	意義	字頻	大考	英檢	多益
❶	picky	[ˋpɪkɪ]	adj.	挑食的	1	1	初級	
	there	[ðɛr]	adv.	有…	1	1	初級	
	lot	[lɑt]	n.	許多				
	food	[fud]	n.	食物	1	1	初級	◎
	eat	[it]	v.	吃	1	1	初級	
❷	never	[ˋnɛvɚ]	adv.	從不	1	1	初級	
	touch	[tʌtʃ]	v.	碰	1	1	初級	◎
	green	[grin]	adj.	綠色的	1	1	初級	
	vegetable	[ˋvɛdʒətəbl]	n.	蔬菜	1	1	初級	◎
❸	hate	[het]	v.	討厭	1	1	初級	
	greasy	[ˋgrizɪ]	adj.	油膩的	4	4	中級	
❹	like	[laɪk]	v.	喜歡	1	1	初級	
	chewy	[ˋtʃuɪ]	adj.	有嚼勁的	8			
❺	detest	[dɪˋtɛst]	v.	厭惡	6			
	rice	[raɪs]	n.	米飯	1	1	初級	
❻	bitter	[ˋbɪtɚ]	adj.	苦的	2	2	初級	
	gourd	[gord]	n.	葫蘆屬植物	6			
	most	[most]	adv.	最	1	1	初級	
❼	soup	[sup]	n.	湯	2	1	初級	
❽	snack	[snæk]	n.	甜點	2	2	初級	◎
❾	fond	[fɑnd]	adj.	喜歡的	3	3	中級	
	sour	[saʊr]	adj.	酸的	2		初級	◎
❿	smell	[smɛl]	n.	味道	1	1	初級	◎
	onion	[ˋʌnjən]	n.	洋蔥	1	2	初級	
⓫	think	[θɪŋk]	v.	認為	1	1	初級	
	stinky	[ˋstɪŋkɪ]	adj.	臭的	8			
	tofu	[ˋtofu]	n.	豆腐	4	2	初級	
	really	[ˋrɪəlɪ]	adv.	很、十分	1	1	初級	
	smelly	[ˋsmɛlɪ]	adj.	難聞的	6			
⓬	ew	[ə]	int.	噁！	2			
	want	[wɑnt]	v.	想要	1	1	初級	◎
	raw	[rɔ]	adj.	生的	1	3	中級	◎
⓭	fishy	[ˋfɪʃɪ]	adj.	有魚腥味的	7			
⓮	hated	[ˋhetɪd]	p.t.	hate（討厭）過去式	6	1	初級	
	pepper	[ˋpɛpɚ]	n.	胡椒屬植物	1	2	初級	
	little	[ˋlɪtl]	adj.	幼小的	1	1	初級	
⓯	fat	[fæt]	n.	肥肉	1	1	初級	
⓰	cold	[kold]	adj.	冷掉的	1	1	初級	
⓱	dislike	[dɪsˋlaɪk]	v.	討厭	3	3	中級	
	fast	[fæst]	adj.	速食的	1	1	初級	

※「紅字單字」於本單元多句出現，「單字級等分析」僅列在「首次出現句」。

MP3 045-02 ❶～❶

❶	你討厭什麼樣的食物？	What kinds of food don't you like? * **What kinds of food...?**（什麼樣的食物…？）
❷	你很多東西不吃嗎？	Is there much you won't eat? * **Is there much...?**（是否有很多…）
❸	你和我一樣不吃青菜嗎？	Do you not eat green vegetables, like me? * **Do you not＋動詞原形...?**（你是否不做…）
❹	你討厭吃肉嗎？	Do you hate meat?
❺	你完全不碰過度加工的食物嗎？	So you completely avoid over-processed food? * **So＋問句?**（那麼，是…囉？） * **over-processed food**（過度加工的食品）
❻	你為什麼討厭吃青菜？	Why do you hate green vegetables?
❼	你討厭吃苦瓜嗎？	Do you hate bitter gourd? * **bitter gourd**（苦瓜）
❽	你受不了魚腥味嗎？	So you can't stand the smell of fish? * **can't stand＋某物**（無法忍受某物）
❾	你從來不吃水果嗎？	Haven't you ever eaten fruit?
❿	你害怕蒜的味道嗎？	Are you afraid of the smell of garlic? * **Are you afraid of...?**（你是否害怕…）
⓫	你對甜食完全沒興趣嗎？	Are you completely immune to the charms of sweets? * **be immune to＋某物**（對某物無動於衷） * **the charms of sweets**（甜食的吸引力）
⓬	你害怕吃肥肉嗎？	Are you avoiding fat? * **avoid＋食物**（拒吃某食物）
⓭	你不喜歡吃酸的東西嗎？	Don't you like things that taste sour? * **Don't you like...?**（你不喜歡…嗎）
⓮	你覺得臭豆腐很臭嗎？	Do you think that stinky tofu smells?
⓯	你都沒吃，食物不合胃口嗎？	You haven't had a bite. Isn't this to your liking? * **haven't had a bite**（從剛才到現在一口都沒吃） * **to one's liking**（合胃口）
⓰	你害怕吃榴槤嗎？	Do you not eat durian?

	單字	音標	詞性	意義	字頻	大考	英檢	多益
❶	kind	[kaɪnd]	n.	種類	1	1	初級	◎
	food	[fud]	n.	食物	1	1	初級	◎
	like	[laɪk]	v.	喜歡	1	1	初級	
❷	there	[ðɛr]	adv.	有…	1	1	初級	
	much	[mʌtʃ]	adv.	許多的	1	1	初級	
	eat	[it]	v.	吃	1	1	初級	
❸	green	[grin]	adj.	綠色的	1	1	初級	
	vegetable	[ˋvɛdʒətəb!]	n.	蔬菜	1	1	初級	◎
❹	hate	[het]	v.	討厭	1	1	初級	
	meat	[mit]	n.	肉類	1	1	初級	
❺	so	[so]	adv.	那麼	1	1	初級	
	completely	[kəmˋplitlɪ]	adv.	完全地	1			
	avoid	[əˋvɔɪd]	v.	避免	1	2	初級	◎
	over-processed	[ˋovəˋprɑsɛst]	adj.	過度加工的				
❼	bitter	[ˋbɪtə]	adj.	苦的	2	2	初級	
	gourd	[gord]	n.	葫蘆屬植物	6			
❽	stand	[stænd]	v.	忍受	1		初級	◎
	smell	[smɛl]	n./v.	味道/發出惡臭	1	1	初級	◎
	fish	[fɪʃ]	n.	魚類	1	1	初級	
❾	ever	[ˋɛvə]	adv.	曾經	1	1	初級	
	eaten	[ˋitn]	p.p.	eat（吃）過去分詞	1	1	初級	
	fruit	[frut]	n.	水果	1	1	初級	
❿	afraid	[əˋfred]	v.	害怕的	1	1	初級	
	garlic	[ˋgarlɪk]	n.	大蒜	2	3	中級	
⓫	immune	[ɪˋmjun]	adj.	無動於衷的	2	6	中高	◎
	charm	[tʃɑrm]	n.	吸引力	2	3	中級	
	sweet	[swit]	n.	甜食	1	1	初級	
⓬	avoiding	[əˋvɔɪdɪŋ]	p.pr.	avoid（避免）現在分詞	1	2	初級	◎
	fat	[fæt]	n.	肥肉	1	1	初級	
⓭	thing	[θɪŋ]	n.	東西	1	1	初級	
	taste	[test]	v.	嘗起來	1	1	初級	◎
	sour	[saʊr]	adj.	酸的	2	1	初級	◎
⓮	think	[θɪŋk]	v.	認為	1	1	初級	
	stinky	[ˋstɪŋkɪ]	adj.	臭的	8			
	tofu	[ˋtofu]	n.	豆腐	4	2	初級	
⓯	had	[hæd]	p.p.	have（吃）過去分詞	1	1	初級	
	bite	[baɪt]	n.	一口	2	1	初級	
	this	[ðɪs]	pron.	這個	1	1	初級	
	liking	[ˋlaɪkɪŋ]	n.	喜好、愛好	6	1	初級	
⓰	durian	[ˋdurɪən]	n.	榴槤				

※「紅字單字」於本單元多句出現，「單字級等分析」僅列在「首次出現句」。

MP3 046-01 ❶ ~ ❸

❶	我的父母親離婚了。	My parents are divorced.
❷	我的父親已經退休。	My father is retired. * be＋形容詞（處於…狀態） * 此句用「現在簡單式」（...is...） 　表示「目前的狀態」。
❸	我必須照顧父母親。	I have to take care of my parents. * take care of（照顧）
❹	我的父親身體不好。	My father's health is not so good.
❺	我的母親已經過世了。	My mother passed away. * pass away（過世） * 此句用「過去簡單式」（...passed...） 　表示「發生在過去的事」。
❻	做決定前，我會找父母親商量。	I consult my parents before I make any decisions. * consult＋某人（請教某人） * before＋子句（…之前） * make a decision（做決定）
❼	我和父親有代溝。	There is a generation gap between my father and me. * There is a generation gap（有代溝） * between A and B（在 A 和 B 之間）
❽	我的母親像我的朋友一樣。	My mother is like my friend. * A is like B（A 像 B 一樣）
❾	父母親贊成我的工作。	My parents approve of my job. * approve of（贊成）
❿	父母親對我很嚴格。	My parents are strict with me. * be strict with＋某人（對某人嚴格）
⓫	我的父母親希望我趕快結婚。	My parents hope that I will get married soon. * 某人＋hope that＋子句（某人希望…） * 子句用「未來簡單式」（...will...） 　表示「在未來將發生的事」。
⓬	父母親從不干涉我的生活。	My parents never interfere in my life. * interfere in（干涉、打擾）
⓭	我的父母親結婚三十年了。	My parents have been married for 30 years. * have been...for＋一段時間（持續…狀態一段時間）

單字級等分析

	單字	音標	詞性	意義	字頻	大考	英檢	多益
❶	parents	[ˋpɛrənts]	n.	parent（雙親）複數	2	1		
	divorced	[dəˋvɔrst]	p.p.	divorce（離婚）過去分詞	3	4	中高	◎
❷	father	[ˋfɑðə]	n.	父親	1	1	初級	
	retired	[ˋrɪtaɪrd]	adj.	退休的	2	4	中高	◎
❸	have	[hæv]	v.	必須	1	1	初級	
	take	[tek]	v.	採取	1	1	初級	◎
	care	[kɛr]	n.	照顧	1	1	初級	◎
❹	health	[hɛlθ]	n.	健康	1	1	初級	◎
	so	[so]	adv.	那麼	1	1	初級	
	good	[gʊd]	adj.	良好的	1	1	初級	◎
❺	mother	[ˋmʌðə]	n.	母親	1	1	初級	
	passed	[pæst]	p.t.	pass（過世）過去式	1	1	初級	◎
	away	[əˋwe]	adv.	消失	1	1	初級	
❻	consult	[kənˋsʌlt]	v.	商量、諮詢	2	4	中級	◎
	make	[mek]	n.	做出	1	1	初級	
	any	[ɛnɪ]	adj.	任何的	1	1	初級	
	decision	[dɪˋsɪʒən]	n.	決定	1	2	初級	◎
❼	there	[ðɛr]	adv.	有…	1	1	初級	
	generation	[ˌdʒɛnəˋreʃən]	n.	世代	1	4	初級	◎
	gap	[gæp]	n.	差距、隔閡	1	3	中級	◎
❽	friend	[frɛnd]	n.	朋友	1	1	初級	
❾	approve	[əˋpruv]	v.	贊成	1	3	中級	◎
	job	[dʒɑb]	n.	工作	1	1	初級	
❿	strict	[strɪkt]	adj.	嚴格的	2	2	中級	◎
⓫	hope	[hop]	v.	希望	1	1	初級	
	get	[gɛt]	v.	變成	1	1	初級	◎
	married	[ˋmærɪd]	p.p.	marry（結婚）過去分詞	1		初級	
	soon	[sun]	adv.	很快	1	1	初級	
⓬	never	[ˋnɛvə]	adv.	從不	1	1	初級	
	interfere	[ˌɪntəˋfɪr]	v.	干涉、打擾	2	4	中級	◎
	life	[laɪf]	n.	生活	1	1	初級	
⓭	year	[ˋjɪr]	n.	年	1	1	初級	

※「紅字單字」於本單元多句出現，「單字級等分析」僅列在「首次出現句」。

046 你的父母親？

MP3 046-02 ❶～❶

❶	你的父親幾歲？	How old is your father? * **How old is**＋某人？（某人年紀多大？）
❷	你的父親退休了嗎？	Is your father retired?
❸	你的父親身體健康嗎？	Is your father healthy?
❹	你必須照顧父母親嗎？	Do you need to take care of your parents? * **Do you...?**（你平常是否…？）
❺	你和母親感情好嗎？	Do you get along with your mother? * **get along with**＋某人（和某人相處融洽）
❻	你和父親有代溝嗎？	Is there a generation gap between you and your father? * **generation gap between A and B** （A 與 B 之間的代溝）
❼	你常和父親聊天嗎？	Do you chat with your father frequently? * **chat with**＋某人（和某人聊天）
❽	你會和父母親商量事情嗎？	Do you discuss things with your parents? * **discuss with**＋某人（和某人討論商量）
❾	你的父母親給你零用錢嗎？	Do your parents give you an allowance?
❿	你和父母親多久聯絡一次？	How often do you contact your parents? * **How often do you...?**（你平常多久一次…？）
⓫	你的父母親結婚幾年了？	How many years have your parents been married? * **How many years have...?**（…持續多少年？）
⓬	你的父母親對你有什麼期望？	What are your parents' expectations for you? * **What are...?**（…是什麼？） * **parents' expectation**（父母的期望） * **for you**（針對你）
⓭	你的母親會催你結婚嗎？	Does your mother urge you to get married soon? * **urge**＋某人＋**to**＋動詞原形（催促某人做某事） * **get married**（結婚）
⓮	你的父母親會干涉你的私生活嗎？	Do your parents interfere in your privacy? * **privacy**（隱私）＝ **private life**
⓯	你的母親喜歡你交的朋友嗎？	Does your mother like the friends you make? * **the friends you make**（你交的朋友）

單字級等分析

	單字	音標	詞性	意義	字頻	大考	英檢	多益
❶	old	[old]	adj.	…歲	1	1	初級	
	father	[ˋfɑðɚ]	n.	父親	1	1	初級	
❷	retired	[ˋrɪtaɪrd]	adj.	退休的	2	4	中高	◎
❸	healthy	[ˋhɛlθɪ]	adj.	健康的	1	2	初級	◎
❹	need	[nid]	v.	需要	1	1	初級	◎
	take	[tek]	v.	採取	1	1	初級	◎
	care	[kɛr]	n.	照顧	1	1	初級	◎
	parents	[ˋpɛrənts]	n.	parent（雙親）複數	2	1		
❺	get	[gæp]	v.	相處/變成	1	1	初級	◎
	along	[əˋlɔŋ]	adv.	一起	1	1	初級	
	mother	[ˋmʌðɚ]	n.	母親	1	1	初級	
❻	there	[ðɛr]	adv.	有…	1	1	初級	
	generation	[ˌdʒɛnəˋreʃən]	n.	世代	1	4	初級	◎
	gap	[gɛt]	n.	差距、隔閡	1	3	中級	◎
❼	chat	[tʃæt]	v.	聊天	2	3	中級	
	frequently	[ˋfrikwəntlɪ]	adv.	頻繁地	1			◎
❽	discuss	[dɪˋskʌs]	v.	討論	1	2	初級	◎
	thing	[θɪŋ]	n.	事情	1	1	初級	
❾	give	[gɪv]	v.	給	1	1	初級	
	allowance	[əˋlaʊəns]	n.	零用錢	3	4	中級	◎
❿	often	[ˋɔfən]	adv.	常常	1	1	初級	
	contact	[kənˋtækt]	v.	聯絡	1	2	初級	◎
⓫	many	[ˋmɛnɪ]	adj.	許多的	1	1	初級	
	year	[jɪr]	n.	年	1	1	初級	
	married	[ˋmærɪd]	p.p.	marry（結婚）過去分詞	1		初級	
⓬	expectation	[ˌɛkspɛkˋteʃən]	n.	期望	1	3	初級	◎
⓭	urge	[ɝdʒ]	v.	催促	1	4	中級	◎
	soon	[sun]	adv.	很快	1	1	初級	
⓮	interfere	[ˌɪntɚˋfɪr]	v.	干涉、打擾	2	4	中級	◎
	privacy	[ˋpraɪvəsɪ]	n.	隱私	2	4	中級	◎
⓯	like	[laɪk]	v.	喜歡	1	1	初級	
	friend	[frɛnd]	n.	朋友	1	1	初級	
	make	[mek]	v.	結交	1	1	初級	

※「紅字單字」於本單元多句出現，「單字級等分析」僅列在「首次出現句」。

🔊 MP3 047-01 ❶～⓮

❶	我只有一個哥哥。	I only have an elder brother.
❷	我有兩個姊姊和一個弟弟。	I have two elder sisters and a younger brother. * **I have...**（我擁有…）
❸	我和兄弟姊妹感情很好。	I have a close relationship with my siblings. * **have a close relationship with**＋某人 　（和某人感情好）
❹	我是大家庭，有很多兄弟姊妹。	I have a big family with many brothers and sisters. * **a big family with**＋家人（包含某種家人的大家庭）
❺	我姊姊很照顧我。	My elder sister takes care of me. * **take care of**（照顧）＝ **look after**
❻	我是獨生子。	I am the only son in my family. * **the only son**（獨生子） * **the only daughter**（獨生女）
❼	我跟兄弟姊妹無話不談。	There are no secrets between me and my siblings. * **There be no**＋名詞（沒有…） * **secrets between A and B**（A 和 B 之間的秘密）
❽	我很希望有個妹妹。	I wish I had a younger sister.
❾	我和兄弟姊妹的性格截然不同。	My personality is totally different from my siblings. * **be totally different from**＋某人（和某人完全不同）
❿	我和妹妹常吵架。	I'm always quarrelling with my younger sister. * **be always**＋動詞-ing（總是發生某件令人厭惡的事） * 此句用「現在進行式」（...am...quarrelling...） 　表示「現階段經常發生、且令人厭惡的事」。
⓫	我和兄弟姊妹經常互相幫忙。	My siblings and I usually help each other.
⓬	我和哥哥是雙胞胎。	My elder brother and I are twins.
⓭	我們兄弟姊妹從事不同的行業。	My siblings and I are engaged in different occupations. * **be engaged in**＋職業（從事某職業）
⓮	我的弟弟妹妹還在唸書。	My younger brother and sister are still studying right now.

	單字	音標	詞性	意義	字頻	大考	英檢	多益
❶	only	[`onlɪ]	adv.	只有	1	1	初級	
	have	[hæv]	v.	擁有	1	1	初級	
	elder	[`ɛldɚ]	adj.	較年長的	2	2	初級	
	brother	[`brʌðɚ]	n.	哥哥	1	1	初級	
❷	two	[tu]	n.	二	1	1	初級	
	sister	[`sɪstɚ]	n.	姐姐、妹妹	1	1	初級	
	younger	[`jʌŋɡɚ]	adj.	young（年輕的）比較級	1	1	初級	
❸	close	[`klos]	adj.	感情好的	1	1	初級	◎
	relationship	[rɪ`leʃən`ʃɪp]	n.	關係	1	2	中級	◎
	sibling	[`sɪblɪŋ]	n.	兄弟姊妹	2			
❹	big	[bɪɡ]	adj.	大的	1	1	初級	
	family	[`fæməlɪ]	n.	家庭	1	1	初級	
	many	[`mɛnɪ]	adj.	許多的	1	1	初級	
❺	take	[tek]	v.	採取	1	1	初級	◎
	care	[kɛr]	n.	照顧	1	1	初級	◎
❻	son	[sʌn]	n.	兒子	1	1	初級	
❼	there	[ðɛr]	adv.	有…	1	1	初級	
	secret	[`sikrɪt]	n.	秘密	1	2	初級	◎
❽	wish	[wɪʃ]	v.	希望	1	1	初級	
	had	[hæd]	p.t.	have（擁有）過去式	1	1	初級	
❾	personality	[ˌpɝsn`ælətɪ]	n.	個性	1	3	中級	
	totally	[`totlɪ]	adv.	完全地	1			◎
	different	[`dɪfərənt]	adj.	不同	1	1	初級	◎
❿	always	[`ɔlwez]	adv.	總是	1	1	初級	
	quarrelling	[`kwɔrəlɪŋ]	p.pr.	quarrel（吵架）現在分詞	2	3	中級	◎
⓫	usually	[`juʒuəlɪ]	adv.	經常	1	1	初級	◎
	help	[hɛlp]	v.	幫助	1	1	初級	
	each	[itʃ]	pron.	每個、各個	1	1	初級	
	other	[`ʌðɚ]	pron.	另一方	1	1	初級	
⓬	twin	[twɪn]	n.	雙胞胎	1	3	中級	◎
⓭	engaged	[ɪn`gedʒd]	p.p.	engage（從事）過去分詞	4	3	中高	◎
	occupation	[ˌɑkjə`peʃən]	n.	職業	2	4	中級	◎
⓮	still	[stɪl]	adv.	仍然	1	1	初級	◎
	studying	[`stʌdɪŋ]	p.pr.	study（唸書）現在分詞	1	1	初級	◎
	right	[raɪt]	adv.	正值	1	1	初級	
	now	[nau]	adv.	現在	1	1	初級	

※「紅字單字」於本單元多句出現，「單字級等分析」僅列在「首次出現句」。

🔵 MP3 047-02 ❶～⓯

❶	你有兄弟姊妹嗎？	Do you have any siblings? * siblings（兄弟姊妹）＝ brothers or sisters
❷	你和兄弟姊妹的感情好嗎？	Do you get along with your brothers and sisters? * get along with＋某人（和某人相處融洽）
❸	你有幾個兄弟姊妹？	How many brothers and sisters do you have? * How many＋可屬名詞?（…有多少？）
❹	你是家裡唯一的小孩嗎？	Are you the only child in your family? * Are you＋身分?（你是否是某身分？）
❺	你和兄弟姊妹經常說話嗎？	Do you often speak to your siblings? * Do you often...?（你是否經常…？）
❻	你的弟弟妹妹還在唸書嗎？	Are your younger brother and sister still studying now?
❼	你的姊姊多大？	How old is your elder sister? * How old is＋某人?（某人年紀多大？）
❽	你會照顧弟弟妹妹嗎？	Do you take care of your younger brother and sister?
❾	你的哥哥姊姊很照顧你嗎？	Do your elder brother and sister look after you? * look after＋某人（照顧某人）
❿	你的兄弟姊妹在工作了嗎？	Are your brothers and sisters working right now? * Are＋某人＋動詞-ing?（某人目前是否正在…？）
⓫	你和兄弟姊妹互相幫忙嗎？	Do you and your siblings help each other? * help each other（互相幫忙）
⓬	你和兄弟姊妹之間有秘密嗎？	Do you keep secrets from your brothers and sisters? * keep secrets from＋某人（和某人之間有秘密）
⓭	你和兄弟姊妹長得像嗎？	Do you look like your brothers and sisters? * A look like B（A長得像B）
⓮	你跟你哥哥是雙胞胎嗎？	Are you and your elder brother twins?
⓯	你會穿姊姊的衣服嗎？	Do you wear your elder sister's clothes?

單字級等分析

	單字	音標	詞性	意義	字頻	大考	英檢	多益
❶	have	[hæv]	v.	擁有	1	1	初級	
	any	[ˈɛnɪ]	adj.	任何的	1	1	初級	
	sibling	[ˈsɪblɪŋ]	n.	兄弟姊妹	2			
❷	get	[gɛt]	v.	相處	1	1	初級	◎
	along	[əˈlɔŋ]	adv.	一起	1	1	初級	
	brother	[ˈbrʌðɚ]	n.	哥哥、弟弟	1	1	初級	
	sister	[ˈsɪstɚ]	n.	姐姐、妹妹	1	1	初級	
❸	many	[ˈmɛnɪ]	adj.	許多的	1	1	初級	
❹	only	[ˈonlɪ]	adj.	唯一的	1	1	初級	
	child	[tʃaɪld]	n.	小孩	1	1	初級	
	family	[ˈfæməlɪ]	n.	家庭	1	1	初級	
❺	often	[ˈɔfən]	adv.	常常	1	1	初級	
	speak	[spik]	v.	說話	1	1	初級	
❻	younger	[ˈjʌŋgɚ]	adj.	young（年輕的）比較級	1	1	初級	
	still	[stɪl]	adv.	仍然	1	1	初級	◎
	studying	[ˈstʌdɪɪŋ]	p.pr.	study（唸書）現在分詞	1	1	初級	◎
	now	[naʊ]	adv.	現在	1	1	初級	
❼	old	[old]	adj.	…歲	1	1	初級	
	elder	[ˈɛldɚ]	adj.	較年長的	2	2	初級	
❽	take	[tek]	v.	採取	1	1	初級	◎
	care	[kɛr]	n.	照顧	1	1	初級	◎
❾	look	[lʊk]	v.	照顧/看起來	1	1	初級	
❿	working	[ˈwɝkɪŋ]	p.pr.	work（工作）現在分詞	2	1	中級	◎
	right	[raɪt]	adv.	正值	1	1	初級	
⓫	help	[hɛlp]	v.	幫助	1	1	初級	
	each	[itʃ]	pron.	每個、各個	1	1	初級	
	other	[ˈʌðɚ]	pron.	另一方	1	1	初級	
⓬	keep	[kip]	v.	保守	1	1	初級	◎
	secret	[ˈsikrɪt]	n.	秘密	1	2	初級	◎
⓮	twin	[twɪn]	n.	雙胞胎	1	3	中級	◎
⓯	wear	[wɛr]	v.	穿	1	1	初級	◎
	clothes	[kloz]	n.	cloth（衣服）複數	1	2	初級	

※「紅字單字」於本單元多句出現，「單字級等分析」僅列在「首次出現句」。

我的情人。

🔵 MP3 048-01 ❶～⓯

❶	我深愛我的男朋友。	I love my boyfriend very much.
❷	我和我的女朋友一見鍾情。	I fell in love with my girlfriend at first sight. * **fall in love at first sight**（一見鍾情）
❸	我的男朋友很體貼。	My boyfriend is very considerate.
❹	我的女朋友是個醋罈子。	My girlfriend is a jealous person. * **jealous person**（愛吃醋的人）
❺	我男朋友是我同事。	My boyfriend is my colleague.
❻	我和男朋友交往五年。	My boyfriend and I have been dating each other for five years. * 某人＋**and I**（我和某人） * **date each other**（交往） * 此句用「現在完成進行式」（...**have been dating**...） 　表示「從過去開始、且直到現在仍持續中的事」。
❼	我跟老婆經常起口角。	My wife and I constantly have quarrels.
❽	我和女朋友是遠距離戀愛。	My girlfriend and I have a long-distance relationship. * **long-distance relationship**（遠距離戀愛）
❾	我和女朋友每天黏在一起。	My girlfriend and I are joined at the hip. * **be joined at the hip**（如膠似漆）
❿	女朋友和我家人感情融洽。	My girlfriend gets along with my family. * **get along with**＋某人（和某人相處融洽）
⓫	我跟女朋友剛分手。	My girlfriend and I just broke up. * **break up**（分手）＝ **separate**
⓬	我和男朋友正是熱戀期。	My boyfriend and I are passionately in love. * **be passionately in love**（正在熱戀）
⓭	老公是我的初戀情人。	My husband was my first love. * **first love**（初戀）
⓮	我跟老公個性完全不同。	My husband and I have totally different personalities. * **have totally different**＋名詞（有完全不同的…）
⓯	老公每天接我上下班。	My husband picks me up from work every day. * **pick me up from work**（接送我上下班）

單字級等分析

	單字	音標	詞性	意義	字頻	大考	英檢	多益
❶	love	[lʌv]	v./n.	喜愛/戀愛	1	1	初級	
	boyfriend	[ˋbɔɪˏfrɛnd]	n.	男朋友	2		中級	
	very	[ˋvɛrɪ]	adv.	十分	1	1	初級	
	much	[mʌtʃ]	adv.	非常	1	1	初級	
❷	fell	[fɛl]	p.t.	fall（變成）過去式	7			
	girlfriend	[ˋgɝlˏfrɛnd]	n.	女朋友	2		中級	
	first	[fɝst]	adj.	第一的	1	1	初級	
	sight	[saɪt]	n.	一眼、看見	1	1	初級	◎
❸	considerate	[kənˋsɪdərɪt]	adj.	體貼的	7	5	中級	◎
❹	jealous	[ˋdʒɛləs]	adj.	嫉妒的	3	3	初級	◎
	person	[ˋpɝsn]	n.	人	1	1	初級	
❺	colleague	[ˋkɑlig]	n.	同事	1	5	中級	◎
❻	dating	[ˋdetɪŋ]	p.pr.	date（交往）現在分詞	3	1	初級	◎
	each	[itʃ]	pron.	每個、各個	1	1	初級	
	other	[ˋʌðɚ]	pron.	另一方	1	1	初級	
	five	[faɪv]	n.	五	1	1	初級	
	year	[jɪr]	n.	年	1	1	初級	
❼	wife	[waɪf]	n.	妻子	1	1	初級	
	constantly	[ˋkɑnstəntlɪ]	adv.	時常地	1			
	have	[hæv]	v.	擁有	1	1	初級	
	quarrel	[ˋkwɔrəl]	n.	吵架	5	3	中級	◎
❽	long-distance	[ˋlɔŋˏdɪstəns]	adj.	遠距離的	3			
	relationship	[rɪˋleʃənˏʃɪp]	n.	戀愛關係	1	2	中級	◎
❾	jointed	[ˋdʒɔɪntɪd]	p.p.	joint（黏在一起）過去分詞	1	1	初級	◎
	hip	[hɪp]	n.	臀部	1	2	初級	
❿	get	[gɛt]	v.	相處	1	1	初級	◎
	along	[əˋlɔŋ]	adv.	一起	1	1	初級	
	family	[ˋfæməlɪ]	n.	家人	1	1	初級	
⓫	just	[dʒʌst]	adv.	剛剛	1	1	初級	
	broke	[brok]	p.t.	break（分手）過去式	4	4	中級	◎
	up	[ʌp]	adv.	結束/接起	1	1	初級	
⓬	passionately	[ˋpæʃənɪtlɪ]	adv.	熱情地	4			
⓭	husband	[ˋhʌzbənd]	n.	丈夫	1	1	初級	
⓮	totally	[ˋtotlɪ]	adv.	完全地	1			◎
	different	[ˋdɪfərənt]	adj.	不同	1	1	初級	◎
	personality	[ˏpɝsnˋælətɪ]	n.	個性	1	3	中級	
⓯	pick	[pɪk]	v.	接某人	1	2	初級	
	work	[wɝk]	n.	工作	1	1	初級	◎
	every	[ˋɛvrɪ]	adj.	每一	1	1	初級	
	day	[de]	n.	天	1	1	初級	

※「紅字單字」於本單元多句出現，「單字級等分析」僅列在「首次出現句」。

MP3 048-02 ❶～❶❺

❶	你有心儀的對象嗎？	Is there someone you are interested in? * Is there someone＋子句？（有…的人嗎？） * be interested in（有好感）
❷	你有女朋友嗎？	Do you have a girlfriend?
❸	你喜歡什麼類型的男生？	What type of guys do you like? * What type of＋名詞＋...?（什麼類型的…？）
❹	你們怎麼認識的？	How did you meet each other? * How did you...?（你當時是如何…？）
❺	你們交往多久了？	How long is your relationship? * How long is＋名詞?（…時間多久了？）
❻	你們感情好嗎？	Do you have a good relationship? * have a good relationship（感情好）
❼	你們每天黏在一起嗎？	Do you two spend every second together? * spend every second together （每分每秒都在一起）
❽	你們常吵架嗎？	Do you fight often? * fight（吵架）＝ quarrel
❾	男朋友什麼特質吸引你？	What is it that attracted you to your boyfriend? * What is it that＋子句?（…的是什麼？） * attract A to B（讓 A 喜歡上 B）
❿	你們吵架通常是誰先低頭？	Who is the first one to apologize when you quarrel? * the first one to apologize（首先道歉的人）
⓫	老公幫你做家事嗎？	Does your husband help you with the household chores? * household chores（家事）
⓬	你們為什麼分手？	Why did you break up? * Why did you＋動詞?（為什麼你們當時…？）
⓭	你最喜歡你老公哪一點？	What do you like most about your husband?
⓮	你最受不了你老婆哪一點？	What can't you bear about your wife? * What can't you...?（什麼是你無法…？）
⓯	你們看起來很登對。	You two look like a perfect match. * look like a perfect match（看起來像天作之合）

	單字	音標	詞性	意義	字頻	大考	英檢	多益
❶	there	[ðɛr]	adv.	有…	1	1	初級	
	someone	[ˈsʌm.wʌn]	pron.	某個人	1	1	初級	
	interested	[ˈɪntərɪstɪd]	p.p.	有興趣的	1	1	初級	◎
❷	have	[hæv]	v.	擁有	1	1	初級	
	girlfriend	[ˈgɝl.frɛnd]	n.	女朋友	2		中級	
❸	type	[taɪp]	n.	類型	1	2	初級	◎
	guy	[gaɪ]	n.	男生	1	2	初級	
	like	[laɪk]	v.	喜歡	1	1	初級	
❹	meet	[mit]	v.	認識	1	1	初級	
	each	[itʃ]	pron.	每個、各個	1	1	初級	
	other	[ˈʌðɚ]	pron.	另一方	1	1	初級	
❺	long	[lɔŋ]	adj.	長的	1	1	初級	
	relationship	[rɪˈleʃənˌʃɪp]	n.	戀愛關係	1	2	中級	◎
❻	good	[gʊd]	adj.	良好的	1	1	初級	◎
❼	two	[tu]	pron.	兩人	1	1	初級	
	spend	[spɛnd]	v.	花費	1	1	初級	◎
	every	[ˈɛvrɪ]	adj.	每一	1	1	初級	
	second	[ˈsɛkənd]	n.	秒鐘	1	1	初級	◎
	together	[təˈgɛðɚ]	adv.	在一起	1	1	初級	
❽	fight	[faɪt]	v.	吵架	1	1	初級	
	often	[ˈɔfən]	adv.	常常	1	1	初級	
❾	attracted	[əˈtræktɪd]	p.t.	attract（吸引）過去式	1	3	中級	◎
	boyfriend	[ˈbɔɪ.frɛnd]	n.	男朋友	2		中級	
❿	first	[fɝst]	adj.	第一個	1	1	初級	
	one	[wʌn]	pron.	一個人	1	1	初級	
	apologize	[əˈpɑlə.dʒaɪz]	v.	道歉	2	4	初級	◎
	quarrel	[ˈkwɔrəl]	v.	吵架	5	3	中級	◎
⓫	husband	[ˈhʌz.bənd]	n.	丈夫	1	1	初級	
	help	[hɛlp]	v.	幫忙	1	1	初級	
	household	[ˈhaʊs.hold]	n.	家庭	1	4	中級	◎
	chore	[tʃor]	n.	家庭雜務	3	4	中級	◎
⓬	break	[brek]	v.	分手	1	1	初級	◎
	up	[ʌp]	adv.	結束	1	1	初級	
⓭	most	[most]	adv.	最	1	1	初級	
⓮	bear	[bɛr]	v.	忍受	1	2	初級	◎
	wife	[waɪf]	n.	妻子	1	1	初級	
⓯	look	[lʊk]	v.	看起來	1	1	初級	
	perfect	[ˈpɝfɪkt]	adj.	完美的	1	2	初級	◎
	match	[mætʃ]	n.	伴侶	1	2	初級	◎

※「紅字單字」於本單元多句出現，「單字級等分析」僅列在「首次出現句」。

049 我的朋友。

❶	我很喜歡交朋友。	I like to make friends. * like to＋動詞原形（喜歡） * make friends（交朋友）
❷	我有很多好朋友。	I have many good friends. * I don't have many good friends.（我的好朋友不多）
❸	我不擅長交朋友。	I am not good at making friends. * be not good at＋動詞-ing（不擅長做某事）
❹	朋友和我有很多共同點。	My friends and I have many things in common. * have many things in common（有很多共同點）
❺	我喜歡和朋友講電話。	I like to chat with my friends on the phone. * chat with＋某人＋on the phone（和某人講電話）
❻	我和朋友爭執後總能和好如初。	My friends and I always make up after we have a quarrel. * make up（和好）、have a quarrel（爭吵）
❼	我和朋友年紀相仿。	My friends and I are about the same age. * about the same age（年紀相仿）
❽	我和朋友有聊不完的話題。	My friends and I can chat forever. * can chat forever（可以聊天聊不完）
❾	我和朋友經常見面。	My friends and I get together frequently. * get together（聚在一起）
❿	我透過網路結交不少朋友。	I've made many friends online.
⓫	我和朋友彼此關心。	My friends and I care about each other.
⓬	我的朋友都很熱情。	All my friends are very enthusiastic.
⓭	我和很多朋友失去聯絡。	I have lost contact with many friends. * 此句用「現在完成式」（...have lost...）表示 「過去某時點發生某事，且結果持續到現在」。 * lose contact with（失去聯絡）
⓮	我有一兩個知心好友。	I have one or two intimate friends. * intimate friend（摯友）
⓯	我和朋友偶爾起爭執。	Sometimes my friends and I get into fights. * Sometimes＋主詞＋動詞（有時候…）

	單字	音標	詞性	意義	字頻	大考	英檢	多益
❶	like	[laɪk]	v.	喜歡	1	1	初級	
	make	[mek]	v.	結交/和好	1	1	初級	
	friend	[frɛnd]	n.	朋友	1	1	初級	
❷	have	[hæv]	v.	擁有	1	1	初級	
	many	[ˈmɛnɪ]	adj.	許多的	1	1	初級	
	good	[gʊd]	adj.	良好的/擅長的	1	1	初級	◎
❸	making	[ˈmekɪŋ]	n.	make（結交）動名詞	2	1	中高	
❹	thing	[θɪŋ]	n.	事物	1	1	初級	
	common	[ˈkɑmən]	adj.	共同的	1	1	初級	◎
❺	chat	[tʃæt]	v.	聊天	2	3	中級	
	phone	[fon]	n.	電話	1	2	初級	◎
❻	always	[ˈɔlwez]	adv.	總是	1	1	初級	
	up	[ʌp]	adv.	結束	1	1	初級	
	quarrel	[ˈkwɔrəl]	n.	爭吵	5	3	中級	◎
❼	about	[əˈbaʊt]	adv.	大約	1	1	初級	
	same	[sem]	adj.	相同的	1	1	初級	
	age	[edʒ]	n.	年齡	1	1	初級	◎
❽	forever	[fɚˈɛvɚ]	adv.	永遠	1	3	中級	
❾	get	[gɛt]	v.	會面、聚集/演變為…	1	1	初級	◎
	together	[təˈgɛðɚ]	adv.	在一起	1	1	初級	
	frequently	[ˈfrikwəntlɪ]	adv.	頻繁地	1			◎
❿	made	[med]	p.p.	make（結交）過去分詞	1	1	初級	
	online	[ˈɑn.laɪn]	adv.	在網路上	1		初級	◎
⓫	care	[kɛr]	v.	關心	1	1	初級	◎
	each	[itʃ]	pron.	每個、各個	1	1	初級	
	other	[ˈʌðɚ]	pron.	另一方	1	1	初級	
⓬	all	[ɔl]	adj.	所有的	1	1	初級	
	very	[ˈvɛrɪ]	adv.	十分	1	1	初級	
	enthusiastic	[ɪn.θjuzɪˈæstɪk]	adj.	熱情的	2	5	中級	◎
⓭	lost	[lɔst]	p.p.	lose（失去）過去分詞	1	2	中高	◎
	contact	[ˈkɑntækt]	n.	聯絡	1	2	初級	◎
⓮	one	[wʌn]	n.	一	1	1	初級	
	two	[tu]	n.	二	1	1	初級	
	intimate	[ˈɪntəmɪt]	adj.	親密的	2	4	中級	◎
⓯	sometimes	[ˈsʌm.taɪmz]	adv.	有時候	1	1	初級	
	fight	[faɪt]	n.	爭吵	1	1	初級	

※「紅字單字」於本單元多句出現，「單字級等分析」僅列在「首次出現句」。

🔵 MP3 049-02 ❶～❺

❶	你有很多好朋友嗎？	Do you have many good friends? * **Do you have＋名詞?**（你是否擁有…？）
❷	你常和朋友聯絡嗎？	Do you speak to your friends frequently?
❸	你喜歡交朋友嗎？	Do you like to make friends?
❹	你和朋友感情好嗎？	Do you have a good relationship with your friends? * **have a good relationship**（感情好）
❺	你會找朋友聊心事嗎？	Will you tell your friend what's on your mind? * **Will you...?**（你是否願意…？）。 * 此句用「未來簡單式問句」（**Will...?**） 　表示「有意願做的事」。 * **what's on your mind**（你的心事）
❻	你有網友嗎？	Do you have any online friends? * **online friend**（網友）
❼	你有外國朋友嗎？	Do you have any foreign friends?
❽	你和朋友興趣相同嗎？	Do you share the same interests as your friends? * **as your friends**（如同你的朋友）
❾	你和朋友多久碰面一次？	How often do you meet with your friends? * **How often do you...?**（你多久做一次…？）
❿	你和朋友會起爭執嗎？	Do you ever have arguments with your friend? * **have arguments**（爭執）＝ **get into fights**
⓫	你和朋友大多怎麼認識的？	How did you meet most of your friends? * **How did you...?**（你當時如何…？）
⓬	你的朋友曾經欺騙你嗎？	Have your friends ever cheated you? * **Have＋某人＋ever...?**（某人是否曾經做…？）
⓭	你的朋友瞭解你嗎？	Do your friends understand you?
⓮	你願意向朋友道歉嗎？	Are you willing to apologize to your friends? * **Are you willing to＋動詞原形?** 　（你是否願意…？）
⓯	你有可以信任的朋友嗎？	Do you have any friends you can trust?

	單字	音標	詞性	意義	字頻	大考	英檢	多益
❶	have	[hæv]	v.	擁有	1	1	初級	
	many	[ˋmɛnɪ]	adj.	許多的	1	1	初級	
	good	[gʊd]	adj.	良好的	1	1	初級	◎
	friend	[frɛnd]	n.	朋友	1	1	初級	
❷	speak	[spik]	v.	說話	1	1	初級	
	frequently	[ˋfrikwəntlɪ]	adv.	頻繁地	1			◎
❸	like	[laɪk]	v.	喜歡	1	1	初級	
	make	[mek]	v.	結交	1	1	初級	
❹	relationship	[rɪˋleʃənˏʃɪp]	n.	關係	1	2	中級	◎
❺	tell	[tɛl]	v.	告訴	1	1	初級	
	mind	[maɪnd]	n.	內心	1	1	初級	◎
❻	any	[ˋɛnɪ]	adj.	任何的	1	1	初級	
	online	[ˋɑnˏlaɪn]	adj.	網路上的	1		初級	◎
❼	foreign	[ˋfɔrɪn]	adj.	外國的	1	1	初級	◎
❽	share	[ʃɛr]	v.	共享	1	2	初級	◎
	same	[sem]	adj.	相同的	1	1	初級	
	interest	[ˋɪntərɪst]	n.	興趣	1	1	初級	◎
❾	often	[ˋɔfən]	adv.	常常	1	1	初級	
	meet	[mit]	v.	見面/認識	1	1	初級	
❿	ever	[ˋɛvɚ]	adv.	曾經	1	1	初級	
	argument	[ˋɑrgjəmənt]	n.	爭執	1	2	中級	◎
⓫	most	[most]	pron.	大部分	1	1	初級	
⓬	cheated	[ˋtʃitɪd]	p.p.	cheat（欺騙）過去分詞	2	2	初級	◎
⓭	understand	[ˏʌndɚˋstænd]	v.	了解	1	1	初級	
⓮	willing	[ˋwɪlɪŋ]	adj.	願意的	1	2	初級	◎
	apologize	[əˋpɑləˏdʒaɪz]	v.	道歉	2	4	初級	◎
⓯	trust	[trʌst]	n.	信任	1	2	初級	◎

※「紅字單字」於本單元多句出現，「單字級等分析」僅列在「首次出現句」。

🔊 MP3 050-01 ❶～❹

❶	我的老闆很有生意頭腦。	My boss is very business savvy. * **business savvy**（很會做生意的）
❷	我的老闆很明理。	My boss is very reasonable.
❸	我的老闆腦筋動很快。	My boss has a keen mind. * **have a keen mind**（有敏銳的頭腦）
❹	我的老闆年輕有為。	My boss is young and promising.
❺	我的老闆白手起家。	My boss started his own business. * **start one's own business**（自己創業）
❻	我的老闆是個腳踏實地的人。	My boss is a practical person.
❼	我的老闆知人善任。	My boss knows how to assign tasks to employees according to their abilities. * **know how to＋動詞原形**（知道如何做某事） * **assign tasks**（指派工作） * **according to...**（依據…）
❽	我的老闆是企業家第二代。	My boss is a second-generation entrepreneur. * **second-generation entrepreneur**（企業家第二代）
❾	我的老闆人脈很廣。	My boss has a broad social network. * **have a broad social network**（社交圈很廣）
❿	我的老闆社交手腕高明。	My boss is good at socializing. * **be good at＋動詞-ing**（擅長做某事）
⓫	我的老闆深受公司員工愛戴。	My boss is deeply respected by his/her employees. * **be deeply respected**（深受愛戴）
⓬	我的老闆非常信任自己的員工。	My boss trusts in his employees very much. * **trust in＋某人**（信任某人）
⓭	我非常敬佩我們老闆。	I admire our boss very much. * **admire＋某人＋very much**（非常敬佩某人）
⓮	我的老闆很愛罵人。	My boss loves to yell at people. * **yell at＋某人**（吼罵某人）

	單字	音標	詞性	意義	字頻	大考	英檢	多益
❶	boss	[bɔs]	n.	老闆	1	2	初級	
	very	[ˋvɛrɪ]	adv.	十分	1	1	初級	
	business	[ˋbɪznɪs]	n.	商業、商務/公司、企業	1	2	初級	◎
	savvy	[ˋsævɪ]	adj.	懂得…的、擅長…的	4			◎
❷	reasonable	[ˋriznəbl]	adj.	明理的	1	3	中級	◎
❸	have	[hæv]	v.	擁有	1	1	初級	
	keen	[kin]	adj.	敏銳的	3	4	中級	◎
	mind	[maɪnd]	n.	頭腦	1	1	初級	◎
❹	young	[jʌŋ]	adj.	年輕的	1	1	初級	
	promising	[ˋprɑmɪsɪŋ]	adj.	有前途的	2	4	中級	◎
❺	started	[ˋstɑrtɪd]	p.t.	start（開創）過去式	1	1	初級	
	own	[on]	adj.	自己的	1	1	初級	
❻	practical	[ˋpræktɪkl]	adj.	務實的	1	3	中級	◎
	person	[ˋpɜsn]	n.	人	1	1	初級	
❼	know	[no]	v.	知道	1	1	初級	◎
	assign	[əˋsaɪn]	v.	指派	1	4	中級	◎
	task	[æsk]	n.	工作	1	2	初級	◎
	employee	[ˌɛmplɔɪˋi]	n.	員工	1	3	中級	◎
	ability	[əˋbɪlətɪ]	n.	能力	1	2	初級	◎
❽	second-generation	[ˋsɛkənd ˌdʒɛnəˋreʃən]	adj.	第二代的	7			
	entrepreneur	[ˌɑntrəprəˋnɜ]	n.	企業家	2		中高	◎
❾	broad	[brɔd]	adj.	廣泛的	1	2	初級	
	social	[ˋsoʃəl]	adj.	社交的	1	2	初級	◎
	network	[ˋnɛtˌwɜk]	n.	網路	1	3	中級	◎
❿	good	[gʊd]	adj.	擅長的	1	1	初級	◎
	socializing	[ˋsoʃəˌlaɪzɪŋ]	n.	socialize（社交）動名詞	3	6	中高	◎
⑪	deeply	[ˋdiplɪ]	adv.	深深地	1			
	respected	[rɪˋspɛktɪd]	p.p.	respect（尊敬）過去分詞	3	2	中高	
⑫	trust	[trʌst]	v.	信任	1	2	初級	◎
	much	[mʌtʃ]	adv.	非常	1	1	初級	
⑬	admire	[ədˋmaɪr]	v.	敬佩	2	3	初級	◎
⑭	love	[lʌv]	v.	喜愛	1	1	初級	
	yell	[jɛl]	v.	吼罵	1	3	中級	◎
	people	[ˋpipl]	n.	person（人）複數	1	1	初級	

※「紅字單字」於本單元多句出現，「單字級等分析」僅列在「首次出現句」。

050 你的老闆？

MP3 050-02 ❶～⓰

❶	你和老闆的關係好嗎？	Do you have a good relationship with your boss?
❷	你的老闆很好溝通嗎？	Is your boss easy to communicate with? * **be easy to communicate with**（容易溝通）
❸	你喜歡你的老闆嗎？	Do you like your boss?
❹	你的老闆會接受員工的意見嗎？	Does your boss accept his/her employees' opinions? * **accept one's opinions**（採納某人的意見）
❺	你的老闆信任你嗎？	Does your boss trust you? * **trust＋某人**（信任某人）
❻	你的老闆欣賞你的才華嗎？	Does your boss appreciate your talent? * **appreciate one's talent**（欣賞某人的才華）
❼	你的老闆每天進公司嗎？	Is your boss in the office every day? * **in the office**（進公司、進辦公室）
❽	你的老闆很囉唆嗎？	Does your boss nag? ＝ Is your boss a nag?
❾	你的老闆通常幾點進公司？	What time does your boss usually arrive at the office? * **What time does＋某人...?**（某人通常幾點…？）
❿	你對你的老闆有什麼感覺？	How do you feel about your boss? * **How do you feel about...?**（你對…感覺如何？）
⓫	你的老闆經常發脾氣嗎？	Does your boss lose his temper often? * **lose one's temper**（發脾氣）
⓬	你的老闆白手起家嗎？	Did your boss start his own business? * **Did＋某人...?**（某人當時是否…？）。 * 此句用「過去簡單式問句」（**Did...?**） 　表示「在過去是否發生某事？」。
⓭	你的老闆是個怎麼樣的人？	What kind of person is your boss? * **What kind of person is＋某人?** 　（某人是什麼樣的人？）
⓮	你瞭解老闆的脾氣嗎？	Do you know your boss's temper?
⓯	你的老闆幾歲？	How old is your boss? * **How old is＋某人?**（某人幾歲…？）
⓰	你的老闆結婚了嗎？	Is your boss married?

	單字	音標	詞性	意義	字頻	大考	英檢	多益
❶	have	[hæv]	v.	擁有	1	1	初級	
	good	[gʊd]	adj.	良好的	1	1	初級	◎
	relationship	[rɪˋleʃənˏʃɪp]	n.	關係	1	2	中級	◎
	boss	[bɔs]	n.	老闆	1	2	初級	
❷	easy	[ˋizɪ]	adj.	容易的	1	1	初級	◎
	communicate	[kəˋmjunəˏket]	v.	溝通	1	3	中級	
❸	like	[laɪk]	v.	喜歡	1	1	初級	
❹	accept	[əkˋsɛpt]	v.	接受	1	2	初級	◎
	employee	[ˏɛmplɔɪˋi]	n.	員工	1	3	中級	◎
	opinion	[əˋpɪnjən]	n.	意見	1	2	中級	◎
❺	trust	[trʌst]	v.	信任	1	2	初級	
❻	appreciate	[əˋpriʃɪˏet]	v.	欣賞	1	3	初級	◎
	talent	[ˋtælənt]	n.	才華	1	2	初級	◎
❼	office	[ˋɔfɪs]	n.	公司、辦公地點	1	1	初級	◎
	every	[ˋɛvrɪ]	adj.	每一	1	1	初級	
	day	[de]	n.	天	1	1	初級	
❽	nag	[næg]	v./n.	囉嗦/囉嗦的人	5	5	中高	
❾	time	[taɪm]	n.	時間	1	1	初級	◎
	arrive	[əˋraɪv]	v.	到達	1	2	初級	◎
❿	feel	[fil]	v.	感覺	1	1	初級	
⓫	lose	[luz]	v.	失去	1	2	初級	◎
	temper	[ˋtɛmpɚ]	n.	脾氣	3	3	中級	◎
	often	[ˋɔfən]	adv.	常常	1	1	初級	
⓬	start	[stɑrt]	v.	開創	1	1	初級	
	own	[on]	adj.	自己的	1	1	初級	◎
	business	[ˋbɪznɪs]	n.	公司、企業	1	2	初級	◎
⓭	kind	[kaɪnd]	n.	種類	1	1	初級	◎
	person	[ˋpɝsn]	n.	人	1	1	初級	
⓮	know	[no]	v.	知道	1	1	初級	◎
⓯	old	[old]	adj.	…歲	1	1	初級	
⓰	married	[ˋmærɪd]	p.p.	marry（結婚）過去分詞	1		初級	

※「紅字單字」於本單元多句出現，「單字級等分析」僅列在「首次出現句」。

051　我的同事。

❶	我跟同事關係很好。	I have a good relationship with my colleagues. * have a good relationship（關係良好） * good（良好）可替換為：average（普通）、bad（惡劣）
❷	我的同事都很好相處。	All my colleagues are easy to get along with. * be easy to＋某事（很好做某事） * get along with（相處）
❸	我的同事都已婚。	All my colleagues are married.
❹	我只認識同部門的同事。	I only know colleagues from my own department. * from＋部門（來自某部門）
❺	我的同事以男性居多。	My colleagues are mostly male.
❻	我和同事會互相幫忙。	My colleagues and I always help each other. * help each other（互相幫忙）
❼	我的同事工作能力很強。	My colleague is quite good at his/her work. * be good at one's work（對自己的工作很拿手）
❽	我的同事是我的最佳拍檔。	My colleague is my best partner. * my best partner（我的最佳拍檔）
❾	我的同事喜歡聊八卦。	My colleagues like to gossip.
❿	我有些同事喜歡打小報告。	Some of my colleagues like to snitch. * some of＋名詞（其中一些…）
⓫	我的同事上班常摸魚。	My colleagues are always slacking off at work. * be always slacking off at work（老是散漫工作） * 此句用「現在進行式」（...are...slacking...） 　表示「現階段經常發生、且令人厭惡的事」。
⓬	我的同事對公司抱怨連連。	My colleagues have repeatedly complained about our company. * 此句用「現在完成式」（...have...complained...） 　表示「過去持續到現在的事」。
⓭	我很多同事最近要離職。	Many of my colleagues are going to quit. * many of＋名詞（其中很多…） * be going to（即將）、jump ship（跳槽） * 此句用「未來簡單式」（...are going to..） 　表示「未排時程、但預定要做的事」。

	單字	音標	詞性	意義	字頻	大考	英檢	多益
❶	have	[hæv]	v.	擁有	1	1	初級	
	good	[ɡʊd]	adj.	良好的/擅長的	1	1	初級	◎
	relationship	[rɪˈleʃənˌʃɪp]	n.	關係	1	2	中級	◎
	colleague	[ˈkɑliɡ]	n.	同事	1	5	中級	◎
❷	all	[ɔl]	adj.	所有的	1	1	初級	
	easy	[ˈizɪ]	adj.	容易的	1	1	初級	◎
	get	[ɡɛt]	v.	相處	1	1	初級	◎
	along	[əˈlɔŋ]	adv.	一起	1	1	初級	
❸	married	[ˈmærɪd]	p.p.	marry（結婚）過去分詞	1		初級	
❹	only	[ˈonlɪ]	adv.	只有	1	1	初級	
	know	[no]	v.	認識	1	1	初級	◎
	own	[on]	n.	自己的	1	1	初級	◎
	department	[dɪˈpɑrtmənt]	n.	部門的	1	2	初級	◎
❺	mostly	[ˈmostlɪ]	adv.	大部分	1	4	中級	
	male	[mel]	adj.	男性的	1	2	初級	
❻	always	[ˈɔlwez]	adv.	總是	1	1	初級	
	help	[hɛlp]	v.	幫助	1	1	初級	
	each	[itʃ]	pron.	每個、各個	1	1	初級	
	other	[ˈʌðɚ]	pron.	另一方	1	1	初級	
❼	quite	[kwaɪt]	adv.	相當	1	1	初級	
	work	[wɜk]	n.	工作	1	1	初級	◎
❽	best	[bɛst]	adj.	最好的	1	1	初級	
	partner	[ˈpɑrtnɚ]	n.	拍檔	1	2	初級	◎
❾	like	[laɪk]	v.	喜歡	1	1	初級	
	gossip	[ˈɡɑsəp]	v.	聊八卦	3	3	中級	◎
❿	some	[sʌm]	pron.	有些	1	1	初級	
	snitch	[snɪtʃ]	v.	告密、打小報告				
⓫	slacking	[ˈslækɪŋ]	p.pr.	slack（散漫）現在分詞	3		中高	◎
	off	[ɔf]	adv.	停滯、不在工作	1	1	初級	
⓬	repeatedly	[rɪˈpitɪdlɪ]	adv.	重複地	2		中級	
	complained	[kəmˈplend]	p.p.	complain（抱怨）過去分詞	1	2	初級	◎
	company	[ˈkʌmpənɪ]	n.	公司、企業	1	2	初級	◎
⓭	many	[ˈmɛnɪ]	pron.	許多的	1	1	初級	
	going	[ˈɡoɪŋ]	p.pr.	go（即將）現在分詞	4	1	初級	
	quit	[kwɪt]	v.	辭職	1	2	初級	◎

※「紅字單字」於本單元多句出現，「單字級等分析」僅列在「首次出現句」。

051　你的同事？

❶	你和同事感情好嗎？	Do you have a good relationship with your colleagues?
❷	你的同事好相處嗎？	Are your colleagues easy to get along with? * **be easy to get along with**（容易相處）
❸	你和同事互動頻繁嗎？	Do you interact with your colleagues frequently? * **interact with**＋某人（和某人互動）
❹	你和同事常有摩擦嗎？	Do you often have disputes with your colleagues? * **have disputes with**＋某人（和某人有爭執）
❺	你的同事男性居多還是女性？	Do you have more male colleagues or female colleagues? * **Do you have more...or...?**（你擁有較多⋯或⋯？）
❻	同事常向你吐苦水嗎？	Do your colleagues spill their complaints to you? * **spill complaints to you**（對你訴說怨言）
❼	你的同事會幫你嗎？	Do your colleagues help you?
❽	你的同事喜歡打小報告嗎？	Do your colleagues like to inform on each other? * **inform on**＋某人（向某人洩密）
❾	你曾受到同事陷害嗎？	Have you ever been framed by your colleagues? * **Have you ever been**＋過去分詞? 　（你是否曾遭受⋯？） * **be framed by**＋某人（被某人誣陷）
❿	你的同事彼此勾心鬥角嗎？	Do your colleagues ever plot against each other? * **plot against**＋某人（密謀中傷某人）
⓫	你的同事愛聊八卦嗎？	Do your colleagues like to gossip?
⓬	你的同事都比你資深嗎？	Are your colleagues senior to you? * **be senior to**＋某人（比某人資深）
⓭	你的同事已婚？還是未婚？	Is your colleague married or single?
⓮	你的同事會在背後說你的壞話嗎？	Do your colleagues talk about you behind your back? * **talk about you behind your back** 　（在你背後道是非） * **behind one's back**（暗中、在某人背後）

	單字	音標	詞性	意義	字頻	大考	英檢	多益
❶	have	[hæv]	v.	擁有	1	1	初級	
	good	[gʊd]	adj.	良好的	1	1	初級	◎
	relationship	[rɪˋleʃənˏʃɪp]	n.	關係	1	2	中級	◎
	colleague	[ˋkɑlig]	n.	同事	1	5	中級	◎
❷	easy	[ˋizɪ]	adj.	容易的	1	1	初級	◎
	get	[gɛt]	v.	相處	1	1	初級	◎
	along	[əˋlɔŋ]	adv.	一起	1	1	初級	
❸	interact	[ˏɪntəˋrækt]	v.	互動	2	4	中級	◎
	frequently	[ˋfrikwəntlɪ]	adv.	頻繁地	1			◎
❹	often	[ˋɔfən]	adv.	常常	1	1	初級	
	dispute	[dɪˋspjut]	n.	爭執	1	4	中級	◎
❺	more	[mor]	adv.	更多	1	1	初級	
	male	[mel]	adj.	男性	1	2	初級	
	female	[ˋfimel]	adv.	女性	1	2	初級	
❻	spill	[spɪl]	v.	傾訴	2	3	中級	◎
	complaint	[kəmˋplent]	n.	抱怨	1	3	中級	◎
❼	help	[hɛlp]	v.	幫忙	1	1	初級	
❽	like	[laɪk]	v.	喜歡	1	1	初級	
	inform	[ɪnˋfɔrm]	v.	告密	1	3	中級	◎
	each	[itʃ]	pron.	每個、各個	1	1	初級	
	other	[ˋʌðə]	pron.	另一方	1	1	初級	
❾	ever	[ˋɛvə]	adv.	曾經	1	1	初級	
	framed	[fremd]	p.p.	frame（陷害）過去分詞	4	4	中級	◎
❿	plot	[plɑt]	v.	密謀	2	4	中級	◎
⓫	gossip	[ˋgɑsəp]	v.	聊八卦	3	3	中級	◎
⓬	senior	[ˋsinjə]	adj.	資深的	1	4	中級	◎
⓭	married	[ˋmærɪd]	p.p.	marry（結婚）過去分詞	1		初級	
	single	[ˋsɪŋgl]	adj.	單身的	1	2	初級	◎
⓮	talk	[tɔk]	v.	講話	1	1	初級	◎
	back	[bæk]	n.	背	1	1	初級	◎

※「紅字單字」於本單元多句出現，「單字級等分析」僅列在「首次出現句」。

052　我的近況。

🔵 MP3 052-01 ❶～❻

❶	我最近很幸運。	I have been very lucky recently. * **I have been very unlucky recently.**（我最近很倒楣） * 此句用「現在完成式」（...have been...） 　表示「過去持續到現在的事」。
❷	我最近過得馬馬虎虎，沒什麼特別的。	I've been all right lately—nothing special. * **be all right**（生活過得還可以）
❸	我大病初癒。	I am just recovering from a serious illness. * **recover from**＋疾病（從某疾病康復） * **serious illness**（重病）。 * 此句用「現在進行式」（...am...recovering...） 　表示「現階段發生的事」。
❹	我最近一直很忙。	I have been busy recently.
❺	我最近累壞了。	I have been exhausted lately.
❻	我最近壓力很大。	I have been under a lot of pressure recently. * **under a lot of pressure**（壓力很大）
❼	我剛搬家。	I just moved. * 此句用「過去簡單式」（...moved...） 　表示「發生在過去的事」。
❽	我剛買新房子。	I've just bought a new house. * **have bought**＋某物（已經買了某物）
❾	我戀愛了。	I've fallen in love.　* **fall in love**（戀愛）
❿	我懷孕了。	I'm pregnant. * 此句用「現在簡單式」（...am...） 　表示「目前的狀態」。
⓫	我最近常常生病。	I've been sick a lot lately.　* **a lot**（經常）
⓬	我剛結婚。	I just got married.　* **get married**（結婚）
⓭	我剛換了新工作。	I just changed jobs. * **change a job**（換工作）＝ switch a job
⓮	我剛當爸爸。	I've just become a father. * **become a father**（成為人父）
⓯	我剛從國外回來。	I just returned from overseas. * **return from**＋某處（從某處回來）

	單字	音標	詞性	意義	字頻	大考	英檢	多益
❶	lucky	[ˈlʌkɪ]	adj.	幸運的	1	1	初級	
	recently	[ˈrisntlɪ]	adv.	最近	1		初級	
❷	all	[ɔl]	adv.	一切	1	1	初級	
	right	[raɪt]	adj.	還可以的	1	1	初級	
	lately	[ˈletlɪ]	adv.	最近	2	4	中級	
	nothing	[ˈnʌθɪŋ]	pron.	沒有事情	1	1	初級	
	special	[ˈspɛʃəl]	adj.	特別的	1	1	初級	◎
❸	just	[dʒʌst]	adv.	剛剛	1	1	初級	
	recovering	[ˈrɪkʌvəɪŋ]	p.pr.	recover（康復）現在分詞	1	3	初級	◎
	serious	[ˈsɪrɪəs]	adj.	嚴重的	1	2	初級	◎
	illness	[ˈɪlnɪs]	n.	疾病	1		中級	
❹	busy	[ˈbɪzɪ]	adj.	忙碌的	1	1	初級	
❺	exhausted	[ɪɡˈzɔstɪd]	adj.	累壞的	3	4	中級	◎
❻	lot	[lɑt]	n.	許多				
	pressure	[ˈprɛʃə]	n.	壓力	1	3	中級	◎
❼	moved	[muvd]	p.t.	move（搬家）過去式	1	1	初級	◎
❽	bought	[bɔt]	p.p.	buy（購買）過去分詞	1	1	初級	
	new	[nju]	adj.	新的	1	1	初級	
	house	[haus]	n.	房子	1	1	初級	
❾	fallen	[ˈfɔlən]	p.p.	fall（變成）過去分詞	3	1	初級	◎
	love	[lʌv]	n.	戀愛	1	1	初級	
❿	pregnant	[ˈprɛɡnənt]	adj.	懷孕的	1	4	中級	
⓫	sick	[sɪk]	adj.	生病的	1	1	初級	◎
⓬	got	[ɡɑt]	p.t.	get（變成）過去式	1	1	初級	◎
	married	[ˈmærɪd]	p.p.	marry（結婚）過去分詞	1		初級	
⓭	changed	[tʃendʒt]	p.t.	change（更換、改變）過去式	4	2	初級	◎
	job	[dʒɑb]	n.	工作	1	1	初級	
⓮	become	[bɪˈkʌm]	p.p.	become（成為）過去分詞	1	1	初級	◎
	father	[ˈfɑðə]	n.	父親	1	1	初級	
⓯	returned	[rɪˈtɜnd]	p.t.	return（返回）過去式	1	1	初級	◎
	overseas	[ˈovəˈsiz]	adv.	國外地	2	1	初級	◎

※「紅字單字」於本單元多句出現，「單字級等分析」僅列在「首次出現句」。

MP3 052-02 ❶～⓰

❶	最近過得如何？	How are you doing?
❷	最近在忙什麼？	What have you been so busy with lately? * **What have you been...?**（你最近的具體行為是…？） * **be busy with**＋某事（忙著做某事）
❸	最近忙嗎？	Have you been busy recently?
❹	你身體好嗎？	How's your health? * **How is**＋名詞?（…狀況如何？）
❺	爛攤子收拾好了嗎？	Has the mess been cleaned up yet? * **Has**＋某事物＋**been...yet?** 　（某事物是否已經…？） * **clean up the mess**（收拾殘局）
❻	最近有什麼好事發生？	Has anything positive happened lately? * **Has**＋某事物＋過去分詞**...?** 　（某事物是否曾經…？） * **anything positive**（任何好事）
❼	你怎麼失蹤了好一陣子？	How come you disappeared for a while? * **How come**＋子句?（怎麼會…？）
❽	你上次的感冒好了嗎？	Have you gotten over the cold you had last time? * **Have you...?**（你是否已經…？） * **get over**＋疾病（某疾病痊癒） * **last time**（上一次）
❾	你怎麼最近看起來很累的樣子？	Why do you look so tired lately?
❿	你的工作順利嗎？	Has work been going smoothly? * **have/has been going**＋副詞（持續進行得很…）
⓫	你買車了嗎？	Did you buy a car?
⓬	你的新工作如何？	How is your new job going?
⓭	你最近怎麼氣色不太好？	How come you don't look so well lately? * **look so well**（看起來氣色很好）
⓮	你搬家了嗎？	Did you move?
⓯	你當媽媽了嗎？	Did you become a mother?
⓰	你最近有出國嗎？	Have you gone abroad recently?

	單字	音標	詞性	意義	字頻	大考	英檢	多益
❶	doing	[`duɪŋ]	p.pr.	do（進行、進展）現在分詞	1	1	初級	
❷	so	[so]	adv.	這麼	1	1	初級	
	busy	[`bɪzɪ]	adj.	忙碌的	1	1	初級	
	lately	[`letlɪ]	adv.	最近	2	4	中級	
❸	recently	[`risntlɪ]	adv.	最近	1		初級	
❹	health	[hɛlθ]	n.	健康	1	1	初級	◎
❺	mess	[mɛs]	n.	一團糟的處境	2	3	中級	◎
	cleaned	[klind]	p.p.	clean（收拾）過去分詞	1	1	初級	
	up	[ʌp]	adv.	完全、徹底	1	1	初級	
	yet	[jɛt]	adv.	尚未	1	1	初級	◎
❻	anything	[`ɛnɪˏθɪŋ]	pron.	任時事物	1	1	初級	
	positive	[`pazətɪv]	adj.	正面的	1	2	初級	◎
	happened	[`hæpənd]	p.p.	happen（發生）過去分詞	1	1	初級	
❼	come	[kʌm]	v.	怎麼會	1	1	初級	
	disappeared	[ˏdɪsə`pɪrd]	p.t.	disappear（消失）過去式	1	2	初級	◎
	while	[hwaɪl]	n.	一段時間	1	1	初級	
❽	gotten	[`gatn]	p.p.	get（痊癒）過去分詞	1	1	初級	◎
	cold	[kold]	n.	感冒	1	1	初級	
	had	[hæd]	p.t.	have（患上）過去式	1	1	初級	
	last	[læst]	adj.	上一次的	1	1	初級	
	time	[taɪm]	n.	次、回	1	1	初級	◎
❾	look	[lʊk]	v.	看起來	1	1	初級	
	tired	[taɪrd]	adj.	疲憊的	1	1	初級	◎
❿	work	[wɝk]	n.	工作	1	1	初級	◎
	going	[`goɪŋ]	p.pr.	go（進行、進展）現在分詞	4	1	初級	
	smoothly	[`smuðlɪ]	adv.	順利地	3			◎
⓫	buy	[baɪ]	v.	購買	1	1	初級	
	car	[kɑr]	n.	車	1	1	初級	◎
⓬	new	[nju]	adj.	新的	1	1	初級	
	job	[dʒɑb]	n.	工作	1	1	初級	
⓭	well	[wɛl]	adj.	氣色好的	1	1	初級	◎
⓮	move	[muv]	v.	搬家	1	1	初級	◎
⓯	become	[bɪ`kʌm]	v.	成為	1	1	初級	◎
	mother	[`mʌðəʳ]	n.	母親	1	1	初級	
⓰	gone	[gɔn]	p.p.	go（去）過去分詞	1	1	初級	
	abroad	[ə`brɔd]	adv.	國外地	2	2	初級	◎

※「紅字單字」於本單元多句出現，「單字級等分析」僅列在「首次出現句」。

053 我最近的心情。

MP3 053-01 ❶～⓰

❶	我最近心情很好。	I have been in a terrific mood as of late. * be in a＋形容詞＋mood（心情…） * as of late（最近） * bad（不好的）、horrible（糟透的）
❷	我的心情不好不壞，沒啥特別的。	I am just so-so, nothing special.
❸	我最近情緒不太穩定。	My moods have been unstable recently.
❹	我陷入低潮。	I am in low spirits. * be in low spirits（處於低潮）
❺	我最近很怕寂寞。	Lately I've been afraid of being lonely. * Lately＋主詞＋動詞（最近…） * be afraid of（害怕） * 此句用「現在完成式」（…have been…） 表示「過去持續到現在的事」。
❻	我這陣子很沮喪。	I have been very depressed lately.
❼	我覺得人生沒意義。	I feel that life is meaningless.
❽	我最近很容易發脾氣。	Lately I've been getting mad easily. * get mad（發脾氣）
❾	我好煩。	I am so annoyed.
❿	我最近對任何事都提不起興趣。	I have been losing interest in everything lately. * lose interest in＋某事（對某事失去興趣）
⓫	我最近常流淚。	I have been crying a lot lately.
⓬	我充滿自信。	I am full of confidence. ＝ I am very self-confident. * be full of＋名詞（充滿…）
⓭	我好像得了憂鬱症。	I think I am suffering from depression. * suffer from＋疾病（罹患某疾病）
⓮	我今天心情跌到谷底。	I am feeling down today. * feel down（感覺很低落）。 * 此句用「現在進行式」（…am feeling…） 表示「現階段發生的事」。
⓯	一切雨過天晴。	Everything has been cleared up. * clear up（解決）
⓰	我充滿鬥志。	I am full of fight.

	單字	音標	詞性	意義	字頻	大考	英檢	多益
❶	terrific	[təˋrɪfɪk]	adj.	很好的	2	2	初級	◎
	mood	[mud]	n.	心情	1	3	中級	◎
	late	[let]	adv.	不久前	1	1	初級	
❷	just	[dʒʌst]	adv.	只是	1	1	初級	
	so-so	[ˋso.so]	adj.	普通的				
	nothing	[ˋnʌθɪŋ]	pron.	沒有事情	1	1	初級	
	special	[ˋspɛʃəl]	adj.	特別的	1	1	初級	◎
❸	unstable	[ʌnˋstebl]	adj.	不穩定的	3			
	recently	[ˋrisntlɪ]	adv.	最近	1		初級	
❹	low	[lo]	adj.	低的	1	1	初級	
	spirit	[ˋspɪrɪt]	n.	精神	1	2	初級	◎
❺	lately	[ˋletlɪ]	adv.	最近	2	4	中級	
	afraid	[əˋfred]	adj.	害怕的	1		初級	
	lonely	[ˋlonlɪ]	adj.	寂寞的	2	2	初級	
❻	very	[ˋvɛrɪ]	adv.	十分	1	1	初級	
	depressed	[dɪˋprɛst]	adj.	沮喪的	2	4	中級	◎
❼	feel	[fil]	v.	覺得	1	1	初級	
	life	[laɪf]	n.	人生	1	1	初級	
	meaningless	[ˋminɪŋlɪs]	adj.	無意義的	3			
❽	getting	[ˋgɛtɪŋ]	p.pr.	get（變成）現在分詞	1	1	初級	◎
	mad	[mæd]	adj.	發狂的	1	1	初級	
	easily	[ˋizɪlɪ]	adv.	容易地	1		中級	
❾	so	[so]	adv.	這麼	1	1	初級	
	annoyed	[əˋnɔɪd]	adj.	煩躁的	4	4	中級	◎
❿	losing	[ˋluzɪŋ]	p.pr.	lose（失去）現在分詞	4	2	初級	◎
	interest	[ˋɪntərɪst]	n.	興趣	1	1	初級	◎
	everything	[ˋɛvrɪ.θɪŋ]	pron.	每件事情	1		初級	
⓫	crying	[ˋkraɪɪŋ]	p.pr.	cry（哭泣）現在分詞	2	1	初級	
	lot	[lɑt]	n.	很多	1	1	初級	
⓬	full	[fʊl]	adj.	充滿的	1	1	初級	
	confidence	[ˋkɑnfədəns]	n.	信心	1	4	初級	◎
	self-confident	[ˋsɛlfˋkɑnfədənt]	adj.	自信的	8			
⓭	think	[θɪŋk]	v.	認為	1	1	初級	
	suffering	[ˋsʌfərɪŋ]	p.pr.	suffer（罹患）現在分詞	2	3	中級	◎
	depression	[dɪˋprɛʃən]	n.	憂鬱症	1	4	中級	◎
⓮	feeling	[ˋfilɪŋ]	p.pr.	feel（感覺）現在分詞	1	1	初級	
	down	[daʊn]	adj.	失落的	1	1	初級	
	today	[təˋde]	adv.	今天	1	1	初級	◎
⓯	cleared	[klɪrd]	p.p.	clear（解決）過去分詞	1	1	初級	◎
	up	[ʌp]	adv.	結束	1	1	初級	
⓰	fight	[faɪt]	n.	鬥志	1	1	初級	

※「紅字單字」於本單元多句出現，「單字級等分析」僅列在「首次出現句」。

MP3 053-02 ❶～❼

❶	你最近心情如何？	How have you been feeling recently? * How have you been...?（你從過去到現在，…如何？）
❷	你心情不好？	Are you in a bad mood? * in a bad mood（心情不好）
❸	你的心情好點沒？	Has your mood improved lately?
❹	你最近常常這麼低落嗎？	Have you often been low-spirited recently?
❺	你走出低潮了嗎？	Have you made it through your rough period? * make it through（度過） * rough period（低潮、難關）
❻	你覺得寂寞嗎？	Do you feel lonesome?
❼	一切雨過天晴了嗎？	Has everything cleared up?
❽	你最近常情緒不穩嗎？	Have your emotions been unstable recently?
❾	你過得快樂嗎？	Do you lead a happy life? * lead a happy life（生活愉快）
❿	你最近常發脾氣嗎？	Have you been losing your temper very easily of late? * lose one's temper（發脾氣）、of late（最近）
⓫	你在煩什麼？	What is annoying you? * What is＋動詞-ing?（正在…的是什麼？） * annoy＋某人（困擾某人）＝ bother＋某人
⓬	你什麼時候變得這麼多疑？	Since when did you become so suspicious? * Since when...?（從什麼時候…？）
⓭	你得了憂鬱症嗎？	Are you suffering from depression?
⓮	你怎麼心事重重的樣子？	Why do you look so upset? * look so upset（看起來很不開心）
⓯	你找回自信心了嗎？	Has your confidence returned yet? * return one's confidence（找回信心）
⓰	你情緒比較穩定了嗎？	Are your emotions more stable now?
⓱	什麼事你這麼開心？	What has made you so happy?

256

	單字	音標	詞性	意義	字頻	大考	英檢	多益
❶	feeling	[`filɪŋ]	p.pr.	feel（感覺）現在分詞	1	1	初級	
	recently	[`risntlɪ]	adv.	最近	1		初級	
❷	bad	[bæd]	adj.	不好的	1	1	初級	
	mood	[mud]	n.	心情	1	3	中級	◎
❸	improved	[ɪm`pruvd]	p.p.	improve（好轉）過去分詞	2	2	初級	◎
	lately	[`letlɪ]	adv.	最近	2	4	中級	
❹	often	[`ɔfən]	adv.	常常	1	1	初級	
	low-spirited	[`lo`spɪrɪtɪd]	adj.	低落的、低潮的				
❺	made	[med]	p.p.	make（度過）過去分詞	1	1	初級	
	rough	[rʌf]	adj.	艱難的	1	3	中級	◎
	period	[`pɪrɪəd]	n.	期間、時期	1	2	初級	◎
❻	feel	[fil]	v.	覺得	1	1	初級	
	lonesome	[`lonsəm]	adj.	寂寞的	6	5	中高	◎
❼	everything	[`ɛvrɪθɪŋ]	pron.	每件事情	1		初級	
	cleared	[klɪrd]	p.p.	clear（解決）過去分詞	1		初級	
	up	[ʌp]	adv.	結束	1		初級	
❽	emotion	[ɪ`moʃən]	n.	情緒	1	2	初級	◎
	unstable	[ʌn`stebl]	adj.	不穩定的	3			
❾	lead	[lid]	v.	度過	1	1	初級	◎
	happy	[`hæpɪ]	adj.	快樂的	1	1	初級	
	life	[laɪf]	n.	生活	1	1	初級	
❿	losing	[`luzɪŋ]	p.pr.	lose（失去）現在分詞	4	2	初級	◎
	temper	[`tɛmpɚ]	n.	脾氣	3	3	中級	◎
	very	[`vɛrɪ]	adv.	十分	1	1	初級	
	easily	[`izɪlɪ]	adv.	容易地	1		中級	
	late	[let]	adv.	不久前	1	1	初級	
⓫	annoying	[ə`nɔɪɪŋ]	p.pr.	annoy（困擾）現在分詞	3	4	中級	◎
⓬	become	[bɪ`kʌm]	v.	變為	1	1	初級	◎
	so	[so]	adv.	這麼	1	1	初級	
	suspicious	[sə`spɪʃəs]	adj.	多疑的	2	4	中級	◎
⓭	suffering	[`sʌfərɪŋ]	p.pr.	suffer（罹患）現在分詞	2	3	中級	◎
	depression	[dɪ`prɛʃən]	n.	憂鬱症	1	4	中級	
⓮	look	[luk]	v.	看起來	1	1	初級	
	upset	[ʌp`sɛt]	adj.	不開心的	2	3	中級	◎
⓯	confidence	[`kɑnfədəns]	n.	信心	1	4	中級	◎
	returned	[rɪ`tɜnd]	p.p.	return（返回）過去分詞	1	1	初級	
	yet	[jɛt]	adv.	尚未	1	1	初級	◎
⓰	more	[mor]	adv.	更加	1	1	初級	
	stable	[`stebl]	adj.	穩定的	2	3	中級	◎
	now	[nau]	adv.	現在	1	1	初級	
	made	[med]	p.p.	make（使得）過去分詞	1	1	初級	

※「紅字單字」於本單元多句出現，「單字級等分析」僅列在「首次出現句」。

MP3 054-01 ❶～❹

❶	我正在找工作。	I am looking for a job. * be looking for＋某物（正在找尋某物） * 此句用「現在進行式」（...am looking...） 　表示「現階段發生的事」。
❷	我正在努力戒煙。	I am trying to give up smoking. * give up＋動詞-ing（戒除…）＝ quit＋動詞-ing * drink（喝酒）
❸	我正在學英文。	I am studying English right now.
❹	我正在減肥。	I am trying to lose some weight. ＝ I am on a diet. * try to＋動詞原形（嘗試）
❺	我正在學開車。	I am learning how to drive. * learn how to＋動詞原形（學習如何做某事） * swim（游泳） * cook（做菜）
❻	我正在整修房子。	I am repairing my house right now.
❼	我正在籌備婚禮。	I am arranging the wedding ceremony right now. * arrange the wedding ceremony（準備婚禮）
❽	我正在準備出國深造。	I am preparing to study abroad. * prepare to＋動詞（準備…） * study abroad（出國念書）
❾	我正在準備搬家。	I am preparing to move.
❿	我正在享受我的假期。	I am enjoying my vacation right now. * enjoy vacation（享受假期） 　＝ have fun on vacation
⓫	我正在抉擇要選哪一間學校。	I am in the process of choosing a school. * be in the process of...（處在…的過程中）
⓬	我正在準備考試。	I am preparing for an exam right now.
⓭	我正在考慮換房子。	I am thinking about moving. * think about＋動詞-ing（考慮做某事）＝ consider
⓮	我正在考慮到海外發展。	I am considering working overseas. * work overseas（到國外工作）

單字級等分析

	單字	音標	詞性	意義	字頻	大考	英檢	多益
❶	looking	[ˋlʊkɪŋ]	p.pr.	look（尋找）現在分詞	5	1	初級	
	job	[dʒɑb]	n.	工作	1	1	初級	
❷	trying	[ˋtraɪɪŋ]	p.pr.	try（嘗試）現在分詞	6	1	初級	
	give	[gɪv]	v.	放棄	1	1	初級	
	up	[ʌp]	adv.	完全、徹底	1	1	初級	
	smoking	[ˋsmokɪŋ]	n.	smoke（抽菸）動名詞	2	1	中級	
❸	studying	[ˋstʌdɪɪŋ]	p.pr.	study（唸書）現在分詞	1	1	初級	◎
	English	[ˋɪŋglɪʃ]	n.	英文	1	1	初級	
	right	[raɪt]	adv.	正值	1	1	初級	
	now	[naʊ]	adv.	現在	1	1	初級	
❹	lose	[luz]	v.	減少	1	2	初級	◎
	some	[sʌm]	adj.	一些	1	1	初級	
	weight	[wet]	n.	體重	1	1	初級	◎
	diet	[ˋdaɪət]	n.	節食	1	3	初級	◎
❺	learning	[ˋlɝnɪŋ]	p.pr.	learn（學習）現在分詞	1	4	中級	
	drive	[draɪv]	v.	開車	1	1	初級	◎
❻	repairing	[rɪˋpɛrɪŋ]	p.pr.	repair（整修）現在分詞	2	3	初級	◎
	house	[haʊs]	n.	房子	1	1	初級	◎
❼	arranging	[əˋrendʒɪŋ]	p.pr.	arrange（籌備）現在分詞	1	2	初級	◎
	wedding	[ˋwɛdɪŋ]	n.	婚禮	1	1	初級	
	ceremony	[ˋsɛrə͵monɪ]	n.	典禮	1	5	中級	◎
❽	preparing	[prɪˋpɛrɪŋ]	p.pr.	prepare（準備）現在分詞	1	1	初級	◎
	study	[ˋstʌdɪ]	v.	唸書	1	1	初級	◎
	abroad	[əˋbrɔd]	adv.	國外地	2	2	初級	◎
❾	move	[muv]	v.	搬家	1	1	初級	
❿	enjoying	[ɪnˋdʒɔɪɪŋ]	p.pr.	enjoy（享受）現在分詞	1	2	初級	
	vacation	[veˋkeʃən]	n.	假期	1	2	初級	◎
⓫	process	[ˋprɑsɛs]	n.	過程	1	3	中級	◎
	choosing	[ˋtʃuzɪŋ]	n.	choose（選擇）動名詞	5	2	初級	◎
	school	[skul]	n.	學校	1	1	初級	
⓬	exam	[ɪgˋzæm]	n.	考試	2	1	初級	
⓭	thinking	[ˋθɪŋkɪŋ]	p.pr.	think（考慮）現在分詞	1	1	中級	
	moving	[ˋmuvɪŋ]	n.	move（搬家）動名詞	3	1	中高	◎
⓮	considering	[kənˋsɪdərɪŋ]	p.pr.	consider（考慮）現在分詞	2	2	中高	◎
	working	[ˋwɝkɪŋ]	n.	work（工作）動名詞	2	1	中級	◎
	overseas	[ˋovɚˋsiz]	adv.	國外地	2	2	初級	◎

※「紅字單字」於本單元多句出現，「單字級等分析」僅列在「首次出現句」。

MP3 054-02 ❶～❻

❶	你最近有什麼計畫？	What plans have you made recently? * **What plans have you...?**（你已經…的計畫是什麼？） * **make a plan**（做出計畫）
❷	你戒酒了沒有？	Have quit drinking yet? * 此句用「現在完成式問句」（**Have quit...?**）表示「過去某時點是否發生某事，且結果持續到現在嗎？」。
❸	你有考慮畢業之後的出路嗎？	Have you thought about what to do after graduation? * 此句用「現在完成式問句」（**Have ...thought...?**）表示「過去到現在是否發生過、經歷過某事？」。 * **what to do**（要做什麼） * **after graduation**（畢業後）
❹	你正在減肥嗎？	Are you on a diet?　* **on a diet**（節食減肥）
❺	你在找工作嗎？	Are you looking for a job? * **job**（工作）可替換為：**house**（房子）
❻	你找到房子了嗎？	Have you found a house yet?
❼	你正在學日文嗎？	Are you studying Japanese?
❽	你在考慮換工作嗎？	Have you thought about changing jobs?
❾	你打算花多久時間學好英文？	How much time do you plan to spend studying English? * **How much time...?**（…是多少時間？）
❿	你開始運動了嗎？	Have you begun exercising? * **begin**＋動詞**-ing**（開始做某事）
⓫	你忙著籌備婚事嗎？	Are you busy with the wedding? * **Are you busy with**＋某事?（你是否在忙某事？）
⓬	你的家人支持你的計畫嗎？	Does your family support your plans?
⓭	你的考試準備得如何？	How is your exam preparation going? * **How is**＋名詞＋**going?**（…進行得如何？）
⓮	你在準備留學的事嗎？	Are you preparing to study abroad?
⓯	你決定到哪一間公司上班了嗎？	Which company have you decided to go to work for?

單字級等分析

	單字	音標	詞性	意義	字頻	大考	英檢	多益
❶	plan	[plæn]	n./v.	計畫	1	1	初級	◎
	made	[med]	p.p.	make（做出）過去分詞	1	1	初級	
	recently	[ˋrisntlɪ]	adv.	最近	1		初級	
❷	quit	[kwɪt]	p.p.	quit（戒除）過去分詞	1	2	初級	◎
	drinking	[ˋdrɪŋkɪŋ]	n.	drink（喝酒）動名詞	2	1	初級	
	yet	[jɛt]	adv.	尚未	1	1	初級	◎
❸	thought	[θɔt]	p.p.	think（考慮）過去分詞	1	1	初級	◎
	do	[du]	v.	做、從事	1	1	初級	
	graduation	[ˌɡrædʒʊˋeʃən]	n.	畢業	2	4	中級	
❹	diet	[ˋdaɪət]	n.	節食	1	3	初級	◎
❺	looking	[ˋlʊkɪŋ]	p.pr.	look（尋找）現在分詞	5	1	初級	
	job	[dʒɑb]	n.	工作	1	1	初級	
❻	found	[faʊnd]	p.p.	find（尋找）過去分詞	1	1	初級	◎
	house	[haʊs]	n.	房子	1	3	中級	◎
❼	studying	[ˋstʌdɪŋ]	p.pr.	study（唸書）現在分詞	1	1	初級	◎
	Japanese	[ˌdʒæpəˋniz]	n.	日語	1		初級	
❽	changing	[ˋtʃendʒɪŋ]	n.	change（更換、改變）動名詞	2	2	初級	◎
❾	much	[mʌtʃ]	adj.	許多的	1	1	初級	
	time	[taɪm]	n.	時間	1	1	初級	
	spend	[spɛnd]	v.	花費	1	1	初級	
	studying	[ˋstʌdɪŋ]	n.	study（唸書）動名詞	1	1	初級	
	English	[ˋɪŋglɪʃ]	n.	英文	1	1	初級	
❿	begun	[bɪˋɡʌn]	p.p.	begin（開始）過去分詞	1	1	初級	
	exercising	[ˋɛksɚˌsaɪzɪŋ]	n.	exercise（運動）動名詞	1	2	初級	◎
⓫	busy	[ˋbɪzɪ]	adj.	忙碌的	1	1	初級	
	wedding	[ˋwɛdɪŋ]	n.	婚禮	1	1	初級	
⓬	family	[ˋfæməlɪ]	n.	家人	1	1	初級	
	support	[səˋport]	v.	支持	1	2	初級	◎
⓭	exam	[ɪgˋzæm]	n.	考試	2	1	初級	
	preparation	[ˌprɛpəˋreʃən]	n.	準備	1	3	中級	◎
	going	[ˋgoɪŋ]	p.pr.	go（進行、進展）現在分詞	4	1	初級	
⓮	preparing	[prɪˋpɛrɪŋ]	p.pr.	prepare（準備）現在分詞	1	1	初級	◎
	study	[ˋstʌdɪ]	v.	唸書	1	1	初級	◎
	abroad	[əˋbrɔd]	adv.	國外地	2	2	初級	◎
⓯	company	[ˋkʌmpənɪ]	n.	公司	1	2	初級	◎
	decided	[dɪˋsaɪdɪd]	p.p.	decide（決定）過去分詞	1	1	初級	◎
	go	[go]	v.	去	1	1	初級	
	work	[wɝk]	v.	工作	1	1	初級	◎

※「紅字單字」於本單元多句出現，「單字級等分析」僅列在「首次出現句」。

MP3　055-01　❶～⓮

❶	我興奮得不得了。	I'm so excited.
❷	我的心情很好。	I'm in a good mood. * in a good mood（心情好） * in a bad mood（心情不好）
❸	我的精神很好。	I feel great. * great（很好的）可替換為： 　energetic（精力旺盛的）
❹	這氣氛真令人陶醉。	This atmosphere intoxicates me. * intoxicate＋某人（令某人陶醉）
❺	我樂歪了！	I'm so happy.
❻	最近我的運氣一直很好。	I've been lucky recently. * 此句用「現在完成式」（…have been…） 　表示「過去持續到現在的事」。
❼	我中了「樂透」，我真是樂透了！	I won the lottery; I am so happy! * win the lottery（中樂透）
❽	聽你這樣說，真是讓我心花怒放。	What you've said makes me feel incredibly happy. * what you've said（你所說的） * make＋某人＋形容詞（讓某人感到…） * incredibly happy（非常開心）
❾	今天是我最快樂的一天。	Today is the happiest day of my life.
❿	人逢喜事精神爽。	Happy occasions give you energy. * give one's energy（神清氣爽）
⓫	我打從心裏替你感到高興。	I'm so happy for you, from the bottom of my heart. * be happy for＋某人（替某人感到高興） * from the bottom of my heart（打從心底）
⓬	考試總算過關，真棒！	I passed the exam, that's great! * pass the exam（通過考試）
⓭	我玩到樂不思蜀。	I had so much fun that I forgot to go back home. * have so much fun（玩得很開心）
⓮	沒想到事情這麼順利。	I never expected to do so well. * never expected to＋動詞原形（沒預料到…） * do well（進行順利）

	單字	音標	詞性	意義	字頻	大考	英檢	多益
❶	so	[so]	adv.	這麼	1	1	初級	
	excited	[ɪkˋsaɪtɪd]	adj.	興奮的	2	2	初級	◎
❷	good	[gʊd]	adj.	良好的	1	1	初級	◎
	mood	[mud]	n.	心情	1	3	中級	◎
❸	feel	[fil]	v.	感覺	1	1	初級	
	great	[gret]	adj.	很好的	1	1	初級	◎
❹	this	[ðɪs]	adj.	這個	1	1	初級	
	atmosphere	[ˋætməs.fɪr]	n.	氣氛	1	4	中級	◎
	intoxicate	[ɪnˋtɑksə.ket]	v.	令人陶醉	7			
❺	happy	[ˋhæpɪ]	adj.	快樂的	1	1	初級	
❻	lucky	[ˋlʌkɪ]	adj.	幸運的	1	1	初級	
	recently	[ˋrisntlɪ]	adv.	最近	1		初級	
❼	won	[wʌn]	p.t.	win（贏得）過去式	1	1	初級	◎
	lottery	[ˋlɑtərɪ]	n.	樂透	3	5	中高	◎
❽	said	[sɛd]	p.p.	say（說）過去分詞	4	1	初級	
	make	[mek]	v.	使得	1	1	初級	
	incredibly	[ɪnˋkrɛdəblɪ]	adv.	極為	2			
❾	today	[təˋde]	n.	今天	1		初級	◎
	happiest	[ˋhæpɪɪst]	adj.	happy（快樂的）最高級	1	1	初級	
	day	[de]	n.	天	1	1	初級	
	life	[laɪf]	n.	生命	1	1	初級	
❿	occasion	[əˋkeʒən]	n.	場合	1	3	中級	◎
	give	[gɪv]	v.	給予	1	1	初級	
	energy	[ˋɛnədʒɪ]	n.	能量	1	2	初級	
⓫	bottom	[ˋbɑtəm]	n.	底部	1	1	初級	◎
	heart	[hɑrt]	n.	心	1	1	初級	
⓬	passed	[pæst]	p.t.	pass（通過）過去式	1	1	初級	
	exam	[ɪgˋzæm]	n.	考試	2	1	初級	
	that	[ðæt]	pron.	那個	1	1	初級	
⓭	had	[hæd]	p.t.	have（擁有）過去式	1	1	初級	
	much	[mʌtʃ]	adj.	許多的	1	1	初級	
	fun	[fʌn]	n.	樂趣	1	1	初級	
	forgot	[fəˋgɑt]	p.t.	forget（忘記）過去式	1	1	初級	
	go	[go]	v.	去	1	1	初級	
	back	[bæk]	adv.	返回	1	1	初級	◎
	home	[hom]	n.	家	1	1	初級	
⓮	never	[ˋnɛvə]	adv.	從不	1	1	初級	
	expected	[ɪkˋspɛktɪd]	p.t.	expect（期待）過去式	2	2	初級	
	do	[du]	v.	進行、進展	1	1	初級	
	well	[wɛl]	adv.	順利地	1	1	初級	◎

※「紅字單字」於本單元多句出現，「單字級等分析」僅列在「首次出現句」。

MP3 055-02 ❶～❹

❶	你最近快樂嗎？	Have you been happy recently? * **Have you been＋**形容詞？（你最近…嗎）
❷	你開心嗎？	Are you having fun? * **have fun**（開心） * 此句使用「現在進行式問句」（**Are you having**…?） 　表示「詢問對方說話當下是否發生某事？」。
❸	你怎麼看起來春風滿面？	Why do you look so cheerful?
❹	什麼事這麼高興？	What makes you so happy like this? * **make＋**某人＋形容詞（讓某人感到…）
❺	要結婚了，開心吧？	Are you happy that you're getting married? * **get married**（結婚）
❻	最近有什麼好事發生嗎？	Any happy thing happened to you recently? * **happy thing**（開心的事） * **happen to＋**某人（發生於某人）
❼	最近看起來氣色很好喔！	You've been looking good these days! * 此句用「現在完成進行式」（…**have been**…） 　表示「現階段持續發生的事」。
❽	一切如你所願，你滿意了吧？	Everything is as you hoped it would be—are you satisfied? * **as you hoped it would be**（如你希望的）
❾	很久沒看到你這麼開心了。	It's been a long time since I've seen you so happy. * **It's been a long time since＋**現在完成式子句 　（自從…，已經過了好久…）
❿	考試過關了，開心吧？	You passed the exam—are you happy?
⓫	要當爸爸了，興奮吧？	Are you excited about being a father? * **be excited about＋**動詞-ing（因為…感到興奮）
⓬	要休假了！開心嗎？	Time for vacation! Happy? * **time for＋**某事（做某事的時間）
⓭	我一直很快樂，你呢？	I'm always happy—what about you?
⓮	升官了，應該很高興吧？	You're happy about your promotion, right? * **be happy about＋**某事（因某事感到高興）

	單字	音標	詞性	意義	字頻	大考	英檢	多益
❶	happy	[ˋhæpɪ]	adj.	快樂的	1	1	初級	
	recently	[ˋrisntlɪ]	adv.	最近	1		初級	
❷	having	[ˋhævɪŋ]	p.pr.	have（擁有）現在分詞	1	1	初級	
	fun	[fʌn]	n.	樂趣	1	1	初級	
❸	look	[lʊk]	v.	看起來	1	1	初級	
	so	[so]	adv.	這麼	1	1	初級	
	cheerful	[ˋtʃɪrfəl]	adj.	興高采烈的、春風滿面的	3	3	中級	
❹	make	[mek]	v.	使得	1	1	初級	
	this	[ðɪs]	pron.	這個	1	1	初級	
❺	getting	[ˋgɛtɪŋ]	p.pr.	get（變成）現在分詞	1	1	初級	◎
	married	[ˋmærɪd]	p.p.	marry（結婚）過去分詞	1		初級	
❻	thing	[θɪŋ]	n.	事物	1	1	初級	
	happened	[ˋhæpənd]	p.t.	happen（發生）過去式	1	1	初級	
❼	looking	[ˋlʊkɪŋ]	p.pr.	look（看起來）現在分詞	5	1	初級	
	good	[gʊd]	adj.	良好的	1	1	初級	◎
	these	[ðiz]	adj.	這些	1	1	初級	
	day	[de]	n.	天	1	1	初級	
❽	everything	[ˋɛvrɪˏθɪŋ]	pron.	每件事情	1		初級	
	hoped	[hopt]	p.t.	hope（希望）過去式	1	1	初級	
	satisfied	[ˋsætɪsˏfaɪd]	adj.	滿意的	2	2	中高	◎
❾	long	[lɔŋ]	adj.	長的	1		初級	
	time	[taɪm]	n.	時間	1	1	初級	◎
	seen	[sin]	p.p.	see（看到）過去分詞	1	1	初級	
❿	passed	[pæst]	p.t.	pass（通過）過去式	1	1	初級	◎
	exam	[ɪgˋzæm]	n.	考試	2	1	初級	
⓫	excited	[ɪkˋsaɪtɪd]	adj.	興奮的	2	2	初級	◎
	father	[ˋfɑðɚ]	n.	父親	1	1	初級	
⓬	vacation	[veˋkeʃən]	n.	假期	1	2	初級	◎
⓭	always	[ˋɔlwez]	adv.	一直	1	1	初級	
⓮	promotion	[prəˋmoʃən]	n.	職位提升	2	4	中級	◎
	right	[raɪt]	int.	對吧	1	1	初級	

※「紅字單字」於本單元多句出現，「單字級等分析」僅列在「首次出現句」。

🔊 MP3 056-01 ❶～❿

❶	是真的嗎？	Is that true?
❷	真是嚇死人了！	That's really scary!
❸	太令人驚訝了！	That's really surprising!
❹	有這回事嗎？	Has such a thing happened? * such a thing（這樣子的事情）
❺	誰說的？	Who said that? * Who said...?（當時是誰說了…？）
❻	別嚇我！	Don't scare me! * Don't＋動詞原形（你別做某事！）
❼	這真是太神奇了。	This is really a miracle.
❽	事情怎麼會變成這樣？	How did it become like this? * How did it...?（當時那是如何…？）
❾	真是不可思議。	That's really amazing.
❿	電影結局真是出乎意料。	This movie ended really unexpectedly. * end＋副詞（結束得…）
⓫	真是怪事年年有。	Strange things happen all the time. * all the time（向來、一直）
⓬	竟然有這種事發生。	Such a thing actually happened.
⓭	真讓我目瞪口呆。	It really amazed me. * amaze＋某人（使某人驚訝）
⓮	我一定是在作夢。	I must be dreaming. * 某人＋must be＋動詞-ing （猜測某人必定在做某事）
⓯	難以相信！	Unbelievable!
⓰	你一定是在說笑吧！	You must be kidding me! * be kidding me（在跟我開玩笑）
⓱	真是嚇出一身冷汗。	Really scared me into a cold sweat. * scare into a cold sweat（嚇出冷汗）
⓲	真是令人歎為觀止。	Absolutely magnificent.
⓳	這事真是好得令人難以置信！	This is really too good to be truc! * too good to be true（美好到不會是真的）

	單字	音標	詞性	意義	字頻	大考	英檢	多益
❶	that	[ðæt]	pron.	那個	1	1	初級	
	true	[tru]	adj.	真的	1	1	初級	
❷	really	[ˋrɪəlɪ]	adv.	很、十分	1		初級	
	scary	[ˋskɛrɪ]	adj.	嚇人的	2	3	中級	
❸	surprising	[səˋpraɪzɪŋ]	adj.	令人驚訝的	1	1	初級	◎
❹	such	[sʌtʃ]	adv.	這樣子	1	1	初級	
	thing	[θɪŋ]	adj.	事情	1	1	初級	
	happened	[ˋhæpənd]	p.p.	happen（發生）過去分詞	1	1	初級	
❺	said	[sɛd]	p.t.	say（說）過去式	4	1	初級	
❻	scare	[skɛr]	v.	驚嚇	2	1	中級	◎
❼	this	[ðɪs]	pron./adj.	這個	1	1	初級	
	miracle	[ˋmɪrəkl̩]	n.	奇蹟	2	3	中級	◎
❽	become	[bɪˋkʌm]	v.	變為	1	1	初級	◎
❾	amazing	[əˋmezɪŋ]	adj.	令人驚訝的	1	3	中級	◎
❿	movie	[ˋmuvɪ]	n.	電影	1	1	初級	
	ended	[ˋɛndɪd]	p.t.	end（結束）過去式	1	1	初級	
	unexpectedly	[ˌʌnɪkˋspɛktɪdlɪ]	adv.	出乎意料地	3			
⓫	strange	[strendʒ]	adj.	奇怪的	1		初級	
	happen	[ˋhæpən]	v.	發生	1	1	初級	
	all	[ɔl]	adj.	一切的、所有的	1	1	初級	
	time	[taɪm]	n.	時間	1	1	初級	◎
⓬	actually	[ˋæktʃʊəlɪ]	adv.	實際上	1		初級	
	happened	[ˋhæpənd]	p.t.	happen（發生）過去式	1	1	初級	
⓭	amazed	[əˋmezd]	p.t.	amaze（使人驚訝）過去式	3	3	中級	◎
⓮	dreaming	[ˋdrimɪŋ]	p.pr.	dream（作夢）現在分詞	7	1	初級	
⓯	unbelievable	[ˌʌnbɪˋlivəbl̩]	adj.	難以置信的	3		中級	
⓰	kidding	[ˋkɪdɪŋ]	p.pr.	kid（開玩笑）現在分詞	6	1	初級	
⓱	scared	[skɛrd]	p.t.	scare（驚嚇）過去式	2		初級	
	cold	[kold]	adj.	冷的	1	1	初級	
	sweat	[swɛt]	n.	汗	2	3	中級	◎
⓲	absolutely	[ˋæbsəˌlutlɪ]	adv.	絕對地、完全地	1		中級	◎
	magnificent	[mægˋnɪfəsənt]	adj.	壯觀的	2	4	中級	◎
⓳	too	[tu]	adv.	過於	1	1	初級	
	good	[gud]	adj.	良好的	1	1	初級	◎

※「紅字單字」於本單元多句出現，「單字級等分析」僅列在「首次出現句」。

MP3 056-02 ❶～❻

❶	看你臉色發青，還好吧？	You look pale, are you okay? * look pale（看起來臉色蒼白）
❷	嚇到你了嗎？你還好吧？	Did I scare you? Are you all right? * Did I...?（我當時是否…） * Are you...?（你目前是否…）
❸	出乎意料之外，不是嗎？	Not what you expected, is it? * not what you expected（並非你當時所預料的）
❹	嚇一跳吧？	Made you jump? * make＋某人＋jump（嚇某人一跳）
❺	你不覺得太意外了嗎？	Don't you think that it's too unexpected?
❻	想都沒想到吧？	You've never thought about that, have you? * have never thought about...（從未想過…）
❼	你不覺得奇怪嗎？	Don't you feel it is strange?
❽	有沒有覺得很驚訝？	Are you surprised?
❾	怎麼樣，令人驚豔吧？	What do you think—pretty amazing, eh?
❿	這點小事就嚇到你啦？	Are you scared of such a tiny thing? * be scare of＋某物（因某物而嚇到）
⓫	你不覺得這事情太不尋常？	Don't you think that this is unusual? * Don't you think that＋子句?（你不認為…嗎？）
⓬	是我太大驚小怪了嗎？	Am I acting too surprised? * act too surprised（大驚小怪、驚訝過頭）
⓭	有什麼不對嗎？	Is there anything wrong?
⓮	如何？這個生日禮物夠特別吧？	What do you think? Is this birthday present special enough?
⓯	有這麼需要小題大作嗎？	Is it really worth making such a big deal over? * be worth＋動詞-ing（值得做…） * make a big deal（小題大作） * over（關於）
⓰	如何？我是不是變漂亮了？	What do you think? Am I prettier?

	單字	音標	詞性	意義	字頻	大考	英檢	多益
❶	look	[lʊk]	v.	看起來	1	1	初級	
	pale	[pel]	adj.	蒼白的	2	3	初級	◎
	okay	[ˋoˋke]	adj.	可以、還好	1	1		
❷	scare	[skɛr]	v.	驚嚇	2	1	中級	◎
	all	[ɔl]	adv.	一切	1	1	初級	
	right	[raɪt]	adj.	還可以的	1	1	初級	
❸	expected	[ɪkˋspɛktɪd]	p.t.	expect（期待）過去式	2	2	初級	◎
❹	made	[med]	p.t.	make（使得）過去式	1	1	初級	
	jump	[dʒʌmp]	v.	跳起	1	1	初級	
❺	think	[θɪŋk]	v.	認為	1	1	初級	
	too	[tu]	adv.	過於	1	1	初級	
	unexpected	[ˌʌnɪkˋspɛktɪd]	adj.	出乎意料的	2		中級	◎
❻	never	[ˋnɛvɚ]	adv.	從不	1	1	初級	
	thought	[θɔt]	p.p.	think（想）過去分詞	1	1	初級	◎
❼	feel	[fil]	v.	覺得	1	1	初級	
	strange	[strendʒ]	adj.	奇怪的	1	1	初級	
❽	surprised	[səˋpraɪzd]	adj.	感到驚訝的	1	1	初級	◎
❾	pretty	[ˋprɪtɪ]	adv.	非常、很	1	1	初級	◎
	amazing	[əˋmezɪŋ]	adj.	令人驚訝的	1	3	中級	◎
❿	scared	[skɛrd]	adj.	害怕的	2		初級	
	such	[sʌtʃ]	adv.	這樣子	1	1	初級	
	tiny	[ˋtaɪnɪ]	adj.	小的	1	1	初級	
	thing	[θɪŋ]	n.	事情	1	1	初級	
⓫	this	[ðɪs]	pron./adj.	這個	1	1	初級	
	unusual	[ʌnˋjuʒʊəl]	adj.	不尋常的	1		中級	◎
⓬	acting	[ˋæktɪŋ]	p.pr.	act（做出舉動）現在分詞	4	1	中高	
⓭	anything	[ˋɛnɪˌθɪŋ]	pron.	任何事情	1	1	初級	
	wrong	[rɔŋ]	adj.	不對的	1	1	初級	◎
⓮	birthday	[ˋbɝθˌde]	n.	生日	1		初級	
	present	[ˋprɛznt]	n.	禮物	1	2	初級	◎
	special	[ˋspɛʃəl]	adj.	特別的	1	1	初級	◎
	enough	[əˋnʌf]	adv.	足夠地	1	1	初級	◎
⓯	really	[ˋrɪəlɪ]	adv.	實際上	1		初級	
	worth	[wɝθ]	adj.	值得的	1	2	初級	◎
	making	[ˋmekɪŋ]	n.	make（做出）動名詞	2	1	中高	
	big	[bɪg]	adj.	大的	1	3	初級	
	deal	[dil]	n.	處理、對待	1	1	初級	◎
⓰	prettier	[ˋprɪtɪɚ]	adj.	pretty（漂亮的）比較級	1	1	初級	◎

※「紅字單字」於本單元多句出現，「單字級等分析」僅列在「首次出現句」。

我感動。

❶	真令人感動。	It's really touching.
❷	真是賺人熱淚。	It really makes people cry. * make＋某人＋動詞原形（讓某人…）
❸	哭得我死去活來。	I cried my eyes out. * cry one's eyes out（痛哭流涕）
❹	他打動了我的心。	He touched my heart. * touch＋某人（使某人感動）＝ move＋某人
❺	我蠻感動的。	I'm really touched. * 某人＋be touched（某人被感動）
❻	他的故事讓我深受感動。	His story really touched me.
❼	快拿面紙給我！	Hurry and pass me a tissue!
❽	聽到這樣悲慘的故事，真是令人鼻酸。	Hearing such a story really puts a lump in your throat. * put a lump in one's throat（讓人哽咽想哭）
❾	我沒有辦法不感動。	I can't help being touched. * can't help＋動詞-ing（忍不住…）
❿	真是可憐！	What a pity!
⓫	我感同身受。	I know exactly how you feel. * I know exactly...（我完全明白…）
⓬	災民們的處境令人感到難過。	The condition of the victims is saddening. * the condition of＋某人（某人的情境）
⓭	他用熱情感動了我。	His enthusiasm touched me.
⓮	好感人的故事。	It's really a touching story.
⓯	這場景真令人感動。	This scene moves people.
⓰	我快哭了。	I'm almost crying. * be almost＋動詞-ing（幾乎…）
⓱	怎麼會有這麼悲慘的事發生？	How could such a tragic thing happen? * such a tragic thing（如此悲慘的事）
⓲	這部戲真是賺人熱淚。	The film's such a tear-jerker.

單字級等分析

	單字	音標	詞性	意義	字頻	大考	英檢	多益
❶	really	[ˋrɪəlɪ]	adv.	很、十分	1		初級	
	touching	[ˋtʌtʃɪŋ]	adj.	感人的	4	1	中高	◎
❷	make	[mek]	v.	使得	1	1	初級	
	people	[ˋpipl̩]	n.	person（人）複數	1	1	初級	
	cry	[kraɪ]	v.	哭泣	1	1	初級	
❸	cried	[kraɪd]	p.t.	cry（哭泣）過去式	1	1	初級	
	eye	[aɪ]	n.	眼睛	1	1	初級	
	out	[aʊt]	adv.	徹底地、大聲地	1	1	初級	
❹	touched	[tʌtʃt]	p.t.	touch（感動）過去式	1	1	初級	◎
	heart	[hɑrt]	n.	心	1	1	初級	
❺	touched	[tʌtʃt]	p.p.	touch（感動）過去分詞	1	1	初級	◎
❻	story	[ˋstorɪ]	n.	故事	1	1	初級	◎
❼	hurry	[ˋhɝɪ]	v.	趕快、催促	2	2	初級	◎
	pass	[pæs]	v.	傳遞	1	1	初級	◎
	tissue	[ˋtɪʃʊ]	n.	面紙	1	3	中級	◎
❽	hearing	[ˋhɪrɪŋ]	n.	hear（聽）動名詞	1	1	中高	
	such	[sʌtʃ]	adv.	這樣子	1	1	初級	
	put	[pʊt]	v.	放置	1	1	初級	
	lump	[lʌmp]	n.	腫塊	3	5	中高	◎
	throat	[θrot]	n.	喉嚨	1	2	初級	
❾	help	[hɛlp]	v.	忍住、抑制	1	1	初級	
❿	pity	[ˋpɪtɪ]	n.	憐憫、同情	3	3	中級	
⓫	know	[no]	v.	知道	1	1	初級	◎
	exactly	[ɪgˋzæktlɪ]	adv.	確切地	1		中級	◎
	feel	[fil]	v.	感覺	1	1	初級	
⓬	condition	[kənˋdɪʃən]	n.	情況	1	3	中級	◎
	victim	[ˋvɪktɪm]	n.	受害者	1	3	中級	◎
	saddening	[ˋsædnɪŋ]	p.pr.	sadden（使難過）現在分詞	5		中級	
⓭	enthusiasm	[ɪnˋθjuzɪ͵æzəm]	n.	熱情	2	4	中級	◎
⓯	this	[ðɪs]	adj.	這個	1	1	初級	
	scene	[sin]	n.	場景、場面	1	1	初級	◎
	move	[muv]	v.	感動	1	1	初級	◎
⓰	almost	[ˋɔl͵most]	adv.	幾乎	1	1	初級	
	crying	[ˋkraɪɪŋ]	p.pr.	cry（哭泣）現在分詞	2	1	初級	
⓱	tragic	[ˋtrædʒɪk]	adj.	悲慘的	2	4	初級	◎
	thing	[θɪŋ]	n.	事情	1	1	初級	
	happen	[ˋhæpən]	v.	發生	1	1	初級	
⓲	film	[fɪlm]	n.	電影	1	1	初級	
	tear-jerker	[ˋtɪr͵dʒɝkɚ]	n.	賺人熱淚的電影或小說				

※「紅字單字」於本單元多句出現，「單字級等分析」僅列在「首次出現句」。

MP3 057-02 ❶～❻

❶	你覺得這部電影感人嗎？	Do you think this movie is touching? * **Do you think (that)**＋子句？（你是否覺得…？）
❷	這本書感人嗎？	Is this book touching?
❸	他這樣說，會影響你的情緒嗎？	Will his words affect your emotions? * **his word**（他所說的話） * **affect one's emotion**（影響情緒）
❹	你被他感動了嗎？	Were you moved by him? * **be moved by**＋某人（被某人感動）
❺	你覺得難過嗎？	Are you feeling sad? * 此句用「現在進行式問句」（**Are…feeling…?**） 　表示「說話當下是否發生某事？」。
❻	被我感動了嗎？	Did I move you?
❼	你在哭嗎？	Are you crying?
❽	怎麼這麼容易感動你啊！	How easily you are moved! * **How**＋副詞＋…!（怎麼如此的…！）
❾	你怎麼啦？	What happened to you?
❿	你的表情看起來怪怪的。	Your expression looks strange.
⓫	大家都說這個劇本很感人，你覺得呢？	Everyone says this script is really touching, don't you think so? * **everyone says**＋子句（大家都說…） * **don't you think so?**（你不這麼覺得嗎？）
⓬	別把感情悶在心裏。	Don't seal your feelings in your heart. * **seal one's feeling**（封閉感情）
⓭	如果想哭就哭吧。	Cry if you want to.
⓮	你不覺得這實在太悲慘了嗎？	Don't you think that it's really tragic? * **Don't you think**＋子句?（你不覺得…嗎？）
⓯	你是鐵石心腸啊？	Do you have a cold heart? * **cold heart**（鐵石心腸）＝ **stone heart**
⓰	你有沒有人性啊？	Don't you have any humanity?

單字級等分析

	單字	音標	詞性	意義	字頻	大考	英檢	多益
❶	think	[θɪŋk]	v.	認為	1	1	初級	
	this	[ðɪs]	adj.	這個	1	1	初級	
	movie	[ˋmuvɪ]	n.	電影	1	1	初級	
	touching	[ˋtʌtʃɪŋ]	adj.	感人的	4	1	中高	◎
❷	book	[bʊk]	n.	書籍	1	1	初級	◎
❸	word	[wɝd]	n.	話語	1	1	初級	
	affect	[əˋfɛkt]	v.	影響	1	3	初級	◎
	emotion	[ɪˋmoʃən]	n.	情緒	1	2	初級	◎
❹	moved	[muvd]	p.p.	move（感動）過去分詞	1	1	初級	◎
❺	feeling	[ˋfilɪŋ]	p.pr.	feel（感覺）現在分詞	1	1	初級	
	sad	[sæd]	adj.	難過的	1	1	初級	
❻	move	[muv]	v.	感動	1	1	初級	◎
❼	crying	[ˋkraɪɪŋ]	p.pr.	cry（哭泣）現在分詞	2	1	初級	
❽	easily	[ˋizɪlɪ]	adv.	容易地	1		中級	
❾	happened	[ˋhæpənd]	p.t.	happen（發生）過去式	1	1	初級	
❿	expression	[ɪkˋsprɛʃən]	n.	表情	1	3	中級	◎
	look	[lʊk]	v.	看起來	1	1	初級	
	strange	[strendʒ]	adj.	奇怪的	1	1	初級	
⓫	everyone	[ˋɛvrɪˏwʌn]	pron.	每個人	1		初級	
	say	[se]	v.	說	1	1	初級	
	script	[skrɪpt]	n.	劇本	2	6	中高	◎
	really	[ˋrɪəlɪ]	adv.	很、十分	1		初級	
	so	[so]	adv.	這麼、如此	1	1	初級	
⓬	seal	[sil]	v.	封閉	2	3	中級	◎
	feeling	[ˋfilɪŋ]	n.	情感	1	1	初級	
	heart	[hɑrt]	n.	心	1	1	初級	
⓭	cry	[kraɪ]	v.	哭泣	1	1	初級	
	want	[wɑnt]	v.	想要	1	1	初級	◎
⓮	tragic	[ˋtrædʒɪk]	adj.	悲慘的	2	4	中級	◎
⓯	have	[hæv]	v.	擁有	1	1	初級	
	cold	[kold]	adj.	冷酷的	1	1	初級	
⓰	any	[ˋɛnɪ]	adj.	任何的	1	1	初級	
	humanity	[hjuˋmænətɪ]	n.	人性	2	4	中級	

※「紅字單字」於本單元多句出現，「單字級等分析」僅列在「首次出現句」。

MP3 058-01 ❶～⓲

❶	我保證一切沒問題。	I promise that everything is okay. * **I promise that＋子句**（我保證…）
❷	我可以勝任。	I can handle that. * **handle**（處理）＝ **deal with**
❸	有我在，別怕！	I'm here, don't be afraid!
❹	交給我準沒錯。	You can count on me. * **count on me**（相信我、託付給我）
❺	我辦得到。	I can do it.
❻	大家都說我很聰明。	Everyone says that I'm very bright. * **everyone says＋子句**（大家都說…）
❼	我有信心。	I have confidence.
❽	我不會辜負你的期望。	I will not let you down. * **let you down**（讓你失望） * 此句用「未來簡單式」（...will...） 　表示「有意願做的事」。
❾	我有把握。	I've got it under control. ＝ I've got this. * **get...under control**（掌控住…）
❿	我有辦法。	I have a plan.
⓫	我相信我一定可以度過難關。	I'm sure I can overcome the difficulties. * **I'm sure＋子句**（我相信…）
⓬	我會解決問題的。	I'll solve the problem. * **solve a problem**（解決問題）
⓭	相信我。	Trust me.
⓮	我會完成老闆交代的任務。	I will complete the task my boss gave me. * **the task my boss gave me**（老闆交代的任務）
⓯	沒那麼困難。	Not so difficult.
⓰	我有百分之百的把握。	I have one hundred percent confidence. * **one hundred percent confidence**（十足的信心）
⓱	我自己就能做好。	I can do it by myself.
⓲	我向你保證。	You have my word. * **my word**（我的承諾）

	單字	音標	詞性	意義	字頻	大考	英檢	多益
❶	promise	[ˋprɑmɪs]	v.	保證	1	2	初級	◎
	everything	[ˋɛvrɪˏθɪŋ]	pron.	每件事情	1		初級	
	okay	[ˋoˋke]	adj.	沒問題的	1	1		
❷	handle	[ˋhændl]	v.	處理	1	2	初級	◎
	that	[ðæt]	pron.	那個	1	1	初級	
❸	here	[hɪr]	adv.	這裡	1	1	初級	
	afraid	[əˋfred]	adj.	害怕的	1	1	初級	
❹	count	[kaʊnt]	v.	相信、託付	1	1	初級	
❺	do	[du]	v.	做	1	1	初級	
❻	everyone	[ˋɛvrɪˏwʌn]	pron.	每個人	1		初級	
	say	[se]	v.	說	1	1	初級	
	very	[ˋvɛrɪ]	adv.	非常	1	1	初級	
	bright	[braɪt]	adj.	聰明的	1	1	初級	
❼	have	[hæv]	v.	擁有	1	1	初級	
	confidence	[ˋkɑnfədəns]	n.	信心		4	中級	◎
❽	let	[lɛt]	v.	讓…	1	1	初級	
	down	[daʊn]	adv.	失望地	1	1	初級	
❾	got	[gɑt]	p.p.	get（搞定）過去分詞	1	1	初級	◎
	control	[kənˋtrol]	n.	掌握	1	2	初級	◎
	this	[ðɪs]	pron.	這個	1	1	初級	
❿	plan	[plæn]	n.	方案、計畫	1	1	初級	
⓫	sure	[ʃʊr]	adj.	確定的	1	1	初級	
	overcome	[ˏovəˋkʌm]	v.	克服	1	4	中級	◎
	difficulty	[ˋdɪfəˏkʌltɪ]	n.	困難	1	2	初級	◎
⓬	solve	[sɑlv]	v.	解決	1	2	初級	◎
	problem	[ˋprɑbləm]	n.	問題	1	1	初級	
⓭	trust	[trʌst]	v.	相信	1	2	初級	◎
⓮	complete	[kəmˋplit]	v.	完成	1	2	初級	◎
	task	[tæsk]	v.	工作、任務	1	2	初級	◎
	boss	[bɔs]	n.	老闆	1	2	初級	
	gave	[gev]	p.t.	give（給）過去式	1	1	初級	
⓯	so	[so]	adv.	這麼	1	1	初級	
	difficult	[ˋdɪfəˏkəlt]	adj.	困難的	1	1	初級	◎
⓰	one	[wʌn]	n.	一	1	1	初級	
	hundred	[ˋhʌndrəd]	n.	一百	1	1	初級	
	percent	[pəˋsɛnt]	n.	百分比	2	4	中級	◎
⓱	myself	[maɪˋsɛlf]	pron.	我自己	1		初級	
⓲	word	[wɝd]	n.	承諾	1	1	初級	

※「紅字單字」於本單元多句出現，「單字級等分析」僅列在「首次出現句」。

058 你有信心嗎？

❶	你可以勝任這份工作嗎？	Can you handle this job? * **Can you...?**（你是否有能力…？）
❷	你辦得到嗎？	Can you do it?
❸	你覺得自己聰明嗎？	Do you think you're smart?
❹	你有信心嗎？	Are you confident?
❺	你有辦法解決問題嗎？	Do you have a plan to solve the problem? * **have a plan to**＋動詞原形（有做某事的辦法）
❻	要不要找人幫忙？	Do you want to look for help? * **look for help**（尋求協助）
❼	你感到害怕嗎？	Do you feel scared?
❽	沒問題吧？	No problem?
❾	是臨時出狀況嗎？	Anything unexpected happen? * **anything unexpected**（意料外的事）
❿	行得通嗎？	Will it work?　* **Will it...?**（是否將會…？）
⓫	你有辦法拿到這個案子嗎？	Do you have any way to get this case? * **have any way**（有任何方法）
⓬	你自己能處理好嗎？	Can you deal with this by yourself? * **deal with**（處理、解決）
⓭	撐得住嗎？	Can you hold on?　* **hold on**（堅持下去）
⓮	你要失去信念了嗎？	Are you losing your faith? * **lose one's faith**（失去信念）
⓯	你能保證嗎？	Do I have your word? * **have one's word**（保證）
⓰	今天能把東西交出來嗎？	Can you make the delivery today? * **make the delivery**（交貨、寄送貨品）
⓱	別裝了，不行就說不行。	Don't pretend; just say no if you can't. * **Don't pretend**（你不要假裝了！）
⓲	有問題就說一聲。	Say something if there's a problem. * **Say...**（你要說出…）、**if there's...**（如果有…）

	單字	音標	詞性	意義	字頻	大考	英檢	多益
❶	handle	[ˋhædl]	v.	處理	1	2	初級	◎
	this	[ðɪs]	adj.	這個	1	1	初級	
	job	[dʒɑb]	n.	工作	1	1	初級	
❷	do	[du]	v.	做	1	1	初級	
❸	think	[θɪŋk]	v.	認為	1	1	初級	
	smart	[smɑrt]	adj.	聰明的	1	1	初級	◎
❹	confident	[ˋkɑnfədənt]	adj.	自信的	2	3	初級	◎
❺	have	[hæv]	v.	擁有	1	1	初級	
	plan	[plæn]	n.	方案、計畫	1	1	初級	◎
	solve	[sɑlv]	v.	解決	1	2	初級	◎
	problem	[ˋprɑbləm]	n.	問題	1	1	初級	◎
❻	want	[wɑnt]	v.	想要	1	1	初級	◎
	look	[lʊk]	v.	尋求	1	1	初級	
	help	[hɛlp]	n.	幫助	1	1	初級	
❼	feel	[fil]	v.	感覺	1	1	初級	
	scared	[skɛrd]	adj.	害怕的	2		初級	
❾	anything	[ˋɛnɪ͵θɪŋ]	pron.	任何事情	1	1	初級	
	unexpected	[͵ʌnɪkˋspɛktɪd]	adj.	出乎意料的	2		中級	◎
	happen	[ˋhæpən]	v.	發生	1	1	初級	
❿	work	[wɜk]	v.	有效果、行得通	1	1	初級	◎
⓫	any	[ˋɛnɪ]	adj.	任何的	1	1	初級	
	way	[we]	n.	方法	1	1	初級	
	get	[gɛt]	v.	拿到	1	1	初級	◎
	case	[kes]	n.	案子	1	1	初級	◎
⓬	deal	[dil]	v.	處理	1	1	初級	◎
	yourself	[jʊɚˋsɛlf]	pron.	你自己	1		初級	
⓭	hold	[hold]	v.	堅持	1	1	初級	
⓮	losing	[ˋluzɪŋ]	p.pr.	lose（失去）現在分詞	4	2	初級	◎
	faith	[feθ]	n.	信念	1	3	中級	◎
⓯	word	[wɜd]	n.	承諾	1	1	初級	
⓰	make	[mek]	v.	做出	1	1	初級	
	delivery	[dɪˋlɪvərɪ]	n.	交貨、寄送	2	3	中級	◎
	today	[təˋde]	adv.	今天	1	1	初級	◎
⓱	pretend	[prɪˋtɛnd]	v.	假裝	2	3	中級	◎
	just	[dʒʌst]	adv.	只要	1	1	初級	
	say	[se]	v.	說	1	1	初級	
⓲	something	[ˋsʌmθɪŋ]	pron.	某些事物	1	1	初級	
	there	[ðɛr]	adv.	有…	1	1	初級	

※「紅字單字」於本單元多句出現，「單字級等分析」僅列在「首次出現句」。

🔵 MP3 059-01 ❶～㉑

❶	我非常生氣。	I'm very angry.
❷	我想打人。	I really want to hit someone.
❸	我不想和你說話。	I don't want to talk to you. * **I don't want to...**（我不想要…）
❹	我不想吃飯。	I don't want to eat anything.
❺	我不想多說。	I don't want to talk.
❻	不要跟我頂嘴！	Don't talk back to me! * **talk back to**＋某人（向某人頂嘴）
❼	少廢話。	Stop talking nonsense. ＝ Cut it out.
❽	別理我。	Leave me alone.
❾	別來煩我！	Get off my back!
❿	讓我靜一靜。	Give me a little peace and quiet.
⓫	滾遠點！	Get out of here! ＝ Get lost!
⓬	小心我揍你。	Careful, or I'll smack you.
⓭	我會報仇的。	I will get revenge. * **get revenge**（報仇）
⓮	少惹我！	Don't push me! ＝ Leave me alone!
⓯	看我會怎麼對付你。	Look how I am dealing with you. * **deal with you**（對付你）
⓰	閃一邊去！	Back off!
⓱	給我記住。	Just remember that.
⓲	畜生！	You beast! ＝ You filthy animal!
⓳	你會有報應的。	You'll pay for that. ＝ You'll get yours. * **pay for**＋某事（為某事付出代價） * 此句用「未來簡單式」（...will...） 　表示「在未來將發生的事」。
⓴	敢碰我一根寒毛試試看！	How dare you try and touch me! * **How dare you**＋動詞（你怎麼膽敢做某事！）
㉑	我再也忍受不了了！	I can't stand it anymore!

單字級等分析

	單字	音標	詞性	意義	字頻	大考	英檢	多益
❶	very	[ˋvɛrɪ]	adv.	十分	1	1	初級	
	angry	[ˋæŋgrɪ]	adj.	生氣的	1	1	初級	
❷	really	[ˋrɪəlɪ]	adv.	很、十分	1		初級	
	want	[wɑnt]	v.	想要	1	1	初級	◎
	hit	[hɪt]	v.	打、揍	1	1	初級	◎
	someone	[ˋsʌm.wʌn]	pron.	某個人	1	1	初級	
❸	talk	[tɔk]	v.	講話	1	1	初級	◎
❹	eat	[it]	v.	吃	1	1	初級	
	anything	[ˋɛnɪ.θɪŋ]	pron.	任何事情	1	1	初級	
❺	back	[bæk]	adv.	回覆	1	1	初級	◎
❼	stop	[stɑp]	v.	停止	1	1	初級	◎
	talking	[ˋtɔkɪŋ]	n.	talk（講話）動名詞	3	1	初級	◎
	nonsense	[ˋnɑnsɛns]	n.	廢話	3	4	中級	
	cut	[kʌt]	v.	剪短	1	1	初級	
	out	[aut]	adv.	去掉/離開	1	1	初級	
❽	leave	[liv]	v.	留下	1	1	初級	◎
	alone	[əˋlon]	adv.	單獨地	1	1	初級	
❾	get	[gɛt]	v.	動身、離去	1	1	初級	◎
	off	[ɔf]	adv.	離開	1	1	初級	
	back	[bæk]	n.	背部、背面	1	1	初級	◎
❿	give	[gɪv]	v.	給予	1	1	初級	
	little	[ˋlɪtl]	adj.	少許的	1	1	初級	
	peace	[pis]	n.	寧靜	1	2	初級	◎
	quiet	[ˋkwaɪət]	n.	安靜	1	1	初級	◎
⓫	here	[hɪr]	n.	這裡	1	1	初級	
	lost	[lɔst]	p.p.	lose（失去蹤影）過去分詞	1	2	中高	◎
⓬	careful	[ˋkɛrfəl]	adj.	小心的	1	1	初級	◎
	smack	[smæk]	v.	用拳頭揍	3	6	中高	
⓭	revenge	[rɪˋvɛndʒ]	n.	報仇	2	4	中級	
⓮	push	[puʃ]	v.	招惹	1	1	初級	
⓯	look	[luk]	v.	注意、留意	1	1	初級	
	dealing	[ˋdilɪŋ]	p.pr.	deal（對付）現在分詞	2	1	中高	◎
⓰	back	[bæk]	v.	退後	1	1	初級	◎
⓱	just	[dʒʌst]	adv.	只是	1	1	初級	
	remember	[rɪˋmɛmbə]	v.	記得	1	1	初級	◎
	that	[ðæt]	pron.	那個	1	1	初級	
⓲	beast	[bist]	n.	野獸	2	3	中級	
	filthy	[ˋfɪlθɪ]	adj.	汙穢的	4			
	animal	[ˋænəml]	n.	動物	1	1	初級	
⓳	pay	[pe]	v.	付出代價	1	3	初級	◎
⓴	dare	[dɛr]	v.	膽敢	2	3	中級	
	try	[traɪ]	v.	嘗試	1	1	初級	
	touch	[tʌtʃ]	v.	觸碰	1	1	初級	◎
㉑	stand	[stænd]	v.	忍受	1	1	初級	◎
	anymore	[ˋɛnɪmɔr]	adv.	不再	1		中高	

※「紅字單字」於本單元多句出現，「單字級等分析」僅列在「首次出現句」。

059　你生氣嗎？

🔘 MP3 059-02 ❶～⓱

❶	你在生氣嗎？	Are you angry right now?
❷	你在生我的氣嗎？	Are you angry with me? * **angry with me**（生我的氣）= **mad at me**
❸	為什麼不說話？	Why don't you speak? * **Why don't you...?**（你現在為什麼不…？）
❹	我做錯了什麼嗎？	Have I done something wrong? * **Have I...?**（我是否曾經做了…？） * 此句用「現在完成式問句」（**Have...done...?**） 　表示「從過去到現在是否經歷某事」。
❺	為什麼不理我？	Why did you ignore me? * **Why did you...?**（你當時為什麼…？）
❻	我又沒有怎麼樣。	I didn't do anything.
❼	想殺我啊？	Want to kill me?
❽	你有什麼好生氣的？	What are you mad about?
❾	想打架嗎？	Do you want to fight me? = You want a piece of me?
❿	眼睛瞪這麼大做什麼？	What are you staring at? * **stare at**（瞪、注視）
⓫	別生我的氣啦！	Don't be mad at me!
⓬	拜託！生什麼氣啊？	Come on! What are you angry for? * **Come on!**（別鬧了！）
⓭	真的生氣了？	Are you really angry?
⓮	這樣就生氣啦？	Do you get angry just like that?
⓯	有這麼嚴重嗎？	Is it really that serious? = Does it really matter?
⓰	我才應該生氣吧？	Shouldn't I be the angry one? * **Shouldn't I...?**（我才是應該…？） * **the angry one**（生氣的那個人）
⓱	你冷靜一點好嗎？	Calm down, will you? * **calm down**（冷靜） * **will you?**（你願意嗎？）

	單字	音標	詞性	意義	字頻	大考	英檢	多益
❶	angry	[ˋæŋgrɪ]	adj.	生氣的	1	1	初級	
	right	[raɪt]	adv.	正值	1	1	初級	
	now	[naʊ]	adv.	現在	1	1	初級	
❸	speak	[spik]	v.	說話	1	1	初級	
❹	done	[dʌn]	p.p.	do（做）過去分詞	1	1	初級	
	something	[ˋsʌmθɪŋ]	pron.	某些事情	1	1	初級	
	wrong	[rɔŋ]	adj.	錯誤的	1	1	初級	◎
❺	ignore	[ɪgˋnor]	v.	忽視	1	2	初級	◎
❻	do	[du]	v.	做	1	1	初級	
	anything	[ˋɛnɪ͵θɪŋ]	pron.	任何事情	1	1	初級	
❼	want	[wɑnt]	v.	想要	1		初級	◎
	kill	[kɪl]	v.	殺	1	1	初級	
❽	mad	[mæd]	adj.	惱火的	1	1	初級	
❾	fight	[faɪt]	v.	打架	1	1	初級	
	piece	[pis]	n.	一部分	1	1	初級	◎
❿	staring	[ˋstɛrɪŋ]	p.pr.	stare（瞪、注視）現在分詞	1	3	中級	◎
⓬	come	[kʌm]	v.	（與 on 連用）別鬧了、少來	1	1	初級	
⓭	really	[ˋrɪəlɪ]	adv.	實際上	1		初級	
⓮	get	[gɛt]	v.	變成	1	1	初級	◎
	just	[dʒʌst]	adv.	只是	1	1	初級	
	that	[ðæt]	pron. /adv.	那個/這麼	1	1	初級	
⓯	serious	[ˋsɪrɪəs]	adj.	嚴重的	1	2	初級	◎
	matter	[ˋmætɚ]	v.	要緊、有關係	1	1	初級	◎
⓰	one	[wʌn]	pron.	一個人	1	1	初級	
⓱	calm	[kɑm]	v.	冷靜	2	2	初級	
	down	[daʊn]	adv.	下來	1	1	初級	

※「紅字單字」於本單元多句出現，「單字級等分析」僅列在「首次出現句」。

MP3 060-01 ❶～⓱

❶	我蠻難過的。	I feel miserable.
❷	真令人感到遺憾。	What a shame. ＝ What a pity.
❸	真讓人傷心。	It really makes you miserable.
❹	我的心好像被挖空了。	My heart seems empty. * seem＋形容詞（似乎…）
❺	我受傷太深。	I've been hurt very deeply. * have been hurt（已經被傷害）
❻	事情怎麼會演變到這樣？	How could it happen like this? * How could it...?（這事怎麼會如此…？） * happen like this（像這樣子發生）
❼	我整天以淚洗面。	I cried all day. * cry all day（哭一整天）。 * 此句用「過去簡單式」（...cried...） 　表示「過去經常如此的事」。
❽	不曉得什麼時候，事情才會過去。	I don't know when it will be over. * I don't know when＋子句（我不知道何時…）
❾	我沒辦法快樂起來。	I can't be happy anymore.
❿	真令人心碎。	It really breaks your heart. * break one's heart（讓人心碎）
⓫	我的心好像被人捅了一刀。	My heart feels like it has been stabbed. * feel like＋子句（感覺像是…） * be stabbed（被刺傷）
⓬	這樣的日子真是難過。	Such days are really difficult. * such days（像這樣的日子）
⓭	我的心好痛。	My heart bleeds.
⓮	真令人心痛。	It really makes my heart bleed.
⓯	最近心情一直很低潮。	My spirits have been low recently. * have been low（一直持續低落）
⓰	生命對我似乎失去了意義。	Life seems meaningless to me. * to me（對我來說）
⓱	我好想他。	I miss him so much.

單字級等分析

	單字	音標	詞性	意義	字頻	大考	英檢	多益
❶	feel	[fil]	v.	感到	1	1	初級	
	miserable	[ˋmɪzərəbl]	adj.	傷心難過的	3	4	中級	◎
❷	shame	[ʃem]	n.	遺憾的事	2	3	中級	◎
	pity	[ˋpɪtɪ]	n.	憐憫、同情	3	3	中級	
❸	really	[ˋrɪəlɪ]	adv.	實際上	1		初級	
	make	[mek]	v.	使得	1	1	初級	
❹	heart	[hɑrt]	n.	心	1	1	初級	
	seem	[sim]	v.	似乎	1	1	初級	◎
	empty	[ˋɛmptɪ]	adj.	空虛的	1	3	初級	◎
❺	hurt	[hɝt]	p.p.	hurt（傷害）過去分詞	1	1	初級	
	very	[ˋvɛrɪ]	adv.	十分	1	1	初級	
	deeply	[ˋdiplɪ]	adv.	深深地	1			
❻	happen	[ˋhæpən]	v.	發生	1	1	初級	
	this	[ðɪs]	pron.	這個	1	1	初級	
❼	cried	[kraɪd]	p.t.	cry（哭泣）過去式	1	1	初級	
	all	[ɔl]	adj.	整個的	1	1	初級	
	day	[de]	n.	天/日子	1	1	初級	
❽	know	[no]	v.	知道	1	1	初級	◎
	over	[ˋovə]	adj.	結束的	1	1	初級	
❾	happy	[ˋhæpɪ]	adj.	快樂的	1	1	初級	
	anymore	[ˋɛnɪmor]	adv.	不再	1		中高	
❿	break	[brek]	v.	打碎	1	1	初級	◎
⓫	stabbed	[stæbt]	p.p.	stab（刺傷）過去分詞	3	3	中級	
⓬	such	[sʌtʃ]	adv.	這樣子	1	1	初級	
	difficult	[ˋdɪfə.kəlt]	adj.	困難的	1	1	初級	◎
⓭	bleed	[blid]	v.	悲傷、心痛	2	3	中級	
⓯	spirit	[ˋspɪrɪt]	n.	精神	1	2	初級	◎
	low	[lo]	adj.	低落的	1	1	初級	
	recently	[ˋrisntlɪ]	adv.	最近	1		初級	
⓰	life	[laɪf]	n.	生命	1	1	初級	
	meaningless	[ˋminɪŋlɪs]	adj.	無意義的	3			
⓱	miss	[mɪs]	v.	想念	1	1	初級	
	so	[so]	adv.	如此	1	1	初級	
	much	[mʌtʃ]	adv.	非常	1	1	初級	

※「紅字單字」於本單元多句出現，「單字級等分析」僅列在「首次出現句」。

MP3 060-02 ❶～❼

❶	感到難過嗎？	Do you feel sad? * sad（傷心的）= miserable = unhappy
❷	傷心嗎？	Heartbroken?
❸	你不快樂嗎？	Are you unhappy?
❹	最近有沒有快樂一點？	Have you grown happier recently? * Have you...?（你是否已經…？） * grow happier（變得更快樂）
❺	要面對這一切並不容易，對吧？	It's not very easy to face everything, is it? * It's not easy to＋動詞原形（…不容易） * face everything（面對一切）
❻	有心事嗎？	Is there anything on your mind? * Is there anything...?（是否有任何事…？）
❼	心情不好嗎？	In a bad mood? * in a good mood（心情好）
❽	發生了什麼事嗎？	Is there anything that has happened?
❾	有什麼我可以幫忙的嗎？	Is there anything that I can help you with?
❿	怎麼把自己搞成這樣不成人形？	Why do you torture yourself like this? * torture oneself（折磨自己）
⓫	還思念著他嗎？	Still miss him?
⓬	想找人聊聊嗎？	Want to talk to someone?
⓭	你也覺得不開心，是嗎？	You feel unhappy too, don't you? * don't you?（不是嗎？）可替換為： 　right?（對吧？）
⓮	想家了嗎？	Miss home? = Homesick?
⓯	沒辦法快樂起來嗎？	Can't seem to cheer yourself up? * Can't seem to＋動詞?（看起來無法…） * cheer oneself up（讓自己開心起來）
⓰	你看起來不太好耶。	Hey, you don't look so good.
⓱	還會流淚嗎？	Still crying?

	單字	音標	詞性	意義	字頻	大考	英檢	多益
❶	feel	[fil]	v.	感覺	1	1	初級	
	sad	[sæd]	adj.	傷心的	1	1	初級	
❷	heartbroken	[ˋhɑrt͵brokən]	adj.	心碎的	7			
❸	unhappy	[ʌnˋhæpɪ]	adj.	不開心的	2		初級	
❹	grown	[gron]	p.p.	grow（變得）過去分詞	6	1	初級	◎
	happier	[ˋhæpɪɚ]	adj.	happy（快樂的）比較級	1	1	初級	
	recently	[ˋrisntlɪ]	adv.	最近	1		初級	
❺	very	[ˋvɛrɪ]	adv.	十分	1	1	初級	
	easy	[ˋizɪ]	adj.	容易的	1	1	初級	◎
	face	[fes]	v.	面對	1	1	初級	
	everything	[ˋɛvrɪ͵θɪŋ]	pron.	每件事情	1		初級	
❻	there	[ðɛr]	adv.	有…	1	1	初級	
	anything	[ˋɛnɪ͵θɪŋ]	pron.	任何事情	1	1	初級	
	mind	[maɪnd]	n.	心	1	1	初級	◎
❼	bad	[bæd]	adj.	不好的	1	1	初級	
	mood	[mud]	n.	心情	1	3	中級	◎
❽	happened	[ˋhæpənd]	p.p.	happen（發生）過去分詞	1	1	初級	
❾	help	[hɛlp]	v.	幫助	1	1	初級	
❿	torture	[ˋtɔrtʃɚ]	v.	折磨	2	5	中高	
	yourself	[juɚˋsɛlf]	pron.	你自己	1		初級	
	this	[ðɪs]	pron.	自己	1	1	初級	
⓫	still	[stɪl]	adv.	仍然	1	1	初級	◎
	miss	[mɪs]	v.	想念	1	1	初級	
⓬	want	[wɑnt]	v.	想要	1	1	初級	◎
	talk	[tɔk]	v.	講話	1	1	初級	◎
	someone	[ˋsʌm͵wʌn]	pron.	某個人	1	1	初級	
⓭	too	[tu]	adv.	也	1	1	初級	
⓮	home	[hom]	n.	家	1	1	初級	
	homesick	[ˋhom͵sɪk]	adj.	想家的	7	2	初級	
⓯	seem	[sim]	v.	似乎	1	1	初級	◎
	cheer	[tʃɪr]	v.	使高興	2	3	初級	◎
	up	[ʌp]	adv.	起來	1	1	初級	
⓰	hey	[he]	int.	嘿	1		初級	
	look	[lʊk]	v.	看起來	1	1	初級	
	so	[so]	adv.	這麼	1	1	初級	
	good	[gʊd]	adj.	良好的	1	1	初級	◎
⓱	crying	[ˋkraɪɪŋ]	p.pr.	cry（哭泣）現在分詞	2	1	初級	

※「紅字單字」於本單元多句出現，「單字級等分析」僅列在「首次出現句」。

061　我失望。

MP3 061-01 ❶～⓳

❶	真令人失望。	It's really disappointing.
❷	太可惜了。	It's too bad. ＝ It's a pity.
❸	我又失敗了。	I've failed again. * have＋過去分詞＋again（再度做了…）
❹	差點就過關了，真是的！	I almost made it, darn it! * make it（成功）、darn it（可惡）
❺	你讓我失望了。	I'm really disappointed in you. * be disappointed in＋某人（對某人感到失望）
❻	真是找錯人了。	That's really not the right person to count on. * the right person to count on （值得信賴的正確人選）
❼	你浪費了我對你的信任。	You wasted my trust in you. * my trust in＋某人（我對某人的信任）
❽	我放棄了。	I give up.　* give up（放棄）
❾	哀莫大於心死。	There is no grief greater than the death of the heart. * there is no A greater than B（沒有比 B 更大的 A）
❿	我再也無所謂了。	It doesn't matter anymore. * not matter anymore（再也不重要）
⓫	我不想再做任何努力了。	I don't want to try anymore.
⓬	沒救了。	It's no use.
⓭	不可能成功了。	It can't be done.
⓮	別再努力了。	Don't bother giving it another try. * Don't bother＋動詞-ing（別再浪費時間做…！）
⓯	好想死喔！	I want to die!
⓰	我不敢相信你又讓我失望了！	I can't believe you've let me down again! * let＋某人＋down（辜負某人）
⓱	沒希望了。	There's no hope.
⓲	我真沒用。	I'm useless.
⓳	我受夠了！	I've had it!　* have had it（受夠了）

	單字	音標	詞性	意義	字頻	大考	英檢	多益
❶	really	[ˋrɪəlɪ]	adv.	很、十分	1		初級	
	disappointing	[ˌdɪsəˋpɔɪntɪŋ]	adj.	令人失望的	3	3	中級	◎
❷	too	[tu]	adv.	過於	1	1	初級	
	bad	[bæd]	adj.	可惜的	1	1	初級	
	pity	[ˋpɪtɪ]	n.	憐憫、同情	3	3	中級	
❸	failed	[feld]	p.p.	fail（失敗）過去分詞	3	2	初級	◎
	again	[əˋgɛn]	adv.	再次	1	1	初級	
❹	almost	[ˋɔl‚most]	adv.	幾乎	1		初級	
	made	[med]	p.t.	make（使成功）過去式	1	1	初級	
	darn	[dɑrn]	int.	可惡	5			
❺	disappointed	[ˌdɪsəˋpɔɪntɪd]	adj.	感到失望的	2	3	中級	◎
❻	that	[ðæt]	pron.	那個	1	1	初級	
	right	[raɪt]	adj.	正確的	1	1	初級	
	person	[ˋpɝsn]	n.	人	1	1	初級	
	count	[kaʊnt]	v.	相信、託付	1	1	初級	
❼	wasted	[ˋwestɪd]	p.t.	waste（浪費）過去式	5			
	trust	[trʌst]	n.	信任	1	2	初級	◎
❽	give	[gɪv]	v.	放棄	1	1	初級	
	up	[ʌp]	adv.	完全、徹底	1	1	初級	
❾	there	[ðɛr]	adv.	有…	1	1	初級	
	grief	[grif]	n.	痛苦	2		中級	◎
	greater	[ˋgretə]	adj.	great（重大的）比較級	1	1	初級	◎
	death	[dɛθ]	n.	死亡	1	4	初級	
	heart	[hɑrt]	n.	心	1	1	初級	
❿	matter	[ˋmætə]	v.	重要、要緊	1	1	初級	◎
	anymore	[ˋɛnɪmɔr]	adv.	不再			中高	
⓫	want	[wɑnt]	v.	想要	1	1	初級	◎
	try	[traɪ]	v./n.	嘗試	1	1	初級	
⓬	use	[juz]	n.	用處	1	1	初級	◎
⓭	done	[dʌn]	p.p.	do（做）過去分詞	1	1	初級	
⓮	bother	[ˋbɑðə]	v.	費心	1	2	初級	◎
	giving	[ˋgɪvɪŋ]	n.	give（給予）動名詞	6	1	初級	
	another	[əˋnʌðə]	adj.	另一個	1			
⓯	die	[daɪ]	v.	死亡	1	1	初級	
⓰	believe	[bɪˋliv]	v.	相信	1	1	初級	◎
	let	[lɛt]	p.p.	讓…	1	1	初級	
	down	[daʊn]	adv.	失望地	1	1	中級	
⓱	hope	[hop]	n.	希望	1	1	初級	
⓲	useless	[ˋjuslɪs]	adj.	沒用的	3		中級	◎
⓳	had	[hæd]	p.p.	have（容忍）過去分詞	1	1	初級	

※「紅字單字」於本單元多句出現，「單字級等分析」僅列在「首次出現句」。

🔊 MP3 061-02 ❶～⓲

❶	你灰心了嗎？	Are you discouraged?
❷	要放棄了嗎？	Want to give up?
❸	不再努力了嗎？	Don't want to try anymore?
❹	很心痛吧？	Really heartbroken, aren't you?
❺	失去鬥志了嗎？	Have you lost your will to fight? * **Have you...?**（你是否已經…？） * **lose one's will to fight**（喪失鬥志）
❻	你覺得無所謂嗎？	Are you apathetic? = Are you indifferent?
❼	你還要繼續支持他嗎？	Are you going to keep supporting him? * **Are you going to＋動詞原形?** （你是否將會…？）
❽	完全沒有機會了嗎？	Is there no chance at all? * **no chance at all**（完全沒機會）
❾	要再試試嗎？	Want to try again? = Want to give it another try? * **give it another try**（再次嘗試）= try again
❿	也許還有機會啊。	There might still be a chance. * **There might be...**（可能會有…）
⓫	還不願意放棄嗎？	Still not giving up?
⓬	真的有這麼糟嗎？	Is it that bad?
⓭	有這麼嚴重嗎？	Is it really that serious?
⓮	還想奮鬥嗎？	Still want to fight on? * **fight on**（繼續奮鬥）
⓯	你還是認為事情不是他做的嗎？	Do you still think that he didn't do it? * **Do you think that＋子句?**（你是否覺得…？）
⓰	還抱希望嗎？	Still have hope?
⓱	你還是相信他嗎？	Do you still believe in him? * **believe in＋某人**（相信某人）
⓲	你認為他真的會來嗎？	Do you think that he really will come?

	單字	音標	詞性	意義	字頻	大考	英檢	多益
❶	discouraged	[dɪsˋkɝɪdʒd]	adj.	沮喪的	3	4	中級	◎
❷	want	[wɑnt]	v.	想要	1	1	初級	◎
	give	[gɪv]	v.	放棄/給予	1	1	初級	
	up	[ʌp]	adv.	完全、徹底	1	1	初級	
❸	try	[traɪ]	v./n.	嘗試	1	1	初級	
	anymore	[ˋɛnɪmor]	adv.	不再	1		中高	
❹	really	[ˋrɪəlɪ]	adv.	很、十分/真的	1		初級	
	heartbroken	[ˋhɑrt͵brokən]	adj.	感到心痛的	7			
❺	lost	[lɔst]	p.p.	lose（失去）過去分詞	1	2	中高	◎
	will	[wɪl]	n.	意志力	1	1	初級	◎
	fight	[faɪt]	v.	奮鬥	1	1	初級	
❻	apathetic	[͵æpəˋθɛtɪk]	adj.	毫不關心的	8			
	indifferent	[ɪnˋdɪfərənt]	adj.	毫不關心的	4	5	中高	
❼	going	[ˋgoɪŋ]	p.pr.	go（即將）現在分詞	4	1	初級	
	keep	[kip]	v.	繼續	1	1	初級	◎
	supporting	[səˋportɪŋ]	n.	support（支持）動名詞	2	2	初級	◎
❽	there	[ðɛr]	adv.	有…	1	1	初級	
	chance	[tʃæns]	n.	機會	1	1	初級	
	all	[ɔl]	n.	完全	1	1	初級	
❾	again	[əˋgɛn]	adv.	再次	1	1	初級	
	another	[əˋnʌðɚ]	adj.	另一個	1	1		
❿	still	[stɪl]	adv.	仍然	1	1	初級	◎
⓫	giving	[ˋgɪvɪŋ]	p.pr.	give（放棄）現在分詞	6	1	初級	
⓬	that	[ðæt]	adv.	這麼	1	1	初級	
	bad	[bæd]	adj.	糟糕的	1	1	初級	
⓭	serious	[ˋsɪrɪəs]	adj.	嚴重的	1	2	初級	◎
⓯	think	[θɪŋk]	v.	認為	1	1	初級	
⓰	have	[hæv]	v.	擁有	1	1	初級	
	hope	[hop]	n.	希望	1	1	初級	
⓱	believe	[bɪˋliv]	v.	相信	1	1	初級	◎
⓲	come	[kʌm]	v.	前來	1	1	初級	

※「紅字單字」於本單元多句出現，「單字級等分析」僅列在「首次出現句」。

❶	我好想你。	I miss you very much.
❷	我沒有朋友。	I don't have any friends. * **I don't have...**（我沒有…）
❸	我想和你說話。	I want to talk to you.
❹	我怕黑。	I'm afraid of the dark. * **I'm afraid of...**（我害怕…）
❺	屋子裡空蕩蕩的。	The house is empty.
❻	整個房子都是你的影子。	There are traces of you all over the house. * **traces of you**（你的痕跡） * **all over**（到處）
❼	你可以過來陪我嗎？	Can you come and stay by my side? * **stay by my side**（陪在我身邊）
❽	四周好安靜，我可以聽到時鐘的滴答聲。	It's really quiet around here; I can hear the clock ticking. * **hear＋名詞＋動詞-ing**（聽見…）
❾	我只聽到自己的心跳聲。	I can only hear my own heart beating. * **I can only＋動詞原形**（我只能夠…）
❿	我總是一個人去看電影。	I always go to the movies alone. * **I always＋做某事＋alone**（我總是一個人做某事）
⓫	沒有人在乎我。	Nobody cares about me. * **care about**（在乎、關心）
⓬	我只有一個人。	I'm only one person.
⓭	我的心沒人瞭解。	Nobody understands what's in my heart. * **what's in my heart**（我心裡所想的事）
⓮	沒有人要和我說話。	There's no one who wants to talk to me. * **There's no one...**（沒有人…）
⓯	我總是一個人吃飯。	I always eat alone.
⓰	沒有人喜歡我。	Nobody likes me.
⓱	我覺得好寂寞。	I'm lonely.
⓲	我和周遭的人好像都沒有關係。	It seems that there's no connection between me and the people around me. * **no connection between A and B**（A 和 B 沒有關聯）

	單字	音標	詞性	意義	字頻	大考	英檢	多益
❶	miss	[mɪs]	v.	想念	1	1	初級	
	very	[ˋvɛrɪ]	adv.	十分	1	1	初級	
	much	[mʌtʃ]	adv.	非常	1	1	初級	
❷	have	[hæv]	v.	擁有	1	1	初級	
	any	[ˋɛnɪ]	adj.	任何的	1	1	初級	
	friend	[frɛnd]	n.	朋友	1	1	初級	
❸	want	[wɑnt]	v.	想要	1	1	初級	◎
	talk	[tɔk]	v.	說話	1	1	初級	◎
❹	afraid	[əˋfred]	adj.	害怕的	1	1	初級	
	dark	[dɑrk]	n.	黑暗	1	1	初級	
❺	house	[haʊs]	n.	屋子	1	1	初級	◎
	empty	[ˋɛmptɪ]	adj.	空無一人的	1	3	初級	◎
❻	there	[ðɛr]	adv.	有…	1	1	初級	
	trace	[tres]	n.	痕跡	2	3	初級	◎
	all	[ɔl]	adv.	完全	1	1	初級	
❼	come	[kʌm]	v.	前來	1	1	初級	
	stay	[ste]	v.	陪伴	1	1	初級	◎
	side	[saɪd]	n.	旁邊	1	1	初級	
❽	really	[ˋrɪəlɪ]	adv.	很、十分	1		初級	
	quiet	[ˋkwaɪət]	adj.	安靜的	1	1	初級	
	here	[hɪr]	n.	這裡	1	1	初級	
	hear	[hɪr]	v.	聽	1	1	初級	
	clock	[klɑk]	n.	時鐘	1	1	初級	◎
	ticking	[ˋtɪkɪŋ]	p.pr.	tick（滴答作響）現在分詞	6			
❾	only	[ˋonlɪ]	adv.	只有	1	1	初級	
	own	[on]	adj.	自己的	1	1	初級	◎
	heart	[hɑrt]	n.	心	1	1	初級	
	beating	[ˋbitɪŋ]	p.pr.	beat（跳動）現在分詞	3	1	**中高**	
❿	always	[ˋɔlwez]	adv.	總是	1	1	初級	
	go	[go]	v.	去	1	1	初級	
	movie	[ˋmuvɪ]	n.	電影	1	1	初級	
	alone	[əˋlon]	adv.	單獨地	1	1	初級	
⓫	nobody	[ˋnobɑdɪ]	pron.	沒有人	1	2	初級	
	care	[kɛr]	v.	關心	1	1	初級	◎
⓬	one	[wʌn]	n./pron.	一/一個人	1	1	初級	
	person	[ˋpɝsn]	n.	人	1	1	初級	
⓭	understand	[ˌʌndɚˋstænd]	v.	瞭解	1	1	初級	
⓯	eat	[it]	v.	吃飯	1	1	初級	
⓰	like	[laɪk]	v.	喜歡	1	1	初級	
⓱	lonely	[ˋlonlɪ]	adj.	寂寞的	2	2	初級	
⓲	seem	[sim]	v.	似乎	1	1	初級	◎
	connection	[kəˋnɛkʃən]	n.	關聯	1	3	**中級**	◎
	people	[ˋpipl]	n.	person（人）複數	1	1	初級	

※「紅字單字」於本單元多句出現，「單字級等分析」僅列在「首次出現句」。

🔵 MP3 062-02 ❶～⓳

❶	想我嗎？	Miss me?
❷	想哭嗎？	Want to cry?
❸	怕黑嗎？	Afraid of the dark?
❹	自己過日子還好嗎？	Do you not mind being alone? * **Do you not mind**＋動詞-ing?（你是否不在意…？） * **be alone**（自己一個人）
❺	要一起用餐嗎？	Want to eat together?
❻	寂寞嗎？	Lonely?
❼	喜歡一個人過生活嗎？	Do you like to live alone? * **Do you like to**＋動詞原形?（你是否喜歡…？）
❽	要我陪你嗎？	Want me to accompany you? * **accompany**＋某人（陪伴某人）
❾	有心愛的人嗎？	Is there anyone you love? * **Is there...?**（是否有…？）
❿	有想做的事嗎？	Is there anything you want to do?
⓫	想交個朋友嗎？	Would you like to make friends with me? * **Would you like to**＋動詞原形?（你是否想要做…？）
⓬	你有朋友嗎？	Do you have any friends?
⓭	你覺得空虛嗎？	Are you feeling empty?
⓮	你不喜歡被打擾嗎？	Do you hate being disturbed? * **Do you hate**＋動詞-ing?（你是否討厭…？）
⓯	你不想被人瞭解嗎？	Don't you want to be understood?
⓰	你不喜歡社交活動嗎？	Do you dislike social activities? * **social activities**（社交活動）
⓱	我想找人聊聊會對你有幫助。	I think it might help you to talk to someone. * **it might help you to**＋動詞原形（…也許能幫助你）
⓲	看來你終究還是獨自一人。	Seems like in the end you're still alone. * **Seems like in the end**＋子句（似乎到最後…）
⓳	我能幫你打起精神嗎？	Can I cheer you up? * **cheer**＋某人＋**up**（使某人打起精神）

單字級等分析

	單字	音標	詞性	意義	字頻	大考	英檢	多益
❶	miss	[mɪs]	v.	想念	1	1	初級	
❷	want	[wɑnt]	v.	想要	1	1	初級	◎
	cry	[kraɪ]	v.	哭泣	1	1	初級	
❸	afraid	[əˋfred]	adj.	害怕的	1	1	初級	
	dark	[dɑrk]	n.	黑暗	1	1	初級	
❹	mind	[maɪnd]	v.	在意	1	1	初級	
	alone	[əˋlon]	adv./adj.	單獨地/單獨的	1	1	初級	
❺	eat	[it]	v.	用餐	1	1	初級	
	together	[təˋgɛðɚ]	adv.	在一起	1	1	初級	
❻	lonely	[ˋlonlɪ]	adj.	寂寞的	2	2	初級	
❼	like	[laɪk]	v.	喜歡/想要	1	1	初級	
	live	[lɪv]	v.	生活	1	1	初級	
❽	accompany	[əˋkʌmpənɪ]	v.	陪伴	1	4	中級	◎
❾	there	[ðɛr]	adv.	有…	1	1	初級	
	anyone	[ˋɛnɪ.wʌn]	pron.	任何人	1	2	初級	
	love	[lʌv]	v.	喜愛	1	1	初級	
❿	anything	[ˋɛnɪ.θɪŋ]	pron.	任何事情	1	1	初級	
	do	[du]	v.	做、從事	1	1	初級	
⓫	make	[mek]	v.	結交	1	1	初級	
	friend	[frɛnd]	n.	朋友	1	1	初級	
⓬	have	[hæv]	v.	擁有	1	1	初級	
	any	[ˋɛnɪ]	adj.	任何的	1	1	初級	
⓭	feeling	[ˋfilɪŋ]	p.pr.	feel（感覺）現在分詞	1	1	初級	
	empty	[ˋɛmptɪ]	adj.	空虛的	1	3	初級	◎
⓮	hate	[het]	v.	討厭	1	1	初級	
	disturbed	[dɪˋstɝbd]	p.p.	disturbs（打擾）過去分詞	5	4	中高	◎
⓯	understood	[ʌndɚˋstud]	p.p.	understand（瞭解）過去分詞	1	1	初級	
⓰	dislike	[dɪsˋlaɪk]	v.	不喜歡	3	3	中級	
	social	[ˋsoʃəl]	adj.	社交的	1	2	初級	◎
	activity	[ækˋtɪvətɪ]	n.	活動	1	3	初級	
⓱	think	[θɪŋk]	v.	認為	1	1	初級	
	help	[hɛlp]	v.	幫忙	1	1	初級	
	talk	[tɔk]	v.	講話	1	1	初級	◎
	someone	[ˋsʌm.wʌn]	pron.	某個人	1	1	初級	
⓲	seem	[sim]	v.	似乎	1	1	初級	◎
	end	[ɛnd]	n.	結果	1	1	初級	
	still	[stɪl]	adv.	仍然	1	1	初級	
⓳	cheer	[tʃɪr]	v.	使打起精神	2	3	初級	◎
	up	[ʌp]	adv.	起來	1	1	初級	

※「紅字單字」於本單元多句出現，「單字級等分析」僅列在「首次出現句」。

🔵 MP3 063-01 ❶～⓰

❶	早知道，我就不會這樣做。	I wouldn't have done it had I known. * **wouldn't have＋過去分詞**（當時不會做某事） * **had I known**（要是我當時知道的話，是 **if I had known** 的倒裝型態）
❷	我後悔死了。	I am really regretful.
❸	後悔也來不及了。	It's too late for regrets. * **be too late**（太遲了）
❹	我是豬頭。	I'm really a fool. ＝ I'm an idiot.
❺	怨不得人。	It can't be blamed on anyone.
❻	你打我、罵我吧！	You can beat me and yell at me for all I care! * **for all I care**（我根本不在乎！）
❼	都怪我。	It's my fault.
❽	事到如今只能怪自己。	At this point I have only myself to blame. * **at this point**（現在這個節骨眼） * **have only myself to blame**（只能怪自己）
❾	我怎麼這麼笨！	How could I be so stupid!
❿	真是天不從人願。	The hopes of man have yet to be fulfilled. * **the hopes of man**（願望） * **have yet to...**（尚未…）
⓫	我後悔當初沒聽朋友的勸告。	I regret ignoring my friend's advice. * **I regret＋動詞-ing**（我後悔做某事）
⓬	我這次真的是學乖了。	I've really learned my lesson this time. * **I've＋過去分詞**（我已經…） * **learn one's lesson**（學到教訓）
⓭	下次，我會多聽聽別人的意見。	Next time, I will listen to others' opinions. * **I will＋動詞原形**（我將會…） * **listen to**（聽從）
⓮	我會努力重新做人。	I will try to be a new person.
⓯	我下次一定不會再犯錯。	I will not make a mistake next time. * **make a mistake**（犯錯）
⓰	我後悔以前沒有好好唸書。	I regret that I didn't study hard before. * **I regret that＋子句**（我後悔…）

	單字	音標	詞性	意義	字頻	大考	英檢	多益
❶	done	[dʌn]	p.p.	do（做）過去分詞	1	1	初級	
	known	[non]	p.p.	know（知道）過去分詞	2	1	初級	◎
❷	really	[ˋrɪəlɪ]	adv.	真的、實在是	1		初級	
	regretful	[rɪˋgrɛtfəl]	adj.	後悔的				
❸	too	[tu]	adv.	過於	1	1	初級	
	late	[let]	adj.	晚的	1	1	初級	◎
	regret	[rɪˋgrɛt]	n./v.	後悔	2	3	初級	
❹	fool	[ful]	n.	傻瓜	2	2	初級	
	idiot	[ˋɪdɪət]	n.	傻瓜	3	5	中高	
❺	blamed	[blemd]	p.p.	blame（責備）過去分詞	1	3	初級	◎
	anyone	[ˋɛnɪˏwʌn]	adv.	任何人	1	2	初級	
❻	beat	[bit]	v.	打	1	1	初級	
	yell	[jɛl]	v.	吼罵	1	3	中級	◎
	all	[ɔl]	n.	所有	1	1	初級	
	care	[kɛr]	v.	在乎	1	1	初級	◎
❼	fault	[fɔlt]	n.	過錯	2	2	初級	◎
❽	this	[ðɪs]	adj.	這個	1	1	初級	
	point	[pɔɪnt]	n.	節骨眼	1	1	初級	◎
	have	[hæv]	v.	擁有/（與 yet to 連用）尚未	1	1	初級	
	only	[ˋonlɪ]	adj.	只有	1	1	初級	
	myself	[maɪˋsɛlf]	pron.	我自己	1		初級	
	blame	[blem]	n.	責怪	1	3	初級	◎
❾	so	[so]	adv.	這麼	1	1	初級	
	stupid	[ˋstjupɪd]	adj.	愚蠢的	1	1	初級	◎
❿	hope	[hop]	n.	希望	1	1	初級	
	man	[mæn]	n.	人	1	1	初級	
	yet	[jɛt]	adv.	尚未	1	1	初級	◎
	fulfilled	[fulˋfɪld]	p.p.	fulfill（實現）過去分詞	2	4	中級	◎
⓫	ignoring	[ɪgˋnorɪŋ]	n.	ignore（不理會）動名詞	1	2	初級	◎
	friend	[frɛnd]	n.	朋友	1	1	初級	
	advice	[ədˋvaɪs]	n.	勸告	1	3	初級	◎
⓬	learned	[ˋlɜnɪd]	p.p.	learn（學到）過去分詞	4	4	中級	
	lesson	[ˋlɛsn]	n.	教訓	1	1	初級	◎
	time	[taɪm]	n.	次、回	1	1	初級	◎
⓭	next	[nɛkst]	adj.	下一	1	1	初級	
	listen	[ˋlɪsn]	v.	聽從	1	1	初級	
	other	[ˋʌðə]	pron.	其他人	1	1	初級	
	opinion	[əˋpɪnjən]	n.	意見	1	2	初級	◎
⓮	try	[traɪ]	v.	嘗試	1	1	初級	
	new	[nju]	adj.	新的	1	1	初級	
	person	[ˋpɜsn]	n.	人	1	1	初級	
⓯	make	[mek]	v.	犯下	1	1	初級	
	mistake	[mɪˋstek]	n.	錯誤	1	1	初級	◎
⓰	study	[ˋstʌdɪ]	v.	唸書	1	1	初級	◎
	hard	[hɑrd]	adj.	認真地	1	1	初級	◎

※「紅字單字」於本單元多句出現，「單字級等分析」僅列在「首次出現句」。

🔊 MP3 063-02 ❶～❶

❶	後悔了吧？	Are you regretful?
❷	知道錯了吧？	Have you realized you were wrong? * **Have you realized (that)**＋子句？ （你是否已經明白…）
❸	早就跟你說不要這樣做。	I've told you before not to do that. * **I've told you before**（我之前告訴過你）
❹	你還是不後悔愛上他？	Do you still not regret loving him? * **regret**＋動詞-ing（後悔做某事）
❺	你後悔當初沒聽朋友的勸告嗎？	Do you regret not taking your friends' advice at the beginning? * **take advice**（採取建議） * **at the beginning**（一開始）
❻	現在說這些是不是太遲了？	Is it too late for saying these things?
❼	你是不是覺得自己太傻了？	Don't you think that you've been too stupid? * **Don't you think that**＋子句?（你不覺得…嗎？） * 子句用「現在完成式」（...have been...） 　表示「過去持續到現在的事」。
❽	每次說你，你都不聽，現在後悔了吧？	You've never listened to me, now do you regret it? * **listen to me**（聽我的）
❾	告訴你那是騙人的，你還不信！	I told you that it was a lie, but you still did not believe me! * **I told you that**＋子句（我當時告訴你…）
❿	現在知道爸媽是為你好了吧？	Now do you know that your father and I are on your side? * **be on your side**（幫助你、為你著想）
⓫	知道老師的用意了吧？	Do you know what your teacher meant?
⓬	後悔了，就趕快改正啊。	If you regret it, then make amends quickly. * **If you**＋動詞，＋動詞（如果你…，就要…） * **make amends**（彌補過錯，amends 字尾永遠有 s）
⓭	你是真心懺悔嗎？	Are you really repentant?
⓮	現在還說這些幹嘛？	Why are you still saying these things?

	單字	音標	詞性	意義	字頻	大考	英檢	多益
❶	regretful	[rɪˋgrɛtfəl]	adj.	後悔的				
❷	realized	[ˋrɪəˌlaɪzd]	p.p.	realize（明白）過去分詞	1	2	初級	◎
	wrong	[rɔŋ]	adj.	錯誤的	1	1	初級	◎
❸	told	[told]	p.t.	tell（告訴）過去式	1	1	初級	
	before	[bɪˋfor]	adv.	以前	1	1	初級	
	do	[du]	v.	做	1	1	初級	
	that	[ðæt]	pron.	那個	1	1	初級	
❹	still	[stɪl]	adv.	仍然	1	1	初級	◎
	regret	[rɪˋgrɛt]	v.	後悔	2	3	初級	
	loving	[ˋlʌvɪŋ]	n.	love（喜愛）動名詞	2	1	中高	
❺	taking	[ˋtekɪŋ]	n.	take（採取）動名詞	4			
	friend	[frɛnd]	n.	朋友	1	1	初級	
	advice	[ədˋvaɪs]	n.	勸告	1	3	初級	◎
	beginning	[bɪˋgɪnɪŋ]	n.	開始	1	1	初級	
❻	too	[tu]	adv.	過於	1	1	初級	
	late	[let]	adj.	晚的	1	1	初級	◎
	saying	[ˋseɪŋ]	n.	say（說）動名詞	3	1	中級	
	these	[ðiz]	adj.	這些	1	1	初級	
	thing	[θɪŋ]	n.	事情	1	1	初級	
❼	think	[θɪŋk]	v.	認為	1	1	初級	
	stupid	[ˋstjupɪd]	adj.	愚蠢的	1	1	初級	◎
❽	never	[ˋnɛvɚ]	adv.	從不	1	1	初級	
	listened	[ˋlɪsnd]	p.p.	listen（聽從）過去分詞	1	1	初級	
	now	[naʊ]	adv.	現在	1	1	初級	
❾	lie	[laɪ]	n.	謊言	1	1	初級	
	believe	[bɪˋliv]	v.	相信	1	1	初級	◎
❿	know	[no]	v.	知道	1	1	初級	◎
	father	[ˋfɑðɚ]	n.	父親	1	1	初級	
	side	[saɪd]	n.	一方、方面	1	1	初級	
⓫	teacher	[ˋtitʃɚ]	n.	老師	1	1	初級	
	meant	[mɛnt]	p.t.	mean（用意）過去式	1	1	初級	◎
⓬	then	[ðɛn]	adv.	那麼	1	1	初級	
	make	[mek]	v.	做出	1	1	初級	
	amends	[əˋmɛndz]	n.	賠罪、賠償	7		中高	
	quickly	[ˋkwɪklɪ]	adv.	快速地	1			
⓭	really	[ˋrɪəlɪ]	adv.	真的	1		初級	
	repentant	[rɪˋpɛntənt]	adj.	懺悔的				

※「紅字單字」於本單元多句出現，「單字級等分析」僅列在「首次出現句」。

064 我覺得無聊。

MP3 064-01 ❶～⓱

❶	無事可做。	I have nothing to do.
❷	只是混日子。	Just fooling around. * **fool around**（遊手好閒、虛度日子）
❸	過一天算一天。	Just taking it one day at a time.
❹	沒什麼大事發生。	Nothing big has happened. * **nothing**＋形容詞（沒有⋯的事情）
❺	每天都一樣。	Every day is the same.
❻	我閒到快抓狂。	I'm so idle I'm about to go crazy. * **so idle (that)**＋子句（過於無所事事，導致⋯） * **be about to**＋動詞原形（即將） * **go crazy**（抓狂）
❼	生活就好像喝白開水一樣。	Life is like drinking a glass of water.
❽	好無聊喔！	It's so boring!
❾	日子真無趣。	Life is monotonous.
❿	好想睡覺。	I really want to sleep.
⓫	我們可以換個話題嗎？	Can we change the subject? * **change the subject**（換個話題）
⓬	再說下去我就要睡著了。	I'm going to fall asleep if you keep talking. * **be going to**（將要）。 * 此句用「未來簡單式」（...am going to...）表示「根據現況預測未來發生的事」。 * **fall asleep**（入睡、睡著）
⓭	課本的內容好無趣。	The textbook is so boring.
⓮	沒什麼事引得起我的興趣。	Nothing interests me. * **interest me**（讓我感興趣）
⓯	沒別的事可聊了嗎？	Is there nothing we can talk about?
⓰	她很單純，但說話很無趣。	She is so innocent but so boring when she speaks. * **be so**＋形容詞（平時很⋯） * **but so**＋形容詞＋**when**＋子句（但在⋯時，很⋯）
⓱	找點新鮮事做做吧！	Find some new things to do!

	單字	音標	詞性	意義	字頻	大考	英檢	多益
❶	have	[hæv]	v.	擁有	1	1	初級	
	nothing	[ˋnʌθɪŋ]	pron.	沒有事情	1	1	初級	
	do	[du]	v.	做	1	1	初級	
❷	just	[dʒʌst]	adv.	只是	1	1	初級	
	fooling	[ˋfulɪŋ]	p.pr.	fool（遊手好閒）現在分詞	2	2	初級	
	around	[əˋraʊnd]	adv.	到處、四處	1	1	初級	
❸	taking	[ˋtekɪŋ]	p.pr.	take（度過）現在分詞	4			
	one	[wʌn]	n.	一	1	1	初級	
	day	[de]	n.	天	1	1	初級	
	time	[taɪm]	n.	次、回	1	1	初級	◎
❹	big	[bɪg]	adj.	大的	1	1	初級	
	happened	[ˋhæpənd]	p.p.	happen（發生）過去分詞	1	1	初級	
❺	every	[ˋɛvrɪ]	adj.	每一	1	1	初級	
	same	[sem]	adj.	相同的	1	1	初級	
❻	so	[so]	adv.	多麼、非常	1	1	初級	
	idle	[ˋaɪdl̩]	adj.	無聊的	3	4	中級	◎
	go	[go]	v.	變為	1	1	初級	
	crazy	[ˋkrezɪ]	adj.	瘋狂的	1	2	初級	
❼	life	[laɪf]	n.	生活	1	1	初級	
	drinking	[ˋdrɪŋkɪŋ]	n.	drink（喝）動名詞	2	1	初級	
	glass	[glæs]	n.	一杯	1	1	初級	
	water	[ˋwɔtɚ]	n.	水	1	1	初級	
❽	boring	[ˋborɪŋ]	adj.	無聊的	2	3	初級	◎
❾	monotonous	[məˋnɑtənəs]	adj.	單調無聊的	7	6	中高	◎
❿	really	[ˋrɪəlɪ]	adv.	真的	1		初級	
	want	[wɑnt]	v.	想要	1	1	初級	◎
	sleep	[slip]	v.	睡覺	1	1	初級	
⓫	change	[tʃendʒ]	v.	更換、改變	1	2	初級	◎
	subject	[ˋsʌbdʒɪkt]	n.	話題	1	2	初級	◎
⓬	going	[ˋgoɪŋ]	p.pr.	go（即將）現在分詞	4	1	初級	
	fall	[fɔl]	v.	變成	1	1	初級	◎
	asleep	[əˋslip]	adj.	睡著的	2	2	初級	
	keep	[kip]	v.	繼續	1	1	初級	◎
	talking	[ˋtɔkɪŋ]	n.	talk（講話）動名詞	3	1	初級	
⓭	textbook	[ˋtɛkst͵bʊk]	n.	課本	2	2	初級	
⓮	interest	[ˋɪntərɪst]	v.	讓…感興趣	1	1	初級	◎
⓯	there	[ðɛr]	adv.	有…	1	1	初級	
	talk	[tɔk]	v.	講話	1	1	初級	◎
⓰	innocent	[ˋɪnəsn̩t]	adj.	單純的	1	3	中級	◎
	speak	[spik]	v.	說話	1	1	初級	
⓱	find	[faɪnd]	v.	尋找	1	1	初級	
	some	[sʌm]	adj.	一些	1	1	初級	
	new	[nju]	adj.	新的	1	1	初級	
	thing	[θɪŋ]	n.	事物	1	1	初級	

※「紅字單字」於本單元多句出現，「單字級等分析」僅列在「首次出現句」。

MP3 064-02 ❶～❽

❶	你沒事做嗎？	Do you have nothing to do?
❷	你太閒了嗎？	Are you too idle?
❸	你的日子都一成不變嗎？	Are your days all the same? * **all the same**（一成不變）
❹	想換個工作嗎？	Want to change jobs? * **change a job**（換工作）= **switch a job**
❺	想去旅行嗎？	Want to go on a trip? * **go on a trip**（去旅行）
❻	你不覺得生活很無趣嗎？	Don't you think your life is boring? * **Don't you think**＋子句?（你不覺得…嗎？）
❼	發什麼呆？	What are you staring into space for? * **What are you**＋動詞?（你做某事的具體行為？） * **stare into space**（發呆、兩眼發直）
❽	你每天都做一樣的事嗎？	Do you do the same thing every day?
❾	想換個話題嗎？	Want to change the subject?
❿	想去學些什麼嗎？	Want to learn something?
⓫	你對這件事沒興趣，是吧？	You are not interested in this, are you? * **be not interest in**＋某事（對某事不感興趣）
⓬	又是這首歌，聽不膩嗎？	This song again—aren't you sick of it? * **aren't you sick of...?**（你不會厭倦…嗎？）
⓭	想來點刺激的嗎？	Want to have some excitement? * **have some excitement**（來點刺激） * **fun**（有趣的事）
⓮	你又在做白日夢啦！	Daydreaming again!
⓯	你沒別的事可做了嗎？	Don't you have other things to do?
⓰	又在混日子？	Fooling around again?
⓱	怎麼整天渾渾噩噩的？	Why have you been muddle-headed all day long? * **Why have you been...?**（為什麼你持續某狀態…？） * **all day long**（一整天）
⓲	有什麼新鮮事嗎？	Anything new?

	單字	音標	詞性	意義	字頻	大考	英檢	多益
❶	have	[hæv]	v.	擁有	1	1	初級	
	nothing	[ˋnʌθɪŋ]	pron.	沒有事情	1	1	初級	
	do	[du]	v.	做	1	1	初級	
❷	too	[tu]	adv.	過於	1	1	初級	
	idle	[ˋaɪdl]	adj.	無聊的	3	4	中級	◎
❸	day	[de]	n.	日子、生活/天	1	1	初級	
	all	[ɔl]	adv. /adj.	完全/整個的	1	1	初級	
	same	[sem]	adj.	同樣的	1	1	初級	
❹	want	[wɑnt]	v.	想要	1	1	初級	◎
	change	[tʃendʒ]	v.	更換、改變	1	2	初級	◎
	job	[dʒɑb]	n.	工作	1	1	初級	
❺	go	[go]	v.	去	1	1	初級	
	trip	[trɪp]	n.	旅行	1	1	初級	◎
❻	think	[θɪŋk]	v.	認為	1	1	初級	
	life	[laɪf]	n.	生活	1	1	初級	
	boring	[ˋborɪŋ]	adj.	無聊的	2	3	初級	◎
❼	staring	[ˋstɛrɪŋ]	p.pr.	stare（注視）現在分詞	1	3	中級	◎
	space	[spes]	n.	空白處	1	1	初級	
❽	thing	[θɪŋ]	n.	事情	1	1	初級	
	every	[ˋɛvrɪ]	adj.	每一	1	1	初級	
❾	subject	[ˋsʌbdʒɪkt]	n.	話題	1	2	初級	◎
❿	learn	[lɝn]	v.	學習	1	1	初級	
	something	[ˋsʌmθɪŋ]	pron.	某些事物	1	1	初級	
⓫	interested	[ˋɪntərɪstɪd]	adj.	有興趣的	1	1	初級	◎
	this	[ðɪs]	pron. /adj.	這個	1	1	初級	
⓬	song	[sɔŋ]	n.	歌曲	1	1	初級	
	again	[əˋgɛn]	adv.	再次	1	1	初級	
	sick	[sɪk]	adj.	厭倦的	1	1	初級	◎
⓭	some	[sʌm]	adj.	一些	1	1	初級	
	excitement	[ɪkˋsaɪtmənt]	n.	刺激	2	2	中級	
⓮	daydreaming	[ˋde͵drimɪŋ]	p.pr.	daydream（做白日夢）現在分詞	6			
⓯	other	[ˋʌðɚ]	adj.	其他的	1	1	初級	
⓰	fooling	[ˋfulɪŋ]	p.pr.	fool（遊手好閒）現在分詞	2	2	初級	
	around	[əˋraʊnd]	adv.	到處、四處	1	1	初級	
⓱	muddle-headed	[ˋmʌdl͵hɛdɪd]	adj.	頭腦迷糊的				
	long	[lɔŋ]	adv.	長久地	1	1	初級	
⓲	anything	[ˋɛnɪ͵θɪŋ]	pron.	任何事情	1	1	初級	
	new	[nju]	adj.	新的	1	1	初級	

※「紅字單字」於本單元多句出現，「單字級等分析」僅列在「首次出現句」。

MP3 065-01 ❶～❶

❶	一定是你做的好事。	You must have done something bad. * must have＋過去分詞（猜測當時一定做了…） * do something bad（做壞事）
❷	我就是不相信。	I just do not believe that.
❸	我憑什麼要相信你？	Why should I believe you? * Why should I...?（為什麼我應該要…？）
❹	我覺得事情不大對勁。	Something's fishy.
❺	我真的沒辦法相信這個事實。	I really can't believe that this is true. * can't believe that＋子句（無法相信…）
❻	這個證據太薄弱。	This evidence is too weak. * weak（不具說服力的）可替換為： 　convincing（具說服力的） * excuse（辯解、說詞）
❼	這是真的嗎？	Is that true?
❽	太奇怪了。	It's too strange.
❾	怎麼會這樣？	How can it be?
❿	很難讓人相信。	It's really hard to convince people. * It's hard to＋動詞原形（難以…）
⓫	一定有人說謊。	Someone must have lied.
⓬	這事情一定有問題。	There must be some problem with this. * must be＋名詞（猜測現在一定是…） * have problem with＋名詞（有問題…）
⓭	我沒有辦法不懷疑你。	I can't help doubting you. * can't help＋動詞-ing（無法不…）
⓮	大家都各說各話。	Everybody speaks for himself. * speak for oneself（各說各話）
⓯	這個理由太牽強。	This reason is too far-fetched. * plausible（似乎說得通的）
⓰	我不知道該相信誰。	I don't know who I can believe.
⓱	你的動機令人懷疑。	Your motives make people doubt. * make＋某人＋動詞原形（讓人…）

	單字	音標	詞性	意義	字頻	大考	英檢	多益
❶	done	[dʌn]	p.p.	do（做）過去分詞	1	1	初級	
	something	[ˈsʌmθɪŋ]	pron.	某些事情	1	1	初級	
	bad	[bæd]	adj.	不好的	1	1	初級	
❷	just	[dʒʌst]	adv.	就是	1	1	初級	
	believe	[bɪˈliv]	v.	相信	1	1	初級	◎
	that	[ðæt]	pron.	那個	1	1	初級	
❹	fishy	[ˈfɪʃɪ]	adj.	令人懷疑的	7			
❺	really	[ˈrɪəlɪ]	adv.	真的	1		初級	
	this	[ðɪs]	pron. /adj.	這個	1	1	初級	
	true	[tru]	adj.	真實的	1	1	初級	
❻	evidence	[ˈɛvədəns]	n.	證據	1	4	中級	◎
	too	[tu]	adv.	過於	1	1	初級	
	weak	[wik]	adj.	不具說服力的	1	1	初級	◎
❽	strange	[strendʒ]	adj.	奇怪的	1	1	初級	
❿	hard	[hɑrd]	adj.	困難的	1	1	初級	
	convince	[kənˈvɪns]	v.	使相信	1	1	初級	◎
	people	[ˈpipl]	n.	person（人）複數	1	4	中級	◎
⓫	someone	[ˈsʌmˌwʌn]	pron.	某些人	1	1	初級	
	lied	[laɪd]	p.p.	lie（說謊）過去分詞	1	1	初級	
⓬	there	[ðɛr]	adv.	有…	1	1	初級	
	some	[sʌm]	adj.	有些	1	1	初級	
	problem	[ˈprɑbləm]	n.	問題	1	1	初級	
⓭	help	[hɛlp]	v.	忍住、抑制	1	1	初級	◎
	doubting	[ˈdaʊtɪŋ]	n.	doubt（懷疑）動名詞	1	1	初級	
⓮	everybody	[ˈɛvrɪˌbɑdɪ]	pron.	每個人	1	2	初級	◎
	speak	[spik]	v.	發言	1		初級	
	himself	[hɪmˈsɛlf]	pron.	他自己	1	1	初級	
⓯	reason	[ˈrizn]	n.	理由	1		初級	
	far-fetched	[ˈfɑrˈfɛtʃt]	adj.	牽強的、可信度低的	1	1	初級	◎
⓰	know	[no]	v.	知道	6			
⓱	motive	[ˈmotɪv]	n.	動機	1	1	初級	
	make	[mek]	v.	使得	2	5	中高	◎
	doubt	[daʊt]	v.	懷疑	1	1	初級	

※「紅字單字」於本單元多句出現，「單字級等分析」僅列在「首次出現句」。

❶	你懷疑他嗎？	Do you doubt him?
❷	你是在考驗我嗎？	Are you testing me?
❸	你不覺得很可疑嗎？	Don't you think it dubious? * dubious（可疑的）＝ questionable ＝ suspicious
❹	你認為有什麼不對的地方嗎？	Do you think anything is wrong? * Do you think...?（你是否覺得…？） * anything is wrong（有任何不對勁的事）
❺	有什麼問題嗎？	Is there a problem? * Is there＋名詞?（是否有…？）
❻	你不再相信我了嗎？	You don't believe me anymore?
❼	那件事難道是他做的？	Is it possible that he was the one who did it? * Is it possible that＋子句?（是否有可能…？） * be the one who...（做某事的人）
❽	你相信這是真的嗎？	Do you believe this is true?
❾	真有這回事嗎？	Has this really happened? * Has＋主詞＋happened?（…是否曾經發生？）
❿	不會是騙人的吧？	It isn't a scam, is it? * fraud（詐騙） * confidence trick（騙局） * phone scam（詐騙電話）
⓫	你總是疑神疑鬼。	You always have unfounded suspicions. * have unfounded suspicions（疑心重、疑神疑鬼）
⓬	不要總是懷疑別人。	Don't doubt people so much. * Don't＋動詞原形（你別做某事！） * doubt people so much（愛懷疑別人）
⓭	別神經質了。	Don't be nervous. * Don't be＋形容詞（你別處在某狀態！）
⓮	你不相信，我也沒辦法。	If you don't believe me, there's nothing I can do. * there's nothing I can do（我無可奈何）
⓯	會不會是你想太多了？	Aren't you thinking too much? * think too much（想太多）

	單字	音標	詞性	意義	字頻	大考	英檢	多益
❶	doubt	[daʊt]	v.	懷疑	1	2	初級	◎
❷	testing	[ˋtɛstɪŋ]	p.pr.	test（考驗、測試）現在分詞	1	2	初級	
❸	think	[θɪŋk]	v.	認為	1	1	初級	
	dubious	[ˋdjubɪəs]	adj.	可疑的	3	6	中高	
❹	anything	[ˋɛnɪˌθɪŋ]	pron.	任何事情	1	1	初級	
	wrong	[rɔŋ]	adj.	不對勁的	1	1	初級	◎
❺	there	[ðɛr]	adv.	有…	1	1	初級	
	problem	[ˋprɑbləm]	n.	問題	1	1	初級	◎
❻	believe	[bɪˋliv]	v.	相信	1	1	初級	◎
	anymore	[ˋɛnɪˌmɔr]	adv.	不再	1		中高	
❼	possible	[ˋpɑsəbl]	adj.	可能的	1	1	初級	◎
	one	[wʌn]	pron.	一個人	1	1	初級	
	did	[dɪd]	p.t.	do（做）過去式	1	1	初級	
❽	this	[ðɪs]	pron.	這個	1	1	初級	
	true	[tru]	adj.	真實的	1	1	初級	
❾	really	[ˋrɪəlɪ]	adv.	真的	1		初級	
	happened	[ˋhæpənd]	p.p.	happen（發生）過去分詞	1	1	初級	
❿	scam	[skæm]	n.	詐騙	4			◎
⓫	always	[ˋɔlwez]	adv.	總是	1	1	初級	
	have	[hæv]	v.	擁有	1	1	初級	
	unfounded	[ʌnˋfaʊndɪd]	adj.	沒有根據的	6			
	suspicion	[səˋspɪʃən]	n.	懷疑	2	3	中級	
⓬	people	[ˋpipl]	n.	person（人）複數	1	1	初級	
	so	[so]	adv.	這麼	1	1	初級	
	much	[mʌtʃ]	adv.	許多地	1	1	初級	
⓭	nervous	[ˋnɝvəs]	adj.	神經質的	1	3	初級	
⓮	nothing	[ˋnʌθɪŋ]	pron.	沒有事情	1	1	初級	
	do	[du]	v.	做	1	1	初級	
⓯	thinking	[ˋθɪŋkɪŋ]	p.pr.	think（想）現在分詞	1	1	中級	
	too	[tu]	adv.	過於	1	1	初級	

※「紅字單字」於本單元多句出現，「單字級等分析」僅列在「首次出現句」。

🔊 MP3 066-01 ❶～❽

❶	我擔心我父親的健康。	I worry about my father's health. * worry about（擔心） * father's（父親的）可替換為：mother's（母親的）
❷	我和父母親無話可說。	There's little I can talk to my parents about. * There's little I can＋動詞（我能夠做…的很少） * There's a lot I can＋動詞（我能夠做…的很多） * talk to＋某人（和某人說話）
❸	我很怕我的小孩會學壞。	I'm afraid my child will pick up bad habits. * be afraid＋子句（害怕…） * 子句用「未來簡單式」（…will…） 　表示「在未來將發生的事」。 * pick up bad habits（染上惡習）
❹	我跟我的孩子有代溝。	There's a generational gap between me and my children. * There's a generational gap（有代溝） * between A and B（A 和 B 之間）
❺	我不知道如何跟孩子溝通。	I don't know how to communicate with my kids. * I don't know how to＋動詞原形 　（我不知道如何做…） * communicate with＋某人（和某人溝通）
❻	我常跟太太吵架。	I often quarrel with my wife. * quarrel with＋某人（和某人吵架）
❼	我們家婆媳問題很嚴重。	There are some serious problems between my wife and my mother. * There are some＋名詞（存在一些…） * problems between my wife and my mother 　（我太太和我母親之間的婆媳問題） * problems between me and my mother-in-law 　（我和婆婆之間的婆媳問題） * mother-in-law（岳母、婆婆） * father-in-law（岳父、公公）
❽	我先生似乎有外遇。	My husband seems to be having an affair. * seem to be＋動詞-ing（似乎正在…） * have an affair（有外遇、出軌） * my husband（我先生） * my wife（我太太）

	單字	音標	詞性	意義	字頻	大考	英檢	多益
❶	worry	[ˋwɝɪ]	v.	擔心	1	1	初級	◎
	father	[ˋfɑðɚ]	n.	父親	1	1	初級	
	health	[hɛlθ]	n.	健康	1	1	初級	◎
❷	there	[ðɛr]	adv.	有…	1	1	初級	
	little	[ˋlɪtl̩]	adj.	少量的	1	1	初級	
	talk	[tɔk]	v.	講話	1	1	初級	◎
	parents	[ˋpɛrənts]	n.	parent（雙親）複數	2	1		
❸	afraid	[əˋfred]	adj.	害怕的	1	1	初級	
	child	[tʃaɪld]	n.	小孩	1	1	初級	
	pick	[pɪk]	v.	學會	1	2	初級	
	up	[ʌp]	adv.	染上	1	1	初級	
	bad	[bæd]	adj.	不好的	1	1	初級	
	habit	[ˋhæbɪt]	n.	習慣	1	2	初級	◎
❹	generational	[͵dʒɛnəˋreʃənl̩]	adj.	世代的	5			
	gap	[gæp]	n.	差距、隔閡	1	3	中級	◎
	children	[ˋtʃɪldrən]	n.	child（小孩）複數	1	1	初級	
❺	know	[no]	v.	知道	1	1	初級	◎
	communicate	[kəˋmjunə͵ket]	v.	溝通	1	3	中級	
	kid	[kɪd]	n.	小孩	1	1	初級	
❻	often	[ˋɔfən]	adv.	常常	1	1	初級	
	quarrel	[ˋkwɔrəl]	v.	吵架	5	3	中級	◎
	wife	[waɪf]	n.	妻子	1	1	初級	
❼	some	[sʌm]	adj.	有些	1	1	初級	
	serious	[ˋsɪrɪəs]	adj.	嚴重的	1	2	初級	◎
	problem	[ˋprɑbləm]	n.	問題	1	1	初級	
	mother	[ˋmʌðɚ]	n.	母親	1	1	初級	
❽	husband	[ˋhʌzbənd]	n.	丈夫	1	1	初級	
	seem	[sim]	v.	似乎	1	1	初級	◎
	having	[ˋhævɪŋ]	p.pr.	have（擁有）現在分詞	1	1	初級	
	affair	[əˋfɛr]	n.	外遇	1	2	初級	◎

※「紅字單字」於本單元多句出現，「單字級等分析」僅列在「首次出現句」。

🔊 MP3 066-01 ❾～⓲

❾	我不放心我父母兩老自己住。	I don't feel comfortable letting my elderly parents live by themselves. * not feel comfortable＋動詞-ing（不放心做…） * let＋某人＋動詞原形（讓某人做…） * elderly parents（年邁的雙親）
❿	我父母一直催我結婚。	My parents keep pressuring me to get married. * keep＋動詞-ing（不斷做…） * pressure me to＋動詞原形（逼迫我做…）
⓫	我父母成天唸著要抱孫子。	My parents nag me all day long to have a child. * nag me all day long to＋動詞原形 　　（整天碎唸我做…） * have a child（生小孩）
⓬	我覺得我弟弟最近怪怪的。	I feel like my little brother's been acting odd recently. * I feel like (that)＋子句（我覺得…） * 子句用「現在完成進行式」（…has been acting...） 　表示「從過去開始，且直到現在仍持續中的事」。 * act odd（行為異常） * little brother（弟弟）、little sister（妹妹）
⓭	我覺得我父母親最近太操勞了。	I feel like my parents have been overworking themselves recently. * overwork＋某人（讓某人工作過勞）
⓮	我怕我先生工作太累了。	I'm afraid that my husband is working too hard. * I'm afraid that＋子句（我害怕…） * work too hard（工作太認真、工作過勞）
⓯	我們家最近氣氛不太好。	The atmosphere in our home isn't very good.
⓰	我姊姊的婚姻出了問題。	My sister has problems in her marriage. * have problems in marriage（婚姻出狀況）
⓱	我跟哥哥常常意見不合。	I often have disagreements with my big brother. * have disagreements（意見不合） * big brother（哥哥）＝ older brother
⓲	我擔心我弟弟畢不了業。	I worry that my brother won't be able to graduate. * I worry that＋子句（我擔心…） * won't be able to＋動詞原形（未來會無法…）

	單字	音標	詞性	意義	字頻	大考	英檢	多益
❾	feel	[fil]	v.	覺得	1	1	初級	
	comfortable	[ˈkʌmfətəbl̩]	adj.	放心的	1	2	初級	◎
	letting	[ˈlɛtɪŋ]	p.pr.	let（讓…）現在分詞	1	1	初級	
	elderly	[ˈɛldəlɪ]	adj.	年邁的	2	3	中級	◎
	parents	[ˈpɛrənts]	n.	parent（雙親）複數	2	1		
	live	[lɪv]	v.	生活	1	1	初級	
	themselves	[ðəmˈsɛlvz]	pron.	他們自己	1		初級	
❿	keep	[kip]	v.	一直	1	1	初級	◎
	pressuring	[ˈprɛʃərɪŋ]	n.	pressure（逼迫）動名詞	1	3	中級	◎
	get	[gɛt]	v.	變成	1	1	初級	◎
	married	[ˈmærɪd]	p.p.	marry（結婚）過去分詞	1		初級	
⓫	nag	[næg]	v.	嘮叨	5	1	中高	
	all	[ɔl]	adj.	整個的	1	5	初級	
	day	[de]	n.	天	1	1	初級	
	long	[lɔŋ]	adv.	長久地	1	1	初級	
	have	[hæv]	v.	生育/擁有	1	1	初級	
	child	[tʃaɪld]	n.	小孩	1	1	初級	
⓬	little	[ˈlɪtl̩]	adj.	小的	1	1	初級	
	brother	[ˈbrʌðə]	n.	哥哥、弟弟	1	1	初級	
	acting	[ˈæktɪŋ]	p.pr.	act（做出舉動）現在分詞	4	1	中高	
	odd	[ɑd]	adj.	怪異的	1	3	中級	◎
	recently	[ˈrisntlɪ]	adv.	最近	1		初級	
⓭	overworking	[ˈovəˈwɜkɪŋ]	p.pr.	overwork（工作過勞）現在分詞	8	5	中高	
⓮	afraid	[əˈfred]	adj.	害怕的	1	1	初級	
	husband	[ˈhʌzbənd]	n.	丈夫	1	1	初級	
	working	[ˈwɜkɪŋ]	p.pr.	work（工作）現在分詞	2	1	中級	◎
	too	[tu]	adv.	過於	1	1	初級	
	hard	[hɑrd]	adv.	認真地	1	1	初級	
⓯	atmosphere	[ˈætməsˌfɪr]	n.	氣氛	1	4	中級	◎
	home	[hom]	n.	家	1	1	初級	
	very	[ˈvɛrɪ]	adv.	十分	1	1	初級	
	good	[gud]	adj.	良好的	1	1	初級	◎
⓰	sister	[ˈsɪstə]	n.	姐姐、妹妹	1	1	初級	
	problem	[ˈprɑbləm]	n.	問題	1	1	初級	◎
	marriage	[ˈmærɪdʒ]	n.	婚姻	1	2	初級	
⓱	often	[ˈɔfən]	adv.	常常	1	1	初級	
	disagreement	[ˌdɪsəˈgrimənt]	n.	意見不合	2	2	中高	
	big	[bɪg]	adj.	大的	1	1	初級	
⓲	worry	[ˈwɜɪ]	v.	擔心	1	1	初級	◎
	able	[ˈebl̩]	adj.	能夠的	1	1	初級	◎
	graduate	[ˈgrædʒuˌet]	v.	畢業	1	3	中級	◎

※「紅字單字」於本單元多句出現，「單字級等分析」僅列在「首次出現句」。

❶	你在擔心父母親的健康嗎？	Do you worry about your parents' health? * **Do you worry about＋名詞?**（你是否擔心…？） * **parents' health**（父母親的健康）
❷	你跟父母親還是無法溝通嗎？	Are you still unable to communicate with your parents? * **Are you unable to＋動詞原形?** 　（你是否無法做…？）v * **Are you able to＋動詞原形?** 　（你是否能夠做…？）
❸	你知道如何跟孩子相處嗎？	Do you know how to get along with your children? * **Do you know how to...?**（你是否知道…的方法？） * **get along with＋某人**（和某人相處融洽） * **siblings**（sibling〔兄弟姊妹〕的複數）
❹	你怕你的孩子交到壞朋友嗎？	Are you afraid that your child will make bad friends? * **Are you afraid that＋子句?**（你是否害怕…？） * **make a bad friend**（交到壞朋友）
❺	你跟你先生常吵架嗎？	Do you often quarrel with your husband? * **Do you often＋動詞?**（你是否經常…？）
❻	你會擔心你太太有外遇嗎？	Do you worry that your wife is having an affair? * **Do you worry that＋子句?**（你是否擔心…？） * 子句用「現在進行式」（...is having...） 　表示「現階段發生的事」。
❼	你擔心你父母會離婚嗎？	Do you worry that your parents will get divorced? * **will get divorced**（未來會離婚）
❽	你太太和你母親之間有婆媳問題嗎？	Are there problems between your wife and your mother? * **Are there problems between you and your mother-in-law?**（你和你婆婆之間有婆媳問題嗎？） * **Are there＋名詞?**（是否存在有…？）
❾	你母親跟你太太還是水火不容嗎？	Do your mother and wife still not get along? * **not get along**（相處不來） * **get along**（相處融洽）

單字級等分析

	單字	音標	詞性	意義	字頻	大考	英檢	多益
❶	worry	[`wɝɪ]	v.	擔心	1	2	初級	◎
	parents	[`pɛrənts]	n.	parent（雙親）複數	1	2	初級	
	health	[hɛlθ]	n.	健康	1	1	初級	
❷	still	[stɪl]	adv.	仍然	3	6	中高	
	unable	[ʌn`ebl̩]	adj.	不能的	1	1	初級	
	communicate	[kə`mjunə‚ket]	v.	溝通	1	1	初級	◎
❸	know	[no]	v.	知道	1	1	初級	
	get	[gɛt]	v.	相處	1	1	初級	◎
	along	[ə`lɔŋ]	adv.	一起	1	1	初級	◎
	children	[`tʃɪldrən]	n.	child（小孩）複數	1		中高	
❹	afraid	[ə`fred]	adj.	害怕的	1	1	初級	◎
	child	[tʃaɪld]	n.	小孩	1	1	初級	
	make	[mek]	v.	結交	1	1	初級	
	bad	[bæd]	adj.	不好的	1	1	初級	
	friend	[frɛnd]	n.	朋友	1	1	初級	
❺	often	[`ɔfən]	adv.	常常	1		初級	
	husband	[`hʌzbənd]	n.	丈夫	4			◎
❻	wife	[waɪf]	n.	妻子	1	1	初級	
	having	[`hævɪŋ]	p.pr.	have（擁有）現在分詞	1	1	初級	
	affair	[ə`fɛr]	n.	外遇	6			
❼	divorced	[də`vɔrst]	p.p.	divorce（離婚）過去分詞	2	3	中級	
❽	there	[ðɛr]	adv.	有…	1	1	初級	
	problem	[`prɑbləm]	n.	問題	1	1	初級	
	mother	[`mʌðɚ]	n.	母親	1	1	初級	

※「紅字單字」於本單元多句出現，「單字級等分析」僅列在「首次出現句」。

🔊 MP3 066-02 ❿〜⓲

❿	你在煩惱家裡的什麼事？	What about your family worries you? * **What about your family＋動詞?** 　（你的家人…的具體內容是什麼？） * **worry＋某人**（使某人擔心）
⓫	你太太不願意跟你父母同住嗎？	Is your wife not willing to live with your parents? * **Is＋某人＋not willing to...?**（某人是否不願意…？） * **live with＋某人**（和某人同住）
⓬	你父母一直催你結婚嗎？	Do your parents keep pressuring you to get married?
⓭	你父母應該急著要抱孫子吧？	Your parents must be eager to have a grandchild, right? * **must be＋形容詞**（猜測　定是…） * **be eager to**（渴望） * **have a grandchild**（有孫子）
⓮	你家最近氣氛不太好嗎？	Is the atmosphere in your home not so good? * **Is＋主詞＋not＋形容詞?**（…是否不…？） * **atmosphere in one's home**（家裡的氣氛）
⓯	你姊姊還是沒找到工作嗎？	Has your sister still not found a job? * **Has＋某人＋not＋過去分詞...?**（某人是否尚未…？） * 此句用「現在完成式問句」（Has...not found...?）表示「過去某時點是否未發生某事，且結果持續到現在嗎？」。
⓰	你不怕孩子會被你爸媽寵壞嗎？	Aren't you afraid that your child will be spoiled by your parents? * **Aren't you afraid that＋子句?**（你不害怕…嗎？） * **be afraid that＋子句**（害怕…） * **be spoiled by＋某人**（被某人寵壞）
⓱	你會擔心孩子的安全問題嗎？	Do you worry about your child's safety? * **worry about＋名詞**（擔心…） * **child's safety**（小孩的安全）
⓲	你放心讓孩子去外地唸書嗎？	Do you feel safe in letting your child attend school in another place? * **feel safe in＋動詞-ing**（放心做…） * **attend school**（就學、上學） * **in another place**（在另一個地方）

單字級等分析

	單字	音標	詞性	意義	字頻	大考	英檢	多益
⑩	family	[ˈfæməlɪ]	n.	家庭	1	1	初級	
	worry	[ˈwɜɪ]	v.	擔心	1	1	初級	◎
⑪	wife	[waɪf]	n.	妻子	1	1	初級	
	willing	[ˈwɪlɪŋ]	adj.	願意的	1	2	初級	◎
	live	[lɪv]	v.	居住	1	1	初級	
	parents	[ˈpɛrənts]	n.	parent（雙親）複數	2	1		
⑫	keep	[kip]	v.	一直	1	1	初級	
	pressuring	[ˈprɛʃərɪŋ]	n.	pressure（逼迫）動名詞	1	3	中級	◎
	get	[gɛt]	v.	變成	1	1	初級	◎
	married	[ˈmærɪd]	p.p.	marry（結婚）過去分詞	1		初級	◎
⑬	eager	[ˈigɚ]	adj.	渴望的	2	3	中級	◎
	have	[hæv]	v.	擁有	1		初級	
	grandchild	[ˈgrænd.tʃaɪld]	n.	孫子	2	1	中級	
	right	[raɪt]	int.	對吧	1	1	初級	
⑭	atmosphere	[ˈætməs.fɪr]	n.	氣氛	1	4	中級	◎
	home	[hom]	n.	家	1	1	初級	
	so	[so]	adv.	非常	1	1	初級	
	good	[gʊd]	adj.	良好的	1	1	初級	◎
⑮	sister	[ˈsɪstɚ]	n.	姐姐、妹妹	1	1	初級	
	still	[stɪl]	adv.	仍然	1	1	初級	◎
	found	[faʊnd]	p.p.	find（尋找）過去分詞	1	3	中級	◎
	job	[dʒɑb]	n.	工作	1	1	初級	
⑯	afraid	[əˈfred]	adj.	害怕的	1	1	初級	
	child	[tʃaɪld]	n.	小孩	1	1	初級	
	spoiled	[spɔɪlt]	p.p.	spoil（寵壞）過去分詞	6	3	中級	◎
⑰	safety	[ˈseftɪ]	n.	安全	1	2	初級	◎
⑱	feel	[ˈfil]	v.	感覺	1	1	初級	
	safe	[sef]	n.	安全的	1	1	初級	◎
	letting	[ˈlɛtɪŋ]	n.	let（讓…）動名詞	1	1	初級	
	attend	[əˈtɛnd]	v.	就學	1	2	初級	◎
	school	[skul]	n.	學校	1	1	初級	
	another	[əˈnʌðɚ]	adj.	另一個	1	1		
	place	[ples]	n.	地方	1	1	初級	◎

※「紅字單字」於本單元多句出現，「單字級等分析」僅列在「首次出現句」。

067 我煩惱情人。

❶	我懷疑我男友劈腿。	I suspect that my boyfriend is cheating on me. * suspect that＋子句（懷疑…） * cheat on me（對我不忠貞、背著我偷吃）
❷	我跟我男友經常意見不合。	I often have disagreements with my boyfriend. * have disagreements（意見不合）
❸	我不知道他對我是不是真心的。	I don't know whether he is sincere to me. * whether＋子句（是否…） * be sincere to＋某人（對某人是真心的）
❹	我女友身邊追求者太多。	Too many men chase my girlfriend.
❺	我男友讓我覺得壓力很大。	My boyfriend puts me under a lot of pressure. * put me under pressure（帶給我壓力）
❻	我最怕我女朋友哭了。	I'm afraid when my girlfriend cries. * be afraid＋子句（害怕…） * when＋子句（…的時候）
❼	我的女友越來越任性。	My girlfriend is getting more and more wild. * 此句用「現在進行式」（...is getting...） 表示「現階段逐漸變化的事」。
❽	我不知道要送她什麼禮物。	I don't know what gift to get her. * what gift to get her（要買給她怎樣的禮物）
❾	我覺得她不喜歡我了。	I feel that she doesn't like me anymore. * feel that＋子句（覺得…）
❿	我的他很愛吃醋。	My boyfriend is jealous.
⓫	我不喜歡他處處管我。	I don't like him trying to control me in every way. * control me（控制我） * in every way（在各方面）
⓬	我怕她拒絕我的求婚。	I'm afraid she will reject my proposal. * reject one's proposal（拒絕求婚）
⓭	我的男朋友遲遲不跟我求婚。	My boyfriend still hasn't proposed to me. * have/has not＋過去分詞（尚未做某事） * propose to＋某人（像某人求婚）
⓮	我不知道如何維持遠距離戀愛。	I don't know how to maintain a long-distance relationship. * maintain a relationship（維持關係） * long-distance relationship（遠距離戀愛）

	單字	音標	詞性	意義	字頻	大考	英檢	多益
❶	suspect	[sə`spɛkt]	v.	懷疑	1	3	中級	◎
	boyfriend	[`bɔɪ.frɛnd]	n.	男朋友	2		中級	
	cheating	[`tʃitɪŋ]	p.pr.	cheat（欺騙）現在分詞	8	2	初級	◎
❷	often	[`ɔfən]	adv.	常常	1	1	初級	
	have	[hæv]	v.	擁有	1	1	初級	
	disagreement	[.dɪsə`grimənt]	n.	意見不合	2	2	中高	
❸	know	[no]	v.	知道	1	1	初級	◎
	sincere	[sɪn`sɪr]	adj.	真心的	3	3	初級	◎
❹	too	[tu]	adv.	過於	1	1	初級	
	many	[`mɛnɪ]	adj.	許多的	1	1	初級	
	men	[mɛn]	n.	man（男人）複數	1	1	初級	
	chase	[tʃes]	v.	追求	2	1	初級	◎
	girlfriend	[`gɝl.frɛnd]	n.	女朋友	2		中級	
❺	put	[pʊt]	v.	施加	1		初級	
	lot	[lɑt]	n.	許多				
	pressure	[`prɛʃɚ]	n.	壓力	1	3	中級	◎
❻	afraid	[ə`fred]	adj.	害怕的	1	1	初級	
	cry	[kraɪ]	v.	哭泣	1	1	初級	
❼	getting	[`gɛtɪŋ]	p.pr.	get（變成）現在分詞	1	1	初級	◎
	more	[mor]	adv.	更加	1	1	初級	
	wild	[waɪld]	adj.	任性的	1	2	初級	
❽	gift	[gɪft]	n.	禮物	1	1	初級	◎
	get	[gɛt]	v.	購買	1	1	初級	◎
❾	feel	[fil]	v.	覺得	1	1	初級	
	like	[laɪk]	v.	喜歡	1	1	初級	
	anymore	[`ɛnɪmɔr]	adv.	不再	1		中高	
❿	jealous	[`dʒɛləs]	adj.	易吃醋的	3	3	初級	◎
⓫	trying	[`traɪɪŋ]	p.pr.	try（嘗試）現在分詞	6	1	初級	
	control	[kən`trol]	v.	控制	1	2	初級	◎
	every	[`ɛvrɪ]	adj.	每一	1	1	初級	
	way	[we]	n.	方面	1	1	初級	
⓬	reject	[rɪ`dʒɛkt]	v.	拒絕	1	2	初級	◎
	proposal	[prə`pozl]	n.	求婚	1	3	中級	◎
⓭	still	[stɪl]	adv.	仍然	1	1	初級	◎
	proposed	[prə`pozd]	p.p.	propose（求婚）過去分詞	2	2	初級	◎
⓮	maintain	[men`ten]	v.	維持	1	2	初級	◎
	long-distance	[`lɔŋ`dɪstəns]	adj.	遠距離的	3			
	relationship	[rɪ`leʃən.ʃɪp]	n.	戀愛關係	1	2	中級	◎

※「紅字單字」於本單元多句出現，「單字級等分析」僅列在「首次出現句」。

MP3 067-02 ❶～⓮

❶	你跟女友發生了什麼問題？	What's the problem between you and your girlfriend? * What's the problem...? （…的具體問題是？）
❷	你怕他不愛你了嗎？	Are you afraid that he doesn't love you anymore? * not like＋人事物＋anymore（不再喜歡某人事物）
❸	你介意她結交異性朋友嗎？	Do you mind if she has a friend of the opposite sex? * mind if＋子句（介意…） * opposite sex（異性）
❹	你覺得你男友不在意你嗎？	Do you feel that your boyfriend doesn't care about you? * care about you（在乎你）
❺	你會為了她吃醋嗎？	Does she make you jealous? * make＋某人＋形容詞（讓某人…）
❻	你們經常意見不合嗎？	Do you two usually disagree?
❼	你害怕有三角戀嗎？	Are you afraid of there being a love triangle? * be afraid（害怕、擔心）＝ be worried ＝ worry * love triangle（三角戀）
❽	你擔心你女友不答應你的求婚嗎？	Are you worried that your girlfriend won't accept your proposal? * be worried that＋子句（擔心…）
❾	你擔心你男友花心嗎？	Do you worry that your boyfriend plays around? * worry that＋子句（擔心…） * play around（對感情不專一、花心）
❿	你會為了送她禮物傷腦筋嗎？	Are you stressed out about what to give her? * be stressed out（感到傷腦筋）
⓫	你擔心遠距離戀愛嗎？	Are you worried about having a long-distance relationship?
⓬	你怕他腳踏兩條船嗎？	Do you feel that he isn't loyal to you? * be not loyal to＋某人（對某人不忠貞）
⓭	你男友讓你覺得有壓力嗎？	Does your boyfriend put you under pressure?
⓮	你覺得你們已經不行了嗎？	Do you feel there is no way for you two to go on? * there is no way（不可能） * go on（繼續在一起）

單字級等分析

	單字	音標	詞性	意義	字頻	大考	英檢	多益
❶	problem	[ˋprɑbləm]	n.	問題	1	1	初級	◎
	girlfriend	[ˋgɝl͵frɛnd]	n.	女朋友	2		中級	
❷	afraid	[əˋfred]	adj.	害怕的	1	1	初級	
	love	[lʌv]	v./n.	喜愛/愛情	1	1	初級	
	anymore	[ˋɛnɪ͵mor]	adv.	不再	1		中高	
❸	mind	[maɪnd]	v.	介意	1	1	初級	◎
	have	[hæv]	v.	擁有	1	1	初級	
	friend	[frɛnd]	n.	朋友	1	1	初級	
	opposite	[ˋɑpəzɪt]	adj.	相對的	1	3	中級	◎
	sex	[sɛks]	n.	性別	1	3	中級	
❹	feel	[fil]	v.	感覺	1	1	初級	
	boyfriend	[ˋbɔɪ͵frɛnd]	n.	男朋友	2		中級	
	care	[kɛr]	v.	在意	1	1	初級	◎
❺	make	[mek]	v.	使得	1	1	初級	
	jealous	[ˋdʒɛləs]	adj.	易吃醋的	3	3	初級	◎
❻	two	[tu]	pron.	兩人	1	1	初級	
	usually	[ˋjuʒʊəlɪ]	adv.	經常	1		初級	◎
	disagree	[dɪsəˋgri]	v.	意見不合、吵架	1	2	中級	◎
❼	there	[ðɛr]	n.	有…	1	1	初級	
	triangle	[ˋtraɪ͵æŋgl]	n.	三角形	3	2	初級	◎
❽	worried	[ˋwɝɪd]	adj.	擔心的	2	1	中級	
	accept	[əkˋsɛpt]	v.	接受	1	2	初級	◎
	proposal	[prəˋpozl]	n.	求婚	1	3	中級	◎
❾	worry	[ˋwɝɪ]	v.	擔心	1	1	初級	◎
	play	[ple]	v.	玩弄	1	1	初級	
	around	[əˋraʊnd]	adv.	四處	1	1	初級	
❿	stressed	[strɛst]	p.p.	stress（傷腦筋）過去分詞	1	2	初級	◎
	out	[aʊt]	adv.	完全、徹底	1	1	初級	
	give	[gɪv]	v.	給予	1	1	初級	
⓫	having	[ˋhævɪŋ]	n.	have（擁有）動名詞	1	1	初級	
	long-distance	[ˋlɔŋˋdɪstəns]	adj.	遠距離的	3			
	relationship	[rɪˋleʃən͵ʃɪp]	n.	戀愛關係	1	2	中級	◎
⓬	loyal	[ˋlɔɪəl]	adj.	忠心的	2	4	中級	◎
⓭	put	[pʊt]	v.	施加	1	1	初級	
	pressure	[ˋprɛʃɚ]	n.	壓力	1	3	中級	◎
⓮	way	[we]	n.	方法	1	1	初級	
	go	[go]	v.	進展	1	1	初級	
	on	[ɑn]	adv.	繼續	1	1	初級	

※「紅字單字」於本單元多句出現，「單字級等分析」僅列在「首次出現句」。

🔊 MP3 068-01 ❶～❸

❶	到新環境我會怕生。	Coming to a new environment, I'm shy around strangers. * **Coming to＋某地**（當我一到某地，是 When I come to 的省略型態） * **around**（在…周遭）
❷	我不敢跟陌生人說話。	I don't dare talk to strangers. * **not dare＋動詞原形**（不敢做某事）
❸	我說話很容易得罪人。	The way I speak easily offends others. * **the way I speak**（我說話的方式）
❹	我最不會應酬了。	I just can't socialize.
❺	我最近常跟朋友吵架。	Lately I've been fighting with my friends a lot. * **Lately＋主詞＋have been...**（最近一直…） * **fight with＋某人**（和某人吵架）
❻	我一緊張舌頭就會打結。	When I'm nervous, I get tongue-tied. * **When I＋動詞, I＋動詞**（當我…的時候，我會…） * **get tongue-tied**（說不出話來）
❼	我每次都不知道要跟人家聊什麼。	I never know what to chat about with people. * **what to chat about**（要聊什麼） * **with people**（和別人）
❽	我常被人惡意中傷。	Other people are often malicious toward me. * **be malicious**（有惡意） * **toward me**（針對我）
❾	我跟我最好的朋友絕交。	I've had a falling-out with my best friend. * **have a falling-out with＋某人**（和某人鬧翻、絕交）
❿	我從小到大都沒什麼朋友。	Ever since I was a child, I've never really had any friends. * **ever since＋子句**（自從） * **I've never...**（我一直沒…）
⓫	我在學校被人排擠。	I was snubbed in school. * **be snubbed**（受到冷落）
⓬	我的生活圈很小。	My world is too small.
⓭	我交不到男朋友。	I never meet any guys. * **I never meet any girls.**（我交不到女友、我遇不到女生）

	單字	音標	詞性	意義	字頻	大考	英檢	多益
❶	coming	[ˋkʌmɪŋ]	p.pr.	come（來到）現在分詞	2	1	中級	
	new	[nju]	adj.	新的	1	1	初級	
	environment	[ɪnˋvaɪrəmənt]	n.	環境	1	2	初級	◎
	shy	[ʃaɪ]	adj.	害羞的	2	1	初級	
	stranger	[ˋstrendʒɚ]	n.	陌生人	1	2	初級	◎
❷	dare	[dɛr]	v.	膽敢	2	3	中級	
	talk	[tɔk]	v.	講話	1	1	初級	◎
❸	way	[we]	n.	方式	1		初級	
	speak	[spik]	v.	說話	1	1	初級	
	easily	[ˋizɪlɪ]	adv.	容易地	1		中級	
	offend	[əˋfɛnd]	v.	冒犯	2	4	中級	
	other	[ˋʌðɚ]	n./adj.	其他人/其他的	1	1	初級	
❹	just	[dʒʌst]	adv.	就是	1	1	初級	
	socialize	[ˋsoʃə͵laɪz]	v.	交際、社交	3	6	中高	◎
❺	lately	[ˋletlɪ]	adv.	最近	2	4	中級	
	fighting	[ˋfaɪtɪŋ]	p.pr.	fight（吵架）現在分詞	2	1	初級	
	friend	[frɛnd]	n.	朋友	1	1	初級	
	lot	[lɑt]	n.	許多				
❻	nervous	[ˋnɝvəs]	adj.	緊張的	1	3	初級	
	get	[gɛt]	v.	變成	1	1	初級	◎
	tongue-tied	[ˋtʌŋ͵taɪd]	adj.	說不出話的				
❼	never	[ˋnɛvɚ]	adv.	從不	1	1	初級	
	know	[no]	v.	知道	1	1	初級	◎
	chat	[tʃæt]	v.	聊天	2	3	中級	
	people	[ˋpipl̩]	n.	person（人）複數	1	1	初級	
❽	often	[ˋɔfən]	adv.	常常	1	1	初級	
	malicious	[məˋlɪʃəs]	adj.	惡意的	5			
❾	had	[hæd]	p.p.	have（擁有）過去分詞	1	1	初級	
	falling-out	[ˋfɔlɪŋ͵aʊt]	n.	鬧翻、絕交				
	best	[bɛst]	adj.	good（良好的）最高級	1	1	初級	
❿	ever	[ˋɛvɚ]	adv.	曾經	1	1	初級	
	child	[tʃaɪld]	n.	小孩	1	1	初級	
	really	[ˋrɪəlɪ]	adv.	真的	1		初級	
	had	[hæd]	p.t.	have（擁有）過去式	1	1	初級	
	any	[ˋɛnɪ]	adj.	任何的	1	1	初級	
⓫	snubbed	[snʌbd]	p.p.	snub（冷落）過去分詞	7			
	school	[skul]	n.	學校	1	1	初級	
⓬	world	[wɝld]	n.	生活圈	1	1	中級	
	too	[tu]	adv.	過於	1	1	初級	
	small	[smɔl]	adj.	小的	1	1	初級	◎
⓭	meet	[mit]	v.	結交	1	1	初級	
	guy	[gaɪ]	n.	男朋友	1	2	初級	

※「紅字單字」於本單元多句出現，「單字級等分析」僅列在「首次出現句」。

MP3 068-02 ❶～❹

❶	你容易交到朋友嗎？	Can you make friends easily? * **Can you＋動詞＋easily?**（你是否能夠輕易…？） * **make friends**（交朋友）
❷	你會怕生嗎？	Are you afraid of strangers? * **be afraid of strangers**（怕生）
❸	你沒辦法很快融入大家嗎？	Do you have a hard time fitting in? * **have a hard time＋動詞-ing**（難以…） * **fit in**（融入…）
❹	你都找不到話題跟人家聊嗎？	Are you unable to find things to chat about? * **Are you unable to＋動詞原形?** 　（你是否無法…？） * **find things to chat about**（找到聊天話題）
❺	你沒交過女朋友嗎？	Have you never had a girlfriend? * **Have you never...?**（你是否沒有…經驗？）
❻	你說話容易得罪人嗎？	Does the way you speak easily offend people?
❼	你不擅言辭嗎？	Are you not good at speaking? * **Are you good at speaking?**（你能言善道嗎？）
❽	你連說話的對象都沒有嗎？	Don't you have anyone to talk to?
❾	你容易和人發生爭執嗎？	Do you get into arguments easily? * **get into arguments**（起爭執）
❿	你不擅長跟人應酬嗎？	Don't you know how to socialize?
⓫	你常常誤解別人的好意嗎？	Do you often misunderstand other people's kindness? * **misunderstand one's kindness**（誤解好意）
⓬	你在學校遭人排擠嗎？	Are you being snubbed in school? * 此句用「現在進行式問句」（Are...being...?） 　表示「詢問對方現階段是否發生某事？」。
⓭	你的生活圈很小嗎？	Is your circle of friends too small? * **circle of friends**（朋友圈）
⓮	你能看穿別人的虛情假意嗎？	Can you see through false displays of affection? * **see through**（看穿） * **false displays of affection**（虛情假意）

	單字	音標	詞性	意義	字頻	大考	英檢	多益
❶	make	[mek]	v.	結交	1	1	初級	
	friend	[frɛnd]	n.	朋友	1	1	初級	
	easily	[ˈizɪlɪ]	adv.	容易地	1		中級	
❷	afraid	[əˈfred]	adj.	害怕的	1	1	初級	
	stranger	[ˈstrendʒə]	n.	陌生人	1	2	初級	◎
❸	have	[hæv]	v.	擁有	1	1	初級	
	hard	[hɑrd]	adj.	困難的	1	1	初級	◎
	time	[taɪm]	n.	時刻	1	1	初級	◎
	fitting	[ˈfɪtɪŋ]	n.	fit（融入）動名詞	4	2	中高	◎
❹	unable	[ʌnˈebl̩]	adj.	不能的	1		中級	◎
	find	[faɪnd]	v.	尋找	1	1	初級	
	thing	[θɪŋ]	n.	事物	1	1	初級	
	chat	[tʃæt]	v.	聊天	2	3	中級	
❺	never	[ˈnɛvə]	adv.	從不	1	1	初級	
	had	[hæd]	p.p.	have（結交）過去分詞	1	1	初級	
	girlfriend	[ˈgɜl.frɛnd]	n.	女朋友	2		中級	
❻	way	[we]	n.	方式	1	1	初級	
	speak	[spik]	v.	說話	1	1	初級	
	offend	[əˈfɛnd]	v.	冒犯	2	4	中級	
	people	[ˈpipl̩]	n.	person（人）複數	1	1	初級	
❼	good	[gʊd]	adj.	擅長的	1	1	初級	◎
	speaking	[ˈspikɪŋ]	n.	speak（說話）動名詞	5	1	初級	
❽	anyone	[ˈɛnɪ.wʌn]	pron.	任何人	1	2	初級	
	talk	[tɔk]	v.	講話	1	1	初級	
❾	get	[gɛt]	v.	引起	1	1	初級	◎
	argument	[ˈɑrgjəmənt]	n.	爭執	1	2	中級	
❿	know	[no]	v.	知道	1	1	初級	◎
	socialize	[ˈsoʃə.laɪz]	v.	交際、社交	3	6	中高	◎
⓫	often	[ˈɔfən]	adv.	常常	1	1	初級	
	misunderstand	[ˈmɪsʌndəˈstænd]	v.	誤解	3	4	中級	◎
	other	[ˈʌðə]	adj.	其他人	1	1	初級	
	kindness	[ˈkaɪndnɪs]	n.	好意	3		中級	
⓬	snubbed	[snʌbd]	p.p.	snub（冷落）過去分詞	7			
	school	[skul]	n.	學校	1	1	初級	
⓭	circle	[ˈsɜkl̩]	n.	圈子	1	2	初級	◎
	too	[tu]	adv.	過於	1	1	初級	
	small	[smɔl]	adj.	小的	1	1	初級	
⓮	see	[si]	v.	看穿	1	1	初級	
	false	[fɔls]	adj.	假意的	1	1	初級	◎
	display	[dɪˈsple]	n.	情感流露	1	2	中級	◎
	affection	[əˈfɛkʃən]	n.	情感	2	5	中級	

※「紅字單字」於本單元多句出現，「單字級等分析」僅列在「首次出現句」。

🔊 MP3 069-01 ❶～⓮

❶	我的工作壓力很大。	My job gives me a lot of stress. * give＋某人＋stress（給某人壓力）
❷	我一直沒有加薪。	I never get raises.　* get raises（加薪）
❸	我的工作老是趕不上進度。	I'm always behind on my work. * be behind on（無法如期完成、落後）
❹	我跟同事處得不好。	I don't get along with my colleagues. * get along with（相處融洽）
❺	我有做不完的工作。	My work never ends.
❻	我沒有一份工作做得長久。	I don't keep jobs for very long. * keep jobs（保住工作）、for long（一段長時間） * 此句用「現在簡單式」（...don't keep...） 　表示「經常如此的事」。
❼	我常被主管叫去訓話。	My manager often calls me in to lecture me. * call me in（叫我進去）、lecture me（對我說教）
❽	我受不了天天要加班。	I can't stand working overtime every day. * can't stand＋動詞-ing（無法忍受…）
❾	我的工作越來越繁重。	My work is getting heavier and heavier. * be getting＋比較級（越來越…）。 * 此句用「現在進行式」（...is getting...） 　表示「現階段逐漸變化的事」。
❿	我最近工作多到忙不過來。	I've been swamped with work recently. * be swamped with＋某事（被某事忙得不可開交） * 此句用「現在完成式」（...have been...） 　表示「過去持續到現在的事」。
⓫	我很怕被公司裁員。	I'm afraid of being laid off. * be laid off（被解雇）
⓬	我的工作常要應付一堆應酬。	My work often requires me to deal with a slew of social engagements. * deal with（應付）、social engagement（應酬）
⓭	我的老闆對我很不滿。	My boss is not satisfied with me.
⓮	工作讓我沒時間陪伴家人。	My work leaves me little time for family. * leave me little time（沒給我太多時間）

單字級等分析

	單字	音標	詞性	意義	字頻	大考	英檢	多益
❶	job	[dʒɑb]	n.	工作	1	1	初級	
	give	[gɪv]	v.	給予	1	1	初級	
	lot	[lɑt]	n.	許多	1	1	初級	
	stress	[strɛs]	n.	壓力	1	2	初級	◎
❷	never	[ˈnɛvɚ]	adv.	從不	1	1	初級	
	get	[gɛt]	v.	獲得/相處	1	1	初級	◎
	raise	[rez]	n.	加薪	1	1	初級	◎
❸	always	[ˈɔlwez]	adv.	總是	1	1	初級	
	work	[wɝk]	n.	工作	1	1	初級	
❹	along	[əˈlɔŋ]	adv.	一起	1	1	初級	
	colleague	[ˈkɑlig]	n.	同事	1	5	中級	◎
❺	end	[ɛnd]	v.	結束	1	1	初級	
❻	keep	[kip]	v.	保住	1	1	初級	
	very	[ˈvɛrɪ]	adj.	非常的	1	1	初級	
	long	[lɔŋ]	n.	長時間	1	1	初級	
❼	manager	[ˈmænɪdʒɚ]	n.	主管	1	3	初級	◎
	often	[ˈɔfən]	adv.	常常	1	1	初級	
	call	[kɔl]	v.	叫喚	1	1	初級	◎
	lecture	[ˈlɛktʃɚ]	v.	說教	2	4	中級	◎
❽	stand	[stænd]	v.	忍受	1	1	中級	◎
	working	[ˈwɝkɪŋ]	n.	work（工作）動名詞	2	1	初級	◎
	overtime	[ˌovɚˈtaɪm]	adv.	超時地	3			◎
	every	[ˈɛvrɪ]	adj.	每一	1	1	初級	
	day	[de]	n.	天	1	1	初級	
❾	getting	[ˈgɛtɪŋ]	p.pr.	get（變成）現在分詞	1	1	初級	◎
	heavier	[ˈhɛvɪɚ]	adj.	heavy（繁重的）比較級	1	1	初級	
❿	swamped	[swɑmpt]	p.p.	swamp（使繁忙）過去分詞	3	5	中高	
	recently	[ˈrisntlɪ]	adv.	最近	1			
⓫	afraid	[əˈfred]	adj.	害怕的	1	1	初級	
	laid	[led]	p.p.	lay（解雇）過去分詞	1	1	初級	
	off	[ɔf]	adv.	離開	1	1	初級	
⓬	require	[rɪˈkwaɪr]	v.	需要	1	2	初級	◎
	deal	[dil]	v.	應付	1	1	初級	◎
	slew	[slu]	n.	大量	5			
	social	[ˈsoʃəl]	adj.	社交的	1	2	初級	◎
	engagement	[ɪnˈgedʒmənt]	n.	約會	2	3	中高	◎
⓭	boss	[bɔs]	n.	老闆	1	2	初級	
	satisfied	[ˈsætɪsˌfaɪd]	adj.	滿意的	2	2	中高	◎
⓮	leave	[liv]	v.	留下	1	1	初級	◎
	little	[ˈlɪtl]	adj.	少量的	1	1	初級	
	time	[taɪm]	n.	時間	1	1	初級	◎
	family	[ˈfæməlɪ]	n.	家人	1	1	初級	

※「紅字單字」於本單元多句出現，「單字級等分析」僅列在「首次出現句」。

MP3 069-02 ❶～⓭

❶	你工作壓力大不大？	Are you under pressure from work? * be under pressure（有壓力） * from work（來自工作）
❷	你的工作忙不過來嗎？	Are you swamped with work?
❸	你最近工作還好吧？	Has your work been okay lately?
❹	你老闆不滿意你的工作表現嗎？	Isn't your boss satisfied with your work? * be satisfied with＋人事物（滿意某人事物）
❺	你最近還是常常加班嗎？	Have you been working overtime a lot lately? * 此句用「現在完成進行式問句」（Has...been working...?）表示「詢問對方某事是否從過去開始、且直到現在仍持續中？」。 * work overtime（加班） * a lot（經常）
❻	你們公司應酬怎麼那麼多？	How can your company have so many social engagements? * How can＋主詞＋動詞?（某主詞怎麼能夠…？） * so many（這麼多的）
❼	你的工作量又增加了嗎？	Has your workload gotten heavier again? * get heavier（變得更沉重）
❽	你都沒休息身體受得了嗎？	You haven't taken any breaks; can your body stand that?　* take a break（休息）
❾	你又想換工作了嗎？	Are you thinking about changing jobs again? * Are you thinking about....?（你是否正在考慮…？） * change a job（換工作）= switch a job
❿	你跟同事相處不好嗎？	Don't you get along with your colleagues?
⓫	你擔心自己被裁員嗎？	Do you worry about being laid off? * Do you worry about....?（你是否會害怕…？）
⓬	工作讓你沒時間陪家人嗎？	Does work leave you little time for your family?
⓭	你常常趕不上工作進度嗎？	Do you often not make progress at work? * not make progress（沒有進度） * at work（工作上）

	單字	音標	詞性	意義	字頻	大考	英檢	多益
❶	pressure	[ˋprɛʃɚ]	n.	壓力	1	3	中級	◎
	work	[wɝk]	n.	工作	1	1	初級	◎
❷	swamped	[swɑmpt]	p.p.	swamp（使繁忙）過去分詞	3	5	中高	
❸	okay	[ˋoˋke]	adj.	還好的	1	1		
	lately	[ˋletlɪ]	adv.	最近	2	4	中級	
❹	boss	[bɔs]	n.	老闆	1	2	初級	
	satisfied	[ˋsætɪs͵faɪd]	adj.	滿意的	2	2	中高	◎
❺	working	[ˋwɝkɪŋ]	p.pr.	work（工作）現在分詞	2	1	初級	◎
	overtime	[͵ovɚˋtaɪm]	adv.	超時地	3			◎
	lot	[lɑt]	n.	許多				
❻	company	[ˋkʌmpənɪ]	n.	公司	1	2	初級	◎
	have	[hæv]	v.	擁有	1	1	初級	
	so	[so]	adv.	這麼	1	1	初級	
	many	[ˋmɛnɪ]	adj.	許多的	1	1	初級	
	social	[ˋsoʃəl]	adj.	社交的	1	2	初級	◎
	engagement	[ɪnˋgedʒmənt]	n.	約會	2	3	中高	◎
❼	workload	[ˋwɝk͵lod]	n.	工作量	5			◎
	gotten	[ˋgɑtn]	p.p.	get（變成）過去分詞	1	1	初級	◎
	heavier	[ˋhɛvɪɚ]	adj.	heavy（繁重的）比較級	1	1	初級	
	again	[əˋgɛn]	adv.	再次	1	1	初級	
❽	taken	[ˋtekən]	p.p.	take（從事、進行）過去分詞	1	1	初級	◎
	any	[ˋɛnɪ]	adj.	任何的	1	1	初級	
	break	[brek]	n.	休息	1	1	初級	◎
	body	[ˋbɑdɪ]	n.	身體	1	1	初級	◎
	stand	[stænd]	v.	忍受	1	1	初級	◎
	that	[ðæt]	pron.	那個	1	1	初級	
❾	thinking	[ˋθɪŋkɪŋ]	p.pr.	think（考慮）現在分詞	1	1	中級	
	changing	[ˋtʃendʒɪŋ]	n.	change（改變、更換）動名詞	2	2	初級	◎
	job	[dʒɑb]	n.	工作	1	1	初級	
❿	get	[gɛt]	v.	相處	1	1	初級	
	along	[əˋlɔŋ]	adv.	一起	1	1	初級	
	colleague	[ˋkɑlig]	n.	同事	1	5	中級	◎
⓫	worry	[ˋwɝɪ]	v.	擔心	1	1	初級	
	laid	[led]	p.p.	lay（解雇）過去分詞	1	1	初級	
	off	[ɔf]	adv.	離開	1	1	初級	
⓬	leave	[liv]	v.	留下	1	1	初級	◎
	little	[ˋlɪtl]	adj.	少的	1	1	初級	
	time	[taɪm]	n.	時間	1	1	初級	◎
	family	[ˋfæməlɪ]	n.	家人	1	1	初級	
⓭	often	[ˋɔfən]	adv.	常常	1	1	初級	
	make	[mek]	v.	做出	1	1	初級	
	progress	[ˋprɑgrɛs]	n.	進展、進度	1	2	初級	◎

※「紅字單字」於本單元多句出現，「單字級等分析」僅列在「首次出現句」。

325

MP3 070-01 ❶～⓬

❶	我覺得錢永遠不夠花。	I feel I never have enough money. * **I feel ＋子句**（我覺得…） * **have enough money**（擁有足夠的錢）
❷	我是個窮光蛋。	I'm as poor as they come. * **as ＋形容詞＋ as they come**（…得不得了、極盡…）
❸	我沒錢繳電話費。	I don't have enough money to pay the phone bill. * **pay a bill**（繳費） * **phone bill**（電話費）、**utilities**（水電費）
❹	我的薪水根本不夠用。	Frankly, my salary isn't enough. * **Frankly, ...**（老實說，…）
❺	我常繳不出房租。	I often can't afford to pay my rent. * **afford to**（負擔得起）
❻	我有付不完的卡費。	I can never pay off my credit card in full. * **pay off ＋費用**（清償某費用） * **credit card**（信用卡）、**in full**（全額）
❼	我被房貸壓得喘不過氣來。	My mortgage payments are crushing me. * **mortgage payment**（房貸）＝ house loan * **car loan**（車貸） * **crush ＋某人**（讓某人苦惱） * **installment payment**（分期付款）
❽	我常常口袋空空。	My pockets are usually empty.
❾	我朋友常向我借錢不還。	My friend often borrows money from me but never pays me back. * **borrow money**（借錢）、**pay back**（還錢）
❿	我常接到紅色炸彈。	I often receive wedding invitations. * **wedding invitation**（喜帖）
⓫	我不想讓家人跟著我吃苦。	I don't want to make my family endure hardships with me. * **endure hardship**（吃苦） * **with me**（和我一起）
⓬	我幾乎每個月都透支。	I overdraw my account nearly every month. * **overdraw one's account**（超支、超提帳戶存款）

	單字	音標	詞性	意義	字頻	大考	英檢	多益
❶	feel	[fil]	v.	覺得	1	1	初級	
	never	[ˋnɛvɚ]	adv.	從不	1	1	初級	
	have	[hæv]	v.	擁有	1	1	初級	
	enough	[əˋnʌf]	adj.	足夠的	1	1	初級	◎
	money	[ˋmʌnɪ]	n.	金錢	1	1	初級	◎
❷	poor	[pʊr]	adj.	貧窮的	1	1	初級	
	come	[kʌm]	n.	到來	1	1	初級	
❸	pay	[pe]	v.	付款	1	3	初級	◎
	phone	[fon]	n.	電話	1	2	初級	◎
	bill	[bɪl]	n.	帳單	1	2	初級	◎
❹	frankly	[ˋfræŋklɪ]	adv.	老實說	2		中高	
	salary	[ˋsælərɪ]	n.	薪水	1	4	中級	◎
❺	often	[ˋɔfən]	adv.	常常	1	1	初級	
	afford	[əˋford]	v.	負擔	1	3	中級	◎
	rent	[rɛnt]	n.	房租	2	3	初級	◎
❻	off	[ɔf]	adv.	完全、徹底	1	1	初級	
	credit	[ˋkrɛdɪt]	n.	信用	1	3	中級	◎
	card	[kɑrd]	n.	卡	1	1	初級	◎
	full	[fʊl]	n.	全額	1	1	初級	
❼	mortgage	[ˋmɔrgɪdʒ]	n.	房貸	2		中級	◎
	payment	[ˋpemənt]	n.	款項	1	1	中級	◎
	crushing	[ˋkrʌʃɪŋ]	p.pr.	crush（使苦惱）現在分詞	5	4	中級	◎
❽	pocket	[ˋpɑkɪt]	n.	口袋、財力	1	1	初級	◎
	usually	[ˋjuʒʊəlɪ]	adv.	經常	1		初級	◎
	empty	[ˋɛmptɪ]	adj.	空無一物的	1	3	初級	◎
❾	friend	[frɛnd]	n.	朋友	1	1	初級	
	borrow	[ˋbɑro]	v.	借入	2	2	初級	◎
	back	[bæk]	adv.	返回	1	1	初級	
❿	receive	[rɪˋsiv]	v.	收到	1	1	初級	◎
	wedding	[ˋwɛdɪŋ]	n.	婚禮	1	1	初級	
	invitation	[ˏɪnvəˋteʃən]	n.	邀請	2	2	初級	◎
⓫	want	[wɑnt]	v.	想要	1	1	初級	
	make	[mek]	v.	使得	1	1	初級	
	family	[ˋfæməlɪ]	n.	家人	1	1	初級	
	endure	[ɪnˋdjʊr]	v.	忍受	2	4	中級	◎
	hardship	[ˋhɑrdʃɪp]	n.	艱難	3	4	中級	◎
⓬	overdraw	[ˋovɚˋdrɔ]	v.	超支				
	account	[əˋkaʊnt]	n.	帳戶	1	3	中級	◎
	nearly	[ˋnɪrlɪ]	adv.	幾乎	1	2	初級	◎
	every	[ˋɛvrɪ]	adj.	每一	1	1	初級	
	month	[mʌnθ]	n.	月	1	1	初級	

※「紅字單字」於本單元多句出現，「單字級等分析」僅列在「首次出現句」。

070　你煩惱金錢嗎？

❶	你覺得錢不夠用嗎？	Do you feel like there's never enough money? * **Do you feel like＋子句?**（你是否覺得…？）
❷	你有房貸壓力嗎？	Do you have pressure from a house loan? * **have pressure from＋貸款**（有某貸款的壓力） * **house loan**（房貸）＝ **mortgage payment**
❸	你的薪水夠你一個月開銷嗎？	Is your salary enough for your monthly expenses? * **be enough for＋某物**（足夠應付…） * **monthly expense**（每月開銷）
❹	你這個月繳不出房租嗎？	Can't you pay your rent this month?
❺	你常會透支嗎？	Do you often overdraw your account?
❻	你常需要包紅包或白包嗎？	Do you often need to give cash gifts for weddings or funerals? * **need to＋動詞原形**（需要） * **give a cash gift**（包禮金）
❼	你的信用卡債還清了嗎？	Have you paid off your credit card debt? * **Have you＋過去分詞?**（你是否已經…？） * **credit card debt**（信用卡債）
❽	你擔心自己存不了錢嗎？	Do you worry that you can't save any money? * **Do you worry that＋子句?**（你是否擔心…？） * **can't save money**（沒辦法存錢）
❾	你擔心沒錢繳水電費嗎？	Do you worry that you won't have enough to pay your utilities?
❿	你擔心家人跟著你吃苦嗎？	Do you worry about making your family endure hardships with you? * **Do you worry about＋動詞-ing?**（你是否擔心…？）
⓫	你煩惱孩子的學費嗎？	Do you worry about your child's tuition? * **Do you worry about＋名詞?**（你是否擔心…？） * **tuition fee**（學雜費）、**dormitory fee**（住宿費） * **lunch money**（午餐費用）
⓬	你擔心戶頭的錢撐不到下個月嗎？	Do you worry that you didn't make enough deposits to last through the month? * **make enough deposits**（存足夠的錢） * **last through＋時間**（撐到…）

	單字	音標	詞性	意義	字頻	大考	英檢	多益
❶	feel	[fil]	v.	覺得	1	1	初級	
	there	[ðɛr]	adv.	有…	1	1	初級	
	never	[`nɛvɚ]	adv.	從不	1	1	初級	
	enough	[ə`nʌf]	adj./adv.	足夠的/足夠地	1	1	初級	◎
	money	[`mʌnɪ]	n.	金錢	1	1	初級	◎
❷	have	[hæv]	v.	擁有	1	1	初級	
	pressure	[`prɛʃɚ]	n.	壓力	1	3	中級	◎
	house	[haus]	n.	房屋	1	1	初級	◎
	loan	[lon]	n.	貸款	1	4	中級	◎
❸	salary	[`sælərɪ]	n.	薪水	1	4	中級	◎
	monthly	[`mʌnθlɪ]	adj.	每月地	2	4	初級	◎
	expense	[ɪk`spɛns]	n.	開銷	1	3	中級	◎
❹	pay	[pe]	v.	付款	1	3	初級	◎
	rent	[rɛnt]	n.	房租	2	3	初級	◎
	this	[ðɪs]	adj.	這個	1	1	初級	
	month	[mʌnθ]	n.	月	1	1	初級	
❺	often	[`ɔfən]	adv.	常常	1	1	初級	
	overdraw	[`ovɚ`drɔ]	v.	超支				
	account	[ə`kaunt]	n.	帳戶	1	3	中級	◎
❻	need	[nid]	v.	需要	1	1	初級	◎
	give	[gɪv]	v.	給予	1	1	初級	
	cash	[kæʃ]	n.	現金	1	2	初級	◎
	gift	[gɪft]	n.	禮品	1	1	初級	◎
	wedding	[`wɛdɪŋ]	n.	婚禮	1	1	初級	◎
	funeral	[`fjunərəl]	n.	喪禮	2	4	中級	◎
❼	paid	[ped]	p.p.	pay（付款）過去分詞	3	3	中高	
	off	[ɔf]	adv.	完全、徹底	1		初級	
	credit	[`krɛdɪt]	n.	信用	1	3	中級	◎
	card	[kɑrd]	n.	卡	1	1	初級	◎
	debt	[dɛt]	n.	債務	1	2	初級	◎
❽	worry	[`wɝɪ]	v.	擔心	1	1	初級	◎
	save	[sev]	v.	儲蓄	1	1	初級	◎
	any	[`ɛnɪ]	adj.	任何的	1	1	初級	
❾	utility	[ju`tɪlətɪ]	n.	水電費	1	6	中高	◎
❿	making	[`mekɪŋ]	n.	make（使得）動名詞	2	1	初級	
	family	[`fæməlɪ]	n.	家人	1	1	初級	
	endure	[ɪn`djur]	v.	忍受	2	4	中級	◎
	hardship	[`hɑrdʃɪp]	n.	艱難	3	4	中級	◎
⓫	child	[tʃaɪld]	n.	小孩	1	1	初級	
	tuition	[tju`ɪʃən]	n.	學費	3	5	中高	◎
⓬	make	[mek]	v.	賺錢	1	1	初級	
	deposit	[dɪ`pɑzɪt]	n.	存款	2	3	中級	◎
	last	[læst]	v	維持	1	1	初級	◎

※「紅字單字」於本單元多句出現，「單字級等分析」僅列在「首次出現句」。

我煩惱外表。

❶	我實在太胖了。	I'm really too fat.
❷	我覺得自己長得不好看。	I don't think I look well. * **I don't think＋子句**（我不認為…）
❸	我常因為身材被取笑。	I'm often made fun of for the way I look. * **be made fun of**（被嘲笑） * **for**（因為）
❹	我的皮膚不夠白。	My skin isn't white enough.
❺	我覺得自己是矮冬瓜。	I think I'm a munchkin.
❻	我的眼睛不夠大。	My eyes are not big enough.
❼	我的腿不夠纖細。	My legs aren't thin enough.
❽	我討厭我的大餅臉。	I hate my moon face. * **hate＋名詞**（討厭…） * **moon face**（月亮臉）
❾	我覺得我的小腹很礙眼。	I think my belly is an eyesore.
❿	我全身上下沒有一個地方能看。	Nowhere on my entire body is nice to look at. * **be nice to look at**（好看的）
⓫	我恨自己是個小胸部。	I hate my small bust size. * **small bust**（小胸部） * **large bust**（大胸部）
⓬	常有人說我是青蛙。	People often say I'm a frog. * **People often say I'm a dog.**（常有人說我是恐龍妹）
⓭	腳太大害我常買不到鞋。	My feet are too big for me to buy shoes that fit. * **too＋形容詞**（太過於…）
⓮	我發福之後很多衣服都穿不下。	After I got fat, a lot of my clothes didn't fit me anymore. * **get fat**（變胖）
⓯	我的臉色太蒼白了。	My face is too pale.
⓰	我的髮型不夠優。	My hairstyle isn't attractive enough. * **be attractive enough**（夠好看、夠迷人）
⓱	我在人群中常被忽略。	I'm often ignored in a crowd. * **in a crowd**（在人群中）

	單字	音標	詞性	意義	字頻	大考	英檢	多益
❶	really	[ˋrɪəlɪ]	adv.	實在	1		初級	
	too	[tu]	adv.	過於	1	1	初級	
	fat	[fæt]	adj.	肥胖的	1	1	初級	
❷	think	[θɪŋk]	v.	認為	1	1	初級	
	look	[lʊk]	v.	看起來/看、注視	1	1	初級	
	well	[wɛl]	adj.	好看的	1	1	初級	◎
❸	often	[ˋɔfən]	adv.	常常	1	1	初級	
	made	[med]	p.p.	make（做出）過去分詞	1	1	初級	
	fun	[fʌn]	n.	嘲笑	1	1	初級	
	way	[we]	n.	方面	1	1	初級	
❹	skin	[skɪn]	n.	皮膚	1	1	初級	◎
	white	[hwaɪt]	adj.	白的	1	1	初級	
	enough	[əˋnʌf]	adv.	足夠地	1	1	初級	◎
❺	munchkin	[ˋmʌnʧkɪn]	n.	小矮人				
❻	eye	[aɪ]	n.	眼睛	1	1	初級	
	big	[bɪg]	adj.	大的	1	1	初級	
❼	leg	[lɛg]	n.	腿	1	1	初級	
	thin	[θɪn]	adj.	纖細的	1	2	初級	◎
❽	hate	[het]	v.	討厭	1	1	初級	
	moon	[mun]	n.	月亮	1	1	初級	
	face	[fes]	n.	臉	1	1	初級	
❾	belly	[ˋbɛlɪ]	n.	肚子	2	3	中級	
	eyesore	[ˋaɪ͵sor]	n.	礙眼的東西				
❿	nowhere	[ˋno͵hwɛr]	pron.	沒有一處	2	5	中級	
	entire	[ɪnˋtaɪr]	adj.	整個的	1	2	初級	◎
	body	[ˋbɑdɪ]	n.	身體	1	1	初級	
	nice	[naɪs]	adj.	美好的	1	1	初級	
⓫	small	[smɔl]	adj.	小的	1	1	初級	◎
	bust	[bʌst]	n.	胸部	3		中高	
	size	[saɪz]	n.	尺寸	1	1	初級	◎
⓬	people	[ˋpipl]	n.	person（人）複數	1	1	初級	
	say	[se]	v.	說	1	1	初級	
	frog	[frɑg]	n.	青蛙	2	1	初級	
⓭	feet	[fit]	n.	foot（腳）複數	1	1	初級	
	buy	[baɪ]	v.	購買	1	1	初級	
	shoes	[ʃuz]	n.	shoe（鞋子）複數	2	1		
	fit	[fɪt]	v.	合身	1	2	初級	◎
⓮	got	[gɑt]	p.t.	get（變成）過去式	1	1	初級	◎
	lot	[lɑt]	n.	許多	1			
	clothes	[kloz]	n.	cloth（衣服）複數	1	2	初級	
	anymore	[ˋɛnɪ͵mor]	adv.	不再	1		中高	
⓯	pale	[pel]	adj.	蒼白的	2	3	初級	◎
⓰	hairstyle	[ˋhɛr͵staɪl]	n.	髮型	6	5	中高	
	attractive	[əˋtræktɪv]	adj.	迷人的	2	3	中級	◎
⓱	ignored	[ɪgˋnord]	p.p.	ignore（忽視）過去分詞	1	2	初級	◎
	crowd	[kraʊd]	n.	人群	1	2	初級	◎

※「紅字單字」於本單元多句出現，「單字級等分析」僅列在「首次出現句」。

071 你煩惱外表嗎？

❶	你不滿意自己的外表嗎？	Aren't you satisfied with your appearance? * Aren't you satisfied with...?（你不滿意…嗎）
❷	你煩惱你的腿不夠細嗎？	Do you worry that your legs are not thin enough? * worry that＋子句（擔心…） * not＋形容詞＋enough（不夠…）
❸	你煩惱自己不夠高嗎？	Do you worry that you're not tall enough?
❹	你煩惱你的臉太大太圓嗎？	Do you worry that your face is too big and round?
❺	你煩惱你的眼睛不夠大嗎？	Do you worry that your eyes are not big enough?
❻	你嫌自己皮膚不夠白嗎？	Do you complain that your skin isn't white enough? * complain that＋子句（抱怨…、嫌棄…）
❼	你介意別人評論你的外表嗎？	Do you mind when others comment on your appearance? * Do you mind...?（你是否介意…？） * comment on＋人事物（評論某人事物）
❽	你不喜歡你的新髮型嗎？	Don't you like your new hairstyle?
❾	你因為腳太小而買不到鞋子嗎？	Do you have a hard time buying shoes because your feet are so small? * have a hard time＋動詞-ing（難以做…）
❿	太胖讓你自卑嗎？	Does being too fat make you feel inferior? * being too fat（過胖這件事） * feel inferior（感覺自卑）
⓫	你會在意自己的氣色好不好嗎？	Do you care if you look well or not? * care if...or not（是否在乎…） * look well（氣色好）
⓬	大胸部讓你很困擾嗎？	Does having a large bust bother you? * having a large bust（有大胸部這件事）
⓭	沒化妝你就不敢出門嗎？	Are you afraid to go outside without makeup on? * be afraid to＋動詞原形（不敢） * go outside（外出） * without makeup on（沒上妝）

	單字	音標	詞性	意義	字頻	大考	英檢	多益
❶	satisfied	[ˈsætɪs.faɪd]	adj.	滿意的	2	2	中高	◎
	appearance	[əˈpɪrəns]	n.	外表	1	2	初級	◎
❷	worry	[ˈwɝɪ]	v.	擔心	1	1	初級	◎
	leg	[lɛg]	n.	腿	1	1	初級	
	thin	[θɪn]	adj.	纖細的	1	2	初級	
	enough	[əˈnʌf]	adv.	足夠地	1	1	初級	◎
❸	tall	[tɔl]	adj.	高的	1	1	初級	◎
❹	face	[fes]	n.	臉	1	1	初級	
	too	[tu]	adv.	過於	1	1	初級	
	big	[bɪg]	adj.	大的	1	2	初級	
	round	[raʊnd]	adj.	圓的	1	1	初級	
❺	eye	[aɪ]	n.	眼睛	1	1	初級	
❻	complain	[kəmˈplen]	v.	抱怨	1	2	初級	◎
	skin	[skɪn]	n.	皮膚	1	1	初級	◎
	white	[hwaɪt]	adj.	白的	1	1	初級	
❼	mind	[maɪnd]	v.	介意	1	1	初級	◎
	other	[ˈʌðɚ]	pron.	其他人	1	1	初級	
	comment	[ˈkɑmɛnt]	v.	評論	1	4	初級	◎
❽	like	[laɪk]	v.	喜歡	1	1	初級	
	new	[nju]	adj.	新的	1	1	初級	
	hairstyle	[ˈhɛr.staɪl]	n.	髮型	6	5	中高	
❾	have	[hæv]	v.	擁有	1	1	初級	
	hard	[hɑrd]	adj.	困難的	1	1	初級	◎
	time	[taɪm]	n.	時刻	1	1	初級	
	buying	[ˈbaɪɪŋ]	n.	bue（購買）動名詞	3	1	初級	
	shoes	[ʃuz]	n.	shoe（鞋子）複數	2	1		
	feet	[fit]	n.	foot（腳）複數	1	1	初級	
	so	[so]	adv.	過於	1	1	初級	
	small	[smɔl]	adj.	小的	1	1	初級	◎
❿	fat	[fæt]	adj.	肥胖的	1	1	初級	
	make	[mek]	v.	使得	1	1	初級	
	feel	[fil]	v.	覺得	1	1	初級	
	inferior	[ɪnˈfɪrɪɚ]	adj.	自卑的	3	3	中級	◎
⓫	care	[kɛr]	v.	在意	1	1	初級	◎
	look	[lʊk]	v.	看起來	1	1	初級	
	well	[wɛl]	adj.	氣色好的	1	1	初級	◎
⓬	having	[ˈhævɪŋ]	n.	have（擁有）動名詞	1	1	初級	◎
	large	[lɑrdʒ]	adj.	大的	1	1	初級	
	bust	[bʌst]	n.	胸部	3		中高	
	bother	[ˈbɑðɚ]	v.	困擾	1	2	初級	◎
⓭	afraid	[əˈfred]	adj.	害怕的	1	1	初級	
	go	[go]	v.	去	1	1	初級	
	outside	[ˈaʊtˈsaɪd]	adv.	外出	1	1	初級	◎
	makeup	[ˈmek.ʌp]	n.	化妝品	2	4		◎
	on	[ɑn]	adj.	有化妝的	1	1	初級	

072 我覺得壓力大。

❶	最近工作多到讓我喘不過氣來。	I have so much work I can't breathe. * **have so much...(that)**＋子句（有太多…，導致…）
❷	真累。	I'm so tired.
❸	我每天都加班到很晚。	I have to work overtime till very late every day. * **have to**（必須）、**work overtime**（加班）、**till**（直到）
❹	我身心俱疲。	My body and mind are tired.
❺	我連假日也要工作。	Even on holidays, I have to work. * **even on**＋日子（甚至在某日子）
❻	我胃痛，吃不下飯。	I can't eat anything, my stomach hurts. * 身體部位＋**hurt**（某身體部位疼痛）
❼	房貸壓力不小。	Having a mortgage is stressful.
❽	我忙到沒時間吃飯。	I am too busy to have meals. * **be too busy to**＋動詞（忙碌到無法做…）
❾	我今天還有幾十通電話要打。	I still have dozens of calls to make today. * **dozens of**（幾十個的）
❿	我的行程已經排到三個月以後了。	My schedule is full for the next three months. * **the next**＋數字＋**months**（之後的…個月）
⓫	我常常腰酸背痛。	I often get a sore waist and an aching back. * **get a sore waist**（腰酸）、**get an aching back**（背痛）
⓬	我很怕被社會淘汰。	I'm afraid of being weeded out from society. * **be weeded out**（被淘汰）、**from society**（從社會中）
⓭	我像蠟燭兩頭燒。	I'm like a candle burning at both ends. * **a candle burning at both ends**（蠟燭兩頭燒）
⓮	我好久沒有好好休息了。	I haven't had a good rest for a long time. * 此句用「現在完成式」（...haven't had...） 表示「過去持續到現在的事」。
⓯	家庭和事業很難兼顧。	It's really difficult to look after both family and career. * **look after both A and B**（兼顧 A 和 B）

	單字	音標	詞性	意義	字頻	大考	英檢	多益
❶	have	[hæv]	v.	擁有/吃/必須	1	1	初級	
	so	[so]	adv.	如此	1	1	初級	
	much	[mʌtʃ]	adj.	許多的	1	1	初級	
	work	[wɜk]	n./v.	工作	1	1	初級	◎
	breathe	[brið]	v.	喘氣	1	3	中級	◎
❷	tired	[taɪrd]	adj.	疲累的	1	1	初級	◎

334

❸	overtime	[ˌovɚ`taɪm]	adv.	超時地	3			◎
	very	[`vɛrɪ]	adv.	十分	1	1	初級	
	late	[let]	adv.	晚地	1	1	初級	◎
	every	[`ɛvrɪ]	adj.	每一	1	1	初級	
	day	[de]	n.	天	1	1	初級	
❹	body	[`bɑdɪ]	n.	身體	1	1	初級	
	mind	[maɪnd]	n.	心靈	1	1	初級	◎
❺	even	[`ivən]	adv.	甚至	1	1	初級	◎
	holiday	[`hɑlə.de]	n.	假日	1	1	初級	
❻	eat	[it]	v.	吃	1	1	初級	
	anything	[`ɛnɪ.θɪŋ]	pron.	任何東西	1	1	初級	
	stomach	[`stʌmək]	n.	胃	1	2	初級	
	hurt	[hɝt]	v.	疼痛	1	1	初級	
❼	having	[`hævɪŋ]	n.	have（擁有）動名詞	1	1	初級	
	mortgage	[`mɔrgɪdʒ]	n.	房貸	2		中級	◎
	stressful	[`strɛsfəl]	adj.	壓力的	3	1		
❽	too	[tu]	adv.	過於	1	1	初級	
	busy	[`bɪzɪ]	adj.	忙碌的	1	1	初級	
	meal	[mil]	n.	一餐	1	2	初級	
❾	still	[stɪl]	adv.	仍然	1	1	初級	◎
	dozen	[`dʌzn]	n.	幾十	1	1	初級	
	call	[kɔl]	n.	電話	1	1	初級	◎
	make	[mek]	v.	打（電話）	1	1	初級	
	today	[tə`de]	adv.	今天	1	1	初級	◎
❿	schedule	[`skɛdʒul]	n.	行程	1	3	中級	◎
	full	[ful]	adj.	滿的	1	1	初級	
	next	[nɛkst]	adj.	接下來	1	1	初級	
	three	[θri]	n.	三	1	1	初級	
	month	[mʌnθ]	n.	月	1	1	初級	
⓫	often	[`ɔfən]	adv.	常常	1	1	初級	
	get	[gɛt]	v.	患上	1	1	初級	◎
	sore	[sor]	adj..	酸的	3	3	初級	◎
	waist	[west]	n.	腰部	2	2	初級	
	aching	[`ekɪŋ]	adj.	疼痛的	5	3	中級	
	back	[bæk]	n.	背部	1	1	初級	◎
⓬	afraid	[ə`fred]	adj.	害怕的	1	1	初級	
	weeded	[`widɪd]	p.p.	weed（淘汰）過去分詞	1	3	中級	◎
	out	[aut]	adv.	出局	1	1	初級	
	society	[sə`saɪətɪ]	n.	社會	1	2	初級	◎
⓭	candle	[`kændl̩]	n.	蠟燭	2	2	初級	
	burning	[`bɝnɪŋ]	p.pr.	burn（燃燒）現在分詞	2	2	中高	
	both	[boθ]	adj.	兩方的	1	1	初級	
	end	[ɛnd]	n.	端末	1	1	初級	
⓮	had	[hæd]	p.p.	have（擁有）過去分詞	1	1	初級	
	good	[gud]	adj.	良好的	1	1	初級	◎
	rest	[rɛst]	n.	休息	1	1	初級	
	long	[lɔŋ]	adj.	長的	1	1	初級	
	time	[taɪm]	n.	時間	1	1	初級	◎
⓯	really	[`rɪəlɪ]	adv.	實在	1		初級	
	difficult	[`dɪfə.kəlt]	adj.	困難的	1	1	初級	◎
	look	[luk]	v.	照顧	1	1	初級	
	family	[`fæməlɪ]	n.	家庭	1	1	初級	
	career	[kə`rɪr]	n.	事業	1	4	初級	◎

※「紅字單字」於本單元多句出現，「單字級等分析」僅列在「首次出現句」。

MP3 072-02 ❶～⓯

❶	你常加班嗎？	Do you work overtime often? * **Do you...often?**（你是否經常…？）
❷	最近很勞累嗎？	Have you been very tired lately?
❸	你有黑眼圈了耶。	You have bags under your eyes.
❹	你假日還要工作啊？	Do you still need to work on weekends? * **need to＋**動詞原形（需要） * **on weekend**（假日時）
❺	要不要出去走走？	Do you want to go for a walk with me? * **go for a walk**（去散步） * **with me**（和我一起）
❻	你一直都這麼努力嗎？	Do you always work this hard?
❼	你這樣會累出病來的。	You will wear yourself out and get sick. * 此句用「未來簡單式」（...will...） 　表示「根據直覺預測未來發生的事」。 * **wear oneself out**（把自己累壞） * **get sick**（生病）
❽	讓自己喘口氣吧？	Give yourself a break, will you? * **will you?**（你願意嗎）
❾	你每天都工作到晚上九點、 十點嗎？	Do you work to nine or ten pm every day?
❿	你要多照顧自己的身體。	You should take care of your health. * **take care of one's health**（照顧身體）
⓫	你會不會壓力太大了？	Are you under too much pressure?
⓬	年紀大了要多注意保養身體。	You should take good care of your health as you get older. * **as＋**子句（在…的時候）
⓭	深呼吸一下吧！	Take a deep breath! * **deep breath**（深呼吸）
⓮	頭還在痛嗎？	Does your head still hurt?
⓯	你透支了嗎？	Are you exhausted?
⓰	有我可以幫忙的嗎？	Is there anything I can help with? * **Is there anything...?**（是否有任何事是…？）

	單字	音標	詞性	意義	字頻	大考	英檢	多益
❶	work	[wɝk]	v.	工作	1	1	初級	◎
	overtime	[ˏovəˋtaɪm]	adv.	超時地	3			◎
	often	[ˋɔfən]	adv.	常常	1	1	初級	
❷	tired	[taɪrd]	adj.	疲累的	1	1	初級	◎
	lately	[ˋletlɪ]	adv.	最近	2	4	中級	
❸	have	[hæv]	v.	擁有	1	1	初級	
	bag	[bæg]	n.	黑眼圈	1	1	初級	
	eye	[aɪ]	n.	眼睛	1	1	初級	
❹	still	[stɪl]	adv.	仍然	1	1	初級	◎
	need	[nid]	v.	需要	1	1	初級	◎
	weekend	[ˋwikˏɛnd]	n.	週末	1	1	初級	
❺	want	[wɑnt]	v.	想要	1	1	初級	◎
	go	[go]	v.	去	1	1	初級	
	walk	[wɔk]	n.	散步	1	1	初級	
❻	always	[ˋɔlwez]	adv.	總是	1	1	初級	
	this	[ðɪs]	adv.	這麼	1	1	初級	
	hard	[hɑrd]	adv.	認真地	1	1	初級	◎
❼	wear	[wɛr]	v.	使疲累	1	1	初級	◎
	yourself	[juəˋsɛlf]	pron.	你自己	1		初級	
	out	[aʊt]	adv.	完全、徹底	1	1	初級	
	get	[gɛt]	v.	變成	1	1	初級	◎
	sick	[sɪk]	adj.	生病的	1	1	初級	◎
❽	give	[gɪv]	v.	給予	1	1	初級	
	break	[brek]	n.	休息	1	1	初級	◎
❾	nine	[naɪn]	n.	九	1	1	初級	
	ten	[tɛn]	n.	十	1	1	初級	
	pm	[ˋpiˋɛm]	adv.	下午	1	4		
	every	[ˋɛvrɪ]	adj.	每一	1	1	初級	
	day	[de]	n.	天	1	1	初級	
❿	take	[tek]	v.	採取	1	1	初級	◎
	care	[kɛr]	n.	照顧	1	1	初級	◎
	health	[hɛlθ]	n.	健康	1	1	初級	◎
⓫	too	[tu]	adv.	過於	1	1	初級	
	much	[mʌtʃ]	adj.	許多的	1	1	初級	
	pressure	[ˋprɛʃə]	n.	壓力	1	3	中級	◎
⓬	good	[gʊd]	adj.	良好的	1	1	初級	◎
	older	[ˋoldə]	adj.	old（老的）比較級	1	1	初級	
⓭	deep	[dip]	adj.	深深的	1	1	初級	
	breath	[brɛθ]	n.	呼吸	1	3	中級	
⓮	head	[hɛd]	n.	頭	1	1	初級	◎
	hurt	[hɝt]	v.	疼痛	1	1	初級	
⓯	exhausted	[ɪgˋzɔstɪd]	adj.	累壞的	3	4	中級	◎
⓰	there	[ðɛr]	adv.	有…	1	1	初級	
	anything	[ˋɛnɪˏθɪŋ]	pron.	任何事情	1	1	初級	
	help	[hɛlp]	v.	幫忙	1	1	初級	

※「紅字單字」於本單元多句出現，「單字級等分析」僅列在「首次出現句」。

073　我贊成。

🔊 MP3 073-01 ❶～❶

❶	我舉雙手贊成。	I completely agree with that. * **agree with**（同意）
❷	我再同意不過了！	I couldn't agree more! * **couldn't agree more**（完全同意） * **couldn't agree less**（完全不同意）
❸	就是這樣！	That's it!
❹	有比這個更好的嗎？	Is there anything better than this?
❺	當然好！	Of course! = Sure! = Certainly!
❻	這真是太棒了！	This is the best!
❼	這個計畫太完美了！	What a perfect plan this is!
❽	算我一份！	Count me in! = I'm in!
❾	漂亮！	Great! = Nice! = Good!
❿	我想這是最好的了。	I think this is the best.
⓫	我沒意見。	It doesn't matter to me. * 某事＋**doesn't matter to**＋某人（某事和某人無關）
⓬	都聽你的！	It's all up to you! = It's your call! * **be up to**＋某人（聽從某人決定）= **be one's call**
⓭	真是超乎我想像的好。	It is beyond my imagination. * **beyond one's imagination**（超乎某人想像） * **imagination**（想像）可替換為：**expectations**（預期）
⓮	放手做吧！	Just do it!
⓯	我投你一票。	You've got my vote. = I will give you my vote.
⓰	你得到我的同意了。	You have my permission. = I give you my approval.
⓱	我這邊沒什麼問題。	There is no problem on my side. * **on my side**（在我這邊）
⓲	就照你說的做吧！	Just do as you suggest! * **suggest**（建議）可替換為：**say**（說）

	單字	音標	詞性	意義	字頻	大考	英檢	多益
❶	completely	[kəmˋpltɪlɪ]	adv.	完全地	1			◎
	agree	[əˋgri]	v.	同意	1	1	初級	◎
	that	[ðæt]	pron.	那個	1	1	初級	
❷	more	[mor]	adv.	更加	1	1	初級	
❹	there	[ðɛr]	adv.	有…	1	1	初級	
	anything	[ˋɛnɪˏθɪŋ]	pron.	任何事情	1	1	初級	
	better	[ˋbɛtɚ]	adj.	good（良好的）比較級	1	1	初級	
	this	[ðɪs]	pron.	這個	1	1	初級	
❺	course	[kors]	adv.	（與 of 連用）當然	1	1	初級	◎
	sure	[ʃur]	adv.	一定	1	1	初級	
	certainly	[ˋsɝtənlɪ]	adv.	沒問題	1		初級	◎
❻	best	[bɛst]	adj.	good（良好的）最高級	1	1	初級	
❼	perfect	[ˋpɝfɪkt]	adj.	完美的	1	2	初級	◎
	plan	[plæn]	n.	計畫	1	1	初級	◎
❽	count	[kaʊnt]	v.	算	1	1	初級	◎
❾	great	[gret]	adj.	極好的	1	1	初級	◎
	nice	[naɪs]	adj.	美妙的	1	1	初級	
	good	[gʊd]	adj.	良好的	1	1	初級	◎
❿	think	[θɪŋk]	v.	認為	1	1	初級	
⓫	matter	[ˋmætɚ]	v.	重要、要緊	1	1	初級	◎
⓬	all	[ɔl]	adv.	完全	1	1	初級	
	up	[ʌp]	adj.	由…決定	1	1	初級	
	call	[kɔl]	n.	決定	1	1	初級	◎
⓭	imagination	[ɪˏmædʒəˋneʃən]	n.	想像	2	3	中級	◎
⓮	just	[dʒʌst]	adv.	就	1	1	初級	
	do	[du]	v.	做	1	1	初級	
⓯	got	[gɑt]	p.p.	get（取得）過去分詞	1	1	初級	◎
	vote	[vot]	n.	支持	1	2	初級	◎
	give	[gɪv]	v.	給予	1	1	初級	
⓰	have	[hæv]	v.	得到	1	1	初級	
	permission	[pɚˋmɪʃən]	n.	允許	2	3	中級	◎
	approval	[əˋpruvl]	n.	同意	1	4	中級	◎
⓱	problem	[ˋprɑbləm]	n.	問題	1	1	初級	◎
	side	[saɪd]	n.	邊、面	1	1	初級	
⓲	suggest	[səˋdʒɛst]	v.	建議	1	3	初級	◎

※「紅字單字」於本單元多句出現，「單字級等分析」僅列在「首次出現句」。

MP3 073-02 ❶～❻

❶	你贊成嗎？	Do you agree?
❷	你有什麼看法？	What is your opinion on this? * on this（關於這個） * opinion（看法）可替換為：point of view（觀點）
❸	你覺得這樣做好嗎？	Do you think this is a good way? * way（方法）可替換為：method（方法）
❹	你覺得這主意如何？	What do you think about this idea? * think about（覺得）
❺	你認為這是最好的方式嗎？	Do you think this is the best method? * the best method（最佳方式）
❻	你同意我說的嗎？	Do you agree with what I said?
❼	我希望可以得到你的許可。	I hope that I can have your permission. * have one's permission（獲得某人允許） 　= receive one's approval
❽	這樣代表你默許了嗎？	Does that mean you agree? * mean (that)＋子句（代表…）
❾	拜託你點個頭嘛！	Please just nod your head and say yes! * nod one's head（點頭） * say yes（同意）
❿	你就將就點嘛！	Can't you be a little more flexible? * a little more＋形容詞（稍微多點…）
⓫	大家都說好，你就答應了吧！	Since everyone has agreed already, would you just say yes?
⓬	希望你能支持我。	I hope you will support me.
⓭	我想不出你有什麼理由拒絕。	I don't think there is any reason for you to refuse.
⓮	我不敢相信你竟然答應了！	I can't believe that you just said yes! * can't believe that＋子句（不敢相信…）
⓯	你在猶豫什麼？	Why do you hesitate? * hesitate（猶豫）可替換為：hang back（猶豫）
⓰	你贊成我就立刻進行。	I will proceed right away if you say yes. * right away（立刻）= straight away

	單字	音標	詞性	意義	字頻	大考	英檢	多益
❶	agree	[əˋgri]	v.	同意	1	1	初級	◎
❷	opinion	[əˋpɪnjən]	n.	看法	1	2	初級	◎
	this	[ðɪs]	pron.	這個	1	1	初級	
❸	think	[θɪŋk]	v.	認為	1	1	初級	
	good	[gʊd]	adj.	良好的	1	1	初級	◎
	way	[we]	n.	方法	1	1	初級	
❹	idea	[aɪˋdiə]	n.	主意	1	1	初級	◎
❺	best	[bɛst]	adj.	good（良好的）最高級	1	1	初級	
	method	[ˋmɛθəd]	n.	方法	1	2	初級	◎
❻	said	[sɛd]	p.t.	say（說）過去式	4	1	初級	
❼	hope	[hop]	v.	希望	1	1	初級	
	have	[hæv]	v.	擁有	1	1	初級	
	permission	[pɚˋmɪʃən]	n.	允許	2	3	中級	◎
❽	mean	[min]	v.	代表	1	1	初級	◎
❾	please	[pliz]	adv.	請	1	1	初級	
	just	[dʒʌst]	adv.	只要	1	1	初級	
	nod	[nɑd]	v.	點頭	1	2	初級	◎
	head	[hɛd]	n.	頭	1	1	初級	◎
	say	[se]	v.	說	1	1	初級	
	yes	[jɛs]	n.	同意	1	1	初級	
❿	little	[ˋlɪtl̩]	adv.	稍微	1	1	初級	
	more	[mor]	adv.	更加	1	1	初級	
	flexible	[ˋflɛksəbl̩]	adv.	願意嘗試改變的、可變通的	2	4	中級	◎
⓫	everyone	[ˋɛrvɪ͵wʌn]	pron.	每個人	1		初級	
	agreed	[əˋgrid]	p.p.	agree（同意）過去分詞	6	1	初級	◎
	already	[ɔlˋrɛdɪ]	adv.	已經	1	1	初級	◎
⓬	support	[səˋport]	v.	支持	1	2	初級	◎
⓭	there	[ðɛr]	adv.	有…	1	1	初級	
	any	[ˋɛnɪ]	adj.	任何的	1	1	初級	
	reason	[ˋrizn̩]	n.	理由	1	1	初級	◎
	refuse	[rɪˋfjuz]	v.	拒絕	1	2	初級	◎
⓮	believe	[bɪˋliv]	v.	相信	1	1	初級	◎
⓯	hesitate	[ˋhɛzə͵tet]	v.	猶豫	2	3	中級	◎
⓰	proceed	[prəˋsid]	v.	進行	1	1	初級	
	right	[raɪt]	adv.	立即	1	1	初級	
	away	[əˋwe]	adv.	直接	1	1	初級	

※「紅字單字」於本單元多句出現，「單字級等分析」僅列在「首次出現句」。

074　我反對。

❶	我不會答應的。	I won't approve of it. ＝ I won't say yes. * approve of（答應）
❷	我無法認同。	I can't agree with that.
❸	我反對。	I disagree. ＝ I don't approve. ＝ I don't agree.
❹	我抵死不從。	I'll die before I agree with that. * I will die before＋子句（在我死之前都不會…）
❺	這不是我希望的。	This is not what I wanted. * what I wanted（我當初想要的）
❻	我不認為這是個好主意。	I don't think it's a good idea. * good idea（好主意）
❼	我不想支持你們。	I don't want to support you.
❽	省省力氣吧！	Save your strength! ＝ Save your energy!
❾	我想不出比這更糟的提議了！	I can't think of any suggestions worse than this. * I can't think of（我想不到…）
❿	我絕不和你同流合污。	I absolutely will not take part in this with you. * take part in（參與）＝ participate in
⓫	門兒都沒有！	No deal! ＝ Don't even think about it!
⓬	不可能說服我的，你放棄吧！	You can't persuade me, give it up!
⓭	不行就是不行，沒什麼好說的。	No means no, there's nothing left to say. * there's nothing left to say（沒有什麼好說的）
⓮	這種事我怎麼可能會答應呢？	How can I possibly agree with that? * How can I...?（我如何能夠…呢）
⓯	我絕對不會改變立場。	I absolutely will not change my position. * change one's position（改變立場）
⓰	我不想再聽你說下去。	I don't want to hear what you have to say anymore. * what you have to say（你想要說的話）
⓱	別想從我這兒得到支持票。	Don't even think about getting my vote. * Don't even think about＋動詞-ing（別想要…！）

	單字	音標	詞性	意義	字頻	大考	英檢	多益
❶	approve	[əˋpruv]	v.	答應	1	3	中級	◎
	say	[se]	v.	說	1	1	初級	
	yes	[jɛs]	n.	同意	1	1	初級	
❷	agree	[əˋgri]	v.	同意	1	1	初級	◎
	that	[ðæt]	pron.	那個	1	1	初級	
❸	disagree	[ˌdɪsəˋgri]	v.	不同意	1	2	中級	◎
❹	die	[daɪ]	v.	死亡	1	1	初級	
❺	this	[ðɪs]	pron.	這個	1	1	初級	
	wanted	[ˋwɑntɪd]	p.t.	want（想要）過去式	5	1	初級	◎
❻	think	[θɪŋk]	v.	認為/想到/考慮	1	1	初級	
	good	[gʊd]	adj.	良好的	1	1	初級	◎
	idea	[aɪˋdiə]	n.	主意	1	1	初級	◎
❼	want	[wɑnt]	v.	想要	1	1	初級	
	support	[səˋport]	v.	支持	1	2	初級	
❽	save	[sev]	v.	節省	1	1	初級	◎
	strength	[strɛŋθ]	n.	力氣	1	3	中級	◎
	energy	[ˋɛnədʒɪ]	n.	能量	1	2	初級	
❾	any	[ˋɛnɪ]	adj.	任何的	1	1	初級	
	suggestion	[səˋdʒɛstʃən]	n.	建議	1	4	中級	◎
	worse	[wɝs]	adj.	bad（糟糕的）比較級	4	1	中級	
❿	absolutely	[ˋæbsəˌlutlɪ]	adv.	絕對	1		中級	◎
	take	[tek]	v.	參與	1	1	初級	
	part	[pɑrt]	n.	部分	1	1	初級	◎
⓫	deal	[dil]	n.	協商	1	1	初級	◎
	even	[ˋivən]	adv.	甚至	1	1	初級	◎
⓬	persuade	[pəˋswed]	v.	說服	2	3	中級	◎
	give	[gɪv]	v.	放棄	1	1	初級	
	up	[ʌp]	adv.	完全、徹底	1	1	初級	
⓭	mean	[min]	v.	代表	1	2	初級	◎
	there	[ðɛr]	adv.	有…	1	1	初級	
	nothing	[ˋnʌθɪŋ]	pron.	沒有事情	1	1	初級	
	left	[lɛft]	p.p.	leave（剩下）過去式	1	1	初級	
⓮	possibly	[ˋpɑsəblɪ]	adv.	可能	1		中級	
⓯	change	[tʃendʒ]	v.	改變	1	2	初級	◎
	position	[pəˋzɪʃən]	n.	立場	1	1	初級	◎
⓰	hear	[hɪr]	v.	聽	1	1	初級	
	have	[hæv]	v.	必須	1	1	初級	
	anymore	[ˋɛnɪˌmor]	adv.	不再	1		中高	
⓱	getting	[ˋgɛtɪŋ]	n.	get（取得）動名詞	1	1	初級	◎
	vote	[vot]	n.	同意	1	2	初級	◎

※「紅字單字」於本單元多句出現，「單字級等分析」僅列在「首次出現句」。

MP3 074-02 ❶～⓮

❶	你反對嗎？	Are you against that? = Are you opposed? * be against＋某事物（反對某事物）
❷	你為什麼反對？	Why don't you agree with that? * Why don't you...?（你為什麼不…？）
❸	你不覺得這個點子很棒嗎？	You don't think it's a good idea?
❹	你不喜歡這個提議嗎？	You don't like this suggestion? * suggestion（建議）= proposal
❺	難道你不再考慮一下？	Why don't you think about it some more? * Why don't you...?（你怎麼不…呢） * think about（考慮） * some more（再多一點）
❻	你不支持我們嗎？	You don't want to support us?
❼	我不敢相信你竟然反對。	I can't believe that you are actually against this. * believe that＋子句（相信…）
❽	請你不要這麼快就說「不」。	Please don't say "no" so quickly. * Please don't＋動詞原形（請別…）
❾	請你不要為了反對而反對。	Please don't oppose this just to oppose it. * oppose＋某事物＋just to oppose it （為了反對某事物而反對）
❿	你上回不是贊成嗎？	Didn't you agree last time? * Didn't you...?（你之前不是…嗎） * last time（上一次）
⓫	你一定要這麼堅持嗎？	Must you be so persistent? * Must you be＋形容詞?（你是否一定要…？） * persistent（堅持的）= insistent
⓬	請你給我一個合理的理由。	Please give me a reasonable reason. * give me a reason（給我一個理由）
⓭	你反對的理由很奇怪。	Your reason for opposing this is strange. * reason for opposing＋某事物（反對某事物的理由） * reason for supporting＋某事物（支持某事物的理由）
⓮	你的反對是有道理的。	Your opposition is reasonable.

單字級等分析

	單字	音標	詞性	意義	字頻	大考	英檢	多益
❶	that	[ðæt]	pron.	那個	1	1	初級	
	opposed	[əˋpozd]	p.p.	oppose（反對）過去分詞	2	4	中高	◎
❷	agree	[əˋgri]	v.	同意	1	1	初級	◎
❸	think	[θɪŋk]	v.	認為/考慮	1	1	初級	
	good	[gʊd]	adj.	良好的	1	1	初級	◎
	idea	[aɪˋdiə]	n.	主意	1	1	初級	◎
❹	like	[laɪk]	v.	喜歡	1	1	初級	
	this	[ðɪs]	adj./pron.	這個	1	1	初級	
	suggestion	[səˋdʒɛstʃən]	n.	建議	1	4	中級	◎
❺	some	[sʌm]	adv.	稍稍、幾分	1	1	初級	
	more	[mor]	adv.	更加	1	1	初級	
❻	want	[wɑnt]	v.	想要	1	1	初級	◎
	support	[səˋport]	v.	支持	1	2	初級	◎
❼	believe	[bɪˋliv]	v.	相信	1	1	初級	◎
	actually	[ˋæktʃʊəlɪ]	adv.	實際上	1		初級	
❽	please	[pliz]	adv.	請	1	1	初級	
	say	[se]	v.	說	1	1	初級	
	no	[no]	n.	否定	1	1	初級	
	so	[so]	adv.	這麼	1	1	初級	
	quickly	[ˋkwɪklɪ]	adv.	快速地	1			
❾	oppose	[əˋpoz]	v.	反對	1	4	中級	◎
	just	[dʒʌst]	adv.	只是	1	1	初級	
❿	last	[læst]	adj.	上一次	1	1	初級	◎
	time	[taɪm]	n.	次、回	1	1	初級	◎
⓫	persistent	[pəˋsɪstənt]	adj.	堅持的	2	6	中高	◎
⓬	give	[gɪv]	v.	給予	1	1	初級	
	reasonable	[ˋriznəbl̩]	adj.	合理的	1	3	中級	◎
	reason	[ˋrizn̩]	n.	理由	1	1	初級	◎
⓭	opposing	[əˋpozɪŋ]	n.	oppose（反對）動名詞	3	4	中級	◎
	strange	[strendʒ]	adj.	奇怪的	1	1	初級	
⓮	opposition	[ˏɑpəˋzɪʃən]	n.	反對	1	6	中級	◎

※「紅字單字」於本單元多句出現，「單字級等分析」僅列在「首次出現句」。

075 我的建議。

MP3 075-01 ❶～❸

❶	我有個提議。	I have a suggestion.
❷	我沒什麼意見。	I don't have an opinion. ＝ That's fine by me.
❸	我想聽聽大家的意見。	I would like to listen to everyone's suggestions. * would like to（想要） * everyone's suggestions（每個人的意見）
❹	我可以提個意見嗎？	May I make a suggestion? * May I＋動詞原形?（請問我是否可以…？）
❺	我在想這麼做是不是比較好？	I am considering whether this is a better way to do it. * whether＋子句（是不是…） * 此句用「現在進行式」（...am considering...）表示「說話當下正在做的事」。
❻	這樣也許行得通。	This way might work. * this way（這個方法）
❼	換個方向想會比較好。	It will be better if we change the direction of our thinking. * will be better（將會更好）、if＋子句（如果…） * direction of thinking（思考方向）
❽	何不試試看？	Why don't you give it a try? ＝ Why not try?
❾	你是否可以考慮一下？	Can you just think about it? * think about（考慮）
❿	我建議找個局外人來評理。	I suggest that we find an outsider to decide which of us is right. * suggest that＋主詞＋(should)＋動詞原形（建議…） * which of us（我們之中的哪一個）
⓫	我建議大家先冷靜下來。	I suggest that everyone calm down first. * calm down（冷靜）
⓬	我想我們各做各的好了。	I think that we should each do our own jobs. * I think that＋子句（我覺得…） * each do our own jobs（我們各做各的事）
⓭	我想不出什麼好建議。	I can't think of any good suggestions. * think of（想出）

	單字	音標	詞性	意義	字頻	大考	英檢	多益
❶	have	[hæv]	v.	擁有	1	1	初級	
	suggestion	[sə`dʒɛstʃən]	n.	建議	1	4	中級	◎
❷	opinion	[ə`pɪnjən]	n.	意見	1	2	初級	◎
	fine	[faɪn]	adj.	沒關係的	1	1	初級	◎
❸	like	[laɪk]	v.	想要	1	1	初級	
	listen	[`lɪsn]	v.	聽	1	1	初級	
	everyone	[`ɛvrɪ.wʌn]	pron.	每個人	1		初級	
❹	make	[mek]	v.	提出	1	1	初級	
❺	considering	[kən`sɪdərɪŋ]	p.pr.	consider（考慮）現在分詞	2	2	中高	◎
	this	[ðɪs]	pron. /adj.	這個	1	1	初級	
	better	[`bɛtɚ]	adj.	good（良好的）比較級	1	1	初級	
	way	[we]	n.	方法	1	1	初級	
	do	[du]	v.	做	1	1	初級	
❻	work	[wɝk]	v.	成功、行得通	1	1	初級	◎
❼	change	[tʃendʒ]	v.	改變	1	2	初級	◎
	direction	[də`rɛkʃən]	n.	方向	1	2	初級	◎
	thinking	[`θɪŋkɪŋ]	n.	think（思考）動名詞	1	1	中級	
❽	give	[gɪv]	v.	給予	1	1	初級	
	try	[traɪ]	n.	嘗試	1	1	初級	
❾	just	[dʒʌst]	adv.	就	1	1	初級	
	think	[θɪŋk]	v.	考慮/覺得/想出	1	1	初級	
❿	suggest	[sə`dʒɛst]	v.	建議	1	3	初級	◎
	find	[faɪnd]	v.	找尋	1	1	初級	
	outsider	[`aʊt`saɪdɚ]	n.	局外人	2	5	中高	
	decide	[dɪ`saɪd]	v.	評斷	1	1	初級	◎
	right	[raɪt]	adj.	正確的	1	1	初級	
⓫	calm	[kɑm]	v.	冷靜	2	2	初級	
	down	[daʊn]	adv.	下來	1	1	初級	
	first	[fɝst]	adv.	首先	1	1	初級	
⓬	each	[itʃ]	adv.	各個	1	1	初級	
	own	[on]	adj.	自己的	1	1	初級	◎
	job	[dʒɑb]	n.	工作	1	1	初級	
⓭	any	[`ɛnɪ]	adj.	任何的	1	1	初級	
	good	[gʊd]	adj.	良好的	1	1	初級	◎

※「紅字單字」於本單元多句出現，「單字級等分析」僅列在「首次出現句」。

075　你的建議？

❶	這件事你有什麼看法？	Do you have any opinion on this matter? * **on this matter**（對於這件事）
❷	你有什麼好建議嗎？	Do you have any good suggestions? * **suggestion**（意見、建議）= **opinion** = **comment**
❸	這是你的建議嗎？	Is this your suggestion?
❹	你覺得這個主意如何？	What do you think of this idea? * **think of**（覺得）可替換為：**think about**（覺得）
❺	你可以幫忙想想辦法嗎？	Can you help think of a solution? * **help**＋動詞原形（幫忙…） * **think of**（想出）= **come up with**
❻	大家一起腦力激盪吧！	Let's brainstorm together! * **Let's**＋動詞原形!（一起做某事吧！）
❼	我很需要你的意見。	I really need your comments. * **need one's comment**（需要意見）
❽	我會尊重你的意見。	I will respect your opinion. * **respect one's opinion**（尊重意見）
❾	謝謝你提供建議。	Thank you for offering your suggestion. * **offer one's suggestion**（提供建議）
❿	你指出了問題的關鍵。	You've pointed out the key point of this problem. * **point out**（指出、指明）、**key point**（關鍵） * 此句用「現在完成式」（...have pointed...）表示「過去某時點發生某事，且結果持續到現在」。
⓫	你的提議真好！	Your proposal is great!
⓬	你的建議解決了大家的難題。	Your recommendation solved everyone's problems. *此句用「過去簡單式」（...solved...）表示「發生在過去的事」。
⓭	你的建議很有可行性。	Your suggestion is quite feasible.
⓮	我想你一定有很多主意吧？	I bet you probably have a lot of ideas. * **I bet**＋子句（我猜測…）
⓯	我等不及要聽你的想法了！	I can't wait to hear your ideas! * **can't wait to**＋動詞原形（等不及…）

	單字	音標	詞性	意義	字頻	大考	英檢	多益
❶	have	[hæv]	v.	擁有	1	1	初級	
	any	[ˋɛnɪ]	adj.	任何的	1	1	初級	
	opinion	[əˋpɪnjən]	n.	意見	1	2	初級	◎
	this	[ðɪs]	adj.	這個	1	1	初級	
	matter	[ˋmætɚ]	n.	事情	1	1	初級	◎
❷	good	[gʊd]	adj.	良好的	1	1	初級	◎
	suggestion	[səˋdʒɛstʃən]	n.	建議	1	4	中級	◎
❹	think	[θɪŋk]	v.	覺得/想出	1	1	初級	
	idea	[aɪˋdiə]	n.	主意	1	1	初級	
❺	help	[hɛlp]	v.	幫助	1	1	初級	
	solution	[səˋluʃən]	n.	辦法	1	2	初級	◎
❻	let	[lɛt]	v.	讓…	1	1	初級	
	brainstorm	[ˋbren͵stɔrm]	v.	腦力激盪	8			
	together	[təˋgɛðɚ]	adv.	一起	1		初級	
❼	really	[ˋrɪəlɪ]	adv.	很、十分	1		初級	
	need	[nid]	v.	需要	1	1	初級	◎
	comment	[ˋkɑmɛnt]	n.	意見	1	4	初級	◎
❽	respect	[rɪˋspɛkt]	v.	尊重	1	2	初級	◎
❾	thank	[θæŋk]	v.	感謝	1	1	初級	
	offering	[ˋɔfərɪŋ]	n.	offer（提供）動名詞	2	6	中高	◎
❿	pointed	[ˋpɔɪntɪd]	p.p.	point（指出）過去分詞	4	1	中高	◎
	out	[aʊt]	adv.	出現	1		初級	
	key	[ki]	adj.	關鍵的	1		初級	◎
	point	[pɔɪnt]	n.	要點	1	1	初級	◎
	problem	[ˋprɑbləm]	n.	問題	1	1	初級	◎
⓫	proposal	[prəˋpozl]	n.	提議	1	3	中級	◎
	great	[gret]	adj.	很好的	1	1	初級	◎
⓬	recommendation	[͵rɛkəmɛnˋdeʃən]	n.	建議	1	6	中高	◎
	solved	[sɑlvd]	p.t.	solve（解決）過去式	1	2	初級	◎
	everyone	[ˋɛvrɪ͵wʌn]	pron.	每個人	1		初級	
⓭	quite	[kwaɪt]	adv.	相當	1	1	初級	
	feasible	[ˋfizəbl]	adj.	可實行的	3	6	中高	◎
⓮	bet	[bɛt]	v.	猜測	1	2	中級	◎
	probably	[ˋprɑbəblɪ]	adv.	可能	1		初級	◎
	lot	[lɑt]	n.	許多				
⓯	wait	[wet]	v.	等待	1	1	初級	◎
	hear	[hɪr]	v.	聽	1	1	初級	

※「紅字單字」於本單元多句出現，「單字級等分析」僅列在「首次出現句」。

MP3 076-01 ❶～⓰

❶	我有麻煩了！	I've got a problem! ＝ I'm in trouble!
❷	誰來救我！	Who can help me?
❸	如果你能幫忙，我會非常感激。	I would appreciate it if you could help me. * **I would＋動詞＋if you could＋動詞** （如果你能…，我會…） * **appreciate＋行為**（感激某行為，此字不可接續「人」）
❹	求求你嘛！	I am begging you! * 此句用「現在進行式」（...am begging...） 表示「說話當下正在做的事」。
❺	你介意我耽誤你一些時間嗎？	Would you mind if I kept you here for a moment? * **Would you mind if＋過去式子句?**（你目前是否介意…， 「if＋過去式子句」表示假設語氣的「如果…」）
❻	我真的走投無路了。	There really is no way out for me. ＝ I have come to a dead end.
❼	你是唯一能幫我的人。	You are the only one who can help me out. * **help me out**（幫我解決困難）
❽	也許我該找別人幫忙。	Perhaps I should look for help from someone else. * **look for**（尋找） * **help from＋某人**（某人的幫助）
❾	我需要找個幫手。	I need to find a helper.
❿	我已經絕望了。	I am hopeless.
⓫	我不知道如何開口求助。	I don't know how to ask for help. * **ask for help**（請求幫忙、求救）
⓬	我不需要別人幫忙。	I don't need help from others.
⓭	沒有人會可憐我的。	Nobody will pity me.
⓮	你別假惺惺了！	Stop pretending! * **Stop＋動詞-ing**（停止做…！）
⓯	我說什麼也不接受你的幫助。	There's no way that I will accept your help. * **There's no way that＋子句**（…是不可能的）
⓰	全世界的人都不幫我！	Nobody in the whole world will help me!

	單字	音標	詞性	意義	字頻	大考	英檢	多益
❶	got	[gɑt]	p.t.	get（陷入）過去式	1	1	初級	◎
	problem	[ˋprɑbləm]	n.	問題	1	1	初級	◎
	trouble	[ˋtrʌbl̩]	n.	問題	1	1	初級	◎
❷	help	[hɛlp]	v./n.	幫忙	1	1	初級	
❸	appreciate	[əˋpriʃɪ͜et]	v.	感激	1	3	初級	◎
❹	begging	[ˋbɛgɪŋ]	p.pr.	beg（乞求）現在分詞	7	2	中級	
❺	mind	[maɪnd]	v.	介意	1	1	初級	◎
	kept	[kɛpt]	p.t.	keep（耽誤）過去式	1	1	初級	◎
	here	[hɪr]	adv.	這裡	1	1	初級	
	moment	[ˋmomənt]	n.	片刻	1	1	初級	
❻	there	[ðɛr]	adv.	有…	1	1	初級	
	really	[ˋrɪəlɪ]	adv.	真的	1		初級	
	way	[we]	n.	方法、路	1	1	初級	
	out	[aʊt]	adv.	擺脫	1	1	初級	
	come	[kʌm]	p.p.	come（來到）過去分詞	1	1	初級	
	dead	[dɛd]	adj.	走投無路的	1	1	初級	
	end	[ɛnd]	n.	盡頭	1	1	初級	
❼	only	[ˋonlɪ]	adj.	只有	1	1	初級	
	one	[wʌn]	pron.	一個人	1	1	初級	
❽	perhaps	[pɚˋhæps]	adv.	也許	1	1	初級	◎
	look	[lʊk]	v.	尋找	1	1	初級	
	someone	[ˋsʌm͵wʌn]	pron.	某個人	1	1	初級	
	else	[ɛls]	adj.	其他的	1	1	初級	
❾	need	[nid]	v.	需要	1	1	初級	◎
	find	[faɪnd]	v.	尋找	1	1	初級	
	helper	[ˋhɛlpɚ]	n.	幫手	4		初級	
❿	hopeless	[ˋhoplɪs]	adj.	絕望的	3		中高	
⓫	know	[no]	v.	知道	1	1	初級	◎
	ask	[æsk]	v.	請求	1	1	初級	
⓬	other	[ˋʌðɚ]	pron.	其他人	1	1	初級	
⓭	nobody	[ˋnobɑdɪ]	pron.	沒有人	1	2	初級	
	pity	[ˋpɪtɪ]	v.	憐憫	3	3	中級	
⓮	stop	[stɑp]	v.	停止	1	1	初級	◎
	pretending	[prɪˋtɛndɪŋ]	n.	pretend（假裝）動名詞	2	3	中級	◎
⓯	accept	[əkˋsɛpt]	v.	接受	1	2	初級	◎
⓰	whole	[hol]	adj.	整個	1	1	初級	◎
	world	[wɝld]	n.	世界	1	1	初級	

※「紅字單字」於本單元多句出現，「單字級等分析」僅列在「首次出現句」。

076　你需要幫忙嗎？

❶	需要幫忙嗎？	Do you need help? = May I help you?
❷	我很樂意幫忙。	I am willing to help you. * **be willing to**（願意）
❸	我可以為你做什麼嗎？	What can I do for you?
❹	我想你可能會需要這個。	I suspect you might need this. * **suspect**＋子句（猜測…）
❺	真的不用幫你嗎？	You really don't need my help?
❻	我想我可以幫得上忙。	I think I can help. = I think I can give you a hand.
❼	你願意接受我的幫助嗎？	Are you willing to accept my help? * **Are you willing to**＋動詞原形? （你是否願意…？）
❽	我不知道該如何幫你。	I don't know how to help you.
❾	讓我試試好嗎？	Let me try, okay?
❿	到時候你就會需要我了。	When the time comes, you will need me. * **When the time comes, ...**（到那個時候，…）
⓫	我不認為你需要我的幫助。	I don't think you need my help. * **I don't think**＋子句（我不覺得…）
⓬	你說什麼我都會盡力而為。	I will do my best to do whatever you ask. * **do one's best**（盡力） * **whatever you ask**（你要求的事）
⓭	請告訴我你的需求。	Please tell me what you need.
⓮	需要什麼，記得告訴我一聲。	Please let me know if you need something. * **let me know**（告訴我）= tell me
⓯	能幫忙是我的榮幸。	It is my pleasure to help you. * **It is my pleasure to**＋動詞原形 （做某事是我的榮幸）
⓰	我不能解決你的問題。	I can't solve your problem. * **solve one's problem**（解決問題）
⓱	也許你並不需要別人的幫助。	You might not anyone's help.

	單字	音標	詞性	意義	字頻	大考	英檢	多益
❶	need	[nid]	v.	需要	1	1	初級	◎
	help	[hɛlp]	n./v.	幫忙	1	1	初級	
❷	willing	[ˋwɪlɪŋ]	adj.	願意的	1	2	初級	◎
❸	do	[du]	v.	做	1	1	初級	
❹	suspect	[səˋspɛkt]	v.	猜測	1	3	中級	◎
	this	[ðɪs]	pron.	這個	1	1	初級	
❺	really	[ˋrɪəlɪ]	adv.	真的	1		初級	
❻	think	[θɪŋk]	v.	認為	1	1	初級	◎
	give	[gɪv]	v.	給予	1	1	初級	
	hand	[hænd]	n.	協助	1	1	初級	
❼	accept	[əkˋsɛpt]	v.	接受	1	2	初級	◎
❽	know	[no]	v.	知道	1	1	初級	◎
❾	let	[lɛt]	v.	讓…	1	1	初級	
	try	[traɪ]	v.	嘗試	1	1	初級	
	okay	[ˋoˋke]	int.	好嗎	1	1		
❿	time	[taɪm]	n.	時間	1	1	初級	◎
	come	[kʌm]	v.	到來	1	1	初級	
⓬	best	[bɛst]	n.	最好	1	1	初級	
	ask	[æsk]	v.	要求	1	1	初級	
⓭	please	[pliz]	adv.	請	1	1	初級	
	tell	[tɛl]	v.	告訴	1	1	初級	
⓮	something	[ˋsʌmθɪŋ]	pron.	某些事情	1	1	初級	
⓯	pleasure	[ˋplɛʒɚ]	n.	榮幸	1	2	初級	◎
⓰	solve	[salv]	v.	解決	1	2	初級	◎
	problem	[ˋprɑbləm]	n.	問題	1	1	初級	◎
⓱	anyone	[ˋɛnɪ.wʌn]	pron.	任何人	1	2	初級	

※「紅字單字」於本單元多句出現,「單字級等分析」僅列在「首次出現句」。

077 我下定決心。

❶	我的心意已決。	I've already made up my mind. = I've already made a decision. * **make up one's mind**（做決定）= **make a decision**
❷	這就是我的決定！	This is my decision!
❸	這個決定對大家都好。	This decision will be good for everyone. * **be good for**＋某人（對某人有好處）
❹	我需要時間考慮。	I need more time to think about it.
❺	我要堅持我的決定。	I have to insist on my decision. * **insist on**（堅持）
❻	沒得商量了！	There's nothing to negotiate! = No deal!
❼	這是我仔細考慮後的決定。	After careful consideration, this is my decision. * **careful consideration**（仔細的考慮）
❽	我常受別人的影響改變決定。	I often change my decisions due to the influence of others. * **due to**＋名詞（因為…）
❾	我做不了主！	I can't make the call! * **call**（決定）= **decision**
❿	我不夠堅持我的想法。	I don't insist enough on my decisions.
⓫	誰能幫我做決定？	Who can help me make the decision? * **help**＋某人＋動詞原形（幫助某人做某事）
⓬	我不會後悔的！	I won't regret it!
⓭	我一定會盡我最大的努力。	I will do my absolute best. = I will give my best effort.
⓮	這事我說了算！	This is final. * 此句表示「不可能改變心意、不得異議」
⓯	誰都不能改變我的決定！	No one can alter my decision! * **alter one's decision**（改變決定） 　= **change one's decision**
⓰	就這麼說定了！	It's decided then! = Decision made!
⓱	我連想都不用想就能決定。	I don't even need to think about this decision.

	單字	音標	詞性	意義	字頻	大考	英檢	多益
❶	already	[ɔlˋrɛdɪ]	adv.	已經	1	1	初級	◎
	made	[med]	p.p.	make（做出）過去分詞	1	1	初級	
	up	[ʌp]	adv.	定下	1	1	初級	
	mind	[maɪnd]	n.	主意	1	1	初級	◎
	decision	[dɪˋsɪʒən]	n.	決定	1	2	初級	◎
❷	this	[ðɪs]	pron. /adj.	這個	1	1	初級	
❸	good	[gʊd]	adj.	良好的	1	1	初級	◎
	everyone	[ˋɛvrɪ.wʌn]	pron.	每個人	1		初級	
❹	need	[nid]	v.	需要	1	1	初級	
	more	[mor]	adj.	many（許多的）比較級	1	1	初級	
	time	[taɪm]	n.	時間	1	1	初級	◎
	think	[θɪŋk]	v.	考慮	1	1	初級	
❺	have	[hæv]	v.	必須	1	1	初級	
	insist	[ɪnˋsɪst]	v.	堅持	1	2	初級	
❻	there	[ðɛr]	adv.	有…	1	1	初級	
	nothing	[ˋnʌθɪŋ]	pron.	沒有事情	1	1	初級	
	negotiate	[nɪˋgoʃɪ.et]	v.	談判、協商	1	4	中級	◎
	deal	[dil]	n.	協商	1	1	初級	
❼	careful	[ˋkɛrfəl]	adj.	仔細的	1	1	初級	◎
	consideration	[kənsɪdəˋreʃən]	n.	考慮	1	3	中級	
❽	often	[ˋɔfən]	adv.	常常	1	1	初級	
	change	[tʃendʒ]	v.	改變	1	2	初級	◎
	due	[dju]	adj.	因為	1	3	初級	◎
	influence	[ˋɪnflʊəns]	n.	影響	1	2	初級	◎
	other	[ˋʌðɚ]	pron.	其他人	1	1	初級	
❾	make	[mek]	v.	做出	1	1	初級	
	call	[kɔl]	n.	決定	1	1	初級	◎
❿	enough	[əˋnʌf]	adv.	足夠地	1	1	初級	◎
⓫	help	[hɛlp]	v.	幫忙	1	1	初級	
⓬	regret	[rɪˋgrɛt]	v.	後悔	2	3	初級	
⓭	do	[du]	v.	做	1	1	初級	
	absolute	[ˋæbsə.lut]	adj.	絕對的	2	4	中級	◎
	best	[bɛst]	n.	最好	1	1	初級	
	give	[gɪv]	v.	給予	1	1	初級	
	best	[bɛst]	adj.	good（良好的）最高級	1	1	初級	
	effort	[ˋɛfɚt]	n.	努力	1	2	初級	◎
⓮	final	[ˋfaɪnl]	adj.	不能更改的	1	1	初級	◎
⓯	one	[wʌn]	pron.	一個人	1	1	初級	
	alter	[ˋɔltɚ]	v.	改變	2	5	中高	◎
⓰	decided	[dɪˋsaɪdɪd]	p.p.	decide（決定）過去分詞	1	1	初級	◎
	then	[ðɛn]	adv.	這麼	1	1	初級	
⓱	even	[ˋivən]	adv.	甚至	1	1	初級	◎

※「紅字單字」於本單元多句出現，「單字級等分析」僅列在「首次出現句」。

🔊 MP3 077-02 **❶** ~ **⓰**

❶	你確定嗎？	Are you sure?
❷	你不會後悔嗎？	Won't you regret it?
❸	你做出決定了嗎？	Have you made your decision yet?
❹	看來你心意堅定。	It seems that you are firm in your decision. * **be firm in one's decision**（心意堅決）
❺	你太優柔寡斷了。	You are too irresolute. * **resolute**（心意堅決的）
❻	大家都在等你的決定。	Everyone is waiting for your decision. * **wait for**（等待）
❼	你怎麼會做這種決定？！	How can you make such a decision?! * **How can you...?**（你怎麼會做…？）
❽	拜託你快做決定吧！	Please make up your mind!
❾	你的決定太冒險了。	Your decision is too risky.
❿	你有可能改變決定嗎？	Is it possible that you may change your decision? * **Is it possible that＋子句？**（…是有可能的嗎）
⓫	你不要匆促下決定。	Don't make your decision hastily. * **make a decision hastily**（匆促決定）
⓬	我信任你的抉擇。	I trust your choice.
⓭	你要不要再考慮一下？	Do you need to think about it again? * **think about it**（考慮）可替換為： 　**consider it**（考慮）
⓮	你這個決定聽起來很不錯。	Your decision sounds good to me. * **sound good**（聽起來不錯） * **sound bad**（聽起來很糟）
⓯	看來是沒有辦法打消你的念頭了。	It seems there's no way to make you give up your idea. * **there's no way to＋動詞**（沒有方法做…） * **make you give up your idea**（讓你打消主意）
⓰	你不該受別人的影響而改變決定。	You should not change your decision due to the influence of others. * **the influence of＋某人**（某人的影響）

	單字	音標	詞性	意義	字頻	大考	英檢	多益
❶	sure	[ʃur]	adj.	確定的	1	1	初級	
❷	regret	[rɪˋgrɛt]	v.	後悔	2	3	初級	
❸	made	[med]	p.p.	make（做出）過去分詞	1	1	初級	
	decision	[dɪˋsɪʒən]	n.	決定	1	2	初級	◎
	yet	[jɛt]	adv.	尚未	1	1	初級	◎
❹	seem	[sim]	v.	似乎	1	1	初級	◎
	firm	[fɜm]	adj.	堅定的	2	2	初級	◎
❺	too	[tu]	adv.	過於	1	1	初級	
	irresolute	[ɪˋrɛzəlut]	adj.	優柔寡斷的				
❻	everyone	[ˋɛvrɪˌwʌn]	pron.	每個人	1		初級	
	waiting	[ˋwetɪŋ]	p.pr.	wait（等待）現在分詞	3	1	初級	◎
❼	make	[mek]	v.	做出	1	1	初級	
	such	[sʌtʃ]	adv.	這種	1	1	初級	
❽	please	[pliz]	adv.	請	1	1	初級	
	up	[ʌp]	adv.	定下/完全、徹底	1	1	初級	
	mind	[maɪnd]	n.	主意	1	1	初級	◎
❾	risky	[ˋrɪskɪ]	adj.	冒險的	2		中高	
❿	possible	[ˋpɑsəbl]	adj.	可能的	1	1	初級	◎
	change	[tʃendʒ]	v.	改變	1	1	初級	◎
⓫	hastily	[ˋhestɪlɪ]	adv.	匆促地	4			
⓬	trust	[trʌst]	v.	信任	1	2	初級	◎
	choice	[tʃɔɪs]	n.	選擇	1	2	初級	◎
⓭	need	[nid]	v.	需要	1	1	初級	◎
	think	[θɪŋk]	v.	考慮	1	1	初級	
	again	[əˋgɛn]	adv.	再次	1	1	初級	
⓮	sound	[saund]	v.	聽起來	1	1	初級	◎
	good	[gud]	adj.	良好的	1	1	初級	◎
⓯	there	[ðɛr]	adv.	有…	1	1	初級	
	way	[we]	n.	方法	1	1	初級	
	give	[gɪv]	v.	放棄	1	1	初級	
	idea	[aɪˋdiə]	n.	念頭	1	1	初級	◎
⓰	due	[dju]	adj.	因為	1	3	初級	◎
	influence	[ˋɪnfluəns]	n.	影響	1	2	初級	◎
	other	[ˋʌðɚ]	pron.	其他人	1	1	初級	

※「紅字單字」於本單元多句出現，「單字級等分析」僅列在「首次出現句」。

MP3 078-01 **❶**～**⓯**

❶	我不懂乁！	I really can't understand!
❷	我不瞭解你在說啥。	I don't understand what you are saying. * what you are saying（你現在在說的事）
❸	我一點頭緒也沒有。	I don't have a clue. * not have a clue（毫無頭緒） = not have the faintest idea
❹	我想我需要翻譯。	I guess I need a translation. * I guess＋子句（我認為…）＝ I think＋子句
❺	可以再解釋清楚一點嗎？	Can you define that more clearly? * define more clearly（解釋得更清楚）
❻	怎麼那麼複雜？	How can it be so complicated?
❼	有誰能說明一下嗎？	Can anyone take a moment to explain? * Can anyone...?（有人可以…嗎） * take a moment（花點時間）
❽	我怎麼想都想不透。	I can't think it through. ＝ I can't figure it out. * think through（想透）＝ figure out
❾	你再說一百次我還是不懂！	You can explain it a hundred times and I still won't understand! * a hundred times（一百次）
❿	真是難懂！	It's really difficult to understand! * be difficult to＋動詞（難以…）
⓫	我想這輩子我都不會明白的！	I don't think I will ever understand that! * I don't think＋子句（我不認為…） * will ever＋動詞（未來會有…的時候）
⓬	我怎麼聽不懂？	Why can't I understand?
⓭	我想我們有代溝。	I think there's a generation gap between us. * generation gap（代溝）
⓮	別打啞謎了！	Don't confuse me like that! * confuse me（把我弄糊塗、讓我搞不清楚）
⓯	你腦袋裡到底裝什麼？	What on earth is in your head? * on earth（究竟、到底）

	單字	音標	詞性	意義	字頻	大考	英檢	多益
❶	really	[ˋrɪəlɪ]	adv.	真的	1		初級	
	understand	[ˏʌndɚˋstænd]	v.	瞭解	1	1	初級	
❷	saying	[ˋseɪŋ]	p.pr.	say（說）現在分詞	3	1	中級	
❸	have	[hæv]	v.	擁有	1	1	初級	
	clue	[klu]	n.	頭緒	2	3	中級	◎
❹	guess	[gɛs]	v.	猜測	1	1	初級	◎
	need	[nid]	v.	需要	1	1	初級	◎
	translation	[trænsˋleʃən]	n.	翻譯	2	4	中級	◎
❺	define	[dɪˋfaɪn]	v.	解釋	1	3	中級	◎
	that	[ðæt]	pron.	那個	1	1	初級	
	more	[mor]	adv.	更加	1	1	初級	
	clearly	[ˋklɪrlɪ]	adv.	清楚地	1			◎
❻	so	[so]	adv.	這麼	1	1	初級	
	complicated	[ˋkɑmpləˏketɪd]	adj.	複雜的	1		中級	◎
❼	anyone	[ˋɛnɪˏwʌn]	pron.	任何人	1	2	初級	
	take	[tek]	v.	花時間	1	1	初級	◎
	moment	[ˋmomənt]	n.	片刻	1	1	初級	◎
	explain	[ɪkˋsplen]	v.	解釋	1	2	初級	◎
❽	think	[θɪŋk]	v.	思考	1	1	初級	
	through	[θru]	adv.	穿過	1	2	初級	◎
	figure	[ˋfɪgjɚ]	v.	想出	1	2	初級	◎
	out	[aʊt]	adv.	出現	1	1	初級	
❾	hundred	[ˋhʌndrəd]	n.	一百	1	1	初級	
	time	[taɪm]	n.	次、回	1	1	初級	◎
	still	[stɪl]	adv.	仍然	1	1	初級	◎
❿	difficult	[ˋdɪfəˏkəlt]	adj.	困難的	1	1	初級	
⓫	ever	[ˋɛvɚ]	adv.	永遠	1	1	初級	
⓭	there	[ðɛr]	adv.	有…	1	1	初級	
	generation	[ˏdʒɛnəˋreʃən]	n.	世代	1	4	初級	◎
	gap	[gæp]	n.	差距、隔閡	1	3	中級	◎
⓮	confuse	[kənˋfjuz]	v.	使混淆	2	3	初級	◎
⓯	earth	[ɝθ]	n.	（與 on 連用）究竟	1	1	初級	
	head	[hɛd]	n.	腦袋	1	1	初級	◎

※「紅字單字」於本單元多句出現，「單字級等分析」僅列在「首次出現句」。

🔘 MP3 078-02 ❶～⓰

❶	我該怎麼說明你才懂？	How can I explain this so that you'll understand? * **How can I...?**（我可以如何…呢）、**so that**（以便）
❷	你聽得懂嗎？	Do you understand?
❸	需要我畫圖說明嗎？	Do I need to draw a picture to describe it? * **draw a picture**（畫圖） * **describe**（描述、說明）可替換為： 　**illustrate**（用圖例說明）
❹	我再加些補充好嗎？	Is it OK if I make some additional remarks? * **Is it OK if**＋子句?（是否可以…呢） * **make additional remarks**（補充說明）
❺	我講得夠不夠清楚？	Did I explain it clearly enough?
❻	可以告訴我你的問題點嗎？	Could you tell me the main point of your question? * **Could you...?**（可以請你…嗎）、**main point**（關鍵）
❼	要不要我再說一次？	Do I need to repeat that again?
❽	這對你來說太困難嗎？	Is this difficult for you? * **be difficult for**＋某人（對於某人很困難）
❾	需要我把它簡化嗎？	Do you need me to simplify it?
❿	我希望你能瞭解。	I hope you can understand.
⓫	你需要翻譯嗎？	Do you need it translated?
⓬	你怎麼那麼遲鈍啊？	How can you be so thick-headed? * **thick-headed**（遲鈍的、慢半拍的）＝**slow-witted**
⓭	我換個方式講好了。	Let me rephrase myself. * **rephrase myself**（換個方式表達我要說的）
⓮	不懂要問。	If you don't know, then ask.
⓯	我再說最後一次！	This is the last time I'll tell you! * **This is the last time**＋子句（這是最後一次…了！）
⓰	我以為你都懂了！	I thought you understood everything! * **I thought**＋子句（我當時認為…） * **understand everything**（全部都理解）

	單字	音標	詞性	意義	字頻	大考	英檢	多益
❶	explain	[ɪkˋsplen]	v.	說明	1	2	初級	◎
	this	[ðɪs]	pron.	這個	1	1	初級	
	understand	[ˌʌndɚˋstænd]	v.	瞭解	1	1	初級	
❸	need	[nid]	v.	需要	1	1	初級	◎
	draw	[drɔ]	v.	畫圖	1	1	初級	◎
	picture	[ˋpɪktʃɚ]	n.	圖片	1	1	初級	◎
	describe	[dɪˋskraɪb]	v.	描述、說明	1	2	初級	◎
❹	ok	[ˋoˋke]	adj.	沒問題的	1		初級	
	make	[mek]	v.	做出	1	1	初級	
	some	[sʌm]	adj.	一些	1	1	初級	
	additional	[əˋdɪʃən!]	adj.	補充的	1	3	中級	◎
	remark	[rɪˋmɑrk]	n.	言論	2	4	中級	◎
❺	clearly	[ˋklɪrlɪ]	adv.	清楚地	1			◎
	enough	[əˋnʌf]	adv.	足夠地	1	1	初級	
❻	tell	[tɛl]	v.	告訴	1	1	初級	
	main	[men]	adj.	主要的	1	2	初級	◎
	point	[pɔɪnt]	n.	要點	1	1	初級	◎
	question	[ˋkwɛstʃən]	n.	問題	1	1	初級	
❼	repeat	[rɪˋpit]	v.	複述	1	2	初級	◎
	that	[ðæt]	pron.	那個	1	1	初級	
	again	[əˋgɛn]	adv.	再次	1	1	初級	
❽	difficult	[ˋdɪfəˌkəlt]	adj.	困難的	1	1	初級	◎
❾	simplify	[ˋsɪmpləˌfaɪ]	v.	簡化	4	6	中級	◎
❿	hope	[hop]	v.	希望	1	1	初級	
⓫	translated	[trænsˋletɪd]	p.p.	translate（翻譯）過去分詞	1	4	中級	◎
⓬	so	[so]	adv.	這麼	1	1	初級	
	thick-headed	[ˋθɪkˋhɛdɪd]	adj.	遲鈍的、慢半拍的				
⓭	let	[lɛt]	v.	讓…	1	1	初級	
	rephrase	[riˋfrez]	v.	換個方式表達				
	myself	[maɪˋsɛlf]	pron.	我自己	1		初級	
⓮	know	[no]	v.	知道	1	1	初級	◎
	then	[ðɛn]	adv.	那麼	1	1	初級	
	ask	[æsk]	v.	詢問	1	1	初級	
⓯	last	[læst]	adj.	上一次	1	1	初級	
	time	[taɪm]	n.	次、回	1	1	初級	
⓰	thought	[θɔt]	p.t.	think（認為）過去式	1	1	初級	◎
	understood	[ˌʌndɚˋstud]	p.t.	understand（瞭解）過去式	1	1	初級	
	everything	[ˋɛvrɪˌθɪŋ]	pron.	每件事情	1		初級	

※「紅字單字」於本單元多句出現，「單字級等分析」僅列在「首次出現句」。

❶	你人真好！	You are a wonderful person!
❷	謝謝！	Thanks!
❸	你是我的英雄！	You are my hero! * **heroine**（女英雄）
❹	辛苦你了！	Thanks for all your hard work! * **Thanks for＋名詞**（謝謝…） * **hard work**（辛苦工作）
❺	我太感動了。	I'm so touched. ＝ I'm so moved.
❻	你的心腸真好。	You have a kind heart.
❼	謝謝你的幫忙！	Thank you for your help!
❽	請接受我的致謝。	Please accept my thanks.
❾	我一定會報答你。	I will definitely pay you back. * 此句用「未來簡單式」（...will...） 　表示「有意願做的事」。 * **pay you back**（報答你）＝ **repay you**
❿	多謝你的費心！	Thank you for your attention!
⓫	你真體貼。	You are so thoughtful.
⓬	我非常喜歡你送的禮物。	I like the gift you gave me very much. * **the gift you gave me**（你送給我的禮物）
⓭	真不知該如何報答你。	I really don't know how I can repay you. * **I really don't know....**（我真的不知道…）
⓮	你的恩情我不會忘記。	I won't forget your kindness.
⓯	我真想給你一個擁抱。	I really want to give you a hug. * **give you a hug**（擁抱你）
⓰	讓我請你吃頓飯好嗎？	Let me treat you to a meal, okay? * **treat you to a meal**（招待你吃飯）
⓱	你真是我的救命恩人。	You really are a lifesaver.
⓲	你不知道你所做的對我意義 重大。	You have no idea how much this means to me. * **have no idea**（不明白） * **how much**（程度有多大）

	單字	音標	詞性	意義	字頻	大考	英檢	多益
❶	wonderful	[ˋwʌndəfəl]	adj.	極好的	1	2	初級	◎
	person	[ˋpɜsn]	n.	人	1	1	初級	
❷	thanks	[θæŋks]	n.	thank（感謝）複數	1			
❸	hero	[ˋhɪro]	n.	英雄	1	2	初級	
❹	all	[ɔl]	adj.	所有的	1	1	初級	
	hard	[hɑrd]	adj.	辛苦的	1	1	初級	◎
	work	[wɜk]	n.	工作	1	1	初級	◎
❺	so	[so]	adv.	太/真的	1	1	初級	
	touched	[tʌtʃt]	p.p.	touch（感動）過去分詞	1	1	初級	◎
	moved	[muvd]	p.p.	move（感動）過去分詞	1	1	初級	◎
❻	have	[hæv]	v.	擁有	1	1	初級	
	kind	[kaɪnd]	adj.	和藹的	1	1	初級	◎
	heart	[hɑrt]	n.	心	1	1	初級	
❼	thank	[θæŋk]	v.	感謝	1	1	初級	
	help	[hɛlp]	n.	幫忙	1	1	初級	
❽	please	[pliz]	adv.	請	1	1	初級	
	accept	[əkˋsɛpt]	v.	接受	1	2	初級	◎
❾	definitely	[ˋdɛfənɪtlɪ]	adv.	一定	1		中高	◎
	pay	[pe]	v.	報答	1	3	初級	◎
	back	[bæk]	adv.	返回	1	1	初級	◎
❿	attention	[əˋtɛnʃən]	n.	照顧	1	2	初級	◎
⓫	thoughtful	[ˋθɔtfəl]	adj.	體貼的	3	4	中級	◎
⓬	like	[laɪk]	v.	喜歡	1	1	初級	
	gift	[gɪft]	n.	禮物	1	1	初級	
	gave	[gev]	p.t.	give（給）過去式	1	1	初級	
	very	[ˋvɛrɪ]	adv.	十分	1	1	初級	
	much	[mʌtʃ]	adv. /adj.	非常/許多的	1	1	初級	
⓭	really	[ˋrɪəlɪ]	adv.	真的	1		初級	
	know	[no]	v.	知道	1	1	初級	◎
	repay	[rɪˋpe]	v.	報答	3	5	中級	◎
⓮	forget	[fəˋgɛt]	v.	忘記	1	1	初級	
	kindness	[ˋkaɪndnɪs]	n.	善意	3		中級	
⓯	want	[wɑnt]	v.	想要	1	1	初級	◎
	give	[gɪv]	v.	給予	1	1	初級	◎
	hug	[hʌg]	n.	擁抱	2	3	中級	◎
⓰	let	[lɛt]	v.	讓…	1	1	初級	
	treat	[trit]	v.	招待	1	2	初級	◎
	meal	[mil]	n.	一餐	1	2	初級	
	okay	[ˋoˋke]	int.	好嗎	1	1		
⓱	lifesaver	[ˋlaɪf.sevə]	n.	救急的人				
⓲	idea	[aɪˋdiə]	n.	了解、明白	1	1	初級	◎
	this	[ðɪs]	pron.	這個	1	1	初級	
	mean	[min]	v.	代表	1	2	初級	◎

※「紅字單字」於本單元多句出現，「單字級等分析」僅列在「首次出現句」。

🔊 MP3 079-02 ❶～⓱

❶	不客氣。	You're welcome. = Don't mention it. = My pleasure.
❷	您過獎了！	I'm flattered! = You flatter me! * be flattered（受到恭維）
❸	那沒什麼啦！	It's nothing!
❹	舉手之勞而已。	I barely lifted a finger. * barely lift a finger（只是舉手之勞）
❺	別放在心上。	Don't worry about it. = Think nothing of it.
❻	我只是盡我所能。	I just did my best.
❼	區區小事，何足掛齒。	Piece of cake, don't mention it. * piece of cake（小事一樁、小意思）
❽	您太客氣了。	You're too kind.
❾	這是我應該做的。	This is the least I can do. * the least I can do（我唯一能做的）
❿	我沒你說的那麼好。	I am not as great as you make me out to be. * as great as...（如同…一樣好） * make＋某人＋out（把某人描述成某個樣子）
⓫	我很高興能幫到你的忙。	I am glad to help you. * be glad to＋動詞原形（樂於做…）
⓬	這一點都不辛苦。	It is not very hard at all.
⓭	你滿意我就開心了。	As long as you are satisfied, I am happy. * as long as＋子句（只要…）
⓮	我才應該謝謝你呢！	It is I who should be thanking you!
⓯	我不求什麼回報。	I don't need any reward.
⓰	你請我看場電影就算扯平！	We can call it even if you treat me to a movie! * call it even（打平、扯平） * treat me to a movie（招待我看電影）
⓱	別這麼說，我會不好意思！	Oh, stop it, you are embarrassing me! * embarrass＋某人（讓某人不好意思）

單字級等分析

	單字	音標	詞性	意義	字頻	大考	英檢	多益
❶	welcome	[ˈwɛlkəm]	adj.	不客氣	1	1	初級	
	mention	[ˈmɛnʃən]	v.	提及	1	3	中級	◎
	pleasure	[ˈplɛʒɚ]	n.	榮幸	1	2	初級	◎
❷	flattered	[ˈflætɚd]	p.p.	flatter（恭維）過去分詞	4	4	中級	
	flatter	[ˈflætɚ]	v.	恭維	4	4	中級	
❸	nothing	[ˈnʌθɪŋ]	pron.	微不足道的事	1	1	初級	
❹	barely	[ˈbɛrlɪ]	adv.	只、僅	1	3	中級	◎
	lifted	[ˈlɪftɪd]	p.t.	lift（舉起）過去式	1	1	初級	◎
	finger	[ˈfɪŋgɚ]	n.	手指	1	1	初級	
❺	worry	[ˈwɝɪ]	v.	擔心	1	1	初級	◎
	think	[θɪŋk]	v.	想	1	1	初級	
❻	just	[dʒʌst]	adv.	只是	1	1	初級	
	did	[dɪd]	p.t.	do（做）過去式	1	1	初級	
	best	[bɛst]	n.	最好	1	1	初級	
❼	piece	[pis]	n.	一塊	1	1	初級	
	cake	[kek]	n.	蛋糕	1	1	初級	
❽	too	[tu]	adv.	過於	1	1	初級	
	kind	[kaɪnd]	adj.	客氣的	1	1	初級	◎
❾	this	[ðɪs]	pron.	這個	1	1	初級	
	least	[list]	n.	最少	1	1	初級	◎
	do	[du]	v.	做	1	1	初級	
❿	great	[gret]	adj.	極好的	1	1	初級	◎
	make	[mek]	v.	描述	1	1	初級	
	out	[aʊt]	adv.	出現	1	1	初級	
⓫	glad	[glæd]	adj.	高興的	1	1	初級	
	help	[hɛlp]	v.	幫忙	1	1	初級	
⓬	very	[ˈvɛrɪ]	adv.	十分	1	1	初級	
	hard	[hɑrd]	adj.	辛苦的	1	1	初級	◎
	all	[ɔl]	n.	完全	1	1	初級	
⓭	long	[lɔŋ]	adv.	只要	1	1	初級	
	satisfied	[ˈsætɪsˌfaɪd]	adj.	滿意的	2	2	中高	◎
	happy	[ˈhæpɪ]	adj.	高興的	1	1	初級	
⓮	thanking	[ˈθæŋkɪŋ]	p.pr.	thank（感謝）現在分詞	1	1	初級	
⓯	need	[nid]	v.	需要	1	1	初級	◎
	any	[ˈɛnɪ]	adj.	任何的	1	1	初級	
	reward	[rɪˈwɔrd]	n.	回報	2	4	中級	◎
⓰	call	[kɔl]	v.	把…視作	1	1	初級	
	even	[ˈivən]	adj.	對等的、相等的	1	1	初級	◎
	treat	[trit]	v.	招待	1	2	初級	◎
	movie	[ˈmuvɪ]	n.	電影	1	1	初級	
⓱	oh	[o]	int.	（表驚訝）哦	1		中級	
	stop	[stɑp]	v.	停止	1	1	初級	◎
	embarrassing	[ɪmˈbærəsɪŋ]	p.pr.	embarrass（使不好意思）現在分詞	3	4	中級	◎

※「紅字單字」於本單元多句出現，「單字級等分析」僅列在「首次出現句」。

365

🔵 MP3 080-01 ❶〜❶❺

❶	誠摯的邀請你。	You are sincerely invited. * 某人＋be sincerely invited（誠摯邀請某人）
❷	歡迎攜伴參加。	Companions are welcome.
❸	請務必出席。	Please be sure to attend. * be sure to＋動詞原形（務必）
❹	請準時入座。	Please take your seat on time. * take one's seat（入座） * on time（準時地）
❺	希望你能前來。	Hope you can participate. * participate（參與）可替換為：attend（出席）
❻	你不會想錯過的！	You wouldn't want to miss this!
❼	我們不能沒有你。	We would be lost without you. ＝ We couldn't manage without you.
❽	你會接受邀約嗎？	Do you accept this invitation? * accept one's invitation（接受邀約）
❾	我們可以配合您的時間。	We can accommodate your schedule. * accommodate（因應）可替換為： adjust to fit（配合）
❿	我們都期待見到你！	We are looking forward to meeting you in person! * be looking forward to＋動詞-ing（期待…） * meet＋某人＋in person（見到…本人）
⓫	你怎麼能不來呢？	How can you not come?
⓬	你不來我會很失望的。	I will be very disappointed if you do not come. * 某人＋be disappointed（某人感到失望）
⓭	你怎麼可以推辭呢？	How could you decline this invitation? * decline one's invitation（婉拒邀約）
⓮	我會發邀請函給你。	I will send the invitation to you. * send the invitation to＋某人（寄邀請函給某人）
⓯	有你在場是我們的榮幸。	It is our honor to have you here. * It is our honor to＋動詞原形（…是我們的榮幸） * have＋某人＋here（有某人在場）

	單字	音標	詞性	意義	字頻	大考	英檢	多益
❶	sincerely	[sɪnˋsɪrlɪ]	adv.	誠懇地	4		中級	◎
	invited	[ɪnˋvaɪtɪd]	p.p.	invite（邀請）過去分詞	8	2	初級	◎
❷	companion	[kəmˋpænjən]	n.	同伴	2	4	中級	◎
	welcome	[ˋwɛlkəm]	adj.	歡迎的	1	1	初級	
❸	please	[pliz]	adv.	請	1	1	初級	
	sure	[ʃʊr]	adj.	務必的	1	1	初級	
	attend	[əˋtɛnd]	v.	出席、參與	1	2	初級	◎
❹	take	[tek]	v.	就座	1	1	初級	◎
	seat	[sit]	n.	座位	1	1	初級	◎
	time	[taɪm]	n.	時間	1	1	初級	◎
❺	hope	[hop]	v.	希望	1	1	初級	
	participate	[parˋtɪsə.pet]	v.	參與	1	3	中級	◎
❻	want	[wɑnt]	v.	想要	1	1	初級	◎
	miss	[mɪs]	v.	錯過	1	1	初級	
	this	[ðɪs]	pron. /adj.	這個	1	1	初級	
❼	lost	[lɔst]	adj.	不知所措的	1	2	中高	◎
	manage	[ˋmænɪdʒ]	v.	安排	1	3	中級	◎
❽	accept	[əkˋsɛpt]	v.	接受	1	2	初級	◎
	invitation	[.ɪnvəˋteʃən]	n.	邀請/邀請函	2	2	初級	◎
❾	accommodate	[əˋkɑmə.det]	v.	因應	2	6	中級	◎
	schedule	[ˋskɛdʒʊl]	n.	時程	1	3	中級	◎
❿	looking	[ˋlʊkɪŋ]	p.pr.	look（期待）現在分詞	5	1	初級	
	meeting	[ˋmitɪŋ]	n.	meet（見到）動名詞	1	2	初級	
	person	[ˋpɝsn]	n.	本人	1	1	初級	
⓫	come	[kʌm]	v.	前來	1	1	初級	
⓬	very	[ˋvɛrɪ]	adv.	十分	1	1	初級	
	disappointed	[.dɪsəˋpɔɪntɪd]	adj.	失望的	2	3	中級	◎
⓭	decline	[dɪˋklaɪn]	v.	婉拒	1	6	中級	◎
⓮	send	[sɛnd]	v.	發送	1	1	初級	
⓯	honor	[ˋɑnə]	n.	榮幸	1	3	中級	◎
	have	[hæv]	v.	讓某人	1	1	初級	
	here	[hɪr]	adv.	這裡	1	1	初級	

※「紅字單字」於本單元多句出現，「單字級等分析」僅列在「首次出現句」。

MP3 080-02 ❶～❿

❶	謝謝，但我不要。	Thanks, but no thanks.
❷	我一定到。	I will definitely be there. = I will be there, of course.
❸	很抱歉，不克前往。	I am sorry that I will be unable to attend. * be sorry that＋子句（抱歉…） * be unable to＋動詞原形（無法）
❹	我受寵若驚！	I am flattered! * flattered（很高興）可替換為： overwhelmed（受寵若驚的）
❺	太突然了，我無法立刻決定。	It's too sudden; I can't make a decision right away. = It's too sudden, I can't make up my mind right now. * make a decision（決定）= make up one's mind
❻	謝謝你的好意。	Thank you for your kindness.
❼	你的盛情難卻。	It would be ungracious not to accept your invitation.
❽	如果可以我一定會去。	I will be there if I can.
❾	我另外有約。	I have another appointment. * appointment（約會）= engagement
❿	我會把當天的時間空下來。	I will set aside some time on that day. * set aside some time（挪出一些時間）
⓫	我想我是沒有藉口推辭了。	I think I have no reason to refuse. * have no reason to＋動詞原形（沒有理由做某事） * refuse（拒絕）可替換為：decline（婉拒）
⓬	你真好！謝謝邀請。	You are really nice! Thank you for your invitation.
⓭	我可以過幾天回覆嗎？	May I reply in a couple of days? = Can I answer in a couple of days?
⓮	我要考慮一下。	I need to think about it. * think about（考慮）
⓯	我很期待那天的到來。	I'm looking forward to that day. * look forward to＋名詞（期待…）

	單字	音標	詞性	意義	字頻	大考	英檢	多益
❶	thanks	[θæŋks]	n.	thank（感謝）複數	1			
❷	definitely	[ˋdɛfənɪtlɪ]	adv.	一定	1		中高	◎
	there	[ðɛr]	adv.	那裡	1	1	初級	
	course	[kors]	adv.	（與 of 連用）當然	1	1	初級	◎
❸	sorry	[ˋsɑrɪ]	adj.	抱歉的	1	1	初級	
	unable	[ʌnˋebl]	adj.	無法的	1		中級	◎
	attend	[əˋtɛnd]	v.	出席、參與	1	2	初級	◎
❹	flattered	[ˋflætəd]	p.p.	flatter（恭維）過去分詞	4	4	中級	
❺	too	[tu]	adv.	過於	1	1	初級	
	sudden	[ˋsʌdn]	adj.	突然的	2	2	初級	◎
	make	[mek]	v.	做出	1	1	初級	
	decision	[dɪˋsɪʒən]	n.	決定	1	2	初級	◎
	right	[raɪt]	adv.	立即	1	1	初級	
	away	[əˋwe]	adv.	直接	1	1	初級	
	up	[ʌp]	adv.	定下	1	1	初級	
	mind	[maɪnd]	n.	主意	1	1	初級	◎
	now	[naʊ]	adv.	現在	1	1	初級	
❻	thank	[θæŋk]	v.	感謝	1	1	初級	
	kindness	[ˋkaɪndnɪs]	n.	好意	3		中級	
❼	ungracious	[ʌnˋgreʃəs]	adj.	不禮貌的				
	accept	[əkˋsɛpt]	v.	接受	1	2	初級	◎
	invitation	[ˏɪnvəˋteʃən]	n.	邀請	2	2	初級	◎
❾	have	[hæv]	v.	擁有	1	1	初級	
	another	[əˋnʌðə]	adj.	另一個	1	1		
	appointment	[əˋpɔɪntmənt]	n.	約會	2	4	中級	◎
❿	set	[sɛt]	v.	挪出	1	1	初級	◎
	some	[sʌm]	adj.	一些	1	1	初級	
	time	[taɪm]	n.	時間	1	1	初級	◎
	that	[ðæt]	adj.	那個	1	1	初級	
	day	[de]	n.	天	1	1	初級	
⓫	reason	[ˋrizn]	n.	理由	1	1	初級	◎
	refuse	[rɪˋfjuz]	v.	拒絕	1	2	初級	◎
⓬	think	[θɪŋk]	v.	認為	1	1	初級	
	really	[ˋrɪəlɪ]	adv.	十分	1	1	初級	
	nice	[naɪs]	adj.	美好的	1	1	初級	
⓭	reply	[rɪˋplaɪ]	v.	回覆	1	2	初級	◎
	couple	[ˋkʌpl]	n.	幾個	1	2	初級	◎
	answer	[ˋænsə]	v.	回覆	1	1	初級	
⓮	need	[nid]	v.	需要	1	1	初級	◎
⓯	looking	[ˋlʊkɪŋ]	p.pr.	look（期待）現在分詞	5	1	初級	

※「紅字單字」於本單元多句出現，「單字級等分析」僅列在「首次出現句」。

🔘 MP3 081-01 ❶～❿

❶	對不起。	Excuse me. = Sorry.
❷	請你原諒。	I beg your pardon. = I beg your forgiveness. * beg one's pardon（請求原諒） 　= beg one's forgiveness
❸	請原諒我。	Please forgive me.
❹	請恕我冒昧。	Please excuse my inappropriate behavior. * inappropriate behavior（不當行為）
❺	請接受我的道歉。	Please accept my apology. * accept one's apology（接受道歉）
❻	我很抱歉。	I am very sorry.
❼	我真不是人！	I am such a jerk!
❽	希望你能諒解。	I hope you can understand.
❾	請原諒我的一時糊塗。	Please forgive me for my stupidity. * forgive me for my＋過失（原諒我的某過失）
❿	請原諒我的無知。	Please forgive me for my ignorance.
⓫	你一定要寬恕我！	You must forgive me!
⓬	請不要掛在心上。	Don't take it to heart. * Don't＋動詞原形（你別做…） * take...to heart（介意…）
⓭	我誠心的向你致歉。	I offer my sincere apologies to you. * I offer my apology to＋某人（我向某人道歉） * sincere apology（誠心的道歉）
⓮	你不知道我有多自責。	You don't know how much I blame myself. * how much（程度有多大） * blame oneself（責怪自己）
⓯	可以再給我一次機會嗎？	Could you give me one more chance? * give me one more chance（再給我一次機會）
⓰	你不原諒我，我就不離開。	I will not leave until you forgive me. * will not（不願意…）、until＋子句（直到…）
⓱	我可以為你做什麼來補償嗎？	What can I do to make up for it? * make up for（彌補）

	單字	音標	詞性	意義	字頻	大考	英檢	多益
❶	excuse	[ɪkˋskjuz]	v.	原諒	2	2	初級	◎
	sorry	[ˋsɑrɪ]	adj.	抱歉的	1	1	初級	
❷	beg	[bɛg]	v.	乞求	2	1	中級	◎
	pardon	[ˋpɑrdn]	n.	原諒	3	2	初級	
	forgiveness	[fɚˋgɪvnɪs]	n.	原諒	3			
❸	please	[pliz]	adv.	請	1	1	初級	
	forgive	[fɚˋgɪv]	v.	原諒	2	2	初級	
❹	inappropriate	[͵ɪnəˋproprɪɪt]	adj.	不適當的	2		中高	
	behavior	[bɪˋhevjɚ]	n.	行為	1	4	中級	◎
❺	accept	[əkˋsɛpt]	v.	接受	1	2	初級	◎
	apology	[əˋpɑlədʒɪ]	n.	道歉	2	4	中級	◎
❼	such	[sʌtʃ]	adv.	真的	1	1	初級	
	jerk	[dʒɝk]	n.	混蛋、蠢蛋	3		中高	◎
❽	hope	[hop]	v.	希望	1	1	初級	
	understand	[͵ʌndɚˋsænd]	v.	瞭解	1	1	初級	
❾	stupidity	[stjuˋpɪdətɪ]	v.	糊塗	5			
❿	ignorance	[ˋɪgnərəns]	n.	無知	3	2	中級	◎
⓬	take	[tek]	v.	介意	1	1	初級	◎
	heart	[hɑrt]	n.	內心	1	1	初級	
⓭	offer	[ˋɔfɚ]	v.	提供	1	2	初級	◎
	sincere	[sɪnˋsɪr]	adj.	誠心的	3	3	初級	◎
⓮	know	[no]	v.	知道	1	1	初級	
	much	[mʌtʃ]	adv.	介意	1	1	初級	
	blame	[blem]	v.	責怪	1	3	初級	◎
	myself	[maɪˋsɛlf]	pron.	我自己	1		初級	
⓯	give	[gɪv]	v.	給予	1	1	初級	
	one	[wʌn]	n.	一	1	1	初級	
	more	[mor]	adj.	另外的、附加的	1	1	初級	
	chance	[tʃæns]	n.	機會	1	1	初級	
⓰	leave	[liv]	v.	離開	1	1	初級	◎
⓱	do	[du]	v.	做	1	1	初級	
	make	[mek]	v.	彌補	1	1	初級	
	up	[ʌp]	adv.	起來	1	1	初級	

※「紅字單字」於本單元多句出現，「單字級等分析」僅列在「首次出現句」。

081 接受／拒絕道歉。

MP3 081-02 ❶ ～ ⓰

❶	沒關係。	It doesn't matter. = It's ok. = It's nothing.
❷	忘了吧！	Forget it! = Let it go!
❸	別在意了。	Don't mention it. = Never mind.
❹	知道錯就好了。	That's fine as long as you realize your mistake. * **as long as**（只要） * **realize mistake**（明白錯誤）
❺	我想你不是故意的。	I am sure you didn't mean it. * **be sure**＋子句（確定⋯）、**mean it**（故意） * 子句用「過去簡單式」（...didn't mean...） 　表示「發生在過去的事」。
❻	我原諒你了。	I forgive you.
❼	我相信你只是一時糊塗。	I am sure you were just confused at the time. * **at the time**（在當時）
❽	我想你一定有你的難處。	I am sure you must have your own difficulties. * **must**＋動詞原形（猜測一定是⋯） * **have difficulties**（有困難、遭遇困難）
❾	以後我們還是好朋友。	We can still continue to be good friends. * **continue to**＋動詞原形（繼續）
❿	真是不可原諒！	This is really unforgivable!
⓫	你怎麼可以那樣做呢？	How could you do that?
⓬	你這麼做對得起我嗎？	How can you face me after what you have done? * **How can you...?**（你如何能夠⋯？） * **what you have done**（你所做過的事）
⓭	我不會輕易放過你的！	I won't let you off easily! * **let you off**（放過你）= **allow you to get off**
⓮	你真是太可惡了！	You really are despicable!
⓯	你要為此付出代價！	You'll pay for this! * **pay for**＋某事（為某事付出代價）
⓰	我這輩子都不會原諒你！	I will never forgive you for the rest of my life! * **for the rest of my life**（在我的餘生）

372

	單字	音標	詞性	意義	字頻	大考	英檢	多益
❶	matter	[ˈmætə]	v.	要緊、有關係	1	1	初級	◎
	ok	[ˈoˈke]	adj.	沒關係的	1	1	初級	
	nothing	[ˈnʌθɪŋ]	pron.	微不足道的事	1	1	初級	
❷	forget	[fəˈgɛt]	v.	忘記	1	1	初級	
	let	[lɛt]	v.	讓…	1	1	初級	
	go	[go]	v.	流逝、成為過往	1	1	初級	
❸	mention	[ˈmɛnʃən]	v.	提及	1	3	中級	◎
	never	[ˈnɛvə]	adv.	從不	1	1	初級	
	mind	[maɪnd]	v.	介意	1	1	初級	◎
❹	that	[ðæt]	pron.	那個	1	1	初級	
	fine	[faɪn]	adj.	足夠的	1	1	初級	◎
	long	[lɔŋ]	adv.	只要	1	1	初級	
	realize	[ˈrɪəˌlaɪz]	v.	瞭解	1	2	初級	◎
	mistake	[mɪˈstek]	n.	錯誤	1	1	初級	◎
❺	sure	[ʃur]	adj.	確信的	1	1	初級	
	mean	[min]	v.	有意做某事	1	2	初級	◎
❻	forgive	[fəˈgɪv]	v.	原諒	2	2	初級	
❼	just	[dʒʌst]	adv.	只是	1	1	初級	
	confused	[kənˈfjuzd]	adj.	糊塗的	3	3	初級	◎
	time	[taɪm]	n.	時刻	1	1	初級	◎
❽	have	[hæv]	v.	擁有	1	1	初級	
	difficulty	[ˈdɪfəˌkʌltɪ]	n.	困難	1	2	初級	◎
❾	still	[stɪl]	adv.	仍難	1	1	初級	◎
	continue	[kənˈtɪnju]	v.	繼續	1	1	初級	◎
	good	[gud]	adj.	良好的	1	1	初級	◎
	friend	[frɛnd]	n.	朋友	1	1	初級	
❿	this	[ðɪs]	pron.	這個	1	1	初級	
	really	[ˈrɪəlɪ]	adv.	真是	1		初級	
	unforgivable	[ˌʌnfəˈgɪvəbl]	adj.	無法原諒的	8			
⓫	do	[du]	v.	做	1	1	初級	
⓬	face	[fes]	v.	面對	1	1	初級	
	done	[dʌn]	p.p.	done（做）過去分詞	1	1	初級	
⓭	off	[ɔf]	adj.	寬恕的、免受的	1	1	初級	
	easily	[ˈizɪlɪ]	adv.	容易地	1		中級	
⓮	despicable	[ˈdɛspɪkəbl]	adj.	可惡的	6			
⓯	pay	[pe]	v.	付出	1	3	初級	◎
⓰	rest	[rɛst]	n.	剩餘的部分	1	1	初級	
	life	[laɪf]	n.	人生	1	1	初級	

※「紅字單字」於本單元多句出現，「單字級等分析」僅列在「首次出現句」。

🔵 MP3 082-01 ❶～⓰

❶	我錯了。	I was wrong.
❷	我真的很抱歉。	I am very sorry. ＝ I am terribly sorry.
❸	我犯了個錯誤。	I made a mistake.
❹	我真是不可原諒。	What I have done is unforgivable.
❺	我真是個大笨蛋。	I really am a big fool. * big fool（大笨蛋）＝ big moron
❻	我真是錯得離譜。	I have made a colossal mistake. * colossal mistake（離譜的錯誤）
❼	要我承認錯誤真不是一件容易的事！	It is really not an easy thing for me to admit that I've made a mistake. * It is not an easy thing to＋動詞（做某事並不容易） * admit that＋子句（承認…）
❽	看吧，我又錯了。	See? I am wrong again.
❾	可以讓我彌補我的過錯嗎？	Will you let me make up for the mistake I've made? * make up for the mistake（彌補錯誤）
❿	事情變得一發不可收拾了。	Things have gotten out of control. * get out of control（失控）
⓫	我一定是昏了頭！	I must have been confused! * must have been＋形容詞 　　（猜測當時一定處於…狀態）
⓬	我真是自私！	I am so selfish!
⓭	我太不用大腦了！	I am so stupid! ＝ I didn't think before I acted! * think before＋某人＋act（某人三思而後行）
⓮	我犯下了滔天大錯。	I made an extremely serious mistake.
⓯	我不敢相信自己這麼糟糕！	I can't believe that I could be so horrible! * can't believe that＋子句（無法相信…）
⓰	我想你一定不想再理我了！	I guess you won't talk to me anymore! * guess＋子句（猜想…） * talk to me（理我、和我講話）

	單字	音標	詞性	意義	字頻	大考	英檢	多益
❶	wrong	[rɔŋ]	adj.	錯誤的	1	1	初級	◎
❷	very	[ˋvɛrɪ]	adv.	十分	1	1	初級	
	sorry	[ˋsɑrɪ]	adj.	抱歉的	1	1	初級	
	terribly	[ˋtɛrəblɪ]	adv.	非常	2			
❸	made	[med]	p.t.	make（犯下）過去式	1	1	初級	
	mistake	[mɪˋstek]	n.	錯誤	1	1	初級	◎
❹	done	[dʌn]	p.p.	do（做）過去分詞	1	1	初級	
	unforgivable	[ˏʌnfɚˋgɪvəbl]	adj.	無法原諒的	8			
❺	really	[ˋrɪəlɪ]	adv.	真的	1		初級	
	big	[bɪg]	adj.	大的	1	1	初級	
	fool	[ful]	n.	笨蛋	2	2	初級	
❻	made	[med]	p.p.	make（犯下）過去分詞	1	1	初級	
	colossal	[kəˋlɑsl]	adj.	離譜的	5			
❼	easy	[ˋizɪ]	adj.	容易的	1	1	初級	◎
	thing	[θɪŋ]	n.	事情	1	1	初級	
	admit	[ədˋmɪt]	v.	承認	1	3	初級	◎
❽	see	[si]	v.	看見	1	1	初級	
	again	[əˋgɛn]	adv.	再次	1	1	初級	
❾	let	[lɛt]	v.	讓…	1	1	初級	
	make	[mek]	v.	彌補	1	1	初級	
	up	[ʌp]	adv.	起來	1	1	初級	
❿	gotten	[ˋgɑtn]	p.p.	get（變成）過去分詞	1	1	初級	◎
	out	[aʊt]	adv.	…之外	1	1	初級	
	control	[kənˋtrol]	n.	控制	1	2	初級	◎
⓫	confused	[kənˋfjuzd]	adj.	糊塗的	3	3	初級	◎
⓬	so	[so]	adv.	真是/這麼	1	1	初級	
	selfish	[ˋsɛlfɪʃ]	adj.	自私的	3		初級	
⓭	stupid	[ˋstjupɪd]	adj.	愚蠢的	1	1	初級	◎
	think	[θɪŋk]	v.	認為	1	1	初級	
	acted	[ˋæktɪd]	p.t.	act（行動）過去式	1	1	初級	
⓮	extremely	[ɪkˋstrimlɪ]	adv.	極度	1		中級	
	serious	[ˋsɪrɪəs]	adj.	嚴重的	1	2	初級	◎
⓯	believe	[bɪˋliv]	v.	相信	1	1	初級	◎
	horrible	[ˋhɔrəbl]	adj.	糟糕的	2	3	初級	◎
⓰	guess	[gɛs]	v.	猜想	1	1	初級	◎
	talk	[tɔk]	v.	理會、講話	1	1	初級	◎
	anymore	[ˋɛnɪˏmor]	adv.	不再	1		中高	

※「紅字單字」於本單元多句出現，「單字級等分析」僅列在「首次出現句」。

🔵 MP3 082-02 ❶〜⓱

❶	沒關係啦！	It doesn't matter! = That's all right! = Never mind!
❷	別自責了。	Don't blame yourself. * blame oneself（自責）
❸	我原諒你了。	I forgive you.
❹	人非聖賢，熟能無過。	Nobody is perfect; everyone makes mistakes.
❺	知道錯就好。	It's enough that you realize you were wrong. * It's enough that＋子句（…已經足夠）
❻	我可以諒解。	I can tolerate that.
❼	下次不要再犯了。	Don't do it again. = Don't make the same mistake again. * make the same mistake（犯下相同錯誤）
❽	沒那麼嚴重啦！	It's not that critical!
❾	你要怎麼補償我？	How are you going to make it up to me? * How are you going to＋動詞?（你打算將來如何…？） * 此句用「未來簡單式」（…are…going to…） 　表示「未排定時程、但預定要做的事」。
❿	我可以理解。	I can understand.
⓫	希望這次你學到教訓了。	I hope that you have learned a lesson from this. * I hope that＋子句（我希望…） * have learned a lesson（已經學到教訓）
⓬	下次眼睛放亮點！	Use your head next time! * use your head（用點腦袋！、用心點！）
⓭	別再這麼迷糊了！	Don't be that foolish again!
⓮	我們還是朋友。	We are still friends. * friends（朋友）可替換為：buddies（好兄弟）
⓯	過去的就讓它過去吧。	Just let the past go. * the past（過去的事）
⓰	別再想了。	Don't think about it anymore.
⓱	我不會記恨的。	I won't bear a grudge. * bear a grudge（記仇、記恨）

	單字	音標	詞性	意義	字頻	大考	英檢	多益
❶	matter	[ˋmætɚ]	v.	要緊、有關係	1	1	初級	◎
	that	[ðæt]	pron. /adv.	那個/那麼	1	1	初級	
	all	[ɔl]	adv.	一切	1	1	初級	
	right	[raɪt]	adj.	沒關係的	1	1	初級	
	never	[ˋnɛvɚ]	adv.	從不	1	1	初級	
	mind	[maɪnd]	v.	介意	1	1	初級	◎
❷	blame	[blem]	v.	指責	1	3	初級	◎
	yourself	[juɚˋsɛlf]	pron.	你自己	1		初級	
❸	forgive	[fɚˋgɪv]	v.	原諒	2	2	初級	
❹	nobody	[ˋnobɑdɪ]	pron.	沒有人	1	2	初級	
	perfect	[ˋpɝfɪkt]	adj.	完美的	1	2	初級	◎
	everyone	[ˋɛvrɪˏwʌn]	pron.	每個人	1		初級	
	make	[mek]	v.	犯下/彌補	1	1	初級	
	mistake	[mɪˋstek]	n.	錯誤	1	1	初級	◎
❺	enough	[əˋnʌf]	adj.	足夠的	1	1	初級	◎
	realize	[ˋrɪəˏlaɪz]	v.	瞭解	1	2	初級	◎
	wrong	[rɔŋ]	adj.	錯誤的	1	1	初級	◎
❻	tolerate	[ˋtɑləˏret]	v.	寬恕	2	4	中級	◎
❼	do	[du]	v.	做	1	1	初級	
	again	[əˋgɛn]	adv.	再次	1	1	初級	
	same	[sem]	adj.	相同的	1	1	初級	
❽	critical	[ˋkrɪtɪkl̩]	adj.	嚴重的	1	4	中級	◎
❾	going	[ˋgoɪŋ]	p.pr.	go（即將）現在分詞	4	1	初級	
	up	[ʌp]	adv.	起來	1	1	初級	
❿	understand	[ˏʌndɚˋstænd]	v.	瞭解	1	1	初級	
⓫	hope	[hop]	v.	希望	1	1	初級	
	learned	[ˋlɝnɪd]	p.p.	learn（學到）過去分詞	4	4	中級	
	lesson	[ˋlɛsn̩]	n.	教訓	1	1	初級	◎
⓬	use	[juz]	v.	使用	1	1	初級	◎
	head	[hɛd]	n.	頭腦	1	1	初級	◎
	next	[nɛkst]	adj.	下一	1	1	初級	
	time	[taɪm]	n.	次、回	1	1	初級	◎
⓭	foolish	[ˋfulɪʃ]	adj.	迷糊的	3	2	初級	
⓮	still	[stɪl]	adv.	仍然	1	1	初級	◎
	friend	[frɛnd]	n.	朋友	1	1	初級	
⓯	just	[dʒʌst]	adv.	就…	1	1	初級	
	let	[lɛt]	v.	讓…	1	1	初級	
	past	[pæst]	n.	過去	1	1	初級	
	go	[go]	v.	流逝、成為過往	1	1	初級	
⓰	think	[θɪŋk]	v.	認為	1	1	初級	
	anymore	[ˋɛnɪˏmor]	adv.	不再	1		中高	
⓱	bear	[bɛr]	v.	記住	1	2	初級	◎
	grudge	[grʌdʒ]	n.	仇恨	6			

※「紅字單字」於本單元多句出現，「單字級等分析」僅列在「首次出現句」。　　377

083　請幫我⋯。

❶	可以幫我一個忙嗎？	Would you give me a hand? * **Would you**＋動詞?（你是否願意⋯呢） * **give me a hand**（幫忙我）＝ **do me a favor** ＝ **help me**
❷	我需要你的協助。	I need your help. ＝ I need a favor from you. ＝ I need your assistance.
❸	你現在有空嗎？	Are you free right now? * **free**（有空閒的）＝ **available**
❹	可憐可憐我吧！	Please have pity on me! * **have pity on**＋某人（同情某人、可憐某人）
❺	求求你啦！	Please!
❻	上回我幫你，這回換你幫我了。	I helped you last time, so this time it's your turn. * **last time**（上一次）、**this time**（這一次） * **be your turn**（輪到你）
❼	你一定要幫我這個忙。	You must help me with this.
❽	我們是朋友吧？	We're friends, aren't we?
❾	沒有你我做不到。	I can't do it without you.
❿	今天我請客，但是你要幫我個忙。	Today I'll treat you, but you need to give me a hand.　* **treat**＋某人（招待某人、請客）
⓫	我只能靠你了！	I am counting on you! * **count on**＋某人（依賴某人、指望某人） * 此句用「現在進行式」（...am counting...）表示「現階段發生的事」。
⓬	我又遇上麻煩了！	I'm in trouble again!
⓭	怎麼辦？沒人幫我！	What should I do? There's no one who'll help me!
⓮	有事請教你。	I need your advice on something.
⓯	你不可以不幫我。	You can't refuse to help me. ＝ You can't say no to me.
⓰	幫忙想想辦法吧！	Help me think of something! * **think of**（想出）＝ **come up with**

單字級等分析

	單字	音標	詞性	意義	字頻	大考	英檢	多益
❶	give	[gɪv]	v.	給予	1	1	初級	
	hand	[hænd]	n.	幫助	1	1	初級	
❷	need	[nid]	v.	需要	1	1	初級	◎
	help	[hɛlp]	n./v.	幫忙	1	1	初級	
	favor	[ˋfevə]	n.	幫助	1	2	初級	◎
	assistance	[əˋsɪstəns]	n.	協助	1	4	中級	◎
❸	free	[fri]	adj.	有空閒的	1	1	初級	
	right	[raɪt]	adv.	正值	1	1	初級	
	now	[naʊ]	adv.	現在	1	1	初級	
❹	please	[pliz]	adv.	請	1	1	初級	
	have	[hæv]	v.	懷有	1	1	初級	
	pity	[ˋpɪtɪ]	n.	同情、憐憫	3	3	中級	
❻	helped	[hɛlpt]	p.t.	help（幫忙）過去式	1	1	初級	
	last	[læst]	adj.	上一	1	1	初級	◎
	time	[taɪm]	n.	次、回	1	1	初級	◎
	this	[ðɪs]	adj./pron.	這個	1	1	初級	
	turn	[tɜn]	n.	輪、次	1	1	初級	◎
❽	friend	[frɛnd]	n.	朋友	1	1	初級	
❾	do	[du]	v.	做	1	1	初級	
❿	today	[təˋde]	adv.	今天	1	1	初級	
	treat	[trit]	v.	招待	1	2	初級	◎
⓫	counting	[ˋkaʊntɪŋ]	p.pr.	count（依賴）現在分詞	4	1	初級	
⓬	trouble	[ˋtrʌbl̩]	n.	麻煩	1	1	初級	◎
	again	[əˋgɛn]	adv.	再次	1	1	初級	
⓭	there	[ðɛr]	adv.	有…	1	1	初級	
	one	[wʌn]	pron.	一個人	1	1	初級	
⓮	advice	[ədˋvaɪs]	n.	建議	1	3	初級	◎
	something	[ˋsʌmθɪŋ]	pron.	某些事情	1	1	初級	
⓯	refuse	[rɪˋfjuz]	v.	拒絕	1	2	初級	◎
	say	[se]	v.	說	1	1	初級	
	no	[no]	n.	否定	1	1	初級	
⓰	think	[θɪŋk]	v.	想出	1	1	初級	

※「紅字單字」於本單元多句出現，「單字級等分析」僅列在「首次出現句」。

🔊 MP3 083-02 ❶〜⓯

❶	沒問題，交給我。	No problem, just leave it to me. * leave it to＋某人（讓某人處理）
❷	我很樂意幫你。	I am glad to do you a favor. * be glad to（樂於…、願意…）＝ be willing to
❸	我想想怎麼解決。	Let me think about how to solve the problem. * think about（考慮）、solve a problem（解決問題）
❹	靜下心來，別急。	Just calm down, don't be in such hurry. * calm down（冷靜）、in such hurry（這麼急）
❺	不好意思，我正在忙…	I'm sorry; I'm in the middle of.... * in the middle of＋某事（正做某事做到一半）
❻	好！你怎麼報答我？	Good! How will you repay me? * repay＋某人（回報某人）
❼	我忙完馬上去幫你。	I'll help you as soon as I am done with my work. * 子句＋as soon as＋子句（…之後，就…） * be done with＋某事（完成某事）
❽	我真的抽不出時間…	I really can't find the time to.... * can't find the time（抽不出時間）
❾	我考慮看看。	Let me think about it.
❿	你找別人幫忙吧！	Find someone else to help you!
⓫	想得美，我不可能幫你。	Don't even think about it, it's impossible for me to help you. * Don't even think about it（想都別想！）
⓬	你應該學會自己解決問題。	You should learn how to solve problems by yourself.
⓭	你總是給我惹麻煩。	You are always making trouble for me. * be always＋動詞-ing（總是在做…） * 此句用「現在進行式」（...are...making）表示「現階段經常發生、且令人厭惡的事」。 * make trouble for＋某人（給某人惹麻煩）
⓮	我為什麼要幫你？	Why should I give you a hand?
⓯	當然！誰叫我們是好朋友。	Of course! We are good friends after all. * after all（畢竟）

	單字	音標	詞性	意義	字頻	大考	英檢	多益
❶	problem	[ˈprɑbləm]	n.	問題	1	1	初級	◎
	just	[dʒʌst]	adv.	就…	1	1	初級	
	leave	[liv]	v.	留給	1	1	初級	◎
❷	glad	[glæd]	adj.	樂意的、願意的	1	1	初級	
	do	[du]	v.	做	1	1	初級	
	favor	[ˈfevɚ]	n.	幫助	1	2	初級	◎
❸	let	[lɛt]	v.	讓…	1	1	初級	
	think	[θɪŋk]	v.	考慮	1	1	初級	
	solve	[sɑlv]	v.	解決	1	2	初級	◎
❹	calm	[kɑm]	v.	冷靜	2	2	初級	
	down	[daʊn]	adv.	下來	1	1	初級	
	such	[sʌtʃ]	adv.	這麼	1	1	初級	
	hurry	[ˈhɝɪ]	n.	急促	2	2	初級	◎
❺	sorry	[ˈsɑrɪ]	adj.	抱歉的	1	1	初級	
	middle	[ˈmɪdl̩]	n.	中間	1	1	初級	
❻	good	[gʊd]	int./adj.	好吧/良好的	1	1	初級	◎
	repay	[rɪˈpe]	v.	回報	3	5	**中高**	◎
❼	help	[hɛlp]	v.	幫忙	1	1	初級	
	soon	[sun]	adv.	不久、很快	1	1	初級	
	done	[dʌn]	p.p.	do（完成）過去分詞	1	1	初級	
	work	[wɝk]	n.	工作	1	1	初級	◎
❽	really	[ˈrɪəlɪ]	adv.	真的	1		初級	
	find	[faɪnd]	v.	抽出	1	1	初級	
	time	[taɪm]	n.	時間	1	1	初級	◎
❿	someone	[ˈsʌmˌwʌn]	pron.	某些人	1	1	初級	
	else	[ɛls]	adj.	其他的	1	1	初級	
⓫	even	[ˈivən]	adv.	甚至	1	1	初級	◎
	impossible	[ɪmˈpɑsəbl̩]	adj.	不可能的	1	1	初級	◎
⓬	learn	[lɝn]	v.	學習	1	1	初級	
	yourself	[jʊɚˈsɛlf]	pron.	你自己	1	1	初級	
⓭	always	[ˈɔlwez]	adv.	總是	1	1	初級	
	making	[ˈmekɪŋ]	p.pr.	make（製造）現在分詞	2	1	**中高**	
	trouble	[ˈtrʌbl̩]	n.	麻煩	1	1	初級	◎
⓮	give	[gɪv]	v.	給予	1	1	初級	
	hand	[hænd]	n.	幫助	1	1	初級	
⓯	course	[kors]	adv.	（與 of 連用）當然	1	1	初級	◎
	friend	[frɛnd]	n.	朋友	1	1	初級	
	all	[ɔl]	n.	一切、全部	1	1	初級	

※「紅字單字」於本單元多句出現，「單字級等分析」僅列在「首次出現句」。

❶	我想和你周轉一下。	I'd like to borrow some money from you. * **borrow money from ＋某人**（向某人借錢）
❷	你有錢可以借我嗎？	Can you lend me some money if you have any?
❸	先借我一萬塊好嗎？	Lend me NT$10,000 first, OK?
❹	先借我錢繳卡費。	Lend me some money first to pay my credit card bills. * **pay a bill**（繳費） * **credit card bills**（信用卡費）
❺	你能借我多少錢？	How much can you lend me? * **How much...?**（…有多少？）
❻	發薪水就還你錢。	I'll pay you back on my payday. * **pay you back**（歸還給你）
❼	我沒有零錢，你有嗎？	I don't have any change, do you?
❽	我忘了帶錢包，先借我一百元。	I forgot my purse, can you spot me NT$100? * **forgot ＋物品**（忘記帶某物品） * **spot me ＋少許金額**（借給我少許金額的錢）
❾	拜託你借我一些錢應急。	Please, lend me some money to meet an urgent need.　* **urgent need**（急用）
❿	我帶的錢不夠，你身上有錢嗎？	I didn't bring enough money; do you have any on you? * **didn't bring enough money**（身上帶的錢不夠）
⓫	借我一些錢吃飯吧？	Will you lend me some money for meals?
⓬	求你幫幫忙，借我十萬元。	I'm begging you for your help; lend me NT$100,000. * **beg ＋某人**（拜託某人）。 * 此句用「現在進行式」（...am begging...）表示「說話當下正在做的事」。
⓭	我的朋友中，就屬你最有錢了。	Of all my friends, you are the richest.
⓮	我保證僅此一次。	I promise that this will be the only time. * **promise that ＋子句**（保證…） * **the only time**（唯一一次）

單字級等分析

	單字	音標	詞性	意義	字頻	大考	英檢	多益
❶	like	[laɪk]	v.	想要	1	1	初級	
	borrow	[ˋbɑro]	v.	借入	2	2	初級	◎
	some	[sʌm]	adj.	一些	1	1	初級	
	money	[ˋmʌnɪ]	n.	金錢	1	1	初級	◎
❷	lend	[lɛnd]	v.	借出	2	2	初級	◎
	have	[hæv]	v.	擁有	1	1	初級	
	any	[ˋɛnɪ]	pron. /adj.	若干、一點/任何的	1	1	初級	
❸	first	[fɝst]	adv.	首先	1	1	初級	
	ok	[ˋoˋke]	int.	好嗎	1	1	初級	
❹	pay	[pe]	v.	付款	1	3	初級	◎
	credit	[ˋkrɛdɪt]	n.	信用	1	3	中級	◎
	card	[kɑrd]	n.	卡	1	2	初級	◎
	bill	[bɪl]	n.	帳單	1	2	初級	◎
❻	back	[bæk]	adv.	返還	1	1	初級	◎
	payday	[ˋpe͵de]	n.	發薪日	6			
❼	change	[tʃendʒ]	n.	零錢	1	2	初級	◎
❽	forgot	[fɚˋgɑt]	p.t.	forget（忘記）過去式	1	1	初級	
	purse	[pɝs]	n.	錢包	2	2	初級	
	spot	[spɑt]	v.	借一點點錢	1	2	初級	◎
❾	please	[pliz]	adv.	請	1	1	初級	
	meet	[mit]	v.	應付	1	1	初級	
	urgent	[ˋɝdʒənt]	adj.	緊急的	2	4	中級	◎
	need	[nid]	n.	需要	1	1	初級	◎
❿	bring	[brɪŋ]	v.	攜帶	1	1	初級	
	enough	[əˋnʌf]	adj.	足夠的	1	1	初級	◎
⓫	meal	[mil]	n.	一餐	1	2	初級	
⓬	begging	[ˋbɛgɪŋ]	p.pr.	beg（乞求）現在分詞	7	2	中級	
	help	[hɛlp]	n.	幫忙	1	1	初級	
⓭	all	[ɔl]	adj.	所有的	1	1	初級	
	friend	[frɛnd]	n.	朋友	1	1	初級	
	richest	[ˋrɪtʃɪst]	adj.	rich（富有的）最高級	1	1	初級	
⓮	promise	[ˋprɑmɪs]	v.	保證	1	2	初級	◎
	this	[ðɪs]	pron.	這個	1	1	初級	
	only	[ˋonlɪ]	adj.	唯一的	1	1	初級	
	time	[taɪm]	n.	次、回	1	1	初級	◎

※「紅字單字」於本單元多句出現，「單字級等分析」僅列在「首次出現句」。

MP3 084-02 ❶～❿

❶	沒問題，你需要多少？	No problem, how much do you need?
❷	需要多少？	How much do you need?
❸	你遇到了什麼困難嗎？	Are you encountering some difficulties? * encounter difficulties（遇到困難）
❹	我馬上去領錢給你。	I'll go withdraw some money for you right now. * withdraw money（提領金錢）＝ take out money
❺	什麼時候可以還我？	When will you pay me back?
❻	我從來不借錢給別人，這是 我的原則。	I never lend money to anyone; this is my principle. * lend money to＋某人（借錢給某人）
❼	我們要先簽個借據。	We have to sign an agreement first. ＝ You have to sign an IOU first. * sign an agreement（簽契約） * sign an IOU（簽借據）
❽	你不是上個月才向我借錢嗎？	Didn't you just borrow money from me last month? * Didn't you...?（你當時不是…嗎）
❾	我的錢都放在定存不能動ㄟ。	All my money is in the deposit account, and I can't take any out. * deposit account（定存帳戶）
❿	一定要還我喔！	You must pay me back!
⓫	我真的沒辦法…	I really can't....
⓬	免談，想都別想！	No way, don't even think about it! * No way（不可能、免談）可替換為： Save your breath（別白費唇舌、省省力氣吧）
⓭	我也沒錢ㄟ！	I don't have any money either!
⓮	拜託，你比我還有錢吧！	Come on, you are richer than I am! * come on（少來了、拜託） ＝ please ＝ get out of here
⓯	我不想借錢給你。	I don't want to lend you money.
⓰	我比你還窮呢！	I'm much poorer than you!
⓱	誰叫你上次不借錢給我？	Why didn't you lend me money last time? * Why didn't you...?（你當時為什麼不做…？）

	單字	音標	詞性	意義	字頻	大考	英檢	多益
❶	problem	[ˋprɑbləm]	n.	問題	1	1	初級	◎
	much	[mʌtʃ]	adv.	許多	1	1	初級	
	need	[nid]	v.	需要	1	1	初級	◎
❸	encountering	[ɪnˋkaʊntəɪŋ]	p.pr.	encounter（遇到）現在分詞	1	4	中級	◎
	some	[sʌm]	adj.	一些	1	1	初級	
	difficulty	[ˋdɪfə.kʌltɪ]	n.	困難	1	2	初級	◎
❹	go	[go]	v.	去	1	1	初級	
	withdraw	[wɪðˋdrɔ]	v.	提款	1	4	中級	◎
	money	[ˋmʌnɪ]	n.	金錢	1	1	初級	◎
	right	[raɪt]	adv.	正值	1	1	初級	
	now	[naʊ]	adv.	現在	1	1	初級	
❺	pay	[pe]	v.	付款	1	3	初級	◎
	back	[bæk]	adv.	返還	1	1	初級	◎
❻	never	[ˋnɛvɚ]	adv.	從不	1	1	初級	
	lend	[lɛnd]	v.	借出	2	2	初級	◎
	anyone	[ˋɛnɪ.wʌn]	pron.	任何人	1	2	初級	
	this	[ðɪs]	pron.	這個	1	1	初級	
	principle	[ˋprɪnsəpl]	n.	原則	1	2	初級	◎
❼	have	[hæv]	v.	必須/擁有	1	1	初級	
	sign	[saɪn]	v.	簽署	1	2	初級	◎
	agreement	[əˋgrimənt]	n.	契約	1	1	中級	◎
	first	[fɝst]	adv.	首先	1	1	初級	
	IOU	[ˋaɪoˋju]	n.	I own you（借據）縮寫				
❽	just	[dʒʌst]	adv.	剛才	1	1	初級	
	borrow	[ˋbɑro]	v.	借入	2	2	初級	◎
	last	[læst]	adj.	上一個	1	1	初級	◎
	month	[mʌnθ]	n.	月	1	1	初級	◎
❾	all	[ɔl]	adj.	所有的	1	1	初級	
	deposit	[dɪˋpɑzɪt]	n.	定存	2	3	中級	◎
	account	[əˋkaʊnt]	n.	帳戶	1	3	中級	◎
	take	[tek]	v.	領錢	1	1	初級	◎
	any	[ˋɛnɪ]	pron. /adj.	若干、一點/任何的	1	1	初級	
	out	[aʊt]	adv.	領出	1	1	初級	
⓫	really	[ˋrɪəlɪ]	adv.	真的	1	1	初級	
⓬	way	[we]	n.	方法、方式	1	1	初級	
	even	[ˋivən]	adv.	甚至	1	1	初級	
	think	[θɪŋk]	v.	考慮	1	1	初級	
⓭	either	[ˋiðɚ]	adv.	也不	1	1	初級	
⓮	come	[kʌm]	v.	（與 on 連用）拜託	1	1	初級	
	richer	[ˋrɪtʃɚ]	adj.	rich（富有的）比較級	1	1	初級	
⓯	want	[wɑnt]	v.	想要	1	1	初級	◎
⓰	poorer	[ˋpʊrɚ]	adj.	poor（貧窮的）比較級	1	1	初級	
⓱	time	[taɪm]	n.	次、回	1	1	初級	◎

※「紅字單字」於本單元多句出現，「單字級等分析」僅列在「首次出現句」。

🔊 MP3 085-01 ❶～❶

❶	這個東西借一下。	Let me borrow this for a while.
❷	這件衣服明天借我穿。	Lend me these clothes for tomorrow. * for＋時間（在某時間）
❸	可以向你借樣東西嗎？	May I borrow something from you? * borrow＋物品＋from＋某人（和某人借某物品）
❹	這本書可以借我嗎？	Can you lend me this book?
❺	外借要錢嗎？	Should I pay you anything to borrow this?
❻	要不要借啦，小氣鬼？	Are you going to lend it to me or not, you cheapskate? * Are you going to＋動詞＋or not? （你現在要不要…？）
❼	外借要辦證件嗎？	Do I need to apply for a certificate to borrow this?　* apply for（申辦）
❽	暫時借用一下，明天還。	I just need to borrow it temporarily—I will return it tomorrow. * need to＋動詞原形（需要）
❾	借我一下原子筆，馬上就還。	Lend me your pen, I'll return it right away. * lend me＋物品（借給我某物品）
❿	我又不是不還，幹麼不借我？	I'm not going to refuse to return it, why not lend it to me? * refuse to return（不肯歸還）
⓫	我想到圖書館借書。	I want to go to the library to check out some books.　* check out a book（從圖書館借書）
⓬	我一向有借有還。	I always return everything I borrow.
⓭	你既然用不上，不如借我。	Since you have no use for it, you might as well lend it to me. * since＋子句（既然…） * have no use for＋某物（用不上某物） * might as well＋動詞（不如…）
⓮	要借不借隨便你。	It's up to you whether or not you'll lend it to me. * be up to you（由你決定） * whether or not＋子句（是否要…）

	單字	音標	詞性	意義	字頻	大考	英檢	多益
❶	let	[lɛt]	v.	讓…	1	1	初級	
	borrow	[ˋbaro]	v.	借出	2	2	初級	◎
	this	[ðɪs]	pron. /adj.	這個	1	1		
	while	[hwaɪl]	n.	一會兒	1	1	初級	
❷	lend	[lɛnd]	v.	借入	2	2	初級	◎
	these	[ðiz]	adj.	這些	1	1	初級	
	clothes	[kloz]	n.	cloth（衣服）複數	1	2	初級	
	tomorrow	[təˋmoro]	n.	明天	1	1	初級	◎
❸	something	[ˋsʌmθɪŋ]	pron.	某樣東西	1	1	初級	
❹	book	[bʊk]	n.	書籍	1	1	初級	◎
❺	pay	[pe]	v.	付款	1	3	初級	◎
	anything	[ˋɛnɪˌθɪŋ]	pron.	任何東西	1	1	初級	
❻	going	[ˋgoɪŋ]	p.pr.	go（即將）現在分詞	4	1	初級	
	cheapskate	[ˋtʃipˌsket]	n.	小氣鬼				
❼	need	[nid]	v.	需要	1	1	初級	◎
	apply	[əˋplaɪ]	v.	申請	1	2	初級	◎
	certificate	[səˋtɪfəkɪt]	n.	單據	2	5	中級	◎
❽	just	[dʒʌst]	adv.	只是	1	1	初級	
	temporarily	[ˋtɛmpəˌrɛrəlɪ]	adv.	暫時地	2		中高	◎
	return	[rɪˋtɜn]	v.	歸還	1	1	初級	◎
❾	pen	[pɛn]	n.	筆	1	1	初級	
	right	[raɪt]	adv.	立即	1	1	初級	
	away	[əˋwe]	adv.	直接	1	1	初級	
❿	refuse	[rɪˋfjuz]	v.	拒絕	1	2	初級	◎
⓫	want	[wɑnt]	v.	想要	1	1	初級	◎
	go	[go]	v.	去	1	1	初級	
	library	[ˋlaɪˌbrɛrɪ]	n.	圖書館	1	2	初級	◎
	check	[tʃɛk]	v.	借閱書籍	1	1	初級	◎
	out	[aʊt]	adv.	借出	1	1	初級	
	some	[sʌm]	adj.	一些	1	1	初級	
⓬	always	[ˋɔlwez]	adv.	一向	1	1	初級	
	everything	[ˋɛvrɪˌθɪŋ]	pron.	每樣東西	1		初級	
⓭	have	[hæv]	v.	擁有	1	1	初級	
	use	[juz]	n.	使用	1	1	初級	◎
	as	[æz]	adv.	如同	1	1	初級	
	well	[wɛl]	adv.	（與 might as 連用）不如…	1	1	初級	◎
⓮	up	[ʌp]	adj.	由…決定	1	1	初級	

※「紅字單字」於本單元多句出現，「單字級等分析」僅列在「首次出現句」。

MP3 085-02 ❶～⓯

❶	你儘管拿去用。	Feel free to use it. * feel free to＋動詞（不用客氣做⋯、儘管做⋯）
❷	沒問題，你用。	No problem, go ahead. * go ahead（請、請用）
❸	記得還我。	Remember to return it back to me.
❹	可以，這原本就是公用的。	Sure, it was for public use originally. * public use（公用）
❺	我不想借你。	I don't want to lend it to you.
❻	你上次向我借的東西還我了嗎？	Have you returned the thing I lent to you last time? * Have you＋過去分詞?（你是否已經⋯？）
❼	說什麼都不借。	No matter what you say, I will not lend anything to you. * no matter what＋主詞＋動詞（不論⋯）
❽	你自己去買！	Go buy it yourself!
❾	你信用不好，不借。	You don't have good credit; I will not lend anything to you. * not have good credit（信用不良、沒信用）
❿	我從來不把東西借給別人。	I never lend anything to anybody.
⓫	這東西不是我的，我不能借你。	I can't lend it to you; it's not mine.
⓬	我現在還要用，下次再借你。	I'm still using it; I will lend it to you next time. * 此句用「現在進行式」（⋯am⋯using⋯） 　表示「說話當下正在做的事」。
⓭	這東西不能外借。	It is not for borrowing. * 某物＋be not for＋動詞-ing（某物不是作為⋯）
⓮	借你我就不能工作了。	I can't work if I lend it to you.
⓯	我已經答應借給別人了。	I've already promised to lend it to someone else. * 此句用「現在完成式」（⋯have⋯promised⋯） 　表示「過去某時點發生某事，且結果持續到現在」。 * promise to＋動詞原形（答應⋯）

	單字	音標	詞性	意義	字頻	大考	英檢	多益
❶	feel	[fil]	v.	感覺	1	1	初級	
	free	[fri]	adj.	自由的、無拘束的	1	1	初級	
	use	[juz]	v./n.	使用	1	1	初級	◎
❷	problem	[ˋprɑbləm]	n.	問題	1	1	初級	◎
	go	[go]	v.	去做	1	1	初級	
	ahead	[əˋhɛd]	adv.	向前	1	1	初級	◎
❸	remember	[rɪˋmɛmbɚ]	v.	記得	1	1	初級	◎
	return	[rɪˋtɝn]	v.	歸還	1	1	初級	◎
	back	[bæk]	adv.	返還	1	1	初級	◎
❹	sure	[ʃur]	adv.	當然、可以	1	1	初級	
	public	[ˋpʌblɪk]	adj.	公共的	1	1	初級	
	originally	[əˋrɪdʒnəlɪ]	adv.	原來	2		中高	◎
❺	want	[wɑnt]	v.	想要	1	1	初級	◎
	lend	[lɛnd]	v.	借入	2	2	初級	
❻	returned	[rɪˋtɝnd]	p.p.	return（歸還）過去分詞	1	1	初級	◎
	thing	[θɪŋ]	n.	物品	1	1	初級	
	lent	[lɛnt]	p.t.	lend（借入）過去式	2	2	初級	
	last	[læst]	adj.	上一	1	1	初級	◎
	time	[taɪm]	n.	次、回	1	1	初級	
❼	say	[se]	v.	說	1	1	初級	
	anything	[ˋɛnɪˌθɪŋ]	pron.	任何東西	1	1	初級	
❽	buy	[baɪ]	v.	購買	1	1	初級	
	yourself	[juɚˋsɛlf]	pron.	你自己	1	1	初級	
❾	have	[hæv]	v.	擁有	1	1	初級	
	good	[gud]	adj.	良好的	1	1	初級	◎
	credit	[ˋkrɛdɪt]	n.	信用	1	3	中級	◎
❿	never	[ˋnɛvɚ]	adv.	從不	1	1	初級	
	anybody	[ˋɛnɪˌbɑdɪ]	pron.	任何人	1	2	初級	
⓫	mine	[maɪn]	pron.	我的	1	2	初級	
⓬	still	[stɪl]	adv.	仍然	1	1	初級	◎
	using	[ˋjuzɪŋ]	p.pr.	use（使用）現在分詞	1	1	初級	◎
	next	[nɛkst]	adj.	下一個	1		初級	
⓭	borrowing	[ˋbɑroɪŋ]	n.	borrow（借出）動名詞	5	2	中高	◎
⓮	work	[wɝk]	v.	工作	1	1	初級	
⓯	already	[ɔlˋrɛdɪ]	adv.	已經	1	1	初級	◎
	promised	[ˋprɑmɪst]	p.p.	promise（答應）過去分詞	4	2	初級	◎
	someone	[ˋsʌmˌwʌn]	pron.	某個人	1	1	初級	
	else	[ɛls]	adj.	其他的	1	1	初級	

※「紅字單字」於本單元多句出現，「單字級等分析」僅列在「首次出現句」。

🔊 MP3 086-01 ❶〜⓲

❶	我很喜歡。	I like it very much.
❷	我會好好珍惜的。	I will be sure to treasure it. * treasure＋物品（珍惜某物品）
❸	我作夢都夢到！	I've dreamt about that! * 此句用「現在完成式」（...have dreamt...） 　表示「過去到現在發生過、經歷過的事」。
❹	我願意用全世界來交換。	I'd give up the whole world for that. * would give up＋物品（願意放棄某物品）
❺	賠上生命我也在所不惜。	Even if it cost me my life, I would not hesitate. * cost＋某人＋某物（花費某人的某物）
❻	我愛死它了！	I love it to death! * love＋某物＋to death（愛死某物）
❼	我想不出還有什麼比這個更棒的了！	I cannot think of anything better than this! * think of（想到）＝ come up with * better than＋某物（比某物更好的）
❽	一看到它我就高興。	As soon as I see it, I feel happy. * as soon as＋子句, 子句（…之後，就會…）
❾	你不覺得這是全世界最棒的嗎？	Don't you think this is the best in the whole world? * Don't you think＋子句?（你不覺得…嗎）
❿	真是迷人！	That is quite charming!
⓫	求求你別將它從我的生命中帶走！	Please do not take it out of my life! * out of＋某事物（從某事物之中）
⓬	多可愛啊！	What a cutie!
⓭	這真是我的救命仙丹！	This really is my lifesaver!
⓮	那就是我想要的！	That's the one that I want!
⓯	你知道它對我有多重要嗎？	Do you know how important it is to me?
⓰	我不能沒有它。	I cannot be without it.
⓱	我一想到就睡不著覺。	When I think about it I can't sleep.
⓲	我恨不得立刻擁有。	I wish I could have it right now. * I wish I could＋動詞原形（可以的話，我希望能…）

	單字	音標	詞性	意義	字頻	大考	英檢	多益
❶	like	[laɪk]	v.	喜歡	1	1	初級	
	very	[ˋvɛrɪ]	adv.	十分	1	1	初級	
	much	[mʌtʃ]	adv.	非常	1	1	初級	
❷	sure	[ʃur]	adj.	必定的	1	1	初級	
	treasure	[ˋtrɛʒɚ]	v.	珍惜	2	2	初級	◎
❸	dreamt	[drɛmt]	p.p.	dream（作夢）過去分詞	1	1	初級	
	that	[ðæt]	pron.	那個	1	1	初級	
❹	give	[gɪv]	v.	放棄	1	1	初級	
	up	[ʌp]	adv.	完全、徹底	1	1	初級	
	whole	[hol]	adj.	整個、全部的	1	1	初級	◎
	world	[wɝld]	n.	世界	1	1	初級	
❺	even	[ˋivən]	adv.	甚至	1	1	初級	◎
	cost	[kɔst]	v.	花費	1	1	初級	◎
	life	[laɪf]	n.	生命	1	1	初級	
	hesitate	[ˋhɛzə.tet]	v.	猶豫	2	3	中級	◎
❻	love	[lʌv]	v.	喜愛	1	1	初級	
	death	[dɛθ]	n.	死亡	1	1	初級	
❼	think	[θɪŋk]	v.	想到	1	1	初級	
	anything	[ˋɛnɪ.θɪŋ]	pron.	任何東西	1	1	初級	
	better	[ˋbɛtɚ]	adj.	good（良好的）比較級	1	1	初級	
❽	soon	[sun]	adv.	不久、很快	1	1	初級	
	see	[si]	v.	看到	1	1	初級	
	feel	[fil]	v.	感到	1	1	初級	
	happy	[ˋhæpɪ]	adj.	高興的	1	1	初級	
❾	this	[ðɪs]	pron.	這個	1	1	初級	
	best	[bɛst]	adj.	good（良好的）最高級	1	1	初級	
❿	quite	[kwaɪt]	adv.	相當	1	1	初級	
	charming	[ˋtʃɑrmɪŋ]	adj.	迷人的	2	3	中級	
⓫	please	[pliz]	adv.	請	1	1	初級	
	take	[tek]	v.	奪走	1	1	初級	◎
	out	[aut]	adv.	取出	1	1	初級	
⓬	cutie	[ˋkjutɪ]	n.	可愛的小動物、可愛的小嬰兒				
⓭	really	[ˋrɪəlɪ]	adv.	真的	1		初級	
	lifesaver	[ˋlaɪf.sevɚ]	n.	救急的物品				
⓮	one	[wʌn]	pron.	一件事物	1	1	初級	
⓯	know	[no]	v.	知道	1	1	初級	◎
	important	[ɪmˋpɔrtnt]	adj.	重要的	1	1	初級	◎
⓱	sleep	[slip]	v.	睡覺	1	1	初級	
⓲	wish	[wɪʃ]	v.	希望	1	1	初級	
	have	[hæv]	v.	擁有	1	1	初級	
	right	[raɪt]	adv.	正值	1	1	初級	
	now	[nau]	adv.	現在	1	1	初級	

※「紅字單字」於本單元多句出現，「單字級等分析」僅列在「首次出現句」。

086   你喜歡嗎？

❶	你有多喜歡？	How much do you like it? * **How much do...?**（…程度有多大？）
❷	你喜歡嗎？	Do you like it?
❸	你覺得怎麼樣？	What do you think? = What's your opinion?
❹	你會接受這個嗎？	Will you accept this? * **Will you...?**（你是否願意…？、你未來是否會…？）
❺	你比較喜歡哪一個？	Which one do you prefer? * **Which one...?**（…是哪一個？）
❻	這是你想要的嗎？	Is this the one you want?
❼	你為它瘋狂嗎？	Are you crazy about it? * **be crazy about...**（為…著迷）= be obsessed with...
❽	你覺得很棒，對吧？	You think it's pretty great, don't you?
❾	你想擁有它嗎？	Do you want to have it?
❿	你就是不能沒有它，對吧？	You just cannot live without it, can you? * **cannot live without** + 某物（沒有某物會無法過活）
⓫	你願意用多少錢買它？	How much would you buy it for? * **How much...?**（…多少錢？）
⓬	你願意拿什麼跟我交換？	What are you willing to exchange with me for it? * **be willing to**（願意）
⓭	你願意割捨哪一個？	Which one would you be willing to give up?
⓮	你想全部擁有，對吧？	You just want to have it all, don't you? * **have** + 某物 + **all**（完全擁有某物）
⓯	你會好好愛惜它嗎？	Will you cherish it dearly? * **cherish** + 某物 + **dearly**（非常珍惜某物）
⓰	你會愛上它嗎？	Will you fall in love with it? * **fall in love with** + 某物（愛上）
⓱	你覺得它適合你嗎？	Do you think it is suitable for you? * **be suitable for** + 某人（適合某人）
⓲	你好像不是很中意的樣子。	It seems like it doesn't appeal to you. * **It seem like** + 子句（好像…） * 某物 + **appeal to** + 某人（某物對某人有吸引力）

單字級等分析

	單字	音標	詞性	意義	字頻	大考	英檢	多益
❶	much	[mʌtʃ]	adv.	程度大小	1	1	初級	
	like	[laɪk]	v.	喜歡	1	1	初級	
❸	think	[θɪŋk]	v.	認為	1	1	初級	
	opinion	[əˈpɪnjən]	n.	意見	1	2	初級	◎
❹	accept	[əkˈsɛpt]	v.	接受	1	2	初級	◎
	this	[ðɪs]	pron.	這個	1	1	初級	
❺	one	[wʌn]	pron.	一件事物	1	1	初級	
	prefer	[prɪˈfɝ]	v.	偏愛	1	2	初級	◎
❻	want	[wɑnt]	v.	想要	1	1	初級	◎
❼	crazy	[ˈkrezɪ]	adj.	瘋狂的	1	2	初級	
❽	pretty	[ˈprɪtɪ]	adv.	非常	1	1	初級	◎
	great	[gret]	adj.	極好的	1	1	初級	◎
❾	have	[hæv]	v.	擁有	1	1	初級	
❿	just	[dʒʌst]	adv.	就是	1	1	初級	
	live	[lɪv]	v.	過活	1	1	初級	
⓫	buy	[baɪ]	v.	購買	1	1	初級	
⓬	willing	[ˈwɪlɪŋ]	adj.	願意的	1	2	初級	◎
	exchange	[ɪksˈtʃendʒ]	v.	交換	1	3	中級	◎
⓭	give	[gɪv]	v.	放棄	1	1	初級	
	up	[ʌp]	adv.	完全、徹底	1	1	初級	
⓮	all	[ɔl]	adv.	全部地	1	1	初級	
⓯	cherish	[ˈtʃɛrɪʃ]	v.	珍惜	4	4	中級	
	dearly	[ˈdɪrlɪ]	adv.	深情地	4			
⓰	fall	[fɔl]	v.	變成	1	1	初級	◎
	love	[lʌv]	n.	戀愛	1	1	初級	
⓱	suitable	[ˈsutəbl̩]	adj.	適合的	2	3	中級	◎
⓲	seem	[sim]	v.	似乎	1	1	初級	◎
	appeal	[əˈpil]	v.	吸引	1	3	中級	◎

※「紅字單字」於本單元多句出現，「單字級等分析」僅列在「首次出現句」。

MP3 087-01 ❶～⓰

❶	我不喜歡。	I don't like it.
❷	我受不了了！	I can't stand it anymore!
❸	他以為他是誰啊？	Who does he think he is? * **Who does she think she is?**（她以為她是誰啊？）
❹	我再也不要跟他說話了。	I don't want to talk to him anymore.
❺	真是噁心！	That's disgusting!
❻	別在我面前提到他。	Do not mention him around me. * **mention**＋人事物（提到某人事物） * **around me**（在我的周遭）
❼	我受不了他的態度。	I can't stand his attitude. * **stand**＋某事物（忍受某事物）
❽	我懶得理她！	I am not in the mood to worry about her! * **be not in the mood to**＋動詞（沒心情做…）
❾	想到就想吐！	When I think about that I want to throw up! * **think about**（想到） * **throw up**（嘔吐）＝ vomit
❿	饒了我吧！	Give me a break! * 此句表示「對於某人所說、所做的事反感」
⓫	窮極無聊！	This is so boring!
⓬	別來煩我！	Leave me alone!
⓭	我恨死她了！	I absolutely hate her! ＝ I hate her so much!
⓮	拜託別找我，我沒興趣。	Please don't count me in, I'm not interested. * **count me in**（把我算進去、讓我成為…裡的一員）
⓯	雞皮疙瘩掉滿地。	I get goose bumps all over my body. * **get goose bumps**（起雞皮疙瘩） * **all over**（到處）
⓰	我已經忍耐到極限。	I've already put up with it as long as I can. * **put up with**（忍受） * **as long as I can**（只要我可以） * 此句用「現在完成式」（...have...put...） 　表示「過去持續到現在的事」。

	單字	音標	詞性	意義	字頻	大考	英檢	多益
❶	like	[laɪk]	v.	喜歡	1	1	初級	
❷	stand	[stænd]	v.	忍受	1	1	初級	◎
	anymore	[ˈɛnɪmor]	adv.	不再	1		**中高**	
❸	think	[θɪŋk]	v.	以為	1	1	初級	
❹	want	[wɒnt]	v.	想要	1	1	初級	◎
	talk	[tɔk]	v.	講話	1	1	初級	
❺	that	[ðæt]	pron.	那個	1	1	初級	
	disgusting	[dɪsˈɡʌstɪŋ]	adj.	噁心的	4			
❻	mention	[ˈmɛnʃən]	v.	提到	1	3	中級	◎
❼	attitude	[ˈætətjud]	n.	態度	1	3	中級	◎
❽	mood	[mud]	n.	心情	1	3	中級	◎
	worry	[ˈwɝɪ]	v.	理會	1	1	初級	◎
❾	throw	[θro]	v.	嘔吐	1	1	初級	
	up	[ʌp]	adv.	吐出/忍住	1	1	初級	
❿	give	[ɡɪv]	v.	給予	1	1	初級	
	break	[brek]	n.	中斷、休息	1	1	初級	◎
⓫	this	[ðɪs]	pron.	這個	1	1	初級	
	so	[so]	adv.	窮極	1	1	初級	
	boring	[ˈborɪŋ]	adj.	無聊的	2	3	初級	◎
⓬	leave	[liv]	v.	留下	1	1	初級	◎
	alone	[əˈlon]	adv.	單獨地	1	1	初級	
⓭	absolutely	[ˈæbsəˌlutlɪ]	adv.	絕對	1		中級	◎
	hate	[het]	v.	討厭	1	1	初級	
	much	[mʌtʃ]	adv.	非常	1	1	初級	
⓮	please	[pliz]	adv.	請	1	1	初級	
	count	[kaʊnt]	v.	算入	1	1	初級	
	interested	[ˈɪntərɪstɪd]	n.	興趣的	1	1	初級	◎
⓯	get	[ɡɛt]	v.	使得、激起	1	1	初級	◎
	goose	[ɡus]	n.	雞皮	2	1	初級	
	bump	[bʌmp]	n.	疙瘩	2	3	中級	◎
	all	[ɔl]	adv.	完全	1	1	初級	
	body	[ˈbɑdɪ]	n.	身體	1	1	初級	
⓰	already	[ɔlˈrɛdɪ]	adv.	已經	1	1	初級	◎
	put	[pʊt]	p.p.	put（忍受）過去分詞	1	1	初級	
	long	[lɔŋ]	adv.	只要	1	1	初級	

※「紅字單字」於本單元多句出現，「單字級等分析」僅列在「首次出現句」。

MP3 087-02 ❶～⓯

❶	你不喜歡嗎？	You don't like that?
❷	你有多討厭它？	How much do you hate it? * **How much...?**（…程度有多大？）
❸	你連看都不看一眼嗎？	You won't even take a look at it? * **take a look at**＋某物（看某物一眼）
❹	你一定要這麼挑剔嗎？	Do you have to be so picky? * **Do you have to be**＋形容詞? （你一定要有…特質嗎）
❺	你真的無法接受嗎？	Are you really unable to accept it? * **Are you unable to...?**（你是否無法…？）
❻	你不能婉轉一點拒絕嗎？	Can't you reject it with a little tact? * **with a little tact**（稍微禮貌一些、婉轉一些）
❼	你真的不願意試試嗎？	You really don't want to give it a try? * **give it a try**（嘗試看看）
❽	你真的覺得那麼糟嗎？	Do you really think it is that terrible?
❾	你真的一點都不考慮嗎？	You really don't even want to give it a little thought? * **give it a little thought**（稍微考慮一下）
❿	這和你期待的不同，對吧？	This is not what you were expecting, is it? * **what you were expecting**（你當時所預期的事）
⓫	你毫無興趣嗎？	Don't you have any interest in it? * **have interest in**＋某物（對某物有興趣）
⓬	你為什麼只看到不好的一面呢？	Why do you only see the bad side? * **bad side**（不好的一面） * **good side**（良好的一面）
⓭	我很意外你竟然不喜歡。	I am surprised that you didn't like it. * **be surprised that**＋子句（對…感到意外）
⓮	這不是你以前的最愛嗎？	Wasn't this your favorite before? * 此句用「過去簡單式問句」（Wasn't...?） 表示「在過去是否處於某狀態、某身分？」。
⓯	你忍耐到極限了嗎？	Have you reached the limits of your patience? * **reach the limit of**＋某物（到達某物的極限）

	單字	音標	詞性	意義	字頻	大考	英檢	多益
❶	like	[laɪk]	v.	喜歡	1	1	初級	
	that	[ðæt]	pron./adv.	那個/那麼	1	1	初級	
❷	hate	[het]	v.	討厭	1	1	初級	
❸	even	[ˋivən]	adv.	甚至	1	1	初級	◎
	take	[tek]	v.	採取	1	1	初級	◎
	look	[lʊk]	n.	看一眼	1	1	初級	
❹	have	[hæv]	v.	必須/擁有	1	1	初級	
	so	[so]	adv.	這麼	1	1	初級	
	picky	[ˋpɪkɪ]	adj.	挑剔的	7			
❺	really	[ˋrɪəlɪ]	adv.	真的	1	1	初級	
	unable	[ʌnˋebl]	adj.	無法的	1		中級	◎
	accept	[əkˋsɛpt]	v.	接受	1	2	初級	◎
❻	reject	[rɪˋdʒɛkt]	v.	拒絕	1	2	初級	◎
	little	[ˋlɪtl]	adj.	些許的	1	1	初級	
	tact	[tækt]	n.	委婉、婉轉	7	6	中高	
❼	want	[wɑnt]	v.	想要	1	1	初級	◎
	give	[gɪv]	v.	給予	1	1	初級	
	try	[traɪ]	n.	嘗試	1	1	初級	
❽	think	[θɪŋk]	v.	認為	1	1	初級	
	terrible	[ˋtɛrəbl]	adj.	糟糕的	1	2	初級	◎
❾	thought	[θɔt]	n.	考慮	1	1	初級	◎
❿	this	[ðɪs]	pron.	這個	1	1	初級	
	expecting	[ɪkˋspɛktɪŋ]	p.pr.	expect（期待）現在分詞	1	2	初級	◎
⓫	any	[ˋɛnɪ]	adj.	任何的	1	1	初級	
	interest	[ˋɪntərɪst]	n.	興趣	1	1	初級	◎
⓬	only	[ˋonlɪ]	adv.	只有	1	1	初級	
	see	[si]	v.	看到	1	1	初級	
	bad	[bæd]	adj.	不好的	1	1	初級	
	side	[saɪd]	n.	面、側	1	1	初級	
⓭	surprised	[səˋpraɪzd]	adj.	感到驚訝的	1	1	初級	◎
⓮	favorite	[ˋfevərɪt]	n.	最愛	1	2	初級	◎
	before	[bɪˋfor]	adv.	以前	1	1	初級	
⓯	reached	[ritʃt]	p.p.	reach（到達）過去分詞	1	1	初級	◎
	limit	[ˋlɪmɪt]	n.	極限	1	1	初級	◎
	patience	[ˋpeʃəns]	n.	耐心	2	3	中級	◎

※「紅字單字」於本單元多句出現，「單字級等分析」僅列在「首次出現句」。

我喜歡／討厭的人。

MP3 088-01 ❶～❸

❶	我喜歡笑口常開的人。	I like people who smile all the time. * people who＋子句（…樣子的人） * all the time（總是）
❷	我喜歡有禮貌的人。	I like people who are polite. * polite（禮貌的）可替換為：gracious（禮貌的）
❸	我喜歡熱心公益的人。	I like people who are enthusiastic about the public welfare. * be enthusiastic about...（熱心於…）＝ be keen on * public welfare（公眾事務、公益）
❹	我喜歡運動型的男生。	I like athletic guys.
❺	我對溫柔的女生特別有好感。	I especially like tender-hearted girls. * especially like＋某人（對某人特別有好感）
❻	我敬佩腳踏實地的人。	I admire people who are practical.
❼	斯文的男生深得我心。	Gentlemanly men always capture my heart. * capture one's heart（深受喜愛）
❽	我討厭沒禮貌的人。	I don't like people who are impolite. * impolite（沒禮貌的）可替換為： 　self-righteous（自視甚高的）、childish（幼稚的）
❾	我討厭不守信用的人。	I hate people who do not keep their promises. * keep one's promises（信守承諾）
❿	我討厭沒有時間觀念的人。	I dislike people who have no sense of punctuality. * have no sense of punctuality（沒有守時觀念）
⓫	我從不跟不擇手段的人打交道。	I refuse to have anything to do with unscrupulous people. * refuse to＋動詞原形（拒絕…） * have anything to do with＋某人（和某人有任何瓜葛） * have nothing to do with＋某人（和某人沒有任何瓜葛）
⓬	自私的人讓我很反感。	Selfish people give me a bad feeling. * 人事物＋give me a bad feeling（某人事物讓我反感） * 人事物＋give me a good feeling（某人事物給我好感）
⓭	我瞧不起馬屁精。	I look down on people who brown-nose. * look down on＋某人（鄙視某人）＝ look down upon

	單字	音標	詞性	意義	字頻	大考	英檢	多益
❶	like	[laɪk]	v.	喜歡	1	1	初級	
	people	[ˈpipl̩]	n.	person（人）複數	1	1	初級	
	smile	[smaɪl]	v.	微笑	1	1	初級	
	all	[ɔl]	adj.	全部的	1	1	初級	
	time	[taɪm]	n.	時間	1	1	初級	◎
❷	polite	[pəˈlaɪt]	adj.	禮貌的	2	2	初級	◎
❸	enthusiastic	[ɪn͵θjuzɪˈæstɪk]	adj.	熱心的	2	5	中級	◎
	public	[ˈpʌblɪk]	adj.	公共的	1	1	初級	
	welfare	[ˈwɛl͵fɛr]	n.	福利	1	4	中級	◎
❹	athletic	[æθˈlɛtɪk]	adj.	運動型的	2	4	中級	◎
	guy	[gaɪ]	n.	男生	1	2	初級	
❺	especially	[əˈspɛʃəlɪ]	adv.	特別	1	2	初級	◎
	tender-hearted	[ˈtɛndəˈhɑrtɪd]	adj.	溫柔的				
	girl	[gɝl]	n.	女生	1	1	初級	
❻	admire	[ədˈmaɪr]	v.	敬佩	2	3	初級	◎
	practical	[ˈpræktɪkl̩]	adj.	腳踏實地的	1	3	中級	◎
❼	gentlemanly	[ˈdʒɛntl̩mənlɪ]	adj.	斯文的				
	men	[mɛn]	n.	man（男生）複數	1	1	初級	
	always	[ˈɔlwez]	adv.	總是	1	1	初級	
	capture	[ˈkæptʃɚ]	v.	擄獲	1	3	中級	◎
	heart	[hɑrt]	n.	心	1	1	初級	
❽	impolite	[͵ɪmpəˈlaɪt]	adj.	不禮貌的			初級	
❾	hate	[het]	v.	討厭	1	1	初級	
	keep	[kip]	v.	信守	1	1	初級	◎
	promise	[ˈprɑmɪs]	n.	承諾	1	2	初級	◎
❿	dislike	[dɪsˈlaɪk]	v.	不喜歡	3	3	中級	
	have	[hæv]	v.	擁有	1	1	初級	
	sense	[sɛns]	n.	觀念	1	1	初級	◎
	punctuality	[͵pʌŋktʃʊˈælətɪ]	n.	守時				
⓫	refuse	[rɪˈfjuz]	v.	拒絕	1	2	初級	◎
	anything	[ˈɛnɪ͵θɪŋ]	pron.	任何事情	1	1	初級	
	do	[du]	v.	有瓜葛	1	1	初級	
	unscrupulous	[ʌnˈskrupjələs]	adj.	不講究道義原則的	7			
⓬	selfish	[ˈsɛlfɪʃ]	adj.	自私的	3	1	初級	
	give	[gɪv]	v.	給予	1	1	初級	
	bad	[bæd]	adj.	不好的	1	1	初級	
	feeling	[ˈfilɪŋ]	n.	感覺	1	1	初級	
⓭	look	[lʊk]	v.	看待	1	1	初級	
	down	[daʊn]	adv.	貶低地	1	1	初級	
	brown-nose	[ˈbraʊn͵noz]	v.	拍馬屁、奉承				

※「紅字單字」於本單元多句出現，「單字級等分析」僅列在「首次出現句」。

🔵 MP3 088-02 ❶～⓯

❶	什麼樣的人令你心動？	What kind of people impress you? * **What kind of…**（什麼樣的…）
❷	你有喜歡的人嗎？	Is there anyone you like? * **Is there anyone you dislike?** （你有討厭的人嗎？）
❸	你喜歡她的個性還是外表？	Do you like her personality or her looks? * **like＋名詞**（喜歡…） * **hate＋名詞**（討厭…）
❹	什麼樣的人令你作嘔？	What kind of people make you sick? * **某人＋make me sick**（某人讓我感到不舒服）
❺	你喜歡幽默的男生嗎？	Do you like funny guys? * **funny**（幽默的）可替換為：**humorous**（幽默的）
❻	你討厭誰？	Who do you dislike?
❼	你喜歡直率的女生嗎？	Do you like forthright girls?
❽	你喜歡的人長得好不好看？	Is the person you like good-looking? * **the person you like**（你喜歡的人）
❾	哪種人最讓你抓狂？	What kind of people drive you crazy? * **drive＋某人＋crazy**（使某人抓狂）
❿	你瞭解你喜歡的人嗎？	Do you understand the people you like?
⓫	你討厭不誠實的人嗎？	Do you hate dishonest people?
⓬	他有那麼好嗎？	Is he really so nice? * **Is he really so bad?**（他有那麼糟嗎？）
⓭	你討厭一個人會怎麼做？	What do you do when you dislike someone?
⓮	他沒有任何優點嗎？	Doesn't he have any virtues? * **Doesn't he have any defects?** （他沒有任何缺點嗎？） * **defect**（缺點）
⓯	他哪裡惹你了？	What has he done to offend you? * **What has he done…?**（他曾經做了什麼…？） * 此句用「現在完成式」（…has…done…） 表示「過去到現在發生過、經歷過的事」。

單字級等分析

	單字	音標	詞性	意義	字頻	大考	英檢	多益
❶	kind	[kaɪnd]	n.	類型	1	1	初級	
	people	[ˈpipl̩]	n.	person（人）複數	1	1	初級	
	impress	[ɪmˈprɛs]	v.	使印象深刻	2	3	中級	◎
❷	there	[ðɛr]	adv.	有…	1	1	初級	
	anyone	[ˈɛnɪˌwʌn]	pron.	任何人	1	2	初級	
	like	[laɪk]	v.	喜歡	1	1	初級	
❸	personality	[ˌpɝsnˈælətɪ]	n.	個性	1	3	中級	
	looks	[lʊks]	n.	外表	1		初級	
❹	make	[mek]	v.	使得	1	1	初級	
	sick	[sɪk]	adj.	不舒服的、作嘔的	1	1	初級	◎
❺	funny	[ˈfʌnɪ]	adj.	幽默的	1	1	初級	
	guy	[gaɪ]	n.	男生	1	2	初級	
❻	dislike	[dɪsˈlaɪk]	v.	不喜歡	3	3	中級	
❼	forthright	[forθˈraɪt]	adj.	直率的	6			
	girl	[gɝl]	n.	女生	1	1	初級	
❽	person	[ˈpɝsn]	n.	人	1	1	初級	
	good-looking	[ˈgʊdˈlʊkɪŋ]	adj.	長相好看的	4		中高	
❾	drive	[draɪv]	v.	驅使	1	1	初級	◎
	crazy	[ˈkrezɪ]	adj.	瘋狂的	1	2	初級	
❿	understand	[ˌʌndɚˈstænd]	v.	瞭解	1	1	初級	
⓫	hate	[het]	v.	討厭	1	1	初級	
	dishonest	[dɪsˈɑnɪst]	adj.	不誠實的	5	2	初級	
⓬	really	[ˈrɪəlɪ]	adv.	真的	1		初級	
	so	[so]	adv.	那麼	1		初級	
	nice	[naɪs]	adj.	美好的	1		初級	
⓭	do	[du]	v.	做	1	1	初級	
	someone	[ˈsʌmˌwʌn]	pron.	某個人	1	1	初級	
⓮	have	[hæv]	v.	擁有	1	1	初級	
	any	[ˈɛnɪ]	adj.	任何的	1	1	初級	
	virtue	[ˈvɝtʃu]	n.	優點	2	4	中級	◎
⓯	done	[dʌn]	p.p.	do（做）過去分詞	1	1	初級	
	offend	[əˈfɛnd]	v.	觸犯	2	4	中級	

※「紅字單字」於本單元多句出現，「單字級等分析」僅列在「首次出現句」。

401

089　我喜歡／討厭的顏色。

❶	我喜歡很多顏色。	I like many colors.
❷	我喜歡明亮的顏色。	I like bright colors.
❸	我沒有特別喜歡的顏色。	I don't have any particular colors that I like.
❹	我只喜歡黑色。	I only like black.
❺	我喜歡黃色。	I like yellow. * **I dislike yellow.**（我討厭黃色）
❻	我喜歡暖色調。	I like warm tones. * **warm tones**（暖色調） * **cool tones**（冷色調）
❼	我最近愛上綠色。	Recently I started liking the color green. * **start＋動詞-ing**（開始…）
❽	我喜歡天空的顏色。	I like the color of the sky. * **the color of＋事物**（某事物的顏色）
❾	紫色是我的最愛。	Purple is my favorite color.
❿	我喜歡彩虹繽紛的顏色。	I like the rich colors of the rainbow.
⓫	我偏愛深色的衣服。	I prefer dark-colored clothing. * **light-colored**（淺色的）
⓬	橘色讓我心情開朗。	Orange makes me feel optimistic. * **make＋某人＋動詞原形**（使某人…） * **feel＋形容詞**（覺得…，感到…）
⓭	我討厭暗的顏色。	I hate gloomy colors.
⓮	粉紅色很襯我的膚色。	Pink is a good shade for my skin. * **for...**（對於…）
⓯	紅色給我溫暖的感覺。	Red gives me a feeling of warmth. * **give a feeling of...**（給我…的感覺）
⓰	我不喜歡穿黑色衣服。	I don't like to wear black clothes.
⓱	我從來不買咖啡色的衣服。	I never buy brown clothing. * **I never＋動詞**（我從來不做…）
⓲	我覺得黑色令人心情沈重。	I think black makes people feel somber. * **I think＋子句**（我覺得…）

	單字	音標	詞性	意義	字頻	大考	英檢	多益
❶	like	[laɪk]	v.	喜歡	1	1	初級	
	many	[ˋmɛnɪ]	adj.	許多的	1	1	初級	
	color	[ˋkʌlə]	n.	顏色	1	1	初級	
❷	bright	[braɪt]	adj.	明亮的	1	1	初級	
❸	have	[hæv]	v.	擁有	1	1	初級	
	any	[ˋɛnɪ]	adj.	任何的	1	1	初級	
	particular	[pəˋtɪkjələ]	adj.	特別的	1	2	初級	◎
❹	only	[ˋonlɪ]	adv.	只有	1	1	初級	
	black	[blæk]	n./adj.	黑色/黑色的	1	1	初級	
❺	yellow	[ˋjɛlo]	n.	黃色	1	1	初級	
❻	warm	[wɔrm]	adj.	溫暖的	1	1	初級	
	tone	[tʌn]	n.	色調	1	1	中級	◎
❼	recently	[ˋrisntlɪ]	adv.	最近	1		初級	
	started	[ˋstɑrtɪd]	p.t.	start（開始）過去式	1	1	初級	
	liking	[ˋlaɪkɪŋ]	n.	like（喜歡）動名詞	6	1	初級	
	green	[grin]	n.	綠色	1	1	初級	
❽	sky	[skaɪ]	n.	天空	1	1	初級	
❾	purple	[ˋpɝpl]	adj.	紫色	2	1	初級	
	favorite	[ˋfevərɪt]	adj.	最喜歡的	1	2	初級	◎
❿	rich	[rɪtʃ]	adj.	多元的、繽紛的	1	1	初級	
	rainbow	[ˋren.bo]	n.	彩虹	3	1	初級	
⓫	prefer	[prɪˋfɝ]	v.	偏愛	1	2	初級	◎
	dark-colored	[ˋdɑrkˋkʌləd]	adj.	深色的				
	clothing	[ˋkloðɪŋ]	n.	衣服	1	2	中級	
⓬	orange	[ˋɔrɪndʒ]	n.	橘色	2	1	初級	
	make	[mek]	v.	使得	1	1	初級	
	feel	[fil]	v.	感覺	1	1	初級	
	optimistic	[.ɑptəˋmɪstɪk]	adj.	開朗樂觀的	2	3	中高	◎
⓭	hate	[het]	v.	討厭	1	1	初級	
	gloomy	[ˋglumɪ]	adj.	陰暗的	4	6	中高	◎
⓮	pink	[pɪŋk]	n.	粉紅色	1	2	初級	◎
	good	[gʊd]	adj.	良好的	1	1	初級	◎
	shade	[ʃed]	n.	某顏色的濃淡色度	2	3	中級	◎
	skin	[skɪn]	n.	皮膚	1	1	初級	◎
⓯	red	[rɛd]	n.	紅色	1	1	初級	
	give	[gɪv]	v.	給予	1	1	初級	
	feeling	[ˋfilɪŋ]	n.	感覺	1	1	初級	
	warmth	[wɔrmθ]	n.	溫暖	2	3	中級	
⓰	wear	[wɛr]	v.	穿著	1	1	初級	◎
	clothes	[kloz]	n.	cloth（衣服）複數	1	2	初級	
⓱	never	[ˋnɛvə]	adv.	從不	1	1	初級	
	buy	[baɪ]	v.	購買	1	1	初級	
	brown	[braʊn]	adj.	咖啡色的	1	1	初級	
⓲	think	[θɪŋk]	v.	認為	1	1	初級	
	people	[ˋpipl]	n.	person（人）複數	1	1	初級	
	somber	[ˋsɑmbə]	adj.	憂鬱的	4			◎

※「紅字單字」於本單元多句出現，「單字級等分析」僅列在「首次出現句」。

089 你喜歡／討厭的顏色？

❶	你喜歡明亮的顏色嗎？	Do you like bright colors?
❷	你討厭什麼樣的顏色？	What colors do you dislike? * **What color...?**（什麼顏色…？）= **Which color...?**
❸	你為什麼喜歡灰色？	Why do you like the color gray? * **the color**＋顏色（某個顏色）
❹	你討厭晦暗的顏色嗎？	Do you hate gloomy colors?
❺	你偏愛深色還是淺色？	Do you prefer dark colors or light colors?
❻	你最喜歡哪一種顏色？	What colors do you like the most?
❼	你喜歡暖色調還是寒色調？	Do you like warm tones or cool tones?
❽	你喜歡黑色還是白色？	Do you like black or white?
❾	你喜歡深藍色還是淺藍色？	Do you like dark blue or light blue? * **dark**＋顏色（深的某顏色） * **light**＋顏色（淺的某顏色）
❿	你覺得哪個顏色最適合你？	Which color do you think suits you best? * **suit**＋某人（適合某人）
⓫	你喜歡買什麼顏色的衣服？	What color clothes do you like to buy? * **What color**＋某物...?（什麼顏色的某物…？）
⓬	你為什麼喜歡紅色？	Why do you like red?
⓭	你喜歡什麼顏色的花？	What color flowers do you like?
⓮	什麼顏色的衣服你絕對不穿？	What color clothing will you never put on? * **will**（願意）、**put on**（穿著）= **wear**
⓯	白色給你什麼感覺？	What do you associate with the color white? * **associate with**＋某物（對某物有聯想） 　= **have an association with**＋某物
⓰	每一種顏色你都喜歡嗎？	Do you like every color?
⓱	每個人對顏色的喜惡很主觀。	Everyone's appreciation of color is subjective. * **everyone's appreciation of**＋某物 　（每個人對某物的欣賞） * **objective**（客觀的）

	單字	音標	詞性	意義	字頻	大考	英檢	多益
❶	like	[laɪk]	v.	喜歡	1	1	初級	
	bright	[braɪt]	adj.	明亮的	1	1	初級	
	color	[ˋkʌlə]	n.	顏色	1	1	初級	
❷	dislike	[dɪsˋlaɪk]	v.	討厭	3	3	中級	
❸	gray	[gre]	n.	灰色	1	1	初級	
❹	hate	[het]	v.	討厭	1	1	初級	
	gloomy	[ˋglumɪ]	adj.	陰暗的	4	6	中高	◎
❺	prefer	[prɪˋfɝ]	v.	偏愛	1	2	初級	◎
	dark	[dɑrk]	adj.	深的	1	1	初級	
	light	[laɪt]	adj.	淺的	1	1	初級	
❻	most	[most]	adv.	最	1	1	初級	
❼	warm	[wɔrm]	adj.	溫暖的	1	1	初級	
	tone	[tʌn]	n.	色調	1	1	中級	◎
	cool	[kul]	adj.	冷色調的	1	1	初級	
❽	black	[blæk]	n.	黑色	1	1	初級	
	white	[hwaɪt]	n.	白色	1	1	初級	
❾	blue	[blu]	n.	藍色	1	1	初級	
❿	think	[θɪŋk]	v.	認為	1	1	初級	
	suit	[sut]	v.	適合	1	2	初級	◎
	best	[bɛst]	adv.	well（良好地）最高級	1	1	初級	
⓫	clothes	[kloz]	n.	cloth（衣服）複數	1	2	初級	
	buy	[baɪ]	v.	購買	1	1	初級	
⓬	red	[rɛd]	n.	紅色	1	1	初級	
⓭	flower	[ˋflauə]	n.	花	1	1	初級	
⓮	clothing	[ˋkloðɪŋ]	n.	衣服	1	2	中級	
	never	[ˋnɛvə]	adv.	從不	1	1	初級	
	put	[put]	v.	穿著	1	1	初級	
⓯	associate	[əˋsoʃɪt]	v.	聯想	1	4	中級	◎
⓰	every	[ˋɛvrɪ]	adj.	每一	1	1	初級	
⓱	everyone	[ˋɛvrɪ͵wʌn]	pron.	每個人	1		初級	
	appreciation	[ə͵priʃɪˋeʃən]	n.	欣賞、鑑賞	2	4	中級	◎
	subjective	[səbˋdʒɛktɪv]	adj.	主觀的	3	6	中高	◎

※「紅字單字」於本單元多句出現，「單字級等分析」僅列在「首次出現句」。

090 打招呼。

🔊 MP3 090-01 ❶～❿

❶	嗨！您好。	Hi! = Hello.
❷	好久不見。	It's been a long time. * 此句用「現在完成式」（...has been...） 　表示「過去持續到現在的事」。
❸	早安。	Good morning.
❹	午安。	Good afternoon.
❺	晚安。	Good evening.
❻	一切都好嗎？	How's everything? * How＋be動詞＋人事物？（某人事物的狀態如何？）
❼	你今天好嗎？	How are you today?
❽	最近過得如何？	How have you been lately?
❾	工作順利嗎？	Is your work going well?　* go well（順利）
❿	嘿！怎麼樣啊？	Hey, what's up?
⓫	最近心情愉快嗎？	Have you been in a good mood lately? * in a good mood（心情愉快）
⓬	吃過飯了嗎？	Have you eaten? * Have you＋過去分詞？（你是否已經…？）
⓭	有什麼好消息要告訴我嗎？	Do you want to tell me something good? * something good（好消息） * something bad（壞消息）
⓮	今天天氣真的很不錯。	The weather is very good today.
⓯	你的家人都好嗎？	How is your family?
⓰	你今天看起來真漂亮。	You look very beautiful today.
⓱	你有心事嗎？	Are you worried about something? * be worried about（擔心）
⓲	之前我們是不是見過面？	Have we met before? * 此句用「現在完成式問句」（Has...met...?） 　表示「從過去到現在是否發生過、經歷過某事」。
⓳	這些日子你跑哪去了？	Where have you been these past few days? * past few days（過去幾天）

	單字	音標	詞性	意義	字頻	大考	英檢	多益
❶	hi	[haɪ]	int.	嗨、您好	1		初級	
	hello	[həˋlo]	int.	嗨、您好	1	1	初級	
❷	long	[lɔŋ]	adj.	長的	1	1	初級	
	time	[taɪm]	n.	時間	1	1	初級	◎
❸	good	[gʊd]	adj.	良好的	1	1	初級	◎
	morning	[ˋmɔrnɪŋ]	n.	早上	1	1	初級	
❹	afternoon	[ˋæftɚˋnun]	n.	下午	1	1	初級	
❺	evening	[ˋivnɪŋ]	n.	晚上	1	1	初級	
❻	everything	[ˋɛvrɪ.θɪŋ]	pron.	每件事情	1		初級	
❼	today	[təˋde]	adv.	今天	1	1	初級	
❽	lately	[ˋletlɪ]	adv.	最近	2	4	中級	
❾	work	[wɝk]	v.	工作	1	1	初級	◎
	going	[ˋgoɪŋ]	p.pr.	go（進行）現在分詞	4	1	初級	
	well	[wɛl]	adv.	順利地	1	1	初級	◎
❿	hey	[he]	int.	嘿	1		初級	
	up	[ʌp]	adv.	發生…、怎麼回事…	1	1	初級	
⓫	mood	[mud]	n.	心情	1	3	中級	◎
⓬	eaten	[ˋitn]	p.p.	eat（吃飯）過去分詞	1	1	初級	
⓭	want	[wɑnt]	v.	想要	1	1	初級	◎
	tell	[tɛl]	v.	告訴	1	1	初級	
	something	[ˋsʌmθɪŋ]	pron.	某些事情	1	1	初級	
⓮	weather	[ˋwɛðɚ]	n.	天氣	1	1	初級	◎
	very	[ˋvɛrɪ]	adv.	非常	1	1	初級	
⓯	family	[ˋfæmlɪ]	n.	家人	1	1	初級	
⓰	look	[lʊk]	v.	看起來	1	1	初級	
	beautiful	[ˋbjutəfəl]	adj.	漂亮的	1	1	初級	
⓱	worried	[ˋwɝɪd]	adj.	擔心的	2	1	中級	◎
⓲	met	[mɛt]	p.p.	meet（見面）過去分詞	1	1	初級	
	before	[bɪˋfor]	adv.	以前	1	1	初級	
⓳	these	[ðiz]	adj.	這些	1	1	初級	
	past	[pæst]	adj.	過去的	1	1	初級	
	few	[fju]	adj.	些許的	1	1	初級	◎
	day	[de]	n.	天	1	1	初級	

※「紅字單字」於本單元多句出現，「單字級等分析」僅列在「首次出現句」。

090　回應打招呼。

❶	您好。	Hello.
❷	是啊，您好嗎？	Yes, how are you?
❸	早安！	Good morning!
❹	午安，要一起用餐嗎？	Good afternoon, do you want to join us for a meal? * **want to**（想要）、**join**＋某人（和某人一起做…）
❺	晚安，您也好嗎？	Good evening, how are you?
❻	我今天心情不錯。	I feel good today. ＝ I'm in a good mood today. * **feel good**（心情很好）＝ **be in a good mood**
❼	我很好。你呢？	I'm fine, and you?
❽	我剛用過餐，你吃過了嗎？	I just had my meal. Have you eaten? * **just**＋動詞過去式（剛剛才做了…）
❾	是啊，太陽終於露臉了。	Yes, the sun has finally come out. * **come out**（（太陽）出來、露臉）
❿	我要結婚了。	I'm getting married. * **get married**（結婚） * 此句用「現在進行式」（...am getting...）表示「已排定時程的個人未來計畫」。
⓫	一切都順利。	Everything is going well.
⓬	是的，我們在艾咪家的聚會上見過一次面。	Yes, we met once at a party at Amy's. * **met once**（見過一次） * **at**＋某人＋**'s**（在某人的家）
⓭	謝謝，你也是。	Thanks, you too.
⓮	託你的福，大家都很好。	Thanks to you, everybody is fine. * **Thanks to**＋人事物（多虧某人事物、託某人事物的福）
⓯	謝謝。不用替我操心。	Thanks. Don't worry about me.
⓰	嗯，最近不太順利。	Yeah, things haven't been too good recently. * **not be too good**（不太好、不太順利）
⓱	我也很高興看到你！	I'm happy to see you, too!
⓲	還不錯。	Not bad.

	單字	音標	詞性	意義	字頻	大考	英檢	多益
❶	hello	[həˋlo]	int.	嗨、您好	1	1	初級	
❷	yes	[jɛs]	int.	是啊	1	1	初級	
❸	good	[gʊd]	adj.	良好的	1	1	初級	◎
	morning	[ˋmɔrnɪŋ]	n.	早上	1	1	初級	
❹	afternoon	[ˋæftɚˋnun]	n.	下午	1	1	初級	
	want	[wɑnt]	v.	想要	1	1	初級	◎
	join	[dʒɔɪn]	v.	加入	1	1	初級	◎
	meal	[mil]	n.	一餐	1	2	初級	
❺	evening	[ˋivnɪŋ]	n.	晚上	1	1	初級	
❻	feel	[fil]	v.	感覺	1	1	初級	
	today	[təˋde]	adv.	今天	1	1	初級	◎
	mood	[mud]	n.	心情	1	3	中級	◎
❼	fine	[faɪn]	adj.	很好的	1	1	初級	◎
❽	just	[dʒʌst]	adv.	剛剛	1	1	初級	
	had	[hæd]	p.t.	have（用餐）過去式	1	1	初級	
	eaten	[ˋitn]	p.p.	eat（吃飯）過去分詞	1	1	初級	
❾	sun	[sʌn]	n.	太陽	1	1	初級	
	finally	[ˋfaɪnlɪ]	adv.	終於	1		初級	
	come	[kʌm]	p.p.	come（出來、露臉）過去分詞	1	1	初級	
	out	[aʊt]	adv.	出現	1	1	初級	
❿	getting	[ˋgɛtɪŋ]	p.pr.	get（變成）現在分詞	1	1	初級	◎
	married	[ˋmærɪd]	p.p.	marry（結婚）過去分詞	1		初級	
⓫	everything	[ˋɛvrɪ.θɪŋ]	pron.	每件事情	1		初級	
	going	[ˋgoɪŋ]	p.pr.	go（進行）現在分詞	4		初級	
	well	[wɛl]	adv.	順利地	1	1	初級	◎
⓬	met	[mɛt]	p.t.	meet（見面）過去式	1	1	初級	
	once	[wʌns]	adv.	一次	1	1	初級	
	party	[ˋpɑrtɪ]	n.	派對	1	1	初級	◎
⓭	thanks	[θæŋks]	n.	thank（感謝）複數	1			
	too	[tu]	adv.	也/過於	1	1	初級	
⓮	everybody	[ˋɛvrɪ.bɑdɪ]	pron.	每個人	1		初級	
⓯	worry	[ˋwɝɪ]	v.	操心	1	1	初級	◎
⓰	yeah	[ˋjɛə]	int.	嗯	1	1	初級	
	thing	[θɪŋ]	n.	事情	1	1	初級	
	recently	[ˋrisntlɪ]	adv.	最近	1		初級	
⓱	happy	[ˋhæpɪ]	adj.	高興的	1	1	初級	
	see	[si]	v.	看到	1	1	初級	
⓲	bad	[bæd]	adj.	不好的	1	1	初級	

※「紅字單字」於本單元多句出現，「單字級等分析」僅列在「首次出現句」。

🔵 MP3 091-01 ❶～❷

❶	再見！	See you around! = Goodbye! = See you later!
❷	掰掰。	Bye-bye.
❸	我會想你的。	I will miss you. ＊此句用「未來簡單式」（...will...）表示「有意願做的事」。
❹	別太想我。	Don't miss me too much.
❺	珍重再見。	Goodbye and take good care of yourself. ＊take good care（好好保重）
❻	祝你一帆風順。	I hope everything goes smoothly.
❼	祝你有美好的一天！	Have a nice day!
❽	好好照顧自己。	Take good care of yourself.
❾	五點見。	I'll see you at five. ＊see＋某人（和某人見面）
❿	晚安。	Good night.
⓫	路上小心。	Take care on the road. = Have a good trip.
⓬	好好過週末喔！	Have a nice weekend!
⓭	戲院門口見。	See you in front of the theater. ＊in front of＋某地（在某地門口、在某地前面）
⓮	有個好夢。	Sweet dreams.
⓯	一夜好眠喔！	Sleep tight!
⓰	記得寫信給我。	Remember to write me. ＊Remember to＋動詞原形（你要記得做…）
⓱	明天見。	See you tomorrow.
⓲	記得回 email 給我。	Remember to email me back.
⓳	記得寫明信片給我。	Remember to send me a postcard.
⓴	記得打電話給我。	Remember to call me.
㉑	玩得開心點！	Have fun!
㉒	要再來喔！	Come again!
㉓	一路順風啊！	Bon voyage!

單字級等分析

	單字	音標	詞性	意義	字頻	大考	英檢	多益
❶	see	[si]	v.	再見	1	1	初級	
	around	[əˋraʊnd]	adv.	回頭、四處	1	1	初級	
	goodbye	[ˏɡʊdˋbaɪ]	int.	再見	2	1		
	later	[ˋletɚ]	adv.	待會	1		初級	
❷	bye-bye	[ˋbaɪˏbaɪ]	int.	掰掰	5	1		
❸	miss	[mɪs]	v.	想念	1	1	初級	
❹	too	[tu]	adv.	過於	1	1	初級	
	much	[mʌtʃ]	adv.	非常	1	1	初級	
❺	take	[tek]	v.	採取	1	1	初級	◎
	good	[ɡʊd]	adj.	良好的	1	1	初級	◎
	care	[kɛr]	n.	照顧	1	1	初級	◎
	yourself	[jʊɚˋsɛlf]	pron.	你自己	1		初級	
❻	hope	[hop]	v.	希望	1	1	初級	
	everything	[ˋɛvrɪˏθɪŋ]	pron.	每件事情	1		初級	
	go	[ɡo]	v.	進行	1	1	初級	
	smoothly	[ˋsmuðlɪ]	adv.	順利地	3			◎
❼	have	[hæv]	v.	擁有	1	1	初級	
	nice	[naɪs]	adj.	美好的	1	1	初級	
	day	[de]	n.	天	1	1	初級	
❾	five	[faɪv]	n.	五點	1	1	初級	
❿	night	[naɪt]	n.	晚上	1	1	初級	
⓫	road	[rod]	n.	路途	1	1	初級	
	trip	[trɪp]	n.	路程	1	1	初級	◎
⓬	weekend	[ˋwikˏɛnd]	n.	週末	1	1	初級	
⓭	front	[frʌnt]	n.	前面	1	1	初級	
	theater	[ˋθɪətɚ]	n.	戲院	1	2	初級	
⓮	sweet	[swit]	adj.	甜美的	1	1	初級	
	dream	[drim]	n.	夢	1	1	初級	
⓯	sleep	[slip]	v.	睡覺	1	1	初級	
	tight	[taɪt]	adv.	睡得安穩地	1	3	中級	◎
⓰	remember	[rɪˋmɛmbɚ]	v.	記得	1	1	初級	◎
	write	[raɪt]	v.	寫信	1	1	初級	
⓱	tomorrow	[təˋmoro]	adv.	明天	1	1	初級	◎
⓲	email	[ˋimel]	v.	寫電子郵件	2	4		
	back	[bæk]	adv.	寄回	1	1	初級	◎
⓳	send	[sɛnd]	v.	寄送	1	1	初級	
	postcard	[ˋpostˏkard]	n.	明信片	3	2	初級	
⓴	call	[kɔl]	v.	打電話	1	1	初級	◎
㉑	fun	[fʌn]	n.	樂趣	1	1	初級	
㉒	come	[kʌm]	v.	前來	1	1	初級	
	again	[əˋɡɛn]	adv.	再次	1	1	初級	
㉓	bon voyage	[bɑn vɔrˋɑdʒ]	int.	（法語）一路順風				

※「紅字單字」於本單元多句出現，「單字級等分析」僅列在「首次出現句」。　411

MP3 091-02 ❶～❿

❶	再見！	Goodbye! = See you around! = See you later!
❷	掰掰。	Bye-bye!
❸	我也會想你的。	I'll miss you, too.
❹	別太想我。	Don't miss me too much.
❺	我會照顧自己的。	I can take care of myself. * take care of oneself（照顧自己）
❻	請不用為我操心。	Don't worry about me, please.
❼	我會寄明信片給你。	I will send you a postcard.
❽	明天見。	See you tomorrow.
❾	我會小心。	I'll be careful.
❿	晚安。	Good night.
⓫	我一到學校就打電話給你。	Once I arrive at school, I will call you. * once＋子句（一旦…）
⓬	等我的消息。	Wait to hear news from me. * hear news（收到消息）、from＋某人（來自某人）
⓭	我又不是不回台北了。	It's not like I am not coming back to Taipei. * It's not like＋子句（並不是…那樣） * 子句用「現在進行式」（...am not coming...） 　表示「已排定時程的個人未來計畫」。
⓮	我怕自己會太想家。	I am afraid that I'll miss home too much. * be afraid that＋子句（害怕…） * miss home（想家）
⓯	我只是出去一個星期，馬上就回來了。	I'm only going away for a week; I'll be right back. * go away（離開家裡一段時間）
⓰	別難過啦！	Don't be so sad!
⓱	謝謝大家來送我。	Thank you, everyone, for seeing me off. * see＋某人＋off（為某人送行）
⓲	大家讓我好感動。	Everyone has really touched me. * 此句用「現在完成式」（...has...touched...）表示 　「過去某時點發生某事，且結果持續到現在」。

	單字	音標	詞性	意義	字頻	大考	英檢	多益
❶	goodbye	[ˌɡʊdˋbaɪ]	int.	再見	2	1		
	see	[si]	v.	再見	1	1	初級	
	around	[əˋraʊnd]	adv.	回頭、四處	1		初級	
	later	[ˋletə]	adv.	待會	1		初級	
❷	bye-bye	[ˋbaɪˌbaɪ]	int.	掰掰	5	1		
❸	miss	[mɪs]	v.	想念	1	1	初級	
	too	[tu]	adv.	過於	1	1	初級	
❹	much	[mʌtʃ]	adv.	非常	1	1	初級	
❺	take	[tek]	v.	採取	1	1	初級	◎
	care	[kɛr]	n.	照顧	1	1	初級	◎
	myself	[maɪˋsɛlf]	pron.	我自己	1		初級	
❻	worry	[ˋwɝɪ]	v.	擔心	1	1	初級	◎
	please	[pliz]	adv.	請	1	1	初級	
❼	send	[sɛnd]	v.	寄送	1	1	初級	
	postcard	[ˋpostˌkɑrd]	n.	明信片	3	2	初級	
❽	tomorrow	[təˋmɔro]	adv.	明天	1	1	初級	◎
❾	careful	[ˋkɛrfəl]	adj.	小心的	1	1	初級	
❿	good	[ɡʊd]	adj.	良好的	1	1	初級	
	night	[naɪt]	n.	夜晚	1	1	初級	
⓫	arrive	[əˋraɪv]	v.	到達	1	2	初級	◎
	school	[skul]	n.	學校	1	1	初級	
	call	[kɔl]	v.	打電話	1	1	初級	◎
⓬	wait	[wet]	v.	等待	1	1	初級	◎
	hear	[hɪr]	v.	收到	1	1	初級	
	news	[njuz]	n.	消息	1	1	初級	◎
⓭	coming	[ˋkʌmɪŋ]	p.pr.	come（前來）現在分詞	2	1	中級	
	back	[bæk]	adv.	返回	1	1	初級	◎
	Taipei	[ˋtaɪˋpe]	n.	台北				
⓮	afraid	[əˋfred]	adj.	害怕的	1	1	初級	
	home	[hom]	n.	家	1	1	初級	
⓯	only	[ˋonlɪ]	adv.	只是	1	1	初級	
	going	[ˋɡoɪŋ]	p.pr.	go（去）現在分詞	4	1	初級	
	away	[əˋwe]	adv.	離開	1	1	初級	
	week	[wik]	n.	一週	1	1	初級	
	right	[raɪt]	adv.	馬上	1	1	初級	
⓰	so	[so]	adv.	這麼	1	1	初級	
	sad	[sæd]	adj.	難過的	1	1	初級	
⓱	thank	[θæŋk]	v.	感謝	1	1	初級	
	everyone	[ˋɛvrɪˌwʌn]	pron.	大家	1		初級	
	seeing	[ˋsiɪŋ]	n.	see（送行）動名詞	7	1	初級	
	off	[ɔf]	adv.	離開	1	1	初級	
⓲	really	[ˋrɪəlɪ]	adv.	很、十分	1		初級	
	touched	[tʌtʃt]	p.p.	touch（感動）過去分詞	1	1	初級	◎

※「紅字單字」於本單元多句出現，「單字級等分析」僅列在「首次出現句」。

MP3 092-01 ❶～⓲

❶	早安！	Good morning!
❷	午安！	Good afternoon!
❸	最近好嗎？	How's it been these days? = How have you been lately? = How is everything?
❹	晚安！（打招呼）	Good evening!
❺	晚安！（道別）	Good night!
❻	最近身體好嗎？	How has your health been these days? * How have / has＋人事物＋been...? （某人事物一直以來的狀態如何？）
❼	你今天氣色不錯ㄟ！	Don't you look great today!
❽	最近都在忙什麼？	What have you been busy with recently? * be busy with＋某事（忙於某事）
❾	最近工作如何？	How's your work been going lately?
❿	有什麼事困擾著你嗎？	Is there anything that's been bothering you recently?　* Is there＋名詞...?（是否有…呢）
⓫	家人好嗎？	How's your family?
⓬	有喜事嗎？	Anything positive happen lately? * anything positive（任何的好事）
⓭	吃飽了嗎？	Are you full? = Are you done?
⓮	今天天氣真好。	The weather is really nice today.
⓯	你好像瘦了？	You've lost some weight, haven't you? * have lost weight（瘦了） * have put on weight（胖了）
⓰	週末去哪裡玩啦？	Where did you go over the weekend? * over（在…期間）
⓱	找個時間到我家坐坐吧？	Would you like to come over to my house sometime?　* come over（前來拜訪、過來坐坐）
⓲	我有事先走，下次再聊。	I have something to do; I'll talk to you later. * talk to you later（改天再聊）

	單字	音標	詞性	意義	字頻	大考	英檢	多益
❶	good	[gʊd]	adj.	良好的	1	1	初級	◎
	morning	[ˋmɔrnɪŋ]	n.	早上	1	1	初級	
❷	afternoon	[ˋæftɚˋnun]	n.	下午	1	1	初級	
❸	these	[ðiz]	adj.	這些	1	1	初級	
	day	[de]	n.	天	1	1	初級	
	lately	[ˋletlɪ]	adv.	最近	2	4	中級	
	everything	[ˋɛvrɪˏθɪŋ]	pron.	每件事情	1		初級	
❹	evening	[ˋivnɪŋ]	n.	晚上	1	1	初級	
❺	night	[naɪt]	n.	夜晚	1	1	初級	
❻	health	[hɛlθ]	n.	健康	1	1	初級	◎
❼	look	[lʊk]	v.	看起來	1	1	初級	
	great	[gret]	adj.	極好的	1	1	初級	◎
	today	[təˋde]	adv.	今天	1	1	初級	
❽	busy	[ˋbɪzɪ]	adj.	忙碌的	1	1	初級	
	recently	[ˋrisntlɪ]	adv.	最近	1		初級	
❾	work	[wɝk]	n.	工作	1	1	初級	◎
	going	[ˋgoɪŋ]	p.pr.	go（進行）現在分詞	4		初級	
❿	there	[ðɛr]	adv.	有…	1	1	初級	
	anything	[ˋɛnɪˏθɪŋ]	pron.	任何事情	1	1	初級	
	bothering	[ˋbɑðɚɪŋ]	p.pr.	bother（打擾）現在分詞	1	2	初級	◎
⓫	family	[ˋfæməlɪ]	n.	家庭	1	1	初級	
⓬	positive	[ˋpɑzətɪv]	adj.	正向的	1	2	初級	◎
	happen	[ˋhæpən]	v.	發生	1	1	初級	
⓭	full	[fʊl]	adj.	吃飽的	1	1	初級	
	done	[dʌn]	p.p.	do（吃飽）過去分詞	1	1	初級	
⓮	weather	[ˋwɛðɚ]	n.	天氣	1	1	初級	◎
	really	[ˋrɪəlɪ]	adv.	真的	1		初級	
	nice	[naɪs]	adj.	良好的	1	1	初級	
⓯	lost	[lɔst]	p.p.	lose（降低）過去分詞	1	2	中高	◎
	some	[sʌm]	adj.	一些	1	1	初級	
	weight	[wet]	n.	體重	1	1	初級	◎
⓰	go	[go]	v.	去	1	1	初級	
	weekend	[ˋwikˏɛnd]	n.	週末	1	1	初級	
⓱	like	[laɪk]	v.	喜歡	1	1	初級	
	come	[kʌm]	v.	前來	1	1	初級	
	house	[haʊs]	n.	家	1	1	初級	◎
	sometime	[ˋsʌmˏtaɪm]	adv.	某個時間	1	1	初級	
⓲	have	[hæv]	v.	擁有	1	1	初級	
	something	[ˋsʌmˏθɪŋ]	pron.	某些事情	1	1	初級	
	do	[du]	v.	做	1	1	初級	
	talk	[tɔk]	n.	聊天	1	1	初級	◎
	later	[ˋletɚ]	adv.	以後	1		初級	

※「紅字單字」於本單元多句出現，「單字級等分析」僅列在「首次出現句」。

🔊 MP3 092-02 ❶～⓱

❶	早啊。	Morning. = Good morning.
❷	晚安。（回應打招呼）	Good evening!
❸	午安。	Good afternoon.
❹	晚安。（回應道別）	Good night!
❺	我很好，你呢？	I am fine, and you?
❻	託您的福，一切都好。	Thanks to you, everything is going fine. * **Thanks to**＋人事物（託某人事物的福）
❼	沒什麼，都是些芝麻蒜皮的小事。	It's nothing, just a few minor things. * **a few**（一些）、**minor thing**（小事情）
❽	你也是啊。	You too. = Likewise.
❾	我升官了。	I got a promotion. * **get a promotion**（升職）、**get a demotion**（降職）
❿	我要結婚了。	I am going to get married.　* **be going to**（即將要）
⓫	老樣子，還在原來的公司。	Everything is the same; I am still at the same company.
⓬	我剛吃過。你呢？	I have just eaten. How about you? * 此句用「現在完成式」（…have…eaten…）表示 　「過去某時點發生某事，且結果持續到現在」。
⓭	是啊，雨總算停了。	That's right, the rain has finally stopped. * **the rain has stopped**（雨已經停了）
⓮	我每個週末爬山。要不要一起去？	I go mountain climbing every weekend. Would you like to join us?
⓯	都很好，我父母親常常提到你。	My parents are fine. They often mention you.
⓰	是啊，我減肥 5 公斤。	Yes, I've lost five kilograms.
⓱	好啊，好久沒和你喝咖啡了。	OK, it's been a while since we've had a cup of coffee together. * **it's been a while**（已經有段時間）、**since**（自從）

	單字	音標	詞性	意義	字頻	大考	英檢	多益
❶	morning	[`mɔrnɪŋ]	n.	早上	1	1	初級	
	good	[gud]	adj.	良好的	1	1	初級	◎
❷	evening	[`ivnɪŋ]	n.	晚上	1	1	初級	
❸	afternoon	[`æftɚ`nun]	n.	下午	1	1	初級	

單字級等分析

❹	night	[naɪt]	n.	夜晚	1	1	初級	
❺	fine	[faɪn]	adj./adv.	很好的/很好地	1	1	初級	◎
❻	thanks	[θæŋks]	n.	thank（感謝）複數	1			
	everything	[ˈɛvrɪˌθɪŋ]	pron.	每件事情	1		初級	
	going	[gʊd]	p.pr.	go（進展）現在分詞	4	1	初級	
❼	nothing	[ˈnʌθɪŋ]	pron.	微不足道的事	1	1	初級	
	just	[dʒʌst]	adv.	只是	1	1	初級	
	few	[fju]	adj.	些許的	1	1	初級	◎
	minor	[ˈmaɪnə]	adj.	較小的、不重要的	1	3	初級	◎
	thing	[θɪŋ]	n.	事情	1	1	初級	
❽	too	[tu]	adv.	也	1	1	初級	
	likewise	[ˈlaɪkˌwaɪz]	adv.	也	2	6	中高	
❾	got	[gɑt]	p.t.	get（取得）過去式	1	1	初級	◎
	promotion	[prəˈmoʃən]	n.	升職	2	4	中級	◎
❿	get	[gɛt]	v.	變成	1	1	初級	◎
	married	[ˈmærɪd]	p.p.	marry（結婚）過去分詞	1		初級	
⓫	same	[sem]	adj.	相同的	1	1	初級	
	still	[stɪl]	adv.	仍然	1	1	初級	◎
	company	[ˈkʌmpənɪ]	n.	公司	1	2	初級	◎
⓬	eaten	[ˈitn]	p.p.	eat（吃）過去分詞	1	1	初級	
⓭	that	[ðæt]	pron.	那個	1	1	初級	
	right	[raɪt]	adj.	沒錯的	1	1	初級	
	rain	[ren]	n.	雨	1	1	初級	
	finally	[ˈfaɪnlɪ]	adv.	總算	1		初級	
	stopped	[stɑpt]	p.p.	stop（停止）過去分詞	8	1	初級	◎
⓮	go	[go]	v.	去	1	1	初級	
	mountain	[ˈmaʊntn]	n.	山	1	1	初級	
	climbing	[ˈklaɪmɪŋ]	n.	climb（爬、攀登）動名詞	3	1	中級	◎
	every	[ˈɛvrɪ]	adj.	每一	1	1	初級	
	weekend	[ˈwikˌɛnd]	n.	週末	1	1	初級	
	like	[laɪk]	v.	想要	1	1	初級	
	join	[dʒɔɪn]	v.	加入	1	1	初級	◎
⓯	parents	[ˈpɛrənts]	n.	parent（雙親）複數	2	1		
	often	[ˈɔfən]	adv.	常常	1	1	初級	
	mention	[ˈmɛnʃən]	v.	提到	1	3	中級	◎
⓰	yes	[jɛs]	int.	是啊	1	1	初級	
	lost	[lɔst]	p.p.	lose（減少）過去分詞	1	2	中高	◎
	five	[faɪv]	n.	五	1	1	初級	
	kilogram	[ˈkɪləˌgræm]	n.	公斤		3	初級	
⓱	ok	[ˈoˈke]	int.	好啊	1	1	初級	
	while	[hwaɪl]	n.	一段時間	1	1	初級	
	had	[hæd]	p.t.	have（喝）過去分詞	1	1	初級	
	cup	[kʌp]	n.	一杯	1	1	初級	
	coffee	[ˈkɔfɪ]	n.	咖啡	1	1	初級	
	together	[təˈgɛðə]	adv.	一起	1	1	初級	

※「紅字單字」於本單元多句出現，「單字級等分析」僅列在「首次出現句」。

MP3 093-01 ❶ ～ ⓯

❶	怎麼一直打哈欠，昨晚熬夜啊？	Why do you keep yawning like that? Did you stay up late last night? * keep yawning（一直打呵欠） * stay up late（熬夜）
❷	大家早安。	Good morning, everyone!
❸	哇，難得看你化妝！	Wow, you hardly ever put on makeup! * hardly ever＋動詞原形（難得做…、很少會做…） * put on makeup（化妝）
❹	上班打卡了嗎？	Did you punch in yet? * punch in（上班打卡） * punch out（下班打卡）
❺	鞋子真漂亮，哪裡買的？	Your shoes are very beautiful. Where did you buy them?
❻	一大早在忙什麼？	What are you so busy with this early in the morning? * this early in the morning（今天一大早）
❼	今天要開會嗎？	Do we have a meeting today? * have a meeting（開會）
❽	穿得真正式，今天要去拜訪客戶嗎？	You are dressed very formally. Are you going to visit clients today? * be dressed formally（穿著正式） * visit a client（拜訪客戶）
❾	要不要來杯咖啡？	Would you like a cup of coffee?
❿	吃過早餐了嗎？	Have you eaten breakfast yet? * Have you＋過去分詞?（你是否已經…？）
⓫	昨晚幾點下班？	What time did you leave the office last night? * What time did you...?（你當時是幾點…？）
⓬	這個月業績如何？	How is your business performance this month? * business performance（業績）
⓭	你今天遇到塞車啦？	Did you get stuck in traffic today? * get stuck in traffic（遇到塞車、被塞在車陣中）
⓮	你今天遲到了？	Were you late today? * Were you...?（你當時是不是…？）
⓯	今天忙嗎？	Are you busy today?

	單字	音標	詞性	意義	字頻	大考	英檢	多益
❶	keep	[kip]	v.	一直	1	1	初級	◎
	yawning	[ˈjɔnɪŋ]	n.	yawn（打呵欠）動名詞	8	3	中級	◎
	that	[ðæt]	pron.	那個	1	1	初級	
	stay	[ste]	v.	保持	1	1	初級	
	up	[ʌp]	adv.	醒著地	1	1	初級	◎
	late	[let]	adv. /adj.	晚地/遲到的	1	1	初級	◎
	last	[læst]	adj.	前一個	1	1	初級	◎
	night	[naɪt]	n.	夜晚	1	1	初級	
❷	good	[gʊd]	adj.	良好的	1	1	初級	
	morning	[ˈmɔrɪŋ]	n.	早上	1	1	初級	
	everyone	[ˈɛvrɪˌwʌn]	pron.	每個人	1		初級	
❸	wow	[waʊ]	int.	哇	2	1	初級	
	hardly	[ˈhɑrdlɪ]	adv.	幾乎不	1	2	初級	
	ever	[ˈɛvɚ]	adv.	曾經	1	1	初級	
	put	[pʊt]	v.	塗抹	1	1	初級	
	makeup	[ˈmekˌʌp]	n.	化妝品	2	4		◎
❹	punch	[pʌntʃ]	v.	打（卡）	2	3	中級	◎
	yet	[jɛt]	adv.	尚未	1	1	初級	◎
❺	shoes	[ʃuz]	n.	shoe（鞋子）複數	2	1		
	very	[ˈvɛrɪ]	adv.	十分	1	1	初級	
	beautiful	[ˈbjutəfəl]	adj.	漂亮的	1	1	初級	
❻	so	[so]	adv.	如此	1	1	初級	
	busy	[ˈbɪzɪ]	adj.	忙碌的	1	1	初級	
	this	[ðɪs]	adv.	這麼	1	1	初級	
	early	[ˈɝlɪ]	adv.	早地	1	1	初級	
❼	have	[hæv]	v.	擁有	1	1	初級	
	meeting	[ˈmitɪŋ]	n.	會議	1	2	初級	
	today	[təˈde]	adv.	今天	1	1	初級	◎
❽	dressed	[drɛst]	p.p.	dress（穿著）過去分詞		2	中高	
	formally	[ˈfɔrmlɪ]	adv.	正式地	2			
	going	[ˈgoɪŋ]	p.pr.	go（進展）現在分詞	4	1	初級	
	visit	[ˈvɪzɪt]	v.	拜訪	1	1	初級	◎
	client	[ˈklaɪənt]	n.	客戶	1	3	中級	◎
❾	like	[laɪk]	v.	想要	1	1	初級	
	cup	[kʌp]	n.	一杯	1	1	初級	
	coffee	[ˈkɔfɪ]	n.	咖啡	1	1	初級	
❿	eaten	[ˈitn]	p.p.	eat（吃）過去分詞	1	1	初級	
	breakfast	[ˈbrɛkfəst]	n.	早餐	1	1	初級	
⓫	time	[taɪm]	n.	時間	1	1	初級	◎
	leave	[liv]	v.	離開	1	1	初級	◎
	office	[ˈɔfɪs]	n.	辦公室	1	1	初級	◎
⓬	business	[ˈbɪznɪs]	n.	生意、業務	1	1	初級	◎
	performance	[pɚˈfɔrməns]	n.	表現	1	3	中級	◎
	month	[mʌnθ]	n.	月	1	1	初級	
⓭	get	[gɛt]	v.	變成	1	1	初級	◎
	stuck	[stʌk]	p.p.	stick（塞住）過去分詞	4	2	中高	◎
	traffic	[ˈtræfɪk]	n.	交通量、車流量	1	2	中級	◎

※「紅字單字」於本單元多句出現，「單字級等分析」僅列在「首次出現句」。

🔵 MP3 093-02 ❶～⓰

❶	早安。	Morning. = Good morning!
❷	是啊，我昨晚又失眠了。	Yes, you're right; I couldn't sleep again last night. *can't sleep（睡不著，couldn't 是過去式）
❸	我已經打卡了。	Yes, I've already punched my card.
❹	我正在準備開會資料。	I am preparing materials for the meeting. *prepare materials（準備資料）
❺	想改變一下造型。	I want to change my style.
❻	是啊，每天都有開不完的會。	Yeah, we have endless meetings every day. *endless meetings（沒完沒了的會議）
❼	等老闆到就開會。	The meeting will begin whenever the boss arrives. *whenever（在…的時候）
❽	吃了一半，一半還在桌上。	I ate half and left the rest on the table. *eat half（吃了一半）、the rest（剩下的部分）
❾	是的，今天約了重要客戶。	Yes, I have an appointment with a major client today. *have an appointment（有約）、major client（大客戶）
❿	沒辦法，車子在半路拋錨。	There was nothing I could have done—my car broke down on the way. *break down（拋錨）、on the way（在路途上）
⓫	好啊，謝謝。	OK, thanks.
⓬	我昨晚十點才離開公司。	I didn't leave my office until ten pm last night. *didn't＋動詞＋until＋時間（在某時間，才做…）
⓭	馬馬虎虎。	So-so.
⓮	很不錯。	Very good.
⓯	是啊，遇到大塞車。	Yes, you're right, I was stuck in a big traffic jam. *be stuck（被塞住）、big traffic jam（交通大塞車）
⓰	我今天有一堆事要處理。	I have a ton of things to deal with today. *a ton of things（一大堆事情）、deal with（處理）

	單字	音標	詞性	意義	字頻	大考	英檢	多益
❶	morning	[`mɔrnɪŋ]	n.	早上	1	1	初級	
	good	[gʊd]	adj.	良好的	1	1	初級	◎
❷	yes	[jɛs]	int.	是啊	1	1	初級	
	right	[raɪt]	adj.	沒錯的	1	1	初級	
	sleep	[slip]	v.	睡覺	1	1	初級	

❷	again	[əˈgɛn]	adv.	再次	1	1	初級	
	last	[læst]	adj.	前一個	1	1	初級	◎
	night	[naɪt]	n.	夜晚	1	1	初級	
❸	already	[ɔlˈrɛdɪ]	adv.	已經	1	1	初級	◎
	punched	[pʌntʃt]	p.p.	punch（打卡）過去分詞	2	3	中級	
	card	[kɑrd]	n.	卡片	1	1	初級	◎
❹	preparing	[prɪˈpɛrɪŋ]	p.pr.	prepare（準備）現在分詞	1	1	初級	◎
	material	[məˈtɪrɪəl]	n.	資料	1	6	初級	◎
	meeting	[ˈmitɪŋ]	n.	會議	1	2	初級	
❺	want	[wɑnt]	v.	想要	1	1	初級	◎
	change	[tʃendʒ]	v.	改變	1	2	初級	◎
	style	[staɪl]	n.	造型	1	3	初級	◎
❻	yeah	[jɛə]	int.	是啊	1	1	初級	
	have	[hæv]	v.	擁有	1	1	初級	
	endless	[ˈɛndlɪs]	adj.	無止盡的	2		中高	
	every	[ˈɛvrɪ]	adj.	每一	1	1	初級	
	day	[de]	n.	天	1	1	初級	
❼	begin	[bɪˈgɪn]	v.	開始	1	1	初級	
	boss	[bɔs]	n.	老闆	1	2	初級	
	arrive	[əˈraɪv]	v.	到達	1	2	初級	◎
❽	ate	[et]	p.t.	eat（吃）過去式	1	1	初級	
	half	[hæf]	adv.	一半地	1	1	初級	
	left	[lɛft]	p.t.	leave（留下）過去式	1	1	初級	
	rest	[rɛst]	n.	剩餘	1	1	初級	
	table	[ˈtebl̩]	n.	桌子	1	1	初級	◎
❾	appointment	[əˈpɔɪntmənt]	n.	約會	2	4	中級	◎
	major	[ˈmedʒɚ]	adj.	重要的	1	3	中級	◎
	client	[ˈklaɪənt]	n.	客戶	1	3	中級	◎
	today	[təˈde]	adv.	今天	1	1	初級	◎
❿	there	[ðɛr]	adv.	有…	1	1	初級	
	nothing	[ˈnʌθɪŋ]	pron.	沒有事情	1	1	初級	
	done	[dʌn]	p.p.	do（做）過去分詞	1	1	初級	
	car	[kɑr]	n.	車子	1	1	初級	◎
	broke	[brok]	p.t.	break（毀壞）過去式	4	4	中級	◎
	down	[daun]	adv.	徹底、完全	1	1	初級	
	way	[we]	n.	路途	1	1	初級	
⓫	ok	[ˈoˈke]	int.	好啊	1	1	初級	
	thanks	[θæŋks]	n.	thank（感謝）複數	1			
⓬	leave	[liv]	v.	離開	1	1	初級	◎
	office	[ˈɔfɪs]	n.	公司	1	1	初級	◎
	ten	[tɛn]	n.	十	1	1	初級	
	pm	[ˈpiˈɛm]	adv.	下午	1	4		
⓭	so-so	[ˈsoˌso]	adj.	馬馬虎虎的				
⓮	very	[ˈvɛrɪ]	adv.	十分	1	1	初級	
⓯	stuck	[stʌk]	p.p.	stick（塞住）過去分詞	4	2	中高	◎
	big	[bɪg]	adj.	大的	1	1	初級	
	traffic	[ˈtræfɪk]	n.	交通量、車流量	2	2	初級	◎
	jam	[dʒæm]	n.	堵塞	2	2	初級	◎
⓰	ton	[tʌn]	n.	一大堆		3	中級	
	thing	[θɪŋ]	n.	事情	1	1	初級	
	deal	[dil]	v.	處理	1	1	初級	◎

※「紅字單字」於本單元多句出現，「單字級等分析」僅列在「首次出現句」。

🔊 MP3 094-01 ❶～⓲

❶	可以和你交換名片嗎？	May we exchange business cards? * **May we＋動詞?**（請問我們是否可以…？） * **exchange business cards**（交換名片）
❷	請問你叫什麼名字？	Excuse me, what is your name? ＝ May I ask your name?
❸	我是瑪莉，想和你認識一下。	I am Mary, and I would like to get to know you. * **would like to**（想要） * **get to know**（認識）
❹	我該怎麼稱呼你？	What should I call you?
❺	你是新的同事嗎？	Are you our new colleague? * **Are you＋身分?**（你是某身分的人嗎）
❻	你有英文名字嗎？	Do you have an English name?
❼	我們會變成好朋友的。	We're going to be good friends. ＝ We'll become good friends.
❽	很高興認識你。	It's nice to meet you.
❾	你來自哪裡？	Where are you from?
❿	你住哪裡？	Where do you live?
⓫	你結婚了嗎？	Are you married?
⓬	你在哪裡工作？	Where do you work?
⓭	你來台灣多久了？	How long have you been in Taiwan? * **How long have you been...?**（你…持續多久了？）
⓮	你來台灣學中文嗎？	Did you come to Taiwan to study Chinese?
⓯	你的興趣是什麼？	What are your interests?
⓰	我覺得你很面熟。	You look familiar to me. * **look familiar**（看起來很面熟） * **to me**（對於我）
⓱	我們見過面嗎？	Have we met before? * **Have we＋過去分詞?**（我們是否曾經…？）
⓲	休閒時都做些什麼？	What do you do in your leisure time? * **in your leisure time**（在你閒暇時）

	單字	音標	詞性	意義	字頻	大考	英檢	多益
❶	exchange	[ɪksˋtʃendʒ]	v.	交換	1	3	中級	◎
	business	[ˋbɪznɪs]	n.	商業、業務	1	2	初級	◎
	card	[kɑrd]	n.	卡片	1	1	初級	◎
❷	excuse	[ɪkˋskjuz]	v.	原諒	2	2	初級	◎
	name	[nem]	n.	名字	1	1	初級	◎
	ask	[æsk]	v.	詢問	1	1	初級	
❸	like	[laɪk]	v.	想要	1	1	初級	
	get	[gɛt]	v.	開始、著手	1	1	初級	
	know	[no]	v.	認識	1	1	初級	◎
❹	call	[kɔl]	v.	稱呼	1	1	初級	
❺	new	[nju]	adj.	新的	1	1	初級	
	colleague	[ˋkɑlig]	n.	同事	1	5	中級	◎
❻	have	[hæv]	v.	擁有	1	1	初級	
	English	[ˋɪŋglɪʃ]	adj.	英文的	1	1	初級	
❼	going	[ˋgoɪŋ]	p.pr.	go（即將）現在分詞	4	1	初級	
	good	[gʊd]	adj.	良好的	1	1	初級	◎
	friend	[frɛnd]	n.	朋友	1	1	初級	
	become	[bɪˋkʌm]	v.	變為	1	1	初級	◎
❽	nice	[naɪs]	adj.	高興的	1	1	初級	
	meet	[mit]	v.	認識	1	1	初級	
❿	live	[lɪv]	v.	居住	1	1	初級	◎
⓫	married	[ˋmærɪd]	p.p.	marry（結婚）過去分詞	1		初級	
⓬	work	[wɜk]	v.	工作	1	1	初級	◎
⓭	long	[lɔŋ]	adj.	長的	1	1	初級	
	Taiwan	[ˋtaɪˋwɑn]	n.	台灣			初級	
⓮	come	[kʌm]	v.	前來	1	1	初級	
	study	[ˋstʌdɪ]	v.	學習	1	1	初級	◎
	Chinese	[ˋtʃaɪˋniz]	n.	中文	1		初級	
⓯	interest	[ˋɪntərɪst]	n.	興趣	1	1	初級	
⓰	look	[lʊk]	v.	看起來	1	1	初級	
	familiar	[fəˋmɪljɚ]	adj.	面熟的	1	3	中級	◎
⓱	met	[mɛt]	p.p.	meet（見面）過去式	1	1	初級	
	before	[bɪˋfor]	adv.	之前	1	1	初級	
⓲	do	[du]	v.	做、從事	1	1	初級	
	leisure	[ˋliʒɚ]	adj.	閒暇的	3	3	中級	◎
	time	[taɪm]	n.	時間	1	1	初級	◎

※「紅字單字」於本單元多句出現，「單字級等分析」僅列在「首次出現句」。

🔊 MP3 094-02 ❶～⓰

❶	我是約翰。	I am John. = My name is John.
❷	大家都叫我妮可。	Everyone calls me Nicole. * **call me**＋名字（用某名字稱呼我）
❸	這是我的名片，請多指教。	This is my business card; your advice is welcome. * **your advice is welcome**（請多指教）
❹	我沒有英文名字。	I don't have an English name.
❺	認識你是我的榮幸。	It's really a pleasure to meet you. * **It's a pleasure to**＋動詞原形（榮幸…）
❻	很高興認識你。	It's nice to meet you.
❼	我對你久仰大名。	I have been looking forward to meeting you. * **have been**＋動詞-ing（一直以來都很…） * **look forward to**（期待）
❽	我們一定會成為好朋友。	We are going to be good friends for sure. * **good friend**（好朋友） * **for sure**（肯定、一定）
❾	業界對你的風評很好。	You have a good reputation in this industry. * **have a good reputation**（名聲很好）
❿	我們一見如故。	I feel like we have known each other for a long time. = I feel like we are old friends. * **feel like**＋子句（感覺…） * **have known**（早已認識） * **old friend**（老朋友）
⓫	聽說你十分幽默。	I heard that you're very humorous.
⓬	我結婚了。	I am married.
⓭	我還是單身。	I am still single.
⓮	真是相見恨晚。	I really wish we had met earlier. * **I wish**＋過去式子句（可以的話，我希望…）
⓯	我來自台灣。	I am from Taiwan.
⓰	我們可以約個時間喝咖啡。	We can make an appointment to have a cup of coffee together. * **make an appointment**（約時間）

	單字	音標	詞性	意義	字頻	大考	英檢	多益
❶	name	[nem]	n.	名字	1	1	初級	◎
❷	everyone	[ˈɛvrɪ.wʌn]	pron.	每個人	1		初級	
	call	[kɔl]	v.	稱呼	1	1	初級	◎
❸	this	[ðɪs]	pron. /adj.	這個	1	1	初級	
	business	[ˈbɪznɪs]	n.	商業、業務	1	2	初級	◎
	card	[kɑrd]	n.	卡片	1	1	初級	◎
	advice	[ədˈvaɪs]	n.	指教	1	3	初級	◎
	welcome	[ˈwɛlkəm]	adj.	歡迎的	1	1	初級	
❹	have	[hæv]	v.	擁有	1	1	初級	
	English	[ˈɪŋglɪʃ]	adj.	英文的	1	1	初級	
❺	really	[ˈrɪəlɪ]	adv.	真的	1		初級	
	pleasure	[ˈplɛʒɚ]	n.	榮幸	1	2	初級	◎
	meet	[mit]	v.	認識	1	1	初級	
❻	nice	[naɪs]	adj.	高興的	1	1	初級	
❼	looking	[ˈlʊkɪŋ]	p.pr.	look（期待）現在分詞	5	1	初級	
	forward	[ˈfɔrwəd]	adv.	將來	1	2	初級	◎
	meeting	[ˈmitɪŋ]	n.	meet（認識）動名詞	1	2	初級	
❽	going	[ˈgoɪŋ]	p.pr.	go（即將）現在分詞	4	1	初級	
	good	[gʊd]	adj.	良好的	1	1	初級	◎
	friend	[frɛnd]	n.	朋友	1	1	初級	
	sure	[ʃʊr]	adj.	肯定的、一定的	1	1	初級	
❾	reputation	[.rɛpjəˈteʃən]	n.	名聲	1	4	中級	◎
	industry	[ˈɪndəstrɪ]	n.	產業	1	2	初級	◎
❿	feel	[fil]	v.	感覺	1	1	初級	
	known	[non]	p.p.	know（認識）過去分詞	2	1	初級	◎
	each	[itʃ]	pron.	每個、各個	1	1	初級	
	other	[ˈʌðə]	pron.	另一方	1	1	初級	
	long	[lɔŋ]	adj.	長的	1	1	初級	
	time	[taɪm]	n.	時間	1	1	初級	◎
	old	[old]	adj.	老的	1	1	初級	
⓫	heard	[hɝd]	p.p.	hear（聽說）過去分詞	1	1	初級	
	very	[ˈvɛrɪ]	adv.	十分	1	1	初級	
	humorous	[ˈhjumərəs]	adj.	幽默的	4	3	初級	
⓬	married	[ˈmærɪd]	p.p.	marry（結婚）過去分詞	1		初級	
⓭	still	[stɪl]	adv.	仍然	1	1	初級	◎
	single	[ˈsɪŋgl]	adj.	單身的	1	2	初級	◎
⓮	wish	[wɪʃ]	v.	希望	1		初級	
	met	[mɛt]	p.p.	meet（認識）過去分詞	1	1	初級	
	earlier	[ˈɝˈlɪr]	adv.	early（早地）比較級	1	1	初級	
⓯	Taiwan	[ˈtaɪˈwɑn]	n.	台灣			初級	
⓰	make	[mek]	v.	做出	1	1	初級	
	appointment	[əˈpɔɪntmənt]	n.	約會	2	4	中級	◎
	cup	[kʌp]	n.	一杯	1	1	初級	
	coffee	[ˈkɔfɪ]	n.	咖啡	1	1	初級	
	together	[təˈgɛðə]	adv.	一起	1	1	初級	

※「紅字單字」於本單元多句出現，「單字級等分析」僅列在「首次出現句」。

MP3 095-01 ❶～❼

❶	你在忙什麼？	What have you been busy with? = What have you been up to?
❷	好久不見！	It's been a long time!
❸	我們已經好幾年沒見啦！	It's been many years since we last saw each other! * see each other（見到彼此）
❹	你一點都沒變！	You haven't changed a bit! * a bit（一點、稍微）
❺	還記得我嗎？	Do you remember me?
❻	怎麼都不聯絡一下？	Why didn't you contact me? * Why didn't you...?（你之前為什麼沒有做…？）
❼	這些年都在忙什麼？	What have you been doing for the past few years? * What have you been doing...?（你一直在做什麼…？）
❽	都聯絡不到你耶。	I haven't been able to get in touch with you at all. * be able to＋動詞原形（能夠…） * get in touch with（聯絡） * at all（完全）
❾	你愈來愈年輕了耶。	You are looking younger and younger. * 此句用「現在進行式」（...are looking...） 　表示「現階段逐漸變化的事」。
❿	還在原來的公司嗎？	Are you still working for the same firm? * firm（公司）= company
⓫	結婚了嗎？	Are you married?
⓬	生孩子了嗎？	Any children? = Do you have any children?
⓭	躲哪去了呀？	Where have you been hiding?
⓮	你搬家了是嗎？	You've moved, right?
⓯	不認得我了呀？	Don't you recognize me?
⓰	你的電話換了是吧？都聯絡不到你耶。	Have you changed phone numbers? I haven't been able to reach you at all. * Have you changed...?（你曾換過…？）
⓱	沒良心的。都沒和我聯絡。	That's messed up! You didn't even contact me. * That's messed up!（真的很糟糕！、很不公平！）

	單字	音標	詞性	意義	字頻	大考	英檢	多益
❶	busy	[ˋbɪzɪ]	adj.	忙碌的	1	1	初級	
	up	[ʌp]	adj./adv.	忙於/完全、徹底	1	1	初級	
❷	long	[lɔŋ]	adj.	長的	1	1	初級	
	time	[taɪm]	n.	時間	1	1	初級	◎
❸	many	[ˋmɛnɪ]	adj.	許多的	1	1	初級	
	year	[jɪr]	n.	年	1	1	初級	
	last	[læst]	adv.	前次	1	1	初級	◎
	saw	[sɔ]	p.t.	see（見面）過去式	3	1	中級	◎
	each	[itʃ]	pron.	每個、各個	1	1	初級	
	other	[ˋʌðə]	pron.	另一方	1	1	初級	
❹	changed	[tʃendʒd]	p.p.	change（改變）過去分詞	4	2	初級	◎
	bit	[bɪt]	n.	一點點、少許	1	1	初級	
❺	remember	[rɪˋmɛmbə]	v.	記得	1	1	初級	
❻	contact	[kənˋtækt]	v.	聯絡	1	2	初級	◎
❼	doing	[ˋduɪŋ]	p.pr.	do（做）現在分詞	1	1	初級	
	past	[pæst]	adj.	過去的	1	1	初級	
	few	[fju]	adj.	些許的	1	1	初級	◎
❽	able	[ˋebl]	adj.	能夠	1	1	初級	◎
	get	[gɛt]	v.	取得	1	1	初級	◎
	touch	[tʌtʃ]	n.	聯繫	1	1	初級	◎
	all	[ɔl]	n.	完全	1	1	初級	
❾	looking	[ˋlʊkɪŋ]	p.pr.	look（看）現在分詞	5	1	初級	
	younger	[ˋjʌŋgə]	adj.	young（年輕的）比較級	1	1	初級	
❿	still	[stɪl]	adv.	仍然	1	1	初級	◎
	working	[ˋwɜkɪŋ]	p.pr.	work（工作）現在分詞	2	1	中級	◎
	same	[sem]	adj.	相同的	1	1	初級	
	firm	[fɜm]	n.	公司	1	2	初級	◎
⓫	married	[ˋmærɪd]	p.p.	marry（結婚）過去分詞	1		初級	
⓬	any	[ˋɛnɪ]	adj.	任何的	1	1	初級	
	children	[ˋtʃɪldrən]	n.	child（小孩）複數	1	1	初級	
	have	[hæv]	v.	生育	1	1	初級	
⓭	hiding	[ˋhaɪdɪŋ]	p.pr.	hide（躲藏）現在分詞	6			
⓮	moved	[muvd]	p.p.	move（搬家）過去式	1	1	初級	◎
	right	[raɪt]	int.	是嗎	1	1	初級	
⓯	recognize	[ˋrɛkəg͵naɪz]	v.	認得	1	3	中級	◎
⓰	phone	[fon]	n.	電話	1	2	初級	◎
	number	[ˋnʌmbə]	n.	號碼	1	1	初級	
	reach	[ritʃ]	v.	聯絡	1	1	初級	◎
⓱	that	[ðæt]	pron.	那個	1	1	初級	
	messed	[mɛst]	p.p.	mess（弄糟）過去分詞	2	3	中級	◎
	even	[ˋivən]	adv.	甚至	1	1	初級	◎

※「紅字單字」於本單元多句出現，「單字級等分析」僅列在「首次出現句」。

🔊 MP3 095-02 ❶～⓰

❶	是啊。	Right. = Yes.
❷	好久不見。	It's been a long time. = Haven't seen you in a long time.
❸	是啊，快十年了。	Yeah, it's been almost ten years.
❹	你也是都沒變。	You haven't changed a bit either. * **haven't changed**（一直都沒變）
❺	你也沒和我聯絡！	You didn't contact me either!
❻	我也聯絡不到你！	I couldn't reach you either!
❼	哪有，變老啦。	Come on, I look a lot older. * **Come on!**（少來！）= **Get out of here!** = **No way!** * **a lot**＋比較級（非常⋯、很⋯）
❽	你的電話我打不通啊。	I couldn't get through to your phone. * **get through to**（打通電話）
❾	都快不認識你了。	I can barely recognize you. * **barely**＋動詞（很難⋯、幾乎無法⋯）
❿	我換工作了。	I changed jobs.
⓫	我已經結婚了。	I got married.
⓬	我現在住美國，很少回台灣。	I live in the U.S. now and seldom come back to Taiwan. * **come back to**（返回）
⓭	你才沒良心呢！結婚也不通知一下。	No way! You're the one who's messed up, getting married and not letting me know! * **messed up**（糟糕的）、**not let me know**（不告訴我）
⓮	我換電話了，所以你聯絡不到我。	You couldn't reach me because I changed my phone number.
⓯	你現在忙嗎，要不要找地方聊聊？	Are you busy right now? Want to find a place to talk? * **Want to...?**（你要不要⋯？）
⓰	把新的聯絡方式給我吧。	Give me your new contact information. * **contact information**（聯絡方式）

	單字	音標	詞性	意義	字頻	大考	英檢	多益
❶	right	[raɪt]	int.	是啊	1	1	初級	
	yes	[jɛs]	int.	是啊	1	1	初級	
❷	long	[lɔŋ]	adj.	長的	1	1	初級	
	time	[taɪm]	n.	時間	1	1	初級	◎
	seen	[sin]	p.p.	see（見面）過去分詞	1	1	初級	

❸	yeah	[jɛə]	int.	是啊	1	1	初級	
	almost	[ˋɔl.most]	adv.	幾乎	1	1	初級	
	ten	[tɛn]	n.	十	1	1	初級	
	year	[jɪr]	n.	年	1	1	初級	
❹	changed	[tʃendʒd]	p.p.	change（改變）過去分詞	4	2	初級	◎
	bit	[bɪt]	n.	一點點、少許	1	1	初級	
	either	[ˋiðɚ]	adv.	也不	1	1	初級	◎
❺	contact	[kənˋtækt]	v.	聯絡	1	1	初級	
❻	**reach**	[ritʃ]	v.	聯絡	1	1	初級	◎
❼	**come**	[kʌm]	v.	少來	1	1	初級	
	look	[lʊk]	v.	看起來	1	1	初級	
	lot	[lɑt]	adv.	非常、很				
	older	[ˋoldɚ]	adj.	old（老的）比較級	1	1	初級	
❽	get	[gɛt]	v.	取得	1	1	初級	◎
	through	[θru]	adv.	通過	1	1	初級	◎
	phone	[fon]	n.	電話	1	2	初級	◎
❾	barely	[ˋbɛrlɪ]	adv.	很難、幾乎無法	1	3	中級	◎
	recognize	[ˋrɛkəg.naɪz]	v.	認得	1	3	中級	◎
❿	changed	[tʃendʒd]	p.t.	change（更換）過去式	4	2	初級	◎
	job	[dʒɑb]	n.	工作	1	1	初級	
⓫	got	[gɑt]	p.t.	get（變成）過去式	1	1	初級	◎
	married	[ˋmærɪd]	p.p.	marry（結婚）過去分詞	1		初級	
⓬	live	[lɪv]	v.	居住	1	1	初級	
	U.S.	[ˋjuˋɛs]	n.	United States（美國）縮寫				
	now	[naʊ]	adv.	現在	1	1	初級	
	seldom	[ˋsɛldəm]	adv.	很少	2	3	初級	◎
	back	[bæk]	adv.	返回	1	1	初級	◎
	Taiwan	[ˋtaɪˋwɑn]	n.	台灣			初級	
⓭	way	[we]	n.	方法、方式	1	1	初級	
	one	[wʌn]	pron.	一個人	1	1	初級	
	messed	[mɛst]	p.p.	mess（弄糟）過去分詞	2	3	中級	◎
	up	[ʌp]	adv.	完全、徹底	1	1	初級	
	getting	[ˋgɛtɪŋ]	p.pr.	get（變成）現在分詞	1	1	初級	◎
	letting	[ˋlɛtɪŋ]	p.pr.	let（讓）現在分詞	1	1	初級	
	know	[ˋno]	v.	知道	1	1	初級	◎
⓮	change	[tʃendʒ]	v.	改變	1	2	初級	◎
	number	[ˋnʌmbɚ]	n.	號碼	1	1	初級	◎
⓯	busy	[ˋbɪzɪ]	adj.	忙碌的	1	1	初級	
	want	[wɑnt]	v.	想要	1	1	初級	◎
	find	[faɪnd]	v.	尋找	1	1	初級	
	place	[ples]	n.	地方	1	1	初級	◎
	talk	[tɔk]	v.	聊天	1	1	初級	◎
⓰	give	[gɪv]	v.	給予	1	1	初級	◎
	new	[nju]	adj.	新的	1	1	初級	
	contact	[ˋkɑntækt]	n.	聯絡	1	1	初級	
	information	[.ɪnfɚˋmeʃən]	n.	資訊	1	4	初級	◎

※「紅字單字」於本單元多句出現，「單字級等分析」僅列在「首次出現句」。　　　429

096　關心與安慰。

🔵 MP3 096-01 ❶～❽

❶	你還好嗎？	Are you all right? = Are you okay?
❷	需要幫忙嗎？	Do you need any help?
❸	有心事嗎？我們可以聊聊。	Is there anything on your mind? We can talk about it. * on your mind（在你心裡） * talk about（聊聊）
❹	你有什麼事要對我說嗎？	Do you have something to say to me? * have something to say（有事要說）
❺	別擔心，事情會好轉的。	Don't worry, everything is going to be fine. * be going to...（將會…）
❻	別老往壞處想嘛！	Stop being so pessimistic! * Stop＋動詞-ing（別再…）
❼	想想愉快的事情吧！	Think about something happy!
❽	要休息一下嗎？	Want to take a rest? * take a rest（休息）
❾	看開一點吧！	Don't take it so hard! * take it hard（想不開）
❿	你看來不太好？	You don't look too good.
⓫	別鑽牛角尖了！	Stop banging your head against a wall! * bang one's head against a wall（徒勞無謂的努力）
⓬	放輕鬆點！	Take it easy! = Relax!
⓭	笑一笑吧！	Smile!
⓮	你遇到什麼麻煩嗎？	Have you run into any trouble? * run into a trouble（遭遇麻煩）
⓯	如果需要幫忙請讓我知道。	Let me know if you need any help. * let me know（告訴我）
⓰	別這樣，你已經盡力了。	Don't act like that; you did your best. * act like...（做出像…的行為） * do one's best（盡力）
⓱	別擔心，我會幫你的。	Don't worry, I'll give you a hand. * give＋某人＋a hand（幫助某人）
⓲	不要拒絕我的關心。	Don't reject my concern. * reject one's concern（拒絕關心）

	單字	音標	詞性	意義	字頻	大考	英檢	多益
❶	all	[ɔl]	adv.	一切	1	1	初級	
	right	[raɪt]	adj.	還可以的	1	1	初級	
	okay	[ˋoˋke]	adj.	還好的	1	1		
❷	need	[nid]	v.	需要	1	1	初級	◎
	any	[ˋɛnɪ]	adj.	任何的	1	1	初級	
	help	[hɛlp]	n.	幫忙	1	1	初級	
❸	there	[ðɛr]	adv.	有…	1	1	初級	
	anything	[ˋɛnɪˏθɪŋ]	pron.	任何事情	1	1	初級	
	mind	[maɪnd]	n.	內心	1	1	初級	◎
	talk	[tɔk]	v.	談話	1	1	初級	◎
❹	have	[hæv]	v.	擁有	1	1	初級	
	something	[ˋsʌmˏθɪŋ]	pron.	某些事情	1	1	初級	
	say	[se]	v.	說	1	1	初級	
❺	worry	[ˋwɝɪ]	v.	擔心	1	1	初級	◎
	everything	[ˋɛvrɪˏθɪŋ]	pron.	每件事情	1		初級	
	going	[ˋgoɪŋ]	p.pr.	go（即將）現在分詞	4	1	初級	
	fine	[faɪn]	adj.	平安無事的	1	1	初級	◎
❻	stop	[stɑp]	v.	停止	1	1	初級	◎
	so	[so]	adv.	如此	1	1	初級	
	pessimistic	[ˏpɛsəˋmɪstɪk]	adj.	悲觀的	4	4	中級	◎
❼	think	[θɪŋk]	v.	認為	1	1	初級	
	happy	[ˋhæpɪ]	adj.	快樂的	1	1	初級	
❽	want	[wɑnt]	v.	想要	1	1	初級	◎
	take	[tek]	v.	採取/看待	1	1	初級	◎
	rest	[rɛst]	n.	休息	1	1	初級	
❾	hard	[hɑrd]	adj.	艱難的、難受的	1	1	初級	◎
❿	look	[lʊk]	v.	看起來	1	1	初級	
	too	[tu]	adv.	過於	1	1	初級	
	good	[gʊd]	adj.	良好的	1	1	初級	◎
⓫	banging	[ˋbæŋɪŋ]	n.	bang（猛撞）動名詞	2	3	中級	
	head	[hɛd]	n.	頭	1	1	初級	◎
	wall	[wɔl]	n.	牆壁	1	1	初級	
⓬	easy	[ˋizɪ]	adj.	輕鬆的	1	1	初級	◎
	relax	[rɪˋlæks]	v.	放鬆	2	3	中級	◎
⓭	smile	[smaɪl]	v.	微笑	1	1	初級	
⓮	run	[rʌn]	p.p.	run（遭遇）過去分詞	1	1	初級	◎
	trouble	[ˋtrʌbl]	n.	麻煩	1	1	初級	◎
⓯	let	[lɛt]	v.	讓…	1	1	初級	
	know	[no]	v.	知道	1	1	初級	◎
⓰	act	[ækt]	v.	做出…行為	1	1	初級	
	that	[ðæt]	pron.	那個	1	1	初級	
	did	[dɪd]	p.t.	do（做）過去式	1	1	初級	
	best	[bɛst]	n.	最好	1	1	初級	
⓱	give	[gɪv]	v.	給予	1	1	初級	
	hand	[hænd]	n.	協助	1	1	初級	
⓲	reject	[rɪˋdʒɛkt]	v.	拒絕	1	2	初級	◎
	concern	[kənˋsɝn]	n.	關心	1	3	初級	◎

※「紅字單字」於本單元多句出現，「單字級等分析」僅列在「首次出現句」。

🔵 MP3 096-02 ❶～⓲

❶	沒事。我很好。	It's nothing, I'm fine.
❷	別管我，讓我靜一靜。	Just leave me alone for a while. * leave me alone（別理會我）、for a while（一段時間）
❸	最近我太太生病了。	My wife has been sick recently.
❹	我會試試看。	I'll give it a try.
❺	如果你願意聽，我是想找個人聊聊。	If you're willing to listen, I'd love to have someone to talk to. * be willing to（願意）、would love to（想要）
❻	我會想出辦法的。	I'll figure it out. ＝ I will find a way.
❼	你說的有道理。	What you've said is reasonable. * what you've said（你曾說過的）
❽	沒辦法，我就是會擔心。	It can't be helped; I'm just a worrier. * it can't be helped（無可避免）
❾	沒關係，我過一陣子就好了。	It's OK, I'll be better soon enough. * soon enough（很快地）
❿	我會振作。	I'll pull myself together. * pull oneself together（讓自己振作）
⓫	我的生活會好轉的。	My life will get better.
⓬	沒辦法，事情就是這樣了。	Nothing to be done—this is it. * nothing to be done（沒別的辦法）
⓭	你就是這麼善體人意。	You are such a thoughtful person.
⓮	你真好。	You're really nice.
⓯	我知道你的好意。	I know you mean well. * mean well（用意良好）
⓰	抱歉，讓你擔心了。	I'm sorry to make you worry.
⓱	謝謝你的關心。	Thanks for your concern.
⓲	我會接受你的建議。	I'll accept your advice.

	單字	音標	詞性	意義	字頻	大考	英檢	多益
❶	nothing	[ˋnʌθɪŋ]	pron.	微不足道的事	1	1	初級	
	fine	[faɪn]	adj.	很好的、沒事的	1	1	初級	◎
❷	just	[dʒʌst]	adv.	就…	1	1	初級	
	leave	[liv]	v.	留下	1	1	初級	◎
	alone	[əˋlon]	adv.	單獨地	1	1	初級	

單字級等分析

	單字	音標	詞性	中文			級等	
❷	while	[hwaɪl]	n.	一段時間	1	1	初級	
❸	wife	[waɪf]	n.	妻子	1	1	初級	
	sick	[sɪk]	adj.	生病的	1	1	初級	◎
	recently	[ˋrisntlɪ]	adv.	最近	1		初級	
❹	give	[gɪv]	v.	給予	1	1	初級	
	try	[traɪ]	n.	嘗試	1	1	初級	
❺	willing	[ˋwɪlɪŋ]	adj.	願意的	1	2	初級	◎
	listen	[ˋlɪsn]	v.	聆聽	1	1	初級	
	love	[lʌv]	v.	想要	1	1	初級	
	have	[hæv]	v.	擁有	1	1	初級	
	someone	[ˋsʌmˏwʌn]	pron.	某個人	1	1	初級	
	talk	[tɔk]	v.	談話	1	1	初級	◎
❻	figure	[ˋfɪgjɚ]	v.	想出、理解	1	2	初級	◎
	out	[aut]	adv.	出現	1	1	初級	
	find	[faɪnd]	v.	尋找	1	1	初級	
	way	[we]	n.	辦法	1	1	初級	
❼	said	[sɛd]	p.t.	say（說）過去式	4	1	初級	
	reasonable	[ˋriznəbl]	adj.	有道理的	1	3	中級	◎
❽	helped	[hɛlpt]	p.p.	help（幫助）過去分詞	1	1	初級	
	worrier	[ˋwɝɪɚ]	n.	容易擔心的人				
❾	ok	[ˋoˋke]	adj.	沒關係的	1	1	初級	
	better	[ˋbɛtɚ]	adj.	good（良好的）比較級	1	1	初級	
	soon	[sun]	adv.	很快	1	1	初級	
	enough	[əˋnʌf]	adv.	足夠地	1	1	初級	◎
❿	pull	[pul]	v.	振作	1	1	初級	
	myself	[maɪˋsɛlf]	pron.	我自己	1		初級	
	together	[təˋgɛðɚ]	adv.	聚集起、起來	1	1	初級	
⓫	life	[laɪf]	n.	生活	1	1	初級	
	get	[gɛt]	v.	變成	1	1	初級	◎
⓬	done	[dʌn]	p.p.	do（做）過去分詞	1	1	初級	
	this	[ðɪs]	pron.	這個	1	1	初級	
⓭	such	[sʌtʃ]	adv.	這麼	1	1	初級	
	thoughtful	[ˋθɔtfəl]	adj.	善解人意的	3	4	中級	◎
	person	[ˋpɝsn]	n.	人	1	1	初級	
⓮	really	[ˋrɪəlɪ]	adv.	很、十分	1		初級	
	nice	[mek]	adj.	良好的	1	1	初級	
⓯	know	[no]	v.	知道	1	1	初級	◎
	mean	[min]	v.	用意	1	2	初級	◎
	well	[wɛl]	adv.	良好地	1	1	初級	◎
⓰	sorry	[ˋsɑrɪ]	adj.	抱歉的	1	1	初級	
	make	[mek]	v.	使得	1	1	初級	
	worry	[ˋwɝɪ]	v.	擔心	1	1	初級	◎
⓱	thanks	[θæŋks]	n.	thank（感謝）複數	1			
	concern	[kənˋsɝn]	n.	關心		3	初級	◎
⓲	accept	[əkˋsɛpt]	v.	接受	1	2	初級	◎
	advice	[ədˋvaɪs]	n.	建議	1	3	初級	◎

※「紅字單字」於本單元多句出現，「單字級等分析」僅列在「首次出現句」。

🔊 MP3 097-01 ❶～❽

❶	別忘了帶雨傘。	Don't forget to bring an umbrella. * **Don't forget to**＋動詞（你不要忘記…）
❷	你又忘了做作業。	You've forgotten to do your homework again. * **have forgotten to**＋動詞（忘了做…）
❸	過馬路要小心！	Be careful crossing the street!
❹	小心！有車。	Watch out! Here comes a car. ＝ Careful, a car! * **Here comes**＋交通工具（有某交通工具行駛過來）
❺	別忘了你昨天說的話。	Don't forget what you said yesterday. * **what you said**（你說過的話）
❻	你總是忘東忘西。	You always forget something.
❼	記得要打電話回來。	Remember to call back.　* **call back**（回電）
❽	不怕一萬，只怕萬一。	Prevention is better than a cure.
❾	別太晚回來。	Don't come home too late.
❿	明天的約會在十點。	Tomorrow's appointment will be at ten o'clock.
⓫	請你多保重。	Please take good care of yourself.
⓬	需要我打電話提醒你嗎？	Do you need me to remind you with a phone call?　* **with a phone call**（以電話的方式）
⓭	想想看，有沒有什麼事忘了？	Think about it, is there anything you've forgotten?
⓮	記得要幫我買東西。	Remember to buy the things for me.
⓯	昨天答應我的事，你忘了嗎？	You promised me yesterday—have you forgotten?
⓰	你知道今天是什麼日子嗎？	Do you know what day it is today? * **what day is...?**（…是什麼樣的日子？）
⓱	是不是快要考試了？	Don't you have a test coming up soon? * **be coming up soon**（即將到來，原句「...a test (that is) coming up soon」，省略代名詞「that」和「be 動詞」）
⓲	所有費用都繳了嗎？	Have you paid all your fees and bills?

	單字	音標	詞性	意義	字頻	大考	英檢	多益
❶	forget	[fɚˋgɛt]	v.	忘記	1	1	初級	
	bring	[brɪŋ]	v.	攜帶	1	1	初級	
	umbrella	[ʌmˋbrɛlə]	n.	雨傘	3	2	初級	
❷	forgotten	[fɚˋgɑtn̩]	p.p.	forget（忘記）過去分詞	4	1	初級	◎
	do	[du]	v.	做	1	1	初級	
	homework	[ˋhom͵wɝk]	n.	功課	2	1	初級	
	again	[əˋgɛn]	adj.	再次	1	1	初級	

❸	careful	[ˋkɛrfəl]	adj.	小心的	1	1	初級	◎
	crossing	[ˋkrɔsɪŋ]	p.pr.	cross（跨越）現在分詞	3	5	中高	
	street	[strit]	n.	馬路	1	1	初級	
❹	watch	[wɑtʃ]	v.	當心	1	1	初級	◎
	out	[aʊt]	adv.	完全、徹底	1	1	初級	
	here	[hɪr]	adv.	這裡	1	1	初級	
	come	[kʌm]	v.	到來	1	1	初級	
	car	[kɑr]	n.	車	1	1	初級	◎
❺	said	[sɛd]	p.t.	say（說）過去式	4	1	初級	
	yesterday	[ˋjɛstəde]	adv.	昨天	1	1	初級	
❻	always	[ˋɔlwez]	adv.	總是	1	1	初級	
	something	[ˋsʌm.θɪŋ]	pron.	某些事情	1	1	初級	
❼	remember	[rɪˋmɛmbə]	v.	記得	1	1	初級	◎
	call	[kɔl]	v./n.	打電話/通話	1	1	初級	◎
	back	[bæk]	adv.	返回	1	1	初級	◎
❽	prevention	[prɪˋvɛnʃən]	n.	預防	2	4	中級	
	better	[ˋbɛtə]	adj.	good（良好的）比較級	1	1	初級	
	cure	[kjʊr]	n.	治療	2	2	初級	◎
❾	home	[hom]	n.	家	1	1	初級	
	too	[tu]	adv.	過於	1	1	初級	
	late	[let]	adv.	晚地	1	1	初級	◎
❿	tomorrow	[təˋmɔro]	n.	明天	1	1	初級	◎
	appointment	[əˋpɔɪntmənt]	n.	約會	2	4	中級	◎
	ten	[tɛn]	n.	十	1	1	初級	
	o'clock	[əˋklɑk]	n.	…點鐘	2	1	初級	
⓫	please	[pliz]	adv.	請	1	1	初級	
	take	[tek]	v.	採取	1	1	初級	◎
	good	[gʊd]	adj.	良好的	1	1	初級	◎
	care	[kɛr]	n.	照顧	1	1	初級	◎
	yourself	[jʊəˋsɛlf]	pron.	你自己	1		初級	
⓬	need	[nid]	v.	需要	1	1	初級	◎
	remind	[rɪˋmaɪnd]	v.	提醒	1	3	初級	◎
	phone	[fon]	n.	電話	1	2	初級	◎
⓭	think	[θɪŋk]	v.	認為	1	1	初級	
	there	[ðɛr]	adv.	有	1	1	初級	
	anything	[ˋɛnɪ.θɪŋ]	pron.	任何事情	1	1	初級	
⓮	buy	[baɪ]	v.	購買	1	1	初級	
	thing	[θɪŋ]	n.	東西	1	1	初級	
⓯	promised	[ˋprɑmɪst]	p.t.	promise（承諾、答應）過去式	4	2	初級	◎
⓰	know	[no]	v.	知道	1	1	初級	◎
	day	[de]	n.	天	1	1	初級	
	today	[təˋde]	n.	今天	1	1	初級	
⓱	have	[hæv]	v.	擁有	1	1	初級	
	test	[tɛst]	n.	考試	1	1	初級	
	coming	[ˋkʌmɪŋ]	p.pr.	come（到來）現在分詞	2	1	中級	
	up	[ʌp]	adv.	出現	1	1	初級	
	soon	[sun]	adv.	很快	1	1	初級	
⓲	paid	[ped]	p.p.	pay（繳費）過去分詞	3	3	中高	◎
	all	[ɔl]	adj.	所有的	1	1	初級	
	fee	[fi]	n.	費用	1	2	初級	◎
	bill	[bɪl]	n.	帳單	1	2	初級	◎

※「紅字單字」於本單元多句出現，「單字級等分析」僅列在「首次出現句」。

🔊 MP3 097-02 ❶～❽

❶	謝謝你的提醒。	Thanks for the reminder.
❷	我會記住的。	I'll keep that in mind. = I'll remember that. * **keep in mind**（記住）
❸	放心，我沒忘。	Don't worry, I haven't forgotten.
❹	別擔心，我知道。	Don't worry, I remember.
❺	謝謝你的提醒，我差點忘了。	Thanks for the reminder; I almost forgot. * **thanks for**＋名詞（謝謝…）
❻	我會把事情記在筆記簿上。	I'll make a note of the matter in my notebook. * **make a note**（寫筆記）
❼	我已經完成了。	I'm already done.
❽	別再嘮叨啦！	Stop babbling. * **Stop**＋動詞-ing（別再…）
❾	沒關係，我會處理。	It's OK, I'll handle it. * **handle**（處理）= **deal with**
❿	我自己會想辦法。	I'll figure it out by myself. * **figure out**（想出辦法）
⓫	我早就準備好了。	I've been ready for a long time. * **have been**＋形容詞（一直…）、**be ready**（準備好）
⓬	別管我！	Leave me alone!
⓭	我一直記得。	I've always remembered that.
⓮	好在有你提醒我。	Fortunately, you reminded me. * **fortunately**（幸好）= **luckily**
⓯	天啊！我怎麼忘記了？	Gosh! How could I forget about that?
⓰	我真是不能沒有你。	I really couldn't live without you. * **couldn't live**（無法生活）、**without you**（沒有你）
⓱	感謝你，我請你吃飯。	Thank you, let me buy you a meal. * **buy**＋某人＋**a meal**（請某人吃飯）
⓲	我真是愈來愈健忘了。	I'm becoming more and more forgetful. * 此句用「現在進行式」（...am becoming...） 表示「現階段逐漸變化的事」。

	單字	音標	詞性	意義	字頻	大考	英檢	多益
❶	thanks	[θæŋks]	n.	thank（感謝）複數	1			
	reminder	[rɪˋmaɪndɚ]	n.	提醒的話	2	5	中級	◎
❷	keep	[kip]	v.	保持	1	1	初級	◎
	that	[ðæt]	pron.	那個	1	1	初級	
	mind	[maɪnd]	n.	內心	1	1	初級	◎
	remember	[rɪˋmɛmbɚ]	v.	記得	1	1	初級	◎
❸	worry	[ˋwɝɪ]	v.	擔心	1	1	初級	◎
	forgotten	[fɚˋgɑtn]	p.p.	forget（忘記）過去分詞	4	1	初級	
❺	almost	[ˋɔl.most]	adv.	幾乎	1	1	初級	
	forgot	[fɚˋgɑt]	p.t.	forget（忘記）過去式	1	1	初級	
❻	make	[mek]	v.	做	1	1	初級	
	note	[not]	n.	筆記	1	1	初級	◎
	matter	[ˋmætɚ]	n.	事情	1	1	初級	◎
	notebook	[ˋnot.bʊk]	n.	筆記本	2	2	初級	◎
❼	already	[ɔlˋrɛdɪ]	adv.	已經	1	1	初級	◎
	done	[dʌn]	p.p.	do（做）過去分詞	1	1	初級	
❽	stop	[stɑp]	v.	停止	1	1	初級	◎
	babbling	[ˋbæblɪŋ]	n.	babble（嘮叨）動名詞	6			
❾	ok	[ˋoˋke]	adj.	沒關係的	1	1	初級	
	handle	[ˋhændl]	v.	處理	1	2	初級	◎
❿	figure	[ˋfɪgjɚ]	v.	想出、理解	1	2	初級	◎
	out	[aʊt]	adv.	出現	1	1	初級	
	myself	[maɪˋsɛlf]	pron.	我自己	1		初級	
⓫	ready	[ˋrɛdɪ]	adj.	準備好的	1	1	初級	◎
	long	[lɔŋ]	adj.	長的	1	1	初級	
	time	[taɪm]	n.	時間	1	1	初級	◎
⓬	leave	[liv]	v.	留下	1	1	初級	◎
	alone	[əˋlon]	adv.	獨自地	1	1	初級	
⓭	always	[ˋɔlwez]	adv.	總是	1	1	初級	
	remembered	[rɪˋmɛmbɚd]	p.p.	remember（記得）過去分詞	1	1	初級	◎
⓮	fortunately	[ˋfɔrtʃənɪtlɪ]	adv.	幸好	2		中級	
	reminded	[rɪˋmaɪndɪd]	p.t.	remind（提醒）過去式	1	3	初級	◎
⓯	gosh	[gɑʃ]	int.	天啊	3			
	forget	[fɚˋgɛt]	v.	忘記	1	1	初級	
⓰	really	[ˋrɪlɪ]	adv.	真的	1		初級	
	live	[lɪv]	v.	過活	1	1	初級	
⓱	thank	[θæŋk]	v.	感謝	1	1	初級	
	let	[lɛt]	v.	讓	1	1	初級	
	buy	[baɪ]	v.	購買	1	1	初級	
	meal	[mil]	n.	一餐	1	2	初級	
⓲	becoming	[bɪˋkʌmɪŋ]	p.pr.	become（變為）現在分詞	1		初級	◎
	more	[mor]	adv.	更加	1	1	初級	
	forgetful	[fɚˋgɛtfəl]	adj.	健忘的		5	中級	

※「紅字單字」於本單元多句出現，「單字級等分析」僅列在「首次出現句」。

098 勸告。

🔊 MP3 098-01 ❶～❶❼

❶	別做壞事。	Don't do bad things.
❷	這樣做不太好。	It's not good to do that.
❸	你會遭到報應。	You will get what you deserve. = What goes around comes around. * **what you deserve**（你應得的報應） 　= **what's coming to you**
❹	這樣做是錯的。	It's wrong to do that.
❺	上帝不會原諒你。	God will not forgive you.
❻	你得做大家的好榜樣。	You have to be a good example for everyone. * **be a good example**（成為好榜樣）
❼	請多多努力。	Please work harder. = Please make an extra effort.
❽	加油！	Go, go! = Come on!
❾	算了，別和他一般見識。	Forget it; don't lower yourself to the same level as him. * **forget it**（算了、別在意） * **lower oneself**（貶低自己） * **the same level as**＋某人（和某人一般見識）
❿	事情過了就算了。	It is past, so let it go. * **let it go**（算了、隨它過去）= **forget it**
⓫	別再吵了。	Knock it off. * **knock it off**（住口、住手）
⓬	再怎樣做也是於事無補。	It's no use doing anything else. * **it's no use**＋動詞-ing（做…是沒用的）
⓭	放棄吧！	Forget it! = Give it up!
⓮	你一定要堅持到底。	You have to stick it out. * **stick it out**（堅持到底）= **go through with it**
⓯	你應該換個工作。	You should change jobs. * **You shouldn't change jobs.**（你不應該換工作）
⓰	你不可以這樣做。	You can't do that.
⓱	你應該換個想法。	You should change your way of thinking. * **way of thinking**（思考方式）

	單字	音標	詞性	意義	字頻	大考	英檢	多益
❶	do	[du]	v.	做	1	1	初級	
	bad	[bæd]	adj.	不好的	1	1	初級	
	thing	[θɪŋ]	n.	事情	1	1	初級	
❷	good	[gʊd]	adj.	良好的	1	1	初級	◎
	that	[ðæt]	pron.	那個	1	1	初級	
❸	get	[gɛt]	v.	得到	1	1	初級	◎
	deserve	[dɪˋzɝv]	v.	應得	1	4	中級	◎
	go	[go]	v.	流轉/逝去	1	1	初級	
	around	[əˋraʊnd]	adv.	循環地	1	1	初級	
	come	[kʌm]	v.	到來	1	1	初級	
❹	wrong	[rɔŋ]	adj.	錯誤的	1	1	初級	◎
❺	god	[gɑd]	n.	神	2	1	初級	
	forgive	[fɚˋgɪv]	v.	原諒	2	2	初級	
❻	have	[hæv]	v.	必須	1	1	初級	
	example	[ɪgˋzæmpḷ]	n.	榜樣	1	1	初級	◎
	everyone	[ˋɛvrɪ.wʌn]	n.	每個人	1		初級	
❼	please	[pliz]	adv.	請	1	1	初級	
	work	[wɝk]	v.	工作	1	1	初級	◎
	harder	[ˋhɑrdɚ]	adv.	hard（努力地）比較級	1	1	初級	◎
	make	[mek]	v.	做出	1	1	初級	
	extra	[ˋɛkstrə]	adj.	額外的	1	2	初級	◎
	effort	[ˋɛfɚt]	n.	努力	1	2	初級	◎
❾	forget	[fɚˋgɛt]	v.	忘記	1	1	初級	
	lower	[ˋloɚ]	v.	降低	1	1	初級	◎
	yourself	[jʊɚˋsɛlf]	pron.	你自己	1		初級	
	same	[sem]	adj.	相同的	1	1	初級	
	level	[ˋlɛvḷ]	n.	水平	1	1	初級	◎
❿	past	[pæst]	n.	過去	1	1	初級	
	let	[lɛt]	v.	讓	1	1	初級	
⓫	knock	[nɑk]	v.	打住	1	2	初級	
	off	[ɔf]	adv.	停止	1	1	初級	
⓬	use	[juz]	n.	用處	1	1	初級	◎
	doing	[ˋduɪŋ]	p.pr.	do（做）現在分詞	1	1	初級	
	anything	[ˋɛnɪ.θɪŋ]	pron.	任何事情	1	1	初級	
	else	[ɛls]	adj.	其他的	1	1	初級	
⓭	give	[gɪv]	v.	放棄	1	1	初級	
	up	[ʌp]	adv.	完全、徹底	1	1	初級	
⓮	stick	[stɪk]	v.	堅持	1	2	初級	◎
	out	[aʊt]	adv.	徹底、到最後	1	1	初級	
⓯	change	[tʃendʒ]	v.	更換	1	2	初級	◎
	job	[dʒɑb]	n.	工作	1	1	初級	
⓱	way	[we]	n.	方式	1	1	初級	
	thinking	[ˋθɪŋkɪŋ]	n.	think（思考）動名詞	1	1	初級	

※「紅字單字」於本單元多句出現，「單字級等分析」僅列在「首次出現句」。

098 回應勸告。

MP3 098-02 ❶～⓲

❶	謝謝你的勸告。	Thanks for your advice. * thanks for＋名詞（謝謝…）
❷	我會三思而後行。	I'll think twice before I act. * think twice before＋某人＋act（某人三思而後行）
❸	你說的也有道理。	What you've said is reasonable. * what you've said（你曾經說過的話）
❹	我會照著你的話去做。	I'll do what you said. * what you said（你當時說過的話）
❺	我也打算這麼做。	That's just what I intend to do. * intend to＋動詞原形（打算…）
❻	我會小心的。	I'll be careful.
❼	我不會這麼做的。	I won't do that.
❽	你把你自己管好吧。	Mind your own business. * mind＋名詞（照顧好…）
❾	只要我喜歡有什麼不可以。	If I like it, then why not?
❿	我自己會負責。	I'll take responsibility for myself. * take responsibility for（負責）
⓫	別管我！	Leave me alone!
⓬	我不怕，我就是要這樣。	I'm not afraid; this is what I want.
⓭	我就是要這樣做。	That's how I'm going to do it, period. * how＋子句（…的方式）
⓮	不關你的事。	It's none of your business. * be none of your business（和你無關、不關你的事）
⓯	我不可能受你影響。	You can't possibly influence me. * influence（影響）＝ affect
⓰	這次我要自己決定。	I want to decide for myself this time. * decide for myself（自己做決定）
⓱	別想改變我的決定。	Don't even think about changing my decision. * change one's decision（改變決定）
⓲	別用大人的口氣對我說話。	Don't speak to me as if I were a child. * as if I were...（好像我現在是…）

單字級等分析

	單字	音標	詞性	意義	字頻	大考	英檢	多益
❶	thanks	[θæŋks]	n.	thank（感謝）複數	1			
	advice	[ədˋvaɪs]	n.	建議	1	3	初級	◎
❷	think	[θɪŋk]	v.	認為	1	1	初級	
	twice	[twaɪs]	adv.	兩次	1	1	初級	◎
	act	[ækt]	v.	行動	1	1	初級	
❸	said	[sɛd]	p.t.	say（說）過去式	4	1	初級	
	reasonable	[ˋriznəbḷ]	adj.	有道理的	1	3	中級	◎
❹	do	[du]	v.	做	1	1	初級	
❺	that	[ðæt]	pron.	那個	1	1	初級	
	just	[dʒʌst]	adv.	正好	1	1	初級	
	intend	[ɪnˋtɛnd]	v.	打算	1	4	中級	◎
❻	careful	[ˋkɛrfəl]	adj.	小心的	1	1	初級	◎
❽	mind	[maɪnd]	v.	照顧	1	1	初級	◎
	own	[on]	adj.	自己的	1	1	初級	◎
	business	[ˋbʊznɪs]	n.	個人事務	1	2	初級	◎
❾	like	[laɪk]	v.	喜歡	1	1	初級	
❿	take	[tek]	v.	負起	1	1	初級	◎
	responsibility	[rɪˏspɑnsəˋbɪlətɪ]	n.	責任	1	3	中級	◎
	myself	[maɪˋsɛlf]	pron.	我自己	1		初級	
⓫	leave	[liv]	v.	留下	1	1	初級	◎
	alone	[əˋlon]	adv.	獨自地	1	1	初級	
⓬	afraid	[əˋfred]	adj.	害怕的	1	1	初級	
	this	[ðɪs]	pron. /adj.	這個	1	1	初級	
	want	[wɑnt]	v.	想要	1	1	初級	◎
⓭	going	[ˋgoɪŋ]	p.pr.	go（即將）現在分詞	4	1	初級	
	period	[ˋpɪrɪəd]	int.	說完了、就這樣	1	2	初級	◎
⓮	none	[nʌn]	pron.	沒有	1	2	初級	
⓯	possibly	[ˋpɑsəblɪ]	adv.	可能	1		中級	
	influence	[ˋɪnflʊəns]	v.	影響	1	2	初級	◎
⓰	decide	[dɪˋsaɪd]	v.	決定	1	1	初級	◎
	time	[taɪm]	n.	次、回	1	1	初級	◎
⓱	even	[ˋivən]	adv.	甚至	1	1	初級	◎
	changing	[ˋtʃendʒɪŋ]	n.	change（改變）動名詞	2	2	初級	◎
	decision	[dɪˋsɪʒən]	n.	決定	1	2	初級	◎
⓲	speak	[spik]	v.	說話	1	1	初級	
	child	[tʃaɪld]	n.	小孩	1	1	初級	

※「紅字單字」於本單元多句出現，「單字級等分析」僅列在「首次出現句」。

🔵 MP3 099-01 ❶～⓲

❶	妳真漂亮。	You are so beautiful.
❷	你真帥。	You are so handsome.
❸	你真的很聰明。	You are really smart.
❹	你可以去當電影明星了。	You could be a movie star with your looks. * movie star（電影明星） * with one's looks（運用長相）
❺	妳看起來只有 25 歲。	You look like you're only 25 years old. * look like...（看起來像…）
❻	我真希望能和妳一樣美。	I really hope that I can be as beautiful as you are. * hope that＋子句（希望） * as beautiful as...（和…一樣美麗）
❼	美女喔！	What a pretty girl! ＝ What a beauty!
❽	看不出來妳已經是三個孩子的媽！	You really don't look like a mother with three children! * with three children（有三個小孩）
❾	帥哥喔！	What a handsome boy!
❿	我真羨慕你的才華。	I really envy your talent. * envy one's talent（羨慕才華）
⓫	你是班上最聰明的學生。	You're the smartest student in this class.
⓬	你太棒了！	You are wonderful! ＝ You are so great!
⓭	做得好！	Good job! ＝ Nice work!
⓮	一定很多人說妳很漂亮。	There must be many people who say that you're really beautiful. * there must be＋名詞（猜測一定有…）
⓯	你讓我們相形失色。	We pale in comparison to you. * in comparison to（相較於）
⓰	妳看起來像她姊姊，不像媽媽。	You look like her sister, not her mother.
⓱	真有你的！	You did a good job! * do a good job（做得好）
⓲	你穿這件衣服比我好看。	This clothing looks better on you than on me. * look better（比較好看）、on you（在你身上）

	單字	音標	詞性	意義	字頻	大考	英檢	多益
❶	so	[so]	adv.	這麼	1	1	初級	
	beautiful	[`bjutəfəl]	adj.	漂亮的	1	1	初級	
❷	handsome	[`hændsəm]	adj.	帥氣的	2	2	初級	
❸	really	[`rɪəlɪ]	adv.	真的/很、十分	1		初級	
	smart	[smɑrt]	adj.	聰明的	1	1	初級	◎
❹	movie	[`muvɪ]	n.	電影	1	1	初級	
	star	[stɑr]	n.	明星	1	1	初級	
	looks	[lʊks]	n.	長相	1	1	初級	
❺	look	[lʊk]	v.	看起來	1	1	初級	
	only	[`onlɪ]	adv.	只有	1	1	初級	
	year	[jɪr]	n.	年齡	1	1	初級	
	old	[old]	adj.	…歲	1	1	初級	
❻	hope	[hop]	v.	希望	1	1	初級	
❼	pretty	[`prɪtɪ]	adj.	美麗的	1	1	初級	◎
	girl	[gɝl]	n.	女孩	1	1	初級	
	beauty	[`bjutɪ]	n.	美女	1	1	中級	
❽	mother	[`mʌðɚ]	n.	母親	1	1	初級	
	three	[θri]	n.	三	1	1	初級	
	children	[`tʃɪldrən]	n.	child（小孩）複數	1	1	初級	
❾	boy	[bɔɪ]	n.	男孩	1	1	初級	
❿	envy	[`ɛnvɪ]	v.	羨慕	4	3	初級	
	talent	[`tælənt]	n.	才能	1	2	初級	◎
⓫	smartest	[`smɑrtɪst]	adj.	smart（聰明的）最高級	1	1	初級	◎
	student	[`stjudnt]	n.	學生	1	1	初級	
	this	[ðɪs]	adj.	這個	1	1	初級	
	class	[klæs]	n.	班級	1	1	初級	
⓬	wonderful	[`wʌndɚfəl]	adj.	極好的	1	2	初級	◎
	great	[gret]	adj.	很棒的	1	1	初級	◎
⓭	good	[gʊd]	adj.	良好的	1	1	初級	
	job	[dʒɑb]	n.	所做的事情	1	1	初級	
	nice	[naɪs]	adj.	美好的	1	1	初級	
	work	[wɝk]	n.	成果	1	1	初級	◎
⓮	there	[ðɛr]	adv.	有	1	1	初級	
	many	[`mɛnɪ]	adj.	許多的	1	1	初級	
	people	[`pipl]	n.	person（人）複數	1	1	初級	
	say	[se]	v.	說	1	1	初級	
⓯	pale	[pel]	v.	失色、黯淡	2	3	初級	◎
	comparison	[kəm`pærəsn]	n.	比較	1	3	中級	◎
⓰	sister	[`sɪstɚ]	n.	姐姐、妹妹	1	1	初級	
⓱	did	[dɪd]	p.t.	do（做）過去式	1	1	初級	
⓲	clothing	[`kloðɪŋ]	n.	衣服	1	2	中級	
	better	[`bɛtɚ]	adj.	good（好看的）比較級	1	1	初級	

※「紅字單字」於本單元多句出現，「單字級等分析」僅列在「首次出現句」。

🔊 MP3 099-02 ❶～⓱

❶	謝謝你的讚美。	Thanks for your praise.
❷	你真有眼光。	You really have good judgment. * **have good judgment**（眼光很好） * **have poor judgment**（眼光很差）
❸	大家都這樣說。	Everybody says that.
❹	沒有啦，你過獎了。	It's nothing; you're making too much of it. * **make too much of**（言過其實、過獎）
❺	你這樣說，我會不好意思的。	I am embarrassed by what you said. * **be embarrassed**（感到不好意思）
❻	再多說幾句好聽的吧。	Say some more things that I like to hear. * **things I like to hear**（我想聽的好話）
❼	別再灌我迷湯了。	Don't flatter me again. * **flatter**＋某人（奉承某人、說某人的好話）
❽	你是真心話嗎？	Do you mean what you said?
❾	你說真的嗎？還是逗我開心？	Do you mean it, or are you just joking around? * **joke around**（開玩笑）
❿	聽你這麼說我心花怒放。	What you said makes me extremely happy. * **make**＋某人＋形容詞（使某人…） * **extremely happy**（心花怒放、非常開心）
⓫	你才是我學習的對象。	You're really a role model I can learn from. * **role model**（模範）＝ **example** * **learn from**＋某人（效法某人）
⓬	我才羨慕你呢！	No, I envy you!
⓭	你比我還棒呢！	You're better than I am!
⓮	別逗我開心了。	Don't make fun of me. ＝ Don't tease me. * **make fun of**（取笑、逗弄）＝ **tease**
⓯	謝謝你的肯定。	Thanks for your recognition.
⓰	你真會說話。	You're just being polite. * 某人＋**be just being polite**（某人太客氣了）
⓱	我沒你說的這麼好。	I'm not as good as you say. * **as good as...**（和…一樣好）

	單字	音標	詞性	意義	字頻	大考	英檢	多益
❶	thanks	[θæŋks]	n.	thank（感謝）複數	1			
	praise	[prez]	n.	讚美	2	2	初級	
❷	really	[ˋrɪəlɪ]	adv.	真的	1		初級	
	have	[hæv]	v.	擁有	1	1	初級	
	good	[gʊd]	adj.	良好的	1	1	初級	◎
	judgment	[ˋdʒʌdʒmənt]	n.	眼光	1	2	中級	◎
❸	everybody	[ˋɛvrɪ.bɑdɪ]	pron.	每個人	1		初級	
	say	[se]	v.	說	1	1	初級	
	that	[ðæt]	pron.	那樣	1	1	初級	
❹	nothing	[ˋnʌθɪŋ]	pron.	沒有事情	1	1	初級	
	making	[ˋmekɪŋ]	p.pr.	make（讚賞）現在分詞	2	1	中高	
	too	[tu]	adv.	過於	1	1	初級	
	much	[mʌtʃ]	adv.	許多地	1	1	初級	
❺	embarrassed	[ɪmˋbærəst]	adj.	感到不好意思的	2	4	初級	◎
	said	[sɛd]	p.t.	say（說）過去式	4	1	初級	
❻	some	[sʌm]	adj.	有些	1	1	初級	
	more	[mor]	adj.	更多的	1	1	初級	
	thing	[θɪŋ]	n.	事情	1	1	初級	
	like	[laɪk]	v.	喜歡	1	1	初級	
	hear	[hɪr]	v.	聽	1	1	初級	
❼	flatter	[ˋflætə]	v.	奉承、說好話	4	4	中級	
	again	[əˋgɛn]	adv.	再次	1		初級	
❽	mean	[min]	v.	用意	1	2	初級	◎
❾	just	[dʒʌst]	adv.	只是/真是、實在	1	1	初級	
	joking	[ˋdʒokɪŋ]	p.pr.	joke（開玩笑）現在分詞	1	1	初級	
	around	[əˋraʊnd]	adv.	四處	1	1	初級	
❿	make	[mek]	v.	使得/嘲笑	1	1	初級	
	extremely	[ɪkˋstrimlɪ]	adv.	極度地	1		中級	
	happy	[ˋhæpɪ]	adj.	開心的	1	1	初級	
⓫	role	[rol]	n.	角色	1	2	初級	
	model	[ˋmɑdl]	n.	模範、典型	1	2	初級	◎
	learn	[lɜn]	v.	學習	1	1	初級	
⓬	envy	[ˋɛnvɪ]	v.	羨慕	4	3	初級	
⓭	better	[ˋbɛtə]	adj.	good（良好的）比較級	1	1	初級	
⓮	fun	[fʌn]	n.	玩笑	1	1	初級	
	tease	[tiz]	v.	取笑、逗弄	2	3	中級	◎
⓯	recognition	[.rɛkəgˋnɪʃən]	n.	認可	1	4	中級	◎
⓰	polite	[pəˋlaɪt]	adj.	客氣的	2	2	初級	◎

※「紅字單字」於本單元多句出現，「單字級等分析」僅列在「首次出現句」。

100 鼓勵。

❶	加油！	Go, go! = Come on!
❷	一定要堅持下去。	You've got to stick it out. * **have got to**（必須）、**stick it out**（堅持到底）
❸	你會成功的。	You'll succeed.
❹	下一次會更好。	Next time will be better.
❺	別洩氣。	Don't feel disappointed.
❻	再試一次。	Try it one more time.
❼	我們對你有信心。	We have confidence in you. * **have confidence in**＋某人（對某人有信心）
❽	我們一起努力。	We can work hard together. * **work hard**（努力做事）
❾	你比我好多了。	You are much better than I am.
❿	比上不足比下有餘啦！	Worse off than some, better off than many! * **worse off than**（比…糟糕）、**better off than**（比…更好）
⓫	沒關係，還有機會。	It's OK, there's still another chance.
⓬	盡力就好。	Your best is good enough. * **your best**（你能做的最大努力）、**good enough**（足夠）
⓭	你已經做得很好了。	You've already done your best. * **have already done...**（已經做了…）
⓮	你很有潛力。	You have a lot of potential. * **a lot of**（許多）
⓯	只差一點就成功了。	You almost succeeded.
⓰	別自暴自棄。	Don't beat yourself up. * **beat oneself up**（過度自責、自暴自棄）
⓱	別放棄啊！	Hang in there! * **hang in**（堅持、撐住）
⓲	失敗為成功之母。	Failure is the mother of success.
⓳	保持下去喔！	Keep it up! = Keep up the good work! * **keep up**（保持）
⓴	你一定可以做到的。	You can do it.

	單字	音標	詞性	意義	字頻	大考	英檢	多益
❶	go	[go]	v.	加油、繼續	1	1	初級	
	come	[kʌm]	v.	加油、繼續	1	1	初級	
❷	got	[gɑt]	p.p.	get（必須）過去分詞	1	1	初級	◎
	stick	[stɪk]	v.	堅持	1	2	初級	◎
	out	[aʊt]	adv.	徹底、到最後	1	1	初級	
❸	succeed	[sək`sid]	v.	成功	1	2	初級	◎
❹	next	[nɛkst]	adj.	下一個	1	1	初級	
	time	[taɪm]	n.	次、回	1	1	初級	◎
	better	[`bɛtɚ]	adj.	good（良好的）比較級	1	1	初級	
❺	feel	[fil]	v.	感到	1	1	初級	
	disappointed	[ˌdɪsə`pɔɪntɪd]	adj.	失望的	2	3	中級	◎
❻	try	[traɪ]	v.	嘗試	1	1	初級	
	one	[wʌn]	n.	一	1	1	初級	
	more	[mor]	adj.	更多的	1	1	初級	
❼	have	[hæv]	v.	擁有	1	1	初級	
	confidence	[`kɑnfədəns]	n.	信心	1	4	中級	◎
❽	work	[wɝk]	v./n.	工作/成果	1	1	初級	◎
	hard	[hɑrd]	adv.	努力地	1	1	初級	◎
	together	[tə`gɛðɚ]	adv.	一起	1	1	初級	
❾	much	[mʌtʃ]	adv.	更為	1	1	初級	
❿	worse	[wɝs]	adj.	bad（不好的）比較級	4	1	中級	
	off	[ɔf]	adv.	更為	1	1	初級	
	some	[sʌm]	pron.	一些	1	1	初級	
	many	[`mɛnɪ]	pron.	許多	1	1	初級	
⓫	ok	[`o`ke]	adj.	沒關係的	1	1	初級	
	there	[ðɛr]	adv.	有…/這裡	1	1	初級	
	still	[stɪl]	adv.	仍然	1	1	初級	◎
	another	[ə`nʌðɚ]	adj.	另一個	1	1	初級	
	chance	[tʃæns]	n.	機會	1	1	初級	
⓬	best	[bɛst]	n.	最好	1	1	初級	
	good	[gʊd]	adj.	良好的	1	1	初級	◎
	enough	[ə`nʌf]	adv.	足夠地	1	1	初級	
⓭	already	[ɔl`rɛdɪ]	adv.	已經	1	1	初級	◎
	done	[dʌn]	p.p.	do（做）過去分詞	1	1	初級	
⓮	lot	[lɑt]	n.	許多	1	1	初級	
	potential	[pə`tɛnʃəl]	n.	潛力		5	中級	◎
⓯	almost	[`ɔl.most]	adv.	幾乎	1	1	初級	
	succeeded	[sək`sidɪd]	p.t.	succeed（成功）過去式	1	2	初級	◎
⓰	beat	[bɛst]	v.	自責	1	1	初級	
	yourself	[jʊ`sɛlf]	pron.	你自己	1		初級	
	up	[ʌp]	adv.	過度地/持續下去	1	1	初級	
⓱	hang	[hæŋ]	v.	堅持	1	2	初級	◎
⓲	failure	[`feljɚ]	n.	失敗	1	2	初級	◎
	mother	[`mʌðɚ]	n.	母親	1	1	初級	
	success	[sək`sɛs]	n.	成功	1	2	初級	◎
⓳	keep	[kip]	v.	保持	1	1	初級	◎
⓴	do	[du]	v.	做到	1	1	初級	

※「紅字單字」於本單元多句出現，「單字級等分析」僅列在「首次出現句」。

100 回應鼓勵。

❶	我會全力以赴的。	I'll do my best.
❷	我不會放棄的。	I will not give up
❸	我不會讓你失望的。	I will not disappoint you. = I will not let you down. * disappoint... （使…失望）= let...down
❹	我會堅持下去。	I'll stick it out to the end.
❺	謝謝你始終這麼支持我。	Thanks for your support from beginning to end. * from beginning to end（自始至終）
❻	謝謝你的鼓勵。	Thanks for your encouragement.
❼	我會再試試的。	I'll give it another try.
❽	為了你，我要好好表現。	For you, I'll do my best. * for（為了）、do one's best（盡全力）
❾	我會繼續努力。	I'll keep on striving. * keep on（繼續）
❿	你說的很對。	What you said is right.
⓫	我太大意了。	I'm too negligent.
⓬	我會試著往好的一面想。	I'll try to look on the bright side. * look on the bright side（往好處想）
⓭	我下次會更努力的。	I'll try harder next time.
⓮	我一定會成功的。	I will succeed.
⓯	我確實已經盡了全力。	I've really done my best.
⓰	聽到你這麼說，我又有信心了。	Hearing what you said has given me confidence again. * Hearing...（聽到…，動名詞當主詞） * what you said（你剛才說的話）
⓱	我決定放棄了。	I decided to give up.
⓲	知道你說的對，可是我做不到。	I know what you said is right, but I just couldn't do it.
⓳	我會試著振作起來的！	I'll try to pull myself together again! * pull oneself together（讓自己振作）
⓴	我要讓你失望了。	I'm going to disappoint you.

	單字	音標	詞性	意義	字頻	大考	英檢	多益
❶	do	[du]	v.	做	1	1	初級	
	best	[bɛst]	n.	最好	1	1	初級	
❷	give	[gɪv]	v.	放棄	1	1	初級	
	up	[ʌp]	adv.	完全、徹底	1	1	初級	
❸	disappoint	[.dɪsə`pɔɪnt]	v.	失望	3	3	中級	◎
	let	[lɛt]	v.	讓…	1	1	初級	
	down	[daʊn]	adv.	失望地	1	1	初級	
❹	stick	[stɪk]	v.	堅持	1	2	初級	◎
	out	[aʊt]	adv.	徹底、到最後	1	1	初級	
	end	[ɛnd]	n.	最後	1	1	初級	
❺	thanks	[θæŋks]	n.	thank（感謝）	1			
	support	[sə`port]	n.	支持	1	2	初級	◎
	beginning	[bɪ`gɪnɪŋ]	n.	開始	1	1	初級	
❻	encouragement	[ɪn`kɝɪdʒmənt]	n.	鼓勵	3	2	中級	◎
❼	another	[ə`nʌðɚ]	adj.	另一個	1	1		
	try	[traɪ]	n./v.	嘗試	1	1	初級	
❾	keep	[kip]	v.	繼續	1	1	初級	◎
	striving	[`straɪvɪŋ]	n.	strive（努力）動名詞	8	4	中級	◎
❿	said	[sɛd]	p.t.	say（說）過去式	4	1	初級	
	right	[raɪt]	adj.	正確的	1	1	初級	
⓫	too	[tu]	adv.	過於	1	1	初級	
	negligent	[`nɛglɪdʒənt]	adj.	粗心大意的	6			
⓬	look	[lʊk]	v.	看見	1	1	初級	
	bright	[braɪt]	adj.	明亮的	1	1	初級	
	side	[saɪd]	n.	面、側	1	1	初級	
⓭	harder	[`hɑrdɚ]	adv.	hard（努力地）比較級	1	1	初級	◎
	next	[nɛkst]	adj.	下一個	1	1	初級	
	time	[taɪm]	n.	次、回	1	1	初級	
⓮	succeed	[sək`sid]	v.	成功	1	2	初級	◎
⓯	really	[`rɪəlɪ]	adv.	確實	1		初級	
	done	[dʌn]	p.p.	do（做）過去分詞	1	1	初級	
⓰	hearing	[`hɪrɪŋ]	n.	hear（聽）動名詞	1	1	中高	
	given	[`gɪvən]	p.p.	give（給予）過去分詞	2	4	中高	◎
	confidence	[`kɑnfədəns]	n.	信心	1	4	中級	◎
	again	[ə`gɛn]	adv.	再次	1	1	初級	
⓱	decided	[dɪ`saɪdɪd]	p.t.	decide（決定）過去式	1	1	初級	◎
⓲	know	[no]	v.	知道	1	1	初級	◎
	just	[dʒʌst]	adv.	只是	1	1	初級	
⓳	pull	[pʊl]	v.	振作	1	1	初級	
	myself	[maɪ`sɛlf]	pron.	我自己	1		初級	
	together	[tə`gɛðɚ]	adv.	聚集起、起來	1	1	初級	
⓴	going	[`goɪŋ]	p.pr.	go（即將）現在分詞	4	1	初級	

※「紅字單字」於本單元多句出現，「單字級等分析」僅列在「首次出現句」。

MP3 101-01 ❶～㉑

❶	新年快樂！	Happy New Year!
❷	情人節快樂！	Happy Valentine's Day!
❸	生日快樂！	Happy birthday!
❹	一路順風。	Bon voyage. ＝ Have a good trip.
❺	母親節快樂！	Happy Mother's Day!
❻	聖誕節快樂！	Merry Christmas!
❼	天作之合。	A match made in heaven. ＝ A perfect couple.
❽	祝福你事業成功。	Best wishes for your business. * **Best wishes for**＋名詞（祝福…、恭喜…）
❾	父親節快樂！	Happy Father's Day!
❿	恭喜你高昇。	Congratulations on your promotion. * **Congratulations on**＋名詞（恭喜…）
⓫	為你的健康舉杯！	To your health!
⓬	祝你青春永駐。	I wish you eternal youth. * **I wish you**＋名詞（祝福你獲得…）
⓭	恭喜啊，喜獲麟兒。	Congratulations on your new son. * **Congratulations on your new daughter.** （恭喜啊，喜獲千金）
⓮	祝你幸福。	I wish you happiness.
⓯	祝你們考試 ALL PASS！	May all of you pass your exams! * **May**＋人事物＋動詞（祝福某人事物…） * **all of you**（你們大家）
⓰	喬遷之喜。	Best wishes for your new home.
⓱	祝你好運。	I wish you luck.
⓲	祝你早日康復。	May you recover soon.
⓳	祝你永遠健康快樂。	I wish you everlasting health and happiness.
⓴	祝你生意興隆。	May your business prosper.
㉑	恭喜啊！！	Good for you!

	單字	音標	詞性	意義	字頻	大考	英檢	多益
❶	happy	[ˈhæpɪ]	adj.	快樂的	1	1	初級	
	new	[nju]	adj.	新的	1	1	初級	
	year	[jɪr]	n.	年	1	1	初級	
❷	valentine	[ˈvæləntaɪn]	n.	情人			初級	
	day	[de]	n.	節日	1	1	初級	
❸	birthday	[ˈbɝθ.de]	n.	生日	1		初級	
❹	bon voyage	[bɑn vɔɪˈɑdʒ]	int.	（法語）一路順風				
	have	[hæv]	v.	擁有	1	1	初級	
	good	[gʊd]	adj.	良好的	1	1	初級	◎
	trip	[trɪp]	n.	旅行	1	1	初級	◎
❺	mother	[ˈmʌðɚ]	n.	母親	1	1	初級	
❻	merry	[ˈmɛrɪ]	adj.	愉快的	3	3	中級	
	Christmas	[ˈkrɪsməs]	n.	聖誕節	1		初級	
❼	match	[mætʃ]	n.	伴侶	1	2	初級	◎
	made	[med]	p.p.	make（撮合）過去分詞	1	1	初級	
	heaven	[ˈhɛvən]	n.	天堂	1	3	中級	
	perfect	[ˈpɝfɪkt]	adj.	最佳的	1	2	初級	◎
	couple	[ˈkʌpl]	n.	伴侶	1	2	初級	◎
❽	best	[bɛst]	adj.	good（良好的）最高級	1	1	初級	
	wish	[wɪʃ]	n./v.	祝福	1	1	初級	
	business	[ˈbɪznɪs]	n.	事業	1	2	初級	
❾	father	[ˈfɑðɚ]	n.	父親	1	1	初級	
❿	congratulation	[kən.grætʃəˈleʃən]	n.	祝賀	4	2		
	promotion	[prəˈmoʃən]	n.	升職	2	4	中級	◎
⓫	health	[hɛlθ]	n.	健康	1	1	初級	◎
⓬	eternal	[ɪˈtɝnl]	adj.	永恆的	3	5	中高	
	youth	[juθ]	n.	年輕、青春	1	2	初級	
⓭	son	[sʌn]	n.	兒子	1	1	初級	
⓮	happiness	[ˈhæpɪnɪs]	n.	幸福	2			
⓯	all	[ɔl]	pron.	所有人	1	1	初級	
	pass	[pæs]	v.	通過	1	1	初級	◎
	exam	[ɪgˈzæm]	n.	考試	2	1	初級	
⓰	home	[hom]	n.	家	1	1	初級	
⓱	luck	[lʌk]	n.	好運	1	2	中級	
⓲	recover	[rɪˈkʌvɚ]	v.	康復	1	3	初級	◎
	soon	[sun]	adv.	快、早	1	1	初級	
⓳	everlasting	[ˌɛvɚˈlæstɪŋ]	adj.	永遠的	7			
⓴	prosper	[ˈprɑspɚ]	v.	昌盛	3	4	中級	◎

※「紅字單字」於本單元多句出現，「單字級等分析」僅列在「首次出現句」。

101　回應祝賀。

❶	謝謝。	Thank you.
❷	你真貼心。	You're really kind.
❸	希望大家都跟你一樣。	I wish everyone were like you. * wish (that)＋過去式子句（可以的話，希望…）
❹	以後還要麻煩你多照顧。	I'm afraid I'll need you to continue to look after me in the future. * I'm afraid＋子句（恐怕…） * look after me（關照我）
❺	你真是有心。	You're so thoughtful.
❻	也同樣祝福你。	Same to you.
❼	謝謝你的禮物。	Thanks for your gift.
❽	人來就好了，別太客氣。	Don't be so polite, just come.
❾	有空常來坐坐。	Come visit whenever you have time.
❿	我今天真的很開心。	I'm really happy today.
⓫	下回就輪到你啦。	Next time it will be your turn. * be one's turn（輪到某人）
⓬	什麼時候換我祝福你呀？	When will it be my turn to offer you my blessings? * offer one's blessing（祝福）
⓭	你的禮物對我來說實在是太珍貴了。	Your present is really too valuable to me. * too valuable（太貴重） * to me（對我來說）
⓮	感謝你特別前來祝賀我。	Thank you for your congratulating me in person. * your congratulating me（你對我的祝賀） * in person（本人親自）
⓯	真不知道怎麼感謝你。	I really don't know how I can thank you.
⓰	你也要加油！	Good luck to you too!
⓱	我感銘在心！	I really appreciate it!
⓲	小小成就，不足掛齒。	It's only a tiny accomplishment, please don't mention it.

	單字	音標	詞性	意義	字頻	大考	英檢	多益
❶	thank	[θæŋk]	v.	感謝	1	1	初級	
❷	really	[ˋrɪəlɪ]	adv.	真的	1		初級	
	kind	[kaɪnd]	adj.	貼心的	1	1	初級	◎
❸	wish	[wɪʃ]	v.	希望	1	1	初級	
	everyone	[ˋɛvrɪˏwʌn]	pron.	每個人	1		初級	
❹	afraid	[əˋfred]	adj.	害怕的	1	1	初級	
	need	[nid]	v.	需要	1	1	初級	◎
	continue	[kənˋtɪnjʊ]	v.	繼續	1	1	初級	◎
	look	[lʊk]	v.	關照	1	1	初級	
	future	[ˋfjutʃə]	n.	未來	1	2	初級	
❺	so	[so]	adv.	真是	1	1	初級	
	thoughtful	[ˋθɔtfəl]	adj.	考慮周到的	3	4	中級	◎
❻	same	[sem]	adj.	相同的	1	1	初級	
❼	thanks	[θæŋks]	n.	thank（感謝）複數	1			
	gift	[gɪft]	n.	禮物	1	1	初級	◎
❽	polite	[pəˋlaɪt]	adj.	客氣的	2	2	初級	◎
	just	[dʒʌst]	adv.	只要	1	1	初級	
	come	[kʌm]	v.	前來	1		初級	
❾	visit	[ˋvɪzɪt]	v.	拜訪	1	1	初級	◎
	have	[hæv]	v.	擁有	1	1	初級	
	time	[taɪm]	n.	時間/次、回	1	1	初級	◎
❿	happy	[ˋhæpɪ]	adj.	開心的	1	1	初級	
	today	[təˋde]	adv.	今天	1	1	初級	◎
⓫	next	[nɛkst]	adj.	下一個	1	1	初級	
	turn	[tɜn]	n.	一輪	1	1	初級	◎
⓬	offer	[ˋɔfə]	v.	獻上	1	2	初級	◎
	blessing	[ˋblɛsɪŋ]	n.	祝福	2	4	中級	
⓭	present	[ˋprɛznt]	n.	禮物	1	2	初級	◎
	too	[tu]	adv.	過於	1	1	初級	
	valuable	[ˋvæljʊəbl]	adj.	珍貴的	1	3	中級	◎
⓮	congratulating	[kənˋgrætʃəˏletɪŋ]	n.	congratulate（祝賀）動名詞	4	4	中級	◎
	person	[ˋpɜsn]	n.	本人	1	1	初級	
⓯	know	[no]	v.	知道	1	1	初級	◎
⓰	good	[gʊd]	adj.	良好的	1	1	初級	◎
	luck	[lʌk]	n.	好運	1	2	中級	
⓱	appreciate	[əˋpriʃɪˏet]	v.	感激	1	3	初級	◎
⓲	only	[ˋonlɪ]	adv.	只是	1	1	初級	
	tiny	[ˋtaɪnɪ]	adj.	微小的	1	1	初級	
	accomplishment	[əˋkɑmplɪʃmənt]	n.	成就	2	4		◎
	please	[pliz]	adv.	請	1	1	初級	
	mention	[ˋmɛnʃən]	v.	提到	1	3	中級	◎

※「紅字單字」於本單元多句出現，「單字級等分析」僅列在「首次出現句」。

MP3 102-01 ❶～❼

❶	嗨，請進。	Hi, please come in.
❷	歡迎歡迎。	Welcome.
❸	希望你會喜歡這個派對。	I hope that you will enjoy my party. * hope that＋子句（希望…）
❹	歡迎來我家玩。	Welcome to my home.
❺	地址好找嗎？	Any problems finding the address? * problem＋動詞-ing（做…有困難）
❻	路上有塞車嗎？	Any traffic on the way here? * on the way＋地點（在前往某地點的路上）
❼	我幫你把外套掛起來。	Let me hang up your coat. * hang up（吊掛起）
❽	你來得真早。	You came early.
❾	很高興你能來。	I'm glad that you could come. * I'm glad that＋子句（我高興…）
❿	其他的人應該也快到了。	The others should be here in a moment. * the others（其餘的人）、in a moment（一會兒）
⓫	這下子全員到齊囉！	Now we have a full house! * have a full house（全員到齊、座無虛席）
⓬	大家都在等你呢！	Everyone is waiting for you! * wait for＋某人（等待某人）
⓭	謝謝你的禮物，你太客氣了！	Thank you for the present, you're too kind!
⓮	你今天一定是全場目光的焦點。	You certainly will be the focus of this party. * 此句用「未來簡單式」（…will…）表示 　「根據直覺預測未來發生的事」。 * certainly（一定）＝ definitely、surely
⓯	你先生沒跟你一起來嗎？	Didn't your husband come with you? * come with＋某人（和某人一起前來）
⓰	你們能來真是我的榮幸。	It's my honor to have you here. * It's my honor to＋動詞原形（…是我的榮幸） * have＋某人＋here（讓某人在場）
⓱	旁邊這位是你太太嗎？	Is the person next to you your wife? * next to you（在你旁邊）

	單字	音標	詞性	意義	字頻	大考	英檢	多益
❶	hi	[haɪ]	int.	嗨	1		初級	
	please	[pliz]	adv.	請	1	1	初級	
	come	[kʌm]	v.	來到	1	1	初級	
	in	[ɪn]	adv.	進入	1	1	初級	
❷	welcome	[ˈwɛlkəm]	adj.	歡迎的	1	1	初級	
❸	hope	[hop]	v.	希望	1	1	初級	
	enjoy	[ɪnˈdʒɔɪ]	v.	享受	1	2	初級	
	party	[ˈpɑrtɪ]	n.	派對	1	1	初級	◎
❹	home	[hom]	n.	家	1	1	初級	
❺	any	[ˈɛnɪ]	adj.	任何的	1		初級	
	problem	[ˈprɑbləm]	n.	問題	1	1	初級	◎
	finding	[ˈfaɪndɪŋ]	p.pr.	find（尋找）現在分詞	1	1	中高	
	address	[əˈdrɛs]	n.	地址	1	1	初級	◎
❻	traffic	[ˈtræfɪk]	n.	塞車	1	2	初級	◎
	way	[we]	n.	路途	1	1	初級	
	here	[hɪr]	adv.	這裡	1	1	初級	
❼	let	[lɛt]	v.	讓…	1	1	初級	
	hang	[hæŋ]	v.	吊、掛	1	2	初級	◎
	up	[ʌp]	adv.	掛起	1	1	初級	
	coat	[kot]	n.	外套	1	1	初級	
❽	came	[kem]	p.t.	come（到來）過去式	1	1	初級	
	early	[ˈɝlɪ]	adv.	早地	1	1	初級	
❾	glad	[glæd]	adj.	高興的	1	1	初級	
❿	other	[ˈʌðɚ]	pron.	其他人	1	1	初級	
	moment	[ˈmomənt]	n.	片刻	1	1	初級	
⓫	now	[nau]	adv.	現在	1	1	初級	
	have	[hæv]	v.	擁有/使得	1	1	初級	
	full	[ful]	adj.	滿的、到齊的	1	1	初級	
	house	[haus]	n.	客席	1	1	初級	◎
⓬	everyone	[ˈɛvrɪˌwʌn]	pron.	每個人	1		初級	
	waiting	[ˈwetɪŋ]	p.pr.	wait（等待）現在分詞	3	1	初級	◎
⓭	thank	[θæŋk]	v.	感謝	1		初級	
	present	[ˈprɛznt]	n.	禮物	1	2	初級	◎
	too	[tu]	adv.	過於	1	1	初級	
	kind	[kaɪnd]	adj.	客氣的	1	1	初級	◎
⓮	certainly	[ˈsɝtənlɪ]	adv.	一定	1		初級	◎
	focus	[ˈfokəs]	n.	焦點	1	2	初級	◎
	this	[ðɪs]	adj.	這個	1	1	初級	
⓯	husband	[ˈhʌzbənd]	n.	丈夫	1	1	初級	
⓰	honor	[ˈɑnɚ]	n.	榮幸	1	3	中級	◎
⓱	person	[ˈpɝsn]	n.	人	1	1	初級	
	wife	[waɪf]	n.	妻子	1	1	初級	

※「紅字單字」於本單元多句出現，「單字級等分析」僅列在「首次出現句」。

102　回應主人的歡迎。

❶	打擾了！	Sorry to bother you!
❷	抱歉，我遲到了！	Sorry I'm late.
❸	謝謝您的邀請。	Thank you for your invitation.
❹	我很高興能參加今天的盛會。	I'm so happy to participate in today's party. *participate in（參加）
❺	這是一點小禮物。	This is a small present.
❻	你們這邊不太好找呢！	It's very hard to find your place!
❼	我不會是最後到的吧？	Am I the last one to arrive? *the last one（最後的人）
❽	這是我太太琳達。	This is my wife Linda.
❾	約翰來了嗎？	Has John arrived yet? *Has＋某人＋過去分詞?（某人是否已經…？）
❿	我帶太太一起來。	I brought my wife with me.
⓫	我等一下有事得先走。	I have to go early; there's something I need to do. *go early（先行離開）
⓬	出門前我把小孩托給我的父母。	I dropped the kids off with my parents before I came here. *drop＋人事物＋off（寄放某人事物）
⓭	我為了這個派對特別打扮一番。	I spent a lot of time dressing up for this party. *spend a lot of time（花很多時間）、dress up（打扮）
⓮	很高興你喜歡我今天的打扮。	I'm glad that you like my outfit.
⓯	我先生有事不能來。	My husband can't come due to a prior commitment. *due to（因為）、prior commitment（更重要的事）
⓰	這個派對看起來很盛大呢！	This party looks very grand.
⓱	我今晚是排除萬難才趕過來的。	I rearranged my whole schedule so I could make it here. *rearrange schedule（更改原定行程）、make it（抵達）

	單字	音標	詞性	意義	字頻	大考	英檢	多益
❶	sorry	[ˋsɑrɪ]	adj.	抱歉的	1	1	初級	
	bother	[ˋbɑðɚ]	v.	打擾	1	2	初級	◎
❷	late	[let]	adj.	遲到的	1	1	初級	◎
❸	thank	[θæŋk]	v.	感謝	1	1	初級	
	invitation	[ˌɪnvəˋteʃən]	n.	邀請	2	2	初級	◎
❹	so	[so]	adv.	非常	1	1	初級	

❹	happy	[ˈhæpɪ]	adj.	高興的	1	1	初級	
	participate	[pɑrˈtɪsə͵pet]	v.	參加	1	3	中級	◎
	today	[təˈde]	n.	今天	1	1	初級	◎
	party	[ˈpɑrtɪ]	n.	派對	1	1	初級	◎
❺	this	[ðɪs]	pron./adj.	這個	1	1	初級	
	small	[smɔl]	adj.	小的	1	1	初級	◎
	present	[ˈprɛznt]	n.	禮物	1	2	初級	◎
❻	very	[ˈvɛrɪ]	adv.	十分	1	1	初級	
	hard	[hɑrd]	adj.	困難的	1	1	初級	◎
	find	[faɪnd]	v.	尋找	1	1	初級	
	place	[ples]	n.	地方	1	1	初級	◎
❼	last	[læst]	adj.	最後的	1	1	初級	
	one	[wʌn]	pron.	一個人	1	1	初級	
	arrive	[əˈraɪv]	v.	到達	1	2	初級	◎
❽	wife	[waɪf]	n.	妻子	1	1	初級	
❾	arrived	[əˈraɪvd]	p.p.	arrive（到達）過去分詞	1	2	初級	◎
	yet	[jɛt]	adv.	尚未	1	1	初級	◎
❿	brought	[brɔt]	p.t.	bring（帶來）過去式	1	1	初級	
⓫	have	[hæv]	v.	必須	1	1	初級	
	go	[go]	v.	離開	1	1	初級	
	early	[ˈɜlɪ]	adv.	先行	1	1	初級	
	there	[ðɛr]	adv.	有…	1	1	初級	
	something	[ˈsʌmθɪŋ]	pron.	一些事情	1	1	初級	
	need	[nid]	v.	需要	1	1	初級	◎
	do	[du]	v.	做	1	1	初級	
⓬	dropped	[drɑpt]	p.t.	drop(託給、寄放)過去式	1	2	初級	◎
	kid	[kɪd]	n.	小孩	1	1	初級	
	off	[ɔf]	adv.	放下	1	1	初級	
	parents	[ˈpɛrənts]	n.	parent（雙親）複數	2	1		
	came	[kem]	p.t.	come（前來）過去式	1	1	初級	
	here	[hɪr]	adv.	這裡	1	1	初級	
⓭	spent	[spɛnt]	p.t.	spend（花費）過去式	6	1	初級	◎
	lot	[lɑt]	n.	許多	1	1		◎
	time	[taɪm]	n.	時間	1	1	初級	◎
	dressing	[ˈdrɛsɪŋ]	n.	dress（打扮）動名詞	3	5	中高	◎
	up	[ʌp]	adv.	穿上地	1	1	初級	
⓮	glad	[glæd]	adj.	高興的	1	1	初級	
	like	[laɪk]	v.	喜歡	1	1	初級	
	outfit	[ˈaʊt͵fɪt]	n.	為特定場合穿的整套服裝	2	6	中高	◎
⓯	husband	[ˈhʌzbənd]	n.	丈夫	1	1	初級	
	come	[kʌm]	v.	前來	1	1	初級	
	due	[dju]	adj.	因為	1	3	中級	◎
	prior	[ˈpraɪɚ]	adj.	更重要的	2	5	中高	◎
	commitment	[kəˈmɪtmənt]	n.	承諾	1	6	中級	◎
⓰	look	[lʊk]	v.	看起來	1	1	初級	◎
	grand	[grænd]	adj.	盛大的	1	1	初級	◎
⓱	rearranged	[͵riəˈrendʒd]	p.t.	rearrange(重新安排)過去式	4			
	whole	[hol]	adj.	整個	1	1	初級	
	schedule	[ˈskɛdʒʊl]	n.	行程	1	3	中級	◎
	make	[mek]	v.	抵達	1	1	初級	

※「紅字單字」於本單元多句出現，「單字級等分析」僅列在「首次出現句」。

457

🔵 MP3 103-01 ❶～⓰

❶	怎麼不找個地方坐下來？	Why don't you find a place to sit down? * **Why don't you...?**（你為什麼不做…？） * **find a place to**＋動詞原形（找個地方做…）
❷	請坐。	Please sit down. ＝ Please take a seat.
❸	來這裡坐，別光站著。	Come sit here; don't just stand there like that.
❹	請不要拘束。	Don't stand on ceremony. ＝ Please don't be uneasy. * **stand on ceremony**（拘謹、客套）
❺	有任何需要儘管跟我說。	Let me know if you need anything. * **let me know**（告訴我）
❻	當自己家一樣，輕鬆點。	Relax, make yourself at home. * **make oneself at home**（當作在自己家一樣放鬆）
❼	你怎麼不過去跟大家聊天？	Why don't you go and socialize with everybody? * **socialize with**＋某人（和某人交談、來往）
❽	你喜歡這種氣氛嗎？	Do you like this kind of atmosphere? * **this kind of**＋人事物（這種…）
❾	只是個簡單的聚會，別緊張。	It's just a simple get-together, don't be nervous. * **simple get-together**（簡單的聚會）
❿	我介紹你給大家認識。	Let me introduce you to everyone. * **introduce you to**＋某人（將你介紹給某人）
⓫	這裡有你認識的人嗎？	Is there anyone you know here? * **Is there**＋人事物?（是否有某人事物？）
⓬	要不要先喝點什麼？	Would you like to have something to drink? * **Would you like to...?**（你要不要…？）
⓭	要不要聽點音樂？	Would you like to listen to some music? * **listen to music**（聽音樂）
⓮	我們都是自己人，別跟我客氣。	We're friends; no need to be polite with me. * **no need to be polite**（不必太客氣） * **be polite with**＋某人（和某人客氣）
⓯	會不會冷？	Are you cold? * **Are you hot?**（會不會熱？）
⓰	你要不要去洗手間？	Would you like to go to the bathroom? * **bathroom**（洗手間）＝ **restroom**

	單字	音標	詞性	意義	字頻	大考	英檢	多益
❶	find	[faɪnd]	v.	尋找	1	1	初級	
	place	[ples]	n.	地方	1	1	初級	◎
	sit	[sɪt]	v.	坐	1	1	初級	
	down	[daʊn]	adv.	（坐）下	1	1	初級	
❷	please	[pliz]	adv.	請	1	1	初級	
	take	[tek]	v.	就座	1	1	初級	◎
	seat	[sit]	n.	座位	1	1	初級	◎
❸	come	[kʌm]	v.	前來	1	1	初級	
	here	[hɪr]	adv.	這裡	1	1	初級	
	just	[dʒʌst]	adv.	只是	1	1	初級	
	stand	[stænd]	v.	站立/拘於	1	1	初級	◎
	there	[ðɛr]	adv.	那裡	1	1	初級	
	that	[ðæt]	pron.	那樣	1	1	初級	
❹	ceremony	[`sɛrə.monɪ]	n.	禮節	1	5	中級	◎
	uneasy	[ʌn`izɪ]	adj.	不自在的	3		中高	
❺	let	[lɛt]	v.	讓…	1	1	初級	
	know	[no]	v.	知道	1	1	初級	◎
	need	[nid]	v.	需要	1	1	初級	◎
	anything	[`ɛnɪ.θɪŋ]	pron.	任何東西	1	1	初級	
❻	relax	[rɪ`læks]	v.	放鬆	2	3	中級	◎
	make	[mek]	v.	使得	1	1	初級	
	yourself	[jʊə`sɛlf]	pron.	你自己	1		初級	
	home	[hom]	n.	家	1		初級	
❼	go	[go]	v.	去	1	1	初級	
	socialize	[`soʃə.laɪz]	v.	和人交談、和人來往	3	6	中高	◎
	everybody	[`ɛvrɪ.bɑdɪ]	pron.	每個人	1		初級	
❽	like	[laɪk]	v.	喜歡/想要	1	1	初級	
	this	[ðɪs]	adj.	這個	1	1	初級	
	kind	[kaɪnd]	n.	種類	1	1	初級	◎
	atmosphere	[`ætməs.fɪr]	n.	氣氛	1	4	中級	◎
❾	simple	[`sɪmpl]	adj.	簡單的	1	1	初級	◎
	get-together	[`gɛt.tə`gɛðə]	n.	聚會	1			
	nervous	[`nɜvəs]	adj.	緊張的	1	3	初級	
❿	introduce	[.ɪntrə`djus]	v.	介紹	1	2	初級	◎
	everyone	[`ɛvrɪ.wʌn]	pron.	每個人	1		初級	
⓫	anyone	[`ɛnɪ.wʌn]	pron.	任何人	1	2	初級	
⓬	have	[hæv]	v.	擁有	1	1	初級	
	something	[`sʌmθɪŋ]	pron.	一些東西	1	1	初級	
	drink	[drɪŋk]	v.	喝	1	1	初級	
⓭	listen	[`lɪsn]	v.	聽	1	1	初級	
	some	[sʌm]	adj.	一些	1	1	初級	
	music	[`mjuzɪk]	n.	音樂	1	1	初級	
⓮	friend	[frɛnd]	n.	朋友	1	1	初級	
	polite	[pə`laɪt]	adj.	客氣的	2	2	初級	◎
⓯	cold	[kold]	adj.	冷的	1	1	初級	
⓰	bathroom	[`bæθ.rum]	n.	洗手間	1	1	初級	

※「紅字單字」於本單元多句出現，「單字級等分析」僅列在「首次出現句」。

459

🔊 MP3 103-02 ❶～⓰

❶	我很好，別擔心我！	I'm fine, don't worry about me!
❷	我覺得很自在。	I feel comfortable. * comfortable（輕鬆自在的）＝ at home
❸	這個派對真是好！	What a great party this is! * great（很好的）可替換為：grand（盛大的）
❹	我根本把這裡當自己家一樣。	I already feel at home right now.
❺	我才不會跟你客氣呢！	I won't stand on ceremony with you!
❻	我需要什麼一定跟你說。	I'll let you know if I need anything.
❼	我第一次參加這種派對。	It's my first time attending a party like this. * It's my first time＋動詞-ing（這是我第一次做…）
❽	我站著就可以了。	Standing is OK for me.
❾	你忙你的，我四處看看。	Go ahead; I'll look around by myself. * go ahead（你忙你的就好）、look around（四處看看）
❿	這裡人真的好多喔！	It's really crowded here!
⓫	我認識的人好像都還沒來。	It seems like none of the people I know has arrived yet. * seem like（似乎）、the people I know（我認識的人） * have / has arrived yet（尚未抵達）
⓬	我覺得有點熱。	I feel a bit hot.　* a bit（稍微、有點）
⓭	人多的地方會令我緊張。	Crowded places make me nervous. * make me＋形容詞（讓我感到…）
⓮	我要借用一下洗手間。	I need to use the restroom.
⓯	我等一下自己找地方坐。	I'll find myself a seat later. * find myself a seat（自己找位子坐）
⓰	我想去陽台透透氣。	I'm going out to the balcony to get some fresh air. * go out（到外面去）、get fresh air（呼吸新鮮空氣）

	單字	音標	詞性	意義	字頻	大考	英檢	多益
❶	fine	[faɪn]	adj.	沒問題的	1	1	初級	◎
	worry	[ˋwɝɪ]	adj.	擔心	1	1	初級	
❷	feel	[fil]	v.	感覺	1	1	初級	
	comfortable	[ˋkʌmfətəbl]	adj.	舒服的	1	2	初級	◎
❸	great	[gret]	adj.	很好的	1	1	初級	◎
	party	[ˋpɑrtɪ]	n.	派對	1	1	初級	◎

	單字	音標	詞性	中文			級等	
❸	this	[ðɪs]	pron.	這個	1	1	初級	
❹	already	[ɔl`rɛdɪ]	adv.	已經	1	1	初級	
	home	[hom]	n.	家	1	1	初級	
	right	[raɪt]	adv.	正值	1	1	初級	
	now	[nau]	adv.	現在	1	1	初級	
❺	stand	[stænd]	v.	拘於	1	1	初級	◎
	ceremony	[`sɛrə.monɪ]	n.	禮節	1	5	中級	
❻	let	[lɛt]	v.	讓…	1	1	初級	
	know	[no]	v.	知道/認識	1	1	初級	◎
	need	[nid]	v.	需要	1	1	初級	◎
	anything	[`ɛnɪ.θɪŋ]	pron.	任何東西	1	1	初級	
❼	first	[fɝst]	adj.	第一的	1	1	初級	
	time	[taɪm]	n.	次、回	1	1	初級	◎
	attending	[ə`tɛndɪŋ]	p.pr.	attend（參加）現在分詞	1	2	初級	◎
❽	standing	[`stændɪŋ]	n.	stand（站立）動名詞	2	1	初級	◎
	ok	[`o`ke]	adj.	沒關係的	1	1	初級	◎
❾	go	[go]	v.	去	1	1	初級	
	ahead	[ə`hɛd]	adv.	向前	1	1	初級	◎
	look	[lʊk]	v.	看	1	1	初級	
	around	[ə`raund]	adv.	四處	1	1	初級	
	myself	[maɪ`sɛlf]	pron.	我自己	1		初級	
❿	really	[`rɪəlɪ]	adv.	真的	1		初級	
	crowded	[`kraudɪd]	adj.	人多的	2	2	初級	◎
	here	[hɪr]	adv.	這裡	1	1	初級	
⓫	seem	[sim]	v.	似乎	1	1	初級	◎
	none	[nʌn]	pron.	沒有	1	2	初級	
	people	[`pipl]	n.	person（人）複數	1	1	初級	
	arrived	[ə`raɪvd]	p.p.	arrive（到達）過去分詞	1	2	初級	◎
	yet	[jɛt]	adv.	尚未	1	1	初級	◎
⓬	bit	[bɪt]	n.	些許	1	1	初級	
	hot	[hɑt]	adj.	熱的	1	1	初級	◎
⓭	place	[ples]	n.	地方	1	1	初級	◎
	make	[mek]	v.	使得	1	1	初級	
	nervous	[`nɝvəs]	adj.	緊張的	1	3	初級	
⓮	use	[juz]	v.	使用	1	1	初級	◎
	restroom	[`rɛst.rum]	n.	洗手間	5	4	初級	
⓯	find	[faɪnd]	v.	尋找	1	1	初級	
	seat	[sit]	n.	位子	1	1	初級	◎
	later	[`letə]	adv.	稍後	1		初級	
⓰	going	[`goɪŋ]	p.pr.	go（去）現在分詞	4	1	初級	◎
	out	[aut]	adv.	出去	1	1	初級	
	balcony	[`bælkənɪ]	n.	陽台	3	2	初級	
	get	[gɛt]	v.	取得	1	1	初級	◎
	some	[sʌm]	adj.	一些	1	1	初級	
	fresh	[frɛʃ]	adj.	新鮮的	1	1	初級	
	air	[ɛr]	n.	空氣	1	1	初級	

※「紅字單字」於本單元多句出現，「單字級等分析」僅列在「首次出現句」。

🔊 MP3 104-01 ❶～⓱

❶	盡量吃，我準備很多菜。	Help yourself; I've prepared lots of dishes. * help yourself（別客氣、你自己取用） * a lot of dishes（很多道菜） * 此句用「現在完成式」（...have prepared...）表示 　「過去某時點發生某事，且結果持續到現在」。
❷	多吃一點，不要客氣。	Eat more; don't be so polite.
❸	有沒有吃飽？	Are you full?
❹	你想吃什麼我幫你拿。	I will get you anything you want.
❺	你怎麼都沒吃？	Why aren't you eating anything? * Why aren't you＋動詞-ing? 　（為什麼你沒有正在…？）
❻	食物合你的胃口嗎？	Does the food suit you all right? ＝ Are you all right with the food? * all right（還可以、差強人意）
❼	你有沒有還沒嘗試的東西？	Is there any food you haven't tried yet?
❽	嚐嚐我的拿手菜吧。	Have a taste of my special dish. * have a taste（吃吃看） * special dish（特製料理）
❾	過來吃點水果吧！	Come over and have some fruit!
❿	我可以抄食譜給你。	I can make a copy of the recipe for you. * make a copy（備份副本）
⓫	要不要吃些點心？	Would you like some dessert? * would like＋名詞（想要…）
⓬	你們有人要喝酒嗎？	Would anyone like a drink?
⓭	甜點會不會太甜？	Is the dessert too sweet for you?
⓮	要不要來杯咖啡？	Would you like a cup of coffee? * juice（果汁）、tea（茶）
⓯	大家都有座位了嗎？	Has everyone found a seat?
⓰	自己拿杯飲料喝吧。	Help yourself to the beverages.
⓱	有人需要紙巾嗎？	Is there anyone who needs a napkin? * wet wipe（濕紙巾）

	單字	音標	詞性	意義	字頻	大考	英檢	多益
❶	help	[hɛlp]	v.	取用	1	1	初級	
	yourself	[juɚˋsɛlf]	pron.	你自己	1		初級	
	prepared	[prɪˋpɛrd]	p.p.	prepare（準備）過去分詞	3	1	中級	◎
	lot	[lɑt]	n.	許多	1			
	dish	[dɪʃ]	n.	菜餚	1	1	初級	
❷	eat	[it]	v.	吃	1	1	初級	
	more	[mor]	adv.	更多	1	1	初級	
	so	[so]	adv.	這麼	1	1	初級	
	polite	[pəˋlaɪt]	adj.	客氣的	2	2	初級	◎
❸	full	[fʊl]	adj.	吃飽的	1	1	初級	
❹	get	[gɛt]	v.	拿	1	1	初級	◎
	anything	[ˋɛnɪˏθɪŋ]	pron.	任何東西	1	1	初級	
	want	[wɑnt]	v.	想要	1	1	初級	◎
❺	eating	[ˋitɪŋ]	p.pr.	eat（吃）現在分詞	2	1	初級	
❻	food	[fud]	n.	食物	1	1	初級	◎
	suit	[sut]	v.	適合	1	2	初級	◎
	all	[ɔl]	adv.	一切	1	1	初級	
	right	[raɪt]	adv.	還可以	1	1	初級	
❼	there	[ðɛr]	adv.	有…	1	1	初級	
	any	[ˋɛnɪ]	adj.	任何的	1	1	初級	
	tried	[traɪd]	p.p.	try（嘗試）過去分詞	1	1	初級	
	yet	[jɛt]	adv.	尚未	7	1	初級	◎
❽	have	[hæv]	v.	吃	1	1	初級	
	taste	[test]	n.	嚐味、一口	1	1	初級	◎
	special	[ˋspɛʃəl]	adj.	特別的	1	1	初級	◎
❾	come	[kʌm]	v.	前往	1	1	初級	
	over	[ˋovɚ]	adv.	從一邊至另一邊	1	1	初級	
	some	[sʌm]	adj.	一些	1	1	初級	
	fruit	[frut]	n.	水果	1	1	初級	
❿	make	[mek]	v.	製作	1	1	初級	
	copy	[ˋkɑpɪ]	n.	副本	1	2	初級	◎
	recipe	[ˋrɛsəpɪ]	n.	食譜	1	4	中級	◎
⓫	like	[laɪk]	v.	想要	1	1	初級	
	dessert	[dɪˋzɝt]	n.	甜點	2	2	初級	◎
⓬	anyone	[ˋɛnɪˏwʌn]	pron.	任何人	1	2	初級	
	drink	[drɪŋk]	n.	酒	1	1	初級	
⓭	too	[tu]	adv.	過於	1	1	初級	
	sweet	[swit]	adj.	甜的	1	1	初級	
⓮	cup	[kʌp]	n.	一杯	1	1	初級	
	coffee	[ˋkɔfɪ]	n.	咖啡	1	1	初級	
⓯	everyone	[ˋɛvrɪˏwʌn]	pron.	每個人	1	1	初級	
	found	[faund]	p.p.	find（尋找）過去分詞	1	3	中級	◎
	seat	[sit]	n.	座位	1	1	初級	◎
⓰	beverage	[ˋbɛvərɪdʒ]	n.	飲料	3	6	中高	◎
⓱	need	[nid]	v.	需要	1	1	初級	◎
	napkin	[ˋnæpkɪn]	n.	紙巾	3	2	初級	

※「紅字單字」於本單元多句出現，「單字級等分析」僅列在「首次出現句」。　　463

MP3 104-02 ❶～❽

❶	你也過來一起吃啊。	Come here and eat with us.
❷	你別忙了。	Don't rush.
❸	你自己也都沒吃東西。	You didn't eat anything either.
❹	你花多少時間準備這些吃的東西啊？	How much time did you spend preparing this food? * How much time...?（…是多少時間？） * spend＋動詞-ing（花時間做…）
❺	這個要怎麼吃呢？	How should I eat this?
❻	每一道菜看起來都好好吃。	Every dish looks delicious. * look＋形容詞（看起來…）
❼	我應該跟你拜師學藝。	I should have you teach me how to cook. * have＋某人＋動詞原形（讓某人做…） * teach me how to＋動詞（教我如何…）
❽	嗯，我不敢吃這個。	Ew, I don't want to eat that.
❾	你可以給我這道菜的食譜嗎？	Can you give me the recipe for this dish?
❿	甜點是你自己做的嗎？	Did you make this dessert?
⓫	我吃得好撐。	I'm stuffed.
⓬	我想再來杯果汁。	I would like one more glass of juice. * would like＋名詞（想要…） * one more（再來一份）
⓭	可以幫我拿一些甜點嗎？	Could you get me some dessert? * get＋某人＋某物（讓某人幫忙拿…）
⓮	我好像喝太多了。	I seem to have drunk too much. * seem to have＋過去分詞（剛剛似乎做了…） * too much（過多）
⓯	請把胡椒粉遞給我。	Please pass the pepper.
⓰	請給我一張紙巾。	Please give me a napkin.
⓱	我自己來，你別忙著招呼我。	I'll help myself; you don't need to wait on me. * help myself（自己取用）、wait on（招呼）
⓲	可以給我一杯水嗎？	Could you give me a glass of water?

單字級等分析

	單字	音標	詞性	意義	字頻	大考	英檢	多益
❶	come	[kʌm]	v.	前來	1	1	初級	
	here	[hɪr]	adv.	這裡	1	1	初級	
	eat	[it]	v.	吃	1	1	初級	
❷	rush	[rʌʃ]	v.	匆匆忙忙	1	2	初級	◎
❸	anything	[ˈɛnɪ̣θɪŋ]	pron.	任何東西	1	1	初級	
	either	[ˈiðɚ]	adv.	也不	1	1	初級	◎
❹	much	[mʌtʃ]	adj./adv.	許多的/許多地	1	1	初級	
	time	[taɪm]	n.	時間	1	1	初級	◎
	spend	[spɛnd]	v.	花費	1	1	初級	◎
	preparing	[prɪˈpɛrɪŋ]	n.	prepare（準備）動名詞	1	1	初級	◎
	this	[ðɪs]	adj./pron.	這個	1	1	初級	
	food	[fud]	n.	食物	1	1	初級	◎
❻	every	[ˈɛvrɪ]	adj.	每一	1	1	初級	
	dish	[dɪʃ]	n.	菜餚	1	1	初級	
	look	[lʊk]	v.	看起來	1	1	初級	
	delicious	[dɪˈlɪʃəs]	adj.	美味的	2	2	初級	◎
❼	have	[hæv]	v.	讓…	1	1	初級	
	teach	[titʃ]	v.	教導	1	1	初級	
	cook	[kʊk]	v.	煮飯	1	1	初級	◎
❽	want	[wɑnt]	v.	想要	1	1	初級	◎
	that	[ðæt]	pron.	那個	1	1	初級	
❾	give	[gɪv]	v.	給予	1	1	初級	
	recipe	[ˈrɛsəpɪ]	n.	食譜	1	4	中級	◎
❿	make	[mek]	v.	製作	1	1	初級	
	dessert	[dɪˈzɝt]	n.	甜點	2	2	初級	◎
⓫	stuffed	[stʌft]	adj.	吃飽的	4	3	中級	◎
⓬	like	[laɪk]	v.	想要	1	1	初級	
	one	[wʌn]	n.	一	1	1	初級	
	more	[mor]	adj.	更多的	1	1	初級	
	glass	[glæs]	n.	一杯	1	1	初級	
	juice	[dʒus]	n.	果汁	1	1	初級	
⓭	get	[gɛt]	v.	拿來	1	1	初級	◎
	some	[sʌm]	adj.	一些	1	1	初級	
⓮	seem	[sim]	v.	似乎	1	1	初級	◎
	drunk	[drʌŋk]	p.p.	drink（喝酒）過去分詞	2	3	中級	
	too	[tu]	adv.	過於	1	1	初級	
⓯	please	[pliz]	adv.	請	1	1	初級	
	pass	[pæs]	v.	傳遞	1	1	初級	◎
	pepper	[ˈpɛpɚ]	n.	胡椒粉	1	2	初級	
⓰	napkin	[ˈnæpkɪn]	n.	紙巾	3	2	初級	
⓱	help	[hɛlp]	v.	取用	1	1	初級	
	myself	[maɪˈsɛlf]	pron.	我自己	1		初級	
	need	[nid]	v.	需要	1	1	初級	◎
	wait	[wet]	v.	招呼	1	1	初級	◎
⓲	water	[ˈwɔtɚ]	n.	水	1	1	初級	

※「紅字單字」於本單元多句出現，「單字級等分析」僅列在「首次出現句」。

105　主人送客。

🔊 MP3 105-01 ❶～⓱

❶	歡迎隨時來玩。	You're always welcome to come over. * be welcome to＋動詞原形（歡迎…） * come over（過來）
❷	以後常來玩喔！	Come here often!
❸	下次一定還要賞臉。	Please come again next time.
❹	謝謝你們肯賞光。	Thank you for coming. * thank you for＋動詞-ing（謝謝你做…）
❺	今天能看到你真的太開心了。	I'm really happy to have seen you today. * have seen you（和你見了面）
❻	真捨不得讓你們走。	It's really hard for me to let you go. * It's hard for me...（我捨不得…、我很難…）
❼	感謝您遠道而來。	Thank you for coming from such a long ways away. * come from a long ways away（遠道而來）
❽	需要幫你們叫車嗎？	Do you need me to call a taxi for you? * call a taxi（叫車）
❾	你們等一下怎麼回去？	How will you get back home? * How will you...?（你們之後要如何…？）
❿	你今天有開車嗎？	Did you drive today?
⓫	我陪你們走出去。	Let me walk you out. * walk＋某人＋out（陪某人去外面走）
⓬	回去路上小心喔！	Be safe on your way home! * on one's way home（在你回家路上）
⓭	你要不要搭他的便車？	Would you like to get a ride with him? * Would you like...?（你想要…嗎）、get a ride（搭便車）
⓮	有沒有東西忘了拿？	Have you forgotten anything?
⓯	你有喝酒不要開車。	You've had a few drinks; don't drive. * have had a few drinks（喝了一些酒） * 此句用「現在完成式」（...have had...）表示「過去某時點發生某事，且結果持續到現在」。
⓰	你可以幫我送她回去嗎？	Can you help me drive her home? * drive＋某人＋home（開車送某人回家）
⓱	要不要先把外套穿上？	Would you like to put on your coat first? * put on（穿上）

	單字	音標	詞性	意義	字頻	大考	英檢	多益
❶	always	[ˈɔlwez]	adv.	隨時	1	1	初級	
	welcome	[ˈwɛlkəm]	adj.	歡迎的	1	1	初級	
	come	[kʌm]	v.	前來	1	1	初級	
	over	[ˈovə]	adv.	從一邊至另一邊	1	1	初級	
❷	here	[hɪr]	adv.	這裡	1	1	初級	
	often	[ˈɔfən]	adv.	常常	1	1	初級	
❸	please	[pliz]	adv.	請	1	1	初級	
	again	[əˈgɛn]	adv.	再次	1	1	初級	
	next	[nɛkst]	adj.	下一	1	1	初級	
	time	[taɪm]	n.	次、回	1	1	初級	◎
❹	thank	[θæŋk]	v.	感謝	1	1	初級	
	coming	[ˈkʌmɪŋ]	n.	come（前來）動名詞	2	1	中級	
❺	really	[ˈrɪəlɪ]	adv.	真的	1		初級	
	happy	[ˈhæpɪ]	adj.	開心的	1	1	初級	
	seen	[sin]	p.p.	see（看）過去分詞	1	1	初級	
	today	[təˈde]	adv.	今天	1	1	初級	◎
❻	hard	[hɑrd]	adj.	困難的	1	1	初級	◎
	let	[lɛt]	v.	讓…	1	1	初級	
	go	[go]	v.	離開	1	1	初級	
❼	such	[sʌtʃ]	adv.	這麼	1	1	初級	
	long	[lɔŋ]	adj.	遠的	1	1	初級	
	way	[we]	n.	路程/路途	1	1	初級	
	away	[əˈwe]	adv.	遙遠地	1	1	初級	
❽	need	[nid]	v.	需要	1	1	初級	◎
	call	[kɔl]	v.	呼叫	1	1	初級	◎
	taxi	[ˈtæksɪ]	n.	計程車	2	1	初級	
❾	get	[gɛt]	v.	抵達/乘上	1	1	初級	◎
	back	[bæk]	adv.	返回	1	1	初級	◎
	home	[hom]	n.	家	1	1	初級	
❿	drive	[draɪv]	v.	開車	1	1	初級	◎
⓫	walk	[wɔk]	v.	陪某人走	1	1	初級	
	out	[aʊt]	adv.	外出	1	1	初級	
⓬	safe	[sef]	adj.	安全的	1	1	初級	◎
⓭	like	[laɪk]	v.	想要	1	1	初級	
	ride	[raɪd]	n.	便車	1	1	初級	
⓮	forgotten	[fəˈgɑtn]	p.p.	forget（忘記）過去分詞	4	1	初級	
	anything	[ˈɛnɪ.θɪŋ]	pron.	任何東西	1	1	初級	
⓯	had	[hæd]	p.p.	have（喝）過去分詞	1	1	初級	
	few	[fju]	adj.	些許的	1	1	初級	◎
	drink	[drɪŋk]	n.	酒	1	1	初級	
⓰	help	[hɛlp]	v.	幫忙	1	1	初級	
⓱	put	[pʊt]	v.	穿上	1	1	初級	
	coat	[kot]	n.	外套	1	1	初級	
	first	[fɝst]	adv.	首先	1	1	初級	

※「紅字單字」於本單元多句出現，「單字級等分析」僅列在「首次出現句」。

🔵 MP3　105-02　❶ ～ ⓰

❶	我們差不多該告辭了。	It's about time for us to leave. * time for... (…的時間)
❷	你一定累了，早點休息吧！	You must be tired right now; don't stay up too late! * must be＋形容詞 (一定…)、stay up late (很晚睡覺)
❸	有時候像這樣聚聚也不錯。	It's really nice to get together like this sometimes.　* get together (聚在一起)
❹	下次還要約我唷！	Be sure to invite me again next time!
❺	你不用出來送我們了。	You don't need to come out with us.
❻	我真希望可以待久一點。	I really wish that I could stay longer. * stay longer (停留更久的時間)
❼	我們先走了。	We're going to take off.　* take off (離開)
❽	外面風大，你趕快進去吧！	It's windy outside; hurry back in the house!
❾	打擾你到這麼晚，真不好意思！	I'm really sorry for bothering you so late! * be sorry for (感到抱歉)
❿	對不起，還要讓你自己善後。	I'm sorry that you'll have to deal with the mess we made. * deal with (解決)、the mess we made (我們造成的髒亂)
⓫	我自己到外面叫車。	I will go outside to call a cab by myself. * cab (計程車) = taxi
⓬	我搭他的便車回去。	I'll get a ride home with him.
⓭	我有開車來。	I drove my car here. * I rode my motorbike here. (我有騎車來)
⓮	我可以搭公車回去。	I can go back by bus.　* MRT (捷運)
⓯	啊！我的外套沒拿！	Ah! I forgot my coat!
⓰	我已經開始期待下次聚會了。	I'm already looking forward to our next get-together.　* look forward to (期待)

	單字	音標	詞性	意義	字頻	大考	英檢	多益
❶	about	[əˈbaʊt]	adv.	差不多	1	1	初級	
	time	[taɪm]	n.	時間/次、回	1	1	初級	
	leave	[liv]	v.	離開	1	1	初級	◎
❷	tired	[taɪrd]	adj.	疲累的	1	1	初級	◎
	right	[raɪt]	adv.	正值	1	1	初級	
	now	[naʊ]	adv.	現在	1	1	初級	

❷	stay	[ste]	v.	保持/停留	1	1	初級	◎
	up	[ʌp]	adv.	醒著地	1	1	初級	
	too	[tu]	adv.	過於	1	1	初級	
	late	[let]	adv.	晚地	1	1	初級	◎
❸	really	[ˋrɪəlɪ]	adv.	很、十分	1		初級	
	nice	[naɪs]	adj.	良好的	1	1	初級	
	get	[gɛt]	v.	聚集/乘上	1	1	初級	◎
	together	[təˋgɛðɚ]	adv.	一起	1	1	初級	
	this	[ðɪs]	pron.	這個	1	1	初級	
	sometimes	[ˋsʌm.taɪmz]	adv.	有時候	1	1	初級	
❹	sure	[ʃur]	adj.	確定的	1	1	初級	
	invite	[ɪnˋvaɪt]	v.	邀請	1	2	初級	◎
	again	[əˋgɛn]	adv.	再次	1	1	初級	
	next	[nɛkst]	adj.	下一個	1	1	初級	
❺	need	[nid]	v.	需要	1	1	初級	◎
	come	[kʌm]	v.	前來	1	1	初級	
	out	[aut]	adv.	外出	1	1	初級	
❻	wish	[wɪʃ]	v.	希望	1	1	初級	
	longer	[ˋlɔŋgɚ]	adv.	long（長地）比較級	1	1	初級	
❼	going	[ˋgoɪŋ]	p.pr.	go（即將）現在分詞	4	1	初級	
	take	[tek]	v.	動身	1	1	初級	◎
	off	[ɔf]	adv.	離開	1	1	初級	
❽	windy	[ˋwɪndɪ]	adj.	風大的	4	2	初級	
	outside	[ˋautˋsaɪd]	adv.	外面	1	1	初級	◎
	hurry	[ˋhɝɪ]	v.	趕快	2	2	初級	◎
	back	[bæk]	adv.	返回	1	1	初級	◎
	house	[haus]	n.	家	1	1	初級	
❾	sorry	[ˋsɑrɪ]	adj.	抱歉的	1	1	初級	
	bothering	[ˋbɑðɚɪŋ]	n.	bother（打擾）動名詞	1	2	初級	◎
	so	[so]	adv.	這麼	1	1	初級	
❿	have	[hæv]	v.	必須	1	1	初級	
	deal	[dil]	v.	解決	1	1	初級	◎
	mess	[mɛs]	n.	髒亂	2	3	初級	
	made	[med]	p.t.	make（製造）過去式	1	1	中級	
⓫	go	[go]	v.	去	1	1	初級	
	call	[kɔl]	v.	呼叫	1	1	初級	◎
	cab	[kæb]	n.	計程車	2	1		◎
	myself	[maɪˋsɛlf]	pron.	我自己	1		初級	
⓬	ride	[raɪd]	n.	便車	1	1	初級	
	home	[hom]	n.	家	1	1	初級	
⓭	drove	[drov]	p.t.	drive（開車）過去式	6			
	car	[kɑr]	n.	車子	1	1	初級	◎
	here	[hɪr]	adv.	這裡	1	1	初級	
⓮	bus	[bʌs]	n.	公車	1	1	初級	
⓯	forgot	[fəˋgɑt]	p.t.	forget（忘記）過去式	1	1	初級	
	coat	[kot]	n.	外套	1	1	初級	
⓰	already	[ɔlˋrɛdɪ]	adv.	已經	1	1	初級	◎
	looking	[ˋlukɪŋ]	p.pr.	look（期待）現在分詞	5	1	初級	
	forward	[ˋfɔrwɚd]	adv.	今後	1	2	初級	◎
	get-together	[ˋgɛt.təˋgɛðɚ]	n.	聚會				

※「紅字單字」於本單元多句出現，「單字級等分析」僅列在「首次出現句」。

🔘 MP3 106-01 ❶～❶

❶	哪裡，招待不周。	I haven't been a good host. * haven't been（一直沒有）、a good host（好主人） * 此句用「現在完成式」（...haven't been...） 　表示「過去持續到現在的事」。
❷	我今天都沒有好好招呼你。	I didn't take such good care of you today. * take good care of（好好招待）
❸	不會啦！一點都不累。	Not at all! I don't feel the least bit tired. * the least bit（一丁點程度）
❹	玩得開心就好。	I'm glad that you had fun. * I'm glad that＋子句（很高興…）、have fun（玩得開心） * 子句用「過去簡單式」（...had...） 　表示「發生在過去的事」。
❺	很高興你有賓至如歸的感覺。	I'm so glad that you felt at home. * feel at home（感覺像在自己家一樣）
❻	一直道謝就太客氣了。	You are very welcome for your many thanks.
❼	過獎了，我也沒做什麼。	I'm flattered; it was nothing. * be flattered（被過獎、受奉承）
❽	哪裡，只是些家常菜。	You're welcome; they were just homemade dishes.　* homemade dish（家常菜）
❾	是你不嫌棄啦！	Well, you must not be too picky! * must not（一定不是）、be too picky（吹毛求疵）
❿	好好招待你是應該的。	Taking good care of you is the least I can do. * the least I can do（我唯一能做的）
⓫	我很高興你喜歡今天的派對。	I'm glad that you liked the party.
⓬	這是我的榮幸。	It's my pleasure.
⓭	謝謝你的稱讚。	Thank you for your praise.
⓮	不好意思，今天還讓你破費。	I'm very sorry about costing you some money today. * sorry about（對不起）、cost you money（讓你破費）
⓯	下次人來就好，別再帶東西了。	Just come here without anything next time. * come without anything（無帶東西前來）

單字級等分析

	單字	音標	詞性	意義	字頻	大考	英檢	多益
❶	good	[gʊd]	adj.	良好的	1	1	初級	◎
	host	[host]	n.	主人	1	4	初級	◎
❷	take	[tek]	v.	採取	1	1	初級	◎
	such	[sʌtʃ]	adv.	這麼	1	1	初級	
	care	[kɛr]	n.	招待	1	1	初級	◎
	today	[təˋde]	adv.	今天	1	1	初級	◎
❸	all	[ɔl]	n.	完全	1	1	初級	
	feel	[fil]	v.	感覺	1	1	初級	
	least	[list]	adj./n.	最少的/最少	1	1	初級	◎
	bit	[bɪt]	n.	些許	1	1	初級	
	tired	[taɪrd]	adj.	疲累的	1	1	初級	◎
❹	glad	[glæd]	adj.	高興的	1	1	初級	
	had	[hæd]	p.t.	have（擁有）過去式	1	1	初級	
	fun	[fʌn]	n.	娛樂、樂趣	1	1	初級	
❺	felt	[fɛlt]	p.t.	feel（感覺）過去式	6	1	初級	
	home	[hom]	n.	家	1	1	初級	
❻	very	[ˋvɛrɪ]	adv.	非常	1	1	初級	
	welcome	[ˋwɛlkəm]	adj.	客氣的	1	1	初級	
	many	[ˋmɛnɪ]	adj.	許多的	1	1	初級	
	thanks	[θæŋks]	n.	thank（感謝）複數	1	1	初級	
❼	flattered	[ˋflætəd]	p.p.	flatter（奉承）過去分詞	4	4	中級	
	nothing	[ˋnʌθɪŋ]	pron.	微不足道	1	1	初級	
❽	just	[dʒʌst]	adv.	只是	1	1	初級	
	homemade	[ˋhomˋmed]	adj.	在家製作的	3			
	dish	[dɪʃ]	n.	菜餚	1	1	初級	
❾	well	[wɛl]	int.	哎呀	1	1	初級	◎
	too	[tu]	adv.	過於	1	1	初級	
	picky	[ˋpɪkɪ]	adj.	挑剔的	7			
❿	taking	[ˋtekɪŋ]	n.	take（採取）動名詞	4			
	do	[du]	v.	做	1	1	初級	
⓫	liked	[laɪkt]	p.t.	like（喜歡）過去式	1	1	初級	
	party	[ˋpɑrtɪ]	n.	派對	1	1	初級	◎
⓬	pleasure	[ˋplɛʒɚ]	n.	榮幸	1	2	初級	◎
⓭	thank	[θæŋk]	v.	感謝	1	1	初級	
	praise	[prez]	n.	稱讚	2	2	初級	
⓮	sorry	[ˋsɑrɪ]	adj.	抱歉的	1	1	初級	
	costing	[ˋkɔstɪŋ]	n.	cost（花費）動名詞		1	中級	◎
	some	[sʌm]	adj.	一些	1	1	初級	
	money	[ˋmʌnɪ]	n.	金錢	1	1	初級	◎
⓯	come	[kʌm]	v.	前來	1	1	初級	
	here	[hɪr]	adv.	這裡	1	1	初級	
	anything	[ˋɛnɪˏθɪŋ]	pron.	任何東西	1	1	初級	
	next	[nɛkst]	adj.	下一個	1	1	初級	
	time	[taɪm]	n.	次、回	1	1	初級	

※「紅字單字」於本單元多句出現，「單字級等分析」僅列在「首次出現句」。

🔊 MP3 106-02 ❶～❽

❶	今晚謝啦！	Thanks for tonight!
❷	謝謝你熱情的款待。	Thank you for your enthusiastic hospitality. * enthusiastic hospitality（熱情款待）
❸	謝謝你邀請我來。	Thank you for your invitation.
❹	謝謝你讓我有個愉快的夜晚。	Thank you for giving me such a pleasant night. * Thank you for＋動詞-ing（謝謝你…）
❺	你真是個稱職的主人。	You're a wonderful host.　* hostess（女主人）
❻	謝謝你費心準備的一切。	Thank you for everything that you've prepared.
❼	謝謝你介紹朋友給我認識。	Thank you for introducing me to new friends. * introduce me to＋某人（介紹某人給我）
❽	你親切的招待讓我賓至如歸。	Your kind hospitality really made me feel at home.　* make＋某人＋feel（讓某人感到）
❾	託你的福，我今天很開心。	Thanks to you, I feel very happy today. * Thanks to＋人事物（幸虧有某人事物）
❿	我玩得非常盡興。	I had a lot of fun today. * have fun（玩得開心）、a lot of（很多）
⓫	派對很成功唷！	What a successful party it was! * What a/an＋形容詞＋名詞...!（真是…！）
⓬	今天真是辛苦你了。	You have really done too much for today. * have done too much（做了很多、付出許多）
⓭	今晚真的是太棒了！	What an amazing night it's been!
⓮	謝謝你的晚餐。	Thank you for your dinner.
⓯	下次讓我招待你吧！	Allow me to reciprocate next time! * allow＋某人＋to＋動詞原形（允許某人…） * reciprocate（回報）＝ repay、recompense
⓰	今天的晚餐很好吃唷！	Today's dinner was really delicious!
⓱	謝謝你精心準備的菜餚。	Thank you for preparing these dishes so painstakingly. * painstakingly（精心地）＝ elaborately
⓲	什麼時候換我款待你？	When can I treat you?

	單字	音標	詞性	意義	字頻	大考	英檢	多益
❶	thanks	[θæŋks]	n.	thank（感謝）複數	1			
	tonight	[təˋnaɪt]	n.	今晚	1	1	初級	
❷	thank	[θæŋk]	v.	感謝	1	1	初級	
	enthusiastic	[ɪn.θjuzɪˋæstɪk]	adj.	熱情的	2	4	中級	◎
	hospitality	[.hɑspɪˋtælətɪ]	n.	招呼、款待	3	6	中高	◎
❸	invitation	[.ɪnvəˋteʃən]	n.	邀請	2	2	初級	◎
❹	giving	[ˋgɪvɪŋ]	n.	give（給予）動名詞	6	1	初級	
	such	[sʌtʃ]	adv.	這麼	1	1	初級	
	pleasant	[ˋplɛzənt]	adj.	愉快的	2	2	初級	
	night	[naɪt]	n.	夜晚	1	1	初級	
❺	wonderful	[ˋwʌndəfəl]	adj.	極好的、稱職的	1	2	初級	◎
	host	[host]	n.	男主人	1	4	初級	◎
❻	everything	[ˋɛvrɪ.θɪŋ]	pron.	每件事情	1		初級	
	prepared	[prɪˋpɛrd]	p.p.	prepare（準備）過去分詞	3	1	中級	◎
❼	introducing	[.ɪntrəˋdjusɪŋ]	n.	introduce（介紹）動名詞	1	2	初級	◎
	new	[nju]	adj.	新的	1	1	初級	
	friend	[frɛnd]	n.	朋友	1	1	初級	
❽	kind	[kaɪnd]	adj.	親切的	1	1	初級	◎
	really	[ˋrɪlɪ]	adv.	真的	1	1	初級	
	made	[med]	p.t.	make（使得）過去式	1	1	初級	
	feel	[fil]	v.	感到	1	1	初級	
	home	[hom]	n.	家	1	1	初級	
❾	very	[ˋvɛrɪ]	adv.	十分	1	1	初級	
	happy	[ˋhæpɪ]	adj.	開心的	1	1	初級	
	today	[təˋde]	adv./n.	今天	1	1	初級	◎
❿	had	[hæd]	p.t.	have（擁有）過去式	1	1	初級	
	lot	[lɑt]	n.	許多	1		初級	
	fun	[fʌn]	n.	娛樂、樂趣	1	1	初級	
⓫	successful	[səkˋsɛsfəl]	adj.	成功的	1	2	初級	
	party	[ˋpɑrtɪ]	n.	派對	1	1	初級	◎
⓬	done	[dʌn]	p.p.	do（做）過去分詞	1	1	初級	
	too	[tu]	adv.	過於	1	1	初級	
	much	[mʌtʃ]	adv.	許多地	1	1	初級	
⓭	amazing	[əˋmezɪŋ]	adj.	令人驚奇的	1	3	中級	◎
⓮	dinner	[ˋdɪnə]	n.	晚餐	1	1	初級	
⓯	allow	[əˋlaʊ]	v.	允許	1	1	初級	◎
	reciprocate	[rɪˋsɪprə.ket]	v.	回報	6			
	next	[nɛkst]	adj.	下一個	1	1	初級	
	time	[taɪm]	n.	次、回	1	1	初級	◎
⓰	delicious	[dɪˋlɪʃəs]	adj.	美味的	2	2	初級	
⓱	preparing	[prɪˋpɛrɪŋ]	n.	prepare（準備）動名詞	1	1	初級	◎
	these	[ðiz]	adj.	這些	1	1	初級	
	dish	[dɪʃ]	n.	菜餚	1	1	初級	
	so	[so]	adv.	如此	1	1	初級	
	painstakingly	[ˋpens.tekɪŋlɪ]	adv.	精心地	6			
⓲	treat	[trit]	v.	款待	1	2	初級	◎

※「紅字單字」於本單元多句出現，「單字級等分析」僅列在「首次出現句」。

🔊 MP3 107-01 ❶～⓱

❶	我要劃位。	I would like to book my seat. * **would like to**（想要）、**book a seat**（訂位、劃位）
❷	這是我的護照和機票。	Here are my passport and plane ticket. * **Here is/are＋物品**（這是某物品）
❸	我要靠走道的座位。	I would like to have an aisle seat.
❹	我有一件託運行李。	I have one piece of baggage to check in. * **baggage**（行李）＝ **luggage**、**check in**（託運）
❺	我不要中間的座位。	I don't want a middle seat.
❻	我要靠窗的座位。	I would like to have a window seat.
❼	我要靠近逃生門的座位。	I would like to have a seat near an emergency exit.　* **emergency exit**（逃生門）
❽	請給我前面的座位。	Please give me a seat near the front.
❾	我需要一份素食餐。	I need a vegetarian meal.
❿	可以給我第一排的座位嗎？	May I have a seat in the first row? * **May I＋動詞?**（我可以…嗎）、**the first row**（第一排）
⓫	我們兩個人要坐一起。	We would like to sit together. * **sit together**（坐在一起）
⓬	我的行李超重了嗎？	Does my luggage exceed the weight limit? ＝ Is my luggage too heavy?　* **weight limit**（限重）
⓭	這是我的會員卡，請幫我累積旅程點數。	This is my membership card; please add my travel mileage to it.　* **travel mileage**（旅程點數）
⓮	這件行李我可以隨身攜帶嗎？	Can this bag be a carry-on?
⓯	何時登機？	When is the boarding time?
⓰	登機門是幾號？	What's the number of the boarding gate?
⓱	我爸爸行動不便，上下飛機需要人幫忙。	My father is disabled, so he needs extra help to get on and off the plane. * **get on and (get) off the plane**（上下飛機）

	單字	音標	詞性	意義	字頻	大考	英檢	多益
❶	like	[laɪk]	v.	想要	1	1	初級	
	book	[bʊk]	v.	預訂	1	1	初級	◎
	seat	[sit]	n.	座位	1	1	初級	◎
❷	here	[hɪr]	adv.	這是	1	1	初級	
	passport	[ˈpæsˌpɔrt]	n.	護照	3	3	中級	◎

單字級等分析

	單字	音標	詞性	中文			級等	
❷	plane	[plen]	n.	飛機	1	1	初級	◎
	ticket	[ˋtɪkɪt]	n.	票券	1	1	初級	◎
❸	have	[hæv]	v.	擁有	1	1	初級	
	aisle	[aɪl]	n.	走道	2	5	中高	◎
❹	one	[wʌn]	n.	一	1	1	初級	
	piece	[pis]	n.	一件	1	1	初級	
	baggage	[ˋbægɪdʒ]	n.	行李	3	3	中級	◎
	check	[tʃɛk]	v.	登記托運	1	1	初級	◎
	in	[ɪn]	adv.	記入	1	1	初級	
❺	want	[wɑnt]	v.	想要	1	1	初級	
	middle	[ˋmɪdl̩]	adj.	中間	1	1	初級	
❻	window	[ˋwɪndo]	n.	窗戶	1	1	初級	
❼	emergency	[ɪˋmɝdʒənsɪ]	n.	緊急	1	3	中級	◎
	exit	[ˋɛksɪt]	n.	出口	2	3	初級	
❽	please	[pliz]	adv.	請	1	1	初級	
	give	[gɪv]	v.	給予	1	1	初級	
	front	[frʌnt]	n.	前面	1	1	初級	
❾	need	[nid]	v.	需要	1	1	初級	◎
	vegetarian	[ˏvɛdʒəˋtɛrɪən]	adj.	素食的	4	4	中級	◎
	meal	[mil]	n.	餐點	1	2	初級	
❿	first	[fɝst]	adj.	第一的	1	1	初級	
	row	[rau]	n.	排、列	1	1	初級	
⓫	sit	[sɪt]	v.	坐	1	1	初級	
	together	[təˋgɛðɚ]	adv.	一起	1	1	初級	
⓬	luggage	[ˋlʌgɪdʒ]	n.	行李	3	3	中級	◎
	exceed	[ɪkˋsid]	v.	超過	2	5	中高	◎
	weight	[wet]	n.	重量	1	1	初級	◎
	limit	[ˋlɪmɪt]	n.	限制	1	2	初級	◎
	too	[tu]	adv.	過於	1	1	初級	
	heavy	[ˋhɛvɪ]	adj.	重的	1	1	初級	
⓭	this	[ðɪs]	pron./adj.	這個	1	1	初級	
	membership	[ˋmɛmbɚˏʃɪp]	n.	會員	2	3	中級	◎
	card	[kɑrd]	n.	卡片	1	1	初級	◎
	add	[æd]	v.	加點、累計	1	1	初級	◎
	travel	[ˋtrævl̩]	n.	旅遊	1	2	初級	◎
	mileage	[ˋmaɪlɪdʒ]	n.	里程數	4	5	中高	◎
⓮	bag	[bæg]	n.	行李	1	1	初級	
	carry-on	[ˋkærɪˏɑn]	n.	隨身行李	7			
⓯	boarding	[ˋbordɪŋ]	n.	board（登機）動名詞	3	2	初級	◎
	time	[taɪm]	n.	時間	1	1	初級	◎
⓰	number	[ˋnʌmbɚ]	n.	號碼	1	1	初級	◎
	gate	[get]	n.	大門	1	2	初級	◎
⓱	father	[ˋfɑðɚ]	n.	父親	1	1	初級	
	disabled	[dɪsˋebld̩]	adj.	殘疾的	2	3	中級	
	extra	[ˋɛkstrə]	adj.	額外的	1	2	初級	◎
	help	[hɛlp]	n.	幫忙	1	1	初級	
	get	[gɛt]	v.	乘上	1	1	初級	◎
	on	[ɑn]	adv.	搭上	1	1	初級	
	off	[ɔf]	adv.	下來	1	1	初級	

※「紅字單字」於本單元多句出現，「單字級等分析」僅列在「首次出現句」。

107　機場櫃臺人員怎麼說？

🔊 MP3 107-02 ❶～⓱

❶	有需要服務的地方嗎？	May I help you?
❷	請告訴我您預訂的班機時間。	Please tell me the time of your flight.
❸	要靠窗還是靠走道的位置？	Would you like a window or an aisle seat? * a window seat（靠窗座位）、an aisle seat（靠走道座位）
❹	我需要您的護照和機票。	I need your passport and plane ticket.
❺	有特別的需要嗎？	Do you have any special needs?
❻	我需要您的身分證明。	I need your identification. * identification（身分證明）= ID
❼	對不起，您的行李超重了。	I'm sorry, your baggage is overweight.
❽	要為您訂素食嗎？	Do we need to order vegetarian meals for you?
❾	要託運行李嗎？	Any baggage to check in?
❿	這班飛機已經客滿了。	This flight is full. = This flight has no empty seats. * empty seat（空位）
⓫	請打開行李接受檢查。	Please open your luggage for inspection.
⓬	十點的飛機，七號登機門。	Boarding gate number seven, departing at ten o'clock.
⓭	您要候補機位嗎？	Would you like to be put on standby? * put on standby（排入候補名單）
⓮	祝您旅途愉快。	Have a nice flight.
⓯	機票已經內含機場稅。	The price of the ticket includes airport tax.
⓰	您要在香港還是澳門轉機？	Will you transfer in Hong Kong or Macao? * 此句用「未來簡單式問句」（Will...?） 　表示「詢問對方是否有意願做某事？」。
⓱	請記得提前半小時登機。	Please remember to board half an hour before takeoff.　* before takeoff（在起飛之前）

	單字	音標	詞性	意義	字頻	大考	英檢	多益
❶	help	[hɛlp]	v.	幫忙	1	1	初級	
❷	please	[pliz]	adv.	請	1	1	初級	
	tell	[tɛl]	v.	告訴	1	1	初級	
	time	[taɪm]	n.	時間	1	1	初級	◎
	flight	[flaɪt]	n.	班機、航班	1	2	初級	◎
❸	like	[laɪk]	v.	想要	1	1	初級	

❸	window	[ˈwɪndo]	n.	窗戶	1	1	初級	
	aisle	[aɪl]	n.	走道	2	5	中高	◎
	seat	[sit]	n.	座位	1	1	初級	◎
❹	need	[nid]	v./n.	需要/需求	1	1	初級	
	passport	[ˈpæs.port]	n.	護照	3	3	中級	◎
	plane	[plen]	n.	飛機	1	1	初級	◎
	ticket	[ˈtɪkɪt]	n.	票券	1	1	初級	◎
❺	have	[hæv]	v.	擁有	1	1	初級	
	special	[ˈspɛʃəl]	adj.	特別的	1	1	初級	◎
❻	identification	[aɪ.dɛntəfəˈkeʃən]	n.	身分證明	2	4	中級	◎
❼	sorry	[ˈsɑrɪ]	adj.	抱歉的	1	1	初級	
	baggage	[ˈbægɪdʒ]	n.	行李	3	3	中級	◎
	overweight	[ˈovɚˌwet]	adj.	超重的	3		初級	
❽	order	[ˈɔrdɚ]	v.	訂餐	1	1	初級	◎
	vegetarian	[ˌvɛdʒəˈtɛrən]	adj.	素食的	4	4	中級	◎
	meal	[mil]	n.	餐點	1	2	初級	
❾	any	[ˈɛnɪ]	adj.	任何的	1	1	初級	
	check	[tʃɛk]	v.	登記托運	1	1	初級	◎
	in	[ɪn]	adv.	記入	1	1	初級	
❿	this	[ðɪs]	adj.	這個	1	1	初級	
	full	[fʊl]	adj.	客滿的	1	1	初級	
	empty	[ˈɛmptɪ]	adj.	空的	1	3	初級	◎
⓫	open	[ˈopən]	v.	打開	1	1	初級	
	luggage	[ˈlʌgɪdʒ]	n.	行李	3	3	中級	◎
	inspection	[ɪnˈspɛkʃən]	n.	檢查	2	4	中高	◎
⓬	boarding	[ˈbordɪŋ]	n.	board（登機）動名詞	3	2	初級	◎
	gate	[get]	n.	大門	1	2	初級	◎
	number	[ˈnʌmbɚ]	n.	號碼	1	1	初級	◎
	seven	[ˈsɛvn]	n.	七	1	1	初級	
	departing	[dɪˈpɑrtɪŋ]	p.pr.	depart（出發）現在分詞	2	4	中級	◎
	ten	[tɛn]	n.	十	1	1	初級	
	o'clock	[əˈklɑk]	n.	…點鐘	2	1	初級	
⓭	put	[pʊt]	v.	排入	1	1	初級	
	standby	[ˈstænd.baɪ]	n.	候補名單	7			
⓮	nice	[naɪs]	adj.	愉快的	1	1	初級	
⓯	price	[praɪs]	n.	價錢	1	1	初級	◎
	include	[ɪnˈklud]	v.	包含	1	2	初級	◎
	airport	[ˈɛr.port]	n.	機場	1	1	初級	◎
	tax	[tæks]	n.	稅	1	3	中級	◎
⓰	transfer	[trænsˈfɚ]	v.	轉機	1	4	中級	◎
	Hong Kong	[ˈhɑŋ ˈkɑŋ]	n.	香港				
	Macao	[məˈkau]	n.	澳門				
⓱	remember	[rɪˈmɛmbɚ]	v.	記得	1	1	初級	◎
	board	[bord]	v.	登機	1	2	初級	◎
	half	[hæf]	n.	一半	1	1	初級	
	hour	[aur]	n.	小時	1	1	初級	
	takeoff	[ˈtek.ɔf]	n.	起飛	4			

※「紅字單字」於本單元多句出現，「單字級等分析」僅列在「首次出現句」。

🔵 MP3 108-01 ❶～⓰

❶	請幫我放一下行李。	Please help me stow this suitcase.
❷	我需要一條毛毯。	I need a blanket.
❸	請問耳機如何使用？	Excuse me, can you tell me how to use the headphones? * **Can you tell me ...?**（可以告訴我…嗎）
❹	可以給我一瓶礦泉水嗎？	May I please have a bottle of mineral water? * **May I (please) have＋物品?**（可以給我某物品嗎） * **mineral water**（礦泉水）
❺	可以給我一杯熱咖啡嗎？	May I have a hot coffee? * **a hot coffee**（熱咖啡）、**an iced coffee**（冰咖啡）
❻	可以給我一杯熱水嗎？	May I please have a cup of hot water? * **hot water**（熱水）、**cold water**（冰水）
❼	我身體不太舒服。	I'm not feeling well. ＝ I don't feel too well. * **feel well**（舒服）
❽	可以給我白酒嗎？	May I please have a glass of white wine? * **white wine**（白酒）、**red wine**（紅酒）
❾	可以給我入境卡嗎？	May I have an incoming passenger form? * **incoming passenger form**（入境表）
❿	可以教我填寫入境卡嗎？	Can you please show me how to fill out the incoming passenger form? * **fill out**（填寫）
⓫	飛機什麼時候降落？	What time does the plane land? * **What time...?**（幾點…？）
⓬	可以給我中文雜誌嗎？	May I please have a Chinese magazine?
⓭	什麼時候開始賣免稅商品？	When will you start selling the duty-free goods? * **When will you...?**（你們什麼時候將會…？） * **start＋動詞-ing**（開始做…） * **duty-free goods**（免稅商品）
⓮	我訂了一份兒童餐。	I ordered a children's meal. * **children's meal**（兒童餐）
⓯	我要買化妝品。	I would like to buy cosmetics. * **duty-free cigarettes**（免稅煙）
⓰	我訂的是素食。	I reserved a vegetarian meal. * **reserve**（預定）＝ **make a reservation for**

	單字	音標	詞性	意義	字頻	大考	英檢	多益
❶	please	[pliz]	adv.	請	1	1	初級	
	help	[hɛlp]	v.	幫忙	1	1	初級	
	stow	[sto]	v.	存放、放置	5			
	this	[ðɪs]	adj.	這個	1	1	初級	
	suitcase	[ˋsut.kes]	n.	行李箱	3	5	中級	◎
❷	need	[nid]	v.	需要	1	1	初級	◎
	blanket	[ˋblæŋkɪt]	n.	毛毯	2	3	初級	◎
❸	excuse	[ɪkˋskjuz]	v.	請問	2	2	初級	◎
	tell	[tɛl]	v.	告訴	1	1	初級	
	use	[juz]	v.	使用	1	1	初級	◎
	headphone	[ˋhɛd.fon]	n.	頭戴式耳機	6	4	中級	
❹	have	[hæv]	v.	擁有	1	1	初級	
	bottle	[ˋbɑtl]	n.	一瓶	1	2	初級	
	mineral	[ˋmɪnərəl]	adj.	礦物的	2	4	中級	◎
	water	[ˋwɔtɚ]	n.	水	1	1	初級	
❺	hot	[hɑt]	adj.	熱的	1	1	初級	
	coffee	[ˋkɔfɪ]	n.	咖啡	1	1	初級	
❻	cup	[kʌp]	n.	一杯	1	1	初級	
❼	feeling	[ˋfilɪŋ]	p.pr.	feel（感覺）現在分詞	1	1	初級	
	well	[wɛl]	adj.	舒服的	1	1	初級	◎
	feel	[fil]	v.	感覺	1	1	初級	
	too	[tu]	adv.	太、過	1	1	初級	
❽	glass	[glæs]	n.	一杯	1	1	初級	
	white	[hwaɪt]	adj.	白色的	1	1	初級	
	wine	[waɪn]	n.	酒、葡萄酒	1	1	初級	
❾	incoming	[ˋɪn.kʌmɪŋ]	adj.	入境的	3			
	passenger	[ˋpæsndʒɚ]	n.	乘客	1	2	初級	◎
	form	[fɔrm]	n.	表格	1	2	初級	◎
❿	show	[ʃo]	v.	示範、解說	1	1	初級	◎
	fill	[fɪl]	v.	填寫	1	1	初級	◎
	out	[aʊt]	adv.	寫完、完畢	1	1	初級	◎
⓫	time	[taɪm]	n.	時間	1	1	初級	◎
	plane	[plen]	n.	飛機	1	1	初級	◎
	land	[lænd]	v.	降落	1	1	初級	◎
⓬	Chinese	[ˋtʃaɪ.niz]	adj.	中文的	1		初級	
	magazine	[.mægəˋzin]	n.	雜誌	1	2	初級	
⓭	start	[stɑrt]	v.	開始	1	1	初級	
	selling	[ˋsɛlɪŋ]	n.	sell（賣）動名詞	3	1	初級	
	duty-free	[ˋdjutɪˋfri]	adj.	免稅的				
	goods	[gʊdz]	n.	商品	2	4	中級	◎
⓮	ordered	[ˋɔrdɚd]	p.t.	order（訂餐）過去式	6	1	初級	◎
	children	[ˋtʃɪldrən]	n.	child（小孩）複數	1	1	初級	
	meal	[mil]	n.	餐點	1	2	初級	
⓯	like	[laɪk]	v.	想要	1	1	初級	
	buy	[baɪ]	v.	購買	1	1	初級	
	cosmetics	[kɑzˋmɛtɪks]	n.	化妝品	4	6		
⓰	reserved	[rɪˋzɝvd]	p.t.	reserve（預訂）過去式	4	3	中高	◎
	vegetarian	[.vɛdʒəˋtɛrɪən]	adj.	素食的	4	4	中級	◎

※「紅字單字」於本單元多句出現，「單字級等分析」僅列在「首次出現句」。

108　空服人員怎麼說？

🔊 MP3　108-02　❶～⓰

❶	歡迎各位搭乘。	Welcome aboard.
❷	您的座位請直走。	Please walk straight ahead to find your seat. * **walk straight ahead**（往前直走）
❸	有什麼需要幫忙的嗎？	Do you need any help?
❹	需要報紙嗎？	Do you need a newspaper?
❺	需要熱茶或咖啡嗎？	Would you like some hot tea or coffee? * **would like＋物品**（想要某物品）
❻	您需要什麼飲料？	What would you like to drink? * **What would you like to...?**（你要做…的具體行為）
❼	請把手機關掉。	Please turn off your cell phone. * **turn off**（關閉）
❽	請問您要牛肉還是豬肉？	Would you like beef or pork? * **Would you like rice or noodles?**（請問要吃飯還是麵）
❾	這是您的素食餐盒。	This is your vegetarian meal.
❿	請繫好安全帶。	Please fasten your seatbelt.
⓫	請把茶杯放在托盤上，我為您倒茶。	Please put your cup on the tray; I will pour some tea for you.
⓬	請把用過的耳機丟進塑膠袋。	Please put your used headphones into the plastic bag.
⓭	飛機遇到亂流，請大家立刻回到座位上。	We are currently experiencing some turbulence; please return to your seat immediately. * **experience turbulence**（遭遇亂流） * 此句用「現在進行式」（...are...experiencing...）表示「說話當下正在做的事」。
⓮	需要毛毯嗎？	Do you need a blanket?
⓯	飛機要降落了，請把椅背豎起來。	The plane is going to land; please put your seat back in the upright position. * **be going to**（即將）、**seat back**（椅背）
⓰	謝謝您的搭乘，下次再見！	Thank you for traveling with us, and see you next time!　* **see you**（再見）

	單字	音標	詞性	意義	字頻	大考	英檢	多益
❶	welcome	[ˋwɛlkəm]	adj.	歡迎的	1	1	初級	
	aboard	[əˋbord]	adv.	登機	2	3	中級	
❷	**please**	[pliz]	adv.	請	1	1	初級	

	單字	音標	詞性	中文			級等	
❷	walk	[wɔk]	v.	走路	1	1	初級	
	straight	[stret]	adv.	筆直地	1	2	初級	◎
	ahead	[ə`hɛd]	adv.	向前	1	1	初級	◎
	find	[faɪnd]	v.	尋找	1	1	初級	
	seat	[sit]	n.	座位	1	1	初級	◎
❸	need	[nid]	v.	需要	1	1	初級	◎
	any	[`ɛnɪ]	adj.	任何的	1	1	初級	
	help	[hɛlp]	n.	幫忙	1	1	初級	
❹	newspaper	[`njuz,pepɚ]	n.	報紙	1	1	初級	
❺	like	[laɪk]	v.	想要	1	1	初級	
	some	[sʌm]	adj.	一些	1	1	初級	
	hot	[hɑt]	adj.	熱的	1	1	初級	
	tea	[ti]	n.	茶	1	1	初級	
	coffee	[`kɔfɪ]	n.	咖啡	1	1	初級	
❻	drink	[drɪŋk]	v.	喝	1	1	初級	
❼	turn	[tɜn]	v.	旋動、擰動	1	1	初級	◎
	off	[ɔf]	adv.	關掉地	1	1	初級	
	cell	[sɛl]	n.	cellular（蜂巢式的）縮寫	1	2	初級	
	phone	[fon]	n.	電話	1	2	初級	◎
❽	beef	[bif]	n.	牛肉	2	2	初級	
	pork	[pork]	n.	豬肉	2	2	初級	
❾	this	[ðɪs]	adj.	這個	1	1	初級	
	vegetarian	[,vɛdʒə`tɛrɪən]	n.	素食的	4	4	中級	
	meal	[mil]	n.	餐點	1	2	初級	
❿	fasten	[`fæsn]	v.	繫上、固定	3	3	中級	◎
	seatbelt	[`sit,bɛlt]	n.	安全帶				
⓫	put	[pʊt]	v.	放置	1	1	初級	
	cup	[kʌp]	n.	杯子	1	1	初級	
	tray	[tre]	n.	托盤	2	3	中級	◎
⓬	used	[juzd]	adj.	用過的	1	2	初級	◎
	headphone	[`hɛd,fon]	n.	頭戴式耳機	6	4	中級	
	plastic	[`plæstɪk]	adj.	塑膠的	1	3	中級	
	bag	[bæg]	n.	袋子	1	1	初級	◎
⓭	currently	[`kɝəntlɪ]	adv.	目前	1			◎
	experiencing	[ɪk`spɪrɪənsɪŋ]	p.pr.	experience（遭遇）現在分詞	1	2	初級	◎
	turbulence	[`tɝbjələns]	n.	亂流	4			◎
	return	[rɪ`tɝn]	v.	返回	1	1	初級	◎
	immediately	[ɪ`midɪɪtlɪ]	adv.	立即	1		中級	◎
⓮	blanket	[`blæŋkɪt]	n.	毛毯	2	3	初級	◎
⓯	plane	[plen]	n.	飛機	1	1	初級	◎
	going	[`goɪŋ]	p.pr.	go（即將）現在分詞	4	1	初級	
	land	[lænd]	v.	降落	1	1	初級	◎
	back	[bæk]	n.	背部	1	1	初級	
	upright	[`ʌp,raɪt]	adj.	豎直	3	5	中高	◎
	position	[pə`zɪʃən]	n.	位置	1	1	初級	◎
⓰	thank	[θæŋk]	v.	感謝	1	1	初級	
	traveling	[`trævlɪŋ]	n.	travel（搭乘）動名詞	4		中級	
	see	[si]	v.	見面	1	1	初級	
	next	[nɛkst]	adj.	下一個	1	1	初級	
	time	[taɪm]	n.	次、回	1	1	初級	◎

※「紅字單字」於本單元多句出現，「單字級等分析」僅列在「首次出現句」。

MP3 109-01 ❶〜❿

❶	請問外國人該排在哪裡？	Excuse me, where is the line for foreigners?
❷	這是本國人士排隊區。	This is the line for citizens only. * for＋某人＋only（專屬某人…）
❸	這是外交人員快速通關管道。	This is the express immigration clearance for diplomatic personnel. * express immigration clearance（快速入境通道） * diplomatic personnel（外交人員）
❹	請問需要檢查哪些證件？	Excuse me, what papers need to be checked? * what papers（哪些證件、什麼樣的證件） * need to＋動詞原形（需要）
❺	對不起，我不懂你的意思。	Excuse me, I don't understand what you mean. * what you mean（你說的意思）
❻	我排錯隊伍了嗎？	Am I in the wrong line? * be in the wrong line（排錯隊伍）
❼	我不知道這些東西要報稅。	I didn't know these things needed to be declared.
❽	請問要到哪裡申報？	Excuse me, where should I go to make a customs declaration? * make a customs declaration（向海關申報）
❾	這些東西需要報稅嗎？	Do these things need to be declared?
❿	這都是我的隨身物品。	These are my personal belongings. * personal belonging（個人隨身物品）
⓫	請問在哪裡取行李？	Excuse me, where can I pick up my baggage? * pick up baggage（領取行李）＝ pick up luggage
⓬	有什麼問題嗎？	Is there a problem?
⓭	有會說中文的人嗎？	Is there anyone who speaks Chinese? * Is there anyone who＋子句（有人…？）
⓮	在幾號行李轉台？	Which luggage carousel is it at? * Which luggage carousel...?（哪一個行李轉台…？）
⓯	我要到免稅商店買香煙和化妝品。	I'm going to buy cigarettes and cosmetics in the duty-free shops. * duty-free shop（免稅商店）
⓰	行李出來了嗎？	Has the baggage come out yet? * Have/Has＋主詞＋過去分詞?（…是否已經…？）

	單字	音標	詞性	意義	字頻	大考	英檢	多益
❶	excuse	[ɪkˋskjuz]	v.	請問	2	2	初級	◎
	line	[laɪn]	n.	隊伍	1	1	初級	◎
	foreigner	[ˋfɔrɪnɚ]	n.	外國人	2	2	初級	
❷	this	[ðɪs]	pron.	這個	1	1	初級	
	citizen	[ˋsɪtəzn]	n.	本國市民	1	2	初級	◎
	only	[ˋonlɪ]	adv.	只、僅	1	1	初級	
❸	express	[ɪkˋsprɛs]	adj.	快速的	1	2	初級	
	immigration	[ˌɪməˋgreʃən]	n.	入境	1	4	中級	
	clearance	[ˋklɪrəns]	n.	通道	4	6	中高	◎
	diplomatic	[ˌdɪpləˋmætɪk]	adj.	外交的	2	6	中高	◎
	personnel	[ˌpɝsnˋɛl]	n.	職員	1	5	中高	◎
❹	paper	[ˋpepɚ]	n.	證件	1	1	初級	◎
	need	[nid]	v.	需要	1	1	初級	◎
	checked	[tʃɛkt]	p.p.	check（檢查）過去分詞	7	1	中高	◎
❺	understand	[ˌʌndɚˋstænd]	v.	瞭解	1	1	初級	
	mean	[min]	v.	表示…的意思	1	2	初級	
❻	wrong	[rɔŋ]	adj.	錯誤的	1	1	初級	◎
❼	know	[no]	v.	知道	1	1	初級	
	these	[ðiz]	adj.	這些	1	1	初級	
	thing	[θɪŋ]	n.	東西	1	1	初級	
	needed	[ˋnidɪd]	p.p.	need（需要）過去分詞	8	1	初級	◎
	declared	[dɪˋklɛrd]	p.p.	declare（申報）過去分詞	7	4	中級	◎
❽	go	[go]	v.	去	1	1	初級	
	make	[mek]	v.	做出	1	1	初級	
	customs	[ˋkʌstəmz]	n.	海關	3	5		◎
	declaration	[ˌdɛkləˋreʃən]	n.	申報	3	5	中級	◎
❿	personal	[ˋpɝsnl]	adj.	個人的	1	2	初級	◎
	belonging	[bəˋlɔŋɪŋ]	n.	所屬物品	4	5	中高	
⓫	pick	[pɪk]	v.	挑選	1	2	初級	
	up	[ʌp]	adv.	起來	1	1	初級	
	luggage	[ˋlʌgɪdʒ]	n.	行李	3	3	中級	◎
⓬	there	[ðɛr]	adv.	有…	1	1	初級	
	problem	[ˋprɑbləm]	n.	問題	1	1	初級	◎
⓭	anyone	[ˋɛnɪˌwʌn]	pron.	任何人	1	2	初級	
	speak	[spik]	v.	說	1	1	初級	
	Chinese	[ˋtʃaɪˋniz]	n.	中文	1		初級	
⓮	carousel	[ˌkæruˋzɛl]	n.	轉台	7			
⓯	going	[ˋgoɪŋ]	p.pr.	go（即將）現在分詞	4	1	初級	
	buy	[baɪ]	v.	購買	1	1	初級	
	cigarette	[ˌsɪgəˋrɛt]	n.	香菸	1	3	中級	
	cosmetics	[kɑzˋmɛtɪks]	n.	化妝品	4	6		
	duty-free	[ˋdjutɪˋfri]	adj.	免稅的				
	shop	[ʃɑp]	n.	商店	1	1	初級	◎
⓰	baggage	[ˋbægɪdʒ]	n.	行李	3	3	中級	◎
	come	[kʌm]	p.p.	come（出來）過去分詞	1	1	初級	
	out	[aut]	adv.	出現	1	1	初級	
	yet	[jɛt]	adv.	尚未	1	1	初級	◎

※「紅字單字」於本單元多句出現，「單字級等分析」僅列在「首次出現句」。

109 海關人員怎麼說？

🔵 MP3 109-02 ❶～⓰

❶	請出示護照。	Please show your passport. * **boarding pass**（登機證存根）
❷	請出示台胞證。	Please show your Mainland Travel Permit for Taiwan residents.
❸	要報稅的東西請拿到這邊。	Please bring the items you would like to declare over here.
❹	入境單填了嗎？	Have you filled out the entry form yet? * 此句用「現在完成式問句」（Have...filled...?）表示「過去某時點是否發生某事，且結果持續到現在嗎？」。
❺	你不能攜帶國外的水果入境。	You are not allowed to bring foreign fruit into the country.
❻	你會停留多久？	How long will you stay?
❼	請經過檢疫區，測量體溫。	Please walk through the quarantine area to have your body temperature measured. * **walk through**（通過）、**have...measured**（測量⋯） * **body temperature**（體溫）
❽	這是你帶的東西嗎？	Did you bring these things with you?
❾	請問你來我們國家的目的？	What's the purpose of your visit to our country? * **What's**＋主詞＋動詞?（⋯的具體行為是什麼？）
❿	古柯鹼是違禁品。	Cocaine is a prohibited item.
⓫	請抬頭讓我比對一下照片。	Please raise your head to let me compare you with your picture. * **compare with**（比對）
⓬	請在黃線之後等候。	Please wait behind the yellow line.
⓭	請到一旁接受檢查。	Please step to the side for inspection. * **step to the side**（站到旁邊）
⓮	護照上的照片是你嗎？	Is the picture in your passport of you?
⓯	歡迎來到我們國家。	Welcome to our country.
⓰	祝你有個愉快的旅程。	Have a nice trip.

	單字	音標	詞性	意義	字頻	大考	英檢	多益
❶	please	[pliz]	adv.	請	1	1	初級	
	show	[ʃo]	v.	出示	1	1	初級	◎
	passport	[ˈpæs.port]	n.	護照	3	3	中級	◎
❷	mainland	[ˈmenlənd]	n.	大陸的	3	5	中級	
	travel	[ˈtrævl]	n.	旅遊	1	2	初級	◎

❷	permit	[ˋpɝmɪt]	n.	許可證	1	3	中級	◎
	Taiwan	[ˋtaɪˋwɑn]	n.	台灣			初級	
	resident	[ˋrɛzədənt]	n.	居民	1	5	中級	◎
❸	put	[pʊt]	v.	放置	1	1	初級	
	item	[ˋaɪtəm]	n.	物品	1	2	初級	◎
	like	[laɪk]	v.	想要	1	1	初級	
	declare	[dɪˋklɛr]	v.	申報	1	4	中級	◎
	over	[ˋovə]	adv.	從一邊到另一邊	1	1	初級	
	here	[hɪr]	adv.	這裡	1	1	初級	
❹	filled	[fɪld]	p.p.	fill（填寫）過去分詞	8	1	初級	◎
	out	[aʊt]	adv.	寫完、完畢	1	1	初級	
	entry	[ˋɛntrɪ]	n.	入境	1	3	中級	◎
	form	[fɔrm]	n.	表單	1	2	初級	◎
	yet	[jɛt]	adv.	尚未	1	1	初級	◎
❺	allowed	[əˋlaʊd]	p.p.	allow（允許）過去分詞	1	1	初級	◎
	bring	[brɪŋ]	v.	攜帶	1	1	初級	
	foreign	[ˋfɔrɪn]	adj.	國外的	1	1	初級	
	fruit	[frut]	n.	水果	1	1	初級	
	country	[ˋkʌntrɪ]	n.	國家	1	1	初級	
❻	long	[lɔŋ]	adv.	長久地	1	1	初級	
	stay	[ste]	v.	停留	1	1	初級	◎
❼	walk	[wɔk]	v.	走過	1	1	初級	
	quarantine	[ˋkwɔrən.tin]	n.	檢疫	6			
	area	[ˋɛrɪə]	n.	區域	1	1	初級	◎
	have	[hæv]	v.	讓…/擁有	1	1	初級	
	body	[ˋbɑdɪ]	n.	身體	1	1	初級	
	temperature	[ˋtɛmprətʃə]	n.	溫度	1	3	初級	◎
	measured	[ˋmɛʒəd]	p.p.	measure（測量）過去分詞	4	4	初級	◎
❽	these	[ðiz]	adj.	這些	1	1	初級	
	thing	[θɪŋ]	n.	物品	1	1	初級	
❾	purpose	[ˋpɝpəs]	n.	目的	1	1	初級	◎
	visit	[ˋvɪzɪt]	n.	拜訪	1	1	初級	◎
❿	cocaine	[koˋken]	n.	古柯鹼	2		中高	
	prohibited	[prəˋhɪbɪtɪd]	adj.	禁止的	7	6	中級	◎
⓫	raise	[rez]	v.	抬起	1	1	初級	◎
	head	[hɛd]	n.	頭	1	1	初級	◎
	let	[lɛt]	v.	讓…	1	1	初級	
	compare	[kəmˋpɛr]	v.	比對	1	2	初級	◎
	picture	[ˋpɪktʃə]	n.	照片	1	1	初級	◎
⓬	wait	[wet]	v.	等待	1	1	初級	◎
	yellow	[ˋjɛlo]	adj.	黃色的	1	1	初級	
	line	[laɪn]	n.	線條	1	1	初級	
⓭	step	[stɛp]	v.	跨於	1	1	初級	◎
	side	[saɪd]	n.	邊、側	1	1	初級	
	inspection	[ɪnˋspɛkʃən]	n.	檢查	2	4	中高	◎
⓯	welcome	[ˋwɛlkəm]	adj.	歡迎的	1	1	初級	
⓰	nice	[naɪs]	adj.	美好的	1	1	初級	
	trip	[trɪp]	n.	旅程	1	1	初級	◎

※「紅字單字」於本單元多句出現，「單字級等分析」僅列在「首次出現句」。

110 行李掛失。

🔊 MP3 110-01 ❶～❺

❶	都半小時了，怎麼還沒有看到我的行李？	It's been half an hour already—how come I haven't seen my baggage yet? * how come（怎麼會） * haven't seen…yet（還沒看見…）
❷	我的行李不見了。	I can't find my luggage.
❸	我少了一件行李。	I'm missing a piece of luggage. * 此句用「現在進行式」（…am missing…）表示「說話當下正在做的事」。 * a piece of（一件）
❹	我的行李箱裡面有我全部的家當。	All my personal belongings are in my suitcase. * personal belongings（個人隨身物品）
❺	遺失行李該找誰幫忙？	Whom should I speak to about lost baggage? * Whom should I＋動詞?（我應該向誰…？） * speak to＋某人（向…說、求助於…）
❻	怎麼樣?發現我的行李了嗎？	Well? Have you found my luggage? * Have you＋過去分詞?（你是否已經…？）
❼	我還沒拿到行李。	I haven't picked up my baggage yet.
❽	請你盡快幫我找到行李。	Please help me find my luggage as soon as possible.　* as soon as possible（盡快）
❾	我的錢都放在行李箱。	All my money is in the suitcase.
❿	找到行李後，請送到飯店給我。	When you find my luggage, please deliver it to the hotel where I'm staying. * when…（在…時）、deliver to（送往） * where I'm staying（我暫住的地方）
⓫	我留下飯店及房號給你。	I will leave the hotel name and room number with you.
⓬	我的行李是藍色的。	My bags are blue.
⓭	這是你的行李嗎？	Is this your luggage?
⓮	行李外有寫我的姓名及電話。	My name and phone number are on my luggage. * on my luggage（行李箱上面）
⓯	這個行李箱和我的一樣，但不是我的。	This suitcase looks the same, but it's not mine. * look the same（看起來一樣）

	單字	音標	詞性	意義	字頻	大考	英檢	多益
❶	half	[hæf]	n.	一半	1	1	初級	
	hour	[aʊr]	n.	小時	1	1	初級	
	already	[ɔl'rɛdɪ]	adv.	已經	1	1	初級	◎
	come	[kʌm]	v.	（與 how 連用）怎麼會	1	1	初級	
	seen	[sin]	p.p.	see（看到）過去分詞	1	1	初級	
	baggage	['bægɪdʒ]	n.	行李	3	3	中級	◎
	yet	[jɛt]	adv.	尚未	1	1	初級	◎
❷	find	[faɪnd]	v.	尋找	1	1	初級	
	luggage	['lʌgɪdʒ]	n.	行李	3	3	中級	◎
❸	missing	['mɪsɪŋ]	p.pr.	miss（遺失）現在分詞	2	3	初級	◎
	piece	[pis]	n.	一件	1	1	初級	◎
❹	all	[ɔl]	adj.	所有的	1	1	初級	
	personal	['pɝsn̩l]	adj.	個人的	1	2	初級	◎
	belonging	[bə'lɔŋɪŋ]	n.	所屬物品	4	5	中高	
	suitcase	['sut‚kes]	n.	行李箱	3	5	中級	◎
❺	speak	[spik]	v.	說	1	1	初級	
	lost	[lɔst]	adj.	遺失的	1	2	中高	◎
❻	well	[wɛl]	int.	怎麼樣	1	1	初級	◎
	found	[faʊnd]	p.p.	find（尋找）過去分詞	1	3	中級	◎
❼	picked	[pɪkt]	p.p.	pick（挑選）過去分詞	1	2	初級	
	up	[ʌp]	adv.	起來	1	1	初級	
❽	please	[pliz]	adv.	請	1	1	初級	
	help	[hɛlp]	v.	幫忙	1	1	初級	
	soon	[sun]	adv.	快、早	1	1	初級	
	possible	['pɑsəbl̩]	adj.	可能的	1	1	初級	◎
❾	money	['mʌnɪ]	n.	金錢	1	1	初級	◎
❿	deliver	[dɪ'lɪvɚ]	v.	運送	1	2	初級	◎
	hotel	[ho'tɛl]	n.	飯店	1	2	初級	
	staying	['steɪŋ]	p.pr.	stay（暫住）現在分詞	1	1	初級	◎
⓫	leave	[liv]	v.	留下	1	1	初級	◎
	name	[nem]	n.	名字	1	1	初級	◎
	room	[rʊm]	n.	房間	1	1	初級	
	number	['nʌmbɚ]	n.	號碼	1	1	初級	◎
⓬	bag	[bæg]	n.	行李	1	1	初級	
	blue	[blu]	adj.	藍色的	1	1	初級	
⓭	this	[ðɪs]	pron. /adj.	這個	1	1	初級	
⓮	phone	[fon]	n.	電話	1	2	初級	◎
⓯	look	[lʊk]	v.	看起來	1	1	初級	
	same	[sem]	adj.	相同的	1	1	初級	
	mine	[maɪn]	pron.	我的	1	2	初級	

※「紅字單字」於本單元多句出現，「單字級等分析」僅列在「首次出現句」。

🔊 MP3 110-02 ❶～❸

❶	行李還沒有全部送出來，請您再等等看。	Please wait a moment; not all the luggage has come out yet. * wait a moment（稍後、且慢）= wait a second
❷	您的行李箱上有做記號嗎？	Was your baggage marked? * Was＋物品＋marked?（某物品是否有被做記號？）
❸	如果您的行李真的遺失，我們會負起賠償的責任。	If your baggage really is lost, we'll take responsibility for compensation. * take responsibility for（負責）= take charge of * compensation（賠償）= indemnification
❹	請問您的行李是什麼顏色的？	Excuse me, what color is your baggage? * what color（哪個顏色、什麼顏色）
❺	請問您少了幾件行李？	How many pieces of baggage have you lost? * How many＋名詞複數型...?（有多少…？）
❻	可以給我看一下您的行李條嗎？	May I see your baggage claim ticket? * baggage claim ticket（行李條）
❼	也許是別人拿錯了您的行李。	It's possible that someone took your bags by mistake. * it's possible that＋子句（可能是…） * by mistake（搞錯）= mistakenly
❽	請留下您的資料，找到行李後我們馬上與您聯絡。	Please leave your contact information; we will contact you as soon as we find your luggage. * leave one's contact information（留下聯絡資訊） * as soon as＋子句（…之後，立即）
❾	您有在行李外寫下姓名及聯絡電話嗎？	Were your name and phone number written on the luggage?
❿	我幫您查看電腦紀錄。	Let me check the computer records for you. * check a record（查詢紀錄）
⓫	不好意思，我們可能弄丟了您的行李。	I'm terribly sorry; we may have lost your luggage. * be terribly sorry（非常抱歉）
⓬	對不起，我們把您的行李送到別的地方去了。	I'm sorry, we delivered your baggage to the wrong place. * deliver to...（送往…）、the wrong place（錯誤地點）
⓭	我們找到您的行李了。	We've found your luggage.

	單字	音標	詞性	意義	字頻	大考	英檢	多益
❶	please	[pliz]	adv.	請	1	1	初級	
	wait	[wet]	v.	等待	1	1	初級	◎
	moment	[`momənt]	n.	片刻	1	1	初級	
	all	[ɔl]	adj.	所有的	1	1	初級	
	luggage	[`lʌgɪdʒ]	n.	行李	3	3	中級	◎
	come	[kʌm]	p.p.	come（出來）過去分詞	1	1	初級	
	out	[aut]	adv.	出現	1	1	初級	
	yet	[jɛt]	adv.	尚未	1	1	初級	◎
❷	baggage	[`bægɪdʒ]	n.	行李	3	3	中級	◎
	marked	[mɑrkt]	p.p.	mark（做記號）過去分詞	3	2	中高	◎
❸	really	[`rɪəlɪ]	adv.	真的	1		初級	
	lost	[lɔst]	p.p.	lost（遺失）過去分詞	1	2	中高	◎
	take	[tek]	v.	擔起	1	1	初級	◎
	responsibility	[rɪ.spɑnsə`bɪlətɪ]	n.	責任	1	3	中級	◎
	compensation	[.kɑmpən`seʃən]	n.	賠償	2	6	中高	◎
❹	excuse	[ɪk`skjuz]	v.	請問	2	2	初級	◎
	color	[`kʌlə]	n.	顏色	1	1	初級	
❺	many	[`mɛnɪ]	adj.	許多的	1	1	初級	
	piece	[pis]	n.	一件	1	1	初級	◎
❻	see	[si]	v.	查看	1	1	初級	
	claim	[klem]	n.	認領	1	2	初級	◎
	ticket	[`tɪkɪt]	n.	票券	1	1	初級	◎
❼	possible	[`pɑsəbl]	adj.	可能的	1	1	初級	◎
	someone	[`sʌm.wʌn]	pron.	某個人	1	1	初級	
	took	[tuk]	p.t.	take（取、拿）過去式	1	1	初級	◎
	bag	[bæg]	n.	行李	1	1	初級	
	mistake	[mɪ`stek]	n.	錯誤	1	1	初級	
❽	leave	[liv]	v.	留下	1	1	初級	
	contact	[`kɑntækt]	n.	聯絡	1	2	初級	◎
	information	[.ɪnfə`meʃən]	n.	資訊	1	4	初級	◎
	contact	[kən`tækt]	v.	聯絡	1	2	初級	◎
	soon	[sun]	adv.	快、早	1	1	初級	
	find	[faɪnd]	v.	尋找	1	1	初級	
❾	name	[nem]	n.	名字	1	1	初級	◎
	phone	[fon]	n.	電話	1	2	初級	◎
	number	[`nʌmbə]	n.	號碼	1	1	初級	◎
	written	[`rɪtn]	adj.	有寫上的	2	1	中高	
❿	let	[lɛt]	v.	讓…	1	1	初級	
	check	[tʃɛk]	v.	檢查	1	1	初級	◎
	computer	[kəm`pjutə]	n.	電腦	1	2	初級	◎
	record	[`rɛkəd]	n.	紀錄	1	2	初級	◎
⓫	terribly	[`tɛrəblɪ]	adv.	非常、十分	2			
	sorry	[`sɑrɪ]	adj.	抱歉的	1	1	初級	
⓬	delivered	[dɪ`lɪvəd]	p.t.	deliver（運送）過去式	1	2	初級	◎
	wrong	[rɔŋ]	adj.	錯誤的	1	1	初級	◎
	place	[ples]	n.	地方	1	1	初級	◎
⓭	found	[faund]	p.p.	find（尋找）過去分詞	1	3	中級	◎

※「紅字單字」於本單元多句出現，「單字級等分析」僅列在「首次出現句」。

MP3 111-01 ❶～⓱

❶	我要預訂一間單人房。	I would like to make a reservation for a single room. = I would like to book a single room. * make a reservation for（預訂）= book * would like to（想要）
❷	這是一個人的價格還是一個房間的價格？	Is the price per person or per room? * Is the price...or...?（價格是…還是…？）、per（每…）
❸	有打折嗎？	Is there any discount?
❹	請問房價多少？	Excuse me, how much is it for a room? * How much is...?（…價格多少？）
❺	請問要如何支付訂金？	Excuse me, how should I pay the deposit? * How should I...?（我應該如何…？）
❻	你們有車來機場接我們嗎？	Will you pick us up from the airport? * Will you...?（你們之後是否會…？）、pick up（接送）
❼	房間有衛浴設備嗎？	Does your room have a bathroom?
❽	要先付訂金嗎？	Do I need to pay a deposit first? * pay a deposit（支付訂金）
❾	這裡是商務旅館還是民宿？	Is it a commercial hotel or a bed and breakfast? * bed and breakfast（民宿）= B&B
❿	房間有空調嗎？	Do your rooms have air conditioning? * air conditioning（空調）
⓫	房間有盥洗用品嗎？	Are your rooms provided with toiletries? * be provided with...（備有…）
⓬	可以用信用卡付款嗎？	Do you take credit cards? * take（接受）= accept
⓭	可以接受美金付款嗎？	Do you accept American currency?
⓮	出發前必須再確認一次嗎？	Do we need to reconfirm before departing? * need to＋動詞原形（需要）
⓯	有供應早餐嗎？	Do you offer breakfast?
⓰	你們的旅館離車站近嗎？	Is your hotel near the train station? * train station（火車站）、MRT station（捷運站）
⓱	從機場怎麼到你們旅館？	How do we get to your hotel from the airport? * How do we...?（我們要如何…？）、get to（抵達）

	單字	音標	詞性	意義	字頻	大考	英檢	多益
❶	like	[laɪk]	v.	想要	1	1	初級	
	make	[mek]	v.	做出	1	1	初級	
	reservation	[ˌrɛzə`veʃən]	n.	預約	2	4	中級	◎
	single	[`sɪŋgl]	adj.	單人的	1	2	初級	◎
	room	[rum]	n.	房間	1	1	初級	
	book	[bʊk]	v.	預定	1	1	初級	◎
❷	price	[praɪs]	n.	價錢	1	1	初級	◎
	person	[`pɜsn]	n.	人	1	1	初級	
❸	there	[ðɛr]	adv.	有…	1	1	初級	
	any	[`ɛnɪ]	adj.	任何的	1	1	初級	
	discount	[`dɪskaʊnt]	n.	折扣	2	3	中級	◎
❹	excuse	[ɪk`skjuz]	v.	請問	2	2	初級	◎
	much	[mʌtʃ]	adj.	許多的	1	1	初級	
❺	pay	[pe]	v.	支付	1	3	初級	◎
	deposit	[dɪ`pɑzɪt]	n.	訂金	2	3	中級	
❻	pick	[pɪk]	v.	用車接送	1	2	初級	
	up	[ʌp]	adv.	接起	1	1	初級	
	airport	[`ɛrˌport]	n.	機場	1	1	初級	◎
❼	have	[hæv]	v.	擁有	1	1	初級	
	bathroom	[`bæθˌrum]	n.	浴室	1	1	初級	
❽	need	[nid]	v.	需要	1	1	初級	◎
	first	[fɜst]	adv.	首先	1	1	初級	
❾	commercial	[kə`mɝʃəl]	adj.	商業的	1	3	中級	◎
	hotel	[ho`tɛl]	n.	旅館	1	2	初級	
	bed	[bɛd]	n.	住宿	1	1	初級	
	breakfast	[`brɛkfəst]	n.	早餐	1	1	初級	
❿	air	[ɛr]	n.	空氣	1	1	初級	
	conditioning	[kən`dɪʃənɪŋ]	n.	調節	3			
⓫	provided	[prə`vaɪdɪd]	p.p.	provide（提供）過去分詞	2		中高	
	toiletries	[`tɔɪlɪtrɪs]	n.	盥洗用品	8			
⓬	take	[tek]	v.	接受	1	1	初級	◎
	credit	[`krɛdɪt]	n.	信用	1	3	中級	◎
	card	[kɑrd]	n.	卡片	1	1	初級	◎
⓭	accept	[ək`sɛpt]	v.	接受	1	2	初級	◎
	American	[ə`mɛrɪkən]	adj.	美國的	1		初級	
	currency	[`kɝənsɪ]	n.	貨幣	2	5	中高	◎
⓮	reconfirm	[ˌrikən`fɝm]	v.	再次確認				
	departing	[dɪ`pɑrtɪŋ]	n.	depart（出發）動名詞	2	4	中級	◎
⓯	offer	[`ɔfə]	v.	提供	1	2	初級	◎
⓰	train	[tren]	n.	火車	1	1	初級	
	station	[`steʃən]	n.	車站	1	1	初級	◎
⓱	get	[gɛt]	v.	抵達	1	1	初級	◎

※「紅字單字」於本單元多句出現，「單字級等分析」僅列在「首次出現句」。

🔊 MP3 111-02 ❶～⓱

❶	歡迎光臨。	Welcome!
❷	您有預約嗎？	Do you have a reservation?
❸	只有套房有衛浴設備。	Only the suites have bathroom facilities.
❹	熱水供應時間是在晚上七點到十二點。	Hot water is available from 7 pm to 12 am.
❺	我們沒有空房了。	We have no vacancy right now. * **We have a vacancy right now.**（我們有一間空房）
❻	我們只剩下四人房。	We only have four-person rooms available. * **single room**（單人房）、**double room**（雙人房）
❼	下午可能有客人退房，您要等等看嗎？	Some our guests might check out this afternoon—would you like to wait?
❽	我們只接受現金付款。	We only accept payment in cash. = We only accept cash.
❾	我們有供應早餐。	We offer breakfast.
❿	樓下健身房可以免費使用。	The gym downstairs is available for free. * 某地＋**downstairs**（樓下的某地）、**for free**（免費）
⓫	您是已經訂房的黃小姐嗎？	Are you the Miss Huang who made a reservation? * **Are you＋人名?**（你是某某人嗎？）
⓬	請先付今天的住宿費。	Please pay your bill for today first.
⓭	我們這裡有腳踏車租借的服務。	We have a bicycle rental service.
⓮	歡迎您下次再來。	Hope you'll come again.
⓯	中午十二點前退房。	Please check out before 12 pm.
⓰	我們的旅館靠近捷運站。	Our hotel is near the MRT Station. * **be near＋**地點（靠近某地點）
⓱	我們的旅館在市區裡，交通非常方便。	Our hotel is centrally located with convenient transportation. * **centrally located**（位於中心地段） * **with convenient transportation**（有便利的交通）

	單字	音標	詞性	意義	字頻	大考	英檢	多益
❶	welcome	[`wɛlkəm]	adj.	歡迎的	1	1	初級	
❷	have	[hæv]	v.	擁有	1	1	初級	
	reservation	[ˌrɛzɚˋveʃən]	n.	預約	2	4	中級	◎
❸	only	[ˋonlɪ]	adv.	只有	1	1	初級	
	suite	[swit]	n.	套房	2	6	中高	◎
	bathroom	[ˋbæθ.rum]	n.	浴室	1	1	初級	

❸	facility	[fəˈsɪlətɪ]	n.	設備	1	4	中級	◎
❹	hot	[hɑt]	adj.	熱的	1	1	初級	
	water	[ˈwɔtɚ]	n.	水	1	1	初級	
	available	[əˈveləbl̩]	adj.	可利用的	1	3	初級	◎
	pm	[ˈpiˈɛm]	adv.	下午	1	4		
	am	[ˈeˈɛm]	adv.	上午	1	4	初級	
❺	vacancy	[ˈvekənsɪ]	n.	空房	4	5	中高	◎
	right	[raɪt]	adv.	正值	1	1	初級	
	now	[naʊ]	adv.	現在	1	1	初級	
❻	four-person	[ˈforˈpɝsn̩]	adj.	四人的				
	room	[rum]	n.	房間	1	1	初級	
❼	some	[sʌm]	adj.	有些	1	1	初級	
	guest	[gɛst]	n.	客人	1	1	初級	
	check	[tʃɛk]	v.	結帳、退房	1	1	初級	◎
	out	[aʊt]	adv.	退出、離開	1	1	初級	
	this	[ðɪs]	adj.	這個	1	1	初級	
	afternoon	[ˈæftɚˈnun]	n.	下午	1	1	初級	
	like	[laɪk]	v.	想要	1	1	初級	
	wait	[wet]	v.	等待	1	1	初級	◎
❽	accept	[əkˈsɛpt]	v.	接受	1	2	初級	◎
	payment	[ˈpemənt]	n.	付款	1	1	中級	◎
	cash	[kæʃ]	n.	現金	1	2	初級	◎
❾	offer	[ˈɔfɚ]	v.	提供	1	2	初級	◎
	breakfast	[ˈbrɛkfəst]	n.	早餐	1	1	初級	
❿	gym	[dʒɪm]	n.	健身房	2	3	初級	◎
	downstairs	[ˌdaʊnˈstɛrz]	adv.	在…樓下	2	1	初級	◎
	free	[fri]	adj.	免費的	1	1	初級	
⓫	Miss	[mɪs]	n.	小姐	1	1	初級	
	made	[med]	p.t.	make（做出）過去式	1	1	初級	
⓬	please	[pliz]	adv.	請	1	1	初級	
	pay	[pe]	v.	付款	1	3	初級	◎
	bill	[bɪl]	n.	費用	1	2	初級	◎
	today	[təˈde]	n.	今天	1	1	初級	◎
	first	[fɝst]	adv.	首先	1	1	初級	
⓭	bicycle	[ˈbaɪsɪkl̩]	n.	腳踏車	1	1	初級	
	rental	[ˈrɛntl̩]	adj.	出租的	2	1	初級	◎
	service	[ˈsɝvɪs]	n.	服務	2	1	中高	◎
⓮	hope	[hop]	v.	希望	1	1	初級	
	come	[kʌm]	v.	前來	1	1	初級	
	again	[əˈgɛn]	adv.	再次	1	1	初級	
⓰	hotel	[hoˈtɛl]	n.	旅館	1	2	初級	
	MRT	[ˈɛmˈɑrˈti]	n.	Mass Rapid Transit（捷運）縮寫		2	初級	◎
	station	[ˈsteʃən]	n.	車站	1	1	初級	◎
⓱	centrally	[ˈsɛntrəlɪ]	adv.	中心地	6			
	located	[ˈloketɪd]	p.p.	locate（位於）過去分詞	1	2	中高	◎
	convenient	[kənˈvinjənt]	adj.	便利的	2	1	初級	◎
	transportation	[ˌtræspɚˈteʃən]	n.	交通	1	4	中級	◎

※「紅字單字」於本單元多句出現，「單字級等分析」僅列在「首次出現句」。

🔊 MP3 112-01 ❶～❿

❶	我想要風景好的房間。	I want a room with a nice view. * with a nice view（有優美的風景）
❷	我要辦理住宿。	I want to check in. * check in（登記入住）
❸	這是我的證件。	This is my ID.
❹	請給我兩張單人床。	Please give me a room with two single beds. * with two single beds（有兩張單人床）
❺	請給我一張大床。	Please give me a room with a king-sized bed.
❻	請給我高樓層的房間。	Please give a room on the upper floors. * the upper floors（高樓層） * the lower floors（低樓層）
❼	住幾天以上住宿有折扣？	How long do I need to stay to get a discount? * How long...?（…多久時間？）
❽	只剩下這間房間了嗎？	Is this room the only one left? * the only one left（僅剩的）
❾	住一晚多少錢？	How much per night?
❿	早餐幾點開始？	When is breakfast available?
⓫	如果不滿意我可以換房間嗎？	Can I change rooms if I'm not satisfied? * Can I＋動詞＋if I...?（如果我…，是否可以…？）
⓬	在幾樓吃早餐？	On what floor is breakfast served? * On what floor is...?（…在哪個樓層？） * be served（…有提供）
⓭	從飯店到市區有車嗎？	Is there any transportation available from the hotel to the city? * transportation available（可利用的運輸工具） * from＋某地＋to＋某地（從…地點，到…地點）
⓮	這裡有賣電話卡嗎？	Do you sell prepaid phone cards here?
⓯	我想多住一晚。	I want to stay one more night. * one more＋名詞（再多一個…）
⓰	請幫我把行李送到房間。	Please send my luggage to my room.
⓱	我想要先看一下房間。	I would like to take a look at the room first. * take a look at＋名詞（看一下…）

單字級等分析

	單字	音標	詞性	意義	字頻	大考	英檢	多益
❶	want	[wɑnt]	v.	想要	1	1	初級	◎
	room	[rum]	n.	房間	1	1	初級	
	nice	[naɪs]	adj.	良好的	1	1	初級	
	view	[vju]	n.	風景	1	1	初級	◎
❷	check	[tʃɛk]	v.	登記	1	1	初級	◎
	in	[ɪn]	adv.	入住	1	1	初級	
❸	this	[ðɪs]	pron./adj.	這個	1	1	初級	
	ID	[ˈaɪˈdi]	n.	identification（證件）縮寫		4		
❹	please	[pliz]	adv.	請…	1	1	初級	
	give	[gɪv]	v.	給予	1	1	初級	
	two	[tu]	n.	二	1	1	初級	
	single	[ˈsɪŋgl]	adj.	單獨的	1	2	初級	◎
	bed	[bɛd]	n.	床	1	1	初級	
❺	king-sized	[ˈkɪŋˈsaɪzd]	adj.	大尺寸的				
❻	upper	[ˈʌpɚ]	adj.	up（高的）比較級	1	2	初級	
	floor	[flor]	n.	樓層	1	1	初級	◎
❼	long	[lɔŋ]	adj.	長的	1	1	初級	
	need	[nid]	v.	需要	1	1	初級	◎
	stay	[stey]	v.	停留	1	1	初級	◎
	get	[gɛt]	v.	取得	1	1	初級	◎
	discount	[ˈdɪskaʊnt]	n.	折扣	2	3	中級	◎
❽	only	[ˈonlɪ]	adj.	只有	1	1	初級	
	one	[wʌn]	n.	一	1	1	初級	
	left	[lɛft]	p.p.	leave（留下）過去分詞	1	1	初級	
❾	much	[mʌtʃ]	adj.	許多的	1	1	初級	
	night	[naɪt]	n.	夜晚	1	1	初級	
❿	breakfast	[ˈbrɛkfəst]	n.	早餐	1	1	初級	
	available	[əˈveləbl]	adj.	可利用的	1	3	中級	◎
⓫	change	[tʃendʒ]	v.	更換	1	2	中高	◎
	satisfied	[ˈsætɪsˌfaɪd]	adj.	滿意的	2	2	中高	◎
⓬	served	[sɝvd]	p.p.	serve（提供）過去分詞	1	1	初級	◎
⓭	there	[ðɛr]	adv.	有…	1	1	初級	
	any	[ˈɛnɪ]	adj.	任何的	1	1	初級	
	transportation	[ˌtrænspɚˈteʃən]	n.	運輸工具	1	4	中級	◎
	hotel	[hoˈtɛl]	n.	旅館	1	2	初級	
	city	[ˈsɪtɪ]	n.	城市	1	1	初級	◎
⓮	sell	[sɛl]	v.	賣	1	1	初級	
	prepaid	[priˈped]	adj.	預付的	7			◎
	phone	[fon]	n.	電話	1	2	初級	◎
	card	[kɑrd]	n.	卡片	1	1	初級	◎
	here	[hɪr]	adv.	這裡	1	1	初級	
⓯	more	[mor]	adj.	更多的	1	1	初級	
⓰	send	[sɛnd]	v.	傳遞	1	1	初級	
	luggage	[ˈlʌgɪdʒ]	n.	行李	3	3	中級	◎
⓱	like	[laɪk]	v.	想要	1	1	初級	
	take	[tek]	v.	採取	1	1	初級	◎
	look	[lʊk]	n.	看一下	1	1	初級	
	first	[fɝst]	adv.	首先	1	1	初級	

※「紅字單字」於本單元多句出現，「單字級等分析」僅列在「首次出現句」。

🔵 MP3 112-02 ❶～❻

❶	歡迎光臨。	Welcome. = Welcome to our hotel.
❷	您有行李嗎？	Do you have any luggage with you?
❸	我查一下電腦紀錄。	Let me check our computer records. * **Let me**＋動詞原形（讓我做…） * **check a record**（查詢紀錄）
❹	一間雙人套房，是嗎？	One double suite, right? * **double suite**（雙人套房）、**single suite**（單人套房）
❺	請給我您的證件。	May I please see a form of ID? * **May I please**＋動詞？（麻煩請讓我做…） * **a form of ID**（身分證明表單）
❻	我沒有看到您的資料。	I don't see any of your information here.
❼	您的訂房日期是七號到十號，共三個晚上。	Your reservation is from the seventh to the tenth, three nights in total. * **from**＋時間＋**to**＋時間（從…時間，到…時間） * **in total**（總共）
❽	這是您的房卡。	This is the keycard for your room.
❾	請填上您的個人資料。	Please fill in your personal information. * **fill in**（填寫） * **personal information**（個人資料）
❿	這是您的早餐券。	This is your breakfast coupon.
⓫	在地下一樓用早餐。	Breakfast is served on B1.
⓬	三樓的房間可以嗎？	Is a room on the third floor OK for you? * **on the**＋序數＋**floor**（在…樓）
⓭	退房的時間在中午十二點前。	Check-out time is at noon. * **check-out time**（退房時間）、**at noon**（正午十二點）
⓮	對房間有什麼特別的要求嗎？	Do you have any special requests for your room? * **have any special requests**（有特殊要求） * **request for**＋某物（對某物的要求）
⓯	服務人員會帶您到房間。	Our staff will show you to your room. * **show**＋某人＋**to**＋某地（帶領某人到某地）
⓰	有任何的需要請打房間的內線。	Please use the phone in your room if you need anything.

	單字	音標	詞性	意義	字頻	大考	英檢	多益
❶	welcome	[ˋwɛlkəm]	adj.	歡迎的	1	1	初級	
	hotel	[hoˋtɛl]	n.	旅館	1	2	初級	
❷	have	[hæv]	v.	擁有	1	1	初級	
	any	[ˋɛnɪ]	adj.	任何的	1	1	初級	
	luggage	[ˋlʌgɪdʒ]	n.	行李	3	3	中級	◎
❸	check	[tʃɛk]	v.	查詢	1	1	初級	◎
	computer	[kəmˋpjutɚ]	n.	電腦	1	2	初級	
	record	[ˋrɛkɚd]	n.	紀錄	1	2	初級	◎
❹	one	[wʌn]	n.	一	1	1	初級	
	double	[ˋdʌbl]	adj.	雙人的	1	2	初級	◎
	suite	[swit]	n.	套房	2	6	中高	◎
	right	[raɪt]	int.	是嗎	1	1	初級	
❺	please	[pliz]	adv.	請…	1	1	初級	
	see	[si]	v.	看	1	1	初級	◎
	form	[fɔrm]	n.	表格	1	2	初級	
	ID	[ˋaɪˋdi]	n.	identification（證件）縮寫		4		
❻	information	[ˌɪnfɚˋmeʃən]	n.	資訊	1	4	初級	◎
	here	[hɪr]	adv.	這裡	1	1	初級	
❼	reservation	[ˌrɛzɚˋveʃən]	n.	預約	2	4	中級	◎
	seventh	[ˋsɛvnθ]	n.	七號	2			
	tenth	[tɛnθ]	n.	十號	3			
	three	[θri]	n.	三	1	1	初級	
	night	[naɪt]	n.	夜晚	1	1	初級	
	total	[ˋtotl]	n.	總共	1	1	初級	◎
❽	this	[ðɪs]	pron.	這個	1	1	初級	
	keycard	[ˋki͵kɑrd]	n.	房卡				
	room	[rum]	n.	房間	1	1	初級	
❾	fill	[fɪl]	v.	填寫	1	1	初級	◎
	in	[ɪn]	adv.	填入	1	1	初級	◎
	personal	[ˋpɜsnl]	adj.	個人的	1	2	初級	
❿	breakfast	[ˋbrɛkfəst]	n.	早餐	1	1	初級	
	coupon	[ˋkupɑn]	n.	禮券	4	5	中高	
⓫	served	[sɝvd]	p.p.	serve（服務）過去分詞	1	1	初級	◎
⓬	third	[θɝd]	adj.	第三的	1	1	初級	
	floor	[flor]	n.	樓層	1	1	初級	◎
	ok	[ˋoˋke]	adj.	可以的	1	1	初級	
⓭	check-out	[ˋtʃɛk͵aʊt]	adj.	退房的		5		
	time	[taɪm]	n.	時間	1	1	初級	◎
	noon	[nun]	n.	正午	2	1	初級	
⓮	special	[ˋspɛʃəl]	adj.	特殊的	1	1	初級	◎
	request	[rɪˋkwɛst]	n.	要求	1	3	中級	◎
⓯	staff	[stæf]	n.	人員	1	3	中級	◎
	show	[ʃo]	v.	帶領	1	1	初級	◎
⓰	use	[juz]	v.	使用	1	1	初級	◎
	phone	[fon]	n.	電話	1	2	初級	◎
	need	[nid]	v.	需要	1	1	初級	◎
	anything	[ˋɛnɪ͵θɪŋ]	pron.	任何東西	1	1	初級	

※「紅字單字」於本單元多句出現，「單字級等分析」僅列在「首次出現句」。

🔊 MP3 113-01 ❶～❼

❶	我想換個房間。	I would like to change rooms.
❷	我的房卡有問題，門打不開。	There is a problem with my keycard—it won't open the door.　* won't（不能夠）
❸	少一組香皂和毛巾。	The room is short one set of soap and towels. * be short＋物品（短少某物品）
❹	旅館有健身房嗎？	Is there a gym in this hotel?
❺	我想點一份三明治。	I want to order a sandwich.
❻	打開水龍頭都沒有熱水。	There is no hot water when I turn on the faucet. * there is no...（沒有…）、turn on（打開）
❼	有免費洗衣的服務嗎？	Is there free laundry service?
❽	冰箱裡的礦泉水是免費的嗎？	Is the mineral water in the fridge free? * mineral water（礦泉水）
❾	房間的空調好像壞了。	The air-conditioner in my room seems to be broken.　* seem to（似乎）
❿	冰箱裡的飲料需要付費嗎？	Do I need to pay for the beverages in the fridge? * pay for...（為…付費）
⓫	可以幫我送兩雙拖鞋來嗎？	Could you please bring up two pairs of slippers? * Could you please＋動詞?（可以請你…嗎）
⓬	怎麼打內線電話？	How do I make a room-to-room call? * How do I...?（我該如何…？）
⓭	請幫我送一些冰塊，謝謝。	Could you please send me some ice cubes? * ice cube（冰塊）
⓮	怎麼打市內電話？	How do I make a local call?
⓯	怎麼打國際電話？	How do I make an international call?
⓰	明天早上七點半請打電話叫我起床。	Please give me a wake-up call at seven-thirty tomorrow morning.　* wake-up call（喚醒電話）
⓱	飯店可以上網嗎？	Is there Internet access at this hotel? * Internet access（網際網路連線、上網）

	單字	音標	詞性	意義	字頻	大考	英檢	多益
❶	like	[laɪk]	v.	喜歡	1	1	初級	
	change	[tʃendʒ]	v.	更換	1	2	初級	◎
	room	[rum]	n.	房間	1	1	初級	
❷	there	[ðɛr]	adv.	有…	1	1	初級	
	problem	[ˈprɑbləm]	n.	問題	1	1	初級	◎

❷	keycard	[ˋki͵kɑrd]	n.	房卡				
	open	[ˋopən]	v.	打開	1	1	初級	
	door	[dor]	n.	房門	1	1	初級	
❸	short	[ʃɔrt]	adj.	缺少的	1	1	初級	◎
	one	[wʌn]	n.	一	1	1	初級	
	set	[sɛt]	n.	一套、一組	1	1	初級	◎
	soap	[sop]	n.	香皂	2	1	初級	
	towel	[ˋtauəl]	n.	毛巾	2	2	初級	
❹	gym	[dʒɪm]	n.	健身房	2	3	初級	◎
	this	[ðɪs]	adj.	這個	1	1	初級	
	hotel	[hoˋtɛl]	n.	旅館	1	2	初級	
❺	want	[wɑnt]	v.	想要	1	1	初級	◎
	order	[ˋɔrdɚ]	v.	點餐	1	1	初級	◎
	sandwich	[ˋsændwɪtʃ]	n.	三明治	2	2	初級	
❻	hot	[hɑt]	adj.	熱的	1	1	初級	
	water	[ˋwɔtɚ]	n.	水	1	1	初級	
	turn	[tɜn]	v.	旋動、擰動	1	1	初級	◎
	on	[ɑn]	adv.	開著、運作中	1	1	初級	
	faucet	[ˋfɔsɪt]	n.	水龍頭	4	3	初級	
❼	free	[fri]	adj.	免費的	1	1	初級	
	laundry	[ˋlɔndrɪ]	n.	洗衣服	2	3	中級	◎
	service	[ˋsɜvɪs]	n.	服務	1	1	初級	◎
❽	mineral	[ˋmɪnərəl]	adj.	礦物的	2	4	中級	◎
	fridge	[frɪdʒ]	n.	冰箱	4	6	中級	
❾	air-conditioner	[ˋɛr͵kənˋdɪʃənɚ]	n.	空調		3	中高	
	seem	[sim]	v.	似乎	1	1	初級	◎
	broken	[brokən]	p.p.	break（故障）過去分詞	1	1	初級	◎
❿	need	[nid]	v.	需要	1	1	初級	◎
	pay	[pe]	v.	付費	1	3	初級	◎
	beverage	[ˋbɛvərɪdʒ]	n.	飲料	3	6	中高	
⓫	please	[pliz]	adv.	請…	1	1	初級	
	bring	[brɪŋ]	v.	攜帶	1	1	初級	
	up	[ʌp]	adv.	向上	1	1	初級	
	two	[tu]	n.	二	1	1	初級	
	pair	[pɛr]	n.	一雙	1	1	初級	◎
	slippers	[ˋslɪpɚs]	n.	slipper（拖鞋）複數	5	2	初級	
⓬	make	[mek]	v.	打電話	1	1	初級	
	room-to-room	[ˋrumtu͵rum]	adj.	房間對房間的				
	call	[kɔl]	n.	電話	1	1	初級	◎
⓭	send	[sɛnd]	v.	傳遞	1	1	初級	
	some	[sʌm]	adj.	一些	1	1	初級	
	ice	[aɪs]	n.	冰	1	1	初級	
	cube	[kjub]	n.	方塊	3	4	中高	
⓮	local	[ˋlokl]	adj.	地區性的	1	2	初級	◎
⓯	international	[͵ɪntɚˋnæʃənl]	adj.	國際的	1	2	初級	◎
⓰	give	[gɪv]	v.	給予	1	1	初級	
	wake-up	[ˋwek͵ʌp]	adj.	喚醒的	4			
	seven-thirty	[ˋsɛvənˋθɜtɪ]	n.	七點半				
	tomorrow	[təˋmɔro]	n.	明天	1	1	初級	◎
	morning	[ˋmɔrnɪŋ]	n.	早上	1	1	初級	
⓱	Internet	[ˋɪntɚ͵nɛt]	n.	網路	1	4	初級	
	access	[ˋæksɛs]	n.	使用	1	4	中級	◎

※「紅字單字」於本單元多句出現，「單字級等分析」僅列在「首次出現句」。

113　飯店服務人員怎麼說？

❶	不好意思，全部房間都客滿了。	I'm very sorry, but all our rooms are full. = I'm very sorry, we have no vacancy.
❷	我們馬上為您安排其他房間。	We will set up another room for you right away. * set up（安排）、another room（另一間房）
❸	我們立即派人幫您處理。	We will send someone on our staff to take care of that for you immediately. * send＋某人（派遣某人）、on our staff（我們員工之一） * take care of（處理、解決）
❹	我們立刻送過去給您。	We will send it to you right away. * send＋某物（遞送某物）
❺	我幫您檢查看看是不是出了問題。	Let me check to see if there's a problem. * if there's a problem（是否出問題）
❻	冰箱的飲料需要付費。	Beverages in the fridge need to be paid for.
❼	洗衣需要另外計費。	There's a separate charge for laundry. * a separate charge（額外的收費）
❽	房客可以免費使用健身中心。	Our guests can use the gym for free.
❾	礦泉水是免費的。	The mineral water is free.
❿	游泳池開放到晚上十點。	The pool is open until ten pm.
⓫	您可以使用房間電話撥打國際電話。	You can use the phone in your room to make international phone calls.
⓬	我們飯店提供無線上網。	We offer wireless Internet access. * wireless Internet access（無線網路連線）
⓭	房間對房間可以直撥房間號碼。	For room-to-room calls, just dial the room number. * for（關於）、room-to-room call（房間對房間的電話）
⓮	好的，我們會準時打電話叫您起床。	All right, we'll give you a prompt wake-up call. * all right（好的、沒問題）

	單字	音標	詞性	意義	字頻	大考	英檢	多益
❶	very	[ˋvɛrɪ]	adv.	十分	1	1	初級	
	sorry	[ˋsɑrɪ]	adj.	抱歉的	1	1	初級	
	all	[ɔl]	adj./ adv.	全部的/完全	1	1	初級	
	room	[rum]	n.	房間	1	1	初級	
	full	[fʊl]	adj.	客滿的	1	1	初級	
	have	[hæv]	v.	擁有	1	1	初級	
	vacancy	[ˋvekənsɪ]	n.	空房間	4	5	中高	◎
❷	set	[sɛt]	v.	安排、設置	1	1	初級	◎

單字級等分析

❷	up	[ʌp]	adv.	出現	1	1	初級	
	another	[əˋnʌðɚ]	adj.	另一個	1	1		
	right	[raɪt]	adv./adj.	立即/沒問題的	1	1	初級	
	away	[əˋwe]	adv.	直接	1	1	初級	
❸	send	[sɛnd]	v.	派遣	1	1	初級	
	someone	[ˋsʌm.wʌn]	pron.	某個人	1	1	初級	
	staff	[stæf]	n.	人員	1	3	中級	◎
	take	[tek]	v.	採取	1	1	初級	◎
	care	[kɛr]	n.	處理	1	1	初級	◎
	that	[ðæt]	pron.	那件事	1	1	初級	
	immediately	[ɪˋmidɪɪtlɪ]	adv.	立即	1		中級	◎
❺	let	[lɛt]	v.	讓…	1	1	初級	
	check	[tʃɛk]	v.	檢查	1	1	初級	◎
	see	[si]	v.	查看	1	1	初級	◎
	there	[ðɛr]	adv.	有…	1	1	初級	
	problem	[ˋprɑbləm]	n.	問題	1	1	初級	◎
❻	beverage	[ˋbɛvərɪdʒ]	n.	飲料	3	6	中高	◎
	fridge	[frɪdʒ]	n.	冰箱	4	6	中級	
	need	[nid]	v.	需要	1	1	初級	◎
	paid	[ped]	p.p.	pay（付費）過去分詞	3	3	中高	◎
❼	separate	[ˋsɛpə.ret]	adj.	個別的	1	2	初級	◎
	charge	[tʃɑrdʒ]	n.	收費	1	2	初級	◎
	laundry	[ˋlɔndrɪ]	n.	洗衣服	2	3	初級	◎
❽	guest	[gɛst]	n.	客人	1	1	初級	
	use	[juz]	v.	使用	1	1	初級	◎
	gym	[dʒɪm]	n.	健身房	2	3	初級	◎
	free	[fri]	adj.	免費的	1	1	初級	
❾	mineral	[ˋmɪnərəl]	adj.	礦物的	2	4	中級	◎
	water	[ˋwɔtɚ]	n.	水	1	1	初級	
❿	pool	[pul]	n.	游泳池	1	1	初級	
	open	[ˋopən]	adj.	有營業的、開放的	1	1	初級	
	ten	[tɛn]	n.	十	1	1	初級	
	pm	[ˋpiˋɛm]	adv.	下午	1	4		
⓫	phone	[fon]	n.	電話	1	2	初級	◎
	make	[mek]	v.	打電話	1	1	初級	
	international	[ˌɪntɚˋnæʃənl]	adj.	國際的	1	2	初級	◎
	call	[kɔl]	n.	電話	1	1	初級	◎
⓬	offer	[ˋɔfɚ]	v.	提供	1	2	初級	◎
	wireless	[ˋwaɪrlɪs]	adj.	無線的	2			
	Internet	[ˋɪntɚ.nɛt]	n.	網路	1	4	初級	
	access	[ˋæksɛs]	n.	使用	1	4	中級	◎
⓭	room-to-room	[ˋrumtu.rum]	adj.	房間對房間的				
	just	[dʒʌst]	adv.	只要	1	1	初級	
	dial	[ˋdaɪəl]	v.	撥打	3	2	初級	◎
	number	[ˋnʌmbɚ]	n.	號碼	1	1	初級	◎
⓮	give	[gɪv]	v.	給予	1	1	初級	
	prompt	[prɑmpt]	adj.	準時的	2	4	中級	◎
	wake-up	[ˋwek.ʌp]	adj.	喚醒的	4			

※「紅字單字」於本單元多句出現，「單字級等分析」僅列在「首次出現句」。

🔊 MP3 114-01 ❶～❶❺

❶	我要不易破的材質。	I want the tougher material. * **tough**（堅韌的）可替換為：**durable**（耐用的）
❷	我要 34 吋，C 罩杯。	I need a size 34C bra. * **I need＋名詞**（我需要…）
❸	我要找棉麻材質的衣服。	I'm looking for cotton-linen clothes. * **be looking for**（正在尋找） * **cotton**（棉）、**linen**（亞麻）
❹	我要吸汗的材質。	I want the moisture-wicking material.
❺	我領圍 14 吋。	My neck size is 14 inches.
❻	我需要滋潤型的乳液。	I need a moisturizing cream. * **moisturizing cream**（滋潤型乳液）
❼	我要成分天然的產品。	I need a product with natural ingredients. * **with＋名詞**（含有…、附帶…） * **natural ingredient**（天然成分） * **man-made**（人工的、人造的）
❽	我要不含油脂的化妝品。	I need oil-free cosmetics.
❾	防曬係數必須在 15 以上。	The SPF has to be above 15. * **have/has to**（必須）、**above＋數字**（大於某數字）
❿	我要透明感好一點的粉底。	I need a facial powder with better transparency. * **transparency**（透明度）可替換為： **covering effect**（遮瑕效果）
⓫	我喜歡尖頭的鞋子。	I like sharp-tipped shoes.
⓬	我需要液態的保養品，不要膏狀的。	I need liquid-based care products, not lotion-based. * **care product**（保養品）
⓭	我喜歡味道清爽一點的香水。	I like the fresher-smelling perfume.
⓮	我喜歡三吋以上的高跟鞋。	I like high heels to be more than three inches. * **more than**（大於、多於）
⓯	我要接近膚色的絲襪。	I need a pair of nude-colored silk stockings. * **a pair of**（一雙）、**silk stockings**（絲襪） * **knee high stockings**（及膝的長筒襪） * **thigh high stockings**（過膝的長筒襪） * **pantyhose**（褲襪）

	單字	音標	詞性	意義	字頻	大考	英檢	多益
❶	want	[wɑnt]	v.	想要	1	1	初級	◎
	tougher	[ˈtʌfɚ]	adj.	tough（堅韌的）比較級	1	4	中級	◎
	material	[məˈtɪrɪəl]	n.	材質	1	6	初級	◎
❷	need	[nid]	v.	需要	1	1	初級	◎
	size	[saɪz]	n.	尺寸	1	1	初級	◎
	bra	[brɑ]	n.	罩杯	3	4	中級	
❸	looking	[ˈlukɪŋ]	p.pr.	look（尋找）現在分詞	5	1	初級	
	cotton-linen	[ˈkɑtnˈlɪnən]	adj.	棉麻的				
	clothes	[kloz]	n.	cloth（衣服）複數	1	2	初級	
❹	moisture-wicking	[ˈmɔɪstʃɚˈwɪkɪŋ]	adj.	吸汗的				
❺	neck	[nɛk]	n.	脖子	1	1	初級	
	inch	[ɪntʃ]	n.	英吋	3	1	初級	
❻	moisturizing	[ˈmɔɪstʃəˌraɪzɪŋ]	adj.	滋潤的			初級	
	cream	[krim]	n.	乳液	1	2	初級	
❼	product	[ˈprɑdəkt]	n.	產品	1	3	初級	◎
	natural	[ˈnætʃərəl]	adj.	天然的	1	2	初級	
	ingredient	[ɪnˈgridɪənt]	n.	成分	1	4	中級	◎
❽	oil-free	[ˈɔɪlˈfri]	adj.	不含油脂的				
	cosmetics	[kɑzˈmɛtɪks]	n.	化妝品	4	6		
❾	SPF	[ˈɛsˈpiˈɛf]	n.	防曬係數、是以下三字的縮寫： sun（陽光） protection（預防） factor（係數）				
	have	[hæv]	v.	必須	1	1	初級	
❿	facial	[ˈfeʃəl]	adj.	臉部的	3	4	中級	
	powder	[ˈpaudɚ]	n.	粉底	2	3	初級	
	better	[ˈbɛtɚ]	adj.	good（良好的）比較級	1	1	初級	
	transparency	[trænsˈpɛrənsɪ]	n.	透明度	4		中高	
⓫	like	[laɪk]	v.	喜歡	1	1	初級	
	sharp-tipped	[ˈʃɑrpˈtɪpt]	adj.	尖頭的				
	shoes	[ʃuz]	n.	shoe（鞋子）複數	2	1		
⓬	liquid-based	[ˈlɪkwɪdˈbest]	adj.	液態的				
	care	[kɛr]	n.	保養	1	1	初級	◎
	lotion-based	[ˈloʃənˈbest]	adj.	膏狀的				
⓭	fresher-smelling	[ˈfrɛʃɚˈsmɛlɪŋ]	adj.	味道清爽一點的				
	perfume	[pɚˈfjum]	n.	香水	3	4	中級	
⓮	high	[haɪ]	adj.	高的	1	1	初級	
	heels	[hils]	n.	heel（高跟鞋）複數	2	3	中級	
	more	[mor]	adv.	多於	1	1	初級	
	three	[θri]	n.	三	1	1	初級	
⓯	pair	[pɛr]	n.	一雙	1	1	初級	◎
	nude-colored	[ˈnjudˈkʌlɚd]	adj.	膚色的				
	silk	[sɪlk]	n.	絲	2	2	中級	
	stockings	[ˈstɑkɪŋs]	n.	stocking（長襪）複數	5	3		

※「紅字單字」於本單元多句出現，「單字級等分析」僅列在「首次出現句」。

114 服務人員怎麼說？

❶	要我幫您量一下尺寸嗎？	Would you like me to take your measurements? * **would like**＋某人＋**to**＋動詞原形（想要某人…） * **take one's measurements**（測量某人的尺寸）
❷	可以告訴我您的尺寸嗎？	Can you tell me your measurements?
❸	您喜歡一般的款式還是流行的？	Would you like the general style or the new fashion style?
❹	要我幫您介紹嗎？	Would you like me to tell you more about it? * **tell you more about it**（介紹更多給你）
❺	您要什麼顏色的口紅？	What kind of lipstick color would you like? * **What kind of**＋名詞**...?**（什麼樣的…？）
❻	您要試試最新的款式嗎？	Would you like to try the newest fashion?
❼	您是乾性肌膚還是油性肌膚？	Do you have dry skin or oily skin? * **have**＋形容詞＋**skin**（是…的肌膚）
❽	您喜歡什麼材質的衣服？	What kind of clothing material would you like? * **clothing material**（衣服材質）
❾	您要一般粉餅還是防曬粉餅？	Would you like the general kind of powder or the UV protection powder? * **UV protection**（防曬）
❿	您需要什麼樣的乳液？	What kind of cream would you like?
⓫	您喜歡清淡的香水還是味道濃郁的？	Would you like perfume with a light, fresh scent or a heavier scent? * **with**＋名詞（含有…、附帶…）
⓬	您喜歡皮製的嗎？	Do you like leather? * **fur**（毛皮）、**wool**（羊毛） * **nylon**（尼龍）、**rubber**（橡膠） * **polyester**（聚酯纖維）、**rayon**（人造絲）
⓭	這個顏色如何？	How do you like this color? * **How do you like...?**（…你覺得如何呢？）
⓮	您要找什麼款式的鞋子？	What kind of shoe style are you looking for? * **be looking for**（正在尋找） * **sharp-tipped**（尖頭的）、**round-tipped**（圓頭的）
⓯	您需要平底鞋還是高跟鞋？	Would you like flat-heeled or high-heeled shoes?

	單字	音標	詞性	意義	字頻	大考	英檢	多益
❶	like	[laɪk]	v.	想要/喜歡/覺得	1	1	初級	
	take	[tek]	v.	測量	1	1	初級	◎
	measurement	[ˋmɛʒəmənt]	n.	尺寸	2	2	中高	◎
❷	tell	[tɛl]	v.	告訴	1	1	初級	
❸	general	[ˋdʒɛnərəl]	adj.	一般的	1	2	初級	◎
	style	[staɪl]	n.	風格、款式	1	3	初級	◎
	new	[nju]	adj.	新的	1	1	初級	
	fashion	[ˋfæʃən]	n.	流行款式	1	3	中級	◎
❹	more	[mor]	adv.	更多	1	1	初級	
❺	kind	[kaɪnd]	n.	種類	1	1	初級	◎
	lipstick	[ˋlɪp.stɪk]	n.	口紅	3	3	中級	
	color	[ˋkʌlə]	n.	顏色	1	1	初級	
❻	try	[traɪ]	v.	嘗試	1	1	初級	
	newest	[ˋnjuɪst]	adj.	new（新的）比較級	1	1	初級	
❼	have	[hæv]	v.	擁有	1	1	初級	
	dry	[draɪ]	adj.	乾性的	1	1	初級	
	skin	[skɪn]	n.	皮膚	1	1	初級	◎
	oily	[ˋɔɪlɪ]	adj.	油性的	5			
❽	clothing	[ˋkloðɪŋ]	n.	衣服	1	2	初級	
	material	[məˋtɪrɪəl]	n.	材料	1	6	中級	◎
❾	powder	[ˋpaudə]	n.	粉餅	2	3	初級	
	UV	[ˋjuˋvi]	n.	ultraviolet（紫外線）縮寫				
	protection	[prəˋtɛkʃən]	n.	保護	1	3	初級	◎
❿	cream	[krim]	n.	乳液	1	2	初級	
⓫	perfume	[pəˋfjum]	n.	香水	2	4	中級	
	light	[laɪt]	adj.	氣味清淡的	1	1	初級	
	fresh	[frɛʃ]	adj.	新鮮的	1	1	初級	
	scent	[sɛnt]	n.	氣味	3	5	中高	◎
	heavier	[ˋhɛvɪə]	adj.	heavy（氣味濃郁的）比較級	1	1	初級	
⓬	leather	[ˋlɛðə]	n.	皮革	2	3	中級	◎
⓭	this	[ðɪs]	adj.	這個	1	1	初級	
⓮	shoe	[ʃu]	n.	鞋子	1	1	初級	
	looking	[ˋlukɪŋ]	p.pr.	look（尋找）現在分詞	5	1	初級	
⓯	flat-heeled	[ˋflætˋhild]	adj.	鞋跟平的				
	high-heeled	[ˋhaɪˋhild]	adj.	鞋跟高的				
	shoes	[ʃuz]	n.	shoe（鞋子）複數	2	1		

※「紅字單字」於本單元多句出現，「單字級等分析」僅列在「首次出現句」。

115 試穿。

❶	可以試穿嗎？	Can I try on the clothes? *try on（試穿）
❷	我覺得還不錯。	I think it's not bad. *not bad（還不錯）
❸	剪裁不夠大方。	The cut doesn't look graceful enough. *look＋形容詞（看起來…）
❹	這個顏色不適合我的膚色。	The color doesn't fit my skin tone. *fit（適合）＝be suitable for
❺	拉鍊不好拉。	The zipper doesn't zip well. *zip well（拉鍊容易拉）
❻	這款設計十分優雅。	The design is very graceful.
❼	我覺得穿起來怪怪的。	I feel weird wearing it.
❽	質料蠻好的。	The material is pretty nice.
❾	是這樣穿沒錯嗎？	Is this the right way to wear it? *right way（正確的方式）
❿	質料不透氣。	The material is airproof.
⓫	腰圍太鬆了。	It's too loose in the waist
⓬	太暴露了。	It's too revealing.
⓭	穿起來很舒服。	It feels comfortable. *It feels uncomfortable.（穿起來不舒服）
⓮	太緊了。	It's too tight.
⓯	好土喔！	It doesn't look cool at all! *look cool（看起來時髦）、at all（完全地）
⓰	好像不太好保養。	It looks difficult to care for. *care for（保養）
⓱	裙子太短了。	The skirt is too short.
⓲	我不能呼吸了！	I can barely breathe!
⓳	這是我一直在找的款式。	This style is what I have been looking for. *have been looking for（一直都在尋找）
⓴	這件我穿起來很好看！	It looks perfect on me! *look perfect（很好看）、on me（在我身上）
㉑	穿這樣我怎麼見人啊！	I can't wear this in public! *in public（在公眾場合）

單字級等分析

	單字	音標	詞性	意義	字頻	大考	英檢	多益
❶	try	[traɪ]	v.	試穿	1	1	初級	
	clothes	[kloz]	n.	cloth（衣服）複數	1	2	初級	
❷	think	[θɪŋk]	v.	認為	1	1	初級	
	bad	[bæd]	adj.	不好的	1	1	初級	
❸	cut	[kʌt]	n.	裁剪樣式	1	1	初級	
	look	[lʊk]	v.	看起來	1	1	初級	
	graceful	[ˈgresfəl]	adj.	大方優雅的	3	4	中級	
	enough	[əˈnʌf]	adv.	足夠地	1	1	初級	◎
❹	color	[ˈkʌlə]	n.	顏色	1	1	初級	◎
	fit	[fɪt]	v.	適合	1	2	初級	◎
	skin	[skɪn]	n.	皮膚	1	1	初級	◎
	tone	[ton]	n.	色調	1	1	中級	◎
❺	zipper	[ˈzɪpə]	n.	拉鍊	4	3	中高	
	zip	[zɪp]	v.	拉拉鍊	4	5	中高	◎
	well	[wɛl]	adv.	良好地	1	1	初級	◎
❻	design	[dɪˈzaɪn]	n.	設計	1	2	初級	◎
	very	[ˈvɛrɪ]	adv.	十分	1	1	初級	
❼	feel	[fil]	v.	感覺	1	1	初級	
	weird	[wɪrd]	adj.	怪異的	2	5	中高	
	wearing	[ˈwɛrɪŋ]	p.pr.	wear（穿上）現在分詞	7	1	初級	◎
❽	material	[məˈtɪrɪəl]	n.	材料	1	6	初級	◎
	pretty	[ˈprɪtɪ]	adv.	非常、頗為	1	1	初級	◎
	nice	[naɪs]	adj.	良好的	1	1	初級	
❾	this	[ðɪs]	pron./adj.	這個	1	1	初級	
	right	[raɪt]	adj.	正確的	1	1	初級	
	way	[we]	n.	方式	1	1	初級	
	wear	[wɛr]	v.	穿上	1	1	初級	◎
❿	airproof	[ˈɛrˌpruf]	adj.	不透氣的				
⓫	too	[tu]	adv.	過於	1	1	初級	
	loose	[lus]	adj.	寬鬆的	2	3	中級	◎
	waist	[west]	n.	腰部	2	2	初級	
⓬	revealing	[rɪˈvilɪŋ]	adj.	暴露的	4	3	中高	◎
⓭	comfortable	[ˈkʌmfətəbl]	adj.	舒服的	1	2	初級	◎
⓮	tight	[taɪt]	adj.	緊的	1	3	中級	
⓯	cool	[kul]	adj.	時髦的	1	1	初級	
	all	[ɔl]	n.	完全	1	1	初級	
⓰	difficult	[ˈdɪfəˌkəlt]	adj.	困難的	1	1	初級	◎
	care	[kɛr]	v.	保養	1	1	初級	◎
⓱	skirt	[skɝt]	n.	裙子	2	1	初級	
	short	[ʃɔrt]	adj.	短的	1	1	初級	
⓲	barely	[ˈbɛrlɪ]	adv.	幾乎無法	1	3	中級	◎
	breathe	[brið]	v.	呼吸	1	3	中級	◎
⓳	style	[staɪl]	n.	款式	1	3	初級	◎
	looking	[ˈlʊkɪŋ]	p.pr.	look（尋找）現在分詞	5	1	初級	
⓴	perfect	[ˈpɝfɪkt]	adj.	完美的	1	2	初級	◎
㉑	public	[ˈpʌblɪk]	n.	公眾場合	1	1	初級	

※「紅字單字」於本單元多句出現，「單字級等分析」僅列在「首次出現句」。

507

🔊 MP3 115-02 ❶～❹

❶	要不要試穿看看？	Would you like to try it on?
❷	不好意思，特價品不能試穿。	Sorry, the products on sale cannot be tried on. * 某物＋on sale（特價的某物）
❸	您比較適合這個顏色。	This color fits you better.
❹	這個顏色很好搭配。	This color goes with everything. * go with everything（百搭、好搭配）
❺	這個款式不會退流行。	This style will never go out of fashion. * go out of fashion（退流行）
❻	質料很棒，您可以摸摸看。	The material is really good—feel it.
❼	這種材質很容易保養。	The material is easy to care for. * be easy to（易於）
❽	我覺得您穿這件衣服很好看。	I think you look great in this. * I think＋子句（我認為…）、in＋衣服(穿著某衣服)
❾	這是我們的暢銷品，前一陣子還缺貨。	This is our best-selling item. In fact, we ran out not too long ago. * run out（缺貨）
❿	這是今年最流行的樣式。	This is the most fashionable style this year.
⓫	這是義大利進口的鞋子。	These shoes are imported from Italy. * be imported from＋國家（進口自某國家）
⓬	您可以試試最新的款式。	You can try the newest style.
⓭	您可以再搭配一件外套。	You can also wear a coat to match it. * wear＋衣服＋to match（再搭配上某衣服）
⓮	這是小牛皮製的。	This is made of calf leather. * be made of...（由…製成）
⓯	還有別的顏色可以選擇。	We also have other colors for you to choose from. * choose from（從中挑選）

	單字	音標	詞性	意義	字頻	大考	英檢	多益
❶	like	[laɪk]	v.	想要	1	1	初級	
	try	[traɪ]	v.	試穿	1	1	初級	
❷	sorry	[ˋsɑrɪ]	adj.	抱歉的	1	1	初級	
	product	[ˋprɑdəkt]	n.	產品	1	3	初級	◎
	sale	[sel]	n.	拍賣、特價	1	1	初級	◎
	tried	[taɪrd]	p.p.	try（試穿）現在分詞	7			
❸	this	[ðɪs]	adj./ pron.	這個	1	1	初級	

單字級等分析

❸	color	[kʌlɚ]	n.	顏色	1	1	初級	
	fit	[fɪt]	v.	適合	1	2	初級	◎
	better	[ˋbɛtɚ]	adv.	well（良好地）比較級	1	1	初級	
❹	go	[go]	v.	搭配/衰退	1	1	初級	
	everything	[ˋɛvrɪˏθɪŋ]	pron.	每件事物	1		初級	
❺	style	[staɪl]	n.	款式	1	3	初級	◎
	never	[ˋnɛvɚ]	adv.	從不	1	1	初級	
	out	[aʊt]	adv.	在…之外/賣光	1	1	初級	
	fashion	[ˋfæʃən]	n.	流行	1	3	中級	◎
❻	material	[məˋtɪrɪəl]	n.	材質	1	6	初級	◎
	really	[ˋrɪəlɪ]	adv.	很、十分	1		初級	
	good	[gʊd]	adj.	良好的	1	1	初級	◎
	feel	[fil]	v.	觸摸	1	1	初級	
❼	easy	[ˋizɪ]	adj.	容易的	1	1	初級	◎
	care	[kɛr]	v.	照顧、保養	1	1	初級	◎
❽	think	[θɪŋk]	v.	認為	1	1	初級	
	look	[lʊk]	v.	看起來	1	1	初級	
	great	[gret]	adj.	極好的	1	1	初級	◎
❾	best-selling	[ˋbɛstˋsɛlɪŋ]	adj.	暢銷的	3			
	item	[ˋaɪtəm]	n.	物品	1	2	初級	◎
	fact	[fækt]	n.	事實	1	1	初級	
	ran	[ræn]	p.t.	run（缺貨）過去式	1	1	初級	◎
	too	[tu]	adv.	太過	1	1	初級	
	long	[lɔŋ]	adv.	長久地	1	1	初級	
	ago	[əˋgo]	adv.	以前	1	1	初級	
❿	most	[most]	adv.	最為	1	1	初級	
	fashionable	[ˋfæʃənəbl]	adj.	流行的	3	3	初級	◎
	year	[jɪr]	n.	年	1	1	初級	
⓫	these	[ðiz]	adj.	這些	1	1	初級	
	shoes	[ʃuz]	n.	shoe（鞋子）複數	2	1		
	imported	[ɪmˋportɪd]	p.p.	import（進口）過去分詞	3	3	初級	◎
	Italy	[ˋɪtlɪ]	n.	義大利				
⓬	newest	[ˋnjuɪst]	adj.	new（新的）最高級	1	1	初級	
⓭	also	[ˋɔlso]	adv.	也…	1	1	初級	
	wear	[wɛr]	v.	穿上	1	1	初級	◎
	coat	[kot]	n.	外套	1	1	初級	◎
	match	[mætʃ]	v.	搭配	1	2	初級	◎
⓮	made	[med]	p.p.	make（製作）過去分詞	1	1	初級	
	calf	[kæf]	n.	小牛	3	5	中高	
	leather	[ˋlɛðɚ]	n.	皮革	2	3	中級	◎
⓯	have	[hæv]	v.	擁有	1	1	初級	
	other	[ˋʌðɚ]	adj.	其他的	1	1	初級	
	choose	[tʃuz]	v.	挑選	1	2	初級	◎

※「紅字單字」於本單元多句出現，「單字級等分析」僅列在「首次出現句」。

116 尺寸。

❶	褲子太長了。	The pants are too long.
❷	大小剛剛好。	It fits me well.　* fit well（很合身）
❸	袖子太短了。	The sleeves are too short.
❹	領口有點緊。	The collar is too tight.
❺	腰圍太鬆了。	It's too baggy in the waist.
❻	腰圍太緊了。	It's too tight in the waist.
❼	拉鍊拉不上來。	I can't zip up the zipper.　* zip up（拉上拉鍊）
❽	扣子扣不起來。	I can't button it up.　* button up（扣上扣子）
❾	我通常穿 M 號的。	I usually wear a medium.　* large（L 號）
❿	尺寸太小了。	The size is too small. * The size is too big.（尺寸太大了）
⓫	我喜歡穿合身的衣服。	I like to wear clothes that fit me well.
⓬	S 號太小，M 號又太大。	The small is too small, but the medium is too big.
⓭	下擺太寬了。	The lower hem is too wide.
⓮	我喜歡穿寬鬆的衣服。	I like to wear loose clothes. * like to＋動詞原形（喜歡）
⓯	有大一號的嗎？	Do you have one in a bigger size? * bigger size（較大尺寸） * smaller size（較小尺寸）
⓰	沒有我的尺寸嗎？	You don't have it in my size? * in my size（我的尺寸）
⓱	有 A 罩杯的嗎？	Do you have one in an A-cup? * in a/an＋尺寸（屬於某尺寸）
⓲	有小一號的嗎？	Do you have one in a smaller size?
⓳	你可以幫我修改嗎？	Could you alter it for me?
⓴	你可以幫我量一下嗎？	Could you measure me? * measure（測量）＝ take one's measurements
㉑	S 號對我來說剛剛好。	S is just my size.

	單字	音標	詞性	意義	字頻	大考	英檢	多益
❶	pants	[pænts]	n.	pant（褲子）複數	3	1	初級	
	too	[tu]	adv.	過於	1	1	初級	
	long	[lɔŋ]	adj.	長的	1	1	初級	
❷	fit	[fɪt]	v.	適合	1	2	初級	◎
	well	[wɛl]	adv.	良好地	1	1	初級	
❸	sleeves	[slivz]	n.	sleeve（袖子）複數	2	3	中級	
	short	[ʃɔrt]	adj.	短的	1	1	初級	◎
❹	collar	[ˋkɑlɚ]	n.	衣領	2	3	中級	
	tight	[taɪt]	adj.	緊的	1	3	中級	◎
❺	baggy	[ˋbægɪ]	adj.	非常寬鬆的	4		中級	
	waist	[west]	n.	腰部	2	2	初級	
❼	zip	[zɪp]	v.	拉拉鍊	4	5	初級	◎
	up	[ʌp]	adv.	拉起/扣起	1	1	初級	
	zipper	[ˋzɪpɚ]	n.	拉鍊	4	3	初級	
❽	button	[ˋbʌtn]	v.	扣子	1	2	初級	◎
❾	usually	[ˋjuʒʊəlɪ]	adv.	經常	1		初級	◎
	wear	[wɛr]	v.	穿上	1	1	初級	◎
	medium	[ˋmidɪəm]	n.	M 號	2	3	初級	◎
❿	size	[saɪz]	n.	尺寸	1	1	初級	◎
	small	[smɔl]	adj./n.	小的/S 號	1	1	初級	◎
⓫	like	[laɪk]	v.	喜歡	1	1	初級	
	clothes	[kloz]	n.	cloth（衣服）複數	1	2	初級	
⓬	big	[bɪg]	adj.	大的	1	1	初級	
⓭	lower	[ˋloɚ]	adj.	low（下面的）比較級	1	2	中級	◎
	hem	[hɛm]	n.	縫邊	4			◎
	wide	[waɪd]	adj.	寬的	1	1	初級	
⓮	loose	[lus]	adj.	寬鬆的	2	3	中級	◎
⓯	have	[hæv]	v.	擁有	1	1	初級	
	one	[wʌn]	pron.	一個	1	1	初級	
	bigger	[ˋbɪgɚ]	adj.	big（大的）比較級	1	1	初級	
⓲	smaller	[ˋsmɔlɚ]	adj.	small（小的）比較級	1	1	初級	◎
⓳	alter	[ˋɔltɚ]	v.	修改	2	5	中高	◎
⓴	measure	[ˋmɛʒɚ]	v.	測量	1	4	初級	◎
㉑	just	[dʒʌst]	adv.	剛好	1	1	初級	

※「紅字單字」於本單元多句出現，「單字級等分析」僅列在「首次出現句」。

🔵 MP3 116-02 ❶～⓲

❶	要不要試試別件？	Would you like to try on another one? * **try on**（試穿）
❷	不好意思，大一號的缺貨。	Sorry, the larger ones are all sold out. * **sell out**（售完、缺貨）
❸	請告訴我您的尺寸。	Please tell me your size.
❹	請試試小一號的。	Try the smaller size.
❺	我們可以幫您修改。	We can alter it for you.
❻	請試試大一號的。	Try the bigger size.
❼	修改不用另外計費。	Alterations are free of charge. * **be free of charge**（不需收費）
❽	可以把褲長放長些。	We can lengthen the pants a bit.
❾	把腰圍改一下就很漂亮了。	A little alteration to the waistline and it'll look great. * **a little**（一些）、**alteration to＋名詞**（修改…）
❿	可以把褲長改短一點。	We can make the pants shorter.
⓫	我們還有其他的尺寸。	We still have some other sizes.
⓬	長度修改到這裡可以嗎？	Is this the length you need?
⓭	我們可以量身訂做。	We can tailor it to your size. * **tailor to one's size**（量身訂做）
⓮	我們可以幫您加個鞋墊。	We can put a pad in your shoes.
⓯	今年都流行比較貼身的設計。	The more skin-tight design is popular this year.
⓰	我們可以幫您調整一下鞋頭。	We can make some adjustments to your shoe tip. * **make some adjustments**（做一些調整）
⓱	穿久了會比較鬆。	It will loosen over time. * **will＋動詞原形**（將會…）、**over time**（隨時間變化）
⓲	我可以幫您墊一個胸墊。	I can insert a bust pad for you. * **bust pad**（胸墊）

	單字	音標	詞性	意義	字頻	大考	英檢	多益
❶	like	[laɪk]	v.	想要	1	1	初級	
	try	[traɪ]	v.	試穿	1	1	初級	
	another	[əˋnʌðɚ]	adj.	另一個	1	1		
	one	[wʌn]	pron.	一件	1	1	初級	
❷	sorry	[ˋsɑrɪ]	adj.	抱歉的	1	1	初級	
	larger	[ˋlɑrdʒɚ]	adj.	large（大的）比較級	1	1	初級	◎

❷	all	[ɔl]	adv.	完全	1	1	初級	
	sold	[sold]	p.p.	sell（賣）過去分詞	1	1	初級	
	out	[aut]	adv.	售完、賣光	1	1	初級	
❸	please	[pliz]	adv.	請…	1	1	初級	
	tell	[tɛl]	v.	告訴	1	1	初級	
	size	[saɪz]	n.	尺寸	1	1	初級	◎
❹	smaller	[ˋsmɔlə]	adj.	small（小的）比較級	1	1	初級	◎
❺	alter	[ˋɔltə]	v.	修改	2	5	中高	◎
❻	bigger	[ˋbɪgə]	adj.	big（大的）比較級	1	1	初級	
❼	alteration	[͵ɔltəˋreʃən]	n.	修改	4			
	free	[fri]	adj.	免費的	1	1	初級	
	charge	[tʃɑrdʒ]	n.	費用	1	2	初級	◎
❽	lengthen	[ˋlɛŋθən]	v.	加長	5	3	中級	◎
	pants	[pænts]	n.	pant（褲子）複數	3	1	初級	
	bit	[bɪt]	n.	些許	1	1	初級	
❾	little	[ˋlɪtl]	adj.	少的	1	1	初級	
	waistline	[ˋwest͵laɪn]	n.	腰圍	8			
	look	[luk]	v.	看起來	1	1	初級	
	great	[gret]	adj.	極好的	1	1	初級	◎
❿	make	[mek]	v.	使得/做出	1	1	初級	
	shorter	[ˋʃɔrtə]	adj.	short（短的）比較級	1	1	初級	◎
⓫	still	[stɪl]	adv.	仍然	1	1	初級	◎
	have	[hæv]	v.	擁有	1	1	初級	
	some	[sʌm]	adj.	一些	1	1	初級	
	other	[ˋʌðə]	adj.	其他的	1	1	初級	
⓬	this	[ðɪs]	adj.	這個	1	1	初級	
	length	[lɛŋθ]	n.	長度	1	2	初級	◎
	need	[nid]	v.	需要	1	1	初級	
⓭	tailor	[ˋtelə]	v.	裁製	3	3	中級	◎
⓮	put	[put]	v.	放置	1	1	初級	
	pad	[pæd]	n.	墊子	2	3	中級	◎
	shoes	[ʃuz]	n.	shoe（鞋子）複數	2			
⓯	more	[mor]	adj.	更加	1	1	初級	
	skin-tight	[ˋskɪn͵taɪt]	adj.	貼身的				
	design	[dɪˋzaɪn]	n.	設計	1	2	初級	◎
	popular	[ˋpɑpjələ]	adj.	流行的	1	2	初級	
	year	[jɪr]	n.	年	1	1	初級	
⓰	adjustment	[əˋdʒʌstmənt]	n.	調整	2	4	中高	◎
	shoe	[ʃu]	n.	鞋子	1	1	初級	
	tip	[tɪp]	n.	尖端	1	2	初級	◎
⓱	loosen	[ˋlusn]	v.	變鬆	3	3	中級	◎
	time	[taɪm]	n.	時間	1	1	初級	
⓲	insert	[ɪnˋsɝt]	v.	塞入	2	4	中級	◎
	bust	[bʌst]	n.	胸部	3			中高	

※「紅字單字」於本單元多句出現，「單字級等分析」僅列在「首次出現句」。

117　殺價。

🔵 MP3 117-01 ❶～⓰

❶	太貴了。	It's too expensive.
❷	算整數吧？	How about making it an even price? * How about＋動詞-ing?（不妨…？）
❸	我就只有這些錢了。	This is all the money I've got.
❹	再便宜一些吧？	Can you go a little lower? * Can you...?（你可以…嗎）、go lower（降價出售）
❺	去掉零頭可以嗎？	How about cutting it to an even amount?
❻	兩件算五百，可以嗎？	Two for five hundred, all right?
❼	別人都賣二百元而已。	Other stores sell it for two hundred.
❽	算便宜點我就多買幾件。	I'll buy more if you give me a lower price. * will buy（願意買）、give me a lower price（算便宜點）
❾	這件衣服有些瑕疵，算便宜點我就買。	This piece of clothing has some flaws; I'll buy it for a discount. * have a flaw（有瑕疵）、have no flaw（沒有瑕疵）
❿	這衣服質料沒有那麼好，應該再便宜點。	The material of the clothes isn't that good. The price should be lower.
⓫	我是老客戶了，還跟我計較這些。	I am your old customer, and you want to haggle with me?　* old customer（老客戶）
⓬	你只剩下這個顏色了，算便宜點我才要買。	This is the only color you have left. I'll take it for a lower price.
⓭	不然你要送我一個小禮物。	Or you can give me a small gift instead. * Or＋子句＋instead（或是以…代替）
⓮	算便宜點，我會介紹朋友來給你買啦！	Give me a better price and I'll bring my friends here. * give me a better price（給個好價錢、算便宜點）
⓯	算便宜一點我就全部買。	I'll buy them all for a lower price. * buy them all（買下全部）
⓰	這好像快退流行了。	This one may go out of fashion soon.

	單字	音標	詞性	意義	字頻	大考	英檢	多益
❶	too	[tu]	adv.	過於	1	1	初級	
	expensive	[ɪkˋspɛnsɪv]	adj.	昂貴的	1	2	初級	◎
❷	making	[ˋmekɪŋ]	n.	make（使得）動名詞	2	1	中高	
	even	[ˋivən]	adj.	整數的	1	1	初級	◎
	price	[praɪs]	n.	價錢	1	1	初級	◎

514

❸	this	[ðɪs]	pron. /adj.	這個	1	1	初級	
	all	[ɔl]	adj./ adv.	全部的/完全	1	1	初級	
	money	[`mʌnɪ]	n.	金錢	1	1	初級	◎
	got	[gɑt]	p.p.	get（掙得）過去分詞	1	1	初級	◎
❹	go	[go]	v.	變為	1	1	初級	
	little	[`lɪtl]	adv.	稍微	1	1	初級	
	lower	[`loɚ]	adj.	low（低的）比較級	1	2	中級	◎
❺	cutting	[`kʌtɪŋ]	n.	cut（降低）動名詞	2	1	中高	
	amount	[ə`maʊnt]	n.	數量	1	2	初級	◎
❻	two	[tu]	n.	二	1	1	初級	
	five	[faɪv]	n.	五	1	1	初級	
	hundred	[`hʌndrəd]	n.	一百	1	1	初級	
	right	[raɪt]	adj.	沒問題的	1	1	初級	
❼	other	[`ʌðɚ]	adj.	其他的	1	1	初級	
	store	[stor]	n.	商店	1	1	初級	◎
	sell	[sɛl]	v.	賣	1	1	初級	
❽	buy	[baɪ]	v.	購買	1	1	初級	
	more	[mor]	adv.	更多	1	1	初級	
	give	[gɪv]	v.	給予	1	1	初級	
❾	piece	[pis]	n.	一件	1	1	初級	◎
	clothing	[`kloðɪŋ]	n.	衣服	1	2	中級	
	have	[hæv]	v.	擁有	1	1	初級	
	some	[sʌm]	adj.	一些	1	1	初級	
	flaw	[flɔ]	n.	瑕疵	2	5	中高	◎
	discount	[`dɪskaʊnt]	n.	折扣	2	3	中級	◎
❿	material	[mə`tɪrɪəl]	n.	材料	1	6	初級	◎
	clothes	[kloz]	n.	cloth（衣服）複數	1	2	初級	
	good	[gʊd]	adj.	良好的	1	1	初級	
⓫	old	[old]	adj.	老的	1	1	初級	
	customer	[`kʌstəmɚ]	n.	客戶	1	2	初級	◎
	want	[wɑnt]	v.	想要	1	1	初級	◎
	haggle	[`hægl]	v.	討價還價	7			
⓬	only	[`onlɪ]	adj.	只有	1	1	初級	
	color	[`kʌlɚ]	n.	顏色	1	1	初級	
	left	[lɛft]	p.p.	leave（留下）過去分詞	1	1	初級	
	take	[tek]	v.	買走	1	1	初級	◎
⓭	small	[smɔl]	adj.	小的	1	1	初級	◎
	gift	[gɪft]	n.	禮物	1	1	初級	◎
	instead	[ɪn`stɛd]	adv.	作為代替	1	3	中級	◎
⓮	better	[`bɛtɚ]	adj.	good（良好的）比較級	1	1	初級	
	bring	[brɪŋ]	v.	帶著	1	1	初級	
	friend	[frɛnd]	n.	朋友	1	1	初級	
	here	[hɪr]	adv.	這裡	1	1	初級	
⓰	one	[wʌn]	pron.	一件	1	1	初級	
	out	[aʊt]	adv.	在⋯之外	1	1	初級	
	fashion	[`fæʃən]	n.	流行	1	3	中級	◎
	soon	[sun]	adv.	很快	1	1	初級	

※「紅字單字」於本單元多句出現，「單字級等分析」僅列在「首次出現句」。

🔊 MP3 117-02 ❶～⓮

❶	我一件只賺十塊錢。	I can only make ten NT on each one.
❷	我是賠本在賣。	I am selling it at below cost. * at（以…價格）、below cost（低於成本） * 此句用「現在進行式」（…am selling…） 　表示「現階段發生的事」。
❸	趕快賣一賣要回家啦！	I'm in a hurry to sell them out.
❹	少算十塊如何。	How about I give you a ten-dollar discount? * How about＋子句?（不妨…？）
❺	三百元，買不買隨便你。	Three hundred, take it or leave it. * take it or leave it（要買就買、不買拉倒）
❻	不然你再多買一件。	How about you buy one more?
❼	不可能再便宜了。	I can't go any cheaper than that. * go cheaper（降價出售）＝ go lower
❽	品質絕對好，不然你可以拿來退。	If the quality isn't what I say it is, I'll give you your money back.
❾	不然你說要算多少？	Exactly how much would you be willing to pay for it? * Exactly how much…?（…到底是要多少錢？）
❿	就是有小瑕疵，才賣你這麼便宜。	The flaw is why I'm offering you such a low price. * 主詞＋is/are＋why…（某主詞是…的原因）
⓫	老客戶才賣你這個價錢。	Only an old customer like you can get this price.
⓬	已經非常便宜了。	It's already very cheap.
⓭	賠錢生意沒人做啦！	Come on, nobody would do business without profit! * do business（做生意）、without profit（沒賺頭）
⓮	你真是殺價高手。	You are truly a good bargainer. * a good bargainer（很會殺價的人）
⓯	要介紹朋友來買喔！	Be sure to bring your friends here!

	單字	音標	詞性	意義	字頻	大考	英檢	多益
❶	only	[ˈonlɪ]	adv.	只有	1	1	初級	
	make	[mek]	v.	賺	1	1	初級	
	ten	[tɛn]	n.	十	1	1	初級	
	each	[itʃ]	adj.	每一個	1	1	初級	
	one	[wʌn]	pron.	一件	1	1	初級	
❷	selling	[ˈsɛlɪŋ]	p.pr.	sell（賣）現在分詞	3	1	初級	

❷	below	[bə'lo]	adj.	低於…的	1	1	初級	◎
	cost	[kɔst]	n.	成本	1	1	初級	◎
❸	hurry	[`hɜɪ]	n.	趕快	2	2	初級	◎
	sell	[sɛl]	v.	賣	1	1	初級	
	out	[aʊt]	adv.	賣完、賣光	1	1	初級	
❹	give	[gɪv]	v.	給予	1	1	初級	
	ten-dollar	[`tɛn'dolə]	adj.	十元的	1	1	初級	
	discount	[`dɪskaʊnt]	n.	折扣	2	3	中級	◎
❺	three	[θri]	n.	三	1	1	初級	
	hundred	[`hʌndrəd]	n.	一百	1	1	初級	
	take	[tek]	v.	買走	1	1	初級	◎
	leave	[liv]	v.	留下	1	1	初級	◎
❻	buy	[baɪ]	v.	購買	1	1	初級	
	more	[mor]	pron.	更多	1	1	初級	
❼	go	[go]	v.	變為	1	1	初級	
	any	[`ɛnɪ]	adv.	絲毫、一些	1	1	初級	
	cheaper	[`tʃipə]	adj.	cheap（便宜的）比較級	1	2	初級	◎
	that	[ðæt]	pron.	那個	1	1	初級	
❽	quality	[`kwɑlətɪ]	n.	品質	1	2	初級	◎
	say	[se]	v.	說	1	1	初級	
	money	[`mʌnɪ]	n.	金錢	1	1	初級	
	back	[bæk]	adv.	退回	1	1	初級	
❾	exactly	[ɪg`zæktlɪ]	adv.	到底	1		中級	◎
	much	[mʌtʃ]	adj.	許多的	1	1	初級	
	willing	[`wɪlɪŋ]	adj.	願意的	1	2	初級	◎
	pay	[pe]	v.	付款	1	3	初級	◎
❿	flaw	[flɔ]	n.	瑕疵	2	5	中高	◎
	offering	[`ɔfərɪŋ]	p.pr.	offer（提供）現在分詞	2	6	中高	◎
	such	[sʌtʃ]	adv.	這麼	1	1	初級	
	low	[lo]	adj.	低的	1	1	初級	
	price	[praɪs]	n.	價格	1	1	初級	◎
⓫	old	[old]	adj.	老的	1	1	初級	
	customer	[`kʌstəmə]	n.	客戶	1	2	初級	◎
	get	[gɛt]	v.	賺到、得到	1	1	初級	◎
	this	[ðɪs]	adj.	這個	1	1	初級	
⓬	already	[ɔl`rɛdɪ]	adv.	已經	1	1	初級	◎
	very	[`vɛrɪ]	adv.	非常	1	1	初級	
	cheap	[tʃip]	adj.	便宜的	1	2	初級	◎
⓭	come	[kʌm]	v.	（與 on 連用）別鬧了、少來	1	1	初級	
	nobody	[`nobɑdɪ]	pron.	沒有人	1	2	初級	
	do	[du]	v.	做	1	1	初級	
	business	[`bɪznɪs]	n.	生意	1	2	初級	
	profit	[`prɑfɪt]	n.	利潤	1	3	中級	◎
⓮	truly	[`trulɪ]	adv.	真是	1		中高	◎
	good	[gʊd]	adj.	擅長的	1	1	初級	◎
	bargainer	[`bɑrgɪnə]	n.	殺價的人	1			
⓯	sure	[ʃʊr]	adj.	必定的	1	1	初級	
	bring	[brɪŋ]	v.	帶著	1	1	初級	
	friend	[frɛnd]	n.	朋友	1	1	初級	
	here	[hɪr]	adv.	這裡	1	1	初級	

※「紅字單字」於本單元多句出現，「單字級等分析」僅列在「首次出現句」。

118 包裝。

❶	請幫我用禮盒包裝。	Please wrap it in a gift box. * wrap＋某物＋in（將某物包裝於…）
❷	請給我有提把的袋子，我比較方便拿。	Please give me a bag with a handle so I can carry it easily. * bag with a handle（提手袋）
❸	我要這一款的紙盒。	I want this type of paper box. * paper box（紙盒）
❹	我需要塑膠袋。	I need a plastic bag. * plastic bag（塑膠袋）
❺	包裝要另外付費嗎？	Is there an extra charge for gift wrapping? * Is there＋名詞?（有…嗎）、extra charge（額外費用） * gift wrapping（禮物包裝）
❻	請幫我把價錢貼標撕掉。	Please tear off the price tag. * tear off（撕除）
❼	我要寫一張卡片放進去。	I want to write a card and put it inside. * 動詞＋and＋動詞（做…然後…） * put＋某物＋inside（將某物放進…）
❽	這是要送給女生的禮物，我想要粉紅色的包裝。	This is a gift for a lady. Please wrap it in pink paper. * for a lady（給女生的）、in＋名詞（以…材料）
❾	我要送禮，請包裝得漂亮一點。	This is a present. Please wrap it nicely. * wrap nicely（包裝得好一點）
❿	如果需要包裝費，就不用了。	I don't want to wrap it if it costs extra. * cost extra（要額外收費）
⓫	請幫我包裝一下。	Please wrap it up for me. * wrap up（包裝起來）
⓬	是自己要用的，就不用包裝了。	This is for my own use—I don't need to wrap it. * for my own use（給自己用的） * need to＋動詞原形（需要）
⓭	有比較特別的包裝方式嗎？	Do you have a more special way to wrap it?
⓮	我不喜歡這樣的包裝，請你重新包一次。	I don't like this wrapping. Please wrap it again.
⓯	請幫我加上緞帶。	Please tie some ribbons to it. * tie ribbons to＋某物（為…加上緞帶）
⓰	包裝得真漂亮。	It looks terrific.
⓱	謝謝你，麻煩你了。	Thank you for the service.

單字級等分析

	單字	音標	詞性	意義	字頻	大考	英檢	多益
❶	please	[pliz]	adv.	請…	1	1	初級	
	wrap	[ræp]	v.	包裝	1	3	中級	◎
	gift	[gɪft]	n.	禮物	1	1	初級	◎
	box	[bɑks]	n.	盒子	1	1	初級	◎
❷	give	[gɪv]	v.	給予	1	1	初級	
	bag	[bæg]	n.	袋子	1	1	初級	
	handle	[ˋhændl̩]	n.	提把	1	2	初級	◎
	carry	[ˋkærɪ]	v.	攜帶、拿	1	1	初級	◎
	easily	[ˋizɪlɪ]	adv.	容易地	1		中級	
❸	want	[wɑnt]	v.	想要	1	1	初級	◎
	this	[ðɪs]	adj./pron.	這個	1	1	初級	
	type	[taɪp]	n.	類型	1	1	初級	
	paper	[ˋpepɚ]	n.	紙	1	1	初級	
❹	need	[nid]	v.	需要	1	1	初級	◎
	plastic	[ˋplæstɪk]	adj.	塑膠的	1	3	中級	
❺	there	[ðɛr]	adv.	有…	1	1	初級	
	extra	[ˋɛkstrə]	adj./adv.	額外的/額外地	1	2	初級	◎
	charge	[tʃɑrdʒ]	n.	收費	1	2	初級	◎
	wrapping	[ˋræpɪŋ]	n.	wrap（包裝）動名詞	6	3	中級	◎
❻	tear	[tɛr]	v.	撕掉	1	2	初級	◎
	off	[ɔf]	adv.	取除	1	1	初級	
	price tag	[praɪs tæg]	n.	價錢標籤				◎
❼	write	[raɪt]	v.	寫	1	1	初級	
	card	[kɑrd]	n.	卡片	1	1	初級	◎
	put	[pʊt]	v.	放置	1	1	初級	
	inside	[ˋɪnˋsaɪd]	adv.	裡面	1	1	初級	
❽	lady	[ˋledɪ]	n.	女士	1	1	初級	
	pink	[pɪŋk]	adj.	粉紅色的	1	1	初級	
❾	present	[ˋprɛznt]	n.	禮物	1	2	初級	◎
	nicely	[ˋnaɪslɪ]	adv.	良好地	3			
❿	cost	[kɔst]	v.	花費	1	1	初級	◎
⓫	up	[ʌp]	adv.	包起	1	1	初級	
⓬	own	[on]	adj.	自己的	1	1	初級	◎
	use	[juz]	n.	使用	1	1	初級	◎
⓭	have	[hæv]	v.	擁有	1	1	初級	
	more	[mor]	adv.	更加	1	1	初級	
	special	[ˋspɛʃəl]	adj.	特別的	1	1	初級	◎
	way	[we]	n.	方法	1	1	初級	
⓮	like	[laɪk]	v.	喜歡	1	1	初級	
	again	[əˋgɛn]	adv.	再次	1	1	初級	
⓯	tie	[taɪ]	v.	綁上	1	1	初級	◎
	some	[sʌm]	adj.	一些	1	1	初級	
	ribbon	[ˋrɪbən]	n.	緞帶	2	3	中級	
⓰	look	[lʊk]	v.	看起來	1	1	初級	
	terrific	[təˋrɪfɪk]	adj.	很好看的	2	2	初級	
⓱	thank	[θæŋk]	v.	感謝	1	1	初級	
	service	[ˋsɝvɪs]	n.	服務	1	1	初級	◎

※「紅字單字」於本單元多句出現，「單字級等分析」僅列在「首次出現句」。

🔊 MP3 118-02 ❶～⓱

❶	請選一個包裝紙的顏色。	Please pick a color of wrapping paper. * wrapping paper（包裝紙）
❷	需要包裝嗎？	Would you like it wrapped? * would like（想要）
❸	我幫您把衣服燙一燙再包起來。	I'll iron your clothes before wrapping them. * iron one's clothes（燙衣服） * before＋動詞-ing（在…之前）
❹	這些都放在一起可以嗎？	Can we have them wrapped together? * wrap together（包在一起）
❺	您要挑張卡片嗎？	Do you need to pick a card?
❻	你要搭配其他的裝飾做包裝嗎？	Are there any decorations you would like to use?　* would like to use（想要使用）
❼	您要用禮盒裝嗎？	Do you need a gift box for it?
❽	要紙袋還是塑膠袋？	Paper or plastic?
❾	要分開包嗎？	Do you want to pack them separately?
❿	您要用有提把的袋子嗎？	Do you need a bag with a handle? * with＋名詞（含有…、附帶…）
⓫	您需要乾燥劑嗎？	Do you need some desiccant?
⓬	價錢要撕掉嗎？	Do you want to tear off the price tag? * tear off（撕除）可替換為：remove（移除）
⓭	您要紙盤和蠟燭嗎？	Would you like some paper plates and candles?　* paper plate（紙盤）
⓮	包裝要另外付費。	There is a surcharge for gift wrapping. * there is a surcharge（要額外收費） * gift wrapping（禮物包裝）
⓯	包裝不用另外付費。	There is no surcharge for gift wrapping. * there is no surcharge（不用額外收費）
⓰	包裝紙要自己選購。	You need to pick and pay for the wrapping paper.　* pick and pay（選購）
⓱	禮品加包裝費一共是五百元。	That will be NT$500 for the gift and wrapping paper.

單字級等分析

	單字	音標	詞性	意義	字頻	大考	英檢	多益
❶	please	[pliz]	adv.	請…	1	1	初級	
	pick	[pɪk]	v.	挑選	1	2	初級	
	color	[ˋkʌlə]	n.	顏色	1	1	初級	
	wrapping	[ˋræpɪŋ]	n.	wrap（包裝）動名詞	6	3	中級	◎
	paper	[ˋpepə]	n.	紙	1	1	初級	◎
❷	like	[laɪk]	v.	想要	1	1	初級	
	wrapped	[ræpt]	p.p.	wrap（包裝）過去分詞	8	3	中級	◎
❸	iron	[ˋaɪən]	v.	熨燙	1	1	初級	
	clothes	[kloz]	n.	cloth（衣服）複數	1	2	初級	
❹	have	[hæv]	v.	讓…	1	1	初級	
	together	[təˋgɛðə]	adv.	一起	1	1	初級	
❺	need	[nid]	v.	需要	1	1	初級	◎
	card	[kɑrd]	n.	卡片	1	1	初級	◎
❻	there	[ðɛr]	adv.	有…	1	1	初級	
	any	[ˋɛnɪ]	adj.	任何的	1	1	初級	
	decoration	[͵dɛkəˋreʃən]	n.	裝飾	3	4	中級	
	use	[juz]	v.	使用	1	1	初級	◎
❼	gift	[gɪft]	n.	禮物	1	1	初級	◎
	box	[bɑks]	n.	盒子	1	1	初級	◎
❽	plastic	[ˋplæstɪk]	n.	塑膠的	1	3	中級	◎
❾	want	[wɑnt]	v.	想要	1	1	初級	◎
	pack	[pæk]	v.	包裝	1	2	初級	◎
	separately	[ˋsɛpərɪtlɪ]	adv.	個別地、分開地	2		中高	◎
❿	bag	[bæg]	n.	袋子	1	1	初級	
	handle	[ˋhædl̩]	n.	提把	1	2	初級	◎
⓫	some	[sʌm]	adj.	一些	1	1	初級	
	desiccant	[ˋdɛsəkənt]	n.	乾燥劑				
⓬	tear	[tɛr]	v.	撕掉	1	2	初級	◎
	off	[ɔf]	adv.	取除	1	1	初級	
	price tag	[praɪs tæg]	n.	價格標籤				◎
⓭	plate	[plet]	n.	盤子	1	2	初級	◎
	candle	[ˋkændl̩]	n.	蠟燭	2	2	初級	
⓮	surcharge	[ˋsɝ͵tʃɑrdʒ]	n.	額外收費	6			◎
⓰	pay	[pe]	v.	付款	1	3	初級	◎
⓱	that	[ðæt]	pron.	那個	1	1	初級	

※「紅字單字」於本單元多句出現，「單字級等分析」僅列在「首次出現句」。

119 結帳。

🔊 MP3 119-01 ❶～⓭

❶	只能用現金嗎？	Do you only take cash? * take＋付款方式（接受某付款方式）
❷	這些總共多少錢？	How much are these in total? * How much...?（…多少錢？）、in total（總共）
❸	這兩件總共多少錢？	How much are these two pieces together? * two pieces together（兩件總共）
❹	這件不是賣三百五十元嗎？	Isn't this one priced at NT$350? * at＋價格（以…價格）
❺	可以刷卡嗎？	Can I use a credit card? ＝ Do you take plastic? * credit card（信用卡）＝ plastic、coupon（禮券）
❻	這件衣服不是打八折嗎？	Isn't this twenty percent off? * 數字＋percent off（減價百分之…） * twenty percent off（減價百分之二十、打八折）
❼	不是有特價嗎？	Don't you have a special discount? * Don't you＋動詞?（你們不是…嗎） * have a discount（有特價、有打折）
❽	不是有贈品嗎？	Doesn't this come with a gift? * come with（附帶）
❾	請幫我分成兩袋，分開結帳。	Please put them into two bags and bill me separately. * bill separately（個別開立帳單、分開結帳）
❿	對不起，我沒有現金。	Sorry, I don't have cash.
⓫	我先結帳，一會兒再過來拿衣服。	I'll pay the bill first and come back to get the clothes later.　* pay the bill first（先結帳）
⓬	我有貴賓卡可以打幾折？	How much of a discount can I get with my VIP card? * How much of＋名詞...?（有多少程度的…？） * with VIP card（用貴賓卡的方式）
⓭	請等一下，我去隔壁提款機提錢。	Hang on a minute, let me withdraw some cash from the ATM next door. * hang on a minute（稍等一下）＝ wait a second * withdraw from…（從…提款）、next door（在隔壁）

	單字	音標	詞性	意義	字頻	大考	英檢	多益
❶	only	[ˋonlɪ]	adv.	只有	1	1	初級	
	take	[tek]	v.	接受	1	1	初級	◎
	cash	[kæʃ]	n.	現金	1	2	初級	◎
❷	much	[mʌtʃ]	adj.	許多的	1	1	初級	
	these	[ðiz]	pron.	這些	1	1	初級	

❷	total	[ˋtotl]	n.	總共	1	1	初級	◎
❸	two	[tu]	n.	二	1	1	初級	
	piece	[pis]	n.	一件	1	1	初級	◎
	together	[təˋgɛðɚ]	adv.	加在一起、總共	1	1	初級	
❹	this	[ðɪs]	adj./pron.	這個	1	1	初級	
	one	[wʌn]	pron.	一個	1	1	初級	
	priced	[praɪst]	p.p.	price（標價）過去分詞	1	1	初級	◎
❺	use	[juz]	v.	使用	1	1	初級	
	credit	[ˋkrɛdɪt]	n.	信用	1	3	中級	◎
	card	[kɑrd]	n.	卡片	1	1	初級	◎
	plastic	[ˋplæstɪk]	n.	塑膠的	1	3	中級	◎
❻	twenty	[ˋtwɛntɪ]	n.	二十	1	1	初級	
	percent	[pɚˋsɛnt]	n.	百分之…	2	4	中級	◎
	off	[ɔf]	adj.	降價、打折	1	1	初級	
❼	have	[hæv]	v.	擁有	1	1	初級	
	special	[ˋspɛʃəl]	adj.	特殊的	1	1	初級	◎
	discount	[ˋdɪskaʊnt]	n.	折扣	2	3	中級	◎
❽	come	[kʌm]	v.	附帶	1	1	初級	
	gift	[gɪft]	n.	禮物	1	1	初級	◎
❾	please	[pliz]	adv.	請…	1	1	初級	
	put	[pʊt]	v.	放置	1	1	初級	
	bag	[bæg]	n.	袋子	1	1	初級	
	bill	[bɪl]	v./n.	開立帳單/帳單	1	2	初級	◎
	separately	[ˋsɛpərɪtlɪ]	adv.	個別地、分開地	2		中高	
❿	sorry	[ˋsɑrɪ]	adj.	抱歉的	1	1	初級	
⓫	pay	[pe]	v.	付款	1	3	初級	◎
	first	[fɝst]	adv.	首先	1	1	初級	
	back	[bæk]	adv.	返回	1	1	初級	◎
	get	[gɛt]	v.	取、拿/得到	1	1	初級	◎
	clothes	[kloz]	n.	cloth（衣服）複數	1	2	初級	
	later	[ˋletɚ]	adv.	稍後	1		初級	
⓬	VIP	[ˋviˋaɪˋpi]	n.	貴賓、是以下三字的縮寫： very（非常） important （重要的） person（人）	5			
⓭	hang	[hæŋ]	v.	稍等	1	2	初級	◎
	minute	[ˋmɪnɪt]	n.	一會、片刻	1	1	初級	◎
	let	[lɛt]	v.	讓…	1	1	初級	
	withdraw	[wɪðˋdrɔ]	v.	提款	1	4	中級	
	some	[sʌm]	adj.	一些	1	1	初級	
	ATM	[ˋeˋtiˋɛm]	n.	自動提款機、是以下三字的縮寫： automated（自動的） teller（出納） machine（機器）	4	4	中高	◎
	next	[nɛkst]	adj.	隔壁的	1	1	初級	
	door	[dor]	n.	戶、門面	1	1	初級	

※「紅字單字」於本單元多句出現，「單字級等分析」僅列在「首次出現句」。

🔵 MP3 119-02 ❶～⓯

❶	我來幫您結帳。	I'll be your cashier. * 此句用「未來簡單式」（...will...） 　表示「有意願做的事」。
❷	對不起，我們只接受現金付費。	Sorry, we only take cash.
❸	黑色的貴五十元。	The black one costs fifty dollars more.
❹	對不起，我們不接受刷卡。	Sorry, we don't take credit cards. * **We take credit cards.**（我們接受刷卡）
❺	有特價的不是這件衣服。	This is not the one that's on sale. * **on sale**（在特價中）
❻	有問題可以拿來換。	You can bring your item back to exchange if there's a problem with it.
❼	七天之內可以退貨。	We have a seven-day return policy.
❽	兩件以上才有特價。	There's only a discount if you buy two or more. * **There is only＋名詞＋if＋子句**（只在…才有…）
❾	特價期間已經過了。	Our sale is over.
❿	總共是二千元。	The total amount is two thousand dollars.
⓫	這也是要結帳的嗎？	Do you want to buy this one too?
⓬	不好意思，您的信用卡被拒絕了。	Sorry, but your credit card was rejected. * **sorry, but＋子句**（抱歉，…） * **One's credit card is rejected**（信用卡被拒絕）
⓭	這是發票及收據。	Here is the invoice and receipt.
⓮	提醒您一下，用禮卷不能找錢喔。	May I remind you that coupons are not exchangeable for cash? * **May I remind you that＋子句**（容我提醒您…） * **not exchangeable**（不可替換的） * **be exchangeable for＋某物**（可替換為某物）
⓯	已經是特價品，貴賓卡不能再打折。	It's already on sale; you can't get a further discount with your VIP card. * **get a discount**（得到折扣）、**further discount**（額外折扣）

	單字	音標	詞性	意義	字頻	大考	英檢	多益
❶	cashier	[kæˈʃɪr]	n.	收銀員	5	6	中級	◎
❷	sorry	[ˈsɑrɪ]	adj.	抱歉的	1	1	初級	
	only	[ˈonlɪ]	adv.	只有	1	1	初級	
	take	[tek]	v.	接受	1	1	初級	◎

單字級等分析

	單字	音標	詞性	中譯			級等	
❷	cash	[kæʃ]	n.	現金	1	2	初級	◎
❸	black	[blæk]	adj.	黑色的	1	1	初級	
	one	[wʌn]	pron.	一件	1	1	初級	
	cost	[kɔst]	v.	花費	1	1	初級	◎
	fifty	[ˈfɪftɪ]	n.	五十	2	1	初級	
	dollar	[ˈdɑlɚ]	n.	元	1	1	初級	
	more	[mor]	adv./pron.	更多	1	1	初級	◎
❹	credit	[ˈkrɛdɪt]	n.	信用	1	3	中級	◎
	card	[kɑrd]	n.	卡片	1	1	初級	◎
❺	this	[ðɪs]	adj.	這個	1	1	初級	
	sale	[sel]	n.	特價	1	1	初級	◎
❻	bring	[brɪŋ]	v.	帶來	1	1	初級	
	item	[ˈaɪtəm]	n.	物品	1	2	初級	◎
	back	[bæk]	adv.	返回	1	1	初級	◎
	exchange	[ɪksˈtʃendʒ]	v.	退換貨	1	3	中級	◎
	there	[ðɛr]	aux.	有…	1	1	初級	
	problem	[ˈprɑbləm]	n.	問題	1	1	初級	◎
❼	have	[hæv]	v.	擁有	1	1	初級	
	seven-day	[ˈsɛvnˈde]	adj.	七天的				
	return	[rɪˈtɜn]	n.	退貨	1	1	初級	◎
	policy	[ˈpɑləsɪ]	n.	方針	1	2	初級	◎
❽	discount	[ˈdɪskaʊnt]	n.	折扣	2	3	中級	◎
	buy	[baɪ]	v.	購買	1	1	初級	
	two	[tu]	pron./n.	兩件/二	1	1	初級	
❾	over	[ˈovɚ]	adj.	結束的	1	1	初級	
❿	total	[ˈtotl]	adj.	總共的	1	1	初級	◎
	amount	[əˈmaʊnt]	n.	數量	1	2	初級	◎
	thousand	[ˈθaʊznd]	n.	一千	1	1	初級	
⓫	want	[wɑnt]	v.	想要	1	1	初級	◎
	too	[tu]	adv.	也	1	1	初級	
⓬	rejected	[rɪˈdʒɛktɪd]	p.p.	reject（拒絕）過去分詞	8	2	初級	◎
⓭	here	[hɪr]	adv.	這裡	1	1	初級	
	invoice	[ˈɪnvɔɪs]	n.	發票	6			◎
	receipt	[rɪˈsit]	n.	收據	3	3	中級	◎
⓮	remind	[rɪˈmaɪnd]	v.	提醒	1	3	初級	◎
	coupon	[ˈkupɑn]	n.	禮卷	2	5	中級	◎
	exchangeable	[ɪksˈtʃendʒəbl]	adj.	可替換的				
⓯	already	[ɔlˈrɛdɪ]	adv.	已經	1	1	初級	◎
	get	[gɛt]	v.	得到	1	1	初級	◎
	further	[ˈfɝðɚ]	adj.	額外的	5	2	初級	
	VIP	[ˈviˈaɪˈpi]	n.	貴賓、是以下三字的縮寫：very（非常）important（重要的）person（人）	5			

※「紅字單字」於本單元多句出現，「單字級等分析」僅列在「首次出現句」。

120 退換貨。

❶	我要換大一號的。	I want to exchange it for a larger size. * **I want to＋動詞**（我想要…）、**exchange for**（交換） * **smaller**（較小的）
❷	我要換長一點的。	I want to exchange it for a longer one. * **shorter**（較短的）
❸	這件衣服我穿起來不好看，我要換別的款式。	This piece of clothing does not fit me. I want to exchange it for another style. * **fit＋某人**（適合某人）
❹	我要換顏色深一點的。	I want to exchange it for a darker one. * **lighter**（顏色較淺的）
❺	我要退錢。	I want a refund.　* **I want＋名詞**（我想要…）
❻	我要換另一件。	I want to exchange it for another one.
❼	這件衣服還沒穿就破了，我要退貨。	This piece of clothing was torn before I wore it. I want a refund. * **this piece of＋某物**（這一件…）
❽	我的發票不見了，可以退貨嗎？	My receipt is gone. Can I still return it?
❾	我想換白色的那件。	I want to exchange it for that white one.
❿	這東西和你們型錄上感覺差太多，我要退貨。	This doesn't look anything like the picture in your catalogue. I want to return it. * **not look anything like**（看起來完全不像） * **in the catalogue**（型錄上）
⓫	為什麼我不能退貨？	Why can't I return this item? * **Why can't I＋動詞?**（為什麼我不能…？）
⓬	其他產品我都不喜歡，我要退錢。	I don't like any of your other products. I want a refund.
⓭	法律規定七日內客戶有權退貨。	Customers have a legal right to return items within seven days of purchasing them. * **legal right**（法律權利） * **within＋時間**（在…時間以內） * **within seven days**（七日以內）
⓮	我要告你們廣告不實。	I want to sue you for running misleading ads. * **suc＋某人＋for＋某事**（因某事控告…） * **run an ad**（刊登廣告）、**misleading ad**（騙人的廣告）

	單字	音標	詞性	意義	字頻	大考	英檢	多益
❶	want	[wɑnt]	v.	想要	1	1	初級	◎
	exchange	[ɪksˋtʃɛndʒ]	v.	交換	1	3	中級	◎
	larger	[ˋlɑrdʒɚ]	adj.	large（大的）比較級	1	1	初級	◎
	size	[saɪz]	n.	尺寸	1	1	初級	◎
❷	longer	[ˋlɔŋgɚ]	adj.	long（長的）比較級	1	1	初級	
	one	[wʌn]	pron.	一個	1	1	初級	
❸	this	[ðɪs]	adj./pron.	這個	1	1	初級	
	piece	[pis]	n.	一件	1	1	初級	◎
	clothing	[ˋkloðɪŋ]	n.	衣服	1	2	中級	
	fit	[fɪt]	v.	適合	1	2	初級	◎
	another	[əˋnʌðɚ]	adj.	另一個	1	1		
	style	[staɪl]	n.	款式	1	3	初級	◎
❹	darker	[ˋdɑrkɚ]	adj.	dark（顏色深的）比較級	1	1	初級	
❺	refund	[ˋri͵fʌnd]	n.	退錢、退貨	4	6	中高	◎
❼	torn	[torn]	p.p.	tear（破損）過去分詞	4	2	初級	◎
	wore	[wor]	p.t.	wear（穿上）過去式	1	1	初級	◎
❽	receipt	[rɪˋsit]	n.	發票	3	3	中級	
	gone	[gɔn]	p.p.	go（遺失）過去分詞	1	1	初級	
	still	[stɪl]	adv.	仍然	1	1	初級	
	return	[rɪˋtɝn]	v.	退貨	1	1	初級	◎
❾	that	[ðæt]	adj.	那個	1	1	初級	
	white	[hwaɪt]	adj.	白色的	1	1	初級	
❿	look	[lʊk]	v.	看起來	1	1	初級	
	anything	[ˋɛnɪ͵θɪŋ]	pron.	任何東西	1	1		
	picture	[ˋpɪktʃɚ]	n.	照片	1	1	初級	◎
	catalogue	[ˋkætəlɔg]	n.	型錄	3	4		
⓫	item	[ˋaɪtəm]	n.	物品	1	2	初級	◎
⓬	like	[laɪk]	v.	喜歡	1	1	初級	
	any	[ˋɛnɪ]	adj.	任何的	1	1	初級	
	other	[ˋʌðɚ]	adj.	其他的	1	1	初級	
	product	[ˋprɑdəkt]	n.	產品	1	3	初級	◎
⓭	customer	[ˋkʌstəmɚ]	n.	客戶	1	2	初級	◎
	have	[hæv]	v.	擁有	1	1	初級	◎
	legal	[ˋligl]	adj.	合法的	1	2	初級	
	right	[raɪt]	n.	權利	1	1	初級	
	seven	[ˋsɛvn]	n.	七	1	1	初級	
	day	[de]	n.	天	1	1	初級	◎
	purchasing	[ˋpɝtʃesɪŋ]	n.	purchase（購買）動名詞	4	5	初級	
⓮	sue	[su]	v.	控告	2		中高	◎
	running	[ˋrʌnɪŋ]	n.	run（刊登）動名詞	2	1	中級	◎
	misleading	[mɪsˋlidɪŋ]	adj.	騙人的	3		中級	◎
	ad	[æd]	n.	advertisement（廣告）縮寫	1	3	中高	◎

※「紅字單字」於本單元多句出現，「單字級等分析」僅列在「首次出現句」。

MP3 120-02 ❶～❹

❶	好，我幫您辦理退貨。	Yes, I'll accept your return. * Sorry, we don't allow returns. (對不起，我們不能退貨) * accept one's return (辦理退貨)
❷	有帶發票嗎？	Did you bring the receipt with you? * bring with (帶著)
❸	這是特價品，不能退錢。	This is an on-sale item. It can't be returned for cash. * on-sale item (特價商品)、return for cash (退錢)
❹	要有發票才能退貨。	We require a receipt for all returns. * require＋某物＋for＋某事 (需要某物才能…)
❺	我們只能換衣服，不能退錢。	We can let you exchange it for something else, but we can't refund your money. * exchange for (交換)、refund＋金錢 (退錢)
❻	這是您自己弄壞的，我們沒有辦法接受退貨。	You have damaged it. We can't accept this return. * have damaged (已經毀壞了)
❼	已經超過七天，不能退貨了。	It has already been over seven days. We can't accept this return. * have been over seven days (已超過七天)
❽	包裝已經打開了不能退貨。	The packaging was open. We can't take it. * take (接受)＝accept
❾	只能更換等價商品。	We can only replace it with something of equal value. * of… (具某種特質)、equal value (相同價格)
❿	買的時候就已經說了「貨出概不退換」。	When you were buying it, we told you that it couldn't be returned. * when＋子句 (在…時候) * 子句用「過去進行式」 (...were buying...) 表示「過去的當下正在做的事」。
⓫	或是補差價購買其他商品。	Or you buy another item and pay for the difference. * pay for (支付)
⓬	已經使用過了就不能退貨。	Once you have used the item you can't return it. * once (只要)、have used (曾經使用)
⓭	我們已經沒有同樣的商品了。	We are out of those items. * be out of (賣光、用光)
⓮	沒有您需要的尺碼了。	We don't have the size you need.

	單字	音標	詞性	意義	字頻	大考	英檢	多益
❶	yes	[jɛs]	int.	好	1	1	初級	
	accept	[əkˋsɛpt]	v.	接受	1	2	初級	◎
	return	[rɪˋtɝn]	n./v.	退貨	1	1	初級	◎
❷	bring	[brɪŋ]	v.	帶來	1	1	初級	
	receipt	[rɪˋsit]	n.	發票	3	3	中級	◎
❸	this	[ðɪs]	pron. /adj.	這個	1	1	初級	
	on-sale	[ɑnˋsel]	adj.	特價的				
	item	[ˋaɪtəm]	n.	商品	1	2	初級	◎
	returned	[rɪˋtɝnd]	p.p.	return（退貨）過去分詞	1	1	初級	◎
	cash	[kæʃ]	n.	現金	1	2	初級	◎
❹	require	[rɪˋkwaɪr]	v.	需要	1	2	初級	◎
	all	[ɔl]	adj.	所有的	1	1	初級	
❺	let	[lɛt]	v.	讓…	1	1	初級	
	exchange	[ɪksˋtʃendʒ]	v.	交換	1	3	中級	◎
	something	[ˋsʌm͵θɪŋ]	pron.	有些物品	1	1	初級	
	else	[ɛls]	adj.	其他的	1	1	初級	
	refund	[rɪˋfʌnd]	v.	退錢	4	6	中高	◎
	money	[ˋmʌnɪ]	n.	金錢	1	1	初級	◎
❻	damaged	[ˋdæmɪdʒd]	p.p.	damage（毀壞）過去分詞	4	2	初級	◎
❼	already	[ɔlˋrɛdɪ]	adv.	已經	1	1	初級	◎
	seven	[ˋsɛvn]	n.	七	1	1	初級	
	day	[de]	n.	天	1	1	初級	
❽	packaging	[ˋpækɪdʒɪŋ]	n.	包裝	3	2	中高	◎
	open	[ˋopən]	adj.	打開	1	1	初級	
	take	[tek]	v.	接受	1	1	初級	◎
❾	only	[ˋonlɪ]	adv.	只有	1	1	初級	
	replace	[rɪˋples]	v.	交換	1	3	中級	◎
	equal	[ˋikwəl]	adj.	相同的	1	1	初級	◎
	value	[ˋvælju]	n.	價格	1	2	初級	◎
❿	buying	[ˋbaɪɪŋ]	p.pr.	buy（購買）動名詞	3	1	初級	
	told	[told]	p.t.	tell（告訴）比較級	1	1	初級	
⓫	buy	[baɪ]	v.	購買	1	1	初級	
	another	[əˋnʌðɚ]	adj.	另一個	1	1		
	pay	[pe]	v.	付款	1	3	初級	◎
	difference	[ˋdɪfərəns]	n.	差價	1	2	初級	◎
⓬	used	[juzd]	p.p.	use（使用）過去分詞	1	2	初級	◎
⓭	out	[aut]	adj.	賣光、用光	1	1	初級	
	those	[ðoz]	adj.	那些	1	1	初級	
⓮	have	[hæv]	v.	擁有	1	1	初級	
	size	[saɪz]	n.	尺寸	1	1	初級	◎
	need	[nid]	v.	需要	1	1	初級	◎

※「紅字單字」於本單元多句出現，「單字級等分析」僅列在「首次出現句」。

MP3 121-01 ❶～⓱

❶	這裡的菜都是單點嗎？	Is everything here à la carte? * set meal（套餐）
❷	有供應套餐嗎？	Do you have set meals?
❸	請給我菜單。	May I have a menu? * May I have＋物品？（請給我某物品）
❹	你們有推出母親節特餐嗎？	Do you have a special menu for Mother's Day? * special menu（特餐、特別菜單） * Mother's Day（母親節）
❺	A 餐和 B 餐有什麼不同？	What's the difference between Set A and Set B? * What is the difference...?（…的具體差異是什麼？）
❻	這道菜會很辣嗎？	Is this dish spicy?　* salty（鹹味重的）
❼	有什麼推薦菜嗎？	Is there anything you can recommend? * recommend（建議）＝ suggest
❽	這道菜是怎麼烹調的？	How is this dish prepared?
❾	你們的招牌菜是什麼？	What's your house special? * house special（招牌菜）
❿	你可以幫我們配菜嗎？	Can you choose some side dishes for us? * side dish（副食、配菜） * choose for（幫忙挑選）
⓫	這是義大利餐廳嗎？	Is this an Italian restaurant? * Japanese restaurant（日本餐廳） * French restaurant（法國餐廳）
⓬	先點這些，不夠我們再點。	That's it for now; we'll order more if it is not enough.
⓭	今天的魚新鮮嗎？	Is the fish fresh today?
⓮	主菜是從這三種中任選一樣嗎？	Does the entrée have to be one of these three? * one of these three（這三個其中之一）
⓯	這些菜夠我們五個人吃嗎？	Are these dishes enough for the five of us?
⓰	我的柳橙汁可以換成西瓜汁嗎？	Can I change my orange juice to a watermelon juice?　* change＋某物＋to＋某物（將…換成…）
⓱	我們想要點甜點。	We would like to order dessert. * would like to＋動詞原形（想要）

	單字	音標	詞性	意義	字頻	大考	英檢	多益
❶	everything	[ˈɛvrɪˌθɪŋ]	pron.	每樣菜餚	1		初級	
	here	[hɪr]	adv.	這裡	1	1	初級	
	à la carte	[ˌɑləˈkɑrt]	adj.	（法文）單點的				
❷	have	[hæv]	v.	擁有/給、拿/必須	1	1	初級	
	set	[sɛt]	n.	一套	1	1	初級	◎
	meal	[mil]	n.	餐點	1	2	初級	
❸	menu	[ˈmɛnju]	n.	菜單	2	2	初級	◎
❹	special	[ˈspɛʃəl]	adj./n.	特別的/特色菜	1	1	初級	◎
	mother	[ˈmʌðɚ]	n.	母親	1	1	初級	
	day	[de]	n.	節日	1	1	初級	
❺	difference	[ˈdɪfərəns]	n.	不同、差異	1	2	初級	◎
❻	this	[ðɪs]	adj./pron.	這個	1	1	初級	
	dish	[dɪʃ]	n.	菜餚	1	1	初級	
	spicy	[ˈspaɪsɪ]	adj.	辣的	3	4	中級	
❼	there	[ðɛr]	adv.	有…	1	1	初級	
	anything	[ˈɛnɪˌθɪŋ]	pron.	任何事物	1	1	初級	
	recommend	[ˌrɛkəˈmɛnd]	v.	推薦	1	5	中級	◎
❽	prepared	[prɪˈpɛrd]	p.p.	prepare（準備、烹調）過去分詞	3	1	中級	◎
❾	house	[haʊs]	n.	店家	1	1	初級	◎
❿	choose	[tʃuz]	v.	選擇	1	2	初級	◎
	some	[sʌm]	adj.	一些	1	1	初級	
	side	[saɪd]	adj.	副食的、配菜的	1	1	初級	
⓫	Italian	[ɪˈtæljən]	adj.	義大利的	1	1	初級	
	restaurant	[ˈrɛstərənt]	n.	餐廳	1	2	初級	
⓬	that	[ðæt]	pron.	那個	1	1	初級	
	now	[naʊ]	n.	現在	1	1	初級	
	order	[ˈɔrdɚ]	v.	點菜	1	1	初級	◎
	more	[mor]	adv.	更多	1	1	初級	
	enough	[əˈnʌf]	adj.	足夠的	1	1	初級	◎
⓭	fish	[fɪʃ]	n.	魚	1	1	初級	
	fresh	[frɛʃ]	adj.	新鮮的	1	1	初級	
	today	[təˈde]	adv.	今天	1	1	初級	◎
⓮	entrée	[ˈɑntre]	n.	主菜	4			
	one	[wʌn]	pron.	一個	1	1	初級	
	these	[ðiz]	adj.	這些	1	1	初級	
	three	[θri]	pron.	三者	1	1	初級	
⓯	five	[faɪv]	n.	五	1	1	初級	
⓰	change	[tʃendʒ]	v.	更換	1	2	初級	◎
	orange	[ˈɔrɪndʒ]	n.	柳橙	2	1	初級	
	juice	[dʒus]	n.	果汁	1	1	初級	
	watermelon	[ˈwɔtɚˌmɛlən]	n.	西瓜	4	2	初級	
⓱	like	[laɪk]	v.	想要	1	1	初級	
	dessert	[dɪˈzɝt]	n.	甜點	2	2	初級	◎

※「紅字單字」於本單元多句出現，「單字級等分析」僅列在「首次出現句」。

121 服務生怎麼說？

MP3 121-02 ❶～❶

❶	需要中文菜單嗎？	Do you need a Chinese menu?
❷	需要我介紹菜單嗎？	Would you like me to introduce our menu?
❸	這是我們的招牌菜。	This is our house special.
❹	要不要點個湯？	Would you like to order soup?
❺	這道菜很受歡迎，要不要試試？	This dish is very popular; would you like to try it?
❻	這是我們的菜單。	Here is our menu.
❼	我們的料理是法式的。	Our cooking is French.
❽	我們都用天然的食材。	We always use natural ingredients.
❾	我可以請廚師少放一些辣椒。	I can ask our chef to add less hot peppers for you. * add less（加少一點）、add more（加多一點）
❿	我們的牛肉鮮嫩多汁，要不要嚐嚐？	Our beef is very tender and juicy; would you like to give a try?　* give a try（試看看）
⓫	需要加點甜點嗎？	Would you like some dessert?
⓬	我們的廚師是五星級飯店的主廚。	Our chef is from a five-star hotel. * from（來自）
⓭	主菜加一百元就變成套餐。	You can add NT$100 to the price of an entrée to make it a set meal.　* add... to...（加⋯在⋯）
⓮	請問需要什麼餐後飲料？	What would you like to drink after your meal? * What would you like to＋動詞...?（你想要⋯的是什麼）
⓯	需要白飯嗎？	Would you like white rice?
⓰	這樣的份量應該足夠了。	A portion this size should be enough. * this size（這個份量）
⓱	我重複一遍您點的菜。	I will repeat what you ordered. * what you ordered（你剛才點的東西）

	單字	音標	詞性	意義	字頻	大考	英檢	多益
❶	need	[nid]	v.	需要	1	1	初級	
	Chinese	[ˋtʃaɪˋniz]	adj.	中文的	1		初級	
	menu	[ˋmɛnju]	n.	菜單	2	2	初級	◎
❷	like	[laɪk]	v.	想要	1	1	初級	
	introduce	[ˌɪntrəˋdjus]	v.	介紹	1	2	初級	◎
❸	this	[ðɪs]	pron. /adj.	這個	1	1	初級	
	house	[haʊs]	n.	店家	1	1	初級	◎

❸	special	[ˋspɛʃəl]	n.	特色菜	1	1	初級	◎
❹	order	[ˋɔrdɚ]	v.	點菜	1	1	初級	◎
	soup	[sup]	n.	湯	2	1	初級	
❺	dish	[dɪʃ]	n.	菜餚	1	1	初級	
	very	[ˋvɛrɪ]	adv.	非常	1	1	初級	
	popular	[ˋpɑpjəlɚ]	adj.	受歡迎的	1	2	初級	
	try	[traɪ]	v./n.	嘗試	1	1	初級	
❻	here	[hɪr]	adv.	這是	1	1	初級	
❼	cooking	[kʊkɪŋ]	n.	料理	2	1	中級	◎
	French	[frɛntʃ]	adj.	法式的	1		初級	
❽	always	[ˋɔlwez]	adv.	總是	1	1	初級	
	use	[juz]	v.	使用	1	1	初級	◎
	natural	[ˋnætʃərəl]	adj.	天然的	1	2	初級	
	ingredient	[ɪnˋgridɪənt]	n.	食材	1	4	中級	◎
❾	ask	[æsk]	v.	要求	1	1	初級	
	chef	[ʃɛf]	n.	主廚	2	5	中高	◎
	add	[æd]	v.	加入	1	1	初級	◎
	less	[lɛs]	adj.	較少的	1	1	初級	
	hot	[hɑt]	adj.	辣的	1	1	初級	
	pepper	[ˋpɛpɚ]	n.	辣椒	1	2	初級	
❿	beef	[bif]	n.	牛肉	2	2	初級	
	tender	[ˋtɛndɚ]	adj.	肉質軟嫩的	2	3	中級	◎
	juicy	[ˋdʒusɪ]	adj.	多汁的	4	2	中級	
	give	[gɪv]	v.	給予	1	1	初級	
⓫	some	[sʌm]	adj.	一些	1	1	初級	
	dessert	[dɪˋzɝt]	n.	甜點	2	2	初級	◎
⓬	five-star	[ˋfaɪvˋstɑr]	adj.	五星級的	7			
	hotel	[hoˋtɛl]	n.	飯店	1	2	初級	
⓭	price	[praɪs]	n.	價錢	1	1	初級	◎
	entrée	[ˋɑntre]	n.	主菜	4			
	make	[mek]	v.	使成為	1	1	初級	
	set	[sɛt]	n.	一套	1	1	初級	◎
	meal	[mil]	n.	套餐/用餐	1	2	初級	
⓮	drink	[drɪŋk]	v.	喝	1	1	初級	
⓯	white	[hwaɪt]	adj.	白色的	1	1	初級	
	rice	[raɪs]	n.	米飯	1	1	初級	
⓰	portion	[ˋporʃən]	n.	一客、一份	1	3	中級	◎
	size	[saɪz]	n.	份量	1	1	初級	◎
	enough	[əˋnʌf]	adj.	足夠的	1	1	初級	◎
⓱	repeat	[rɪˋpit]	v.	複述	1	2	初級	◎
	ordered	[ˋɔrdɚd]	p.t.	order（點菜）過去式	6	1	初級	◎

※「紅字單字」於本單元多句出現，「單字級等分析」僅列在「首次出現句」。

122   用餐。

MP3 122-01 ❶∼❼

❶	我們沒點這道菜。	We didn't order this.
❷	這家餐廳的口味不錯。	This restaurant has good food.
❸	請問這道菜怎麼吃？	May I ask how this dish should be eaten? * **May I ask how**＋子句？（可以請問要如何…嗎）
❹	這家餐廳的氣氛很好。	This restaurant's atmosphere is very good.
❺	這家餐廳的服務很好。	This restaurant has very good service.
❻	請給我辣椒醬。	Please pass me the hot sauce. * **pass me**＋某物（遞給我某物）、**hot sauce**（辣椒醬）
❼	這家餐廳的餐點都很健康。	All of this restaurant's meals are healthy.
❽	這盤海鮮很新鮮。	This seafood dish is very fresh.
❾	請問這是什麼醬汁？	Excuse me, what kind of sauce is this? * **excuse me**（請問一下）、**what kind of**（什麼樣的）
❿	這道菜很有異國風味。	This dish has an exotic flavor.
⓫	這道菜很適合配生啤酒。	This dish goes well with draft beer. * **go well with...**（和…很搭）、**draft beer**（生啤酒）
⓬	吃不完可以打包嗎？	Can we wrap up what we haven't finished? * **Can we...?**（我們可以…嗎）、**wrap up**（打包） * **what we haven't finished**（我們沒吃完的東西）
⓭	可以給我們刀叉嗎？	Could you please give us a fork and knife?
⓮	可以再給我們一副碗筷嗎？	Could we please have a bowl and chopsticks?
⓯	可以幫我們加個水嗎？	Could you please fill our water glasses?
⓰	我們還有一道菜沒上。	We still have one more course that has not been served yet.
⓱	可以上甜點了。	You can bring us dessert.

	單字	音標	詞性	意義	字頻	大考	英檢	多益
❶	order	[ˋɔrdə]	v.	點菜	1	1	初級	◎
	this	[ðɪs]	pron. /adj.	這個	1	1	初級	
❷	restaurant	[ˋrɛstərənt]	n.	餐廳	1	2	初級	
	have	[hæv]	v.	擁有	1	1	初級	
	good	[gʊd]	adj.	良好的	1	1	初級	◎
	food	[fud]	n.	食物	1	1	初級	◎
❸	ask	[æsk]	v.	詢問	1	1	初級	

❸	dish	[dɪʃ]	n.	菜餚	1	1	初級	
	eaten	[`itn]	p.p.	eat（吃）過去分詞	1	1	初級	
❹	atmosphere	[`ætməs.fɪr]	n.	氣氛	1	4	中級	◎
	very	[`vɛrɪ]	adv.	十分	1	1	初級	
❺	service	[`sɜvɪs]	n.	服務	1	1	初級	◎
❻	pass	[pæs]	v.	傳遞	1	1	初級	◎
	hot	[hɑt]	adj.	辣的	1	1	初級	
	sauce	[sɔs]	n.	醬料	1	2	中級	
❼	all	[ɔl]	pron.	全部	1	1	初級	
	meal	[mil]	n.	餐點	1	2	初級	
	healthy	[`hɛlθɪ]	adj.	健康的	1	2	初級	◎
❽	seafood	[`si.fud]	n.	海鮮	3			
	fresh	[frɛʃ]	adj.	新鮮的	1	1	初級	
❾	excuse	[ɪk`skjuz]	v.	請問	2	2	初級	◎
	kind	[kaɪnd]	n.	種類	1	1	初級	
❿	exotic	[ɛg`zɑtɪk]	adj.	異國的	2	6	中高	
	flavor	[`flevə]	n.	口味	2	3	中級	
⓫	go	[go]	v.	搭配	1	1	初級	
	well	[wɛl]	adv.	良好地	1	1	初級	◎
	draft	[dræft]	adj.	桶裝的	1	4	中級	◎
	beer	[bɪr]	n.	啤酒	1	2	初級	
⓬	wrap	[ræp]	v.	打包	1	3	中級	◎
	up	[ʌp]	adv.	包起	1	1	初級	
	finished	[`fɪnɪʃt]	p.p.	finish（吃完）過去分詞	3	1	中級	◎
⓭	please	[pliz]	adv.	請…	1	1	初級	
	give	[gɪv]	v.	給予	1	1	初級	
	fork	[fɔrk]	n.	叉子	2	1	初級	
	knife	[naɪf]	n.	刀子	1	1	初級	
⓮	bowl	[bol]	n.	碗	1	1	初級	
	chopsticks	[tʃɑp.stɪks]	n.	chopstick（筷子）複數	7	2		
⓯	fill	[fɪl]	v.	注入	1	1	初級	◎
	water	[`wɔtə]	n.	水	1	1	初級	
	glass	[glæs]	n.	杯子	2	1	中級	
⓰	still	[stɪl]	adv.	仍然	1	1	初級	◎
	one	[wʌn]	n.	一	1	1	初級	
	more	[mor]	adj.	更多的	1	1	初級	
	course	[kors]	n.	一道菜	1	1	初級	◎
	served	[sɜvd]	p.p.	serve（端上）過去分詞	1	1	初級	◎
	yet	[jɛt]	adv.	尚未	1	1	初級	◎
⓱	bring	[brɪŋ]	v.	帶上	1	1	初級	
	dessert	[dɪ`zɜt]	n.	甜點	2	2	初級	◎

※「紅字單字」於本單元多句出現，「單字級等分析」僅列在「首次出現句」。

🔊 MP3 122-02 ❶～⓯

❶	沙拉吧可以自己取用。	Help yourself to the salad bar. * **help oneself**（自行取用）
❷	上菜了，請小心。	Here you go; be careful. * **here you go**（這是您點的東西）
❸	刀叉在餐台的下方。	Knives and forks are underneath the table. * **underneath**＋某物（在某物的下面）
❹	這是您需要的調味醬。	Here is the sauce you asked for. * **ask for**（要求）
❺	這盤菜是免費招待的。	There is no charge for this dish. = This dish is on the house. * **no charge**（免費）、**on the house**（店家免費招待）
❻	這是我們廚師的拿手菜。	This is our chef's specialty. * **one's specialty**（某人的拿手菜）
❼	菜都到齊了嗎？	Have all your dishes been served yet? * 此句用「現在完成式問句」（Have...been...?）表示 「過去某時點是否發生某事，且結果持續到現在嗎？」。
❽	請等一下，您的菜馬上送過來。	Please wait a second; I'll bring your meal right away. * **right away**（立刻）
❾	需要辣椒醬或是醬油嗎？	Do you need either hot sauce or soy sauce? * **either A or B**（A 或 B）
❿	湯涼了，要再加熱一下嗎？	The soup is cold; would you like it warmed up a bit? * **warm up a bit**（稍微加熱）
⓫	餐盤放在桌上我會來收。	Just leave your dishes on the table; I'll pick them up. * **pick up**（收拾乾淨）
⓬	請問您需要甜點或是飲料嗎？	Excuse me, would you like any dessert or beverages?
⓭	需要我幫您服務嗎？	Can I help you with anything? * **help**＋某人＋**with**（幫忙某人…）
⓮	剩下的菜需要打包嗎？	Would you like to wrap up your leftovers? * **would like**（想要）、**wrap up leftovers**（打包剩菜）
⓯	還滿意我們的菜色嗎？	How was your meal?

	單字	音標	詞性	意義	字頻	大考	英檢	多益
❶	help	[hɛlp]	v.	取用	1	1	初級	
	yourself	[jʊəˋsɛlf]	pron.	你自己	1		初級	
	salad	[ˋsæləd]	n.	沙拉	1	2	初級	
	bar	[bɑr]	n.	吧檯	1	1	初級	

❷	here	[hɪr]	adv.	這是	1	1	初級	
	go	[go]	v.	到、來	1	1	初級	
	careful	[ˋkɛrfəl]	adj.	小心的	1	1	初級	◎
❸	knife	[naɪf]	n.	刀子	1	1	初級	
	fork	[fɔrk]	n.	叉子	2	1	初級	
	table	[ˋtebl̩]	n.	桌子	1	1	初級	◎
❹	sauce	[sɔs]	n.	醬料	1	2	中級	
	asked	[æskt]	p.t.	ask（要求）過去式	1	1	初級	
❺	there	[ðɛr]	adv.	有…	1	1	初級	
	charge	[tʃɑrdʒ]	n.	費用	1	2	初級	◎
	this	[ðɪs]	adj./pron.	這個	1	1	初級	
	dish	[dɪʃ]	n.	菜餚	1	1	初級	
	house	[haʊs]	n.	店家	1	1	初級	◎
❻	chef	[ʃɛf]	n.	主廚	2	5	中高	◎
	specialty	[ˋspɛʃəltɪ]	n.	拿手菜	2	6	中高	◎
❼	all	[ɔl]	adj.	全部的	1	1	初級	
	served	[sɝvd]	p.p.	serve（端上）過去分詞	1	1	初級	◎
	yet	[jɛt]	adv.	尚未	1	1	初級	◎
❽	please	[pliz]	adv.	請…	1	1	初級	
	wait	[wet]	v.	等待	1	1	初級	◎
	second	[ˋsɛkənd]	n.	片刻	1	1	初級	◎
	bring	[brɪŋ]	v.	帶來	1	1	初級	
	meal	[mil]	n.	餐點	1	2	初級	
	right	[raɪt]	adv.	立即	1	1	初級	
	away	[əˋwe]	adv.	馬上	1	1	初級	
❾	need	[nid]	v.	需要	1	1	初級	◎
	hot	[hɑt]	adj.	辣的	1	1	初級	
	soy	[sɔɪ]	n.	醬油	3	2		
❿	soup	[sup]	n.	湯	2	1	初級	
	cold	[kold]	adj.	冷的	1	1	初級	
	like	[laɪk]	v.	想要	1	1	初級	
	warmed	[wɔrmd]	p.p.	warm（加熱）過去分詞	1	1	初級	
	up	[ʌp]	adv.	加溫/拾起/包起	1	1	初級	
	bit	[bɪt]	n.	稍微	1	1	初級	
⓫	just	[dʒʌst]	adv.	就	1	1	初級	
	leave	[liv]	v.	留下	1	1	初級	◎
	pick	[pɪk]	v.	收拾	1	2	初級	
⓬	excuse	[ɪkˋskjuz]	v.	請問	2	2	初級	
	any	[ˋɛnɪ]	adj.	任何的	1	1	初級	
	dessert	[dɪˋzɝt]	n.	甜點	2	2	初級	◎
	beverage	[ˋbɛvərɪdʒ]	n.	飲料	3	6	中高	◎
⓭	anything	[ˋɛnɪ͵θɪŋ]	pron.	任何事情	1	1	初級	
⓮	wrap	[ræp]	v.	打包	1	3	中級	◎
	leftover	[ˋlɛft͵ovɚ]	n.	剩菜	4			

※「紅字單字」於本單元多句出現，「單字級等分析」僅列在「首次出現句」。

🔵 MP3 123-01 ❶～⓰

❶	這盤菜的份量好少。	The portions of this meal are too small. * portion of＋名詞（…的份量）
❷	湯裡面有蚊子。	There is a mosquito in my soup. * there is/are＋名詞（有…）
❸	好鹹喔。	It's too salty. * sour（味道酸的）、sweet（味道甜的） * bitter（苦的）、astringent（味道澀澀的）
❹	這道菜和照片上的差太多了。	This dish does not look like the picture. * not look like（看起來不像）
❺	好辣喔。	It's too spicy. * numb（麻麻的）、pungent（味道很嗆的、嗆鼻的）
❻	食材不太新鮮。	The food is not very fresh. * not very fresh（不太新鮮）可替換為： 　stale（不新鮮的、走味的）
❼	這道菜不好吃。	This dish tastes bad. * taste bad（不好吃）、taste good（好吃）
❽	肉煮得太老了，咬不動。	The meat is overcooked, I can't chew it. * be overcooked（煮得太老、煮過頭）
❾	桌巾怎麼這麼髒？	How come the tablecloth is so dirty? * How come＋子句？（怎麼會…？）
❿	我們已經等了快半個小時了。	We've waited for almost half an hour. * have waited for（持續等待）
⓫	餐具好像不太乾淨。	The tableware doesn't look very clean.
⓬	餐廳好吵喔。	It's too noisy in this restaurant.
⓭	水的味道怪怪的。	The water tastes weird. * weird（奇怪的）＝ strange ＝ funny
⓮	為什麼最後一道菜遲遲不來？	Why has our last dish not been served yet? * Why has＋主詞＋not been...yet? 　（為什麼某主詞還沒…？）
⓯	這裡的服務生態度很差。	The waiters here have bad attitudes. * have bad attitudes（態度惡劣）
⓰	我們先來的，為什麼菜上得比較晚？	We arrived first—why is our meal being served so late?　* arrived first（當時較早抵達）

單字級等分析

	單字	音標	詞性	意義	字頻	大考	英檢	多益
❶	portion	[`porʃən]	n.	一客、一份	1	3	中級	◎
	this	[ðɪs]	adj.	這個	1	1	初級	
	meal	[mil]	n.	餐點	1	2	初級	
	too	[tu]	adv.	過於	1	1	初級	
	small	[smɔl]	adj.	小的	1	1	初級	◎
❷	there	[ðɛr]	adv.	有…	1	1	初級	
	mosquito	[məs`kɪto]	n.	蚊子	3	2	初級	
	soup	[sup]	n.	湯	2	1	初級	
❸	salty	[`sɔltɪ]	adj.	鹹的	4	2	中級	
❹	dish	[dɪʃ]	n.	菜餚	1	1	初級	
	look	[lʊk]	v.	看起來	1	1	初級	
	picture	[`pɪktʃɚ]	n.	照片	1	1	初級	◎
❺	spicy	[`spaɪsɪ]	adj.	辣的	3	4	中級	
❻	food	[fud]	n.	食物	1	1	初級	◎
	very	[`vɛrɪ]	adv.	十分	1	1	初級	
	fresh	[frɛʃ]	adj.	新鮮的	1	1	初級	
❼	taste	[test]	v.	嘗起來	1	1	初級	◎
	bad	[bæd]	adj.	不好的	1	1	初級	
❽	meat	[mit]	n.	肉	1	1	初級	
	overcooked	[͵ovɚ`kʊkt]	p.p.	overcook（煮過頭）過去分詞	8			
	chew	[tʃu]	v.	咀嚼	2	3	中級	
❾	come	[kʌm]	v.	（與 how 連用）怎麼會	1	1	初級	
	tablecloth	[`tebl͵klɔθ]	n.	桌巾	5		中級	◎
	so	[so]	adv.	這麼	1	1	初級	
	dirty	[`dɝtɪ]	adj.	髒的	2	1	初級	
❿	almost	[`ɔl͵most]	adv.	幾乎	1	1	初級	
	waited	[`wetɪd]	p.p.	wait（等待）過去分詞	1	1	初級	◎
	half	[hæf]	n.	一半	1	1	初級	
	hour	[aʊr]	n.	小時	1	1	初級	
⓫	tableware	[`tebl͵wɛr]	n.	餐具			中高	
	clean	[klin]	adj.	乾淨的	1	1	初級	
⓬	noisy	[`nɔɪzɪ]	adj.	吵鬧的	3	1	初級	
	restaurant	[`rɛstərənt]	n.	餐廳	1	2	初級	
⓭	water	[`wɔtɚ]	n.	水	1	1	初級	
	weird	[wɪrd]	adj.	奇怪的	2	5	中高	
⓮	last	[læst]	adj.	最後的	1	1	初級	◎
	served	[sɝvd]	p.p.	serve（端上）過去分詞	1	1	初級	◎
	yet	[jɛt]	adv.	尚未	1	1	初級	◎
⓯	waiter	[`wetɚ]	n.	男服務生	2	2	初級	◎
	here	[hɪr]	adv.	這裡	1	1	初級	
	have	[hæv]	v.	擁有	1	1	初級	
	attitude	[`ætət͵jud]	n.	態度	1	3	中級	◎
⓰	arrived	[ə`raɪvd]	p.t.	arrive（到達）過去式	1	2	初級	◎
	first	[fɝst]	adv.	最先地	1	1	初級	
	late	[let]	adv.	晚地	1	1	初級	◎

※「紅字單字」於本單元多句出現，「單字級等分析」僅列在「首次出現句」。

🔊 MP3 123-02 ❶～⓰

❶	對不起，我幫您問一下廚房。	I'm sorry, I'll check with our kitchen for you. * **will check with...**（稍後會向…確認）
❷	對不起，我們幫您重新出菜。	I'm sorry, we'll bring you a new order. * **bring a new order**（重新出菜）
❸	對不起，這道菜烹調時間要久一點。	I'm sorry, this dish needs some more time to cook. * **need some more time to＋動詞原形** （需要久一點的時間…）
❹	不合口味嗎？	It doesn't appeal to your tastes? * **appeal to one's taste**（合胃口）
❺	您覺得太辣了嗎？	Do you think it is too spicy? * **Do you think＋子句**（您覺得…）
❻	我幫您換一副餐具。	I'll bring you a new set of utensils. * **a set of**（一副）
❼	對不起，我馬上幫您更換。	I'm sorry, I will change that for you immediately.
❽	菜馬上就來了。	Your food is on its way. * **on one's way**（馬上會到）
❾	對不起讓您久等。	I'm sorry for keeping you waiting. * **keep＋某人＋waiting**（讓某人久等）
❿	不好意思，我們會盡力改進。	I'm terribly sorry; we'll do our best to improve. * **do one's best**（盡力） * 此句用「未來簡單式」（...will...） 表示「有意願做的事」。
⓫	對不起，我們遺漏了這道菜。	I'm sorry, we forgot about your dish. * **forget about**（遺漏、忘記）
⓬	如果份量不夠，我再幫您補充一些。	If the portion is not big enough, I'll bring you some more.
⓭	對不起，今天客人實在太多了。	I'm sorry, we are very busy today.
⓮	對不起，這個服務生今天第一天上班。	I'm sorry; this is the waiter's first day. * **one's first day**（上班第一天） * **waitress**（女服務生）
⓯	這些小菜由我們免費招待。	These side dishes are on the house. * **on the house**（店家免費招待）
⓰	謝謝您的建議。	Thank you for your suggestion.

	單字	音標	詞性	意義	字頻	大考	英檢	多益
❶	sorry	[ˋsɑrɪ]	adj.	抱歉的	1	1	初級	
	check	[tʃɛk]	v.	確認	1	1	初級	
	kitchen	[ˋkɪtʃɪn]	n.	廚房	1	1	初級	◎
❷	bring	[brɪŋ]	v.	帶來	1	1	初級	
	new	[nju]	adj.	新的	1	1	初級	
	order	[ˋɔrdɚ]	n.	所點的菜	1	1	初級	◎
❸	this	[ðɪs]	adj.	這個	1	1	初級	
	dish	[dɪʃ]	n.	菜餚	1	1	初級	
	need	[nid]	v.	需要	1	1	初級	◎
	some	[sʌm]	adv. /adj.	一些	1	1	初級	
	more	[mor]	adj./ pron.	更多	1	1	初級	
	time	[taɪm]	n.	時間	1	1	初級	◎
	cook	[kʊk]	v.	煮、烹調	1	1	初級	◎
❹	appeal	[əˋpil]	v.	符合	1	3	中級	◎
	taste	[test]	n.	胃口	1	1	初級	◎
❺	think	[θɪŋk]	v.	認為	1	1	初級	
	too	[tu]	adv.	過於	1	1	初級	
	spicy	[ˋspaɪsɪ]	adj.	辣的	3	4	中級	
❻	set	[sɛt]	n.	一副	1	1	初級	◎
	utensil	[juˋtɛnsl̩]	n.	餐具	5	6	中高	◎
❼	change	[tʃendʒ]	v.	更換	1	2	初級	◎
	immediately	[ɪˋmidɪɪtlɪ]	adv.	馬上	1		中級	◎
❽	food	[fud]	n.	食物	1	1	初級	◎
	way	[we]	n.	途中	1	1	初級	
❾	keeping	[ˋkipɪŋ]	n.	keep（讓…）動名詞	8	1	初級	◎
	waiting	[ˋwetɪŋ]	n.	wait（等待）動名詞	3	1	初級	◎
❿	terribly	[ˋtɛrəblɪ]	adv.	非常	2			
	do	[du]	v.	做	1	1	初級	
	best	[bɛst]	n.	最好	1	1	初級	
	improve	[ɪmˋpruv]	v.	改善	1	2	初級	◎
⓫	forgot	[fɚˋgɑt]	p.t.	forget（忘記）過去式	1	1	初級	
⓬	portion	[ˋporʃən]	n.	一客、一份	1	3	中級	◎
	big	[bɪg]	adj.	量多的	1	1	初級	
	enough	[əˋnʌf]	adv.	足夠地	1	1	初級	◎
⓭	very	[ˋvɛrɪ]	adv.	十分	1	1	初級	
	busy	[ˋbɪzɪ]	adj.	忙碌的	1	1	初級	
	today	[təˋde]	adv.	今天	1	1	初級	
⓮	waiter	[ˋwetɚ]	n.	男服務生	2	2	初級	◎
	first	[fɝst]	adj.	第一個的	1	1	初級	
	day	[de]	n.	天	1	1	初級	
⓯	these	[ðiz]	adj.	這些	1	1	初級	
	side	[saɪd]	n.	副食的、配菜的	1	1	初級	
	house	[haʊs]	n.	店家	1	1	初級	◎
⓰	thank	[θæŋk]	v.	感謝	1	1	初級	
	suggestion	[səˋdʒɛstʃən]	n.	建議	1	4	中級	◎

※「紅字單字」於本單元多句出現，「單字級等分析」僅列在「首次出現句」。

MP3 124-01 ❶～⓱

❶	我要買單。	Check, please. = May I have the bill, please? * check（帳單）= bill
❷	可以刷卡嗎？	Can I pay by credit card? * pay by（用…付錢）、credit card（信用卡）
❸	只接受現金嗎？	Do you only accept cash? * accept（接受）= take
❹	總共多少錢？	How much is the total? * How much is / are＋名詞?（…是多少錢？）
❺	錢好像不太對…	The amount does not seem right....
❻	零錢不用找了，謝謝。	Keep the change, thanks. * keep the change（不用找零、零錢你留著）
❼	請給我看一下帳單明細。	Please give me a detailed check. * detailed check（帳單明細）
❽	這不是我們的帳單。	This is not our check.
❾	有含一成服務費嗎？	Does it already include the ten percent service charge? * include＋名詞（包含…）、service charge（服務費）
❿	小菜是多少錢？	How much are the side dishes? * side dish（小菜）
⓫	可以找零錢給我嗎？	May I have the change? * May I have...?（請給我…）
⓬	你算錯帳了。	You made a mistake on this bill. = There is an error on this check. * made a mistake（剛剛弄錯了）
⓭	可以分開找錢給我們嗎？	Can you give us the change separately? * give the change separately（個別找零）
⓮	白飯一碗多少？	How much for a bowl of white rice? * a bowl of（一碗）
⓯	我這裡有折價餐券。	I have a discount meal coupon. * discount meal coupon（折價餐券）
⓰	不是三千塊錢嗎？	Isn't it three thousand dollars?
⓱	我這裡有一張兌換券。	I have a coupon for a free meal.

542

	單字	音標	詞性	意義	字頻	大考	英檢	多益
❶	check	[tʃɛk]	n.	帳單	1	1	初級	
	please	[pliz]	adv.	請…	1	1	初級	
	have	[hæv]	v.	取、拿	1	1	初級	
	bill	[bɪl]	n.	帳單	1	2	初級	◎
❷	pay	[pe]	v.	付款	1	3	初級	◎
	credit	[`krɛdɪt]	n.	信用	1	3	中級	◎
	card	[kɑrd]	n.	卡片	1	1	初級	◎
❸	only	[`onlɪ]	adv.	只有	1	1	初級	
	accept	[əkˋsɛpt]	v.	接受	1	2	初級	◎
	cash	[kæʃ]	n.	現金	1	1	初級	◎
❹	much	[mʌtʃ]	adj.	許多的	1	1	初級	
	total	[`totl]	n.	總共	1	1	初級	◎
❺	amount	[əˋmaunt]	n.	數量	1	2	初級	◎
	seem	[sim]	v.	似乎	1	1	初級	
	right	[raɪt]	adj.	正確的	1	1	初級	
❻	keep	[kip]	v.	留著	1	1	初級	◎
	change	[tʃendʒ]	n.	零錢	1	2	初級	◎
	thanks	[θæŋks]	n.	thank（感謝）複數	1			
❼	give	[gɪv]	v.	給予	1	1	初級	
	detailed	[`diˋteld]	adj.	細節的	2	3	中級	◎
❽	this	[ðɪs]	adj.	這個	1	1	初級	
❾	already	[ɔlˋrɛdɪ]	adv.	已經	1	1	初級	◎
	include	[ɪnˋklud]	n.	包含	1	2	初級	◎
	ten	[tɛn]	n.	十	1	1	初級	
	percent	[pəˋsɛnt]	n.	百分之…	2	4	中級	◎
	service	[`sɜvɪs]	n.	服務	1	1	初級	◎
	charge	[tʃɑrdʒ]	n.	費用	1	2	初級	◎
❿	side	[saɪd]	adj.	副食的、配菜的	1	1	初級	
	dish	[dɪʃ]	n.	菜餚	1	1	初級	
⓬	made	[med]	p.t.	make（弄出）過去式	1	1	初級	
	mistake	[mɪˋstek]	n.	錯誤	1	1	初級	◎
	there	[ðɛr]	adv.	有…	1	1	初級	◎
	error	[`ɛrə]	n.	錯誤	1	2	初級	
⓭	separately	[`sɛpərɪtlɪ]	adv.	個別地	2		中高	
⓮	bowl	[bol]	n.	碗	1	1	初級	
	white	[hwaɪt]	adj.	白色的	1	1	初級	
	rice	[raɪs]	n.	米飯	1	1	初級	
⓯	discount	[`dɪskaunt]	n.	折扣	2	3	中級	◎
	meal	[mil]	n.	餐點	1	2	初級	
	coupon	[`kupɑn]	n.	禮券	4	5	中高	◎
⓰	three	[θri]	n.	三	1	1	初級	
	thousand	[`θauznd]	n.	一千	1	1	初級	
	dollar	[`dɑlə]	n.	元	1	1	初級	◎
⓱	free	[fri]	adj.	免費的	1	1	初級	

※「紅字單字」於本單元多句出現，「單字級等分析」僅列在「首次出現句」。

🔊 MP3 124-02 ❶〜⓱

❶	這是您的帳單。	This is your check. = Here is your check.
❷	需要開收據嗎？	Do you need a receipt?
❸	還要加上三碗白飯的費用。	I still need to add three bowls of white rice to the bill. * **add...to the bill**（加上…在帳單裡）
❹	可以給我您公司的統一編號嗎？	Can I please have your company's unified invoice number? * **Can I please have...?**（請給我…、請告訴我…） * **unified invoice number**（統一編號）
❺	我們有收一成的服務費。	We put in a ten percent service charge. * **put in**（加上）、數字＋**percent**（…成、百分之…）
❻	這張折價券可以使用。	You can use this discount coupon.
❼	一次消費只能使用一張折價券。	You can only use one coupon at a time. * **at a time**（一次）
❽	這張折價券過期了。	This discount coupon has expired.
❾	您需要分開結帳嗎？	Do you need separate checks? * **separate checks**（個別的帳單）
❿	剛才離開的客人已經幫您結帳了。	Your check has already been paid by the guest who just left. * **have/has been paid**（已經被付清）、**by**（經由）
⓫	對不起，我算錯帳了。	I'm so sorry, I miscalculated the bill.
⓬	請問您有零錢嗎？	Excuse me, do you have any change? * **excuse me**（不好意思、請問）
⓭	請簽名。	Please sign your name.
⓮	這是您的發票。	Here is your receipt.
⓯	這是折價券，您下次可以使用。	This is a discount coupon you may use next time.
⓰	謝謝光臨。	Thank you for coming.
⓱	歡迎下次再來。	Please come again.

	單字	音標	詞性	意義	字頻	大考	英檢	多益
❶	this	[ðɪs]	pron. /adj.	這個	1	1	初級	
	check	[tʃɛk]	n.	帳單	1	1	初級	◎
	here	[hɪr]	adv.	這裡	1	1	初級	
❷	need	[nid]	v.	需要	1	1	初級	◎

❷	receipt	[rɪˋsit]	n.	收據	3	3	中級	◎
❸	still	[stɪl]	adv.	還要	1	1	初級	◎
	add	[æd]	v.	加	1	1	初級	◎
	three	[θri]	n.	三	1	1	初級	
	bowl	[bol]	n.	碗	1	1	初級	
	white	[hwaɪt]	adj.	白色的	1	1	初級	
	rice	[raɪs]	n.	米飯	1	1	初級	
	bill	[bɪl]	n.	帳單	1	2	初級	◎
❹	please	[pliz]	adv.	請…	1	1	初級	
	have	[hæv]	v.	持有	1	1	初級	
	company	[ˋkʌmpənɪ]	n.	公司	1	2	初級	◎
	unified	[ˋjunə͵faɪd]	adj.	統一的	3	6	中高	◎
	invoice	[ˋɪnvɔɪs]	n.	發票	6			◎
	number	[ˋnʌmbɚ]	n.	編號	1	1	初級	◎
❺	put	[pʊt]	v.	加上	1	1	初級	
	ten	[tɛn]	n.	十	1	1	初級	
	percent	[pɚˋsɛnt]	n.	百分之…	2	4	中級	◎
	service	[ˋsɝvɪs]	n.	服務	1	1	初級	◎
	charge	[tʃɑrdʒ]	n.	費用	1	2	初級	◎
❻	use	[juz]	v.	使用	1	1	初級	◎
	discount	[ˋdɪskaʊnt]	n.	折扣	2	3	中級	◎
	coupon	[ˋkupɑn]	n.	禮券	4	5	中高	◎
❼	only	[ˋonlɪ]	adv.	只有	1	1	初級	
	one	[wʌn]	n.	一	1	1	初級	
	time	[taɪm]	n.	次、回	1	1	初級	
❽	expired	[ɪkˋspaɪrd]	p.p.	expire（過期）過去分詞	3	6	中高	◎
❾	separate	[ˋsɛpə͵ret]	adj.	個別的	1	2	初級	◎
❿	already	[ɔlˋrɛdɪ]	adv.	已經	1	1	初級	
	paid	[ped]	p.p.	pay（付款）過去分詞	3	3	中高	◎
	guest	[gɛst]	n.	客人	1	1	初級	
	just	[dʒʌst]	adv.	剛剛	1	1	初級	
	left	[lɛft]	p.t.	leave（離開）過去式	1	1	初級	
⓫	sorry	[ˋsɑrɪ]	adj.	抱歉的	1	1	初級	
	miscalculated	[ˋmɪsˋkælkjə͵letɪd]	p.t.	miscalculate（計算錯誤）過去式	8			
⓬	excuse	[ɪkˋskjuz]	v.	請問	2	2	初級	◎
	any	[ˋɛnɪ]	adj.	任何的	1	1	初級	
	change	[tʃendʒ]	n.	零錢、硬幣	1	2	初級	◎
⓭	sign	[saɪn]	v.	簽名	1	2	初級	◎
	name	[nem]	n.	名字	1	1	初級	◎
⓯	next	[nɛkst]	adj.	下一	1	1	初級	
⓰	thank	[θæŋk]	v.	感謝	1	1	初級	
	coming	[ˋkʌmɪŋ]	n.	come（前來）動名詞	2	1	中級	
⓱	come	[kʌm]	v.	前來	1	1	初級	
	again	[əˋgɛn]	adv.	再次	1	1	初級	

※「紅字單字」於本單元多句出現，「單字級等分析」僅列在「首次出現句」。

125 換錢。

MP3 125-01 ❶～⓱

❶	我要換錢打電話。	I need some change to make a phone call. * **make a phone call**（打電話）
❷	我想換美金。	I'd like to exchange this into U.S. dollars. * **exchange A into B**（將 A 換成 B） * **U.S. dollars**（美金）、**Japanese yen**（日圓） * **Euro**（歐元）、**Great Britain pound**（英鎊） * **South Korean won**（韓圓） * **Australian dollar**（澳幣）
❸	哪裡可以換零錢？	Where can I get change? * **get change**（獲得零錢）
❹	可以和你換零錢嗎？	Can I get change from you?
❺	請問需要什麼證件？	What kind of ID do you need?
❻	請幫我把錢換開。	Please change the money into small bills for me. * **change A into B**（將 A 換成 B）
❼	請全部換給我零錢。	Please change all my money into coins.
❽	今天的匯率是多少？	What's the exchange rate for today? * **What's**＋某數字相關名詞?（…是多少？） * **exchange rate**（匯率）
❾	可以換新台幣嗎？	Can I exchange this into New Taiwan dollars? * **Renminbi**（人民幣）、**Hong Kong dollar**（港幣）
❿	哪裡有換鈔機？	Where can I find a coin machine? * **coin machine**（兌幣兌鈔機）
⓫	紙鈔可以打電話嗎？	Can I use a bill to make a phone call?
⓬	需要手續費嗎？	Is there a service charge? * **service charge**（手續費）
⓭	可以給我一些百元鈔票嗎？	Can you give me some hundred-dollar bills? * 數字＋**-dollar**（…面額的）
⓮	請換零錢給我。	Please give me some coins.
⓯	這台機器會找零嗎？	Does this machine give change? * **give change**（找零）
⓰	可以到商店換錢嗎？	Can I get change in the store?
⓱	搭公車需要準備零錢嗎？	Do I need change to take a bus? * **take a bus**（搭公車）

單字級等分析

	單字	音標	詞性	意義	字頻	大考	英檢	多益
❶	need	[nid]	v.	需要	1	1	初級	◎
	some	[sʌm]	adj.	一些	1	1	初級	
	change	[tʃendʒ]	n./v.	零錢/交換	1	2	初級	◎
	make	[mek]	v.	撥打	1	1	初級	
	phone	[fon]	n.	電話	1	2	初級	◎
	call	[kɔl]	n.	通話	1	1	初級	◎
❷	like	[laɪk]	v.	想要	1	1	初級	
	exchange	[ɪks`tʃendʒ]	v./n.	兌換	1	3	中級	◎
	this	[ðɪs]	pron. /adj.	這個	1	1	初級	
	U.S.	[`ju`ɛs]	n.	United States（美國）縮寫				
	dollar	[`dɑlə]	n.	元	1	1	初級	◎
❸	get	[gɛt]	v.	獲得	1	1	初級	
❺	kind	[kaɪnd]	n.	種類	1	1	初級	◎
	ID	[`aɪ`di]	n.	identification（證件）縮寫		4		
❻	please	[pliz]	adv.	請…	1	1	初級	
	money	[`mʌnɪ]	n.	金錢	1	1	初級	◎
	small	[smɔl]	adj.	面額小的	1	1	初級	◎
	bill	[bɪl]	n.	鈔票	1	2	初級	◎
❼	all	[ɔl]	adj.	所有的	1	1	初級	
	coin	[kɔɪn]	n.	硬幣	2	2	初級	
❽	rate	[ret]	n.	比率	1	3	中級	◎
	today	[tə`de]	n.	今天	1	1	初級	◎
❾	new	[nju]	adj.	新的	1	1	初級	
	Taiwan	[`taɪ`wɑn]	n.	台灣			初級	
❿	find	[faɪnd]	v.	尋找	1	1	初級	
⓫	use	[juz]	v.	使用	1	1	初級	◎
⓬	there	[ðɛr]	adv.	有…	1	1	初級	
	service	[`sɝvɪs]	n.	服務	1	1	初級	◎
	charge	[tʃɑrdʒ]	n.	費用	1	2	初級	◎
⓭	give	[gɪv]	v.	給予	1	1	初級	
	hundred-dollar	[`hʌndred`dɑlə]	adj.	百元的				
⓯	machine	[mə`ʃin]	n.	機器	1	1	初級	
⓰	store	[stor]	n.	商店	1	1	初級	◎
⓱	take	[tek]	v.	搭乘	1	1	初級	◎
	bus	[bʌs]	n.	公車	1	1	初級	

※「紅字單字」於本單元多句出現，「單字級等分析」僅列在「首次出現句」。

125 服務人員怎麼說？

MP3 125-02 ❶～⓰

❶	你要怎麼換錢？	How would you like your money? * **How would you like...?**（你想要如何…？）
❷	你要換多少錢？	How much money do you want to exchange? * **How much money...?**（…多少金額？）
❸	你要換十元還是一元？	Do you want your money changed into tens or ones?
❹	請給我你的護照。	Please let me see your passport.
❺	你要換美金還是日圓？	Would you like your money exchanged into U.S. dollars or Japanese yen?
❻	這裡也可以換新台幣。	We can exchange money into New Taiwan dollars here, too.
❼	不能用零錢打卡式電話。	You cannot use coins for prepaid card phones. * **prepaid card phone**（電話卡式的電話）、**bill**（鈔票） * **payphone**（投幣式公共電話）
❽	搭公車要自備零錢。	You need change to take a bus. * **buy…from a vending machine**（從販賣機購買…） * **buy capsule toys**（購買扭蛋）
❾	手續費是 5%。	The service charge is five percent. * **service charge**（手續費）
❿	這是你的收據。	Here is your receipt. * **Here is**＋名詞（這是…）
⓫	我看看有沒有零錢。	Let me see if I have any change. * **let me see if**＋子句（讓我查看是否…）
⓬	你還需要多少零錢？	How much more change do you need?
⓭	我沒有零錢。	I don't have any change.
⓮	五張一元和一張五元可以嗎？	Can I give you five ones and one five?
⓯	我只有兩張十元。	I only have two tens.
⓰	我沒有那麼多零錢。	I don't have that much change.
⓱	我沒辦法換錢給你，你找別人問問看。	I can't give you any change; try asking someone else. * **try**＋動詞-ing（試著做…）、**someone else**（其他人）
⓲	這是我身上全部的零錢了。	This is all the change I have. * **This is all**＋名詞＋**I have**（這是我所有的…）

548

	單字	音標	詞性	意義	字頻	大考	英檢	多益
❶	like	[laɪk]	v.	想要	1	1	初級	
	money	[ˈmʌnɪ]	n.	金錢	1	1	初級	◎
❷	much	[mʌtʃ]	adv.	許多的	1	1	初級	
	want	[wɑnt]	v.	想要	1	1	初級	◎
	exchange	[ɪksˋtʃendʒ]	v.	兌換	1	3	中級	◎
❸	changed	[tʃendʒd]	p.p.	change（交換）過去分詞	4	2	初級	◎
	ten	[tɛn]	n.	十元	1	1	初級	
	one	[wʌn]	n.	一元	1	1	初級	
❹	please	[pliz]	adv.	請…	1	1	初級	
	let	[lɛt]	v.	讓…	1	1	初級	
	see	[si]	v.	查看	1	1	初級	
	passport	[ˈpæs.port]	n.	護照	3	3	中級	◎
❺	exchanged	[ɪksˋtʃendʒd]	p.p.	exchange（兌換）過去分詞	1	3	初級	◎
	U.S.	[ˋjuˋɛs]	n.	United States（美國）縮寫				
	dollar	[ˈdɑlɚ]	n.	元	1	1	初級	◎
	Japanese	[ˌdʒæpəˈniz]	n.	日本	1		初級	
	yen	[jɛn]	n.	日圓	4		中高	
❻	new	[nju]	adj.	新的	1	1	初級	
	Taiwan	[ˈtaɪˋwɑn]	n.	台灣			初級	
	here	[hɪr]	adv.	這裡	1	1	初級	
	too	[tu]	adv.	也	1	1	初級	
❼	use	[juz]	v.	使用	1	1	初級	◎
	coin	[kɔɪn]	n.	硬幣	2	2	初級	◎
	prepaid	[priˈped]	adj.	預付的	7			◎
	card	[kɑrd]	n.	卡片	1	1	初級	◎
	phone	[fon]	n.	電話	1	2	初級	◎
❽	need	[nid]	v.	需要	1	1	初級	◎
	change	[tʃendʒ]	n.	零錢	1	2	初級	◎
	take	[tek]	v.	搭乘	1	1	初級	◎
	bus	[bʌs]	n.	公車	1	1	初級	
❾	service	[ˈsɝvɪs]	n.	服務	1	1	初級	◎
	charge	[tʃɑrdʒ]	n.	費用	1	2	初級	◎
	five	[faɪv]	n.	五個/五元	1	1	初級	
	percent	[pɚˋsɛnt]	n.	百分之…	2	4	中級	◎
❿	receipt	[rɪˋsit]	n.	收據	3	3	中級	◎
⓫	have	[hæv]	v.	擁有	1	1	初級	
	any	[ˈɛnɪ]	adj.	任何的	1	1	初級	
⓮	give	[gɪv]	v.	給予	1	1	初級	
⓯	only	[ˈonlɪ]	adv.	只有	1	1	初級	
	two	[tu]	n.	二	1	1	初級	
⓰	that	[ðæt]	adv.	那麼	1	1	初級	
⓱	try	[traɪ]	v.	嘗試	1	1	初級	
	asking	[ˈæskɪŋ]	n.	ask（詢問）動名詞	5	1	初級	
	someone	[ˈsʌmˏwʌn]	pron.	某個人	1	1	初級	
	else	[ɛls]	adj.	其他的	1	1	初級	
⓲	this	[ðɪs]	pron.	這個	1	1	初級	
	all	[ɔl]	adj.	所有的	1	1	初級	

※「紅字單字」於本單元多句出現，「單字級等分析」僅列在「首次出現句」。

126 問路。

❶	請告訴我怎麼回麗晶飯店。	Can you please tell me how to get back to the Regent Hotel from here? * **Can you please tell me...?**（請告訴我…、請問…） * **get back to**（返回）、**from here**（從這裡）
❷	我迷路了。	I am lost.
❸	請問這裡是哪裡？	Excuse me, where is this place? * **excuse me**（不好意思、請問）
❹	請問哪裡可以搭計程車？	Can you please tell me where I can find a taxi? * **taxi**（計程車）= **cab**
❺	請問最近的公車站要往哪裡走？	Excuse me, which way is the nearest bus station? * **Which way is＋地點?**（某地點是在哪個方向？） * **bus station**（公車站）
❻	請問捷運站在哪一個方向？	Excuse me, which way is the MRT station? * **MRT station**（捷運站）
❼	請問火車站在哪裡？	Excuse me, where is the train station? * **train station**（火車站）
❽	什麼時候要左轉呢？	When should I turn left?
❾	請問我在地圖上的哪裡？	Excuse me, where am I on this map? * **Where am I?**（我在哪裡？）、**on a map**（在地圖上）
❿	直走就會到我的目的地嗎？	If I keep going straight, will I reach my destination? * **keep＋動詞ing**（一直）、**go straight**（直走） * **reach the destination**（抵達目的地）
⓫	直走之後呢？	And after going straight ahead?
⓬	請問還有幾站？	Excuse me, how many stations are left? * **How many＋名詞複數型...?**（有多少…？）
⓭	右轉還是左轉？	Turn right, or turn left?
⓮	第幾個十字路口該左轉？	At which crossroads should I turn left? * **at**（位在…地點）
⓯	我必須過馬路嗎？	Do I need to cross the road? * **cross the road**（過馬路）
⓰	走路到得了嗎？	Can I walk there? = Can I get there on foot? * **walk there**（走路到那裡）、**on foot**（用走路的方式）

	單字	音標	詞性	意義	字頻	大考	英檢	多益
❶	please	[pliz]	adv.	請…	1	1	初級	
	tell	[tɛl]	v.	告訴	1	1	初級	
	get	[gɛt]	v.	抵達	1	1	初級	◎
	back	[bæk]	adv.	返回	1	1	初級	◎
	hotel	[hoˋtɛl]	n.	旅店	1	2	初級	
	here	[hɪr]	n.	這裡	1	1	初級	
❷	lost	[lɔst]	adj.	迷路的	1	2	中高	◎
❸	excuse	[ɪkˋskjuz]	v.	請問	2	2	初級	◎
	this	[ðɪs]	adj.	這個	1	1	初級	
	place	[ples]	n.	地方	1	1	初級	◎
❹	find	[faɪnd]	v.	發現、找到	1	1	初級	
	taxi	[ˋtæksɪ]	n.	計程車	2	1	初級	
❺	way	[we]	n.	方向	1	1	初級	
	nearest	[ˋnɪrɪst]	adj.	near（鄰近的）最高級	3			
	bus	[bʌs]	n.	公車	1	1	初級	
	station	[ˋsteʃən]	n.	車站	1	1	初級	◎
❻	MRT	[ˋɛmˋɑrˋti]	n.	Mass Rapid Transit（捷運）縮寫		2	初級	◎
❼	train	[tren]	n.	火車	1	1	初級	
❽	turn	[tɜn]	v.	轉彎	1	1	初級	◎
	left	[lɛft]	adv.	向左側	1	1	初級	
❾	map	[mæp]	n.	地圖	1	1	初級	
❿	keep	[kip]	v.	繼續	1	1	初級	◎
	going	[ˋgoɪŋ]	n.	go（去、走）動名詞	4	1	初級	
	straight	[stret]	adv.	筆直地	1	2	初級	◎
	reach	[ritʃ]	v.	到達	1	1	初級	◎
	destination	[ˌdɛstəˋneʃən]	n.	目的地	2	5	中級	◎
⓫	ahead	[əˋhɛd]	adv.	向前	1	1	初級	◎
⓬	many	[ˋmɛnɪ]	adj.	許多的	1	1	初級	
	left	[lɛft]	p.p.	leave（剩下）過去分詞	1	1	初級	
⓭	right	[raɪt]	adv.	向右側	1	1	初級	
⓮	crossroad	[ˋkrɔsˌrod]	n.	十字路口	4			
⓯	need	[nid]	v.	需要	1	1	初級	◎
	cross	[krɔs]	v.	穿越	1	2	初級	
	road	[rod]	n.	馬路	1	1	初級	
⓰	walk	[wɔk]	v.	走路	1	1	初級	
	there	[ðɛr]	adv.	那裡	1	1	初級	
	foot	[fʊt]	n.	走路、步行	1	1	初級	

※「紅字單字」於本單元多句出現，「單字級等分析」僅列在「首次出現句」。

🔊 MP3 126-02 ❶～⓰

❶	你走錯方向了。	You took a wrong turn. * take a wrong turn（走錯路）
❷	有公車可以到那裡。	There is a bus that goes there. * go there（開往那裡）
❸	往前直走就到了。	Go straight ahead and you'll be there. * will be＋某地（將會位在某地）
❹	你可以搭捷運過去。	You can take the MRT to get there.
❺	搭計程車只要十分鐘。	It only takes ten minutes to get there by cab. * 某事＋take＋時間（某事花費…時間） * by＋交通工具（搭乘某交通工具）
❻	過馬路後往前走就看到了。	Cross the street, then walk straight ahead and you'll see it.
❼	向右轉、再左轉就到了。	Make a right turn and then a left turn and you'll be there. * make a turn（轉彎）
❽	直走後看到紅綠燈右轉。	Go straight ahead and make a right at the traffic light. * make a right（右轉） * at the traffic light（在紅綠燈處）
❾	你現在在地圖的這裡。	On the map, you are right here. * on the map（地圖上）
❿	前面最大的建築物就是火車站。	The train station is the largest building in front of you. * in front of（在…前面）
⓫	你可以在這一站下車。	You can get off at this station. * get off（下車）
⓬	直走五分鐘就到了。	Go straight along this road for five minutes and you'll be there. * along this road（沿著這條路）
⓭	下一站你就要下車了。	You should get off at the next station.
⓮	坐計程車過去比較方便。	It would be easier to take a taxi there. * would（可能）、be easier to（更容易）
⓯	不會很遠，走路只要五分鐘。	It is not that far from here, only a five-minute walk. * from here（離這裡） * 數字＋-minute walk（…分鐘路程）
⓰	你必須轉好幾趟車。	You need to transfer a few times. * a few times（好幾次）

552

	單字	音標	詞性	意義	字頻	大考	英檢	多益
❶	took	[tʊk]	p.t.	take（採取）過去式	1	1	初級	◎
	wrong	[rɔŋ]	adj.	錯誤的	1	1	初級	◎
	turn	[tɜn]	n.	轉彎	1	1	初級	◎
❷	there	[ðɛr]	adv.	那裡	1	1	初級	
	bus	[bʌs]	n.	公車	1	1	初級	
	go	[go]	v.	前往/去、走	1	1	初級	
❸	straight	[stret]	adv.	筆直地	1	2	初級	◎
	ahead	[əˋhɛd]	adv.	向前	1	1	初級	
❹	take	[tek]	v.	搭乘	1	1	初級	◎
	MRT	[ˋɛmˋorˋti]	n.	Mass Rapid Transit（捷運）縮寫		2	初級	◎
	get	[gɛt]	v.	抵達/下車	1	1	初級	◎
❺	only	[ˋonlɪ]	adv.	只有	1	1	初級	
	ten	[tɛn]	n.	十	1	1	初級	
	minute	[ˋmɪnɪt]	n.	分鐘	1	1	初級	◎
	cab	[kæb]	n.	計程車	2	1		◎
❻	cross	[krɔs]	v.	穿越	1	2	初級	
	street	[strit]	n.	馬路	1	1	初級	
	then	[ðɛn]	adv.	然後	1	1	初級	
	walk	[wɔk]	v./n.	走路/路程	1	1	初級	
	see	[si]	v.	看到	1	1	初級	
❼	make	[mek]	v.	做出	1	1	初級	
	right	[raɪt]	adj.	右邊的	1	1	初級	
	left	[lɛft]	adj.	左邊的	1	1	初級	
❽	right	[raɪt]	n.	右轉	1	1	初級	
	traffic	[ˋtræfɪk]	n.	交通	1	2	初級	◎
	light	[laɪt]	n.	燈	1	1	初級	
❾	map	[mæp]	n.	地圖	1	1	初級	
	right	[raɪt]	adv.	恰好、就	1	1	初級	
	here	[hɪr]	adv./n.	這裡	1	1	初級	
❿	train	[tren]	n.	火車	1	1	初級	
	station	[ˋsteʃən]	n.	車站	1	1	初級	◎
	largest	[lɑrdʒɪst]	adj.	large（大的）最高級	1	1	初級	◎
	building	[ˋbɪldɪŋ]	n.	建築物	1	1	初級	◎
	front	[frʌnt]	n.	前面	1	1	初級	
⓫	off	[ɔf]	adv.	下來	1	1	初級	
	this	[ðɪs]	adj.	這個	1	1	初級	
⓬	road	[rod]	n.	馬路	1	1	初級	
	five	[faɪv]	n.	五	1	1	初級	
⓭	next	[nɛkst]	adj.	下一個	1	1	初級	
⓮	easier	[ˋizɪə]	adj.	easy（容易的）比較級	1	1	初級	◎
	taxi	[ˋtæksɪ]	n.	計程車	2	1	初級	
⓯	that	[ðæt]	adv.	這麼	1	1	初級	
	far	[fɑr]	adj.	遠的	1	1	初級	
	five-minute	[ˋfaɪvˋmɪnɪt]	adj.	五分鐘的				
⓰	need	[nid]	v.	需要	1	1	初級	◎
	transfer	[trænsˋfɝ]	v.	轉乘	1	4	中級	◎
	few	[fju]	adj.	少許的	1	1	初級	◎
	time	[taɪm]	n.	次、回	1	1	初級	◎

※「紅字單字」於本單元多句出現，「單字級等分析」僅列在「首次出現句」。

MP3 127-01 ❶～❹

❶	請問哪裡可以買到電話卡？	Can you please tell me where I can buy a phone card? * **Can you please tell me...?**（請問…） * **phone card**（電話卡）
❷	請問附近哪裡有公共電話？	Excuse me, is there a public phone around here? * **excuse me**（請問）、**public phone**（公共電話） * **around**＋地點（在…附近）
❸	請問打市內電話要多少錢？	Excuse me, how much does it cost to make a local call? * **How much...?**（…多少錢？）、**local call**（市內電話）
❹	市內電話要怎麼打？	How can I make a local call? * **How can I...?**（我要如何…？）
❺	電話卡要多少錢？	How much does a prepaid phone card cost?
❻	請問打長途電話要多少錢？	Excuse me, how much does it cost to make a long-distance call? * **long-distance call**（長途電話）
❼	國際電話要怎麼打？	How can I make an international call? * **international call**（國際電話）
❽	公共電話可以打國際電話嗎？	Can a public phone be used to make an international call? * **be used to**＋動詞原形（用於…）
❾	長途電話要怎麼打？	How can I make a long-distance call?
❿	這個電話壞掉了嗎？	Is this phone broken? * **Does this phone malfunction?**（這個電話故障了嗎？）
⓫	叫消防隊要打幾號？	What number should I dial to reach the fire department? * **What number...?**（…幾號？）、**dial to**（撥打給…） * **fire department**（消防局）、**ambulance**（救護車）
⓬	公共電話能打對方付費電話嗎？	Can I use a public phone to make a collect call? * **collect call**（對方付費電話）
⓭	有免費的公共電話嗎？	Are there any toll-free payphones? * **toll-free payphone**（免付費公共電話）
⓮	我的手機沒電了，可以借用你的嗎？	My mobile phone's battery is dead; can I borrow yours? * **mobile phone**（手機）、**a battery is dead**（電池沒電）

單字級等分析

	單字	音標	詞性	意義	字頻	大考	英檢	多益
❶	please	[pliz]	adv.	請…	1	1	初級	
	tell	[tɛl]	v.	告訴	1	1	初級	
	buy	[baɪ]	v.	購買	1	1	初級	
	phone	[fon]	n.	電話	1	2	初級	◎
	card	[kɑrd]	n.	卡片	1	1	初級	◎
❷	excuse	[ɪkˋskjuz]	v.	請問	2	2	初級	◎
	there	[ðɛr]	adv.	有…	1	1	初級	
	public	[ˋpʌblɪk]	adj.	公共的	1	1	初級	
	here	[hɪr]	n.	這裡	1	1	初級	
❸	much	[mʌtʃ]	adv.	許多地	1	1	初級	
	cost	[kɔst]	v.	花費	1	1	初級	◎
	make	[mek]	v.	打電話	1	1	初級	
	local	[ˋlokl̩]	adj.	地區性的	1	2	初級	◎
	call	[kɔl]	n.	電話	1	1	初級	◎
❺	prepaid	[priˋped]	adj.	預付的	7			◎
❻	long-distance	[ˋlɔŋˋdɪstəns]	adj.	長途的	3			
❼	international	[͵ɪntɚˋnæʃənl̩]	adj.	國際的	1	2	初級	◎
❽	used	[juzd]	p.p.	use（使用）過去式	1	2	初級	◎
❿	this	[ðɪs]	adj.	這個	1	1	初級	
	broken	[ˋbrokən]	p.p.	break（故障）過去分詞	1	1	初級	
⓫	number	[ˋnʌmbɚ]	n.	號碼	1	1	初級	
	dial	[ˋdaɪəl]	v.	撥打	3	1	初級	
	reach	[ritʃ]	v.	聯繫	1	1	初級	
	fire	[faɪr]	n.	火災	1	1	初級	◎
	department	[ˋdɪpɑrtmənt]	n.	局、署	1	2	初級	
⓬	use	[juz]	v.	使用	1	1	初級	◎
	collect	[kəˋlɛkt]	adj.	受話人付費的	1	2	初級	◎
⓭	any	[ˋɛnɪ]	adj.	任何的	1	1	初級	
	toll-free	[͵tolˋfri]	adj.	免付電話費的	6			◎
	payphone	[ˋpefon]	n.	公共電話				
⓮	mobile	[ˋmobɪl]	adj.	行動的	2	3	中級	◎
	battery	[ˋbætərɪ]	n.	電池	2	4	中級	
	dead	[dɛd]	n.	電力耗盡的	1	1	初級	
	borrow	[ˋbɑro]	v.	借入	2	2	初級	◎

※「紅字單字」於本單元多句出現，「單字級等分析」僅列在「首次出現句」。

🔊 MP3 127-02 ❶～⓮

❶	大馬路旁都有公共電話。	There are always payphones beside major roads. * payphone（公共電話）= public phone
❷	先撥區域號碼，再撥對方的電話號碼。	Dial the area code first, and then dial the phone number of the person you want to call. * area code（區域碼）、and then（然後）
❸	你可以到便利商店買電話卡。	You can buy phone cards at convenience stores.
❹	電話卡有各種面額。	The value of prepaid phone cards varies.
❺	每一通市內電話一美元。	One dollar per local call. * per（每一…）
❻	電話卡大部分都是一百元的面額。	The value of most prepaid phone cards is 100 dollars.
❼	插入卡片，再直撥電話號碼。	Insert the card and then dial the phone number directly.
❽	你可以用我的手機。	You can use my cell phone.
❾	你可以不投錢，直撥 110 或 119。	You can dial 110 or 119 directly without inserting any coins. * dial＋號碼＋directly（直撥某號碼） * without＋動詞-ing（沒有…）、insert a coin（投幣）
❿	長途電話比較貴。	Long-distance calls are more expensive.
⓫	話機上有特別註明的，才能打國際電話。	Only specially marked phones can be used to make international calls. * specially marked（特殊標示的）、be used to（被用於）
⓬	這台電話不適用這種卡片。	This type of card cannot be used with this phone.
⓭	打國際電話要撥國碼。	When making international calls, you need to dial the country code. * country code（國碼）
⓮	你的電話卡金額不夠了。	You do not have enough value on your calling card. * calling card（電話卡）= (prepaid) phone card

	單字	音標	詞性	意義	字頻	大考	英檢	多益
❶	there	[ðɛr]	adv.	有…	1	1	初級	
	always	[ˋɔlwez]	adv.	總是	1	1	初級	
	payphone	[ˋpeˌfon]	n.	公共電話				
	major	[ˋmedʒɚ]	adj.	主要的	1	3	初級	◎
	road	[rod]	n.	馬路	1	1	初級	
❷	dial	[ˋdaɪəl]	v.	撥打	3	2	初級	◎
	area	[ˋɛrɪə]	n.	地區	1	1	初級	◎

❷	code	[kod]	n.	代碼	1	4	中級	◎
	first	[fɝst]	adv.	首先	1	1	初級	
	then	[ðɛn]	adv.	然後	1	1	初級	
	phone	[fon]	n.	電話	1	2	初級	◎
	number	[ˋnʌmbɚ]	n.	號碼	1	1	初級	◎
	person	[ˋpɝsn]	n.	人	1	1	初級	
	want	[wɑnt]	v.	想要	1	1	初級	◎
	call	[kɔl]	v./n.	打電話/電話	1	1	初級	◎
❸	buy	[baɪ]	v.	購買	1	1	初級	
	card	[kɑrd]	n.	卡片	1	1	初級	◎
	convenience	[kənˋvinjəns]	n.	便利	2	4	中級	◎
	store	[stor]	n.	商店	1	1	初級	
❹	value	[ˋvælju]	n.	金額	1	2	初級	
	prepaid	[priˋped]	adj.	預付的	7			◎
	vary	[ˋvɛrɪ]	v.	有各式各樣	1	3	中級	◎
❺	one	[wʌn]	n.	一	1	1	初級	
	dollar	[ˋdɑlɚ]	n.	美元/元	1	1	初級	◎
	local	[ˋlokl]	adj.	地區性的	1	2	初級	◎
❻	most	[most]	adj.	大部分的	1	1	初級	
❼	insert	[ɪnˋsɝt]	v.	插入	2	4	中級	◎
	directly	[dəˋrɛktlɪ]	adv.	直接	1		中高	
❽	use	[juz]	v.	使用	1	1	初級	◎
	cell	[sɛl]	adj.	cellular（蜂巢式的）縮寫	1	2	初級	
❾	inserting	[ɪnˋsɝtɪŋ]	n.	insert（插入）動名詞	2	4	中級	◎
	any	[ˋɛnɪ]	adj.	任何的	1	1	初級	
	coin	[kɔɪn]	n.	硬幣	2	2	初級	◎
❿	long-distance	[ˋlɔŋˋdɪstəns]	adj.	長途的	3			
	more	[mor]	adv.	更加	1	1	初級	
	expensive	[ɪkˋspɛnsɪv]	adj.	昂貴的	1	2	初級	◎
⓫	only	[onlɪ]	adv.	只有	1	1	初級	
	specially	[ˋspɛʃəlɪ]	adv.	特別地	3		中高	
	marked	[ˋmɑrkt]	p.p.	mark（註明）過去分詞	3	2	中高	◎
	used	[juzd]	p.p.	use（使用）過去分詞	1	1	初級	
	make	[mek]	v.	打電話	1	1	初級	◎
	international	[͵ɪntɚˋnæʃənl]	adj.	國際的	1	2	初級	◎
⓬	this	[ðɪs]	adj.	這個	1	1	初級	
	type	[taɪp]	n.	類型	1	1	初級	◎
⓭	making	[ˋmekɪŋ]	p.pr.	make（打電話）現在分詞	2	1	中高	
	need	[nid]	v.	需要	1	1	初級	◎
	country	[ˋkʌntrɪ]	n.	國家	1	1	初級	
⓮	have	[hæv]	v.	擁有	1	1	初級	
	enough	[əˋnʌf]	adj.	足夠的	1	1	初級	◎
	calling	[ˋkɔlɪŋ]	n.	call（打電話）動名詞	4	1	初級	◎

※「紅字單字」於本單元多句出現，「單字級等分析」僅列在「首次出現句」。

MP3 128-01 ❶～❶

❶	我已經打電話叫計程車了。	I've already called a taxi. * taxi（計程車）= cab
❷	我要到桃園機場。	I want to go to Taoyuan Airport.
❸	我要到這上面的地址。	I want to get to this address. * get to（到達）
❹	這是我住的飯店地址，請帶我到飯店。	This is the address of the hotel I'm staying in; please take me there. * I'm staying in（我目前下榻）
❺	請快一點，我在趕時間。	Please hurry up; I'm really in a rush. * in a rush（趕時間）
❻	請走不會塞車的路。	Please take a road that will avoid traffic. * avoid traffic（避開其他車子）
❼	司機先生，請問你知道怎麼走嗎？	Excuse me sir, do you know how to get there? * excuse me sir（先生，請問一下）
❽	是不是走錯路了？	Did we go the wrong way? * Did we...?（我們剛剛是否…？）
❾	請在下一個紅綠燈讓我下車。	Please let me off at the next traffic light. * let me off（讓我下車）、at（在…地點）
❿	這樣子好像繞了遠路。	It seems like this is the long way.
⓫	請把車轉進第一個巷子。	Please turn down the first alley. * turn down（轉向、轉往）
⓬	計程車資是多少錢起跳？	How much is the initial taxi fare? * initial taxi fare（計程車起跳車資）
⓭	我在前面的巷口下車，謝謝。	I want to get off at the alley up ahead, thanks. * get off（下車）、up ahead（前面的）
⓮	計程車有夜間加成嗎？	Do the cabs have a late night surcharge? * late night surcharge（夜間加成收費）
⓯	請開張收據給我。	May I please have a receipt? * May I (please) have＋物品?（請給我某物品）

	單字	音標	詞性	意義	字頻	大考	英檢	多益
❶	already	[ɔlˋrɛdɪ]	adv.	已經	1	1	初級	◎
	called	[kɔld]	p.p.	call（呼叫）過去分詞	4	1	初級	◎
	taxi	[ˋtæksɪ]	n.	計程車	2	1	初級	
❷	want	[wɑnt]	v.	想要	1	1	初級	◎
	go	[go]	v.	去	1	1	初級	
	Taoyuan	[ˋtɑʊˏjʊɑn]	n.	桃園				
	airport	[ˋɛrˏport]	n.	機場	1	1	初級	◎

❸	get	[gɛt]	v.	抵達/下車	1	1	初級	◎
	this	[ðɪs]	adj./pron.	這個	1	1	初級	
	address	[ə`drɛs]	n.	住址	1	1	初級	◎
❹	hotel	[ho`tɛl]	n.	飯店	1	2	初級	◎
	staying	[`steɪŋ]	p.pr.	stay（暫留）現在分詞	1	1	初級	◎
	please	[pliz]	adv.	請…	1	1	初級	
	take	[tek]	v.	帶領	1	1	初級	◎
	there	[ðɛr]	adv.	那裡	1	1	初級	
❺	hurry	[`hɜɪ]	v.	趕快	2	2	初級	◎
	up	[ʌp]	adv.	增強、增大/向前	1	1	初級	
	really	[`rɪəlɪ]	adv.	真的	1		初級	
	rush	[rʌʃ]	n.	急忙、緊急	1	2	初級	◎
❻	road	[rod]	n.	路	1	1	初級	
	avoid	[ə`vɔɪd]	v.	避免	1	2	初級	◎
	traffic	[`træfɪk]	n.	車流量/交通	1	2	初級	◎
❼	excuse	[ɪk`skjuz]	v.	請問	2	2	初級	◎
	sir	[sɜ]	n.	先生	1	1	初級	
	know	[no]	v.	知道	1	1	初級	◎
❽	wrong	[rɔŋ]	adj.	錯誤的	1	1	初級	◎
	way	[we]	n.	路	1	1	初級	
❾	let	[lɛt]	v.	讓…	1	1	初級	
	off	[ɔf]	adv.	下來	1	1	初級	
	next	[nɛkst]	adj.	下一個	1	1	初級	
	light	[laɪt]	n.	燈	1	1	初級	
❿	seem	[sim]	v.	似乎	1	1	初級	◎
	long	[lɔŋ]	adj.	長的	1	1	初級	
⓫	turn	[tɜn]	v.	轉彎	1	1	初級	◎
	first	[fɜst]	adj.	第一個	1	1	初級	
	alley	[`ælɪ]	n.	巷子	2	3	中級	
⓬	much	[mʌtʃ]	adj.	許多的	1	1	初級	
	initial	[ɪ`nɪʃəl]	adj.	起始的	1	4	中級	◎
	fare	[fɛr]	n.	車資	2	3	中級	◎
⓭	ahead	[ə`hɛd]	adv.	向前	1	1	初級	◎
	thanks	[θæŋks]	n.	thank（感謝）複數	1			
⓮	cab	[kæb]	n.	計程車	2	1		◎
	have	[hæv]	v.	擁有	1	1	初級	
	late	[let]	adj.	晚的	1	1	初級	
	night	[naɪt]	n.	夜晚	1	1	初級	
	surcharge	[`sɜ.tʃɑrdʒ]	n.	加成收費	6			
⓯	receipt	[rɪ`sit]	n.	收據	3	3	中級	◎

※「紅字單字」於本單元多句出現，「單字級等分析」僅列在「首次出現句」。

🔊 MP3 128-02 ❶～⓲

❶	請問您要去哪裡？	Where would you like to go?
❷	你有飯店的名片借我看一下嗎？	Could I have a look at the hotel's business card? * **Could I...?**（我是否能…？）、**have a look**（看一下）
❸	是在火車站附近嗎？	Is it near the train station?
❹	要不要繞到對面？	Should I turn around to the other side? * **turn around**（調頭）、**to the other side**（往另一邊）
❺	想走哪一條路過去？	What road would you like to take to get there? * **What road...?**（哪條路…？）、**get there**（到達那裡）
❻	這條巷子太窄，車子進不去。	This alley is too narrow; the car can't fit through it.　* **fit through**（通過、行駛過）
❼	你知道怎麼走嗎？	Do you know how to get there?
❽	要在這裡下車嗎？	Do you want to get off here?　* **get off**（下車）
❾	我知道在哪裡。	I know where it is.
❿	這條路是捷徑。	This way is a shortcut.
⓫	走這條路比較不塞車。	There will be less traffic this way. * **there will be**（將會有）、**less traffic**（較少車子） * 此句用「未來簡單式」（...will...）表示 　「根據直覺預測未來發生的事」。
⓬	我找錢給你。	Let me give you your change.
⓭	前面就到了。	It is just ahead.
⓮	快不了，塞車了。	There's a traffic jam; we can't go any faster. * **traffic jam**（塞車）、**go faster**（行駛更快）
⓯	尖峰時間，到處都塞車。	It is rush hour; there is traffic everywhere. * **rush hour**（尖峰時間）
⓰	需要收據嗎？	Need a receipt?
⓱	應該就在這附近了。	It should be around here.
⓲	你要不要打電話問朋友怎麼走？	Would you like to call your friend to ask directions?　* **ask directions**（問路）

	單字	音標	詞性	意義	字頻	大考	英檢	多益
❶	like	[laɪk]	v.	想要	1	1	初級	
	go	[go]	v.	去/變為	1	1	初級	
❷	have	[hæv]	v.	執行、做某動作	1	1	初級	

❷	look	[lʊk]	n.	看一下	1	1	初級	
	hotel	[hoˋtɛl]	n.	飯店	1	2	初級	
	business	[ˋbɪznɪs]	n.	商業、業務	1	2	初級	◎
	card	[kɑrd]	n.	卡片	1	1	初級	
❸	train	[tren]	n.	火車	1	1	初級	
	station	[ˋsteʃən]	n.	車站	1	1	初級	◎
❹	turn	[tɝn]	v.	轉彎	1	1	初級	◎
	around	[əˋraʊnd]	adv.	向相反方向	1	1	初級	
	other	[ˋʌðɚ]	adj.	其他的	1	1	初級	
	side	[saɪd]	n.	邊、側	1	1	初級	
❺	road	[rod]	n.	路	1	1	初級	
	take	[tek]	v.	行駛	1	1	初級	◎
	get	[gɪv]	v.	抵達/下車	1	1	初級	◎
	there	[ðɛr]	n./adv.	那裡/有…	1	1	初級	
❻	this	[ðɪs]	adj.	這個	1	1	初級	
	alley	[ˋælɪ]	n.	巷子	2	3	中級	
	too	[tu]	adv.	過於	1	1	初級	
	narrow	[ˋnæro]	adj.	窄的	1	2	初級	◎
	car	[kɑr]	n.	車子	1	1	初級	◎
	fit	[fɪt]	v.	適合	1	2	初級	◎
❼	know	[no]	v.	知道	1	1	初級	
❽	want	[wɑnt]	v.	想要	1	1	初級	◎
	off	[ɔf]	adv.	下來	1	1	初級	
	here	[hɪr]	adv./n.	這裡	1	1	初級	
❿	way	[we]	n.	路	1	1	初級	
	shortcut	[ˋʃɔrt.kʌt]	n.	捷徑	4		中級	
⓫	less	[lɛs]	adj.	較少的	1	1	初級	
	traffic	[ˋtræfɪk]	n.	車子	1	2	初級	◎
⓬	let	[lɛt]	v.	讓…	1	1	初級	
	give	[gɪv]	v.	給予	1	1	初級	
	change	[tʃendʒ]	n.	找零的錢	1	2	初級	◎
⓭	just	[dʒʌst]	adv.	就…	1	1	初級	
	ahead	[əˋhɛd]	adv.	向前	1	1	初級	◎
⓮	jam	[dʒæm]	n.	塞車	2	2	初級	
	any	[ˋɛnɪ]	adv.	絲毫、若干	1	1	初級	
	faster	[ˋfæstɚ]	adv.	fast（快速地）比較級	2			
⓯	rush	[rʌʃ]	adj.	尖峰的	1	2	初級	◎
	hour	[aʊr]	n.	時間	1	1	初級	
	everywhere	[ˋɛvrɪ.hwɛr]	adv.	到處	1		初級	
⓰	need	[nid]	v.	需要	1	1	初級	◎
	receipt	[rɪˋsit]	n.	收據	3	3	中級	◎
⓲	call	[kɔl]	v.	打電話	1	1	初級	◎
	friend	[frɛnd]	n.	朋友	1	1	初級	
	ask	[æsk]	v.	尋找	1	1	初級	
	direction	[dəˋrɛkʃən]	n.	方向	1	2	初級	◎

※「紅字單字」於本單元多句出現，「單字級等分析」僅列在「首次出現句」。

129 接電話。

🔊 MP3 129-01 ❶ ～ ❼

❶	喂。	Hello.
❷	我就是。	Speaking. = This is she / he.
❸	請問您是哪一位？	May I ask who is calling? = May I ask who this is, please?
❹	喂，我是約翰。	Hello, this is John. * this is＋某人（我是某人，電話用語）
❺	你好，請問你要找哪一位？	Hello, who are you looking for? * be looking for（正在尋找）
❻	我們有兩位林小姐。	We have two Miss Lins here.
❼	你要找哪一位林小姐？	Which Miss Lin are you calling for? * be calling for（來電尋找…）
❽	我幫你把電話轉給她。	I will transfer your call to her. = I will put you through to her. * transfer one's call to＋某人（轉接給某人） * put＋某人＋through（幫某人轉接）
❾	你要找陳小姐是嗎？	You are looking for Miss Chen, right?
❿	抱歉，我現在不方便講電話。	Sorry; I can't take your call right now. * take one's call（接聽某人電話）
⓫	你介意再說一次剛剛的話嗎？	Would you mind repeating what you just said? * Would you mind＋動詞-ing?（你是否介意…？） * what you just said（你剛才說的話）
⓬	請稍等。	Please wait a moment. = Hold on, please.
⓭	我幫你轉客服部。	I will transfer your call to the customer service department.
⓮	抱歉，我聽不清楚你說的話。	Excuse me, I can't hear you clearly. * hear＋某人＋clearly（聽清楚某人講話）
⓯	等一下回你電話。	I'll call you back later. = I'll give you a call later.
⓰	我在講另外一支電話。	I am on another call right now. * on another call（在另一通電話中）
⓱	這裡是 B 公司，有什麼可以為您服務的嗎？	This is B Company, how may I help you? * this is＋某公司（這裡是某公司，電話用語）

	單字	音標	詞性	意義	字頻	大考	英檢	多益
❶	hello	[hə`lo]	int.	喂	1	1	初級	
❷	speaking	[`spikɪŋ]	p.pr.	speak（說話）現在分詞	5	1	初級	
	this	[ðɪs]	pron.	這是	1	1	初級	
❸	ask	[æsk]	v.	詢問	1	1	初級	
	calling	[`kɔlɪŋ]	p.pr.	call（打電話）現在分詞	4	1	初級	◎
	please	[pliz]	adv.	請…	1	1	初級	
❺	looking	[`lʊkɪŋ]	p.pr.	look（尋找）現在分詞	5	1	初級	
❻	have	[hæv]	v.	擁有	1	1	初級	
	two	[tu]	n.	兩個	1	1	初級	
	Miss	[mɪs]	n.	小姐	1	1	初級	
	here	[hɪr]	adv.	這裡	1	1	初級	
❽	transfer	[træns`fɝ]	v.	轉接	1	4	中級	◎
	call	[kɔl]	n./v.	電話/打電話	1	1	初級	◎
	put	[pʊt]	v.	為…接通	1	1	初級	
	through	[θru]	adv.	轉至	1	2	初級	◎
❾	right	[raɪt]	int./ adv.	是嗎/正值	1	1	初級	
❿	sorry	[`sɔrɪ]	adj.	抱歉的	1	1	初級	
	take	[tek]	v.	接聽	1	1	初級	◎
	now	[naʊ]	adv.	現在	1	1	初級	
⓫	mind	[maɪnd]	v.	介意	1	1	初級	◎
	repeating	[rɪ`pitɪŋ]	n.	repeat（複述）動名詞	6	2	初級	
	just	[dʒʌst]	adv.	剛剛	1	1	初級	
	said	[sɛd]	p.t.	say（說）過去式	4	1	初級	
⓬	wait	[wet]	v.	等待	1	1	初級	◎
	moment	[`momənt]	n.	片刻	1	1	初級	
	hold	[hold]	v.	等候	1	1	初級	
⓭	customer	[`kʌstəmɚ]	n.	客戶	1	2	初級	◎
	service	[`sɝvɪs]	n.	服務	1	1	初級	◎
	department	[dɪ`pɑrtmənt]	n.	部門	1	2	初級	◎
⓮	excuse	[ɪk`skjuz]	v.	請問	2	2	初級	◎
	hear	[hɪr]	v.	聽見	1	1	初級	
	clearly	[`klɪrlɪ]	adv.	清楚地	1			◎
⓯	back	[bæk]	adv.	返回	1	1	初級	◎
	later	[letɚ]	adv.	稍後	1		初級	
	give	[gɪv]	v.	給予	1	1	初級	
⓰	another	[ə`nʌðɚ]	adj.	另一個	1	1		
⓱	company	[`kʌmpənɪ]	n.	公司	1	2	初級	◎
	help	[hɛlp]	v.	協助	1	1	初級	

※「紅字單字」於本單元多句出現，「單字級等分析」僅列在「首次出現句」。

MP3 129-02 ❶～❶

❶	可以麻煩史密斯先生聽電話嗎？	May I speak to Mr. Smith? * May I speak to＋某人？（麻煩請找某人，電話用語） ＝ I would like to speak to＋某人.
❷	喂，我是湯姆。	Hello, this is Tom.
❸	你好，請問琳達在嗎？	Hello, is Linda there?
❹	大衛在嗎？	Is David there?
❺	請幫我轉客服部。	Please transfer me to the customer service department. * customer service department（客服部） * human resources department（人資部） * marketing department（行銷部） * sales department（業務部）
❻	我想跟王先生講話。	I would like to speak to Mr. Wang.
❼	喂，比利嗎？	Hello, Billy, is that you?
❽	我是他同事。	I am his colleague. * classmate（同學）、friend（朋友）
❾	請接分機 15。	Extension 15, please.
❿	電話可以借我用一下嗎？	May I use your phone? * May I＋動詞…?（請問我可以…嗎）
⓫	你在忙嗎？	Are you busy right now?
⓬	我是 XYZ 公司的吳大衛。	This is David Wu of XYZ Company.
⓭	我有急事要找林先生。	I would like to speak to Mr. Lin regarding an urgent matter. * regarding（關於）、urgent matter（要緊的事情）
⓮	我要找你們老闆。	I would like to speak to your boss.
⓯	我把你吵醒了嗎？	Did I wake you up? ＝ Did I wake you?
⓰	你剛剛打電話找我嗎？	Did you just call me? * Did you...?（你剛才有…嗎）
⓱	希望我沒有打擾到你。	I hope that I didn't disturb you.
⓲	很抱歉這麼晚打電話給你。	I am very sorry for calling you so late. * late（時間晚的）可替換為：early（時間早的）

	單字	音標	詞性	意義	字頻	大考	英檢	多益
❶	speak	[spik]	v.	說話	1	1	初級	
	Mr.	[ˋmɪstɚ]	n.	先生		1	初級	
❷	hello	[həˋlo]	int.	喂	1	1	初級	
	this	[ðɪs]	pron.	這是	1	1	初級	
❸	there	[ðɛr]	adv.	那裡	1	1	初級	
❺	please	[pliz]	adv.	請…	1	1	初級	
	transfer	[trænsˋfɚ]	v.	轉接	1	4	中級	◎
	customer	[ˋkʌstəmɚ]	n.	客戶	1	2	初級	◎
	service	[ˋsɚvɪs]	n.	服務	1	1	初級	◎
	department	[dɪˋpɑrtmənt]	n.	部門	1	2	初級	◎
❻	like	[laɪk]	v.	想要	1	1	初級	
❼	that	[ðæt]	pron.	那位	1	1	初級	
❽	colleague	[ˋkɑlig]	n.	同事	1	5	中級	◎
❾	extension	[ɪkˋstɛnʃən]	n.	分機	2	5	中級	◎
❿	use	[juz]	n.	使用	1	1	初級	
	phone	[fon]	n.	電話	1	2	初級	◎
⓫	busy	[ˋbɪzɪ]	adj.	忙碌的	1	1	初級	
	right	[raɪt]	adv.	正值	1	1	初級	
	now	[naʊ]	adv.	現在	1	1	初級	
⓬	company	[ˋkʌmpənɪ]	n.	公司	1	2	初級	◎
⓭	urgent	[ˋɚdʒənt]	adj.	要緊的	2	4	中級	◎
	matter	[ˋmætɚ]	n.	事情	1	1	初級	◎
⓮	boss	[bɔs]	n.	老闆	1	1	初級	
⓯	wake	[wek]	v.	喚醒	1	2	初級	
	up	[ʌp]	adv.	起來	1	1	初級	
⓰	just	[dʒʌst]	adv.	剛剛	1	1	初級	
	call	[kɔl]	v.	打電話	1	1	初級	◎
⓱	hope	[hop]	v.	希望	1	1	初級	
	disturb	[dɪsˋtɚb]	v.	打擾	2	4	中級	◎
⓲	very	[ˋvɛrɪ]	adv.	十分	1	1	初級	
	sorry	[ˋsɑrɪ]	adj.	抱歉	1	1	初級	
	calling	[ˋkɔlɪŋ]	n.	call（打電話）動名詞	4	1	初級	◎
	so	[so]	adv.	這麼	1	1	初級	
	late	[let]	adv.	晚地	1	1	初級	◎

※「紅字單字」於本單元多句出現，「單字級等分析」僅列在「首次出現句」。

130 告知對方打錯電話。

🔊 MP3 130-01 ❶～⓰

❶	你可能撥錯電話號碼了。	You might have the wrong number. * might（可能）、have the wrong number（打錯電話）
❷	沒有這個人。	There is nobody by that name here. * by＋名字（叫…名字）
❸	這支電話是我新申請的。	I've only recently started using this number. * have recently started（最近開始） * start＋動詞-ing（開始…）
❹	你說你要找誰？	Who did you say you are calling? * Who did you say...?（你剛才說是誰…？）
❺	你打錯了。	You have the wrong number.
❻	我們公司沒有林小姐。	There is no Miss Lin in our company. * there is no...（沒有…）
❼	我們這邊是住家。	This is a residential number. * residential（住家的）可替換為：business（公司）
❽	號碼沒錯，但沒有你要找的人。	The number you dialed is correct, but there's nobody by that name here. * the number you dialed（你剛才撥的號碼）
❾	她已經離職了。	She is no longer working here. * no longer＋動詞-ing（不再…）
❿	他已經不使用這個電話號碼了。	He doesn't use this number anymore. = He is no longer using this number.
⓫	他已經不住在這裡了。	He doesn't live here anymore.
⓬	他的分機號碼改了。	His extension number has changed. * 此句用「現在完成式」（...has changed）表示 　「過去某時點發生某事，且結果持續到現在」。
⓭	我不是你要找的人。	I am not the person you are looking for. * be looking for（正在尋找）
⓮	林小姐的分機是 17。	Miss Lin's extension number is 17. * extension number（分機號碼） * switchboard（電話總機）
⓯	找他要打另一支電話號碼。	You'll have to call another number to speak to him.　* have to（必須）
⓰	你說的號碼完全不對。	The number you said is completely wrong.

	單字	音標	詞性	意義	字頻	大考	英檢	多益
❶	have	[hæv]	v.	擁有/必須	1	1	初級	
	wrong	[rɔŋ]	adj.	錯誤的	1	1	初級	◎
	number	[ˋnʌmbɚ]	n.	號碼	1	1	初級	◎
❷	there	[ðɛr]	adv.	有…	1	1	初級	
	nobody	[ˋnobɑdɪ]	pron.	沒有人	1	2	初級	
	that	[ðæt]	adj.	那個	1	1	初級	
	name	[nem]	n.	名字	1	1	初級	◎
	here	[hɪr]	adv.	這裡	1	1	初級	
❸	only	[ˋonlɪ]	adv.	剛剛	1	1	初級	
	recently	[ˋrisntlɪ]	adv.	最近	1		初級	
	started	[ˋstɑrtɪd]	p.p.	start（開始）過去分詞	1	1	初級	
	using	[ˋjuzɪŋ]	n.	use（使用）動名詞	1	1	初級	◎
	this	[ðɪs]	adj./pron.	這個	1	1	初級	
❹	say	[se]	v.	說	1	1	初級	
	calling	[ˋkɔlɪŋ]	p.pr.	call（打電話）現在分詞	4	1	初級	◎
❻	Miss	[mɪs]	n.	小姐	1	1	初級	
	company	[ˋkʌmpənɪ]	n.	公司	1	2	初級	◎
❼	residential	[ˌrɛzəˋdɛnʃəl]	adj.	居住的	2	6	**中高**	◎
❽	dialed	[ˋdaɪəld]	p.t.	dial（撥打）過去式	3	2	初級	◎
	correct	[kəˋrɛkt]	adj.	正確的	1	1	初級	◎
❾	longer	[ˋlɔŋgɚ]	adv.	（與 no 連用）不再	1	1	初級	
	working	[ˋwɝkɪŋ]	p.pr.	work（工作）現在分詞	2	1	**中級**	◎
❿	use	[juz]	v.	使用	1	1	初級	
	anymore	[ˋɛnɪmor]	adv.	不再	1		**中高**	
	using	[ˋjuzɪŋ]	p.pr.	use（使用）現在分詞	1	1	初級	◎
⓫	live	[lɪv]	v.	居住	1	1	初級	
⓬	extension	[ɪkˋstɛnʃən]	n.	分機	2	5	**中級**	◎
	changed	[tʃendʒd]	p.p.	change（更換）過去分詞	4	2	初級	◎
⓭	person	[ˋpɝsn]	n.	人	1	1	初級	
	looking	[ˋlʊkɪŋ]	p.pr.	look（尋找）現在分詞	5	1	初級	
⓯	call	[kɔl]	v.	打電話	1	1	初級	◎
	another	[əˋnʌðɚ]	adj.	另一個	1	1		
	speak	[spik]	v.	說話	1	1	初級	
⓰	said	[sɛd]	p.t.	say（說）	4	1	初級	
	completely	[kəmˋplitlɪ]	adv.	完全地	1			

※「紅字單字」於本單元多句出現，「單字級等分析」僅列在「首次出現句」。

130 確認是否打錯電話。

❶	請問你的電話號碼是幾號？	Sorry, may I ask what your phone number is? * **May I sak...?**（請問…）
❷	你撥打幾號？	What number did you dial? * **What number did you...?**（你剛才…的是幾號？）
❸	請問你用這支號碼多久了？	Excuse me, how long have you been using this phone number? * **How long have you been using...?**（你持續用了多久…）
❹	你這支電話是最近申請的嗎？	Have you just recently started using this number?
❺	你那邊是 ABC 公司嗎？	Is this the ABC company? * **Is this...?**（你那邊是…嗎，電話用語）
❻	你確定你沒撥錯號碼？	Are you sure that you didn't dial the wrong number? * **be sure that**＋子句（確信…）
❼	你的電話號碼是 1234-1234 嗎？	Is your phone number 1234-1234?
❽	可以跟你確認一下電話號碼嗎？	May I double-check the phone number with you? * **May I...?**（請問我可以…嗎） * **double-check with**＋某人（跟…確認）
❾	請問是黃先生府上嗎？	Excuse me, is this the Huangs' residence? * **the**＋某姓氏＋**s'**（某姓氏一家人）
❿	請問是林小姐嗎？	Excuse me, is this Miss Lin?
⓫	喂，剛剛有人打我手機嗎？	Hello, did someone just call my mobile phone? * **Did someone**＋動詞**...?**（剛才是否有某人…？） * **mobile phone**（手機）
⓬	喂，客服專線是這支號碼嗎？	Hello, is this the customer service number? * **customer service number**（客服專線）
⓭	這個分機不是陳小姐的嗎？	Isn't this Miss Chen's extension number? * **extension number**（分機號碼）
⓮	我打錯了嗎？怎麼是你接電話？	Did I dial the wrong number? How come it is you who are answering the phone? * **How come...?**（怎麼會…？） * **answer the phone**（接聽電話）= pick up the phone * **hang up the phone**（掛斷電話）= put down the phone * **be on the phone**（在電話中） * **slam down the phone**（怒掛電話）

	單字	音標	詞性	意義	字頻	大考	英檢	多益
❶	sorry	[ˋsɑrɪ]	adj.	抱歉的	1	1	初級	
	ask	[æsk]	v.	詢問	1	1	初級	
	phone	[fon]	n.	電話	1	2	初級	◎
	number	[ˋnʌmbɚ]	n.	號碼/專線	1	1	初級	◎
❷	dial	[ˋdaɪəl]	v.	撥打	3	2	初級	◎
❸	excuse	[ɪkˋskjuz]	v.	請問	2	2	初級	◎
	long	[lɔŋ]	adv.	長久地	1	1	初級	
	using	[ˋjuzɪŋ]	p.pr.	use（使用）現在分詞	1	1	初級	◎
	this	[ðɪs]	adj./pron.	這個	1	1	初級	
❹	just	[dʒʌst]	adv.	剛剛	1	1	初級	
	recently	[ˋrisntlɪ]	adv.	最近	1		初級	
	started	[ˋstɑrtɪd]	p.p.	start（開始）過去分詞	1	1	初級	
	using	[ˋjuzɪŋ]	n.	use（使用）動名詞	1	1	初級	◎
❺	company	[ˋkʌmpənɪ]	n.	公司	1	2	初級	◎
❻	sure	[ʃur]	adj.	確信的	1	1	初級	
	wrong	[rɔŋ]	adj.	錯誤的	1	1	初級	◎
❽	double-check	[ˋdʌblˋtʃɛk]	v.	確認				
❾	residence	[ˋrɛzədəns]	n.	住家	2	5	中級	◎
❿	Miss	[mɪs]	n.	小姐	1	1	初級	
⓫	hello	[həˋlo]	int.	喂	1	1	初級	
	someone	[ˋsʌm.wʌn]	pron.	某個人	1	1	初級	
	call	[kɔl]	v.	打電話	1	1	初級	◎
	mobile	[ˋmobɪl]	adj.	行動的	2	3	中級	◎
⓬	customer	[ˋkʌstəmɚ]	n.	客戶	1	2	初級	◎
	service	[ˋsɝvɪs]	n.	服務	1	1	初級	◎
⓭	extension	[ɪkˋstɛnʃən]	n.	分機	2	5	中級	◎
⓮	come	[kʌm]	v.	（與how連用）怎麼會	1	1	初級	
	answering	[ˋænsɚɪŋ]	p.pr.	answer（接聽）現在分詞	3	1	初級	

※「紅字單字」於本單元多句出現，「單字級等分析」僅列在「首次出現句」。

🔊 MP3 131-01 ❶～⓰

❶	他現在不方便接電話。	He can't come to the phone right now. * **can't come to the phone**（不方便接電話）
❷	你要在線上等候嗎？	Would you like to stay on the line? * **stay on the line**（在電話線上等候）= hold
❸	他今天休假。	He is taking a day off today. * **take a day off**（請一天假） * 此句用「現在進行式」（...is taking...）表示「現階段發生的事」。
❹	他現在在開會。	He is in a meeting right now.
❺	琳達不在。	Linda is not here right now.
❻	我請他回你電話。	I will ask him to call you back. * **call back**（回電） * 此句用「未來簡單式」（...will...）表示「有意願做的事」。
❼	她現在在電話中。	She is on the phone right now. * **on the phone**（在電話中）
❽	林先生還沒有進公司。	Mr. Lin hasn't come into the office yet. * **come into the office**（進公司）
❾	愛咪還沒回來。	Amy hasn't come back yet.
❿	你要找的人不在座位上。	The person you're looking for is not at his desk right now. * **at one's desk**（在座位上）
⓫	請問他幾點會進公司？	When will he come in?
⓬	他外出了，他出去拜訪客戶了。	He is out; he went to see some clients. * **see a client**（拜訪客戶）= visit a client
⓭	他什麼時候回來？	When will he be back?
⓮	李先生這個禮拜出差。	Mr. Lee is going on a business trip this week. * **go on a business trip**（出差）
⓯	有什麼辦法可以聯絡到他嗎？	Is there any way to contact him? * **Is there＋名詞...?**（有…嗎） * **contact**（聯絡）= reach、get
⓰	他大概再一個小時才會回來。	He probably will be back in another hour. * **probably will＋動詞原形**（可能之後會…） * **in another hour**（一小時以後）

	單字	音標	詞性	意義	字頻	大考	英檢	多益
❶	come	[kʌm]	v.	前去接聽/前來	1	1	初級	
	phone	[fon]	n.	電話	1	2	初級	◎
	right	[raɪt]	adv.	正值	1	1	初級	
	now	[naʊ]	adv.	現在	1	1	初級	
❷	like	[laɪk]	v.	想要	1	1	初級	
	stay	[ste]	v.	等候	1	1	初級	◎
	line	[laɪn]	n.	線上	1	1	初級	◎
❸	taking	[ˈtekɪŋ]	p.pr.	take（從事）現在分詞	4			
	day	[de]	n.	一日	1	1	初級	
	off	[ɔf]	adj.	休假的	1	1	初級	
	today	[təˈde]	adv.	今天	1	1	初級	◎
❹	meeting	[ˈmitɪŋ]	n.	會議	1	2	初級	
❺	here	[hɪr]	adv.	這裡	1	1	初級	
❻	ask	[æsk]	v.	請求	1	1	初級	
	call	[kɔl]	v.	打電話	1	1	初級	◎
	back	[bæk]	adv. /adj.	返回	1	1	初級	◎
❽	come	[kʌm]	p.p.	come（前來）過去分詞	1	1	初級	
	office	[ˈɔfɪs]	n.	公司	1	1	初級	◎
	yet	[jɛt]	adv.	尚未	1	1	初級	◎
❿	person	[ˈpɜsn]	n.	人	1	1	初級	
	looking	[ˈlʊkɪŋ]	p.pr.	look（尋找）現在分詞	5	1	初級	
	desk	[dɛsk]	n.	座位	1	1	初級	◎
⓬	out	[aʊt]	adj.	不在辦公室	1	1	初級	
	went	[wɛnt]	p.t.	go（離開）過去式	1	1	初級	
	see	[si]	v.	拜訪	1	1	初級	
	some	[sʌm]	adj.	一些	1	1	初級	
	client	[ˈklaɪənt]	n.	客戶	1	3	中級	◎
⓮	going	[ˈɡoɪŋ]	p.pr.	go（去）現在分詞	4	1	初級	
	business	[ˈbɪznɪs]	n.	商業、商務	1	2	初級	◎
	trip	[trɪp]	n.	旅行	1	1	初級	◎
	this	[ðɪs]	adj.	這個	1	1	初級	
	week	[wik]	n.	禮拜	1	1	初級	
⓯	there	[ðɛr]	adv.	有…	1	1	初級	
	any	[ˈɛnɪ]	adj.	任何的	1	1	初級	
	way	[we]	n.	方式	1	1	初級	
	contact	[kənˈtækt]	v.	聯繫	1	2	初級	◎
⓰	probably	[ˈprɑbəblɪ]	adv.	可能	1		初級	◎
	another	[əˈnʌðə]	adj.	另一個	1	1		
	hour	[aʊr]	n.	小時	1	1	初級	

※「紅字單字」於本單元多句出現，「單字級等分析」僅列在「首次出現句」。

131 處理對方留言。

🔊 MP3 131-02 ❶～❹

❶	你要請他回電嗎？	Would you like to have him call you back? * **Would you like to...?**（你想要…？） * **have＋某人＋動詞原形**（請求某人做某事） * **call＋某人＋back**（回電給某人） 　= **return one's call**
❷	請問你找他有什麼事情嗎？	May I ask what you are calling him about? * **May I ask...?**（請問…？）、**about**（關於）
❸	有什麼我可以為你轉達的嗎？	Is there any message I can pass on for you? * **pass on**（轉達）= **relay**
❹	要我告訴湯姆你找他嗎？	Would you like me to tell Tom that you called? * **tell＋某人＋that＋子句**（告訴某人…）
❺	你要留言嗎？	Would you like to leave a message? * **leave a message**（留下留言）
❻	請問你哪裡找？	May I ask who is calling?
❼	我會幫你轉告他。	I will pass your message on to him. = I will let him know. * **pass one's message on**（轉達留言）、**to**（向、給）
❽	你方便留一下聯絡方式嗎？	Would you like to leave a contact number? * **contact number**（聯絡電話）
❾	請告訴我你的電話號碼。	Please tell me your phone number. * **tell＋某人＋名詞**（告訴某人…）
❿	我等一下要外出，請她打我手機。	I'm going out in a minute; please tell her to call my mobile number. * **be going out**（現在要外出）、**in a minute**（馬上）
⓫	你可以請他回電嗎？	Could you have him call me back?
⓬	我是約翰的母親，請告訴他我找他。	This is John's mother; please tell him that I called.
⓭	請琳達盡快回電給我。	Please have Linda give me a call as soon as possible. * **give me a call**（給我電話、打給我） * **as soon as possible**（儘快）
⓮	他多晚回我電話都沒關係。	It does not matter how late he returns my call. * **it does not matter＋子句**（不要緊…、沒關係…） 　= **it is no matter＋子句**

572

	單字	音標	詞性	意義	字頻	大考	英檢	多益
❶	like	[laɪk]	v.	想要	1	1	初級	
	have	[hæv]	v.	使某人…	1	1	初級	
	call	[kɔl]	v./n.	打電話	1	1	初級	◎
	back	[bæk]	adv.	返回	1	1	初級	
❷	ask	[æsk]	v.	詢問	1	1	初級	
	calling	[`kɔlɪŋ]	p.pr.	call（打電話）現在分詞	4	1	初級	◎
❸	there	[ðɛr]	adv.	有…	1	1	初級	
	any	[`ɛnɪ]	adj.	任何的	1	1	初級	
	message	[`mɛsɪdʒ]	n.	留言	1	2	初級	◎
	pass	[pæs]	v.	轉達	1	1	初級	◎
❹	tell	[tɛl]	v.	告訴	1	1	初級	
	called	[kɔld]	p.t.	call（打電話）過去式	4	1	初級	◎
❺	leave	[liv]	v.	留下	1	1	初級	◎
❼	let	[lɛt]	v.	讓…	1	1	初級	
	know	[no]	v.	知道	1	1	初級	◎
❽	contact	[`kɑntækt]	n.	聯絡	1	2	初級	◎
	number	[`nʌmbɚ]	n.	號碼	1	1	初級	◎
❾	please	[pliz]	adv.	請…	1	1	初級	
	phone	[fon]	n.	電話	1	2	初級	◎
❿	going	[`goɪŋ]	p.pr.	go（去、離開）現在分詞	4	1	初級	
	out	[aut]	adv.	外出	1	1	初級	
	minute	[`mɪnɪt]	n.	片刻	1	1	初級	◎
	mobile	[`mobɪl]	adj.	行動的	2	3	中級	◎
⓬	this	[ðɪs]	pron.	這是	1	1	初級	
	mother	[`mʌðɚ]	n.	母親	1	1	初級	
⓭	give	[gɪv]	v.	給予	1	1	初級	
	soon	[sun]	adv.	早、快	1	1	初級	
	possible	[`pɑsəbl]	adv.	可能地	1	1	初級	◎
⓮	matter	[`mætɚ]	v.	要緊	1	1	初級	◎
	late	[let]	adv.	晚地	1	1	初級	◎
	return	[rɪ`tɝn]	v.	回覆	1	1	初級	◎

※「紅字單字」於本單元多句出現，「單字級等分析」僅列在「首次出現句」。

132 轉達有人來電。（1）

❶	林先生剛剛有回你電話。	Mr. Lin just called you back. * call＋某人＋back（回電給某人） ＝ return one's call
❷	你不在座位時，手機有響。	Your mobile phone rang while you were away from your desk. * mobile phone（手機）＝ cell phone * away from one's desk（離開座位）
❸	剛剛有人打來找你。	Someone just called you.
❹	我不在時有人打來嗎？	Did anyone call while I was out? * Did anyone＋動詞...?（剛才有誰…嗎） * while I was out（我外出時） * 此句用「過去簡單式問句」（Did...?） 表示「在過去是否發生某事？」。
❺	你母親要你回電話給她。	Your mother wants you to call her back. * want＋某人＋to＋動詞原形（想要某人…）
❻	陳先生現在在 1 線電話上。	Mr. Chen is on line one now. * on line＋數字（在電話的第…線上） * on the phone（在電話中） * leave a phone off the hook（無將聽筒掛上） * The number is engaged now.（此電話正通話中）
❼	這是林小姐的電話號碼。	This is Miss Lin's phone number. * phone number（電話號碼）
❽	林先生請你撥他手機。	Mr. Lin asked you to call his cell number. * ask＋某人＋to＋動詞原形（要求某人…） * call one's cell number（打手機給某人） * cell number（手機號碼）＝ mobile number
❾	你不在時，有個女生打電話找你。	A woman called for you while you were out. * call for＋某人（來電找某人） * 此句用「過去簡單式」（...called...） 表示「發生在過去的事」。
❿	一堆人留言要你回電話。	A bunch of people left messages for you to call them back. * a bunch of＋人（一群人、一票人） * leave a message for＋某人（留下留言給某人）

	單字	音標	詞性	意義	字頻	大考	英檢	多益
❶	Mr.	[ˋmɪstɚ]	n.	先生		1	初級	
	just	[dʒʌst]	adv.	剛剛	1	1	初級	
	called	[kɔld]	p.t.	call（打電話）過去式	4	1	初級	◎
	back	[bæk]	adv.	返回	1	1	初級	◎
❷	mobile	[ˋmobɪl]	adj.	行動的	2	3	中級	◎
	phone	[fon]	n.	電話	1	2	初級	◎
	rang	[ræŋ]	p.t.	ring（鈴聲響起）過去式	1	1	初級	
	away	[əˋwe]	adj.	離開的	1	1	初級	
	desk	[dɛsk]	n.	座位	1	1	初級	◎
❸	someone	[ˋsʌm͵wʌn]	pron.	某個人	1	1	初級	
❹	anyone	[ˋɛnɪ͵wʌn]	pron.	任何人	1	2	初級	
	call	[kɔl]	v.	打電話	1	1	初級	◎
	out	[aʊt]	adj.	外出的、不在的	1	1	初級	
❺	mother	[ˋmʌðɚ]	n.	母親	1	1	初級	
	want	[wɑnt]	v.	想要	1	1	初級	◎
❻	line	[laɪn]	n.	線上	1	1	初級	◎
	one	[wʌn]	n.	一	1	1	初級	
	now	[naʊ]	adv.	現在	1	1	初級	
❼	this	[ðɪs]	pron.	這個	1	1	初級	
	Miss	[mɪs]	n.	小姐	1	1	初級	
	number	[ˋnʌmbɚ]	n.	號碼	1	1	初級	◎
❽	asked	[æskt]	p.t.	ask（請求、要求）過去式	1	1	初級	
	cell	[sɛl]	adj.	cellular（蜂巢式的）縮寫	1	2	初級	
❾	woman	[ˋwʊmən]	n.	女生	1	1	初級	
❿	bunch	[bʌntʃ]	n.	一群、一票	1	3	中級	
	people	[ˋpipl̩]	n.	person（人）複數	1	1	初級	
	left	[lɛft]	p.t.	leave（留下）過去式	1	1	初級	
	message	[ˋmɛsɪdʒ]	n.	訊息	1	2	初級	◎

※「紅字單字」於本單元多句出現，「單字級等分析」僅列在「首次出現句」。

🔊 MP3 132-01 ⑪～⑱

⑪	林小姐在公司，她請你回電話。	Miss Lin is in her office now, and she asks that you call her back. * in one's office（在公司） * ask that＋子句（請求…）、call back（回電）
⑫	強尼下午有打電話找你。	Johnny called for you this afternoon. * call for＋某人（打電話找某人）
⑬	你太太請你儘速回電。	Your wife asked you to phone her as soon as possible. * ask＋某人＋to＋動詞原形（要求某人…） * phone（打電話）＝ call * as soon as possible（儘快）、husband（丈夫）
⑭	林小姐說晚一點會再來電。	Miss Lin said that she would call you again later. * said that...（剛才說…） * would（will〔將會〕的過去式） * call again（再次來電）
⑮	你開會時，A公司的林小姐有來電。	Miss Lin from A company called while you were in the meeting. * 某人＋from＋某公司（某公司的某人） * while…（當…的時候，在…的同時） * in the meeting（開會中）
⑯	打電話找你的留言我放在你桌上了。	I put your phone messages on your desk. * put＋某物＋on（放某物於…上面）
⑰	珍妮打了好幾通電話找你。	Jenny has already called you several times. * several times（好幾次） * 此句用「現在完成式」（...has...called...）表示「過去到現在發生過、經歷過的事」。
⑱	剛才有人找你，不過沒有留言就掛斷了。	Someone just called for you, but they hung up without leaving a message. * hang up（掛上電話）＝ put down * without＋動詞-ing（沒有做…） * leave a message（留下留言） * take a message（記下留言） * convey a message（傳達留言） * pick up a phone（接起電話）

單字級等分析

	單字	音標	詞性	意義	字頻	大考	英檢	多益
⑪	Miss	[mɪs]	n.	小姐	1	1	初級	
	office	[ˋɔfɪs]	n.	公司	1	1	初級	◎
	now	[naʊ]	adv.	現在	1	1	初級	
	ask	[æsk]	v.	請求	1	1	初級	
	call	[kɔl]	v.	打電話	1	1	初級	◎
	back	[bæk]	adv.	返回	1	1	初級	◎
⑫	called	[kɔkd]	p.t.	call（打電話）過去式	4	1	初級	◎
	this	[ðɪs]	adj.	這個	1	1	初級	
	afternoon	[ˋæftɚ͵nun]	n.	下午	1	1	初級	
⑬	asked	[æskt]	p.t.	ask（請求）過去式	1	1	初級	
	phone	[fon]	v./n.	打電話/電話	1	2	初級	◎
	soon	[sun]	adv.	早、快	1	1	初級	
	possible	[ˋpɑsəb!]	adv.	可能地	1	1	初級	◎
⑭	said	[sɛd]	p.t.	say（說）過去式	4	1	初級	
	again	[əˋgɛn]	adv.	再次	1	1	初級	
	later	[ˋletɚ]	adv.	稍後	1		初級	
⑮	company	[ˋkʌmpənɪ]	n.	公司	1	2	初級	◎
	meeting	[ˋmitɪŋ]	n.	會議	1	2	初級	
⑯	put	[pʊt]	p.t.	put（放置）過去式	1	1	初級	
	message	[ˋmɛsɪdʒ]	n.	留言	1	2	初級	◎
	desk	[dɛsk]	n.	桌子	1	1	初級	
⑰	called	[kɔld]	p.p.	call（打電話）過去分詞	4	1	初級	◎
	several	[ˋsɛvərəl]	adj.	幾個的	1	1	初級	
	time	[taɪm]	n.	次、回	1	1	初級	◎
⑱	someone	[ˋsʌm͵wʌn]	pron.	某個人	1	1	初級	
	just	[dʒʌst]	adv.	剛剛	1	1	初級	
	hung	[hʌŋ]	p.t.	hang（掛）過去式	8	2	初級	◎
	up	[ʌp]	adv.	掛上	1	1	初級	
	leaving	[ˋlivɪŋ]	n.	leave（留下）動名詞	6	1	初級	◎

※「紅字單字」於本單元多句出現，「單字級等分析」僅列在「首次出現句」。

MP3 132-02 ❶～❾

❶	我不在時有人找我嗎？	Did anyone call for me while I was out? * call for me（打電話找我）= call me * while I was out（我外出時、我不在時）
❷	對方沒說他是誰嗎？	Did he say who he was? * Did she say who she was?（對方沒說她是誰嗎） * Did he say who＋過去式子句? （他剛才有說…是誰嗎）
❸	他有留姓名跟電話嗎？	Did he leave his name and phone number? * leave one's name（留姓名） * leave one's phone number（留電話） * contact information（聯絡資訊）
❹	你記得他大概什麼時候打的嗎？	Do you remember when he called? * Do you remember when＋過去式子句? （你記得剛剛是什麼時候…嗎） * 此句用「現在簡單式問句」（Do...?） 表示「目前是否為某狀態？」。
❺	他幾點打來的？	When did he call? * When did he...?（他剛才是什麼時候…）
❻	他有說是哪一間公司的人嗎？	Did he say which company he was from? * Did he say...?（他剛才有說…嗎） * which company（哪一間公司） * from＋某公司（來自某公司）
❼	他有說會再打來嗎？	Did he say that he would call again? * Did he say that...?（他剛才有說…嗎） * would（will〔將會〕的過去式） * call again（再次來電）
❽	她的聲音聽起來怎麼樣？	What did her voice sound like? * What did＋主詞＋動詞?（當時…是什麼樣的？） * sound like（聽起來像） * like（像、相似）
❾	我母親是下午打給我的嗎？	Did my mother call me this afternoon? * this afternoon（今天下午） * this morning（今天早上） * this evening（今天晚上）

單字級等分析

	單字	音標	詞性	意義	字頻	大考	英檢	多益
❶	anyone	[ˈɛnɪ.wʌn]	pron.	任何人	1	2	初級	
	call	[kɔl]	v.	打電話	1	1	初級	◎
	out	[aʊt]	adj.	外出的、不在的	1	1	初級	
❷	say	[se]	v.	說	1	1	初級	
❸	leave	[liv]	v.	留下	1	1	初級	◎
	name	[nem]	n.	名字	1	1	初級	◎
	phone	[fon]	n.	電話	1	2	初級	◎
	number	[ˈnʌmbɚ]	n.	號碼	1	1	初級	◎
❹	remember	[rɪˈmɛnbɚ]	v.	記得	1	1	初級	◎
	called	[kɔld]	p.t.	call（打電話）過去式	4	1	初級	◎
❻	company	[ˈkʌmpənɪ]	n.	公司	1	2	初級	◎
❼	again	[əˈgɛn]	adv.	再次	1	1	初級	
❽	voice	[vɔɪs]	n.	聲音	1	1	初級	◎
	sound	[saʊnd]	v.	聽起來	1	1	初級	◎
❾	mother	[ˈmʌðɚ]	n.	母親	1	1	初級	
	this	[ðɪs]	adj.	這個	1	1	初級	
	afternoon	[ˈæftɚˈnun]	n.	下午	1	1	初級	

※「紅字單字」於本單元多句出現，「單字級等分析」僅列在「首次出現句」。

132 詢問是否有人來電。（2）

⑩	早上你有幫我代接電話嗎？	Did you take any calls for me this morning? * **Did you**＋動詞...?（你當時是否做了…？） * **take calls**（接聽電話） * **for me**（為我、幫我） * **this morning**（今天早上）
⑪	是不是吉米打來的？	Was it Jimmy that just called? * **Was it**＋某人...?（當時是某人…嗎）
⑫	吉米有說找我什麼事嗎？	Did Jimmy say why he was calling me? * **say why**＋子句（說…的原因） * 子句用「過去進行式」（ **...was calling...** ） 　表示「過去的當下正在做的事」。
⑬	李先生有打電話找我嗎？	Has Mr. Lee called for me? * **Has**＋某人＋**called**...?（某人是否曾經…？） * **call for me**（打電話找我） * 此句用「現在完成式問句」（ **Has...called...?** ） 　表示「從過去到現在是否發生過、經歷過某事」。
⑭	剛剛是林小姐找我嗎？	Did Miss Lin just call for me?
⑮	他有說他在公司還是在家裡嗎？	Did he say whether he was in the office or at home? * **Did he say**...?（他剛才有說…嗎） * **whether A or B**（A還是B） * **in the office**（在公司）＝ **in the company** * **at home**（在家）
⑯	對方有要我回電話嗎？	Did he ask me to call him back? * **ask**＋某人＋**to**＋動詞原形（要求某人…） * **call**＋某人＋**back**（回電給某人） 　＝ **return one's call**
⑰	他一句話都沒說就掛電話了嗎？	Did he hang up without saying a word? * **hang up**（掛掉電話）＝ **put down** * **without saying a word**（一個字都沒說）
⑱	我不認識什麼 ABC 公司的彼特先生。	I don't know any Mr. Peter from ABC company. * **don't know**＋某人（不認識某人） * **from**＋某公司（來自某公司）

	單字	音標	詞性	意義	字頻	大考	英檢	多益
❿	take	[tek]	v.	接聽	1	1	初級	◎
	any	[ˋɛnɪ]	adj.	任何的	1	1	初級	
	call	[kɔl]	n./v.	電話/打電話	1	1	初級	◎
	this	[ðɪs]	adj.	這個	1	1	初級	
	morning	[ˋmɔrnɪŋ]	n.	早上	1	1	初級	
⓫	just	[dʒʌst]	adv.	剛剛	1	1	初級	
	called	[kɔld]	p.t.	call（打電話）過去式	4	1	初級	◎
⓬	say	[se]	v.	說	1	1	初級	
	calling	[ˋkɔlɪŋ]	p.pr.	call（打電話）現在分詞	4	1	初級	◎
⓭	called	[kɔld]	p.p.	call（打電話）過去分詞	4	1	初級	◎
⓮	Miss	[mɪs]	n.	小姐	1	1	初級	
⓯	office	[ˋɔfɪs]	n.	公司	1	1	初級	◎
	home	[hom]	n.	家裡	1	1	初級	
⓰	ask	[æsk]	v.	要求、請求	1	1	初級	
	back	[bæk]	adv.	返回	1	1	初級	◎
⓱	hang	[hæŋ]	v.	掛掉	1	2	初級	◎
	up	[ʌp]	adv.	掛上	1	1	初級	
	saying	[ˋseɪŋ]	n.	say（說）動名詞	3	1	中級	
	word	[wɝd]	n.	字、一句話	1	1	初級	
⓲	know	[no]	v.	知道	1	1	初級	◎
	Mr.	[ˋmɪstɚ]	n.	先生		1	初級	
	company	[ˋkʌmpənɪ]	n.	公司	1	2	初級	◎

※「紅字單字」於本單元多句出現，「單字級等分析」僅列在「首次出現句」。

🔊 MP3 133-01 ❶～❾

❶	這位是我們公司的新進人員。	This is our new employee. * **This is＋人**（我身旁這位是某人） * **employee**（員工）可替換為：**colleague**（同事） * **new employee**（新來的員工、新任的員工） 　可替換為：**freshman**（新鮮人、新手）
❷	你們認識嗎？	Do you know each other? * **Do you know...?**（你們認識…嗎） * **each other**（彼此）
❸	瑪麗從今天起擔任祕書的職務。	As of today, Mary will be our new secretary. * **as of today**（從今天起） * **as of yesterday**（到昨日止） * **某人＋will be our＋職位**（某人將擔任我們的…）
❹	你見過史密斯先生嗎？	Have you met Mr. Smith yet? * **Have you...yet?**（你是否有…經驗） * 此句用「現在完成式問句」（**Have...met...?**）表示 　「從過去到現在是否發生過、經歷過某事」。
❺	你要不要自我介紹一下？	Would you like to introduce yourself a bit? * **Would you like to...?**（你要不要…？） * **introduce oneself**（介紹自己） * **a bit**（稍微）
❻	林先生，我介紹我同事給您認識。	Mr. Lin, allow me to introduce to you my colleague. * **allow me to＋動詞**（請讓我做…） * **introduce to A＋B**（向A介紹B）
❼	他是職場新鮮人。	He is a rookie in the job market. * **rookie**（新人、菜鳥）＝ **newcomer**、**novice** * **a rookie in＋領域**（某領域的新手、某領域的菜鳥） 　＝ **a newcomer to＋領域** * **job market**（職場）
❽	他是我們公司最負責任的員工。	He is the most responsible employee in our company. * **the most responsible**（最負責的，responsible的最高級）
❾	他是我的上司。	He is my boss. * **boss**（上司、主管）＝ **supervisor** * **subordinate**（部下，部屬）＝ **inferior** * **coworker**（同事）＝ **associate**

	單字	音標	詞性	意義	字頻	大考	英檢	多益
❶	new	[nju]	adj.	新來的、新任的	1	1	初級	
	employee	[ˌɛmplɔɪˋi]	n.	員工	1	3	中級	◎
❷	know	[no]	n.	知道	1	1	初級	◎
	each	[itʃ]	pron.	每個、各個	1	1	初級	
	other	[ˋʌðɚ]	pron.	另一方	1	1	初級	
❸	today	[təˋde]	n.	今天	1	1	初級	◎
	secretary	[ˋsɛkrəˌtɛrɪ]	n.	秘書	1	2	初級	◎
❹	met	[mɛt]	p.p.	meet（見過）過去分詞	1	1	初級	
	Mr.	[ˋmɪstɚ]	n.	先生		1	初級	
	yet	[jɛt]	adv.	尚未	1	1	初級	◎
❺	like	[laɪk]	v.	想要	1	1	初級	
	introduce	[ˌɪntrəˋdjus]	v.	介紹	1	2	初級	◎
	yourself	[juɚˋsɛlf]	pron.	你自己	1		初級	
	bit	[bɪt]	n.	些許	1	1	初級	
❻	allow	[əˋlau]	v.	允許	1	1	初級	
	colleague	[ˋkɑlig]	n.	同事	1	5	中級	◎
❼	rookie	[ˋrʊkɪ]	n.	新人、菜鳥	2			
	job	[dʒɑb]	n.	工作	1	1	初級	
	market	[ˋmɑrkɪt]	n.	市場	1	1	初級	◎
❽	most	[most]	adv.	最為	1	1	初級	
	responsible	[rɪˋspɑnsəbl̩]	adj.	負責的	1	2	初級	◎
	company	[ˋkʌmpənɪ]	n.	公司	1	2	初級	◎
❾	boss	[bɔs]	n.	上司、主管	1	2	初級	

※「紅字單字」於本單元多句出現，「單字級等分析」僅列在「首次出現句」。

MP3 133-01 ⑩～⑱

⑩	帶你認識一下公司同事。	Let me take you to meet our colleagues. * take＋某人＋to＋動詞（帶某人去…）
⑪	這位是我們公司的業務。	This is our company's salesperson. * This is＋人（我身旁這位是某人） * accountant（會計）、manager（經理） * consultant（顧問）、assistant（助理）
⑫	這位史密斯先生是管理部的主管。	Mr. Smith here is the chief of the management department. * 某人＋here is...（這邊這位某人是…） * the chief of＋部門（某部門主管） * management department（管理部） * human resource department（人資部） * procurement department（採購部） * research and development department（研發部）
⑬	旁邊這位是負責業務的大衛。	This man beside me is David, who is in charge of sales. * be in charge of（負責）＝ be responsible for
⑭	我先介紹你給大家認識。	First, I want to introduce you to everyone. * First, ...（首先…） * introduce A to B（向 B 介紹 A）
⑮	這位是以後負責帶你的林小姐。	This is Miss Lin, who is going to be in charge of training you. * 某人＋, who＋子句（某人是…） * 子句用「未來簡單式」（...is going to...） 　表示「未排定時程、但預定要做的事」。 * in charge of＋動詞-ing（負責做…）
⑯	這是跟你同部門的琳達。	This is Linda, who is in the same department as you are.　* as（和…一樣）
⑰	先帶你去各部門拜碼頭。	Let me take you around to each department first. * take you around（帶你四處看看） * each＋名詞單數型（各個…）
⑱	他有非常豐富的工作經驗。	He has extensive work experience. * extensive（充分的）可替換為： 　wide（廣泛的）、considerable（相當多的） * work experience（工作經驗）

	單字	音標	詞性	意義	字頻	大考	英檢	多益
⑩	let	[lɛt]	v.	讓…	1	1	初級	
	take	[tek]	v.	帶領	1	1	初級	
	meet	[mit]	v.	認識	1	1	初級	
	colleague	[ˋkɑlig]	n.	同事	1	5	中級	◎
⑪	this	[ðɪs]	pron. /adj.	這個	1	1	初級	
	company	[ˋkʌmpənɪ]	n.	公司	1	2	初級	◎
	salesperson	[ˋselz͵pɚsn]	n.	業務人員	7	1	中級	
⑫	Mr.	[ˋmɪstɚ]	n.	先生		1	初級	
	here	[hɪr]	adv.	這裡	1	1	初級	
	chief	[tʃif]	n.	主管	1	1	初級	
	management	[ˋmænɪdʒmənt]	n.	管理	1	3	初級	◎
	department	[dɪˋpɑrtmənt]	n.	部門	1	2	初級	◎
⑬	man	[mæn]	n.	男生	1	1	初級	
	charge	[tʃɑrdʒ]	n.	負責	1	2	初級	◎
	sales	[selz]	n.	業務	1			◎
⑭	first	[fɜst]	adv.	首先	1	1	初級	
	want	[wɑnt]	v.	想要	1	1	初級	◎
	introduce	[͵ɪntrəˋdjus]	v.	介紹	1	2	初級	◎
	everyone	[ˋɛvrɪ͵wʌn]	pron.	每個人	1		初級	
⑮	Miss	[mɪs]	n.	小姐	1	1	初級	
	going	[ˋgoɪŋ]	p.pr.	go（即將）現在分詞	4	1	初級	
	training	[ˋtrenɪŋ]	n.	train（培訓）動名詞	1	1	中級	◎
⑯	same	[sem]	adj.	相同的	1	1	初級	
⑰	around	[əˋraʊnd]	adv.	四處	1	1	初級	
	each	[itʃ]	adj.	各個	1	1	初級	
⑱	have	[hæv]	v.	擁有	1	1	初級	
	extensive	[ɪkˋstɛnsɪv]	adj.	充分的	2	5	中級	◎
	work	[wɜk]	n.	工作	1	1	初級	◎
	experience	[ɪkˋspɪrɪəns]	n.	經驗	1	2	初級	◎

※「紅字單字」於本單元多句出現，「單字級等分析」僅列在「首次出現句」。

MP3 133-02 ❶～❿

❶	初次見面，你好嗎？	This is the first time we've met; how are you? * the first time we've met（我們初次見面） * How are you?（你好嗎，問候用語）
❷	你好，我是負責業務的約翰。	Hello, I am John, and I'm in charge of sales. * in charge of（負責）＝ be responsible for * marketing（行銷）、planning（企畫） * finance（財務）、general affairs（總務） * customer service（客服）、quality control（品管）
❸	你好嗎？我是珍・史密斯。	How are you? I am Jane Smith.
❹	這是我的名片，請多指教。	This is my business card; your suggestions are welcome. * business card（名片） * your suggestions are welcome（請多指教） * suggestion（建議）＝ advice
❺	很高興認識你。	It's really nice to meet you. * It is nice to＋動詞原形（很高興…）
❻	歡迎加入我們。	We're so happy you joined us! * be so happy (that)＋子句（很高興…） 　＝ be so glad (that)＋子句 * join our team（加入我們的團隊）
❼	你好，請多指教。	Hello, your advice is welcome. * your advice is welcome（請多指教） 　＝ your suggestions are welcome
❽	很高興能跟你成為同事。	I'm really happy to be your colleague. * be happy to＋動詞原形（很高興…） 　＝ be glad to＋動詞原形 * colleague（同事）＝ coworker、associate
❾	工作上有任何問題都可以問我。	You can ask me any question about work. * ask me＋某事（詢問我某事） * any＋名詞單數型（任何一個…） * question about＋名詞（關於…的問題）
❿	久仰大名。	I've heard a lot about you. * have heard a lot（曾經聽聞許多） * about you（關於你） * 此句用「現在完成式」（...have heard...） 　表示「過去到現在發生過、經歷過的事」。

單字級等分析

	單字	音標	詞性	意義	字頻	大考	英檢	多益
❶	this	[ðɪs]	pron.	這個	1	1	初級	
	first	[fɜst]	adj.	第一的	1	1	初級	
	time	[taɪm]	n.	次、回	1	1	初級	◎
	met	[mɛt]	p.p.	meet（見面）過去分詞	1	1	初級	
❷	hello	[hə`lo]	int.	你好	1	1	初級	
	charge	[tʃɑrdʒ]	n.	負責	1	2	初級	◎
	sales	[selz]	n.	銷售	1			◎
❹	business	[`bɪznɪs]	n.	商業、商務	1	2	初級	◎
	card	[kɑrd]	n.	卡片	1	1	初級	◎
	suggestion	[sə`dʒɛstʃən]	n.	建議	1	4	中級	◎
	welcome	[`wɛlkəm]	adj.	歡迎的	1	1	初級	
❺	really	[`rɪəlɪ]	adv.	很、十分	1		初級	
	nice	[naɪs]	adj.	美好的	1	1	初級	
	meet	[mit]	v.	認識	1	1	初級	
❻	so	[so]	adv.	非常	1	1	初級	
	happy	[`hæpɪ]	adj.	高興的	1	1	初級	
	joined	[dʒɔɪnd]	p.t.	join（加入）過去式	1	1	初級	◎
❼	advice	[əd`vaɪs]	n.	建議	1	3	初級	◎
❽	colleague	[`kɑlig]	n.	同事	1	5	中級	◎
❾	ask	[æsk]	v.	詢問	1	1	初級	
	any	[`ɛnɪ]	adj.	任何的	1	1	初級	
	question	[`kwɛstʃən]	n.	問題	1	1	初級	
	work	[wɜk]	n.	工作	1	1	初級	◎
❿	heard	[hɜd]	p.p.	hear（聽聞）過去分詞	1	1	初級	
	lot	[lɑt]	n.	許多				

※「紅字單字」於本單元多句出現，「單字級等分析」僅列在「首次出現句」。

🔘 MP3 133-02 ⓫～⓱

⓫	你好，我是今天第一天上班的珍妮。	Hello, I am the new girl, Jennie. * the new girl（新來的人，女生用語） * the new guy（新來的人，男生用語）
⓬	我是個菜鳥，請多擔待。	Please excuse me, I am a newcomer. * please excuse me（請多多包容我） * excuse me（請多擔待、請多包涵） * newcomer（新人）＝ freshman、rookie * senior（資深人士、前輩） * veteran（老手、經驗老到的人）
⓭	我會盡快進入工作狀況。	I'll do my best to settle into a work routine. * do one's best（盡全力） * settle into（習慣、適應） * work routine（例行的工作流程、常態的工作程序） * 此句用「未來簡單式」（...will...） 　表示「有意願做的事」。
⓮	我會努力工作，不給大家添麻煩。	I'll work hard to avoid causing extra work for anyone. * work hard（努力工作） * avoid＋動詞-ing（避免…、以免…） * cause extra work（添麻煩、增添額外的工作量）
⓯	叫我珍就可以了。	You can call me Jane. * call＋某人＋名字（稱呼某人…）
⓰	今後請多多關照。	I'm looking forward to your guidance. * look forward to＋名詞（期待…） * guidance（指導、關照）可替換為： 　direction（指導、教導）、instruction（教誨） * 此句用「現在進行式」（...am looking...） 　表示「說話當下正在做的事」。
⓱	日後我們應該有很多合作機會。	We should have many opportunities to work together in the future. * should（應該、大概） * have many opportunities（有很多機會） 　＝ have many chances * work together（合作、共事） * in the future（在未來）

單字級等分析

	單字	音標	詞性	意義	字頻	大考	英檢	多益
⑪	hello	[hə`lo]	int.	你好	1	1	初級	
	new	[nju]	adj.	新來的、新任的	1	1	初級	
	girl	[gɝl]	n.	女生	1	1	初級	
⑫	please	[pliz]	adv.	請…	1	1	初級	
	excuse	[ɪk`skjuz]	v.	包容	2	2	初級	◎
	newcomer	[`nju`kʌmɚ]	n.	新人	3		中級	
⑬	do	[du]	v.	做	1	1	初級	
	best	[bɛst]	n.	最好	1	1	初級	
	settle	[`sɛtl̩]	v.	習慣、適應	1	2	中級	◎
	work	[wɝk]	n./v.	工作	1	1	初級	
	routine	[ru`tin]	n.	程序	1	3	中級	◎
⑭	hard	[hɑrd]	adv.	認真地	1	1	初級	◎
	avoid	[ə`vɔɪd]	v.	避免、以免	1	2	初級	◎
	causing	[`kɔzɪŋ]	n.	cause（造成）動名詞	1	1	初級	◎
	extra	[`ɛkstrə]	adj.	額外的	1	2	初級	◎
	anyone	[`ɛnɪ.wʌn]	pron.	任何人	1	2	初級	
⑮	call	[kɔl]	v.	打電話	1	1	初級	◎
⑯	looking	[`lʊkɪŋ]	p.pr.	look（期待）現在分詞	5	1	初級	
	forward	[`fɔrwəd]	adv.	今後、將來	1	2	初級	◎
	guidance	[`gaɪdn̩s]	n.	指導、關照	2	3	中級	◎
⑰	have	[hæv]	v.	擁有	1	1	初級	
	many	[`mɛnɪ]	adj.	許多的	1	1	初級	
	opportunity	[.ɑpə`tjunətɪ]	n.	機會	1	3	初級	◎
	together	[tə`gɛðɚ]	adv.	一起	1	1	初級	
	future	[`fjutʃɚ]	n.	未來	1	2	初級	

※「紅字單字」於本單元多句出現，「單字級等分析」僅列在「首次出現句」。

🔘 MP3 134-01 ❶～❿

❶	你可以幫我請病假嗎？	Can you help me ask for a sick leave? * **Can you help me＋動詞原形?**（你可以幫我做…嗎） * **ask for a leave**（請假）、**sick leave**（病假）
❷	我後天請喪假。	I'm taking a bereavement leave the day after tomorrow. * **take a leave**（請假）、**bereavement leave**（喪假） * **marriage leave**（婚假）、**maternity leave**（產假） * **the day after tomorrow**（後天） * 此句用「現在進行式」（...am taking...） 　表示「已排定時程的個人未來計畫」。
❸	我明天請半天假。	I'm taking a half-day leave tomorrow. * **half-day leave**（半天假）
❹	我明天請事假。	I'm taking a personal day tomorrow. * **take a personal day**（請事假） * **casual leave**（臨時事假）
❺	我可以請一個禮拜的假嗎？	Can I request a one-week leave? * **request a leave**（請假）＝ **ask for a leave** ＝ **take a leave** * **one-week leave**（一星期的假）
❻	我要請年假。	I want to take my annual leave. * **annual leave**（年假）
❼	我在等頭兒准假。	I'm waiting for my boss to approve my leave of absence. * **be waiting for**（正在等待） * **approve**（核准）＝ **accept** * **leave of absence**（休假）＝ **leave**
❽	休假期間他是我的職務代理人。	He'll fill in for me while I'm away on vacation. * **fill in for me**（接替我的工作）、**while**（在…時候） * **on vacation**（休假期間）
❾	我請假這段期間，萬事拜託了。	Please take good care of everything for me while I am on leave. * **take good care of**（好好處理、好好負責） * **on leave**（休假中）
❿	他早上有打電話來請假。	He called this morning to ask for a leave of absence.　* **this morning**（今天早上）

	單字	音標	詞性	意義	字頻	大考	英檢	多益
❶	help	[hɛlp]	v.	幫忙	1	1	初級	
	ask	[æsk]	v.	請求	1	1	初級	
	sick	[sɪk]	adj.	生病的	1	1	初級	◎
	leave	[liv]	n.	休假	1	1	初級	◎
❷	taking	[ˈtekɪŋ]	p.pr.	take（請假）現在分詞	4			
	bereavement	[bəˈrivmənt]	n.	失去親人	8			
	day	[de]	n.	天	1	1	初級	
	tomorrow	[təˈmɔro]	n.	明天	1	1	初級	◎
❸	half-day	[ˈhæfˈde]	adj.	半天的				
❹	personal	[ˈpɝsnl]	adj.	個人的、私人的	1	2	初級	◎
❺	request	[rɪˈkwɛst]	v.	請求	1	3	中級	
	one-week	[ˈwʌnˈwik]	adj.	一週的				
❻	want	[wɑnt]	v.	想要	1	1	初級	◎
	take	[tek]	v.	請假/負責	1	1	初級	◎
	annual	[ˈænjuəl]	adj.	一年的	1	4	中級	
❼	waiting	[ˈwetɪŋ]	p.pr.	wait（等待）現在分詞	3	1	初級	◎
	boss	[bɔs]	n.	老闆	1	2	初級	
	approve	[əˈpruv]	v.	核准	1	3	中級	◎
	absence	[ˈæbsns]	n.	缺席	1	2	中級	◎
❽	fill	[fɪl]	v.	接替	1	1	初級	◎
	away	[əˈwe]	adj.	不在的、離開的	1	1	初級	
	vacation	[veˈkeʃən]	n.	假期	1	2	初級	◎
❾	please	[pliz]	adv.	請…	1	1	初級	
	good	[gud]	adj.	良好的	1	1	初級	◎
	care	[kɛr]	n.	處理、照料	1	1	初級	◎
	everything	[ˈɛvrɪˌθɪŋ]	pron.	每件事情	1		初級	
❿	called	[kɔld]	p.t.	call（打電話）過去式	4	1	初級	◎
	this	[ðɪs]	adj.	這個	1	1	初級	
	morning	[ˈmɔrnɪŋ]	n.	早上	1	1	初級	

※「紅字單字」於本單元多句出現，「單字級等分析」僅列在「首次出現句」。

134 必須請假／有同事請假。（2）

🔊 MP3 134-01 ⑪~⑱

⑪	我想申請留職停薪。	I would like to apply for unpaid leave. * **would like to**（想要） * **apply for unpaid leave**（申請留職停薪） * **unpaid leave**（無薪假）
⑫	我可以提早一個小時離開公司嗎？	May I leave the office an hour early? * **May I＋動詞...?**（請問我可以…嗎） * **leave the office**（下班、離開公司） * **時間＋early**（提早…時間）
⑬	我們公司請假規定很多。	Our company has a lot of rules about taking time off. * **have a lot of...**（有很多…） * **rules about...**（關於…的規定） * **take time off**（請假）、**time off**（休假）
⑭	我想請假到月底。	I would like to request a leave of absence till the end of the month. * **request a leave**（請假）＝ **ask for a leave** ＝ **take a leave** * **leave of absence**（休假） * **till**（直到）、**the end of the month**（這個月底）
⑮	我已經把請假單交給主管。	I've already submitted my leave application form to my boss. * **submit an application form**（呈交申請表） * **leave application form**（請假單） * **boss**（上司、主管）＝ **supervisor**
⑯	他最近常常請假。	Lately he has been asking for a lot of time off. * **lately**（最近）＝ **recently**、**of late** * **ask for**（請求、要求）＝ **request** * **ask for a lot of time off**（常請假、請很多假） * 此句用「現在完成進行式」（...has been asking...）表示「現階段持續發生的事」。
⑰	他常請假讓老闆不太高興。	He often asks for time off, which upsets his boss. * **upset＋某人**（使某人生氣）
⑱	他下個月開始請長假。	He will take a long leave of absence beginning next month. * **will**（將會）、**take a long leave of absence**（請長假） * **beginning next month**（從下個月起）

	單字	音標	詞性	意義	字頻	大考	英檢	多益
⑪	like	[laɪk]	v.	想要	1	1	初級	
	apply	[əˋplaɪ]	v.	申請	1	2	初級	◎
	unpaid	[ʌnˋped]	adj.	未付薪水的	4			
	leave	[liv]	n./v.	休假/離開	1	1	初級	◎
⑫	office	[ˋɔfɪs]	n.	公司	1	1	初級	◎
	hour	[aʊr]	n.	小時	1	1	初級	
	early	[ˋɝlɪ]	adv.	提早	1	1	初級	
⑬	company	[ˋkʌmpənɪ]	n.	公司	1	2	初級	◎
	have	[hæv]	v.	擁有	1	1	初級	
	lot	[lɑt]	n.	許多				
	rule	[rul]	n.	規定	1	1	初級	◎
	taking	[ˋtekɪŋ]	n.	take（請假）動名詞	4			
	time	[taɪm]	n.	時間	1	1	初級	◎
	off	[ɔf]	adj.	休假的	1	1	初級	
⑭	request	[rɪˋkwɛst]	v.	請求	1	3	中級	◎
	absence	[ˋæbsns]	n.	缺席	1	2	中級	
	end	[ɛnd]	n.	結尾	1	1	初級	
	month	[mʌnθ]	n.	月	1	1	初級	
⑮	already	[ɔlˋrɛdɪ]	adv.	已經	1	1	初級	◎
	submitted	[səbˋmɪtɪd]	p.p.	submit（呈交）過去分詞	2	5	中高	
	application	[ˌæpləˋkeʃən]	n.	申請	1	4	中級	◎
	form	[fɔrm]	n.	表單	1	2	初級	◎
	boss	[bɔs]	n.	主管、老闆	1	2	初級	
⑯	lately	[ˋletlɪ]	adv.	最近	2	4	中級	
	asking	[ˋæskɪŋ]	p.pr.	ask（請求）現在分詞	5	1	初級	
⑰	often	[ˋɔfən]	adv.	常常	1	1	初級	
	ask	[æsk]	v.	請求	1	1	初級	
	upset	[ʌpˋsɛt]	v.	使…生氣	2	3	中級	◎
⑱	take	[tek]	v.	請假	1	1	初級	◎
	long	[lɔŋ]	adj.	長的	1	1	初級	
	beginning	[bɪˋgɪnɪŋ]	p.pr.	begin（開始）現在分詞	1	1	初級	
	next	[nɛkst]	adj.	下一個	1	1	初級	

※「紅字單字」於本單元多句出現，「單字級等分析」僅列在「首次出現句」。

MP3 134-02 ❶～❾

❶	誰來幫我一下？	Is there anyone who can help me? = Who can help me out here? = Who can give me a hand? * **Is there＋名詞...?**（有沒有…？） * **help me**（幫忙我）= help me out = give me a hand
❷	我自己忙不過來。	I can't handle it by myself. * **can't handle＋某事物**（處理不了某事物） * **by myself**（靠自己）
❸	我需要一個人幫忙影印。	I need someone to make copies for me. * **need＋某人＋to＋動詞原形**（需要某人去…） * **make copies**（影印） * **for me**（幫我、為了我）
❹	你願意協助我處理這個案子嗎？	Can you help me deal with this case? * **Can you...?**（你可以…嗎、你願意…嗎） 　= Could you...? = Would you...? * **help＋某人＋動詞原形**（幫某人做…） * **deal with**（處理）= cope with
❺	可以幫我看一下我的電腦嗎？	Could you have a look at my computer for me? * **have a look at**（看一下）= take a look at
❻	可以幫我看一下這份企畫案嗎？	Would you take a look at this proposal for me?
❼	可以幫我把這些資料輸入電腦嗎？	Can you help me input this data into the computer? * **input**（輸入）= enter * **input＋某物＋into the computer**（將…輸入電腦） 　= key＋某物＋into the computer
❽	麻煩你在主管面前幫我美言幾句。	Please put in a good word to your manager for me. * **put in a good word**（美言、說好話） 　= say a good word
❾	可以拜託你一件事嗎？	Can I request a favor from you? * **request a favor from you**（拜託你一件事、請你幫忙） * **do one's favor**（幫助某人） * **owe＋某人＋a favor**（欠某人一個人情）

單字級等分析

	單字	音標	詞性	意義	字頻	大考	英檢	多益
❶	there	[ðɛr]	adv.	有…	1	1	初級	
	anyone	[ˈɛnɪˌwʌn]	pron.	任何人	1	2	初級	
	help	[hɛlp]	v.	幫助	1	1	初級	
	out	[aʊt]	adv.	擺脫	1	1	初級	
	here	[hɪr]	adv.	這裡	1	1	初級	
	give	[gɪv]	v.	給予	1	1	初級	
	hand	[hænd]	n.	協助	1	1	初級	
❷	handle	[ˈhændl̩]	v.	處理	1	2	初級	◎
	myself	[maɪˈsɛlf]	pron.	我自己	1		初級	
❸	need	[nid]	v.	需要	1	1	初級	◎
	someone	[ˈsʌmˌwʌn]	pron.	某個人	1	1	初級	
	make	[mek]	v.	做	1	1	初級	
	copy	[ˈkɑpɪ]	n.	影印、拷貝	1	2	初級	◎
❹	deal	[dil]	v.	處理	1	1	初級	◎
	this	[ðɪs]	adj.	這個	1	1	初級	
	case	[kes]	n.	案子	1	1	初級	
❺	have	[hæv]	v.	執行、做某動作	1	1	初級	
	look	[lʊk]	n.	看一下	1	1	初級	
	computer	[kəmˈpjutɚ]	n.	電腦	1	2	初級	
❻	take	[tek]	v.	採取	1	1	初級	◎
	proposal	[prəˈpozl̩]	n.	企劃、提案	1	3	中級	◎
❼	input	[ˈɪnˌpʊt]	v.	輸入	2	4	中級	
	data	[ˈdetə]	n.	資料	1	2	初級	◎
❽	please	[pliz]	adv.	請…	1	1	初級	
	put	[pʊt]	v.	表述	1	1	初級	
	good	[gʊd]	adj.	良好的	1	1	初級	◎
	word	[wɝd]	n.	話語	1	1	初級	
	manager	[ˈmænɪdʒɚ]	n.	主管、經理	1	3	初級	◎
❾	request	[rɪˈkwɛst]	v.	請求、拜託	1	3	中級	◎
	favor	[ˈfevɚ]	n.	幫忙	1	2	初級	◎

※「紅字單字」於本單元多句出現，「單字級等分析」僅列在「首次出現句」。

❿	你願意陪我一起去拜訪客戶嗎？	Would you accompany me to visit this client? * Would you...?（你願意…嗎） * accompany me（陪我） * visit a client（拜訪客戶）= see a client
⓫	我需要借助你的專業技能。	I need to borrow your professional skills. * need to＋動詞原形（需要） * borrow one's skills（借助某人的技能） * professional skills（專業技能）
⓬	你可以幫我打幾個電話嗎？	Can you help me make some phone calls? * Can you help me＋動詞...?（你可以幫我做…嗎） * make a phone call（打一通電話）
⓭	可以幫我傳真這份文件嗎？	Can you fax this document for me? * fax＋某文件（傳真某文件） * for me（幫我、為了我）
⓮	有任何需要儘管說。	Don't hesitate to tell me if you need anything. * Don't hesitate to...（別客氣…、儘管…） * hesitate to＋動詞原形（猶豫、遲疑） * if＋主詞＋動詞（要是…、如果…） * if you need anything（如果你有任何需要）
⓯	我可以幫你什麼嗎？	What can I do for you? * What can I do...?（我可以做什麼…嗎） * for you（幫你、為了你）
⓰	有我幫得上忙的地方嗎？	Is there anything that I can help with? * Is there anything...?（有沒有任何事是…？） * help with（幫忙）
⓱	你可以幫忙聯絡幾個客戶嗎？	Would you help me to contact some clients? * help＋某人＋(to)＋動詞（幫某人做…） * contact（聯絡）= reach
⓲	你要不要多找幾個同事幫忙？	Do you want to look for a few more coworkers to help out? * want to＋動詞原形（想要） * look for＋人（尋求某人） * a few more（再多一些） * coworker（同事）= colleague、associate * help out（幫忙處理）

	單字	音標	詞性	意義	字頻	大考	英檢	多益
❿	accompany	[ə`kʌmpənɪ]	v.	陪伴	1	4	中級	◎
	visit	[`vɪzɪt]	v.	拜訪	1	1	初級	◎
	this	[ðɪs]	adj.	這個	1	1	初級	
	client	[`klaɪənt]	n.	客戶	1	3	中級	◎
⓫	need	[nid]	v.	需要	1	1	初級	◎
	borrow	[`bɑro]	v.	借助	2	2	初級	◎
	professional	[prə`fɛʃənl]	adj.	專業的	1	4	中級	◎
	skill	[skɪl]	n.	技能	1	1	初級	◎
⓬	help	[hɛlp]	v.	幫忙	1	1	初級	
	make	[mek]	v.	撥打	1	1	初級	
	some	[sʌm]	adj.	一些	1	1	初級	
	phone	[fon]	n.	電話	1	2	初級	◎
	call	[kɔl]	n.	通話	1	1	初級	◎
⓭	fax	[fæks]	v.	傳真	3	3	中級	◎
	document	[`dɑkjəmənt]	n.	文件	1	5	初級	◎
⓮	hesitate	[`hɛzəˌtet]	v.	猶豫、遲疑	2	3	中級	◎
	tell	[tɛl]	v.	告訴	1	1	初級	
	anything	[`ɛnɪˌθɪŋ]	pron.	任何事情	1	1	初級	
⓯	do	[du]	v.	做	1	1	初級	
⓰	there	[ðɛr]	adv.	有…	1	1	初級	
⓱	contact	[kən`tækt]	v.	聯絡	1	2	初級	◎
⓲	want	[wɑnt]	v.	想要	1	1	初級	◎
	look	[lʊk]	v.	尋求	1	1	初級	
	few	[fju]	adj.	些許的	1	1	初級	
	more	[mor]	adj.	更多的	1	1	初級	
	coworker	[`koˌwɜkə]	n.	同事				
	out	[aʊt]	adv.	擺脫	1	1	初級	

※「紅字單字」於本單元多句出現，「單字級等分析」僅列在「首次出現句」。

135 接待訪客。

❶	您好，請問您要找哪一位？	Hello, may I ask who you are looking for? * **May I ask...?**（請問…？）、**look for**（尋找）
❷	您有預約嗎？	Do you have an appointment? * **have an appointment**（有預約）
❸	歡迎您大駕光臨。	Thank you for your visit.
❹	他的辦公室在這個方向。	His office is this way. * **this way**（這邊、這個方向）
❺	讓您久等了。	Sorry to keep you waiting for so long. * **Sorry to...**（抱歉…） * **keep you＋動詞-ing**（讓你一直…） * **wait for so long**（等候多時、久等）
❻	請問有什麼事嗎？	May I help you?
❼	我們老闆已經等您很久了。	Our boss has been waiting for you. * 此句用「現在完成進行式」（...has been waiting...）表示「從過去開始、且直到現在仍持續中的事」。
❽	請您稍待片刻。	Please wait here for a moment.
❾	這邊請。	This way, please.
❿	我帶您到會客室。	Let me show you to the reception room. * **show＋某人**（為某人帶路） * **reception room**（會客室）
⓫	抱歉，他現在有客人。	I'm sorry, he is meeting with a client right now. * **be meeting**（正在開會）、**with＋某人**（和某人）
⓬	請坐這裡。	Have a seat here, please. ＝ Sit here, please.
⓭	不好意思，林先生有事外出。	I'm very sorry; Mr. Lin is out.
⓮	下次請您先預約時間。	Next time please make an appointment first. * **next time**（下次）、**make an appointment**（約時間）
⓯	請喝咖啡。	Have some coffee, please.
⓰	他現在不方便會客。	He is not available to receive visitors at the moment. * **be not available to＋動詞原形**（不方便做…） * **receive visitors**（接待客人、會客） * **at the moment**（現在）

	單字	音標	詞性	意義	字頻	大考	英檢	多益
❶	hello	[hə`lo]	int.	您好	1	1	初級	
	ask	[æsk]	v.	詢問	1	1	初級	
	looking	[`lʊkɪŋ]	p.pr.	look（尋找）現在分詞	5	1	初級	
❷	have	[hæv]	v.	擁有/就座/喝	1	1	初級	
	appointment	[ə`pɔɪntmənt]	n.	約會	2	4	中級	◎
❸	thank	[θæŋk]	v.	感謝	1	1	初級	
	visit	[`vɪzɪt]	n.	拜訪	1	1	初級	◎
❹	office	[`ɔfɪs]	n.	辦公室	1	1	初級	◎
	this	[ðɪs]	adj.	這個	1	1	初級	
	way	[we]	n.	方向	1	1	初級	
❺	sorry	[`sɑrɪ]	adj.	抱歉的	1	1	初級	
	keep	[kip]	v.	讓…一直	1	1	初級	◎
	waiting	[`wetɪŋ]	p.pr.	wait（等待）現在分詞	3	1	初級	◎
	so	[so]	adv.	這麼	1	1	初級	
	long	[lɔŋ]	n.	長時間	1	1	初級	
❻	help	[hɛlp]	v.	幫忙	1	1	初級	
❼	boss	[bɔs]	n.	老闆	1	2	初級	
	waiting	[`wetɪŋ]	p.pr.	wait（等待）現在分詞	3	1	初級	◎
❽	please	[pliz]	adv.	請…	1	1	初級	
	wait	[wet]	v.	等待	1	1	初級	◎
	here	[hɪr]	adv.	這裡	1	1	初級	
	moment	[`momənt]	n.	片刻/時刻	1	1	初級	
❿	let	[lɛt]	v.	讓…	1	1	初級	
	show	[ʃo]	v.	帶領	1	1	初級	
	reception	[rɪ`sɛpʃən]	n.	接待	2	4	中級	
	room	[rum]	n.	房間	1	1	初級	
⓫	meeting	[`mitɪŋ]	p.pr.	meet（開會）現在分詞	1	2	初級	
	client	[`klaɪənt]	n.	客戶	1	3	中級	
	right	[raɪt]	adv.	正值	1	1	初級	
	now	[naʊ]	adv.	現在	1	1	初級	
⓬	seat	[sit]	n.	座位	1	1	初級	◎
	sit	[sɪt]	v.	坐	1	1	初級	
⓭	very	[`vɛrɪ]	adv.	十分	1	1	初級	
	Mr.	[`mɪstə]	n.	先生		1	初級	
	out	[aʊt]	adj.	外出的、不在的	1	1	初級	
⓮	next	[nɛkst]	adj.	下一個	1	1	初級	
	time	[taɪm]	n.	次、回	1	1	初級	◎
	make	[mek]	v.	執行、做	1	1	初級	
	first	[fɚst]	adv.	預先	1	1	初級	
⓯	some	[sʌm]	adj.	一些	1	1	初級	
	coffee	[`kɔfɪ]	n.	咖啡	1	1	初級	
⓰	available	[ə`veləbl]	adj.	有空閒的	1	3	初級	◎
	receive	[rɪ`siv]	v.	接待	1	1	初級	◎
	visitor	[`vɪzɪtə]	n.	客人	1	2	初級	◎

※「紅字單字」於本單元多句出現，「單字級等分析」僅列在「首次出現句」。

135　主動拜訪。

MP3 135-02 ❶～❹

❶	我是 ABC 公司的業務，想要拜訪你們老闆。	I am a salesperson with ABC Company, and I would like to visit your boss. * salesperson with＋公司（某公司的業務人員） * would like to（想要）
❷	不好意思，可以幫我通報一下嗎？	I'm sorry, could you let him know I've arrived? * let him know＋子句（告訴他…） * I've arrived（我到了）
❸	你跟他說大衛他就知道了。	Just tell him that David is here; he will know what you mean. * will（應該會）、what you mean（你的意思）
❹	我是順道過來拜訪的。	I happened to be in the neighborhood, so I stopped by to visit you. * happen to（恰巧）、in the neighborhood（在附近） * stop by（順道拜訪）
❺	我沒有事先預約。	I haven't made an appointment. * haven't＋過去分詞（並未做…） * make an appointment（預約）
❻	我有打過電話預約。	I made an appointment over the phone. * over＋工具（透過某工具）
❼	他今天都不會再進公司嗎？	Will he not be in the office for the rest of the day? * Will he not...?（他之後不會…了嗎） * be in the office（進公司） * the rest of the day（今天剩餘的時間）
❽	那我改天再登門拜訪。	OK, I'll come some other day. * some other day（改天）
❾	他現在方便會客嗎？	Is he available to meet with visitors right now? * Is＋某人＋available...?（某人方便…嗎）
❿	請問他大概還要多久才會有空？	Around what time will he be available? * around（大約）、what time...?（幾點…？）
⓫	我跟他約三點，不過我早到了。	My appointment with him is for three pm, but I've arrived early.　* arrive early（提早到達）
⓬	麻煩你為我帶路。	Please show me the way. * show＋某人＋the way（幫…帶路）
⓭	沒關係，我等他。	That's fine, I will wait for him.　* will（願意）
⓮	請問可以坐這邊嗎？	Excuse me, may I sit here?

600

	單字	音標	詞性	意義	字頻	大考	英檢	多益
❶	salesperson	[ˋselz͵pɚsn]	n.	業務	7	1	中級	
	company	[ˋkʌmpənɪ]	n.	公司	1	2	初級	◎
	like	[laɪk]	v.	想要	1	1	初級	
	visit	[ˋvɪzɪt]	v.	拜訪	1	1	初級	◎
	boss	[bɔs]	n.	老闆	1	2	初級	
❷	sorry	[ˋsɑrɪ]	adj.	抱歉的	1	1	初級	
	let	[lɛt]	v.	讓…	1	1	初級	
	know	[no]	v.	知道	1	1	初級	◎
	arrived	[əˋraɪvd]	p.p.	arrive（抵達）過去分詞	1	2	初級	◎
❸	just	[dʒʌst]	adv.	就…	1	1	初級	
	tell	[tɛl]	v.	告訴	1	1	初級	
	here	[hɪr]	adv.	這裡	1	1	初級	
	mean	[min]	v.	用意	1	2	初級	◎
❹	happened	[ˋhæpənd]	p.t.	happen（碰巧）過去式	1	1	初級	
	neighborhood	[ˋnebɚ͵hʊd]	n.	鄰近地區	1	3	中級	
	stopped	[stɑpt]	p.t.	stop（順道拜訪）過去式	8	1	初級	◎
❺	made	[med]	p.p.	make（執行、做）過去分詞	1	1	初級	
	appointment	[əˋpɔɪntmənt]	n.	約會	2	4	中級	◎
❻	made	[med]	p.t.	make（執行、做）過去式	1	1	初級	
	phone	[fon]	n.	電話	1	2	初級	◎
❼	office	[ˋɔfɪs]	n.	公司	1	1	初級	◎
	rest	[rɛst]	n.	剩餘	1	1	初級	
	day	[de]	n.	一天	1	1	初級	
❽	ok	[ˋoˋke]	int.	好吧	1	1	初級	
	come	[kʌm]	v.	前來	1	1	初級	
	some	[sʌm]	adj.	一些	1	1	初級	
	other	[ˋʌðɚ]	adj.	其他的	1	1	初級	
❾	available	[əˋveləbl]	adj.	有空閒的	1	3	初級	◎
	meet	[mit]	v.	接見	1	1	初級	
	visitor	[ˋvɪzɪtɚ]	n.	客人	1	2	初級	◎
	right	[raɪt]	adv.	正值	1	1	初級	
	now	[nau]	adv.	現在	1	1	初級	
❿	time	[taɪm]	n.	時間	1	1	初級	◎
⓫	three	[θri]	n.	三	1	1	初級	
	pm	[ˋpiˋɛm]	adv.	下午	1	4		
	early	[ˋɝlɪ]	adv.	提早	1	1	初級	
⓬	please	[pliz]	adv.	請…	1	1	初級	
	show	[ʃo]	v.	帶領	1	1	初級	◎
	way	[we]	n.	路	1	1	初級	
⓭	fine	[faɪn]	adj.	沒關係的	1	1	初級	◎
	wait	[wet]	v.	等待	1	1	初級	◎
⓮	excuse	[ɪkˋskjuz]	v.	請問	2	2	初級	◎
	sit	[sɪt]	v.	坐	1	1	初級	

※「紅字單字」於本單元多句出現，「單字級等分析」僅列在「首次出現句」。

MP3 136-01 ❶～❹

❶	請問您是 X 公司的史密斯先生嗎？	Excuse me; are you Mr. Smith of X company? * excuse me（請問、不好意思）
❷	公司派我來機場接您。	My company sent me here to pick you up. * send＋某人（派遣某人） * pick＋某人＋up（接送某人）
❸	您好，我是 ABC 公司的陳大衛。	Hello, I am David Chen of ABC company.
❹	我一直等候您大駕光臨。	I've been waiting for your arrival. * wait for（等候） * your arrival（您的光臨、您的抵達）
❺	麻煩您在這裡等我。	Please wait here.
❻	一路上還好吧？	Did you have a good flight? * Did you...?（你剛才是…嗎） * have a good flight（搭機旅途愉快）
❼	您在台灣期間由我負責接待您。	I am responsible for taking care of you during your stay in Taiwan. * be responsible for（負責）＝ be in charge of * take care of（接待） * during one's stay（在某人停留時）
❽	我幫您拿一些行李吧。	Let me help you carry some of your baggage. * help＋某人＋動詞原形（幫某人坐…）
❾	歡迎您來到台灣。	Welcome to Taiwan. * welcome to＋某地（歡迎來到…）
❿	希望您在台灣期間過得愉快。	Hope you have a pleasant time in Taiwan. * have a pleasant time（有愉快時光、過得愉快）
⓫	我先為您說明今明兩天的行程。	First let me explain the itinerary of today and tomorrow. * let me explain（為您解說） * the itinerary of＋日期（某日期的行程）
⓬	我去把車子開過來。	I will pull the car over here. * pull over（開〔車〕到路邊）
⓭	我先帶您到飯店休息。	I'll go ahead and drive you to the hotel so you can rest.　* go ahead（開始）、drive you（開車載你）
⓮	旅途一切順利嗎？	Is everything on your trip going smoothly? * on one's trip（旅途中）、go smoothly（進行順利）

	單字	音標	詞性	意義	字頻	大考	英檢	多益
❶	excuse	[ɪkˋskjuz]	v.	請問	2	2	初級	◎
	Mr.	[ˋmɪstɚ]	n.	先生		1	初級	
	company	[ˋkʌmpənɪ]	n.	公司	1	2	初級	
❷	sent	[sɛnt]	p.t.	send（派遣）過去式	1	1	初級	
	here	[hɪr]	adv.	這裡	1	1	初級	
	pick	[pɪk]	v.	接送	1	2	初級	
	up	[ʌp]	adv.	接起	1	1	初級	
❸	hello	[həˋlo]	int.	您好	1	1	初級	
❹	waiting	[ˋwetɪŋ]	p.pr.	wait（等候）現在分詞	3	1	初級	◎
	arrival	[əˋraɪvl]	n.	抵達	2	3	中級	◎
❺	please	[pliz]	adv.	請…	1	1	初級	
	wait	[wet]	v.	等候	1	1	初級	◎
❻	have	[hæv]	v.	擁有	1	1	初級	
	good	[gʊd]	adj.	良好的	1	1	初級	◎
	flight	[flaɪt]	n.	搭機、飛行	1	2	初級	◎
❼	responsible	[rɪˋspɑsəbl]	adj.	負責的	1	2	初級	◎
	taking	[ˋtekɪŋ]	n.	take（採取）動名詞	4			
	care	[kɛr]	n.	照料	1	1	初級	◎
	stay	[ste]	n.	停留	1	1	初級	◎
	Taiwan	[ˋtaɪwɑn]	n.	台灣			初級	
❽	let	[lɛt]	v.	讓…	1	1	初級	
	help	[hɛlp]	v.	幫忙	1	1	初級	
	carry	[ˋkærɪ]	v.	提、拿	1	1	初級	◎
	some	[sʌm]	adj.	一些	1	1	初級	
	baggage	[ˋbægɪdʒ]	n.	行李	3	3	中級	◎
❾	welcome	[ˋwɛlkəm]	adj.	歡迎的	1	1	初級	
❿	hope	[hop]	v.	希望	1	1	初級	
	pleasant	[ˋplɛzənt]	adj.	愉快的	2	2	初級	
	time	[taɪm]	n.	時光	1	1	初級	◎
⓫	first	[fɝst]	adv.	首先	1	1	初級	
	explain	[ɪkˋsplen]	v.	說明	1	2	初級	◎
	itinerary	[aɪˋtɪnəˏrɛrɪ]	n.	行程	5			◎
	today	[təˋde]	n.	今天	1	1	初級	◎
	tomorrow	[təˋmoro]	n.	明天	1	1	初級	
⓬	pull	[pʊl]	v.	停車	1	1	初級	
	car	[kɑr]	n.	車子	1	1	初級	◎
	over	[ˋovɚ]	adv.	從一邊至另一邊	1	1	初級	
⓭	go	[go]	v.	去	1	1	初級	
	ahead	[əˋhɛd]	adv.	向前	1	1	初級	◎
	drive	[draɪv]	v.	開車	1	1	初級	◎
	hotel	[hoˋtɛl]	n.	飯店	1	2	初級	◎
	rest	[rɛst]	v.	休息	1	1	初級	
⓮	everything	[ˋɛvrɪˏθɪŋ]	pron.	每件事情	1		初級	
	trip	[trɪp]	n.	旅行	1	1	初級	◎
	going	[ˋgoɪŋ]	p.pr.	go（進行）現在分詞	4	1	初級	
	smoothly	[ˋsmuðlɪ]	adv.	順利地	3			◎

※「紅字單字」於本單元多句出現，「單字級等分析」僅列在「首次出現句」。

🔵 MP3 136-02 ❶～❹

❶	你好，我是 X 公司的麥可‧史密斯。	Hello, I'm Michael Smith of X company.
❷	謝謝你來接我。	Thank you for picking me up. * pick＋某人＋up（接送某人）
❸	這樣麻煩你真不好意思。	I'm very sorry to bother you with this. * sorry to＋動詞原形（抱歉⋯） * bother you（麻煩你）
❹	你的車停哪？	Where did you park your car? * Where did you＋動詞?（你剛才做⋯是在哪？） * park a car（停車）
❺	行李我自己拿就可以了。	I can carry my luggage. * luggage（行李）＝ baggage
❻	我在這裡等你開車過來嗎？	Should I just wait for you to drive over here? * Should I⋯?（我應該⋯嗎）、over here（到這裡）
❼	這真是趟漫長的旅程。	This seems like an endless journey. * seem like（似乎是） * endless journey（漫長的旅程）
❽	我想先回飯店休息。	I would like to go to the hotel to rest. * would like to（想要）
❾	你可以先帶我去吃點東西嗎？	Can you take me to get a bite to eat? * get a bite to eat（隨便吃點東西）
❿	你可以先告訴我今天的行程嗎？	Can you tell me about today's schedule first? * about（關於）、today's schedule（今日行程）
⓫	接下來幾天是你負責接待我嗎？	Are you going to be my guide for the next few days? * Are you going to⋯?（接下來你會⋯嗎） * the next few days（之後這幾天） * 此句用「未來簡單式問句」（Are...going to...?）表示「詢問對方是否有某預定計畫？」。
⓬	我這幾天要如何跟你聯絡？	How can I contact you for the next few days? * How can I⋯?（我要如何⋯？）
⓭	我想直接去你們公司。	I want to go directly to your company. * go directly to＋某地（直接去）
⓮	你明天早上會來接我嗎？	Are you going to pick me up tomorrow morning? * tomorrow morning（明天早上）

	單字	音標	詞性	意義	字頻	大考	英檢	多益
❶	hello	[həˋlo]	int.	你好	1	1	初級	
	company	[ˋkʌmpənɪ]	n.	公司	1	2	初級	◎
❷	thank	[θæŋk]	v.	感謝	1	1	初級	
	picking	[ˋpɪkɪŋ]	n.	pick（接送）動名詞	8	2	初級	
	up	[ʌp]	adv.	接起	1	1	初級	
❸	very	[ˋvɛrɪ]	adv.	十分	1	1	初級	
	sorry	[ˋsɑrɪ]	adj.	抱歉的	1	1	初級	
	bother	[ˋbɑðɚ]	v.	麻煩	1	2	初級	◎
❹	park	[pɑrk]	v.	停車	1	1	初級	
	car	[kɑr]	n.	車子	1	1	初級	◎
❺	carry	[ˋkærɪ]	v.	提、拿	1	1	初級	◎
	luggage	[ˋlʌgɪdʒ]	n.	行李	3	3	中級	◎
❻	just	[dʒʌst]	adv.	就…	1	1	初級	
	wait	[wet]	v.	等候	1	1	初級	◎
	drive	[draɪv]	v.	開車	1	1	初級	◎
	over	[ˋovɚ]	adv.	從一邊至另一邊	1	1	初級	
	here	[hɪr]	adv.	這裡	1	1	初級	
❼	seem	[sim]	v.	似乎	1	1	初級	◎
	endless	[ˋɛndlɪs]	adj.	漫長的、無盡的	2		中高	
	journey	[ˋdʒɝnɪ]	n.	旅程	1	3	中級	◎
❽	like	[laɪk]	v.	想要	1	1	初級	
	go	[go]	v.	去	1	1	初級	
	hotel	[hoˋtɛl]	n.	飯店	1	2	初級	
	rest	[rɛst]	n.	休息	1	1	初級	
❾	take	[tek]	v.	帶領	1	1	初級	◎
	get	[gɛt]	v.	獲取	1	1	初級	◎
	bite	[baɪt]	n.	一口的量	2	1	初級	
	eat	[it]	v.	吃	1	1	初級	
❿	tell	[tɛl]	v.	告訴	1	1	初級	
	today	[təˋde]	n.	今天	1	1	初級	◎
	schedule	[ˋskɛdʒʊl]	n.	行程	1	3	中級	◎
	first	[fɝst]	adv.	首先	1	1	初級	
⓫	going	[ˋgoɪŋ]	p.pr.	go（即將）現在分詞	4	1	初級	
	guide	[gaɪd]	n.	嚮導	1	1	初級	◎
	next	[nɛkst]	adj.	接下來的	1	1	初級	
	few	[fju]	adj.	些許的	1	1	初級	◎
	day	[de]	n.	天	1	1	初級	
⓬	contact	[kənˋtækt]	v.	聯繫	1	2	初級	◎
⓭	want	[wɑnt]	v.	想要	1	1	初級	◎
	directly	[dəˋrɛktlɪ]	adv.	直接地	1		中高	◎
⓮	pick	[pɪk]	v.	接送	1	2	初級	
	tomorrow	[təˋmɔro]	n.	明天	1	1	初級	◎
	morning	[ˋmɔrnɪŋ]	n.	早上	1	1	初級	

※「紅字單字」於本單元多句出現，「單字級等分析」僅列在「首次出現句」。

MP3 137-01 ❶～❽

❶	我想找時間到貴公司拜訪。	I want to take some time to pay a visit to your company. * take some time（找個時間、花點時間） * pay a visit（拜訪） * to＋地點（前往某地點）
❷	您好，我是接替傑克職務的人。	Hello, I am the person who replaced Jack. * the person who＋動詞...（…的人） * replace＋某人（接替某人） 　＝ take over for＋某人
❸	請問什麼時候方便過去拜訪您？	May I ask when would be a suitable time to visit you? * May I ask when...?（請問什麼時候…？） * would be（大概會是） * suitable time（方便的時間） * visit＋人／地點（拜訪某人／某地點）
❹	這是我的名片，請多指教。	This is my business card; I look forward to working with you in the future. * business card（名片） * look forward to working with you in the future（請多指教） * look forward to＋動詞-ing（期待） * work with you（和你共事） * in the future（在未來）
❺	您好，我是 LKK 公司的吳大衛。	Hello, I'm David Wu from LKK company. * from＋公司（來自某公司）
❻	我主要負責業務方面的工作。	I'm mainly responsible for business matters. * mainly responsible for（主要負責） * business matters（業務事宜）
❼	以後將由我繼續為貴公司服務。	I will continue to serve your company in the future. * will continue to＋動詞原形（將會繼續） * serve＋人事物（服務某人事物）
❽	有任何需要請跟我說。	Please let me know if you need anything. * please let me know（請告訴我） * if＋主詞＋動詞（要是…、如果…）

	單字	音標	詞性	意義	字頻	大考	英檢	多益
❶	want	[wɑnt]	v.	想要	1	1	初級	◎
	take	[tek]	v.	花費	1	1	初級	◎
	some	[sʌm]	adj.	一些	1	1	初級	
	time	[taɪm]	n.	時間	1	1	初級	◎
	pay	[pe]	v.	致以（拜訪）	1	3	初級	◎
	visit	[`vɪzɪt]	n.	拜訪、訪問	1	1	初級	◎
	company	[`kʌmpənɪ]	n.	公司	1	2	初級	◎
❷	hello	[hə`lo]	int.	您好	1	1	初級	
	person	[`pɝsn]	n.	人	1	1	初級	
	replaced	[rɪ`plest]	p.t.	replace（接替）過去式	1	3	中級	◎
❸	ask	[æsk]	v.	詢問	1	1	初級	
	suitable	[`sutəbl̩]	adj.	方便的	2	3	中級	◎
❹	this	[ðɪs]	pron.	這個	1	1	初級	
	business	[`bɪznɪs]	n.	商業、商務	1	2	初級	◎
	card	[kɑrd]	n.	卡片	1	1	初級	◎
	look	[lʊk]	v.	期待	1	1	初級	
	forward	[`fɔrwəd]	adv.	今後、將來	1	2	初級	◎
	working	[`wɝkɪŋ]	n.	work（工作）動名詞	2	1	中級	◎
	future	[`fjutɚ]	n.	未來	1	2	初級	
❻	mainly	[`menlɪ]	adv.	主要	2		中級	◎
	responsible	[rɪ`spɑnsəbl̩]	adj.	負責的	1	2	初級	◎
	matter	[`mætɚ]	n.	事宜	1	1	初級	◎
❼	continue	[kən`tɪnjʊ]	v.	繼續	1	1	初級	◎
	serve	[sɝv]	v.	服務	1	1	初級	◎
❽	please	[pliz]	adv.	請…	1	1	初級	
	let	[lɛt]	v.	讓…	1	1	初級	
	know	[no]	v.	知道	1	1	初級	◎
	need	[nid]	v.	需要	1	1	初級	◎
	anything	[`ɛnɪˌθɪŋ]	pron.	任何事情	1	1	初級	

※「紅字單字」於本單元多句出現，「單字級等分析」僅列在「首次出現句」。

🔊 MP3 137-01 ❾～❻

❾	很抱歉臨時來打擾您。	I'm very sorry to trouble you at the last minute. * **be sorry to**＋動詞（抱歉…） * **trouble**＋某人（造成某人的麻煩） 　＝ **make troubles for**＋某人 * **at the last minute**（在最後一刻、在緊要關頭時） 　＝ **at the last moment**
❿	我是剛剛打電話來的懷特。	I'm White, the one who just called. * **the one who**＋動詞（做…的某人）
⓫	請問怎麼稱呼？	May I ask your name? * **May I ask**＋名詞?（請問…）
⓬	我們的報價是同業中最便宜的。	Our price quotes are the cheapest in the business. * **price quote**（報價） * **in the business**（在這個產業中、在同業中） 　＝ **in the industry**
⓭	方便給我一張您的名片嗎？	May I have your business card? * **May I have**＋名詞?（請給我…） * **business card**（名片） * **contact information**（聯絡資訊）
⓮	希望能爭取跟貴公司合作的機會。	I really hope that we can have the opportunity to cooperate with your firm. * **really hope that**＋子句（非常希望…） * **have the opportunity**（有機會） 　＝ **have the chance** * **cooperate with**＋人事物（和某人事物合作） 　＝ **collaborate with**＋人事物 * **firm**（公司）＝ **company**
⓯	您是史密斯先生吧？久仰大名。	Are you Mr. Smith? I've heard a lot about you. * **Are you**＋名字?（你叫某名字嗎、你是…嗎） * **have heard a lot**（曾經聽聞許多） * **about you**（關於你）
⓰	希望有幸能為貴公司服務。	I really hope that we have the opportunity to serve your company. * **serve your company**（服務貴公司）

單字級等分析

	單字	音標	詞性	意義	字頻	大考	英檢	多益
❾	very	[ˋvɛrɪ]	adv.	十分	1	1	初級	
	sorry	[ˋsɑrɪ]	adj.	抱歉的	1	1	初級	
	trouble	[ˋtrʌbl]	v.	造成…的麻煩	1	1	初級	◎
	last	[læst]	adj.	最後的、緊要關頭的	1	1	初級	◎
	minute	[ˋmɪnɪt]	n.	時刻	1	1	初級	◎
❿	one	[wʌn]	pron.	一個人	1	1	初級	
	just	[dʒʌst]	adv.	剛剛	1	1	初級	
	called	[kɔld]	p.t.	call（來電）過去式	4	1	初級	◎
⓫	ask	[æsk]	v.	詢問	1	1	初級	
	name	[nem]	n.	名字	1	1	初級	◎
⓬	price	[praɪs]	n.	價格	1	1	初級	◎
	quote	[kwot]	n.	報價	1	3	中級	◎
	cheapest	[ˋtʃipɪst]	adj.	cheap（便宜的）最高級	1	2	初級	◎
	business	[ˋbɪznɪs]	n.	產業、行業/商業、商務	1	2	初級	◎
⓭	have	[hæv]	v.	擁有	1	1	初級	
	card	[kard]	n.	卡片	1	1	初級	◎
⓮	really	[ˋrɪəlɪ]	adv.	很、非常	1	1	初級	
	hope	[hop]	v.	希望	1	1	初級	
	opportunity	[ˌɑpɚˋtjunətɪ]	n.	機會	1	3	初級	◎
	cooperate	[koˋɑpəˌret]	v.	合作	2	4	中級	◎
	firm	[fɝm]	n.	公司	1	2	初級	◎
⓯	Mr.	[ˋmɪstɚ]	n.	先生	1	1	初級	
	heard	[hɝd]	p.p.	hear（聽聞）過去分詞	1	1	初級	
	lot	[lɑt]	n.	許多	1			
⓰	serve	[sɝv]	v.	服務	1	1	初級	◎
	company	[ˋkʌmpənɪ]	n.	公司	1	2	初級	◎

※「紅字單字」於本單元多句出現，「單字級等分析」僅列在「首次出現句」。

🔊 MP3 137-02 ❶〜❽

❶	要不要我先幫您估個價？	Would you mind if I made an assessment for you first? * **Would you mind if**＋過去式子句?（你會介意…嗎） * **make an assessment**（估價） * **initial assessment**（初步估價）
❷	請問您有什麼需要？	May I ask what it is that you need? * **May I ask what it is that...?**（請問…是什麼？） * **that you need**（你需要的）
❸	您是希望降折扣嗎？	You're looking for a discount, right? * **be looking for**（正在尋求、正在期待） * **...., right?**（…，對吧？） * 此句用「現在進行式」（...are looking...） 表示「現階段發生的事」。
❹	您希望我們給您多少的折扣？	How much of a discount would you like us to offer? * **How much of**＋名詞...?（…是多少？） * **like**＋某人＋**to**＋動詞原形（想要某人…） * **offer a discount**（提供折扣）＝ **give a discount** * **obtain a discount**（取得折扣）
❺	您的要求我們會優先考量。	Your requests will be our top priority. * **will be**（總是、會是） * **top priority**（優先考量、當務之急） * 此句用「未來簡單式」（...will...） 表示「某人經常性的習慣」。
❻	您有任何要求都可以提出來討論。	Go ahead and bring up any requests that you would like to discuss. * **go ahead**（開始進行） * **bring up**（提出、說出來） * **request**（要求、需求）＝ **need** * **request**＋**that**＋子句（…的要求） * **would like to**（想要）
❼	您需要詳細的價目表嗎？	Do you need a detailed price list? * **price list**（價目表）
❽	請務必讓我們知道您的需求。	Please let us know what you need. * **what you need**（你的需求）

	單字	音標	詞性	意義	字頻	大考	英檢	多益
❶	mind	[maɪnd]	v.	介意	1	1	初級	◎
	made	[med]	p.t.	make（做）過去式	1	1	初級	
	assessment	[əˈsɛsmənt]	n.	估價	1	6	中高	◎
	first	[fɜst]	adv.	首先	1	1	初級	
❷	ask	[æsk]	v.	詢問	1	1	初級	
	need	[nid]	v.	需要	1	1	初級	◎
❸	looking	[ˈlʊkɪŋ]	p.pr.	look（尋求）現在分詞	5	1	初級	
	discount	[ˈdɪskaʊnt]	n.	折扣	2	3	中級	◎
	right	[raɪt]	int.	對吧	1	1	初級	
❹	much	[mʌtʃ]	adj.	許多的	1	1	初級	
	like	[laɪk]	v.	想要	1	1	初級	
	offer	[ˈɔfə]	v.	提供	1	2	初級	◎
❺	request	[rɪˈkwɛst]	n.	要求、需求	1	3	中級	◎
	top	[tɑp]	adj.	最高的	1	1	初級	◎
	priority	[praɪˈɔrətɪ]	n.	優先	1	5	中高	
❻	go	[go]	v.	去	1	1	初級	
	ahead	[əˈhɛd]	adv.	向前、直接	1	1	初級	◎
	bring	[brɪŋ]	v.	提出	1	1	初級	
	up	[ʌp]	adv.	出來	1	1	初級	
	any	[ˈɛnɪ]	adj.	任何	1	1	初級	
	discuss	[dɪˈskʌs]	v.	討論	1	2	初級	◎
❼	detailed	[ˈdiˈteld]	adj.	詳細的	2	3	中級	◎
	price	[praɪs]	n.	價錢	1	1	初級	◎
	list	[lɪst]	n.	表單	1	1	初級	◎
❽	please	[pliz]	adv.	請…	1	1	初級	
	let	[lɛt]	v.	讓…	1	1	初級	
	know	[no]	v.	知道	1	1	初級	◎

※「紅字單字」於本單元多句出現，「單字級等分析」僅列在「首次出現句」。

❾	請問您希望何時簽約？	When would you like to sign the agreement? * **When would you like to...?**（你想要什麼時候…？） * **sign the agreement**（簽約）= sign the contract * **adhere to the agreement**（遵守合約）
❿	您有其他的考量嗎？	Do you have any other considerations? * **Do you have＋名詞?**（你是否有…？） * **have other considerations**（有其他考量） * **take into consideration**（納入考量）
⓫	付款方式您可以自由選擇。	You are free to choose the type of payment. * **free to＋動詞原形**（任意…、自由…） * **the type of＋名詞**（…的方式） * **the type of payment**（付款方式）
⓬	您是考慮成本的問題嗎？	Are you considering the problem of cost? * **Are you＋動詞-ing...?**（你是在…嗎） * **consider**（考慮、斟酌）= think about * **the problem of＋名詞**（…的問題）
⓭	付款期限我們可以再商量。	We can discuss the payment terms later. * **payment terms**（付款期限） * **delivery terms**（交貨期限）
⓮	您不用擔心品質問題。	You don't need to worry about the quality. * **not need to**（不需要、不必） * **worry about**（擔心）
⓯	售後服務的問題您不用擔心。	You don't need to worry about after-sale service. * **after-sale service**（售後服務） * **be under warranty**（於保固期內）
⓰	我們隨時有專人為您服務。	Our expert staff is always at your service. * **expert staff**（專人） * **at your service**（隨時為你效勞） * 此句用「現在簡單式」（...is...） 表示「經常如此的事。
⓱	您是擔心價格會調漲嗎？	Are you worried about the increase in price? * **be worried about**（擔心）= worry about * **increase in price**（漲價） * **decrease in price**（降價）

單字級等分析

	單字	音標	詞性	意義	字頻	大考	英檢	多益
❾	like	[laɪk]	v.	想要	1	1	初級	
	sign	[saɪn]	v.	簽署	1	2	初級	◎
	agreement	[ə`grimənt]	n.	合約	1	1	中級	◎
❿	have	[hæv]	v.	擁有	1	1	初級	
	any	[`ɛnɪ]	adj.	任何的	1	1	初級	
	other	[`ʌðə]	adj.	其他的	1	1	初級	
	consideration	[kənsɪdə`reʃən]	n.	考慮	1	3	中級	◎
⓫	free	[fri]	adj.	任意的、自由的	1	1	初級	
	choose	[tʃuz]	v.	選擇	1	2	初級	◎
	type	[taɪp]	n.	方式	1	2	初級	◎
	payment	[`pemənt]	n.	付款	1	1	中級	◎
⓬	considering	[kən`sɪdərɪŋ]	p.pr.	consider（考慮）現在分詞	2	2	中高	◎
	problem	[`prɑbləm]	n.	問題	1	1	初級	◎
	cost	[kɔst]	n.	成本	1	1	初級	◎
⓭	discuss	[dɪ`skʌs]	v.	討論	1	2	初級	◎
	term	[tɝm]	n.	期限	1	2	初級	◎
	later	[`letə]	adv.	以後、之後	1		初級	
⓮	need	[nid]	v.	需要	1	1	初級	◎
	worry	[`wɝɪ]	v.	擔心	1	1	初級	◎
	quality	[`kwɑlətɪ]	n.	品質	1	2	初級	◎
⓯	after-sale	[`æftə.sel]	adj.	售後的				
	service	[`sɝvɪs]	n.	服務	1	1	初級	◎
⓰	expert	[`ɛkspɝt]	n.	專家	1	2	初級	◎
	staff	[stæf]	n.	人員	1	3	中級	◎
	always	[`ɔlwez]	adv.	隨時、一直	1	1	初級	
⓱	worried	[`wɝɪd]	adj.	擔心的	2	1	中級	◎
	increase	[`ɪnkris]	n.	增加	1	2	初級	◎
	price	[praɪs]	n.	價格	1	1	初級	◎

※「紅字單字」於本單元多句出現，「單字級等分析」僅列在「首次出現句」。

MP3 138-01 ❶～❼

❶	您會考慮長期跟我們合作嗎？	Would you consider working with us for the long term? * **Would you＋動詞...?**（你願意…嗎） * **consider＋動詞-ing**（考慮做…） * **work with**（共事、合作） * **long term**（長期）、**short tem**（短期）
❷	林先生，您好嗎？好久不見。	How are you, Mr. Lin? It's been a long time. * **How are you?**（你好嗎，問候用語） * **It's been a long time.**（好久不見）
❸	百忙之中勞您抽空見我，非常感謝。	I appreciate that you've found some time in your full schedule to see me. * **appreciate that＋子句**（感激…） * 子句用「現在完成式」（...have found...）表示「過去某時點發生某事，且結果持續到現在」。 * **find some time**（抽空、抽出時間） * **in one's full schedule**（在百忙之中）
❹	希望貴公司再給我們一次機會。	We hope that your firm will give us another chance. * **hope that＋子句**（希望…） * **another chance**（再一次機會） * **firm**（公司）＝ **company**
❺	請問您何時會做出決定？	When will you make the decision, may I ask? * **When will you...?**（你之後什麼時候會…？） * **make the decision**（做決定） * **..., may I ask?**（請問…）
❻	希望您好好考慮，我等您的答覆。	Hope you will think about it; I'm looking forward to your answer. * **Hope＋主詞＋動詞**（我希望…） * **think about**（考慮）＝ **consider** * **look forward to＋名詞**（期待…） * **answer**（答覆）＝ **reply**
❼	如果還有任何問題，請與我聯絡。	Please contact me if you have any further questions about that. * **contact me**（與我聯絡） * **further questions**（其他問題）、**about**（關於）

	單字	音標	詞性	意義	字頻	大考	英檢	多益
❶	consider	[kənˋsɪdɚ]	v.	考慮	1	2	初級	◎
	working	[ˋwɝkɪŋ]	n.	work（工作）動名詞	2	1	中級	◎
	long	[lɔŋ]	adj.	長期的	1	1	初級	
	term	[tɝm]	n.	期限	1	2	初級	◎
❷	Mr.	[ˋmɪstɚ]	n.	先生		1	初級	
	time	[taɪm]	n.	時間	1	1	初級	◎
❸	appreciate	[əˋpriʃɪˏet]	v.	感激	1	3	初級	◎
	found	[faʊnd]	p.p.	find（抽出）過去分詞	1	3	中級	◎
	some	[sʌm]	adj.	一些	1	1	初級	
	full	[fʊl]	adj.	滿的	1	1	初級	
	schedule	[ˋskɛdʒʊl]	n.	行程	1	3	中級	◎
	see	[si]	v.	見面	1	1	初級	
❹	hope	[hop]	v.	希望	1	1	初級	
	firm	[fɝm]	n.	公司	1	2	初級	◎
	give	[gɪv]	v.	給予	1	1	初級	
	another	[əˋnʌðɚ]	adj.	再一次的	1	1		
	chance	[tʃæns]	n.	機會	1	1	初級	
❺	make	[mek]	v.	做出	1	1	初級	
	decision	[dɪˋsɪʒən]	n.	決定	1	2	初級	◎
	ask	[æsk]	v.	詢問	1	1	初級	
❻	think	[θɪŋk]	v.	考慮	1	1	初級	
	looking	[ˋlʊkɪŋ]	p.pr.	look（期待）現在分詞	5	1	初級	
	forward	[ˋfɔrwɚd]	adv.	今後、將來	1	2	初級	◎
	answer	[ˋænsɚ]	n.	答覆	1	1	初級	
❼	please	[pliz]	adv.	請…	1	1	初級	
	contact	[kənˋtækt]	v.	聯絡	1	2	初級	◎
	have	[hæv]	v.	擁有	1	1	初級	
	any	[ˋɛnɪ]	adj.	任何的	1	1	初級	
	further	[ˋfɝðɚ]	adj.	進一步的	5	2	初級	◎
	question	[ˋkwɛstʃən]	n.	問題	1	1	初級	
	that	[ðæt]	pron.	那件事	1	1	初級	

※「紅字單字」於本單元多句出現，「單字級等分析」僅列在「首次出現句」。

🔵 MP3 138-01 ❽～⓱

❽	我要來跟您簽約。	I've come to sign a contract with you. * have＋過去分詞（已經…） * come to＋動詞（決定要…） * sign a contract（簽約）
❾	明天給您答覆可以嗎？	Can I give you the answer tomorrow? * give an answer（給予回覆）＝ offer an answer
❿	我會盡可能完成您的所有要求。	I'll try my best to fulfill all of your requests. * try one's best（盡全力） * fulfill one's requests（達成要求、完成要求） * 此句用「未來簡單式」（…will…） 　表示「有意願做的事」。
⓫	我會跟公司反應您的意見。	I'll relay your feedback to our company. * relay your feedback（回饋你的意見）
⓬	我們非常有誠意要跟您做生意。	We would sincerely like to do business with you. * would sincerely like to＋動詞（誠心誠意要…） * do business（做生意）
⓭	上次您反應的事情我們做了調整。	We've already made some adjustments in response to the suggestions you gave last time. * make some adjustments（做一些調整） * in response to（因應） * the suggestions you gave（你之前提供的建議） * last time（上一次）
⓮	您要不要先看一下合約？	Would you like to see the contract first? * would like to（想要） * contract（合約）＝ agreement
⓯	這是新的報價單。	This is the new price list.　* price list（價目表）
⓰	合約內容有問題嗎？	Are there any questions about the content of the agreement? * Are there＋名詞複數…?（是否有…？） * the content of the agreement（合約內容）
⓱	抱歉，打擾您這麼久。	I'm very sorry to have bothered you for so long. * sorry to have＋過去分詞（抱歉一直…） * have bothered for so long（打擾這麼久）

單字級等分析

	單字	音標	詞性	意義	字頻	大考	英檢	多益
❽	come	[kʌm]	p.p.	決定要	1	1	初級	
	sign	[saɪn]	v.	簽署	1	2	初級	◎
	contract	[ˋkɑntrækt]	n.	合約	1	3	初級	
❾	give	[gɪv]	v.	給予	1	1	初級	
	answer	[ˋænsɚ]	n.	答覆	1	1	初級	
	tomorrow	[təˋnɔro]	adv.	明天	1	1	初級	
❿	try	[traɪ]	v.	努力	1	1	初級	
	best	[bɛst]	n.	最好	1	1	初級	
	fulfill	[fʊlˋfɪl]	v.	達成、完成	2	4	中級	◎
	all	[ɔl]	pron.	全部	1	1	初級	
	request	[rɪˋkwɛst]	n.	要求	1	3	中級	◎
⓫	relay	[rɪˋle]	v.	轉達	3	6	中高	
	feedback	[ˋfid͵bæk]	n.	意見	2	6	中級	◎
	company	[ˋkʌmpənɪ]	n.	公司	1	2	初級	◎
⓬	sincerely	[sɪnˋsɪrlɪ]	adv.	誠心誠意地	4		中級	◎
	like	[laɪk]	v.	想要	1	1	初級	
	do	[du]	v.	做、從事	1	1	初級	
	business	[ˋbɪznɪs]	n.	生意	1	2	初級	◎
⓭	already	[ɔlˋrɛdɪ]	adv.	已經	1	1	初級	◎
	made	[med]	p.p.	make（做出）過去分詞	1	1	初級	
	some	[sʌm]	adj.	一些	1	1	初級	
	adjustment	[əˋdʒʌstmənt]	n.	調整	2	4	中高	◎
	response	[rɪˋspɑns]	n.	因應	1	3	中級	◎
	suggestion	[səˋdʒɛstʃən]	n.	建議	1	4	中級	◎
	gave	[gev]	p.t.	give（給予）過去式	1	1	初級	
	last	[læst]	adj.	上一個	1	1	初級	◎
	time	[taɪm]	n.	次、回	1	1	初級	◎
⓮	see	[si]	v.	看	1	1	初級	
	first	[fɝst]	adv.	首先	1	1	初級	
⓯	this	[ðɪs]	pron.	這個	1	1	初級	
	new	[nju]	adj.	新的	1	1	初級	
	price	[praɪs]	n.	價格	1	1	初級	◎
	list	[lɪst]	n.	清單	1	1	初級	◎
⓰	there	[ðɛr]	adv.	有…	1	1	初級	
	any	[ˋɛnɪ]	adj.	任何的	1	1	初級	
	question	[ˋkwɛstʃən]	n.	問題	1	1	初級	
	content	[ˋkɑntɛnt]	n.	內容	1	4	中級	◎
	agreement	[əˋgrimənt]	n.	合約	1	1	中級	◎
⓱	very	[ˋvɛrɪ]	adv.	十分	1	1	初級	
	sorry	[ˋsɑrɪ]	adj.	抱歉的	1	1	初級	
	bothered	[ˋbɑðɚd]	p.p.	bother（打擾、麻煩）過去分詞	1	2	初級	◎
	so	[so]	adv.	這麼	1	1	初級	
	long	[lɔŋ]	n.	長時間	1	1	初級	

※「紅字單字」於本單元多句出現，「單字級等分析」僅列在「首次出現句」。

617

MP3 138-02 ❶～❾

❶	不要緊，歡迎你來。	That's OK, you're welcome. * That's OK.（沒關係、不要緊）＝ That's fine.
❷	平時很謝謝你們公司的幫忙。	Thank you for your firm's steady assistance. * Thank you for＋名詞（謝謝你們的…） * firm（公司）＝ company * steady assistance（長期持續的幫忙）
❸	沒關係，我上一個訪客才剛離開。	That's fine; my last visitor has just left. * last＋名詞（前一個…） * have / has left（已經離開）
❹	你好，找我有什麼事情嗎？	Hello, what can I do for you? * do for＋某人（為某人做…）
❺	我記得我今天沒跟你約吧？	I don't remember having an appointment with you for today. * remember＋動詞-ing（記得…） * have an appointment（有約、預約會面） * cancel an appointment（取消預約、取消會面）
❻	今天怎麼會來？	Why did you come here today? * Why did you...?（為什麼你稍早前會…？）
❼	我等一下要開會，請長話短說。	I have a meeting coming up, so please make it short. * have a meeting（開會） * coming up（即將到來）、so（因此） * make it short（長話短說）
❽	希望你盡快幫我解決這個問題。	I hope that you can help me solve this problem as soon as possible. * I hope that＋子句（我希望…） * help＋某人＋動詞原形（幫某人做…） * solve a problem（解決問題） * as soon as possible（盡快）
❾	上次談的價錢你評估了嗎？	Have you evaluated the price we discussed last time? * Have you＋過去分詞...?（你已經…了嗎） * evaluate the price（評估價格） * we discussed（我們之前談的） * last time（上一次）

	單字	音標	詞性	意義	字頻	大考	英檢	多益
❶	that	[ðæt]	pron.	那個	1	1	初級	
	ok	[ˋoˈke]	adj.	不要緊的	1	1	初級	
	welcome	[ˋwɛlkəm]	adj.	歡迎的	1	1	初級	
❷	thank	[θæŋk]	v.	感謝	1	1	初級	
	firm	[fɝm]	n.	公司	1	1	初級	◎
	steady	[ˋstɛdɪ]	adj.	長期持續的	2	3	中級	◎
	assistance	[əˋsɪstəns]	n.	幫忙	1	4	中級	◎
❸	fine	[faɪn]	adj.	沒關係的	1	1	初級	◎
	last	[læst]	adj.	前一個	1	1	初級	◎
	visitor	[ˋvɪzɪtə]	n.	訪客	1	2	初級	◎
	just	[dʒʌst]	adv.	剛剛	1	1	初級	
	left	[lɛft]	p.p.	leave（離開）過去分詞	1	1	初級	
❹	hello	[həˋlo]	int.	你好	1	1	初級	
	do	[du]	v.	做	1	1	初級	
❺	remember	[rɪˋmɛmbə]	v.	記得	1	1	初級	◎
	having	[ˋhævɪŋ]	n.	have（擁有）動名詞	1	1	初級	
	appointment	[əˋpɔɪntmənt]	n.	約會	2	4	中級	◎
	today	[təˋde]	n./adv.	今天	1	1	初級	◎
❻	come	[kʌm]	v.	前來	1	1	初級	
	here	[hɪr]	adv.	這裡	1	1	初級	
❼	have	[hæv]	v.	擁有	1	1	初級	
	meeting	[ˋmitɪŋ]	n.	會議	1	2	初級	
	coming	[ˋkʌmɪŋ]	p.pr.	come（到來）現在分詞	2	1	中級	
	up	[ʌp]	adv.	接近、靠前	1	1	初級	
	please	[pliz]	adv.	請…	1	1	初級	
	make	[mek]	v.	使得	1	1	初級	
	short	[ʃɔrt]	adj.	簡短的	1	1	初級	◎
❽	hope	[hop]	v.	希望	1	1	初級	
	help	[hɛlp]	v.	幫忙	1	1	初級	
	solve	[sɑlv]	v.	解決	1	2	初級	◎
	this	[ðɪs]	adj.	這個	1	1	初級	
	problem	[ˋprɑbləm]	n.	問題	1	1	初級	◎
	soon	[sun]	adv.	快、早	1	1	初級	
	possible	[ˋpɑsəbl]	adv.	可能地	1	1	初級	◎
❾	evaluated	[ɪˋvæljuˌetɪd]	p.p.	evaluate（評估）過去分詞	1	4	中級	◎
	price	[praɪs]	n.	價格	1	1	初級	◎
	discussed	[dɪsˋkʌst]	p.t.	discuss（討論）過去式	1	2	初級	◎
	time	[taɪm]	n.	次、回	1	1	初級	◎

※「紅字單字」於本單元多句出現，「單字級等分析」僅列在「首次出現句」。

❿	我打算終止我們的合作關係。	I plan to terminate the cooperative relations between us. * plan to＋動詞原形（打算） * terminate a relation（結束關係） * cooperative relations（合作關係） * between us（在我們之間）
⓫	我不想跟你們公司合作。	I don't want to work with your company. * don't / doesn't want to＋動詞原形（不想要） * work with（合作）= cooperate with * company（公司）= firm
⓬	你什麼時候可以給我答案？	When can you give me your reply? * When can you...?（你什麼時候可以…？） * give one's reply（給予答覆） * reply（答覆）= answer
⓭	我目前沒有換廠商的打算。	I currently don't have any plans to change suppliers. * currently（目前）= presently * not have any plans to（不打算…）
⓮	我考慮看看。	Let me think about it. * think about（考慮）
⓯	我上次已經清楚表達我的立場。	I already made my position very clear last time. * make my position（表達我的立場） * 此句用「過去簡單式」（...made...） 　表示「發生在過去的事」。
⓰	你們公司可不可以拿出點誠意？	Could your firm show a little sincerity? * Could＋主詞＋動詞?（可以請…嗎） * your firm（你們公司） * show a little sincerity（拿出一點點誠意） * show a complete sincerity（拿出最大的誠意） * sincerity（誠意）= good faith
⓱	不好意思，又讓你跑一趟。	I'm sorry to make you come here one more time. * sorry to＋動詞原形（抱歉…） * make＋某人＋動詞原形（讓某人…） * one more time（再一次）

	單字	音標	詞性	意義	字頻	大考	英檢	多益
⑩	plan	[plæn]	v./n.	打算	1	1	初級	◎
	terminate	[ˈtɝmə.net]	v.	終止、結束	3	6	中高	◎
	cooperative	[koˈɑpə.retɪv]	adj.	合作的	2	4	中級	
	relation	[rɪˈleʃən]	n.	關係	1	2	中級	◎
⑪	want	[wɑnt]	v.	想要	1	1	初級	◎
	work	[wɝk]	v.	工作	1	1	初級	◎
	company	[ˈkʌmpənɪ]	n.	公司	1	2	初級	◎
⑫	give	[gɪv]	v.	給予	1	1	初級	
	reply	[rɪˈplaɪ]	n.	答覆	1	2	初級	◎
⑬	currently	[ˈkɝəntlɪ]	adv.	目前	1			◎
	have	[hæv]	v.	擁有	1	1	初級	
	any	[ˈɛnɪ]	adj.	任何的	1	1	初級	
	change	[tʃendʒ]	v.	更換	1	2	初級	◎
	supplier	[səˈplaɪɚ]	n.	供應商	2		中高	◎
⑭	let	[lɛt]	v.	讓…	1	1	初級	
	think	[θɪŋk]	v.	考慮	1	1	初級	
⑮	already	[ɔlˈrɛdɪ]	adv.	已經	1	1	初級	◎
	made	[med]	p.t.	make（表明）過去式	1	1	初級	
	position	[pəˈzɪʃən]	n.	立場	1	1	初級	
	very	[ˈvɛrɪ]	adv.	十分	1	1	初級	
	clear	[klɪr]	adj.	明確的	1	1	初級	◎
	last	[læst]	adj.	上一個	1	1	初級	◎
	time	[taɪm]	n.	次、回	1	1	初級	◎
⑯	firm	[fɝm]	n.	公司	1	2	初級	◎
	show	[ʃo]	v.	展現、拿出	1	1	初級	◎
	little	[ˈlɪtl̩]	adj.	一點點的	1	1	初級	
	sincerity	[sɪnˈsɛrətɪ]	n.	誠意	4	4	中高	
⑰	sorry	[ˈsɑrɪ]	adj.	抱歉的	1	1	初級	
	make	[mek]	v.	讓…	1	1	初級	
	come	[kʌm]	v.	前來	1	1	初級	
	here	[hɪr]	adv.	這裡	1	1	初級	
	one	[wʌn]	n.	一	1	1	初級	
	more	[mor]	adj.	更多的	1	1	初級	

※「紅字單字」於本單元多句出現，「單字級等分析」僅列在「首次出現句」。

🔊 MP3 139-01 ❶～❿

❶	這是我的名片，上面有我的聯絡方式。	This is my business card; on the front is my contact info. * **business card**（名片）= **name card** * **on the front**（在正面） * **on the back**（在背面） * **contact info**（聯絡方式）
❷	我公司的電話是 2927-0000。	My company's phone number is 2927-0000. * **company's phone number**（公司電話號碼） * **cell number**（手機號碼）= **mobile number**
❸	我留我的聯絡方式給您。	Let me leave my contact info for you. * **Let me**＋動詞原形（讓我…）
❹	我沒有分機。	I don't have an extension. * **extension number**（分機號碼） * **switchboard**（電話總機）
❺	我手機會隨時開著。	My cell phone is always on. * **off**（關閉的狀態） * 此句用「現在簡單式」（...is...） 　表示「經常如此的事」。
❻	我的分機是 17。	My extension is 17.
❼	您也可以打手機找我。	You also can reach me through my cell number. * **reach**＋某人（用電話或信件聯絡某人） * **through**（利用、透過） * **through my cell number**（打手機給我）
❽	這是我的電子郵件信箱。	This is my email address. * **email address**（電子信箱地址） * **fax number**（傳真號碼）
❾	有事情可以透過電子郵件聯絡。	You can contact me via email if anything occurs. * **contact**＋某人（聯絡某人） * **via**＋工具（透過某工具） * **if anything occurs**（有事情的話） * **occur**（發生）= **happen**
❿	我留我的電子信箱給您。	Let me write down my email address for you. * **write down...**（寫下…）

	單字	音標	詞性	意義	字頻	大考	英檢	多益
❶	this	[ðɪs]	pron.	這個	1	1	初級	
	business	[ˋbɪznɪs]	n.	商業、商務	1	2	初級	◎
	card	[kɑrd]	n.	卡片	1	1	初級	◎
	front	[frʌnt]	n.	正面	1	1	初級	
	contact	[ˋkɑntækt]	n.	聯絡	1	2	初級	◎
	info	[ˋɪnfo]	n.	information（資訊）縮寫	4			
❷	company	[ˋkʌmpənɪ]	n.	公司	1	2	初級	◎
	phone	[fon]	n.	電話	1	2	初級	◎
	number	[ˋnʌmbɚ]	n.	號碼	1	1	初級	◎
❸	let	[lɛt]	v.	讓…	1	1	初級	
	leave	[liv]	v.	留下	1	1	初級	◎
❹	have	[hæv]	v.	擁有	1	1	初級	
	extension	[ɪkˋstɛnʃən]	n.	電話分機	2	5	中級	◎
❺	cell	[sɛl]	adj.	cellular（蜂巢式的）縮寫	1	2	初級	
	always	[ˋɔlwez]	adv.	隨時、一直	1	1	初級	
	on	[ɑn]	adj.	開啟的狀態	1	1	初級	
❼	also	[ˋɔlso]	adv.	也	1	1	初級	
	reach	[ritʃ]	v.	聯絡	1	1	初級	◎
❽	email	[ˋimel]	n.	電子郵件	2	4		
	address	[əˋdrɛs]	n.	信箱地址	1	1	初級	◎
❾	contact	[kənˋtækt]	v.	聯絡	1	2	初級	◎
	anything	[ˋɛnɪˌθɪŋ]	pron.	任何事情	1	1	初級	
	occur	[əˋkɝ]	v.	發生	1	2	初級	◎
❿	write	[raɪt]	v.	寫下	1	1	初級	
	down	[daʊn]	adv.	書面形式地、在紙上	1	1	初級	

※「紅字單字」於本單元多句出現，「單字級等分析」僅列在「首次出現句」。

MP3 139-01 ⑪～⑱

⑪	不好意思，我剛好沒帶名片。	I'm sorry, I ran out of name cards. = I'm sorry, I don't have my business card with me. * run out of（用完） * name card（名片）= business card * with me（在我身上、帶在身上）
⑫	我常不在公司，請用手機與我聯絡。	I am seldom in my office, so please contact me through my cell phone. * in one's office（在…的公司）、so（因此） * through one's cell phone（透過手機） * 此句用「現在簡單式」（...am...） 表示「經常如此的事」。
⑬	您有紙筆嗎？我抄電話給您。	Do you have a pen and paper? Let me write down my phone number for you. * Let me＋動詞原形（讓我…） * phone number（電話號碼）
⑭	我上班時間 Skype 都會開著。	I log into Skype while working. * log into（登入（網站、電腦系統）） * log out（登出（網站、電腦系統）） * while＋動詞-ing（在…的時候） * while working（上班時、工作時）
⑮	上班時間您可以打電話到公司。	You can call me at my office during working hours. * call me at my office（打我公司的電話） * during working hours（在上班時間）
⑯	這個號碼是我的專線。	This number is my private line. * private line（專線、私人專線）
⑰	請在上班時間聯絡我。	Please contact me during office hours. * during office hours（在上班時間） * office hours（上班時間）= working hours
⑱	下班後我的手機會關機。	I will turn off my mobile after work. * turn off（關機）、turn on（開機） * after work（下班後） * 此句用「未來簡單式」（...will...） 表示「某人經常性的習慣」。

	單字	音標	詞性	意義	字頻	大考	英檢	多益
⑪	sorry	[ˈsɑrɪ]	adj.	抱歉的	1	1	初級	
	ran	[ræn]	p.t.	run（消耗）過去式	1	1	初級	◎
	out	[aʊt]	adv.	用盡	1	1	初級	
	name	[nem]	n.	名字	1	1	初級	◎
	card	[kɑrd]	n.	卡片	1	1	初級	◎
	have	[hæv]	v.	擁有	1	1	初級	
	business	[ˈbɪznɪs]	n.	商業、商務	1	2	初級	◎
⑫	seldom	[ˈsɛldəm]	adv.	很少	2	3	初級	◎
	office	[ˈɔfɪs]	n.	公司/辦公、上班	1	1	初級	
	please	[pliz]	adv.	請…	1	1	初級	
	contact	[kənˈtækt]	v.	聯絡	1	2	初級	◎
	cell	[sɛl]	adj.	cellular（蜂巢式的）縮寫	1	2	初級	
	phone	[fon]	n.	電話	1	1	初級	◎
⑬	pen	[pɛn]	n.	筆	2	1	初級	
	paper	[ˈpepə]	n.	紙	1	1	初級	◎
	let	[lɛt]	v.	讓…	1	1	初級	
	write	[raɪt]	v.	寫下	1	1	初級	
	down	[daʊn]	adv.	書面形式地、在紙上	1	1	初級	
	number	[ˈnʌmbə]	n.	號碼	1	1	初級	◎
⑭	log	[lɔg]	v.	登入	2	2	中級	
	working	[ˈwɜkɪŋ]	p.pr.	work（工作）現在分詞	2	1	中級	◎
⑮	call	[kɔl]	v.	打電話	1	1	初級	
	working	[ˈwɜkɪŋ]	adj.	工作的	2	1	中級	◎
	hour	[aʊr]	n.	時間	1	1	初級	
⑯	this	[ðɪs]	adj.	這個	1	1	初級	
	private	[ˈpraɪvɪt]	adj.	私人的	1	2	初級	◎
	line	[laɪn]	n.	專線	1	1	初級	◎
⑱	turn	[tɜn]	v.	旋動、擰動	1	1	初級	◎
	off	[ɔf]	adv.	關上的狀態	1	1	初級	
	mobile	[ˈmobɪl]	n.	手機	2	3	中級	◎
	work	[wɜk]	n.	工作	1	1	初級	◎

※「紅字單字」於本單元多句出現，「單字級等分析」僅列在「首次出現句」。

MP3 139-02 ❶～❾

❶	請問我怎麼和您聯絡？	How can I contact you? * How can I...?（我要如何…？） * contact（連絡）= reach
❷	方便留一下您的聯絡方式嗎？	Would you mind leaving your contact info? * Would you mind＋動詞-ing...?（你方便…嗎） * one's contact info（某人的聯絡方式）
❸	可以再跟我說一次您的電話嗎？	Could you please tell me your phone number one more time? * Could you please...?（可以請你…嗎） * tell me＋名詞（告訴我…） * phone number（電話號碼） * cell number（手機號碼）= mobile number * one more time（再一次）
❹	我可以用電子郵件跟您聯繫嗎？	Can I contact you via email? * Can I...?（我可以…嗎）= May I...? * via（利用、透過） * via email（用電子郵件的方式） * via phone（用電話的方式）
❺	您有電子信箱嗎？	Do you have an email account? * Do you have＋名詞?（你有沒有…？） * email account（電子郵件帳號）
❻	您有備用的電子信箱嗎？	Do you have a backup email account? * backup account（備用的帳號）
❼	打到公司找曾小姐就可以了嗎？	Can I just dial your company's number to call Miss Tseng? * dial＋電話號碼（撥打某電話號碼） * company's number（公司電話號碼） * call＋某人（打電話找某人）
❽	您有分機嗎？	Do you have an extension?
❾	請等一下，我拿筆寫下您的電子信箱。	Please wait a second, let me grab a pen to write your email address down. * wait a second（稍等、等一下）= wait a moment * let me＋動詞原形（讓我…） * grab＋某物＋to＋動詞原形（匆匆地拿某物去…） * write...down（寫下…）

	單字	音標	詞性	意義	字頻	大考	英檢	多益
❶	contact	[kənˋtækt]	v.	聯絡	1	2	初級	◎
❷	mind	[maɪnd]	v.	介意	1	1	初級	◎
	leaving	[ˋlivɪŋ]	n.	leave（留下）動名詞	6	1	初級	◎
	contact	[ˋkɑntækt]	n.	聯絡	1	2	初級	◎
	info	[ˋɪnfo]	n.	information（資料）簡寫	4			
❸	please	[pliz]	adv.	請…	1	1	初級	
	tell	[tɛl]	v.	告訴	1	1	初級	
	phone	[fon]	n.	電話	1	2	初級	◎
	number	[ˋnʌmbə]	n.	號碼	1	1	初級	◎
	one	[wʌn]	n.	一	1	1	初級	
	more	[mor]	adj.	更多的	1	1	初級	
	time	[taɪm]	n.	次、回	1	1	初級	◎
❹	email	[ˋimel]	n.	電子郵件	2	4		
❺	have	[hæv]	v.	擁有	1	1	初級	
	account	[əˋkaʊnt]	n.	帳號	1	3	中級	◎
❻	backup	[ˋbæk͵ʌp]	adj.	備用的	2			◎
❼	just	[dʒʌst]	adv.	就	1	1	初級	
	dial	[ˋdaɪəl]	v.	撥打	3	2	初級	◎
	company	[ˋkʌmpənɪ]	n.	公司	1	2	初級	◎
	call	[kɔl]	v.	打電話	1	1	初級	◎
	Miss	[mɪs]	n.	小姐	1	1	初級	
❽	extension	[ɪkˋstɛnʃən]	n.	電話分機	2	5	中級	◎
❾	wait	[wet]	v.	等候	1	1	初級	
	second	[ˋsɛkənd]	n.	片刻	1	1	初級	
	let	[lɛt]	v.	讓…	1	1	初級	
	grab	[græb]	v.	快速地去拿、匆匆地拿	1	3	中級	
	pen	[pɛn]	n.	筆	2	1	初級	
	write	[raɪt]	v.	寫下	1	1	初級	
	address	[əˋdrɛs]	n.	信箱地址	1	1	初級	◎
	down	[daʊn]	adv.	書面形式地、在紙上	1	1	初級	

※「紅字單字」於本單元多句出現，「單字級等分析」僅列在「首次出現句」。

🔊 MP3 139-02 ⑩～⑱

⑩	名片上有您的手機嗎？	Is your cell number on your business card? * **Is your cell number on＋名詞?** 　（你的手機號碼有在…上面嗎） * **on one's business card**（在名片上面） * **business card**（名片）＝ **name card**
⑪	我可以用 Skype 與您保持聯絡嗎？	Can I keep in touch with you via Skype? * **keep in touch**（保持聯絡）＝ **keep in contact** * **with＋某人**（和某人） * **via＋工具**（透過某工具）
⑫	您會使用視訊會議的功能嗎？	Can you use the video conference function? * **Can you use...?**（你能使用…嗎、你會用…嗎） * **video conference**（視訊會議）
⑬	您用 Skype 嗎？	Do you use Skype? * **Do you use＋名詞?**（你平常會用…嗎） * 此句用「現在簡單式問句」（**Do...?**） 　表示「詢問是否經常有如此的事？」。
⑭	請告訴我您的手機號碼。	Please tell me your mobile number. * **Please tell me＋名詞**（請告訴我…） * **mobile number**（手機號碼）＝ **cell number**
⑮	晚上找您也是撥這支電話嗎？	Is this also the number to call you at night? * **Is this also＋名詞...?**（這個也是…嗎） * **the number to call you at night** 　（晚上打給你的號碼） * **at night**（在晚上）
⑯	什麼時間跟你聯絡比較方便？	When is the best time to contact you? * **When is...?**（什麼時候是…？） * **the best time**（最適當的時間） 　＝ **the most suitable time** * **contact**（聯絡）＝ **get in touch with**
⑰	您還有其他聯絡方式嗎？	Do you have any other contact info? * **Do you have...?**（你有沒有…？） * **any other＋名詞**（其他的…） * **contact info**（聯絡方式）＝ **contact way**
⑱	您還有其他的電話號碼嗎？	Do you have any other phone numbers?

	單字	音標	詞性	意義	字頻	大考	英檢	多益
❿	cell	[sɛl]	adj.	cellular（蜂巢式的）縮寫	1	2	初級	
	number	[`nʌmbɚ]	n.	號碼	1	1	初級	◎
	business	[`bɪznɪs]	n.	商業、商務	1	2	初級	◎
	card	[kɑrd]	n.	卡片	1	1	初級	◎
⓫	keep	[kip]	v.	保持	1	1	初級	◎
	touch	[tʌtʃ]	n.	聯絡	1	1	初級	◎
⓬	use	[juz]	v.	使用	1	1	初級	◎
	video	[`vɪdɪˌo]	n.	視訊	1	2	初級	
	conference	[`kɑnfərəns]	n.	會議	1	4	中級	◎
	function	[`fʌŋkʃən]	n.	功能	1	2	初級	◎
⓮	please	[pliz]	adv.	請…	1	1	初級	
	tell	[tɛl]	v.	告訴	1	1	初級	
	mobile	[`mobɪl]	adj.	行動的	2	3	中級	◎
⓯	this	[ðɪs]	pron.	這個	1	1	初級	
	also	[`ɔlso]	adv.	也	1	1	初級	
	call	[kɔl]	v.	打電話	1	1	初級	◎
	night	[naɪt]	n.	夜晚	1	1	初級	
⓰	best	[bɛst]	adj.	最適當的	1	1	初級	
	time	[taɪm]	n.	時間	1	1	初級	◎
	contact	[kənˋtækt]	v.	聯絡	1	2	初級	◎
⓱	have	[hæv]	v.	擁有	1	1	初級	
	any	[ˋɛnɪ]	adj.	任何的	1	1	初級	
	contact	[`kɑntækt]	n.	聯絡	1	2	初級	◎
	info	[ˋɪnfo]	n.	information（資料）縮寫	4			
⓲	other	[ˋʌðɚ]	adj.	其他的	1	1	初級	
	phone	[fon]	n.	電話	1	2	初級	◎

※「紅字單字」於本單元多句出現，「單字級等分析」僅列在「首次出現句」。

🔵 MP3 140-01 ❶～❽

❶	我想向您介紹本公司的產品。	I would like to introduce our company's product to you. * **would like to**（想要） * **introduce＋某物＋to＋某人**（介紹某物給某人）
❷	這款是我們本月的主打商品。	This design is what we're promoting this month. * **what we're promoting**（我們目前主力推廣的） * **major product**（主打產品） * **this month**（這個月）
❸	這是我們公司最暢銷的產品。	This is our company's most popular product. ＝ This is our company's hottest product.
❹	這是我們的最新產品。	This is our newest product.
❺	這項產品頗受好評。	This product has received several positive reviews. * **receive positive reviews**（得到好評） * **receive negative reviews**（得到負評） * **several reviews**（不少的評價） * 此句用「現在完成式」（...has received...）表示「過去某時點發生某事，且結果持續到現在」。
❻	這個商品下個月即將上市。	This product will go on the market next month. ＝ This product will be available on the market next month. * **go on the market**（上市）＝ **be available on the market** * **next month**（下個月）
❼	這是我們獨家研發的產品。	This is our exclusively developed product. * **exclusively developed**（獨家研發的） * **innovative product**（創新產品）
❽	它經過改良後更臻完善。	It is nearing perfection after so much improvement. * **near perfection**（接近完美） * **after＋名詞**（在…之後） * **after so much improvement**（在多次改良後） * 此句用「現在進行式」（...is nearing...）表示「現階段發生的事」。

	單字	音標	詞性	意義	字頻	大考	英檢	多益
❶	like	[laɪk]	v.	想要	1	1	初級	
	introduce	[ˌɪntrəˋdjus]	v.	介紹	1	2	初級	◎
	company	[ˋkʌmpənɪ]	n.	公司	1	2	初級	◎
	product	[ˋprɑdəkt]	n.	產品	1	3	初級	◎
❷	this	[ðɪs]	adj./pron.	這個	1	1	初級	
	design	[dɪˋzaɪn]	n.	款式	1	2	初級	◎
	promoting	[prəˋmotɪŋ]	p.pr.	promote（推廣、推銷）現在分詞	1	3	中級	◎
	month	[mʌnθ]	n.	月	1	1	初級	
❸	most	[most]	adv.	最為	1	1	初級	
	popular	[ˋpɑpjələ]	adj.	熱門的	1	2	初級	
	hottest	[ˋhɑtɪst]	adj.	hot（熱門的）最高級	1	1	初級	
❹	newest	[ˋnjuɪst]	adj.	new（新的）最高級	1	1	初級	
❺	received	[rɪˋsivd]	p.p.	receive（得到）過去分詞	6	1	初級	◎
	several	[ˋsɛvərəl]	adj.	不少的	1	1	初級	◎
	positive	[ˋpɑzətɪv]	adj.	正面的	1	2	初級	◎
	review	[rɪˋvju]	n.	評價	1	2	初級	◎
❻	go	[go]	v.	進入	1	1	初級	
	market	[ˋmɑrkɪt]	n.	市場	1	1	初級	◎
	next	[nɛkst]	adj.	下一個	1	1	初級	
	available	[əˋveləbḷ]	adj.	可利用的	1	3	初級	◎
❼	exclusively	[ɪkˋsklusɪvlɪ]	adv.	獨家地	2		中高	◎
	developed	[dɪˋvɛləpt]	p.p.	develop（研發）過去分詞	2	2	中高	◎
❽	nearing	[ˋnɪrɪŋ]	p.pr.	near（接近）現在分詞	1	1	初級	
	perfection	[pəˋfɛkʃən]	n.	完美	3	4	中級	
	so	[so]	adv.	如此	1	1	初級	
	much	[mʌtʃ]	adj.	許多的	1	1	初級	
	improvement	[ɪmˋpruvmənt]	n.	改良	1	2	中級	◎

※「紅字單字」於本單元多句出現，「單字級等分析」僅列在「首次出現句」。

🔊 MP3 140-01 ❾～❻

❾	這個產品我們主打年輕人市場。	We are promoting this product mainly to the youth market. * promote＋某物＋to＋某人（推銷某物給某人） * mainly to＋某人（主要鎖定某人） * youth market（年輕人市場） * silver market（銀髮族市場） * 此句用「現在進行式」（...are promoting...）表示「現階段發生的事」。
❿	操作人性化是本產品的特色。	User-friendliness is this product's feature. * feature（特色）＝ characteristic * environmental friendliness（環保）
⓫	價格便宜是它最大的優勢。	A low price is its biggest advantage. * low price（低價、價格便宜） * high price（高價、價格昂貴） * advantage（優點）＝ strong point * disadvantage（缺點）＝ defect
⓬	這是目前最受歡迎的款式。	This is currently our most popular design. * currently（目前）＝ presently
⓭	它已經在網路上引起熱烈討論。	It has provoked fervent discussion on the Internet. * have / has provoked（已經導致、已經引發） * provoke discussion（導致討論、引發討論） * fervent discussion（熱烈的討論） * on the Internet（在網路上）
⓮	這項商品堪稱本公司的代表作。	This product can be considered our company's signature work. * be considered＋名詞（被認為是…） 　＝ be thought of as＋名詞、be viewed as＋名詞 * signature work（代表作）
⓯	它的功能十分強大。	It has strong functions. * have / has＋形容詞＋functions（具有…功能） * multiple（多樣化的）
⓰	我們的產品在國外也賣得不錯。	Our products also sell well abroad. * sell well（銷售良好） * sell badly（銷售不佳）

單字級等分析

	單字	音標	詞性	意義	字頻	大考	英檢	多益
❾	promoting	[prə`motɪŋ]	p.pr.	promote（推廣、推銷）現在分詞	1	3	中級	◎
	this	[ðɪs]	adj./pron.	這個	1	1	初級	
	product	[`prɑdəkt]	n.	產品	1	3	初級	◎
	mainly	[`menlɪ]	adv.	主要地	2		中級	
	youth	[juθ]	n.	年輕人	1	2	初級	
	market	[`mɑrkɪt]	n.	市場	1	1	初級	◎
❿	user-friendliness	[`juzə`frɛndlɪnɪs]	n.	操作人性化				
	feature	[`fitʃə]	n.	特色	1	3	中級	◎
⓫	low	[lo]	adj.	低的	1	1	初級	
	price	[praɪs]	n.	價格	1	1	初級	◎
	biggest	[`bɪgɪst]	adj.	big（大的）最高級	1	1	初級	
	advantage	[əd`væntɪdʒ]	n.	優點	1	3	初級	
⓬	currently	[`kɝəntlɪ]	adv.	目前	1			◎
	most	[most]	adv.	最為	1	1	初級	
	popular	[`pɑpjələ]	adj.	有名的	1	2	初級	
	design	[dɪ`zaɪn]	n.	款式	1	2	初級	◎
⓭	provoked	[prə`vokt]	p.p.	provoke（導致、引發）過去分詞	2	6	中高	◎
	fervent	[`fɝvənt]	adj.	熱烈的	6			
	discussion	[dɪ`skʌʃən]	n.	討論	1	2	初級	◎
	Internet	[`ɪntə,nɛt]	n.	網路	1	4	初級	
⓮	considered	[kən`sɪdəd]	p.p.	consider（認為）過去分詞	1	2	初級	◎
	company	[`kʌmpənɪ]	n.	公司	1	2	初級	◎
	signature	[`sɪgnətʃə]	n.	特徵、代表	2	4	中級	◎
	work	[wɝk]	n.	作品	1	1	初級	
⓯	have	[hæv]	v.	擁有	1	1	初級	
	strong	[strɔŋ]	adj.	強大的	1	1	初級	
	function	[`fʌŋkʃən]	n.	功能	1	2	初級	◎
⓰	also	[`ɔlso]	adv.	也	1	1	初級	
	sell	[sɛl]	v.	銷售	1	1	初級	
	well	[wɛl]	adv.	良好地	1	1	初級	◎
	abroad	[ə`brɔd]	adv.	國外地	2	2	初級	◎

※「紅字單字」於本單元多句出現，「單字級等分析」僅列在「首次出現句」。

140　客戶需要的產品？（1）

❶	您需要怎樣的產品呢？	What kind of product do you want? * **What kind of**＋名詞...?（什麼樣的…？）
❷	您的預算大概是多少？	Approximately how much is your budget? * **Approximately how much is...?**（…大約是多少？） * **low-end price**（最底價）
❸	這項產品不符合您的需求嗎？	Doesn't this product meet your needs? * **meet your needs**（滿足你的需求） 　＝ **satisfy your needs**、**fulfill your needs**
❹	您比較注重實用性是嗎？	You are concerned with practicality, right? * **be concerned with**（注重、關心） * **functionality**（功能性） * **uniqueness**（獨特性）
❺	您要不要看我們的產品型錄？	Would you like to take a look at our product catalogue? * **Would you like to...?**（你要不要…？） * **take a look at**（看一下） * **product catalogue**（產品型錄）
❻	請問您需要哪些功能？	What functions do you need, may I ask? * **What functions...?**（什麼樣的功能…？） * **..., may I ask?**（請問…）
❼	您希望功能及外觀兩者兼顧嗎？	Are you hoping to consider both function and appearance? * **hope to**＋動詞原形（希望…） * **consider both A and B**（兼顧A和B）
❽	您有指定品牌嗎？	Do you have a designated brand? * **designated brand**（指定品牌） * **brand**（品牌）可替換為：**manufacturer**（製造商）
❾	外型是你選購產品的重點嗎？	Is the external appearance the key point for you when buying products? * **external appearance**（外觀）、**key point**（關鍵） * **when buying products**（在購買產品時）
❿	需要我為您推薦嗎？	Do you need me to make a recommendation for you? * **need**＋某人＋**to**＋動詞原形（需要某人做…） * **make a recommendation**（推薦）

	單字	音標	詞性	意義	字頻	大考	英檢	多益
❶	kind	[kaɪnd]	n.	種類	1	1	初級	◎
	product	[ˋprɑdəkt]	n.	產品	1	3	初級	◎
	want	[wɑnt]	v.	想要	1	1	初級	◎
❷	approximately	[əˋprɑksəmɪtlɪ]	adv.	大約	1		中高	◎
	much	[mʌtʃ]	adj.	許多的	1	1	初級	
	budget	[ˋbʌdʒɪt]	n.	預算	1	3	中級	◎
❸	this	[ðɪs]	adj.	這個	1	1	初級	
	meet	[mit]	v.	滿足	1	1	初級	
	need	[nid]	n./v.	需求/需要	1	1	初級	◎
❹	concerned	[kənˋsɝnd]	p.p.	concern（注重）過去分詞	1	3	中高	◎
	practicality	[ˌpræktɪˋkælətɪ]	n.	實用性	6		中高	
	right	[raɪt]	int.	是吧	1	1	初級	
❺	like	[laɪk]	v.	想要	1	1	初級	
	take	[tek]	v.	採取	1	1	初級	◎
	look	[lʊk]	n.	看一下	1	1	初級	
	catalogue	[ˋkætəlɔg]	n.	型錄	3	4		
❻	function	[ˋfʌŋkʃən]	n.	功能	1	2	初級	◎
	ask	[æsk]	v.	詢問	1	1	初級	
❼	hoping	[ˋhopɪŋ]	p.pr.	hope（希望）現在分詞	1	1	初級	
	consider	[kənˋsɪdɚ]	v.	考慮	1	2	初級	◎
	appearance	[əˋpɪrəns]	n.	外表	1	2	初級	◎
❽	have	[hæv]	v.	擁有	1	1	初級	
	designated	[ˋdɛzɪɡˌnetɪd]	p.p.	designate（指定）過去分詞	3	6	中高	◎
	brand	[brænd]	n.	品牌	1	2	中級	◎
❾	external	[ɪkˋstɝnəl]	adj.	外觀的	2	5	中高	
	key	[ki]	adj.	關鍵的	1	1	初級	◎
	point	[pɔɪnt]	n.	要點	1	1	初級	◎
	buying	[ˋbaɪɪŋ]	p.pr.	buy（購買）現在分詞	3	1	初級	
❿	make	[mek]	v.	做出	1	1	初級	
	recommendation	[ˌrɛkəmɛnˋdeʃən]	n.	推薦	1	6	中高	◎

※「紅字單字」於本單元多句出現，「單字級等分析」僅列在「首次出現句」。

⑪	這項產品非常符合您的需要。	This product definitely meets your requirements. * definitely（肯定、絕對）= surely * meet your requirements（符合你的需要） = meet your needs * fundamental requirement（基本的需要） * minimum requirement（最低限度的需要）
⑫	我比較建議您選購這個商品。	I would suggest that you buy this product. * would（覺得、認為，婉轉表達想法的用語） * suggest that＋主詞＋(should)＋動詞原形（建議…）
⑬	您的產品想要強調什麼呢？	What does your product try to emphasize? * What do / does＋主詞＋動詞...?（…的是什麼？） * emphasize（強調）= stress
⑭	您有設計圖嗎？	Do you have the design drawings? * Do you have＋名詞?（你有沒有…？） * design drawing（設計圖）
⑮	您想給消費者怎樣的感受？	What kind of feeling do you want to convey to the consumers? * What kind of feeling...?（什麼樣的感覺…？） * want to＋動詞原形（想要…）、convey to...（傳達給…） * consumer（消費者）可替換為：customer（顧客） * feeling（感覺）可替換為：experience（體驗）
⑯	您希望抓住哪個年齡的客層？	What age group of customers are you hoping to appeal to? * What age group of customers...? （什麼樣的顧客年齡層…？） * age group of customers（顧客年齡層） * infant（嬰兒）、preschooler（學齡前的兒童） * schoolchild（學童）、teenager（青少年） * adult（成人）、middle age（中年人） * the elderly（老年人）= senior citizen * appeal to（吸引）
⑰	您偏好哪種材質呢？	What is your preferred material? * What is / are＋名詞?（…是什麼？、…是哪一種？） * preferred material（偏好的材質）、color（顏色）

	單字	音標	詞性	意義	字頻	大考	英檢	多益
⓫	this	[ðɪs]	adj.	這個	1	1	初級	
	product	[ˋprɑdəkt]	n.	產品	1	3	初級	◎
	definitely	[ˋdɛfənɪtlɪ]	adv.	肯定、絕對	1		中高	◎
	meet	[mit]	v.	符合	1	1	初級	
	requirement	[rɪˋkwaɪrmənt]	n.	需要	1	2	中級	◎
⓬	suggest	[səˋdʒɛst]	v.	建議	1	3	初級	◎
	buy	[baɪ]	v.	購買	1	1	初級	
⓭	try	[traɪ]	v.	試圖	1	1	初級	
	emphasize	[ˋɛmfə͵saɪz]	v.	強調	1	3	初級	◎
⓮	have	[hæv]	v.	擁有	1	1	初級	
	design	[dɪˋzaɪn]	n.	設計	1	2	初級	◎
	drawing	[ˋdrɔɪŋ]	n.	圖畫	1	2	中級	
⓯	kind	[kaɪnd]	n.	種類	1	1	初級	◎
	feeling	[ˋfilɪŋ]	n.	感覺	1	1	初級	
	want	[wɑnt]	v.	想要	1	1	初級	◎
	convey	[kənˋve]	v.	表達	2	4	中級	◎
	consumer	[kənˋsjumɚ]	n.	消費者	1	4	中級	◎
⓰	age	[edʒ]	n.	年齡	1	1	初級	◎
	group	[grup]	n.	族群	1	1	初級	◎
	customer	[ˋkʌstəmɚ]	n.	顧客	1	2	初級	◎
	hoping	[ˋhopɪŋ]	p.pr.	hope（希望）現在分詞	1	1	初級	
	appeal	[əˋpil]	v.	吸引	1	3	中級	◎
⓱	preferred	[prɪˋfɝd]	p.p.	prefer（偏好）過去分詞	3	2	初級	◎
	material	[məˋtɪrɪəl]	n.	材質	1	6	初級	◎

※「紅字單字」於本單元多句出現，「單字級等分析」僅列在「首次出現句」。

141 說明交貨時間。（1）

❶	我們即將完成。	We are about finished with it. * be about finished（即將完成） * be finished with＋某事（完成、做完）
❷	我們保證如期交貨。	We guarantee on-time delivery. * guarantee（保證）＝ promise * on-time delivery（準時交貨） 　＝ delivery as scheduled * on-time（準時的）、as scheduled（如期）
❸	明天交貨沒問題。	Delivery tomorrow is no problem. * no problem（沒問題、不成問題）
❹	交貨時間可以商量嗎？	Can we talk about the delivery time? * Can we...?（我們可以…嗎） * talk about（討論、商量） * delivery time（交貨時間）
❺	我們目前進度落後。	We are currently behind schedule. * behind schedule（進度落後） * ahead of schedule（進度超前）
❻	恐怕得向您延後交貨時間。	I'm afraid of that we probably will have to delay the time of your delivery. * I'm afraid of that＋子句（恐怕…） * 子句用「未來簡單式」（...will...）表示 　「根據直覺預測未來發生的事」。 * probably（可能）＝ likely * have to＋動詞原形（不得不） * delay（延後）＝ postpone
❼	我們的交貨期限通常是一個禮拜。	Our delivery time is usually one week. * be usually＋時間（通常花費的時間）
❽	我們盡量幫您趕趕看。	We'll try our best to do that for you. * try one's best（竭盡全力） * do that for＋某人（為某人做…）
❾	您給我們的期限真的很短。	The deadline you gave is really short. * the deadline you gave（你當初給的期限） * make the deadline（於期限內趕上） 　＝ meet the deadline
❿	我們需要一個月的生產時間。	We need one month's time for production. * need＋時間＋for＋某事（某事需花…時間）

638

單字級等分析

	單字	音標	詞性	意義	字頻	大考	英檢	多益
❶	about	[ə'baʊt]	adv.	即將	1	1	初級	
	finished	['fɪnɪʃt]	p.p.	finish（完成）過去分詞	3	1	中級	◎
❷	guarantee	[,gærən'ti]	v.	保證	1	4	中級	◎
	on-time	['ɑn'taɪm]	adj.	準時的				
	delivery	[dɪ'lɪvərɪ]	n.	交貨	2	3	中級	◎
❸	tomorrow	[tə'mɔro]	adv.	明天	1	1	初級	
	problem	['prɑbləm]	n.	問題	1	1	初級	
❹	talk	[tɔk]	v.	討論、商量	1	1	初級	
	time	[taɪm]	n.	時間	1	1	初級	◎
❺	currently	['kɝəntlɪ]	adv.	目前	1			◎
	schedule	['skɛdʒʊl]	n.	進度	1	3	中級	◎
❻	afraid	[ə'fred]	adj.	害怕的	1	1	初級	
	probably	['prɑbəblɪ]	adv.	可能	1	1	初級	◎
	have	[hæv]	v.	必須	1	1	初級	
	delay	[dɪ'le]	v.	延後	2	2	初級	◎
❼	usually	['juʒʊəlɪ]	adv.	通常	1		初級	◎
	one	[wʌn]	n.	一	1	1	初級	
	week	[wik]	n.	禮拜	1	1	初級	
❽	try	[traɪ]	v.	努力、試圖	1	1	初級	
	best	[bɛst]	n.	最好	1	1	初級	
	do	[du]	v.	做	1	1	初級	
	that	[ðæt]	pron.	那個	1	1	初級	
❾	deadline	['dɛd,laɪn]	n.	期限	2	4	中級	◎
	gave	[gev]	p.t.	give（給）過去式	1	1	初級	
	really	['rɪəlɪ]	adv.	真的	1	1	初級	
	short	[ʃɔrt]	adj.	短暫的	1	1	初級	◎
❿	need	[nid]	v.	需要	1	1	初級	◎
	month	[mʌnθ]	n.	月	1	1	初級	
	production	[prə'dʌkʃən]	n.	製造、生產	1	4	初級	◎

※「紅字單字」於本單元多句出現，「單字級等分析」僅列在「首次出現句」。

MP3 141-01 ⓫ ～ ⓲

⓫	機器故障，恐怕無法如期出貨。	I'm afraid that we can't make the delivery on time due to a mechanical malfunction. * be afraid that（恐怕）＝ be afraid of that * make the delivery（交貨）、on time（準時） * due to＋名詞（因為…） * mechanical malfunction（機器故障）
⓬	我們三天內會送達。	We will make the delivery within three days. * within＋天數（在某天數內）
⓭	延誤交貨時間，真是抱歉。	I'm very sorry for the delayed delivery. * be sorry for＋名詞（對…感到抱歉） * delayed delivery（延遲的交貨）
⓮	這批貨最快要下禮拜才會到。	This batch of products will be delivered next week. * a batch of＋名詞複數形（一批…、一組…） * will be delivered（將被遞送） * next week（下星期）
⓯	我們今天下午 3 點會交貨。	We will make the delivery at three o'clock this afternoon. * at＋1、2、3、…9＋o'clock（於…點鐘） * this afternoon（今天下午） * tomorrow afternoon（明天下午）
⓰	我們可以分批交貨嗎？	May we deliver in batches? * May we＋動詞…?（請問我們可以…嗎） * deliver in batches（分批交貨） * in batches（以分批的方式）
⓱	如果有庫存，明天就可以交貨。	We can make the delivery tomorrow if we have the item in stock. * if（假如） * in stock（有庫存、有現貨） * out of stock（沒有庫存、沒有現貨）
⓲	交貨時間要問我們老闆。	We have to ask our boss about the delivery time. * have to＋動詞原形（必須） * ask＋某人＋about＋某事（向…詢問某件事情） * about（關於）

	單字	音標	詞性	意義	字頻	大考	英檢	多益
⑪	afraid	[ə`fred]	adj.	害怕的	1	1	初級	
	make	[mek]	v.	做出	1	1	初級	
	delivery	[dɪ`lɪvərɪ]	n.	交貨	2	3	中級	◎
	time	[taɪm]	n.	時間	1	1	初級	
	due	[dju]	adj.	因為	1	3	中級	◎
	mechanical	[mə`kænɪkl]	adj.	機器的	2	4	中級	◎
	malfunction	[mæl`fʌŋʃən]	n.	故障	6			
⑫	three	[θri]	n.	三	1	1	初級	
	day	[de]	n.	天	1	1	初級	
⑬	very	[`vɛrɪ]	adv.	十分	1	1	初級	
	sorry	[`sɑrɪ]	adj.	抱歉的	1	1	初級	
	delayed	[dɪ`led]	p.p.	delay（延遲）過去分詞	5	2	初級	◎
⑭	this	[ðɪs]	adj.	這個	1	1	初級	
	batch	[bætʃ]	n.	一批、一組	3	5	中高	
	product	[`prɑdəkt]	n.	產品	1	3	初級	◎
	delivered	[dɪ`lɪvəd]	p.p.	deliver（遞送）過去分詞	1	2	初級	◎
	next	[nɛkst]	adj.	下一個	1	1	初級	
	week	[wik]	n.	禮拜	1	1	初級	
⑮	o'clock	[ə`klɑk]	n.	…點鐘	2	1	初級	
	afternoon	[ˌæftə`nun]	n.	下午	1	1	初級	
⑯	deliver	[dɪ`lɪvə]	v.	遞送	1	2	初級	◎
⑰	tomorrow	[tə`mɔro]	adv.	明天	1	1	初級	◎
	have	[hæv]	v.	擁有	1	1	初級	
	item	[`aɪtəm]	n.	品項	1	2	初級	◎
	stock	[stɑk]	n.	庫存	1	6	中級	◎
⑱	ask	[æsk]	v.	詢問	1	1	初級	
	boss	[bɔs]	n.	老闆	1	2	初級	

※「紅字單字」於本單元多句出現，「單字級等分析」僅列在「首次出現句」。

MP3 141-02 ❶～❿

❶	你預定何時交貨？	When do you plan to make the delivery? * **When do you...?**（你什麼時候會…？） * **plan to** ＋動詞原形（打算） * **make the delivery**（交貨）
❷	產品進度如何？	What is the current production schedule? * **production schedule**（生產進度）
❸	你們什麼時候可以出貨？	What time can you make the delivery? * **What time can you...?**（你什麼時候可以…？）
❹	你自己說一個交貨期限給我。	Just give me a deadline for your delivery. * **give me a deadline**（告訴我最後期限）
❺	你們已經出貨了嗎？	Have you made the delivery yet? * **Have you** ＋過去分詞**...?**（你（們）已經…了嗎）
❻	趕得上交貨截止日吧？	Can you meet the delivery deadline? * **meet the deadline**（於期限內趕上） 　＝ **make the deadline** * **delivery deadline**（交貨期限）
❼	你能保證如期交貨嗎？	Can you guarantee to make the delivery as scheduled? * **guarantee to** ＋動詞原形（保證） 　＝ **promise to** ＋動詞原形 * **make the delivery as scheduled**（如期交貨）
❽	為什麼一再延期？	Why has the delivery been postponed again and again? * **Why has** ＋主詞＋過去分詞**...?**（為什麼…一直…？） * **postpone**（延期、延後）＝ **delay** * **again and again**（一再地、再三地） * 此句用「現在完成式」（**...has...been...**）表示 　「過去到現在發生過、經歷過的事」。
❾	貨還要多久才能送到？	How long will it take you to make the delivery? * **How long will...?**（之後…還要多久？） * **it takes** ＋某人＋**to** ＋動詞原形 　（某人花費…時間去…）
❿	星期五前可以交貨嗎？	Could the delivery be made before Friday? * **before** ＋日期（在某日期之前）

	單字	音標	詞性	意義	字頻	大考	英檢	多益
❶	plan	[plæn]	v.	打算	1	1	初級	◎
	make	[mek]	v.	做出	1	1	初級	
	delivery	[dɪˋlɪvərɪ]	n.	出貨	2	3	中級	◎
❷	current	[ˋkɝnɛt]	adj.	目前的	1	3	初級	◎
	production	[prəˋdʌkʃən]	n.	製造、生產	1	4	初級	◎
	schedule	[ˋskɛdʒul]	n.	進度	1	3	中級	◎
❸	time	[taɪm]	n.	時間	1	1	初級	◎
❹	just	[dʒʌst]	adv.	就…	1	1	初級	
	give	[gɪv]	v.	給予	1	1	初級	
	deadline	[ˋdɛd͵laɪn]	n.	期限	2	4	中級	◎
❺	made	[med]	p.p.	make（做出）過去分詞	1	1	初級	
	yet	[jɛt]	adv.	尚未	1	1	初級	◎
❻	meet	[mit]	v.	趕得上、如期	1	1	初級	
❼	guarantee	[͵gærənˋti]	v.	保證	1	4	中級	◎
	scheduled	[ˋskɛdʒuld]	p.p.	schedule（預定）過去分詞	3	3	中級	◎
❽	postponed	[postˋpondɪd]	p.p.	postpone（延期）過去分詞	3	3	初級	◎
	again	[əˋgɛn]	adv.	再次	1	1	初級	
❾	long	[lɔŋ]	adv.	長久地	1	1	初級	
	take	[tek]	v.	花費（時間）	1	1	初級	◎
❿	Friday	[ˋfraɪ͵de]	n.	星期五	1	1	初級	

※「紅字單字」於本單元多句出現，「單字級等分析」僅列在「首次出現句」。

🔊 MP3 141-02 ⑪～⑱

⑪	不準時交貨，我就退貨。	I will reject the delivery if it isn't on time. * reject the delivery（退貨、拒絕收貨） * accept the delivery（收貨） * on time（準時）
⑫	可以馬上出貨給我嗎？	Can you make a delivery for me right now? * make the delivery（交貨） * for me（幫我、為了我） * right now（現在）
⑬	你們現在完成多少了？	How much have you completed? * How much have you＋過去分詞?（有多少已經…?） * 此句用「現在完成式」（…have…completed…） 　表示「過去某時點發生某事，且結果持續到現在」。
⑭	我一定要在月底前收到東西。	I have to receive the products by the end of this month. * have to（必須、一定要） * by（在…之前） * the end of this month（這個月底） * the end of next month（下個月底）
⑮	我希望盡快收到貨品。	I hope that I can receive the goods as soon as possible. * I hope that＋子句（我希望…） * goods（貨品、商品）＝ products * as soon as possible（盡快）
⑯	你們現在有庫存嗎？	Do you have any stocks available now? ＝ Do you have any reserves available now? * have any stocks（有任何庫存） * stock（庫存、存貨）＝ reserve * in stock（有庫存、有現貨） * out of stock（沒有庫存、沒有現貨）
⑰	難道不能加班幫我趕一下？	Is it possible for you to work overtime for me? * Is it possible to＋動詞原形?（有可能…嗎） * work overtime（加班）
⑱	我急著要這個貨品。	I really need the merchandise in a hurry. * I really need＋名詞（我真的很需要…） * in a hurry（緊急、趕快）

	單字	音標	詞性	意義	字頻	大考	英檢	多益
⑪	reject	[rɪˋdʒɛkt]	v.	拒絕	1	2	初級	◎
	delivery	[dɪˋlɪvərɪ]	n.	交貨	2	3	中級	◎
	time	[taɪm]	n.	時間	1	1	初級	◎
⑫	make	[mek]	v.	做出	1	1	初級	
	right	[raɪt]	adv.	正值	1	1	初級	
	now	[nau]	adv.	現在	1	1	初級	
⑬	much	[mʌtʃ]	adv.	許多地	1	1	初級	
	completed	[kəmˋplitɪd]	p.p.	complete（完成）過去分詞	4			
⑭	have	[hæv]	v.	必須/擁有	1	1	初級	
	receive	[rɪˋsiv]	v.	收到、領取	1	1	初級	◎
	product	[ˋprɑdəkt]	n.	商品	1	3	初級	◎
	end	[ɛnd]	n.	結尾	1	1	初級	
	this	[ðɪs]	adj.	這個	1	1	初級	
	month	[mʌnθ]	n.	月	1	1	初級	
⑮	hope	[hop]	v.	希望	1	1	初級	
	goods	[gudz]	n.	貨品、商品	2	4	中級	
	soon	[sun]	adv.	早、快	1	1	初級	
	possible	[ˋpɑsəbl̩]	adv./adj.	可能地	1	1	初級	◎
⑯	any	[ˋɛnɪ]	adj.	任何的	1	1	初級	
	stock	[stɑk]	n.	庫存、存貨	1	6	中級	◎
	available	[əˋveləbl̩]	adj.	可取得的	1	3	初級	◎
	reserve	[rɪˋzɝv]	n.	庫存、存貨	2	3	中級	◎
⑰	work	[wɝk]	v.	工作	1	1	初級	
	overtime	[ˏovəˋtaɪm]	adv.	超時地	3			◎
⑱	really	[ˋrɪəlɪ]	adv.	真的	1		初級	
	need	[nid]	v.	需要	1	1	初級	◎
	merchandise	[ˋmɝtʃənˏdaɪz]	n.	商品	3	6	中高	◎
	hurry	[ˋhɝɪ]	n.	緊急、趕快	2	2	初級	◎

※「紅字單字」於本單元多句出現，「單字級等分析」僅列在「首次出現句」。

142 品質保證。

❶	我辦事，您放心。	Don't worry about what I'm handling. * worry about（擔心） * what I'm handling（我所負責的事）
❷	我們在業界是有口碑的。	We have a good reputation in this industry. * good reputation（好口碑） * in the industry（在業界）
❸	別間公司絕對做不出這種品質。	Other companies could never match our quality.　* could never match（絕比不上）
❹	我們的產品絕對不輸其他同業。	Our products are at least as good as those of other companies in the industry. * at least as good as…（不會輸…、至少和…一樣好） * those of other companies（其他公司的產品，those 是代替「products」的代名詞）
❺	貨品保證毫無瑕疵。	We guarantee that there's no fault in the goods. * guarantee＋子句（保證…） * there's no fault（沒有瑕疵）
❻	我們公司的產品您可以放心。	You can rest assured about our company's products.　* rest assured（放心、有信心）
❼	我們絕不賣假貨。	We never sell fake products. * fake product（假貨）＝ counterfeit
❽	品質絕對與您當初看的樣品一樣。	The quality is absolutely the same as the sample you saw. * absolutely（絕對）＝ surely * the same as…（和…一樣） * the sample you saw（你當初看的樣品）
❾	我們公司提供一年保固。	Our company provides a one-year warranty. * one-year warranty（一年保固） * be under warranty（在保固期內）
❿	本公司產品保證原裝進口。	Our company's product is guaranteed to be the original import. * be guaranteed to＋動詞原形（保證） * original import（原裝進口）
⓫	我們有提供免費維修服務。	We provide free maintenance service. * maintenance service（維修服務）
⓬	我們廠內有嚴格的商品控管。	We have a strict process of quality control in our factory.　* quality control（品質控管）

	單字	音標	詞性	意義	字頻	大考	英檢	多益
❶	worry	[ˈwɝɪ]	v.	擔心	1	1	初級	
	handling	[ˈhædlɪŋ]	p.pr.	handle（負責）現在分詞	2			◎
❷	have	[hæv]	v.	擁有	1	1	初級	
	good	[gʊd]	adj.	良好的	1	1	初級	◎
	reputation	[ˌrɛpjəˈteʃən]	n.	口碑	1	4	中級	◎
	this	[ðɪs]	adj.	這個	1	1	初級	
	industry	[ˈɪndəstrɪ]	n.	產業	1	2	初級	◎
❸	other	[ˈʌðɚ]	adj.	其他的	1	1	初級	
	company	[ˈkʌmpənɪ]	n.	公司	1	2	初級	◎
	never	[ˈnɛvɚ]	adv.	從不	1	1	初級	
	match	[mætʃ]	v.	比得上	1	2	初級	◎
	quality	[ˈkwɑlətɪ]	n.	品質	1	2	初級	◎
❹	product	[ˈprɑdəkt]	n.	產品	1	3	初級	◎
	least	[list]	n.	最少	1	1	初級	
	those	[ðoz]	pron.	那些	1	1	初級	
❺	guarantee	[ˌgærənˈti]	v.	保證	1	4	中級	◎
	there	[ðɛr]	adv.	有…	1		初級	
	fault	[fɔlt]	n.	瑕疵	2	2	初級	
	goods	[gʊdz]	n.	貨品、商品	2	4	中級	
❻	rest	[rɛst]	v.	放心	1	1	初級	
	assured	[əˈʃʊrd]	adj.	有信心的	5	4	中高	◎
❼	sell	[sɛl]	v.	販賣	1	1	初級	
	fake	[fek]	adj.	假的	2	3	中級	◎
❽	absolutely	[ˈæbsəˌlutlɪ]	adv.	絕對	1		中級	◎
	same	[sem]	adj.	相同的	1	1	初級	
	sample	[ˈsæmpl̩]	n.	樣品	1	2	初級	◎
	saw	[sɔ]	p.t.	see（看）過去式	3	1	中級	◎
❾	provide	[prəˈvaɪd]	v.	提供	1	2	初級	◎
	one-year	[ˈwʌnˌjɪr]	adj.	一年的				
	warranty	[ˈwɔrəntɪ]	n.	保固	4	6	中高	◎
❿	guaranteed	[ˌgærənˈtid]	p.p.	guarantee（保證）過去分詞	4	4	中高	◎
	original	[əˈrɪdʒɪnl̩]	adj.	原裝的	1	3	中級	◎
	import	[ˈɪmport]	n.	進口	2	3	初級	◎
⓫	free	[fri]	adj.	免費的	1	1	初級	
	maintenance	[ˈmentənəns]	n.	維修	2	5	中高	◎
	service	[ˈsɝvɪs]	n.	服務	1	1	初級	◎
⓬	strict	[strɪkt]	adj.	嚴格的	2	2	中級	◎
	process	[ˈprɑsɛs]	n.	過程	1	3	中級	◎
	control	[kənˈtrol]	n.	控管	1	2	初級	◎
	factory	[ˈfæktərɪ]	n.	工廠	1	1	初級	◎

※「紅字單字」於本單元多句出現，「單字級等分析」僅列在「首次出現句」。

MP3 142-02 ❶～❸

❶	您用得滿意嗎？	Are you satisfied with its performance? * be satisfied with（滿意）
❷	請問您覺得哪裡需要改進？	Where do you think it needs improvement? * Where do you...?（哪些地方是…？） * need improvement（需要改進）
❸	我們有沒有需要修正的地方？	Is there anything we need to correct? * Is there anything...?（有任何…的嗎） * correct（修改）＝ amend
❹	您滿意這次的產品嗎？	Are you satisfied with the merchandise this time?　* this time（這一次）
❺	我們的工作效率您滿意嗎？	Are you satisfied with our work efficiency? * work efficiency（工作效率）
❻	您覺得我們公司的配合度如何？	How do you feel about our company's coordination? * How do you feel about...?（你覺得…如何？）
❼	您滿意我們提供的服務嗎？	Are you satisfied with the service we've provided? * the service we've provided（我們到目前提供的服務）
❽	我們日後還有合作機會嗎？	Will there be any other chances for us to cooperate in the future? * Will there be...?（未來會有…嗎） * any other＋名詞（其他的） * in the future（未來、日後）
❾	這次合作您還滿意嗎？	Are you satisfied with our cooperation?
❿	已經交貨的商品您覺得如何？	What do you think about the delivered product? * What do you think about…?（你覺得…如何？） * the delivered product（已交貨的產品）
⓫	您覺得成效如何？	What do you think of the result? * think of（覺得）
⓬	您驗收後覺得如何呢？	How do you feel after checking on the delivery? * check on（驗收、檢驗）
⓭	多謝您的誇讚，我們會繼續努力。	Thanks for your praise; we will keep trying our best. * Thanks for＋名詞（謝謝…） * praise（稱讚）＝ compliment * keep＋動詞-ing（持續…）

	單字	音標	詞性	意義	字頻	大考	英檢	多益
❶	satisfied	[ˋsætɪs.faɪd]	adj.	滿意的	2	2	中高	◎
	performance	[pəˋfɔrməns]	n.	表現	1	3	中級	◎
❷	think	[θɪŋk]	v.	認為	1	1	初級	
	need	[nid]	v.	需要	1	1	初級	◎
	improvement	[ɪmˋpruvmənt]	n.	改進	1	2	中級	◎
❸	there	[ðɛr]	adv.	有…	1	1	初級	
	anything	[ˋɛnɪ.θɪŋ]	pron.	任何地方	1	1	初級	
	correct	[kəˋrɛkt]	v.	修正	1	1	初級	◎
❹	merchandise	[ˋmɝtʃən.daɪz]	n.	商品	3	6	中高	◎
	this	[ðɪs]	adj.	這個	1	1	初級	
	time	[taɪm]	n.	次、回	1	1	初級	◎
❺	work	[wɝk]	n.	工作	1	1	初級	
	efficiency	[ɪˋfɪʃənsɪ]	n.	效率	2	4	中級	
❻	feel	[fil]	v.	覺得	1	1	初級	
	company	[ˋkʌmpənɪ]	n.	公司	1	2	初級	◎
	coordination	[ko.ɔrdṇˋeʃən]	n.	配合度	3			
❼	service	[ˋsɝvɪs]	n.	服務	1	1	初級	◎
	provided	[prəˋvaɪdɪd]	p.p.	provide（提供）過去分詞	2		中高	
❽	any	[ˋɛnɪ]	adj.	任何的	1	1	初級	
	other	[ˋʌðɚ]	adj.	其他的	1	1	初級	
	chance	[tʃæns]	n.	機會	1	1	初級	
	cooperate	[koˋɑpə.ret]	v.	合作	2	4	中級	◎
	future	[ˋfjutʃɚ]	n.	未來	1	2	初級	
❾	cooperation	[ko.ɑpəˋreʃən]	n.	合作	1	4	中級	◎
❿	delivered	[dɪˋlɪvɚd]	p.p.	deliver（遞送）過去分詞	1	2	初級	◎
	product	[ˋprɑdəkt]	n.	產品	1	3	初級	◎
⓫	result	[rɪˋzʌlt]	n.	成效、成果	1	2	初級	
⓬	checking	[ˋtʃɛkɪŋ]	n.	check（驗收、檢驗）動名詞	6	1	初級	◎
	delivery	[dɪˋlɪvərɪ]	n.	所交的貨	2	3	中級	◎
⓭	thanks	[θæŋks]	n.	thank（感謝）複數	1			
	praise	[prez]	n.	感激	2	2	初級	
	keep	[kip]	v.	繼續	1	1	初級	◎
	trying	[ˋtraɪɪŋ]	n.	try（努力）動名詞	6	1	初級	
	best	[bɛst]	n.	最好	1	1	初級	

※「紅字單字」於本單元多句出現，「單字級等分析」僅列在「首次出現句」。

🔵 MP3 143-01 ❶～⓫

❶	我喜歡買名牌。	I love buying name brands. * love＋動詞-ing（喜歡做…） * name brand（名牌、名牌產品）
❷	我存錢就是為了買名牌。	I save up for name brands. * save up（存錢） * for＋某事物（為了某事物…）
❸	我相信名牌的品質。	I trust the quality of name brands. * trust（信賴）＝ believe in * the quality of＋某物（某物的品質）
❹	我喜歡名牌的設計。	I like the design of name brands. * figure（外形）、pattern（樣式） * motif（設計的基調）、tone（色調）
❺	我最愛 LV。	LV is my favorite. * 名詞＋is / are my favorite（我最愛…）
❻	名牌包包永不退流行。	Name-brand bags will never go out of fashion. * name-brand bag（名牌包包） * go out of fashion（過時、退流行）
❼	名牌服飾配件的顏色特別鮮豔。	The colors of name-brand accessories are particularly bright. * particularly（特別地）＝ especially * dark（色彩深暗的）
❽	30 歲時我買了第一個 Gucci 包。	I bought my first Gucci bag at age thirty. * at age＋數字（在…歲的時候）
❾	我從不用名牌。	I've never had a name-brand item before. * have never had（不曾擁有） * name-brand item（名牌產品）
❿	我會分期付款買名牌。	I pay for name-brand items in installments. * pay for＋某物（支付某物的費用） * in installments（以分期付款的方式） * installment plan（分期付款的購買方式） * pay off（一次付清）
⓫	聽說亞洲人最愛用名牌。	It's said that Asians are name brands' top customers. * It's said that＋子句（據說…） * top customer（最大的客戶）

	單字	音標	詞性	意義	字頻	大考	英檢	多益
❶	love	[lʌv]	v.	喜歡	1	1	初級	
	buying	[ˋbaɪɪŋ]	n.	buy（購買）動名詞	3	1	初級	
	name	[nem]	adj.	知名的	1	1	初級	◎
	brand	[brænd]	n.	品牌	1	2	中級	◎
❷	save	[sev]	v.	保存	1	1	初級	◎
	up	[ʌp]	adv.	存起	1	1	初級	
❸	trust	[trʌst]	v.	信任	1	2	初級	
	quality	[ˋkwɑlətɪ]	n.	品質	1	2	初級	
❹	like	[laɪk]	v.	喜歡	1	1	初級	
	design	[dɪˋzaɪn]	n.	設計	1	2	初級	◎
❺	favorite	[ˋfevərɪt]	n.	最喜歡的東西	1	2	初級	◎
❻	name-brand	[ˋnemˋbrænd]	adj.	名牌的				
	bag	[bæg]	n.	包包	1	1	初級	
	never	[ˋnɛvɚ]	adv.	從不	1	1	初級	
	go	[go]	v.	衰退	1	1	初級	
	out	[aʊt]	adv.	在…範圍外	1	1	初級	
	fashion	[ˋfæʃən]	n.	流行	1	3	中級	◎
❼	color	[ˋkʌlɚ]	n.	顏色	1	1	初級	
	accessory	[ækˋsɛsərɪ]	n.	配件	3	6	中高	◎
	particularly	[pɚˋtɪkjələlɪ]	adv.	特別地	1		中級	◎
	bright	[braɪt]	adj.	色彩鮮艷的	1	1	初級	
❽	bought	[bɔt]	p.t.	buy（購買）過去式	1	1	初級	
	first	[fɝst]	adj.	第一個	1	1	初級	
	age	[edʒ]	n.	年齡	1	1	初級	◎
	thirty	[ˋθɝtɪ]	n.	三十	2	1	初級	
❾	had	[hæd]	p.p.	have（擁有）過去分詞	1	1	初級	
	item	[ˋaɪtəm]	n.	品項	1	2	初級	◎
	before	[bɪˋfor]	adv.	以前	1	1	初級	
❿	pay	[pe]	v.	付款	1	3	初級	◎
	installment	[ɪnˋstɔlmənt]	n.	分期付款	4	6	中高	◎
⓫	said	[sɛd]	p.p.	say（說）過去分詞	4	1	初級	
	Asian	[ˋeʃən]	n.	亞洲人	1		初級	
	top	[tɑp]	adj.	最大的	1	1	初級	◎
	customer	[ˋkʌstəmɚ]	n.	客戶	1	2	初級	◎

※「紅字單字」於本單元多句出現，「單字級等分析」僅列在「首次出現句」。

⑫	二手名牌的銷路也不差。	The secondhand name-brand item market is active as well. * secondhand（二手的）可替換為： 　used（使用過的）、pre-owned（二手的） * an active market（熱絡的市場） * as well（也、同樣）
⑬	名牌在歐洲價格比較便宜。	The prices of name-brand items are lower in Europe.
⑭	很多六年級生都是名牌愛用者。	Many people born in the 70s are name brand lovers. * people born in＋年代（生於⋯年代的人） * in the 70s（1970年代） * 某事物＋lover（某事物的愛好者）
⑮	有些名牌仿冒品看起來幾可亂真。	Some name brand imitations look just like the real thing. * look just like（看起來非常像） * real thing（真品） * imitation（仿冒品）可替換為：fake product（假貨）
⑯	很多年輕人分期付款買名牌。	Many young people pay for name brands in installments. * pay for＋某物（支付某物的費用） * pay...in installments（分期付款） * pay by credit card（刷卡付款）
⑰	一不小心就會買到名牌仿冒品。	There's a good possibility of accidentally getting an imitation name brand. * There's a good possibility of＋動詞-ing（很可能⋯） * good possibility（很大的可能性） * accidentally（不小心）＝ incidentally * get（購買到）＝ buy * imitation name brand（冒牌貨、名牌仿冒品）
⑱	名牌讓很多人變得比較有自信。	Name-brand items make many people more confident. * make＋某人＋形容詞（使某人感到⋯） * self-confidence（自信） * lack of self-confidence（缺乏自信）

	單字	音標	詞性	意義	字頻	大考	英檢	多益
⑫	secondhand	[ˈsɛkəndhænd]	adj.	二手的				◎
	name-brand	[ˈnemˋbrænd]	adj.	名牌的				
	item	[ˈaɪtəm]	n.	品項	1	2	初級	◎
	market	[ˈmɑrkɪt]	n.	市場	1	1	初級	◎
	active	[ˈæktɪv]	adj.	熱絡的	1	2	初級	◎
	as	[æz]	adv.	如同	1	1	初級	
	well	[wɛl]	adv.	也	1	1	初級	◎
⑬	price	[praɪs]	n.	價格	1	1	初級	
	lower	[ˈloɚ]	adj.	low（便宜的）比較級	1	2	中級	◎
	Europe	[ˈjurəp]	n.	歐洲	2		初級	
⑭	many	[ˈmɛnɪ]	adj.	許多的	1	1	初級	
	people	[ˈpipl̩]	n.	person（人）複數	1	1	初級	
	born	[bɔrn]	p.p.	bear（出生）過去分詞	1	1	初級	
	name	[nem]	adj.	知名的	1	1	初級	◎
	brand	[brænd]	n.	品牌	1	2	中級	◎
	lover	[ˈlʌvɚ]	n.	愛好者	1	2	初級	
⑮	some	[sʌm]	adj.	一些	1	1	初級	
	imitation	[ˌɪməˈteʃən]	n.	仿冒品	3	4	中級	
	look	[lʊk]	v.	看起來	1	1	初級	
	just	[dʒʌst]	adv.	就…	1	1	初級	
	real	[ˈriəl]	adj.	真的	1	1	初級	
	thing	[θɪŋ]	n.	物品	1	1	初級	
⑯	young	[jʌŋ]	adj.	年輕的	1	1	初級	
	pay	[pe]	v.	付款	1	1	初級	
	installment	[ɪnˈstɔlmənt]	n.	分期付款	4	6	中高	◎
⑰	there	[ðɛr]	adv.	有…	1	1	初級	
	good	[gʊd]	adj.	十足的、充分的	1	1	初級	◎
	possibility	[ˌpɑsəˈbɪlətɪ]	n.	可能性	1	2	中級	◎
	accidentally	[ˌæksəˈdɛntl̩ɪ]	adv.	不小心	3			
	getting	[ˈgɛtɪŋ]	n.	get（購買）動名詞	1	1	初級	◎
⑱	make	[mek]	v.	使得	1	1	初級	
	more	[mor]	adv.	更加	1	1	初級	
	confident	[ˈkɑnfədənt]	adj.	自信的	2	3	初級	◎

※「紅字單字」於本單元多句出現，「單字級等分析」僅列在「首次出現句」。

🔊 MP3 143-02 ❶～❾

❶	哇！LV 的新款包包？	Wow! Is that the new LV bag? * **Is that＋名詞?**（那是…嗎） * **accessory**（飾品）、**bracelet**（手鐲） * **handbag**（手提包）、**wallet**（皮夾） * **classic bag**（經典款皮包）
❷	你喜歡用名牌嗎？	Are you fond of name brands? * **be fond of**（喜歡） * **be averse to**（嫌惡）
❸	你常買名牌嗎？	Do you buy name-brand items often? * **name-brand item**（名牌產品）＝ **name brand** * 此句用「現在簡單式問句」（Do...?） 　表示「詢問是否經常有如此的事？」。
❹	你有 LV 的包包嗎？	Do you have any LV bags? * **Do you have...?**（你擁有…嗎）
❺	為什麼有人喜歡追求名牌？	Why do some people like to pursue name brands? * **Why do＋主詞＋動詞...?**（為什麼…會做…？） * **some people**（有些人） * **like to＋動詞原形**（喜歡做…）＝ **like＋動詞-ing** * **pursue＋人事物**（追求某人事物）
❻	你捨得花大錢買名牌嗎？	Are you willing to pay an arm and a leg for name-brand items? * **Are you willing to...?**（你願意…嗎） * **pay an arm and a leg**（花大錢、付出昂貴代價）
❼	這雙鞋子是哪個牌子的？設計真獨特。	Which brand is this pair of shoes? Its design is unique. * **Which brand is...?**（哪一個品牌…？） * **this pair of＋名詞**（這一雙…） * **common**（大眾化的）
❽	名牌真的比較好用嗎？	Are those name-brand items really more practical?
❾	你會分期付款買名牌嗎？	Do you pay for name-brand items in installments? * **pay for＋某物**（支付某物的費用） * **in installments**（以分期付款的方式）

單字級等分析

	單字	音標	詞性	意義	字頻	大考	英檢	多益
❶	wow	[waʊ]	int.	哇	2		中級	
	that	[ðæt]	pron.	那個	1	1	初級	
	new	[nju]	adj.	新的	1	1	初級	
	bag	[bæg]	n.	包包	1	1	初級	
❷	fond	[fɑnd]	adj.	喜歡的	3	3	中級	
	name	[nem]	adj.	知名的	1	1	初級	◎
	brand	[brænd]	n.	品牌	1	2	中級	◎
❸	buy	[baɪ]	v.	購買	1	1	初級	
	name-brand	[ˋnemˋbrænd]	adj.	名牌的				
	item	[ˋaɪtəm]	n.	品項	1	2	初級	◎
❹	have	[hæv]	v.	擁有	1	1	初級	
	any	[ˋɛnɪ]	adj.	任何的	1	1	初級	
❺	some	[sʌm]	adj.	一些	1	1	初級	
	people	[ˋpipl̩]	n.	person（人）複數	1	1	初級	
	like	[laɪk]	v.	喜歡	1	1	初級	
	pursue	[pɚˋsu]	v.	追求	1	2	中級	◎
❻	willing	[ˋwɪlɪŋ]	adj.	願意的	1	2	初級	◎
	pay	[pe]	v.	付出代價/支付	1	3	初級	◎
	arm	[ɑrm]	n.	手臂	1	1	初級	
	leg	[lɛg]	n.	腿	1	1	初級	
❼	this	[ðɪs]	adj.	這個	1	1	初級	
	pair	[pɛr]	n.	一雙	1	1	初級	◎
	shoes	[ʃuz]	n.	shoe（鞋子）複數	2	1		
	design	[dɪˋzaɪn]	n.	設計	1	2	初級	◎
	unique	[juˋnik]	adj.	獨特的	1	4	初級	◎
❽	those	[ðoz]	adj.	這些	1	1	初級	
	really	[ˋrɪəlɪ]	adv.	真的	1		初級	
	more	[mor]	adv.	比較	1	1	初級	
	practical	[ˋpræktɪkl̩]	adj.	實用的	1	3	中級	◎
❾	installment	[ɪnˋstɔlmənt]	n.	分期付款	4	6	中高	◎

※「紅字單字」於本單元多句出現，「單字級等分析」僅列在「首次出現句」。

🔊 MP3 143-02 ⑩～⑱

⑩	你能分辨出真假名牌嗎？	Can you tell the difference between the real and the fake name-brand items? * tell the difference（分辨、看出差異） 　= be aware of the difference * between A and B（A和B之間）
⑪	這是真品還是仿冒品？	Is it real or an imitation? * Is it A or B?（這是 A 還是 B？） * real thing（真品） * imitation（仿冒品）可替換為：duplicate（複製品）
⑫	你會上網買名牌嗎？	Do you shop for name-brand items online? * shop for＋某物（購買某物） * shop online（網路購物） * bricks-and-mortar store（實體店家）
⑬	你會買二手名牌嗎？	Do you buy secondhand name-brand items? * buy（購買）= purchase
⑭	你最喜歡哪個名牌？	Which name brand is your favorite? * Which name brand is...?（哪一個名牌是…？）
⑮	你買過名牌仿冒品嗎？	Have you bought an imitation name-brand item before? * Have you bought...?（你有買過…的經驗嗎） * 此句用「現在完成式問句」（Have...bought...?） 　表示「從過去到現在是否發生過、經歷過某事」。 * imitation name brand（冒牌貨、名牌仿冒）
⑯	你為什麼不愛名牌？	Why don't you like name brands? * Why don't you…?（你為什麼不…？）
⑰	你喜歡全身名牌的感覺嗎？	Do you like the feeling of being decked out in name-brand items from head to toe? * like the feeling of...（喜歡…的感覺） * be decked out（打扮、穿著） * in name-brand items（用名牌產品） * from head to toe（全身上下、從頭到腳）
⑱	你可以接受多少錢的名牌？	What's your budget for a name-brand item? * What's your budget for＋物品? 　（你對某物品的預算是多少？）

	單字	音標	詞性	意義	字頻	大考	英檢	多益
⑩	tell	[tɛl]	v.	分辨、看出	1	1	初級	
	difference	[ˈdɪfərəns]	n.	差異	1	2	初級	◎
	real	[ˈriəl]	adj.	真的	1	1	初級	
	fake	[fek]	adj.	假的	2	3	中級	◎
	name-brand	[ˈnemˈbrænd]	adj.	名牌的				
	item	[ˈaɪtəm]	n.	品項	1	2	初級	◎
⑪	imitation	[ˌɪməˈteʃən]	n.	仿冒品	3	4	中級	
⑫	shop	[ʃɑp]	v.	購物	1	1	初級	
	online	[ˈɑnˌlaɪn]	adv.	在網路上	1		初級	◎
⑬	buy	[baɪ]	v.	購買	1	1	初級	
	secondhand	[ˈsɛkəndhænd]	adj.	二手的				◎
⑭	name	[nem]	adj.	知名的	1	1	初級	◎
	brand	[brænd]	n.	品牌	1	2	中級	◎
	favorite	[ˈfevərɪt]	adj.	最喜歡的東西	1	1	初級	◎
⑮	bought	[bɔt]	p.p.	buy（購買）過去分詞	1	1	初級	
	before	[bɪˈfor]	adv.	以前	1	1	初級	
⑯	like	[laɪk]	v.	喜歡	1	1	初級	
⑰	feeling	[ˈfilɪŋ]	n.	感覺	1	1	初級	◎
	decked	[dɛkt]	p.p.	deck（打扮）過去分詞		3	中級	
	out	[aʊt]	adv.	完全、徹底	1	1	初級	
	head	[hɛd]	n.	頭	1	1	初級	◎
	toe	[to]	n.	腳趾	2	2	初級	
⑱	budget	[ˈbʌdʒɪt]	n.	預算	1	3	中級	◎

※「紅字單字」於本單元多句出現，「單字級等分析」僅列在「首次出現句」。

🔊 MP3 144-01 ❶～❽

❶	沒有醜女人，只有懶女人。	There are no ugly women, only lazy ones.
❷	台灣的女生超愛用面膜。	Girls in Taiwan love beauty masks. * **beauty mask**（面膜）
❸	皮膚的清潔工作最重要。	Cleanliness is the most important thing for skin care.
❹	很多人喜歡天然的保養品。	Many people are fond of natural skin care products. * **be fond of**（喜歡）、**skin care product**（保養品）
❺	擦乳液可以保護皮膚。	Lotion will help protect your skin.
❻	夏天出門一定要擦防曬。	You must wear sunscreen when you're out during the summer. * **wear sunscreen**（擦防曬）
❼	聽說按摩臉部會改善肌肉鬆弛。	It's said that massaging your face will improve flabby muscles. * **It's said that**＋子句（據說…） * **flabby muscles**（鬆弛的肌肉）
❽	一到夏天美白產品就熱賣。	Skin whitening products are popular in summer. * **skin whitening**（美白）
❾	去角質會讓皮膚更細緻。	Exfoliating will give skin a fine texture. * **fine texture**（細緻膚質）
❿	很多女生認為皮膚白就是漂亮。	Some girls equate beauty with fair skin. * **equate A with B**（把A和B畫上等號）
⓫	皮膚脫皮，就是太乾燥了。	If your skin flakes off, it's too dry. * **flake off**（剝落）
⓬	很多人做了拉皮手術。	Many people get facelifts. * **get a facelift**（做臉部拉皮手術）
⓭	多吃水果蔬菜是最簡單的美容方法。	Eating more fruits and vegetables is the simplest way to beauty. * **way**（方法）= method

	單字	音標	詞性	意義	字頻	大考	英檢	多益
❶	there	[ðɛr]	adv.	有…	1	1	初級	
	ugly	[ˈʌɡlɪ]	adj.	醜陋的	2	2	初級	◎
	women	[ˈwɪmɪn]	n.	woman（女人）複數	1	1	初級	
	only	[ˈonlɪ]	adv.	只有	1	1	初級	
	lazy	[ˈlezɪ]	adj.	懶惰的	3	1	初級	
	one	[wʌn]	pron.	一人	1	1	初級	
❷	girl	[ɡɝl]	n.	女孩	1	1	初級	
	Taiwan	[ˈtaɪˈwɑn]	n.	台灣			初級	
	love	[lʌv]	v.	喜愛	1	1	初級	

❷	beauty	[ˋbjutɪ]	n.	美容/美麗	1	1	中級	
	mask	[mæsk]	n.	面膜	2	2	初級	
❸	cleanliness	[ˋklɛnlɪnɪs]	n.	清潔	6			
	most	[most]	adv.	最為	1	1	初級	
	important	[ɪmˋpɔrtnt]	adj.	重要的	1	1	初級	◎
	thing	[θɪŋ]	n.	事物	1	1	初級	
	skin	[skɪn]	n.	皮膚	1	1	初級	◎
	care	[kɛr]	n.	保養	1	1	初級	◎
❹	many	[ˋmɛnɪ]	adj.	許多的	1	1	初級	
	people	[ˋpipl]	n.	person（人）複數	1	1	初級	
	fond	[fɑnd]	adj.	喜歡的	3	3	中級	
	natural	[ˋnætʃərəl]	adj.	自然的	1	2	初級	
	product	[ˋprɑdəkt]	n.	產品	1	3	初級	◎
❺	lotion	[ˋloʃən]	n.	乳液	4	4	中級	
	help	[hɛlp]	v.	幫助	1	1	初級	
	protect	[prəˋtɛkt]	v.	保護	1	2	初級	◎
❻	wear	[wɛr]	v.	塗抹	1	1	初級	◎
	sunscreen	[ˋsʌn.skrin]	n.	防曬乳	4			
	out	[aut]	adj.	外出的	1	1	初級	
	summer	[ˋsʌmɚ]	n.	夏天	1	1	初級	
❼	said	[sɛd]	p.p.	say（據說）過去分詞	4	1	初級	
	massaging	[məˋsɑʒɪŋ]	n.	massage（按摩）動名詞	3	5	中高	
	face	[fes]	n.	臉部			初級	
	improve	[ɪmˋpruv]	v.	改善	1	2	初級	◎
	flabby	[ˋflæbɪ]	adj.	鬆弛的	8			
	muscle	[ˋmʌsl]	n.	肌肉	1	3	中級	◎
❽	whitening	[ˋhwaɪtnɪŋ]	n.	whiten（變白）動名詞	8			
	popular	[ˋpɑpjəlɚ]	adj.	熱門的	1	2	初級	
❾	exfoliating	[ɛksˋfolɪ.etɪŋ]	n.	exfoliate（去角質）動名詞				
	give	[gɪv]	v.	給予	1	1	初級	
	fine	[faɪn]	adj.	纖細的	1	1	初級	◎
	texture	[ˋtɛkstʃɚ]	n.	膚質	2	6	中高	◎
❿	some	[sʌm]	adj.	一些	1	1	初級	
	equate	[ɪˋkwet]	v.	打…畫上等號	3	5	中高	
	fair	[fɛr]	adj.	白皙的	1	2	初級	
⓫	flake	[flek]	v.	剝落	3	5	中高	
	off	[ɔf]	adv.	掉下	1	1	初級	
	too	[tu]	adv.	過於	1	1	初級	
	dry	[draɪ]	adj.	乾燥的	1	1	初級	
⓬	get	[gɛt]	v.	接受做	1	1	初級	◎
	facelift	[ˋfeslɪft]	n.	臉部拉皮手術				
⓭	eating	[ˋitɪŋ]	n.	eat（吃）動名詞	2	1	初級	
	more	[mor]	adj.	更多的	1	1	初級	
	fruit	[frut]	n.	水果	1	1	初級	
	vegetable	[ˋvɛdʒətəbl]	n.	蔬菜	1	1	初級	◎
	simplest	[ˋsɪmplɪst]	adj.	simple（簡單的）最高級	1	1	初級	◎
	way	[we]	n.	方法	1	1	初級	

※「紅字單字」於本單元多句出現，「單字級等分析」僅列在「首次出現句」。

🔵 MP3 144-02 ❶～⓰

❶	你用名牌保養品嗎？	Do you use name-brand skin care products?
❷	你擔心變老嗎？	Are you afraid of getting old? * **Are you afraid of＋動詞-ing…?**（你害怕…嗎）
❸	你有做什麼特別的保養嗎？	Do you have any particular skin maintenance method? * **skin maintenance**（保養）＝ **skin care**
❹	你常注意美容資訊嗎？	Do you pay much attention to beauty news? * **pay attention to**（注意）
❺	你每個月花多少錢買保養品？	How much do you pay for beauty products each month? * **How much…?**（…多少錢？）
❻	你的臉色暗沉嗎？	Do you have a dull complexion?
❼	你相信面膜的功效嗎？	Do you trust those beauty masks?
❽	你也認為皮膚白就是漂亮嗎？	Do you think that fair skin equals beauty? * **Do you think that＋子句?**（你認為…嗎）
❾	你有毛孔粗大的問題嗎？	Are you troubled by large pores? * **Are you troubled by…?**（你有…的困擾嗎）
❿	皮膚太乾燥怎麼辦？	What if your skin is too dry? * **What if＋主詞＋動詞…?**（要是…該怎麼辦？）
⓫	出現小細紋該怎麼辦？	What should I do when fine lines appear? * **What should I do…?**（我該做什麼…？） * **fine line**（細微紋路、小細紋）
⓬	如何防止臉部肌肉鬆弛？	How can I prevent flabby facial muscles? * **How can I＋動詞…?**（我該如何…？）
⓭	怎樣讓肌膚白回來？	How can I get my skin white again?
⓮	如何青春永駐？	How can I stay young?
⓯	粉刺要怎麼處理？	What should I do about acne?
⓰	出現魚尾紋了，怎麼辦？	What am I going to do about my crow's feet? * **be going to**（接下來要）、**crow's feet**（魚尾紋）

	單字	音標	詞性	意義	字頻	大考	英檢	多益
❶	use	[juz]	v.	使用	1	1	初級	
	name-brand	[ˋnemˋbrænd]	adj.	名牌的				
	skin	[skɪn]	n.	皮膚	1	1	初級	◎
	care	[kɛr]	n.	保養	1	1	初級	◎
	product	[ˋprɑdəkt]	n.	產品	1	3	初級	◎
❷	afraid	[əˋfred]	adj.	害怕的	1	1	初級	

❷	getting	[ˋgɛtɪŋ]	n.	get（變成）動名詞	1	1	初級	
	old	[old]	adj.	老的	1	1	初級	
❸	have	[hæv]	v.	擁有	1	1	初級	
	any	[ˋɛnɪ]	adj.	任何的	1	1	初級	
	particular	[pɚˋtɪkjəlɚ]	adj.	特別的	1	2	初級	◎
	maintenance	[ˋmentənəns]	n.	保養	2	5	中高	◎
	method	[ˋmɛθəd]	n.	方法	1	2	初級	◎
❹	pay	[pe]	v.	給予	1	3	初級	
	much	[mʌtʃ]	adj.	許多的	1	1	初級	
	attention	[əˋtɛnʃən]	n.	注意	1	2	初級	◎
	beauty	[ˋbjutɪ]	n.	美容	1	1	中級	
	news	[njuz]	n.	資訊	1	1	初級	◎
❺	each	[itʃ]	adj.	每一個	1	1	初級	
	month	[mʌnθ]	n.	月	1	1	初級	
❻	dull	[dʌl]	adj.	暗沉的	2	2	中級	◎
	complexion	[kəmˋplɛkʃən]	n.	膚色	4	6	中高	
❼	trust	[trʌst]	v.	相信	1	2	初級	◎
	those	[ðoz]	adj.	這些	1	1	初級	
	mask	[mæsk]	n.	面膜	2	1	初級	
❽	think	[θɪŋk]	v.	認為	1	1	初級	
	fair	[fɛr]	adj.	白皙的	1	2	初級	
	equal	[ˋikwəl]	v.	等同於	1	1	初級	◎
❾	troubled	[ˋtrʌbld]	p.p.	trouble（困擾）過去分詞	2	1	中高	◎
	large	[lɑrdʒ]	adj.	大的	1	1	初級	◎
	pore	[por]	n.	毛孔	5		中高	
❿	too	[tu]	adv.	過於	1	1	初級	
	dry	[draɪ]	adj.	乾燥的	1	1	初級	
⓫	do	[du]	v.	做	1	1	初級	
	fine	[faɪn]	adj.	纖細的	1	1	初級	◎
	line	[laɪn]	n.	紋路	1	1	初級	◎
	appear	[əˋpɪr]	v.	出現	1	1	初級	◎
⓬	prevent	[prɪˋvɛnt]	v.	預防	1	3	中級	◎
	flabby	[ˋflæbɪ]	adj.	鬆弛的	8			
	facial	[ˋfeʃəl]	adj.	臉部的	3	4	中級	
	muscle	[ˋmʌsl]	n.	肌肉	1	3	中級	◎
⓭	get	[gɛt]	v.	變成	1	1	初級	◎
	white	[hwaɪt]	adj.	白皙的	1	1	初級	
	again	[əˋgɛn]	adv.	再次	1	1	初級	
⓮	stay	[ste]	v.	保持	1	1	初級	◎
	young	[jʌŋ]	adj.	年輕的	1	1	初級	
⓯	acne	[ˋækɪnɪ]	n.	粉刺	6	5	中高	
⓰	going	[ˋgoɪŋ]	p.pr.	go（即將）現在分詞	4	1	初級	
	crow	[kro]	n.	烏鴉	4	2	中級	
	feet	[fit]	n.	foot（腳）複數	1	1	初級	

※「紅字單字」於本單元多句出現，「單字級等分析」僅列在「首次出現句」。

MP3 145-01 ❶～❾

❶	減肥彷彿成了全民運動。	It seems that weight loss has become a civic movement. * **It seems that**＋子句（似乎…、彷彿…） * **weight loss**（減肥） * **a civic movement**（全民運動） * 此句用「現在完成式」(**…has become**…) 表示「過去某時點發生某事，且結果持續到現在」。
❷	減肥的方法太多了。	There are all kinds of ways to lose weight. * **all kinds of ways**（有太多方法） * **lose weight**（減肥） * **way**（方法）＝ **method**
❸	身體一胖穿衣服就不好看。	Once you gain weight, your clothes don't look as good on you. * **Once...**（一旦…，只要…） * **gain weight**（變胖） * **look as good on**＋某人（在某人身上好看）
❹	一星期瘦 0.5 公斤最理想。	It'd be perfect if you could lose half a kilo per week. * **It'd be perfect if**＋子句（…是理想的） * **per week**（每一星期）
❺	減肥成功後，千萬不要再復胖。	Once you get rid of the fat, be sure it doesn't come back. * **get rid of**（擺脫） * **be sure (that)**＋子句（切記、務必） * **come back**（回復原狀）
❻	醫院現在也有推出專門的減重班。	Even hospitals are promoting weight-loss programs now. * **weight-loss program**（減重課程）
❼	減肥藥可不能亂吃。	Don't just take any diet pills. * **take pills**（服藥） * **diet pills**（減肥藥）
❽	台灣有很多減肥減出問題的案例。	There are many weight-loss issues in Taiwan. * **weight-loss issue**（減重案例）
❾	你說吃肉也可以減肥？	Did you say that eating meat can help burn off fat? * **Did you say that**＋子句（你剛才是說…嗎） * **burn off**（燃燒掉）

單字級等分析

	單字	音標	詞性	意義	字頻	大考	英檢	多益
❶	seem	[sim]	v.	似乎	1	1	初級	◎
	weight	[wet]	n.	體重	1	1	初級	◎
	loss	[lɔs]	n.	減少	1	2	初級	◎
	become	[bɪˋkʌm]	p.p.	become（變為）過去分詞	1	1	初級	◎
	civic	[ˋsɪvɪk]	adj.	全民的	2	5	中高	◎
	movement	[ˋmuvmənt]	n.	運動、活動	1	1	初級	◎
❷	there	[ðɛr]	adv.	有…	1	1	初級	
	all	[ɔl]	adj.	所有的	1	1	初級	
	kind	[kaɪnd]	n.	種類	1	1	初級	
	way	[we]	n.	方法	1	1	初級	
	lose	[luz]	v.	減少	1	2	初級	◎
❸	gain	[gen]	v.	增加	1	2	初級	◎
	clothes	[kloz]	n.	cloth（衣服）複數	1	2	初級	
	look	[lʊk]	v.	看起來	1	1	初級	
	good	[gʊd]	adj.	良好的	1	1	初級	
❹	perfect	[ˋpɝfɪkt]	adj.	美好的	1	1	初級	◎
	half	[hæf]	n.	一半	1	1	初級	
	kilo	[ˋkɪlo]	n.	kilogram（公斤）縮寫				
	week	[wik]	n.	禮拜	1	1	初級	
❺	get	[gɛt]	v.	變成	1	1	初級	◎
	rid	[rɪd]	p.p.	rid（擺脫）過去分詞	2	3	中級	
	fat	[fæt]	n.	脂肪、肥胖	1	1	初級	
	sure	[ʃʊr]	adj.	確定的	1	1	初級	
	come	[kʌm]	v.	到來	1	1	初級	
	back	[bæk]	adv.	返回	1	1	初級	◎
❻	even	[ˋivən]	adv.	甚至	1	1	初級	◎
	hospital	[ˋhɑspɪtl̩]	n.	醫院	1	2	初級	◎
	promoting	[prəˋmotɪŋ]	p.pr.	promote（宣傳、推銷）現在分詞	1	3	中級	◎
	weight-loss	[ˋwetˏlɔs]	adj.	減重的				
	program	[ˋprogræm]	n.	課程	1	3	初級	◎
	now	[naʊ]	adv.	現在	1	1	初級	
❼	just	[dʒʌst]	adv.	就…	1	1	初級	
	take	[tek]	v.	服用	1	1	初級	◎
	any	[ˋɛnɪ]	adj.	任何的	1	1	初級	
	diet	[ˋdaɪət]	n.	減肥	1	3	初級	◎
	pill	[pɪl]	n.	藥粒	2	3	中級	
❽	many	[ˋmɛnɪ]	adj.	許多的	1	1	初級	
	issue	[ˋɪʃʊ]	n.	案例	1	5	中級	◎
	Taiwan	[ˋtaɪˋwɑn]	n.	台灣			初級	
❾	say	[se]	v.	說	1	1	初級	
	eating	[ˋitɪŋ]	n.	eat（吃）動名詞	2	1	初級	
	meat	[mit]	n.	肉類	1	1	初級	
	help	[hɛlp]	v.	幫助	1	1	初級	
	burn	[bɝn]	v.	燃燒	1	2	初級	
	off	[ɔf]	adv.	燒掉	1	1	初級	

※「紅字單字」於本單元多句出現，「單字級等分析」僅列在「首次出現句」。

145   減肥…。（2）

❿	我還是覺得自己可以再瘦一點。	I still think there's room for me to lose a little weight. * **there is room for me to**＋動詞原形（我還有餘裕做…） * **lose weight**（減肥）
⓫	我一定可以減肥成功。	I'm definitely going to cut down my weight to the ideal standard. * **definitely**（明確地、肯定地）＝ **certainly** * **be going to**＋動詞原形（即將） * **cut down**（削減） * **ideal standard**（理想標準）
⓬	去瘦身中心減肥好貴喔！	It's too expensive to go to a weight-loss center. * **It's too expensive to**＋動詞原形（做某事很昂貴） * **weight-loss center**（瘦身中心）
⓭	為了穿上這件洋裝，我決定要減肥。	I've decided to lose enough weight to be able to put on this dress. * **decide to**＋動詞原形（決定） * **be able to**＋動詞原形（能夠） * **put on**（穿上）
⓮	太瘦並不健康。	It's not good to be too thin. * **It's not good to**＋動詞原形（…並不好） * **It's good to**＋動詞原形（…是好的）
⓯	肥胖是不健康的前兆。	Obesity is a sign of unhealthiness. * **obesity**（肥胖）＝ **fatness** * **a sign of…**（…的徵兆）
⓰	減肥要有意志力才能成功。	It takes willpower to lose weight. * **It takes willpower to**＋動詞原形（做…需要意志力）
⓱	很多減肥廣告都誇大不實。	Many ads about weight loss are fake. * **weight loss**（減肥） * **an ad about...**（一個…的廣告） * **fake**（不實的）可替換為：**false**（謬誤的） * **run a misleading ad**（廣告不實）
⓲	很多減肥書都不實用。	Many books about weight loss are not that practical. * **practical**（實用的）可替換為：**workable**（可行的）

單字級等分析

	單字	音標	詞性	意義	字頻	大考	英檢	多益
❿	still	[stɪl]	adv.	仍然	1	1	初級	◎
	think	[θɪŋk]	v.	認為	1	1	初級	
	there	[ðɛr]	adv.	有…	1	1	初級	
	room	[rum]	n.	餘裕	1	1	初級	
	lose	[luz]	v.	減少	1	2	初級	◎
	little	[ˈlɪtl̩]	adj.	少許的	1	1	初級	
	weight	[wet]	n.	體重	1	1	初級	◎
⓫	definitely	[ˈdɛfənɪtlɪ]	adv.	明確地、肯定地	1		中高	◎
	going	[ˈgoɪŋ]	p.pr.	go（即將）現在分詞	4	1	初級	
	cut	[kʌt]	v.	減少	1	1	初級	
	down	[daʊn]	adv.	降下	1	1	初級	
	ideal	[aɪˈdiəl]	adj.	理想的	2	3	中級	◎
	standard	[ˈstændəd]	n.	標準	1	2	初級	◎
⓬	too	[tu]	adv.	過於	1	1	初級	
	expensive	[ɪkˈspɛnsɪv]	adj.	昂貴的	1	2	初級	◎
	go	[go]	v.	去	1	1	初級	
	weight-loss	[ˈwetˌlɔs]	adj.	減肥的				
	center	[ˈsɛntə]	n.	中心	1	1	初級	
⓭	decided	[dɪˈsaɪdɪd]	p.p.	decide（決定）過去分詞	1	1	初級	◎
	enough	[əˈnʌf]	adj.	足夠的	1	1	初級	◎
	able	[ˈebl̩]	adj.	能夠的	1	1	初級	◎
	put	[pʊt]	v.	穿上	1	1	初級	
	this	[ðɪs]	adj.	這個	1	1	初級	
	dress	[drɛs]	n.	洋裝	1	2	初級	
⓮	good	[gʊd]	adj.	良好的	1	1	初級	◎
	thin	[θɪn]	adj.	瘦的	1	2	初級	◎
⓯	obesity	[oˈbisətɪ]	n.	肥胖	3			
	sign	[saɪn]	n.	徵兆	1	2	初級	◎
	unhealthiness	[ʌnˈhɛlθɪnɪs]	n.	不健康				
⓰	take	[tek]	v.	需要	1	1	初級	◎
	willpower	[ˈwɪlˌpaʊə]	n.	意志力	8			
⓱	many	[ˈmɛnɪ]	adj.	許多的	1	1	初級	
	ad	[æd]	n.	advertisement（廣告）縮寫	1	3	中高	◎
	loss	[lɔs]	n.	減少	1	2	初級	◎
	fake	[fek]	adj.	不實的	2	3	中級	◎
⓲	book	[bʊk]	n.	書籍	1	1	初級	◎
	that	[ðæt]	adv.	那麼	1	1	初級	
	practical	[ˈpræktɪkl̩]	adj.	實用的	1	3	中級	◎

※「紅字單字」於本單元多句出現，「單字級等分析」僅列在「首次出現句」。

MP3 145-02 ❶～❿

❶	最近發福了嗎？	Have you put on some weight lately? * **Have you＋過去分詞＋lately?**（你最近…嗎） * **put on weight**（體重增加） * **lately**（最近）＝ **recently**
❷	斷食減肥法會不會很辛苦？	Is cutting down on your diet a burden? * **cut down on**（削減）
❸	每個台灣人都覺得自己需要減肥嗎？	Do Taiwanese people all feel like they need to lose weight? * **feel like＋子句**（想要、覺得） * **need to＋動詞原形**（需要） * **lose weight**（減肥）
❹	秤秤看你現在多重。	Check how much you weigh now. * **check one's weight**（量體重） 　＝ **measure one's weight** * **How much do you weigh?**（你的體重多少？）
❺	電視購物頻道上的減肥藥真的有效嗎？	Are those weight-loss medicines on the TV shopping channel effective? * **weight-loss medicine**（減肥藥） 　＝ **weight-loss medications**、**diet pills** * **TV shopping channel**（電視購物頻道）
❻	究竟有多少方法可以減肥啊？	How many ways on earth are there to lose weight? * **on earth**（究竟、到底）＝ **in the world**
❼	你減重成功了嗎？	Have you lost weight successfully? * 此句用「現在完成式問句」（Have…lost…?）表示 　「過去某時點是否發生某事,且結果持續到現在嗎?」。
❽	減肥可別傷了健康。	Don't harm your health while losing weight. * **harm one's health**（傷害健康） * **while＋動詞-ing**（做某事的同時）
❾	減肥後是不是很容易復胖？	Is it easy to gain weight again after losing weight? * **It is easy to＋動詞原形**（某事很容易發生） * **gain weight again**（復胖）
❿	瘦身中心有效嗎？	Does the weight-loss center help? * **weight-loss center**（瘦身中心）

666

單字級等分析

	單字	音標	詞性	意義	字頻	大考	英檢	多益
❶	put	[pʊt]	p.p.	put（增加）過去分詞	1	1	初級	
	some	[sʌm]	adj.	一些	1	1	初級	
	weight	[wet]	n.	體重	1	1	初級	◎
	lately	[ˋletlɪ]	adv.	最近	2	4	中級	
❷	cutting	[ˋkʌtɪŋ]	n.	cut（減少）動名詞	2	1	中高	
	down	[daʊn]	adv.	降下	1	1	初級	
	diet	[ˋdaɪət]	n.	減肥	1	3	初級	◎
	burden	[ˋbɝdn]	n.	困難的事	1	3	中級	◎
❸	Taiwanese	[ˌtaɪwəˋniz]	adj.	台灣的	4		初級	
	people	[ˋpipl]	n.	person（人）複數	1	1	初級	
	all	[ɔl]	adv.	都…	1	1	初級	
	feel	[fil]	v.	覺得	1	1	初級	
	need	[nid]	v.	需要	1	1	初級	◎
	lose	[luz]	v.	減少	1	2	初級	
❹	check	[tʃɛk]	v.	測量	1	1	初級	◎
	much	[mʌtʃ]	adv.	許多地	1	1	初級	
	weigh	[we]	v.	秤…重量	1	1	中級	
	now	[naʊ]	adv.	現在	1	1	初級	
❺	those	[ðoz]	adj.	那些	1	1	初級	
	weight-loss	[ˋwetˏlɔs]	adj.	減肥的				
	medicine	[ˋmɛdəsn]	n.	藥物	1	2	初級	◎
	TV	[ˋtiˋvi]	n.	television（電視）縮寫		2	初級	
	shopping	[ˋʃɑpɪŋ]	n.	shop（購物）動名詞	1	1	中級	
	channel	[ˋtʃænl]	n.	頻道	1	3	初級	
	effective	[ɪˋfɛktɪv]	adj.	有效果的	1	2	初級	◎
❻	many	[ˋmɛnɪ]	adj.	許多的	1	1	初級	
	way	[we]	n.	方法	1	1	初級	
	earth	[ɝθ]	n.	世界、世間	1	1	初級	
	there	[ðɛr]	adv.	有…	1	1	初級	
❼	lost	[lɔst]	p.p.	lose（減少）過去分詞	1	2	中高	◎
	successfully	[səkˋsɛsfəlɪ]	adv.	成功地	2			
❽	harm	[hɑrm]	v.	傷害	2	3	中級	
	health	[hɛlθ]	n.	健康	1	1	初級	◎
	losing	[ˋluzɪŋ]	p.pr.	lose（減少）現在分詞	4	2	初級	◎
❾	easy	[ˋizɪ]	adj.	容易的	1	1	初級	◎
	gain	[gen]	v.	增加	1	2	初級	
	again	[əˋgɛn]	adv.	再次	1	1	初級	
	losing	[ˋluzɪŋ]	n.	lose（減少）動名詞	4	2	初級	◎
❿	center	[ˋsɛntɚ]	n.	中心	1	1	初級	◎
	help	[hɛlp]	v.	有幫助	1	1	初級	

※「紅字單字」於本單元多句出現，「單字級等分析」僅列在「首次出現句」。

⑪	怎樣的人容易變胖？	What kind of person tends to gain weight? * **What kind of**＋人事物（什麼類型的人事物） * **tend to**（傾向、易於）＝ **be inclined to** * **gain weight**（變胖）
⑫	快樂就好，幹麼這麼在意身材？	What's all the fuss about your figure so long as you can choose to be happy? * **What's all the fuss about**…（為何要對…小題大作） * **so long as**（只要） * **you can choose to be happy**（你能夠開心） * **figure**（身材）＝ **shape** * **keep one's figure**（保持身材） * **choose to**＋動詞原形（選擇）
⑬	吃減肥藥會不會有副作用？	Will there be any side effects to taking the weight-loss medicine? * **side effect**（副作用） * **take the weight-loss medicine**（服用減肥藥）
⑭	台灣似乎有為數不少關於減肥的書。	Seems there're quite a few books about weight loss in Taiwan. * **seem**＋子句（似乎…） * **quite a few**（相當不少的） * **a book about**…（一本關於…的書）
⑮	你成功瘦了幾公斤？	How many kilograms have you lost? * **How many kilograms…?**（…多少公斤？） * 此句用「現在完成式」（…have...lost…）表示「過去某時點發生某事，且結果持續到現在」。
⑯	你又不胖，幹麼減肥？	Lose weight? Why bother! You're not fat. * **lose weight**（減肥） * **Why bother!**（何必呢！）
⑰	哪一種減肥方法最有效？	What is the most effective way to lose weight? * **the most effective way to**＋動詞原形（做…最有效的方法）
⑱	醫院有教人如何減肥嗎？	Does the hospital teach people how to lose weight? * **teach**＋某人＋**how to**＋動詞原形（教某人如何…）

單字級等分析

	單字	音標	詞性	意義	字頻	大考	英檢	多益
⓫	kind	[kaɪnd]	n.	種類	1	1	初級	◎
	person	[ˋpɝsn]	n.	人	1	1	初級	
	tend	[tɛnd]	v.	傾向、易於	1	3	中級	◎
	gain	[gen]	v.	增加	1	2	初級	◎
	weight	[wet]	n.	體重	1	1	初級	◎
⓬	all	[ɔl]	adj.	所有的	1	1	初級	
	fuss	[fʌs]	n.	小題大作、大驚小怪	4	5	中高	◎
	figure	[ˋfɪgjɚ]	n.	身材	1	2	初級	◎
	long	[lɔŋ]	adv.	只要	1	1	初級	
	choose	[tʃuz]	v.	選擇	1	2	初級	◎
	happy	[ˋhæpɪ]	adj.	快樂的	1	1	初級	
⓭	there	[ðɛr]	adv.	有…	1	1	初級	
	any	[ˋɛnɪ]	adj.	任何的	1	1	初級	
	side	[saɪd]	adj.	附帶的、次要的	1	2	初級	
	effect	[ɪˋfɛkt]	n.	作用	1	1	初級	◎
	taking	[ˋtekɪŋ]	n.	take（服用）動名詞	4			
	weight-loss	[ˋwetˏlɔs]	adj.	減肥的				
	medicine	[ˋmɛdəsn]	n.	藥物	1	2	初級	◎
⓮	seem	[sim]	v.	似乎	1	1	初級	◎
	quite	[kwaɪt]	adv.	相當	1	1	初級	
	few	[fju]	adj.	些許的	1	1	初級	
	book	[bʊk]	n.	書籍	1	1	初級	
	loss	[lɔs]	n.	減少	1	2	初級	◎
	Taiwan	[ˋtaɪˋwɑn]	n.	台灣			初級	
⓯	many	[ˋmɛnɪ]	adj.	許多的	1	1	初級	
	kilogram	[ˋkɪləˏgræm]	n.	體重		3	初級	
	lost	[lɔst]	p.p.	lose（減少）過去分詞	1	2	中高	◎
⓰	lose	[luz]	v.	減少	1	2	初級	◎
	bother	[ˋbɑðɚ]	v.	困擾	1	2	初級	◎
	fat	[fæt]	adj.	肥胖的	1	1	初級	
⓱	most	[most]	adv.	最為	1	1	初級	
	effective	[ɪˋfɛktɪv]	adj.	有效的	1	2	初級	◎
	way	[we]	n.	方法	1	1	初級	
⓲	hospital	[ˋhɑspɪtl]	n.	醫院	1	2	初級	◎
	teach	[titʃ]	v.	教導	1	1	初級	
	people	[ˋpipl]	n.	person（人）複數	1	1	初級	

※「紅字單字」於本單元多句出現，「單字級等分析」僅列在「首次出現句」。

146　整型…。（1）

MP3 146-01 ❶～❽

❶	韓國有很多人工美女。	South Korea has many man-made beauties. * **South Korea**（南韓） * **man-made**（人工的）＝ **artificial** * **natural**（自然的、天然的）
❷	我還是不敢嘗試整型。	I still don't dare to give plastic surgery a try. * **dare to**＋動詞原形（敢做…、有膽做…） * **give**＋某事＋**a try**（嘗試做某事） * **plastic surgery**（整型手術）
❸	很多人整型後變得有自信。	Many people become more confident after having plastic surgery. * **become**＋形容詞（變得…） * **after**＋動詞-**ing**（在…之後） * **have plastic surgery**（做整型手術）
❹	我老了一定會去拉皮。	I'm going to tighten my skin when I get older. * **I'm going to...**（我預計要…） * **tighten one's skin**（拉皮） * **get older**（變老、年紀變大） * 此句用「未來簡單式」（...**be going to**...） 　表示「未來排定時程、但預定要做的事」。
❺	整型失敗的例子其實不少。	Actually, there are many failed examples of plastic surgery. * **there are many**＋名詞（有很多…） * **failed example**（失敗的案例） * **successful example**（成功的案例） * **typical example**（典型的案例）
❻	整型是變美最快的方法。	Plastic surgery is the fastest way to become beautiful. * **the fastest way to**＋動詞原形（最快速的方法…） * **shortcut**（捷徑）
❼	現在的整型手術可以做得很自然。	Plastic surgery nowadays can be done very naturally. * **nowadays**（現今）＝ **at present**
❽	其實有些整型手術費用不高。	Actually, some plastic surgery operations are not that expensive. * **plastic surgery operation**（整型手術）

670

	單字	音標	詞性	意義	字頻	大考	英檢	多益
❶	south	[sauθ]	adj.	南部的	1	1	初級	
	Korea	[ko`riə]	n.	韓國	3		初級	
	have	[hæv]	v.	擁有	1	1	初級	
	many	[`mɛnɪ]	adj.	許多的	1	1	初級	
	man-made	[`mæn͵med]	adj.	人造的	4		中級	
	beauty	[`bjutɪ]	n.	美女	1	1	中級	
❷	still	[stɪl]	adv.	仍然	1	1	初級	◎
	dare	[dɛr]	v.	敢做⋯、有膽做⋯	2	3	中級	
	give	[gɪv]	v.	給予	1	1	初級	
	plastic	[`plæstɪk]	adj.	整型的	1	3	中級	◎
	surgery	[`sɝdʒərɪ]	n.	手術	1	4	中級	◎
	try	[traɪ]	n.	嘗試	1	1	初級	
❸	people	[`pipl]	n.	person（人）複數	1	1	初級	
	become	[bɪ`kʌm]	v.	變得	1	1	初級	◎
	more	[mor]	adv.	更加	1	1	初級	
	confident	[`kɑnfədənt]	adj.	自信的	2	3	初級	
	having	[`hævɪŋ]	n.	have（動〔手術〕）動名詞	1	1	初級	
❹	going	[`goɪŋ]	p.pr.	go（預計）現在分詞	4		初級	
	tighten	[`taɪtn]	v.	拉緊	2	3	中級	
	skin	[skɪn]	n.	皮膚	1	1	初級	◎
	get	[gɛt]	v.	變成	1	1	初級	
	older	[`oldɚ]	adj.	old（老的）比較級	1	1	初級	
❺	actually	[`æktʃʊəlɪ]	adv.	實際上	1		初級	
	there	[ðɛr]	adv.	有⋯	1	1	初級	
	failed	[feld]	adj.	失敗的	3	2	初級	◎
	example	[ɪg`zæmpl]	n.	案例	1	1	初級	◎
❻	fastest	[`fæstɪst]	adj.	fast（快速的）最高級	3			
	way	[we]	n.	方法	1	1	初級	
	beautiful	[`bjutəfəl]	adj.	漂亮的	1	1	初級	
❼	nowadays	[`nauə͵dez]	adv.	現今	3	4	中級	
	done	[dʌn]	p.p.	do（做）過去分詞	1	1	初級	
	very	[`vɛrɪ]	adv.	十分	1	1	初級	
	naturally	[`nætʃərəlɪ]	adv.	自然地	1		中級	
❽	some	[sʌm]	adj.	一些	1	1	初級	
	operation	[͵ɑpə`reʃən]	n.	手術	1	4	初級	◎
	that	[ðæt]	adv.	那麼	1	1	初級	
	expensive	[ɪk`spɛnsɪv]	adj.	昂貴的	1	2	初級	◎

※「紅字單字」於本單元多句出現，「單字級等分析」僅列在「首次出現句」。

MP3 146-01 ❾～⓰

❾	很多人割雙眼皮。	Many people have plastic surgery to get double-fold eyelids. * **have plastic surgery to get double-fold eyelids**（割雙眼皮） * **have plastic surgery**（做整型手術） * **get double-fold eyelids**（得到雙眼皮）
❿	很多學生利用暑假整型。	Many students get plastic surgery during summer vacation. * **during**（在⋯期間） * **get plastic surgery**（接受整型手術） * **summer vacation**（暑假） * **winter vacation**（寒假）
⓫	整型手術讓許多人美夢成真。	Plastic surgery makes many people's dreams come true. * **make＋某人＋動詞原形**（讓某人⋯） * **dreams come true**（實現夢想）
⓬	隆鼻的人也不少。	There are many people who have had nose jobs. * **have had nose jobs**（曾經隆鼻、有隆鼻經驗）
⓭	整型手術幾個小時就能完成。	Plastic surgery can be done in a couple of hours. * **a couple of hours**（幾個小時）
⓮	抽脂是熱門的整型項目。	Liposuction is the most popular form of plastic surgery. * **breast implants**（豐胸手術） * **hair transplantation**（植髮手術） * **orthognathic surgery**（正顎手術） * **injection of botulinum toxin**（注射肉毒桿菌）
⓯	選擇整型醫生時要多比較。	It's good to shop around for plastic surgeons before choosing one. * **shop around**（貨比三家、多做比較） * **plastic surgeon**（整型醫生） * **before＋動詞-ing**（在⋯之前）
⓰	我覺得人工美女看起來還是怪怪的。	I think man-made beauties still look strange. * **man-made beauty**（人工美女） * **look strange**（看起來怪怪的）

	單字	音標	詞性	意義	字頻	大考	英檢	多益
❾	many	[`mɛnɪ]	adj.	許多的	1	1	初級	
	people	[`pipl]	n.	person（人）複數	1	1	初級	
	have	[hæv]	v.	動（手術）	1	1	初級	
	plastic	[`plæstɪk]	adj.	整型的	1	3	中級	◎
	surgery	[`sɝdʒərɪ]	n.	手術	1	4	中級	◎
	get	[gɛt]	v.	得到/接受（手術）	1	1	初級	◎
	double-fold	[`dʌbl`fold]	adj.	雙眼皮的				
	eyelids	[`aɪ.lɪds]	n.	eyelid（眼皮）複數	4	5	中高	
❿	student	[`stjudnt]	n.	學生	1	1	初級	
	summer	[`sʌmɚ]	n.	夏季	1	1	初級	
	vacation	[ve`keʃən]	n.	假期	1	2	初級	◎
⓫	make	[mek]	v.	使得	1	1	初級	
	dream	[drim]	n.	夢想	1	1	初級	
	come	[kʌm]	v.	變成	1	1	初級	
	true	[tru]	adj.	真實的	1	1	初級	
⓬	there	[ðɛr]	adv.	有…	1	1	初級	
	had	[hæd]	p.p.	have（動〔手術〕）過去分詞	1	1	初級	
	nose	[noz]	n.	鼻子	1	1	初級	
	job	[dʒɑb]	n.	手術作業	1	1	初級	
⓭	done	[dʌn]	p.p.	do（做）過去分詞	1	1	初級	
	couple	[`kʌpl]	n.	幾個	1	2	初級	◎
	hour	[aʊr]	n.	小時	1	1	初級	
⓮	liposuction	[`lɪpo.sʌkʃən]	n.	抽脂				
	most	[most]	adv.	最為	1	1	初級	
	popular	[`pɑpjəlɚ]	adj.	熱門的	1	2	初級	
	form	[fɔrm]	n.	類型	1	2	初級	◎
⓯	good	[gʊd]	adj.	良好的	1	1	初級	◎
	shop	[ʃɑp]	v.	逛、打聽比較	1	1	初級	◎
	around	[ə`raʊnd]	adv.	四處	1	1	初級	
	surgeon	[`sɝdʒən]	n.	外科醫生	2	4	中級	◎
	choosing	[`tʃuzɪŋ]	n.	choose（選擇）動名詞	5	2	初級	◎
	one	[wʌn]	pron.	一人	1	1	初級	
⓰	think	[θɪŋk]	v.	認為	1	1	初級	
	man-made	[`mæn.med]	adj.	人造的	4		中級	
	beauty	[`bjutɪ]	n.	美女	1	1	中級	
	still	[stɪl]	adv.	還是	1	1	初級	◎
	look	[lʊk]	v.	看起來	1	1	初級	
	strange	[strendʒ]	adj.	奇怪的	1	1	初級	

※「紅字單字」於本單元多句出現，「單字級等分析」僅列在「首次出現句」。

MP3 146-02 ❶~❿

❶	你做過整型手術嗎？	Have you ever had plastic surgery? * **Have you ever…?**（你是否曾經…） * **have plastic surgery**（做整型手術） * 此句用「現在完成式問句」（Have…had…?）表示「從過去到現在是否發生過、經歷過某事」。
❷	你會嘗試整型嗎？	Would you give plastic surgery a try? * **Would you＋動詞…?**（你願意…嗎、你想…嗎） * **give＋某事＋a try**（嘗試做某事）
❸	你贊成整型嗎？	Do you agree with plastic surgery? * **agree with**（贊成） * **disagree with**（不贊成） * **oppose to**（反對）
❹	你最想改變哪一個部位？	Which part of your body would you like to change most? * **Which part of your body…?**（哪一個身體部位是…？） * **would like to＋動詞＋most**（最想要做…）
❺	你想豐胸嗎？	Would you like to have breast implants? * **breast implants**（豐胸手術）
❻	你想割雙眼皮嗎？	Would you like to have double-fold eyelids? * **double-fold eyelids**（雙眼皮）
❼	你想隆鼻嗎？	Would you like to have a nose job? * **nose job**（隆鼻手術）
❽	整型會讓你更有自信嗎？	Will plastic surgery make you more confident? * **make＋某人＋形容詞**（讓某人…） * 此句用「未來簡單式問句」（Will…?）表示「詢問對方根據直覺預測未來是否會發生某事」。
❾	你覺得整型有危險嗎？	Do you think there's any danger to plastic surgery? * **Do you think…?**（你認為…嗎） * **there's any danger**（有任何危險）
❿	你擔心整型可能會有後遺症嗎？	Do you worry about the possible side effects of plastic surgery? * **worry about**（擔心、害怕） * **possible**（可能的）可替換為：**potential**（潛在的） * **side effect**（副作用）

	單字	音標	詞性	意義	字頻	大考	英檢	多益
❶	ever	[ˋɛvɚ]	adv.	曾經	1	1	初級	
	had	[hæd]	p.p.	have（動〔手術〕）過去分詞	1	1	初級	
	plastic	[ˋplæstɪk]	adj.	整型的	1	3	中級	◎
	surgery	[ˋsɝdʒərɪ]	n.	手術	1	4	中級	◎
❷	give	[gɪv]	v.	給予	1	1	初級	
	try	[traɪ]	n.	嘗試	1	1	初級	
❸	agree	[əˋgri]	v.	同意	1	1	初級	◎
❹	part	[pɑrt]	n.	部位	1	1	初級	◎
	body	[ˋbɑdɪ]	n.	身體	1	1	初級	
	like	[laɪk]	v.	想要	1	1	初級	
	change	[tʃendʒ]	v.	改變	1	2	初級	◎
	most	[most]	adv.	最為	1	1	初級	
❺	have	[hæv]	v.	動（手術）	1	1	初級	◎
	breast	[brɛst]	n.	胸部	1	3	中級	
	implant	[ɪmˋplænt]	n.	植入	3			
❻	double-fold	[ˋdʌblˋfold]	adj.	雙眼皮的				
	eyelids	[ˋaɪ.lɪds]	n.	eyelid（眼皮）複數	4	5	中高	
❼	nose	[noz]	n.	鼻子	1	1	初級	
	job	[dʒɑb]	n.	手術作業	1	1	初級	
❽	make	[mek]	v.	使得	1	1	初級	
	more	[mor]	adv.	更加	1	1	初級	
	confident	[ˋkɑnfədənt]	adj.	自信地	2	3	初級	◎
❾	think	[θɪŋk]	v.	認為	1	1	初級	
	there	[ðɛr]	adv.	有…	1	1	初級	
	any	[ˋɛnɪ]	adj.	任何的	1	1	初級	
	danger	[ˋdendʒɚ]	n.	危險	1	1	初級	◎
❿	worry	[ˋwɝɪ]	v.	擔心	1	1	初級	◎
	possible	[ˋpɑsənl]	adj.	可能的	1	1	初級	◎
	side	[saɪd]	adj.	附帶的、次要的	1	1	初級	
	effect	[ɪˋfɛkt]	n.	效果	1	2	初級	◎

※「紅字單字」於本單元多句出現，「單字級等分析」僅列在「首次出現句」。

🎵 MP3 146-02 ⑪～⑰

⑪	整型失敗你會怎麼樣？	What would you do if the plastic surgery failed? * **What would you...if...?**（假設…，你會怎麼辦？） * 主詞＋would＋動詞原形＋if＋主詞＋動詞過去式 　（假設…的話，…） * **fail through**（化為泡影） * **screw up**（搞砸）
⑫	家人贊成你整型嗎？	Does your family agree with you having plastic surgery? * **agree with**（贊成、同意） * **disapprove of**（不贊成、不同意） * **have plastic surgery**（做整型手術）
⑬	你不能接受自己既有的樣子嗎？	Can't you accept the way you look right now? * **Can't you...?**（你無法…嗎） * **the way you look**（你的外表） * **right now**（現在、目前） * **accept**（接受）可替換為：**put up with**（忍受、容忍）
⑭	你有朋友動過整型手術嗎？	Do you have any friends who have had plastic surgery? * **have had plastic surgery**（曾經整型） 　＝ **have undergone plastic surgery**
⑮	整型的費用很高嗎？	Is the price of plastic surgery high? ＝ Does plastic surgery cost much? * **the price of**＋名詞（…的價錢） * **cost much**（花費很高） * **low**（價格低的）
⑯	你認識知名的整型醫生嗎？	Do you know any famous plastic surgeons? * **famous**（有名的）＝ **well-known** * **physician**（內科醫生）
⑰	怎樣才能找到合格的整型醫生？	How can you find a qualified plastic surgeon? * **How can you...?**（你要如何…？） * **unqualified**（不合格的） * **qualification**（資格、核准） * **perform a surgery**（施行手術）

	單字	音標	詞性	意義	字頻	大考	英檢	多益
⑪	do	[du]	v.	做	1	1	初級	
	plastic	[ˋplæstɪk]	adj.	整型的	1	3	中級	◎
	surgery	[ˋsɝdʒərɪ]	n.	手術	1	4	中級	◎
	failed	[feld]	p.t.	fail（失敗）過去式	3	2	初級	◎
⑫	family	[ˋfæməlɪ]	n.	家人	1	1	初級	
	agree	[əˋgri]	v.	同意	1	1	初級	◎
	having	[ˋhævɪŋ]	n.	have（動〔手術〕）動名詞	1	1	初級	
⑬	accept	[əkˋsɛpt]	v.	接受	1	2	初級	◎
	way	[we]	n.	方式	1	1	初級	
	look	[lʊk]	v.	看起來	1	1	初級	
	right	[raɪt]	adv.	正值	1	1	初級	
	now	[naʊ]	adv.	現在	1	1	初級	
⑭	have	[hæv]	v.	擁有	1	1	初級	
	any	[ˋɛnɪ]	adj.	任何	1	1	初級	
	friend	[frɛnd]	n.	朋友	1	1	初級	
	had	[hæd]	p.p.	have（動〔手術〕）過去分詞	1	1	初級	
⑮	price	[praɪs]	n.	價格	1	1	初級	◎
	high	[haɪ]	adj.	價錢高的	1	1	初級	
	cost	[kɔst]	v.	花費	1	1	初級	◎
	much	[mʌtʃ]	adv.	許多地	1	1	初級	
⑯	know	[no]	v.	認識	1	1	初級	◎
	famous	[ˋfeməs]	adj.	有名的	1	2	初級	◎
	surgeon	[ˋsɝdʒən]	n.	外科醫生	2	4	中級	◎
⑰	find	[faɪnd]	v.	尋找	1	1	初級	
	qualified	[ˋkwɑləˏfaɪd]	adj.	合格的	3		中級	◎

※「紅字單字」於本單元多句出現，「單字級等分析」僅列在「首次出現句」。

147　八卦···。（1）

❶	很多人愛看八卦新聞。	Many people like to read gossip columns. * like to＋動詞原形（喜歡） * gossip columns（八卦專欄）
❷	很多人愛聊八卦。	Many people like to gossip.
❸	八卦風近幾年非常盛行。	Gossip has grown very popular over the past few years. * have grown very popular（變為盛行） * over the past few years（最近這幾年）
❹	電視新聞也越來越八卦。	There has been more and more gossip on the TV news. * more and more gossip（越來越八卦） * TV news（電視新聞）
❺	蘋果日報是台灣第一份八卦報紙。	The Apple Daily was the first gossip newspaper in Taiwan. * gossip newspapers（八卦報紙） * weekly（週刊）、biweekly（雙週刊、半週刊） * monthly（月刊）、quarterly（季刊） * semiyearly（半年刊）、yearly（年刊、年鑑）
❻	藝人的八卦往往引起熱烈討論。	The gossip on entertainers often gives rise to enthusiastic discussion. * gossip on＋某人（某人的八卦） * give rise to（引起） * enthusiastic discussion（熱烈討論）
❼	同一件八卦，不同媒體有不同的報導。	Different media have different reports on the same gossip. * have a report on＋某事（報導某事）
❽	名人的緋聞也是大家注意的焦點。	The love affairs of celebrities are also focuses of interest. * love affair（緋聞） * focuses of interest（眾所注目的焦點）
❾	狗仔隊最愛偷拍名人隱私。	Paparazzi love to take sneak shots at celebrities' privacy. * love to＋動詞原形（喜愛） * take a sneak shot（偷拍照片） * take a photo（拍照）

單字級等分析

	單字	音標	詞性	意義	字頻	大考	英檢	多益
❶	many	[`mɛnɪ]	adj.	許多的	1	1	初級	
	people	[`pipl]	n.	person（人）複數	1	1	初級	
	like	[laɪk]	v.	喜歡	1	1	初級	
	read	[rid]	v.	閱讀	1	1	初級	
	gossip	[`gɑsəp]	n./v.	八卦/聊八卦、流言蜚語	3	3	中級	◎
	column	[`kɑləm]	n.	專欄	1	3	中級	◎
❸	grown	[gron]	p.p.	grow（發展為）過去分詞	6	1	初級	◎
	very	[`vɛrɪ]	adv.	十分	1	1	初級	
	popular	[`pɑpjələ]	adj.	盛行的	1	2	初級	
	past	[pæst]	adj.	過去的	1	1	初級	
	few	[fju]	adj.	少許的	1	1	初級	◎
	year	[gɪv]	n.	年	1	1	初級	
❹	there	[ðɛr]	adv.	有…	1	1	初級	
	more	[mor]	adj.	更多的	1	1	初級	
	TV	[`ti`vi]	n.	television（電視）縮寫		2	初級	
	news	[njuz]	n.	新聞	1	1	初級	◎
❺	apple	[`æpl]	n.	蘋果	1	1	初級	
	daily	[`delɪ]	n.	日報	1	2	初級	◎
	first	[fɝst]	adj.	第一個	1	1	初級	
	newspaper	[`njuz‚pepɚ]	n.	報紙	1	1	初級	
	Taiwan	[`taɪ`wɑn]	n.	台灣			初級	
❻	entertainer	[‚ɛntɚ`tenɚ]	n.	藝人	4		中級	◎
	often	[`ɔfən]	adv.	常常	1	1	初級	
	give	[gɪv]	v.	給予	1	1	初級	
	rise	[raɪz]	n.	增長	1	1	初級	◎
	enthusiastic	[ɪn‚θjuzɪ`æstɪk]	adj.	熱烈的	2	5	中級	◎
	discussion	[dɪ`skʌʃən]	n.	討論	1	2	初級	◎
❼	different	[`dɪfərənt]	adj.	不同的	1	1	初級	◎
	media	[`midɪə]	n.	medium（媒體）複數	1	3	中高	◎
	have	[hæv]	v.	擁有	1	1	初級	
	report	[rɪ`port]	n.	報導	1	1	初級	◎
	same	[sem]	adj.	相同的	1	1	初級	
❽	love	[lʌv]	n./v.	愛情/喜愛	1	1	初級	
	affair	[ə`fɛr]	n.	緋聞	1	2	初級	◎
	celebrity	[sɪ`lɛbrətɪ]	n.	名人	2	5	中高	◎
	also	[`ɔlso]	adv.	也	1	1	初級	
	focus	[`fokəs]	n.	焦點	1	2	初級	◎
	interest	[`ɪntərɪst]	n.	興趣	1	1	初級	◎
❾	paparazzi	[‚pɑpə`rɑtsɪ]	n.	paparazzo（狗仔隊）複數	6			
	take	[tek]	v.	拍攝	1	1	初級	◎
	sneak	[snik]	adj.	偷偷摸摸的	2	5	中級	
	shot	[ʃɑt]	n.	照片	1	1	初級	◎
	privacy	[`praɪvəsɪ]	n.	隱私	2	4	中級	◎

※「紅字單字」於本單元多句出現，「單字級等分析」僅列在「首次出現句」。

147　八卦…。（2）

⑩	很多八卦新聞都是鬼扯。	Much gossip is simply made up. * **much**＋不可數名詞（很多的…） * **simply**（僅、只）＝ **just** * **be made up**（被捏造出的、虛構出來的）
⑪	醜聞見光讓很多人身敗名裂。	Public scandals cause many people to lose their good standing and reputation. * **public scandal**（公眾的醜聞） * **cause**＋某人＋**to**＋動詞原形（造成某人…） * **lose one's good standing**（喪失地位） * **lose one's good reputation**（名譽掃地）
⑫	由八卦報導的存在，可見今日媒體的自由。	The existence of gossip reports is evidence of the freedom of the modern media. * **the existence of...**（…的存在） * **evidence**（證據）可替換為：**proof**（證明） * **the freedom of the modern media**（現代媒體自由）
⑬	狗仔隊真是唯恐天下不亂。	It is the paparazzi's pleasure to see a chaotic world. * **It is**＋某人's＋**pleasure to...**（…是某人的樂事） * **chaotic world**（天下大亂）
⑭	沒人愛看，就不會有八卦報導出現。	If there were no one who loved to read gossip reports, they would not exist. * **If**＋主詞＋動詞過去式，主詞＋**would**＋動詞原形（假設…的話，…） * **gossip report**（八卦報導）
⑮	無聊時我才看八卦雜誌。	I read gossip magazines when I am bored. * **gossip magazine**（八卦雜誌） * **when I am bored**（我無聊的時候）
⑯	這些八卦報導真是讓人心碎。	These gossip reports are really heartbreaking. * **heartbreaking**（令人傷心的）可替換為： 　**heartrending**（令人心碎的、揪心的）
⑰	八卦報導侵犯了許多人的隱私。	Gossip reports really invade many people's privacy.　* **invade privacy**（侵犯隱私）
⑱	我覺得政府應該約束一下媒體。	I think that the government should restrict the media.　* **think that**＋子句（認為…）

	單字	音標	詞性	意義	字頻	大考	英檢	多益
❿	much	[mʌtʃ]	adj.	許多的	1	1	初級	
	gossip	[ˈgɑsəp]	n.	八卦	3	3	中級	◎
	simply	[ˈsɪmplɪ]	adv.	只、僅	1	2	初級	◎
	made	[med]	p.p.	make（編造）過去分詞	1	1	初級	
	up	[ʌp]	adv.	出現	1	1	初級	
⓫	public	[ˈpʌblɪk]	adj.	眾所皆知的	1	1	初級	
	scandal	[ˈskændl]	n.	醜聞	2	5	中高	
	cause	[kɔz]	v.	造成	1	1	初級	◎
	many	[ˈmɛnɪ]	adj.	許多的	1	1	初級	
	people	[ˈpipl]	n.	person（人）複數	1	1	初級	
	lose	[luz]	v.	失去	1	2	初級	◎
	good	[gʊd]	adj.	良好的	1	1	初級	◎
	standing	[ˈstændɪŋ]	n.	地位	2	1	初級	◎
	reputation	[ˌrɛpjəˈteʃən]	n.	名譽	1	4	中級	◎
⓬	existence	[ɪgˈzɪstəns]	n.	存在	1	3	中級	
	report	[rɪˈport]	n.	報導	1	1	初級	◎
	evidence	[ˈɛvədəns]	n.	證據	1	1	初級	
	freedom	[ˈfridəm]	n.	自由	1	2	初級	
	modern	[ˈmɑdən]	adj.	現代的	1	2	初級	◎
	media	[ˈmidɪə]	n.	medium（媒體）複數	1	3	中高	◎
⓭	paparazzi	[ˌpɑpəˈrɑtsɪ]	n.	paparazzo（狗仔隊）複數	6			
	pleasure	[ˈplɛʒə]	n.	樂事	1	2	初級	◎
	see	[si]	v.	看到	1	1	初級	
	chaotic	[keˈɑtɪk]	adj.	混亂的	3		中高	
	world	[wɝld]	n.	世界	1	1	初級	
⓮	there	[ðɛr]	adv.	有…	1	1	初級	
	one	[wʌn]	pron.	一人	1	1	初級	
	loved	[lʌvd]	p.t.	love（喜愛）過去式	3	1	初級	
	read	[rid]	v.	閱讀	1	1	初級	
	exist	[ɪgˈzɪst]	v.	存在	1	2	初級	◎
⓯	magazine	[ˌmægəˈzin]	n.	雜誌	1	2	初級	
	bored	[bɔrd]	adj.	無聊的	3	3	初級	◎
⓰	really	[ˈrɪəlɪ]	adv.	真是	1		初級	
	heartbreaking	[ˈhɑrtˌbrekɪŋ]	adj.	令人傷心的	5		中級	
⓱	invade	[ɪnˈved]	v.	侵犯	2	4	中級	◎
	privacy	[ˈpraɪvəsɪ]	n.	隱私	2	4	中級	◎
⓲	think	[θɪŋk]	v.	認為	1	1	初級	
	government	[ˈgʌvənmənt]	n.	政府	1	2	初級	◎
	restrict	[rɪˈstrɪkt]	v.	限制、約束	2	3	中級	◎

※「紅字單字」於本單元多句出現，「單字級等分析」僅列在「首次出現句」。

MP3 147-02 ❶～❿

❶	你喜歡看八卦報導嗎？	Do you like to read the gossip news? * **like to＋動詞原形**（喜歡） * **gossip news**（八卦報導）
❷	這一期壹週刊的封面人物是誰？	Who is on the cover of this issue of Next magazine? * **Who is...?**（…的是誰？） * **on the cover**（在封面上） * **this issue**（本期、這一期）= latest issue
❸	你相信八卦雜誌所寫的嗎？	Do you believe the articles in gossip magazines? * **gossip magazine**（八卦雜誌）
❹	最近最熱門的八卦是什麼？	What has been the most popular gossip recently? * **What has been...?**（持續…的是什麼？） * **recently**（最近）= lately
❺	誰是這次緋聞的男主角？	Who is the leading man in this love affair? * **the leading man**（男主角） * **the leading woman**（女主角） * **love affair**（緋聞）
❻	最熱門的八卦主角是誰？	Who is the hottest gossip topic? * **gossip topic**（八卦主題、八卦主角）
❼	為什麼那麼多人愛看八卦新聞？	Why are there so many people who love to read gossip? * **Why are there＋名詞...?**（為什麼會有…？） * **love to＋動詞原形**（喜愛）
❽	最近最勁爆的新聞是什麼？	What is the most explosive sexy news these days? * **explosive sexy news**（勁爆的新聞） * **these days**（這幾天）
❾	難道沒有別的東西可以報導嗎？	Isn't there anything else to report? * **Isn't there...?**（沒有…了嗎） * **anything else**（其他的東西）
❿	你對八卦新聞有什麼想法？	What do you think about gossip columns? * **think about＋名詞**（關於…有什麼想法） * **gossip columns**（八卦專欄）

	單字	音標	詞性	意義	字頻	大考	英檢	多益
❶	like	[laɪk]	v.	喜歡	1	1	初級	
	read	[rid]	v.	閱讀	1	1	初級	
	gossip	[ˈgɑsəp]	n.	八卦	3	3	中級	◎
	news	[njuz]	n.	新聞	1	1	初級	◎
❷	cover	[ˈkʌvə]	n.	封面	1	1	初級	◎
	this	[ðɪs]	adj.	這個	1	1	初級	
	issue	[ˈɪʃʊ]	n.	期數	1	5	中級	◎
	next	[nɛkst]	adj.	下一個	1	1	初級	
	magazine	[ˌmægəˈzin]	n.	雜誌	1	2	初級	
❸	believe	[bɪˈliv]	v.	相信	1	1	初級	◎
	article	[ˈɑrtɪkl̩]	n.	文章	1	2	初級	◎
❹	most	[most]	adv.	最為	1	1	初級	◎
	popular	[ˈpɑpjələ]	adj.	熱門的	1	2	初級	
	recently	[ˈrisntlɪ]	adv.	最近	1		初級	
❺	leading	[ˈlidɪŋ]	adj.	最重要的、主角的	1	1	中級	◎
	man	[mæn]	n.	男人	1	1	初級	
	love	[lʌv]	n./v.	愛情/喜愛	1	1	初級	
	affair	[əˈfɛr]	n.	緋聞	1	2	初級	◎
❻	hottest	[ˈhɑtɪst]	adj.	hot（熱門的）最高級	1	1	初級	
	topic	[ˈtɑpɪk]	n.	主題、主角	1	2	初級	◎
❼	there	[ðɛr]	adv.	有…	1	1	初級	
	so	[so]	adv.	那麼	1	1	初級	
	many	[ˈmɛnɪ]	adj.	許多的	1	1	初級	
	people	[ˈpipl̩]	n.	person（人）複數	1	1	初級	
❽	explosive	[ɪkˈsplosɪv]	adj.	勁爆的	2	4	中級	
	sexy	[ˈsɛksɪ]	adj.	有趣的、吸引人的	2	3	中級	
	these	[ðiz]	adj.	這些	1	1	初級	
	day	[de]	n.	天	1	1	初級	
❾	anything	[ˈɛnɪˌθɪŋ]	pron.	任何事情	1	1	初級	
	else	[ɛls]	adj.	其他的	1	1	初級	
	report	[rɪˈport]	v.	報導	1	1	初級	◎
❿	think	[θɪŋk]	v.	認為	1	1	初級	
	column	[ˈkɑləm]	n.	專欄	1	3	中級	◎

※「紅字單字」於本單元多句出現，「單字級等分析」僅列在「首次出現句」。

147 你覺得八卦…？（2）

⑪	你同情那些被放大檢視的公眾人物嗎？	Do you sympathize with these public figures under scrutiny? * sympathize with＋某人（同情） 　＝ have sympathy with＋某人 * public figure（公眾人物） * under scrutiny（被放大檢視、備受矚目）
⑫	你覺得有人在乎真相嗎？	Do you think there is anyone who cares about the truth? * Do you think...?（你認為…嗎） * there is anyone（有任何人） * care about（在乎、關心）
⑬	你覺得公眾人物應該保有自己的隱私嗎？	Do you think that public figures should have their privacy protected? * have＋名詞＋過去分詞（讓…受到…） * have...protected（讓…受到保護）
⑭	你覺得八卦報導是社會的亂源嗎？	Do you think gossip news is the origin of social chaos? * gossip news（八卦報導） * social chaos（社會亂象）
⑮	你想誰是下一個話題主角？	Who do you think will be the next hot topic? * Who do you think...?（你認為…是誰？） * hot topic（熱門話題、話題主角）
⑯	你對狗仔隊的看法如何？	What is your view on the paparazzi? * view on＋人事物（對某人事物的看法） 　＝ opinion on＋人事物
⑰	你覺得藝人的緋聞值得大肆報導嗎？	Do you think that it's worth it to report so exhaustively on entertainers' love affairs? * be worth it to＋動詞原形（值得…） 　＝ be worth＋動詞ing * report on＋名詞（報導…） * so exhaustively（如此詳盡地） * love affair（緋聞）
⑱	又愛看，又要罵，你這是在幹嘛？	Love to read, love to criticize—what do you think you're doing? * love to＋動詞原形（喜愛）

	單字	音標	詞性	意義	字頻	大考	英檢	多益
⑪	sympathize	[ˈsɪmpəˌθaɪz]	v.	同情	5	5	中級	◎
	these	[ðiz]	adj.	這些	1	1	初級	
	public	[ˈpʌblɪk]	adj.	公眾的	1	1	初級	
	figure	[ˈfɪgjɚ]	n.	人物	1	2	初級	◎
	scrutiny	[ˈskrutnɪ]	n.	放大檢視、備受矚目	2		中高	
⑫	think	[θɪŋk]	v.	認為	1	1	初級	
	there	[ðɛr]	aux.	有…	1	1	初級	
	anyone	[ˈɛnɪˌwʌn]	pron.	任何人	1	2	初級	
	care	[kɛr]	v.	關心	1	1	初級	◎
	truth	[truθ]	n.	真相	1	2	初級	
⑬	have	[hæv]	v.	讓…	1	1	初級	
	privacy	[ˈpraɪvəsɪ]	n.	隱私	2	4	中級	◎
	protected	[prəˈtɛktɪd]	p.p.	protect（保護）過去分詞	3	2	初級	◎
⑭	gossip	[ˈgɑsəp]	n.	八卦	3	3	中級	◎
	news	[njuz]	n.	新聞	1	1	初級	
	origin	[ˈɔrədʒɪn]	n.	起源	1	3	中級	
	social	[ˈsoʃəl]	adj.	社會的	1	2	初級	◎
	chaos	[ˈkeɑs]	n.	亂象	2	6	中高	
⑮	next	[nɛkst]	adj.	下一個	1	1	初級	
	hot	[hɑt]	adj.	熱門的	1	1	初級	
	topic	[ˈtɑpɪk]	n.	主題、主角	1	2	初級	◎
⑯	view	[vju]	n.	看法	1	1	初級	◎
	paparazzi	[ˌpɑpəˈrɑtsɪ]	n.	paparazzo（狗仔隊）複數	6			
⑰	worth	[wɝθ]	adj.	值得的	1	2	初級	◎
	report	[rɪˈport]	v.	報導	1	1	初級	◎
	so	[so]	adv.	如此	1	1	初級	
	exhaustively	[ɪgˈzɔstɪvlɪ]	adv.	詳盡地				
	entertainer	[ˌɛntɚˈtenɚ]	n.	藝人	4		中級	◎
	love	[lʌv]	n./v.	愛情/喜愛	1	1	初級	
	affair	[əˈfɛr]	n.	緋聞	1	2	初級	◎
⑱	read	[rid]	v.	閱讀	1	1	初級	
	criticize	[ˈkrɪtɪˌsaɪz]	v.	批評	1	4	中級	◎
	doing	[ˈduɪŋ]	p.pr.	do（做）現在分詞	1	1	初級	

※「紅字單字」於本單元多句出現，「單字級等分析」僅列在「首次出現句」。

❶	台北的捷運很方便。	The MRT system in Taipei is really convenient. * the MRT system（捷運系統）
❷	上下班時間捷運十分擁擠。	It's very crowded during rush hour. * during（在…期間） * rush hour（尖峰時間） * off-peak hour（離峰時間）
❸	搭捷運上班的人很多。	There are many people who take the MRT to work. * take the MRT（搭乘捷運） * to work（去上班） * to school（去上課）
❹	捷運改變了我們的生活。	The MRT system has changed our lives. * 此句用「現在完成式」（...has changed...）表示「過去某時點發生某事，且結果持續到現在」。 * change one's life（改變生活）
❺	捷運後轉乘公車半價優待。	There's a 50% discount on bus fare if you transfer from the MRT. * 50% discount（半價、打對折） * bus fare（公車票價） * if＋子句（如果…） * transfer from...（從…轉乘）
❻	建造捷運花了很長的時間。	It took a long time to build the MRT. * take a long time（花很長的時間） * build the MRT（興建捷運）
❼	很多人搭捷運後轉乘公車。	Many people transfer to buses after taking the MRT.　* transfer to buses（轉乘公車）
❽	幾乎大家都用悠遊卡搭捷運。	Almost everyone uses EasyCards to take the MRT. * use＋某物＋use＋動詞原形（用某物去做…）
❾	台北捷運偶爾 24 小時營業。	The Taipei MRT system is occasionally open for twenty-four hours. * occasionally（偶爾）＝ once in a while * open for twenty-four hours（全天營業）

	單字	音標	詞性	意義	字頻	大考	英檢	多益
❶	MRT	[ˈɛmˌɑrˈti]	n.	Mass Rapid Transit（捷運）縮寫		2	初級	◎
	system	[ˈsɪstəm]	n.	系統	1	3	初級	◎
	Taipei	[ˈtaɪˈpe]	n.	台北				
	really	[ˈrɪəlɪ]	adv.	很、十分	1		初級	
	convenient	[kənˈvinjənt]	adj.	方便的	2	2	初級	◎
❷	very	[ˈvɛrɪ]	adv.	十分	1	1	初級	
	crowded	[ˈkraʊdɪd]	adj.	擁擠的	2	2	初級	
	rush	[rʌʃ]	adj.	尖峰的	1	2	初級	
	hour	[aʊr]	n.	時間/小時	1	1	初級	
❸	there	[ðɛr]	adv.	有…	1	1	初級	
	many	[ˈmɛnɪ]	adj.	許多的	1	1	初級	
	people	[ˈpipl̩]	n.	person（人）複數	1	1	初級	
	take	[tek]	v.	搭乘	1	1	初級	◎
	work	[wɜk]	v.	工作	1	1	初級	◎
❹	changed	[tʃendʒd]	p.p.	change（改變）過去分詞	4	2	初級	◎
	life	[laɪf]	n.	生活	1	1	初級	
❺	discount	[ˈdɪskaʊnt]	n.	折扣	2	3	中級	◎
	bus	[bʌs]	n.	公車	1	1	初級	
	fare	[fɛr]	n.	車資	2	3	中級	◎
	transfer	[trænsˈfɜ]	v.	轉乘	1	4	中級	◎
❻	took	[tʊk]	p.t.	take（花費）過去式	1	1	初級	◎
	long	[lɔŋ]	adj.	長久的	1	1	初級	
	time	[taɪm]	n.	時間	1	1	初級	◎
	build	[bɪld]	v.	興建	1	1	初級	
❼	taking	[ˈtekɪŋ]	n.	take（搭乘）動名詞	4			
❽	almost	[ˈɔlˌmost]	adv.	幾乎	1	1	初級	
	everyone	[ˈɛvrɪˌwʌn]	adj.	每個人	1		初級	
	use	[juz]	v.	使用	1	1	初級	◎
❾	occasionally	[əˈkeʒənl̩ɪ]	adv.	偶爾	1			
	open	[ˈopən]	adj.	營業的	1	1	初級	
	twenty-four	[ˈtwɛntɪˈfor]	adj.	二十四	1			

※「紅字單字」於本單元多句出現，「單字級等分析」僅列在「首次出現句」。

148　捷運…。（2）

🔘 MP3 148-01 ⑩～⑱

⑩	假日時，可以帶腳踏車搭捷運。	You can take your bike on the MRT during holidays. * take（攜帶）= bring * on the MRT（在捷運上） * during holidays（在假日期間）
⑪	捷運站的標示混亂，讓人搞不清楚。	The signs in the MRT stations are confusing. * MRT station（捷運站） * direction sign（方向標示） * warning sign（警告標示）
⑫	有些捷運車廂禁用手機。	In some cars of the MRT, the use of cell phones is prohibited. * cell phone（手機）= mobile phone * the use of＋某物（某物的使用） * be prohibited（被禁止）
⑬	台北捷運以顏色區分路線。	The Taipei MRT lines are distinguished by color. * be distinguished by＋名詞（藉由…區分） * route map（路線圖） * single route map（單一路線圖） * line identity sign（路線辨識標示）
⑭	捷運有夜間婦女候車區。	The MRT station has a "Night Time Waiting Area" for women. * Night Tine Waiting Area（夜間候車區） * for women（給女性用）
⑮	台北車站是主要的捷運交會站。	Taipei Main Station is the main transfer station. * transfer station（轉乘車站）
⑯	台北捷運票價最低 20 元。	The lowest fare of the MRT is NT$20. * highest（價格最高的，high 的最高級） * fare map（票價圖）
⑰	捷運末班車大概是晚上十二點。	The last train boards at about twelve pm. * the last train（末班車） * board at＋時間（在…時進站搭載乘客）
⑱	捷運首班車大概是早上五點。	The first train boards at about five am. * the first train（首班車）

	單字	音標	詞性	意義	字頻	大考	英檢	多益
⑩	take	[tek]	v.	攜帶	1	1	初級	◎
	bike	[baɪk]	n.	腳踏車	1	1	中級	
	MRT	[ˈɛmˈɑrˈti]	n.	Mass Rapid Transit（捷運）縮寫		2	初級	◎
	holiday	[ˈhɑləˌde]	n.	假日	1	1	初級	
⑪	sign	[saɪn]	n.	標誌	1	2	初級	◎
	station	[ˈsteʃən]	n.	車站	1	1	初級	◎
	confusing	[kənˈfjuzɪŋ]	adj.	令人混淆的	3	3	中高	
⑫	some	[sʌm]	adj.	一些	1	1	初級	
	car	[kɑr]	n.	車廂	1	1	初級	◎
	use	[juz]	n.	使用	1	1	初級	◎
	cell	[sɛl]	adj.	cellular（蜂巢式的）縮寫	1	2	初級	
	phone	[fon]	n.	電話	1	2	初級	◎
	prohibited	[prəˈhɪbɪtɪd]	p.p.	prohibit（禁止）過去分詞	7	6	中級	◎
⑬	Taipei	[ˈtaɪˈpe]	n.	台北				
	line	[laɪn]	n.	路線	1	1	初級	◎
	distinguished	[dɪˈstɪŋgwɪʃt]	p.p.	distinguish（區分）過去分詞	2	4	中級	
	color	[ˈkʌlə]	n.	顏色	1	1	初級	
⑭	have	[hæv]	v.	擁有	1	1	初級	
	night	[naɪt]	n.	夜晚	1	1	初級	
	time	[taɪm]	n.	時間	1	1	初級	◎
	waiting	[ˈwetɪŋ]	n.	wait（等待）動名詞	3	1	初級	◎
	area	[ˈɛrɪə]	n.	區域	1	1	初級	◎
	women	[ˈwɪmɪn]	n.	woman（女人）複數	1	1	初級	
⑮	main	[men]	adj.	主要的	1	2	初級	◎
	transfer	[trænsˈfɝ]	n.	轉乘	1	4	中級	◎
⑯	lowest	[ˈloɪst]	adj.	low（價格低的）最高級	1	1	初級	
	fare	[fɛr]	n.	車資	2	3	中級	◎
⑰	last	[læst]	adj.	最後的	1	1	初級	◎
	train	[tren]	n.	班車	1	1	初級	
	board	[bord]	v.	進站搭載乘客	1	2	初級	◎
	about	[əˈbaʊt]	adv.	大約	1	1	初級	
	twelve	[twɛlv]	n.	十二	2	1	初級	
	pm	[ˈpiˈɛm]	adv.	下午	1	4		
⑱	first	[fɝst]	adj.	首班的	1	1	初級	
	five	[faɪv]	n.	五	1	1	初級	
	am	[ˈeˈɛm]	adv.	早上	1	4	初級	

※「紅字單字」於本單元多句出現，「單字級等分析」僅列在「首次出現句」。

MP3 148-02 ❶～❿

❶	你覺得搭捷運比公車方便嗎？	Do you think the MRT system is more convenient than the bus? * **Do you think＋子句…?**（你覺得…？） * **A is＋比較級＋than B**（A比B更…）
❷	你家附近有捷運站嗎？	Is there an MRT station near your place? * **Is there＋名詞…?**（有沒有…？） * **MRT station**（捷運站） * **near your place**（在你住處附近） * **in your neighborhood**（在你家鄰近地區）
❸	悠遊卡搭捷運有優惠嗎？	Is there a discount for taking the MRT with an EasyCard? * **a discount for＋某事物**（對某事物的折扣） * **take the MRT**（搭乘捷運） * **with an EasyCard**（使用悠遊卡）
❹	晚上搭乘捷運安全嗎？	Is it safe to take the MRT at night? * **Is it safe to＋動詞…?**（…是否安全？） * **at night**（在晚上） * **in the early morning**（在清晨）
❺	捷運首班車是幾點？	What time is the first train of the MRT? * **What time is＋名詞?**（…是幾點？） * **the first train**（首班車） * **the last train**（末班車）
❻	你覺得捷運的票價太貴嗎？	Do you think the MRT fare is too expensive? * **the MRT fare**（捷運票價）
❼	紙鈔能購買捷運車票嗎？	Can I buy an MRT ticket with bills? * **MRT ticket**（捷運車票） * **with bills**（使用鈔票）
❽	搭乘捷運要如何買票？	How do I buy a ticket to take the MRT? * **How do I＋動詞…?**（我要如何做…？）
❾	你覺得台北捷運舒適嗎？	Do you think the Taipei MRT is comfortable?
❿	你覺得捷運改變了台北人的生活嗎？	Do you feel that the MRT system has changed the lifestyles of people living in Taipei? * **Do you feel that＋子句**（你覺得…嗎） * **change the lifestyle**（改變生活方式） * **people living in Taipei**（住在台北的人）

單字級等分析

	單字	音標	詞性	意義	字頻	大考	英檢	多益
❶	think	[θɪŋk]	v.	認為	1	1	初級	
	MRT	[ˈɛmˈɑrˈti]	n.	Mass Rapid Transit（捷運）縮寫		2	初級	◎
	system	[ˈsɪstəm]	n.	系統	1	3	初級	◎
	more	[mor]	adv.	更加	1	1	初級	
	convenient	[kənˈvinjənt]	adj.	方便的	2	2	初級	◎
	bus	[bʌs]	n.	公車	1	1	初級	
❷	there	[ðɛr]	adv.	有…	1	1	初級	
	place	[ples]	n.	住處	1	1	初級	◎
❸	discount	[ˈdɪskaʊnt]	n.	折扣	2	3	中級	◎
	taking	[ˈtekɪŋ]	n.	take（搭乘）動名詞	4			
❹	safe	[sef]	adj.	安全的	1	1	初級	◎
	take	[tek]	v.	搭乘	1	1	初級	◎
	night	[naɪt]	n.	夜晚	1	1	初級	
❺	time	[taɪm]	n.	時間	1	1	初級	◎
	first	[fɝst]	adj.	首班的	1	1	初級	
	train	[tren]	n.	班車	1	1	初級	
❻	fare	[fɛr]	n.	車資	2	3	中級	◎
	too	[tu]	adv.	過於	1	1	初級	
	expensive	[ɪkˈspɛnsɪv]	adj.	昂貴的	1	2	初級	◎
❼	buy	[baɪ]	v.	購買	1	1	初級	
	ticket	[ˈtɪkɪt]	n.	車票	1	1	初級	◎
	bill	[bɪl]	n.	鈔票	1	2	初級	◎
❾	Taipei	[ˈtaɪˈpe]	n.	台北				
	comfortable	[ˈkʌmfətəbl]	adj.	舒服的	1	2	初級	◎
❿	feel	[fil]	v.	覺得	1	1	初級	
	changed	[tʃendʒd]	p.p.	change（改變）過去分詞	4	2	初級	◎
	lifestyle	[ˈlaɪfˌstaɪl]	n.	生活方式	2		中高	◎
	people	[ˈpipl]	n.	person（人）複數	1	1	初級	
	living	[ˈlɪvɪŋ]	p.pr.	live（居住）現在分詞	1	1	中高	

※「紅字單字」於本單元多句出現，「單字級等分析」僅列在「首次出現句」。

MP3 148-02 ⑪〜⑰

⑪	你覺得捷運的路線標示清楚嗎？	Do you think the line sign is clear enough? * line sign（路線標示） * 形容詞＋enough（足夠…） * confusing（令人困惑的）
⑫	你覺得台灣要興建更多捷運嗎？	Would you prefer there to be a more extensive MRT system in Taiwan? * Would you prefer...?（你會希望…嗎） * MRT system（捷運系統）
⑬	悠遊卡的錢不夠了，要怎麼加值呢？	How do I add money to my EasyCard when there's not enough stored on it? * How do I...?（我要如何…？） * add money（加值） * not enough stored（沒有儲值足額） * on（在…上面）
⑭	每一種公車都接受悠遊卡嗎？	Does every bus take EasyCard? * take EasyCard（接受悠遊卡付款）
⑮	目前只有台北市有捷運嗎？	Is Taipei the only city that has an MRT system at the moment? * Is Taipei＋名詞?（台北是…嗎） * the only city（唯一的城市） * have（擁有）可替換為：be equipped with（具備） * at the moment（目前）
⑯	捷運周邊有熱門景點或餐廳嗎？	Are there any hot spots or restaurants around the MRT? * Are there＋名詞複數形...?（有沒有…？） * hot spot（熱門景點） * around＋地點（在某地點附近） * station information map（車站位置圖） * exit information map（出口資訊圖）
⑰	你知道捷運曾發生色狼事件嗎？	Did you know that there was once a "groper incident" in the MRT station? * Did you know that＋子句?（你之前知道…嗎） * there was（以前有，was 是過去式） * groper incident（色狼事件） * assault incident（攻擊事件） * report a crime to the police（報警）

	單字	音標	詞性	意義	字頻	大考	英檢	多益
⑪	think	[θɪŋk]	v.	認為	1	1	初級	
	line	[laɪn]	n.	路線	1	1	初級	◎
	sign	[saɪn]	n.	標示	1	2	初級	◎
	clear	[klɪr]	adj.	清楚的	1	1	初級	◎
	enough	[əˋnʌf]	adv.	足夠地	1	1	初級	◎
⑫	prefer	[prɪˋfɝ]	v.	偏愛	1	2	初級	◎
	there	[ðɛr]	adv.	有…	1	1	初級	
	more	[mor]	adv.	更多的	1	1	初級	
	extensive	[ɪkˋstɛnsɪv]	adj.	廣大的、更多的	2	5	中級	◎
	MRT	[ˋɛmˋɑrˋti]	n.	Mass Rapid Transit（捷運）縮寫	1	2	初級	◎
	system	[ˋsɪstəm]	n.	系統	1	3	初級	◎
	Taiwan	[ˋtaɪˋwɑn]	n.	台灣			初級	
⑬	add	[æd]	v.	加值	1	1	初級	◎
	money	[ˋmʌnɪ]	n.	金錢	1	1	初級	◎
	stored	[stord]	p.p.	store（儲存）過去分詞	5	1	初級	◎
⑭	every	[ˋɛvrɪ]	adj.	每一個	1	1	初級	
	bus	[bʌs]	n.	公車	1	1	初級	
	take	[tek]	v.	搭乘	1	1	初級	◎
⑮	Taipei	[ˋtaɪˋpe]	n.	台北				
	only	[ˋonlɪ]	adj.	唯一的	1	1	初級	
	city	[ˋsɪtɪ]	n.	城市	1	1	初級	◎
	have	[hæv]	v.	擁有	1	1	初級	
	moment	[ˋmomənt]	n.	當前	1	1	初級	
⑯	any	[ˋɛnɪ]	adj.	任何的	1	1	初級	
	hot	[hɑt]	adj.	熱門的	1	1	初級	
	spot	[spɑt]	n.	景點	1	2	初級	◎
	restaurant	[ˋrɛstərənt]	n.	餐廳	1	2	初級	◎
⑰	know	[no]	v.	知道	1	1	初級	◎
	once	[wʌns]	adv.	曾經	1	1	初級	
	groper	[ˋgropɚ]	n.	伸出鹹豬手的色狼				
	incident	[ˋɪnsədnt]	n.	事件	1	4	中級	◎
	station	[ˋsteʃən]	n.	車站	1	1	初級	◎

※「紅字單字」於本單元多句出現，「單字級等分析」僅列在「首次出現句」。

🔵 MP3 149-01 ❶〜⓯

❶	今天天氣真好！	What a wonderful day today!
❷	今天天氣總算放晴了。	It's finally clearing up today. * clear up（放晴）
❸	我喜歡涼爽的天氣。	I like cool weather. * warm（溫暖的）
❹	最近早晚溫差大。	There's been a big difference in temperature between day and night recently. * a big difference in temperature（溫差大） * 此句用「現在完成式」（...has been...）表示「過去持續到現在的事」。
❺	今年夏天特別熱。	It's been particularly hot this summer.
❻	氣象預報經常不準。	The weather forecast is often inaccurate. * weather forecast（氣象預報）
❼	梅雨季節即將開始。	The rainy season is about to begin. * rainy season（梅雨季）、be about to（即將）
❽	昨天的最低溫在淡水。	The coldest temperatures yesterday were in Danshui.
❾	七、八月最常出現颱風。	Typhoons occur most frequently between July and August.
❿	最近常有豪雨特報。	There have been many heavy-rain alerts lately. * heavy-rain alert（豪雨特報）
⓫	聽說這星期都會下雨。	I heard that it's going to rain for the whole week. * I heard that＋子句（我之前聽說…）
⓬	氣象預報說週末有機會下雪。	The weather forecast says that there's a good chance it will snow this weekend. * there's a good chance（很有可能、機率很大）
⓭	今天氣溫高達攝氏 40 度。	The temperature reached forty degrees Celsius today. * reach＋溫度（高達某溫度）
⓮	台灣的氣候十分潮濕。	It's pretty humid here in Taiwan.
⓯	今天沒有風，感覺很悶熱。	It's windless and sultry today.

	單字	音標	詞性	意義	字頻	大考	英檢	多益
❶	wonderful	[ˋwʌndɚfəl]	adj.	極好的	1	2	初級	◎
	day	[de]	n.	一天/白天	1	1	初級	
	today	[təˋde]	adv.	今天	1	1	初級	◎
❷	finally	[ˋfaɪnlɪ]	adv.	總算	1		初級	
	clearing	[ˋklɪrɪŋ]	p.pr.	clear（放晴）現在分詞	3	1	中高	◎
	up	[ʌp]	adv.	起來	1	1	初級	

單字級等分析

❸	like	[laɪk]	v.	喜歡	1	1	初級	
	cool	[kul]	adj.	涼爽的	1	1	初級	
	weather	[ˈwɛðɚ]	n.	天氣	1	1	初級	◎
❹	there	[ðɛr]	adv.	有…	1	1	初級	
	big	[bɪg]	adj.	大的	1	1	初級	
	difference	[ˈdɪfərəns]	n.	差異	1	2	初級	◎
	temperature	[ˈtɛmprətʃɚ]	n.	溫度	1	3	初級	◎
	night	[naɪt]	n.	夜晚	1	1	初級	
	recently	[ˈrisntlɪ]	adv.	最近	1	1	初級	
❺	particularly	[pɚˈtɪkjələlɪ]	adv.	特別	1		中級	◎
	hot	[hɑt]	adj.	熱的	1	1	初級	
	this	[ðɪs]	adj.	這個	1	1	初級	
	summer	[ˈsʌmɚ]	n.	夏天	1	1	初級	
❻	forecast	[ˈforˌkæst]	n.	預報	3	4	中級	◎
	often	[ˈɔfən]	adv.	常常	1	1	初級	
	inaccurate	[ɪnˈækjərɪt]	adj.	不準確的	4	1		
❼	rainy	[ˈrenɪ]	adj.	降雨的	3	1	初級	
	season	[ˈsizn]	n.	季節	1	1	初級	◎
	about	[əˈbaʊt]	adv.	即將	1	1	初級	
	begin	[bɪˈgɪn]	v.	開始	1	1	初級	
❽	coldest	[ˈkoldɪst]	adj.	cold（低溫的）最高級	1	1	初級	
	yesterday	[ˈjɛstɚde]	adv.	昨天	1	1	初級	
	Danshui	[ˈdɑnʃuɪ]	n.	淡水				
❾	typhoon	[taɪˈfun]	n.	颱風		2	初級	
	occur	[əˈkɝ]	v.	出現	1	2	初級	◎
	most	[most]	adv.	最為	1	1	初級	
	frequently	[ˈfrikwentlɪ]	adv.	頻繁地	1			◎
	July	[dʒuˈlaɪ]	n.	七月	1		初級	
	August	[ˈɔgəst]	n.	八月	1	1	初級	
❿	heavy-rain	[ˈhɛvɪˈren]	adj.	豪雨的				
	alert	[əˈlɝt]	n.	特報	2	4	中級	◎
	lately	[ˈletlɪ]	adv.	最近	2	4	中級	
⓫	heard	[hɝd]	p.t.	hear（聽聞）過去式	1	1	初級	
	going	[ˈgoɪŋ]	p.pr.	go（即將）現在分詞	4	1	初級	
	rain	[ren]	v.	下雨	1	1	初級	
	whole	[hol]	adj.	整個的	1	1	初級	◎
	week	[wik]	n.	星期	1	1	初級	
⓬	say	[se]	v.	說	1	1	初級	
	good	[gʊd]	adj.	良好的	1	1	初級	◎
	chance	[tʃæns]	n.	機會	1	1	初級	
	snow	[sno]	v.	下雪	1	1	初級	
	weekend	[ˈwikˈɛnd]	n.	週末	1	1	初級	
⓭	reached	[ritʃt]	p.t.	reach（達到）過去分詞	1	1	初級	◎
	forty	[ˈfɔrtɪ]	n.	四十	2	1	初級	
	degree	[dɪˈgri]	n.	度數	1	2	初級	◎
	Celsius	[ˈsɛlsɪəs]	n.	攝氏		5	中高	
⓮	pretty	[ˈprɪtɪ]	adv.	相當、十分	1	1	初級	◎
	humid	[ˈhjumɪd]	adj.	潮濕的	4	2	初級	
	here	[hɪr]	adv.	這裡	1	1	初級	
	Taiwan	[ˈtaɪˈwɑn]	n.	台灣			初級	
⓯	windless	[ˈwɪndlɪs]	adj.	無風的				
	sultry	[ˈsʌltrɪ]	adj.	悶熱的	6			

※「紅字單字」於本單元多句出現，「單字級等分析」僅列在「首次出現句」。

🔊 MP3 149-02 ❶～⓯

❶	今天天氣如何？	How's the weather today? * How's＋人事物（某人事物狀態如何？）
❷	最近常下雨嗎？	Has it rained often lately?
❸	最近早晚溫差大嗎？	Is there a big difference in temperature between day and night? * between day and night（早晚、日夜之間）
❹	你每天看氣象預報嗎？	Do you watch the weather forecast every day? * weather forecast（氣象預報） * weather report（氣象報告）
❺	有颱風嗎？	Is there a typhoon? * hurricane（颶風）、cyclone（氣旋） * tornado（龍捲風）、windstorm（風暴）
❻	今天的氣象報告怎麼說？	What does the weather report say?
❼	週末的天氣適合去爬山嗎？	Will the weather be good for us to go mountain climbing this weekend? * be good for＋某人＋to＋動詞原形（適合某人做⋯） * go mountain climbing（爬山）
❽	已經進入了梅雨季節了嗎？	Is it already the rainy season? * rainy season（雨季）、dry season（旱季）
❾	有機會下雪嗎？	Is there a possibility that we'll get snow? * there is a possibility（有機會） * get snow（可能下雪）
❿	上海的天氣和台灣一樣嗎？	Is it the same weather in Shanghai as it is here in Taiwan? * Is it the same weather...as...?（⋯的天氣和⋯一樣嗎） * as（如同）
⓫	你習慣台灣的氣候嗎？	Are you used to the weather in Taiwan? * Are you used to＋名詞...?（你習慣⋯嗎）
⓬	天氣什麼時候放晴？	When will it clear up? * clear up（放晴）
⓭	這裡的冬天經常下雪嗎？	Does it snow often here in the wintertime? * summertime（夏季）
⓮	你喜歡夏天還是冬天？	Do you like summer or winter?
⓯	明天的降雨機率是多少？	What's the chance of rain tomorrow? * What's the chance of...?（⋯的機率是多少？）

單字級等分析

	單字	音標	詞性	意義	字頻	大考	英檢	多益
❶	weather	[`wɛðɚ]	n.	天氣	1	1	初級	◎
	today	[tə`de]	adv.	今天	1	1	初級	◎
❷	rained	[rend]	p.p.	rain（下雨）過去分詞	1	1	初級	
	often	[`ɔfən]	adv.	常常	1	1	初級	
	lately	[`letlɪ]	adv.	最近	2	4	中級	
❸	there	[ðɛr]	adv.	有…	1	1	初級	
	big	[bɪg]	adj.	大的	1	1	初級	
	difference	[`dɪfərəns]	n.	差異	1	2	初級	◎
	temperature	[`tɛmprətʃɚ]	n.	溫度	1	3	初級	◎
	day	[de]	n.	白天/一天	1	1	初級	
	night	[naɪt]	n.	夜晚	1	1	初級	
❹	watch	[wɑtʃ]	v.	觀看	1	1	初級	◎
	forecast	[`for.kæst]	n.	預報	3	4	中級	◎
	every	[`ɛvrɪ]	adj.	每一	1	1	初級	
❺	typhoon	[taɪ`fun]	n.	颱風		2	初級	
❻	report	[rɪ`port]	n.	報告	1	1	初級	
	say	[se]	v.	說明	1	1	初級	
❼	good	[gʊd]	adj.	適合的	1	1	初級	◎
	go	[go]	v.	去	1	1	初級	
	mountain	[`maʊntn]	n.	山	1	1	初級	
	climbing	[`klaɪmɪŋ]	n.	climb（攀爬）動名詞	3	1	中級	◎
	this	[ðɪs]	adj.	這個	1	1	初級	
	weekend	[`wik`ɛnd]	n.	週末	1	1	初級	
❽	already	[ɔl`rɛdɪ]	adv.	已經	1	1	初級	◎
	rainy	[`renɪ]	adj.	雨天的	3	2	初級	
	season	[`sizn]	n.	季節	1	1	初級	◎
❾	possibility	[.pɑsə`bɪlətɪ]	n.	機會	1	2	中級	◎
	get	[gɛt]	v.	變為	1	1	初級	◎
	snow	[sno]	n./v.	下雪	1	1	初級	
❿	same	[sem]	adj.	相同的	1	1	初級	
	Shanghai	[`ʃæŋhaɪ]	n.	上海				
	here	[hɪr]	adv.	這裡	1		初級	
	Taiwan	[`taɪ`wɑn]	n.	台灣			初級	
⓫	used	[juzd]	p.p.	use（習慣）過去分詞	1	2	初級	◎
⓬	clear	[klɪr]	v.	放晴	1	1	初級	◎
	up	[ʌp]	adv.	起來	1	1	初級	
⓭	wintertime	[`wɪntɚ.taɪm]	n.	冬季	8			
⓮	like	[laɪk]	v.	喜歡	1	1	初級	
	summer	[`sʌmɚ]	n.	夏天	1	1	初級	
	winter	[`wɪntɚ]	n.	冬天	1	1	初級	
⓯	chance	[tʃæns]	n.	機率	1	1	初級	
	rain	[ren]	n.	降雨	1	1	初級	
	tomorrow	[tə`mɔro]	adv.	明天	1	1	初級	◎

※「紅字單字」於本單元多句出現，「單字級等分析」僅列在「首次出現句」。

❶	我從沒買過樂透。	I've never played the lottery. * have never＋過去分詞（沒有…的經驗） * play the lottery（買樂透、下注樂透彩）
❷	我每星期買樂透。	I play the lottery every week.
❸	買樂透可以自己選號。	You can pick your own lottery numbers. * pick（挑選）＝ choose、select * lottery number（樂透號碼）
❹	也可以由電腦選號。	Or you can choose numbers with a computer. * with＋工具、手段（運用某工具、經由某手段）
❺	樂透彩可以增加政府的收入。	The lottery can increase the government's revenue. * increase one's revenue（增加收入）可替換為： 　raise one's revenue（提升收入）
❻	中了樂透我一定馬上辭職。	I'll quit once I hit the jackpot. * 主詞＋will＋動詞＋once＋現在式子句（一旦…，就…） * hit the jackpot（中頭獎、贏到大獎） * jackpot winner（頭獎得主）、prize（獎金）
❼	我每期都槓龜。	I miss the jackpot every time. * miss the jackpot（沒中大獎、槓龜）
❽	樂透彩造就很多百萬富翁。	The lottery has made many multimillionaires. * make many multimillionaire（造就許多百萬富翁）
❾	一張樂透彩五十元。	The cost of each ticket is fifty NT. * the cost of＋某物（某物的花費）
❿	我中過兩次樂透。	I've won the lottery twice. * have won（曾經贏過）
⓫	如果這次沒人中獎，獎金就累積到下次。	If no one hits the jackpot, then it carries over to next time. * carry over（累積、保留）
⓬	樂透彩是合法的。	The lottery is legal.
⓭	這一期的頭彩獎金已經累計到十億元。	This time the jackpot is up to one billion NT. * up to（上看、累計） * million（百萬）、trillion（兆）
⓮	有人告訴我這組號碼中獎機率高。	Someone told me this combination is sure to win. * someone told me（有人之前告訴我） * be sure to＋動詞原形（必定…）
⓯	這間彩券行曾經開出過頭獎。	Someone hit the jackpot from this vendor before.

	單字	音標	詞性	意義	字頻	大考	英檢	多益
❶	never	[`nɛvə]	adv.	從不	1	1	初級	
	played	[pled]	p.p.	play（下注、簽賭）過去分詞	1	1	初級	
	lottery	[`lɑtərɪ]	n.	樂透	3	5	中高	◎
❷	play	[ple]	v.	下注、簽賭	1	1	初級	
	every	[`ɛvrɪ]	adj.	每一	1	1	初級	
	week	[wik]	n.	禮拜	1	1	初級	
❸	pick	[pɪk]	v.	挑選	1	2	初級	
	own	[on]	adj.	自己的	1	1	初級	◎
	number	[`nʌmbə]	n.	號碼	1	1	初級	
❹	choose	[tʃuz]	v.	選擇	1	2	初級	◎
	computer	[kəm`pjutə]	n.	電腦	1	2	初級	
❺	increase	[ɪn`kris]	v.	增加	1	2	初級	◎
	government	[`gʌvənmənt]	n.	政府	1	2	初級	◎
	revenue	[`rɛvə.nju]	n.	收入	1	6	中高	◎
❻	quit	[kwɪt]	v.	辭職	1	1	初級	◎
	hit	[hɪt]	v.	中獎	1	1	初級	◎
	jackpot	[`dʒæk.pɑt]	n.	頭獎、大獎	7			
❼	miss	[mɪs]	v.	錯過、沒中	1	1	初級	
	time	[taɪm]	n.	次、回	1	1	初級	◎
❽	made	[med]	p.p.	make（造就）過去分詞	1	1	初級	
	many	[`mɛnɪ]	adj.	許多的	1	1	初級	
	multimillionaire	[`mʌltəmɪljə`nɛr]	n.	買萬富翁	7			
❾	cost	[kost]	n.	花費	1	1	初級	◎
	each	[itʃ]	adj.	每一個	1	1	初級	◎
	ticket	[`tɪkɪt]	n.	票券	1	1	初級	◎
	fifty	[`fɪftɪ]	n.	五十	2	1	初級	
❿	won	[wʌn]	p.p.	win（贏得）過去分詞	1	1	初級	◎
	twice	[twaɪs]	adv.	兩次	1	1	初級	◎
⓫	one	[wʌn]	pron. /n.	一人／一	1	1	初級	
	then	[ðɛn]	adv.	那時	1	1	初級	
	carry	[`kærɪ]	v.	累積、保留	1	1	初級	◎
	next	[nɛkst]	adj.	下一個	1	1	初級	
⓬	legal	[`ligl]	adj.	合法的	1	2	初級	◎
⓭	this	[ðɪs]	adj.	這個	1	1	初級	
	up	[ʌp]	adj.	上升至…	1	1	初級	
	billion	[`bɪljən]	n.	十億	1	3	中級	
⓮	someone	[`sʌm.wʌn]	pron.	某個人	1	1	初級	
	told	[told]	p.t.	tell（告訴）過去式	1	1	初級	
	combination	[.kɑmbə`neʃən]	n.	一組號碼	1	4	中級	◎
	sure	[ʃur]	adj.	一定的	1	1	初級	
	win	[wɪn]	v.	中獎	1	1	初級	◎
⓯	vendor	[`vɛndə]	n.	攤商	2	6	初級	◎
	before	[bɪ`for]	adv.	之前	1	1	初級	

※「紅字單字」於本單元多句出現，「單字級等分析」僅列在「首次出現句」。

MP3 150-02 ❶～⓯

❶	哪裡可以買到樂透？	Where can I get a lottery ticket? * get（購買到）= buy、purchase
❷	你買過樂透嗎？	Have you bought any lottery tickets? * Have you＋過去分詞...?（你有…的經驗嗎）
❸	你自己選號嗎？	Do you pick the numbers yourself?
❹	你用電腦選號嗎？	Do you let the computer pick the numbers for you?
❺	你一次買幾張樂透彩券？	How many tickets do you get at a time? * How many＋名詞複數形...?（…數量有多少？） * at a time（一次）
❻	你每星期買樂透嗎？	Do you put money into the lottery every week? * put money into＋某物（把錢花在某物上）
❼	樂透什麼時候開獎？	When are they going to run the lottery? * be going to（預計） * run the lottery（樂透開獎）
❽	樂透的獎金是多少？	How much is the prize of the lottery? * How much is...?（…是多少錢？）
❾	樂透是合法活動嗎？	Is the lottery a legal activity? * legal activity（合法活動）
❿	樂透之外，還有其他的彩券嗎？	Are there any other kinds of raffles besides the lottery? * other kinds of＋名詞（其他種類的…） * besides（除了…以外）
⓫	樂透要如何對獎？	How do I check to see if I've won? * if（是否）= whether
⓬	樂透一張多少錢？	How much is it for one lottery ticket?
⓭	台灣人熱衷樂透嗎？	Are Taiwanese people into the lottery? * into（熱衷、著迷）
⓮	有沒有明牌可以告訴我？	Is there a sign from God that can tell me the winning numbers? * a sign from God（神明的指示） * the winning numbers（會中獎的號碼）
⓯	你中過樂透獎嗎？	Have you ever won the lottery? * win a lottery（中樂透）

	單字	音標	詞性	意義	字頻	大考	英檢	多益
❶	get	[gɛt]	v.	購買	1	1	初級	◎
	lottery	[ˋlɑtərɪ]	n.	樂透	3	5	**中高**	◎
	ticket	[ˋtɪkɪt]	n.	票券	1	1	初級	◎
❷	bought	[bɔt]	p.p.	buy（購買）過去分詞	1	1	初級	
	any	[ˋɛnɪ]	adj.	任何的	1	1	初級	
❸	pick	[pɪk]	v.	挑選	1	2	初級	◎
	number	[ˋnʌmbɚ]	n.	號碼	1	1	初級	
	yourself	[juɚˋsɛlf]	pron.	你自己	1		初級	
❹	let	[lɛt]	v.	讓…	1	1	初級	
	computer	[kəmˋpjutɚ]	n.	電腦	1	2	初級	
❺	many	[ˋmɛnɪ]	adj.	許多的	1	1	初級	
	time	[taɪm]	n.	次、回	1	1	初級	◎
❻	put	[put]	v.	投入	1	1	初級	
	money	[ˋmʌnɪ]	n.	金錢	1	1	初級	
	every	[ˋɛvrɪ]	adj.	每一	1	1	初級	
	week	[wik]	n.	禮拜	1	1	初級	
❼	going	[ˋgoɪŋ]	p.pr.	go（預計）現在分詞	4	1	初級	
	run	[rʌn]	v.	開獎	1	1	初級	◎
❽	much	[mʌtʃ]	adj.	許多的	1	1	初級	
	prize	[praɪz]	n.	獎金	2	2	初級	◎
❾	legal	[ˋligl̩]	adj.	合法的	1	2	初級	◎
	activity	[ækˋtɪvətɪ]	n.	活動	1	3	初級	
❿	there	[ðɛr]	adv.	有…	1	1	初級	
	kind	[kaɪnd]	n.	種類	1	1	初級	◎
	other	[ˋʌðɚ]	n.	其他的	1	1	初級	
	raffle	[ˋræfl̩]	n.	彩券、獎券				
⓫	check	[tʃɛk]	v.	核對	1	1	初級	◎
	see	[si]	v.	明白	1	1	初級	
	won	[wʌn]	p.p.	win（贏得）過去分詞	1	1	初級	◎
⓬	one	[wʌn]	n.	一個	1	1	初級	
⓭	Taiwanese	[ˌtaɪwəˋniz]	adj.	台灣的	4		初級	
	people	[ˋpipl̩]	n.	person（人）複數	1	1	初級	
⓮	sign	[saɪn]	n.	指示	1	2	初級	◎
	god	[gɑd]	n.	神明	2	1	初級	
	tell	[tɛl]	v.	告訴	1	1	初級	
	winning	[ˋwɪnɪŋ]	adj.	中獎的	2	1	**中高**	◎
⓯	ever	[ˋɛvɚ]	adv.	曾經	1	1	初級	

※「紅字單字」於本單元多句出現，「單字級等分析」僅列在「首次出現句」。

MP3 151-01 ❶～❿

❶	我喜歡自助旅行。	I like to travel on my own. * **travel on my own**（自助旅行） 　= **travel independently** * **on one's own**（獨自、自己） * **backpacker**（背包客）
❷	跟團比較方便。	It's more convenient to go with a group. * **it's convenient to**＋動詞原形（方便…） * **go with a group**（跟團）
❸	我通常參加旅行團。	I usually go with travel groups. * **travel group**（旅行團）
❹	我每年出國旅遊一次。	I go abroad for touring every year. * **go abroad for touring**（出國旅行） 　= **travel abroad**
❺	出國旅遊安全最重要。	Safety is the top concern when going abroad. * **top concern**（首要考量） * **go abroad**（出國）
❻	出國前最好先訂好旅館。	You'd better take care of the hotel reservation before leaving the country. * **You'd better**＋動詞原形（你最好要做…） * **take care of**（處理好） * **hotel reservation**（飯店訂房） * **before leaving the country**（在離境之前）
❼	自助旅行未必比較便宜。	Traveling independently does not necessarily cost less. * **do / dese not necessarily**（未必…） * **cost less**（花費較少）
❽	出國前最好先收集一些旅遊資訊。	You'd better gather together some travel information before going abroad. * **gather together**（收集）
❾	很多人利用年節出國旅遊。	Many people go abroad during the New Year's holiday. * **the New Year's holiday**（春節、新年假期）
❿	旅遊品質是一分錢一分貨。	When you travel, you get what you pay for * **you get what you pay for**（一分錢一分貨） * **what you pay for**（你付費的東西）

	單字	音標	詞性	意義	字頻	大考	英檢	多益
❶	like	[laɪk]	v.	喜歡	1	1	初級	
	travel	[ˋtrævl]	v./n.	旅遊	1	2	初級	◎
	own	[on]	adj.	獨自的	1	1	初級	◎
❷	more	[mor]	adv.	更加	1	1	初級	
	convenient	[kənˋvinjənt]	adj.	方便的	2	2	初級	◎
	go	[go]	v.	去	1	1	初級	
	group	[grup]	n.	團體	1	1	初級	
❸	usually	[ˋjuʒʊəlɪ]	adv.	經常	1		初級	◎
❹	abroad	[əˋbrɔd]	adv.	出國地	2	2	初級	◎
	touring	[ˋtʊrɪŋ]	n.	tour（旅遊）動名詞	5	2	初級	◎
	every	[ˋɛvrɪ]	adj.	每一	1	1	初級	
	year	[jɪr]	n.	年	1	1	初級	
❺	safety	[ˋseftɪ]	n.	安全	1	2	初級	◎
	top	[tɑp]	adj.	首要的	1	1	初級	
	concern	[kənˋsɜn]	n.	考量	1	3	初級	◎
	going	[ˋgoɪŋ]	p.pr.	go（去）現在分詞	4	1	初級	
❻	better	[ˋbɛtɚ]	adv.	最好	1	1	初級	
	take	[tek]	v.	採取	1	1	初級	◎
	care	[kɛr]	n.	處理	1	1	初級	◎
	hotel	[hoˋtɛl]	n.	飯店	1	2	初級	◎
	reservation	[ˏrɛzɚˋveʃən]	n.	預約	2	4	中級	◎
	leaving	[ˋlivɪŋ]	n.	leave（離開）動名詞	6	1	初級	◎
	country	[ˋkʌntrɪ]	n.	國家	1	1	初級	
❼	traveling	[ˋtrævlɪŋ]	n.	travel（旅遊）動名詞	4		中級	
	independently	[ˏɪndɪˋpɛndəntlɪ]	adv.	獨自地	3			
	necessarily	[ˋnɛsəsɛrɪlɪ]	adv.	必定	1		中級	◎
	cost	[kɔst]	v.	花費	1	1	初級	◎
	less	[lɛs]	adv.	較少地	1	1	初級	
❽	gather	[ˋgæðɚ]	v.	聚集	1	2	初級	◎
	together	[təˋgæðɚ]	adv.	一起	1	1	初級	
	some	[sʌm]	adj.	一些	1	1	初級	
	information	[ˏɪnfɚˋmeʃən]	n.	資訊	1	4	初級	◎
	going	[ˋgoɪŋ]	n.	go（去）動名詞	4	1	初級	
❾	many	[ˋmɛnɪ]	adj.	許多的	1	1	初級	
	people	[ˋpipl]	n.	person（人）複數	1	1	初級	
	new	[nju]	adj.	新的	1	1	初級	
	holiday	[ˋhɑləˏde]	n.	假期	1	1	初級	
❿	get	[gɛt]	v.	得到、獲得	1	1	初級	◎
	pay	[pe]	v.	付費	1	3	初級	◎

※「紅字單字」於本單元多句出現，「單字級等分析」僅列在「首次出現句」。

🔊 MP3 151-01 ⑪～⑱

⑪	我會上網查旅遊資訊。	I go online to search for travel information. * **go online**（上網） * **search for**（搜尋）
⑫	網路上有時候可以買到廉價機票。	You can sometimes get cheap airline tickets online. * **get an airline ticket**（購買機票） * **book an airline ticket**（訂機票） * **airline ticket**（機票） * **train ticket**（火車票）
⑬	國內旅遊的費用並不便宜。	The cost of domestic tourism isn't cheap at all. * **domestic tourism**（國內旅遊） * **international tourism**（國際旅遊） * **at all**（根本、絲毫）
⑭	旅途中永遠有未知的事發生。	There'll always be surprises along the journey. * **along the journey**（在旅途中） * 此句用「未來簡單式」（...will...）表示 　「根據直覺預測未來發生的事」。
⑮	我喜歡精緻旅遊，不喜歡走馬看花。	I prefer having a nice trip to giving only a passing glance at things. * **prefer A to B**（喜歡A大於B） * **have a nice trip**（精緻旅遊） * **give only a passing glance at things**（走馬看花） * **give a passing glance**（匆匆瞥一眼）
⑯	七、八月是旅遊旺季。	July and August are the peak season for tourism. * **peak season**（旺季） * **low season**（淡季）
⑰	旅遊旺季的團費更高。	The charge during peak season will be higher. * **charge**（花費）= **cost** * **during peak season**（在旺季時）
⑱	最近很風行世界遺跡的主題旅遊。	The world ruins tour has been very popular recently. * **would ruin**（世界遺跡） * **ancient architecture**（古代建築） * 此句用「現在完成式」（...has been...） 　表示「過去持續到現在的事」。

單字級等分析

	單字	音標	詞性	意義	字頻	大考	英檢	多益
⑪	go	[go]	v.	去	1	1	初級	
	online	[ˋɑnˌlaɪn]	adv.	網路地	1		初級	◎
	search for	[sɝtʃ fɔr]	v.	搜尋				◎
	travel	[ˋtrævl]	n.	旅遊	1	2	初級	◎
	information	[ˌɪnfɚˋmeʃən]	n.	資訊	1	4	初級	◎
⑫	sometimes	[ˋsʌmˌtaɪmz]	adv.	有時候	1	1	初級	
	get	[gɛt]	v.	購買	1	1	初級	◎
	cheap	[tʃip]	adj.	便宜的	1	2	初級	◎
	airline	[ˋɛrˌlaɪn]	n.	航線	1	2	初級	
	ticket	[ˋtɪkɪt]	n.	票券	1	1	初級	◎
⑬	cost	[kɔst]	n.	費用	1	1	初級	◎
	domestic	[dəˋmɛstɪk]	adj.	國內的	1	3	中級	◎
	tourism	[ˋtʊrɪzəm]	n.	旅遊	2	3	中級	◎
	all	[ɔl]	n.	完全	1	1	初級	
⑭	there	[ðɛr]	adv.	有…	1	1	初級	
	always	[ˋɔlwez]	adv.	永遠、總會	1	1	初級	
	surprise	[səˋpraɪz]	n.	驚喜、意想不到的事	1	1	初級	◎
	journey	[ˋdʒɝnɪ]	n.	旅途	1	3	中級	◎
⑮	prefer	[ˋprɪfɝ]	v.	偏好	1	1	初級	◎
	having	[ˋhævɪŋ]	n.	have（擁有）動名詞	1	1	初級	
	nice	[naɪs]	adj.	細緻的	1	1	初級	
	trip	[trɪp]	n.	旅遊	1	1	初級	◎
	giving	[ˋgɪvɪŋ]	n.	give（給予）動名詞	6	1	初級	
	only	[ˋonlɪ]	adj.	僅僅	1	1	初級	
	passing	[ˋpæsɪŋ]	adj.	短暫的	2	1	中高	◎
	glance	[glæns]	n.	瞥一眼	1	1	中級	◎
	thing	[θɪŋ]	n.	東西	1	1	初級	
⑯	July	[dʒuˋlaɪ]	n.	七月	1		初級	
	August	[ˋɔgəst]	n.	八月	1	1	初級	
	peak	[pik]	n.	高峰、最高點	1	3	中級	◎
	season	[ˋsizn]	n.	季節	1	1	初級	◎
⑰	charge	[tʃɑrdʒ]	n.	收費	1	2	初級	◎
	higher	[ˋhaɪɚ]	adj.	high（高的）比較級	1	1	初級	
⑱	world	[wɝld]	n.	世界	1	1	初級	
	ruin	[ˋruɪn]	n.	遺產	2	4	初級	
	tour	[tʊr]	n.	旅遊	1	2	初級	◎
	very	[ˋvɛrɪ]	adv.	十分	1	1	初級	
	popular	[ˋpɑpjələ]	adj.	風行的	1	2	初級	
	recently	[ˋrisntlɪ]	adv.	最近	1		初級	

※「紅字單字」於本單元多句出現，「單字級等分析」僅列在「首次出現句」。

🔊 MP3 151-02 ❶～❿

❶	你喜歡旅遊嗎？	Do you like to travel? * **Do you like...?**（你喜歡…嗎）
❷	你去過哪幾個國家？	Which countries have you been to? * **Which countries...?**（哪些國家是…？） * **have been to**（曾經去過、曾經前往）
❸	你最喜歡哪個地方？	What's your top choice? * **What's＋名詞?**（哪個是…？） * **top choice**（首選、最喜歡的地方）
❹	你今年有旅遊計畫嗎？	Have you got any travel plans for this year? * **Have you＋過去分詞...?**（你已經…了嗎） * **get a travel plan**（訂定旅行計畫）
❺	你最想去哪一個國家旅遊？	Which country is your top choice?
❻	你多久安排一趟出國旅遊？	How often do you arrange trips abroad? * **How often do you...?**（你多久一次…呢？） * **arrange a trip**（安排旅遊、規畫旅遊） 　＝ **organize a trip**
❼	這趟旅遊你花了多少錢？	How much did you pay for this trip? * **How much did you...?**（你當時花了多少錢…？） * **pay for＋某事物**（為某事物而花費）
❽	你會避開旅遊旺季嗎？	Do you avoid the peak travel season? * **avoid＋名詞**（避免…） * **peak travel season**（旅遊旺季） * **low travel season**（旅遊淡季）
❾	這次你的旅遊預算是多少？	What's your budget for this trip? * **What's your budget for...?**（對於…的預算是多少？） * **one's budget for＋某事物**（某事物的預算） * **within one's budget**（在預算範圍內） * **exceed one's budget**（超出預算）
❿	你喜歡跟團還是自助旅行？	Do you prefer going with a group or going by yourself? * **prefer A or B**（比較喜歡A還是B） * **go with a group**（跟團前往） * **go by oneself**（獨自前往） * **escorted tour**（跟團旅行） * **package tour**（套裝行程旅行）

	單字	音標	詞性	意義	字頻	大考	英檢	多益
❶	like	[laɪk]	v.	喜歡	1	1	初級	
	travel	[ˈtrævl̩]	v./n.	旅遊	1	2	初級	◎
❷	country	[ˈkʌntrɪ]	n.	國家	1	1	初級	
❸	top	[tɑp]	adj.	首選的、最喜歡的	1	1	初級	◎
	choice	[tʃɔɪs]	n.	選擇	1	2	初級	◎
❹	got	[gɑt]	p.p.	get（訂定）過去分詞	1	1	初級	◎
	any	[ˈɛnɪ]	adj.	任何的	1	1	初級	
	plan	[plæn]	n.	計畫	1	1	初級	◎
	this	[ðɪs]	adj.	這個	1	1	初級	
	year	[jɪr]	n.	年	1	1	初級	
❻	often	[ˈɔfən]	adv.	經常	1	1	初級	
	arrange	[əˈrendʒ]	v.	安排	1	2	初級	◎
	trip	[trɪp]	n.	旅遊	1	1	初級	◎
	abroad	[əˈbrɔd]	adv.	國外地	2	2	初級	◎
❼	much	[mʌtʃ]	adv.	許多地	1	1	初級	
	pay	[pe]	v.	花費	1	3	初級	◎
❽	avoid	[əˈvɔɪd]	v.	避免	1	2	初級	◎
	peak	[pik]	n	高峰、最高點	1	3	中級	◎
	season	[ˈsizn̩]	n	季節	1	1	初級	◎
❾	budget	[ˈbʌdʒɪt]	n	預算	1	3	中級	◎
❿	prefer	[prɪˈfɝ]	v.	偏好	1	2	初級	◎
	going	[ˈgoɪŋ]	n.	go（去）動名詞	4	1	初級	
	group	[grup]	n.	團體	1	1	初級	
	yourself	[juəˈsɛlf]	pron.	你自己	1		初級	

※「紅字單字」於本單元多句出現，「單字級等分析」僅列在「首次出現句」。

🔊 MP3 151-02 ⑪～⑱

⑪	你喜歡國內旅遊還是國外旅遊？	Do you prefer domestic travel or foreign tours? * **Do you prefer A or B?**（你比較喜歡 A 或 B？） * **domestic travel**（國內旅遊） * **foreign tour**（國外旅遊）
⑫	這次旅遊你打算去多久？	For how long do you plan to go this time? * **For how long…?**（…會有多久時間？） * **plan to＋動詞原形**（打算、計畫） * **this time**（這一次）
⑬	國內旅遊會比較便宜嗎？	Will a domestic tour be cheaper? * **Will＋主詞＋動詞?**（…可能嗎） * **more expensive**（較昂貴的）
⑭	自助旅行是不是很危險？	Is it dangerous to travel on one's own? * **Is it＋形容詞＋to＋動詞?**（做某行為是否很…？） * **travel one one's own**（自助旅行） * **on one's own**（獨自，自己） * **safe**（安全的）
⑮	台灣每年很多人出國旅遊嗎？	Do a lot of Taiwanese people travel abroad every year? * **a lot of＋人事物**（很多某人事物） * **travel abroad**（出國旅行） * **every year**（每年）
⑯	你能推薦品質好的旅行社嗎？	Can you recommend any good-quality travel agencies? * **Can you recommend…?**（你能推薦…嗎） * **recommend**（推薦）＝ suggest、advise * **travel agencies**（travel agency〔旅行社〕的複數）
⑰	台灣人為什麼喜歡去日本旅遊？	Why do Taiwanese people like to take trips to Japan? * **like to＋動詞原形**（喜歡） * **take a trip**（旅遊） * **to**（前往、到）
⑱	你覺得旅遊最有趣的事是什麼？	What do you find most interesting about traveling? * **What do you find…?**（你發覺什麼是…？） * **about**（關於）

	單字	音標	詞性	意義	字頻	大考	英檢	多益
⑪	prefer	[prɪˋfɝ]	v.	偏好	1	2	初級	◎
	domestic	[dəˋmɛstɪk]	adj.	國內的	1	3	中級	◎
	travel	[ˋtrævl]	n./v.	旅遊	1	2	初級	◎
	foreign	[ˋfɔrɪn]	adj.	國外的	1	1	初級	◎
	tour	[tʊr]	n.	旅遊	1	2	初級	◎
⑫	long	[lɔŋ]	adv.	長久地	1	1	初級	
	plan	[plæn]	v.	計畫	1	1	初級	◎
	go	[go]	v.	去	1	1	初級	
	this	[ðɪs]	adj.	這個	1	1	初級	
	time	[taɪm]	n.	次、回	1	1	初級	◎
⑬	cheaper	[ˋtʃipɚ]	adj.	cheap（便宜的）比較級	1	2	初級	◎
⑭	dangerous	[ˋdendʒərəs]	adj.	危險的	1	2	初級	
	one	[wʌn]	pron.	一人	1	1	初級	
	own	[on]	adj.	獨自的	1	1	初級	◎
⑮	lot	[lɑt]	n.	許多				
	Taiwanese	[ˌtaɪwəˋniz]	adj.	台灣人的	4		初級	
	people	[ˋpipl]	n.	person（人）複數	1	1	初級	
	abroad	[əˋbrɔd]	adv.	國外地	2	2	初級	◎
	every	[ˋɛvrɪ]	adj.	每一	1	1	初級	
	year	[jɪr]	n.	年	1	1	初級	
⑯	recommend	[ˌrɛkəˋmɛnd]	v.	推薦	1	5	中級	◎
	any	[ˋɛnɪ]	adj.	任何的	1	1	初級	
	good-quality	[ˋgʊdˋkwɑlətɪ]	adj.	優良的				
	agency	[ˋedʒənsɪ]	n.	機構	1	4	中級	◎
⑰	like	[laɪk]	v.	喜歡	1	1	初級	
	take	[tek]	v.	執行、做	1	1	初級	◎
	trip	[trɪp]	n.	旅遊	1	1	初級	◎
	Japan	[dʒəˋpæn]	n.	日本	3		初級	
⑱	find	[faɪnd]	v.	發覺	1	1	初級	
	most	[most]	adv.	最為	1	1	初級	
	interesting	[ˋɪntərɪstɪŋ]	adj.	有趣的	1		中級	
	traveling	[ˋtrævlɪŋ]	n.	travel（旅遊）動名詞	4		中級	

※「紅字單字」於本單元多句出現，「單字級等分析」僅列在「首次出現句」。

MP3 152-01 ❶～❾

❶	我最近睡得很安穩。	Lately I've been sleeping soundly. * **lately**（最近）= **recently** * **sleep soundly**（睡得很熟、睡得很安穩） * 此句用「現在完成進行式」（**...have been sleeping...**）表示「從過去開始、且直到現在仍持續中的事」。
❷	病況算是控制住了。	I have the condition under control for now. * **under control**（在掌控中） * **out of control**（失控） * **one's condition gets better**（病況好轉） * **one's condition gets worse**（病況惡化）
❸	我盡量讓自己的生活變得規律。	I'm trying to keep more regular hours. * **be trying to**＋動詞原形（盡量） * **keep regular hours**（維持規律生活、作息正常）
❹	我還是經常頭痛。	I still get headaches constantly. * **get headaches**（頭痛） * **suffer from headaches**（受頭痛之苦） * **constantly**（時常地、不斷地）= **again and again**
❺	我今天的精神很好。	I'm full of vitality today. * **be full of**（充滿）
❻	肥胖是不健康的前兆。	Obesity is a sign of unhealthiness. * **a sign of unhealthiness**（不健康的徵兆） * **unhealthiness**（不健康）= **poor health** * **thinness**（瘦弱）
❼	年紀大了不能熬夜。	Avoid staying up late once you reach a certain age. * **avoid**＋動詞-ing（避免做…） * **stay up**（熬夜） * **once**＋子句（一旦…） * **reach a certain age**（到了特定的年紀）
❽	每天五種蔬果身體會更健康。	Eating five kinds of fruits and vegetables every day makes you healthy. * **make**＋某人＋形容詞（使某人…）
❾	失眠在台灣已經成為很多人的問題。	Insomnia has become a problem for many people in Taiwan. * **become a problem**（成為問題） * **for many people**（對很多人來說）

單字級等分析

	單字	音標	詞性	意義	字頻	大考	英檢	多益
❶	lately	[ˋletlɪ]	adv.	最近	2	4	中級	
	sleeping	[ˋslipɪŋ]	p.pr.	sleep（睡覺）現在分詞	3	1	初級	
	soundly	[ˋsaʊndlɪ]	adv.	安穩地	6			
❷	have	[hæv]	v.	使得	1	1	初級	
	condition	[kənˋdɪʃən]	n.	病情	1	3	中級	◎
	control	[kənˋtrol]	n.	控制	1	2	初級	◎
	now	[naʊ]	n.	現在	1	1	初級	
❸	trying	[ˋtraɪɪŋ]	p.pr.	try（盡力）現在分詞	1	1	初級	
	keep	[kip]	v.	保持	6	1	初級	◎
	more	[mor]	adv.	更加	1	1	初級	
	regular	[ˋrɛgjələ]	adj.	規律地	1	2	初級	◎
	hour	[aʊr]	n.	時間、小時	1	1	初級	
❹	still	[stɪl]	adv.	仍然	1	1	初級	◎
	get	[gɛt]	v.	患有	1	1	初級	◎
	headache	[ˋhɛd͵ek]	n.	頭痛	2		初級	◎
	constantly	[ˋkɑnstəntlɪ]	adv.	時常地、不斷地	1			
❺	full	[fʊl]	adj.	充滿地	1	1	初級	
	vitality	[vaɪˋtælətɪ]	n.	活力、精神	4	6	中高	◎
	today	[təˋde]	adv.	今天	1	1	初級	
❻	obesity	[oˋbisətɪ]	n.	肥胖	3			
	sign	[saɪn]	n.	前兆	1	2	初級	
	unhealthiness	[ʌnˋhɛlθɪnɪs]	n.	不健康				
❼	avoid	[əˋvɔɪd]	v.	避免	1	2	初級	◎
	staying	[ˋsteɪŋ]	n.	stay（保持）動名詞	1	1	初級	◎
	up	[ʌp]	adv.	醒著地	1	1	初級	
	late	[let]	adv.	晚地	1	1	初級	◎
	reach	[ritʃ]	v.	到達	1	1	初級	◎
	certain	[ˋsɝtən]	adj.	特定的	1	1	初級	◎
	age	[edʒ]	n.	年紀	1	1	初級	◎
❽	eating	[ˋitɪŋ]	n.	eat（吃）動名詞	2	1	初級	
	five	[faɪv]	n.	五	1	1	初級	
	kind	[kaɪnd]	n.	種類	1	1	初級	◎
	fruit	[frut]	n.	水果	1	1	初級	
	vegetable	[ˋvɛdʒətəbl]	n.	蔬菜	1	1	初級	◎
	every	[ˋɛvrɪ]	adj.	每一	1	1	初級	
	day	[de]	n.	天	1	1	初級	
	make	[mek]	v.	使人	1	1	初級	
	healthy	[ˋhɛlθɪ]	adj.	健康的	1	2	初級	◎
❾	insomnia	[ɪnˋsɑmnɪə]	n.	失眠	4			
	become	[bɪˋkʌm]	p.p.	become（成為）過去分詞	1	1	初級	◎
	problem	[ˋprɑbləm]	n.	問題	1	1	初級	◎
	many	[ˋmɛnɪ]	adj.	許多的	1	1	初級	
	people	[ˋpipl]	n.	person（人）複數	1	1	初級	
	Taiwan	[ˋtaɪˋwɑn]	n.	台灣			初級	

※「紅字單字」於本單元多句出現，「單字級等分析」僅列在「首次出現句」。

152 健康…。（2）

⑩	最近經常腰酸背痛。	I've been getting pains in my waist and back for some time. * have been＋動詞-ing（一直持續發生…） * get pains in one's waist and back（腰酸背痛） * for some time（有一段時間）
⑪	各種污染是讓人不健康的主因。	All this pollution is a major cause of unhealthiness. * all this＋名詞（所有的…） * major cause（主要原因） * air pollution（空氣污染）、water pollution（水質污染） * noise pollution（噪音污染）、 　thermal pollution（熱污染）
⑫	人過三十身體差很多。	You can't keep the same shape once you pass thirty. * keep the same shape（維持同樣強健的體魄） * once（一旦）、pass＋年齡（超過某年齡）
⑬	癌症算是現代人的文明病。	Cancer's a disease of modern civilization. * a disease of＋名詞（…的疾病） * modern civilization（現代文明）
⑭	經常運動讓你身體健康。	Regular exercise keeps you healthy. * regular exercise（規律運動） * keep＋某人＋形容詞（使某人保持…）
⑮	健康是人生最大的財富。	Health is the greatest wealth in life.
⑯	老年人要多補充鈣質。	The elderly must replenish their calcium more. * the youth（年輕人） * replenish＋營養（補充某營養） * protein（蛋白質）、vitamin（維生素） * mineral（礦物質）、sodium（鈉） * carbohydrate（碳水化合物）
⑰	女生要多補充鐵質。	Women need to increase their iron intake. * increase an intake（增加攝取） * reduce an intake（減少攝取） * 物質＋intake（攝取某物質）
⑱	身體太累時可以吃一些營養補給品加強。	Get some nutritional supplements when you're tired. * nutritional supplement（營養補給品）

	單字	音標	詞性	意義	字頻	大考	英檢	多益
⑩	getting	[ˋgɛtɪŋ]	p.pr.	get（患有）現在分詞	1	1	初級	◎
	pain	[pen]	n.	痛苦	1	2	初級	◎
	waist	[west]	n.	腰部	2	2	初級	
	back	[bæk]	n.	背部	1	1	初級	
	some	[sʌm]	adj.	一些	1	1	初級	
	time	[taɪm]	n.	時間	1	1	初級	◎
⑪	all	[ɔl]	adj.	所有的	1	1	初級	
	this	[ðɪs]	adj.	這個	1	1	初級	
	pollution	[pəˋluʃən]	n.	汙染	2	4	初級	◎
	major	[ˋmedʒɚ]	adj.	主要的	1	3	初級	◎
	cause	[kɔz]	n.	原因	1	1	初級	◎
	unhealthiness	[ʌnˋhɛlθɪnɪs]	n.	不健康				
⑫	keep	[kip]	v.	保持	1	1	初級	◎
	same	[sem]	adj.	相同的	1	1	初級	
	shape	[ʃep]	n.	身材	1	1	初級	◎
	pass	[pæs]	v.	超過	1	1	初級	◎
	thirty	[ˋθɝtɪ]	n.	三十歲	2	1	初級	
⑬	cancer	[ˋkænsɚ]	n.	癌症	1	2	初級	◎
	disease	[dɪˋziz]	n.	疾病	1	3	中級	◎
	modern	[ˋmadɚn]	adj.	現代的	1	2	初級	◎
	civilization	[ˌsɪvləˋzeʃən]	n.	文明	2	4	中級	◎
⑭	regular	[ˋrɛgjəlɚ]	adj.	規律的	1	2	初級	◎
	exercise	[ˋɛksɚˏsaɪz]	n.	運動	1	2	初級	◎
	healthy	[ˋhɛlθɪ]	adj.	健康的	1	2	初級	◎
⑮	health	[hɛlθ]	n.	健康	1	1	初級	◎
	greatest	[ˋgretɪst]	adj.	great（巨大的）最高級	1			
	wealth	[wɛlθ]	n.	財富	1	3	中級	◎
	life	[laɪf]	n.	人生	1	1	初級	
⑯	elderly	[ˋɛldɚlɪ]	adj.	年長的、老年的	2	3	中級	◎
	replenish	[rɪˋplɛnɪʃ]	v.	補充、補給	5			
	calcium	[ˋkælsɪəm]	n.	鈣質	3	6	中高	
	more	[mor]	adv.	更多	1	1	初級	
⑰	women	[ˋwɪmɪn]	n.	woman（女人）複數	1	1	初級	
	need	[nid]	v.	需要	1	1	初級	◎
	increase	[ɪnˋkris]	v.	增加	1	2	初級	◎
	iron	[ˋaɪɚn]	n.	鐵質	1	1	初級	
	intake	[ˋɪnˏtek]	n.	攝取	3		中高	◎
⑱	get	[gɛt]	v.	吃	1	1	初級	◎
	nutritional	[njuˋtrɪʃənl]	adj.	營養的	3			
	supplement	[ˋsʌpləmənt]	n.	補給品	2	6	中高	◎
	tired	[taɪrd]	adj.	疲累的	1	1	初級	◎

※「紅字單字」於本單元多句出現，「單字級等分析」僅列在「首次出現句」。

MP3 152-02 ❶〜⓫

❶	最近好嗎？	How have you been lately? * How have you been…?（你一直以來的狀態如何？） * lately（最近）＝ recently
❷	最近精神好點了嗎？	Have you been more energetic? * Have you been＋形容詞?（你一直處在…狀態嗎）
❸	病情好點了嗎？	Are you getting any better? * get better（好轉） * get worse（惡化） * 此句用「現在進行式問句」（Are…getting…?） 　表示「詢問對方現階段是否發生某事？」。
❹	你還是經常熬夜嗎？	Do you still stay up late often? * Do you still…?（你目前仍然會…嗎） * stay up（熬夜）
❺	你的生活規律嗎？	Do you keep regular hours? * keep regular hours（維持規律生活、作息正常）
❻	你有經常在做運動嗎？	Do you exercise regularly? * exercise regularly（定期地運動、規律地運動）
❼	你有定期做健康檢查嗎？	Do you get health examinations regularly? * get a health examination（做健康檢查） 　＝ get a physical examination * premarital examination（婚前健檢） * employee medical exam（就職體檢） * personal medical history（個人病史）
❽	有去看醫生嗎？	Have you gone to the doctor? * Have you＋過去分詞…?（你已經…了嗎） * go to the doctor（看醫生）
❾	你去看病醫生怎麼說？	What did the doctor say? * What did＋主詞＋動詞?（當時…的是什麼？）
❿	最近睡得好嗎？	Have you been sleeping well lately? * sleep well（睡得好） * 此句用「現在完成進行式問句」（Have…been sleeping…?）表示「詢問對方某事是否從過去開始、且直到現在仍持續中？」。
⓫	你最近是不是很累？	You've been pretty tired lately, haven't you? * You have been…, haven't you?（你一直…，對吧？） * have been＋形容詞（一直處於…狀態）

	單字	音標	詞性	意義	字頻	大考	英檢	多益
❶	lately	[ˈletlɪ]	adv.	最近	2	4	中級	
❷	more	[mor]	adv.	更加	1	1	初級	
	energetic	[ˌɛnɚˈdʒɛtɪk]	adj.	充滿活力的	3	3	中級	
❸	getting	[ˈgɛtɪŋ]	p.pr.	get（變成）現在分詞	1	1	初級	◎
	any	[ˈɛnɪ]	adv.	絲毫	1	1	初級	
	better	[ˈbɛtɚ]	adj.	well（安好的）比較級	1	1	初級	
❹	still	[stɪl]	adv.	仍然	1	1	初級	◎
	stay	[ste]	v.	保持	1	1	初級	◎
	up	[ʌp]	adv.	醒著地	1	1	初級	
	late	[let]	adv.	晚地	1	1	初級	◎
	often	[ˈɔfən]	adv.	常常	1	1	初級	
❺	keep	[kip]	v.	保持	1	1	初級	◎
	regular	[ˈrɛgjələ]	adj.	定期的、規律的	1	2	初級	◎
	hour	[aʊr]	n.	時間、小時	1	1	初級	◎
❻	exercise	[ˈɛksɚˌsaɪz]	v.	運動	1	2	初級	◎
	regularly	[ˈrɛgjələlɪ]	adv.	定期地、規律地	2			
❼	get	[gɛt]	v.	接受做	1	1	初級	◎
	health	[hɛlθ]	n.	健康	1	1	初級	
	examination	[ɪɡˌzæməˈneʃən]	n.	檢查	2	1	中級	
❽	gone	[gɔn]	p.p.	go（去）過去分詞	1	1	初級	
	doctor	[ˈdɑktɚ]	n.	醫生	1	1	初級	◎
❾	say	[se]	v.	說	1	1	初級	
❿	sleeping	[ˈslipɪŋ]	p.pr.	sleep（睡眠）現在分詞	3	1	初級	
	well	[wɛl]	adv.	良好地	1	1	初級	◎
⓫	pretty	[ˈprɪtɪ]	adv.	相當、很	1	1	初級	◎
	tired	[taɪrd]	adj.	疲累的	1	1	初級	◎

※「紅字單字」於本單元多句出現，「單字級等分析」僅列在「首次出現句」。

152 你覺得健康…？（2）

⑫	身體好點了嗎？	You feel better now? * feel better（感覺比較好）
⑬	你有覺得哪裡不舒服嗎？	Is there anywhere on your body that feels uncomfortable? * Is there anywhere...?（有沒有哪裡…？） * on your body（在你身上） * feel uncomfortable（覺得不舒服）
⑭	要不要我陪你去看醫生？	Do you want me to go to the doctor with you? * want＋某人＋動詞原形?（想要某人做…） * go to the doctor（看醫生） * with you（和你一起）
⑮	你要不要休息一下？	Do you want to take a little rest? * Do you want to＋動詞原形...?（你想要…嗎） * take a rest（休息） * little（稍微、少許）可替換為：short（短暫的）
⑯	你以前身體會有這種感覺嗎？	Have you felt like this before? * Have you＋過去分詞...?（你有…經驗嗎） * like this（像這樣子）
⑰	現代人罹患癌症的人愈來愈多？	Are there more and more people getting cancer in modern times? * Are there＋名詞...?（是否有…？） * more and more（越來越多） * get cancer（罹患癌症） * in modern times（在現代） * a disease of modern civilization（現代文明病） * diabetes（糖尿病）、heart disease（心臟病） * stroke（中風）、osteoporosis（骨質疏鬆症）
⑱	你有吃營養補給品嗎？	Are you taking any nutritional supplements? * take nutritional supplements（服用營養補給品） * take medicines（服用藥物） * 此句用「現在進行式問句」（Are...taking...?）表示「詢問對方現階段是否發生某事？」。
⑲	最困擾你的疾病是什麼？	Which of your illnesses bothers you the most? * Which of＋名詞複數形...?（多個…中，哪個是…?） * bother the most（最困擾）

	單字	音標	詞性	意義	字頻	大考	英檢	多益
⑫	feel	[fil]	v.	感覺	1	1	初級	
	better	[ˈbɛtɚ]	adj.	well（安好的）比較級	1	1	初級	
	now	[naʊ]	adv.	現在	1	1	初級	
⑬	there	[ðɛr]	adv.	有…	1	1	初級	
	anywhere	[ˈɛnɪ.hwɛr]	pron.	任何地方	1	2	初級	
	body	[ˈbɑdɪ]	n.	身體	1	1	初級	
	uncomfortable	[ʌnˈkʌmfɚtəbl̩]	adj.	不舒服的	2		中高	
⑭	want	[wɑnt]	v.	想要	1	1	初級	◎
	go	[go]	v.	去	1	1	初級	
	doctor	[ˈdɑktɚ]	n.	醫生	1	1	初級	◎
⑮	take	[tek]	v.	採取	1	1	初級	◎
	little	[ˈlɪtl̩]	adj.	稍微、少許的	1	1	初級	
	rest	[rɛst]	n.	休息	1	1	初級	
⑯	felt	[fɛlt]	p.p.	feel（感覺）過去分詞	6	1	初級	
	this	[ðɪs]	pron.	這個	1	1	初級	
	before	[bɪˈfor]	adv.	以前	1	1	初級	
⑰	more	[mor]	adj.	更多的	1	1	初級	
	people	[ˈpipl̩]	n.	person（人）複數	1	1	初級	
	getting	[ˈgɛtɪŋ]	p.pr.	get（罹患）現在分詞	1	1	初級	◎
	cancer	[ˈkænsɚ]	n.	癌症	1	2	初級	◎
	modern	[ˈmɑdɚn]	adj.	現代的	1	2	初級	◎
	time	[taɪm]	n.	時代	1	1	初級	◎
⑱	taking	[ˈtekɪŋ]	p.pr.	take（吃、服用）現在分詞	4			
	any	[ˈɛnɪ]	adj.	任何的	1	1	初級	
	nutritional	[njuˈtrɪʃənl̩]	adj.	營養的	3			
	supplement	[ˈsʌpləmənt]	n.	補給品	2	6	中高	◎
⑲	illness	[ˈɪlnɪs]	n.	疾病	1		中級	
	bother	[ˈbɑðɚ]	v.	困擾	1	2	初級	◎
	most	[most]	adv.	最為	1	1	初級	

※「紅字單字」於本單元多句出現，「單字級等分析」僅列在「首次出現句」。

153 政治…。（1）

🔊 MP3 153-01 ❶～❿

❶	我無黨無派。	I have no political affiliation. * **have no political affiliation**（沒有政治黨派） 　＝ **be not affiliated to political parties**
❷	我沒有加入任何政黨。	I haven't joined any political party. * **haven't joined**（尚未加入） * **political party**（政黨） * **establish a political party**（建立政黨） * **leave a political party**（退出政黨）
❸	許多人熱衷政治。	Many people are passionate about politics. * **be passionate about**＋人事物（熱衷於） 　＝ **be enthusiastic about**＋人事物
❹	現在的年輕人越來越不關心政治。	Young people nowadays show more and more indifference to politics. * **show indifference to**＋人事物（毫不關心某人事物） 　＝ **show no concern about**＋人事物 * **more and more**＋名詞（越來越…） * **indifference**（不關心、不感興趣）＝ **apathy**
❺	有些人對政治漠不關心。	Some people are apathetic about politics. * **be apathetic about**（毫不關心）可替換為： 　＝ **be casual about**（漫不經心）
❻	許多政治人物令人失望。	Many politicians disappoint people. * **disappoint**＋某人（使某人失望） 　＝ **let**＋某人＋**down**
❼	每一個政黨都有各自的支持者。	Each party has its own supporters. * **have its own supporters**（有自己的支持者）
❽	我支持執政黨。	I support the ruling party. * **I support the opposition party.**（我支持在野黨）
❾	政治和黑金常常扯上關係。	Politics is often linked to corruption. * **be linked to**（與…有關） 　＝ **be related to**、**have relation to**
❿	政局會影響經濟。	The political situation will affect the economy. * **political situation**（政治局面、政治形勢） * **affect**＋人事物（影響某人事物） 　＝ **have influence on**＋人事物

	單字	音標	詞性	意義	字頻	大考	英檢	多益
❶	have	[hæv]	v.	擁有	1	1	初級	
	political	[pəˋlɪtɪk!]	adj.	政治的	1	3	中級	
	affiliation	[ə.fɪlɪˋeʃən]	n.	隸屬關係	3			◎
❷	joined	[dʒɔɪnd]	p.p.	join（加入）過去分詞	1	1	初級	◎
	any	[ˋɛnɪ]	adj.	任何的	1	1	初級	
	party	[ˋpɑrtɪ]	n.	政黨	1	1	初級	
❸	many	[ˋmɛnɪ]	adj.	許多的	1	1	初級	
	people	[ˋpip!]	n.	person（人）複數	1	1	初級	
	passionate	[ˋpæʃənɪt]	adj.	熱衷的	2	5	中高	◎
	politics	[ˋpɑlətɪks]	n.	政治	1	3	中級	
❹	young	[jʌŋ]	adj.	年輕的	1	1	初級	
	nowadays	[ˋnauə.dez]	adv.	現代	3	4	中級	
	show	[ʃo]	v.	展現	1	1	初級	◎
	more	[mor]	adj.	更多的	1	1	初級	
	indifference	[ɪnˋdɪfərəns]	n.	不關心、不感興趣	3	5	中高	
❺	some	[sʌm]	adj.	一些	1	1	初級	
	apathetic	[.æpəˋθɛtɪk]	adj.	毫不關心的	8			
❻	politician	[.pɑləˋtɪʃən]	n.	政治人物	1	3	中級	
	disappoint	[.dɪsəˋpɔɪnt]	v.	使失望	3	3	中級	◎
❼	each	[itʃ]	adj.	每一	1	1	初級	
	own	[on]	adj.	自己的	1	1	初級	
	supporter	[səˋportɚ]	n.	支持者	1		中級	
❽	support	[səˋport]	v.	支持	1	2	初級	◎
	ruling	[ˋrulɪŋ]	adj.	執政的	2	1	中高	
❾	often	[ˋɔfən]	adv.	常常	1	1	初級	
	linked	[lɪŋkt]	p.p.	link（有關聯）過去分詞	5	2	初級	◎
	corruption	[kəˋrʌpʃən]	n.	貪汙、賄賂	2	6	中高	◎
❿	situation	[.sɪtʃʊˋeʃən]	n.	局面、形勢	1	3	中級	◎
	affect	[əˋfɛkt]	v.	影響	1	3	初級	◎
	economy	[ɪˋkɑnəmɪ]	n.	經濟	1	4	中級	◎

※「紅字單字」於本單元多句出現，「單字級等分析」僅列在「首次出現句」。

🔊 MP3 153-01 ⑪～⑱

⑪	台灣每四年舉行一次總統大選。	A presidential election is held in Taiwan once every four years. * presidential election（總統選舉） * 事件＋be held（舉行某事件） * once every＋時間（每隔某時間一次） * presidential candidate（總統候選人）
⑫	綠、藍、橘是台灣三大政黨的代表顏色。	Green, blue and orange are the representative colors of three major political parties in Taiwan. * representative color（代表顏色） * political party（政黨）
⑬	投票是公民權利。	Voting is a civic right. * civic right（公民的權利）、association（結社） * assembly（集會）、parade（遊行）
⑭	在野黨和執政黨總是對立。	The opposition party is always against the ruling party. * opposition party（在野黨）、ruling party（執政黨） * against（敵對的）
⑮	許多政治人物愛作秀。	Many politicians love to show off. * love to＋動詞原形（喜愛） * show off（賣弄、作秀）
⑯	真正替人民做事的政治人物實在不多。	There are not many politicians who really serve the people. * serve the people（為人民服務） 　＝ work for the people
⑰	賄選是違法的。	Vote-buying is illegal. * bribery（行賄、受賄）、break the law（違法）
⑱	解決兩岸問題需要很高的政治智慧。	Solving the cross-straits problem will take great political wisdom. * solve a problem（解決問題）、take＋名詞（需要…） * political wisdom（政治手腕、政治智慧）

	單字	音標	詞性	意義	字頻	大考	英檢	多益
⓫	presidential	[ˋprɛzədɛnʃəl]	adj.	總統的	1	6	中級	
	election	[ɪˋlɛkʃən]	n.	選舉	1	3	初級	◎
	held	[hɛld]	p.p.	hold（舉辦）過去分詞	1	1	初級	
	Taiwan	[ˋtaɪˋwɑn]	n.	台灣			初級	
	once	[wʌns]	adv.	一次	1	1	初級	
	every	[ˋɛvrɪ]	adj.	每一	1	1	初級	
	four	[for]	n.	四	1	1	初級	
	year	[jɪr]	n.	年	1	1	初級	
⓬	green	[grin]	n.	綠色	1	1	初級	
	blue	[blu]	n.	藍色	1	1	初級	
	orange	[ˋɔrɪndʒ]	n.	橘色	2	1	初級	
	representative	[rɛprɪˋzɛntətɪv]	adj.	代表性的	1	3	中級	◎
	color	[ˋkʌlɚ]	n.	顏色	1	1	初級	
	three	[θri]	n.	三	1	1	初級	
	major	[ˋmedʒɚ]	adj.	主要的	1	3	初級	◎
	political	[pəˋlɪtɪkl]	adj.	政治的	1	3	中級	
	party	[ˋpɑrtɪ]	n.	政黨	1	1	初級	◎
⓭	voting	[ˋvotɪŋ]	n.	vote（投票）動名詞	2	2	初級	◎
	civic	[ˋsɪvɪk]	adj.	公民的	2	5	中高	
	right	[raɪt]	n.	權力	1	1	初級	
⓮	opposition	[ˌɑpəˋzɪʃən]	n.	反對	1	6	中級	◎
	always	[ˋɔlwez]	adv.	總是	1	1	初級	
	ruling	[ˋrulɪŋ]	adj.	執政的	2	1	中高	◎
⓯	many	[ˋmɛnɪ]	adj.	許多的	1	1	初級	
	politician	[ˌpɑləˋtɪʃən]	n.	政治人物	1	3	中級	
	love	[lʌv]	v.	喜愛	1	1	初級	
	show	[ʃo]	v.	賣弄、作秀	1	1	初級	◎
	off	[ɔf]	adv.	秀出	1	1	初級	
⓰	there	[ðɛr]	adv.	有…	1	1	初級	
	really	[ˋrɪəlɪ]	adv.	真的	1		初級	
	serve	[sɝv]	v.	服務	1	1	初級	◎
	people	[ˋpipl]	n.	person（人民）複數	1	1	初級	
⓱	vote-buying	[ˋvotˋbaɪɪŋ]	n.	賄選、買票				
	illegal	[ɪˋligl]	adj.	非法的	1		中級	◎
⓲	solving	[ˋsɑlvɪŋ]	n.	solve（解決）動名詞	4	2	初級	◎
	cross-straits	[ˋkrɔsˋstrets]	adj.	海峽兩岸的				
	problem	[ˋprɑbləm]	n.	問題	1	1	初級	◎
	take	[tek]	v.	需要	1	1	初級	◎
	great	[gret]	adj.	很大的	1	1	初級	◎
	wisdom	[ˋwɪzdəm]	n.	手腕、智慧	2	3	中級	◎

※「紅字單字」於本單元多句出現，「單字級等分析」僅列在「首次出現句」。

🔊 MP3 153-02 ❶～❿

❶	你熱衷政治嗎？	Are you passionate about politics? * be passionate about＋人事物（熱衷於） * passionate（熱衷的）可替換為： 　apathetic（不關心的）
❷	你支持哪一個政黨？	Which political party do you support? * Which＋名詞...?（…的是哪一個…？） * political party（政黨）
❸	你支持執政黨還是在野黨？	Do you support the ruling party or the opposition party? * ruling party（執政黨） * opposition party（在野黨）
❹	你對政治完全沒興趣嗎？	Are you not interested in politics at all? * be interested in（有興趣）＝ have interest in * interested（有興趣的）可替換為： 　indifferent（不感興趣的） * at all（根本、完全）
❺	每次選舉你都前往投票嗎？	Do you vote in every election? * every election（每次的選舉） * presidential election（總統選舉） * municipal election（市長選舉）
❻	你今年有投票嗎？	Did you vote this year? * Did you...?（你之前有做…嗎）
❼	你曾被賄選嗎？	Have you ever sold your vote? * Have you ever...?（你是否曾經…？） * sell one's vote（被賄選、出售選票）
❽	你贊成統一還是獨立？	Do you support either unification or independence? * either A or B（A或B）
❾	你相信政治人物的話嗎？	Do you believe what politicians say? * Do you believe...?（你相信…嗎） * what＋某人＋say（某人說的話）
❿	你覺得民意代表真的為民喉舌嗎？	Do you think that the public representatives really speak for the people? * Do you think that＋子句...?（你認為…嗎） * public representative（民意代表） * speak for the people（為民喉舌）

	單字	音標	詞性	意義	字頻	大考	英檢	多益
❶	passionate	[ˈpæʃənɪt]	adj.	熱衷的	2	5	中高	◎
	politics	[ˈpɑlətɪks]	n.	政治	1	3	中級	
❷	political	[pəˈlɪtɪkl]	adj.	政治的	1	3	中級	
	party	[ˈpɑrtɪ]	n.	政黨	1	1	初級	◎
	support	[səˈport]	v.	支持	1	2	初級	◎
❸	ruling	[ˈrulɪŋ]	adj.	執政的	2	1	中高	◎
	opposition	[ˌɑpəˈzɪʃən]	n.	反對	1	6	中級	
❹	interested	[ˈɪntərɪstɪd]	adj.	有興趣的	1	1	初級	
	all	[ɔl]	n.	完全	1	1	初級	
❺	vote	[vot]	v./n.	投票/選票	1	2	初級	◎
	every	[ˈɛvrɪ]	adj.	每一	1	1	初級	
	election	[ɪˈlɛkʃən]	n.	選舉	1	3	初級	◎
❻	this	[ðɪs]	adj.	這個	1	1	初級	
	year	[jɪr]	n.	年	1	1	初級	
❼	ever	[ˈɛvɚ]	adv.	曾經	1	1	初級	
	sold	[sold]	p.p.	sell（出售）過去分詞	1	1	初級	
❽	unification	[ˌjunəfəˈkeʃən]	n.	統一	4		中高	
	independence	[ˌɪndɪˈpɛndəns]	n.	獨立	1	2	中級	◎
❾	believe	[bɪˈliv]	v.	相信	1	1	初級	◎
	politician	[ˌpɑləˈtɪʃən]	n.	政治人物	1	3	中級	
	say	[se]	v.	說	1	1	初級	
❿	think	[θɪŋk]	v.	認為	1	1	初級	
	public	[ˈpʌblɪk]	adj.	公眾的、民意的	1	1	初級	
	representative	[rɛprɪˈzɛntətɪv]	n.	代表	1	3	中級	◎
	really	[ˈrɪəlɪ]	adv.	真的	1		初級	
	speak	[spik]	v.	代言	1	1	初級	
	people	[ˈpipl]	n.	person（人民）複數	1	1	初級	

※「紅字單字」於本單元多句出現，「單字級等分析」僅列在「首次出現句」。

153 你覺得政治…？（2）

⑪	你最欣賞的政治人物是誰？	Who is your favorite politician? * Who is＋名詞?（…是誰？）
⑫	你贊成兩岸三通嗎？	Do you agree to the "three direct links" between Taiwan and China? * agree to（同意、贊成） * disagree to（不同意、不贊成） * three direct links（三通） * between Taiwan and China（兩岸、台灣和中國）
⑬	你關心立法問題嗎？	Are you concerned about legislative issues? * be concerned about（關心） 　= show concerns about＋人事物 * legislative issue（立法問題）
⑭	你常看 call-in 節目嗎？	Do you often watch those call-in shows? * watch a show（觀看電視節目） * call-in show（叩應節目） * show（電視節目）= program
⑮	你曾在 call-in 節目發表意見嗎？	Have you ever voiced your opinion on a call-in show? * Have you ever...?（你是否曾經…？） * voice one's opinion（發表意見） 　= express one's opinion
⑯	你曾參與示威遊行嗎？	Have you participated in a protest march? * participate in（參加）= take part in * protest march（示威遊行）= demonstration * hold a protest march（舉行示威遊行）
⑰	你們國家是由人民直選總統嗎？	Is your president elected directly by your people? * 某人＋be elected directly（被直選出來） * direct democracy（直接民主制） * representative democracy（代議民主制） * by（經由）
⑱	你有興趣從政嗎？	Do you have any interest in politics? * have interest in（有興趣）= be interested in * stand as a candidate（擔任候選人） * run for（參加競選）

單字級等分析

	單字	音標	詞性	意義	字頻	大考	英檢	多益
⑪	favorite	[ˈfevərɪt]	adj.	最喜歡的	1	2	初級	◎
	politician	[ˌpɑləˈtɪʃən]	n.	政治人物	1	3	中級	
⑫	agree	[əˈgri]	v.	同意	1	1	初級	◎
	three	[θri]	n.	三	1	1	初級	
	direct	[dəˈrɛkt]	adj.	直接的	1	1	初級	◎
	link	[lɪŋk]	n.	連結	1	2	初級	
	Taiwan	[ˈtaɪˈwɑn]	n.	台灣			初級	
	China	[ˈtʃaɪnə]	n.	中國	4	3	初級	
⑬	concerned	[kənˈsɝnd]	p.p.	concern（關心）過去分詞	1	3	中高	◎
	legislative	[ˈlɛdʒɪsˌletɪv]	adj.	立法的	2	6	中高	
	issue	[ˈɪʃʊ]	n.	問題	1	5	中級	◎
⑭	often	[ˈɔfən]	adv.	常常	1	1	初級	
	watch	[wɑtʃ]	v.	觀看	1	1	初級	◎
	those	[ðoz]	adj.	這些	1	1	初級	
	call-in	[ˈkɔlˈɪn]	adj.	叩應的	7			
	show	[ʃo]	n.	節目	1	1	初級	◎
⑮	ever	[ˈɛvɚ]	adv.	曾經	1	1	初級	
	voiced	[vɔɪst]	p.p.	voice（發表）過去分詞	1	1	初級	◎
	opinion	[əˈpɪnjən]	n.	意見	1	2	初級	◎
⑯	participated	[pɑrˈtɪsəˌpetɪd]	p.p.	participate（參與）過去分詞	1	3	中級	◎
	protest	[ˈprotɛst]	n.	抗議	2	4	中級	◎
	march	[mɑrtʃ]	n.	遊行	2	3	初級	
⑰	president	[ˈprɛzədənt]	n.	總統	1	2	初級	◎
	elected	[ɪˈlɛktɪd]	p.p.	elect（選出）過去分詞	2	2	初級	◎
	directly	[dəˈrɛktlɪ]	adv.	直接地	1		中高	◎
	people	[ˈpipl]	n.	person（人民）複數	1	1	初級	
⑱	have	[hæv]	v.	擁有	1	1	初級	
	any	[ˈɛnɪ]	adj.	任何的	1	1	初級	
	interest	[ˈɪntərɪst]	n.	興趣	1	1	初級	◎
	politics	[ˈpɑlətɪks]	n.	政治	1	3	中級	

※「紅字單字」於本單元多句出現，「單字級等分析」僅列在「首次出現句」。

🔊 MP3 154-01 ❶～❽

❶	今天我接到一通詐騙電話。	I received a fraudulent phone call today. * receive a phone call（接到電話） * fraudulent phone call（詐騙電話） * phone scam gang（電話詐騙集團）
❷	治安越來越差了。	Public security is getting worse and worse. * public security（治安） * be getting＋比較級（變得越來越…） * worse and worse（越來越糟糕） * 此句用「現在進行式」（...is getting...） 　表示「現階段逐漸變化的事」。
❸	詐騙案件越來越多。	Fraud is becoming more and more frequent. * fraud（詐騙）＝ swindling * more and more（越來越…） * frequent（頻繁、常見）＝ common
❹	應召場所到處充斥。	Prostitution is everywhere. * sex offense（妨害風化罪）
❺	超商在晚上經常被搶。	Convenience stores usually get robbed at night. * convenience store（便利商店） * get robbed（被搶劫） * robbery（搶劫案件） * at night（夜間）
❻	現在的歹徒是愈來愈囂張了。	These days criminals are getting more and more insolent. * criminal（歹徒、犯人）可替換為： 　lawbreaker（違法者） * catch a criminal（逮捕犯人）
❼	現在的歹徒連警察也敢殺。	Criminals nowadays even dare to kill police officers. * dare to＋動詞原形（膽敢…） * police officer（警察）
❽	手機和網路讓犯罪變得更容易。	Mobile phones and the Internet make it easier to commit crimes. * mobile phone（手機）＝ cell phone * make it easier to＋動詞（讓…變得容易） * commit a crime（犯罪） * cybercrime（網路犯罪）

	單字	音標	詞性	意義	字頻	大考	英檢	多益
❶	received	[rɪˋsiv]	p.p.	receive（接收、收到）過去分詞	6	1	初級	◎
	fraudulent	[ˋfrɔdʒələnt]	adj.	詐騙的	5			◎
	phone	[fon]	n.	電話	1	2	初級	◎
	call	[kɔl]	n.	一通電話、通話	1	1	初級	◎
	today	[təˋde]	adv.	今天	1	1	初級	◎
❷	public	[ˋpʌblɪk]	adj.	公共的	1	1	初級	
	security	[sɪˋkjʊrətɪ]	n.	安全	1	3	中級	◎
	getting	[ˋgɛtɪŋ]	p.pr.	get（變成）現在分詞	1	1	初級	◎
	worse	[wɝs]	adj.	bad（糟糕的）比較級	4	1	中級	
❸	fraud	[frɔd]	n.	詐騙	2	6	中高	◎
	becoming	[bɪˋkʌmɪŋ]	p.pr.	become（變為）現在分詞	1	1	初級	
	more	[mor]	adv.	更佳	1	1	初級	
	frequent	[ˋfrikwənt]	adj.	頻繁的、常見的	2	3	中級	◎
❹	prostitution	[͵prɑstəˋtjuʃən]	n.	賣淫、色情業	3		中高	
	everywhere	[ˋɛvrɪ͵hwɛr]	n..	無所不在、到處都是	1		初級	
❺	convenience	[kənˋvinjəns]	n.	便利	2	4	中級	◎
	store	[stor]	n.	商店	1	1	初級	◎
	usually	[ˋjuʒʊəlɪ]	adv.	經常	1		初級	
	get	[gɛt]	v.	被⋯	1	1	初級	
	robbed	[rɑbd]	p.p.	rob（搶劫）過去分詞	2	3	初級	
	night	[naɪt]	n.	夜晚	1	1	初級	
❻	these	[ðiz]	adj.	這些	1	1	初級	
	day	[de]	n.	天	1	1	初級	
	criminal	[ˋkrɪmənl]	n.	歹徒、犯人	1	3	中級	◎
	insolent	[ˋɪnsələnt]	adj.	囂張的、目中無人的				
❼	nowadays	[ˋnaʊə͵dez]	adv.	現在	3	4	中級	
	even	[ˋivən]	adv.	甚至	1	1	初級	◎
	dare	[dɛr]	v.	膽敢	2	3	中級	
	kill	[kɪl]	v.	殺害	1	1	初級	
	police	[pəˋlis]	n.	警方	1	1	初級	
	officer	[ˋɔfəsɚ]	n.	警官	1	1	初級	◎
❽	mobile	[ˋmobɪl]	adj.	行動的	2	3	中級	◎
	Internet	[ˋɪntɚ͵nɛt]	n.	網路	1	4	初級	
	make	[mek]	v.	使得	1	1	初級	
	easier	[ˋiziɚ]	adj.	easy（容易的）比較級	1	1	初級	◎
	commit	[kəˋmɪt]	v.	犯（罪）	1	4	中級	◎
	crime	[kraɪm]	n.	犯罪	1	2	初級	

※「紅字單字」於本單元多句出現，「單字級等分析」僅列在「首次出現句」。

🔊 MP3 154-01 ❾～⓰

❾	很多壞人都逍遙法外。	Many lowlifes stay out of the law's reach. * stay out of the law's reach（逍遙法外） * out of（在…之外）
❿	綁票現在是司空見慣。	Nowadays kidnapping is a common occurrence. * murder（謀殺案）、homicide（殺人罪） * larceny（竊盜）、conversion（侵占） * extortion（勒索）、gambling（賭博）
⓫	輟學的青少年造成不少治安問題。	Juveniles who drop out of school cause many of the problems in public security. * drop out of school（輟學） * skip a class（翹課） * cause a problem（造成問題） * public security（治安）
⓬	晚上最好不要在外面逗留。	It's better not to stay outside at night. * It's better not to＋動詞原形（最好別做…） * stay outside（在外逗留） * at night（夜間）
⓭	現代人要學會自我保護。	Modern people have to learn to protect themselves. * have to＋動詞原形（必須） * learn how to＋動詞原形（學習如何…） * protect oneself（自我保護） * self-defense（自衛，正當防衛）
⓮	夜歸單身女子要特別小心。	Any woman returning home alone at night needs to be especially careful. * woman returning home alone（獨自回家的女性） * need to＋動詞原形（必須） * be especially careful（特別留意）
⓯	警民合作非常重要。	Cooperation between civilians and police is very important. * cooperation between A and B（A和B的合作）
⓰	很多社區自組巡邏隊。	Many communities have formed their own patrol teams. * form a team（組織隊伍）＝ organize a team * patrol team（巡邏隊）

	單字	音標	詞性	意義	字頻	大考	英檢	多益
❾	many	[ˋmɛnɪ]	adj.	許多的	1	1	初級	
	lowlife	[ˋlo͵laɪf]	n.	壞人				
	stay	[ste]	v.	停留、待	1	1	初級	◎
	out	[aʊt]	adv.	在…之外	1	1	初級	
	law	[lɔ]	n.	法律	1	1	初級	◎
	reach	[ritʃ]	n.	觸及	1	1	初級	◎
❿	nowadays	[ˋnaʊə͵dez]	adv.	現在	3	4	中級	
	kidnapping	[ˋkɪdnæpɪŋ]	n.	綁架	3	6	中級	
	common	[ˋkɑmən]	adj.	常見的	1	1	初級	◎
	occurrence	[əˋkɝəns]	n.	事件	3	5	中高	
⓫	juvenile	[ˋdʒuvənl]	n.	青少年	2	5	中高	◎
	drop	[drɑp]	v.	中止	1	2	初級	◎
	school	[skul]	n.	學校	1	1	初級	
	cause	[kɔz]	v.	造成	1	1	初級	◎
	problem	[ˋprɑbləm]	n.	問題	1	1	初級	◎
	public	[ˋpʌblɪk]	adj.	公共的	1	1	初級	
	security	[sɪˋkjʊrətɪ]	n.	安全	1	3	中級	◎
⓬	better	[ˋbɛtɚ]	adj.	最好…	1	1	初級	
	outside	[ˋaʊtˋsaɪd]	adv.	外面地	1	1	初級	◎
	night	[naɪt]	n.	夜晚	1	1	初級	
⓭	modern	[ˋmɑdɚn]	adj.	現代	1	2	初級	◎
	people	[ˋpipl]	n.	person（人）複數	1	1	初級	
	have	[hæv]	v.	必須	1	1	初級	
	learn	[lɝn]	v.	學習	1	1	初級	
	protect	[prəˋtɛkt]	v.	保護	1	2	初級	◎
	themselves	[ðəmˋsɛlvz]	pron.	他們自己	1		初級	
⓮	any	[ˋɛnɪ]	adj.	任何的	1	1	初級	
	woman	[ˋwʊmən]	n.	女人	1	1	初級	
	returning	[rɪˋtɝnɪŋ]	p.pr.	return（返回）現在分詞	6	1	初級	◎
	home	[hom]	n.	家	1	1	初級	
	alone	[əˋlon]	adv.	獨自地	1	1	初級	
	need	[nid]	v.	需要	1	1	初級	◎
	especially	[əˋspɛʃəlɪ]	adv.	特別	1	2	初級	
	careful	[ˋkɛrfəl]	adj.	留意的	1	1	初級	
⓯	cooperation	[ko͵ɑpəˋreʃən]	n.	合作	1	4	中級	◎
	civilian	[sɪˋvɪljən]	n.	公民	2	4	中級	
	police	[pəˋlis]	n.	警方	1	1	初級	
	very	[ˋvɛrɪ]	adv.	十分	1	1	初級	
	important	[ɪmˋpɔrtnt]	adj.	重要的	1	1	初級	
⓰	community	[kəˋmjunətɪ]	n.	社區	1	4	中級	
	formed	[fɔrmd]	p.p.	form（組織）過去分詞	1	2	初級	◎
	own	[on]	adj.	自己的	1	1	初級	◎
	patrol	[pəˋtrol]	n.	巡邏	2	5	中高	
	team	[tim]	n.	隊伍	1	2	初級	

※「紅字單字」於本單元多句出現，「單字級等分析」僅列在「首次出現句」。

❶	你覺得社會治安好嗎？	Do you think public security is good or not? * public security（社會治安） * be...or not（是否…）
❷	為什麼治安越來越差？	Why is public security getting worse and worse? * Why is＋主詞＋動詞-ing?（為什麼…變得越來越…？） * worse and worse（越來越糟糕）
❸	你家有裝保全嗎？	Do you have a security system in your home? * security system（保全系統）
❹	你覺得警察能保護人民嗎？	Do you think the police can protect the people? * Do you think＋子句…?（你覺得…？）
❺	你這麼晚回家安全嗎？	Is it safe for you to return home so late? * be safe to＋動詞原形（做…是安全的） * return home（回家）
❻	夜晚你敢一個人出門嗎？	Do you dare to go out alone at night? * Do you dare to＋動詞原形＋…?（你敢…嗎？） * go out alone（獨自出門） * at night（夜間）
❼	你家附近的治安好嗎？	Is the public security around your neighborhood good? * around your neighborhood（在你家附近） * around（在…附近）
❽	報警有用嗎？	Is making a report to the police any use? * make a report（報案）
❾	你接過詐騙集團的電話嗎？	Have you ever received a phone call from scammers? * Have you ever...?（你是否曾經…？） * a phone call from＋某人（某人打來的電話） * phone scam gang（電話詐騙集團） * fraudulent call（詐騙電話）＝ phone scam
❿	你曾經受騙匯款給詐騙集團嗎？	Were you ever tricked into remitting money to swindlers? * Were you ever＋過去分詞...?（你以前有被…嗎） * trick into（欺騙、詐欺） * be tricked into（被欺騙、被詐欺） * remit money to＋某人（匯款給某人）

	單字	音標	詞性	意義	字頻	大考	英檢	多益
❶	think	[θɪŋk]	v.	認為	1	1	初級	
	public	[ˋpʌblɪk]	adj.	公共的	1	1	初級	
	security	[sɪˋkjʊrətɪ]	n.	安全/保全	1	3	中級	◎
	good	[gʊd]	adj.	良好的	1	1	初級	◎
❷	getting	[ˋgɛtɪŋ]	p.pr.	get（變成）現在分詞	1	1	初級	◎
	worse	[wɝs]	adj.	bad（糟糕的）比較級	4	1	中級	
❸	have	[hæv]	v.	擁有	1	1	初級	
	system	[ˋsɪstəm]	n.	系統	1	3	初級	◎
	home	[hom]	n.	家	1	1	初級	
❹	police	[pəˋlis]	n.	警方	1	1	初級	
	protect	[prəˋtɛkt]	v.	保護	1	2	初級	◎
	people	[ˋpipl]	n.	person（人民）複數	1	1	初級	
❺	safe	[sef]	adj.	安全的	1	1	初級	◎
	return	[rɪˋtɝn]	v.	返回	1	1	初級	◎
	so	[so]	adv.	這麼	1	1	初級	
	late	[let]	adv.	晚地	1	1	初級	◎
❻	dare	[dɛr]	v.	膽敢	2	3	中級	
	go	[go]	v.	去	1	1	初級	
	out	[aʊt]	adv.	外出地	1	1	初級	
	alone	[əˋlon]	adv.	獨自地	1	1	初級	
	night	[naɪt]	n.	夜晚	1	1	初級	
❼	neighborhood	[ˋnebɚͺhʊd]	n.	鄰近地區	1	3	中級	
❽	making	[ˋmekɪŋ]	n.	make（做出）動名詞	2	1	中高	
	report	[rɪˋport]	n.	報案	1	1	初級	◎
	any	[ˋɛnɪ]	adj.	任何的	1	1	初級	
	use	[juz]	n.	作用	1	1	初級	◎
❾	ever	[ˋɛvɚ]	adv.	曾經	1	1	初級	
	received	[rɪˋsivd]	p.p.	receive（接收、收到）過去分詞	6	1	初級	◎
	phone	[fon]	n.	電話	1	2	初級	◎
	call	[kɔl]	n.	一通電話、通話	1	1	初級	◎
	scammer	[ˋskæmɚ]	n.	詐騙份子				
❿	tricked	[trɪkt]	p.p.	trick（欺騙、詐欺）過去分詞	2	2	初級	◎
	remitting	[rɪˋmɪtɪŋ]	n.	remit（匯款）動名詞				◎
	money	[ˋmʌnɪ]	n.	金錢	1	1	初級	◎
	swindler	[ˋswɪndlɚ]	n.	詐騙份子				

※「紅字單字」於本單元多句出現，「單字級等分析」僅列在「首次出現句」。

MP3 154-02 ⑪～⑱

⑪	你家附近常有警察巡邏嗎？	Do the police often patrol your neighborhood? * patrol＋地區（巡邏某地區） * arrest＋犯人（逮捕某犯人） * investigate＋地區（調查某地區）
⑫	聽說又發生銀行搶案？	I heard that another bank was robbed today. * I heard that＋子句（我之前聽說…） * another bank（另一間銀行） * was robbed（之前被搶劫、剛被搶劫） * venue（犯案地點）
⑬	你認為警察能破案嗎？	Do you think the police can solve crimes? * Do you think＋子句…?（你覺得…？） * solve a crime（破案、解決案件） * investigate a crime（調查案件） * prevent a crime（預防案件）
⑭	今天發生警匪槍戰嗎？	Were there any shootouts between the criminals and police today? * Were there any＋名詞…?（之前是不是有…？） * shootout（槍戰）可替換為：conflict（衝突） * between the criminals and police（警匪之間）
⑮	為什麼破案率這麼低？	Why is the crime-solving rate so low? * Why is＋主詞＋形容詞?（為什麼…很…？） * crime-solving rate（破案率） * crime rate（犯罪率） * high（比率高的）
⑯	又有人在超商被搶嗎？	Has someone been robbed in a convenience store again? * convenience store（便利商店） * crime clock（犯罪時鐘、週期） * recidivist（慣犯）
⑰	你曾經被搶嗎？	Have you been robbed before? * Have you been＋過去分詞…?（你有被…的經驗嗎）
⑱	你讓孩子自己上下學嗎？	Do you let your children go to and from school alone? * let＋某人＋動詞原形（讓某人…） * go to and from school（上下學） * commute（通勤）

	單字	音標	詞性	意義	字頻	大考	英檢	多益
⑪	police	[pə`lis]	n.	警方	1	1	初級	
	often	[`ɔfən]	adv.	常常	1	1	初級	
	patrol	[pə`trol]	v.	巡邏	2	5	中高	
	neighborhood	[`nebɚ.hud]	n.	鄰近地區	1	3	中級	
⑫	heard	[hɝd]	p.t.	heard（聽聞）過去式	1	1	初級	
	another	[ə`nʌðɚ]	adj.	另一個	1	1		
	bank	[bæŋk]	n.	銀行	1	1	初級	◎
	robbed	[rɑbd]	p.p.	rob（搶劫）過去分詞	2	3	初級	
	today	[tə`de]	adv.	今天	1	1	初級	◎
⑬	think	[θɪŋk]	v.	認為	1	1	初級	
	solve	[sɑlv]	v.	解決	1	2	初級	◎
	crime	[kraɪm]	n.	犯罪	1	2	初級	
⑭	there	[ðɛr]	adv.	有…	1	1	初級	
	any	[`ɛnɪ]	adj.	任何的	1	1	初級	
	shootout	[`ʃut.aʊt]	n.	槍戰	5			
	criminal	[`krɪmən!]	n.	歹徒、犯人	1	3	中級	◎
⑮	crime-solving	[`kraɪm`sɑlvɪŋ]	adj.	破案的				
	rate	[ret]	n.	比率	1	3	中級	◎
	so	[so]	adv.	這麼	1	1	初級	
	low	[lo]	adj.	比率低的	1	1	初級	
⑯	someone	[`sʌm.wʌn]	pron.	某個人	1	1	初級	
	convenience	[kən`vinjəns]	n.	便利	2	4	中級	◎
	store	[stor]	n.	商店	1	1	初級	◎
	again	[ə`gɛn]	adv.	再次	1	1	初級	
⑰	before	[bɪ`for]	adv.	以前	1	1	初級	
⑱	let	[lɛt]	v.	讓…	1	1	初級	
	children	[`tʃɪldrən]	n.	child（孩子）複數	1	1	初級	
	go	[go]	v.	去	1	1	初級	
	school	[skul]	n.	學校	1	1	初級	
	alone	[ə`lon]	adv.	獨自地	1	1	初級	

※「紅字單字」於本單元多句出現，「單字級等分析」僅列在「首次出現句」。

155 貧與富⋯。（1）

🔊 MP3 155-01 ❶～❼

❶	有錢人一餐可以花上幾萬元。	The rich can spend tens of thousands on a meal. * the rich（富人）、the poor（窮人） * spend＋金錢＋on＋某物（因某物花⋯錢） * tens of thousands（好幾萬） * spend extravagantly（揮霍金錢）
❷	現在社會笑貧不笑娼。	Society nowadays laughs at the poor, not the streetwalker. * laugh at＋某人物（嘲笑某人物） 　＝ jeer at＋某人物
❸	有些人連小孩的營養午餐費都繳不出來。	Some people can't even pay their children's lunch money. * lunch money（午餐費用） * dormitory fee（住宿費） * tuition fee（學雜費）
❹	納稅人都是辛苦的薪水階級。	The taxpayers make up the hard-working salaried class. * make up（組成） * be made up of（由⋯組成） * salaried class（領薪階級）
❺	社會上貧富差距越來越大。	The gap between the poor and the rich is getting wider and wider in our society. * the gap between the poor and the rich（貧富差距） * be getting＋比較級（變得越來越⋯） * wider and wider（越來越大、越來越寬）
❻	窮人家的孩子沒機會受到更好的教育。	Children of the poor don't have the opportunity to receive a better education. * have the opportunity（擁有機會） 　＝ have the chance * receive education（接受教育）
❼	很多人因為活不下去而自殺。	Many people have committed suicide because they couldn't handle their lives. * have＋過去分詞（已經做了⋯） * commit suicide（自殺） * handle one's life（自理生活）

	單字	音標	詞性	意義	字頻	大考	英檢	多益
❶	rich	[rɪtʃ]	adj.	富有的	1	1	初級	
	spend	[spɛnd]	v.	花費	1	1	初級	◎
	ten	[tɛn]	n.	十	1	1	初級	
	thousand	[ˋθauznd]	n.	一千	1	1	初級	
	meal	[mil]	n.	一餐	1	2	初級	
❷	society	[səˋsaɪətɪ]	n.	社會	1	2	初級	◎
	nowadays	[ˋnauə.dez]	adv.	現今	3	4	中級	
	laugh	[læf]	v.	嘲笑	1	1	初級	
	poor	[pur]	adj.	貧窮的	1	1	初級	
	streetwalker	[ˋstrit.wɔkɚ]	n.	阻街女郎、流鶯				
❸	some	[sʌm]	adj.	一些	1	1	初級	
	people	[ˋpipl]	n.	person（人）複數	1	1	初級	
	even	[ˋivən]	adv.	甚至	1	1	初級	◎
	pay	[pe]	v.	繳費	1	3	初級	◎
	children	[ˋtʃɪldrən]	n.	child（小孩）複數	1	1	初級	
	lunch	[ˋlʌntʃ]	n.	午餐	1	1	初級	
	money	[ˋmʌnɪ]	n.	金錢	1	1	初級	◎
❹	taxpayer	[ˋtæks.peɚ]	n.	納稅人	2		中高	
	make	[mek]	v.	組成	1	1	初級	
	up	[ʌp]	adv.	起來	1	1	初級	
	hard-working	[.hɑrdˋwɜkɪŋ]	adj.	辛苦工作的	4		中級	
	salaried	[ˋsælərɪd]	adj.	領薪的	8	4	中級	◎
	class	[klæs]	n.	階級	1	1	初級	
❺	gap	[gæp]	n.	差距	1	3	中級	◎
	getting	[ˋgɛtɪŋ]	p.pr.	get（變為）現在分詞	1	1	初級	◎
	wider	[ˋwaɪdɚ]	adj.	wide（寬廣的）比較級	1	1	初級	
❻	have	[hæv]	v.	擁有	1	1	初級	
	opportunity	[.ɑpɚˋtjunətɪ]	n.	機會	1	3	初級	◎
	receive	[rɪˋsiv]	v.	接受	1	1	初級	◎
	better	[ˋbɛtɚ]	adj.	good（良好的）比較級	1	1	初級	
	education	[.ɛdʒuˋkeʃən]	n.	教育	1	2	初級	◎
❼	many	[ˋmɛnɪ]	adj.	許多	1	1	初級	
	committed	[kəˋmɪtɪd]	p.p.	commit（犯下）過去分詞	3	4	中級	◎
	suicide	[ˋsuə.saɪd]	n.	自殺	1	3	中級	◎
	handle	[ˋhændl]	v.	處理	1	2	初級	◎
	life	[laɪf]	n.	生活	1	1	初級	

※「紅字單字」於本單元多句出現，「單字級等分析」僅列在「首次出現句」。

🔊 MP3 155-01 **❽ ～ ⓰**

❽	很多人三餐不繼。	Many people live in want. * live in want（生活貧困）
❾	有些窮人因媒體報導而獲得幫助。	Some poor people get help because of media reports. * get help（獲得幫助） * because of＋名詞（因為…） * media report（媒體報導） * government subsidy（政府補助）
❿	物價越來越高，等於薪水越來越薄。	Rising commodity prices equal smaller salaries. * commodity price（物價） * high commodity price（高物價） * low commodity price（低物價） * smaller salary（較少的薪水）
⓫	很多人沒有房子可住。	Many people don't have a house to live in. * live in（居住）
⓬	有人追求名牌，有人連衣服都沒得穿。	Some people seek luxury while others don't even have a shirt on their back. * some…, others…（有人…，有人…） * seek（追求）＝ pursue * while（反之、然而） * not have a shirt on one's back（身上沒衣服穿） * on one's back（在身上）
⓭	我沒有錢，但我很快樂。	I don't have money, but I'm happy.
⓮	街頭流浪漢愈來愈多。	There are more and more vagrants on the street. * more and more（越來越多） * on the street（街上） * vagrant（流浪漢，遊民）＝ homeless people
⓯	會捐錢幫助別人的，往往不是最有錢的人。	People who donate money to help others often are not the richest people. * donate money（捐錢） * help others（幫助別人）
⓰	有人很有錢，是因為他們真的很努力。	Some people are rich due to hard work. * due to＋名詞（因為…） * get rich（變有錢） * hard work（努力）

	單字	音標	詞性	意義	字頻	大考	英檢	多益
❽	many	[ˈmɛnɪ]	adj.	許多的	1	1	初級	
	people	[ˈpipl̩]	n.	person（人）複數	1	1	初級	
	live	[lɪv]	v.	生活/居住	1	1	初級	
	want	[wɑnt]	n.	短缺	1	1	初級	◎
❾	some	[sʌm]	adj.	一些	1	1	初級	
	poor	[pʊr]	adj.	貧窮的	1	1	初級	
	get	[gɛt]	v.	獲得	1	1	初級	◎
	help	[hɛlp]	n./v.	幫助	1	1	初級	
	media	[ˈmidɪə]	n.	媒體	1	3	中高	◎
	report	[rɪˈport]	n.	報導	1	1	初級	◎
❿	rising	[ˈraɪzɪŋ]	adj.	高漲的	2	1	初級	◎
	commodity	[kəˈmɑdətɪ]	n.	日用品、商品	2	5	中高	
	price	[praɪs]	n.	價格	1	1	初級	◎
	equal	[ˈikwəl]	v.	等同	1	1	初級	◎
	smaller	[ˈsmɔlə]	adj.	small（少量的）比較級	1	1	初級	◎
	salary	[ˈsælərɪ]	n.	薪水	1	4	中級	◎
⓫	have	[hæv]	v.	擁有	1	1	初級	
	house	[haʊs]	n.	房子	1	1	初級	◎
⓬	seek	[sik]	v.	追求	1	3	初級	◎
	luxury	[ˈlʌkʃərɪ]	n.	奢侈品	2	4	中級	◎
	other	[ˈʌðə]	pron.	其他人	1	1	初級	
	even	[ˈivən]	adv.	甚至	1	1	初級	◎
	shirt	[ʃɜt]	n.	上衣	1	1	初級	
	back	[bæk]	n.	背脊	1	1	初級	◎
⓭	money	[ˈmʌnɪ]	n.	金錢	1	1	初級	◎
	happy	[ˈhæpɪ]	adj.	快樂的	1	1	初級	
⓮	there	[ðɛr]	adv.	有…	1	1	初級	
	more	[mor]	adj.	更多的	1	1	初級	
	vagrant	[ˈvegrənt]	n.	流浪漢、遊民				
	street	[strit]	n.	街頭	1	1	初級	
⓯	donate	[ˈdonet]	v.	捐獻	2	6	中級	◎
	often	[ˈɔfən]	adv.	常常	1	1	初級	
	richest	[ˈrɪtʃɪst]	adj.	rich（富有的）最高級	1	1	初級	
⓰	rich	[rɪtʃ]	adj.	富有的	1	1	初級	
	due	[dju]	adj.	因為	1	3	中級	◎
	hard	[hɑrd]	adj.	努力的	1	1	初級	◎
	work	[wɜk]	n.	工作	1	1	初級	◎

※「紅字單字」於本單元多句出現，「單字級等分析」僅列在「首次出現句」。

155　你覺得貧與富…？（1）

❶	台灣的貧富差距愈來愈大了嗎？	Is the gap between rich and poor widening? * Is＋主詞＋動詞-ing?（…是否正在…？） * M-shaped society（M型社會） * shorten（變小、變狹窄）
❷	羨慕有錢人嗎？	Do you envy the rich?
❸	為什麼有些人那麼有錢？	Why are some people so rich? * Why is / are＋主詞＋形容詞?（為什麼…很…？）
❹	為什麼有那麼多流浪漢？	Why are there so many homeless people? * Why are there＋名詞?（為什麼會有…？） * homeless people（流浪漢、遊民）= vagrant * homeless shelter（遊民收容所）
❺	台灣有完善的社會福利制度嗎？	Does Taiwan have a well-developed social welfare system? * social welfare system（社會福利制度） * social welfare policy（社會福利政策） * unemployment benefit（失業救濟） * financial aid（經濟援助）
❻	你定期捐款給慈善團體嗎？	Do you regularly donate to charity? * Do you regularly＋動詞?（你是否定期…？） * donate to＋某單位（捐款、捐贈給某單位） * donate food（捐贈食物） * donate blood（捐血）
❼	你覺得政府應該多照顧窮人嗎？	Do you think that the government should take better care of the poor? * Do you think that＋子句?（你認為…嗎） * take better care of（更妥善照顧）
❽	你覺得要對富人課更重的稅嗎？	Do you think that it is necessary to levy higher taxes on the rich? * it is necessary to＋動詞（必須做…） * levy...on＋某人（對某人徵收…稅） * higher taxes（更重的稅、更高的稅） * lower taxes（更輕的稅、更低的稅）
❾	這是一個金錢決定一切的年代嗎？	Is this the era of "money talks?" * the era＋某事物（某事物的年代） * money talks（金錢萬能、有錢好辦事）

	單字	音標	詞性	意義	字頻	大考	英檢	多益
❶	gap	[gæp]	n.	差距	1	3	中級	◎
	rich	[rɪtʃ]	adj.	富有的	1	1	初級	
	poor	[pʊr]	adj.	貧窮的	1	1	初級	
	widening	[ˋwaɪdnɪŋ]	p.pr.	widen（變大、變寬廣）現在分詞	6	2	初級	◎
❷	envy	[ˋɛnvɪ]	v.	羨慕、嫉妒	4	3	初級	
❸	some	[sʌm]	adj.	一些	1	1	初級	
	people	[ˋpipl̩]	n.	person（人）複數	1	1	初級	
	so	[so]	adv.	那麼	1	1	初級	
❹	there	[ðɛr]	adv.	有…	1	1	初級	◎
	many	[ˋmɛnɪ]	adj.	許多的	1	1	初級	
	homeless	[ˋhomlɪs]	adj.	無家可歸的、流浪的	2		中高	
❺	Taiwan	[ˋtaɪˋwɑn]	v.	台灣			初級	
	have	[hæv]	v.	擁有	1	1	初級	
	well-developed	[ˋwɛldɪˋvɛləpt]	adj.	完善的、發展健全的	7			
	social	[ˋsoʃəl]	adj.	社會的	1	1	初級	◎
	welfare	[ˋwɛl.fɛr]	n.	福利	1	4	中級	◎
	system	[ˋsɪstəm]	n.	制度	1	3	初級	◎
❻	regularly	[ˋrɛgjələlɪ]	adv.	定期地	2			◎
	donate	[ˋdonet]	v.	捐獻	2	6	中級	◎
	charity	[ˋtʃærətɪ]	n.	慈善團體、慈善機構	2	4	中級	◎
❼	think	[θɪŋk]	v.	認為	1	1	初級	◎
	government	[ˋgʌvənmənt]	n.	政府	1	2	初級	◎
	take	[tek]	v.	採取	1	1	初級	◎
	better	[ˋbɛtə]	adj.	good（妥善的）比較級	1	1	初級	◎
	care	[kɛr]	n.	照顧	1	1	初級	◎
❽	necessary	[ˋnɛsə.sɛrɪ]	adj.	必需的	1	2	初級	
	levy	[ˋlɛvɪ]	v.	徵稅	5		中高	
	higher	[ˋhaɪə]	adj.	high（重的、高的）比較級	1	1	初級	
	tax	[tæks]	n.	稅金	1	3	中級	◎
❾	this	[ðɪs]	pron.	這個	1	1	初級	
	era	[ˋɪrə]	n.	年代	1	4	中級	
	money	[ˋmʌnɪ]	n.	金錢	1	1	初級	◎
	talk	[tɔk]	v.	說話	1	1	初級	◎

※「紅字單字」於本單元多句出現，「單字級等分析」僅列在「首次出現句」。

MP3 155-02 ⑩～⑱

⑩	窮人真的是因為不夠努力嗎？	Is it true that the poor don't work hard enough? * **Is it true that**＋子句…？（…是真的嗎） * **work hard**（努力）
⑪	富人難道有罪？	Is it possible that the rich are at fault? * **Is it possible that**＋子句?（…可能嗎、可以說…嗎） * **at fault**（有過錯的）
⑫	社會貧富差距太大時會出現什麼問題？	What problems will occur if the gap between rich and poor is too wide? * **What problems will…?**（…將會是什麼問題？） * **occur**（出現）可替換為： **arise**（產生）、**come up**（出現） * **if**（如果、要是）
⑬	你會捐錢給路邊的乞丐嗎？	Do you give change to beggars on the roadside? * **give change to**＋某人（給某人零錢、硬幣） * **on the road side**（路邊）
⑭	你覺得你的生活富裕嗎？	Do you feel like your life is rich? * **feel like**（感覺、覺得）
⑮	窮人注定會窮苦一生嗎？	Are the poor destined to be poor for their whole lives? * **be destined to**（注定） * **the poor**（窮人） * **whole life**（一生、一輩子）
⑯	金錢萬能嗎？	Is money omnipotent?
⑰	有錢人一定比窮人快樂嗎？	Are the rich definitely happier than the poor? * **Are the rich…than the poor?** 　（有錢人會比窮人…嗎） * **definitely**（肯定、絕對）＝ surly
⑱	衡量貧富的標準只有金錢嗎？	Is money the only way to measure rich and poor? * **the only way**（唯一的方式） * **measure**（衡量、評估）可替換為： **define**（給…下定義） * **rich and poor**（富有和貧窮）

	單字	音標	詞性	意義	字頻	大考	英檢	多益
⑩	true	[tru]	adj.	真的	1	1	初級	
	poor	[pʊr]	adj.	貧窮的	1	1	初級	
	work	[wɜk]	v.	工作	1	1	初級	◎
	hard	[hɑrd]	adv.	努力地	1	1	初級	◎
	enough	[əˋnʌf]	adv.	足夠地	1	1	初級	◎
⑪	possible	[ˋpɑsəbl̩]	adj.	可能的	1	1	初級	◎
	rich	[rɪtʃ]	adj.	富有的/生活富裕的	1	1	初級	
	fault	[fɔlt]	n.	過錯	2	2	初級	◎
⑫	problem	[ˋprɑbləm]	n.	問題	1	1	初級	◎
	occur	[əˋkɜ]	v.	發生	1	2	初級	◎
	gap	[gæp]	n.	差距	1	3	中級	◎
	too	[tu]	adv.	過於	1	1	初級	
	wide	[waɪd]	adj.	大的、寬廣的	1	1	初級	
⑬	give	[gɪv]	v.	給予	1	1	初級	
	change	[tʃɛndʒ]	n.	零錢、硬幣	1	2	初級	◎
	beggar	[ˋbɛgə]	n.	乞丐	5	3	中級	
	roadside	[ˋrod.saɪd]	n.	路邊	3			
⑭	feel	[fil]	v.	感覺、覺得	1	1	初級	
	life	[laɪf]	n.	生活/人生	1	1	初級	
⑮	destined	[ˋdɛstɪnd]	p.p.	destine（注定）過去分詞		6	中高	
	whole	[hol]	adj.	整個	1	1	初級	◎
⑯	money	[ˋmʌnɪ]	n.	金錢	1	1	初級	◎
	omnipotent	[ɑmˋnɪpətənt]	adj.	萬能的、無敵的				
⑰	definitely	[ˋdɛfənɪtlɪ]	adv.	肯定、絕對	1			◎
	happier	[ˋhæpɪə]	adj.	happy（快樂）比較級	1	1	初級	
⑱	only	[ˋonlɪ]	adj.	唯一的	1	1	初級	
	way	[we]	n.	方式	1	1	初級	
	measure	[ˋmɛʒə]	v.	衡量、評估	1	4	初級	◎

※「紅字單字」於本單元多句出現，「單字級等分析」僅列在「首次出現句」。

741

MP3 156-01 ❶～❽

❶	家庭是青少年問題的起因。	The family is the origin of the juvenile problem. * origin（起因）= cause * juvenile problem（青少年問題）
❷	現在的青少年都太早熟了。	Youth today mature too early. * mature too early（早熟）
❸	社會應該幫助中輟生重返校園。	Society should help dropout students return to school. * dropout student（中輟生） * drop out of school（輟學） * return to school（重返校園）
❹	教條式的規範青少年很難接受。	Young people do not take well to dogmatic discipline. * not take well（難以接受、難以適應） * dogmatic discipline（教條式的規範）
❺	我不知道如何和我的孩子溝通。	I don't know how to communicate with my children. * not know how to＋動詞（不知道如何做…） * communicate with（溝通）
❻	很多青少年都有翹家的經驗。	Many youths have had the experience of running away from home. * have had（曾經有過） * the experience of＋動詞-ing（…的經驗） * run away from home（逃家）
❼	現在的青少年要面對的問題比過去更多。	Youth nowadays are facing far more problems than before. * far more＋名詞（更多…） * than before（比起以前） * 此句用「現在進行式」（...are facing...）表示「現階段發生的事」。
❽	部分青少年對毒品沒有抵抗力。	Some young people don't have the strength to avoid drugs. * have the strength（有能力） * avoid drugs（遠離毒品） * inject drugs（注射毒品）、drug addiction（毒癮）

單字級等分析

	單字	音標	詞性	意義	字頻	大考	英檢	多益
❶	family	[ˈfæməlɪ]	n.	家庭	1	1	初級	
	origin	[ˈɔrədʒɪn]	n.	起因	1	3	中級	◎
	juvenile	[ˈdʒuvənl]	n.	青少年	2	5	中高	◎
	problem	[ˈprɑbləm]	n.	問題	1	1	初級	◎
❷	youth	[juθ]	n.	青少年	1	2	初級	
	today	[təˈde]	adv.	現在	1	1	初級	◎
	mature	[məˈtʃur]	v.	變成熟	2	3	中級	◎
	too	[tu]	adv.	過於	1	1	初級	
	early	[ˈɜlɪ]	adv.	早地	1	1	初級	
❸	society	[səˈsaɪətɪ]	n.	社會	1	2	初級	◎
	help	[hɛlp]	v.	幫助	1	1	初級	
	dropout	[ˈdrɑpˌaut]	n.	輟學	3			
	student	[ˈstjudnt]	n.	學生	1	1	初級	
	return	[rɪˈtɜn]	v.	返回	1	1	初級	◎
	school	[skul]	n.	學校	1	1	初級	
❹	young	[jʌŋ]	adj.	年輕的	1	1	初級	
	people	[ˈpipl]	n.	person（人）複數	1	1	初級	
	take	[tek]	v.	接受、適應	1	1	初級	◎
	well	[wɛl]	adv.	良好地	1	1	初級	◎
	dogmatic	[dɔgˈmætɪk]	adj.	教條式的	7			
	discipline	[ˈdɪsəplɪn]	n.	規範	1	4	中級	◎
❺	know	[no]	v.	知道	1	1	初級	
	communicate	[kəˈmjunəˌket]	v.	溝通	1	3	中級	
	children	[ˈtʃɪldrən]	n.	child（小孩）複數	1	1	初級	
❻	many	[ˈmɛnɪ]	adj.	許多的	1	1	初級	
	had	[hæv]	p.p.	have（擁有）過去分詞	1	1	初級	
	experience	[ɪkˈspɪrɪəns]	n.	經驗	1	2	初級	◎
	running	[ˈrʌnɪŋ]	n.	run（逃跑）動名詞	2	1	中級	◎
	away	[əˈwe]	adv.	遠離	1	1	初級	
	home	[hom]	n.	家	1	1	初級	
❼	nowadays	[ˈnauəˌdez]	adv.	現今	3	4	中級	
	facing	[ˈfesɪŋ]	p.pr.	face（面對）現在分詞	8	1	初級	
	far	[fɑr]	adv.	很、極為	1	1	初級	
	more	[mor]	adj.	更多的	1	1	初級	
	before	[bɪˈfor]	adv.	以前	1	1	初級	
❽	some	[sʌm]	adj.	一些	1	1	初級	
	have	[hæv]	v.	擁有	1	1	初級	
	strength	[strɛŋθ]	n.	能力	1	3	中級	◎
	avoid	[əˈvɔɪd]	v.	遠離	1	2	初級	◎
	drug	[drʌg]	n.	毒品	1	2	初級	

※「紅字單字」於本單元多句出現，「單字級等分析」僅列在「首次出現句」。

MP3 156-01 ❾～⓱

❾	現在的青少年簡直是目無尊長。	Young people nowadays are simply rude. * **rude**（失禮的）= **impolite**
❿	青少年需要家長與老師更多關心。	Youth need more care from parents and teachers. * **need more care**（需要更多的關懷） * **from**＋某人（來自某人）
⓫	青少年對性有許多錯誤的觀念。	There are many mistaken ideas that juveniles have about sex. * **There is / are**＋名詞（有…） * **mistaken idea**（錯誤的想法） * **have**＋形容詞＋**ideas about**＋某物 　（對某物有…想法）
⓬	青少年時期朋友的影響力很大。	The friends of one's youth are very influential. * **one's youth**（某個人的青少年時期） * **peer**（同儕） * **peer pressure**（同儕壓力）
⓭	很多少女靠援交賺生活費。	Many young girls make a living by prostitution. * **make a living**（謀生、賺錢） * **by**（以…方式）
⓮	不健全的家庭容易教育出問題青年。	Unhealthy families often produce troubled youths. * **unhealthy family**（不健全的家庭） * **produce**（產生、招致）= **cause** * **troubled youth**（問題青年）
⓯	培養正當興趣對青少年很重要。	It's important for young people to have healthy interests. * **It's important for**＋某人＋**to...**（…對某人很重要） * **healthy interest**（良好興趣、正當興趣）
⓰	很多年輕少女都有墮胎經驗。	Many young girls have had abortions. * 此句用「現在完成式」（...have had...）表示 　「過去到現在發生過、經歷過的事」。
⓱	父母應該多關心自己的孩子。	Parents should be more concerned with their own kids. * **be concerned with**（關心、關懷）= **care for**

	單字	音標	詞性	意義	字頻	大考	英檢	多益
❾	young	[jʌŋ]	adj.	年輕的	1	1	初級	
	people	[ˋpipḷ]	n.	person（人）複數	1	1	初級	
	nowadays	[ˋnaʊə͵dez]	adv.	現今	3	4	中級	
	simply	[ˋsɪmplɪ]	adv.	非常	1	2	初級	◎
	rude	[rud]	adj.	失禮的	1	2	初級	
❿	youth	[juθ]	n.	青少年/青少年時期	1	2	初級	
	need	[nid]	v.	需要	1	1	初級	◎
	more	[mor]	adj./adv.	更多的/更加	1	1	初級	
	care	[kɛr]	n.	關懷	1	1	初級	◎
	parents	[ˋpɛrənts]	n.	parent（雙親）複數	2	1		
	teacher	[ˋtitʃɚ]	n.	老師	1	1	初級	
⓫	there	[ðɛr]	adv.	有…	1	1	初級	
	many	[ˋmɛnɪ]	adj.	許多的	1	1	初級	
	mistaken	[mɪˋstekən]	adj.	錯誤的	5	1	中高	◎
	idea	[aɪˋdiə]	n.	想法	1	1	初級	◎
	juvenile	[ˋdʒuvənḷ]	n.	青少年	2	5	中高	◎
	have	[hæv]	v.	擁有	1	1	初級	
	sex	[sɛks]	n.	性	1	3	中級	
⓬	friend	[frɛnd]	n.	朋友	1	1	初級	
	one	[wʌn]	n.	一個	1	1	初級	
	very	[ˋvɛrɪ]	adv.	十分	1	1	初級	
	influential	[͵ɪnflʊˋɛnʃəl]	adj.	有影響力的	2	4	中級	◎
⓭	girl	[gɝl]	n.	少女	1	1	初級	
	make	[mek]	v.	謀生、賺取	1	1	初級	
	living	[ˋlɪvɪŋ]	n.	生計	1	1	中高	
	prostitution	[͵prɑstəˋtjuʃən]	n.	賣淫	3		中高	
⓮	unhealthy	[ʌnˋhɛlθɪ]	adj.	不健全的、不良的	4		初級	
	family	[ˋfæməlɪ]	n.	家庭	1	1	初級	
	often	[ˋɔfən]	adv.	常常	1	1	初級	
	produce	[prəˋdjus]	v.	產生、招致	1	2	初級	◎
	troubled	[ˋtrʌbḷd]	adj.	問題的	2	1	中高	◎
⓯	important	[ɪmˋpɔrtnt]	adj.	重要的	1	1	初級	
	healthy	[ˋhɛlθɪ]	adj.	健康的	1	2	初級	◎
	interest	[ˋɪntərɪst]	n.	興趣	1	1	初級	◎
⓰	had	[hæd]	p.p.	have（擁有）過去分詞	1	1	初級	
	abortion	[əˋbɔrʃən]	n.	墮胎	1	5	中高	
⓱	concerned	[kənˋsɝnd]	adj.	關心的、關懷的	1	3	中高	◎
	own	[on]	adj.	自己的	1	1	初級	◎
	kid	[kɪd]	n.	孩子	1	1	初級	

※「紅字單字」於本單元多句出現，「單字級等分析」僅列在「首次出現句」。

MP3 156-02 ❶～❾

❶	現在的年輕人出了什麼問題？	What is the problem with young people nowadays? * **problem with**＋某人（某人的困擾） * **what is wrong with**＋某人（某人哪裡不對勁） * **what is matter with**＋某人（某人怎麼回事）
❷	現在的年輕人為什麼動不動就自殺？	Why do more young people nowadays commit suicide? * **commit suicide**（自殺） * **commit a crime**（犯罪）
❸	為什麼青少年問題越來越嚴重？	Why is the youth problem getting more and more serious? * **be getting**＋比較級（變得越來越…） * **more and more**（越來越） * 此句用「現在進行式」（…is…getting…）表示「現階段逐漸變化的事」。
❹	不知道青少年為什麼愛飆車。	We really don't know why young people love joyriding. * **not know why**＋子句（不知道為什麼…） * **love**＋動詞ing（喜愛）
❺	真不知道現在的青少年在想什麼。	I really don't know what teenagers today are thinking.
❻	現在的青少年壓力太大了嗎？	Are young people nowadays under too much pressure? * **under too much pressure**（承受太大壓力）
❼	要如何加強青少年的性教育？	How can sexual education for the youth be strengthened? * **sexual education**（性教育） * **strengthen the education**（加強教育）
❽	為什麼小孩有心事都不對我說？	Why do my kids not want to tell me what is on their minds? * **Why do**＋主詞＋**not**＋動詞…?（為什麼…不做…？） * **want to**＋動詞原形（想要） * **what is on one's mind**（某人的心事）
❾	你能和你的孩子溝通嗎？	Can you communicate with your child? * **communicate with**（溝通）

	單字	音標	詞性	意義	字頻	大考	英檢	多益
❶	problem	[`prɑbləm]	n.	問題	1	1	初級	◎
	young	[jʌŋ]	adj.	年輕的	1	1	初級	
	people	[`pipl]	n.	person（人）複數	1	1	初級	
	nowadays	[`nauə.dez]	adv.	現今	3	4	中級	
❷	more	[mor]	adj./adv.	更多的/更加	1	1	初級	
	commit	[kə`mɪt]	v.	犯下	1	4	中級	◎
	suicide	[`suə.saɪd]	n.	自殺	1	3	中級	◎
❸	youth	[juθ]	n.	青少年	1	2	初級	
	getting	[`gɛtɪŋ]	p.pr.	get（變成）現在分詞	1	1	初級	◎
	serious	[`sɪrɪəs]	adj.	嚴重的	1	2	初級	◎
❹	really	[`rɪəlɪ]	adv.	真的	1		初級	
	know	[no]	v.	知道	1	1	初級	◎
	love	[lʌv]	v.	喜愛	1	1	初級	
	joyriding	[`dʒɔɪraɪdɪŋ]	n.	joyride（飆車）動名詞				
❺	teenager	[`tin.edʒɚ]	n.	青少年	1	2	初級	◎
	today	[tə`de]	adv.	當今、目前	1	1	初級	◎
	thinking	[`θɪŋkɪŋ]	p.pr.	think（想）現在分詞	1	1	中級	
❻	too	[tu]	adv.	過於	1	1	初級	
	much	[mʌtʃ]	adj.	許多的	1	1	初級	
	pressure	[`prɛʃɚ]	n.	壓力	1	3	中級	◎
❼	sexual	[`sɛkʃuəl]	adj.	性的	1	3	中級	◎
	education	[.ɛdʒʊ`keʃən]	n.	教育	1	2	初級	◎
	strengthened	[`strɛŋθənd]	p.p.	strength（加強）過去分詞	2	4	中級	◎
❽	kid	[kɪd]	n.	小孩	1	1	初級	
	want	[wɑnt]	v.	想要	1	1	初級	◎
	tell	[tɛl]	v.	告訴	1	1	初級	
	mind	[maɪnd]	n.	內心	1	1	初級	◎
❾	communicate	[kə`mjunə.ket]	v.	溝通	1	3	中級	
	child	[tʃaɪld]	n.	小孩	1	1	初級	

※「紅字單字」於本單元多句出現，「單字級等分析」僅列在「首次出現句」。

🔘 MP3 156-02 ❿～⓲

❿	為什麼青少年會染上毒癮？	Why do teenagers become addicted to drugs? * **become addicted to**（上癮、成癮） * **drug addition**（毒癮）
⓫	我不知道我的孩子究竟在想什麼。	I don't know what my child is thinking at all. * **not know...at all**（完全不知道…）
⓬	怎麼樣才能讓孩子跟我溝通？	How can I get my kids to communicate with me? * **How can I＋動詞原形...?**（我該如何…？） * **get＋某人＋to＋動詞原形**（讓某人做…） * **communicate with**（溝通）
⓭	為什麼青少年嚮往加入幫派？	Why do juveniles look forward to joining a gang? * **look forward to＋動詞ing**（期待做…） * **join a gang**（加入幫派）
⓮	為什麼那麼多青少年徹夜不歸？	Why are there so many young people who don't return home at night? * **Why are there＋名詞...?**（為什麼會有…？） * **return home**（回家） * **at night**（夜間）
⓯	家長和老師做錯了什麼嗎？	Have parents and teachers done something wrong? * **do something wrong**（做錯事） * 此句用「現在完成式問句」（Have...done...?）表示「過去某時點是否發生某事，且結果持續到現在嗎？」。
⓰	網咖是青少年問題的幫兇嗎？	Are Internet cafés part of the youth problem? * **Internet café**（網咖） * **be part of＋某物**（某物的一部分）
⓱	為什麼有那麼多中輟生？	Why are there so many high school students who drop out of school? * **high school student**（高中生） * **drop out of school**（輟學）
⓲	這一代的年輕人為何無法忍受挫折？	Why can't the youth of this generation endure frustration? * **of this generation**（這一代的） * **endure frustration**（忍受挫折） * **sense frustration**（挫折感）

	單字	音標	詞性	意義	字頻	大考	英檢	多益
❿	teenager	[ˈtin.edʒɚ]	n.	青少年	1	2	初級	◎
	become	[bɪˈkʌm]	v.	變為	1	1	初級	◎
	addicted	[əˈdɪktɪd]	adj.	上癮的		6	中高	◎
	drug	[drʌg]	n.	毒品	1	2	初級	
⓫	know	[no]	v.	知道	1	1	初級	◎
	child	[tʃaɪld]	n.	小孩	1	1	初級	
	thinking	[ˈθɪŋkɪŋ]	p.pr.	think（想）現在分詞	1	1	中級	
	all	[ɔl]	n.	完全	1	1	初級	
⓬	get	[gɛt]	v.	讓…	1	1	初級	◎
	kid	[kɪd]	n.	小孩	1	1	初級	
	communicate	[kəˈmjunə.ket]	v.	溝通	1	3	中級	
⓭	juvenile	[ˈdʒuvənl]	n.	青少年	2	5	中高	◎
	look	[lʊk]	v.	期待	1	1	初級	
	forward	[ˈfɔrwɚd]	adv.	今後、將來	1	2	初級	
	joining	[ˈdʒɔɪnɪŋ]	n.	join（加入、入會）動名詞	1	1	初級	◎
	gang	[gæŋ]	n.	幫派	1	3	中級	
⓮	there	[ðɛr]	adv.	有…	1	1	初級	
	so	[so]	adv.	這麼	1	1	初級	
	many	[ˈmɛnɪ]	adj.	許多的	1	1	初級	
	young	[jʌŋ]	adj.	年輕的	1	1	初級	
	people	[ˈpipl]	n.	person（人）複數	1	1	初級	
	return	[rɪˈtɜn]	v.	返回	1	1	初級	◎
	home	[hom]	n.	家	1	1	初級	
	night	[naɪt]	n.	夜晚	1	1	初級	
⓯	parents	[ˈpɛrənts]	n.	parent（雙親）複數	2	1		
	teacher	[ˈtitʃɚ]	n.	老師	1	1	初級	
	done	[dʌn]	p.p.	do（做）過去分詞	1	1	初級	
	something	[ˈsʌmθɪŋ]	pron.	某些事情	1	1	初級	
	wrong	[rɔŋ]	adj.	錯誤的	1	1	初級	◎
⓰	Internet	[ˈɪntɚ.nɛt]	n.	網路	1	4	初級	
	café	[kəˈfe]	n.	咖啡店	3	2	中級	
	part	[pɑrt]	n.	一部分	1	1	初級	◎
	youth	[juθ]	n.	青少年	1	2	初級	
	problem	[ˈprɑbləm]	n.	問題	1	1	初級	◎
⓱	high	[haɪ]	adj.	中學的	1	1	初級	
	school	[skul]	n.	學校	1	1	初級	
	student	[ˈstjudnt]	n.	學生	1	1	初級	
	drop	[drɑp]	v.	中止	1	2	英檢	◎
	out	[aʊt]	adv.	在…之外	1	1	初級	
⓲	this	[ðɪs]	adj.	這個	1	1	初級	
	generation	[.dʒɛnəˈreʃən]	n.	世代	1	1	初級	◎
	endure	[ɪnˈdjʊr]	v.	忍受	2	2	中級	◎
	frustration	[.frʌsˈtreʃən]	n.	挫折	2	3	中高	◎

※「紅字單字」於本單元多句出現，「單字級等分析」僅列在「首次出現句」。

❶	70％的人都是上班族。	About 70% of people belong to the commuter class. * **belong to**（屬於） * **commuter class**（上班族、領薪階級）
❷	領薪是上班族最期待的。	Payday is the most highly anticipated day for working people. * **highly anticipated**（相當受期待的）
❸	加班是上班族的夢魘。	Working overtime is the nightmare of the commuter class. * **working overtime**（加班） * **the nightmare of＋**某人（某人的夢魘）
❹	跳槽是上班族的定律。	Switching companies is the law of the commuter class. * **switch companies**（跳槽） * **the law of＋**某人事物（某人事物的定律、常態）
❺	有些上班族也有業績壓力。	Some working people have to deal with the stress of performance expectations. * **deal with**（解決、處理） * **stress of...**（來自…的壓力） * **performance expectation**（預期達到的業績） * **performance evaluation**（業績考核）
❻	我大學畢業後就成為上班族。	I became part of the commuter class after I graduated from college. * **become part of...**（成為…的一部分） * **graduate from...**（從…畢業） * **after graduation**（畢業後）
❼	上班族必須按時上下班。	A member of the commuter class must be punctual at work. * **be punctual at work**（準時上下班）
❽	上班族過勞死的問題時有耳聞。	The problem of karoshi, or death from overwork, has been heard of among the commuter class from time to time. * **or**（也可稱為） * **has been heard of**（一直有所耳聞） * **among**（在…之中） * **from time to time**（有時候、偶爾）

	單字	音標	詞性	意義	字頻	大考	英檢	多益
❶	about	[ə`baut]	adv.	大約	1	1	初級	
	people	[`pipl]	n.	person（人）複數	1	1	初級	
	belong	[bə`lɔŋ]	v.	屬於	1	1	初級	
	commuter	[kə`mjutɚ]	n.	通勤族	3	5	中高	◎
	class	[klæs]	n.	階級	1	1	初級	
❷	payday	[`pe,de]	n.	發薪日	6			
	most	[most]	adv.	最為	1	1	初級	
	highly	[`haɪlɪ]	adv.	非常、相當	1	4	中級	
	anticipated	[æn`tɪsə,petɪd]	adj.	受期待的	4	6	中高	◎
	day	[de]	n.	一天	1	1	初級	
	working	[`wɜkɪŋ]	adj.	工作的	2	1	中級	◎
❸	working	[`wɜkɪŋ]	n.	work（工作）動名詞	2	1	中級	◎
	overtime	[,ovɚ`taɪm]	adv.	超時地	3			◎
	nightmare	[`naɪt,mɛr]	n.	夢魘	2	4	中級	
❹	switching	[`swɪtʃɪŋ]	n.	switch（跳槽）動名詞	6	3	中級	◎
	company	[`kʌmpənɪ]	n.	公司	1	2	初級	◎
	law	[lɔ]	n.	定律	1	1	初級	◎
❺	some	[sʌm]	adj.	一些	1	1	初級	
	have	[hæv]	v.	必須	1	1	初級	
	deal	[dil]	v.	處理	1	1	初級	◎
	stress	[strɛs]	n.	壓力	1	1	初級	◎
	performance	[pɚ`fɔrməns]	n.	業績	1	3	中級	◎
	expectation	[,ɛkspɛk`teʃən]	n.	預期	1	3	中級	
❻	became	[bɪ`kem]	p.t.	become（成為）過去式	1	1	初級	◎
	part	[pɑrt]	n.	部分	1	1	初級	◎
	graduated	[`grædʒu,etɪd]	p.t.	graduate（畢業）過去式	7	3	中級	◎
	college	[`kɑlɪdʒ]	n.	大學	1	3	初級	◎
❼	member	[`mɛmbɚ]	n.	成員	1	2	初級	◎
	punctual	[`pʌŋktʃuəl]	adj.	準時的		6	中級	◎
	work	[wɜk]	n.	工作	1	1	初級	◎
❽	problem	[`prɑbləm]	n.	問題	1	1	初級	
	karoshi	[`karoʃi]	n.	（日文）過勞死				
	death	[dɛθ]	n.	死亡	1	1	初級	
	overwork	[`ovɚ`wɜk]	n.	過度工作	1	1	初級	
	heard	[hɜd]	p.p.	hear（聽聞）過去分詞	1	1	初級	
	time	[taɪm]	n.	時候	1	1	初級	

※「紅字單字」於本單元多句出現，「單字級等分析」僅列在「首次出現句」。

157　上班族…。（2）

❾	商業午餐是針對上班族設計的。	Commercial lunch menus are designed for the commuter class. * commercial lunch menus（商業午餐） * be designed for...（為…而設計） * commuter class（上班族、領薪階級）
❿	週休二日是上班族的福音。	The weekend is the blessing of the commuter class. * the blessing of＋某人（某人的恩賜、福音）
⓫	上班族的職業病也不少。	Commuters also have their share of occupational illnesses. * have one's share of...（有共同的…） * occupational illness（職業病） 　= occupational disease
⓬	很多上班族搭捷運上班。	Many people of the commuter class go to work by MRT. * go to work（上班通勤） * by MRT（搭乘捷運） * public transportation（公共運輸）
⓭	上班族必須忍受擁擠的捷運。	The commuter class has to put up with the crowded MRT. * have to（必須） * put up with（忍受）
⓮	上班族隨時面臨裁員減薪的壓力。	The commuter class always faces the pressures of layoffs and pay cuts. * face pressure（面對壓力） * withstand pressure（承受壓力） * pay cuts（減薪）
⓯	聊八卦是上班族的娛樂之一。	Gossip is one type of entertainment for the commuter class. * one type of（其中一種） * entertainment for＋某人（某人的娛樂）
⓰	大多數的上班族每天忙到不可開交。	Most members of the commuter class perpetually have more work than they can finish. * have more work than...（工作量大於…）

單字級等分析

	單字	音標	詞性	意義	字頻	大考	英檢	多益
⑨	commercial	[kə`mɝʃəl]	adj.	商業的	1	3	中級	◎
	lunch	[lʌntʃ]	n.	午餐	1	1	初級	
	menu	[`mɛnju]	n.	菜單	2	2	初級	◎
	designed	[dɪ`zaɪnd]	p.p.	design（設計）過去分詞	1	1	初級	◎
	commuter	[kə`mjutɚ]	n.	通勤族	3	5	中高	◎
	class	[klæs]	n.	階級	1	1	初級	
⑩	weekend	[`wik`ɛnd]	n.	週末	1	1	初級	
	blessing	[`blɛsɪŋ]	n.	恩賜、福音	2	4	中級	
⑪	also	[`ɔlso]	adv.	也	1	1	初級	
	have	[hæv]	v.	擁有/必須	1	1	初級	
	share	[ʃɛr]	n.	共通點	1	2	初級	◎
	occupational	[.akjə`peʃənl]	adj.	職業的	3			
	illness	[`ɪlnɪs]	n.	疾病	1		中級	
⑫	many	[`mɛnɪ]	adj.	許多的	1	1	初級	
	people	[`pipl]	n.	person（人）複數	1	1	初級	
	go	[go]	v.	去	1	1	初級	
	work	[wɝk]	v./n.	工作	1	1	初級	◎
	MRT	[`ɛm`ar`ti]	n.	Mass Rapid Transit（捷運）縮寫		2	初級	◎
⑬	put	[pʊt]	v.	忍受	1	1	初級	
	crowded	[`kraʊdɪd]	adj.	擁擠的	2	2	初級	◎
⑭	always	[`ɔlwez]	adv.	總是、隨時	1	1	初級	
	face	[fes]	v.	面對	1	1	初級	
	pressure	[`prɛʃɚ]	n.	壓力	1	3	中級	◎
	layoff	[`le.ɔf]	n.	裁員	3			
	pay	[pe]	n.	薪水	1	3	初級	◎
	cut	[kʌt]	n.	減少	1	1	初級	
⑮	gossip	[`gasəp]	n.	八卦	3	3	中級	
	one	[wʌn]	n.	一	1	1	初級	
	type	[taɪp]	n.	種類	1	2	初級	◎
	entertainment	[.ɛntɚ`tenmənt]	n.	娛樂	1	4	中級	◎
⑯	most	[most]	adj.	多數的	1	1	初級	
	member	[`mɛmbɚ]	n.	成員	1	2	初級	◎
	perpetually	[pɚ`pɛtʃʊəlɪ]	adv.	不斷地、持續地	5			
	more	[mor]	adj.	更多的	1	1	初級	
	finish	[`fɪnɪʃ]	v.	完成	1	1	初級	◎

※「紅字單字」於本單元多句出現，「單字級等分析」僅列在「首次出現句」。

MP3 157-02 ❶～❽

❶	畢業後你希望當一個上班族嗎？	Do you want to be part of the commuter class after graduating from school? * want to＋動詞原形（想要） * be part of（身為一員） * commuter class（上班族、領薪階級） * graduate from school（從學校畢業）
❷	你是個快樂的上班族嗎？	Are you a contented member of the commuter class? * contented（心滿意足的）＝ satisfied * be contented with＋某物（對…感到滿意的）
❸	你是個愛聊八卦的上班族嗎？	Are you a commuter who likes to gossip? * like to＋動詞原形（喜歡）
❹	你擔心裁員減薪嗎？	Do you worry about layoffs and pay cuts? * worry about＋名詞（擔心…） 　＝ be concerned about * pay cuts（減薪）
❺	你有上班族的職業病嗎？	Do you have an occupational disease common among the commuter class? * occupational disease（職業病） 　＝ occupational illness * common among...（在…之中常見的）
❻	你成為上班族多久了？	How long have you been a member of the commuter class? * How long have you been...? 　（你身為…持續多久？） * 此句用「現在完成式」（...have...been...） 　表示「過去持續到現在的事」。
❼	如果可以選擇，你寧願不上班嗎？	Would you rather not go to work if you could choose not to? * Would you＋動詞＋if you could＋動詞? 　（假設你可以…，你會…嗎） * would rather（寧願、寧可） * choose not to（選擇不要…）
❽	你擔心自己過勞嗎？	Do you worry about being overworked? * worry about＋動詞-ing（擔心…）

	單字	音標	詞性	意義	字頻	大考	英檢	多益
❶	want	[wɑnt]	v.	想要	1	1	初級	◎
	part	[pɑrt]	n.	一部分	1	1	初級	◎
	commuter	[kə`mjutɚ]	n.	通勤族	3	5	中高	◎
	class	[klæs]	n.	階級	1	1	初級	
	graduating	[`grædʒʊ,etɪŋ]	n.	graduate（畢業）動名詞	1	3	中級	◎
	school	[skul]	n.	學校	1	1	初級	
❷	contented	[kən`tɛntɪd]	adj.	心滿意足的	8			
	member	[`mɛmbɚ]	n.	成員	1	2	初級	◎
❸	like	[laɪk]	v.	喜歡	1	1	初級	
	gossip	[`gɑsəp]	v.	聊八卦	3	3	中級	
❹	worry	[`wɝɪ]	v.	擔心	1	1	初級	◎
	layoff	[`le,ɔf]	n.	裁員	3			
	pay	[pe]	n.	薪水	1	3	初級	◎
	cut	[kʌt]	n.	減少	1	1	初級	
❺	have	[hæv]	v.	擁有	1	1	初級	
	occupational	[,ɑkjə`peʃənl]	adj.	職業的	3			
	disease	[dɪ`ziz]	n.	疾病	1	3	中級	◎
	common	[`kɑmən]	adj.	常見的	1	1	初級	◎
❻	long	[lɔŋ]	adv.	長久地	1	1	初級	
❼	rather	[`ræðɚ]	adv.	寧願、寧可	1	2	初級	◎
	go	[go]	v.	去	1	1	初級	
	work	[wɝk]	v.	工作	1	1	初級	◎
	choose	[tʃuz]	v.	選擇	1	2	初級	◎
❽	overworked	[,ovɚ`wɝkt]	adj.	過勞的、工作過度的	6	5	中高	

※「紅字單字」於本單元多句出現，「單字級等分析」僅列在「首次出現句」。

157 你覺得上班族…？（2）

❾	你做好退休規畫了嗎？	Have you already made your retirement plan? * **Have you already＋過去分詞?**（你已經…了嗎） * **make a plan**（規畫） * **retirement plan**（退休規畫）
❿	為了薪水，你不得已才上班嗎？	Are you working with no motive other than a paycheck? * **with no motive other than...**（除了…以外別無動機） * **other than**（除此之外）
⓫	你擔心自己喪失競爭力嗎？	Do you worry about losing your competitiveness? * **worry about＋名詞**（擔心…）＝ **be worried about** * **lose one's competitiveness**（失去競爭力）
⓬	你覺得職場上男女平等嗎？	Do you think that gender equality exists in the workforce? * **Do you think that＋子句?**（你覺得…嗎） * **gender equality**（男女平等） * **in the workforce**（職場上）
⓭	你擔心長江後浪推前浪嗎？	Do you worry about being outdone by younger generations? * **be outdone**（被超越） * **younger generation**（年輕一輩）
⓮	你討厭規律的上班生活嗎？	Do you hate having a regular working life? * **hate＋動詞-ing**（討厭…） * **regular working life**（規律的上班生活）
⓯	沒有工作你會沒安全感嗎？	Would you feel insecure if you were unemployed? * **Would you＋動詞＋if you＋過去式動詞?**（假設…，你會…嗎）
⓰	你有職業倦怠嗎？	Do you feel tired of your job? * **feel tired of**（厭倦） * **job burnout**（職業倦怠）
⓱	一旦失業你打算做什麼？	What would you do if you became unemployed one day? * **become＋形容詞**（變成…） * **one day**（有一天）

單字級等分析

	單字	音標	詞性	意義	字頻	大考	英檢	多益
❾	already	[ɔlˋrɛdɪ]	adv.	已經	1	1	初級	
	made	[med]	p.p.	make（準備）過去分詞	1	1	初級	
	retirement	[rɪˋtaɪrmənt]	n.	退休	1	4	中高	◎
	plan	[plæn]	n.	計畫	1	1	初級	◎
❿	working	[ˋwɝkɪŋ]	p.pr.	work（工作）現在分詞	2	1	中級	◎
	motive	[ˋmotɪv]	n.	動機	2	5	中高	◎
	other	[ˋʌðɚ]	adj.	其他的	1	1	初級	
	paycheck	[ˋpe.tʃɛk]	n.	薪水	3			
⓫	worry	[ˋwɝɪ]	v.	擔心	1	1	初級	◎
	losing	[ˋluzɪŋ]	n.	lose（喪失）動名詞	4	2	初級	◎
	competitiveness	[kəmˋpɛtətɪvnɪs]	n.	競爭力	3			
⓬	think	[θɪŋk]	v.	認為	1	1	初級	
	gender	[ˋdʒɛndɚ]	n.	性別	1	5	中高	
	equality	[iˋkwɑlətɪ]	n.	平等	2	4	中級	◎
	exist	[ɪgˋzɪst]	v.	存在	1	2	初級	◎
	workforce	[ˋwɝk.fors]	n.	職場	3		中高	◎
⓭	outdone	[ˋaʊtˋdʌn]	p.p.	outdo（超越）過去分詞	6	5	中高	
	younger	[ˋjʌŋgɚ]	adj.	young（年輕的）比較級	1	1	初級	
	generation	[.dʒɛnəˋreʃən]	n.	世代	1	4	初級	◎
⓮	hate	[het]	v.	討厭	1	1	初級	
	having	[ˋhævɪŋ]	n.	have（擁有）動名詞	1	1	初級	
	regular	[ˋrɛgjəlɚ]	adj.	規律的	1	2	初級	◎
	working	[ˋwɝkɪŋ]	adj.	上班的	2	1	中級	◎
	life	[laɪf]	n.	生活	1	1	初級	◎
⓯	feel	[fil]	v.	感到	1	1	初級	
	insecure	[.ɪnsɪˋkjʊr]	adj.	沒安全感的	4		中高	
	unemployed	[.ʌnɪmˋplɔɪd]	adj.	失業的	3		中高	
⓰	tired	[taɪrd]	adj.	厭倦的	1	1	初級	◎
	job	[dʒɑb]	n.	工作	1	1	初級	
⓱	do	[du]	v.	做	1	1	初級	
	became	[bɪˋkem]	p.t.	become（變為）過去式	1	1	初級	◎
	one	[wʌn]	n.	一	1	1	初級	
	day	[de]	n.	天	1	1	初級	

※「紅字單字」於本單元多句出現，「單字級等分析」僅列在「首次出現句」。

158 失業…。（1）

❶	失業率越來越高。	The unemployment rate is getting higher and higher. * **unemployment rate**（失業率） * **employment rate**（就業率） * **be getting＋比較級**（變得越來越…）
❷	許多公司進行縮編，精簡人力。	Many companies are in the process of laying off and downsizing. * **in the process of＋動詞-ing**（在進行…） * **lay off**（解雇）
❸	很多人一直找不到工作。	Many people can't find a job at all. * **find a job**（找工作） * **at all**（根本、完全） * **job opportunity**（工作機會）
❹	父母親失業，很多家庭陷入經濟危機。	Many families fall into economic crisis due to the parents being out of work. * **fall into**（陷入某種情況） * **economic crisis**（經濟危機） * **due to＋主詞＋動詞-ing**（因為…） * **out of work**（失業、沒有工作）
❺	中年失業令人同情。	Middle-aged unemployment is a pitiable situation. * **middle-aged unemployment**（中年失業） * **pitiable situation**（令人同情的處境）
❻	工廠外移到大陸，許多員工被裁員。	Many employees are laid off due to factories having moved to mainland China. * **due to＋名詞**（因為…） * **have moved**（已經搬遷）
❼	失業經常是自殺的原因之一。	Unemployment is often one of the reasons for suicide. * **one of the reason for＋某事物**（某事物的原因之一） * **commit suicide**（自殺）
❽	公司惡性倒閉，員工都沒領到薪水。	Employees haven't received their salaries due to vicious company shutdowns. * **receive one's salary**（得到薪水） * **vicious shutdown**（惡性倒閉）

	單字	音標	詞性	意義	字頻	大考	英檢	多益
❶	unemployment	[ˌʌnɪmˈplɔɪmənt]	n.	失業	2	6	中高	◎
	rate	[ret]	n.	比率	1	3	中級	◎
	getting	[ˈɡɛtɪŋ]	p.pr.	get（變成）現在分詞	1	1	初級	◎
	higher	[ˈhaɪə]	adj.	high（比率高的）比較級	1	1	初級	
❷	many	[ˈmɛnɪ]	adj.	許多的	1	1	初級	
	company	[ˈkʌmpənɪ]	n.	公司	1	2	初級	◎
	process	[ˈprɑsɛs]	n.	過程	1	3	中級	◎
	laying	[ˈleɪŋ]	n.	lay（解雇）動名詞	1	1	初級	
	off	[ɔf]	adv.	停止、無工作	1	1	初級	
	downsizing	[ˈdaʊnˈsaɪzɪŋ]	n.	downsize（縮編人員）動名詞	7			◎
❸	people	[ˈpipl̩]	n.	person（人）複數	1	1	初級	
	find	[faɪnd]	v.	找到	1	1	初級	
	job	[dʒɑb]	n.	工作	1	1	初級	
	all	[ɔl]	n.	完全	1	1	初級	
❹	family	[ˈfæməlɪ]	n.	家庭	1	1	初級	
	fall	[fɔl]	v.	陷入	1	1	初級	
	economic	[ˌikəˈnɑmɪk]	adj.	經濟的	1	4	中級	◎
	crisis	[ˈkraɪsɪs]	n.	危機	1	2	初級	
	due	[dju]	adj.	因為	1	3	中級	◎
	parents	[ˈpɛrənts]	n.	parent（雙親）複數	2	1		
	out	[aʊt]	adv.	在…之外、沒有	1	1	初級	
	work	[wɝk]	n.	工作	1	1	初級	◎
❺	middle-aged	[ˈmɪdl̩ˌedʒd]	adj.	中年的	3		中高	
	pitiable	[ˈpɪtɪəbl̩]	adj.	令人同情的				
	situation	[ˌsɪtʃʊˈeʃən]	n.	處境	1	3	中級	◎
❻	employee	[ˌɛmplɔɪˈi]	n.	員工	1	3	中級	◎
	laid	[led]	p.p.	lay（解雇）過去分詞	1	1	初級	
	factory	[ˈfæktərɪ]	n.	工廠	1	1	初級	◎
	moved	[muvd]	p.p.	move（搬遷）過去分詞	1	1	初級	◎
	mainland	[ˈmenlənd]	n.	大陸	3	5	中級	
	China	[ˈtʃaɪnə]	n.	中國	4	3	初級	
❼	often	[ˈɔfən]	adv.	常常	1	1	初級	
	one	[wʌn]	pron.	一個	1	1	初級	
	reason	[ˈrizn̩]	n.	原因	1	1	初級	◎
	suicide	[ˈsuəˌsaɪd]	n.	自殺	1	3	英檢	◎
❽	received	[rɪˈsivd]	p.p.	receive（得到）過去分詞	6	1	初級	◎
	salary	[ˈsælərɪ]	n.	薪水	1	4	中級	◎
	vicious	[ˈvɪʃəs]	adj.	惡性的	3	6	中高	◎
	shutdown	[ˈʃʌtˌdaʊn]	n.	倒閉	5			

※「紅字單字」於本單元多句出現，「單字級等分析」僅列在「首次出現句」。

🔊 MP3 158-01 ❾～⓰

❾	失業會造成嚴重的社會問題。	Unemployment will cause serious social problems. * cause a problem（造成問題） * social problem（社會問題）
❿	政府舉辦了失業勞工訓練課程。	The government has a training program for unemployed laborers. * training program（訓練課程） * unemployed laborer（失業勞工）
⓫	我擔心中年失業。	I'm worried that I'll be unemployed when I am middle-aged. * be worried that＋子句（擔心⋯）
⓬	我每個月領失業救濟金。	I receive an unemployment relief check every month. * unemployment relief check（失業救助金） * every month（每個月）
⓭	我寄了很多履歷表，但是都沒有回音。	I've already sent my resume to many companies, but I haven't received any replies at all. * send one's resume（投履歷） * receive a reply（收到回覆） * job interview（求職面試）
⓮	我沒有任何證照，很難找工作。	I don't have any certificates, so it's really hard for me to find a job. * so（因此） * it is hard to...（難以⋯）
⓯	公司發給我三個月的遣散費。	My company compensated me for my dismissal with three months' pay. * compensate me for my dismissal（給我遣散費） * compensate＋某人＋for＋某事（因某事補償某人） * with（以⋯方式）
⓰	失業後有人選擇自行創業。	Some people choose to start their own businesses after becoming unemployed. * choose to＋動詞原形（選擇） * start one's own business（自行創業） * become unemployed（失業）

	單字	音標	詞性	意義	字頻	大考	英檢	多益
❾	unemployment	[ˌʌnɪmˈplɔɪmənt]	n.	失業	2	6	中高	◎
	cause	[kɔz]	v.	造成	1	1	初級	◎
	serious	[ˈsɪrɪəs]	adj.	嚴重的	1	2	初級	◎
	social	[ˈsoʃəl]	adj.	社會的	1	2	初級	◎
	problem	[ˈprɑbləm]	n.	問題	1	1	初級	◎
❿	government	[ˈgʌvənmənt]	n.	政府	1	2	初級	◎
	have	[hæv]	v.	擁有	1	1	初級	
	training	[ˈtrenɪŋ]	n.	訓練	1	1	中級	◎
	program	[ˈprogræm]	n.	課程	1	3	初級	◎
	unemployed	[ˌʌnɪmˈplɔɪd]	adj.	失業的	3		中高	
	laborer	[ˈlebərə]	n.	勞工	3			
⓫	worried	[ˈwɝɪd]	adj.	擔心的	2	1	中級	◎
	middle-aged	[ˈmɪdl̩ˌedʒd]	adj.	中年的	3		中高	
⓬	receive	[rɪˈsiv]	v.	收到	1	1	初級	
	relief	[rɪˈlif]	n.	補助	1	3	中級	◎
	check	[tʃɛk]	n.	支票	1	1	初級	◎
	every	[ˈɛvrɪ]	adj.	每一	1	1	初級	
	month	[ˈmʌnθ]	n.	月	1	1	初級	
⓭	already	[ɔlˈrɛdɪ]	adv.	已經	1	1	初級	◎
	sent	[sɛnt]	p.p.	send（遞送）過去分詞	1	1	初級	
	resume	[ˈrɛzjuˌme]	n.	履歷	2	5	中高	◎
	many	[ˈmɛnɪ]	adj.	許多的	1	1	初級	
	company	[ˈkʌmpənɪ]	n.	公司	1	2	初級	◎
	received	[rɪˈsivd]	p.p.	receive（收到）過去分詞	6	1	初級	◎
	any	[ˈɛnɪ]	adj.	任何的	1	1	初級	
	reply	[rɪˈplaɪ]	n.	回覆	1	2	初級	◎
	all	[ɔl]	n.	完全	1	1	初級	
⓮	certificate	[səˈtɪfəkɪt]	n.	證照	2	5	中級	◎
	really	[ˈrɪəlɪ]	adv.	很、十分	1	1	初級	
	hard	[hɑrd]	adj.	困難的	1	1	初級	◎
	find	[faɪnd]	v.	找到	1	1	初級	
	job	[dʒɑb]	n.	工作	1	1	初級	
⓯	compensated	[ˈkɑmpənˌsetɪd]	p.t.	compensate（賠償）過去式	2	6	中高	◎
	dismissal	[dɪsˈmɪsl̩]	n.	解雇	4		中高	
	three	[θri]	n.	三	1	1	初級	
	pay	[pe]	n.	薪水	1	3	初級	◎
⓰	some	[sʌm]	adj.	一些	1	1	初級	
	people	[ˈpipl̩]	n.	person（人）複數	1	1	初級	
	choose	[tʃuz]	v.	選擇	1	2	初級	◎
	start	[stɑrt]	v.	創立	1	1	初級	
	own	[on]	adj.	自己的	1	1	初級	◎
	business	[ˈbɪznɪs]	n.	公司、企業	1	2	初級	◎
	becoming	[bɪˈkʌmɪŋ]	n.	become（變為）動名詞		1	初級	◎

※「紅字單字」於本單元多句出現，「單字級等分析」僅列在「首次出現句」。

🔵 MP3 158-02 ❶～❾

❶	你為什麼失業？	Why are you unemployed?
❷	你失業多久了？	How long have you been unemployed? * **How long have you been...?**（你持續…多久？） * **an employment period**（一段失業期） * **long-term unemployment**（長期失業）
❸	你被老闆炒魷魚了？	Did you get fired by your boss? * **Did you...?**（你當時是…嗎） * **get fired**（被炒魷魚、被解雇） * **fire**（解雇）＝ **lay off**
❹	你有領到失業救濟金嗎？	Have you claimed any unemployment relief funds? * **Have you＋過去分詞...?**（你已經…了嗎） * **unemployment relief fund**（失業救濟金） * **claim a fund**（索取資金） * **claim**（索取）可替換為：**apply for**（申請）
❺	台灣的失業率高嗎？	Is the unemployment rate high in Taiwan? * **unemployment rate**（失業率） * **unemployed population**（失業人口） * **low**（比率低的）
❻	國外的失業率比台灣高嗎？	Are the unemployment rates of foreign countries higher than Taiwan's? * **Are / Is...higher than...?**（…是否高於…？） * **foreign country**（外國）
❼	你有找工作嗎？	Have you looked for a job? * **look for a job**（找工作）
❽	你有領到遣散費嗎？	Did you get compensated for your dismissal? * **get compensated for...**（得到…的補償費用） * **dismissal**（遣散、解雇）＝ **layoff**
❾	政府有實際措施解決失業問題嗎？	Are there any practical methods that the government has proposed to solve the unemployment problem? * **Are there＋名詞...?**（是否有…？） * **practical method**（實際措施、實際方法） * **propose to＋動詞原形**（提出來做…） * **solve a problem**（解決問題）

單字級等分析

	單字	音標	詞性	意義	字頻	大考	英檢	多益
❶	unemployed	[ˌʌnɪmˈplɔɪd]	adj.	失業的	3		中高	
❷	long	[lɔŋ]	adv.	長久地	1	1	初級	
❸	get	[gɛt]	v.	被…	1	1	初級	◎
	fired	[faɪrd]	p.p.	fire（解雇）過去分詞	7	1	初級	◎
	boss	[bɔs]	n.	老闆	1	2	初級	
❹	claimed	[klemd]	p.p.	claim（索取）過去分詞	1	2	初級	◎
	any	[ˈɛnɪ]	adj.	任何的	1	1	初級	
	unemployment	[ˌʌnɪmˈplɔɪmənt]	n.	失業	2	6	中高	◎
	relief	[rɪˈlif]	n.	救濟、幫助	1	3	中級	◎
	fund	[fʌnd]	n.	資金	1	3	中級	◎
❺	rate	[ret]	n.	比率	1	3	中級	◎
	high	[haɪ]	adj.	比率高的	1	1	初級	
	Taiwan	[ˈtaɪˈwɑn]	n.	台灣			初級	
❻	foreign	[ˈfɔrɪn]	adj.	外國的	1	1	初級	◎
	country	[ˈkʌntrɪ]	n.	國家	1	1	初級	
	higher	[ˈhaɪɚ]	adj.	high（比率高的）比較級	1	1	初級	
❼	looked	[lʊkt]	p.p.	look（尋找）過去分詞	1	1	初級	
	job	[dʒɑb]	n.	工作	1	1	初級	
❽	compensated	[ˈkɑmpənˌsetɪd]	p.p.	compensate（補償）過去分詞	2	6	中高	◎
	dismissal	[dɪsˈmɪsl̩]	n.	遣散、解雇	4		中高	
❾	there	[ðɛr]	adv.	有…	1	1	初級	
	practical	[ˈpræktɪkl̩]	adj.	實際的	1	3	中級	◎
	method	[ˈmɛθəd]	n.	措施	1	2	初級	◎
	government	[ˈgʌvənmənt]	n.	政府	1	2	初級	◎
	proposed	[prəˈpozd]	p.p.	propose（提出）過去分詞	2	2	初級	◎
	solve	[sɑlv]	v.	解決	1	2	初級	◎
	problem	[ˈprɑbləm]	n.	問題	1	1	初級	◎

※「紅字單字」於本單元多句出現，「單字級等分析」僅列在「首次出現句」。

🔵 MP3 158-02 ⑩ ～ ⑰

⑩	失業了沒收入你怎麼辦？	What will you do if you're unemployed and without any income? * **What will you do if...?**（如果…，你將會做什麼？） * **without income**（沒有收入）
⑪	政府對失業勞工有任何補助嗎？	Are there any subsidies the government gives to the unemployed? * **give subsidies to**＋某人（給某人補助、津貼） * **receive subsidies**（收到補助） * **lose subsidies**（失去補助） * **the unemployed**（失業的人）
⑫	需要我幫忙找工作嗎？	Do you need my help in looking for work? * **need my help**（需要我的幫忙） * **in**＋動詞-ing（在…方面） * **look for**（找尋）＝ **find**
⑬	你將個人資料放到網路上了嗎？	Have you posted your personal information on the Internet? * **personal information**（個人資料） * **on the Internet**（網路上） * **autobiography**（自傳）、**resume**（履歷） * 此句用「現在完成式問句」(Have...posted...?)表示「過去某時點是否發生某事，且結果持續到現在嗎？」。
⑭	你上過徵才網站找工作嗎？	Have you ever accessed a recruiting website to look for a job? * **Have you ever...?**（你是否曾經…？） * **access a website**（進入網站） * **recruiting website**（徵才網站） * **employment agency**（人力銀行）
⑮	你急著找新工作嗎？	Are you anxiously trying to find a new job? * **Are you**＋動詞-ing...?（你現在正在做…嗎） * **try to**＋動詞原形（試圖）、**vacancy**（職缺、空缺）
⑯	家庭生活還過得去嗎？	Is your family life tolerable?
⑰	你是家裡唯一的經濟支柱？	Are you the only breadwinner in your family? * **only breadwinner**（唯一的經濟支柱）

	單字	音標	詞性	意義	字頻	大考	英檢	多益
❿	do	[du]	v.	做	1	1	初級	
	unemployed	[ˌʌnɪmˋplɔɪd]	adj.	失業的	3		中高	
	any	[ˋɛnɪ]	adj.	任何的	1	1	初級	
	income	[ˋɪn͵kʌm]	n.	收入	1	2	初級	◎
⓫	there	[ðɛr]	adv.	有…	1	1	初級	
	subsidy	[ˋsʌbsədɪ]	n.	補助、津貼	2		中高	◎
	government	[ˋgʌvənmənt]	n.	政府	1	2	初級	◎
	give	[gɪv]	v.	給予	1	1	初級	
⓬	need	[nid]	v.	需要	1	1	初級	◎
	help	[hɛlp]	n.	幫忙	1	1	初級	
	looking	[ˋlʊkɪŋ]	n.	look（尋找）動名詞	5	1	初級	
	work	[wɝk]	n.	工作	1	1	初級	◎
⓭	posted	[ˋpostɪd]	p.p.	post（張貼）過去分詞	1	2	初級	◎
	personal	[ˋpɝsn̩l]	adj.	個人的	1	2	初級	◎
	information	[ˌɪnfəˋmeʃən]	n.	資料	1	4	初級	◎
	Internet	[ˋɪntə͵nɛt]	n.	網路	1	4	初級	
⓮	ever	[ˋɛvə]	adv.	曾經	1	1	初級	
	accessed	[ˋæksɛst]	p.p.	access（進入）過去分詞	1	4	中級	◎
	recruiting	[rɪˋkrutɪŋ]	adj.	徵才的	3	6	中高	◎
	website	[ˋwɛb͵saɪt]	n.	網站	2	4	中高	◎
	look	[lʊk]	v.	尋找	1	1	初級	
	job	[dʒɑb]	n.	工作	1	1	初級	
⓯	anxiously	[ˋæŋkʃəslɪ]	adv.	焦急地	4			
	trying	[ˋtraɪŋ]	p.pr.	try（試圖）現在分詞	6		初級	
	find	[faɪnd]	v.	尋找	1	1	初級	
	new	[nju]	adj.	新的	1	1	初級	
⓰	family	[ˋfæməlɪ]	n.	家庭	1	1	初級	
	life	[laɪf]	n.	生活	1	1	初級	
	tolerable	[ˋtɑlərəbl̩]	adj.	還可以的、還過得去的	6	4	中級	
⓱	only	[ˋonlɪ]	adj.	唯一的	1	1	初級	
	breadwinner	[ˋbrɛd͵wɪnə]	n.	負擔生計的人	8			

※「紅字單字」於本單元多句出現，「單字級等分析」僅列在「首次出現句」。

檸檬樹出版社
Lemon Tree Publishing House

虹系列 07

實用英語會話大全：
字頻/大考/英檢/多益，四類字級解析應用版

初版 1 刷　2018 年 8 月 7 日

作者	王琪
封面設計・版型設計	陳文德・洪素貞
英語審訂	郝凱楊（NICHOLAS B. HAWKINS）
責任編輯	郭哲維
協力編輯	簡子媛
發行人	江媛珍
社長・總編輯	何聖心
出版者	檸檬樹國際書版有限公司 檸檬樹出版社
	E-mail：lemontree@booknews.com.tw
	地址：新北市 235 中和區中安街 80 號 3 樓
	電話・傳真：02-29271121・02-29272336
法律顧問	第一國際法律事務所 余淑杏律師
	北辰著作權事務所 蕭雄淋律師
全球總經銷・印務代理	知遠文化事業有限公司
網路書城	http://www.booknews.com.tw 博訊書網
	電話：02-26648800　傳真：02-26648801
	地址：新北市222深坑區北深路三段155巷25號5樓
港澳地區經銷	和平圖書有限公司
	電話：852-28046687　傳真：850-28046409
	地址：香港柴灣嘉業街12號百樂門大廈17樓
定價	台幣 599 元／港幣 200 元
劃撥帳號・戶名	19726702・檸檬樹國際書版有限公司
	・單次購書金額未達300元，請另付50元郵資
	・信用卡・劃撥購書需7-10個工作天

實用英語會話大全 / 王琪作. --
初版. -- 新北市：檸檬樹, 2018.08
面；　公分. -- (虹系列；7)
ISBN 978-986-94387-3-5 (精裝附光碟片)

1. 英語　2. 會話

805.188　　　　　　　　　　107008580